TED ALLBEURY

TED ALLBEURY

NO PLACE TO HIDE

THE JUDAS FACTOR

CHILDREN OF TENDER YEARS

THE SEEDS OF TREASON

THE CROSSING

OCTOPUS BOOKS

No Place to Hide first published in Great Britain in 1984 by New English Library
The Judas Factor first published in Great Britain in 1984 by New English Library
Children of Tender Years first published in Great Britain in 1985 by
New English Library
The Seeds of Treason first published in Great Britain in 1986 by
New English Library
The Crossing first published in Great Britain in 1987 by New English Library

This edition first published in Great Britain in 1988 by

The Octopus Group Limited
Michelin House
81 Fulham Road
London SW3 6RB

ISBN 0 7064 3806 X

Printed and bound in the United Kingdom by William Clowes Limited, Beccles

CONTENTS

NO PLACE TO HIDE

With love to Thys Ockersen – citizen of Amsterdam – the most civilized city in Europe.

Law is a regulation in accord with reason, issued by a lawful superior for the common good.

THOMAS AQUINAS, *Summa Theologicae*

CHAPTER ONE

The man was tall, just over six feet, and his face, chest and shoulders were a deep brown. The tan that comes from wind as well as sun. He was in his early forties, his black hair already beginning to streak with grey, but his body was firm and well muscled. He was wearing a pair of khaki shorts, and shoes without socks. Down the slope of the hill from the small wooden house he could see three cars parked by the stall where they sold the eggs and produce from the small-holding.

They had lived there for nearly two years, earning a bare living from the tourists heading for South Hero from mainland Burlington. They came in their hundreds to Lake Champlain and many of them stopped at the stall to buy stores for their week's holiday. In the spring and fall the trees and foliage of Vermont brought visitors from all over the States. The leaves were already beginning to turn gold and red but there would be another two months before they packed up the stall for the winter.

The locals on the other small scattered farmsteads had been good to them right from the start, helping him to repair the ramshackle clapboard house, letting him join the local farm cooperative so that he could buy poultry food, fertilizer and seed at discount, digging them out from the snow that first terrible winter.

There was another hour's light and he turned to go back to the barn and the tractor. There was something wrong with the linkage on the PTO and it would save him 40 dollars if he could put it right himself. With neither mechanical nor farming skills he had to learn from instruction manuals and textbooks, and despite the practical difficulties that came from ignorance he had found peace and calm from the new life. He often wondered whether the peace came from the farm or from the girl. She would go on selling until it was too dark to see. He smiled to himself as he worked. For a girl who loathed capitalism, cities, governments and the establishment she nevertheless enjoyed selling their produce. The fact that she was young and pretty helped, but she swore that it was the reputation of their fresh eggs and luscious organically-grown fruit that made the tourists come back for more.

He went round the poultry arks before the light went, closing them for the night and taking half a dozen eggs for their own meal from the nesting boxes.

He was soaping his body under the shower when he heard her come into the house and a few minutes later he walked into the living room, a towel round his waist.

She was twenty-three, twenty-four in two month's time, and she was strikingly pretty. Even prettier than when he had first met her when she was barely twenty. She turned to look at him.

'I took 352 dollars, honey. Everything's gone. I've got two people coming back tomorrow for more eggs.'

'Well done, kid. I'll do an early egg-collection tomorrow. They're doing well, those hybrids. Averaging 200 eggs a bird and still two months to go. And all top size with strong white shells.'

She laughed softly as she looked up at his face. 'I never thought you'd stick it. I knew you'd try – but I thought you'd miss so much.'

'Like what?'

She shrugged. 'Theatres . . .'

'I never went to the theatre. It bores me stiff. I prefer the movies.'

She laughed. 'We've been to the movies three times in fourteen, no, fifteen months. That's all. What about England? Don't you miss England?'

'I never think about it, let alone miss it. That's all over.'

'What about your daughters?'

She regretted saying it the moment it was said. Those muscles stiffening at the sides of his mouth and the pulse beating by his left eye. But if she didn't ask he could think she wasn't aware or didn't care.

'They're better off without me.' He paused, shaking his head like a dog coming out of water, as if to shake away the thoughts in his mind. 'How about I do us an omelette. I've brought in some eggs.'

'OK. Suits me fine.'

He stood with his hands on his hips looking at her face.

'How about you, honey. Are you bored?'

'Me? You're crazy. I'm the confirmed dropout, it's you who's the city slicker.'

He shrugged. 'It's fine longing for the simple life when you're in New York or London. Or Amsterdam for that matter. But it ain't necessarily the same when you've actually got it.'

'It's great, Johnny. I love it, every minute of it.'

'What do you love?'

'Jesus. Everything. No crowds, no muggers, no guys trying to push me drugs because they want to screw me. No self-important creeps in offices playing God so I can earn a hundred bucks a week.' She paused and then said, softly, 'I always meant it, Johnny. This is where I belong.' She smiled. 'And here I've got you. And I love you, mister. You're the only really honest person I've met. And you're the only man who's ever actually listened to what I say.'

She slid her warm arms around his neck and kissed him avidly, her young body pressed to his.

It seemed a long time and a long way from those sleazy rooms in Amsterdam. The blue pills to fight off the depression, the temptation to call it a day in the dark, cold waters of the Amstel river.

CHAPTER TWO

He had recognized the face as soon as he saw him but he couldn't place him for several minutes. At first he assumed it was one of their distant neighbours, and then the penny dropped. His name was Logan or Cogan. Something like that. And the last time he had seen him Logan had been one of the agents on a refresher course he was instructing at Moulton House. He'd been talking to them about covert room searches without a full back-up team. Logan had asked him some questions about under-carpet pressure pads. It all seemed a long time ago but it must be only a couple of years. Maybe three.

There had been a hold up on the road from the mainland across the lake to the island. A big Dodge truck had broken down and two patrolmen were trying to sort out the shambles as impatient weekend trippers vented their frustration by revving engines and blaring horns. He had walked back down the line of cars to talk to old man Swenson, and Logan had been at the wheel of an elderly Chev saloon.

As he walked back to his own car he looked across the lake to where the orchards of South Hero were bathed in the evening sun. After nearly two years of peace he had tended to assume that either they didn't know where he was, or that they had decided to leave him alone. But they hadn't sent Logan all the way from London to Vermont just to sample the fresh apple cider and apple and pumpkin pie that South Hero was famous for. He sighed as he got back in the car.

When the long tail-back of vehicles eventually moved on he didn't turn off to the cabin road but went on past South Hero, through Keeler Bay and on up to Grand Isle. The dark blue Chevy followed about a quarter of a mile behind. Rennie drove fast into the next corner and turned sharp left to the Lovell's barn, cut the engine and looked in the driving mirror. The SIS man drove past, staring ahead, but Rennie waited until it was dark before he turned back down the road to South Hero and the farmstead.

There were 62 typed pages in the cardboard box-file. He had written it all out by hand and then typed it himself on the second-hand Olivetti Lettera. The writing had taken him four days and three nights. It was checking the dates that took the time. And the typing had taken a week.

On the outskirts of Winooski he slowed down at the long row of single-storey shops and offices, and then he saw what he was looking for. The hand-painted sign said, 'DIY Xeroxing 10¢ a sheet'. He pulled in and stopped the car. The old man who owned the general store offered to let his daughter do the copying but Rennie thanked him and did it himself. It took him until well past lunch-time before the seven sets of copies were done. He bought stout brown envelopes and put a set in each and sealed them from a roll of Scotch tape, crossing the length and breadth of each envelope three times.

He drove to the next public phone. What he wanted was a young attorney who'd be eager for the business and wouldn't want to ask a lot of questions. He called the operator and gave the story of trying to trace this newly qualified lawyer from Yale or Harvard, he couldn't remember which. The operator didn't know the background details of any lawyers but from the new subscribers' list she gave him the phone numbers and addresses of the two newest attorneys in Winooski.

He chose the nearest. A Howard Bernstein, whose place was over a dry-cleaning store. An elderly secretary announced his arrival and he was shown in straightaway to the inner office.

Bernstein looked about thirty, soberly dressed in a dark grey suit and a dark red tie, but his face was the face of a shrewd and eager operator. The rows of law-books behind him looked brand-new as he waved Rennie to the comfortable leather chair in front of his desk.

'What can I do for you Mr . . . ?'

'Novaks. Paul Novaks. I just want to put some documents into safe-keeping.'

Bernstein smiled. 'Wouldn't a safe-box at one of the banks be cheaper, Mr Novaks?'

'Well there's a possibility that there could be a question of forwarding the documents to certain people if . . . if it became necessary.'

'Are those the documents? The ones you've got there?'

'Yes. They're already addressed to various organizations. You'd just have to post them if you were asked to.'

'Sounds simple enough. How long are you likely to want them kept here?'

'Indefinitely.'

'And you would pay periodically, I take it?'

'No. I'd like to make a once-and-for-all payment. I'd got in mind two thousand dollars.'

Bernstein tried not to look surprised. 'Why did you come to me, Mr Novaks?'

'Somebody recommended you.'

Bernstein's face showed some disbelief. 'Who was that?'

'I don't remember.'

'I see. Well I don't see any problem. I'll give you a receipt for the documents and a receipt for the money.'

Bernstein held out his hand and Rennie put all but two of the packets on his desk. Bernstein glanced at the address of the top one. It just said, 'The Editor, The Washington Post, 1150, 15th St NW, Washington DC.' Bernstein glanced briefly back at Rennie, then pulled over his pad and picked up a pen.

Rennie said, 'I don't need a receipt for the documents nor for the fee. I'll be paying cash.'

Bernstein shrugged and watched as Rennie counted out twenty used hundred-dollar bills. He made no attempt to count them himself but said, 'You'd be calling for the documents personally when you want them?'

'No. It probably wouldn't be me. It would be a girl who'd come for them. Or maybe she'd just phone you.'

'I see. Could I have the lady's name?'

'She'd just give you a message. Only she would know the message so there'd be no doubt she was the right person.'

Bernstein picked up his pen. 'I'd better take the message down and put it with the documents.'

'No. I don't want that. It's just a simple message. I'd like you to remember it.'

'What is it?'

'She'll say she wants the documents sent off, and when you ask her to identify herself she'll say, "Should old acquaintance be forgot and never brought to mind".'

Bernstein looked at Rennie's face. 'What if something happens to me?' he said quietly. 'I could get knocked over by a car.'

'I'll take the risk, Mr Bernstein.'

Bernstein was aware of the fact that his client had not expressed any hope that he might not be hit by a car and as he looked at his visitor's face he realized that what had at first sight seemed soft, brown, spaniel's eyes were, in fact, hard and strangely compelling. For a moment he hesitated and then he said, 'D'you live around these parts, Mr Novaks?'

'I'm just visiting. Passing through.' And Rennie stood up, proffering his hand to the lawyer. Bernstein's hand was dry and his grip strong and Rennie felt confident that the young man would carry out conscientiously the instructions he had given him.

Rennie drove down to Burlington and booked a seat on the Delta evening flight to Washington.

Rennie stood looking out at the lights and bustle of the city from the window of the hotel bedroom. He hated being away from the peace of the small farm. And he hated being away from her. But he knew it had to be done. The loneliness was the price of the insurance policy. But being alone in a hotel bedroom reminded him of what it used to be like. In Berlin and Paris, Hamburg and Bangkok, Beirut and Tel Aviv, Brazil and Addis Ababa. And Amsterdam of course. A week or two planning, moving from one hotel to another, then a few hours aimlessly hanging about until it was time to do whatever had to be done. Checking watches, a last look at a street map and instinctively reaching to touch the pistol in the holster under his left arm. The pistol that was now wrapped in oily rags and a plastic bag under the straw and floorboards of one of the poultry arks. It had 'Smith and Wesson' engraved on its barrel. Model 39-2. But it was a long way from its original specification. Three hundred pounds' worth of mods that had made it a killer's weapon and the Guttersnipe sight that made its accuracy almost incredible for a hand-gun.

There were crumpled pages of notepaper in the wastepaper basket by the small table and he turned from the window and walked back to the chair and sat down as he switched on the bedside lamp. The brief note to the ambassador asking him to forward the packet in the diplomatic bag was already done and sealed in its envelope. It was the letter to Paynter that was the problem. Rennie wasn't a natural letter-writer and he was uncertain about what he should say. He was torn between anger and the need to make it work. He tried to imagine Paynter's reaction as he sat in his office and read the letter and then his detailed documentation of every 'dirty-tricks' operation that he had carried out personally for SIS. It was almost another hour before he started writing the note for the last time.

TO: G.S.PAYNTER. DEP. DIR. SPECIAL SERVICES
FROM: J.H. RENNIE.
Enclosed is a copy of the material that will be sent to the media by third parties if there should be any harassment of any kind of myself or the girl. J.H.R.

He read it through a dozen times, tempted to add to the threat or express his anger at what they had done to his life. But he had been in the business a long time and he knew it was enough.

CHAPTER THREE

He stood listening in the silence of the woods. And as he waited, the woods came slowly back to life. Two wood-pigeons cooing softly, the flutter of wings in the tops of the trees, and far away in the distance the faint sound of a dog barking. Then he could hear it, the cracking of dry twigs and branches as Hartmann headed towards him, running away from Williams who was probably more scared than Hartmann himself. But not so scared he wouldn't carry out his orders. Williams had taken a double-first at St Anthony's. Russian and German. But he had been hopeless at even the mildest rough stuff so they'd put him behind a desk to evaluate documents in peace and quiet.

But Attwood in Hamburg had gone down with his annual dose of amoebic dysentery and Williams had been sent out to help him with Hartmann. He had been quite good on the planning and analysis but when, inevitably, it had come to putting on the pressure Williams couldn't take it.

Rennie could hear Hartmann's heavy breathing as the German clambered over fallen tree trunks, weeping in desperation as he cursed the thorns that snatched at his clothes. He could see him now, looking at the ground, stumbling as he ran, no thought of looking to see if there was anyone else but Williams. He let him almost pass the tree and then reached out, confidently and efficiently, and one strong arm locked round Hartmann's fat neck from behind. Hartmann tried to scream but no sound came from his lips as the hard wrist jerked back against his throat. There was always a temptation to say something before you did it. Explain why it was happening. That they hadn't got away with it. But it wasn't professional. When it had gone that far there was no point in underlining whatever mistake they had made. No point in sermonizing.

As Hartmann's large plump body wriggled in the grip of Rennie's right arm. Rennie's left arm came up, the hand gently cupping the German's chin to measure the distance. Then the thumb slid up, along the angle of the jaw to the nerve behind the ear, the folds of flabby flesh parting reluctantly until he could feel the apex of the bone. His shoulders shook with the effort as his thumb pressed against the nerve and he staggered back a step under the weight of Hartmann's unconscious body. Then Hartmann's body seemed to ripple, every muscle moving involuntarily, and there was the stench as his bowels voided noisily.

As he lowered Hartmann's body to the wet leaves Williams arrived, panting, the gun in his hand, staring down at Hartmann's corpse before he looked up at Rennie's face.

'Is he dead?'

'Of course he's dead.'

'How did it happen?'

Rennie said softly, 'It didn't *happen*, Roger. I *did* it.'

'What are we going to do with him?'

'We'll leave him here.'

'But he could lie here for days before somebody finds him.'

'So what. He's dead and that's all that matters.'

Williams shook his head slowly. 'I've never understood you, Johnny. None of you people. How the hell do you sleep at nights?'

'Go through his clothes and see if there's anything you want for the office.'

For ten minutes Williams gingerly slid his hand into various pockets and checked the contents. Then he stood up, holding out Hartmann's wallet.

'D'you want this?'

'Why should I?'

'There's nearly three thousand D-marks in it.'

'I don't steal from dead bodies, Roger. Put it back where it came from . . . and if there's nothing you want then we'd better get moving. Back to the car.'

They were sitting in the flat in Grosse Bleicher, the curtains flapping slowly at the open window in the soft summer breeze that came off the Binnen Alster. The noise of the traffic just audible.

Williams looked at Rennie's face and said, 'Don't you ever get sick of it . . . all the violence?'

'It isn't all violence. In fact, there's very little violence.'

'But all the messing about. Finding out how to pressure them. Trying to find out if they screw young boys, or underaged girls, all the perversions. The filth that people get up to.'

Rennie shrugged. 'It isn't always that sort of thing. That's just your nasty mind. Some of them are selling things they shouldn't be selling. Sophisticated missiles to crazy governments. Like Gadaffi, for instance. Forging documents so that a Red Brigade loony can assassinate some country's Foreign Minister just for a few paragraphs in the world's press. Or the IRA shooting fathers in front of their wives and kids. Why do you always have to let your heart bleed for the villains?'

'Is that what they tell you when they're training you?'

'I didn't need telling. It's my country I'm protecting. A damn good country. The best in the world in my opinion. You don't keep your freedom if you won't fight for it. Every minute of every hour there's a dozen bastards planning to bring us down. To hand us over to foreigners of some kind or another.'

'Is it really that black and white? Hartmann for instance.'

'My God, Roger. How can you say that? Franz Ludwig Hartmann was a Nazi. Right from the start. Not when you had to be a Nazi to keep your job, but in 1933. He bought out Jewish businesses for a song. Took their heirlooms in return for documents that were supposed to get them to the USA. Except that most of them ended up in Dachau or Belsen or some other bloody camp.

'When the war ends he's a rich man. He bribes all and sundry to hide his identity. Moves up here to Hamburg. Gets elected to the Town Council, then to Bonn. Is appointed to a sensitive committee that deals with NATO secrets. The Russians trace him, blackmail him, and he passes over every document he can lay hands on that's of any importance. What did you want us to do? Tell him not to be a naughty boy?'

'But it's the Germans' business, surely. And the due process of law.'

'The Germans knew, for Christ's sake. But it would have meant one more scandal for an already shaky party. They've had enough scandals of Soviet agents in Cabinet offices. And he had friends in the right places. He'd spent tens of thousands of dollars seeing that he had friends in the right places.

'Of course they were going to deal with him. It was just a question of timing, they said. That was three months ago.'

'But they'll know we did it.'

'Of course they will. And they'll be delighted that we've got rid of the problem for them. They've got plenty more problems where he came from and they'd be only too glad for us to solve them the same way.'

'Were you recruited straight into SIS?'

'No, I read law, practised for a year, and then I did four years in the army. SAS.'

'It doesn't worry you, the dirty tricks?'

'I'm not employed to worry, my friend. I've got every faith in the people above me who decide these things. Whatever they give me to do, I do. You can't have a discussion group about democracy and fair play every five minutes when you're dealing with bastards like Hartmann.'

'And due process of law? That doesn't count for anything?'

Rennie smiled. 'Some High Court judge once said that the judges were there not to administer justice but to administer the law. Why should we go through all that humbug when we know what they've done and what they deserve?'

'You think that the law is humbug?'

'In these sorts of things, yes. Just expensive barristers running up the bills. A hundred thousand quid of the public's money to try and prove that a well-known terrorist really is a terrorist. It would be laughable if it wasn't so serious.'

'You never have any doubts?'

Rennie shook his head slowly. 'Never. Why should I? The people who give me my assignments are responsible for the security of the country. If they say that's what is needed, I do it. To the very best of my ability.'

'You'd carry out any order they gave you?'

'Of course.'

'Say they're wrong sometime and some innocent guy ends up floating in the canal face down?'

'That's not for me to decide. I can't know everything they know.'

'So even if you knew the guy was innocent you'd knock him off?'

'If those were my orders, yes. They don't go after innocent men. Why the hell should they?'

'Maybe he's innocent but they just don't like him. Or maybe they're mistaken.'

'Too bad.'

'D'you sleep at nights OK?'

'Like a log.'

'They must love you, Johnny.'

'They respect me and I respect them. Loyalty counts for a lot. Chaps like you are always full of doubts. Never sort yourselves out. You should remember what Cromwell told his men.'

'What was that?'

'Know what you fight for, and love what you know.'

'Sounds ghastly. When are you going back to London?'

'Have you got a Canadian passport I can use?'

'United States do?'

'OK. In that case I'll go tomorrow.'

'D'you fancy a night out with a couple of pretty girls?'

'No thanks.'

'You still carrying a torch for Mary?'

'No way.' Rennie shook his head vigorously.

'Let's go eat at the Four Seasons.'

'OK.'

CHAPTER FOUR

Bora Glen village lies between what the locals call The Gowls and Big Torr, the two massive hills whose valley points towards the Forth estuary. The village streets have been cobbled since the 1660s and the architecture of even its humbler homes was decided by the local orange-tinted stone and the Dutch tiles that came over to the Fife harbours on boats from the Low Countries.

The Rennies' house was at the northern end of the village where the road led to the awe-inspiring gorge formed by the rift in the Ochil Hills. It had always been known as the Little Manse although it had never housed a minister when James Rennie moved in with his new bride. The deep and misshapen scar on James Rennie's left cheek was a permanent reminder of the last months of World War I. On his release from hospital the shortage of trained teachers had led to his appointment as headmaster of the village school. He was almost forty when he married the much younger girl who bore him their only child, a son. The school provided both primary and secondary education for nearly two hundred children from the villages that were scattered along the valley and the hills. Not even the rose-pink spectacles of nostalgia had ever persuaded an alumnus to admit to a moment's pleasure in his time at the school. But their successes at the university in Edinburgh and in their future lives had made a reputation for the ex-captain headmaster. Four rugby caps for Scotland, a bishop, a raft of cabinet ministers; city money-men gladly sent cheques when the school appealed for funds; but they never went back.

John Hamish Rennie had been afraid of his father until he was eight years old. Physically and mentally afraid. The sight of his father's tall, gaunt frame approaching could bring him near to fainting. He was aware that his father despised his spindly weak body and his ineptitude at both learning and games. He spoke only when spoken to but that was not unusual in those parts.

It all changed with the chickens. His father kept a dozen Rhode Island Reds in a shed in the back-garden and on a Friday evening in the summer before his ninth birthday he had been picking flowers for his mother when his father called him over. He was inside the chicken shed.

His father said, without turning to look at him, 'Hold the door open, laddie, and give me some light.'

As he held the door his father stooped and grabbed a hen's legs, its wings flapping as he tucked it under his arm. Two big hands twisted in opposite directions on the chicken's neck and held it until the twitching body was still. His father turned and held out the dead hen. 'Take it to your mother, boy. Tell her I'll pluck it later.' He held the boy's arm and looked at his pale face as he shrank back. 'Ye're no' frightened of a dead hen, are ye, lad?'

'Yes, father.'

The man looked intently at the boy's face and then said quietly. 'Come straight back here when ye've handed over the bird.'

'Yes, father.'

When the boy returned his father had another hen tucked under his arm. He pointed at its neck.

'Take hold of its neck with both hands.'

And as the boy's hands closed round the thin warm neck his father said, 'Go on. Wring its neck. Twist like I did. Hard.'

The bird squawked and shrieked and struggled under the man's arm. Then its neck went limp. As the boy stood there he looked up at his father's face. His father was smiling and he said softly, 'Well done, laddie. Take it to the kitchen then I want to see you in my study. Wash your hands first.'

His father had lit the old oil-lamp in his study and he sat in the big oak upright chair alongside the circular mahogany table. He beckoned the boy over and he stood in front of the man.

'What do you think of ma face, laddie? Here.' And he pointed at the massive scar.

'I'm sorry about it, sir.'

'You know how I got it?'

'In the Great War, sir. A piece of a shell.'

'Ugly isn't it?'

The boy stood silent.

His father said softly, 'I'm proud of that scar, laddie. Look at the wee box on the table.'

The boy reached out for the small leather box and his father said, 'Go on. Open it.'

The boy looked at the mauve stripe on the white ribbon and the metal cross with a crown on each spur. He looked back at his father's face.

'Do you know what it is?'

'It's a medal, sir.'

'It's a Military Cross and that's why I'm proud of my ugly face. The King himself gave it to me. At Buckingham Palace. Your mother was with me. D'you know why I'm showing it to you today?'

'No, sir.'

'Because when I asked you if you were scared of a dead hen you told me the truth. And because you wrung the chicken's neck when I told you. You *were* scared, weren't you?'

'Yes, sir.'

'But you're not scared to do it again, are you?'

'No, sir.'

'Would you do it again if I told you to right now?'

The boy nodded. 'I would, sir.'

The man pointed at the medal in its case. 'Take it. It's yours now. And don't ever be scared again. Not of any thing nor any man. You understand?'

The boy nodded and his father reached out and handed him the medal and its case. As the boy turned to go the man said sharply, 'Boy.' And the boy turned. His father was smiling with the only side of his face that was capable of responding. He said softly, 'I'm proud of you, boy. Not that you killed the chicken but that you killed your own fear.'

Johnny Rennie gathered up just enough credits to get a university place. He took his Law finals twice and just passed on the second attempt. He got a half-blue for boxing and had a trial for the Scottish fifteen. He had two years with a firm of Edinburgh solicitors and was moderately successful but totally bored by what he saw as the fiddling detail of the law. It took too long to do so little and he felt it was on the side of the criminal rather than the victim. At the end of the two years he resigned from the practice and applied for a commission in the SAS.

But a commission in SAS has to be earned not applied for, and he reported at the depôt in Hereford as a private after three months' basic infantry training with the Black Watch. His toughness and tenacity were noted during his training and he was accepted as a sergeant at the end of the course. He was commissioned at the end of two years. His indifference to pain and his unquestioning loyalty and respect for his superiors were noted but there were some who worried that his attitude and personality bordered on the psychopathic. But the SAS psychologists found him normal enough and that was the end of the doubts.

When an unofficial request came through from the Ministry of Defence for an officer with certain qualifications that were not put in writing he had been offered the transfer to the Foreign Office and SIS. He had been interviewed by a number of people – long, testing interviews – and then he was re-trained and inducted into the service. Again there were doubts by some of his new masters but his unquestioning loyalty and courage gradually persuaded most of them that their fears were unfounded. SIS was more used to men who argued and debated than men who unquestioningly did what they were asked to do; and doubts or not, John Rennie was respected and highly valued by his immediate superiors.

CHAPTER FIVE

The wrought-iron gate squealed on its hinges as Rennie went up the short garden path to the porch of what had once been his home, a Victorian semi in one of the leafy but dusty Chiswick streets beyond the tube station.

He pressed the bell and then stood back as if he were some door-to-door salesman trained to stand back to avoid looking aggressive.

She was wearing a bright red sweater and a black skirt that he hadn't seen before.

'You're early,' she said.

'On the dot actually, my dear. And how are you keeping?'

She ignored the question and stood aside so that he could enter the hallway. He stood there respectfully as she closed the front door and brushed past him, leading the way to the front living room.

He waited until she sat before sitting down himself. He wondered if it was accidental or something to do with Women's Lib that she chose to sit in 'his' old chair.

'How are the girls?'

'They're fine. They break up on Thursday. Their reports are on the table for you to see.'

'How have they done?'

She shrugged. 'Not bad. You may think otherwise.'

'Have you heard from Cowley?'

He saw her mouth go thin and pursed before she spoke.

'That's hardly your business now, Johnny. We *are* divorced if you remember.'

She was conscious of his brown eyes on her face. Those brown eyes that had always seemed to know what was going on in her mind. Except for that one solitary episode.

'You deserved better than him, my dear. He's a rascal.'

The old-fashioned word stuck in her mind. Cowley was a shit. A charming shit. Rascals belonged in Thomas Hardy novels. But it was typical of her ex-husband's vocabulary. She had wondered sometimes when it had happened if he wouldn't challenge Cowley to a duel. Pistols at dawn on Chiswick Common.

'Would you like a cup of tea?'

'Yes. I think I would. Very kind of you to offer.'

He sat reading the girls' school reports until she came back with a tray. As she put it down beside him he noticed that there was just one cup and a plate of biscuits.

He looked up at her. 'Elizabeth seems to be doing all right but young Mary seems to be resting on her laurels.'

'She's been a bit out of sorts recently. She'll make it up before long.'

'Out of sorts? What does that mean?'

She brushed a strand of blonde hair from her cheek as she looked at him. 'She's very fond of you. Johnny. They both are. But Mary's taken it all a bit to heart. She'll get over it. But it takes time.'

He stood up. And she knew that she had annoyed him. He didn't say so but she knew that for him she was the cause of any disturbance or unhappiness.

'I'd better be off,' he said brusquely. 'I'll call for them on Saturday at ten if that's agreeable to you. I'll have a little talk with Mary then.'

'You haven't had your tea.'

'See you on Saturday. I can see myself out.'

As Mary Rennie sat sewing buttons on to school dresses, glancing from time to time at the Wimbledon highlights, she wondered what kind of woman could have done better with John Hamish Rennie than she had done. Twelve years of marriage. Two of them in army married quarters. No great ups and downs. Not particularly boring. No problems of health or money. A straightforward, honest man who took his responsibilities seriously. Who was protective to her and the girls. Polite to the point of punctiliousness. An opener of car doors. Decisive and self-confident, an ideal husband. All her friends said so, and there was no doubt that some of them envied her the quite handsome man who had put her on a pedestal.

She would never understand why she had got involved with Guy Cowley. He wasn't even her kind of man. And on reflection it wasn't even vaguely romantic. Sometimes she was almost ready to admit that it was nothing more than boredom with a husband who gave her no cause for complaint. But to admit that openly would cost her dignity. It was the behaviour of a wilful schoolgirl, not an adult woman.

Cowley had chatted her up in the supermarket. Carrying the heavy cardboard box with her groceries back to her car. Admiring her hair and her clothes, smiling that smooth, charming smile with the dimples and the cleft in the chin. He'd been there the next week, all too obviously waiting for her, laughing and unabashed when she had accused him. He had taken her for a mid-morning coffee at the White Hart. Somehow he had found out her name and where she lived and when he had phoned ten days later she had been too flustered just to hang up. He had invited himself round for a coffee. He had chatted amiably with the standard lacing of compliments and that had been all.

But gradually she came to look forward to the Friday encounters at Sainsbury's, and the coffee at the hotel. It was like meeting an old friend. She had kidded herself that it was romantic. A kind of rerun of *Brief Encounter*. But she had said nothing to her husband of the meetings and when Cowley had asked her if she had told her husband and she had said no she realized from the smile on his face that in that moment they had become fellow-conspirators. And he knew that too.

She knew that she was flattered by his interest, and by the end of three months of meetings it had seemed both inevitable and exciting when she had gone to his rooms by the bank one Friday morning. And half an hour later she was aware of a sense of pleasurable defiance of her husband as she lay naked on the bed with Cowley. Afterwards he had talked vaguely of divorce and marriage and that had brought her down to earth. The thought of being with him permanently suddenly revolted her, and the thought of him with her two children seemed outrageous. She had never been back to Sainsbury's even now that she was divorced.

She had felt only a moment's surprise when her husband had confronted her.

There are people whose mistakes and sins, no matter how small, are always inevitably exposed, and she was one of those people.

For the first time in her life she had realized why her husband was so successful in his job. No anger, no abuse, just the continual calm probing. After her admission of the facts, the questions about motive. Why had she done it? Why that particular man? What were his attractions? Did she love the man? Did he love her? Was he going to stand by her once they were divorced? Her answers had been negative, and pathetic enough to have perhaps moved most other men. She told him that she had no complaints. No discontents. It had been an accident. A slow-motion nightmare like those TV action-replays of missed goals. She had always been aware of his almost ruthless attitude to the outside world, but with her and the girls he had always been different. Kind and considerate. But it was obvious that for him she was now part of that outside world and was to be treated accordingly.

He hadn't asked her if she wanted a divorce. For him it just flowed as a natural and automatic outcome of that single act of infidelity. He had expressed no sympathy for her, nor indignation or disappointment on his part. It was no more emotional than the ending of a business partnership, and strangely enough she had been carried along, even sustained, by that impersonal approach.

There had been no quarrel about financial things. The house remained his property but she was given a lifetime's lease at a peppercorn rent, and half his earnings went for her upkeep and that of the girls. He showed no embarrassment when he visited the house to pick up or deliver the girls and expressed no nostalgia or regret for old times.

And strangely enough the lack of emotion seemed to work out quite well with the two girls. It was almost as if he had not really ceased to be their father and her husband, but was merely away for even longer than in the days when they were married. He seemed to exert an influence on them all even when he wasn't there.

Just once, before the divorce finally went through, she had tentatively questioned his attitude. Was it really necessary for them to part? They could be at arm's length and uncommitted, but together for the girl's sake. It had been like arguing with a mathematician about the validity of the square on the hypotenuse. A vow had been made and the vow had been broken. With this particular kind of vow its breaching meant divorce. That was the law so far as Rennie was concerned. A simple straightforward formula. To question its inevitability was as pointless as trying to swim up Niagara Falls.

What seemed strange to her was that none of them appeared to have suffered unduly. His rigid attitude seemed to her to expunge her guilt, and life went on much as usual for all of them. She had asked him once if he ever thought of marrying again and it was obvious from his reactions that the thought had never entered his mind. Not that the answer was no, but just that he had never actually thought about it. He had frowned, shaken his head dismissively, and continued talking about the estimates for fixing the guttering on the conservatory.

She thought of him quite often and the image was always the same one. The rather handsome young man standing to attention in his best barathea uniform and polished Sam Browne, pale-blue parachute wings over the pocket. For her he always seemed to be standing to attention in uniform, even when he was wearing a sports jacket and slacks.

CHAPTER SIX

There was a portrait of Disraeli on the panelled wall behind the long mahogany table, and through the half-windows came the faint sounds of one of the Guards' regiments on their way to the Mall. The yelps of warrant officers' commands and the thud of the bass drum and the strains of 'Highland Laddie'.

The two men sat opposite each other at one end of the table. Fredericks in a black jacket and pin-stripes despite the heat, and Paynter in a light-weight two-piece. Fredericks had one of those pseudo-tired voices, the words precisely chosen but their definition diffused by the affected drawl. Despite the impression of casualness his eyes were alert and constantly observant. His manner he saw as a form of disguise. The casual drawl could give the impression that it represented what went on in that well-trained mind. It wasn't wise to let casual observers know one's real thoughts. It came to him naturally but had been refined by the daily contact with his Foreign Office colleagues. Fredericks was Foreign Office–SIS liaison, and Paynter was SIS, responsible for operations that were tactfully described as 'not conveniently fitting into the standard departmental hierarchy'. They had known one another for years and had been contemporaries at Oxford, Fredericks at Balliol and Paynter at St Anthony's. Normally when they met the atmosphere was civilized and relaxed but this day they were both subdued. It was Fredericks who broke the long silence.

'Have SDECE been cooperating?'

'It's hard to tell, Freddie. They haven't *done* anything but I don't think that's their fault. There's just nothing to go on. Except for the woman who thinks she saw him wave down a taxi nobody saw a thing.'

'Is there any significance in the fact that they called *Le Figaro* rather than *Le Monde*?'

'No. We're not even sure that they didn't call *Le Monde*. We daren't ask or it might come out in public.'

'And all they said was what?'

'"We've got Mason", and they gave the number on his ID card.'

'And it was said in French?'

'Yes. The voice analysis said there were Turkish overtones, whatever that means.'

Fredericks sighed. 'If somebody has lifted him what does he know?'

'The usual mixed bag of operations. He's been on all sorts of things over the last five years. It depends on who's got him as to what he could give them that could be useful.'

'What was he actually doing in Paris?'

'Trying to patch things up with his wife. She'd started divorce proceedings against him.'

'On what grounds?'

'Incompatibility. Irretrievable breakdown of the marriage. Nothing spectacular.'

'Has anybody interviewed her?'

'No. We don't think she even knows he's not around. He wasn't staying with her, he'd taken a room for a couple of weeks.'

'Has his room been searched thoroughly?'

'No. We just asked the French for it to be sealed and that's what they've done. We didn't want to look too concerned.'

'Will the French keep it quiet?'

'I think they will. I asked my opposite number to put the lid on it. He was very cooperative. They don't like this sort of thing. They're not recognizing officially that he's even a missing person.'

'Have you talked to the Turkish desk?'

'Yes. But without more information they can't help us. There are hundreds of dissident groups in Turkey. Could be any one of them. I don't want to go down that route until there's some real reason to.' He paused. 'Are the FO getting the wind-up?'

Fredericks shrugged. 'I'd say touchy rather than windy. But they're pros. They're used to the ups and downs.'

'Where will you be tonight?'

'At the Travellers until about seven and then at home.'

'Town or country home?'

Fredericks half-smiled. 'Town. Keep in touch no matter how little there is. If he's been lifted we'll hear from them before long. You'd better check whether we've got any political Turks in jail.'

'We have. Seven of the bastards. They're in the Scrubs. The governor would love to see the back of them.'

Fredericks looked across at Paynter. 'Do you ever get tired of all this, Hugo?'

'Of what, exactly?'

'The contrast. The smooth diplomats on the surface and the violence underneath it all.'

Paynter smiled. 'I sometimes wish I was a diplomat instead of what I am.'

'D'you think the public has any idea of what goes on in their name?'

'I don't imagine they think about it for a moment. They've got their mortgages to worry about.' He smiled. 'And the greenfly on the roses. Their kids' education and next year's holiday on the Algarve.'

Fredericks nodded. 'Sometimes when Angie is giving one of our routine dinner parties at the flat I look at them. Ambassadors and First Secretaries, MPs and visiting Senators and minor dictators, and I'm terribly tempted to say out loud what their governments are really doing. Financing dissidents to stir up trouble, training and arming assassins to murder some politician of a rival party or an unfriendly country. Infiltration to destabilize a whole country. And for what? A few years of power or money in a Swiss bank account. Tens, maybe hundreds of thousands of their countrymen killed or starving in some banana republic.

'And they sit there, Hugo, as smooth as they come. Babbling away about some resolution in the UN, how much they've just paid for half a dozen new suits, whether their wives or mistresses prefer Madame Rochas to Chanel Number Five and complaining that their illegally parked cars are towed away by the police. And all the time their minds are really on whether they should fund the IRA or the PLO or the latest group of Islamic lunatics. It doesn't seem credible. They're such bloody hypocrites. All of them. Us included.'

'Maybe you should come back into SIS, Freddie. There's no hypocrisy for us. We do the dirty deeds and that's the end of it. No philosophizing.'

Fredericks looked towards the windows and sighed. 'Sometimes I'd like to leave it all and be a monk. In some silent order preferably.'

Paynter laughed softly and stood up. 'You'd always be arguing with the abbot. You need a holiday, Freddie. That's all that's the matter with you.'

There was no further information from Paris that night and Fredericks and Paynter met again in Fredericks's office at ten the following morning. Fredericks stood at the window and Paynter was aware of the handsome profile backlit from the sunshine outside. It was a Saturday and Fredericks had relaxed from the pin-stripes to a tweed suit. He looked every inch the actor that he had once aimed to be. For several minutes he was silent and then turned to look at Paynter.

'The Minister has been told. Wanted to know what SIS were doing about it. I told him there was nothing to go on. That it might even be a hoax. Suggested very, very diplomatically that the embassy could keep a watching brief on it.' Fredericks sighed. 'That caused an immediate eruption, and Carter was told to signal the ambassador and ensure that they showed no interest.

'I weaseled a bit and said that I only meant that the SIS staff at the embassy could nose around a little and that earned me a tirade about the shortcomings of SIS and the countless embarrassments that they caused to our embassies everywhere.' Fredericks shrugged and sighed. 'Why don't you send somebody over from here? Make it a sort of free-lance assignment. Never contacts the embassy and plays it very low-key.'

'I've already told someone to stand by.'

'Who?' Fredericks swung round to look at Paynter.

'John Rennie.'

Fredericks pursed his lips. 'Isn't there anybody else?'

'Not who's suitable. You've never given Rennie his due. Why don't you?'

'God knows. I can't put my finger on it . . .'

'There must be something.'

'He's such a zombie, Hugo.'

'What's that mean in Foreign Office semantics these days?'

'Inflexible. Unimaginative. And a thug.'

Paynter smiled wryly. 'For inflexible read patriotic, for unimaginative read loyal, and for thug . . .' He shrugged. 'Well, it's thugs he has to deal with most of the time. We don't intend sending lambs to the slaughter if that's what you want.'

'But he's so right-wing you could justifiably say that he's a Fascist.'

Paynter laughed. 'Nonsense. Rennie isn't the slightest bit interested in any kind of politics. Not even vaguely . . .' He paused. 'We've all sworn and signed to protect Queen and Country from their enemies . . . the only thing you don't like about him is that unlike the rest of us he actually means it. Every word of it. No dodging. No interpreting. The Queen's commission and all that.'

'But he's so bloody naïve.'

'He's not, actually. He's just loyal. Maybe a bit too black and white in his judgements but he's utterly dependable. And that's more than you can say for some of your Foreign Office friends.'

'Oh God. Don't let's go over Burgess and Maclean and all that *galère* again.'

'I don't mean them. I mean some of your contemporaries. Very sophisticated.

Very intellectual. And I wouldn't trust them an inch.'

Fredericks smiled and said quietly, 'You're right of course. We're just swapping prejudices. I guess what I'm looking for doesn't exist.'

Paynter shrugged. 'If they've got complex, searching minds they'll never be totally committed. Rennie's a bit Beau Geste and the Union Jack and all that, but he knows what he's doing and he does it well. Don't let's beat him over the head with his virtues. We need 'em. I wish I'd got more like him. I'd sleep a lot better of nights.'

'I ought not to comment. It's not my business.' Fredericks half-smiled. 'What a funny world. I'm getting more stick-in-the-mud every day. When did it all start getting out of hand? It used not to be like this.'

'I think it started when they killed Jack Kennedy. It was like some kind of signal that if that was possible then anything was possible. It was a sort of bench-mark.'

Fredericks nodded. 'As Antony said, "Cry 'Havoc!' and let slip the dogs of war".' He paused and grimaced. 'Let's have a drink. What do you want, Glenlivet or Jamieson Ten Year Old?'

'Jamieson's, but no water or soda, thanks.'

CHAPTER SEVEN

Paynter had allocated Rennie an office, and after his briefing, Rennie sat at the small table reading Mason's file, his sports jacket draped over the back of the issue chair, his shirt sleeves rolled up.

Most SIS field agents would have complained at being assigned to such a wild-goose chase, but Rennie took it as a compliment to his abilities. And in a way it was.

Mason was 42, married to a French girl of 26. He had been on assignments in Hong Kong, Brazil, Sydney, Johannesburg, and Addis Ababa in the last five years. He had not been to Turkey either on duty or holiday and the only Arab country he had been to was a brief three-day visit to Cairo eight years ago. And that was only for a routine check on the embassy security system.

The brief notes on Mason's marital troubles he found interesting. Mason didn't speak good French and when he was away his young wife paid visits to Paris and had been seen with several different men in nightclubs and discos. Mason had not been officially told that his wife was under surveillance but somebody had obviously tipped him off. There was an unsubstantiated suggestion that he had reacted violently. Then there had been a series of reconciliations and more quarrels. The girl had no criminal or subversive connections and it looked as if her behaviour was a mixture of genuine loneliness and an incipient promiscuity. She had started the divorce action in London as that was their technical domicile and she was now a British subject, which she apparently resented.

Rennie found it difficult to understand how a man could want to be reconciled with a woman who behaved like that. Why did he wait for her to divorce him? Why didn't he just walk right out and divorce her? They had made a mutual promise, a contract even, and the woman had broken the contract. What use was that kind of woman to a man?

He knew Harry Mason reasonably well. He had great charm and some of his work had been brilliant. But there must be a flaw in his character somewhere. Maybe it was that flaw that had got him into this mess. And it may be that the mess was part of his private life and nothing to do with his SIS work. But in that case why the cryptic telephone call to the French newspaper? And why did they quote his field identity number?

Rennie closed the file and spoke to Paynter's secretary on the internal phone. Paynter could see him right away.

Paynter finished talking and put down the phone and looked questioningly at Rennie.

'I've read the file, Hugo.'

'What did you think of it?'

'It's either something connected with his private life or it's something bigger than it looks.'

'Well, whichever it is we've got to find him. Are you planning to go over to Paris?'

'I don't think it will do much good but I planned to go tomorrow if you can lay on funds, tickets and facilities in time.'

'I'll tell Harris to get you whatever you want.' Paynter stood up to end the interview. 'Keep me in touch.'

'I'll be taking a transceiver and I'll leave a schedule with Signals so you can contact me too.'

'Take care.'

Rennie smiled as he left, but said nothing.

The SDECE man helped him carry his kit up the creaking wooden stairs, and on the top landing Rennie waited as the Frenchman broke the official seal and unlocked the heavy padlock that had been temporarily fixed to the door. Almost ceremoniously he handed Rennie the normal door-key as if it absolved him from any further involvement in the British problem. Rennie invited him inside but the Frenchman pleaded urgent work waiting for him back at his office.

It was one large room and the air was stale and still. There was a divan against the wall in the far corner. An old-fashioned wardrobe, a chest of drawers, a table with a plastic top and two tubular chairs. Facing the door was a curtain on a curved rail that marked off the kitchen which consisted of a small, chipped enamel sink, a draining-board and a box turned on its end that had a few cloths and bottles on its centre shelf. Two empty jam jars held a small clutter of cutlery and on the shelves of a crudely-made, open, triangular, corner-cupboard there were a few packets and tins and a cheap combined tin- and bottle-opener.

Rennie unpacked one of his bags and took out the leather case that housed the transceiver. He had to reset the voltage wheel before he slid the plug into the travel convertor plug that fitted the two-pin socket by the bed. He pressed the buttons and watched as the LEDs ran through the frequencies until he found the one he wanted. He pressed the memory button and then tuned the night-time frequency and entered that in the memory too. He looked at his watch. There were five minutes to go until the scheduled time. 1300 hours GMT, plus the date in minutes, and 2300 hours GMT with the same addition.

He switched on and turned the switch to 'Receive' and the blips came through at half-volume. He turned the volume down and left the radio warming up. Its micro-circuitry needed no warming up as the older equipment did, but it was a habit that was hard to break.

London acknowledged dead on time and he tapped out his location on the built-in key. When the radio was back in its case he looked around for somewhere to conceal it. There was nowhere suitable and in the end he edged the divan away from the wall and placed the radio in the corner angle and shoved the divan back against the wall.

He knew that despite its bareness he would have to search the room, but its depressing stillness tempted him to go out first for a meal or a snack. He looked at his watch. It was twenty minutes to midnight. He was not a man to succumb to temptation.

Rennie carried out the search as if it were a demonstration of technique on an agents' course. Two hours later he looked at the small display of the fruits of his search laid out on the plastic table. One thing was certain, they gave no clues to what had happened although they were indications that Mason had actually used the room. But that had never really been in doubt. He had paid for the room in his own name, and had given the address to the SIS man based at the embassy.

There was a crumpled gold pack of Stuyvesants with two cigarettes still inside it. A parking ticket for the long-stay carpark at Heathrow. A ball-point pen that was sticky as if it had been used to stir a cup of coffee or tea. A 10p coin and two blank pages ripped from a diary for that year and the month of May.

Rennie ignored his hunger, undressed slowly and lay on the creaking divan bed. He slept soundly until seven the next morning.

Mason's room was in the 10ème in an old house in a back street near the Gare du Nord, and Rennie took a taxi to the address near the Metro station St Philippe du Roule.

There were geraniums in clay pots on the steps up to the door and the front door was open. The card under the top bell said 'Mme Mason'. He walked up to the third floor and pushed the well-polished brass bell. She looked younger than her 26 years. Blonde and pretty, and frail-looking in a pale blue peignoir embroidered with dark blue irises.

'Mrs Mason?'

'Who are you?' She spoke with only a trace of a French accent.

'I'm a colleague of your husband, Mrs Mason. Could I speak to you for a few moments?'

'There's no point. I won't change my mind. I told Harry that.'

'It's not about your domestic problems, Mrs Mason.'

'I don't understand.'

'I'm trying to contact him. I think you could help.'

For a moment she hesitated and then she opened the door wider and stood aside to let him in. The room was spacious and the furnishings elegant. Plain white walls and polished wood floors. She pointed to a comfortable armchair. 'Do sit down please.' She looked at him, curiosity in her eyes. 'What is it you want?'

'My name's Rennie, Mrs Mason, John Rennie. As I said, I'm a colleague of Harry's and I'm trying to contact him.'

'He doesn't live here,' she said quietly. 'He's got a room somewhere near the Gare du Nord.'

'Yes. I've been there but he's not there.'

'Maybe he was asleep or shopping or something.'

'When did you see him last?'

'It was nearly two weeks ago.'

'Did he seem OK?'

She sighed. 'Do you know him well?'

'I used to know him well. I haven't seen him for a couple of years.'

'He was upset because of our situation.'

'The divorce proceedings?'

'Yes.'

'How upset was he?'

She looked towards the window for a few seconds and then back at Rennie. 'He was very upset.' She paused. 'You said you were a colleague of his. Does that mean you do the same kind of work that he does?'

'Tell me what you think he does.'

'He always says he works for the Foreign Office. The English Foreign Office, but I think it is more than that.'

'In what way more?'

'I think he did secret work. Like the SDECE here in France.'

'What makes you think that?'

'He was always leaving me. Going off suddenly. Sometimes I didn't hear from him for weeks. He brought me back things from foreign places. He was away more than he was with me. And when he confronted me about going out with other men it was obvious that I had been watched very carefully. He knew so much.'

'Was he violent towards you?'

'Only the first time, and when I told him of the divorce. Then he threatened me.'

'What did he threaten you with?'

'He said he would kill me if I left him.'

'Did you believe that?'

'Half I believed it.'

'Are you scared of him?'

'Yes.' She said it calmly, as if it needed no explanation.

'Did you mention the threat to any of your men friends?' She shook her head and he knew she was lying, but he let it go.

'Would you mind telling me why you wanted a divorce?'

She shrugged. 'He put his job before me. He left me alone for weeks on end. I was lonely so I went out with other people.'

'What kind of man was your husband?'

'Maybe you know better than I do.'

'Tell me what you think.'

'He was attractive . . . and charming . . . but he didn't understand. He said I was a whore . . . he didn't understand that I was so lonely.'

'But you don't have to sleep with a man just because he takes you out.'

She shrugged. 'In Paris you do. I think in London is the same.'

'Maybe Harry was lonely too. Wishing he was with you.'

'He could have changed his job and been with me every day. He preferred his job to me.'

'In our kind of job we have no choice but to go off at a moment's notice. We can't tell our wives or friends where we are going or what we are doing. They would be put in danger if they were told. And other people's lives can depend on a quick response when it's needed. It isn't just Harry.'

'He could have got another job. He's got a degree.'

'It's not just a job, Mrs Mason. It's more a calling. A bit like a priest, I suppose.'

'Maybe. But priests don't marry.'

'Do you expect to see Harry again soon?'

'No. I told him not to come back again. And my solicitor had sent him a letter to say that he shouldn't pester me.'

'Can you remember the last thing he said to you?'

'Yes. Very well. He was standing outside the door here and he said I was a whore but he loved me. He was crying.'

'Can I ask you one more question?'

'Yes.'

'The men you went around with. Were they all Frenchmen?'

'All except one.'

'What nationality was he?'

'He was an Arab but I don't know which Arab country he came from.'

'Can you remember his name?'

'His first name was Khalim. I don't know his other name.'

'What was he like? Was he a tough sort of fellow?'

She smiled. 'No. He was charming. Very attractive. Very wealthy and he was here on a visit. Not at all tough. He was well-educated. I think he had been to Cambridge or Oxford. He spoke perfect English and French.'

Rennie stood up. He was almost certain that he had wasted his time. 'It was very kind of you to speak to me, Mrs Mason. I hope things work out for you and Harry one way or another.'

Rennie didn't wait for the radio schedule but used the scrambler at the embassy to phone London and ask for copies of the surveillance reports on Mason's wife to be sent over. They arrived in the evening diplomatic bag and Humphries, SIS's man based at the embassy, brought them to his room.

As he poured Humphries a whisky from his duty-free bottle he said, 'Who did the surveillance on Mrs Mason?'

Humphries shrugged. 'I did most of it. A new guy from London did the rest. Phillips I think his name was.'

'When was all this done?'

'Eight, nine months ago roughly. I don't remember. It didn't have any priority.'

'Who initiated it?'

'Paynter. He was worried about a wife getting mixed up with the wrong people.'

'Was she?'

'Was she what?'

'Getting mixed up with undesirables?'

'They were the usual Paris creeps. Her family's got plenty of money. And she was opening her legs for most of them. They weren't political, if that's what you mean. Just socialites. The French equivalent of Sloane Rangers, but older.'

'Were they all French?'

'So far as I can remember.'

I thought there was an Arab as well.'

'Not that I came across anyway.'

'Did you know Mason?'

'I met him several times.'

'What did you think of him?'

'He was OK. A bit . . . I don't know the word . . . a bit undecided. No . . . it was more than that. A bit uncommitted. He was crazy about that two-timing wife of his and I think that put him off his stroke most of the time.'

'What kind of places did these guys take her to?'

'Oh God. From four star to the gutter. London raised hell about my expenses. I sometimes had to use locals, in some of the places I would have been recognized. Some were the best in town but most of them were dives.'

'I may want to look over one or two. Could you spare the time to come with me? My French is terrible.'

'I'm OK for the next week but after that we've got a security audit at the embassy and I'll be on the hop all the time.'

'I'll phone you tomorrow morning. Another drink?'

'No thanks. I'll get back and close down.'

Rennie spent the evening reading the surveillance reports and noting the places and, when they were identified, the names of the men Mrs Mason had been seen with.

He and Humphries had visited six of the places over two nights and Humphries had had long boozy chats with bartenders, trying to find out if they had ever heard of a wealthy man named Khalim. There had been no response. Nightclub bartenders don't talk indiscreetly about their patrons even if they know their identities.

They were sitting in a dingy club in a side-street off the Boulevard des Capucines. The music was deafening and the flashing lights were almost hypnotic as they sat finishing their drinks, shaking their heads amiably but decisively at a succession of girls who came to their table.

'There's one other way, you know, Humphries.'

'What's that?'

'The Immigration people will have records of foreigners entering the country. She said the Arab was just visiting. Could you get a look at the records for this period? Just the visitors from Arab countries. They're probably categorized so that they can be passed to SDECE.'

'I don't have any contact with Immigration. The embassy's bound to. But they'll be very sticky. They like to pretend I don't exist.'

'How about the Deuxième Bureau?'

'I'd stand a better chance there. Especially if I could offer a trade.'

'See what you can do tomorrow.'

'OK. I'll try.'

Humphries was waiting outside Mason's room when Rennie got back from lunch.

'Any luck?'

'I think so. I've made some notes.'

Rennie unlocked the door and waved Humphries inside. As they sat at the tatty table Humphries pulled a folded sheet of paper from his inside pocket. 'They wouldn't cooperate unless I told them the name I was looking for. Said they wouldn't cooperate if it was just a fishing expedition. I gave them a description. What Mason's wife had told you. Wealthy, handsome and all that and when I said his first name was Khalim they said they knew who I meant.'

'Well done. Tell me what you've got.'

Humphries unfolded the paper and read from his notes.

'Khalim Abu Said. Forty-three years old. Born in Jerusalem. Now living in Amsterdam. Describes himself as a merchant. Net worth unknown but certainly a multi-millionaire. Was at Oxford, Balliol, and two years at the London School of Economics. Firsts in everything and played tennis for his college. Married with two children. A boy and a girl. Has some sort of diplomatic status as semi-official consul for several Arab states. Including Libya. Has diplomatic passports for Saudi Arabia and . . . believe it or not . . . the USA.' Humphries looked up at Rennie. 'That's about it, Johnny. Hope it's enough.'

'It's a good lead. Thanks. Did they squeeze you for anything?'

'No. Not a thing. I've got the feeling they knew why we were looking for Khalim Said.'

'What makes you think they knew?'

'When I was leaving the guy smiled and said, "Let us know what happens."'

Rennie said, 'Thanks for your help. I'll be leaving tomorrow.'

The phone rang for a long time before Fleur Mason answered. He'd asked for just ten minutes of her time and very reluctantly she'd agreed to see him at six that evening.

She was wearing a vivid green dress and he was aware of her beautiful neck and shoulders as he noticed the pearls she was wearing. When they were both seated he said, 'The other day you told me that your husband threatened to kill you if you left him. Did you really believe him?'

She looked down at the ring on her finger before she replied. 'As a man I didn't think that he would kill me. Not even in his anger and depression. But because of his work I wondered if I might be mistaken.'

'Do you still have any affection for him?'

For several moments she closed her eyes, thinking. Then she said slowly, 'Affection, yes. Love, no. He was a very nice man in many ways. Like I said, it was his job and the leaving me was the problem.'

'Would you be upset if something happened to him?'

'I don't understand. Is he ill?'

'No. But I think he might be in some danger.'

'From to do with his job?'

'Possibly. I'm trying to find out. I very much need your help.'

'How on earth can I help?' Her shrug was very French.

'Would you answer me two questions absolutely truthfully? Personal questions.'

'Of course.'

'The Arab you mentioned, Khalim. Did you sleep with him?'

It was several seconds before she said softly, 'Yes, I slept with him twice.'

'Did you talk about your husband and the divorce?'

'Only in passing.' She shrugged. 'He asked if I was married and I told him of the divorce.'

'Did you tell him why you were divorcing Harry?'

'A little.'

'Please tell me. It's very important.'

She shrugged. 'I told him the facts. The truth.'

'What did he say?'

'He seemed sympathetic to Harry. Said that men in that kind of work had to make sacrifices for their cause, for their country.'

'Did he ask any more about Harry's job?'

'Just how long he does it. Where we lived in London. Just gossip. I don't remember. It didn't seem important.'

'Did Khalim say where he lived?'

'No. But he said he was just a visitor to Paris.'

'He hasn't contacted you since?'

'No.'

Rennie stood up. 'Thanks for your help. I won't trouble you again.'

She stood up and walked with him to the door. As he opened it she said, 'What has happened to him, to Harry?'

'I don't know. Maybe nothing. Don't worry.'

He was conscious of her standing at the door, watching him as he clattered down the stairs.

CHAPTER EIGHT

The reports had come back in 24 hours from the SIS stations in Damascus, Teheran, Baghdad, Riyadh and Cairo, but there was nothing. Khalim Abu Said was exactly what he appeared to be, a millionaire several times over, an acceptable person in most Arab states and he had semi-diplomatic status. And he had no known connection with terrorist groups. There was no reliable SIS source of information in Tripoli and no request had been put to the SIS people in Holland.

Paynter was edgy and doubtful. 'There's nothing to go on, Johnny. His only connection is that he slept with Mason's wife.'

'And he asked about Mason's job.'

'That could be just the usual flannel. Trying to look interested in the girl before he got her into bed.'

'Or confirming what he already knew about Mason.'

'I think you're just clutching at straws.'

'He's the only straw we've got.'

'And that's about all there is to make him interesting. For me it's not really enough.' Paynter paused. 'Why are you so keen?'

'Just instinct and experience.'

'Let's wait a couple more days. If we don't hear anything by then you can go over and check him out. At least he'd be eliminated.' He sighed. 'I'm just wondering if we aren't off on a wild-goose chase and Mason's just gone off somewhere to lick his marital wounds. Where are you going to be over the rest of the weekend?'

'I'll be at the flat. The girls are with me for the weekend.'

'I'll contact you if anything comes in. Collins in admin wants to see you to go over your Paris expenses. But leave that until Monday if you want.'

Collins was an old hand and not unncessarily tough with field agents' expenses unless they tried it on. He usually accepted Rennie's expenses without reference to him but as Rennie sat down Collins said, 'There's no way I can apportion these expenses, Johnny. You haven't given an indication of what they're for.'

Rennie shrugged. 'Just put it down as routine surveillance.'

'What? Nearly five hundred quid in six days.'

'I've spent five hundred quid in an hour before now.'

'Sure. But for a specific operation. What the hell was this?'

'Ask Paynter.'

'Why all the mystery? Just give me a code name. I don't need to know what it was about.'

'Just ask Paynter. He'll give you something. We just don't want anything on the record. Not yet anyway.'

Collins shrugged and sighed his exasperation. 'I'll put it down to the embassy audit. They won't notice.'

There were only two bedrooms in Rennie's flat and the two girls had to sleep in the same bed which, with the perversity of children, they loved.

'It's time, girls. Get undressed and I'll come in and say goodnight.'

'Will you read to us. Just a little bit?'

It was Mary who smiled as she asked, her head to one side, her brown eyes on his face.

'If you're quick I will. Don't forget to do your teeth.'

'I forgot my toothbrush, daddy. Can I use yours?'

He looked at the small girl. They were so different from one another. Elizabeth meticulous and tidy and already a bit of a loner. And the little one, Mary, eager and excitable, desperately untidy but equally desperately loving and affectionate.

'No,' he said. 'That's unhygienic. Give them an extra clean when you get back home.'

As he washed up the tea things he could hear the normal laughing and shouting that went with bed-times when they were with him. It seemed strange to him. Their mother was mild and vague but they never messed about when it was bed-time at home. But with him, the disciplinarian, they seemed always to have known that they could get away with it. Then they were calling that they were ready. As he sat on the bed he said, 'Who's going to choose?'

Mary sat up quickly. 'It's my turn.'

'What do you want, sweetie?'

'I want . . . I want . . . "Bed in Summer" by Robert Louis Stevenson. The book's on the little table there.'

He reached for the book, found the poem and read it to them. Then he closed the book. As he leaned forward to kiss the little one she said, 'Beth told me to ask you something.'

He leaned back looking at Elizabeth. 'Why don't you ask me yourself?'

She blushed and Mary said, 'She was scared to. She said you wouldn't be cross if I asked you.'

He shrugged. 'OK. Ask me.'

The small voice said, 'Why aren't you at home with us any more? We miss you.' She looked at her sister. 'We both do, don't we, Beth?' Her sister nodded vigorously.

'What did your mother tell you?'

'She just said you'd had a disagreement and to ask you if we wanted to know more.'

Rennie hesitated and then he was back in his normal skin again. He said matter-of-factly, 'When people get married they make some promises. Your mother didn't keep one of them.'

'Momma always keeps her promises.' Elizabeth's face was red with embarrassment and challenge. 'She's a very nice mother.'

Rennie nodded. 'Of course she is. The very best. Anyway. . . . Don't worry about us. We're OK. And we both love you. All the love there is.'

He kissed them both and left the door half open so that they could see the light from the hall.

He switched on the TV and poured himself a drink, changing channels to the ITV news before he sat down. He didn't absorb what was on the screen. He was trying to think what better answer he could have given. He had told the truth but it wasn't enough. And the whole truth was not for children. Maybe the whole truth wasn't for anybody. As with his work, the public didn't need to know about the things that had to be done to protect them.

They spent the Sunday morning at the Zoo and when it started to rain he took them in a taxi to the Science Museum and the Natural History Museum. Then tea at the hotel in Sloane Square.

When they arrived back at their home he told the taxi-driver to wait and walked up the path to the door. She had seen them arrive and was standing at the open door.

'Johnny. A man phoned. He said he'd been trying to contact you. Would you ring him right away.'

'What's his name?'

'I think it was Payne or Paynter. I've written it out and his telephone number. It's on the pad by the telephone.'

'Do you mind if I use your phone?'

'Of course not. Do you want to pay off the taxi?'

'I'll see what Paynter wants. I might need the taxi.'

There was barely one ring before the phone was lifted at the other end.

'Hugo Paynter speaking.'

'It's Johnny, Hugo. I got your message to phone you.'

'They've been in touch, Johnny. They've got him. They even knew my unlisted phone number.'

'Who are they?'

'Can you come round to my place now?'

'Yes. I'll be there in about fifteen minutes.'

'I'll be waiting for you.'

Paynter's man, Wharton, answered his ring. An ex-Hong Kong policeman, his expressionless eyes looked over Rennie and then he stood aside, and as Rennie walked in Paynter appeared in a faded but elegant denim safari suit.

'Ah, Johnny. Let's go upstairs to my study.'

Paynter poured them each a whisky and sat down facing Rennie.

'They phoned me here. A local call from a pay-phone. It looks like you could be right. They said they'd got Mason.' He paused and said softly. 'They want us to release four men we've got in jail. The men are all Arabs. Known terrorists. Not yet been brought before the courts. They've given us two weeks to agree a deal.'

'Did they say who they were?'

'Yes. He said he was speaking on behalf of...' He looked at his notes. '*El Jihad el Islami*, an Iranian group sponsored by the ayatollahs. It means "The holy Islamic war".'

'Why do they give us so long? Fourteen days. Kidnappers usually want a decision inside a couple of days.'

'They want something else apart from the release of the terrorists. In fact I'm not sure that they're all that interested in us releasing their mates.'

'What else do they want?'

Paynter sighed and leaned back in his chair. 'Seems that they've got hold of some Israeli equipment. They don't know how to use it. They want us to train them.'

'What kind of equipment?'

Paynter looked at his notes again. 'It's all electronic surveillance equipment. Battlefield stuff. Jamming equipment. Intercept equipment. But their main problem is a remotely piloted plane. Israeli made, called Mastiff. It's not the latest Israeli RPV but it could be useful to the PLO.'

'Are these people PLO?'

'No. But I'd guess that they're probably backed by the Syrians who control what's left of the PLO. We don't have much on them on the files. But they sound like a mixed bunch of thugs from Syria, Iran, and Libya, being used by Islamic fanatics.'

'Can we do what they want?'

'Yes. But if the Israelis found out that we'd been training Arab terrorists to use Israeli equipment against them they'd raise hell all over the place. Including Washington.'

'And if we don't do what they want, they bury Mason.'

Paynter shook his head. 'No. More than that in a way. Apparently they've made Mason write out a description of all his assignments over the last five years. If we don't play ball it'll be sent to the press. Here, Europe and the States.'

'So we just deny them. Say they're fakes. Hitler's Diaries stuff.'

'Not if they've still got Mason. They could offer the press interviews with him.'

'So what have the brass decided?'

'We'll play ball. At least it's going to take time that we can be using for our own purposes. The equipment isn't British-made. We need to check what information we have. We'd have to go to wherever it's being kept, and that's probably in the Lebanon. And we need to check it over before it can be used. We can spin the time out for weeks.'

'How do we contact these people?'

'The usual story. Don't phone us we'll phone you. There's one other thing. I phoned Lambert in Aterdam. He phoned me back about an hour ago. We had to talk in parables but the long and short of it is that your friend Khalim Said was reported to have been in Teheran a month ago. He went to Damascus on the way back.'

'Have you put Lambert in the picture?'

'No. I haven't told him anything. I want you to deal with it.'

'Why not Lambert?'

'For several reasons. Lambert doesn't come under me. Secondly he's a desk type not a . . .' he hesitated. '. . . not one of us. And thirdly Mason's one of my men. It's up to us to get him out.'

'Are these people going to leak it to the media?'

'No. They threatened to kill Mason if we told the press.'

'Why should they do that? They usually love the publicity. That's half the reason why they bomb and kill.'

'I'd say they want that equipment in service for some operation that's only in the planning stage.'

'What do you want me to do?'

Paynter shrugged. 'I want you to find out where they're holding him and get him back.'

'What resources do I get?'

'Anything you want. Within reason money no object. Men and equipment. Say what you want and it's yours. But until you know more, keep it very low-key. When you have to move then be as discreet as you can short of risking losing him. We don't want anyone to get even a faint whiff of what's going on. I've alerted Facilities already. They're standing by. I've told them to lay on dollars and guilders for tonight if necessary.'

'I'll need to do some background checking before I go over.'

'Where will you start?'

'With Khalim Said.'

'Do your best for us, Johnny.'

Rennie just smiled and nodded as he stood up. But he was well aware of the extra courtesy of his boss when he escorted him down to the front door himself.

Rennie spent the night at his office making notes of the basics that he would need. Paynter saw him at ten o'clock, marking his cooperation by walking through to Rennie's office. He pulled out a chair and sat opposite him.

'You look done in, Johnny. How much sleep did you get?'

'None. I'll sleep while you're looking into what I need in Amsterdam.'

'OK. Tell me.'

'I want a twenty-four-hour radio network. A system that covers voice and CW.'

'Do you want an operator for CW?'

'It would help.'

'OK.'

'I want an introduction to somebody, preferably a woman, who mixes in Khalim Said's set. A way in to him. She doesn't need to know anything about the operation.'

'Not easy. I'll see what pressure we can put on the embassy to cooperate.'

'I want a really sound cover. Something that will stand up to a check.'

'No problem.'

'I want surveillance equipment and an operator. I want him to check that I'm not bugged as well. I want a guy who can get through electronic security, and I want weapons. A PPK for me, with silencer. Machine pistols, say four, and maybe more later on. I'll let you know.

'I want credit references with two different Dutch banks and money available in four banks, one British. And I want a personal contact in Amsterdam, round the clock. Messages, maybe help, and no questions asked.'

'I'll get people working on it.' Paynter held out his hand. 'Let me have your notes as a check. Get some sleep and contact me when you're ready. My girl will know where I am. I'll tell her to give you top priority.'

'I want time to see my girls before I go.'

Paynter looked blank. 'Girls? – ah yes – your daughters. Of course. I'm sure you can manage that. And on family things, if you get over here a time or two you might grab me some of that lovely Dutch asparagus. There's a place at Schiphol that sells it. Wonderful stuff.'

CHAPTER NINE

Rennie took the early B-Cal flight to Amsterdam and at Schiphol he hung around until all the other passengers on the flight had passed through immigration and collected their baggage from the conveyor. His two bags were the only ones left still circling on the belt. He took a taxi to de Bijenkorf and when it had gone he carried his bags across to the Krasnapolsky and booked in for a week.

It took him two days to find what he wanted and at the real-estate office on the Damrak he paid three months' rental in advance on the apartment on the Prinsengracht.

There was a large living room, one double bedroom and a single bedroom. The kitchen and bathroom were modern and well fitted out. The furnishings of the rooms were better than he had expected. It was owned by a Dutch diplomat who was working at the UN in New York. He spent a morning rigging the radio in the smaller bedroom, and tested out the network to London. He decided that he could get by in the first few days without a radio operator.

In every city where Rennie had ever operated there was always one man he could call on for information and help. They were never diplomats, and seldom British. More often than not they were criminals. Swaggering, arrogant, ruthless men with a network of information on places and people, able to carry out surveillance and act as go-betweens and lead him to any kind of specialist from forgery to burglary. They knew more about the secrets of their cities than its government and police. The man he hoped to find in Amsterdam was Jan Branders.

He checked through the telephone directory but there was no entry for Jan Branders. Plenty of Branders but not the kind of addresses where Jan would hang out. Jan Branders had been one of his informers in Surinam before the military coup in 1980. A pale-brown Creole, he had been toally reliable for the few months that Rennie had been there and it was Rennie and SIS who had helped him escape to Holland when the sergeants took over. A hundred thousand Surinamese had fled the small country just before independence in 1975 but Jan Branders would never have made it on his own. The military had offered a tempting reward for his capture. He had been an officer of the band of several hundred mercenaries who had invaded Surinam from French Guiana to liberate the country. Only Jan Branders and five others escaped capture. Like all Surinamese he had been a Dutch national before independence and Rennie had heard that he was now part of the underworld that controlled the girls and drugs over the small bridge from the Damrak. And that was where he'd have to look for him.

The houses and buildings of the red-light district of Amsterdam are as old and historic as the rest of the city, and despite the ruthlessness of the men who control it the area has a kind of innocence despite its activities. The girls sitting bathed in the purple or orange lights in the windows catered for every taste. A few were young and pretty, most were bored-looking and in their thirties, and a few were stout motherly figures whose attractions would appeal only to the most Freudian tastes.

It was almost ten o'clock as Rennie wended his way through the narrow alleyways to the canals. There was a small coffeeshop between two sex cinemas and Rennie sat at the counter aware of the eyes that watched him from the other tables, from the men lounging as lookouts at the open door, and from the cobbled street. Outsiders were not welcome. They belonged in the cobbled streets, browsing in sex-shops or staring at the girls. The coffeeshop was for locals and they resented any intrusion. The chatter went on in half a dozen languages, none of them Dutch.

When he ordered a second coffee the coloured man behind the counter said quietly, 'You Engelse?'

Rennie smiled and nodded. 'I'm looking for a friend.'

The man didn't look up as he filled Rennie's cup. 'Is plenty friends in the windows.'

Rennie paused over a five-guilder note. 'I'm looking for Jan Branders.'

'Who he?' the man said without interest.

'An old friend of mine.'

The man pushed over his coffee and the change from the note.

'Keep the change.'

The man left the coins lying there and walked over to speak to a group of three men at the table in the corner. Five minutes later a man got on to the stool next to him. The man behind the counter handed him a cafe-filtre in a metal holder without being asked. The man's dark skin was pock-marked and the pale line of a knife scar ran from the side of his mouth to behind his ear. Without looking at Rennie he said, 'What you want, mijnheer – smack?'

Rennie turned to look at his face. The eyes were black, the whites laced with blood vessels. 'I'm looking for a friend.'

'Who the friend, man?'

'His name's Jan Branders.'

'Why you look here?'

'He lives in this area.'

'Who say he lives here.'

Rennie said, smiling. 'I do.' And without turning Rennie was aware of a man moving on to the stool on the other side of him. And a voice said, 'You come outside now, mister.'

Rennie shook his head and a big brown hand closed on his upper arm. He looked at the second man's face. He was white, bald at the front but not more than twenty-five or six with a round pudding face and a rash of raw spots that were oozing yellow pus. As Rennie looked at him he clamped his hand over the man's fingers on his arm and squeezed them tightly together. In the cracked mirror behind the bar he saw a third man move up behind him, and a voice said softly, *'He, hoe maak jy het, Johnny?'* As he turned the voice said something in

Dutch and the men on either side of him moved away. And Jan Branders moved on to one of the empty stools.

He was smiling as he said, 'What in hell you doing here?'

Rennie looked back without smiling. 'Looking for you. Why the gorillas?'

'Gorillas? What is gorillas?'

'The two apes sitting each side of me.'

'Oh them?' he smiled. 'They friends of mine. They think maybe you from narcotics squad. What they call it? – *agent provocateur?*'

'Where can we talk?'

'Is OK here?'

'Not for me. Where can we go?'

'What is about?'

'Money. Information.'

Jan Branders smiled. 'Money OK. Information forgetting.' He paused. 'You know Jewish Historical Museum by Nieuw Markt?'

'I can find it.'

'OK. I meet you there in ten minutes, yes?'

'OK.'

The coffeeshop had been almost silent as they talked, and the chatter started again as Rennie went up the steps to the door.

As he walked across the bridges and through to the Gelderskade he was glad to be one of the crowd again. But as he turned right towards the museum the crowds thinned and the groups in the shop entrances were Surinamese and Javanese, and a few Chinese in the small shops that were still open.

He walked slowly round the museum building and finally stood between two parked cars. He saw Jan Branders walking across the square towards him, his hands in his jacket pockets. It wasn't the kind of welcome he had expected. Then Branders was standing in front of him staring at his face.

'You look younger, Johnny.'

Rennie shrugged. 'And you look older. Why the Mafia welcome?'

'You picked one of the drug places to have your coffee. That's where all the big deals are done. You were lucky you asked for me so soon. They usually throw strangers in the canal. The police don't interfere too much on the three canals down here.'

'Where can we talk?'

'If you want to talk about drugs is better you forget it.'

'I don't. I want to talk about a man. An Arab.'

'There's no Arab down these parts. I doubt if there are any in the whole city.'

'What about drugs from Iran and Afghanistan, and Pakistan?'

'When the drugs get here they have nobody but us.'

'There *is* an Arab in Amsterdam. He lives in a place on Nieuwe Leliestraat. His name's in the telephone book, Khalim Said. I want to find out about him.'

'What you want to find out?'

'Anything. Everything. And I want a room on the canals here where nobody knows who I am. And nobody cares.'

For long moments Jan Branders was silent. Looking over Rennie's shoulder at the people in the square. Finally he turned back to look at Rennie.

'Tell me what you're doing here.'

'Find out about Khalim Said for me and then maybe I'll tell you. But it's nothing to do with drugs, I promise you.'

'You swear that?'

'I swear it.'

Jan Branders smiled. 'I believe. You worry me too much coming out of the night like this.' He looked at his watch. 'I take you my place. Let's go. You keep with me all time.'

As they walked past the drug-pushers they shuffled out of the way, some of them saying a few words to Branders as they passed. He didn't respond to any of them. They came to a small, children's playground. A few yards further on Jan Branders turned round and made his way back down the street to a small alleyway on the right. A pretty coloured girl in a white leotard sat inside a lighted window and Jan Branders pushed a key into a door painted black. As it opened he pulled Rennie inside. There was a smell of incense or joss-sticks in the darkness and when Branders switched on the light there was a set of steep stairs facing them.

He followed up six flights of stairs past doors with double locks and no sounds from inside. Just once a door opened and a Chinese girl looked out; seeing Branders she closed the door again.

At the top of the stairs Jan turned keys in two separate locks, reached inside and switched on a light and waved Rennie inside.

The big room was nothing like he had expected. Plain white walls and white leather furniture. Even the carpet was white. It was straight out of *Vogue, House and Garden*, or some Swiss design magazine.

He turned to Branders. 'It's beautiful, Jan,' he smiled. 'You must be doing well.'

Branders was taking off his tatty rabbit-skin jacket, tossing it on to one of the big white leather armchairs. He walked over to a teak cabinet on the far wall.

'What you wish? Whisky, genever, English gin, vodka?'

Rennie smiled. 'Have you got a tomato juice?'

'Is only tinned.'

'That's fine.'

Branders bent down and opened the cupboard doors and took out two cans and a can-opener.

As Branders opened the cans and poured out the juice he said, 'You still with the same old mob, Johnny?'

'Yes.'

'That why you over here?'

'Yes.'

Branders handed him the drink and sat down facing Rennie.

'Tell me about your Arab.'

'He lives in a house on Nieuwe Leliestraat. Just beyond the small art gallery. He's rich. He's important, and I want to know all there is to know about him.'

'You got a photo of him?'

'No.'

'How much you pay for this?'

'Just for basic information and background . . . say two hundred guilders to start.'

'And why you want a room in the red-light district?'

'I want somewhere I can use that nobody knows about.'

'You mean police?'

'I mean everybody. Including my people.'

Branders nodded; he understood the need for such a place.

'I can let you have couple of rooms in Warmoesstraat. Is on edge of red-light area but not inside. Inside is not possible. You know Warmoesstraat? Is where you come over Old Bridge from the Damrak. There's a police station down the street.' He paused. 'You want to see it now?'

'If it's not too late for you.' Rennie paused. 'You look a bit tired.'

Branders finished the tomato juice and stood up, reaching for his jacket. 'Let's go.'

They crossed the two bridges and down the narrow alleyway, past the sex cinema and the peep-show and turned left into Warmoesstraat. He remembered it now he had seen it again. It was a narrow one-way street of shops, small hotels and the inevitable sex cinemas. There was a narrow pavement on one side of the street and a continuous line of parked cars on the opposite side. Jan Branders stopped a few houses beyond the bright yellow sign that said, 'Gay Cinema Adonis'. It was starting to rain.

As Branders stopped he searched his pockets for the key to the outer door and then realized that it wasn't locked. At the side of the door was a wooden plaque fastened to the wall and burned into its surface was a Chinese hieroglyph and the letters 'Jan B'. There was a smell of disinfectant as they walked up two flights of stairs and then Branders unlocked a door and waved Rennie into the darkness. When the light went on he saw a dingy room. Peeling paint on the brick walls, and plasterboard walls that marked off a small room with a bed. Along the far wall a stone sink. In the centre of the room was a cheap wooden table covered in worn oilcloth. The rest of the furnishings were cheap chairs and two roughly-made cupboards. Over the sink was a print of Princess Juliana. It reminded him suddenly of Mason's room in Paris.

Branders stood looking around the room as if it were as strange and new to him as it was to Rennie.

'Is OK for you, Johnny?'

Rennie turned and nodded. 'It's fine, Jan. How much?'

'Give me six hundred guilder and is yours for one year.'

'Can I pay you in sterling?'

'Anything except pesetas.'

'Are you sure that's enough?'

'I tell you if I need more sometime. You gonna live here?'

'No. I'll be here from time to time. I've got a place on the Prinsengracht.'

Branders gave him two keys. 'One for street. One for door here.'

'How can I contact you?'

'Go to my place. Ring bell three short and one long time. If I don't come down you go away.'

'Can you have lunch with me tomorrow?'

'What is lunch?'

'Midday.'

'OK. What time and where?'

'Twelve. You say where.'

'OK. Twelve at Restaurant Schiller in Rembrandtsplein. You know it?'

'I'll find it.'

'Is very busy. Is best you book for a table.'

'I'll bring the money for you.'

Branders shrugged his indifference, nodded, and walked out of the room. Rennie could hear his footsteps on the stairs and the sound of the street door closing. He looked around the room again. It was a depressing room, but it was just what he wanted. An escape hatch. If things went wrong he could abandon the apartment on Prinsengracht and hole up here until things quietened down.

In an area like this people didn't care who you were or what you were doing. And being seen around by the locals could provide a useful alibi. It was somewhere he could meet the kind of people who'd look out of place on the Prinsengracht. He could keep the team's weapons here if it was necessary. In a dozen cities around the world Rennie had had similar hideaways and they had sometimes saved him from arrest, and at least twice had saved his life, because he was able to disappear from his usual territory. And because even SIS didn't know where he was. A few minutes later he walked through to the Damrak and waved down a taxi. It wasn't far to the Prinsengracht but suddenly he felt very tired.

Rennie slept until ten and shaved and dressed slowly. He found a bookshop and bought two street maps of Amsterdam, a paperback guide in English and a Berlitz phrase book.

The rain of the previous evening had cleared and the sky was blue. He walked over the Old Bridge and down Warmoesstraat past the rooms. It all looked slightly more civilized in daylight. Locals shopping and bicycles leaning against walls. A car or two threaded its way cautiously down the street. At the far end workmen were fitting a sign over an empty shop. He had forgotten to book the table at the restaurant and took a taxi to Rembrandtsplein. There was one vacant table. He ordered a coffee and told the waitress that he was waiting for a friend.

Branders came a quarter of an hour early and they ordered the soup of the day and fish. Branders was dressed in jeans and a check shirt and hadn't shaved, but he seemed at home in the restaurant. The waitress had chatted to him in Dutch as if they knew one another well.

When they got to the fish Branders said quietly, 'Your Arab. Age is early forties. Like you say he is very rich. All his business is big contracts. Gover'ment contracts. Engineering. Construction. Hospitals, hotels, cars, tractors. He gets piece of action from both sides. All legal and in writing.

'His wife is Italian girl from Milan. Twenty-seven years old. Very, very pretty. Name Gabriella. Two childs. Boy seven, girl four or five. Not sure. He has many friends but not many people at their house. Two servants. One Dutch woman for wife and childs. An Indian for house and drive car. A Filipino cook comes in every day. Seven days a week.

'No drugs. No girls. No boys. Genuine Islam. Makes Haj to Mecca every year. He's a straight guy.'

'Any contact with terrorists?'

Branders shrugged. 'Would take time to find that out. He don't look like that sort of guy.' He shrugged again. 'But with Arabs who can tell?' He pronounced Arabs the American way and he went on: 'Arabs most of the time quiet people like my people, but sometimes they go crazy. You seen my people when they explode.'

Rennie said casually, 'Have you heard any rumours of Arab terrorists moving into this area?'

'Are you after terrorists, Johnny?'

For a moment Rennie hesitated. Then he nodded. 'There's a group of Arabs holding one of our men. I want to get him back.'

'You mean they kidnapped him?'

'Yes.'

'If they did that they'll do a deal, Johnny. They'll want money to fund their operations.'

'They don't want money, Jan. They've already said what they want.'

'What is it?'

'I can't tell you, but we don't want to go along with it. I've got to get our guy back as soon as possible.'

'You got people to help you?'

'They'll come over when I want them.'

'How much you pay for some help?'

'Tell me what you want.'

Branders looked intently at Rennie's face for several moments and then looked down at his coffee as he stirred it slowly. Without looking up he said, 'You think I forget you saved my life, yes?'

'That was a long time ago, Jan. Forget it.'

'I never forget, my friend. Is maybe other mens would have got me out but they would want in return. Money, drugs – they want something. And I would have paid. Being glad to pay. You ask me nothing. In fac' you give me hundert pounds sterling to give me a start.' He smiled. 'With your money I buy drugs. I make nice profit. Soon I make big, big money. I got money in banks all over the world. Dollars, yen, D-marks, Swiss francs, gold and diamonds.' Branders smiled. 'Same as you do. In Amsterdam is more than twenty people work for me now.' He nodded. 'I pay you any way you like. Cash, girls, drugs or . . . I help you any way you want. I've not forgot what you did for me. They would have killed you too.'

Rennie smiled. 'Forget it, Jan. Nobody's ever gonna kill me.'

Branders grinned. 'You still know all those tricks?'

'And more. I never stop learning.'

'So what you want me to do next?'

'Can you have the Arab watched. I want a pattern of his day. Where he goes. What the family does. What kind of protection does he have at the house?'

'You going in after him?'

'Not if there's some other way.'

'He don't look like terrorist to me.'

'He isn't. But he's the go-between.'

'OK. Give me your address in Prinsengracht.' When he saw Rennie's face he laughed softly. 'I not come myself, I send somebody better.'

Rennie smiled. 'How long do you need?'

'One day. Maybe two to make sure. If you are in the rooms in Warmoesstraat you put a white chalk cross on the wooden sign by the door. When you leave you wipe off.'

Rennie paid the bill and as they walked past the bar to the outer door Branders said, 'How your wife?'

'We're divorced, Jan. About a year ago.'

Branders nodded without comment. 'If you want girl you tell me. No problem.'

'Thanks.'

Branders looked across the square and a car parked by the public telephone boxes moved out and came forward as Branders stepped into the road. The rear door opened and Branders nodded to Rennie as he got inside.

A note had been pushed under the door at the flat on Prinsengracht. It was from Lambert, the SIS man based at the Amsterdam consulate at Johannes

Vermeerstraat. Lambert wanted him to phone as soon as possible.

Rennie dialled the number and the telephonist put him through to Lambert. Lambert suggested a meeting by the bank in the Central Station in half an hour.

Rennie bought a *Daily Mail* at the papershop in the station and walked along the passage to the bank. He stood looking at the headlines. The usual strikes, a bomb attack on an Israeli settlement on the West Bank and a pop-star fined £50 for possession of a gram of marijuana. A bored sermon from the magistrate and the usual claim by the pop-star to reporters outside the court that marijuana was less harmful than gin or cigarettes. And then Lambert arrived.

'Hi, Johnny.'

'Hi. What's the panic?'

'No panic, but I had a mysterious message a couple of days ago from Paynter. Said I was to find you a lead to this Arab named Khalim Said. Preferably a woman. Said it was urgent so I've been scouting around.'

'What have you got?'

'Her name's Adele Palmer. Twenty-seven or eight. Divorced. British subject. Owns a gallery not far from your place. Attractive, intelligent, easy-going and she's been a friend of the Said family for a year or so.'

'What kind of tale can I give her?'

'Whatever your cover is. I don't want to know. Paynter told me to ask you no questions. There's no problem with her, her father was in SOE and then in SIS. He retired about five years ago. Heart trouble of some sort. I've used her from time to time to get me routine information. We both pretend it's so that HM Consuls can invite the right people to his dinner parties. Or at least know what they've been up to if he *has* to ask them for some reason or other. And we help her in various ways.

'If you want, I can contact her and tell her that you'd like to get alongside Khalim Said and that we'd like her to fix it. She'll want to be assured that it's all in a good cause and that Said isn't being involved in anything.'

Rennie half-smiled. 'She sounds OK to me. Will you phone me when you've arranged for me to meet her?'

'Sure. Is it urgent?'

'Yes.'

'I don't want to know what you're up to but I hope it isn't going to have repercussions on us or the embassy in The Hague.'

'It shouldn't. If it looks like blowing up I'll warn you, if there's time.'

'It's bloody difficult operating out of the consulate. You'd think I was KGB rather than SIS.'

Rennie shrugged. 'You should be used to that by now. Anyway, thanks for the contact. I'll keep away from you as much as I can.'

'If you're desperate you can use my direct line to London. It's got scrambler facilities.'

'Thanks.'

Lambert hesitated for a moment as if he was embarrassed and then said, 'Cheers,' and walked back towards the main entrance of the station.

Rennie walked to the entrance and stood in the shadow of one of the pillars as he watched Lambert get into a taxi.

If you were part of SIS's 'dirty-tricks' set-up you didn't trust anyone. Not even those who were supposed to be on your side. Trust anyone and you could easily end up face-down in some canal or with a knife in your back in some alleyway. There was a scar that ran from his shoulder to his belly that was a constant reminder of what could happen if you trusted when you shouldn't. But Johnny Rennie had never been scared since he was a boy. His natural characteristics and his training made fear seem a waste of time. He was a hunter not the hunted. There were no niceties or Queensberry Rules in his life. Sitting ducks were there to be shot. It wasn't competitive. Once the target was in your sights you pulled the trigger, or tightened the noose, whatever the situation called for. You didn't get into fights because you were trained to kill not fight. Fighting was for amateurs.

He walked down the Damrak and turned off to the sleazy room in Warmoesstraat. He bought food and a few pieces of crockery and cutlery, a frying pan and two saucepans and took them back to the room.

There was one small window and in the late afternoon sun the room looked less forbidding. He spent an hour cleaning it up and then walked back to his apartment.

The phone was ringing as he let himself in. It was Lambert. He'd talked to the woman and there was no problem. She could be contacted anytime he wanted. Lambert gave him her gallery and private numbers and the address of the gallery. She lived over the premises.

CHAPTER TEN

The gallery was on a corner, and as Rennie walked in, a woman sitting at a small teak desk smiled as she looked him over.

'I'm guessing that you're English. Please look around. The prices are on the little white stars on the frames.'

'Are you Adele Palmer?'

'Yes.'

'I'm John Rennie.'

'Please feel free to look around, Mr Rennie.'

'Mr Lambert at the consulate said he'd mentioned my name to you.'

'Of course. How silly of me. It didn't register.' She stood up and walked over to him. 'Peter Lambert said you wanted an introduction to a friend of mine.'

'I'd be much obliged if you could do that.'

The brown eyes looked him over and then she said, 'Khalim Said is a special friend of mine. His family too. I don't want to pry but I take it that your motives for meeting him are – what shall I say? – above-board. Not to his detriment.'

Rennie's face was impassive as he said, 'You don't need to worry, Ms Palmer.'

'How would you like to do this?'

'As casually as you can. Do you see them often?'

'Most days I pop in for an hour or so in the evening.'

'Perhaps I could take you to dinner tonight or tomorrow. I could be a friend of yours from England and we drop in to see them after we have eaten.'

'Let me phone them and see it it's convenient.'

She spoke in Italian and he guessed she was speaking to the Arab's wife. There was a lot of girlish laughter and then she put her hand over the phone.

'Gabriella says why don't we eat with them tonight.'

'Fine. What time shall I call for you?'

'About eight OK?'

'Of course.'

She spoke again on the telephone and then hung up. She smiled. 'See you at eight. It's in walking distance from here. About ten minutes.

'I'll call for you at a quarter to.'

'OK. Ring the bell on the side door. My name's on the card.'

'Thanks for your help.'

'Not at all.'

Rennie wore his one and only good suit and took a taxi because of the flowers. Adele Palmer was obviously surprised and pleased and insisted on putting them into a vase before they left.

Her living room was feminine and cosy and on the wall there was a drawing in *sanguine* of a naked girl. An Annigoni. The photographs clustered on an antique table were all of females and Rennie was aware of the oblique but obvious message. It made things easier.

It was still sunny, and the narrow Amsterdam streets looked at their best. Rennie was seldom aware of his surroundings apart from their effect on whatever he was doing, but he found the medieval houses and streets strangely appealing. Amsterdam was a city that represented many things that he admired. There was nothing contrived or phoney about its beauty or its people. the city and its inhabitants seem to have moved through the centuries calmly, without being caught up in the race for skyscrapers and neon lights.

A servant answered the door and Gabriella Said was waiting for them at the top of the stairs. She looked younger than he had expected and she was strikingly beautiful. He had expected a typically extrovert Italian girl but she was both shy and gentle, her large brown eyes constantly on her husband's face. And she admired, smiling, the bunch of roses that Rennie had brought for her before she led them into the large living room.

Khalim Said was tall and not quite handsome, but his face was alive and his black eyes alert. He smiled easily with an almost boyish laugh. His skin was no darker than would come from a season's tan at St Tropez and the slightly aquiline nose could make a casual observer assume that he was a Jew. There was black hair on the backs of his hands but his long tapering fingers were almost white with carefully manicured nails. The movements of his hands and arms were surprisingly graceful for a man. Each gesture, even the most ordinary, seemed to be choreographed and controlled. But it was obviously instinctive and natural and not contrived. His English was fluent and without any foreign accent, but he interposed an Arabic word from time to time when he was speaking to his wife.

The music coming from the concealed speakers was a slow, languorous guitar, a mixture of Spain and North Africa. Long, haunting strands of single notes without chords, reminiscent of de Falla and 'Nights in the Gardens of Spain'.

After the meal they sat in the tiled living room, Said and his wife together on a brocade settee, her long slim fingers just touching his brown hand as they all chatted together. Eventually Said looked at Rennie, smiling as he said, 'I know it's terribly bad manners to ask, Mr Rennie, but I'm curious. What do you do?'

Rennie smiled back. 'Guess.'

Said looked intently at Rennie's face before he spoke. Then he said, slowly and thoughtfully, 'If I didn't know already that you are a civilian I would have said that you were a soldier.'

Rennie laughed. 'Why that?'

'You look four-square on the world from those brown eyes of yours. And there is something about your mouth that says you are used to giving orders and having them obeyed. I see no doubts in your face. It's an honest face but a cautious face.' Said laughed. 'And now tell me that you are a poet who writes of love, and stars in the evening sky.'

Rennie shook his head, still smiling. 'Like most men I served in the army a long time ago but I'm not a professional soldier. I work for a firm of solicitors in London.'

'I'm surprised. Very surprised. Do you defend people or prosecute them?'

'Neither. I'm an investigator.'

'How interesting. Tell me. Why do solicitors need investigators?'

'Most solicitors use free-land investigators. The firm that I work for is quite large. So it's more economical to employ someone full-time.'

'And what do you investigate?'

Rennie shrugged. 'Documents, relationships, suspected fraud, missing persons, stolen valuables.' He paused. 'Anything and everything.'

'It must be very satisfactory to help the innocent. But what if you suspect your company's client is guilty?'

Rennie laughed. 'My company's clients are never guilty. Anyway, that's for a court to decide and by the time it gets to court my work is almost always over.'

'What are you looking for in Amsterdam, may I ask?'

'I'm afraid I can't say very much. It's a missing person – a girl.'

'How sad that a daughter should leave her home and family.' Said shrugged. 'But we live in a time of turmoil. As if the whole world is bubbling like a cauldron on a fire.'

'Can I ask you something, Mr Said?'

'Khalim, please. Of course.'

'Where did you learn such perfect English?'

Said laughed, his strong teeth exposed for a moment, and Rennie realized then how attractive he must be to women. It wouldn't have been all that difficult for him to ease Fleur Mason into bed.

'I went to university in England and business school in the USA. My American friends say it's a genuine Oxford accent and my English friends say it's obviously Bostonian.' He paused. 'It's a language I love. It's like Arabic in a way. Gentle and descriptive. Made for poets and story-tellers.'

Adele interrupted. 'Tell us an Arabic story, Khalim. Please.'

Said laughed. 'You westerners are terrible. You've been deceived by all those stories of Scheherazade. Magic carpets and belly-dancers. We're not like that any more. We never were, for that matter.' He looked at Rennie and then at Adele. 'Tell me – what is an Arab? How do you define it?'

Adele said briskly, 'Someone who believes in Mohammed. A Moslem – or is it a Muslim?'

Said shook his head. 'There are Christian Arabs and Jewish Arabs.' He smiled and looked at Rennie. 'Your definition, Mr Rennie?'

'People who live in an Arab country.'

Said was quiet for a moment. 'Would you say Israel was an Arab country . . . I was born there.'

Rennie said quietly, 'I imagine that you see it still as an Arab country.'

'I do. And it is of course. My family have been there for at least three hundred years. Until the British gave our land and our homes to the Jews to salve their consciences about the gas-chambers.'

'But the Arabs could have stayed.'

'So why am I here? Why aren't I in Jerusalem in the home where I was born? Why are my mother and father dead, and my sister living in Detroit? Tell me.'

Adele said softly, 'Don't get upset, Khalim. Let's forget it. Let's talk about art or music. Anything but that.'

Said's wife said something to him softly, in Arabic, but he shook his head.

'It has to be said. It was done. It is part of history.' He took a deep breath. 'My father was a judge – a *Khadi.* We had a big house and several hundred acres of orange and lemon groves. Bought and paid for by my grandfather and his father. We had Jews in Palestine long before the Mandate and long before the UN gave our land to the Jews. But there were at least two Palestinians for every Jew. The Jews were a minority in an Arab land.

'In 1948 Palestine was partitioned and part became Israel. No Palestinian was asked if he agreed. It was just done. Palestine was not just colonized. Six hundred thousand Palestinians were evicted from their homes. There was no compensation. We were evicted and looted. By force. Against our will and against all natural justice. But the figures are just figures. What they represent was countless personal tragedies. The burning of villages, bulldozing homes and property, killings of innocent people, massacres of whole communities. Women and girls raped. Respected public figures deliberately humiliated.

'We moved from the official judge's house in Tel Aviv to the family home in Jerusalem. My father counselled calmness and restraint. Two years later he was shot in the gardens of our home. So was my mother. My sister was already in Damascus. In one day they wiped out my family's history. With guns and hatred.'

Said brushed a tear from his eye and the others sat in silence. There was nothing to say. If there was, they didn't know what it was.

It was Adele who broke the silence. 'Let me play you something, Khalim, and then we'll go,' she said quietly.

Khalim nodded and sighed as he stood up and followed her through the wide archway.

Adele pushed the silk scarf back over her shoulder and sat down at the piano. She played a few random quiet chords and then she sang in a childish voice, thin, quavering but sweet. And Khalim smiled at last as he recognized the words of the Brahms lullaby – '*Guten Abend, Gute Nacht, von Rosen bedacht . . .*'

It was as nearly right for their mood as anything could have been.

They were all conscious of the tension but Adele chattered quietly with Gabriella and kissed Khalim gently as they said their goodbyes.

As they walked back together towards the gallery they were silent for most of the time and then Adele said, 'Arabs must hate us Europeans.'

'There's a lot of Europeans hate the Arabs. Their record isn't all that good.'

'In what way?'

'Killings. The Munich Olympics. The PLO. Bombing and shelling civilians. The Arab countries all put their own interests first. There could have been a Palestinian state on the West Bank years ago. And what have any of the Arab States done for their people? Without oil they'd be back in the deserts. And the oil won't last for ever.'

'But what right had anybody to give other people's land and houses to the Israelis?'

'None. But it wasn't the British who gave it away, it was the UN.'

'But they didn't have any right to do that either.'

'Too true. But it's done, and now all the Palestinians are trying to do is put the clock back. And they won't be able to do it. Nobody can. History has moved on. They should do a deal and settle somewhere and make that a new Palestine.'

'But you can't expect them just to forget what's been done to them.'

'They have to learn to forget. It's the only way. All over the world nations have done terrible things to other nations. The Danes and the Normans and Romans to Britain. Britain to the Irish. Someday you have to cry halt to the bitterness or the killing goes on for centuries until it has nothing to do with the original crimes. The world's got tired of the Palestinians. They're just killing for the sake of it. Murdering just to keep themselves in the news. But there's people all over the world doing just the same. Kampuchea, El Salvador, Nicaragua, all over Africa, and the Arabs aren't news any more.'

'But a man like Khalim would understand all that. And he obviously still cares.'

'D'you want a drink before you turn in? It might take your mind off tonight.'

'Where can we go at this time of night?'

'I'll take you for a drink at The Pulitzer and then walk you home.'

'Fine,' she paused. 'Did you like Khalim?'

Rennie smiled. 'I liked them both and they obviously count you as one of the family.'

Then they were at the hotel. From the corner of his eye Rennie could see a man leaning casually against the wall by the door of his own flat.

As Rennie walked back towards his flat he tried to reconstruct the layout of the Said apartment. But his mind was hindered by the thought of the man lounging by his own front door. He stopped at the corner that led the side street into the Prinsengracht. The man was still there. He could see the glow from his cigarette in the darkness.

As he walked across the bridge the man came towards him and Rennie saw the glowing arc as the man flicked his cigarette over the rails alongside the canal. The man stood squarely in front of him, blocking his path, and as Rennie raised his arm to push him aside the man said gruffly, '*Ik kom van Jan Branders*.' He paused and said slowly, 'You come . . . with . . . me . . . to . . . Jan . . . now . . . he waits . . . for you.'

'Where is Jan?'

The man turned and pointed towards the church and said, 'Kom.'

Without waiting to see if Rennie followed him the man turned and walked along the street towards the church. There was nobody outside the church and the man walked on ahead. At Noorder Markt he stopped and Rennie saw the headlights of a car flash briefly in the side street.

As he approached he saw Jan Branders at the wheel of the black Mercedes. Jan leaned across and opened the passenger door, and Rennie got in.

Branders smiled. 'You tekking out ladies already, my friend?'

Rennie didn't respond. 'What is it, Jan?'

Branders looked away, staring through the windscreen towards the canal. 'I got problems and you got problems.'

'What's my problem?'

Jan laughed softly, 'Your problem is I got problem.'

'I'm tired, Jan. Let's get on with it.'

Branders reached inside his jacket, took out an envelope and handed it to Rennie. 'Is report on what Said family do . . . like you asked. Is from inside. All correct.'

'Thanks. Is that the problem?'

'No. No, my friend. Is difficult to tell you of problem.'

'Why?'

'I think I know who got your man.'

'Where is he?' Rennie said quickly.

'Slow, slow. I said *who* got him not where he is.'

'So who's got him?'

'Is one Arab is boss but like you they come to Surinamese for help.'

'Tell me more.'

'Surinamese is my countrymen, old friend. You want for me to get them in jail?'

Rennie sighed. 'Just tell me where he is and leave it to me. There's no question of jail.'

Branders shook his head. 'I told you I don't know where he is. All I know is one Arab and four, five Surinamese got a white man as prisoner.'

'How did you find this out?'

'I sent word out. It came back to me.'

'D'you think it's true?'

Jan Branders laughed softly, 'Nobody tell lie to me, Johnny. Is better dead they do that.'

'Is he in Amsterdam?'

'No.'

'In Holland?'

'Yes.'

'What else do you know?'

'I know they have him on a boat. And that's all I know.'

'Can you find out more?'

'I don't think so. Maybe money would work but I don't think so. If my man say more they kill him for sure.'

'So why did he tell you this much?'

'He owe me plenty from way back. I make him talk. He scared of me now but much more he is scared of the Arab and the others.'

'How does he know what he knows?'

'The Surinam men are addicts. Heroin and opium. My man is their supplier.'

'Can I talk with your man?'

'No. Definitely no. Never.' Branders shook his head vehemently.

Rennie took a deep breath. 'Well . . . thank you, Jan, for what you've told me. And for the report. If you hear any more that you feel you can tell me I'd be very grateful for your help.'

Jan Branders turned his head quickly to look at Rennie. 'You think I know more than I tell you, don't you?'

'Yes.'

Branders looked away and sat silent for several moments.

'If I hear more I contact you. If you get in trouble – use my name.'

Rennie patted Branders's hand on the steering-wheel and let himself out of the car.

CHAPTER ELEVEN

The phone rang several times before Rennie turned in his bed and reached out to lift the phone.

'Rennie.'

'I'm booked in at the Amstel, Johnny. How about you come over?'

It was Paynter and Rennie said, 'I'll be about an hour. You booked in your name?'

'Of course.'

'See you later.' And Rennie hung up.

The taxi pulled up at the foot of the steps of the Amstel Hotel and a doorman opened the door for Rennie and helped him out.

Rennie found it typical of Paynter to have booked in at the Amstel. It was a cross between the Connaught and the Ritz. Quiet, impressive, old-fashioned, and luxurious by any standards.

The hall-porter phoned Paynter's room and Paynter asked for him to go up.

'Room 329, sir. The lift's on the left. Thank you, sir.'

Paynter opened the door before he knocked and pointed to the table in the window.

'I've got coffee for us both. Sit yourself down.'

As Rennie stirred his coffee Paynter said, 'You've only had a few days. How are things going?'

'I've met Khalim Said and his wife. And I can confirm that Mason is being held in Holland. I don't know where but he's on a boat. There's an Arab in charge and the others are Surinamese.'

'You've not been wasting your time, have you? How did you get on to Mason?'

'An old contact. A Surinamese.'

'Is this the chap you raised hell about way back when you wanted to get him out?'

'That's the one.'

'Well, my news is not so startling but it's useful. We sent two ordnance and electronics chaps out to Damascus and they were taken down to a place called Rayak in the Beka'a valley, just over the Syrian border in Lebanon.

'We don't really know who we're dealing with but it's a mixed bag of Syrians and Iranians. They've got this RPV, a remote piloted vehicle, that's got some fault in its electronics and also they don't know how to operate it. They've got their own electronics guy watching our chaps like a hawk, but he's got no experience on anything as sophisticated as this.

'They've offered our chaps money, girls, the lot. All on the side. Swiss bank accounts and all the trimmings and we've told them to look cooperative within reason.

'But there's two snags. The first is that our communication with our two fellows is pretty tenuous and secondly we suspect that we can't trust either the Syrians or the Iranians to keep to the bargain.'

'Why didn't the Arabs get the Russians to fix the equipment?'

Paynter shrugged. 'Probably don't want the Russians to know they've got it.'

'How important is it to the Arabs? The equipment.'

'It's very important. It could help them give the Israeli ground forces a real beating.'

'What does it do?'

'You know me, Johnny. Can hardly fix a fuse. But from what they tell me they can shuffle these things around just on a lorry. It's a pilotless plane. They launch the bloody thing on a battle front and it sends back high-resolution TV pictures covering sixteen square miles. Shows everything on the ground. You can guide it where you want and bring it back. The Israeli ground forces have always relied on surprise and they'd be sitting ducks for any guerrillas if they had this little gadget.'

'And if our guys fix this, will they release Mason, d'you think?'

'Well, one of the technicians we sent is an Arab-speaker and we think he's trying to hint that they're just using us. Unfortunately the Arabs are deliberately using a dialect where he can only get a rough idea of what they're saying to one another. I wouldn't trust the bastards myself.'

'So we have to operate here like they aren't going to deliver.'

'Looks a bit like it. Maybe I'll know more in the next few days. But have a contingency plan in mind for a last resort.'

'And Said is definitely involved?'

'Oh sure. All the messages from our two chaps come back through him. He contacts us daily. I generally speak to him myself. Smooth, charming and amiable. Tries to give the impression that it's all something he'd rather have no hand in. Above this sort of caper.' Paynter laughed. 'Doesn't stop him from putting on all the pressure he can. Was terribly hurt and indignant when I asked him if his friends in the Lebanon were to be trusted to keep their part of the bargain.'

'I'd guess he genuinely doesn't like it all that much. He's the wrong type for this kind of business.'

'Maybe. But the fact is he does it. And it's facts that count in my book.' He reached over to his open case on the bed. 'Got some mail for you.' As he handed over a manilla envelope he said, 'Anything else you want while I'm over here?'

'Nothing at the moment.'

He stood up and Rennie took the hint. They shook hands and Paynter escorted him to the door.

CHAPTER TWELVE

He saw the crowd of young people and the flashing light on the police van as he came over the canal bridge. He could hear the shouting and cursing in half a dozen languages as he approached the crowd. Then he realized who they were. They were young squatters from the basements of the two empty houses opposite his room, and the police were evicting them. Suddenly the crowd broke away, running down the streets towards the lights at the far end. All except a girl who sat on the cobbles clutching a small bundle, her head bowed over her drawn-up knees.

A policeman said something to her and she looked up slowly, her face deathly pale in the moonlight. And slowly and clearly she said, in English, 'Why don't you fuck off, you bastards.'

As the policeman reached for her thin arm Rennie bent down towards the girl and said, 'What's the matter?'

'Tell those pigs to leave me alone.'

Rennie straightened up and looked at the policeman. Shaking his head, as he said, 'Can I help? What's the problem? I'm afraid I can't speak Dutch.' He paused. 'Has she committed an offence?'

The policeman shrugged. 'We have orders from the court to evict the squatters. We can't let her go back in the house again.'

'Let me talk to her. I'll see that she doesn't go back in.'

'Are you a tourist, mijnheer?'

Rennie nodded towards the house. 'I live here, officer. I've got rooms in that house.'

The policeman shouted in Dutch to one of the other policemen who said something brief in reply. He turned back to Rennie. 'If she is here in one hour she will be taken into custody.' He frowned and said, 'She is not safe in these streets at this hour.'

'I'll look after her.'

'OK. But you must warn her or she will be taken as a vagrant.'

When the police van had reversed out of the street Rennie looked down at the girl. Her head was resting on her knees, one hand on the small cheap plastic hold-all beside her on the cobbles.

He crouched down beside her and said, 'Are you English?'

She shook her head.

'American?'

The girl lifted her face slowly and looked at Rennie.

'Just leave me alone.'

'You heard what he said, they'll pick you up if you stay here.'

She shrugged her thin shoulders. 'So what.'

'Have you eaten?' It was the only thing he could think of to say.

She just looked away towards the lights at the far end of the street and said nothing. Rennie put his hand gently on her bony shoulder.

'I live in the house there. Come and have a coffee and a sandwich.'

He stood up slowly, taking her hand. For a moment she hesitated and then she stood up unsteadily, her eyes closed. Rennie put his arm round her and walked her to the door of the house.

When he switched on the light in his room he saw how ill she looked. The white face, the brown patches under her eyes and the almost bloodless lips. Now that she was inside the room she seemed to have lost her defiance. She sat obediently when he pointed to the chair, and when he came back with a cheese sandwich, a cold sausage and mugs of coffee she sat with him at the rickety table and ate slowly without talking or looking at him.

'Where do you live?'

She shook her head.

'What's that mean?'

'I don't live anywhere. I just bum around.'

'Where are you from?'

'Are you English?' As the girl looked at him he realized that she was on some drug. Her pupils were dilated and her breathing was shallow.

'Yes.'

She shrugged. 'I nearly went to London instead of this place. London sounds grim.'

'Look, girl, it's nearly 3 a.m. There's a bed in the next room. I'll fix myself up out here. Get some sleep and then you can decide what you want to do.'

'What's your name?'

'Johnny.'

'OK. But I got bad news for you, Johnny. I don't screw just for a bed.'

The girl saw the aggression in Rennie's eyes as he said, 'There's a key in the bedroom door, honey. It works just as well from the inside.' He stood up, collecting the dirty crockery from the table. As she picked up her plastic hold-all she half-smiled as she walked to the bedroom.

He fried four eggs and grilled half a dozen narrow strips of lean bacon. And when he had poured the coffee into the mugs he knocked on the bedroom door.

'Time to eat, girl. It's getting cold.'

Rennie didn't wait for an answer, he expected her to do as she was told.

Five minutes later she joined him at the table. And as she ate he covertly looked at her. Her long lank hair looked as if it hadn't been washed in weeks and her skin was pallid, her hands shaking as she held the knife and fork. But he saw that she must have been very pretty before she let herself go. She ate slowly and reluctantly as if she found the food distasteful. She didn't look at him as she ate and when she had finished she put her bony hands around the warm mug as if to warm them before she lifted the mug to her mouth.

'What's your name, girl?'

'Joanna. Joanna de Vries.'

'You speak very good English.'

For the first time she looked at his face. 'I'm not Dutch. I'm American. My grandparents were Dutch.'

'How old are you?'

'Twenty.'

'Are you on holiday here?'

'No. I live here.'

'What do you do?'

'I don't understand?'

'What's your job?'

She shook her head. 'I don't have a work permit.'

'How do you get by? For food and things.'

She shrugged. 'I share with other squatters. I've got some savings. Not much. But I manage.'

'You like it here?'

'Not really.'

'So why stay?'

'I've nowhere else to go.'

'What about your home back in the States?'

'They don't want me.' She sighed and hesitated. 'My father. He threw me out.'

Rennie collected up the plates and cutlery and walked over to the sink. As he washed them in the bowl he thought about the girl. She looked ill, and he wondered if she was a confirmed addict. But she would fit in well with his cover of looking for a missing girl. As he dried his hands he turned and looked at her. She was still sitting at the table, her head bowed, her hands around the mug.

'What were you planning to do today?'

She shrugged. 'I don't know. I'll go looking for the squatters. They'll have found some place by now.'

'Are they friends of yours?'

'No. They're just squatters.'

He sat down at the table facing her and said softly, 'Are you on drugs, Joanna?'

'Only hash. I was never much into anything else. Anyway I can't afford the real stuff any more.'

'I shan't be using my rooms for a couple of days. Would you like to stay here and rest up for a bit?'

'I can't pay. There's not enough for that.'

'You don't have to pay. There's food and a bed. Just help yourself.'

'Why? Why are you helping me?'

Rennie shrugged. 'No particular reason. But you obviously need some help.'

'I'm no good in bed, if that's what you want. They all say that.'

For long moments Rennie looked at the girl's face. And for the first time he noticed the clear blue of her eyes. The same blue as his daughter's eyes. He smiled and said, 'Just clear up the place a bit for me. That's all. And you don't have to do even that unless you want to.'

He stood up and took the two spare keys that he'd had made from the ring and put them on the table. 'The big one's for the street door. I'm not sure when I'll be back. Two, maybe three days. If you go, leave the keys on the table.'

'What's your name?'

'John. John Rennie.'

As he opened the door he turned and looked at her. 'Take care of yourself. See you.'

Her eyes were looking at the mug in her hands and she didn't look at him as he left.

Adele Palmer had invited him to the opening of a new artist's show at the gallery and the whole Said family was there. Khalim, Gabriella, their son Jamal and the little girl, Nadia.

The pictures were modern, not the kind of work that Rennie could admire or even understand but there were a dozen red 'sold' stars already on the frames. Said had bought two and was enthusiastic about them, chatting knowledgeably to the girl artist. The pictures he had bought were presents for a member of the Saudi royal family and Said was sure that they would certainly lead to other purchases.

Rennie had invited them all to drinks that night but the children's nurse had her day off and they invited him and Adele back to their apartment instead.

They all walked back together to the Saids' apartment, the Saids holding hands and walking ahead. Adele Palmer said quietly, 'Are you married, Johnny?'

'Divorced.'

'Any children?'

'Two daughters.'

'How old are they?'

'Round about the same age as Khalim's kids.'

'Do you see them at all?'

'Most weekends.'

'Do you miss them when you're away?'

It was several seconds before Rennie replied. 'I never spend time regretting things that can't be changed. Only fools do that.'

Adele Palmer smiled. 'Fools and women.'

Rennie nodded. 'Yes. And women. It's their nature. Too much time to think and dwell on things.'

He was quite unconscious of the jibe at his character.

After they had eaten they stayed talking at the table. About the show at the gallery. Music. Films and books. It was Adele who had brought up the subject of Arabic script and Said's eyes had lit up as he talked.

'For us Arabs the word is everything. And that beautiful script is part of the word. Just twelve basic shapes and a few dots and there is art as well as communication. That's what we have from the Qur'ān. The Qur'ān is the word. It rules all good Muslims' lives. It's our rock.' He looked at Rennie, smiling. 'Do words mean a lot to you, Johnny?'

'Not like they do to you.'

'But think of the influence that English words have had on the whole world.'

'Like what?'

'Like Dickens who made us all aware of the plight of the poor. *Uncle Tom's Cabin* and the slaves. Your beautiful translation of the Scriptures. You don't have to be a Christian to appreciate the wisdom of the Bible. Think of the Sermon on the Mount. Nobody has ever said in so few words, and more beautifully, how a man should live.'

Rennie smiled. 'Do you really believe that the meek will inherit the earth?'

Adele Palmer laughed softly. 'He's got you there, Khalim.'

Said turned quickly towards her. 'No. No. You cannot take just one precept and criticize it.' He looked back at Rennie. 'Take the big conflicts of the world today. Communism and Christianity. If you read the words with understanding there is almost no difference between them. They would both work – but nobody tries to make them work. The Russians are not communists and the West are not Christians. If it were not for people either belief would work.'

'And what about the Jews and the Arabs. The Talmud and the Qur'ān?'

Gabriella held up her hand. 'No. Please no more. It's all been said so many times. But nobody listens.'

Said smiled. 'Just one more sentence, my love. The last word privilege of a host.'

She shrugged and smiled, reaching out for his hand, holding it as he turned back to look at Rennie.

'The problem with us, the Jews and the Arabs, is not our differences. The problem *is* . . . that we are too alike. We understand each other too well. We are like children of the same parents, quarrelling like siblings. We are from the same forebears, we lived in the same lands, our language is almost the same. Remember what I said about the word. There is not much difference between saying "shalom" and saying "salaam alyekum".'

'So why the fighting, the assassinations, the bombings of innocent people?'

'You want to remember something. The Qur'ān is the Old Testament, not the New. The Jews spread all over the world. The Arabs stayed in their lands. Our lands were taken from us by outsiders and given to the Jews. What we fight for now is justice. The West has pushed us back to the old laws. An eye for an eye. A tooth for a tooth.'

'But there could be a State of Palestine on the West Bank right now.'

Said shook his head disparagingly. 'Just imagine that after the war the United Nations had said that there are a lot of Jews in Bradford so we give them Yorkshire and Lancashire as a Jewish state. People's land and houses are taken and they are driven out of where they lived for decades. Then later, to keep others quiet the Jews say, OK. Stop being a nuisance. We give you a small piece back. A piece we were never given originally but we took by force. A piece of Derbyshire. We say we give you Derbyshire and we keep the rest. Would the English not fight back? Tell me, honestly.'

Rennie shook his head. 'There's a point beyond which you don't go. A line you don't cross.'

'What point, Johnny? What line?'

'Killing innocent women and children. Assassinating people just to get a headline in some crummy newspaper.'

'Is that how you see the Arabs?'

'No. But when the Palestinians said they would kill every Israeli – man, woman and child – they went back into the dark ages and the world isn't willing to go back with them into that dark night.'

'So what should we do?'

'Talk. Negotiate.'

'We tried that right at the start. Nobody listened.'

'They'll listen now. It's the PLO who won't listen.'

Said shook his head, trying to smile. 'We shan't solve the problem tonight, Johnny. It's a mad world we've all made and . . .' He paused. '. . . I saw a musical in London years ago called *Stop the World I Want to Get Off*. I think I would like that. To stop the world for a week so that we can all think again about what we want.'

'What do *you* want, Khalim?' Rennie said quietly.

Said leaned back in his chair, closing his eyes, thinking. Then he opened his eyes and leaned forward, looking at Rennie.

'I would like it to be evening. The sun just going down. To walk in a garden with Gabriella and our two children. And say to them, "Pick an orange off one of the trees as I did when I was a child. As my father did. And his father. And all the way back. In this same garden where I belong and you belong."' Said looked at Rennie and sighed. 'Is that asking too much? Or should the garden stay as it is now, occupied by an Israeli anti-riot squad. I love that place, Johnny. It's where I belong.' Said turned suddenly to Adele Palmer. 'Give me your cure for being sad. Play me some music. Be like David in the Bible playing to calm King Saul.'

Adele smiled and walked over to the Steinway. She looked towards the window wondering what to play and then she looked, smiling, towards Khalim Said. She saw Gabriella smile as she played and sang softly, '*J'attendrai. Le jour et la nuit j'attendrai toujours . . . ton retour . . .*' When she finished, Khalim walked over and kissed the top of her head.

As Rennie walked back with her to the gallery she tucked her arm in his. 'I wonder why Khalim is so defensive with you.'

'Is he?'

'In all the time I've known him he's never talked about Arab affairs. Not even Arab art. But both times with you he's got wound up about it all.'

'I hope it's not me.'

'You certainly didn't start it. Maybe it's because you're British.'

'You're British too.'

She laughed. 'But I'm only a woman.'

She waited for him to agree but he didn't respond. As they stood at her door she said, 'When you want some company, just pop in. Anytime.'

'That's very kind of you. I will.'

She smiled at the formal schoolboyish response, kissed him on the cheek and let herself in to her flat.

It was drizzling as he walked over the bridge into Warmoesstraat. He wondered if the girl would still be there.

As he opened the door she was standing there with the man. She was wearing only her skirt and the man's hand was between her legs. He saw the thin piece of cord and the syringe on the table. As he closed the door the man turned from the girl, hands on hips, his chin thrust out aggressively. He was in his middle-forties with a shaven head. Tall and heavily built with a black moustache that made him look faintly Victorian. Rennie guessed from the look of him that he was a Turk.

The man said, 'What you fuckin' here, mister?'

Rennie opened the door behind him, pointing as he said quietly, 'Get out.'

The man flexed his biceps and grinned as he said, 'You wanna try me to go, man?' And when Rennie didn't answer the man lurched forward, his right arm reaching out to Rennie's face with his thick fingers splayed apart. Rennie kicked him hard between the legs, and as the man's heavy body bent over, Rennie's knee smashed up under his jaw. He fell heavily, one hand clutching for support from the table and then the room shook as his body hit the floor. The girl was cowering against the wall, one hand to her face as she watched Rennie open the door and drag the man's body to the landing outside.

His face was white with anger as he walked back to the table and picked up the syringe. He heard the girl cry out as he thrust the needle deep into the man's big backside before he lifted him on to his shoulder and walked down the stairs, the man's feet banging on each stair until they reached the hall. Rennie opened the front door and shoved the man's body into the cobbled street.

The girl was sitting at the table, her whole body shaking as she looked at him. Her voice quavered as she said, 'That was a terrible thing to do.'

Rennie frowned. 'What thing?'

'All of it. Especially the syringe.'

'Who was he?'

'His name's Franco. He's a Turk.'

'A friend of yours?'

She sighed. 'No. He's just a pusher.'

'What does he deal in?'

'Anything. Everything.'

Rennie reached out for the small plastic envelope, and licked his finger before touching the off-white powder and bringing it to the tip of his tongue. It was cocaine.

'How much did you pay for this?'

She shrugged. 'I hadn't paid him.' She looked at his face. 'Why were you so . . . violent with him?'

'Me? For God's sake. It was he who started the violence. He probably isn't used to people who hit back. He's a bully, girl. A thug.'

'But you did it so . . .' She shrugged. '. . . clinically. Smoothly.'

Rennie shrugged. 'What did you want? An exhibition bout?'

'You must be terribly strong.'

'You could have done that, my dear. Never wait for a man to grab you. Kick him hard in the groin and the police can do the rest.'

'But the syringe.'

'He's got to learn his lesson, girl. We all have to. Pushing drugs is a dangerous game. And the danger's not always on the side of the victims. It happens both ways. You'd better put your sweater on and make us some coffee.'

'Don't I get taught a lesson too.'

Rennie pulled out the rickety chair and sat down at the table, his arms folded as he leaned back looking at the girl. 'What is it you want? One more lecture on the stupidity of taking drugs? You must have had plenty of those already. And it obviously hasn't convinced you, has it?'

'It isn't like you think.'

'Tell me what it's like.'

She sighed. 'It's an escape. An escape from the world. Money and power and corruption. Politicians, governments, police – all the people who pressure people into doing what *they* want.'

'But if you didn't have law and order you'd have anarchy. The thugs like Franco would take over and the weak would go to the wall.'

'You mean people like me?'

'Yes. But not just you. Most people are weak in the face of threats and violence.'

'You're not weak.'

'Maybe not. It's easier for a man. And I've sorted out what I believe in. How I'm going to be – you haven't done that yet. But you will.'

'What makes you think that?'

'I know you will. I can tell.'

'Are you married?'

'Divorced.'

'Any children?'

'Yes. Two girls.'

'They're very lucky.'

'Why?'

She sighed. 'You don't agree with me but you don't put me down. At least you listen. And you're encouraging. You're the only person who's ever said anything encouraging or hopeful about me. My father thinks I'm disgusting. He wouldn't have me in the house.'

'He's just not very mature. That's all.'

'Oh he is. He's a very important man in our area. Very successful businessman with his own business. Big house, heated pool and all the trimmings.'

Rennie smiled. 'None of that makes him mature. Some of the most childish men I know are successful businessmen and stinking rich.'

'What's your job?'

'I work for a firm of lawyers as an investigator.'

'What are you doing in Amsterdam?'

He shrugged. 'Looking for someone.'

'Why are you in this dump? Why not a four-star hotel?'

'You don't find missing people in four-star hotels, my dear.'

'Do you want me to leave?'

'Do you want to?'

'No. I like it here.'

'Why?'

She smiled. 'I feel safe here with you.' She paused. 'I won't be a nuisance.'

'OK. We do a deal. You stay and you keep the place a bit tidy.'

'No rules? No regulations?'

'No. No rules, kid. Just relax.' As he stood up he reached inside his jacket and brought out a bundle of Dutch currency. 'We need to stock up. Get what you think we'll need for the next week. Can you cook?'

'I've never tried.'

'Buy a cookbook and start learning.'

She smiled as she stood up unsteadily, and as she passed his chair on her way to the bedroom her hand lightly touched his shoulder.

Back at the Prinsengracht apartment Rennie was reading through Jan Branders's report on the daily routines of the Said family when the phone rang. It was Paynter calling from the consulate.

'Just had an interesting call from London, Johnny. The Syrian embassy phoned the Law Society and asked for the name of a firm of solicitors big enough to have their own investigator. They were given four names. All four of them were contacted by the embassy and in each case they asked specifically if they had an investigator named John Rennie. There were broad hints that they might be putting business to whatever firm he worked for.'

'Did Langridge cover me OK?'

'Of course. His clerk had been well briefed and so had he. And he's done it for us before.' Paynter laughed. 'Spoke highly of your talents and experience and said you were overseas at the moment looking for a missing person on behalf of one of their clients.'

'That must have been instigated by Khalim.'

'Yes. So much for him not wanting to be involved too deeply.'

'Thanks for letting me know.'

'There was another query from Finance. Do you want to add a voluntary contribution to your pension scheme? They've made some new deal with the insurance company so that you can increase your pension by a separate policy funded by you. Let them know sometime if you're interested. There's some bumph on the way to you.'

'I'll drop them a note when I've seen it.'

'Cheers.'

'Bye.'

CHAPTER THIRTEEN

Most days Rennie paid brief visits to the rooms at Warmoesstraat. He tried different routes and timed them carefully. The girl seemed more relaxed and she talked to him about her family. Her father sounded a bit of a tyrant but her mother and sister sounded quite normal. She didn't try to blame her father or anyone else for her wayward behaviour and there was obviously a quite strong character underneath the hippie front. He wondered what he would do if Beth or young Mary turned out like this girl. Not that he expected them to, but these were funny times, especially for young people. He hoped that he'd be more constructive than the girl's father had been and he hoped that there would be somebody around who might bother to look for the virtues in his small girls.

On that particular day they had talked late into the night and his walk back to Prinsengracht was even less inviting than a night in the ramshackle chair.

It was five o'clock when Rennie finally gave up trying to sleep. He let himself out quietly and walked through the almost empty streets back to the Prinsengracht. It was going to be a warm day and already there were clouds of midges dancing over the canals. He slept until nine o'clock and lay in the warm bath for half an hour listening to Radio 4 on long-wave. London seemed far away.

As he sipped his second cup of coffee the door-bell rang. The three short and one long rings that Jan Branders had told him to use at his place. He tied his bath robe as he walked to the door.

Jan Branders was standing there, unshaven and red-eyed. There was a bloody bandage around his right hand and Rennie said quietly, 'Come in.' He could see the pain on Branders's face as he slumped down into the nearest armchair.

'What have you done to your hand?'

'Got it cut.'

'Have you seen a doctor?'

Branders shook his head.

'Who bandaged it up?'

'One of the girls.'

Rennie reached for the bandaged hand. There was a big area of dark, dried blood, but the stain on the palm was wet and bright red in the centre. The bandage had been fastened with a gilt safety-pin. As he peeled off the bandage he saw the wound. It was a deep knife cut from the base of the thumb right across the palm. It was deep and gaping, and the white glint of bone showed through in several places. He looked up at Branders's face. His eyes were closed and his brown skin was grey.

'You need a doctor, Jan,' he said quietly but firmly. 'You need stitches in this. I'll get a taxi and go with you.'

'I gotta talk with you first. You got big trouble.'

'We'll talk later. Just sit there while I get dressed.'

Before he dressed Rennie checked the Yellow Pages and called a taxi. As he dressed hurriedly he called out.

'Where's the nearest doctor, d'you know, Jan?'

'Not in town. They tell the *politie*.'

'Is there a doctor on the canals?'

'Yes.'

'We'll go there.' The door-bell rang and he called out. 'I'll answer it – don't move.'

Branders gave the taxi-driver an address and the man didn't look any too happy. But ten minutes later he pulled up outside a house on the Ouderzijds Voorburgwal. There was a girl in a white bra and panties already sitting in the window. Jan pointed at the stone steps and Rennie paid off the driver and got Branders unsteadily up the steps, leaving a trail of blood spots as they went. At the top of the steps Jan pressed the middle button of three with his closed fist and seconds later the door clicked open.

On the first floor the door was open and a Chinese man stood waiting for them to go in. Inside the small room Jan spoke to him in Dutch and the man nodded as he looked at the hand, holding it gently. Then he took Branders behind a green curtain.

Twenty minutes later Branders came out, looking less pale and with his hand properly bandaged. The doctor said slowly to Rennie, 'To keep warm. Not use for three days. Have given injection of iron for loss of blood.'

Rennie nodded and when he took out a bundle of notes the old man smiled and waved it aside. Rennie looked at Branders.

'Can you walk with me to your place?'

'I'm OK now, Johnny. We better talk together. Have coffees.'

'Whatever you want, Jan.'

The old man watched them go slowly down the stairs and out on to the street.

Five minutes later they were sitting at a table in the sleazy coffeeshop where they had first met. Branders looked at Rennie for a long time before he spoke.

'These mens who got your man. The Arab is a bad man. Real bad.' He took a deep breath. 'He killed my man when he got back. Cut out his tongue alive. Cut off his dick and put in his mouth. Cut open his belly and let him die slow.'

'How do you know this, Jan?'

'One of the Arab's men was scared and came back to tell me. They send killer to get him. I send him out of Netherlands.'

'How did you get cut?'

'When he find him gone he come for me.'

'Where is he now?'

'He drinking canal water. Was very bad for his health.'

'What's happening at the boat?'

'They make your man write. Every day they beat him up and afterwards he write.' Branders glanced quickly around the coffeeshop and lowered his voice. 'Whatever you are doing with those Arab . . . that Arab . . . you not trust him. He laugh at your people. Make jokes of the English. He say too much of gentlemans. You think is games but is war. All that he say them. Surinam men real scared of him. They do all he say – Jesus . . .' Branders's mouth grimaced with pain and he closed his eyes until the spasm of pain had passed.

'You know where the boat is, don't you?'

'OK. I know.'

'Tell me.'

'They kill your man if anyone find them. The Arab say so. They cut his throat and watched him bleed to death like sacrificial sheep.'

'Tell me, Jan. Where is it?'

'You heard of Loosdrechtse lake?'

'No. Where is it?'

'Is big big lake north of Utrecht. The boat is on Hilversum canal. Just east of village called Vreeland. Is windmill on canal. Three boats together north of windmill. Their boat is middle boat. Big, heavy canal boat. Name of *Het Vlaamsche Leeuw*.'

'What's that mean?'

'Is meaning *The Flemish Lion*. Is a Belgian boat.'

'They could move it somewhere else.'

'No. I ask. Is no engine. And not safe to move even with tractor or horses.'

'When you say he jokes about the English what does he joke about?'

'He say you don' understand Arabs. You make some deal but when you do your part they not do for their bargain.'

'You're sure that's what he means?'

'Quite, quite sure. Hundert pro cent.'

'Thanks for telling me.'

Branders shook his head slowly. 'Go home, Johnny. Is bad scene for you here.'

'You know me better than that, Jan. Just let me keep the room and we're all square. No obligations either side. OK?'

'OK for me. You still my buddy.'

'Let me walk to your place with you.'

'No. I got business to talk here.' He smiled. 'Nice clean business of white powder and brown paradise for pipe-smokers.'

Rennie stood up. 'Thanks, Jan. And if you ever need me just phone the consulate. Ask for Lambert, he'll put you in touch.'

Branders nodded and signalled to the man behind the counter for more coffee.

Almost without thinking Rennie walked back slowly to the room in Warmoesstraat. As he turned the key in the lock and pushed open the door he saw a man sitting at the table. A well-dressed man in his fifties.

CHAPTER FOURTEEN

As Rennie walked in and closed the door the man stood up.

'I guess you must be Rennie. John Rennie.'

'Who are you?'

'My name's de Vries. Johan de Vries.'

'Who let you in?'

'My daughter let me in.'

'I see. You're Joanna's father?'

'Indeed I am.'

'Where is she?'

'I don't know. She was angry at me coming here. Angry that I had found out where she was holed-up. She walked out on me.'

'Sit down, Mr de Vries,' Rennie said amiably. 'No need to stand. Would you like a cup of coffee?'

'You're a pretty cool customer, Rennie. Not what I expected, I might say.'

Rennie sat down facing de Vries. 'What were you expecting, Mr de Vries?'

'Somebody younger, I guess. One of those long-haired bums she's always hung around with.'

'And why are you still here?'

'Don't try and bluff me, Rennie. I know your kind. You may be a bit smoother than the others but you're all tarred with the same brush. Drugs, sex, crime, you don't deceive me.'

Rennie said quietly, 'I think you'd better leave, Mr de Vries, or you might not like being thrown into the street in broad daylight.'

'You lay a hand on me, my friend, and I'll have you in jail in an hour.'

Rennie looked at the man's flushed face. He was a pathetic figure. A bluffer as well as a tyrant. But he was a sad figure at the same time. He wanted to protect his daughter from the unknown forces that he was sure her life implied. To him it wasn't a question of her loneliness or helplessness but a fantasy of sexual orgies laced with drugs. And the crime that supplied the money to buy the drugs. Rennie said quietly, 'What made you come to see her?'

'You picked her up in the street when she was with some squatters, didn't you?'

'That's one way of putting it. Go on.'

'One of those kids was from our town. He told me she was facing charges as a drug-peddlar and she'd signed a statement saying she had no money to defend herself. I phoned our embassy in The Hague and they put me in touch with the consul here in Amsterdam. He suggested I appoint a lawyer to defend her. I wanted to talk with her and see if I was wasting my time and money again.'

'How did you find her?'

'The kid told me where they'd been squatting and he saw her go off with you. Right opposite, he said. And he was right.'

'And what are you going to do now, Mr de Vries?'

'I've told her she's brought shame on her whole family. It's time she faced up to life.'

'What does that mean exactly – "face up to life"?'

'When she's served her sentence she'd better get back to the States and start earning a living like everybody else has to do. I'd been working for two, three years by the time I was her age. Contributing to the family funds. Going to classes at night. Not bumming around like some kid from the wrong side of the tracks.'

'You said that to her?'

'I certainly did.'

'More or less those words?'

'Exactly those words.'

Rennie looked at the man's angry face. 'Not the best way of solving the problem, if you don't mind me saying so.'

'And what would you do if you were me, Mr Rennie?'

'If you mean what would I do if I was her father then I'd use my influence with the American consul here in Amsterdam and the embassy in The Hague and get the charge withdrawn. That's what I'd do first anyway.'

'And would it work? Would the authorities here play ball?'

'Despite what people say, drug peddling is a serious charge in this city, but I'm sure they wouldn't get a conviction. I'd guess I'd want to talk to the public prosecutor if she was my daughter.'

'You said you'd do that first. What else would you do?'

Rennie looked at de Vries as he spoke. 'I'd make her an allowance so that she's not totally dependent on other people. And I'd try to convince her that I loved her just as much as I love her kid sister.'

'She's talked to you about her family?'

'Yes. A lot.'

'And you see me as a hard-nosed father who's thrown her out and left her destitute, eh?'

'No. Let me be frank, Mr de Vries. I don't like you, and I don't like your attitude, and I'm not surprised that your daughter left home. I see you as a man who was brought up with a set of rules governing relationships and behaviour. Good rules. Nothing wrong with the rules. Except that they have to be applied with a lot of love and affection.' Rennie paused. 'I guess you are a very busy man, Mr de Vries. Maybe your younger daughter was easier to deal with, more amenable. And maybe you'd never been told what to do if someone you loved wouldn't go along with the rules. Not just your rules but any rules.'

De Vries looked at Rennie intently. 'You're an odd kind of man, Mr Rennie.'

De Vries waited for Rennie to ask him why he thought he was odd but Rennie didn't respond. He wasn't interested in what de Vries thought of him.

De Vries said, 'I suppose you sleep with my daughter?'

'You must suppose what you want, mister.'

'Do you sleep with her?'

'You're not entitled to ask me that, Mr de Vries. You gave up that right a couple of years back. Maybe even before. But I understand why you ask so I'll tell you. No. I don't sleep with your daughter, and I never have done.'

'Why answer me if you think I'm not entitled to ask?'

'Because you're wondering if you should take my advice about what to do. If I sleep with her you can dismiss the advice as coming from an interested party. A party with an axe to grind. Without that you've got to at least consider what I said. And maybe change your whole thinking about your daughter.'

'I heard from several people who've been over here and come back home that she'd been sleeping around.'

'Did they also tell you she was desperately lost and unhappy despite her tough front?'

'She was arrogant enough when she was speaking to me.'

'She's twenty, nearly twenty-one, and she hates being ordered about by anybody. She knows that she only has to do what you say, knuckle under, and she can be back in the big house with the servants and the money and all the rest of it. So why doesn't she just give in?'

'That's what I ask myself.'

'And?'

'And what?'

'And what's your answer? Why doesn't she just give up?'

'I guess she's stubborn and stupid. She doesn't know what the real world is all about.'

'How old are you, Mr de Vries?'

'I'm fifty-seven.'

'Let me tell you something, Mr de Vries. Your girl Joanna knows more about what the real world is like than you do.' Rennie paused. 'Maybe more than you'll ever know,' he said quietly.

'You say that because you're on her side. You believe in the rubbish she believes in. Anti-everything that makes society work.'

Rennie shifted in his chair and stared back at de Vries with barely concealed anger. 'You know nothing about my views. In fact I go along with most of your views. The only difference is that I accept that most other people don't share them. You want to fight your own daughter – beat her into submission. Not by argument but by blackmail. Moral blackmail. No home, no mother, no family, no money – unless you toe your dear daddy's line. You're as bad as the drug pushers, Mr de Vries. You want a daughter of twenty who thinks like a mature man. Heaven help her.'

Rennie stood up and de Vries stood up too. Slowly and uncertainly. And as they stood facing one another de Vries said softly, 'I loathe you, Rennie. I hate your guts.' He paused. 'But I'll do what you say.'

'You never asked me if she was innocent of the drug-pushing charge, did you?'

'No.'

'You assumed she was guilty?'

'I assumed that the authorities wouldn't have charged her unless they had convincing evidence.'

'That shows how little you know of the real world, mister. Your daughter's never pushed a speck of any drug in her life.'

'How do you know?'

'Because I asked her.'

'And you believed her?'

'What a father.' Rennie shook his head slowly. 'God help her. She's mixed up and unhappy but I'll tell you this . . . she's one of the most honest people I've ever met. I'd bet my last dollar that you tell more lies in business in week than she's ever told in her life. No wonder she's mixed up.'

De Vries opened his mouth to speak, changed his mind and stood up, walking to the door, banging it behind him without looking back.

It was almost midnight when she came back. He said nothing about her father but for once she offered to make the coffee. He heard her humming softly to herself as she waited for the water to boil. It was one of the tunes the girls liked. From some film. Something about 'Over the rainbow'.

As she put the coffee in front of him and sat down she was smiling and it was the first time he'd ever seen her smile genuinely. She laughed as she said, 'I understand you had a confrontation with my father.'

'How did you know?'

'I went to the Amstel where he's staying. I apologized for what I said to him earlier.'

'Good girl. Never lose your temper. If you're in the right you don't need to. If you're in the wrong you can't afford to.'

She smiled. 'And here endeth the second lesson. You certainly made an impression. Purple Hearts and Congressional medals barely good enough.' She reached out and put her hand on his. 'You're a good man, Johnny Rennie. I hope that somebody's being good to you.'

Rennie looked at his watch. 'Time you were in bed, honey. It's tomorrow already.'

The next morning he was awake early, stiff from his night in the uncomfortable chair, thinking instead of sleeping. Thinking of what Jan Branders had told him. Trying not to think of what it meant he had to do.

He made breakfast, knocked on the bedroom door and when they had eaten he took her for a walk in the sun.

He bought her an ice-cream cone and they sat on a bench in the sunshine in the small square. Now that she was eating and resting, her face and her body had already changed. The pallor and the brown patches under her eyes had gone and her face was beginning to fill out. She looked younger now and the big heavy-lidded blue eyes were clear and beautiful. Her hands still trembled as she held the ice-cream but it was only her hands. She turned to look at him, smiling.

'You still think I'm an anarchist?'

'You are, Joanna. Not a cartoon one with a bomb in your hand and a striped jersey, but an anarchist all the same.'

'I don't want to change anything. I just don't want to be part of it myself.'

'Part of what?'

'A corrupt society.'

'It's a tough world, kid. Always was and always will be.'

'But why should it be? Why should people be so rotten?'

Rennie laughed softly. 'Who've you got in mind this time?'

She sighed. 'You know what I mean.'

'Tell me.'

'Why do politicians have to be corrupt? Why do educated men spend their energies selling people rubbish they don't need? Why don't people care about the losers? Why are money and success the only things that matter?'

'As long as you recognize that that's what it's like, you won't get hooked. You're much the same as them anyway.'

'How on earth do you make that out?'

'Don't sound so surprised. They're turned out by power and money and you're turned on by grass and coke. What's the difference?'

'What I do doesn't hurt anyone but me.'

'When a politician gets a pay-off for giving a construction job to an old friend that's what he says to himself. Somebody's got to build the road so why not old Joe? And don't kid yourself that taking drugs doesn't hurt anyone but you. It does and you know it.'

'And the people who advertise and sell junk we don't need?'

'What junk for instance?'

'Junk food. Dish-washers, stupid cosmetics.'

'They sell junk food because people are busy at their jobs and haven't got time to prepare old-fashioned food. That's why they need dish-washers too. To save time.'

'Save time to do what?'

'Go to ball-games, swim, play with their kids.'

'You're a good arguer, Johnny Rennie. I wish I knew how to argue back. But winning an argument doesn't mean you're right. It just means you're a good arguer.'

'Tell me what you'd really like for yourself.'

She looked up at the sun and then at the children by the fountain.

'I'd like to live somewhere quiet. A small farm. Just getting by. Doing nobody any harm. Just growing good food for people to eat.'

'I'd say your old man would stake you to that if he thought it would make you happy.'

She leaned towards him, smiling. 'How did you make him change his mind about me and like me?'

'He always liked you. Loved you in his own way. But suddenly his pet lamb turned into a carnivore and snarled at him. He didn't know what to do. Didn't want to shoot it so he chained it up. Which made it worse. I'd guess he's shed a lot of tears about you in his time.'

'But he doesn't love me properly or he wouldn't have thrown me out.'

Rennie looked at his watch. 'Time to get back, honey. I'll see you in a couple of days. How are our housekeeping funds?'

'I've got enough for at least two weeks.'

Rennie stood up, reached for her hand and pulled her gently to her feet. She slid her arm in his as they walked back to the rooms.

He opened the shutters on the window and then looked out on the cobbled street and over to where the sun was setting behind the church tower. When he turned she was looking at him and she said softly, 'Don't you ever have any doubts, Johnny?'

'About what?'

'About life. How to think. How to behave. How to react to other people.'

'No. I just do what I think is right.'

'How do you decide what's right?'

'I don't decide. I just know. You know too. Just as well as I do.'

'So why am I like I am?'

Rennie shrugged. 'You wanted to make sure that the wrong way wasn't more fun.' He paused. 'You can't kid either of us that squatting in an Amsterdam alley is the equivalent of that quiet life in the country you talked about.' He smiled. 'But you'll be OK, kid, don't worry. You'll work it out.'

'How do you know?'

'You're too bright to want to end up in the gutter.'

'What should I do next?'

'Sit down and think. About the world and about yourself.' He paused. 'And think, perhaps, of looking at England. It's got advantages for a girl like you. The language and the people. The Dutch are tolerant but in a different sort of way. Anyway. Think about it.'

'Would you do something to help me?'

'Yes.'

'You didn't ask what it was.'

'Tell me.'

'My father wants to apologize to you. He asked if you'll see him in the Amstel tomorrow morning before he leaves. He said he'd stay in in case you can.'

'I'll see what I can do.'

She walked over to him and looked at his face. 'When will you be coming back here?'

'I'm not sure. A couple of days maybe.'

'It's better when you're here. I get lonely when you're not here. You're so different. You're sane and – I don't know – honest.'

'Don't depend on me, girl. Just stand on your own two feet. Be independent.' Impulsively he kissed her forehead. 'I'll be back.'

De Vries had a luxury suite at the Amstel Hotel and when Rennie gave his name in at reception he was expected and escorted to the second floor immediately.

The American was standing looking out of the window as Rennie walked in and he turned quickly.

'I'm grateful to you for coming, Mr Rennie. A coffee or a drink?' De Vries's hand hovered over the service bell but Rennie shook his head.

'Do sit down, Mr Rennie. Perhaps you wouldn't object to me calling you Johnny?' De Vries had got his confidence back and he didn't wait for an answer. He sat down facing Rennie. 'You know, Johnny, I owe you an apology. I jumped to conclusions. The wrong conclusions. I wanted the chance to apologize.'

'Don't worry, Mr de Vries. You were very worried about your daughter's situation.'

'Let me say I followed your advice. The charges have been withdrawn and I gather they weren't going to take them further anyway. But it's not just an apology I owe you. I want to thank you for what you've done for my daughter. She was very angry when I told her my suspicions.' He paused. 'I wish that she felt about me as she does about you.'

Rennie shrugged. 'She probably will. Just give her time.'

'You're a very unusual man, Mr Rennie – Johnny. You gave a young girl shelter and food and asked nothing in return. You don't know what an effect it has had on that girl. She's seen a man, a good-looking man, an attractive active man who's got standards. She told me about her talks with you. That you've never criticized her crazy way of life or the stupid things she does. I'm afraid I wasn't wise enough to take that attitude.' He shrugged. 'But that's water under the bridge now. She doesn't admit it but she's beginning to change her thinking. I can tell. Still anti-everything but calm about it.' De Vries gave an embarrassed shrug. 'So. I want to ask if there's anything I can do to repay you. To show my thanks.'

'Are you friends with one another now?'

'She's very cautious but on my side we're friends.'

'Will she be able to write home to her mother and sister?'

'I've told her she can be just how she wants to be and if some time she wanted to come home then there'd be the fattest calf on the spit that Pittsburgh's ever seen. No explanations. No judgements on my part. I'd just love to see her back.'

'Well that's payment enough for me, Mr de Vries.'

'That's not really what I meant – but let me say this – if there's ever a good turn you need, Johnny, I'd be flattered if you turned to me. I've learned my lesson and I'm grateful. You've got a permanent invitation and welcome at my house.'

'Well, thank you and congratulations. I'm glad it's turned out well for both of you. I'll keep an eye on her while I'm around.'

De Vries walked with him down to the hotel foyer and shook his hand enthusiastically.

CHAPTER FIFTEEN

He phoned London and Paynter agreed to a meeting, but Paynter didn't want the meeting in his office. He seemed uncertain and on edge and finally he opted for the old familiar meeting-place – a bench in St James's Park.

They sat opposite the island and Paynter was affecting an interest in the ducks. Rennie said quietly, 'What do you want to do?'

'You've eliminated the idea of offering him money, I gather.'

'He's got more money than the total SIS budget for the next ten years.'

'I've never met a rich man who wasn't greedy for more, Johnny.'

'Not Khalim Said, I assure you.'

'What about physical pressure? You grab him and give him the works.'

'The people holding Mason wouldn't give a damn whatever we did to Said.'

'Would he himself?'

Rennie shrugged. 'He's not hero material if that's what you mean. But it would be pointless. He could scream his head off and the others wouldn't give a damn.'

'So what are we left with?'

'You tell me.'

'You know what we have to go for as well as I do.'

'So don't beat around the bush, tell me what you want me to do.'

'We'll have to lift his kids, put pressure on him that way, so that he uses his influence on the higher-up Arabs who are backing these people.'

'Or I could move in on the gang holding Mason and wipe them out. Get Mason and whatever documents they've got at the same time.'

'You know that isn't a runner. Apart from the diplomatic outcry they could have copies of Mason's stuff lodged somewhere else.'

Rennie shrugged. 'So, like I said originally, we swear that the documents are fakes.'

'And every journalist in London clamouring for an interview with Mason.'

'Threaten him with the Official Secrets Act.'

'He'd cave in under the pressure like he had with the kidnappers.'

'So let me deal with Mason on the spot. We can say that he got in the crossfire or they killed him so we couldn't prove they were faked.'

'Crossfire,' Paynter rasped. 'There ain't gonna be any crossfire, Johnny. The whole point of what we've been doing is to keep it quiet.'

Rennie shrugged, putting his hand on his thighs preparatory to standing up. 'OK. I'll take the children. But I'll need a few days to work out a plan.'

Paynter half-smiled. 'You mean you haven't already worked it out?'

Rennie sighed. 'Yes. But I need to go over it again.' He stood up. 'Anything else while I'm over here?'

'No.' Paynter stood up too, not looking at Rennie as he said quietly, 'I'll see that you get appropriate recognition when this is over, Johnny. You can rely on that.'

'I'll walk back with you and get a pool car to take me to the airport.'

Paynter grinned and patted Rennie's shoulder. 'No way. We'll get a taxi in Horse Guards. And a pool car can take you to Gatwick. Never walk when you can ride. That's the one bit of training I always remember.'

Rennie sat with his small hold-all at a table by the self-service counter at Gatwick, and emptied two packets of sugar into his coffee.

As he sipped the hot sweet mixture he looked at the people in the cafeteria. Working people, families on their way to Majorca and Benidorm. Construction workers and oil-men on their way back to the Gulf. A handful of businessmen clutching briefcases as they ate stale sausage rolls. Infrequent travellers or they'd have fixed themselves up in one of the so-called VIP lounges. He wondered if they valued their hum-drum routine lives where their only worries were the mortgage, their children's 'O' levels and keeping their jobs.

Not that he envied them their peaceful pursuits, he would have hated to live their lives. But he wondered what they would think if they knew about the things he did. They wouldn't envy him. They probably wouldn't even vaguely understand. They didn't care about the country they lived in. They were fond of the royals in the same way that they idolized a football team or some scruffy pop group. They probably couldn't name two members of the Cabinet or even their own Member of Parliament. They didn't believe in a God so why should they believe in anything? They hadn't always been like that, but nowadays they relied on the state for everything. But they didn't value what was done for them. It was always 'their' responsibility to protect them and care for them. And if they could avoid paying the taxes that it cost to cosset them they did it without a moment's feeling of guilt. Jack Kennedy had been right when he said, 'Ask not what your country can do for you but what you can do for your country.' Never for a moment did Rennie's thoughts extend as far as questioning the fact that what he was doing for his country at the moment was planning the cold-blooded kidnapping of two small children. It was something they wanted him to do. The people who cared for Britain. The people who knew what had to be done.

He remembered that he hadn't asked Paynter to send Ryan over and he walked to a call-box and left a message for Paynter.

CHAPTER SIXTEEN

Ryan flew in the next day and Rennie put him up in the spare bedroom, but they worked all day and through most of the night. Ryan's team were specialists at dealing with kidnap incidents. Ryan himself was both tough and intelligent. The four other members of his team included an expert car-driver and a psychologist. Ryan and his men spent their whole time studying kidnappings and their perpetrators whether the objectives were merely ransoms or political. They were consulted by the police and the military, and from time to time they advised friendly governments faced with a political kidnapping.

Rennie took him to see the outside of the Said apartment and Ryan had paced out the surrounding streets and alleyways. Back at the Prinsengracht he had made Rennie describe everything that he could recall of the layout and furnishings of the place.

For an hour Ryan went carefully through Jan Branders's report on the Said family's daily routine. By mid-afternoon he was already to talk, the street maps laid out on the table in front of him.

'Who did this report on the family's movements, Johnny?'

Rennie shrugged. 'A friend of mine.'

'Wouldn't make "O" level English, whoever he is.'

'How's your Taki Taki?'

'What the hell's that?'

'It's his language. He's Surinamese.'

'Is he reliable?'

'He's reliable enough but he's not a trained observer.'

'It's the times that matter to me. Will those be accurate?'

'Yes. They're local times of course, not GMT.'

'The best time to pick up those children is in the morning when the car comes to take them to school. The school will assume they're not coming and that could give us all day before the balloon goes up.' Ryan paused. 'And that brings me to the main question. Will Said bring in the Dutch police, d'you reckon?'

'It's hard to say. My guess is that he won't. Not at first anyway. He'll be scared of prejudicing his diplomatic status here if anything comes out about what he's been involved in. But he's very fond of his children. That might make him panic and call in the police.'

'So we pick up the two kids. Stash them away. Contact him. Tell him the only way he'll get them back is for Mason to be released unharmed. What about a time limit?'

'What do you think? A week?'

'Not longer anyway. These things begin to start falling apart after four or five days no matter how well planned they are.'

'It must seem odd for you, to be on the other side for once.'

'Not really. I always have to think as if I were on the other side when we're acting against them. And interrogating them afterwards you learn a lot about what they were thinking and the effect your own moves had on them at the time.'

'Is this going to be tougher or easier than the usual kidnappings?'

'Picking them up should be easy. Keeping them under wraps shouldn't be difficult unless the police are drawn in and the media get hold of it. This is a small country. Everybody knows everybody. And when you're dealing with fanatics you can't rely on previous experience.'

Rennie nodded. 'We've got two lots of fanatics here. The psychopath who's actually holding Mason, and the lunatics back in Damascus who are supposed to be in charge. Will the Arab on the boat do what Khalim Said tells him to do? Will he do what even his masters tell him to do? It's going to be tricky.'

Ryan half-smiled. 'I'm afraid that's going to be your problem, Johnny. I'm only responsible for the washing up.'

'When can you start?'

'I'll move out of here tomorrow and find myself a place. I'll want a day's observation myself and then I'll get my chaps over and brief them. Say four days from today, five at the worst.'

'The sooner the better, Pat. It must be getting a bit hairy on that boat.'

'OK. I'll phone Paynter from the consulate now and get my chaps over tonight. I'll find them a place outside Amsterdam while I'm waiting.'

'Do you need funds?'

'No. We've got our own sources over here already. Paynter fixed that yesterday.' Ryan stood up, stretching his arms. 'I'll move out myself tomorrow if you can put up with me tonight.'

'You're welcome to use this place any time you want, Pat. You know that.'

'See you later then.' As Ryan walked to the door he turned. 'Is it OK to give Lambert this address and the telephone number?'

'He's got them already.'

Ryan nodded, looked at his watch and closed the door quietly behind him.

Ryan came back just after eight that evening. He didn't say much about what he'd been doing but Rennie gathered that he'd spoken to Paynter and had already found a place for his team well out of the city.

As they sat at the table drinking coffee Ryan said, 'That was wonderful smoked salmon, Johnny. I must take some back with me when this caper's over.'

'How's that beautiful wife of yours?'

'She's fine. Wouldn't approve of this little lot though.'

'Why not?'

Ryan shrugged. 'Not many women would go along with kidnapping kids.'

'Do you know Mason?'

'I've met him a time or two. Nice enough chap but a bit wet I thought.'

'Have you met his wife?'

'No. I've seen a photograph. A real cracker.'

'You know they're splitting up? Divorce and all that.'

'No. I hadn't heard.' He shrugged. 'Happens to the best in this game.'

'Khalim Said, the children's father, went to Paris quite deliberately intending to screw Mason's wife just to check that he was SIS and a suitable guy for them to kidnap.'

Ryan laughed. 'An original story anyway. Mind you, she looked a bit of a sex-pot in the photo.'

'It wasn't difficult to get her into bed but in case you had doubts you might as well know that Said isn't some innocent bystander. He's asked for it. And he's the go-between for the Arabs.'

Ryan shook his head. 'I don't have any doubts. It's all the same to me, Johnny. I couldn't care less about what he's been up to.'

'We're going to need portable transceivers so that you and I can keep in touch.'

'My technical guy's bringing four pairs over, they'll be here in the morning.'

The phone rang and Rennie picked up the receiver.

'It's Paynter, Johnny. Can you hear me OK?'

'Yes. Loud and clear.'

'I had a message through about an hour ago from our friends in foreign parts. Looks like your Surinam chap was right, and they're going to renege. Not said it in so many words but strong indications that way. Tell your Irish friend there that the sooner he gets cracking the better. It's beginning to fall apart. OK?'

'Understood.'

He heard the click as Paynter hung up and as he replaced the receiver he said to Ryan, 'A message from Paynter. He's had a tip-off from our boys on the spot that the Arabs are going to renege on the deal. He asks that you act as soon as possible.' He paused. 'If they intend reneging they'll wipe out Mason before they pack it in.'

Ryan nodded. 'I'll pack my bags and meet my chaps in at Schiphol. They're coming in on a chartered plane from Biggin Hill.' He stood up, leaning on the back of his chair. 'I'll send my guy round here about eleven tomorrow morning. He'll go over the portable with you in case it's one you don't know.'

At 5 a.m. the phone rang. It was Ryan, sounding very much awake.

'Johnny?'

'Yep.'

'Tomorrow's the day. There'll be no contact today from us to you so make the best of it because you'll be stuck in your place after that. Or somewhere we can always contact you. The equipment's coming your way about now, OK?'

'OK. Best of British.'

Ryan laughed softly and hung up.

CHAPTER SEVENTEEN

As he opened the door of the room he just stood there amazed. She was putting some flowers in a vase and she smiled as she saw the surprise on his face. The sleazy room had been transformed. The walls painted, the whole place cleaned, and pictures from magazines pinned up on a cork display board fastened to the wall.

She laughed. 'Don't overdo it. It's only a lick of paint.'

'It must have taken you ages.'

'One day and half one night. I never want to see another can of white paint in all my life. The cleaning down took most time. It hadn't been stripped since God knows when.'

As he closed the door he said, 'It's a marvellous job. Makes me want to move in right away.'

The blue eyes looked at his face and she said softly, 'I wish you would.' When she saw his indifference she became brisk again. 'Tea, coffee or hot chocolate?'

'Hot chocolate.'

As they drank from brand-new mugs she said, 'Where do you stay when you're not here?'

'Oh. Here and there. Nowhere special.'

'What do you do?'

'See the sights, look around.' He paused. 'And what have you been doing apart from painting and decorating?'

'Father gave me some money and I've been making a list of jobs I might like to have a go at.'

'Such as?'

'Nursing, social worker, probation officer, teacher...' She blushed. '... things like that.'

'You'd be good at any one of those. What's the next step?'

'Getting some training.'

'Here or in the States?'

'I thought I would have a last couple of months here in Amsterdam and go back home at the end of September.'

Rennie smiled. 'You know, I'm proud of you. You've really sorted yourself out. And quickly. Well done.'

'It's mostly been you.'

'Not me, girl. What makes you think that?'

'I don't really know. You believe in everything I hate. Governments, the Establishment, laws, rules, obeying . . . all that. But somehow it doesn't matter. All that matters is that you're so terribly honest. And you don't try and force people to think your way. You don't even try to persuade them. That's really something.'

'I'm going to take you for a nice lunch, so if you've got to fix anything fix it now.'

'Where are we going?'

'To the Schiller. Do you know it?'

'I've seen it from the outside. It looks nice.'

They walked from the restaurant to the Dam square and sat on the steps watching the crowds stroll by in the sunshine. An hour later he walked her back to Warmoesstraat, left her there and headed back to Prinsengracht. He was in bed by nine o'clock.

CHAPTER EIGHTEEN

Gabriella Said clutched her dressing-gown around her with one hand and waved to the children with the other. The taxi-driver put the car in gear and drove off on the usual route to the school. When he eventually turned right into the narrow alley that led to the bridge he stopped and waited for the big Mercedes to come across the bridge. When it stopped he signalled to it to move aside so that he could pass. He was too intent on the blockage ahead of him to notice the man who came from behind.

As the man opened the car door the driver turned to curse him and only then did he see the gun. As he looked up the cotton-wool pad covered his mouth and nose. He was almost unconscious as he was dragged out and carried to the big Mercedes.

A man came from each rear door at the children. A hand over each mouth and a prick in the arm that they barely noticed.

The taxi engine was still running and one of the men swung it into the open gates by the old flour mill. By the time the taxi-driver had been dumped in his own car boot and the children pushed on to the back-seat of the Mercedes only two minutes had elapsed.

The big Merc continued over the last few feet of the bridge, turned towards the Central Station then south to Rembrandtsplein down Utrechtsestraat to Frederiksplein across to Westeinde. Then it was straight on to the Utrechtse bridge and the A2. As they passed the Overamstel sports complex it was 9.20 a.m. Ryan glanced at his watch again as they turned west off the highway just before Breukelen. Four kilometres further on, the roadsign pointed north to Joostendam. The car bumped over the rutted road and turned into the open gate of the ramshackle farmhouse and stopped. Ryan could just see the sails of the distant windmill catching the sun.

At two o'clock the carpenter who rented one of the two garages in the old flour mill had phoned the traffic police to complain about the parked taxi that was stopping him from getting his car out of the garage.

The taxi was owned by a radio-taxi company and they sent one of their staff to bring it in. By the time he arrived the traffic police had discovered the unconscious driver in the boot of the taxi and had radioed the BAR who were on their way over.

Rennie's phone rang at 4 p.m. and when he picked it up Ryan's voice said quietly, 'Done. All OK. You can start.'

In the small bedroom Rennie turned the switch on the ICOM to transmit and tapped out the two-word code for Paynter to go ahead.

Khalim Said picked up the phone and spoke in Dutch but the reply was in English.

'Mr Khalim Said?'

'Yes.'

'Where are your children, Mr Said?'

'They're at school.'

'I'm afraid not, Mr Said. Your children are a long way from home. Would you like to see them again?'

'What do you mean. My children are . . .'

'Don't argue, Mr Said. Answer my question. Do you want to see your children again. Alive?'

Said felt the room revolving as he reached for a chair and sat down heavily. 'What is all this? I don't understand.'

'But you do, Mr Said, you have been talking to a friend of mine in London. About a Mr Mason, yes? A friend of my friend. And now I talk to you about your children. Would you like to make an exchange? There's not much time left. If you go to the police, things could be very bad for your kids. Think about it, Mr Said.'

And the speaker hung up. Said dialled for the operator and asked them to trace the number of his caller.

'That's not possible, sir. We don't have records of numbers of dialled calls for incoming calls.'

Said tried to stand up, his legs shaking as his wife came into the room with a tray of coffee cups and cream. She put it down quickly and hurried over to him as he sat down weakly.

'What is it, love? What is it?' She saw the beads of perspiration on his face, his chest rising and falling rapidly. 'I'll call the doctor. Keep quite still.'

Said groaned. 'No. No. The children . . . don't.'

She smiled. 'The children are all right. They'll be on their way home now.'

He shook his head slowly, gasping as he said, 'They've taken them. Kidnapped them.'

She stood frozen but unbelieving. 'Don't say such things, Khalim.'

'They just phoned . . . said they had the children . . . my God, I don't believe it . . .' He looked at her, shaking his head as tears rolled slowly down his cheeks. '. . . but it's true.'

'And they demand money, yes? We pay them quickly. Tonight. Phone them back now. Say yes whatever they want . . . we will give them.'

'Get me a brandy, Gabbie.'

He closed his eyes, not opening them until he had taken the first sip from the glass she put into his hand. As the brandy worked he drank the rest of the glass.

'Sit down, Gabbie. We've got to talk.'

She pulled up a gilt chair and reached for his hand. 'Stay calm, Khalim. Stay calm.'

'I'm helpless, Gabbie. As helpless as if I had ropes around me. They offer the children in exchange for a man. A man who is held prisoner by other people. People I don't control.'

'I don't understand, Khalim. What man? What other people?'

'The man is called Mason. He is an Englishman. The men who have him are Arabs under orders from Damascus.'

'Why do they have him?'

'They got hold of some high-technology war equipment made by the Israelis. They couldn't make it work. They kidnapped Mason so that his friends would show them how to use it.'

'But what has this got to do with you?'

'I acted as a go-between for them, passing their messages to Mason's friends in London and passing their replies back to Damascus.'

'But why you?'

'Because I speak English and understand the English. Because I have diplomatic status. Because they trust me.'

'Who is this Mason?'

He sighed heavily as he looked at her face. 'He's an English Secret Service man.'

For a moment she frowned and then her face was white with anger. 'You must be mad. You risk the safety of all your family for those madmen in Damascus. You sacrifice our children to make a piece of equipment work. Why? Why? Why did you have anything to do with it?'

His brown eyes pleaded as he looked at her face. 'They asked me, my love. I'm a Palestinian. They are my people. I had to do what I could.'

'You fool.' She whispered. 'You stupid, stupid fool. A few soft words of flattery and your family can be put at risk. What kind of man are you?'

'You can't understand what it would have meant for me to refuse. It would have been a betrayal.'

'You disgust me.' She burst into tears, brushing his arms away as he reached out to comfort her. She walked slowly around the room sobbing, shaking her head slowly, her hands covering her face.

He reached for her diary to check the number and then dialled. As always, the girl answered.

'Can I help you?'

'I want to speak to Mr Paynter.'

'I'm afraid he's not available at the moment.'

'When is he available?'

'Maybe I can help you. What is it about?'

'I want you to get a message to Mr Paynter. Tell him I must speak to him urgently. It's a matter of life and death. You understand?'

'And your name, sir?'

'Said. Khalim Said.'

'I'll pass on your message, sir.'

In London Paynter put down the parallel receiver.

'Well done.' He grinned. 'I was right. You could hear the panic in his voice. The bastards don't like it when they're on the receiving end themselves.' He looked at his watch. 'Let him sweat for half an hour and we'll call him back. Should just catch the highlights of the Test Match. Give me a shout in my office when it's time.'

'Right, sir.'

Paynter dialled the number and smiled as the receiver at the other end was picked up on the first ring.

'Mr Khalim?'

'Yes.'

'Paynter here. You called me.'

'I want my children, Paynter. I want them back in twenty-four hours.'

'I don't understand. Why phone me about your children?'

'They've been taken, Paynter. Kidnapped.'

'That must be very disturbing. How can I help you?'

'It's your people, you bastard. They want me to free Mason in exchange for my children.'

'I see.' He waited. 'Seems a very sensible idea to me. Are you making the necessary arrangements?'

'It's not in my control, Paynter. You know that. I was just an intermediary.'

'Not quite, Mr Khalim,' Paynter said softly, 'You played your part.'

'I only passed messages back and forth. Nothing more.'

'I was thinking of Mason's wife, Mr Said. The girl in Paris. Remember?'

There were several moments of silence and then the Arab said, 'Are you going to help, Paynter? Or do I go to the police?'

'You'd have a lot to explain to the Dutch police, Mr Said. Abuse of your diplomatic status, involvement in kidnapping an Englishman, attempting to blackmail the British government. The world press would have a wonderful time . . . and you would still have the problem of your children.' He paused. 'Why don't you have a word with your friends in Damascus? I understand they've got what they wanted. The equipment is working. They will want to keep their side of the bargain, I'm sure. You said several times that they could be trusted. Men of honour, you said. Remember? I have tapes of all our conversations if you need reminding.'

'What do you want me to do, you bastard?'

'Come, come, Mr Said. Vulgarity won't get us anywhere. It sounds as if it would be wise to go along with what these people say, or they might feel that what was good enough for Mason was good enough for your children.'

'What does that mean?'

'You suggested that your friends might get impatient and kill poor Mason. The people who hold your children might be equally impatient.'

'You mean you would kill my children in cold blood?'

'I resent that comment, Mr Said. I resent it very much. You asked for advice and I gave it. Your problem has nothing to do with me. You have involved yourself in a very dangerous situation. I assume you did that voluntarily. It hasn't worked out as you expected and it's up to you to solve the problem. Not me.'

'Damascus might not do as I ask.'

'I'm sure they will, Mr Said. At least you should try. And quickly too.'

'If I can arrange this, you will cooperate?'

'I'm in no position to cooperate but if the other parties referred to me I should recommend they assist you in any way they could.'

'I curse you, Paynter. In the name of my family, I curse you.'

And Said hung up, aware of his wife standing silently watching him from the doorway. He looked at his watch. It was one o'clock in the morning in Damascus but he reached for the phone.

For half an hour he pleaded and cursed in gutter Arabic, angered by the coolness and calmness of the two men he spoke to.

An hour later as he sat exhausted in the armchair the phone rang and a different voice, a voice with a faint accent said, 'Are you ready to make the exchange, Said?'

His voice was hoarse from shouting as he said, 'For God's sake, I'm not in control of Mason. There are others to persuade.'

'You'd better hurry up, my friend. Your little girl is getting rather upset. We can't wait around much longer. Maybe another twenty-four hours.'

And the line went dead.

Paynter phoned Rennie and gave him a cryptic description of his conversation with Said and no sooner had Rennie hung up than the door-bell rang. It was Ryan, looking worried.

'We've got a problem, Johnny. I'm not sure what to do.'

'Sit down. Whisky or gin?'

'Whisky.'

As Rennie handed him the drink he said, 'What's the problem?'

'It's the girl, Nadia. When she came to, she was obviously in a bit of a state. Trembling and crying. We put Josh on to smoothing her down a bit. He's got five kids of his own and knows how to joke them out of a mood. But she doesn't speak much English. She speaks mainly Dutch and a bit of Italian and Arabic, so he didn't get far.

'She wouldn't eat anything. We put her to bed and tonight she was awake. At least she'd got her eyes open . . . and that's how she's been ever since. She's breathing OK, her temperature's normal but she doesn't speak or move or show any signs of recognition of anybody. We brought her brother in but she didn't respond.'

'What do you think it is?'

'I don't know. It's like she's in coma. I'm not a medic but it looks like some kind of trauma to me.'

'Have you tried sitting her up, moving her around?'

'She's just limp like a rag doll.'

'How's the boy?'

'He's OK. Being very Brit and stiff upper lip. Seeing his sister like that upset him but he tried not to show it.'

'What have you got in mind?'

'Give her another day, maybe two, and if she doesn't improve we'd better fly in one of our own doctors.' He was silent for a moment. 'How much longer is it going to take?'

'It's stuck at the moment. Said's mates in Damascus are the ones who have to break the log-jam. They won't like losing face.'

Ryan stood up. 'I'd better get back. I'll keep in touch if there's any development you need to know. By the way, Paynter said in London that it might be necessary to tape an appeal from his kids to play to him. I've got a Uher if you need it?'

'Forget it, Pat. That's Paynter's thinking, not mine. We haven't sunk that low yet.'

'See you soon.'

'OK.'

Adele Palmer was just opening the gallery when he got there the next morning.

He smiled. 'Any chance of taking you out for a meal today?'

Her face was pale and her eyes red-rimmed and he guessed that Said or Gabriella had told her the news.

She sighed. 'Thanks for the invitation, Johhny. But I'm afraid I'm not in the mood.'

'What's the matter?'

For a moment he thought she was going to tell him and then she said, 'I promised to stay with Gabbie tonight.'

'Let's take them for a meal too.'

Her lips trembled and a tear rolled down one cheek. She could barely speak as she said softly. 'Something dreadful's happened, Johnny. Gabbie's out of her mind.'

'What's happened?'

'I promised not to tell anyone.' She looked towards the window for long moments and then back to his face. 'Would you help them if they asked you to?'

'How can I say, Adele, when I don't know what it's all about?'

'Would you do something for me . . . walk round the block ten minutes while I phone Gabbie.'

'Sure. Is ten minutes enough?'

'Yes. Ample.'

Rennie walked slowly in the sunshine and after the ten minutes were up he went back to the gallery. Adele Palmer seemed to have recovered her composure.

'I spoke to Khalim and Gabriella. She had suggested they talk to you.' She looked at his face. 'You said you were in Amsterdam to find a missing person. Is that true?'

He nodded. 'Yes.'

'Do you swear that?'

'If you insist. Yes. But why does it matter?'

She took a deep breath and exhaled slowly as if she were building up her courage. 'Gabriella wants to see you. She's coming here in a few minutes. Against Khalim's wishes. He says he will divorce her if she speaks to you about her problem.'

'What's the problem?'

'She wants you to find her children. They've been kidnapped. She will pay you herself. Anything you ask. Will you help her? She's desperate.'

'Let me talk to her first.'

'Please help her, Johnny. I can't bear to see her so distressed.' She looked over his shoulder. 'Here she is. Be kind.'

The pupils of Gabriella's eyes were so dilated that her brown eyes looked almost black. She was wearing a white summer dress. Adele brought a chair over for her to sit on.

'I've told Johnny, Gabbie.'

Rennie said softly, 'Tell me about Khalim. Why did he forbid you to talk to me? Maybe he has a good reason. Maybe he is in control of the situation and an outsider could spoil it.'

'He's not in control. He is helpless. Let me tell you what has happened.'

She told him everything she knew and when she had finished he said, 'Let me go and speak to Khalim. You stay here with Adele.'

Five minutes later he was at Said's apartment. It was a long time after he pressed the bell that the cook answered the door. He nodded to her, ignoring her protests and walked through into the living room. Said was sitting with the telephone on his knees. He shook his head at Rennie.

'I don't want you to help, Mr Rennie.'

'I haven't offered you my help, Khalim. Gabriella has told me what happened. She's with Adele. She asked me to find the children but I said I would want to speak to you first.'

Khalim shrugged exaggeratedly. 'Why pass up a chance of making money?'

'Can we talk?'

'There's no point.'

'Can we talk?'

'I can't stop you.'

'You only have to ask me to leave, Khalim, and I'll leave.'

'There is nothing anyone can do. Not me, not you, not anyone else.'

'May I sit down?'

Khalim pointed at a chair and when Rennie was sitting, facing Khalim, he said, 'Do you know where the Englishman is being held?'

'Yes. He's on a boat on the Hilversum canal just above a boating lake called Loosdrechtse.'

'Could you take me there if it was necessary?'

'Yes.'

'Could you show me on a map where it is?'

'Yes.'

'How many of your men are at the boat?'

'They're not my men, Rennie. They're . . . not . . . my men.' Khalim was almost screaming.

'How many men, Khalim?'

'So far as I know there are five.'

'All Arabs?'

'No. Only one Arab. He is in charge.'

'Would he obey an order from you?'

'Of course not. He would laugh at me.'

'Who put him in charge?'

'The people in Damscus.'

'What did they say when you spoke to them?'

'They were cool. Said they would consider it and let me know.'

'When will they let you know?'

'God knows. They didn't say.'

'How did you leave it?'

'I cursed them. I swore that if they didn't do it I would never lift a finger again for Palestine or any Arab country.' He shrugged. 'I reacted like a camel-driver not a diplomat.'

'How important are they? How near the top?'

Said shrugged. 'Three steps down. Thereabouts.'

'What other governments are involved? What about the ayatollahs?'

'They know. They supplied most of the funds but they're not involved otherwise.'

'Could you prove that Damascus and Teheran are involved?'

'Not on paper.'

'But you could give details of who approached you?'

'Yes.'

'Gabbie said that the Arab who's got Mason wouldn't carry out their orders. Do the people in Damascus know that?'

'I'm sure they do. But now they don't want to lose face by having their orders refused.'

'This chap in London that Gabbie mentioned, Paynter. Have you got a number where you can call him?'

'Yes.'

'Do you want me to help you?'

'How can you, Johnny? Nobody can help me.'

Rennie saw that Said was beginning to soften.

'I think I can. In fact I'm sure I can.'

'Why should you get involved?'

'Do you want me to help or don't you? I'm used to dealing with this sort of situation. I could have your kids back in a couple of days.'

'What could you do?'

'The first thing is for you and Gabriella to move out to a hotel. Somewhere out of the centre. The Amstel would do fine.'

'Why, for God's sake? I've got to be here for the phone.'

'Your friends in Damascus will be getting scared that you might bring in the police or talk to the press. They'd never live it down. They'll want to wipe you out. Both of you.'

Khalim looked aghast. 'They are friends of mine.'

'Why did you get involved with this, Khalim?'

'For the sake of my country, Palestine.'

'And that's the way they'll square their consciences when they have you both killed. It'll all be in a good cause.'

'And if we move out?'

'I'll take over here. I'll negotiate with Paynter.'

'I suppose you're used to this sort of thing because of your job?'

'Yes. And you're emotionally involved. They know that. They know how vulnerable you are.'

'Let me go and talk with Gabbie.'

An hour later Rennie was back at Prinsengracht. Khalim, Gabbie and the servants had moved out to the Amstel Hotel before he left. Said had shown him on an ANWB map where the boat was moored. He dialled his number for Paynter and waited as the lines clicked through. Paynter himself answered.

'Paynter speaking.'

'It's Rennie.'

'Jesus. I've been going crazy trying to contact you. What the hell's going on?'

'Said's officially appointed me to take over the negotiation for him.'

'You're joking.'

'I'm not. He's desperate but his friends in foreign parts aren't in a hurry. Apart from that, their representative here is unlikely to carry out their orders. He's a nutter. He likes what he's doing.'

'How do you know all this, Johnny? And how, why, did you get Said to hand over?'

'I haven't got time to explain. I'm worried that the nutter might blow it all up by finishing off our mutual friend.'

'So who are you going to negotiate with?'

'Nobody.'

There were several seconds' silence and then Paynter said, 'Go on.'

'I'm going to deal with the nutter myself. Soonest.'

'So you know where our friend is then?'

'Within a mile or so. I'll find him OK.'

'I don't like all this, Johnny. It sounds real crazy.'

'It is. But it's the only way.'

'I could try asking the FO to put pressure on Damascus. They'd blow their tops but they might cooperate.'

'It would take too long. And Damascus would just say they didn't know what we were talking about.'

'Well, on your head be it. But for Christ's sake keep it low-key. If it becomes public the balloon will really go up. Understood?'

'Understood.'

Rennie walked back to Said's place intending to see if there was any hard evidence of Said's connection with Mason's kidnapping in case it was ever needed to satisfy a court or an internal enquiry. But a few moments after he arrived the door-bell rang. For a moment he hesitated and then he walked through the short hall passage and opened the front door.

There was a police car outside and two uniformed policemen.

CHAPTER NINETEEN

The older policeman said, 'Mijnheer Said?'

Rennie shook his head. 'He's not here. Can I help you?'

'Maybe. We'd like to talk with somebody.'

The two policemen followed him into the sitting room, glancing around it before they sat.

'We are from BAR, the Criminal Investigation Section of the Amsterdam police. We're investigating a murder.'

'How can I help?'

'Where is Mr Said?'

'He's away for a few days. I'm not sure where they are. Touring I think. I'm just looking after the flat for them.'

'Where are his children?'

'They are with him so far as I know. But what does all this have to do with a murder?'

'A taxi-driver was attacked and made unconscious with some chemical. He had a weak heart. He never recovered consciousness and he died late last night.'

He waited for Rennie to comment but when he sat silent the policeman went on. 'We checked with the company who employ him and it seems he had a regular trip every day to take the Said children to school. We know from his girlfriend that he intended to pick them up as usual the morning he was attacked.

'When was this?'

'Three days ago.'

'The Said children haven't been to school all this week.'

'We know that. We checked at the school. May I ask your name?'

'Rennie. John Rennie.'

'Are you English?'

'Yes.'

'What are you doing here in Amsterdam?'

'I'm here on business. I'm employed by a large firm of solicitors in London.'

'We found children's fingerprints in the taxi. We'd like to compare them with the Said children's prints. When will they be back?'

'They said five or six days.'

'Will you be in contact with Mr Said?'

'He said he would phone to say when they are on their way back.'

'Perhaps you would ask him to contact us as soon as possible.'

Both policemen stood up. The older man said, 'Did Mr Said seem worried when you last saw him?'

'I wouldn't say that. Why should he be worried?'

'There was a theory we had. It doesn't seem likely but it would fit what we know.'

'What was the theory?'

The policeman smiled. 'Policemen's theories should never be for publication. Thank you for your help.'

Again they looked casually but intently around the room as they left. After Rennie let them out it was almost ten minutes before he heard their car start up. He abandoned the search and headed back to Prinsengracht.

Back at his own flat he gathered together things he needed – binoculars, maps, the portable transceiver – and then took the parts of the pistol from the inside of the lead-lined, spare radio-case. He assembled it slowly and carefully. He had only twenty rounds in the two magazines. But if they weren't enough then it would no longer be his problem. He cut sandwiches and wrapped them in a damp cloth and ate two boiled eggs as he looked at the large-scale map. It would be quicker to drive down the A2 and turn off east onto the road to the big Loosdrechtse lake and then go up towards the windmill. But that's the way they would expect anyone to come. If he took the road to Weesp and then south to Nederhorst he would go through the town and leave the car well before the windmill.

He slept soundly for four hours and then washed and shaved slowly and carefully. The car-hire offices were only just opening when he arrived. He filled in the form, showed them his passport and paid the deposit.

He stopped in the suburbs and bought a butcher's knife, some wide medical adhesive plaster and two short lengths of nylon boat rope. He also bought a thermos and had it filled with coffee at a restaurant, and his last purchases were a kilo of pears and some bread, and a copy of that day's *De Telegraaf*. There was a paragraph about a dead taxi-driver but so far as he could make out there was no suggestion that it was murder.

As he got to Weesp itself he saw a man on a cycle with fishing-rods tied to the crossbar and the wicker basket on the carrier at the back. He walked the streets for ten minutes before he found it. It was a hardware shop that had fishing rods in a case by the door. He had never fished in his life but the owner of the shop showed him what to buy and how to assemble the rod with its line, hook and old-fashioned centre-pin reel. He bought a keep-net, a small folding canvas stool and a tin of worms.

He parked the car just under a kilometre from the windmill. There was a sign that pointed to the next village – Vreeland.

The sky was blue but there was a breeze disturbing the water of the canal, bending the reeds and grass as he walked along the bank. There was a sort of embankment that rose up five or six feet before sloping down to the fields on the other side. The slopes were covered with a mass of field poppies and clumps of white marguerites.

Kneeling at the top of the embankment he focused the binoculars on the centre boat of the three. As Jan had said it was big and ugly, designed to draw coal-barges, not as a pleasure boat. It was about fifty feet long, very wide, and low in the water with a wooden wheelhouse at the far end with flaking white paint. In front of the wheelhouse was a crude ventilator stack. He could just make out the painted name on the bow – *Het Vlaamsche Leeuw – The Flemish Lion.* There was a man sitting on a wooden chair outside the wheelhouse; Rennie watched as he lit a cigarette. The nearest boat was a GRP launch about 27 feet long and the canvas covers were all tied down. The furthest boat was only just visible, almost two hundred metres from the gang's boat.

Rennie went down the embankment into the field and walked along about three hundred metres. Crawling up the embankment he lay prone at the top, pulling out the lens hoods of the binoculars to cut off any reflection before he peered out through the tall green stalks of cow-parsley that fringed the top of the bank.

There were two men visible now on the boat. The man who was smoking had his head back against the wheelhouse and his eyes were closed, and Rennie guessed that it wasn't just tobacco that he was smoking. His skin was a light brown and he had a pock-marked clean-shaven face. The man standing in front of him was obviously the Arab. He wore just a towel around his waist. His hair was black and he had a moustache and beard and his lean smooth body was much darker. He was standing with his hands on his hips and Rennie could faintly hear his angry voice as he shouted at the man who was smoking.

There was no sign of the other men for almost an hour, then one of them came into sight from the direction of the windmill and as Rennie refocused he saw that it was two men, one on a cycle and the other walking alongside.

Rennie realized that they must be very confident that they had not been traced. It was all very casual and undisciplined. His mind went back to those early days of training. Have a clear plan of what you intend to do. Then do it. It was a dictum he believed in. Some people liked complex plans with variations for all eventualities. People always remarked on how easily he carried out his missions. Experience had told him that it always was easy provided your intention was clear. If it wasn't easy it seldom worked. And if it did there were more casualties than there need be.

He had only one objective. To kill the Arab. He was the key. When the others saw him die it would be enough. They were thugs but they were neither fanatics nor psychopaths. It wasn't their cause. They were just hired hands. Unreliable hands from the look of them.

The two men went on board with a cardboard box that looked as if it held groceries, leaving the cycle lying on the grass of the embankment.

Somebody drew back one of the curtains on the portholes but Rennie could see nothing inside. A radio was switched on and he could hear the drone of an announcement and then music, rock or reggae, he didn't know which.

He made his way back along the field almost up to the lock gates. There was only one thing he wanted to know now and that was the layout of the wheelhouse and the way down to the interior of the boat.

Sitting on the canal bank he assembled the rod and the line and the reel, sticking the point of the hook into the cork handle as the man in the shop had shown him. With his haversack over one shoulder and the rod over the other he started the walk back towards the boats.

As he approached the boats he stopped every few yards and looked at the water as if he were judging his chances of a fish. As he walked alongside the boat the Arab was sitting on a box on the small aft deck. Rennie nodded to him as he passed but the Arab ignored him as he carried on wiping his neck with a cloth.

There were no doors on the wheelhouse and there were double swing doors leading down below decks.

He settled down on the side of the canal just ahead of the third boat, two hundred yards away from *The Flemish Lion*. Slowly and carefully he baited the hook, cast the float a few feet into the canal and settled down on the small canvas seat.

At midday he ate the sandwiches and poured a drink from the thermos into its plastic cap. Just once he heard a shout from the boat but otherwise there was silence. A few passing barges created a gentle wash that sent a small wave through the reeds at the edge of the canal. As the heat shimmered on the water he moved to the shade of the embankment lying back as if he were sleeping. From the extra height he could see the whole of the after-deck and the wheelhouse. There was one man, asleep, sitting on a coil of rope, leaning back against the rails on the far side. He counted twelve slats on the boarding plank and the distance to the steps leading below deck was about seven feet.

As the sun began to set he gathered together his things and walked back along the towpath. The Arab was just coming up from below decks and he stopped for a moment, glancing at Rennie, as he shook the sleeping man awake.

Rennie passed by without turning his head and when he next looked back the boats were invisible in the evening mist that rose from the canal.

He turned the car by the old lock-gates and backed it slowly down the towpath for about fifty yards so that it was a little nearer the boat and facing the right way for when he wanted to leave.

He wrapped the nylon rope around his waist and tied it loosely and took only the knife and the gun and the roll of adhesive plaster as he walked back down the canal.

When he saw the lights from the wheelhouse he went up over the embankment into the fields. Ten minutes later he crawled slowly to the top of the embankment and he was where he expected to be. Right opposite the boat. He looked at his watch in the darkness and pressed the small button that illuminated the dial. It was 9.15. Over three hours before he intended to make a move.

Rennie lay on his back looking up at the stars. It would have been so much easier to have done this right at the start, once Jan had said where he could find the boat. Just knock off the Arab, take Mason, and the party would have been over. Except that those high-born goons in Damascus didn't know then that they'd got a mutineer on the good ship *Flemish Lion*. And nobody could guess how they would have reacted when their sacrificial goat had been released. Who could know what Mason had written and whether or not they had it to use on the media to square the account? If they couldn't come out winners they could make sure that the Brits were losers too. It was one of those doomed operations where all you could do was count the cards as they fell, and hope that you could take a trick with a ten and a jack when it was getting towards the end of the game. But it was what they wanted. Paynter and the high-ups. It wasn't their fault that it had been such a shambles. If the Arabs hadn't got Mason they'd have got somebody else. But it was good thinking to have picked on Mason. A man who'd taken a beating because he'd married the wrong kind of girl. Somebody else might have taken his pill rather than talk.

And Khalim Said. He might be a good diplomat and even a good businessman but it was fatal for a man to walk away from his own character. When they had conned Khalim Said into seducing Fleur Mason as proof of his patriotism he may well have thought of Jerusalem and Palestine while he was performing but it had involved him up to his neck. He'd probably expected that that was the big sacrifice and would be the end of the matter. And when they insisted that he become the go-between he wouldn't have needed to be told of the subtle hold they now had on him. A word from some anonymous voice from Damascus in Gabriella's ear would have been enough to tear them apart. Khalim Said wasn't cut out for the realities of what went on under all the diplomatic hypocrisy. He could probably fine-tune some diplomatic manoeuvring but when it came down to the real world he was a lamb sent to the slaughter.

Despite the day's sun it was beginning to turn cold. He would have been glad of a drink from the Thermos but it would have got in the way. The rope, the plaster, the gun and the knife were the essentials. And it was a time for essentials.

Moving back to the crest of the embankment he peered towards the boat. There was a figure in the shadows where the gangplank rested on the canal bank. Whoever it was was smoking and he coughed before shuffling back up the gangplank to the after-deck. It was the Arab, and Rennie watched as the man walked across to the far rails and spat into the canal.

For a moment Rennie hesitated, then he drew back the slide on the pistol, tightened the silencer and slipped up the safety catch. Some ducks fluttered and quacked on the far side of the canal as Rennie went on all fours down the embankment, moving silently to the shadow where the Arab had been standing a few minutes before. There was the sweet smell of dope in the air. He backed off a little so that he could see the deck. The man was still leaning over the rails and Rennie slid the pistol back into his side-pocket and took the knife from his inside jacket pocket. He eased off his shoes and crouched as he went up the gangplank and across the deck. The Arab didn't turn until he was three feet away: he saw the knife in Rennie's hand and as he opened his mouth to shout Rennie's left hand smashed sideways against his wind-pipe and his right hand rammed the knife into the man's bare chest. He felt it jar and turn against a rib but it went on its way right up to the handle until he felt the gush of warm blood over the back of his hand. He lowered the Arab to the deck and cursed himself for not bringing a torch.

Halfway down the companion-way he pushed open the double doors and kept them open with his shoulders. The stench of humanity and dope fumes was nauseating. With one hand he felt around for a light switch and couldn't find one. His hand closed over the butt of the pistol in his pocket and, taking it out, he fired one shot into the darkness. The crack echoed round for long seconds and then a light came on. It was one of the Surinamese, naked, peering across the saloon from the corridor that seemed to lead to the cabins.

He beckoned the man forward. He was way out high, stumbling his uncertain way across the saloon. He was panting, his eyes rolling as Rennie said, 'Waar is Engelsman?'

The man pointed to the far end of the passageway. Rennie turned him and prodded him with the gun, pushing the man ahead of him. A cabin door opened and a brown face looked out. Rennie slammed the cabin door against the face and the man screamed with pain.

Mason was lying on filthy blankets on the bunk. A light was on, the switch taped over. He looked terrible. 'What's going on?' he whispered.

'It's Rennie, Mason, John Rennie. Take my gun and get off the boat and wait for me.'

Mason staggered as he tried to get to his feet and Rennie took his arm and pushed him towards the passageway. Rennie kept the gun. Mason couldn't have held it, let alone fired it.

There were seven cabins and only three were occupied. One with the man nursing the smashed nose, rocking slowly on his bunk. In the other two the men were out cold. When Rennie looked around he saw the stubby pipes and little brown pellets in saucers.

He locked the half-mobile Surinamese in one of the cabins and headed for the wheelhouse. Mason was lying on the embankment. There was no point in tying up the men, they wouldn't be active for hours and even then they wouldn't have recovered enough to do anything.

Mason cowered back as Rennie stood over him and Rennie realized that Mason wasn't going to be able to walk. It was almost a mile to the car.

Rennie knelt beside him, and Mason turned his face away. He struggled a little as Rennie lifted him on to his shoulder and stood up. Mason was sickeningly light. Rennie hurried as fast as he could along the towpath in case someone had heard the shot and reported it.

Twice he had to stop and lower Mason to the grassy embankment and the second time Mason vomited.

He laid Mason on the back seat of the car and then walked round to the boot and unlocked it. He took out the portable transceiver, switched on and pressed the call button. There was no response and Rennie looked at his watch. It was 1.15 a.m. On the third attempt there was a reply and a voice said, 'Pyramid.'

Rennie said, 'Is "R" there? This is Sandwich calling. It's urgent.'

'Hold on. He'll call you back.'

Rennie switched off the acoustic indicator and turned the pointer to 'Visual' and less than a minute later the red light was blinking and the LED showed 'SPK'.

'Sandwich speaking. Can you hear me?'

'Loud and clear.'

'The two pixies to go to their home address for ten hundred hours. Understood?'

'Understood. Will deliver. Quack advisable, situation deteriorating.'

'Maybe I'll be there. Don't recognize me. Out.'

'Roger.'

The journey back to Amsterdam seemed interminable. But the roads were almost free of any other traffic. Just a few lorries heading for the markets.

He parked the car a hundred yards from his apartment. The Prinsengracht was empty, but as the army always said, 'Time spent in reconnaissance is seldom wasted.'

Inside the apartment everything was exactly as he had left it.

Mason was conscious and Rennie drove the car right up to the open door of the apartment and carried him inside. He put him gently on to the big soft sofa. Rennie carefully undressed him and bathed his face and body. There were welts across his ribs and belly and his scrotum looked like a raw red balloon. When he had carried Mason to one of the beds he looked at his watch. He would phone Said at 6.30. Meanwhile he would report to London and then have a bath.

The duty officer took his call. They would contact Paynter immediately. He had given orders to be woken whenever Rennie called. He could expect a return call inside fifteen minutes. Five minutes later the phone rang.

'Is that you, Johnny?'

'Yes. It's done. Mason's with me. We'll be returning our small friends to their owners this morning.'

'That's bloody marvellous, Johnny. Congratulations. First class. Was it difficult?'

'No. If it had been difficult it wouldn't have worked.'

'My God, I'm relieved. It's been hanging over everything like a big black cloud. When will you be back?'

'Do you want me to debrief Mason while he's here?'

'Might be easier. More likely to talk now than later. No time to concoct some cock and bull story. How is he?'

'In pretty bad shape but he'll be OK in a few days.'

'Well, again, congratulations. It won't be forgotten, I assure you. Bloody marvellous.'

'OK. See you.'

'Take care.'

Rennie hung up and closed his eyes, putting his hands up to his face, rubbing it slowly to relax the muscles.

When he had bathed and shaved he went in to look at Mason. Rennie had little sympathy for agents who succumbed to pressure and talked when they were caught. There was always the option of that small yellow pill and oblivion. Not even the old agony of prussic acid, but a painless micro-second to nothingness. But Mason's body had been systematically abused. The work of a sadist not an opponent seeking information. His mouth gaped open, his breathing stertorous. But given a few days he would be fit to send to London if somebody went with him. If he could sleep for twenty-four hours he would be fit enough to talk.

At 6.30 a.m. he phoned the Amstel and the porter put him through to the Said's suite. Said's voice was a monotone.

'Khalim Said.'

'Said, this is John Rennie. The children will be back at your place at ten o'clock. I suggest you and Gabriella go over as soon as it's convenient.'

There was a long silence. 'You mean that? It's not just a hope?'

'No. They'll be there at ten.'

Rennie heard Said say something in Arabic and it sounded like some sort of prayer. Then Said said quietly, 'I can't believe it, Johnny. How did you do it? Can I wake Gabbie and tell her?'

'Of course you can. I'll go over and wait for you both.'

Rennie let himself into the Said's apartment and twenty minutes later they arrived with the servants. Khalim Said hugged him, smiling and excited. Gabriella still looked pale and stunned. Not quite believing, and not quite back out of her nightmare. She walked aimlessly from room to room. Touching things, adjusting a cushion, moving an ornament, then standing, sighing, arms folded across her chest, looking towards the windows but seeing nothing.

A little later Said took Rennie into his small study.

'Tell me how you did it, Johnny?'

'Just forget it, Khalim. Just be glad that they're back.'

'Did you have to pay a ransom?'

'No. Just forget it. The Englishman has been handed over to his friends and that's the end of it all.'

'But how can I repay you, Johnny?'

'Just do what I say. Forget it. All of it.' Rennie told him about the police and their questions about the children, and told Said to stick to the same story. The kids were with them on tour. He went on, 'I'm going back to my place now.'

'Whatever you say, Johnny.'

'Can I give you some advice?'

'Of course.'

'Don't talk to the children about what happened until they've settled back in their usual routine. If they want to talk let them talk but don't ask them questions.'

'I'll do just what you say, and Johnny, how can I thank you for what you've done?'

'Like I told you, Khalim. Just forget it.'

Rennie slept for six hours and then tried to contact Ryan on the portable. There was no response, not even the hum of a carrier wave. They were probably already on their way to Schiphol, maybe even back in London.

He drove the car round to the Saids' apartment. Said himself let him in. The elation had gone and he looked distraught. 'What's the matter, Khalim?'

'It's Nadia. She just doesn't speak. She just sits there and looks at us. Gabbie's right at the end of her tether. I just don't know what to do.'

For a few moments Rennie stood with his eyes closed, thinking. When he opened them he said, 'Have you got a flat or a house in any other country, Khalim?'

'Yes. I've got a house just outside Los Angeles, a flat in Geneva and a house in Amman.'

Rennie nodded. 'I think you all need a change of scene. You need medical advice. Whatever doctor you use you'll need to tell him as much as he needs to know about what's happened. If you use a Dutch doctor he's going to feel a conflict of interest between his discretion to you and his patriotic duty. It would only need a hint to the authorities and the whole thing could blow up. I suggest you go to your place in California and find a good physician there.'

'We can't go on like this, Johnny. I thought it would be a day of celebration but it's been dreadful. Not just little Nadia, but Gabbie too. I can't take any more.'

'What do you want to do? Would you like me to fix your flight arrangements for you?'

Said closed his eyes, slowly shaking his head. 'How soon can you get away?'

'Where to?'

'To the States.'

'Let me come up and use your phone. You put Gabbie in the picture. How long do you need to get ready?'

'We can leave in half an hour. We have all we need in the other house.'

Rennie looked at his watch as he dialled the airport. It was 8.20. There was a KLM flight to New York via Shannon at midnight and Rennie used Said's American Express card to book their places.

He arranged for a taxi to pick the Saids up at ten and walked over to where Gabbie was sitting alone on the couch. She was shivering violently as if she had an ague and as he bent down to speak to her she waved him away.

Khalim was talking to the servants and Rennie said, 'The tickets are at the KLM desk at Schiphol. I hope things improve out there.'

Rennie held out his hand and Said took it in both of his. There were tears in his eyes. He shrugged hopelessly. 'Thanks, Johnny. Thanks for everything.'

Rennie smiled and said softly, '*Salaam alyekum.*'

CHAPTER TWENTY

He made Mason sip slowly at a cup of warm broth from a can. It would be a couple of days before he'd start talking to him about what had happened. When Mason was in bed Rennie phoned London and Paynter got him transferred to the medical section. He described Mason's condition as best he could and they told him how to treat his wounds and the sort of diet he would need.

It was three days before Mason was fit to talk of his experiences and it was obvious that there were periods that he couldn't remember at all. The one bright spot was Mason's insistence that all the names and dates and operations that he'd written down had been entirely fictitious. They had no way of checking on anything and he had realized that. What he had written would have been useless to them. The only hard information he had given them was Paynter's name and telephone number. Rennie went over this point with Mason again and again. In the end he believed him. Mason was basically fit now and the improvement in his physical condition was noticeable. It was Mason himself who broached the subject of his return to London.

'What do they intend to do when I get back to London, Johnny?'

'I guess they'll give you at least a couple of weeks' leave.'

'I mean after that. Will they chuck me out?'

'There's been no hint of that.'

'They won't like it that I gave them Paynter's identity and telephone number.'

'Maybe not but there were mitigating circumstances.'

'How d'you mean?'

Rennie sighed. 'You were at a low ebb when they got you. Your private problems.'

'Does she know what happened to me?'

'No. She doesn't even know you went missing. She just knew I was trying to contact you.'

'Do you think she'd be sympathetic if she knew what they'd done to me?'

Rennie sighed. 'Yes. I'm sure she would be. But not in the way you want. She said nothing unpleasant about you but you've got to get used to the fact that it's over.' He looked at Mason and said quietly, 'She's burned her bridges and yours. There's no going back.'

'You mean the other men?'

'Not just that. She closed her mind to any reconciliation way back. She signalled that when she moved back to Paris. She was closing the door on London, and you.'

'I still love her.'

'Look, Harry. Forget her. It's over. And you'd never have succeeded anyway. Not even if you'd given up your job. There would have been some other excuse.'

'You didn't like her then?'

'No I didn't. She's very pretty but she's French and selfish. And she's far tougher than you are. And she's a woman. If they let you down once they'll do it again, no matter what they say.'

'You're a hard nut, Johnny, aren't you?'

'I know what will work and what won't. I don't kid myself. I face the facts and you should do the same. There's plenty of pretty girls who are far more suitable for you than that one. You'll look back on all this one day when you're happily married and you'll thank God that you escaped.'

Mason half-smiled, his lip trembling. 'Find me one, Johnny.'

'It's time you were in bed. I'm going round to see a friend of mine. Don't answer the door-bell or the phone. I'll be back in about an hour.'

The lights were on in Adele Palmer's flat and he rang the bell and waited. She was in her dressing-gown when she opened the door.

'Am I disturbing you?'

She shook her head. 'No. Come in and have a drink.' She sighed as he followed her up the stairs. 'I could do with some company.'

Without asking she poured them both a whisky and sat down facing him. 'Khalim phoned me this morning.'

'How are things with them?'

'You haven't heard?'

'No.'

'Little Nadia's in some sort of mental home. From what I can gather she's no more than a zombie now. They found an Italian-speaking psychiatrist. Gabbie thinks he's good but Nadia doesn't recognize Khalim or Gabriella. The medics are bandying around words like "catatonic state". And Gabbie blames it all on Khalim. She's asked him to move out. Says the marriage is over.'

'How's he taking it?'

'It's the last straw for him. He's right at the end of his tether.'

'Did you visit them when they were at the hotel?'

'Only once. That was enough. It was obvious that there was nothing I could do to improve things. She seemed to blame Khalim for everything that had happened.' She paused. 'You know, I used to see them as the perfect couple. Lively, intelligent, gentle and loving. I'd have bet my last guilder on them never breaking up. And now. In ten days it's as good as finished. How the hell can that happen, Johnny? Was it Khalim's fault?'

It was a long time before Rennie answered and then he said quietly, 'I guess indirectly it was. Would you like to go out for a meal?'

She smiled. 'Thanks, but no. All this depresses me terribly.'

'Don't think about it. If you want to help when the time's ripe you'll need to be calm and bright. Your usual self. Stay on dry land. If you get in the quagmire with them you won't be able to help them out. You'll sink with them.'

She smiled. 'How about I do us a fry-up?'

Rennie smiled back. 'I'd enjoy that.'

Rennie sent his notes on the debriefing of Mason back to Paynter through Lambert at the consulate and the diplomatic bag.

The following day he walked across to the room in Warmoesstraat. He half expected that she would have left already but she was there, and she was obviously delighted to see him.

'I thought you must have gone back to England already. Tea, coffee or hot chocolate?'

He smiled. 'Hot chocolate if you've got it.'

She looked at his face. 'Has anything happened?'

Why do you ask that?'

'I'm not sure. I think it's your eyes. They generally look all shiny and alive. They look a bit sad. In fact your whole face looks sad. What is it?'

'Nothing that you and a mug of hot chocolate won't cure.'

She said over her shoulder from the sink, 'I heard from my father a couple of days ago. Said to give you his good wishes if you were still around.'

'That's nice of him. What have *you* been doing?'

'Thinking mainly. Like you said I should.'

She put the two mugs of hot chocolate on the table and sat down facing him, smiling with pleasure as she looked at him.

'It's great to see you again. What have *you* been doing? Or shouldn't I ask?'

He smiled. 'Tell me what you've been thinking about?'

'I thought about you as well as me.'

'How did I make out?'

She laughed. 'You came out of it fine. You always do. Not on all counts but on most.'

'Tell me more.'

'Which bits do you want to hear?'

'The failings. The minus factors.'

She wrinkled her nose. 'They're not exactly failings. More like things that don't fit.'

'So tell me.'

'Part of you really scares me. Sometimes your eyes look like spaniel's eyes but sometimes they're so hard they send shivers down my spine. The way you dealt with that crummy drug-pusher that night. Not just throwing him out but sticking that syringe in his backside. All the way in. My God that must have really hurt him. That's one side. The other's you with me. You pick me up from the gutter, literally the gutter. You give me a bed and food. You don't try to get me into bed. I thought at first you might be a queer.' She laughed softly, 'But by the second day I'd given up that theory.

'I must be a prime example of everything you despise. A squatter, a feckless girl, into the drug scene. Agin authority, spouting my half-baked ideas on how the world should be run. And you actually listened. And discussed it. God knows why you bothered. I must have been a real pain in the neck.' She paused and said softly, 'And yet in your "macho" sort of way you're really quite kind and gentle.

'It's an impossible combination but that's how it is. And I like it.'

'How are you going to put me right?'

She laughed. 'Now you're being sarcastic and that's not fair.'

'I'm not. I want to know. Seriously.'

'What do you do, Johnny? How do you earn your living?'

He shook his head. 'I plead the Fifth and the Fourteenth.'

'OK. You're not going to tell me. But I think that whatever you do you're being wasted.'

'I'll tell my bosses what you think.'

'I can't imagine you have a boss.'

'Why not?'

'I can't imagine you doing anything you don't want to do.'

'Like what?'

She shrugged. 'Something dishonest. Something that's not right. Something you don't like doing.'

'And how did *you* come out of all the thinking?'

She grinned. 'I decided that my ideas were right. But my arguments are no good. What I think is just instinct. I need to justify it better.'

'How are you going to do that?'

'I bought a pile of paperbacks from the American Discount Book Store. Books on politics and economics and social sciences.'

'I'd better start sharpening up my arguments. When are you going back home?'

'I decided in the end not to go home until Christmas but that depends on you.'

'Go on.'

'Can I use this room as long as that?'

'The rent's paid to next June. You can stay as long as you want.'

As he stood up she said softly, 'When shall I see you again?'

'Maybe tomorrow or the day after.'

Rennie checked that Mason was sleeping, poured himself a whisky and settled down in the armchair, his long legs stretched out, his head resting on the back of the chair.

As he had crossed back over the bridge to the Damrak he knew he wanted to get away from Amsterdam. Right now. Mason was fit enough to travel and the operation was over. There was no reason to stay any longer. But as he sat there in the comfortable chair he knew that there were other reasons why he had to go. He wanted to get away from Adele Palmer and Joanne de Vries. Not because he didn't enjoy their company but because of what they said. He needed to get back into his world. A man's world, where he knew the rules and customs, and where self-analysis was only for the weak. He didn't want to spend another minute with people who trusted him.

For the first time in his life John Hamish Rennie was at odds with himself. And it was the outsiders who had caused it. Why the hell should they saddle him with virtues he didn't possess? Virtues that he admired. Honesty, truthfulness and all the rest of it. And his little sermons to Said and the two women. They were what they needed to be told but he wasn't the one who should be telling them. But why not? And Rennie already knew the answer to that question and didn't like it. He found it disturbing.

In the last two weeks he had got back Mason, but that was his job. And as part of his job he had killed a man and brought the Said family to the verge of ruin. A broken marriage and a demented girl in a mental institution. He had lied glibly and half-lied without hesitating, and had been praised and thanked by one and all. By Paynter, by the two girls, and Said himself. There was something wrong when your victims thanked you for what you had done to them.

But it was part of the game. It was what he had been trained for. It was what he was good at. So what was wrong with that? What was wrong was that the outsiders should see him as a knight in shining armour, and despite all his rationalizing what they saw was what he wanted to be. And what, in his private life, he was. In all his time with SIS he had been secure in the knowledge that what he did was not only in a good cause but was right in itself. If there was violence then it was against people of violence. But was Said a man of violence? Were two small children part of violence? Could you still be called honest if the honesty was only in your personal life? Did the end really justify the means? John Rennie was disturbed and depressed by the thoughts of what he had become. He wasn't sure what he was going to do about it, but instinct told him that something had to be done.

Early the next morning he wrote a letter to Jan Branders explaining that the girl would be using the room in Warmoesstraat until the end of December. He thanked Jan for his help and enclosed five thousand guilders. He found a free taxi by the Westerkerk and gave the driver ten guilders to deliver the letter. The man raised his eyebrows when he saw the name and address but nodded and said it would be there in ten minutes.

Rennie booked them on the British Caledonian afternoon flight and started packing his gear. They were over Gatwick just before 5 p.m.

As the landing gear thudded down it was as if they were putting the final full stop at the end of the Amsterdam story. He had been in two minds about saying goodbye to Adele and Joanna and in the end he had decided against it. He wasn't sure why.

CHAPTER TWENTY-ONE

Paynter met them in at Gatwick himself and a pool car drove them all to the Hilton where they had been booked in for the night.

Mason was obviously ill at ease with Paynter and he went straight to his room for the night. Paynter went up with Rennie to his room.

Paynter opened the small room-bar and poured them each a drink. As he looked across at Rennie he lifted his glass.

'Cheers, Johnny. Good to see you back.'

'Cheers.'

'You look pretty knackered. How d'you feel?'

'Tired. A bit out of rhythm.'

Paynter nodded and stood up, putting his empty glass on top of the TV. Rennie said, 'You got my report about the Said family?'

Paynter hunched his shoulders. 'Serve the bugger right. He was bloody well asking for it and he got it. Where the chicken got the chopper. In the neck.' He walked to the door and opened it, pausing. 'Don't bother to come in tomorrow. When are you moving back to your place?'

'Tomorrow.'

'I'll contact you there. We'll have a meeting with Fredericks the next day. You've met Fredericks haven't you?'

'He's the FO liaison chap, isn't he?'

'Yes. Very influential. And a good brain.' He smiled. 'He was holding his breath a bit while you were in Amsterdam.'

'So was I.'

Paynter laughed. 'See you in a couple of days.'

It felt strange when he opened the door of his flat. It was warm and smelled of dust and on the sink there was still the cup and saucer that he had left drying there.

Slowly, as if it was some kind of therapy, he unpacked his bags. Putting things back where they belonged, pushing clothes for washing into the plastic basket and laying out the equipment he had to return to HQ on the dining table.

It looked strange now. Just metal boxes with knobs and switches and dials. Inert and lifeless, clinical and innocent.

He spent an hour in the supermarket and cleaned out his refrigerator before packing it with new supplies. He was cleaning out the cupboards when Paynter rang to give him the time and room number of the next day's meeting.

As he vacuumed the carpets in the rooms he knew very well what he was doing. All the cleaning was to give him time to think. Something that he could do without concentrating while he tried to clear his mind.

By mid-evening he had sorted out his priorities. He came to the harsh conclusion that he had been just as weak as Khalim Said. He had gone along with thinking that he didn't agree with. He had crossed the invisible line that marked the difference between loyalty and subservience. Maybe not subservience exactly, but somewhere near it. Paynter and the others were entitled to decide what the ends should be but it had always been up to him to decide the means.

When he had sat in the park that day with Paynter he had known beforehand what was going to be suggested. He had put up a couple of hurdles for Paynter to jump and he'd jumped them effortlessly. And from then on he was in the business of kidnapping children. He hadn't joined SIS to do that. And when he had gone along with it it was the equivalent of Khalim Said's seduction of Mason's wife. Bad thinking. Bad morality. And what was worse was that it hadn't been necessary. He could have gone in and got Mason without the kidnapping. But Paynter wanted the easy way. Just in case it worked.

But there was no need to make a song and dance of it. All he had to do was to mark his distance from such things. Formally and irrevocably so that they would know where he stood. Loyal still, patriotic still, but his own man. And now, when they were all full of congratulations, was the time to clear the air. They would probably share his views. At worst they'd know where he stood.

He was relieved once he had made the decision but still uneasy about what had triggered it. Why should it have taken the naive words of a dropout girl to focus his mind? Why should he have given a second thought to what she said? But he remembered the blue eyes and the look on her face as she listed his virtues in ignorance of the realities of his character. He had know in those moments that if one of them wasn't facing real life it was him not her. Out of the mouths of babes and dropouts.

Rennie wondered why the meeting was to be at the Foreign Office and when he was shown up to Fredericks's office he knew it was more than a routine debriefing meeting. The messenger knocked and a voice called out for them to go in. The man opened the door and said, 'Mr Rennie, sir.'

Fredericks was sitting at his desk and Paynter was standing by the window, looking out towards the river. Fredericks pointed to one of the chairs by the desk. 'Do sit down, Rennie,' he said quietly.

Paynter nodded to Rennie as he walked over slowly and took the other chair. 'I wanted Mr Fredericks to hear from you directly how it went.'

Rennie took a deep breath. 'Before I do that I'd like to make a statement.' And Rennie realized that his voice was louder and harsher than he had meant it to be.

Paynter looked up quickly. 'About what?'

'About the operation.'

Paynter frowned. 'Is this really necessary, Rennie? This is only an informal debriefing.'

'Whatever it is I'd like to make my statement.'

Paynter waved his hand languidly. 'By all means. But don't be too long. We're all busy people as you well know.'

'Right. I'll make it brief. I want to dissociate myself from this operation.'

'*This* operation. It's all over now surely.' Paynter said curtly.

'Not for me it isn't. I'm talking of a matter of principle.'

Paynter smiled. 'Ah . . . principles. That word always worries me. What was it somebody said – "It's easier to create principles than live up to them." I think it was Adlai Stevenson. Anway . . .' He waved his hand again. '. . . do carry on.'

'I've made my statement. I've nothing to add.'

Fredericks looked up from his pad at Rennie. 'For my benefit, Mr Rennie, perhaps you can tell me what this is all about.'

Rennie looked at Paynter but his face showed neither encouragement nor concern as he looked back at him. Rennie looked at Fredericks and said quietly, 'It'll be easier if I give you my report.'

Fredericks shrugged briefly. 'If that's what you want, Mr Rennie.'

'My team found out where Mason was being held but it wasn't possible to get him out without an actual attack on the place where he was being held. I was told from London that that was out.

'After a meeting in London with Mr Paynter it was concluded that the only way of getting Mason back was to put pressure on Khalim Said. And that the only pressure that would be effective was the kidnapping of his two young children. I was instructed – ordered – to go ahead and do that.

'This was done under my supervision, but only after some action against the kidnappers was Mason rescued and Said's children were returned to him. He has no proof that SIS was involved in kidnapping his children nor does he know how Mason was released. I debreifed Mason in Amsterdam and escorted him back to London two days ago.' Rennie leaned back in his chair. 'Those are the basic details. I'll be making a full report when I'm back at the office.'

Paynter said, 'There seems to . . .'

Fredericks silenced Paynter with a shake of his head and then looked across at Rennie.

'It sounds a well-planned and well-executed operation, Mr Rennie, if I might say so, as a mere bystander, so to speak. So tell me now why you want to be dissociated from it.'

For long moments Rennie sat silent and then, looking at Fredericks directly, he said, 'I've never disputed or even questioned an order from Mr Paynter or anyone else I have worked for in SIS. I didn't see it as either my role or within my status to question orders. But when it came to lifting the two children I was reluctant. Mr Paynter knows that. But when I was told to do it, I did it. I want to make clear that I'll never carry out an order in future that I find abhorrent. And if anybody wants my resignation they can have it right now.'

Fredericks spoke very quietly. 'I can imagine that this operation must have been a great strain on you, Mr Rennie. However, I don't think anybody should start leaping to decisions or making threats. You are a valuable and much respected member of your department, Mr Rennie, and you views will be borne in mind.' Fredericks paused. 'Am I right in thinking that it was the taking of the children that you disliked?'

'Yes. And the consequences.'

'What consequences, Mr Rennie? I took it that the children were back with their father, safe and sound.'

'Safe, Mr Fredericks, but not sound.'

'You'd better explain, perhaps.'

'They've gone to the States to get away from their memories of what happened. The little girl is in a mental hospital under the daily care of an analyst. I understand the technical term is "trauma". The Arab's marriage is virtually over.'

Paynter said angrily, 'For Christ's sake, Johnny. The Arab was in it up to his neck. It works both ways, you know. Kidnapping and threats are a dangerous operation. Sometimes the danger ends up coming back at you. He should have thought about his family before he got mixed up in it. It's all very well bemoaning your fate when it goes wrong on you. That's what they all do.'

Rennie made as if to stand up but Fredericks waved him down. 'How about you have some leave, Rennie? Go and get some sun. Somewhere warm.'

'Have you finished with me, sir?'

'Of course.' Fredericks looked at Paynter. 'We have, haven't we?'

Paynter nodded, his face still flushed with anger. When Rennie had left, Fredericks said. 'It won't do to antagonize him. Let him cool off. You too. We'll have to think how to get him back into line.'

'A little harassment won't do Master Rennie any harm.'

'Maybe not, but you'd better not lean too heavily or you'll be getting a note of resignation on your desk some bright morning.'

Paynter stood up slowly. 'Maybe that's not a bad idea either. He's not going to be as useful to me in future whatever he does.'

'Oh come on. It was you who told me how good he was when I criticized him. One kick over the traces doesn't mean he's suddenly no good.'

'Maybe. Maybe not. Are your people satisfied with how it went?'

'They're *not* my people. I'm in both camps. Liaison not partisanship. All I do is act as a humble interpreter. One side to the other. But, yes. The FO are relieved that there were no diplomatic repercussions. I suggested an MBE for Rennie. The January list.' He smiled. '"Services to foreign trade."'

Paynter only half-smiled as he walked to the door.

CHAPTER TWENTY-TWO

It was almost a week before Rennie got around to checking his mail. There was a pile of a dozen or so letters on the table and three letters that had been addressed to him at SIS's security Post Office box number. He opened those first.

One was a note from Finance asking for a meeting about his expenses in Holland; one was a slip confirming the tax-free payment of his salary cheque to the merchant bank; and the third was notification that he was due for an official medical.

The other mail was mainly bills and reminders. There were a few mail-shots offering pension schemes and one from a book-club with a special offer. The one that mattered was an official letter from his landlord giving him two months' notice to quit the flat. He put it aside for his solicitor to deal with. He was sure there was at least a year to go on his lease.

He phoned Macalister but he was in court and he made an appointment to see one of the other partners. He took a taxi to Regent Street and walked up to the third-floor reception. The girl phoned through to Mr Cooper and then pointed the way down the corridor. For a moment he thought he had heard the girl say 'Yes, Mr Macalister' on the telephone as he went through the swing doors.

Mr Cooper was young and dapper and he pointed to the chair in front of his desk.

'I understand that it's a lease problem, Mr Rennie?'

'Yes. But there shouldn't be a problem. The lease isn't up for another thirteen months.'

'May I see the lease and the letter?'

Rennie handed them to him and sat waiting as the solicitor read the contract then the letter. Eventually he looked up from the document at Rennie.

'The clause they quote – clause fourteen brackets three. You understand what that means?'

'It means the period of the letting. Two years in my case.'

'I'm afraid not. This is what's called a "periodic tenancy". The two years is the maximum period of tenancy. You pay your rent monthly, don't you?'

'Yes. But that was because the landlord said he preferred it that way.'

'I'm sure he does, but from that it follows that the landlord only needs to give you a month's notice to quit. Apart from that, according to the lease you accepted that the landlord was not a company but a person, and was a resident landlord.'

'He's just got a room upstairs.'

'Is it occupied?'

'Yes, there's a girl there. He stays there sometimes during the week.'

'Well I'm afraid that makes it even more difficult. If you try and contest it you could probably hang on for three months. But you'd end up paying his costs as well as your own. It's not worth it.'

'Is there any point in me having a word with Mr Macalister? He checked it over for me.'

Cooper shook his head. 'It wouldn't make any difference. The clause is there and you signed the lease.' He leaned back in his chair and stared at Rennie. 'Of course you could always sue us for negligence if you feel it wasn't done to your instructions.' He paused. 'I suspect it wouldn't succeed. But that's up to you.'

Rennie stood up and Cooper gave him back the documents and saw him to the door.

The medical took a day and a half of being attached to one instrument after another, and he had a psychiatric test and a long interview with a psychologist. They were all full-time SIS specialists. Medicals were compulsory and at random intervals.

Rennie was dressed and waiting when the medical supervisor came in with his file.

'Don't stand up, please. I just want to go over a few things and have a word with you. By the way, are you operational at the moment?'

'No. I'm on leave.'

'Well now.' The supervisor looked at the notes pinned to the file cover. 'Physical fine. Muscle tone excellent, blood OK. But a couple of things. Your blood pressure is a bit over your normal and your reflexes are a bit slow. I'll give you a few pills to bring it down but the reflexes I'm afraid we can't help. They'll probably come back, but I suggest you take it easy for a month or two.' He put the file on the floor then his foot on the file as he leaned back to look at Rennie.

'I'm a bit worried about the psychiatrist's report. Have you got any pressures at the moment?'

'Just the usual pressures that anybody has.'

'Nothing more than that?'

'I don't think so.'

'The report says . . .' He watched Rennie's face as he spoke. '. . . "marked indecision" and "some indications of paranoia". What would you say about those comments?'

Rennie half-smiled and shrugged. 'I took a short psychology course during my training and I can remember being told that the classification of paranoia was not a matter of persecution complex as lay people call it, but of chronic symptoms of extraordinary behaviour from a feeling of being persecuted. So it seems unlikely that your chap can have observed me over a period long enough to describe anything as chronic. And I'd like to know what the extraordinary behaviour is that he's observed.'

The supervisor smiled. 'I'm afraid the misdescription was mine. I used paranoia in its lay sense – persecution complex. The psychologist merely noted that a number of your replies indicated a hidden resentment of something or other – possibly an overdone resentment of any form of criticism.'

Rennie shrugged. 'I never take too much notice of what other people think of me. I worked out my own lifestyle a long time ago.'

The supervisor nodded. 'OK. Well, just bear it in mind.' He reached for a pad on his desk. 'I'll give you a prescription for the blood pressure. It looks a temporary thing, and it's certainly nothing to worry about.'

The following weekend he took the girls to the Planetarium on the Saturday afternoon, and when they returned to where he had parked his car it had gone.

He reported the theft to the police and gave them his name, address and telephone number.

They were playing rummy that evening when the police called him and told him that his car had not been stolen but towed away for causing an obstruction. He would have to claim it personally at the Elephant and Castle police pound. It was not manned on a Sunday so it would not be available until Monday morning. He hung up and sat there for several minutes before the girls called him back to get on with the game. Two days earlier his car had been festooned with three different parking tickets.

After paying the fine and claiming the car Rennie spent the Monday and Tuesday at Century House working on his day-by-day report on the Amsterdam operation. He phoned Paynter on the internal phone several times but he wasn't available.

On the Wednesday evening he ate a snack at the Special Forces Club and then strolled back to the flat down Sloane Street towards Sloane Square. As he waited for some cars to pass before crossing the road to Peter Jones a girl asked him how to get to the Markham Arms. He was not a frequenter of pubs and there were several in the King's Road so he hesitated as he tried to work out which one was the Markham Arms. As the girl stood there waiting for an answer a man touched his arm and as he turned to look at him the man showed him an identity card. 'Sergeant Davies, mister. Vice Squad. I'm charging you under the Justices of the Peace Act. Breaching the peace.'

Rennie reached in his pocket and brought out his own identity card. 'My name's Rennie. This is my ID card. I'm afraid you've got the wrong person.'

The man shook his head. 'That won't help you, sir. I'm still charging you.'

'For what?'

'Like I said – breaching the peace. Accosting WPC Coleman for sex.' And he pointing at the girl.

'You must be out of your mind, sergeant. She merely asked me how to get to one of the pubs in King's Road.'

'You'll have an opportunity of telling the magistrates your version of events, Mr Rennie. Meantime I'd like your full name and address please.'

Paynter was available the first time he called him the following morning, and Rennie wondered what his reaction would be. He seemed amiable and friendly, talking on the phone as he waved Rennie to a chair. As he hung up he looked across at Rennie, smiling.

'Sorry I've been so elusive the last few days. My girl says you've phoned several times. I thought you were on leave.'

'I am, officially. I wanted to get my log over and done with.'

'Don't fret about it, Johnny. You're more important to us than a bloody report.' He smiled. 'Fredericks tells me that the FO have approved a rather nice little surprise for you next January one.'

'Thanks. But if that means what I think it means then there are problems.'

'What are the problems? Maybe we can help sort them out.'

Rennie told him about the encounter with the police and the problem concerning his flat. Paynter noted down names, addresses and telephone numbers and dates, and leaned back in his chair. 'Leave it to me, Johnny. We'll teach those bastards a lesson. The Met *and* the landlord. Believe me, their feet won't touch.' He stood up. 'Forget it. All of it. Leave it to your uncle. When you're part of the family as you are they ain't gonna play games and get away with it. The cheeky bastards. I've got to push off now, I'm afraid. Trouble in Brazil. Old Lawson's got his knickers in a twist and we've got to organize some help. Call me tomorrow about three. And I'll tell you what I've done.'

Rennie had just come back from the canteen when Paynter walked into his office and pulled up a chair. He looked at some notes on a card as he spoke.

'Abject apologies from the Metropolitan Police. They've been doing a blitz on kerb-crawlers and others in the Sloane Square area. Afraid that it was going to become a new spot for girls. Sergeant Davies has been kicked up the arse for being over-enthusiastic and the record's been wiped out. So that's that.' Paynter turned over the card. 'Your landlord would be very happy for you to stay the full term of your lease at the present rental.' Paynter grinned at Rennie. 'He felt his wife might not be too happy if she heard about the little bird who he keeps in his place up the stairs.'

Paynter tore up the card, searched for the wastepaper basket and threw the pieces away. Then he looked at Rennie, smiling as he stood up. 'There aren't many benefits we get in the old firm but putting on a bit of pressure where it counts is something we *can* do.'

CHAPTER TWENTY-THREE

Paynter stood on the steps of the Reform with Fredericks and watched the rain lashing down.

Fredericks turned and said, 'Let's go back inside and have a coffee until it's cleared. I'll ring for a pool car to pick us up.'

They sat on the balcony and a club servant brought the coffee things on a tray, and as Paynter poured, Fredericks said, 'I gather your little scheme worked with friend Rennie.'

'Yes. No problem. It always works. A bit of pressure and then the magic wand.'

'You don't think he rumbled what was going on? He's an old hand. Probably seen it happen to others.'

Paynter grinned. 'That's the beauty of it. If they don't cotton on to what's happening they're impressed and grateful for what we do for them. And the relief of everything going back to normal. If they *do* suspect that it's a put-up job it gives them pause to think. If that's what can happen just as a warning, what might happen if it was for real? If they're clever enough to work it out, they get the message. Loud and clear. Play ball and life goes on its merry way. Play silly buggers and they need to keep wondering when the next load of bricks is going to drop on them.'

Fredericks sipped his coffee and then, leaning forward, he said, 'The odd thing is that I'd have bet my last pound on you never needing to do that sort of thing to Rennie. He's never questioned anything, and God knows you've given him some pretty rough assignments in the last few years.'

'I agree. His attitude was always that what happened to the opposition was exactly what they deserved. And he was the department's avenging angel seeing that they got their just desserts.' He shrugged. 'Ah well. It's a lesson learned. For me as well as him.' He smiled. 'Like the Bible says, "Put not your trust in princes, nor in any child of man: for there is no help in them."'

Fredericks half-smiled. 'The Book of Common Prayer, actually. I should keep him in London for a bit if I were you. Easier to keep an eye on him.'

'True.'

'Ah. There's Grainger with the car, let's get going.'

Although Paynter had been close to Rennie for years and had frequently defended his unquestioning loyalty against criticism from SIS's intellectuals, he had totally misread Rennie's reaction to the minor harassments that had been used to bring him to heel. Rennie had been suspicious when his car had collected so many parking tickets and then finally been towed away. When the Metropolitan Police had been used to pressure him by invoking an Act of Parliament drawn up in 1361 his suspicions were confirmed. When he went to Paynter it was a piece of routine so far as Rennie was concerned. He was neither disturbed by what they had done nor concerned about what else would be done. It was a routine response to a move in an official game of chess. It was a nuisance that he wanted to put a stop to. When the department had 'put things right' that would be the end of the matter. That was how they worked. He had to seem grateful for their help or worried about what might happen if he didn't toe the line. But he wasn't grateful, he was resentful at being treated to such a juvenile charade. But if that was what they wanted he was willing to go along with the ritual until he had worked out what he wanted to do. It was no more than a minor irritation compared with his own growing torment of doubt.

Rennie was never aware before of dreaming but his sleep now was fitful and disturbed. Disturbed by dreams of his childhood and his father, and sometimes he dreamed of things he had done, men he had killed, men he had pressured to breaking point. They weren't nightmares. They no more frightened him now than the actual events had done. What disturbed him was that they were uncontrollable. He could neither avoid them nor stop them. They just happened. And always there was the face of Paynter somewhere in the dream. Not menacing but smiling. An amused smile. Not part of the incident but an observer of the dream

In his rational daytime thoughts Rennie tried to separate his doubts. His continued doubts about himself, and his doubts about his attitude to Paynter and the department. Perhaps they were right and, like they said, all he needed was a rest in the sun. And the things he did had to be done by someone. The Americans, the French, the Germans, the Arabs and the Israelis – they all had people who did those things. They were heroes not villains. They risked their lives just as he did, for their country. The world had changed, diplomacy was no longer enough. The moment one country started the rough stuff the others had to respond. They may wish, like the British, that they didn't have to, but if they didn't they'd go down into anarchy or surrender. International politics had become a jungle where only the fit and ruthless survived. The things he did were to hold the ring so that governments and diplomats could negotiate and manoeuvre and make it look as if civilization still mattered.

If his thinking on all this was wrong then what was left? This had been his life for too long to be able to just walk out. And what would he do? How would he earn a living? And where would Paynter find a replacement? It took years of experience to be able to do the things he did, efficiently and purposefully. He may not owe Paynter anything personally, but what about his loyalty to the things Paynter represented? You can't just walk away from your country and all that it represents. Decency, tolerance, democracy and all the other vague things that he cared about. That picture that he always kept in his mind: all those young people singing 'Land of Hope and Glory' at the last night of the Proms. That was what it was all about. He would be rejecting all of them too.

A dozen times a day he rationalized his thoughts until there were no doubts left. He would carry on as he always had. Loyal to the things he believed in. But no sooner was the decision made than his thoughts went back to Khalim Said and his wife and the little girl. He could take a deep breath and accept that it was just one of those unfortunate things that happen when a man like Said gets mixed up in matters that he doesn't really understand. And for God's sake, surely Said was old enough and sophisticated enough to realize what he was doing. Why should *he* be immune to the consequences of what he put his hand to? What right did he have to expect that there would be no day of reckoning or that his family would not be involved? He had gone to Paris deliberately to check on Mason. He had slept with Mason's wife. Not even out of desire or lust, but cold-bloodedly, just to check that he was what the fanatics wanted. Where was the dignity and Islamic justification for that? The thoughts about Khalim Said were only fleeting elusive thoughts but they always seemed enough to crumble his resolve to indecision again.

Rennie was well aware that Fredericks and some of the others saw him as no more than a thug. A ruthless thug who was respected or tolerated only because of his being on their side. But Rennie was indifferent to what they thought. He knew where he stood. The people he fought were men of evil and Rennie saw evil as being an actuality. Evil was as real as goodness. As positive as virtue. As definable as any other human characteristic.

What made that evil in the first place was no concern of his. His only concern was that evil should be vanquished. Cleanly, ruthlessly as a surgeon's knife removes a malignant growth from an otherwise healthy body. It was not romantic. He was not a knight in shining armour, he was the protector of all those ordinary people who had no idea of the forces ranged against them. The subversives who worked in every field to bring the country to ruin. The assassins who murdered and then looked to British courts for justice and mercy. The abusers of society. The infiltrators who so crudely turned striking workers into a fighting rabble and then complained about the police interfering with their 'democratic' rights.

Back on duty Paynter briefed him on the details of an MP who was being set up by a small group of Greek Cypriots. The Cypriots weren't looking for a protagonist in the Commons – the MP was also the owner and chairman of an electronics company which designed and manufactured components for surface-to-air missiles. The Greek Cypriots were planning a free-enterprise and 'unofficial' strike against the Turkish aircraft that zoomed lazily in and out of the northern half of Cyprus that the Turks had invaded and occupied. The missiles would jack up the stakes high enough to make the UN take notice of their government's case. They had the missiles already but they didn't know how to operate them. But there were several men employed by Roger Lumley who could teach them how.

The SIS evaluation was that the Cypriots had come to the conclusion that money wouldn't work – Lumley was making a pile on contracts for the British government and half a dozen others including Egypt and Brazil. Ill-informed, they had gone off on a wild-goose chase through gossip from a Cypriot waiter at the restaurant he regularly used. Gossip had suggested that Roger Lumley was homosexual. And gossip had been wrong. A patriotic young Cypriot was now nursing a badly bruised face and a gap in his teeth. Roger Lumley had been a divisional welterweight champion during his army service.

Special Branch had better sources of Cypriot and Greek gossip than the ill-assorted group and had watched with passing interest the machinations of the patriots holed up in one room over a topless bar in D'Arblay Street in Soho. For some administrative reason the operation had been passed over by MI5 to SIS.

'What we're interested in,' Paynter said, 'is not pulling in this gang of amateurs but keeping tabs on Lumley. They'll keep on at him because their masters have told them to, and we'd like to see how Lumley reacts when they find out the chink in his armour.'

'Any idea what the chink might be?'

Paynter shrugged. 'Five seem to think they were on the right lines with sex. But girls not boys.'

'Why? It seems a bit obvious and traditional.'

'Yes. If he was just an industrialist it wouldn't matter. But against an MP they can use sex things more easily. The poor bastard would have all the usual hassle with the media. Local party chairman swearing eternal loyalty and then the committee meetings where the other contenders for the seat put the knife in for the sake of the morals of the constituency. The poor sod always loses out in the end. Anyway, it's an interesting exercise. Should keep you going for a couple of months.'

'Why don't they go down the line a bit and use one of Lumley's technicians?'

'I'd guess for several reasons. Like I said, an MP is still open to blackmail. He may wish he could defy them but he knows that as an MP the scandal will finish him no matter how it ends up.

'And a technician can't just swan off to Ankara or Famagusta just for the hell of it. No – they're right in going for Lumley. He's a sitting duck once they've got something on him.'

'Is this a solo or do I have a team?'

'Well, start solo and see me if you feel it's worth expanding a bit. There's a name in the file. A Ministry of Defence bod who knows Lumley well. Could be useful as a lead to meeting Lumley.'

It was two weeks later when Fredericks phoned Paynter to see him in his office. As Paynter sat down Fredericks passed him a page from a magazine.

'Have you seen that? It's an early copy of this week's *Newsweek*. Washington sent it over in last night's bag. Don't read it all now. Just the bit that's side-lined.'

Paynter turned the page the right way round and read the two paragraphs that had been marked with an orange high-lighter.

> . . . no doubt the debate in Congress will include some voices asking if nothing was learned from the shambles of Watergate and the 'dirty tricks' department of the CIA.
>
> Rumour has it that even England's usually discreet MI6 is not above taking a leaf from the CIA books. Recent unreported MI6 operations in the

Netherlands and Australia bear an uncanny likeness to the pre-Watergate habits of our own intelligence services. Old habits certainly die hard so far as 'dirty tricks' are concerned.

There is also the question of whether such operations receive an official 'blind eye' or . . .

Paynter looked up as he finished reading.

'Just fishing, I'd say. Seeing if anyone rises to the bait. And the thing in Australia was ASIO not us.'

'No cunsultation with us? No advice?' Fredericks's voice was sharp.

'Not officially anyway. And certainly nothing in writing.'

'And the Netherlands reference?'

'Could be a shot in the dark.'

'Oh come on. Who the hell has been up to anything in the Netherlands in the last four years that could reasonably be described as dirty tricks? Somebody's talked and I know who I suspect.'

'Who?'

For the first time in years Paynter saw Fredericks lose his temper. His voice cracking with anger. 'Don't bullshit *me*, Paynter. I have to respond to this piece. What do you expect me to do?'

'Say it's a shot in the dark.'

'You must be out of your mind. I've personally put my name to a recommendation for an MBE for Rennie in the next Honours List.'

'Did you say what it was for?'

'Of course I bloody well did. They're not given out with the rations despite what the public thinks. I didn't give details but I mentioned a very delicate operation in Amsterdam.' He paused. 'And only a few weeks back the chap was sitting right here in this office saying he wanted to be dissociated from the operation.' Fredericks paused. 'Has he put in his resignation like he threatened?'

'No. He hasn't even mentioned it again. I put that bit of mild harassment on him and he came into line. He was just strung up from the operation.'

'Rennie's not the kind who gets strung-up from operations. You know that as well as I do. You were always on about his loyalty and dependability. You wished you had more like him. Remember?'

'Have you borne in mind that it could be somebody else? Khalim Said for instance.'

'I read Rennie's full report. According to that Said had got troubles enough of his own, and apart from that Rennie was sure that Said never connected him with SIS. Said's got too much to lose by talking about that affair.'

'Do you want me to do a discreet internal check before I take action against Rennie? There were others involved, you know.'

'Look Hugo. I've never trusted Rennie. You know my views on him. He's a ruthless, tough bastard and you've found him useful. But you were just as surprised as I was when he put on his little act in this office, disassociating himself from the operation. You were sure you knew him inside out, but you were wrong. He's a loner and he doesn't lay his cards down on the table. I didn't trust him way back and I don't trust him now. You can say I'm prejudiced and maybe I am. But I'm right as well. So let's stop playing games.'

'What do you want me to do?'

Fredericks leaned forward and said quietly, 'I want you to put the real bite on that bastard. Show him that if he breathes one word out of place he's going to get the full treatment. And put somebody on to keepng an eye on him. Not a team. He'd spot that. But give him the works.'

'What will you tell the FO people?'

'That's my worry. You just do your part and don't let the bastard make any more waves than he has done already.'

'Do you want me to confront him about this piece?'

'Oh Jesus. No, no, no.' Fredericks's anger overflowed. 'Just do what I've told you. And keep me in touch, especially if you have any doubts.'

'I'll do that.'

CHAPTER TWENTY-FOUR

Paynter sat in the first-floor coffee place at the Hilton and watched Mason getting out of the lift. He still looked pale and unwell but Paynter needed to keep the Amsterdam operation in as closed a circle as he could. And that meant using Mason.

He smiled amiably as Mason shed his coat and sat down at the table.

'What'll you have?' He had in mind coffee or tea but he hid his annoyance as Mason asked for a Bloody Mary. He realized that Mason looked a Bloody Mary type. A bit on the wet side despite his good looks. When the drink had been brought he pulled his chair nearer to Mason's.

'I've got a bit of a problem, Mason. I need your help.'

Mason smiled. 'Glad to be wanted. I've felt a bit spare and unloved since I got back.'

'Well, that's natural. But oddly enough the problem comes out of that business in Amsterdam.'

Mason pursed his lips. 'Not my favourite place, Amsterdam.'

'I'm sure it isn't. But the problem's here in London. Your friend Rennie as a matter of fact.'

Mason sighed. 'I don't think he sees me as a friend these days. I'm a bit of a broken reed in his eyes.'

Paynter ignored the plea and went on. 'There was a piece in one of the American magazines. Mainly about dirty tricks in the CIA but it made a fleeting mention of SIS and dirty tricks. It specifically mentioned a recent SIS operation in the Netherlands.'

'Good grief. Now what?'

'Now nothing. If we can keep the lid on it. But Rennie turned a bit wet about the Amsterdam operation. Has he said anything to you?'

'No. He's avoided me. But I know he was put out about the Arab's kid and the wife. I think he had in mind that sort of thing happening to his own daughters.'

'Did he now? Did he say that?'

'No. But when he was debriefing me, before I got back here, it was obvious that it stuck in his gullet. Made him a bit sharp with me. Because I talked.'

'I see. Anyway, we're worried that he might have leaked the story because he didn't like what he had to do.'

Mason shook his head, frowning. 'That isn't the kind of thing Rennie would do. I'd stake my life on that. He's dead straight, is Rennie. If he wanted to raise hell he'd do it head on.'

'You sound like a Rennie fan. Are you?'

'I suppose I am in a way. I admire him. He's tough and he's got bags of courage. Never seen him back down. And in his own peculiar way he's straight as a die.'

'You may be right. Maybe he didn't leak. But somebody did. And I want you to keep an eye on Rennie for me. I'm going to post you to him as an assistant on the job he's doing now.'

Mason shrugged. 'If that's what you want.'

'I'll notify him tomorrow.'

Mason nodded and finished his drink. And then Paynter remembered.

'How's things with your wife now? Any progress?'

There were tears at the edges of Mason's eyes, as always at any mention of his wife, but he brushed them away with the back of his hand. 'She's started the divorce. I wanted to defend it but Legal said no. It could mean things coming out in court or using the Official Secrets Act to prevent it. They didn't want either to happen.'

'Is there anything we could do? Explain to her that it was only your work kept you away?'

'She knows it was that. But she's not the kind of girl who goes for that sort of stuff. And she's French not British, despite the passport. It's gone too far. I've had it so far as she's concerned.'

'I'm sorry. Very sorry. Maybe you'll meet someone else with more understanding. I hope so. And you're a good-looking chap, you know.'

Mason half-smiled. 'I don't want anyone else. I want her.'

'I understand.' He stood up. 'I'll contact you tomorrow when I've spoken to Rennie.' He paused. 'Can I give you a lift anywhere?'

'No. I'll hang on here for a bit and have another noggin.'

Rennie had been formal but not unfriendly when Mason reported to him.

'There's not much happening, Mason. It's a bit of a wild-goose chase in my opinion, but a new face will be useful. I've been in every porn shop in Soho trying to keep an eye on these birds.' He smiled. 'I think whoever's backing them and funding them is being taken for a ride.'

'What are they like?'

'A pretty hairy bunch. There's one smoothie who wears the good clothes. He's trying to get alongside Lumley's secretary at the moment. She's in her fifties. The old retainer. Been with him for years but I think the Cypriot's making some progress all the same. Her cleaning lady's from Cyprus and he's doing the dutiful nephew bit.'

Rennie took Mason to see the various cafes and clubs frequented by the Cypriots, and drove him over to see the outside of Lumley's plant on the industrial estate on Purley Way. They also drove past the small semi-detached house in Waddon where Lumley's secretary lived. As they drove off Mason said, 'Is Lumley married?'

'Yes. But not very happily from what I've heard. She's a bit of a virago. But they keep up appearances.'

'Is he likely to fall for girl-bait?'

'Guessing, I'd say yes. He's got a thing for very young girls. He has sex with a girl in the typing pool at his works – looks like strictly business for both parties. And he also finances a young married woman who lives in South Croydon. She used to work for him and he visits her frequently in the daytime. If it was carefully done I'd say he'd fall all right.'

'Any signs of them finding a suitable girl?'

'Well, they've had dozens of girls at their rooms in Soho. All young and pretty. Those we've been able to identify are Maltese or Cypriots and they may be looking them over for pushing at Lumley. One of the prettiest is definitely a hooker. But I'd guess they'd all play if there was incentive enough. They'd be able to offer her a chance to be a patriot and earn a few quid at the same time. Their problem is getting her alongside Lumley. But he has been known to visit one or two shady clubs in Soho. Shouldn't be too difficult to get them together but not so easy to raise the proposition about the missiles.'

'Anything you'd like me to do tomorrow?'

'Yes. See if you can put together a list of the chaps at Lumley's place who are capable of showing those goons how to fire a missile. Take your time on it but keep in touch, even if it's only a nil report.'

'OK. Where shall I contact you?'

'Office or flat, it doesn't matter.'

Back at the office there was a message on Rennie's desk to ring his wife as soon as possible.

Rennie rang several times but there was no reply. He looked at his watch. It was nearly six and they ought to be there. It was a schoolday and homework to be done. He decided that he'd drive over and see what she wanted. And it was a chance to see the girls.

It was dark when he pulled up at the house and there were no lights on in any of the windows. He rang the bell and waited. But there was no response. He walked round to the back of the house. The curtains weren't drawn and the house was obviously empty. Walking back to the porch he opened his wallet and took out the small slip of plastic, hesitated and then put it back. It might be legally his house but he wasn't entitled to break in.

There were lights on in the houses on both sides. He decided on the Crasters. Craster was something in banking or insurance and had always nodded when he had seen Rennie picking up the girls. It was Craster himself who answered the door.

'Hello, old man. What can I do for you?'

'I had a message to phone my ex-wife as soon as possible. I couldn't get an answer so I came over. But the place is empty. I wondered if you knew where they were.'

'I don't I'm afraid. But hold on. Fran might know.' He turned and called out, 'Fran.'

She was wiping her hands on a teacloth as she hurried down the hall.

'What is it, Frankie? Oh hello. Mr Rennie, isn't it?'

Craster said, 'Wondered if you knew where Mrs Rennie and the girls are. She phoned him to contact her but there's nobody there.'

Mrs Craster looked intently at Rennie's face. 'It's not some domestic quarrel, is it?'

'Fran . . .' Craster said angrily, '. . . whatever next. How can you say such a thing? Mr Rennie and . . .'

'Be quiet, Frank.' She turned to Rennie. 'She was very upset about something. She fetched the girls from school at lunch-time and I saw them leave about an hour later in a taxi. They had suitcases with them. She looked terribly agitated.'

'Which direction did the taxi go?'

Mrs Craster pointed. 'Down towards the main street. I hope she's not poorly.'

'Would you allow me to use your telephone? She might have gone to her mother's.'

Craster waved him inside. 'Of course. Come in.' He pointed towards the glass-topped table. 'Help yourself. Give us a call when you've finished.'

Mrs Winfield, Mary's mother, had been shocked by the divorce. She was a staunch admirer of Rennie, and with Mary not wanting her mother to know about her lapse with Cowley the explanations had been unconvincing. But she still sent him cards at Christmas and on his birthday. He dialled the number and after several rings he heard her quavering voice.

'Who is that?'

'It's Johnny, mother. Is Mary with you?'

He heard the phone clatter at the other end and then his ex-wife's breathless voice. She was almost whispering.

'Is that you, Johnny?'

'Yes. What's going on? I got a message to ring you. I got no answer so I . . .'

'Johnny. I'm scared.'

'Of what?'

'Can you come over,' she whispered. 'I don't want the girls to hear.'

'You mean come over now, tonight?'

'Yes. Please come, Johnny. Please help me.'

'Of course I will. Just relax and I'll be there in about forty-five minutes.'

He hung up and called out to the Crasters, told them that Mary was at her mother's and headed for his car.

Mrs Winfield lived in a detached house in Purley, near where he had been with Mason earlier that day when they were looking at Lumley's factory. There were lights on all over the house and as he walked up the garden path Mary was standing at the open door. She looked pale, and even in the dim light he could see that she had been crying.

'Oh Johnny. Thank God you've come. I've been out of my mind all day. I phoned but you were out. Don't go in, the girls are still up.'

'Tell me what's the matter,' Rennie said quietly.

'I fainted, Johnny. I've never fainted in my life before.'

'Let's walk round the block. Leave the door.'

'Is it safe, d'you think?'

'Of course it is. Come on.'

He waited until they were several houses away and then stopped by a street light and turned her so that he could look at her. Her whole body was shaking.

'Now tell me what's happened.'

'I took the girls to school and was back just after nine. About ten there was a knock on the door. When I opened it there were two men there, a young one and an old one. And there was a van in the road. I asked them what they wanted and the older man took off his hat and said he'd brought the coffins. I think I was kind of dazed and I said I didn't understand. He said to come and look, and I went out to the van. There were three coffins there on a strip of foam. A large one and two small ones . . .' She burst into tears and he put his hands on her shoulders.

'Go on, Mary.'

She took a deep breath as she looked up at his face. 'They had labels on them. Glued on. One said, "Mary Rennie" and others just said "Elizabeth" and "Mary". I walked back to the house and the old man came with me. He gave me an envelope. There was a note inside. It was typed, and it said "Be very quiet and very careful". I looked at it and I must have passed out. When I came to I was in the kitchen and the old man was wiping my face with a cloth. He was very concerned. I told him to take the coffins away. That it was all a mistake.'

'Where's the note?'

'I don't know. I looked for it afterwards but I couldn't find it.'

'Go on.'

'I phoned you and left the message and I didn't know what to do. I panicked and phoned mother. She said come over and I fetched the girls from school. They helped me pack and I called a taxi and we came over.'

'Did you tell the girls what had happened?'

'Oh God, no. But they could see I was worried and they're terribly upset. Was I a fool about it all?'

'No. Of course not. People play these tricks from time to time. Practical jokes. But they're not very funny for the folk on the receiving end. I'll come back in and chat to the girls. Wipe your eyes and tell them it was a stupid joke by one of my friends. Go back home when you feel like it. It won't happen again. I'll sort out whoever's done this idiotic thing.'

'But who would do such a terrible thing. It's the kind of thing gangsters do to one another in New York, isn't it?'

Rennie smiled. 'More like Chicago. Don't worry about who did it. I'll soon find out and there'll be no such nonsense again.'

She smiled up at him. 'You know, you're a good man, Johnny Rennie. A real rock.' She hunched her shoulders. 'Let's go in. I feel fine all of a sudden.'

Rennie stayed until after ten, playing Scrabble with the two girls and afterwards reading them a story in bed. They caught the relief of their mother and grandmother and were back to normal long before they went to bed. Mrs Winfield gave him a thermos of coffee to take with him and was obviously relieved that all had turned out well in the end.

It took Rennie an hour and a half to find Mason's place in Pimlico. He had the top floor of a Victorian house in one of the rundown streets off the Embankment. It was several minutes before Mason opened the door. He was wearing just an old blue shirt and a pair of slippers, standing there unsteadily, trying to work out who it was. Rennie could smell the booze on his breath. Then Mason said slowly, slurring his words, 'Well hello, Johnny. The balloon gone up? Third World War and all that?'

'Can I come in, Mason?'

'By all means. Welcome to my humble abode.'

Mason staggered slightly as he drew out a chair by the table and sat down heavily opposite Rennie.

'A drinkie, old man?'

'No thanks. I need your help, Mason. Will you listen carefully while I explain.'

'Something serious is it?'

'Important to me anyway.'

Mason stood up, swaying slightly. 'In that case let me dip the old head in a drop of cold water. Let's clear the brain for action, eh?'

Five minutes later Mason came back. His face ruddy, hair combed, and wearing an ancient bath-robe. He moved sharply and seemed to have recovered.

'Forgive the shambles and the stupor. What's cooking?'

'Can this be between just you and me?'

'Of course it can.'

'Is that a promise?'

Mason half-smiled. 'Do you trust my promises, Johnny?'

'Yes. Why shouldn't I?'

'I'm the man who talked, remember? One twist of my balls and I called it a day. You debriefed me so you know all about it. No hero me. No stiff upper lip. Just a couple of screams and I blew the gaff.'

'Harry, you were in no fit state to resist anyone. You'd already been through the mincer with Fleur in Paris.'

Mason sighed and then said softly, 'She was very beautiful, Johnny. And I loved her very much. It did influence me. I felt the department had caused my troubles. I begged them for a home posting. Just for a year to give me time with her. But no. They wouldn't. I didn't feel I owed the department all that much loyalty.'

'I met Fleur when I was trying to find you. She *is* beautiful. But like I told you before, being with her wouldn't have solved the problem. I'm not just guessing. I know.'

'How do you know?'

'I fell in love with a Fleur when I was first in the army. In the end I walked away. I knew we'd never last.'

'Why?'

'She was much younger than me. And very beautiful. Even priests turned their heads to have another look. We both thought we loved one another, but I knew in my heart that we didn't fit.'

'Why not?'

'I was jealous of other men. Every man. Old men, her uncles, passing strangers. The lot. She knew I was jealous and I think she liked it. But she did nothing to calm me down. She knew she was beautiful and she knew that all men found her attractive. We got engaged and I thought that would change it all. It didn't of course. She was out with a couple of men behind my back. One was my company commander. Both men were married so there was nothing in it for her except the conquest.' Rennie smiled. 'I sat down one night and wrote myself an "appreciation report", as if it was some campaign I was in. Typical army thinking. There was no doubt about the conclusion. There was nothing in it for me. Not a damn thing. So I walked out. I was desperately unhappy for a week. Terribly tempted to phone her. But after a week I realized it was a relief. I felt normal again.'

'And you've never regretted it?'

'No way. Just faintly embarrassed that I ever got into it in the first place.'

Mason leaned forward, looking at Rennie. 'You can't have liked telling me this. The guy who's got his lifestyle all worked out. The black and white man. No greys.'

'I've told you because I know you'll understand. And it might help you. I've never told anyone else.'

'Thanks for telling me.' He sighed heavily. 'Sometimes when I've thought exactly the same. And for an hour or so I feel relieved to be out of it. No more jealousy. No more imagining her with other men. Maybe it'll go in the end.'

'It will, Harry. It will. I promise.'

'We were talking about promises. Yes, I promise, Johnny.'

Rennie took a deep breath. 'When I came back from Amsterdam I told Paynter that I didn't like the kidnapping of Said's children and the consequences. They put on a little harassment to keep me in line. I went through the "help me" ritual and it was all stopped. But it's started again. I don't know why. But this time it's for real.' He paused. 'Three coffins were delivered at my ex-wife's house today. One had her name on it and the other two were in the names of my daughters. My wife was half out of her mind.'

Mason shook his head in disbelief. 'The shits.' He sighed. 'I know why they're doing it.'

'Tell me.'

'You won't let on that I told you?'

'This is just between you and me, like I said. It applies both ways. Me as well as you.'

'There was a piece in an American magazine. About the CIA and dirty tricks and there was a brief dig at an SIS dirty tricks operation in the Netherlands. It only came in two or three days ago. They think you leaked it to the press. Did you?'

'Of course I didn't. I never meet any press people anyway. I haven't told anyone outside the people concerned in the department.'

'Paynter told me about it. I said it wasn't you. What are you going to do?'

'I'm putting in my resignation tonight. It'll be on Paynter's desk in the morning.'

'For God's sake, Johnny. That'll make things worse. They'll do their nuts in case you talk any more.'

'That's their worry. As far as I'm concerned I've had enough. I don't trust them any more. Not their honour, nor their integrity, nor their motives. I wouldn't lift a finger for them ever again.'

'Would you talk?'

'No. Definitely not. Not unless they really put me in a corner.'

'What do you want me to do?'

'I think they've worked out that my dislike of what had to be done to Said's children shows where my Achilles' heel is. My family. That's why we had today's little game. I want to ask if you'll keep an eye on Mary and the two girls for me. Will you do that?'

'Yes. Of course I will.'

Rennie took out a card from his jacket pocket and handed it to Mason. 'I've put down various telephone numbers where you should be able to contact me.'

'Do you want to kip down here for the night?'

'Thanks, but I've got things to do before I sleep.'

Rennie typed out the brief letter of resignation on his portable and read it again and again before he signed it.

To: Paynter G.S. Dir. Sp. Services
From: Rennie J.H.

With this letter I give the required thirty-one days' notice of my resignation from SIS. With accumulated leave amounting to forty days I suggest that the department accepts that leave in lieu of both notice and attendance at HQ.

J.H. Rennie.

It was almost three o'clock in the morning when he drove to Century House. Showing his card at the security checks he made his way up to his office.

As he sat at his desk he unhooked the two keys from his key-ring and tucked them into an official envelope. Paynter's office and his secretary's office were both locked and Rennie left the two envelopes with the security guard in the outer office.

Back at the flat he undressed slowly and lay on the bed, wide-awake, trying to slow down his brain as the pictures and words of the day crowded and jostled obscenely in his mind.

He had never imagined such a situation and he was mentally unprepared. One half of his mind was totally in control. He wanted no more of such people. The other half was a confused observer of the shambles. Barely believing what was happening and vaguely fearful of what the outcome would be.

Rennie was not a man used to doubts. The action of writing out his resignation and delivering it had relieved his tension momentarily, but now it was done he realized that he had no idea what he was going to do next. The whole framework of his life had just gone. Not with a burst of gunfire or the flash of a knife as it went for his ribs, but just melted away like the fade-out at the end of a film. The adrenalin had been used up and his whole body ached as if he had been in a fight. He could feel the lethargy of exhaustion taking hold of his body and mind. He wanted to rouse himself, get up and start taking decisive action. But there was no will to move and no action to take.

It was the phone ringing that woke him. He looked at his watch. It was eleven-thirty. As he picked up the phone it all flooded back as he heard Paynter's voice. Amiable and calm. Would he pop in during the afternoon just to clear up a few things. The Lumley business, his pension and so on. He arranged to see Paynter at four.

CHAPTER TWENTY-FIVE

Paynter saw him not in his office, but in one of the small conference rooms on the top floor. Rennie suspected that the room had been chosen because it was wired for recording. He saw no signs of mikes or switches but that didn't mean a thing.

Paynter came bustling in, Rennie's letter of resignation in his hand. He sat facing Rennie, smiling as he looked at him.

'You don't mean this, Johnny, do you? You're just having me on. Making a point.'

'I may be making a point but don't kid yourself about me meaning it. I mean it all right.'

Still looking amiable Paynter said, 'Is there anything – anything at all – that I can do to dissuade you? It'll be a real blow to the department to lose you. Nobody's irreplaceable but you're as near irreplaceable as you can get.'

Rennie shook his head decisively and Paynter was aware of the anger in Rennie's eyes.

'Well – if that's how you feel. I've checked with Finance. You'll be entitled to a pension of four-fifths of present salary. It becomes subject to tax, I'm afraid, but it *is* index-linked. That's some consolation.'

Rennie made to stand up and Paynter said, 'I really am sorry about all this, Johnny. Are you sure you're all right? How was your medical?'

'OK.'

'What if I suggested six months' leave on full pay?'

'I'd tell you to stuff it.'

Paynter pulled a face. 'Well in that case all I can say is thanks for all you've done and good luck for the future.' He paused. 'But I'd be very remiss if I didn't tell you that we're all very concerned about the state you've been in for the last few weeks.'

'Is that all?'

'Yes.'

Paynter put out his hand and Rennie ignored it, turning and walking to the door without looking back.

He saw Mason downstairs by the desk. He looked worried as Rennie walked over to him.

'How did you get on with Paynter? He told me you'd resigned. Seemed to accept it. Sad loss but you were rather disturbed at the moment.'

'He did accept it. A bit of soft soap but not aggressive.'

'Don't worry. I'll keep an eye on the family if you're not available. Any idea what you're going to do?'

'No. I haven't given it a thought as yet.'

'You won't have any problem getting a job with some big company, not with your experience.'

'I hope you're right.'

Rennie phoned Mary and mentioned Harry Mason as help if he was not around when she called, and reassured her that there would be no more trouble like yesterday's.

He was uneasy about his meeting with Paynter. He had gone there prepared for threats and bluster and a bit of table thumping, but Paynter had been reasonable enough bearing in mind the circumstances. Maybe he *was* a bit strung-up at the moment and not thinking straight. But instinct told him otherwise, and all his training and experience led him to trust his highly-developed animal instincts rather than logic or contradictory facts.

For two days he dealt with his accumulated bills and tidied his rooms. He read the 'Situations Vacant' ads in *The Times* and the *Daily Telegraph* but not with any great interest. He could live quite well enough on his pension. And like most SIS field agents he had lived virtually free of all expense and had money in several foreign banks. If it wasn't for the two girls he'd move to Spain or buy a boat and live on board. Cruising the Med.

Both Paynter and Fredericks interviewed the specialist. Careful not to tread too heavily in the mine-infested area of medical ethics, even if they did own the specialist, lock, stock and barrel. The medical chaps would always do what you wanted provided you served it up in an acceptable way. They were used to digging out bullets and stitching up wounds without asking too many questions, and they knew the problems that went with what the department classified as LMF. Lack of Moral Fibre. The mental disturbances of men who had talked or cracked under pressure. And they were just as used to the aberrant behaviour of men who had stuck it out and not talked, but who went to pieces once the pressure was off.

Fredericks avoided any part of the actual discussion, sitting silent and aloof, not even taking off his coat as Paynter pursued his various points. It wasn't the sort of thing he wanted to be involved in. But he considered it his duty to hear what was decided.

The doctor looked at his notes and then at Paynter. 'I listened to the tape of your last conversation with him. I don't think it has any significance either way. You were friendly and considerate and he was – let's say aloof – but he showed no signs of paranoia.'

Paynter nodded. 'That tape was just to establish that prior to anything that might subsequently happen we had treated him reasonably. No antagonism from our side.'

'If you used section 135 of the Mental Health Act the police can remove a mentally ill person from any premises. If you use section 136 any policeman can detain any person found in a public place who he reasonably believes to be mentally disturbed.'

'And after that?'

'He can be held by the police for seventy-two hours and that would give you time to apply to a court for a compulsory admission.' The doctor looked with raised eyebrows at Paynter's face and said softly, 'I assume you'd use your usual devices with the Home Office and that would be that. From what you've told me there's no problem of next-of-kin. Ex-wife is not next-of-kin and the children are too young. You could even consider Crown Court level *in camera* and get indefinite detention without right to review.'

'And how long can we hold him?'

'Provided that it is a recognized mental institution he can be held permanently. And a compulsory patient can be treated against his will.'

'Is our place at Loch Gar a recognized mental institution?'

'Of course.'

And then Fredericks interrupted. 'Are you saying, doctor, that an ordinary policeman with no medical knowledge can seize a citizen in a public place just because he, an unqualified person, considers that citizen mentally disordered?'

'Yes. That's what I'm saying.'

'And he never has to justify the arrest before any court?'

'Exactly. That's what the Mental Health Act 1959 provides for. Some people have suggested that the Act gives an unnecessarily wide power to the police.'

'Is it ever used?'

'Oh, yes. Regularly. Especially in the Greater London area.'

Paynter interrupted. 'If I made arrangements regarding the police, would you attend when the arrest took place?'

'There's no legal need to have a doctor there.'

'I know. You explained that. But just as a back-up.'

The doctor shrugged. 'If that's what the department wished then I'd attend. As you know, when he had his medical at your instigation I taped my talk with him and that establishes my section's concern about signs of paranoia.'

Fredericks sniffed. 'I'd have said he was a psychopath myself.'

The doctor smiled, rather patronizingly. 'On what evidence?'

'The work he did. He was a thug. Killing people ruthlessly.'

'Ah, but he didn't do it out of enjoyment. He killed because people he repected, people in authority, required him to do so. From what you've told me about recent events he is showing acute remorse for the kidnapping of that Arab's children. No psychopath ever shows remorse. He may pretend to if he's caught and he thinks it will help him, but that isn't the case with Rennie. No. Rennie's not a psychopath.'

Paynter said, 'What is he then?'

The doctor said quietly, 'A tough, puritanical man, but otherwise quite normal.'

'No paranoia even?'

'None at all. He feels harassed by authority but that's for a very simple reason. He *is* being harassed by authority. That's why we're here today, gentlemen. We're off the record. I understand your problems and the law provides you with a solution. But let's not be mealy-mouthed about it.'

'Right,' said Fredericks, standing up abruptly. 'I must get on my way. I'll leave you two to discuss the details.'

It was midday on Tuesday when Mary phoned him. She sounded tense.

'Is anything the matter?'

'No, Johnny. Nothing at all. I just wanted to have a word with you.'

'I'll be picking the girls up on Saturday. Will that do?'

'I'd like to see you today.'

'OK. I'll come over this evening and see you all.'

'I'd like to see you now. You remember the coffee place you sometimes take the girls to in the High Street?'

'Yes. You mean . . .'

She interrupted quickly. 'I'll be waiting for you there.' And the phone went dead.

She was sitting in the far corner, her back to the restaurant and the windows, and she looked up at him as he pulled out a chair and sat down.

'Can I ask you something, Johnny, something personal?'

'Sure.'

'Do you ever think about the times when you and I were happy?'

'I try not to. But Elizabeth sometimes behaves like you and that reminds me of you when I first met you.'

'I think about you a lot. What a fool I was. Not being responsible. Behaving like a silly schoolgirl. I've tried to hate you, but I've never succeeded. I'm stuck with liking you. And admiring you, even when I don't agree with you. Johnny Rennie – foursquare on to the world.'

'Why are you telling me this?'

'Because I care about you . . .' She shivered involuntarily. '. . . and to try and pluck up the courage to give you some bad news.'

'What's the bad news?'

'The man you told me about, Harry Mason? Is he reliable?'

'In most ways, yes.'

'Is he a friend of yours?'

'He works with me. I asked him to keep an eye on you if I wasn't around. I mentioned it to you on the phone. Two of the telephone numbers I gave you were his. Home and office.'

'He came to the house this morning. He asked me to warn you about something your people were planning against you.'

'Tell me.'

'A man named Paynter has arranged for you to be taken into custody by a policeman and a doctor. They'll claim that you're insane, and you'll be sent to a place in Scotland. A mental home that's run by your people for their own purposes.'

'The one at Loch Gar.'

'Yes. I think that *was* the name he gave.'

'They'd need evidence to do that.'

'They don't. He told me how they intend to do it.'

'Tell me.'

She gave him a garbled but understandable account of what she had been told.

'Did he say when they plan to do this?'

'Paynter told him it would be on a Saturday so that if there was any struggle it would look like they were arresting a drunk. Mason thought it would be this coming Saturday.'

'Anything else?'

'He said that your phone was almost certainly tapped by now and that I wasn't to discuss it on the phone. He was very upset about it all. He didn't like it. And he was very scared about what would happen to him if they found out that he'd warned you.'

'Must have taken a lot of courage on his part.'

'What are you going to do?'

'It's best I don't tell you, Mary,' Rennie said quietly. 'Then if they ask you, you don't know anything.'

'Mason said you'd leave the country.'

'Can I ask you to do something for me?'

And for the first time in her life she saw tears in his eyes.

'Of course I will. Anything.'

He spoke very slowly. 'If I have to leave the country I'd never be able to come back or they'd have no alternative but to wipe me out. Will you explain some way to the girls that I didn't desert them. That I love them both dearly. And when they're grown up they can come and see me if they want to. Wherever I am.'

And a tear spattered on to the menu he was holding.

'I'll tell them, Johnny. That means you'll go, doesn't it?'

'Probably.'

'They must be terrible people, Johnny. Real animals.'

He half-smiled. 'Until a few weeks back I was one of them, Mary. I'm in no position to criticize.'

'Do you need any money?'

'No. I've got money in various places. More than enough. I've already made arrangements for my pension to be paid directly to you. If they ask you about phoning today, don't deny it. Say we arranged to meet here but I never turned up. And say you had wanted to talk to me about more maintenance and you thought I'd rumbled that and was trying to dodge meeting you.'

She reached out and put her hand on his. 'It seems crazy to be sitting in this crummy little cafe talking about these sorts of things. I can't believe that this is the last time I'll see you.'

'I'll keep in touch but not using my name, and if it's a letter the post-mark won't be relevant and I'll havc to bcat around thc bush with what I say. Thcy'll put a check on all your mail for quite a time.'

'You'd better go, Johnny. You'll have so many things to do.'

He nodded and stood up, and for a moment she hoped he might kiss her. 'You promise to square me off with the girls?'

'Of course I will.'

He nodded and walked away and she saw his eyes checking the other tables and the windows as he went towards the door.

Rennie took a taxi to the nearest Central Line tube station and a train to Redbridge. He waved down a passing taxi which dropped him at the corner of one of the small roads behind Cranbrook Park.

Harry Parks's house was like most of the othes. Semi-detached, Victorian and well looked after. As he walked up the stone steps to the front door he saw the lace curtains twitch and guessed that he had been spotted. Harry Parks opened the door before Rennie pressed the bell.

'Come on in, skipper. Lovely to see you.'

Harry took him into the living room and pointed to one of the heavy armchairs.

'What you doin' nowadays, Johnny?'

'The same old thing.' He smiled. 'I need your help.'

'Just say the word, chief. What can I do for you?'

'I want a passport, Harry. Canadian or United States. Doesn't matter which. But it's got to be the real thing and I've got to have it in twenty-four hours.'

'Jesus. You always was the one for the impossible.'

'Can you do it, Harry?'

'Yeah, but it'll cost. Will the department pay?'

'How much?'

'Five hundred quid for the passport and say another hundred for the work. Getting the real thing ain't that easy now I'm retired, and they cost a packet, either of those.'

'How long do you want?'

'Cash?'

'Yes. I'll go down to the bank and draw it out now.'

'Have you got photos?'

'No.'

'Doesn't matter. I can do them upstairs in the studio.'

'So when?'

'You can take it with you today if you'll accept the United States one. I've got one all ready. Let me take a snap or two, and you go and get the cash and get something to read while you're waiting.'

Upstairs in the studio Rennie sat on the straight-backed chair and Harry Parks measured the distance from the camera lens to his nose. 'Want to get it spot on, skipper. No time for developing and enlarging or reducing. Got to stick to Polaroid.'

Harry took a series of photographs checking each one as it formed, measuring until there were two that could be cut to the correct size.

The local Barclays near Ilford Broadway phoned his Chelsea branch and cleared the transaction before they counted out a thousand pounds in ten-pound notes. He signed for the money and tucked the four bundles of notes into his inside jacket pocket.

For an hour he sat in the park watching some schoolboys playing cricket and then he walked back to Harry Parks's house. Harry Parks had been one of the department's specialists, a talented commercial artist whose skills had been commandeered in wartime and who afterwards had stayed on with SIS. He could produce the right paper, inks, typing, embossing for any kind of document. Ration cards, army orders, security passes, driving licences and all the rest of the forged material that an intelligence organization needs. And even after his retirement there had been tricky jobs that only Harry could do to a standard that would pass even the most rigorous scientific and complex tests. A chain-smoker, he suffered from chronic bronchitis and lived alone in the house crowded with furniture, framed paintings stacked in piles against every wall and upright surface. His pictures sold readily in local shops and cafes. There had been talk years ago of a wartime love-affair and an illegitimate son but nobody had ever heard any details.

Harry Parks took him upstairs again to the studio and he sat there watching him work on the passport. He worked at a small table with a swivel lamp and a magnifying glass on a stand. On a trolley alongside him were rows of small bottles of inks and colouring ranged in the order of the standard spectrum.

As he worked, Harry said over his shoulder, 'There's an Israeli immigration stamp. D'you want me to take it out? You won't get into an Arab country with this as it is.'

'No. That's OK, Harry. Just leave it. What's my new name?'

'Novaks. Paul Novaks. Born in Pine City, Minnesota. That OK?'

'That's fine. What's the occupation?'

'Says engineer but I can change that if you want.'

'No, that'll do.'

'How's old whatshisname – Peters, Paynter?'

'Paynter. Oh he's still going strong.'

'A sharp bugger he was. If I did a passport for him he always gave it to one of his men first time.' Harry laughed. 'Just to make sure it was OK.'

'He's still much the same. Do they still use you?'

'They did give me odd jobs for a couple of years but I don't hear from them nowadays. As you know they've got a whole bunch of people they use for this kind of work.'

'D'you miss it?'

'No. I make a decent living from the paintings.' He paused. 'How's your old lady?'

'She's fine. We're divorced.'

Harry Parks didn't look up from his work. 'You chaps never stay married long, do you? Either they get fed up hanging around or you've got some little piece in Berlin or Rio de Janeiro. Younger and prettier. Can't blame you. I'd do it myself if I was away all the time.'

It was eleven o'clock before the passport was finished and Rennie counted out seven hundred pounds in ten-pound notes.

'That's very decent of you, Johnny. I'll come down with you and lock up for the night.'

On the doorstep Harry Parks said, 'Take care of yourself, Johnny. Don't let 'em grind you down.'

Rennie smiled. 'You too, Harry.'

It was past one when the taxi dropped him at Sloane Square. The streets were empty as he walked down the deserted King's Road to his rooms. He walked on past thc door and then crossed the road, walking back again slowly, checking shop entrances as he went. He realized that if they were already watching him at least it wasn't yet a twenty-four hour surveillance. And that was a good sign.

For the rest of the night he sat at the small table listing the things he had to do. It was a long list and it was already light as he got undressed.

CHAPTER TWENTY-SIX

By noon Rennie had drawn all the money from his London bank accounts, and changed it into dollars and dollar traveller's cheques. He had bought one-way airline tickets in the name of Paul Novaks to Paris, Hamburg, Brussels and Toronto. When he had decided where to go the others could be cashed in. The instructions to his overseas banks had been written and posted and he had sold his car for spot cash to a dealer in Battersea.

In the afternoon he bought clothes at Simpson's and Marks and Spencer's and travel-luggage to pack them in. He left the packed cases a couple of hours later at the left-luggage office at Victoria Station.

Back at his rooms he checked again to see if there was anything that was essential to take. His two passports he carried with him permanently, along with his wallet. The tickets were in a plastic folder and the money was in a canvas hold-all. There was nothing to stop him from leaving. Except for two things. He wanted to find out if they really would have come for him and put him away, and secondly, he didn't know where to go.

The only people he knew well anywhere in the world were SIS people. It had always been safer that way. Outsiders wanted to know too much about you. What was your job? What were you doing in wherever you happened to be? SIS men didn't ask questions. They didn't want to know. They provided a place to sleep and a meal. They knew doctors who would sew up a knife wound without asking questions and they could give you a raft of telephone numbers of pretty girls. They could find you a safe place to hide if you were on the run. But not if you were on the run from London. Once you were not one of the 'old firm', even if you'd only retired, you were, at best, just one more outsider.

He moved out from his rooms in darkness at three o'clock the next morning and booked in at a small hotel in Victoria. He spent most of the next few days sleeping and resting and trying not to be aware of the sickening feeling at the pit of his stomach. The feeling that came from the dawning realization that this wasn't an operation. It was the real thing. He was spending his last few days in the country that he had worked for, holed up in a room in a cheap hotel. Mary and the girls were taken care of but it was unlikely that he would ever see them again. No more trips to the Zoo. No more games of Scrabble. No more stories to be read. No more eager young arms around his neck in reward for some small treat. For the first time in his life John Hamish Rennie was very near the end of his tether. Habit and inbred characteristics were just about keeping his mind on an even keel. But only just. He was very near the end of his mental resources.

He paid three days' rental for a car at a small hire firm in Southwark, and loaded his luggage from the locker at the station. Once they knew he was away they'd check the big hire companies first.

At six o'clock he found a small parking space just off Lower Sloane Street and he walked to the pub that almost faced his rooms. From time to time he glanced out of the steamed-up windows, his fingers wiping a small area clear, but he didn't expect them to come until ten or eleven.

From ten o'clock he watched continuously, a glass of beer in one hand and a ham sandwich in the other. They came at ten twenty-five. Two of them and a driver, in the big Jag from the pool. One was a uniformed policeman and the other was a man he had seen somewhere before. The policeman would be on loan from Special Branch. And as they went inside Rennie remembered the tall one. He was the supervisor at the medical section. And he recalled all that bullshit about paranoia. They must have had some sort of contingency plan all worked out even then. Something on the record to establish that he was unstable. Five minutes later the light went on in his rooms.

A passing constable on foot patrol stopped at the car, opened the door and spoke to the driver, obviously complaining about the car being parked on yellow lines and on a bus route. He saw the constable take out his notebook and then the driver showed him something. Probably his ID card. The notebook was tucked back into the pocket and the constable nodded and moved on.

Rennie walked out of the side entrance of the pub and back to his rented car. Two hours later he cashed in his airline tickets at Gatwick and booked a seat on the early-morning plane to Amsterdam. He used his United States passport and booked in for the night at the airport Hilton in the name of Paul Novaks. He tried to sleep but spent most of the night pacing the room. Several times he picked up the phone to change his flight to some other place than Amsterdam. He knew Berlin better and Rome too. And there was the sunshine of the Spanish coast from Malaga to Alicante. But in those few weeks he had felt strangely at home in Amsterdam. Despite what he had been involved in, there was a sanity about the people and a calmness about those medieval buildings that gave him comfort. And there was the room and the girl. He could try it for a few weeks. She would be someone to talk to.

Just once he started dialling the number of his old house before he slammed down the receiver. The temptation to talk to the girls just one last time was constantly there. But it was self-indulgence and by now the phone would be tapped. Rennie found it almost impossible to accept the role of being the hunted not the hunter. Always before there had been the righteous cause to give a patina of innocence to deception and subterfuge, but without that it all seemed degrading and inhuman. His mind was no longer decisive and his reactions changed constantly from blazing anger to despair, from guilt to humiliation. He didn't belong in this strange new scenario.

At Schiphol he took a taxi to Warmoesstraat and slowly unloaded his bags. It took two journeys to get them to the top of the stairs. He walked down slowly and paid off the driver. When he turned to look up the stairs it seemed as if they were moving.

The ascent up the narrow wooden stairs seemed interminable and he could feel the sweat pouring down his face as he stood outside the door. It seemed to take a long time for his hand to find the brass handle. As his fingers closed round it the door opened and he was vaguely aware of the girl standing there. He leaned against the door-jamb, his hand feeling for some support, and not finding any his body slid down to the floor as his knees slowly gave way.

As he tried to work out where he was, he saw her standing looking out of the window and as the bed creaked she turned quickly to look at him. He was vaguely aware of her hand stroking his face before he passed out again. He tried to speak but no words came out.

When he woke again the light was on in the room and she was sitting on the bed beside him, holding his hand.

'How're you feeling, Johnny? Just nod if you're feeling better.'

His mouth and lips were dry and his voice was a croak as he tried to smile as he said, 'I'm fine.'

'You idiot,' she said, 'you're not fine. And I've been so worried.' He could see tears in her eyes.

'What's going on?' he said.

'You passed out two days ago. I got a doctor. He said you were suffering from exhaustion. What the hell have you been doing to get into this state?'

He shrugged. 'Just wear and tear.'

She shook her head in disbelief. 'You're going to drink a bowl of soup. Not tinned. The real stuff.'

The doctor called in twice during the next week. Probing in slow precise English as to what might have caused his patient's collapse, and getting nowhere.

After the second visit she had walked down to the street with the doctor.

'How is he, doctor?'

'He's a very storng man so physically there's nothing to worry about. But mentally I'm not sure.'

'In what way?'

'To be perfectly frank – I don't know. But there's something wrong there. Something stored up. There's a big, big scream inside that man. Some day it's going to come out. And I don't know what will happen then.'

'What could help him?'

The doctor shrugged. 'Getting him to talk. He won't talk to me. He's obviously experienced at hiding his feelings. He's better at evading questions than I am at asking them.' He turned and looked at the girl. 'Maybe you could do it.'

'But I don't know what to ask.'

'I don't think you need to know anything. You just need to get him to talk. It's a bit like cutting open a boil to let out the pus.' He paused as he looked at her face. 'You're fond of him, aren't you?'

'Yes. I care about him a lot.'

'I think that that's why you might succeed where I've failed.' He looked down the street and then back to the girl's face. 'I'm only guessing, but I think I'm right – I don't think anyone has cared for that man for a long, long time. Something, or somebody, has drained his batteries over the years. Maybe you could charge them for him.'

'I'll try.'

The doctor smiled. 'I'm sure you will contact me if you feel he needs anything.'

'I will.'

'Good luck.'

'Thank you.'

By the end of the week Rennie was fit enough to go for short walks in the autumn sunshine, sitting in small nearby cafes, drinking coffee and eating cream cakes.

The girl was trying desperately not to hurry any attempt to persuade him to talk, or to choose a wrong moment. Although they chatted as they ate and drank she was aware that his responses were strained and only made with great effort. She was also aware of his unease when they were away from the room, his eyes roving over the people they passed as if he were looking for someone. Although he was physically much fitter he seemed to be retreating mentally a little more each day. When they were back in the room he lay on the bed, his eyes closed, but he wasn't asleep, and when he opened his eyes he just lay there inert, staring unseeing at the ceiling.

As his condition deteriorated she asked the doctor to call again. He stayed for almost half an hour and afterwards he talked to her on the stairs.

'I've left some pills for him. He says he won't take them. They're Valium and they could probably calm him down. See if you can persuade him to take them. It's important that he should.'

'What's the matter with him, do you think?'

'It's obviously depression. Not just feeling down but clinical depression. I want to break it up. It could give him a chance to relax and stop all those wheels grinding away so relentlessly in his mind.' He paused. 'If you could get him to talk . . . to unburden himself a little, it could help a lot.'

'I've been afraid of making things worse.'

'You won't do that. He's too deep inside himself already. He should really be in hospital. I suggested it but he wouldn't cooperate.' He paused. 'I'm very worried about him.'

'Tell me.'

For several moments the doctor was silent and then he said quietly, 'I'd say that he was potentially suicidal.'

'Oh God.'

'Are you sure that you can cope with him on your own? I could consider having him removed to a clinic whether he agrees or not.'

'Oh don't do that. I can cope. I'm sure I can.'

'OK. But if you change your mind let me know.'

'I won't change my mind.'

The doctor nodded and made his way down the narrow stairs.

She had persuaded him to take the pills for two days and when they had finished their evening meal and they were drinking their coffee she said softly, 'Will you tell me what went wrong, Johnny?'

She half expected a dismissive shake of the head but he put down his cup and looked at her across the table.

'I guess I owe you an explanation, sweetie, after all the trouble I've caused.'

'You don't *owe* me anything and you've been no trouble. I'd just like to help, that's all.'

'It would take a long time to explain. And it's all a bit mixed up.'

'I've got all the time in the world for you, John Rennie, so tell me what it's all about.'

It was past midnight when he finished telling her. Not only the recent events in Amsterdam but of the years before. She asked very few questions but she reached out and covered his hand with hers when he sometimes came to a halt or found something difficult to explain. When he stopped she said softly, 'We're a bit alike, you and I, aren't we?'

'In what way?'

'Inside we're both terrible puritans. Not liking the world we see around us. But in practice we both indulge in the very things we quite genuinely despise. You in your dirty-tricks, and me in my dope and squatting and general bumming around.'

'I guess so. But yours does no harm to other people. Mine's on a different scale.'

She smiled. 'You were very cross with me once when I said that me smoking hash did nobody any harm but me.'

'I'm sorry.'

'Don't be sorry, Johnny. What I've done isn't worth talking about. What about you? What are you going to do?'

'Do you mind if I hang on here for a bit while I sort myself out?'

'You don't have to ask me, Johnny, *I'm* the visitor, not you. This is your place.'

'Tell me something, Joanna. You said to me once that you didn't like the society we live in because it doesn't care about its losers. What did you mean by that? Do you mean that if a man doesn't make an effort to support himself that the state should do it for him?'

'No. I mean that there are tens of thousands of people in the USA and Europe who try very hard to succeed but for one reason or another – genes or environment or maybe ill-health – they don't make it. I don't think it's right that those people and their families should be without food or shelter or medical care. And it's not the state that should help them. The state is a myth. It's the rest of us who should help them. And willingly, not grudgingly. And we should care about people in other countries who die because they lack basic medicine and food. Babies die who could live for a month on what we throw away in a couple of days.'

'Are you describing Communism?'

'Yes,' she said, defiantly. 'The snag is, that if you believe Communism would work everybody assumes you are pro-Moscow. The Russians aren't Communists at all. They're just tyrants, dictators. With love it would work.' She paused and said lamely, 'I'm sure it would, Johnny.' She hesitated for a moment and then she said, 'What made you so sure that the establishment was always right? Especially when you had a grandstand view of the things they got up to.'

'I think it was reaction against the people who wanted to bring the country down by revolution and force.'

'What attracted you to that kind of work in the first place?'

'It's a gradual process. You don't just decide that that's what you want to do. They look out all the time for people who could be useful in one way or another. You're asked to do something, and if you do it well you're given something else to do. You kind of drift into it. It seems like that anyway but in fact it's very carefully controlled. Testing you out without you knowing it.'

'But you must have liked it or you wouldn't have stayed. And you wouldn't have been successful.'

'It's not a question of liking it. You see what's going on behind the scenes and you want to play your part in stopping it.'

'But isn't it all rather phoney or exaggerated? Is all that much really happening?'

Rennie shrugged. 'Right now some man at one of the KGB schools will be under training for a mission to find out some industrial secret in a plant in Cardiff or London or somewhere in Britain. Another man will be looking over a list of people who run so-called peace movements. Deciding how to penetrate them and turn the protest into violence and subversion. Thousands of highly-trained people spend all their working hours planning how to destroy the whole fabric of society in Britain. And others will be doing the same for every country in the non-Soviet world. There's no question of exaggeration. It's fact. It suits some people to pretend it isn't happening. But it is. And I wish it wasn't. That's why I wanted to do my bit to stop it.'

'But isn't it up to ordinary people to decide what they want? They won't be conned by a few Russians.'

Rennie smiled. 'The Russians don't do the conning themselves, they just control and direct the people who do it.'

'What people?'

'All sorts of people. People who openly rant and rave in public about everything the government does. And the really dangerous ones. The quiet ones who weasel their way into any group of people who have a genuine grievance.

'Groups against the bomb, civil liberty groups, strikers with a genuine grievance. As soon as they start, the undercover people move in and encourage violence. The general public end up losing sympathy with the causes but the media people, newspapers and TV, give the spoilers space and air-time to put over their picture of class-hatred and defiance of the law. The media call it balance. But it isn't. It just sells newspapers. If you had anything good to say about the country or the government, they wouldn't be interested. They want scandal and violence.'

'But if they don't convince the public, what does it matter?'

'It matters because they are trying to destroy the public faith in democracy. If some clerk in a government office leaks a secret document to the press, he says he did it in the public interest and the newspaper claims that too. The fact that the clerk signed the Official Secrets Act swearing to maintain confidentiality is seen as a restriction on civil liberties. It's not just that they do it, but they pretend that their breach of the Act is from the highest motives.

'And behind all these dupes are the real manipulators. The quiet ones who never speak in public but whose role is to keep the political pot boiling. And behind them the KGB and all the others who murder and blackmail in order to destroy us.'

'What made you change your mind about all this?'

'I don't think I did change my mind about it. I still think somebody has to fight them. All of them. But not me any more.'

'Why?' she said quietly.

For several moments he didn't speak. Then he sighed and said, 'It started with you when you said how honest I was. The woman at the gallery, Adele Palmer, said the same. For some reason it set me thinking. I realized that in my private life I was honest. Genuinely honest. But in my work there was no room for honesty. I justified that by accepting that somebody had to do what I did. To protect society. The public.' He sighed. 'And for some reason my rationalizing started falling apart . . . I don't know why.'

'I do.'

'Tell me then.'

'It was the little girl. The Arab's daughter. For you that was going too far.'

'If I want to stay honest in your eyes then I have to say no . . . it wasn't just that. In fact until I was telling you tonight about all that had happened, I wasn't really sure what the turning point was.'

'What was it, Johnny? Tell me.'

'I didn't like the kidnapping of Said's children. There were other ways of dealing with the problem. And in the end the kidnapping didn't help in getting Mason back. No . . . what really brought it home was the incident with the coffins. Not just the sadism, the cruelty, but the fact that they did it to *my* family. That may sound just selfish but it isn't. It was a signpost for me that they had too much power. They didn't have to justify what they did to anybody. They just had to give an order to somebody and it was done. Whoever did it wouldn't have questioned what they were asked to do. It was just a job. And they did it. Just like I had done it so many times. The Nazis on trial at Nuremberg gave that as their excuse. They were just obeying orders.' He paused and said softly, 'Those people who were my masters were more sophisticated than I was. And I guess that I've just grown up. What was tolerable for me as a young man isn't tolerable now I'm older.' He paused. 'Or maybe I'm still busy rationalizing my own behaviour. Who knows.'

'Does it help to have talked about it?'

'I'm not sure. I think so. It's a relief to have said it aloud instead of it churning around inside my head.'

'You are honest, Johnny. Don't doubt that. It's a nasty world we live in especially the bit you've been living in.'

'And what are we all going to do about it, honey?'

She shook her head. 'I don't know, Johnny. You can't just go around telling people to be nice to one another.'

'That's what Jesus Christ did.'

'Sure. And look what they did to *him*.'

'So it's all hopeless?'

'No way. It's not hopeless.'

'Tell me what we have to do.'

'We have to live our lives so that we are never tempted to do anyone any harm. We give up all forms of aggression as individuals. Greed, ambition, indifference are all a kind of personal aggression. We just have to live quietly and lovingly.'

'On that small farm you wanted. Just enough to get by.'

She smiled. 'Funny you remembering that. But you're right. That's one way.' She shrugged. 'It would suit me.'

'Truly, or is it just a dream thing?'

'It's a dream thing all right. But it's real for me.'

'So why not do it?'

She sighed. 'I couldn't do it alone. I'd be scared.'

'So do it with me.'

She lifted her head and looked at his face as she said softly, 'Don't tease me, Johnny.'

'I'm not teasing. I mean it. Seriously.'

'You mean you could turn your back on all your old life? The excitement. The power. The people you know.'

'I've done that already, my dear. I've nothing to lose. I've lost already.'

'But on your own you could see the world.'

'I've seen the world – I didn't like the look of it.'

She looked at his face for a long time and then said quietly, 'I'd love it, Johnny. I wouldn't be a nuisance.'

'So why are there tears in your eyes?'

'Because I love you, Johnny Rennie. I've loved you for forty-nine days. And it all seems to good to be true.'

'Where shall we have our farm?'

'We'd have to raise a loan first.'

'I've got all the money we'll need. So where do we go?'

'You say. I'll go wherever you say.'

Rennie put his hand in his jacket pocket and took out the two passports. One British, one United States. He pointed at the green one. 'That's the only one I can use. So let's go to your place.'

'Where in the States?'

'Have you ever been to Vermont?'

'No.'

'Let's go there then.'

'Do you like it there?'

'I've never been there.'

She laughed. 'So why choose Vermont?'

'A long time ago I heard a song – I think it was Glenn Miller – it was called "Moonlight in Vermont". I've always remembered it, and I've always wanted to go there. It sounded special.'

She smiled. 'My dream – the little farm. Your dream – Vermont. It sounds a great combination.'

'Let's start planning.'

She looked at him quizzically, her head to one side just like young Mary sometimes did. 'Do you like me at all, Johnny?'

'Yes. More than like.'

'But not love?'

'You once said you liked it when I came here. That it made you feel safe. I feel that about you. I like being with you. And I feel safe with you.'

'Safe from what?'

'Safe from hurt. Safe from the rest of the world.'

She smiled. 'That's not a bad start, is it?'

'For me it's pretty good. I hope it is for you.'

'It is, Johnny Rennie. It is.'

It was already turning from autumn to winter and there was a cold wind as he walked over the bridge, and then he saw her, running towards him, her long blonde hair streaming out behind her like a palomino's mane.

She was panting as she got up to him, smiling as she waved a large brown envelope.

'He's found what we wanted, Johnny. It's perfect.'

'Who's found what?'

'It's a long letter from daddy. He's found us a place. In Vermont. On Lake Champlain. There's photographs and maps and everything. Even the name is romantic.'

'What's the name?'

'South Hero. Isn't that great?'

He smiled. 'Let's go and have a board meeting.'

They had done the calculations, pored over the maps and field plans and had tried hard not to be over-influenced by the beautiful scenery in the photographs. But Johan de Vries had done a good job. It was exactly what they wanted. She could barely keep still, she was so pleased and excited.

'Shall I phone him tonight, Johnny? We could go to one of the hotels and use an international kiosk.'

'Yes. Let's do that. He'll be delighted to know you'll be back so soon.'

'There's just one thing,' and her face looked serious.

'What's that?'

'I want us to do something before we decide. I want us to look down the other end of the telescope.'

'How do we do that?'

'I want us to be honest with one another. I want both of us to look at it from the other's point of view. And say out loud what we think are the snags. Not for ourselves but for the other one.'

He looked at her fondly and reached out for her hand. 'Tell me why we should do that?'

'Because I think there are a lot of disadvantages for you in all this. And none for me. You ought to think about them before we plunge.'

For long moments he looked at her face and then he said softly, 'I love you, Joanna de Vries.'

'Do you mean that, Johnny?'

'I do.'

'What would be your description of loving someone?'

He shrugged. 'A very simple one. That you would rather anything bad happened to you than to the other person.'

'So,' she smiled. 'Let's be Devil's Advocates for each other. You start.'

He sighed. 'There are three disadvantages for you that I'm aware of. The first is that I would like to ask you to marry me. But I can't. With my phoney passport and no supporting documents we'd be caught at first base. That's unfair on you and not too good for your parents.'

She nodded. 'Go on.'

'Secondly, you might get tired of me. I'm much older than you for one thing and . . .'

'Forget that,' she said. 'It's rubbish.'

'And thirdly you might find the life boring or too much hard work,' he paused. 'And one more thing I've just remembered. We could never be sure that I wasn't going to be exposed.'

'The only bit that matters to me is the marrying bit. But that could come right in time. There's ways of putting these things right. Daddy might be able to help. But I'd like us to pretend to be married so far as the outsde world is concerned. Just a wedding ring and me with your name.'

'I'm sorry that it has to be so messy but that's fine with me. What about the other snags?'

She shook her head. 'They don't matter. None of them.'

'Your turn in the box then.'

'I've only got two points. One is big and the other one's sort of medium. Let me do the medium one first. You've been terribly down because of what's happened to you. Do you think when you've recovered properly and you're fit that you won't miss your old work?'

'I won't miss it for a moment. They wouldn't have me back anyway. They'd sooner cut my throat.'

'Maybe. But other intelligence services would be glad to have you. I bet the CIA would have you like a shot.'

He shook his head vehemently. 'Forget it. What's the other thing?'

It was several seconds before she spoke. 'Is there any chance you still love your ex-wife?'

'No. She's a good mother and a nice lady but she's not for me.'

'And the girls? I know you love them.'

'Yes,' he said quietly, 'I love the girls and I'll be sad sometimes when I think about them. 'I shall miss them terribly. I do already. But I think you're forgetting something fundamental.'

'What's that?'

'Once they decided to certify me as insane there was no choice left for me. I had no choice but to leave or go into a mental institution. It's better this way. If things work out I might see the girls again some day.'

'You don't think SIS or whatever they're called would forgive you?'

He smiled. 'It's a nice gentle word "forgive". No, they're not designed for forgiving. And I don't want their forgiveness.'

'I want you to be so happy, Johnny.'

He leaned across the table and for the first time ever he kissed her on the lips.

Johan de Vries met them at Kennedy and drove them the next day to the small farmstead at South Hero. When they went to the realtor to complete the deal he smiled as he gave Rennie the big buff envelope. The farmstead had already been bought by Johan de Vries and the deeds were in the names of Paul Novaks and his wife Joanna Veronica Novaks. The realtor, enjoying his role of Fairy Prince, found it entirely fitting that Joanna Veronica Novaks should burst into tears.

CHAPTER TWENTY-SEVEN

The typescript and its packing lay untidily on Fredericks's desk. He was no longer responsible for FO/SIS liaison. He had been transferred to the Foreign Office with a two-grade promotion. He stood with his hands in his trouser pockets, rocking slowly on his heels.

'Why haven't you consulted Mayhew on this? It's nothing to do with me.'

'I thought you might have a view.'

'I do, dear boy, I do. But it's not my domaine any longer. It's yours – and Mayhew's.'

'I'd be obliged if you gave me your views. Unofficially of course.'

Fredericks smiled but not with his eyes. 'Are you scared of what Mayhew might start? A cosy little Commission of Enquiry to keep his new friends in the FO happy. A show of his independence from SIS. Is that it?'

'Yes.'

'Well at least you're frank about it. Some wouldn't be.' He waved towards the untidy package on his desk. 'How damaging would it be?'

'Very damaging.'

'More than Mason's?'

'Oh far worse. Mason wasn't dirty-tricks.'

Fredericks pursed his lips in disapproval of the phrase. 'Is it accurate?'

'There are some errors on dates but nothing more than that.'

Fredericks sighed and looked at his neat black shoes. 'Probably compiled from memory.' He looked up quickly at Paynter. 'D'you think he'd use it?'

'I'm sure he would.'

'Did your chap trace where he is?'

'No. He's still looking. I called a halt as soon as I got this stuff. It's a small area and I've no doubt we could trace him in the next few weeks. But he's probably using some other name.'

'Well he's got you by the short and curlies, my friend. No doubt about that. He was on our – your side of the fence when Mason was scribbling away for those wretched Arabs. He saw the panic that caused.'

'So what do we do?'

Fredericks laughed sharply. 'We don't do anything. But if I were you, I'd take every paper on that operation and shove it in the shredder. Then cremate it. And if there's any chance of sending up a smoke-signal to your old friend Rennie – then do it. And don't go near him ever again.' Fredericks raised his eyebrows in dismissal and Paynter got up, gathered up the package and headed across the thick carpet to the door.

At the door he turned and said, 'Thanks for your help, Freddie.' Fredericks ignored him, looking out of the window, watching the Scots Guards march past. The band was playing 'Auld Lang Syne'.

THE JUDAS FACTOR

This book is for Dr Martin Robards – consultant paediatrician at Pembury Hospital, Kent – whose skill and care over many years has made it possible for my daughter Lisa who had Still's Disease, to be transformed from a five year old with permanently painful swollen joints to a happy, active and very beautiful fifteen year old. It comes with love from us all.

TED ALLBEURY

CHAPTER ONE

The pianist was playing 'Ain't Misbehavin'' and if he'd been listening Fats Waller wouldn't have been offended. But if he *had* been listening he'd have been the only one in the club who was.

The girl looked across the table as the man refilled her wine glass.

'*Are* you a Jew, Charles?'

The man didn't look up as he filled his own glass slowly and carefully.

'No. What made you ask?'

'Daddy says you are in his letter.'

'Good old Daddy. Cheers.'

He held up his glass to her before he drank.

'You can't just dismiss it like that. He's been checking on you. I told you he would.'

'Did he check on your husband before he married you?'

'That's different. Our families knew one another. We moved in the same social circles.'

'The ones where husbands beat up their wives?'

He saw the flush on her cheeks. It had been unsporting but she'd asked for it. And he was irritated by the question. Her grey eyes were antagonistic as she looked at his face.

'You're not much help. I'm only trying to get things straightened out.'

He reached over the table and put his hand gently on hers. 'I'm sorry, Judy. I'm not being difficult but it's pointless you trying to convince him. He wants you to go back to your husband. Your father-in-law is an influential man and it doesn't do your father's career a lot of good when his daughter lights out to do her own thing. And if she ends up with another man he ain't going to call for champagne and hope that she'll be happier the second time around.'

'You'd like him if you met him. He's only trying to protect me.'

'How old are you, sweetie?'

'You know how old I am. I'm twenty-nine.'

'Maybe it's time you decided things for yourself.'

'I *have* decided, Charles. You know that. As soon as I can get a divorce I want to marry you. You're what I want.'

He looked across at her face and said softly, 'Why do you want me?'

She shrugged her shoulders, and half-smiled. 'You're my rock, Charles. My protector. I'd be lost without you.'

'D'you want to dance?'

She looked round the smoke filled room of the club and then back at his face. She shook her head slowly. 'Why do you hang on to this place?'

He smiled. 'Greed. It makes me money.'

For a moment she looked back at him, and then hesitantly she opened her handbag and passed him an envelope. He saw the US stamp and the New York postmark. It was addressed to her. He guessed it was from her father. He looked up at her.

'D'you want me to read it?'

She nodded, and he took the single page out and folded it open. The New York address of her parents was embossed on the expensive paper. He was the UN representative of what had once been a small part of the British Empire. The handwriting was neat and clenched up, with Greek 'e's and a lot of underlining.

MA CHÈRE JUDY,

Needless to say, I have been much disturbed by the news in your letters. You seem to have swallowed everything this man says, 'holus-bolus'. I have had some of his 'facts' checked out. I understand from *English* friends of mine that he has grossly exaggerated his position at the Foreign Office. For many years he was employed on minor consular activities, mainly the issuing of passports and trade documents. The lowest of the low.

As for his self-styled linguistic abilities, nobody who left school aged fifteen is capable of learning foreign languages. He *claims* to speak Polish and Russian, no doubt aware that these are languages you are not able to test him on. You remember Kretski, the Ambassador at the Polish Embassy when I was in London? Get him to invite you both to one of their minor receptions. He would check his languages for you.

Whilst I find it is correct that he has not been married I find this in itself suspicious. A man of his age must have very 'good' reasons for being single. As for what you referred to as his being owner of a popular night club my heart *sinks*. If it were the best in London, is this the background you wish to be part of? And when I am told on good authority that it is in fact a tenth-rate club in Soho, patronized by the criminal element and prostitutes, I wonder how you could be so easily deceived by this man. You make him out to be some sort of Sir Galahad. I see him more as a typical central European, Jew-boy entrepreneur. Is this where your expensive education has led you? Your previous diversions during your marriage were at least with people from your own circle, but this '*nostalgie de la boue*' is, quite frankly, inexplicable.

Why don't you come over to New York for a few months and consider, without pressure, your position? Your mother and I are 'ad idem' on all this.'

YOUR LOVING FATHER

Anders slowly folded the letter, slid it back into its envelope and reached over to put it beside her plate. He lit a cigarette before he spoke.

'There's food for thought there, my love.'

'He's only trying to help me.'

'Or somebody. When are you going to fix for us to go to Weymouth Street?'

'Weymouth Street? Why Weymouth Street?'

'That's where the Polish Embassy is.'

Her eyes brightened. 'You mean you'll go there with me?'

'I don't mind jumping through a couple of hoops if it'll make you happy.'

'I love you, Charles.'

'And I love you.'

'I'd better be going. I promised to call in at the French Embassy after dinner. The Couve de Mourvilles are over for the week and I was at school with their daughter when Daddy was in Paris.'

'I'll walk out with you for a taxi.'

She blushed. 'I'm going by tube.'

In his lap, out of sight, he took out five ten-pound notes from his wallet and folding them over he passed them to her.

'I can't keep taking money off you, Charles. I really can't.'

He stood up and moved her chair back as she stood too, and they walked up the dimly lit stairs to the grubby foyer and out into the street. He walked with her through to Charing Cross Road and waved down a taxi that had just dropped a fare at Leicester Square underground station. He kissed her as he held open the door and stood waiting until the taxi drove off.

He looked at his watch. It was almost ten o'clock and he crossed the street and walked through to Leicester Square. The square was crowded. The usual group of dropouts, a police car with its blue lamp flashing, its occupants sitting and watching. Their faces had that strange immobility that policemen's faces have when they are waiting for something to happen, contemplating the people walking by, wondering whether it would be a drunken fight or an unconscious heroin addict that they had to deal with first. It was too early for knifings and gang fights, and break-ins would come over the radio.

Anders was walking against the stream, but he was in no hurry. He wasn't going anywhere. He just felt a need to be out in the world. Not having to talk, not having to think. Walking amongst strangers who weren't part of his life, and for whom he had not the slightest responsibility. At Piccadilly Circus he just stood. Watching the traffic and the people. The touts, the pimps and the pushers, and the well-dressed middle-class who had just come out of the cinema, still humming the tunes from the re-run of *Gigi*.

Tadeusz Charles Anders was a big-built man, but his six feet one inch made his broad shoulders look less broad and his big face look less aggressive. He wasn't handsome, but he was certainly attractive. It was an old-fashioned manly face that could have earned him good money in Hollywood. A John Wayne face. Lived in, with hard eyes but a benevolent mouth, and hair that was black and wiry. Those who looked carefully at faces would have said that it wasn't an English face. And they would have been right. His father had been Polish and his mother a Scot, and the two sets of flamboyant genes showed not only in his face but in his temperament. There was no doubt that the Polish genes were dominant, and they and a few other factors in his early life had been responsible for his troubles in SIS. They valued and used his physical strength, even his wild outbreaks of anger when provoked. But as an established officer of SIS they saw him as a potential source of embarrassment. He was the stuff that Parliamentary Questions are made of. He still worked for them, and it was SIS cash that had funded the setting up of his club. As an undercover man he was invaluable. Available for operations that were never minuted, which could be denied as having anything to do with MI6 and the Foreign Office. And the sleazy club acted as a letter-drop, a safe-house and a meeting place.

Tad Anders had been born in the small Northumbrian town of Morpeth, the son of a refugee from Poland who had joined the Free Polish Army. Captain Anders had been killed in the assault on Monte Cassino and from that time the boy's mother had tried to be both father and mother. Born in poverty in Glasgow she had the gift of counting her blessings. There was a considerable Polish colony in Morpeth and young Anders learned Polish at the little Polish school, and spent his free time with other children of his age. He was good at games and bright at his school-work, and was welcome in many homes.

His mother was a teacher at the local primary school. She was a patient, competent teacher, but it was obvious to all that her son was the centre of her life. It was equally obvious that his mother's love and devotion were appreciated by the boy. He did the man's jobs around the house and was consulted about the household budget. She didn't spoil him, although it was an easy-going relationship on both sides. They were able to take each other's affection for granted.

In the summer after his eighteenth birthday they had the letter offering him a place at Newcastle University. Neither of them realized what a climactic effect that brief, formal note would have on both their lives.

Maggie Anders' virtues were not altogether rare for nothern England and the Border counties, but they were rare enough to be prized, particularly when they went hand in hand with a lively personality and an attractive woman. There had been several interested men but she had never let their interest prosper beyond an arm's-length friendliness. She accepted invitations to agricultural shows and sometimes a play or concert in Newcastle but the men were never invited to her home. She liked them all or she wouldn't have accepted their invitations, but there was one, a man who farmed near Alnwick, who was her particular favourite. He was a calm, patient, smiling man whose wife had been killed in a road accident towards the end of the war. They had met at the house of a mutual friend and had taken to each other instantly. It had been almost a year before they met again and there had been only a score or so of meetings since. But when she told him the good news in the letter from the University he had asked her to marry him. And with her son well on the way to independence she had accepted.

Maggie had waited two days before she told the boy, after they had finished their evening meal together. She made it clear that it would never make any difference to them – they'd always be the same.

The wedding was a few weeks later and Tadeusz was to stay with his aunt while the couple had a few days honeymoon in Edinburgh. There were many people at the wedding from both Alnwick and Morpeth, for the couple were much liked and respected. The boy stood with his aunt and nieces as the couple were photographed on the church steps. Like the others, he saw the tears on Maggie's cheeks, but unlike the others he couldn't bear that she was smiling too. And her new husband had his arm round her.

Everything he had went into the old army kit-bag, including his father's medals from the small glass-fronted showcase. He went down to London the same day and two days later he was starting his recruit training at Caterham barracks, saying 'Yes, trained soldier' and 'No, trained soldier' to his three-month seniors in the Coldstream Guards. He had remembered a sign on the Great North Road, just a few miles from Morpeth: Coldstream 22 miles. He didn't reveal his true name and age until he was commissioned.

In some ways the army is a quite kindly orphanage, and it liked the courage and ability of the young lieutenant who absorbed so readily all they had to teach him. Because of his Polish he was transferred to the Intelligence Corps who sent him on a Russian course and by the usual process of snakes and ladders he became one of the more experienced and valued officers in SIS, the Secret Intelligence Service, MI6. Singleness of purpose was the phrase most often used by his various superiors. He never saw nor heard of his mother again. He never talked about his childhood and almost succeeded in never thinking about it. He felt he'd learned a lesson about women from his mother, and he was glad he'd learned it early. No woman would ever again get the chance to bring back that sudden cold that gripped his limbs, the feeling of darkness and a rushing wind. The feeling that the lights had all gone out. Loneliness.

He was well liked by men and women. Despite his looks, his vitality and his obvious intelligence, for some reason men never saw him as a rival. For the same reasons, many young women saw him as a husband, and even more saw him as a lover.

Anders bought a Final edition of the *Evening Standard* and looked at the front page. They were going to re-open the Suez Canal in June. Turning to the Stop Press he checked the result of the last race at Sandown. Crown Prince had won by a length at 11–1 so Chalky White had been right. He said he'd had it from the horse's 'connections' and they obviously knew what they were talking about. It was beginning to drizzle and he turned and walked back towards the club.

He walked up Charing Cross Road and turned into one of the alleys just before Great Newport Street. The red neon sign outside the club door announced that it was the entrance to the Kama Sutra Club, and a flashing arrow pointed the way.

Inside the door was a small reception area complete with a well-worn flowered Wilton carpet that went well with the blistered brown paint on the walls. On the far wall were two rows of crude hooks for jackets and coats, and on the left was a reception counter with a black GPO phone and a red internal phone. On the wall behind the counter was a faded, handwritten notice that said Members Only. And taking pride of place were two centrefolds from girlie magazines Sellotaped to an otherwise empty notice board.

Anders stopped to talk to the young man behind the counter.

'How are we doing tonight, Tony?'

'Pretty good, Mr Anders. We're already full and Joe's had to send out for more bottles.'

'Is Candy in?'

'Yes. She came in with Mr White.'

Anders smiled. 'Come to spend his winnings, I expect.'

The narrow stairs were uncarpeted and uneven but they were familiar, and Anders walked down slowly to the main club room. It held twenty-one tables with a bar along the length of one wall and in the corner was a dais that held the piano and its stool. It was a small Bechstein grand. The Bechstein had been the only way to bribe and keep Baldy Morton, the black American who plied his solitary, unheeded talent night after night. He loved the Bechstein, and that, and the fact that he hadn't got a work permit, were the reasons why he first came to the club. By now it was more than that. He liked Tad Anders, who appreciated his talent.

The air was heavy with cigar smoke, and the barman and the two girls were edging their way busily between tables with trays of glasses and empty bottles. The club members had the usual things in common. Few of them earned their livings honestly and most of them had plenty of money. And most of them were happy extroverts who spent their money freely on booze and girls. That was why they came to the club. There were at least half a dozen who had done breakins for Tad at unlikely places for not much more than his goodwill. Admittedly, they would have been horrified if they had know they were unwittingly helping SIS. He got on well with most of them. They were ruthless and hard in their crimes but generous with their families and friends. The next day was a public holiday and the club would be virtually empty. The underworld treated holidays with proper respect, and they'd all be in their beds with their wives or other people's wives. Or walking around deserted buildings with nylon stockings over their faces, trying to remember where the Wages Office had been on the sketch done by one of the charladies.

Anders played his ration of being 'mine host', wandering from table to table, chatting with those he knew well, and exchanging an amiable nod with those he didn't recognize. And in the far corner was Candy Price, on her own, laughing at the mildly obscene references to her figure from the four men at the next table. He pulled up a chair and sat down facing her.

'Where's Chalky?'

'Gone to the loo.'

'How's your ma?'

'Same as usual. Up and down. How're you?'

'Same as your ma, up and down.'

'I hear madam was here tonight. She put you down as usual?'

He offered her a cigarette and leaned forward to light it for her and then leaned back and lit his own. She put her knee against his under the table. Candy came from Bethnal Green. Eighteen years old, blonde and pretty, with a figure that had been known to cause street accidents. She smiled across at him, not put off by his lack of response to her question.

'What d'you want me to say to Chalky?'

'About what?'

'Don't be stupid, lovie. Do I go back with him to his place or do you want me to stay the night?'

'What do *you* want to do?'

'I don't need the bread.'

'So?'

'So I'd rather stay with you.'

Candy Price had fallen for Tad Anders the first time she had seen him. It was serious and for real, and she showed her affection in the only ways she knew. She slept with him without payment and she bought him small presents. Sometimes a packet of Stuyvesants, sometimes a tie or a shirt that had taken her eye. Anders looked back at the big blue eyes that were watching his face. For once she wasn't all smiles.

'How about you stay the night and we go down to the coast tomorrow? We could take your old lady if you want.'

She reached across and touched his hand.

'I love you, Tad. I love you so much.'

'How are you going to deal with Chalky?'

She shrugged. 'God knows. He won't be a problem. He's half cut already.'

'Give me a ring on the bar phone when you're free.'

'OK.'

He stood up, took a last look around the room and then walked along the narrow corridor, past the toilets to the far stairs that took him up to his own living quarters and the two offices. The back office had a heavy steel door behind the wooden door and a complex locking device. The contrast with the rest of the club was extreme. The walls were panelled with rosewood, and the armchairs and three-seater settee were in soft tan leather. Good reproductions of French Impressionists were framed on three walls and the long wall was completely shelved from end to end. The upper shelves were packed with books and on the lowest shelf was a Technics hi-fi system and racks of cassettes. There were two digital GPO telephones and a red internal telephone. On the narrow wall beside the right-hand window was a photograph of a girl, a blonde. She was very beautiful, and she was smiling into the camera. A gentle, loving smile. Across the bottom right-hand corner, in a larger feminine scrawl, it said '*Je t'aime infiniment – ta Marie-Claire.*' Tad Anders only looked at that photograph when he was depressed. Not because it cheered him up, but it gave him a logical reason for any inexplicable lowering of his spirits.

As he poured himself a whisky he turned on the hi-fi and the chimes of Big Ben rang out to herald the midnight news bulletin. He turned it off impatiently and he could hear the dull roar of the traffic in the Charing Cross Road.

He was asleep on the leather settee when the telephone rang. It was Candy Price and she was waiting for him downstairs. It was three-fifteen.

She was leaning over the piano in the deserted club and Baldy was playing softly and slowly, singing the words in his thin negro voice, and the girl with her chin cupped in her hands was listening intently. It was the melody she always asked for – 'Gettin' sentimental over you'. When his hands left the keys he looked up smiling at Anders.

'I still got the Dorsey version of that.'

The girl looked at the two men. From one face to the other. She wished she could have had brothers like them. Or even a father.

'Play Tad's tune for him, Baldy. The French one he likes.'

The negro looked up at Anders' face because he knew what the song meant for him. When Anders shrugged and nodded the negro played, and the second time around he came in at the end. '. . . *le temps passe et cours en battant tristement dans mon coeur si lourd . . . et pourtant, j'attendrai ton retour.*' Then very gently he closed the lid of the piano and stood up.

'Time for us chickens to roost, boss. See you day after tomorrow.'

'Night, Baldy. Take care.'

Anders and the girl sat on the beach on a damp, striped bath towel, and the old lady sat in a deckchair. They had lunched at a small restaurant in the High Street in Battle, on their way through to Bexhill. Candy's mother wasn't old, she was only fifty next October, but her body was grossly misshapen by arthritis. In spite of her bent back and her distorted hands and legs she was a cheerful woman whose life in the East End of London had inured her to the inevitable burdens that were the lot of the poverty-stricken generation that had grown up before and during the war. Uncomplaining despite the chronic pain, she was a good judge of people although she seldom aired her views. She liked Tad Anders.

Although she had never been told outright how her daughter earned a living she had a good idea of what went on. She was neither approving nor shocked. The girl was too pretty not to be a target for men. It had been like that when Candy was still at school. But Tad Anders was almost like a son. Easy-going, cheerful, protective, he was genuinely caring, and God knows there was no need to ingratiate himself with her in order to sleep with her daughter. She was used to Italians and East-End Jews and Tad Anders was very like them. A loner, who knew what he wanted and who took time to watch life going by. Her girl would come to no harm with this man, and that was more than she could say about most of them. She didn't see him as a husband; not because he was unavailable, but because girls who lived the kind of life that Candy lived always went on a few years too long, until they could no longer pick and choose. She had seen it all before, but there was no point in talking about it. When you are young and pretty, and the men are like bees round a honey pot, you can't believe that it could ever end.

Candy Price, in a white bikini, sat humming quietly to herself as she painted her toenails in Shocking Pink. When she had finished the paint job she fanned her toes with the *Daily Mail* until the lacquer had set hard. Then she sighed contentedly and lay back on the towel.

Anders sat looking across the beach out to sea where a long low tanker barely moved on the horizon; a Royal Navy frigate lay hull-down a mile or so behind the tanker. And when they had been up on the promenade he'd seen the long, thin grey smudge that was the coast of France. He had turned his eyes away deliberately because everything French reminded him of Marie-Claire Foubert and the nightmare in the dark, on the banks of the Thames at Marlow. It was years ago now, but it had been the end of a piece of his life when the Russians had thrown her bruised and battered body into the river. He had been standing under the tree in the moonlight, his hand on the Russian's throat as he made him talk, when he learned that it was too late and the girl was already dead. And beside himself with grief and rage, he had hunted Rudenko until he had him cornered in the churchyard. Mac had led him away and the doctor had given him an injection.

It had been two days and nights before he came to in his bed, and Mac had been sitting there, solemn-faced and concerned. And it had been Mac who told him that he was being taken off the SIS establishment and given the undercover option. They had suggested a club as his cover and they had been generous with money. When he had asked why he was being dismissed Mac had sighed and asked if he didn't really already know. When he swore that he didn't, Mac had looked at his face for a long time before he spoke, and then he had told him that even though his shots had gone home, and Rudenko was dying, Anders had carved a great slit in his belly and pulled out his guts on to the damp night grass. There would be no enquiry and no comeback, but he was definitely out. SIS were not unused to violence but his kind of violence was politically dangerous. They would use it when it was necessary, but he was no longer part of the apparatus of the house in Queen Anne's Gate. He didn't remember doing it but Mac was a friend who had no reason to lie. And he said he had seen it, and taken quick action to protect both Anders and SIS. He had still been in coma when they buried Marie-Claire in the same churchyard of All Saints, and for almost two years his devil had frequently driven him in despair to the churchyard in Marlow to look at her grave. It was a ritual that gave him no peace or consolation. He drove down in reckless haste, parked the car by the church, walked into the churchyard and stared transfixed at the river. It was only when he eventually realized that he never actually looked at her grave that he stopped the frantic neurotic journeys.

Anders had made no protest at their decision, and had accepted the option they offered. His life with SIS was all he knew. But he always considered they had been unfair. Marie-Claire was his girl, and Rudenko had let his men rape her before they killed her and threw her body in the river. It had been a piece of cold, deliberate revenge against him by Rudenko when he saw his operation falling apart. That surely made the circumstances different and unusual, but even Mac hadn't hesitated in going along with their decision. He was useful but dangerous, and that was the end of it for them. But they showed no embarrassment when they briefed him to do the things that went against their grain, and they took it for granted that he himself had no such scruples. He sensed that they no longer even considered him to be an Englishman. He was a Pole, their Slav, to counter the other Slavs from Dzerdzhinski Square.

He turned to look at the girl's face and even though her eyes were closed she said, 'What is it, Tad?'

'Nothing. I was just looking at you.'

She shrugged up on to one elbow and half closed her eyes against the sun as she looked at his face.

'Are you OK?'

'I'm fine. How about you?'

'Another half-hour and we'll head back, yes?'

'Whatever you say, sweetie.'

He had taken a round-about route along narrow country lanes to get to Battle and he had glanced briefly at the old thatched cottage as he passed. There was blossom on the apple trees and it looked calm and welcoming with the orange light of the setting sun on the diamond-paned windows. He was sure that the girl hadn't noticed him looking.

CHAPTER TWO

Although it was only the first week in September, Radio Moscow's weather bulletin that morning had reported that there had been light falls of snow during the night in Leningrad and warned of possible snowfalls in Moscow by that evening.

There were only six people sitting in the chairs facing the man standing at the lectern. He was not tall, but his dark eyes dominated his face and his audience. He was leaning with his arms on the old wooden lectern as he looked at them all intently. His voice was soft and educated with a faint trace of a Leningrad accent. He pushed aside the light on its swivel so that he could lean further forward, as if the few extra inches might make a difference.

'. . . and one last thing I want to say to you. Go search for people who are hurt by fate or nature – the ugly, those suffering from an inferiority complex, craving power and influence but defeated by unfavourable circumstances . . . The sense of belonging to an influential, powerful organization will give them a feeling of superiority over the handsome and prosperous people around them. For the first time in their lives they will experience a sense of importance . . . It is sad indeed, and humanly shallow – but we are obliged to profit from it.'

There was a long silence as his dark eyes scanned their faces, and then he stood up straight. He nodded towards them. 'Goodnight, comrades.' And there was a clatter of feet as they all stood up as he walked to the door and left the room. General Pavl Anatolevich Sudotplatov was the commander of *Spetsburo* Number One: the KGB's special unit entrusted with peacetime sabotage and murder. His audience had just completed their final three years' training as field operatives for whichever Soviet Intelligence service might choose to use them.

At least one would go to the Red Army's Intelligence service, the GRU; one would probably operate under the direct control of the Politburo; and the others would stay with the newly founded KGB. All of them were already commissioned officers. They had another week of final indoctrination when they would be shown what were some of the most closely guarded secrets of the Soviet Union.

They were given only fifteen minutes in the laboratory known as the *Kamera*, whose staff spent their time and hundreds of thousands of roubles perfecting methods of killing human beings by devices and poisons that had no antidotes, and left no traces in the victim's body. Their short transit through the laboratory required the students to walk between chalked guide-lines to prevent them accidentally touching some innocent-looking lethal artefact. There were few official visitors to the *Kamera*. Even inside the Politburo which authorized it, and the KGB who operated it and used its research, it was feared rather than respected.

Vasili Pavlovich Burinski was one of the group who ended up on the KGB's payroll. He had been trained at three KGB schools with all their normal thoroughness. Apart from his intelligence training he spoke fluent German and good English. His father had been a full colonel in the Red Army, a career officer who had commanded an artillery regiment that had helped to defend Moscow, and fired the first barrage into beleaguered Berlin. He had lost an arm and an eye in the last week before the city fell and had been promoted to Major General. His wife had been killed in the siege of Leningrad and he now had a small government apartment in the centre of Moscow and a *dacha* in the pine woods just off the Volokolamskoye Highway beyond the Arkhangelskoye Estate. With no interest in politics, his only interest in life had been the educating and bringing up of his only child. When his son had left Moscow University and had been chosen for training at the Frunze Academy he had been lonely, but happy that his son would follow in his military footsteps. When Vasili had been transferred to the KGB he hid his anger and disappointment. If you were a career officer in the Red Army you needed to be a committed Soviet to find virtue in the KGB. If you were not so committed you despised and subconsciously feared them. General Burinski kept his views to himself but his anger came from the fact that it was the first time in their lives that his son and he had a subject they studiously avoided. His disappointment showed only in his never enquiring about his son's work or his progress. His love and concern were as obvious as they had always been but the talk was always of chess and books and the countryside.

Burinski was the only one of the new intake who was taken back to the *Kamera* again. There was a long row of offices in the compound, away from the main building, and it was there that he was interviewed.

The man who interviewed him was a short, thickset KGB man in his late fifties. Burinski recognized the type. A committed Soviet who had survived from the days of the OGPU, the NKVD and all the other upheavals that finally produced the KGB. Dedicated and experienced, they carried out their orders with unquestioning obedience. Burinski saw the file on the desk with his own name stencilled on the front. It was thicker than he expected and he wondered what it could contain to be so full.

'And how is your father, comrade Burinski?'

'I haven't seen him for three months, comrade Major, but he seems well enough from his letters.'

'A pity he never joined the Party.'

'He's not interested in politics. The Red Army was always the whole of his life.'

'And you? What are your interests?'

'My work.'

Karpov nodded, not so much in approval as a sign that he recognized the correct and standard response to his question.

'It's been suggested that you are capable of carrying out special tasks for the *Spetsburo*. What do you think?'

'I'll do whatever the Bureau orders me to do.'

Karpov half-smiled and leaned back in his chair.

'Easy to say, young man. I've heard people make that sort of rash statement before, and then when they're told what they have to do they back down.'

He waited for the younger man to answer, but he sat there in silence, his blue eyes arrogant and challenging. Karpov reached for a file from a metal trolley behind him.

'There is a man named Krause. Doctor Emil Krause. He's a judge of the West Berlin High Court. A fanatical anti-Soviet who has handed out long terms of imprisonment to some of our people who have been trapped over there. We'd like you to bring him back into East Berlin so that we can talk with him.' He slid the file across the desk to Burinski. 'Read it and come back with a plan, tomorrow.'

Burinski reached for the file, and Karpov said, 'It doesn't go outside the compound, my friend. There's a room put aside for you in Block F.'

Burinski's plan had been approved and he had spent two weeks in East Berlin, crossing several times into West Berlin, checking Krause's movements and a route back to the Wall. In the third week Burinski and a KGB man from Karlshorst had stopped Krause in the street, and in open daylight they had bundled him into a black Mercedes on the Kurfürstendamm and driven straight to the Brandenburger Tor. The barrier opened to let them through, and then closed behind them. Krause had been flown to Moscow in a military plane the same night.

The American and British commanders jointly protested vigorously against the kidnapping to the Soviet authorities who indignantly denied any knowledge of Dr Krause or his abduction. It was nearly five years later when the Soviet Red Cross announced the death of Dr Krause in an unnamed Soviet prison. It was a piece of outrageous impudence that expressed the mounting arrogance of the men in the Kremlin.

Burinski's next two assignments were both kidnappings. One in Vienna, and the other, more complex, in Paris. The abduction in Paris had required the use of one of the *Kamera*'s special drugs.

After three years he was posted to East Berlin, and his new operations were more precise. The targets were defectors from the Eastern bloc countries and leading anti-Communist figures in West Germany as well as West Berlin. And they were to be killed, not kidnapped. He had had special training at the *Kamera* laboratories on their secret murder weapons. Weapons that left no trace of killing. No wounds, no blood, no medical symptoms even after an autopsy. And the weapons themselves were not like weapons but cigarette cases, a toothpaste tube and sometimes merely a tablet or a powder.

They had shown Burinski a light metal tube that looked like a cigar container, and a sectional drawing showing how the device worked. Then they told him about blood vessels, with slides on a screen of normal blood vessels and the contracted blood vessels of a woman who had died of a heart attack, and they explained about the gas and the antidote pill.

The instructor and one of the scientists drove out with him to the nearby woods. The big German Shepherd was on a chain. At the woods they gave him the antidote pill and watched him slip it into his mouth. They warned him again that it worked very quickly. Less than fifteen seconds, and its effects only lasted three minutes. The dog was chained to a tree and it wagged its tail as he approached. Two feet away from the dog he pressed the button on the steel tube and heard the glass ampoule shatter as it was struck by the needle. There was no other sound and for a moment he thought the device had failed. Then the dog shuddered terribly, its legs gave, and for a few seconds it convulsed silently, its paws frantically scattering the fallen leaves. In less than thirty seconds it was dead. Coldly and precisely the scientist explained once again how the weapon caused all the body's blood vessels to contract, instantly stopping the heart. But in ten minutes, as the effects of the drug wore off, the vessels would dilate again and even the most rigorous autopsy would diagnose that death was caused by a heart attack. The diagnosis would be correct and there would be no evidence to indicate that it was prussic acid vapour that had induced the attack.

Burinski walked back slowly to the car. He felt faint, but was determined not to show that he had been affected in even the slightest way by the demonstration. But he remembered the green moss and lichen on the weather side of the tree and the red of the fallen leaves. And the fact that every part of the dog had quivered while it was dying, its muzzle and neck, its chest and belly, and the long muscles in its haunches and hind legs had rippled as if they were liquid. For the first time he realized why even the top men feared the *Spetsburo*. He feared them now himself. What had happened to the dog could happen to him.

Burinski watched Yushenko every day for nearly three weeks. The defector had got himself a job as a repair mechanic for a typewriter company in Cologne. The West Germans had given him a new name and new documents but Moscow had identified him long before they sent in Burinski. He lived in a small flat in an inexpensive block off Salzgasse and led a quiet, regular life. He left for work every morning at 7.30 and spent the day in the workshop, eating sandwiches and reading the daily paper at his lunch-time break. At 5 p.m. he left promptly, bought a packet of American cigarettes and groceries at a neighbourhood shop and was home by 5.30.

The exception to this routine was Friday nights, when Yushenko left his flat as soon as it was dark and walked up to the Hohenzollernring, where he picked up one of the girls and went home with her. In the three weeks that Burinski had been watching it was always a different girl, but they were always girls who had a place nearby. Yushenko would stay for an hour and then walk back to his flat.

It was nine o'clock when Yushenko walked out of the building and made his way through the side streets to the St Apostoln church and then past the museum to Rudolfplatz. There were no girls there when Yushenko arrived and he looked at his watch and walked slowly down Hohenzollernring towards the savings bank building. There were two girls by the carpet shop and Yushenko spoke to one of them, and a few moments later they walked off together. As they stood at the edge of the pavement Burinski thought for a horrible moment that they were going to take a taxi, but they were only waiting for cars to pass so that they could cross the wide street. He watched them enter Lindenstrasse and then followed them. Down one of the side streets the girl stopped at a newspaper shop, and using a key she let them both in to a narrow passageway that led to a flight of stairs. He saw the light go on behind the curtains of the second floor window and settled down to wait.

There was no traffic in the narrow street, but a few pedestrians meant that he had to move on from time to time, looking in the unlit shop windows without straying too far. He was actually level with the newspaper shop when Yushenko eventually came out and Burinski crossed the narrow street towards him. Yushenko was lighting a cigarette and Burinski took out his cigarettes as he went up to him and asked for a light. In the flare of the lighter Burinski saw that Yushenko's face was deeply lined and his skin covered with a rash. As his cigarette glowed he gripped the tube in his jacket pocket and took it out as he slid the tablet into his mouth. He said very softly '*Spasiba, tovarich Yushenko.*' He saw the look of horror on Yushenko's face then he lifted the tube and pressed the button. The effect was immediate, the defector's hands went to his chest as he collapsed in the shop doorway, and as Burinski walked away he heard the man's shoes scrabbling frenziedly on the paving stones. It made him think for a moment of dry autumn leaves, and lichen on the trunk of a tree.

Burinski phoned the safe-house from the car park on the Ring road and they drove him to the airport at Wahn where he was given a ticket for the internal flight to West Berlin that left an hour later. He wondered if he dared telephone Inge to meet him. He decided against it. They probably monitored all calls to East Berlin automatically.

It was past midnight when he landed at Berlin but there was a KGB car waiting for him. He phoned Inge before he left the airport. She sounded pleased to hear from him and said she would get a bath and a meal ready for him. Her flat was only ten minutes walk from his headquarters in Lichtenburg.

Karpov was waiting for him. He was a Lieutenant-Colonel now, and he had flown in from Moscow especially to see Burinski. He was obviously pleased with Burinski's mission. It seemed that Moscow were pleased too. Karpov brought confirmation of Burinski's promotion to captain. He reported what had happened but Karpov obviously already knew. Bonn had already lodged an angry protest with Moscow who had routinely denied all knowledge of the affair. There was little to say as they sat drinking their coffee.

'D'you want a driver to take you home?'

'No thanks. I'll walk.'

'It's a long walk to your place, my boy.'

For a moment he hesitated, and then he said, 'I'm making a call first.'

'Who is it? The dark-haired girl?'

'Yes.'

'Why not a nice Soviet girl? There's plenty of pretty ones here at Karlshorst. Why pick a German?'

Burinski shrugged. 'I didn't pick her for her nationality, comrade Colonel. I find her attractive, and pleasant company.'

'She's a German, comrade. Don't trust her. Don't risk a promising career for a pretty face and a pair of big tits. We can find you plenty of those in Moscow.'

Karpov stood up and held out his hand, and as Burinski took it Karpov said, 'But at least she provides good background for your cover as an East German.

As Burinski walked slowly through the deserted streets he knew that he must have been under surveillance all the time since he had been in East Berlin. He took it for granted that there would have been routine checks: KGB officers were as suspect as anyone else, maybe more. Were they really warning him off, or just being their usual bloody-minded selves where all foreigners were concerned? The German Democratic Republic might be the Soviet Union's most important ally but it didn't make Moscow like Germans, wherever they came from.

Inge was smiling as she opened the door and she was wearing a white frothy *peignoir*. She must have been asleep before he called from the airport but she had made up her face and looked sleepily glamorous.

They kissed passionately, and ten minutes later he was lying back in the warm bath as she made him an omelette. Before drying himself he slid on his bathrobe, walked back into the living room and took the small parcel from his plastic Scandinavian Airline's bag. He walked into the kitchen and put the package on the table.

'Something from Paris for you.'

He was amused at her excitement as she eagerly tore off the flowered paper. It was a small phial of Chanel No. 5, and she was delighted.

CHAPTER THREE

Inge Laufer worked as a secretary at the offices of the East German Press Service. She wasn't a member of the Party, but nobody cared too much about the political leanings of secretaries and typists. But two days after Burinski had come back she was called to the office of the Editor-in-Chief.

She had never been in his office before. It was large and modern with two TV sets, a radio, a tape-recorder and a Telex. He was a burly man with grey hair and she had heard that he'd been a Party member since before the war. He waved her to a chair in front of his desk.

'Fraülein Laufer?'

'Yes, sir.'

'How long have you been working for us?'

'Three years six months.'

'Do you like your work?'

'Yes.'

'You're working for the news desk, yes?'

'Yes, sir.'

'There's a possibility of promotion as secretary to the News Editor himself. Are you interested?'

'Yes, of course.'

'It's a career post, you understand. Not a job.'

'I don't understand.'

'Your work would have to take precedence over everything else. Over your social life for instance.'

'My social life is very limited already, Herr Lemke.'

But she knew now where they were heading.

'So I understand. But you'd be willing to forgo these outside . . . relationships and concentrate on your work here.'

'I'm afraid not.'

'You're not interested in the promotion, then?'

'Oh yes, I'm interested, but not at that price.'

'Is the relationship that important to you?'

'I think so.'

'You aren't sure?'

'He's asked me to marry him. I haven't answered him.'

'You know what he does?'

'He works for the Ministry of the Interior.'

'What as?'

'I've no idea.'

He sighed and leaned back in his chair.

'Fraülein Laufer, you surely don't need me to put it more bluntly, but you would be wise to drop this relationship. Not crudely or suddenly. You're an attractive young girl. You must have had such situations before. Suitors who don't interest you, and you gently put them to one side. You could be tactful. Just let it fade quietly away.'

She smiled. 'You flatter me, Herr Lemke. With five women to every man what you describe doesn't happen in the Democratic Republic.'

'So?'

'So if I have to choose between the man and the promotion I should choose the man.'

'Well. At least we know where we stand. Thank you.'

'So no promotion?' she said as she stood up.

'I'll think about it.'

She walked back slowly to her desk in the newsroom, angry and disturbed. Who the hell did they think they were, deciding every aspect of everybody's life? And doing it so blandly, as if they took obedience for granted. You didn't just carry out orders, you were expected to obey even vague hints. It was bad enough that the Russians lived in their cloud-cuckoo land, but what she couldn't understand was how Germans like Lemke could go along with it. He wasn't uninformed, he saw uncensored news items from all over the world, but he was still willing to send out the clap-trap that went for news items, as if he thought they would be believed. Not even the East German public believed them. They heard the real news on their radios. So who did they think they were deceiving? Even the Russian public took the official news with a pinch of salt. Did the Party really think that because the Allies had drawn a line on a map and divided Germany in two that half the Germans had lost the power to think? She never discussed politics with Burinski but she knew from some of the things he said that he followed the Party line. He must be more important than he made out, and working for the Ministry of the Interior could cover anything from controlling the price of vegetables to the police. And she'd noticed the small printed label on the bottom of the Chanel No. 5 that said it was bought at the duty free shop at Wahn airport, not Paris. He hadn't actually said that he had bought it in Paris. She remembered the words – 'Something from Paris for you.' And it *was* from Paris originally. Not a lie, but not the truth.

CHAPTER FOUR

Burinski took three days of his accumulated leave, Inge was on leave from the Friday night, and they borrowed a car and drove down to the Harz mountains, to Wernigerode.

The German Democratic Republic, East Germany, is a small country – about half the size of the State of Oregon, or half the size of Great Britain, according to viewpoint. Twenty-five kilometres from the centre of Berlin, and the harsh realities of the Wall and the rival powers of occupation, the landscape changes to a countryside of quiet plains and thickly-forested mountains. Mainly rural and, like farming all over the world, only obliquely touched by occupying forces or even wars, the majority of its people had no wish to cross the barbed-wire frontiers. They lived their lives indifferent to governments and decrees and ideologies, much more concerned with weather and good husbandry. They worked hard and had nothing to fear. They no more thought of joining the Communist Party than they had the Nationalist Socialist Party of Adolf Hitler. They were not enthusiasts about anything, not even the Soviet Union's hybrid wheats and barleys that were claimed to crop forty percent heavier than traditional strains.

It was against this background that Inge Laufer grew up. A farmer's daughter, she could milk a cow, harness a plough-horse, drive a tractor and bake bread. She had completed all but the last half-year at the Hochschule in Weimar. That was when the Russians had come. Her father farmed two hundred acres, and as the Russians settled into the city there had been talk of breaking up the farms into fifty-acre holdings, but it never came to anything. The Russians needed all the foodstuffs they could get, and apart from a few hot-heads and sycophants there had been no local clamour to take farms over.

The phone was ringing as Anders opened the door to his flat. It was Peter Nicholson.

'Tad, I've just had a phone call from one of our chaps. I've told him to come straight to you. He's in trouble – bleeding quite a bit – should be with you in a few minutes. His name's Mason. Jerry Mason. Will you look after him until I get there? I'll bring a doctor as soon as I can lay hands on one . . . OK?'

'What's he look like?'

'Young, dark hair, Zapata moustache. I must go.'

'See you.'

Anders hung up and walked down the stairs, along the corridor and up the stairs to the reception area. He switched on the light and opened the double door. A man was sitting on one of the dustbins, one arm hugging his chest, his head back against the brick wall. He had dark hair and a moustache. Anders walked forward and stood in front of the man.

'What's the matter?'

'Find Anders . . . at the club . . . please?'

'I'm Anders.'

'Nicholson said . . .' The man tried to suppress a thin cry of pain and failed. Anders put his own hand on the back of the man's hand where it was pressed to his side inside his sports jacket. The man's hand was wet and warm and slippery with blood. Anders slid one hand under the man's knees and put his arm round his shoulders. The man was heavier than he expected and inside the reception area he rested him for a moment on the desk as he kicked the door to behind him.

The man was unconscious as Anders lowered him gently on to his leather couch. With scissors from the kitchen he sliced off half the man's jacket and then his shirt. Gently shifting the man's hand he saw the wound. The slug had hit the bottom rib and sliced across the soft flesh of his belly to leave a six-inch long flap of loose flesh that was seeping blood. Anders propped the man up against two cushions and covered the wound with a towel soaked in cold water. A few minutes later he heard the bell ringing downstairs.

Nicholson had a tall gangling man with him in evening dress and as he led them along the corridor to the stairs and his room Nicholson said, 'How bad is he, Tad?'

'Fair amount of blood lost. I'd say he's in shock.'

Anders and Nicholson stood in silence as they watched the doctor lift off the sopping wet towel and peer at the wound. He checked the wounded man's pulse with his wristwatch and then stood up.

'It wasn't a bullet. Somebody struck him with a knife. Hit his rib and it slid downwards and across his abdomen, slicing open the skin . . . looks as if he might have lost up to half a pint of blood.'

'What does he need?' asked Nicholson.

'He needs to go into hospital . . . needs some blood, a thorough check and some sewing up. I don't think anything vital has been touched but we'll soon find out.'

Nicholson shook his head. 'He can't go into a general ward.'

'I'll take him to my place in Welbeck Street. But he'll need some blood first and some temporary patching up. We can't move him as he is.'

Nicholson looked worried. 'We'll have to put a guard on him while he's with you.'

'That's no problem. We usually have that with your people.'

'Can you fix it now and get the blood over? He's 'O' group.'

The doctor turned towards Anders. 'Can I use your phone?'

Anders nodded. 'The one on the left. The grey one. Just dial.'

Fifteen minutes later two medical orderlies slid the unconscious man on to a stretcher and Nicholson and the doctor followed Anders to the waiting private ambulance. The doctor climbed in with the wounded man.

The first light of the false dawn was already stirring the pigeons, and empty vans from the Home Counties were heading for the markets. It looked as if it were going to be a very hot day.

Anders made coffee for himself and Nicholson and they sat together in the small bright kitchen.

'What had your chap Mason been up to, Peter?'

'He's been checking on an Armenian named Kanassian. He's got a warehouse on the river at Blackfriars. Buys and sells oriental carpets. High-class stuff, and genuine, but we had a quiet look at his bank balances. There's not much there and we think he's a banker for the KGB. They provide the carpets. He sells them, and the money goes to fund KGB operations here.'

'What happened last night?'

'A month ago we established a positive link between the Soviet Embassy and Kanassian. We discovered a KGB dead-letter box. They were using a loose coping stone on the embankment near the Festival Hall. Kanassian was seen using it. We didn't pick him up but we checked the package he had left. It was a newspaper cutting . . . just a couple of inches of a single column with the racing results from Sandown Park. And – of course – a microdot. The microdot gave details of cash deposits in lockers at the main London railway stations. We left everything as it was but it was decided that we'd have a look at Kanassian's warehouse and his living quarters. He lives there too. That's what Mason was doing last night. I don't know what happened but he phoned me from a call-box by Leicester Square underground station. I sent him round to you.'

'Why so much secrecy now?'

Nicholson shrugged. 'We didn't have a warrant and we want to find out what happened before we take any action.'

'Did he go alone?'

'Yes.'

Anders raised his eyebrows. 'You guys never learn, do you?'

'What's that mean?'

'It's crazy sending out one man when you already know the KGB are involved. It needs a proper set-up. A full recce, radio support and a back-up team. You've blown Mason. And you've closed down their operation when you'd have got far more just letting it run until you'd got it fully evaluated. You could probably have turned Kanassian and used him.'

'I doubt it.'

'How much money was there in the lockers?'

'Just over seventy thousand.'

'Dollars or pounds?'

'Pounds.'

'Have you collared it?'

'They're doing that now.'

'And Kanassian?'

'We'll deport him when we know from Mason what went on.'

'Why don't you knock him off? Teach them a lesson.'

'Is it justified?'

'Oh for Christ's sake, Peter. Anything's justified with those bastards.'

'Would you do it yourself?'

'Sure. Providing you ask me to.'

'Maybe we will. Let's wait until I can talk with Mason.'

And that was how they left it.

Burinski booked two rooms in a small inn at the edge of the town and they lazed the days away. It was on the second day, when they were sitting at the edge of the forest looking over the quiet valley that she told him of the pressures at her office.

He smiled and shrugged. 'They did the same to me.'

'Why are they doing it? Why do we matter so much?'

He turned to look at her. She was very beautiful and her big brown eyes were clear and honest.

'Have you decided yet?'

'Decided what?' She smiled.

'Don't tease. You know what I mean.'

'Do you still want to marry me?'

'You know I do.'

'They might try and stop us.'

He shrugged. 'They'll try, maybe, but they won't refuse in the end.'

She looked at his face, intently. 'Who are the "they" we're talking about?'

'Your bosses and mine.'

'Herr Lemke couldn't give a damn who I marry. It will have come from your people at the Ministry.'

'You're probably right.' He smiled at her and said softly, 'So what's your answer?'

She looked away from him, gazing over the valley, touching a limp stem of red campion to her mouth. Without turning to look at him she said. 'The answer's yes; if you're sure that's what you want.'

He reached out for her hand. 'When?'

She laughed gently and looked at him. 'Whenever you want.'

He stood up and pulled her up alongside him. He turned her, kissing her gently, her body against his, warm and soft.

'I'll start things moving as soon as we get back to Berlin.'

And suddenly the mere name of the city was grim and grey and menacing.

After they had made love in her bed that night he had gone back to his own room next door. He pulled up a chair to thc small window, lit a cigarette and looked out. He could see the outline of the pine trees in the light of the moon, and he wished that he could stay there for the rest of his life. He knew he'd have to tell her before they actually got married, and she would know he had lied. Lied about almost everything, except that he loved her. She wouldn't believe that he only lied because it was his duty to lie. His duty to his calling, and his duty to his country. She never recognized such loyalties. She wasn't committed as he was. Tomorrow was their last full day. He would tell her tomorrow. He looked at his watch. It was one o'clock. Tomorrow was already today.

He put it off again and again. Hoping to find the right opening that would lead to it naturally. But no such opening came. They visited the museum in the morning, and in the afternoon they walked again to the place where they had sat the previous day. She seemed so happy, and so sure that they were both going to be happy. And she insisted on gathering a bag of the big pine cones to take back with them. She said they were good weather guides. She was counting them, moving them from the heap beside her into the red canvas bag.

Eventually she turned, smiling. 'Fifty-seven.'

'Are you warm enough here?'

'Yes, of course I am. And I've got a sweater in my bag. What about you?'

'Will you listen very carefully?' And his voice trembled. 'I've got something I want to tell you.'

'You sound very solemn all of a sudden,' she said softly.

He looked away from her face, focusing his eyes on the red canvas bag.

'I'm not German, Inge. I'm a Russian. And I'm a captain in the KGB.'

Compelled to see her reaction he looked back to her face. She had closed her eyes as if she had received a blow and when she opened them she sighed before she spoke. And tears rimmed her eyes.

'They won't let us marry. They'll just send you back to Moscow.'

'But what about you?'

'What do you mean?'

'Are you disappointed that I'm a Russian?'

She looked at him calmly. 'I never loved you because you were German. That just doesn't matter.'

'What does matter?'

'They pressured both of us. But it was only a nudge compared with what they'll do when you tell them you want to marry me.'

'But if they don't object, you'd still marry me?'

'I fell in love with a man. It makes no difference to me whether you're German, Russian or Chinese. You're just you as far as I'm concerned.'

'What about the other thing?'

She smiled. 'You mean the KGB?'

'Yes.'

'If you like playing cowboys and Indians that's up to you.'

'It's more than that, Inge, my work . . .'

She held up her hand to silence him. 'I don't want to hear. Whatever you do you must feel that it's right to do it. That's enough for me.'

'You really mean that?'

'Of course.'

'You're very generous. You haven't pointed out that I told you a pack of lies.'

'Moscow lives on lies. How could you be different and survive?'

'For God's sake don't say anything like that if they talk to you about us marrying.'

She smiled. 'Are you afraid they might send me to the Gulag?'

'It's not a joke, Inge. The Gulag really does exist.'

She smiled. 'Hadn't you better tell me your name? Your real name?'

He sighed. 'It's terrible when I hear you say that.' He half-smiled, embarrassed. 'Maybe you won't like it.'

'Try me.'

'Vasili Pavlovich Burinski.'

He sounded defensive, and she leaned forward and kissed him gently.

'Vasili Pavlovich Burinski, I love you.'

He pulled her to him fiercely, and with his head resting on her shoulder he said, 'I love you so much, Inge. I was so worried about telling you, but you've made it so easy.'

She stroked his shoulder gently, soothing him as mothers soothe their children.

Karpov had flown in from Moscow the day after Burinski reported that he wanted to marry Inge Laufer. Karpov's attitude had ranged from the fatherly to the recriminating. From despair to barrack-room male chauvinism. There was probably nothing wrong with the girl, but why oh why marry a foreigner when there were millions, literally millions, of Russian girls to choose from? Girls who would be proud of his rank and the organization he served. For that matter why marry at all, why load your shoulders with all that responsibility? Sow some wild oats by all means, but for God's sake you don't have to buy it outright. What he needed was a couple of weeks' leave in Moscow to remind himself of what pretty girls were like. Karpov himself would see that he had a special selection.

It wasn't an aggressive interview. There were no threats and Karpov didn't say that the marriage was impossible. He nagged and derided but he said nothing against the girl herself beyond the fact that she was a foreigner. They had obviously done a lot of checking on her but there was nothing in Karpov's harangue to indicate that anything negative had been discovered.

After they had lunched together Karpov had a private telephone conversation with Moscow, and when he sent for Burinski again the atmosphere was relaxed. Moscow, he said, were not too happy about his request. Apart from the fact that she was a foreigner the girl was not a Party member and seemed to have no political convictions at all. That was a dangerous vacuum in the background of the wife of a KGB officer. On the other hand Moscow wanted him to be content, and if this marriage was what he wanted they would agree, with certain provisos. He would never discuss his work with her. Not even a cover story. She would have to accept that his work was closed to her and she would not interfere in any way. Moscow would also arrange for her to see the Party at work in the Republic. She would visit various works and schools, hospitals and research laboratories so that she could absorb the efforts that were being made to make East Germany economically and socially advanced. It was also accepted that marrying her would give a genuine basis to Burinski's cover story of being an East German. Nevertheless, he would have to play his part. It would be up to him to help make her at least a supporter of the Party line if not an enthusiast. Burinski assured him that he would do everything possible to repay their faith in him.

There was no comment and no pressures on Inge at the office of the Presse Dienst but she was vaguely aware of glances in her direction by senior people who would normally have ignored her.

Ten days later, permission came through from Moscow for them to marry. Karpov broke the good news, hedged about again with warnings of dire consequences if the girl did not conform to accepted Party behaviour for Soviet officials' wives. They were allowed to marry in church in Inge's home village just outside Weimar and her parents were impressed by her young husband. They had a three-day honeymoon before they went back to East Berlin, where they were given privileged married quarters in a block that housed senior officials of the Red Army Intelligence Staff and the East Germans' Intelligence service, MfS.

The two Germans sat on one side of the table and Peter Nicholson on the other. The room was thick with smoke and Kiefer was lighting yet another cigarette. He threw the used match at the ashtray and missed, and left the match to smoke on the polished table top. Gierecke reached for it and put it in the tray. They had been talking for two hours; and the dead-lock was solid.

It was Kiefer who broke the silence. 'Would it help if we came to London, Herr Nicholson?'

'By all means. You'd be very welcome but it would make no difference. What you are asking puts it into the political field. It's no longer just a counter-intelligence matter. They couldn't possibly agree.'

Gierecke sighed. 'Our agreement was made a long time ago. Nearly ten years. Neither party could have foreseen a situation like this. Surely London must understand that?'

'There's every sympathy with your situation, but to extend the present arrangements could have all sorts of repercussions.'

'Meantime we just sit on our backsides while they send over professional assassins who are safely back over the border in a couple of hours.' Gierecke shook his head slowly. 'Bonn couldn't let this go on.'

Nicholson shrugged. 'That would be a question for the two governments to sort out.'

Kiefer lit another cigarette. 'Their people in East Berlin must be expecting some reaction, for God's sake.'

'That could be why they are doing this. Just to make us react. So that they have an excuse for another blockade of Berlin. Or something even more provocative. Imagine what a propaganda victory they would have if anything went wrong. West Germans being sent into East Berlin or East Germany as revenge killers? You would be totally exposed and isolated. The rest of Europe and the Americans couldn't possibly support you.'

Gierecke spoke very softly. 'So why don't you people look after it?'

Nicholson shook his head. 'There's no possibility of that. If something went wrong it could be catastrophic. They would really have an excuse to attack West Berlin. You've heard what Radio Moscow is saying already: West Berlin is being used as a base for the Americans and the British to launch their spies into the Democratic Republic. And if something goes wrong we've handed the proof to them on a silver salver. And whatever they did in West Berlin half the world would say we had got what we deserve and the other half would hold its breath and say nothing.'

'What do they have to do, Herr Nicholson, before we retaliate? Two more assassinations? Four? A member of the West German cabinet? Where do you draw the line? Or can they go on killing as they please?'

'We can put British Army units with your Frontier Police and we'll feed you all the information we get out of Moscow and Berlin that could help you deal with them when they come over.'

Kiefer smiled. A cold contemptuous smile. 'If you gave us the whole of the Rhine Army it would make no difference.'

Nicholson didn't rise to the bait. 'I suggest, gentlemen, that we report back to our chiefs and leave it to them to decide what to do.'

It was the soft-spoken Gierecke who said the words he had hoped he wouldn't hear. 'You won't expect our cooperation in Berlin from now onwards, will you?'

'Is that official?'

'Yes.'

'You're quite sure? If I pass that on it will hinder rather than help.'

'It's official, Herr Nicholson, make no mistake about that.'

'I assume your people discussed the implications of withdrawing cooperation with SIS?'

Gierecke nodded. 'Extensively.'

Nicholson sighed. 'May I ask at what level the discussion took place?'

'Top level BfV, and a representative from the Chancellor's office, the Foreign Ministry and the Opposition.' Gierecke paused. 'It's not a bluff, Herr Nicholson, I assure you.'

'I'll go back to London and report on our meeting. Would you be available for a further meeting at the end of the week?'

'We're available at any time.'

Back in London Nicholson reported to French.

'D'you think they mean it, Peter, about withdrawing cooperation?'

'I do.'

'Including Berlin?'

'Yes. They're very bitter about it. Gierecke drove me back to the airport and he told me that it was possible that they would take unilateral action if we didn't do something about it.'

'D'you think they will?'

'I don't think so. But I wouldn't bet on it. I suspect they'll be letting off steam at Cabinet level before long.'

'They have already. The West German Ambassador had an hour with the Foreign Secretary late last night. There was no threat of going it alone, but they were very steamed up and the Minister was sympathetic but adamant.'

'They've got a good case. They haven't got a chance of picking up a trained professional who slips over the border after an unknown victim, kills and is back home an hour or two later. Whoever was facing the problem would have no choice. If they did it without our agreement or the American's they'd be out in the snow even if they were successful.'

Sir Arthur pursed his lips as he looked across his desk at Nicholson. 'What would you propose if, in the end, something had to be done?'

'We couldn't possibly let the Germans do it. It would have to be us. I can only think of one sensible solution.'

'Anders?'

'Yes.'

CHAPTER FIVE

For seven or eight weeks Burinski was given desk work at the intelligence centre in Normannenstrasse and he and his wife were taken on escorted visits to schools, factories, trade-union meetings and government departments. Their escorts were always experts in the field concerned, who were able to explain and answer their questions. And comparisons were drawn with what was being done for the people in West Berlin and West Germany. Burinski was impressed and his wife made few comments and asked no questions.

When he tried to discuss the visits with her she wouldn't be drawn. She never disagreed with what he said but she never agreed either. She just listened, half-smiling, as he praised the benefits that the East Germans got from adopting the Soviet system. It was after a visit to a tyre plant that he provoked her into a reply. He didn't intend to provoke her; they were sitting together after their evening meal and he read out the production figures from the handouts they'd been given, and then he'd looked at her smiling.

'The same production as the Americans. Same output per man and with cheaper costs. Those are facts, Inge, not propaganda.'

'I'm sure you're right, Vasili.'

He smiled back at her. 'You don't believe it, do you?'

She shrugged. 'There's football on TV if you want it.'

'Why don't you believe, Inge?'

She sighed. 'There's no way of knowing whether the figures are true or phoney. And that isn't the point.'

'What is the point?'

'Those tyres all go to the Soviet Union. You'd have to get it on the black market if you wanted one and you were German. About a month's pay is the going rate.'

'Are you sure?'

She reached out and put her hand gently on his as it lay on the arm of his chair. 'We don't have to quarrel about things like this Vasili. None of it matters.'

'But I want to know what you think.'

'Do you mean that? Really mean it?'

'Of course I do.'

'I'll tell you. Then let's not ever discuss these things again.'

'OK.'

She took a deep breath. 'Hitler started the war against the Soviet Union. We lost it, and now we're paying for it. In the first few months we paid the Red Army. They looted and raped and sent convoys back to Russia loaded with the loot. Everything you could imagine. Wooden doors, toilets, carpets, furniture, everything. No German old enough to remember is ever going to forget those days. Now it's all done officially. You use paper and forms to loot us now and there's no more raping of women. It's just factories and farms being raped now. We do as we're told because arguing can get you in jail. There is no freedom of speech, no democracy, no political opposition, and we're kept in East Berlin by the Wall. Maybe we deserve it, whether we do or not we've got it.'

'Does that mean you hate all Russians?'

'Of course it doesn't. I love *you*, and I've met many Russians I like. You've all got the same dictatorship that we have. The only difference is that the Russians never had anything better. But we did.'

'Is there nothing good that we've done in the Republic?'

'That's not the point, Vasili. We're an occupied country. And we're occupied by a dictatorship. The news is censored and distorted. We don't have news, we have propaganda. We can only hear the real news from other countries on our radios. We know our news is a pack of lies and we just have to pretend we've been fooled. It's all a pretence. We've *not* been fooled. We were once part of the real world and living in this . . . this deception, is degrading.'

'But before the Revolution there were serfs in Russia, and now . . .'

'Oh, Vasili, the Russians must work out their own destiny in their own way. But you don't really think that the Georgians, the Khazakhstanis, the Uzbeks, the Ukrainians and all the rest of them would stay in the Soviet Union for a day if they had the chance to be independent, do you?'

'But they are represented in the Praesidium.'

'Of course. By men who can be trusted to do what the Politburo wants.'

'But conditions are so much better now. There is food, houses, education, work for all. The Soviets have done all this.'

'Let's forget it, my love. Don't let's argue.'

He smiled. 'You had no answer, did you?'

'To what?'

'To what I said. The improvements since the Tsar.'

She shook her head, smiling. 'You're saying that things have improved in sixty years. Of course they have. They've improved everywhere in the world. But what have the Russians got? A shortage of everything, from pots and pans to milk and butter – but plenty of nuclear bombs.'

'We have to defend ourselves, Inge.'

'Rubbish.'

Then she saw the hurt look on his face. 'I was going to tell you some news tomorrow, but maybe I'll tell you now. You and I are going to have a baby.'

He looked so surprised, and then so pleased that their differences were swept away in an orgy of planning from names to baby clothes.

They never talked about politics again, but the fact that they didn't, that there were things that couldn't be discussed, made it's own sharp point. There were sometimes items in news bulletins that were so obviously distorted that he would glance guiltily towards her, and occasionally she smiled back at him without comment. As time went by he was sometimes the one to smile first.

Karpov was on one of his routine visits but it was only on his last day in Berlin that he called Burinski to his temporary office. He pointed to a chair, a brown file cover in his hand.

'How's your Dutch, Burinski?'

'I don't speak Dutch, comrade Karpov.'

'Well, you'll get by with German. I'm sending you to Holland for a couple of days. Have you heard of a town called Arnhem?'

'No, comrade Colonel.'

'It's not far from the German frontier. I want you to attend a funeral.'

Burinski sat silently. There was nothing to say.

'You'll have to leave tonight. There's an Aeroflot flight to Warsaw at seven o'clock. You'll have fresh documents before you leave. You take the KLM flight to Amsterdam that gets you there just before midnight. You phone the home of our cultural attaché, Andreyev. He will send a car for you. It will be driven by a Dutch woman. You'll sleep at her apartment and she'll take you to Arnhem in the afternoon. She'll take you to a church. You'll attend the funeral of a Jugoslav named Djuranovic. You'll go on your own to the funeral. I want you to observe all that goes on. Particularly the people who are there. Afterwards the Dutch woman will pick you up outside the church and she will tell you of the arrangements for you to come back to Berlin. Any questions?'

'What do you want me to look for?'

'What I said. Everything. Watch what happens. Study the people. Particularly the principal ones. That's your brief.'

Karpov stood up to signal that the interview was over but when Burinski was at the door Karpov said, 'I hear your wife is pregnant, comrade. My congratulations. Maybe she should have it in Moscow to make sure that it's a genuine Soviet.'

Karpov was smiling, but his hard grey eyes were intent on Burinski's reactions.

'I think my wife wants to have the baby in Weimar to be near her parents.'

Karpov shrugged. 'Bear it in mind, comrade Burinski, bear it in mind. These things get noticed.'

And Karpov nodded his final dismissal.

The coffin was carried by six men from the hearse, through the arched gate to the churchyard. There were twelve people following the coffin. Only one of them was well-dressed, a man with a shaven head and a pale, impassive face. He glanced briefly at Burinski and then joined the others as they walked into the church.

It was a short service, without ceremony. A prayer, a hymn, an oration in a foreign language that Burinski guessed was Serbo-Croat, a final prayer, then what sounded like a national anthem as the coffin was carried down the aisle. It was a small church and a small graveyard long and narrow, with a gentle slope down a gravel path to a line of cypress trees.

A lean old man stood holding a shiny spade at the side of the freshly dug grave. He doffed his workman's cap as the coffin approached and stood back so that the mourners could gather round the graveside. There was only one woman. An elderly woman in black, with the tanned, leathery face of a gypsy. She held a small bunch of red and white carnations in her hand. Six or seven blooms.

The priest stood at the head of the open grave and as the coffin was lowered he intoned a prayer in Latin. The priest was a big, tall man, dark-skinned with bright blue eyes, and the light breeze lifted his thin hair as he bent down to throw a handful of soil into the grave. Four or five men nearest the grave did the same. The woman in black threw in the carnations and the priest signalled to the grave-digger to fill in the grave. The heap of clay soil was on the far side of the grave and as the first clods thudded on to the coffin the priest spoke again in the foreign tongue and this time it wasn't a prayer, it was a speech, an oration. The man spoke with passion as a plane flew overhead, the noise obliterating his words. And faces were lifted to the sky in irritation. As the noise abated, the priest finished his speech and the mourners followed him back to the church where they stood in small groups. And only the well-dressed man with the shaven head watched Burinski as he walked alone to the gate.

He walked along the country road towards the village and a few minutes later the Dutch woman pulled up the car alongside him.

His orders were to take a commercial flight from Schiphol, Amsterdam to Heathrow, London, where an embassy car and a colleague would be waiting for him.

It seemed a pointless journey. The car and the junior KGB man picked him up at Heathrow and drove him to the embassy. Burinski stayed there for three days. They escorted him on walks through Kensington Gardens, he saw Buckingham Palace and Karl Marx's grave in Highgate cemetery, but that was all. Sightseeing trips but not even a mention of the funeral in Arnhem. And then, with only two hours notice, the flight back to Prague and then on to East Berlin. Karpov was back in Moscow and nobody mentioned his trip. For a few weeks he was occupied in the usual office duties of a KGB administrative officer. Checking documents and signals traffic, and for a few days, interrogating a low-grade West German agent who had been picked up in Magdeburg.

Karpov phoned him from Moscow, not mentioning his journey to Holland but congratulating him on the interrogation. There was a special mission he was to carry out and after that he would be given more interrogations of German-speakers so that he could be in Berlin when the child was born. He recognized that he was being officially absolved from persuading Inge that their child should be born in the Soviet Union. There would be some reason behind it all, but he had no idea what it was.

The special assignment came earlier than he had expected. It was late one afternoon when the signal arrived from Moscow saying that he was to fly there the next day.

Karpov himself met him in at Sheremetyevo and he was surprised when they drove through Moscow and out to the *Kamera* compound outside the city. The *Kamera* was seldom used for actual briefings. He was shown to a small, narrow room in one of the wooden huts where he left his single case, and then he was escorted back to Karpov's office.

Karpov took him over to a trestle table along one wall of the office and one by one he turned over seven photographs so that they lay face upwards, as if he were a gambler turning up his cards.

'Have you ever seen any of those before? Look carefully.'

They were photographs of seven faces. Five men and two women. Burinski looked at each one carefully and then for a long time at two of them. Eventually he pointed at the two. The first and the sixth in the row.

'I think I've seen those two before.'

'Where?'

'At the funeral in Holland.'

'Go on.'

'The man has shaved his head. But I'm sure he was there. And I think this woman was there. But she's much older now. I'd say twenty years older.'

'So how do you know it's the same one?'

'Her eyes. They were very fiery eyes. She looks like a gypsy woman. I'd say she was sixty. Here she was younger but it's still the same eyes and she still looks like a gypsy.'

'Tell me about the man.'

'He was different from the others. Well-dressed. Tall, maybe one eight-five or even a little more. Angry looking. Or maybe stern is the right word. It was almost as if he were the boss or the leader of the people who were there.'

Karpov moved across to his desk and pointed to a chair as he opened a drawer in his desk with his other hand. He took out a small thin phial and put it carefully on the desk in front of him.

'I want you to see this, Burinski.' He held it up towards Burinski. 'This phial is made of lead. It's practically solid lead. There are a few drops of liquid inside it. If the smallest drop touches your skin you'll die. It'll take quite a time. Whatever medical treatment they give you will make no difference, because they won't know what's the matter with you. Not even when you're dead and they do an autopsy.' He put the lead phial carefully back in his drawer and took out a piece of paper. It was a draughtsman's section through something, with dimensions, and arrows with numbers. He pushed it across the desk so that Burinski could see it closer. 'That's a section through the spike of an umbrella. A special umbrella that's been produced by *Kamera* staff. The bottom of the spike unscrews. You put the phial in here. Doesn't matter which end goes in first. When you touch the release button on the handle the hypodermic needle pierces the phial and extends about half a centimetre. A prick from that will be enough. Understood?'

Burinski nodded. 'Yes, comrade Major.' His voice was low and uncertain.

'They'll show you how to use it. They've got dummies for you to practise on, and when they say you're ready you'll go to London. Your target is the man you saw at the funeral. The well-dressed man with the shaven head. You'll be given assistance in contacting him, and I'll be talking to you again before you leave.'

'Who is the man, comrade Major?'

Karpov shook his head. 'An enemy of the State. You don't need to know more. It should take no more than ten days at the most. You'll be back in good time for your wife's confinement.'

'Yes, comrade Colonel.'

And when he was standing he saluted. They were both in uniform and you didn't have to salute in special establishments. But something compelled Burinski to salute just to relieve his own tension.

From where they were standing on Chiswick Common they could see both Woodstock Road and Bath Road. Some mornings Vojnovic came the longer way to the underground station at Turnham Green. The house where he lived was at the far end of Abinger Road. A pleasant Victorian semi-detached house with bay windows up and down and a small front garden that had been paved over. There was only a handful of cultivated gardens in the road. The more political refugees from Slav countries have neither the time nor the inclination for gardening. Putting Eastern Europe to rights is a full-time occupation.

It seemed strange to Burinski at first to see the shaven-headed man in these different surroundings. He heard Polish, Czech, Croat and Ukrainian spoken in these suburban London streets while they were carrying out the surveillance, but the speakers looked as English as the English themselves. Sometimes there was a small giveaway. Men who still wore trilby hats, and women who wore chiffon scarves as they had once worn them in Buda or Warsaw.

Augustin Vojnovic worked at a small import-export company with offices over a printing press in Hammersmith. Every morning including Saturday he walked from Abinger Road to Turnham Green station and took the underground. It was only three stops to Hammersmith Broadway and a five-minute walk to the office.

The assignment had not been difficult: Vojnovic had already been under surveillance and his habits were regular. The only problem was which end of his journey to deal with him. There were advantages both ways. The crowds at the station in the morning gave excellent cover, but Burinski's instinct was for the other end of the journey, and on the open street rather than inside the station.

Panov, under orders from the Embassy, treated him as the expert and merely provided assistance where his English was insufficient or his lack of knowledge of England would make him noticed. Panov was also responsible for checking that they themselves were not under surveillance. He was a Tass man, an efficient journalist who worked out of the main offices in the Press Centre just off Fleet Street. He lived in Highgate and was well dug-in in the student fraternity and with the left-wing intellectuals. He was in no hurry to be posted away from London, particularly to Moscow. It was the first time he had positively assisted in a KGB operation and he wanted it to go smoothly. KGB commendations could help careers and provide extra privileges.

Then they saw Vojnovic, his old-fashioned raincoat over his arm, his black briefcase in his other hand. He walked briskly, a soldierly walk, head held high and eyes to the front. As he went in to the station they crossed the main road. They had already bought weekly season tickets and they followed Vojnovic up the crowded stairway on to the eastbound platform. They travelled in the same carriage and walked slowly a few yards behind him in the crowds at Hammersmith. As usual he stopped at the small newsagents and bought a single packet of Gauloise's before carrying on to his office.

When they were sitting in the small snackbar just off Hammersmith Broadway Panov said, 'We've only got another two days, comrade.'

'I'll do it today. This evening. That's the best time.'

'But I thought . . .'

'You'd better make the travel arrangements for me right now. I'll be finished here by six-thirty. I'll show you where I shall want the car. It'll be by the dance hall.'

They eventually took a train to Hampstead and a taxi to Panov's place just off Highgate High Street. Panov went out to use a public telephone to make the travel arrangements and order a car and driver.

Burinski sat alone, the umbrella on the table alongside him as he read a tattered copy of *Anna Karenina*. He had always meant to read it but had somehow never got round to it. It was better than he had expected. It was one of his father's favourites. That and *War and Peace*. From time to time he put the book down, reached out for the umbrella and, holding it carefully he looked again at the little grey button on the handle. There was a terrible temptation to touch it, to press it. A temptation that increased as the hours passed.

Panov was back by midday, with cold meat and salad for their meal. At three o'clock they walked to the crossroads at Southwood Lane. A grey Volkswagen was waiting for them.

All three of them sat silently in the Volkswagen at the back of the playing fields at Hammersmith moving on from time to time to avoid the traffic wardens. At five o'clock Burinski got out. A few moments later Panov followed him, his eyes on the umbrella. He guessed it was some sort of weapon but he had no idea how it was to be used.

Burinski wanted to be able to walk in the same direction as Vojnovic but there were no shop windows to cover his loitering. There was a big public building and he stood near the entrance checking his watch as if he were waiting for someone.

It was five-thirty exactly when Vojnovic came through the door that the offices shared with the jobbing printer. He paused on the pavement, glancing up at the sky, then turned to walk to the station. Five paces behind, Burinski pressed the button and felt the slight jolt of the mechanism working. Increasing his stride until he was just behind his victim, he touched the umbrella spike to the back of the man's leg. Vojnovic turned his head quickly, frowning, and Burinski walked on and past him.

There was a woman traffic warden leaning down at the Volkswagen window, talking to the driver. As Burinski got to the car, the warden said something as she turned to walk away. Burinski could tell that it was some form of admonishment but he had no idea what it meant.

Panov pushed forward the front seat so that Burinski could get in the car and seconds later the car moved off. There were three or four people looking down at the man on the pavement; another person, a man, was crouching down undoing Vojnovic's shirt at the neck, then they were past. They turned into Goldhawk Road, crossed King Street and took the Great West Road in the direction of Heathrow.

Panov waited with him at the terminal until the SAS flight to Stockholm was called. Only then did Burinski carry out the *Kamera*'s final instruction and grind the spike of the umbrella against the concrete floor before handing it to Panov. And later that night it was pushed into the junk and rubble in a demolition company's yellow skip outside a deserted site in Aldgate.

At Bromma a man from the Stockholm Embassy had passed him his air ticket to East Berlin on a flight that left just after midnight. There was only half an hour to wait.

Karpov himself was waiting for Burinski at Schönefeld and listened attentively as he reported on his mission. Interested enough to put a few questions to him, nodding a tentative approval from time to time.

Vojnovic was unconscious for five hours before he came to in the emergency ward at Hammersmith Hospital. He complained of stomach pains and was treated for acute gastritis. But by the third day the treatment was obviously failing and he was put in a room on his own. Apart from the severe stomach pains nothing seemed wrong. Although he was unsteady on his feet he was able to walk to the toilets unaided. On the fourth day he was lethargic and weak but there were no medical indications of any disease or infection.

It was the sixth day when the situation changed drastically. When the duty nurse turned back the sheets to wake him she took one look and then, covering him again, she reported to the ward sister who telephoned for the duty doctor.

Vojnovic's breathing was shallow but even. As the ward sister and the doctor looked at his body they saw that it was criss-crossed with dark brown stripes and there were black and blue swellings on his face as well as his body. A thick, yellow secretion oozed from his eyelids and ran down his cheeks, and small pinheads of blood had seeped through the pores down one side of his body.

The doctor reached out and gently touched his chest, his belly and the side of his neck. The skin was dry, shrunken, and burning hot.

He turned to the ward sister who looked shocked. 'He's been poisoned. Get our emergency service to locate Professor O'Connor. He should be at St Thomas's. Otherwise try his home and his practice in Wimpole Street. Tell them that it's very urgent.'

The ward sister came back a few minutes later and stood beside him. 'Patsy's tracing him. Is there anything we can do for the man?'

'Not until I've spoken to O'Connor. Watch.'

He reached forward and touched Vojnovic's scalp where his hair had sprouted while he was in the hospital. The stubble came away from the dry scalp as if were dust.

'I'd say that it's thallium poisoning. And that means we had better notify the police if it's confirmed.'

'Why?'

'Thallium's a very rare toxic metal. It couldn't have been ingested accidentally. I doubt if even any hospital lab in London has any.'

'Who would have it?'

He turned to look at her and said softly, 'One of the secret government labs. O'Connor will know.'

A young man came hurrying in. Professor O'Connor was on the phone.

O'Connor came over himself an hour later and examined their patient. He confirmed that it was almost certainly thallium poisoning, wrote out a programme of treatment and telephoned himself to one of the Assistant Commissioners at Scotland Yard. He was given another number to contact and the AC laid on a police escort for bringing the antidotes by plane and motor cycle from Cornwall.

The antidotes arrived by RAF fighter at Northolt, and the police brought them the rest of the way. They were being administered six hours after the diagnosis. According to O'Connor the prognosis was reasonable provided there were no other complications.

Long before the antidotes arrived a uniformed police guard had been mounted outside Vojnovic's room.

O'Connor telephoned the number he had been given by Scotland Yard. It was a Cambridge number and the man he spoke to, Sir Arthur French, was only mildly interested until he asked the victim's name. When O'Connor said it was a

Slav name he was asked to go over his comments again.

When Peter Nicholson showed his SIS identity card to the doctor in charge he was refused access to Vojnovic's room. The patient was unconscious and was not to be disturbed. Nicholson did not insist on access that night.

After three days it was obvious that Vojnovic was dying. O'Connor came across twice a day to go over the results of the various tests. Vojnovic's white corpuscles were being swiftly and fatally destroyed, his bones were decaying, his saliva glands atrophying and his blood turning to plasma. In the early hours of the fourth morning he died.

CHAPTER SIX

Sir Arthur French stood in the shelter of the station canopy at Leicester Square underground and looked up at the sky. The rain was teeming down, but there was a good patch of blue way over towards St Paul's. It was the third week of April so you could still expect the traditional showers. As he stood there, waiting for the rain to abate he wondered what Meynell would have to say. Meynell had talked with O'Connor and was concerned that SIS should be aware of the implications. And Luther Meynell wasn't a panic merchant. Nevertheless, he *had* suggested that the meeting should not be held at any of the official places. He had also suggested that Nicholson from the Soviet desk, and perhaps Anders, should also attend.

The rain stopped, but French put up his umbrella to hide his face as he walked up Charing Cross Road. It was a reflex rather than a real precaution. There were probably fewer than a couple of dozen people outside the security services who could identify him as the current head of MI6, and most of those would be members of foreign Intelligence services. But he was a cautious man and that caution was the main reason for his appointment. Some said that he was a bit of an old maid, a nagger, but there had been enough slap-happy administration in the service for the Foreign Office to prefer to put the clock back to the good old days.

In fact, Sir Arthur French was no more cautious than his appointment called for. It was he who had offered the funding for Anders' club to ensure that a valuable talent was not completely lost to SIS. It was merely that before he made certain types of decisions he liked to hear the opinion of others whose judgement he valued. And if the operation concerned was in any way offbeat he wanted somebody to check that it wasn't straying beyond its brief. Those who appointed him were well satisfied. Those who worked with him sometimes wondered what sort of man he really was.

On the steps of the club he shook the rain from his umbrella before turning to go inside. His eyes took in the general tattiness, and then Anders came up the stairs.

'Good afternoon, sir. Your other guests haven't arrived yet, would you rather wait here until they come, or go through to my place?'

'I think perhaps your place. Can somebody wait for them?'

'Of course.'

Anders used the internal phone and told Jacky to come up and wait for the two other guests. As Sir Arthur followed Anders down the stairs he said, 'You don't feel a coat of paint might improve the appearance in the . . . er . . . foyer?'

Anders laughed. 'It would, sir, but the customers would hate it. They never really notice what the place is like. The lights are low anyway, and they like everything to stay the same. They're a bit like children.'

'Do you get police in here, checking?'

Anders hesitated. Sorting out acceptable truth from shocking truth. Half a dozen policemen of various ranks were unofficial members of the club. There was an understanding that they were totally off duty and his more traditional members could ignore them, like herds of gazelle grazing contentedly under the gaze of lions who had already killed.

'They pop in from time to time. They're no problem.'

Anders unlocked both locks on the door to his suite and went in with Sir Arthur who accepted a Vichy water and looked at the spines of the books on the shelves.

'You've got a very catholic taste in books, Mr Anders. Are you a reader or a collector?'

Before Anders could reply there was a knock on the door. It was Peter Nicholson and Luther Meynell.

'Hello Tad. Are we first?'

'No. Come in. I'll leave you to it. You know where the drinks are. Help yourselves and use the red phone if you want anything. Ask for me.'

'Right. Thanks.'

Luther Meynell poured himself a double whisky and Nicholson took a sherry.

Luther Meynell had a strong face, but his deep-set eyes and his downward curving mouth gave it a touch of grimness that was deceptive. He was a serious man but not grim. Not too far back there had been a Jewish grandma, a strong-willed woman who had moved her family from Berlin to Bermondsey and had prospered in the fur trade in London's East End. Born in 1930 into a middle-class family in Hampstead, Luther Meynell had the same determination. It was addressed not to commerce but to learning, and eventually to teaching. Even at Cambridge he wasn't sure whether his final interest would be languages or science.

His natural aptitude for languages he took for granted, and after graduating he had done his National Service in the Intelligence Corps. Commissioned almost immediately, he had been a captain by the time his service was over. Against his expectations he had enjoyed his time in the Army. His fellow officers were intelligent, with lively minds, and when he had been offered a permanent post in the Foreign Office he had taken only twenty-four hours to think about it before he accepted. The urge to the academic life was still there, but the job in MI6 appealed to him.

He had that rare ability to reduce complex problems to their simplest equation, and exercising that talent on significant problems appealed to him. Although his talent had been much in demand it had not led to startling advancement. In SIS in the late fifties and early sixties, internal politics and personal relationships had too often controlled promotion. When, in 1972 he had been offered a chair at his old college he hadn't hesitated. He had taken early retirement and a reduced pension, and with the unanimous good wishes of his colleagues he had gone off to teach.

By then he had a family. Two girls. His choice of a wife had surprised his friends. She was younger than he, a strikingly pretty short-story writer of considerable talent. Perhaps his young wife was the only person who knew that behind that rather immobile face and incisive mind there was a sensitivity that he deliberately kept hidden. It was a sensitivity that made him reach for solutions in deeds rather than words. You didn't console the drowning. You fished them out.

When he had made himself comfortable Meynell turned to look at French. 'I arranged with Professor O'Connor to attend the autopsy. It was done at St Thomas's because they had facilities he needed.' He paused. 'It took over a week, Arthur. It was very meticulously done. And I'm afraid there's no doubt that it was murder. And, I suppose, more assassination than murder.'

'How can you be sure of that?'

'Only a government laboratory could have supplied either the know-how or the material. According to O'Connor we couldn't have done it ourselves. We could now. But you'd have to have scientists specifically briefed to find a means of killing a man without leaving any evidence. And they would need to have access to all available written information to come up with this particular solution. Even then I would estimate that it must have taken them at least two years to achieve this . . . this terrible success. It's complex, expensive, almost fool-proof, and incredibly vicious.'

'Tell us more, Luther.'

Meynell hesitated for a moment. It wasn't easy to describe to non-scientists. Whatever you said it would be slightly inaccurate.

'Well let's start with thallium. From the Greek *thallos* – a green shoot. Shoot like plants have. Called thallium because it has a brilliant green stripe in its spectrum. It's a rare metal, found in very small quantities in iron and copper pyrites. It's bluish-white in colour and looks a bit like lead. It has one other property. It's highly toxic. However, there are antidotes against thallium poisoning. We used them all to treat this man but we were on a wild goose chase. We were doing exactly what we were meant to do. We were wasting vital hours. I'm not sure that we could have done anything even if we had known what the real problem was.'

'What was the real problem?'

'The thallium had been subjected to intense atomic radiation which causes the metal to disintegrate into tiny particles. We still don't know how it was introduced into the man's body, and I suspect we never will, but as soon as it was in him, perhaps by food or drink, the radio-active particles disintegrated completely and permeated his system with deadly radiation.' Meynell paused. 'Who was he, Arthur?'

'A Jugoslav. He had worked for the KGB and then changed his mind. He defected about three years ago with his family. He wasn't a normal defector because he was still a convinced Communist. But he'd changed his mind about Moscow and decided that Tito was right to be independent. Obviously Tito's people were suspicious and he wasn't sure what their reaction would be if he went back. We let him stay here. He filled in a few holes for us. More confirmation than revelation, and he was building his bridges back to Jugoslavia. He headed a group of Serbo-Croats in Europe who were pro-Tito. They weren't all that effective but I suspect they raised the blood-pressure a bit in Moscow.'

'So Moscow have him murdered to discourage others.'

'It seems like it.'

Nicholson shifted in his chair but said nothing. Not so much from diffidence but because he was conscious of his youth compared with the other two.

'Can we prove this, Luther?'

'It depends what you mean by prove. We have enough factual information recorded to convince any competent forensic scientist. But if you mean the public then forget it. Start using words like thallium and they'll turn the page. And they're used to stories about dirty tricks by the KGB. Even if they believe them it doesn't surprise them.'

'But sending someone to London to assassinate a man just to *décourager les autres* is outrageous by any standards.'

'Is it? Even after the Arabs?'

'For us it's very different from the Arabs. The KGB are professionals. They know we won't knuckle under on this sort of issue. They see the Arabs as fanatics. Lunatics. And they're not far wrong. But to me this is a very dangerous precedent.'

'Of course. But you're a professional. You know the rules and you know these chaps are breaking the rules. But all that is meaningless to the public.'

Nicholson turned to look at his boss. 'If we let them get away with this, God knows where it will stop. They can start putting *us* on the list. It's not difficult for them here but our chances of retaliating in Moscow are almost nil.'

French raised his eyebrows. 'So what do you suggest?'

'I don't know. I'd need to think about it. But right now my mind goes to the guy downstairs.'

'You mean Anders?'

'Yes.'

'What do you think, Luther?'

'Maybe Peter's right. But I suggest we all think about it for a couple of days.' He turned to look at French. 'Are you going to be up at the cottage at the weekend?'

'I expect so.'

'Perhaps we could meet then.'

'OK. I'll call you tomorrow to fix a time.'

Peter Nicholson stayed behind after the other two had left. Anders and he were more of an age, and although they were very different kinds of men they got on well together.

Peter Nicholson was thirty-eight, with an actor's handsome face. He had toyed with the idea of an acting career in his last year at Winchester and during his time at Oxford. He was almost too handsome not to be an actor. It was a Roman emperor's face with large features. Men noticed his eyes but women noticed the full sensuous mouth. A tendency towards corduroy suits only emphasised the theatricality of his face. When he walked in the street young women openly stared and, recovering their composure, discovered that they were lost and turned to the handsome man for help in directing them on their way. And in restaurants homosexual waiters clamoured to serve him. Although he was aware of his good looks he was genuinely indifferent to the heads that turned, and the overt flattery.

His father was a High Court judge. Handsome, but not so extravagantly handsome as his eldest son, his face looked saturnine under his judge's wig. And guilt-ridden prisoners in the dock saw menace in the thick black eyebrows and piercing eyes. The less guilty were more aware of the judge's total absorption in what was being said. With two sons and three daughters Mr Justice Nicholson lived a full, rather Victorian life between the small flat in Chelsea and the sprawling manor house in Sussex. It was a civilized life with a wide circle of interesting friends and acquaintances, the only criterion he and his wife applied when issuing a second invitation was their guest should have an enquiring lively mind. A family friend had likened it all to a modern version of the Bloomsbury set.

Peter Nicholson had taken Winchester and Oriel College in his stride, seemingly immune to the barbarities of English public schools, and capable of enjoying both the academic and social life at Oxford. He came from a privileged family and it gave him a kind of invisible armour against the world. His wife came from a similar background of privilege, wealth and the arts. Beautiful, French and chic she brought a sharp dressing to his rather mellow life. He had been recruited into SIS during his last year at Oxford and his promotions had been slow as they weighed him up. He had met his wife Fleur during his two years in Paris but when he was posted to Moscow it was almost another three years before they met again. Two months later they were married in the church at Perigueux and after a short honeymoon he had gone back to Oriel for an advanced Russian course. Nicholson had been Deputy Head of the Russian desk at SIS for nearly three years.

Nicholson poured himself another sherry.

'I saw your Judy last week.'

'Which judy was that?'

Nicholson laughed. 'You cheeky bastard. The one *called* Judy.'

'Oh. Where was she?'

'A dinner party. At the Fawcetts'. She was there with her husband but neither of them looked too happy about it. Has she gone back to him?'

'Not that I know of.' Anders sighed. 'How did she look?'

'And oh what ails thee knight at arms, alone and palely loitering et cetera, et cetera. She looked attractive, a bit drawn, rather haunted eyes, and she was trying very hard to be the life and soul of the party. Or maybe just the centre of attention.' He looked at Anders' face. 'I'd say she was high as a kite and that it wasn't just on grass.'

'And her husband?'

'Much as usual. Po-faced. Pompous. The successful barrister. Holding his breath in case his wife was so far gone that she started using four-letter words to show how with-it she is.'

'Did she?'

'No. She flaked out about ten-thirty. Everybody was very understanding.' Nicholson sighed. 'Why the hell do you waste your time with a bunch like that?'

'Only one of them.'

'Oh, Tad. Don't play God or the knight in shining armour. She's one of them, tough as steel, eye on the main chance and utterly selfish. There's hundreds of 'em around. They're poison, Tad.'

'She needs help.'

'Sure she does. But not your kind of help. She needs a psychiatrist or a kick up the backside. Why get mixed up with them, Tad? Her whole family are a bunch of creeps and I'll bet she gave that husband of hers a rough ride.'

'He seems to be coming back for more.'

'He's a Catholic. He's got to, but I bet he isn't enjoying it.'

'D'you want to go downstairs for a bit?'

'If he'll play my tunes.' Nicholson grinned.

'What tunes?'

'"Manhattan" for me and "La Mer" for my old lady.'

'How is she?'

'Everybody's fine.' He put his hand on Anders' shoulder. 'I wish I could get you fixed up nice and cosy.'

Sir Arthur French went back to his flat in Albany and boiled an egg, made some toast and poured coffee from the Cona. When he had finished eating he cleared away, washed up and walked back into the sitting room.

It was too late to ring Mrs Griggs, his housekeeper at the cottage. He reached out for the copy of Verlaine's *Romances sans Paroles* and walked slowly to his bedroom. The cottage was just outside Cambridge on the Trumpington Road, and once upon a time he'd been happy there. Sometimes he envied Verlaine, who had had the courage to shoot at his rival. Only a wound in the wrist and it hadn't done any good. But it had improved his poetry. He wondered what it was that had made Vera despise him. It had been a difficult time, and he had tried very hard. To no avail. There had been a series of men before she went off with the shifty solicitor from Bury St Edmunds. Sir Arthur had been glad when it was all over. It had caused him pain but not grief, and it had taught him a lesson. He now shared Somerset Maugham's jaundiced view of women, and valued his freedom more than that short year of happiness.

CHAPTER SEVEN

Luther Meynell stood with his hands in his pockets looking out of the window of French's small study next to his bedroom. A dark female thrush stood on the lawn just below the window. Her thin legs braced, her head to one side, then savagely attacking the lawn, tugging at a fat, wet worm. Creatures ordered their lives so much better than men, he thought. The decades, even the centuries, had made no difference to them. A seventeenth-century thrush would have led a life no different from the one on the lawn. But seventeenth-century man, and now twentieth-century man . . . He turned impatiently away from the window. His thoughts were being diverted.

He walked back to the table, touched the brown folder, then reached for the cup and slowly sipped what was left of the cold coffee. He walked out to the small landing, the cup still in his hand.

'Arthur? Are you there Arthur?'

'Coming.'

Sir Arthur French was wearing a pair of plastic gloves and a flowered pinafore, and Luther Meynell wondered what would happen to a Director of the KGB who appeared in such a garb. It was both endearing and rather frightening, and, he thought, very typically British.

'Let's sit down and talk, Arthur.'

They sat facing each other across the small mahogany table, the file pushed to one side.

'Your people have done a first-class job with so little to go on. The first two proposals are right out, to my mind. They're just revenge operations. And Moscow may not even recognize them as such. We don't learn anything and we may not make our point. But the third scheme is a possible. The one using Anders. The right experience and the right temperament. A lot of useful information for us and a real lesson for them, not only for the top boys but for any other operatives they might be thinking of using in the future. But the suggestion of a public trial isn't on. The media would have a field-day. The public would love it, of course: British agent goes into enemy territory and brings back assassin to justice. That would last a couple of days and then you'd have a pompous leader in *The Times* – can we complain about Arab kidnappings – encouraging retaliation – murder in the streets of London. You could end up with a vote of censure in the UN if they played their cards well.'

'What about Anders himself?'

'Ideal. It's lucky you kept him on.'

'Your suggestion, my friend.'

Meynell shrugged. 'He'll need some back-up.'

'I can't let many people in on it. It's got to be off the record. Private enterprise on Anders' part. No official knowledge of what was going on. And if he makes a cock-up it's all his. I don't want to know.'

Meynell smiled and shrugged. 'He must be used to that by now, Arthur. Official hypocrisy.'

'There's no other way, Luther.'

'Of course not. It's just that the Russians do it better.'

'Yes. I suppose they do. The blessings of dictatorships. How about a sherry before you go?'

'No thanks. We've got guests this evening – why don't you join us? It's informal. Only a handful.'

'No. Odd men are always a damn nuisance. Thanks all the same.'

'Don't be ridiculous, it's just a cold spread and a debate about whether small really is beautiful. You'd enjoy it.'

He saw French hesitate and chipped in. 'We'll expect you at eight. Pullover and slacks. OK?'

'I'll look forward to it.'

As Luther Meynell cycled back the two miles to his own home he felt sad for the lonely man who had once been his chief. He hoped that he was better at choosing undercover men than he was at choosing wives. A schoolboy would have seen that the beautiful Vera was vain to the point of mania, and would need her ego polished by a dozen men to hold her neuroses in check. But intelligent men seemed as prone as fools to wrong judgements about pretty women. When he chose his pretty Patsy it hadn't been because he *needed* someone but because he *wanted* her, and that was a very different thing. It would be a good discussion point at a Saturday night get-together. Need is negative, want is positive. Discuss.

Anders recognized Peter Nicholson's voice immediately.

'Can I come over and see you, Tad?'

'Sure. When?'

'You tell me.'

'Right now if you want. We don't open for another couple of hours.'

'OK. I'll come right over.'

'Is it business or pleasure?'

He heard Nicholson's soft laugh. 'You crazy loon. Can you imagine me coming to that dump for pleasure?'

Anders smiled as he hung up. It was nearly an hour before Nicholson arrived. Anders noticed that he was carrying a brief-case. They walked along the corridor and up to his rooms.

'D'you want a drink, Peter?'

'After we've talked, if I get a second chance.'

Nicholson took out a pale green file cover and a large brown envelope and placed them on the coffee table.

'It's a briefing, Tad.'

'Where?'

'We're not sure but it looks like Berlin. East Berlin.'

'Is this the Jugoslav murder thing?'

'Yes. What have you heard?'

'Nothing. I just read the very brief reports in the papers. They seemed a bit guarded and low-key so I assumed that it was KGB. What happened?'

Nicholson tipped up the brown envelope and a dozen or so photographs slid out. Some black and white, and some Polaroid colour prints. He took out two or three of the colour prints.

'A bit grainy and the colours not absolutely accurate but enough for you to see what happened.'

Nicholson sat silently as Anders looked slowly and carefully at the photographs, until without looking up he said, 'How did they do it?'

He listened intently as Nicholson explained what they had been told. When he finished Anders looked up at his face.

'And you want me to knock him off?'

'No. We want you to bring him back.'

'Who is he?'

'We're pretty sure he's a guy named Burinski. A traffic warden saw a man get into a Volkswagen just after the Jugoslav went down. It was parked on a double-yellow line and she'd taken its number but the driver was a foreigner and she'd let him go after the passenger got in. We traced the car. It was hired but we did a bit of ferreting and discovered that it had been hired by a Russian named Panov. He works as a journalist at the Tass set-up.

'He was obviously scared and we put the frighteners on him and then dangled a few carrots. He likes it in the West and we let him phone his office and say he'd got the flu. We've got someone with him at his rooms.

'He's given us all he knows about this guy Burinski. It seems Burinski is KGB. Vasili Burinski. Early thirties. Married with one kid. Son of a retired Red Army General and it looks like he's an operator with the *Spetsburo*. Lives in East Berlin and based at the MfV HQ in Normannenstrasse. We've got an artist's impression of him that Panov swears is a good likeness. That's about all we've got at the moment.'

'How the hell do I get him out, for God's sake? Why do I have to bring him back?'

'We want to find out a number of things, Tad. Was this a one-off emergency job? Are they planning more? Are they testing out our reaction? There's a lot we want to know. There's no obvious reason why it should be an emergency. The Jugoslav wasn't that important. There's hundreds like him all over the world. Not ex-KGB maybe, but dissidents organizing other dissidents. They aren't a real danger to the Soviet Union, not even in their twisted minds.'

'Maybe they struck at that level so that we wouldn't react too strongly.'

'Could be. But whatever the reason was, our masters have decided that he's going to be lifted and brought back here.'

'What back-up do I get?'

'As little as possible. I'll give you all the technical help you need and I'll get as much background as I can. But when you're there it'll be you on your own. It's absolutely unofficial. We know nothing about it. We've never heard of you. It's all just a KGB frame-up.' He paused. 'I'm sorry, Tad. But you know how it is. Even if you were still in the old firm it would be much the same. We couldn't acknowledge you or lift a finger. The KGB would know we were bluffing, just the same as they do, but with you it has to be for real. We really would have to abandon you if anything went wrong.'

'Who will be my contact in Berlin?'

'Andy Pritchett.'

'Jesus. That's a good start. Why him?'

'Because he's there. I know you don't like him, but he's tough and efficient and he knows his way around Berlin.'

'Has he been told?'

'Not yet.'

'Why don't you use him instead of me?'

Nicholson half-smiled. 'You're fishing for compliments. He doesn't speak Russian and . . .' he shrugged. '. . . he's just not the right man for the job. You are.'

'Let me think about it, Peter. I'm not sure I want it.'

'Why not?'

'There's too much to go wrong. Especially on a freelance basis. When I've got him over the frontier or through the Wall I've still got the West Germans to contend with. I'm going to need a hell of a lot of documentation for the other side of the Wall. Passport, travel documents, visas. Different nationalities and different names. And a lot of money. Dollars, krugerrands, sovereigns, the lot.'

'That's no problem, Tad. I don't understand why you're so . . . cautious – or whatever it is.'

'I'm cautious, friend, because of what's happened in the past. I cleared up an operation completely but because I went over the top for personal reasons I was thrown out. No talking, no discussion, no beating round the bush. I came to from the drugs and the second they were sure I could hear, they told me the good news. I was dangerous, they said, but I had my uses. All was not lost. So here I am, in my tatty little club where you all hold your skirts aside so that they don't catch the germs. But it's my leather couch that guys lie on while I fish a slug out of a shoulder or a leg. My bed that men sleep in when it's all got too much. And it's me you turn to when you need things doing that are just a bit too slimy for the good boys to touch.'

Nicholson looked at Anders for a long time before he spoke.

'That was all a long time ago, Tad. I hadn't realized that it still irked you. That was stupid of me. Stupid of all of us. Nobody wanted to do it. And it was Mac who told you because he was your friend. It must have seemed terribly unfair to you. You obviously *still* feel it was unfair. There wasn't any other way. Both SIS and 5 were in total disfavour with the politicians. The frogman thing with Crabb at Portsmouth still hung over us like a big black warning. When Macmillan moved Dick White from head of 5 to head of SIS it was a punishment as well as a warning.' He sighed, 'I'm sorry, Tad. I really am.'

'We'd better meet again tomorrow. What time?'

'I'll come about ten if that'll suit you.'

'OK.'

Anders walked with him to the street door but he didn't answer when Nicholson said. 'Ciao.'

In the taxi Nicholson sat with his head back against the top of the seat. He had seen tears round the edges of Tad Anders' eyes. And Anders wasn't the kind of man for tears. He would talk to Luther and Arthur French about it. Anders was big and tough, and a born loner, but they'd obviously taken him too much for granted. Everybody assumed that it was all water under the bridge. A single dud event that had had to happen. Long forgotten. But they were wrong. They had all taken it for granted that time would heal the wound for Tad Anders. But it hadn't. It sounded like time had made it worse. He must loathe them all. Taking him for granted. Happily using him to do their dirty work. Condescending to him in that tatty club. The old family retainer put out to graze, to be visited for a cup of tea when you happened to be in the vicinity. God, how stupid they'd been.

Anders was shaving when the internal phone rang. He looked at his watch on the hook at the edge of the mirror. It was 7.45, a quarter of an hour before they officially opened. As he lifted the phone Jacky said, 'Miss Judy's here to see you, Mr Anders.'

'Bring her up, Jacky. You can leave the desk.'

'Right, sir.'

Anders still used a blade and soap and he stood waiting for her with his face half smooth half lather. She was smiling and she looked pretty, and she smelled of Madame Rochas as she put up her mouth to be kissed. She stood looking up at his face, her arms round his neck, her body close to his.

'Why haven't you phoned me, Charles?'

'You said not to, sweetie.'

'Did I? How stupid. Maybe you misunderstood.'

'Maybe. Anyway, nice to see you. D'you want a sherry?'

'You finish shaving and I'll help myself.'

'OK. You do that. The evening paper's on the settee.'

When he had shaved and put on his tie and jacket he joined her on the settee. But he noticed that it wasn't sherry she was drinking. It was a large neat whisky and the bottle was on the table, alongside her glass.

'What have you been doing?'

She screwed up her nose, thinking. 'Nothing much. I've been trying to get a job.'

'What kind of job?'

'Oh, modelling, anything a bit glam would do.'

'I heard you were back with your husband.'

'Who told you that?'

'Does it matter?'

She shrugged irritably. 'I'm not, actually. I just met him a few times to talk, that's all.'

'How did you get on?'

'As usual. Bloody awful.'

'What happened?'

'He told me the conditions if I wanted to go back.'

'What were they?'

'I go to confession every week. I learn how to cook. I keep proper household accounts to be examined weekly. I get no cash dress allowance, just credit at two stores. No cheque book. No trips on my own. A regular medical check for alcohol and drugs and I adopt what he calls "a proper supportive role as his wife".'

'What did you think of all that?'

'I told him to get stuffed. What do you think of it?'

Anders smiled. 'It sounds like Monty's surrender document to the Germans.'

'D'you want to make love to me, Tad?'

'Why don't you stay the night?'

'I can't.'

'Why not?'

'He's having me watched. He'd got a whole sheaf of reports from a detective agency. He read me out a letter from his solicitor that said if I was out with a man after midnight the court would look on it in an unfavourable light. Why on earth should a barrister need a solicitor to tell him what the law is?'

'It's called getting things on the record. And reading it out is just to scare you.'

'It depresses me.'

'Why?'

'All of it depresses me. I feel lonely. An outcast. And I haven't really done much to deserve it.'

He took her hand and walked with her to his bedroom. As he undressed she pulled up her skirt and opened her legs as he lay alongside her.

'D'you like touching me there, Tad?'

'You know I do.'

'Do it to me, Tad. Do it to me now. Quickly.'

And when it was over she said softly, 'Was I good?'

'You were wonderful honey.'

'How about you get me another drink?'

As he sat on the edge of the bed and watched her drink the whisky he was sorry for her. He knew exactly how she felt.

'I'd better go, Tad.'

'Come down in the club and let Baldy play you a couple of tunes.'

She shook her head. 'I don't like it down there.'

'You'll be with me.'

She looked up at his face. 'Tad?'

'What is it?'

'I'm broke, Tad, will you lend me some money?'

He felt suddenly cold but he said, 'Of course I will. How much do you need?'

'Is a hundred too much?'

'No. Is it enough?'

'Yes.'

He walked with her to Charing Cross Road and waited until he was able to wave down a taxi for her. She got in and gave an address in Belgrave Square and only as the taxi pulled away did she remember and turn to wave to him. Her eyes looked as if she were already somewhere far away.

They talked for four hours and the table was covered with maps and papers that overflowed on to the floor.

'What do you feel about it, Tad?'

'Frankly it stinks. But if you're desperate then I'll do it, but it ought to be done properly. A full back-up team, a radio net, safe-house in East Berlin, route back properly planned and support people on the other side of the wall. There's no proper surveillance, all I can do is go straight in and out. And God knows how I get an unwilling man through the check point.'

'Let's go and have some lunch and talk about it again this afternoon.'

'OK. But why the hurry on this job?'

'He might get posted back to Moscow or somewhere that's even less accessible than Berlin.'

'Any chance of surveillance before I go in?'

'It's possible. Let's go and eat.'

They walked through Soho and ate at Leoni's, and by the time they were back at Anders' place he had thawed out enough for Nicholson to get down to positive planning.

'Let's go over the minimum you need, Tad, to give it a better than fifty-fifty chance.'

'I need someone over the other side. Preferably with accommodation and access to a vehicle. I need a radio net back to Pritchett and I need the documentation we've discussed. And I need the money already over there so that I don't have to take it in myself.'

'Why do you need a vehicle? You'd never get it through the check point with a body in it. Not even if you drugged him.'

'I won't be coming through the check point.'

'Tell me more.'

'Any check point is out unless you've got a full operation.'

'So where?'

'I want to use the place we've got in the Harz mountains.'

'I'll have to apply, Tad. And they're terribly uptight about using that.'

'It's that or a blind attempt up on the Baltic coast. There's no other way.'

'Let me check on it. I'll see what I can do. The other things you mentioned should be OK. We've had difficulty getting cash through recently but I think we can do it. How much do you need?'

'At least five thousand. Pounds not dollars. Eight would be better.'

'If I can fix those things how soon can you go?'

'Four hours' notice will be enough.'

CHAPTER EIGHT

Anders sat with his canvas bag between his feet. The Lufthansa girl had offered to put it up on the rack for him but he'd told her it was all the luggage he had and she let him bend the rules. She was obviously aware that he had been escorted by Airport security to the aircraft. It was Friday night and Gatwick was beginning its heavy weekend holiday traffic. There were eight planes ahead of them, waiting to take their turn on the main runway. It had been raining for most of the afternoon but the sky was cloudless now, a pale blue, and the watery sun cast long shadows from the equipment around the loading-bay.

It was nearly forty minutes before the under-carriage thudded into its housing and there were lights in the tiny model houses on the ground. Almost without thinking, Anders slid his right hand inside his jacket to check that the pistol was in place. He squeezed the base of the soft leather holster and felt the butt rise up under his arm and his thumb stretched out to touch lightly the grid on the safety-catch. Sir Arthur himself had got him clearance at both ends.

The plane was half empty. Berlin had its tourists, but not enough from London to fill a plane on a Friday evening, and the two seats beside him were both empty.

Nicholson had worked hard to get him everything he had asked for. There was only five thousand but it was mainly gold coin and the rest was dollars. It would be available night or day from the bookshop in Unter den Linden. The password was '*Abschied*' and the response was '*Servus*'. The contact man was Willi Kraus and there was a bed for him at the garage workshop. Anders had worked with Willi two or three times before. He was stolid and efficient and there would be no problems there. Luther Meynell had phoned him that morning and wished him luck in his guarded professorial way. And Nicholson had brought a message from French to say that Stoppard would keep an eye on the club for him until he was back. They had allowed seven days from start to finish, not counting the evening flight.

He had phoned Judy two days running but there had been no reply. Candy had stayed with him the last two nights. He had told her he was going to visit his father's family in Poland. She had asked him about them. What they did, and the details of their families, and he had felt ashamed when she bought two dolls for his nieces. There was something wrong with his life since Marie-Claire. Up to then his life had seemed always to be under control.

He had been successful as an SIS officer. Not spectacularly successful, but he had done what was asked of him and had been part of a team. His private life had been uneventful. Girlfriends, but with neither party too intense or dependent.

Marie-Claire had changed all that. It was as if she had opened some magic door from his ordinary world and taken him into a garden. But that tombstone in the church at Marlow had marked the end of all that. Sometimes he thought that in fact it had ended his life. Nothing had really gone right since then. It was like the seven lean years in the Bible. Which meant that there was still another year to go. His routine, controlled life in SIS had gone overnight. He was now what they officially referred to as a 'special category operator'. No longer part of a team, no longer a member of that special club whose members know what is really going on in the world. Almost no longer British. Just a Polish hoodlum who spoke good English. Like Kipling's description – 'the lesser breeds without the law'. Without consciously intending it, Anders had wrapped the tatty club around him like a protective cloak. It was his only home, and over the years he had come to have more in common with the criminal extroverts he mixed with every night than with his former colleagues. They passed no moral judgements and if he had asked it of them they would have arranged, without any question, the elimination of anyone who threatened his peace of mind. But if they never saw him again he would be forgotten in a couple of months. He didn't belong with them. They tolerated him amiably, as SIS tolerated him. He lived from day to day. He no longer had ambitions or even expectations. He had somehow lost the art of living, he just existed. He had money and he had his health, and most of the time that was enough. But there were times when he had to escape. And the cottage outside Battle was his retreat. He had told nobody about it and he was sure that even SIS were not aware of its existence. But in two or three days of peace and sleep he could charge the batteries of his mind to face going back to his grey, grim world.

The cottage was isolated but he was never lonely there. His books and his music were all that he needed. And his thoughts. In that private limbo his life had a future. He had no idea what it was, but as more normal mortals have their vague dream of heaven, he had vague dreams of a better future, and tried to find the patience to await its arrival. No doubt the people who knew him in his other life would have found it incredible. That was because they looked without seeing. But in a way it was no more strange to dream of merely being happy than to dream of being a painter in Tahiti, the owner of a pub in Devon, or winning the Pools.

Anders was asleep by the time they passed over the ragged coastline of Holland. Ten minutes out from Tegel and the captain's announcement that they were on time for landing had woken him. Like most SIS field agents he was used to snatching sleep when he could, and he could come out of even the deepest sleep to instant awareness. He moved his right foot to check that the bag was still there, slid his hand inside his jacket and went through the reflex routine of checking his pistol, and then leaned back, relaxed in his seat. He wished that it wasn't to be Pritchett as his back-up in Berlin. He wasn't sure why he didn't like the man. He was competent and amiable, but there was a cockiness there that bordered on arrogance. Self-confidence was a plus in their game, but over-confidence could be fatal. But he wouldn't be all that dependent on Pritchett.

Andy Pritchett was sitting on a red stool in the airport bar, sipping a malt whisky and gazing at the sweater of a young blonde on the other side of the circular bar. She'd got a bedroom look in her big blue eyes but he guessed she was just practising. She wasn't more than eighteen.

Andrew Pritchett had never lacked for either girlfriends or bedfellows and they weren't always synonymous. In his middle thirties, with only a wisp of blonde hair between him and baldness he had one of those worn, bag-eyed faces that had suddenly come into fashion with the new men in Hollywood. Not plain, and certainly not ugly, but the deep lines from nose to mouth and the aggressive piercing grey eyes gave him an openly macho image that, despite women's lib, girls and women still seemed to find attractive.

He didn't fancy this operation with Anders. Unless they'd been holding out on him it didn't seem well enough prepared. Not enough background and not enough planning. Gung-ho operations worked in wartime, but in Berlin now the pieces were all laid out very carefully on the chess board, and the rules of the game were precise. There was no room for amateurs when you were playing games with the KGB. And what made it worse was that Anders didn't like him. He wasn't sure why, but others had said that it was resentment: that they both operated in the same violent area of SIS but Anders had been pushed outside while he was still on the establishment. It probably *had* been unfair but if you put up a black like Anders had done you could expect to get your head chopped off. And they hadn't done that. They'd just shuffled him to one side. His own life and career had been even more unorthodox than Anders' but he had kept just inside the rules. And that didn't include literally slicing up a man's belly and pulling his guts out. Especially when the man was already dead or dying. Maybe it was like people had said. Once a Slav always a Slav, and despite Anders' upbringing and his mother's genes it was the Slav bit that came out in crises. The Slav bit was pretty useful. But not in a civil servant. And cut the cake whichever way you fancied, SIS was part of the Foreign Office and they *were* all civil servants. Index-linked pensions and all.

Pritchett ordered another double whisky and sat there sipping it slowly and thinking. His whole life seemed to have been a progress through the criminal calendar. Thrown out of Eton for putting the girl from the sweetshop in the family way. Four years crewing on luxury yachts, the last two running guns from Marseilles to Crete, Tunisia, Turkey and Libya. A year as chucker-out at a St Tropez night-club and more girl trouble. Knife trouble. His knife. Then the job as a salesman of Rolls-Royces and Bentleys in Rome, when, after a few months, he'd been invited by the owner to meet a friend in a café on the Via Veneto. And a week later he was being interviewed in a private room at the Connaught. An interview that saw him recruited into SIS. Or, to be more exact, recruited to an established post in the Foreign Office. He was always amazed that people saw him as prone to violence and as having an exaggerated independence of authority.

His father was delighted that his son was what he referred to as a member of the Foreign Office, and he did nothing to disturb the old man's peace of mind. As vicar of a small village in the West Country his father was the kindest man he had ever known. Nothing that he had ever done had forfeited the old man's love. Married in middle-age to a charming younger woman, he was an elderly father, but when Andy Pritchett's mother had died in a sanatorium when he was ten, the Reverend Anthony Pritchett had become father and mother to the young boy. He was probably neither a very good father nor a competent mother, but every minute of his life was devoted to the boy. There was almost no discipline, and his father had never read Spock. But they walked for miles through the countryside and the old man knew every wildflower and animal and how they lived. And in the evenings they read together. Not the books he had at the village school, but anything from Thomas Hardy to Plato. He was always amazed when he was older, how much his mind had retained. At the time it had seemed to leave him untouched, but by some mental osmosis, poems and opinions would float into his mind to match some place or feeling. There were those, sharp-tongued village matrons, who said that the boy had been thoroughly spoilt. But if he had been, then the loving gentle father had equally bequeathed him the self-confidence and independence that made his life a happy game in which he excelled. He needed no life-belt of constant reassurance from other people, neither did he suffer from a conforming mind. Possibly immoral, certainly amoral, Andy Pritchett was a happy, healthy, young man who enjoyed most days of his life.

Pritchett had one more whisky before the landing of the flight from London was announced. As he stood up he glanced around the bar and the restaurant. It was one of his favourite places for picking up new girls. There were few people at that time of night. The flights from Frankfurt and Paris were not due for another hour.

He stood watching through the glass windows as the handful of passengers went through customs and immigration. Anders was one of the first half dozen. He saw him look up, his eyes scanning the arrivals area. He gave no sign of recognition and when he came through the exit doors Pritchett turned and walked towards the street entrance. There was the usual hubbub of people clamouring for taxis, the British distinguishable because they were forming a queue, the Berliners because they were piling into every taxi before it even reached the queue. He waited for the town coach to pass and then walked to the parking lot, threading his way through Mercs and BMWs to a black Volkswagen. He started the engine and sat there waiting. He turned to look for Anders and saw him still standing at the airport exit, reading the front page of a newspaper. Whatever others were doing Anders wasn't leaving things to chance. He was doing what you should do. Waiting to see that all your flight companions had left. A few minutes later Anders looked at his watch, yawned and picked up his bag from between his feet.

As Anders opened the passenger door he heaved his bag on to the back seat.

'Welcome to Berlin, Tad.'

'Thanks. How are things?'

'Much as usual. Except for your thing. I've got a bit more background to give you. How about a meal?'

'Have you eaten already?'

'No. I waited for you.'

'How about we treat ourselves to Kempinski's?'

Pritchett grinned. 'Eat and drink for tomorrow we die, eh?'

'Not if I can help it, friend.'

They had eaten at Kempinski's and then strolled down the Kurfürstendamm and back to Fazanenstrasse where Pritchett had parked his car.

Pritchett's flat was on the top floor of a modern block just to the east of Potsdammerstrasse. The sitting room was comfortably furnished. Very male and very Pritchett. A beautiful nude in *sanguine* by Annigoni had pride of place on the main wall. There were unframed photographs of boats in sunny harbours and girls in bikinis. A row of framed targets with frayed bulls were strung along the top of a set of mahogany bookshelves and a copy of *Playboy*'s German edition was open on the leather couch. There were two clocks on the end of one of the bookshelves. One showed local time and the other looked like Moscow time.

'D'you want a decent night's sleep, Tad, or would you rather get working?'

'Let's do a couple of hours, anyway, Andy.'

'I've got the stuff laid out in here.'

They sat side by side at the dining room table, Pritchett with his elbow on the table, his chin cradled in his hand, as he looked sideways at Anders.

'You don't look all that bright, Tad, are you OK?'

'I'm fine.'

'Maybe we should leave this junk till tomorrow?'

'No, I'm OK.'

Pritchett reached out and pulled a small pile of photographs towards them.

'There's the lovely boy himself. Vasili Pavlovich Burinski. Middle to late thirties. There he is again, coming out of the block where he lives. There he is with his wife. He works from an office in the Intelligence block in Normannenstrasse. I can show you a whole pile of photographs of that block. Inside and out, aerial views, architects' plans, the lot. But I suggest you keep well away, the surveillance there is red hot.

'Then four or five shots of him in the street. A bit grainy but he's recognizable. The blue file is four days' surveillance but it doesn't tell you much. He's KGB. I'm not sure of his rank but it's not more than captain. The buff file is accumulated background on him from routine sources. Nothing very exciting, except that he not only did a *Spetsburo* course but seems to have stayed with them. I don't know why you and London are interested in him but I'd say he's a pretty tough cookie.'

'Does he have any personal protection, surveillance or anything like that?'

'Not that's been seen, but it hasn't been a thorough surveillance on our part. You know that, don't you?'

Anders nodded. 'How about Willi Kraus? Is he going to be cooperative?'

'Yes. He's obviously a fan of yours. He's got a car that will get you out of Berlin and another at Magdeburg. He's going to respray and renumber the first one and drive it back to Berlin himself. He's really putting his head on the chopping block for you.'

'What about the set-up in Goslar?'

Pritchett shrugged. 'They're very touchy as you know.'

'Touchy? On what grounds, for God's sake? They're put there to do a job.'

'I know. But they complain all the time that we're over-doing it. When they first set it up things were a lot different. There was more discontent in East Germany. More poverty and more hatred of the Russians and the puppet government. That's all changed. They're comparatively well off now. They still hate the Russians but they've learned how to deal with them. And the penalties for frontier guards are really tough now. Mandatory death sentences if there's hard evidence.

'Ten years' ago we were bringing through four or five bodies a week. About two a month is all we can do now. The Goslar unit has politicals as its main remit, and sticking in another body, two with you, puts the whole programme back a month or more.'

'Nicholson's gone into all that and he gave orders that we had top priority.'

'I know. But up to yesterday they were still protesting that you should use a chopper or bring him through the Wall. That's the usual way out for our East Berlin bodies.'

'What was Nicholson's reaction to the protests?'

'He gave them a flea in their ears. A direct order, but he gave them authorization to charge it to general funds.'

'How much does it cost these days?'

Pritchett smiled. 'It's not like the old days, Tad, when a couple of hours in the cabin with the girl and a hundred dollars could get half a dozen bodies across. Have a guess at what it costs now?'

'I've no idea. Tell me.'

'Well, for a start you have to cover three men now. East German frontier guards are never the same two men together. There's always a shift between the two being on together again. So three is the smallest number we need to be sure. And even then we have to rely on two days to get someone over. It's a basic three hundred dollars a week for each guard. And a thousand bucks each for every crossing. And girls are thrown in by the dozen.'

'The unit has agreed though?'

'Of course. They take their orders from Nicholson.'

'What contact do I have with them?'

'Willi Kraus knows the drill. Goslar have got a man in Magdeburg, an agricultural machinery salesman, and he'll take you to a farm in a small place called Tanne right on the border. You'll be there one night. Two at the most.'

'Do you liaise with the document section?'

'Yes.'

'I want them to check all my documents and make sure they're OK and up to date.'

'Give them to me when you turn in and I'll take them across myself and they can do them during the night.'

'I'll have tomorrow here to get acclimatized and then go over the next morning.'

'Fine. Let's have a drink before you turn in.'

It was just after one o'clock when Anders pulled the duvet up to his shoulders and he was asleep almost immediately. But an hour later he was awake. He got slowly out of bed and walked to the window, pulling the curtains aside. The apartment block was high enough for him to see across to the Tiergarten.

Despite the lateness the lights of the city were still bright enough to be reflected on the low-lying clouds. Just beyond the black silhouette of the treetops in the Tiergarten he could see the floodlights on the golden figure of the Winged Victory and there were lights on the huge edifice of the Brandenburger Tor. There were fewer lights on the other side of the wall. There were lights at Check-Point Charlie but the barriers were across on both sides. There was a jeep by the Allied control post and a big Merc with a flag on its bonnet. It was too far away to see what flag it was.

Anders was at home in Berlin, he had always been successful on Berlin operations. And he liked the Berliners who lived permanently on the edge of disaster but still found the courage to defy the Soviets and poke fun at the Allies who were there to defend them. They knew all too well that Berlin was not defensible against a Soviet or East German attack: their only real defence was that such an attack would mean World War III had started. They didn't dwell on the likelihood of that disaster. It hadn't been all that many years since Berlin had been a heap of rubble, yet now, a trifle theatrically maybe, they lived successfully on the tightrope. Perhaps the only thing that depressed Berliners was the Wall. Ugly, man-made, it epitomized the differences between the East and the West. Not just the contrived differences of politics and economics but the real and fundamental differences between two kinds of people. Some said it only represented the difference between two sets of rules and that the people were much the same. But, without dwelling on it, most people felt that the differences were total and eternal.

Anders, because he had a Slav background but a western upbringing was often asked what the fundamental differences were, and he had no answer. But he knew that the Wall was a genuine and realistic monument to those differences. It depressed him, and Check-Point Charlie depressed him most of all. He knew its mechanics inside out. He had been through it, both ways, scores of times. Legally and illegally. There was no element of fear in his revulsion. But despite its floodlights Check-Point Charlie looked like a black hole to Anders, a void that led down into the earth, out of the real world into nothingness.

He leaned forward, resting his forehead on the coldness of the window, his eyes closed. And he wished that he was somewhere else. In the club in Soho, in the small house in Morpeth, chopping logs for firewood in the small back-yard. There must be some other work he could do. Something ordinary like other men did. But he groaned because he knew that all that he was good at were the things that he did. He turned sharply as he heard Pritchett's voice.

'What is it, Tad? What's the matter?'

'What do you mean?'

'I heard you talking so I came in. Is there anything I can do?'

'No. I'm OK.'

But Pritchett switched on the light and walked over to him putting his hand on Anders' arm.

'Lie down, Tad. Just rest if you can't sleep.'

He led Anders to the bed and watched, concerned, as he lay back. Pritchett sat on the edge of the bed.

'Do you want me to phone London and get them to call the operation off until you're fitter?'

'No. I'm OK, Andy. Just a fit of the blues.'

'Anything special?'

'No. Like I said, just a passing fit of the blues.'

'I know the feeling.'

Anders turned his head to look at Pritchett. 'I can't see you getting the heebie-jeebies, Andy.'

'Why not?'

'You're not that kind of guy.'

Pritchett half-smiled. 'You think I'm too dumb to have doubts?'

'I didn't mean that.'

'What did you mean?'

'You're all of a piece. You know what you're doing and you get on with it and enjoy it.'

Pritchett laughed softly. 'Those are almost the exact words Peter Nicholson used about you when he was briefing me on this operation. But I wouldn't expect him to understand about you or me. He's a desk wallah, not an operator.'

'So what gives you the blues?'

'God knows. I don't often get that way. No more than I guess you do. But every now and again. I can't remember where I am or why I'm there. And when it all comes back I wish I was somewhere else.'

'Where do you wish you were?'

Pritchett smiled. 'There's this garden. A country garden. Lawns and herbaceous borders and a wooden bench under an apple tree. And there's a girl walking towards me in a dress with flowers on. I don't have any idea what she looks like except that she's breathtakingly beautiful and she's my wife. She's holding a little girl's hand and the little girl's name is Emma. She's our daughter. And there's a brown labrador dog. Fade to music. Vera Lynn singing "We'll meet again". Produced and directed by Andrew Pritchett in conjunction with Thames TV and SIS.'

Anders leaned up on his elbows, smiling, shaking his head. 'And I'd have bet my last dollar that your idea of heaven would be screwing the chorus of the best musical in town.'

Pritchett laughed. 'That ain't a dream, Tad, that's grim reality. And most of the time I like my reality. So do you, you stupid sod. You're a bit worse than the rest of us because you've got that Slav blood in your veins.' He looked at Anders and winked. 'Get to sleep, honey-chile and dream about those pretty hookers who float around your club.'

Anders nodded. 'OK.' And he nodded again. 'Thanks for the revelations.'

'That's OK. See you later.'

Nicholson stirred in his sleep and then opened his eyes. There was moonlight at the windows and somewhere far away the telephone was ringing. He leaned up on one elbow, testing the moral fibre of the caller. There were ten double rings before it cut off in mid-ring.

Fleur's face was turned towards him, her head back on the pillow, a thick swatch of long blonde hair curved over her shoulder to where her hand lay loosely at her neck. She was frowning in her sleep as if sleeping required the same intensity of effort that she gave to everything else that she did. Then the telephone started again.

There was enough moonlight in the hall not to need to switch on the light and he sat on the bottom stair and reached for the phone. It was Pritchett.

'Where are you calling from, Andy?'

'Berlin. My flat.'

'What can I do for you?'

'I'm worried about Anders, and this operation.'

'Why?'

'First of all I don't think it's been properly assessed. It's too chancy. Too hit and miss. It needs far more back-up than it's getting.'

There was a long pause. 'You may be right, Andy, but it's all we can give it at the moment.'

'So postpone it for a week or two.'

'We can't do that. You know the circumstances. We've promised Bonn to give our friends a bloody nose and we've got to do it . . . You said "first of all". What else is there?'

'I don't think Anders is in the right mood for going over.'

'What on earth does that mean?'

'He's not on top form.'

'You mean he's ill?'

'No. Jesus, it's hard to describe. You need to be all wound-up and raring to go to be successful on these sort of trips. And he's not. He's discouraged.'

'About what?'

'Nothing specific. Just things. His batteries are down.'

'Has he complained, or what?'

'No. He's not the complaining type.'

'There's nothing wrong this end, so far as I know.'

'It's nothing to do with things being wrong, Peter, it's . . . oh God, how can I explain . . . I think you people take him too much for granted. He's on his own in that bloody club. You use him and the club when it suits you but he isn't in the swim. He doesn't get promotions. Nobody's responsible for his morale. He's not made part of the team, the club.'

'He *isn't* part of the club, Andy. It's a pity, but that's how it is. We can't wet-nurse a grown man. Anyway, knowing Anders he'd probably tell us to get stuffed.'

'So what? It's the job of senior people to look after the understrappers.'

'So what do you want me to do? I can't postpone it, that's for sure. Is there anything else I can do?'

'Maybe not right now, but when he's back keep alongside him. Not just when you need him. He's not a bloody gorilla.'

Nicholson said softly. 'What's that mean?'

'I'll have to go, Peter. I've got things to do.'

'OK. Keep in touch.'

Nicholson sat on the stairs looking across the panelled hall. He could just see the reflection from the windows on one edge of the gilt frame of the painting of his father in his judge's wig and robes. Maybe Pritchett's protests were as much on his own behalf as on Anders'. There was always some moaning and groaning from field operators. Sometimes justified, but more often not much more than routine petulance against those who, as they saw it, sat safely in offices moving the pieces around the board. It was understandable. If you were the pawn sacrificed in some early gambit you didn't cheer the ultimate check-mate no matter how subtly it was achieved.

He looked at his watch. It was five o'clock and the moonlight had darkned into the faint summer dawn. He would spend some time with Anders when he was back. It always looked as if Pritchett and Anders led easy-going Bohemian lives that were to be faintly envied rather than pitied. Anders was outside the magic circle but nobody emphasized the fact. Perhaps they did, unconsciously, draw an imaginary line between gentlemen and players but it wasn't intentional and it wasn't the result of official policy. And Pritchett was on the establishment so he had no reason to feel that *he* was out in the cold. He would discuss it with French or maybe Meynell. He stood up, cursed softly as his foot slid on a rug on the polished floor, and walked through to the kitchen and switched on the lights.

It was warm enough to walk out and drink his coffee on the bench in the garden. It was going to be a fine day and people were coming for the weekend. People they both liked. Successful people with no axes to grind, who did things that were worthwhile doing. He had been so lucky with Fleur. Not just beautiful, but alive and capable, running the house and family with French efficiency. Demanding of everyone except of him, because for her he could do no wrong. Please God let it all last. Let nothing go wrong. Let no child be struck down. We do no harm to anyone, let none happen to us. He smiled to himself. It sounded like the prayers he said when he was a small boy. But he realized now that he owed his happy childhood more to his parents than to God. Not ostentatiously loving but always observant and instantly aware of subdued spirit or a shadow on a face.

He remembered the long pieces in the Sunday papers about his father. The terror of the Old Bailey. The judge who addressed the hardest criminal as 'Mister' and explained carefully and scrupulously why he was being sent down for the maximum number of years, as if he were sure to be interested in how the decision was arrived at and the subtle beauty of the law. And the same man bending to listen, wiping the sweat from his face after a set of tennis, intent on what the child was saying. A pause to consider what had been said, then 'Well

Peter, that's an interesting problem. What you have to look for is justice. You and Michael agreed to share, and now he refuses and says that it was unfair. Was it? You have an agreement, but *was* it fair? He's two years younger than you. Did he really understand what he was agreeing to? Did you, perhaps, know things that he didn't know because he was younger? Or is he just a bad loser trying to back off from his word? Think about it, boy. The law of contract or natural justice. An interesting problem. I know you'll enjoy solving it. Let's have a look at the raspberries and see if that netting has worked.'

He never tried to ape his father with his own family but he instinctively used what he had learned as a boy in a happy family, and when he failed with the three girls Fleur succeeded. Not with logic or appeals to fair play but a mixture of Lycée strictness and taking advantage of being loved and admired. She was a gem, a treasure.

CHAPTER NINE

Anders was up at seven and the world seemed normal and sunny again. The few hours rest, or something, had chased his depression away.

After breakfast he went over the route to Magdeburg and Tanne again on the maps, and read through the background files on Burinski. Pritchett went across for his documents.

The information in Burinski's file was sparse but he sounded like a typical KGB hit-man. The only hard fact was that the journalist, Panov, had sworn that Burinski was the man who had killed the Jugoslav. But Burinski was a common enough name. Was this Burinski the right one? He matched Panov's description: his KGB background and training also fitted; and there were minor descriptive details from two or three unsolved political murders in West Germany that also fitted. The fact that Panov had said the assassin was the son of a Red Army general seemed to make the identification conclusive.

The surveillance sheets only indicated how difficult a kidnap was going to be. Burinski was only on the street when he went to his office and when he returned home. The rest of the day he was in his office, and once home there appeared to be no evening visits. Only once in four days' surveillance had he emerged during an evening, and that was for a matter of minutes when he walked to the corner of the street and posted a letter.

With only two opportunities a day for a pick-up the choice was simple but against all normal tactics. Although a morning pick-up with all the daylight hours for the getaway had advantages, in Burinski's case it was out. His non-appearance at his office would be noticed immediately. It would have to be the afternoon, and that meant driving after dark when there was less traffic on the roads and road-blocks were not visible in advance.

He would watch Burinski himself tomorrow and check the timings, and the next day would have to be the day. It was a Friday, and Burinski's weekend movements had not been under surveillance. And almost certainly he would be expected by his wife and the alarm would be given right away. Anders needed at least twenty minutes to get clear of the city. They would not suspect a kidnapping until they had gone through all the standard routines for delayed husbands: shopping, meetings, girlfriends on the side, hospital checks and arrest records at local police stations. And once kidnapping was a possibility for a man like Burinski they would go for the obvious way out, the Wall. Simultaneously they would be checking his flat for evidence of possible defection. If he was lucky they could be in Magdeburg before the hunt was really on.

Then Pritchett was back with the documents.

'All OK, Tad, but they've put in a couple of extras.' He pushed two pieces of paper across the table. 'This one is a new requirement for visitors to areas within twenty miles of the border. It covers all three of you and it's valid for thirty days from yesterday. This is a medical card covering Burinski in case you decide to drug him. Classifies him as an epileptic sometimes requiring sedation. The card gets you drugs on an emergency basis. Not for you to use but to explain why he's under sedation. They say the rest are first-class and half of them are genuine.'

'Thanks. I'm going through Charlie with one of the guided tours at eleven. I'll be back about four.' He smiled as he stood up. 'I just want to sniff the breeze.'

Pritchett smiled. 'I hope you're not going through with that bulge under your arm. 'They've got metal detectors on all the time.'

'I'll leave it in the thing beside my bed.'

'I'll put it in my safe.'

Anders went through Check-Point Charlie with the other tourists from the travel agency. The courier collected their passports and fifteen minutes later the coach was through and turned into Friedrichstrasse. They covered the usual sights of the TV tower, Marx-Engelsplatz and Alexanderplatz. And then they had the usual free hour for shopping, with the coach parked at the Brandenburg Gate. He walked up Unter den Linden, took a coffee at a pavement table and afterwards strolled up to the bookshop. It was there, right in the centre of the second row of books. A secondhand copy of Lukàcs' *Geschichte und Klassenbewusstsein*. The original 1923 edition. And the card with the handwritten price – seventeen Ostmarks. He walked slowly back to the coach and chatted in English to the driver about the problems of driving licences and petrol supplies in the Democratic Republic.

It was mid-evening when Pritchett came back. He had that day's surveillance report on Burinski and nothing had changed. Burinski had left his office at 17.05 and had gone into his flat at 17.21. He had been carrying a leather briefcase, an evening paper, and an unidentifiable package.

They ate at Café Wien and then went to see *Kramer v Kramer* at the Astor. Not being fathers they were less moved than the majority of the audience and were unconvinced about ladies who fought legal battles and then gave back the prize money. But a couple of hours in the Black Horse put things back in perspective. Andy Pritchett was at home because he was obviously a regular, and Anders felt at home working out the profit margins. But they were both in demand by girls for dancing, and were experienced enough to turn aside a wide repertoire of propositions without incurring wrath or wounding maidenly pride.

They walked back to the flat in good spirits and were sound asleep just after midnight.

Anders paid the 6.50 marks for his visa, bought his compulsory ration of Ostmarks and was passed through the check point. He had nothing except the clothes he stood up in and he bought a shirt and a spare pair of socks at an

Intershop before taking the S-bahn to the Lichtenburg Station. It took him fifteen minutes to find Burinski's block in Rüdigenstrasse and he timed the walk to the MfS headquarters in Normannenstrasse. Despite the sunshine it looked more like a prison than offices, a dark brown concrete structure with its windows set in long monotonous rows. He only glanced at it as he walked by but he wondered why they had allowed the down-pipes to be mounted on the front of the building. An invitation to break-ins, but maybe the surveillance was too good to tempt anyone to try. There were four uniformed men just inside the big glass-panelled doors.

There was a church in a small square on Burinski's usual route and that was where he'd pick him up. There would be long shadows in the later afternoon from the church itself and from the trees in the churchyard, and the car could wait on the south side and come round as soon as Burinski crossed the square. Then a half circle and straight down the main road to the underpass at Biesdorf.

There was a taxi on the stand by the Rathaus and he took it to the main Ostbahnhof station. He walked inside the station. It was crowded with people and there were long queues at the ticket stations. He looked at his watch. It was midday. There was something odd and he couldn't think what it was. He went back to the station entrance and waited at the lights until they changed. Crossing the street he walked slowly down Mühlenstrasse and turned left. He could hear the siren blasts of barges on the river and at the bridge he saw the Germans-only checkpoint at Oberbaumbrücke. Twenty minutes later he walked past Willi Kraus's workshop. It was up a cobbled yard between two warehouses, a battered notice said W KRAUS AUTO REPARATUREN. Anders walked on up to the corner of Rudolfstrasse and turned to look back. He could hear the roar of traffic in the main street the other side of the warehouses, but in Warschauer Platz itself there was only a youth on a bicycle and a girl with a pram. He stood there for about ten minutes before walking back and turning into the cobbled yard up to the corrugated iron doors. A small door with a battered brass knob was let into the main door, and he turned the knob, opened the door and bent his head and lifted his leg to go through the small opening.

The garage was silent and empty, and there was only a faint light from the long, dirt-encrusted windows on the far wall. In the far corner he saw the glow of a coke fire in a brazier with a crude metal canopy above it. He pushed the door to behind him and walked into the building, his footsteps echoing from the metal roof. There was a small glazed-in office in the far corner and he made his way slowly past stripped down car engines and a litter of spare parts.

The office was empty but when he touched the cigarette butt in the ashtray it was still warm. He stood half inside the office doorway looking around the garage, his eyes more accustomed to the dim light. Willi Kraus was standing behind the small door at the entrance. Smiling, a big wrench held loosely in his hand. He reached out his arm and the lights came on. He turned, opened the small door, looked out and then closed it, turning the key in the lock. He walked over still smiling, his hand held out.

'Good to see you again.'

'Good to see you too. Where do you want me?'

Kraus nodded towards the office. Inside, he moved the old-fashioned swivel chair to one side, pulled back the threadbare greasy carpet and reached down. He tugged twice and then a square of the floorboards swung up with a waft of dank, stale air. There was a steel ladder that went down vertically into the darkness.

Kraus laughed softly, 'It's not as bad as it looks but it isn't the Hilton.' He took a rubber torch from his desk. 'Take this and go on down. I'll close this up when you flash the torch. I'll be down in half an hour.' He smiled. 'Make yourself at home.'

The square hole was barely big enough to take Anders' broad shoulders and the torch in his hand made the descent more difficult. He estimated that he was ten foot down when his feet met the concrete base. He flashed the torch and as the cover swung down overhead he shone the torch on each side of him. The door was at his back and he reached behind him awkwardly to open it. As it opened a light came on and he heard the soft purr of an air-conditioner. He turned his body slowly and entered the underground room.

The room was larger than he expected, about eight feet by six feet. There was an ex-Wehrmacht camp bed and canvas wash-basin, a cane arm-chair, a small table with a battery radio and two small white cupboards hung on the wall. An electric boiling ring and a small heap of crockery and cutlery were on a metal shelf over the bed. The walls, floor and ceiling were concrete roughly painted white, and in the far corner of the ceiling was a white plastic grille over the air-conditioner; a wire trailed down loosely to a plug and socket near the floor. Despite the air-conditioning the walls and ceiling were covered with droplets of condensation, and apart from the dankness there was a smell that he recognized but couldn't identify. A faintly acrid smell.

The cane chair creaked as he sat down. There were two or three paperbacks on the small table and he looked through them and picked one out. It was an Ed McBain, *Würger an Bord*. It was almost an hour before Kraus came down to join him. He had a cellophane-wrapped parcel of sandwiches tucked inside his jacket.

'We'd better eat, Tad. We shan't get much chance tomorrow.' He put the sandwiches on the table. 'Help yourself, I'd better let Pyramid know you're here.' Pyramid was Pritchett's code name.

Kraus knelt down and reached under the camp-bed to bring out a battered leather case, and when he lifted the lid Anders saw the neat black transceiver. It was an Israeli Elta, a model he hadn't seen before, with an LED display and a neat rubber hand-mike. And as Kraus switched on the set Anders recognized the elusive smell. It was ozone generated by the radio set that the small air-conditioner hadn't dispersed. Pritchett responded immediately and Kraus just said 'Cairo OK.' Pritchett acknowledged and that was it.

Anders went over the timetable and plans for the next day and they turned in just after eight. Kraus insisted that Anders took the camp bed, and slept himself in the wicker chair with his feet on the table. They both slept soundly and Kraus woke Anders at five o'clock. At six Kraus left to pick up the car.

By 7.30 they had driven to the church and Anders had shown him where he wanted the car and then they had parked the car two blocks away and walked back on foot. As if to a timetable, Burinski came out of Schottstrasse and passed the church without even glancing at Anders or Kraus. He had nodded to a woman who passed him and then he was over into the bottom end of Normannenstrasse. There was no difficulty in identifying him: he was exactly like the descriptions and the photographs.

Anders made no attempt to follow Burinski and they walked back to the car and drove back to Kraus's place. Anders took the S-bahn back to Friedrichstrasse and strolled down to Unter den Linden. The book was still there in the window but he walked on, bought a paper and took a table at one of the cafés. He was tempted by the *hühnersuppe* on the menu but hot liquids never went well with the tension of an active operation. He stuck to coffee and toast. Better an empty belly than a queasy one.

He paid his bill and looked at his watch as he waited for his change. It was 1.15. The notice on the bookshop door said that it was closed for lunch fom 1 until 2. He reached out and pressed the brass bell button twice. One short and one long. His initial in Morse. There were no lights on in the shop and it was several minutes before he saw the old man's solemn face as he pulled back the bolts and turned the key. He opened the door slightly, Anders said softly, '*Abschied*,' and the old man nodded, his face impassive as he responded. '*Servus*.'

As Anders walked into the shop the old man walked past him into a small section that was curtained off. When he came out a few minutes later he was carrying a small plastic airlines bag with the logo of Berolina Travel on its side. The old man dumped it unceremoniously on the counter and looked up at Anders' face. 'It's heavier than it looks, friend.'

'How is she, Max?'

'She's still in hospital.'

'What's the prognosis?'

The old man shook his head slowly but didn't reply. He touched Anders' shoulder gently as he let him out of the door. 'Thanks for remembering.'

There were half a dozen taxis at the Brandenburger Tor. He let the first one go and took the second to the Oberbaum Bridge and walked the rest of the way back to Kraus's place. The BMW was already in the cobbled entrance facing the right way.

They went over the Berlin street map again to cover the two alternatives. Either way they had to do almost a complete half circle of the city and most of it was on the autobahn. They decided to stick to their original plan and take the long route and turn off the autobahn to Beelitz and use the secondary roads to Magdeburg and then the twisting minor roads by passing Quedlinburg and up the mountain road to Tanne. But the man in Magdeburg would know the safest route.

Anders gave Kraus the forged identity card, the travel passes, petrol coupons, zone pass and worker's holiday pass for the Trades Union recreation centre at Wernigerode. Kraus had bought a used spare tyre in addition to the spare wheel and Anders slid the canvas bag into the cavity of the tyre. And then it was time to go.

He allowed fifteen minutes for traffic delays and they arrived four minutes early. Anders waited in the car on the south side of the church, breathing deeply and evenly, then, with his hand on the car door he said, 'When you see Burinski, wait until he's half way across the square, count five seconds, and come round. Open the back door as wide as it will go as soon as you're alongside me, and the second I'm inside put your foot down until we're out of the square. Leave him to me no matter what's happening. Understood?'

Kraus nodded and Anders got out and walked the long way round the churchyard. As soon as he turned the corner he saw Burinski and he slowed until Burinski started crossing the square. He heard the car engine start and the squeak of the shock absorbers as it moved. Then it was as if they had rehearsed it a dozen times. As the car came alongside him Burinski turned to look, the rear door was open and in one movement Anders had pinioned the Russian's arms and they fell together into the rear of the car. Burinski went in backwards and his head took a crack from the roof of the car, but he put up his knee to fend off Anders. As the car moved off Anders felt the door against his foot which was still outside and he knelt on Burinski's groin to quieten him as he swung his foot inside. The Russian's head was half under the front seat, his face contorted with pain, and Anders grabbed at the lapels of the man's jacket, bunching them together tightly at his throat.

'Don't move or make a noise, Burinski. I don't want to hurt you.'

The Russian turned his head but couldn't move it from under the metal seat frame. His eyes were hard with anger and he said. 'Whoever you are, you must be out of your mind. You're going to suffer for this.'

Kneeling on Burinski's chest Anders reached in his pocket for the adhesive tape. 'Don't worry, comrade. It's your turn first so keep nice and quiet.'

He saw the shock on Burinski's face as he spoke in Russian not German and he reached forwards and spread the tape firmly across Burinski's mouth. Turning him on one side he roped his hands behind him and then roped his legs.

As he sat back on the seat they were just approaching the Post Office on Strasse der Befreiung. Anders saw a big black Mercedes come hurtling out of the side street. Kraus frantically spun the wheel and then the police car came up from behind hitting them at full speed, turning them sideways until they smashed into the black Mercedes. Then two cars skidded to a halt alongside them and uniformed men poured out. As the rear door was wrenched open, Anders had only a fleeting sight of the club before it struck the base of his skull.

CHAPTER TEN

The office was small, with a desk pushed back against the wall. There were two men looking at him: a tall man in civilian clothes and an older man in a KGB uniform.

Ander's hands were handcuffed to the chair behind his back and an ache at the base of his skull throbbed with pain to the beat of his heart.

'What's your name?'

'It's on my documents.'

The tall man closed his eyes. 'What's your name?'

'Anderson'.

'Forename.'

'Theo.'

'Have you any explanation to offer for your hooliganism?'

Anders shook his head.

'Who sent you?'

Anders sat silently, his eyes deliberately unfocused. The civilian had spoken German but the KGB man used Russian.

'Kraus has already told us what we need to know.'

Anders looked down at the floor. It was a ritual he knew so well. They were waiting for him to ask why they were questioning him if they already knew everything. Anything to get him talking. It was a standard ploy. As old as the hills, and it never worked with professionals.

When he looked up, the tall civilian was leaning back lazily against the wall, his arms folded, half-smiling as he looked at Anders' face. He spoke very quietly.

'Anders, Tadeusz Anders. SIS officer. And they send you in like a lamb to the slaughter. Why, Anders? What have you done that they want to throw you away? And poor Kraus and the old man, Steiner, at the bookshop. His wife dying slowly in hospital. Which one of you do they want to get rid of? Closing your eyes won't change the facts, my friend.'

The tall man nodded to the KGB man who unlocked the handcuffs from Anders' wrists, put them in his pocket and left the office. The tall man stretched out a long leg, hooked his foot round the leg of a wooden chair and sat down.

'My name's Kalin, Anders. Colonel Kalin, KGB. If we can talk together in a civilized fashion we can bear that in mind when you come up for trial.' He paused and looked with raised eyebrows at Anders' face. 'You've committed almost every criminal act in the book except rape.' He sighed theatrically. 'If you and I can't talk here in Berlin I'll have to send you to Moscow.' He shrugged. 'You don't need me to paint a picture of what happens to non-talking foreign agents in the Lubyanka. It isn't quite as crude as it used to be but modern technology is just as painful and far more efficient. You'll talk in the end, but it's up to you how long it takes.'

Anders stared back at Kalin but said nothing. The Russian sat there silently, watching Anders' face. It was almost five minutes before he spoke again.

'There's no point in wasting time, Anders. I might as well send you to Moscow and let them get started. It is genuinely a matter of indifference to me. If you'll talk with me, well and good. If you want to do it the hard way, so be it.' He looked at the thin gold watch on his wrist. 'I'll give you five minutes, Anders. If you haven't started by then, I shall press the bell and that will be that. Understood?'

Anders closed his eyes and fought the urge to touch the ache in his neck. His eyes were still closed as he heard the Russian stand up and take a few paces, and a few minutes later two armed guards in East German army uniforms pulled him up out of the chair and walked him down the empty corridor to a heavy-duty lift. He counted eight floors before the lift stopped and then he was in a brightly lit corridor with cells on each side. He was shoved into number 17 and keys turned in the heavy locks outside. There was a ceiling light in a metal frame and a bed with one blanket, and a bucket in one corner. And then the light went out. He had no idea what time it was. He guessed that he hadn't been unconscious for more than an hour. But it didn't really matter.

The next morning he was given four slices of sausage and a small piece of stale bread, and an hour later the cell door opened and Kalin stood there looking more like an actor than a KGB man. Elegant blue suit, a white shirt and a white tie, and a strong smell of aftershave.

Kalin stood there looking at Anders' unshaven haggard face and he noticed the arrogant, defiant eyes. He opened his mouth to speak, then shook his head and turned away.

Two hours later Anders was at Gatow under escort, and the car avoided the terminal buildings and circled the airfield. It stopped alongside a plane and one of his escorts pointed to the almost vertical metal steps that led into the aircraft.

It was a small military transport plane and all the seats were occupied by troops from an artillery unit going to Moscow on leave. One or two glanced in his direction but a sergeant had spoken to them and obviously warned them off.

Anders' hands were separately handcuffed to the metal arms of the seat and once the plane was airborne the guards left him and sat in the empty area behind him. The plane flew very low, constantly changing course and he guessed that the pilot was cooperating with ground defence and radar units in a routine testing of defences. But the low altitude produced a turbulence that made the ninety-minute journey bruising and unpleasant because he couldn't use his hands to brace himself, and it was a relief when the aircraft banked slowly and he could see the airfield below. It was far too small to be Sheremetyevo, Moscow's international airport. The plane lurched and came in slowly and as its wheels touched down he saw the sign. It was the Red Air Force field at Domodyedovo.

The soldiers picked up their gear and clattered down the metal steps and he watched them form up and march off towards the long low buildings. It was almost twenty minutes before the handcuffs were unlocked and he was shoved towards the open door. It was beginning to rain as he stood on the tarmac with the guards and then he saw the black Zil heading towards them from the cluster of airport buildings.

The guards handed over a small linen bag that he guessed contained his documents and then the two KGB men took him over. They sat each side of him on the back seat and only once did they speak, to give directions to the driver when they were held up by traffic at Sadovniki on the outskirts of Moscow. And then they were on Varsavskoje Sosse, with the Moskva river on their right.

Ten minutes later they had crossed the two bridges over the island and once they were on Karl Marx Prospekt he knew where they were going. He had half expected they were heading for the KGB's newer headquarters on the outer ring-road but it was going to be Dzerdzhinski Square and the Lubyanka.

The rain was lashing down as the car pulled up outside the grim building that filled one side of the square and the uniformed men hurried him up the steps to get out of the rain. But Anders knew that getting soaked to the skin was going to be the least of his worries in the next few days.

The room was stark. The whitewashed walls had no pictures, no decoration and there was no furniture apart from four hardwood chairs and the metal chair that was bolted to the floor just off centre.

Anders was surprised that Kalin was already there. Even in uniform he looked theatrical, as if he had just come from a rehearsal of *Der Rosenkavalier*. But the melting brown eyes were a hunter's eyes as he looked at Anders sitting on the metal chair. Kalin sat on a chair facing him and two men stood behind Anders' chair.

'Now, Mr Anders, I suggest you start talking. Tell me who was in charge of your operation and what you were ordered to do.'

Anders sat there in silence and a few seconds later Kalin's nod was as imperceptible as the nod of an experienced bidder at a Sotheby's art sale. A hand clawed into Anders' hair, wrenching back his head until his body arched to relieve the pain and a solid rocklike fist crashed against the side of his face. He lashed out with his legs and arms, jerking his head from the man's grip on his hair, and half-blinded he reached for a chair and swung it at the two shadowy figures. The heavy iron-tipped boot caught his kneecap and as he fell he heard a man laugh and felt a violent shattering blow against his body, and as he hit the concrete floor another, and another, and then everything dissolved into blackness.

Somewhere far away there were children singing 'What a friend we have in Jesus', and then it faded away and there were the shouts of a drill-sergeant on the square at Catterick and Luther Meynell was wishing him luck, telling him to take care. And there was a star slowly growing bigger until it was a bulb covered by a metal grille and it was in the ceiling above him. And there was a man looking down at him from a long way away.

A hand took hold of him roughly and he groaned as it pulled him to a sitting position and his hand went to the left side of his chest.

'Are you ready to talk now, Anders?'

The voice echoed painfully in his head and he wasn't sure what the words meant but he shook his head slowly and his stomach flexed as the vomit streamed from his mouth. His eyes were closed and he heard somebody curse him in Russian as he sank back against the wall.

It was a normal office. Carpeted and unfurnished with a modern teak desk, a well-polished table, and six matching chairs. There was a bowl of anemones in the centre of the table at the far end. And both Kalin and Burinski were in civilian clothes.

Kalin lit a cigarette and Anders noticed the pack. It was export Benson and Hedges. It was Kalin who spoke first.

'Mr Anders. All three of us are professionals. Experienced, well-trained, well aware of what goes on in our rather special world. But there are rules in our special world and one of the rules is that you don't talk. At least you don't talk for forty-eight hours so that the others in your network can disperse to try and avoid arrest. You've been in our hands for nine days.' He half-smiled. 'And you haven't talked. However, there are other rules and one of those is that you get every last item of information from a captured enemy agent.'

Kalin paused and tapped the ash of his cigarette into the china ashtray and then looked back at Anders.

'We can't afford to admire courage, Mr Anders. However, I want to make a suggestion to you. Answer me one question. Just one. And I'll make arrangements for the old man and Kraus to be released. And when you are brought before the court we will arrange for the charges to be reduced so that your sentence is also reduced. You can expect twenty-five years in a labour camp as things stand. And a public trial. If you cooperate the sentence could be halved. If you cooperated fully of course then even more lenient arrangements could be made. Do you understand?'

Anders sat silent and unmoving. After a minute's silence Kalin said, 'Mr Anders. There is a point when courage becomes no more than chest-beating and flag-waving. Posturing from the theatre. We are none of us heroes, none of us James Bonds, but men doing a job. Your service serves your country, mine serves the Soviet Union. We do our work. We know each other's names and habits. Our training is much the same. We are much the same kind of people. When it is necessary we are ruthless. When it is necessary we use violence. Not only us, but your people too. It's regrettable in human terms, but that is what our masters require us to do.

'Is it really necessary for me to give the orders for more brutality and the special drugs and the latest technical devices? Do you really need to force me to play these games? I assure you that I have no wish to give such orders. If you force me to, then that is that.'

Kalin's big brown eyes were not hard as he waited for a reply. Anders was conscious of the almost tangible silence in the room.

'What's the question?'

Kalin sighed with relief and stubbed out his cigarette. It was a mistake. It had an air of getting down to business. Quiet victory over a gallant loser.

'Just one simple question, Mr Anders.' He paused. 'Why Burinski?'

Anders looked back at Kalin and slowly shook his head. Kalin closed his eyes in theatrical despair but when he opened them they were no longer those melting spaniel's eyes of a few minutes earlier. And his voice was hard with restrained anger when he spoke.

'I don't understand you, Anders. Just one question. Why in God's name are you so stupid? We've got theories, and sooner or later we'll find out the answer.'

'Not from me you won't.' And Anders gasped as speaking sent a surge of pain through his chest.

'Why not? Tell me why not.'

'You know why not, Kalin.'

'Tell me.'

'Nothing you could do or say would make me talk. But if I had considered talking it wouldn't be sitting here with my ribs caved in and my jawbone showing through my skin.'

Kalin smiled. 'And your people never use violence? You yourself never use violence?'

'I'm not objecting to the violence.'

'What, then? What are you objecting to?'

'Because you're stupid, Kalin. You're too used to interrogating frightened Soviet citizens. You're handsome and elegant but under all that, you're just a bloody animal. It hasn't crossed your dim mind that it hurts me to breathe, let alone talk. You're not a professional, Kalin. You're a bully boy.'

A thin red stream of saliva and blood flowed from Anders' mouth, over his unshaven chin, dripping slowly on to his filthy shirt. His face was grey with pain and his thick beard was matted with dried vomit and blood. And the hand on his knee was tembling violently. But not from fear.

He saw Kalin reach forward and press one of the buttons on the panel on his desk. The two guards came in from the corridor and shoved him out of the door. As the walls and ceiling in the corridor tilted and swung they dragged him back to his cell.

Meynell had cycled over, and French, Peter Nicholson and Pritchett had travelled up together by car.

French had arranged for Mrs Griggs to open up the cottage and prepare sandwiches and a flask of coffee for them. French himself passed round the sandwiches and poured the coffee. Luther Meynell was aware that apart from himself nobody was looking at anyone else. His diagnosis was guilt. They were an odd mixture. Andy Pritchett, who ignored the handle on his Spode cup and looked as if he would have preferred an army mug. Nicholson, who looked as though he wished he wasn't there. Leaning back in his chair, his head turned to look abstractedly towards the window, his coffee untouched after the first tentative sip. And French himself, Sir Arthur. A neat man, checking the cushion on his chair before he sat down, almost more conscious of his responsibilities as host than the purpose of their hastily arranged meeting.

'Well, gentlemen,' French said. 'We all know why we're here. I'm sorry it had to be in such a rush, but there you are.'

'How long have they had him, Arthur?'

They all looked at Meynell. It was a relief to be with someone who wasn't directly involved in the shambles. Meynell was a sound man. He'd got a shrewd mind and he'd been in the business. He wouldn't want to pin it on anyone. Just find a solution.

'We think he was taken almost immediately. Five days and a few hours.'

'Any ideas on how they got on to him so quickly?'

'Not as yet.'

Nicholson interrupted, speaking quietly. 'I'd say it was lack of preparation, Luther. Too much of a hurry and not enough surveillance.'

'What do you think, Andy?' Luther turned to look at Pritchett.

'I agree with what Peter said. It was spur of the moment stuff and maybe Burinski was more important than we thought. The two men I used for surveillance are pretty low-grade, but they were all I had available. The one who passed me most of the information hasn't contacted us for payment. Maybe they spotted what he was doing and picked him up. He'd talk. Or maybe he was already working for them, doubling with us.'

Meynell raised his eyebrows. 'Where is Anders now?'

Nicholson sighed. 'He was in Berlin for two days. We know that for certain. Maybe he was there longer. But we know he's not there now. I've had an indication that he's in Moscow. That fits the usual pattern. It probably means that he didn't talk in Berlin so they've taken him to Moscow for the treatment.'

'Have we made any diplomatic complaints, Arthur?'

'No. It isn't on. We wouldn't do that for an established agent and we certainly can't do it for an unofficial.'

'Can we make an unofficial approach? The lawyer fellow in Berlin, perhaps.'

Pritchett interrupted. 'If you do and Anders is holding out with his cover story he'd be exposed immediately.'

Nicholson shook his head. 'He must have been caught red-handed, Andy. They don't need any confirmation of what he was up to. All they'll want to know is why we were doing it.' He turned and looked at French. 'I think we *should* make an unofficial approach, sir. I really do. I think we should offer an exchange and I think we should do it quickly. We owe him that.'

'Why, Peter?'

'Because we rushed him into it. We spent days when we should have spent weeks or even months.'

'I agree, sir.'

French ignored Pritchett's words. Oblique criticism from the Deputy Head of the Soviet desk was one thing. Criticism from field agents was another. He looked directly at Nicholson.

'Who have we got, Peter?'

Nicholson rested his head on the back of the chair, his eyes closed as he thought. When he opened his eyes he shook his head.

'Nothing, Arthur. Two who are far too important to trade, and a dozen routine people.'

'Offer more than one, then,' Meynell said.

Nicholson looked at French. 'Do you want me to have a go, Arthur?'

It was several silent minutes before French responded.

'I just don't know. I'll have to think about it. We could be pouring petrol on the blaze. However unofficial it may be they'll use it against us if it suits their purpose.'

'Your phone's ringing, Sir Arthur. Shall I answer it?'

'No thanks, Pritchett. I'll do it.'

French was back in a few minutes. 'It's for you, Peter. The office.'

When Nicholson came back he put a note into French's hand as he walked past him to his chair. French read the note and looked up. 'Gentlemen, Peter's just had confirmation from his people. Anders *is* in Moscow.'

Meynell shifted in his chair. 'I think you should make unofficial contact, Arthur. You needn't mention names or cases. Just dip your toe in and test the water. If it's a blank refusal you've lost nothing. If they're open to talks you could establish a shopping list that doesn't pinpoint Anders. Say four names from each side. Possibles. The usual ritual.'

French turned to Nicholson. 'Will you do that, Peter.'

'Yes, sir.'

Paul Degens looked more like an American than a German. In his middle fifties, he had a big, handsome face and the body of a retired professional sportsman. No longer all muscle, but still heavy and strong. With alert blue eyes, a pleasant sensual mouth and a thick crop of wavy hair, there was a touch of Harvard Business School about him.

In fact he had been a major in a German parachute regiment until he was severely wounded in the attack on Crete. Invalided out of the army he had finished his law training and gone into practice on his own, specializing in company law. The successful practice lasted less than six months when it disappeared with everything else in the cloud of smoke and rubble that was Berlin in 1945. When, in the fullness of time, the first Russian soldier had been tried by a German court for rape, Degens had defended him. Despised by his countrymen, he had defended the Russian ably and successfully. Three months after the 'not guilty' verdict had been passed two things happened that changed the whole of Degens' life. The Russian *Kommandatura* and the East German authorities paid him a six-figure annual retainer as their adviser on German Law, and he married the rape victim.

Two decades later he spoke good English and poor but fluent Russian, and seldom appeared in court except to represent any of the surviving companies who had employed him when he started his first practice.

His office was typical of a successful Berlin lawyer. Expensive, well-made, solid furniture, and the lived-in look that men who work long hours sometimes create. He wore a well-cut mid-grey suit that added to his bulk but didn't detract from his business-like aura.

Paul Degens was the man to whom governments came when they wanted to exchange one prisoner for another. Whether it was a U-2 pilot, a dissident or a spy, Paul Degens was the man you talked to. Provided that the Soviet Union was involved on one side or the other. And like most foreigners who appeared to be trusted by Moscow, and with access to top politicians and the Intelligence services he was less trusted by all the other countries who used his services. He asked for and received no fee for these services, but made no secret of the fact that he was paid a substantial retainer by Moscow and East Berlin as a legal adviser.

Nicholson had dealt with Degens before. He liked him as a man, and found him helpful, tactful and totally discreet. He made no attempt to clothe himself in any spurious authority, neither did he use words like 'intermediary' or 'honest broker'. He was no more and no less than what the facts indicated. A competent lawyer who had access to both sides. He negotiated when it was helpful but he didn't drive bargains, that was up to his principals. Nobody had ever claimed that he had told a lie, exaggerated or misinformed them. He had once made a genuine error to the Russians' disadvantage and they valued him enough to go along with the arrangements he had made.

Degens looked at Nicholson, his hands clasped on his desk, the knot of his tie pulled down from his shirt collar.

'So far as I know they are not indicating any desire to exchange at the moment but I'll check just to make sure.'

'How long will that take?'

'If my contact is available, ten minutes. Otherwise it could take me an hour or two to contact an alternative.'

'Would you be willing to try?'

'Of course. Would you like to wait?'

'If that's convenient to you.'

'Certainly. No, don't get up. I'll get my secretary to bring you a coffee. There are magazines there on the side-table. I'll be as quick as I can.'

The coffee came, and Nicholson browsed through a *New Yorker* and a copy of *Playboy*. It was almost half an hour before Degens came back, closing the door carefully and getting back behind his desk before he spoke.

'It's much as I thought, but they mentioned a Russian named Gorlinski. Andrei Gorlinski. I think they would be interested in talking about him.'

'Is there any way I could indicate interest without naming the prisoner we are interested in?'

'No. I don't want to be involved in a poker game. If both parties start fishing for reactions we end up in a Middle East bazaar situation. The Soviets have responded to you. They've named their interest. You have to do the same if you want to pursue it further.'

'My interest is a man named Anders. He was arrested in Berlin and taken to Moscow. He's in the . . . I guess it doesn't matter where he is. I would exchange Gorlinski for that man.'

Degens slid his hand inside his jacket and pulled out a folded piece of paper. He unfolded it and read it carefully twice. Then he looked up at Nicholson.

'Moscow gave me a list of names of people they would not be willing to consider for exchange. Mr Anders' name is not on that list so it looks as if it might be possible.'

'Do you want me to confirm Gorlinski in writing?'

'No. I assume you have the authority to commit your service or you wouldn't be here.'

'So what next?'

Degens looked at his wristwatch, and then at Nicholson.

'I can phone now, if you wish.'

'I'd be glad if you would.'

Degens smiled. 'That word "glad" always puzzles me. In the dictionary it gives the meaning as *froh* or *erfreut*, but they mean happy or pleased. What's the difference between glad and pleased?'

Nicholson smiled back. 'Glad is a milder word than pleased. Less enthusiastic. A smile but not flag-waving.'

'A word you could use when you didn't want to seem as if you would be very pleased.'

Nicholson laughed. '*Touché*. Very discerning of you to notice. It was instinctive, not deliberate.'

'Of course. But I'm a lawyer and even full-stops and commas matter to me. I may be longer this time. You are welcome to stay, or otherwise we could meet later this evening.'

'I'll stay on. Or . . .'

Degens smiled and interrupted. 'No. You staying does not indicate to the other party or me that you are anxious to finalize the arrangements. The other party will not know, and for me I assume the best. That you are conscientious and that Mr Anders is a colleague of yours. I should be anxious for a man's release if he were a friend of mine.'

It was a shorter wait. Degens was back in ten minutes. And once again he didn't speak until he was sitting behind his desk, as if that was a symbol of truth and straight dealing.

'That's OK, Mr Nicholson. They are agreeable. The exchange would be made here in Berlin in a few week's time. Maybe a little longer. I'll pass on the details when I have them.'

'Thank you for your help, Dr Degens.'

'Don't thank me, Mr Nicholson. I'm just a messenger-boy. Where can I contact you?'

'Through the consulate. Ask for Mr Treadgold.'

'Ah yes. I know Mr Treadgold. I expect you are already occupied this evening or I would invite you for a meal.'

'Thank you. I shall fly back tonight.'

'Have a good journey.' Degens held out his hand and Nicholson took it.

'Again, thanks for your help.'

Degens smiled and shook his head as he opened his office door.

CHAPTER ELEVEN

Anders lay still on the concrete slab, looking up at the ceiling. There was more light than usual, and he guessed that it must have snowed in the night and it was the reflection from the snow that lit the grey paint on the ceiling, and the dull metal of the circular light that was set into the concrete.

He knew that sooner or later he would have to move, and the pain in his ribs and kneecap was bearable now, but if he moved it would be back like a raging flood and he would be tempted to ask for the morphine. The plaster along his jaw hung down to touch his neck, and the stench from the suppurating wound was still offensive despite the antibiotic; the pain from the open wound pulsed with the beat of his heart. He closed his bloodshot eyes against the light, and lay quietly for several minutes until, without conscious decision, he clenched his teeth and sat up, swinging his feet to the ground. He groaned, his eyes still closed, as the pain in his chest and leg flared up like a forest fire. And as he sat there he heard the steel shutter pushed aside in the cell door. Then the rattle of the heavy keys in the two locks.

Anders opened his good eye to turn to look as someone came into his cell. It was Burinski and he was in his uniform. He looked clean and smart, but uneasy as he walked over towards Anders.

'Are you feeling better?'

Anders didn't reply but his good eye watched Burinski's face intently. Something had changed. He could tell it. Was it a change for the good or were things going to get worse?

'I've arranged for you to be transferred to the hospital. Do you agree?'

Despite the pain Anders managed a half-smile.

'A psychiatric ward, comrade? And a tape-recording that I agreed to go?'

'No. The prison hospital.'

Burinski stood there awkwardly and Anders realized that he was just a messenger boy. Burinski didn't know himself why there was a change of attitude. He was a spaniel bringing a bone, wagging its tail and waiting for a pat on the head.

Then the keys rattled again in the door and a man came in. He was dressed like a doctor. A white coat and a stethoscope round his neck; and a smell of strong disinfectant. But in the Lubyanka Prison that didn't mean he *was* a doctor. It meant only what was visible. A man dressed as a doctor. He stood looking Anders over and then he said with a heavy Georgian accent: 'Are you able to walk?'

Anders nodded, but it was an act of useless defiance. He couldn't walk. He couldn't even stand up. For a moment the doctor stood there and then he walked to the door and spoke through the grille to the guard. When he came back he said to Burinski, 'What injuries has he got?'

'I don't know.'

The doctor gave him a brief look of disgust and turned back to Anders.

'Have you had drugs?'

Anders nodded. 'Morphine.'

'Antibiotics?'

'Two days.'

The pain in Anders chest was spreading and mounting because he had spoken and there were beads of perspiration on his forehead and his cheeks. He was unconscious before the two orderlies came with the wheeled stretcher and in the operating room the doctor carefully cut the clothes from Anders' body. He shook his head slowly as he saw the white rib-bone where it pierced the skin and the huge swelling on the left knee. He sliced and sewed for four hours before Anders was wheeled to a hospital cell.

Anders was kept under heavy sedation for a week but when he finally surfaced he realized that the treatment he had been given had been efficient and effective. On the tenth day the doctor had told him to get out of bed and there had been no more than bearable pain in his chest. Although his knee was not articulating freely the swelling had gone down, and the wound along his jawline was almost healed.

The next day Burinski came to visit him, bringing a couple of English newspapers and that day's *Pravda*. He sat on the edge of Anders' bed and was obviously eager to talk. Was there anything else he wanted? Was he satisfied with the medical treatment? Anders ignored the questions.

'What is it you want, Burinski?'

'I want to help you.'

'Don't bullshit me, comrade, you're wasting your time.'

'Why shouldn't I want to help you?'

'Two reasons, my friend. First of all you've got no reason to help me, and secondly, you haven't got the authority to help me even if you wanted to.'

Burinski looked uneasy and Anders guessed that the conversation was being taped.

'You're being moved in a few days. Outside Moscow. A kind of . . .' Burinski sighed as he sought for the right word, '. . . recuperation. A chance to recover.'

'Why the sudden concern?'

'They're not inhuman, you know. They respect your courage.'

Anders smiled. 'They're wasting their time, Burinski. The soft touch won't work with me. They ought to know that.'

'It will be just you and me. No more interrogation of any kind.'

Anders lay looking at Burinski, wondering why the KGB had seen him as an assassin. There was no doubt that he had murdered the men they had picked as his targets, but there was a flaw in his character, a fundamental weakness under the dedication. They had trained him and used him, but you needed more than that. You needed either conviction or an inborn lust for killing. Burinski had neither. And right now the flaw was showing through. He was under some pressure. There was something they wanted, and it was Burinski's job to get it. Anders wondered what it could be.

The next day Burinski brought clothes for him to wear and a carton of English cigarettes and a lighter. Two days later Burinski brought a leather case and said they were leaving. There had been no formalities, they had just walked to the lift and gone down to street level, along a narrow corridor to the main doors and then they were at the top of the main steps in Dzerdzhinski Square. It was a grey spring day. A Moscow spring day, and although it was mid-morning cars had their lights on and there was frost or light snow on the buildings, and a big black Volga M124 its engine running, at the foot of the steps.

Burinski sat with him in the back of the car as the driver threaded his way through the city. The only thing Anders recognized was Sokolniki Park and he guessed they were heading almost due east. When they crossed the outer ring road the signs said 'Gorenki 5km'. As they turned off the main road they took a road marked 'Balasicha' and at the start of a pine forest they took a rutted road that eventually brought them to a lake. There were half a dozen well-built log houses alongside the lake, and at the far end was a stone-built house with a high wall and heavy iron gates. The gates were opened as they drove up, and inside was a wooden hut on wheels and half a dozen armed soldiers. The gardens were large and well maintained, mainly lawns and well-established trees. A Red Army lieutenant waved them on to the house.

The house itself was smaller than it had appeared from outside and an elderly woman held open the door and bowed her head as they walked inside. Burinski took him up the wide oak staircase and showed him his room. It was spotlessly clean and sparsely furnished with solid peasant furniture. A bed, a chest, a wardrobe, a worktable and two carved armchairs. There were bars on the small window.

Not even after a week had Anders discovered the purpose of the changed treatment. Burinski seemed almost as much a prisoner as he was, but on the second Sunday Burinski had surprised him as they walked together in the garden, the snow squeaking crisply as they walked under the bare trees.

'My wife's coming to join us. She's arriving tomorrow.'

'Is she KGB too?'

Burinski sighed. 'No. Anyway, she's German not Russian.'

Anders half-smiled. 'Why don't you come clean, Burinski and tell me what it's all about?'

'I'm not sure what it *is* all about.'

'So what do you *think* it's all about? Why is your wife involved?'

'Oh, that's just me. I hate being away from her. She means a lot to me. It's a favour just to keep me happy.'

'You still haven't answered. What do you think it is?'

'I think they're considering an exchange of prisoners.'

Anders stopped walking and turned to look at Burinski.

'You mean me?'

'Yes.'

'What makes you think that?'

'London offered an exchange almost as soon as we picked you up.'

'I don't believe it.'

'They offered one of our people in exchange.'

'How long have they been negotiating?'

'Ever since we got you.'

'That's why you've been patching me up?'

'Yes. I expect so.'

'Who's holding things up?'

'Nobody. It's just a question of ironing out the snags.'

'What snags?'

'I don't know. I've not been told.'

Burinski's wife, obviously pregnant, arrived the next day, and the three of them had eaten their meals together. After a few days Anders realized that for all Burinski's ruthlessness he was the weaker partner in the marriage, obviously very dependent on his young wife. Anders realized too from several remarks that she made that she was not one of Moscow's admirers. She made no open criticism but she had smiled her disbelief at several propaganda items on the TV news. She had a different kind of self-confidence from Burinski's rather macho arrogance. A self-confidence that came from a shrewd, informed mind. He wasn't surprised to learn that she worked in a news office.

On the few occasions when he was alone with her she had asked him no awkward questions. He guessed that she knew that he was a foreigner and under some kind of restraint but she made no attempt to probe. She was a jazz enthusiast and she talked knowledgeably. An Oscar Peterson, Earl Hines fan. She had talked too about her parents and the farm, and what it was like when she was a girl, but he got the impression that the best time in her life was now. She obviously genuinely cared for her husband. There were times when she was almost excusing his rôle, but otherwise her comments lacked the ring of conviction that she usually had with all her views.

Alone in his room at night Anders wondered why SIS had offered to do a deal. They never did that. Once you were in the bag you didn't exist. They'd never heard of you. And even if an exchange took place the initiative always came from Moscow. And right to the bitter end London claimed that their man was no more than an innocent businessman falsely entrapped by the machinations of the KGB. It was odder still to acknowledge a man who wasn't on the establishment. They knew him too well to think that he'd crack and talk. Maybe Meynell had suggested it and put pressure on Sir Arthur. But why? Maybe Burinski was mistaken, or maybe the whole scenario was phoney, a ruse to build him up and then deflate him by the disappointment. Yet by now they'd have some background stuff on him from the Embassy in London and they'd at least know that he wasn't likely to be vulnerable to that kind of ploy. And when the KGB wanted an exchange they usually wanted it over quickly. It seldom took longer than a week from first approach to the final exchange. They must have been negotiating for nearly three months.

From time to time Anders thought about Judy and Candy and the club. They would probably have put in somebody to hold the fort at the club. Joey would be able to look after the day to day running. Candy would be worried, pulling underground strings to find out if he had been spirited away by the police. He had no idea what Judy's reaction would be. It would almost certainly be introspective. She would either see it as a desertion, or proof that her father's warnings about his unsuitability were well-founded. Facing the facts he guessed that it was unlikely that she would worry on his account. For Judy, when one life-boat foundered you looked around for another.

Burinski had gone to Moscow for the day. Anders and the girl walked in the garden in the morning under the watchful eyes of the guards. The snow had gone and there were the first signs of spring. The sky was still grey and the air was cold, but there were thin tentative shoots of new grass on the lawns, and a sheen on the reticulated bark of the silver birches that spoke of the end of the season dormancy. They lunched together and, as if the burgeoning world outside had touched their spirits, they had been relaxed and the girl had been mildly flirtatious. Not seriously, but as if for the first time she saw him as a man. The old *babushka* had cleared the table but they sat there talking and she had told him a mildly anti-Soviet Berlin joke that made him smile. She looked back at his face.

'You know, that's the first time I've ever seen you smile.'

He shrugged. 'I haven't had much to smile about lately.'

'How did you get hurt?'

He put his finger to his lips to warn her that the room would be bugged. 'I got hit by a car.'

She nodded her understanding.

'Did my husband tell you that I'm pregnant?'

'No. But I noticed. When is it due?'

'End of June according to the doctor.'

'D'you want a boy or a girl?'

'I want a boy like Vasili.' She laughed. 'And he wants a girl like me.' She shook her head, smiling with pleasure. 'I don't really mind. Shall we go for another walk in the garden before it gets dark?'

'Why not? I'll get my coat and meet you in the hall.'

He walked her away from the trees and the wooden benches until they were clear of anything that could conceal a microphone.

'Can I call you Inge?'

'Of course.'

'Don't ever say anything critical or private in an official building, especially a KGB one. They're all wired for surveillance. You're the wife of a KGB officer so you're pretty safe, but it all goes down on your record. It can be used some day if they want to.'

She stood with her hands in her coat pockets, her coat collar turned up and her eyes were on his face.

'Why do you warn me?'

'Why shouldn't I?'

'I think you're a prisoner. You can't possibly care what happens to me.'

'Why not?'

'Why should you?'

'You're a human being. And you don't look like you particularly want to be a martyr.'

'You must be very sure of yourself.'

'Why?'

'To care about anyone else when you're in danger yourself. Especially the wife of your . . . enemy.'

'Your husband's not my enemy. Rival, maybe. The enemy are the men in the Politburo. But they're everybody's enemy. Yours as well as mine.'

'Will it ever change?'

'I shouldn't think so. Not substantially.'

'Will there be a nuclear war in the end?'

'I don't think so. The Kremlin may want to take over the world but they want it all in one piece, just as it is, with everything working, not a radioactive desert.'

She sighed. 'I hope you're right.' She paused. 'Are you married?'

'No.'

'Divorced?'

'No.'

'Girl friend?'

He half-smiled. 'I've not heard from her. Who knows?'

'You don't really like women, do you?'

'I like them a lot. But I can get by without one. I don't rely on them to make my life.'

'Maybe you'll fall one day.' She smiled.

'Maybe. I hope not.'

'That's a terrible thing to say.'

He laughed. 'Why?'

'I don't really know. But it's unnatural somehow.'

'The birds and the bees and the survival of the species?'

'No. Just love and friendship and trust.'

He looked at her face. She was quite pretty. He didn't want to hurt her or spoil her dreams.

'We'd better go back, or the Red Army will be getting agitated.'

They walked back in silence as they approached the house Burinski's car came through the main gates and the girl waited for him as Anders walked into the house and up to his room. He didn't know it but it was almost the last night he was to spend in the house.

The next day Burinski arranged for them to walk outside the garden of the house, across the fields and up the slope to the woods on the brow of the hill.

At the edge of the woods they found a felled tree trunk and sat together looking across towards the house and the lake. Burinski seemed more relaxed than usual and his wife said, 'Go on, Vasili. Say it.'

Burinski turned to look at Anders. 'I want to thank you for warning my wife against being indiscreet. She's German and she doesn't understand these things.'

'I do, Vasili. I understand all right. What I can't understand is how millions of people tolerate it.' Her voice was insistent.

Burinski smiled. 'We don't think about it. We're used to it. It's like the weather. And ninety-nine per cent of those millions have no complaints against the Party. They complain about shortages but there's no country in the world where the people don't complain about something or other.' He turned to look at Anders. 'Isn't that so, Mr Anders?'

'There is a difference, of course.'

'What's that.'

'Their complaints are listened to. They can throw out the politicians every four years and shortages of food and goods seldom happen. In the Soviet Union it's permanent.'

Burinski smiled. 'You just don't like Russians.'

'Not true. I just don't like the Soviet system. And despite what you say, most Russians don't like it either. They tolerate it because it's a dictatorship and they have no choice.'

'How is it you speak such good Russian?'

'My father was Polish. I found Russian fairly easy. How did you learn your German?'

'School. University and . . . service courses. What does your father do?'

'He's dead. He was in the Free Polish Army. He was killed at Monte Cassino.'

'My father was a career soldier. He's retired now.'

'Where does he live?'

'Just outside Moscow.'

'D'you see much of him?'

'No.' Burinski shrugged. 'We don't see eye to eye on many things.'

'Have they told you to pump me on my background?'

Burinski looked shocked. 'Good God no. I was just chatting. Anyway they've got your background on file.'

'Have you read it?'

'Not all of it. Part of it is restricted.'

'Why are we talking like this? You must have a reason.'

Burinski shrugged. 'No special reason. I was just grateful that you warned Inge.'

'No more than that?'

'They are puzzled about you, and interested.'

'Puzzled about what?'

'That somebody so senior in SIS should have been sent on such an unplanned mission. They wonder why. They wonder if you were deceived in some way.' Burinski looked at Anders' face. 'They have been trying to decide whether it would be sensible to suggest you should be offered a senior rank to work for us. Not against the British.'

Anders half-smiled. 'And what did they decide?'

'That I was to see if you were interested even slightly. If you were then somebody very senior would talk with you. You would be offered at least colonel in the KGB.'

'I'm not interested, Burinski. You'd better tell them that.'

'I told them already that you would not be interested. I think it was their view too. But they insisted I make an approach.'

'Are you permanently in Moscow now?'

'No. When you leave I shall be going back to Berlin with Inge.'

Anders looked past Burinski to his wife. 'I guess you'll be glad to go back.'

She shrugged. 'It's been interesting seeing Moscow but, yes, Moscow makes East Berlin seem like civilization, and God knows it isn't. But when I got to Moscow it was like there was a power-cut or somebody had switched off all the lights.' She put her hand on Burinski's arm. 'We're being unkind aren't we, Vasili?'

'Yes. But I understand. We'll have to get back to the house, my love.'

She linked her arms in theirs and they walked slowly back down the hill. Before they came in sight of the house she put her hands back in the pockets of her coat.

They ate together that evening and watched a sports programme on TV. Burinski, for once, kept to his orders and switched off before the news came on.

For the next three days they walked together away from the house. There had been no more talk of politics or political systems and Burinski had asked him no more questions about his background. It was obvious that Inge was the centre of Burinski's life, and Anders wondered what the girl would think if she knew that her husband was a professional assassin for the regime she so obviously despised. She probably wouldn't believe it when eventually she found out, because you would have to have been in the business to believe it and notice the give-away signs. The eyes that looked around without moving, the quick reflexes, the sudden change from normal body movements to complete stillness, the almost imperceptible holding of his breath as he listened, and the barely controlled swagger as he walked when he was relaxed and at ease.

There was an ornamental iron bench under one of the apple trees and they sat there in the pale spring sunlight after their walk. Burinski had been called to Moscow again.

She turned to look at Anders. 'The scar on your jaw has almost blended into your skin.' She smiled. 'But I'm sure your girlfriend will notice it.'

Anders smiled. 'Maybe.'

'Tell me about her. What is she like?'

Anders looked away towards the house and was silent for several moments. The girl said, 'Have I offended you?'

'No. I was just thinking. I've got two girlfriends and I was wondering which one to describe.'

'Are they both alike?'

'No. They're very different. One is sophisticated. From a well-known family in her own small country. The other is younger, prettier and from a working-class family.'

'Tell me about the sophisticated one.'

'She's married. Unhappily. She's a Roman Catholic. The family are mildly important but not wealthy. They care a lot about public opinion and status and that sort of thing. She's attractive but not pretty. She has a drink problem and maybe a drug problem.'

'What's her name?'

'Judy.'

'And the other one?'

'She's very young and very pretty. Very loving and . . .' he shrugged. '. . . I don't know more than that.'

'But you don't love either of them?'

Anders smiled. 'It's worse than that, Inge. I love both of them.'

'What do you love about the Judy girl?'

'I feel great sympathy for her. She looks as though she's always had everything but she hasn't. They were not loving people, they were cold-hearted and only concerned with appearances. She drinks to escape from thinking about her life.

She has no talents, no skills, no means to earn a living. She's alone and quite defenceless.'

For a moment she was silent then she said softly. 'You're a strange man, Mr Anders. You don't understand women, do you?'

Anders half-smiled. 'You tell me.'

'You're a very strong man. Very tough. So strong that you can afford to be loving. Inside you are loving, but for some reason you don't want it to come out. Why?'

Anders shrugged and said nothing.

'Was there a girl before these?'

'Yes.'

'What happened?'

Anders shook his head without speaking. The girl said, 'Some time in your life some woman, some girl, must have hurt you very much. I wonder who it was. And now you have two girls. One who is a lame dog you protect out of sympathy, and one who loves you even though you don't love her back. Maybe some day a man will feel sympathy for the loving girl who is not loved back. Maybe it will be you.'

Anders stood up. 'We should be getting back.'

'Have I offended you?'

'No.'

'Angered you?'

'No.'

'I do it only out of affection and because you cared about me and my husband enough to warn me that I was being stupid.'

'Forget it, Inge. In a sane country it wouldn't be necessary.'

'If I don't have a chance to talk to you again, I hope you are happy when you get back.'

Anders nodded and the girl was disappointed at his lack of response.

He was deeply asleep when they roused him and he woke with a start to see one of the guard sergeants standing by his bed.

'You leave in half an hour, comrade.'

'Where for?'

'Half an hour,' the sergeant said, ignoring the question.

At Sheremetyevo a KGB man in civilian clothes took him over from the two Red Army officers and he was escorted across the tarmac to the big Aeroflot jet. It was still dark and the cabin clock showed the local time as 06.00 hours.

When they landed at Schönefeld there was a car waiting on the apron and an hour later they were making their way through the centre of East Berlin. Except when Anders had needed to use the toilets on the aircraft the KGB man had not spoken a word. At the far end of Unter den Linden he had been transferred to a van. He was put into the back, his left foot handcuffed to his left hand and to a ring on the floor of the van. He had noticed the squat dish-aerial revolving slowly on top of the van's roof and the KGB man had spoken half a dozen numbers into a walkie-talkie before he locked the heavy steel door that left the interior in complete darkness.

For almost ten minutes the van waited and Anders could hear nothing; not even the traffic in the busy street; then the engine started and the van moved off slowly. It made no turn and Anders guessed they must be approaching the Brandenburger Tor. A few minutes later the engine was cut and the vehicle rolled on silently, slowly pulling to the left as it braked smoothly.

Anders heard the van door slam to and then there was silence again. Slowly his head went down until it was resting on his free arm across his knees; his eyes closed, and he slept.

The KGB man had already unlocked the handcuffs before Anders came to, and when he opened his eyes he saw that the door was open and two Red Army soldiers were standing in the road at the front of the short metal steps. One of them reached up for his arm as he stumbled on the first step and Anders roughly pushed the helping hand aside. He took a deep breath as he stood unsteadily in the road. It was obviously the early hours of the morning. There were no civilians about and he noticed then that there were no East German *Volkspolizei* or Frontier Police who usually manned the Germans-only checkpoint at the Brandenburg Gate. Apart from the KGB man there were only half a dozen Red Army soldiers, their Kalashnikovs held loosely with the sling looped across one arm.

Then suddenly the lights went on, flooding the whole area where they were standing. The KGB man took his arm and pushed him to the big circle of light where two floodlights merged, and spoke softly into his small transceiver. He paused, listening, then spoke again, and a torch flashed three times from the darkness ahead of them. Still holding Anders' arm he pushed him forward, walking slowly towards the guard hut, and another set of lights came on on the other side of the barrier.

Anders saw the balding head and the wispy hair above Andy Pritchett's belligerent face. A man in a dark anorak stood beside him as they both walked slowly towards the barrier. The KGB man muttered again into his small radio and Anders saw Pritchett doing the same. As he was pushed forward the man in the anorak crossed a few feet away, smiling towards his KGB colleagues.

Anders saw Pritchett's eyes on the scar along his jaw and then he held out his hand. It was cold and damp as Anders took it and Pritchett said softly. 'The green Volkswagen's ours. Keep moving.'

CHAPTER TWELVE

They had coffee from a thermos as the driver headed for Tegel, and at the airport they had a meal. As he pushed aside his empty plate Anders said, 'Who's been looking after the club?'

'I have. And Stoppard.'

'How're things?'

'No problems.' He smiled. 'Except your little blonde. She's been raising hell in all directions. And a girl named Judy rang a few times early on.'

Anders nodded. 'Who suggested the deal?'

Pritchett avoided his eyes. 'No idea, Tad.'

'Who briefed you, for instance?'

'Skip it, Tad. Wait till we get back. It's not safe to talk here.'

'You mean the KGB might discover they've let me out.'

Pritchett saw the anger in Anders' eyes but made no effort to placate him. 'Just cool it, Tad. If you want to beef, you've got the wrong guy.'

'Who's the right guy?'

'For Christ's sake, what's the problem? They got you out and that's more than they'd normally do for any of us.'

'Where are we going?'

'London.'

'Where?'

'You'd better wait and see. They'll want to debrief you. I'm not in the picture.'

Then the Tannoy was calling their flight and they walked to the gate.

At Gatwick Nicholson was waiting with a Rover 2000, and Pritchett went off to get his own car from the multi-storey. Nicholson looked tired but amiable and when Anders asked him where they were going he didn't hesitate. 'Tunbridge Wells.'

The house at Tunbridge Wells was one of SIS's safe-houses. It was one of the big Victorian houses in Broadwater Down. Set in its own large grounds, it was one of the few that had not been turned into four or five large flats. SIS used it for a variety of purposes when top security and physical security were essential. From the outside it looked like the rest of the houses, but inside it was a mass of electronics, recording gear and weapons. A plain-clothes CI section was permanently based at the house. They did one-month stints and were not allowed out of the house in daylight hours.

Anders sat without talking, absorbing the information, working out the implications. They were on the main A21 at Farnborough before he spoke again.

'Who's debriefing me, Peter?'

'I am.'

'How long will it take?'

'Not long I should think. Providing you cooperate.'

'Why was Pritchett doing the strong, silent man bit?'

Nicholson laughed softly. 'Was he? Protocol I suppose. The debriefing officer's privilege and all that.'

'How's the club?'

'God knows, Tad. I wouldn't be seen dead in it. You know that. Not my scene at all. They'll have kept it going, you can be sure of that. But they won't be using it as a safe-house without you being there.'

'Can I make a couple of phone calls?'

'Get some sleep in. Let's have a chat and see how it goes, eh?'

Anders didn't reply. They were by-passing Sevenoaks, and the signs were for Tonbridge and Hastings. As he gazed silently out of the window he could see the light of the false dawn silhouetting the hills to the east. There were few vehicles on the road and they were all heading in the opposite direction, for London. Then they turned off the main road on to the feeder for Tunbridge Wells. Fifteen minutes later they were turning left at the Pantiles into the Frant road and at the top of the hill they turned into Broadwater Down. The safe-house was about three hundred yards up on the left, and Nicholson turned into the gravel drive and parked by the double garage at the side of the house. They both got out, Nicholson reaching into the back seat of the car for his bag, Anders looking up at the pink dawn behind the trees. He looked without thinking at his wrist to check the time and then remembered that his watch had gone in the first few days of interrogation.

'Have you got any kit, Tad?'

'No.'

'Nothing?'

'No.'

'The bastards. Let's go in.'

Anders slept until midday and when he woke he saw that someone must have come down from the club. A suit, some shirts and a pair of jeans were laid out on the other single bed.

He was sitting on the edge of his bed when the phone on the bedside table rang. As he put the receiver to his ear a male voice said, 'Press the scrambler button please, Mr Anders.' He pressed the button and recognized Luther Meynell's voice.

'Welcome back, Tad. How are you feeling?'

'It makes a change to hear somebody say welcome back.'

'Give them time, Tad. I expect they've been mainly concerned with getting you back to London.'

'Was it you who suggested the exchange?'

'It was a joint decision. Is there anything I can do to help?'

'Maybe I could come up and see you for a couple of days after the debriefing.'

'Splendid idea. Give me a call as soon as you're ready.'

'I'll do that, Luther. And thanks for the call.'

'Take care of yourself.'

'I will.' And he hung up and cleared the scrambler button.

There was shaving kit and towels on the shelf over the washbasin and he was shaving when Peter Nicholson came in in his dressing gown and slippers.

'What woke you, Tad? I could have slept for a week.'

'I don't know. I think there were some church bells, or maybe I imagined it. And then Luther Meynell phoned.'

'Well it is Sunday, and there's a church up the road a bit. How're you feeling?'

'My mind's still in Moscow but I'll survive.'

'Are you fit enough to talk?'

'Sure. Let's get it over.'

They had breakfast together and Nicholson kept the talk to neutral subjects like pay-scales, promotions and postings, and a problem they'd got at government level in Bonn. After the breakfast things had been cleared away by an orderly Nicholson reached for his briefcase and put it on the table. He opened it, took out a pad and a pen and looked across the table at Anders.

'Have you any objection to having our talk recorded?'

'No. If you think it's necessary.'

'OK. Let's start,' Nicholson paused. 'Where did they pick you up, Tad?'

'In the car.'

'Whereabouts?'

'Just before the underpass. I don't remember the name. I'd need a map.'

'Have you got any idea of how they got on to you?'

'Only theories.'

'Tell me.'

'I think one of Pritchett's men doing the survey was a double agent.'

'He would have known we were interested in Burinski. But he couldn't have known about you or what we intended to do.'

'I think they put a special surveillance on Burinski's flat and on Normannenstrasse. I think they checked on anyone who went near his flat. And I did something stupid that put them on to me.'

'What was that?'

'When I'd checked his flat I checked the square I had in mind, then I walked along to the office building in Normannenstrasse. There's a taxi stand near there. I took a taxi. The only one that was there. I should have known it was a plant. With their surveillance resources it must have been easy after that.'

'Who interrogated you?'

'A KGB colonel named Kalin.'

'Jesus. Have you seen his file?'

'No. I'd never heard of him.'

'Who beat you up?'

'Two KGB thugs. They didn't introduce themselves.'

'But Kalin gave the order.'

'Yes.'

'He started off as an actor but he did rather nasty things to two or three of his girlfriends and the KGB took him over to save prosecution, and to use his nastier talents.'

'You'd better ask the sixty-four thousand dollar question.'

'What's that?'

Anders shrugged impatiently. 'Did I talk?'

Nicholson looked at Anders' face and then said softly. 'OK. Did you talk?'

'No.'

'How long did they put you through the mincer?'

'Most of it was done on one day. The beating up. They interrogated me off and on for ten days.'

'Then what happened?'

'They started giving me hospital treatment. I suppose the negotiations had started. Then they sent me to a safe-house in the country outside Moscow with Burinski and his wife.'

'Burinski? Is he an interrogator as well?'

'No. He didn't interrogate me, anyway.'

'What happened there?'

'Nothing. I think they were just fattening me up to send back.'

'Why was Burinski's wife there?'

'I think it was just personal. Burinski's very fond of her.'

'She wasn't a KGB swallow trying to lure you into her bed?'

Anders smiled. 'She's six months or maybe seven months pregnant. And she's German.'

'What sort of questions did you get?'

'The usual stuff. Tell uncle all about it first and then when they'd done me over Kalin offered a deal. Answer just one question and Kraus and old Max would go free and I'd only do five years in the Gulag for being a good boy.'

'What was the question?'

'Why Burinski?'

'What did you tell them?'

'Same as before, nothing.'

The telephone rang and Nicholson reached out and picked up the receiver.

'Nicholson . . . yes, he's with me now . . . it's up to you. I'd suggest right now . . . OK.'

When he had hung up he looked at Anders. 'They've sent a quack down from London to check that you're OK. He's here now. I suggested that he got cracking straight away.' Nicholson looked at him. 'Off the record, Tad, how do you feel? Are you all right in yourself?'

'How do I look?'

'Truth or . . .'

'Truth.'

'You look terrible. I'm not sure I would have recognized you in a crowd. If the doctor says things are reasonably under control I suggest you relax for the rest of the day and tomorrow I'll come down and pick you up and you stay with us over the weekend. We'll leave the debriefing for a few days.'

'What day is it today?'

'Thursday.'

'Is it an order that I stay with you?'

'Of course not. I just thought you might like it. I should like it. So would Fleur.'

'OK. Thanks. I'd like to come.'

Fleur Nicholson had a vague idea of what her husband did. It was accepted SIS practice that once a man was as senior as Nicholson some explanation should, or could, be given to his wife. Wives needed to know why it sometimes happened that their husbands didn't come home that night, to allay their fears until they heard the familiar voice calling from Helsinki, Hong Kong or Washington. A few wives were excluded. Those who were not born British were excluded for their own protection. Those who were promiscuous, tyrants or neurotics were not told for their husband's sake. It was emphasised that their husband's job was responsible and secret and that knowing too much could endanger their husbands and their colleagues. Most wives responded well, but for even the most level-headed there was a period, months or even longer, when they felt as women feel when their homes have been burgled. There had been an intruder and it was hard to decide whether the intruder was SIS or this man who used to be her husband. A strange new man who wasn't any more just a diplomat at the Foreign Office, but a man who lived in a shadowy world where she didn't belong. He was no longer the young man she had met at the tennis-club or a college dance. He had successfully kept it all secret from her, and maybe if he could do that there were other things he could hide from her that were not SIS. For some months he wasn't her husband, and they weren't a pair. Even the fact that he was more important than she had known, more valued by other people, was disturbing.

But Fleur Nicholson, being a Frenchwoman and realistic, had taken it in her stride. If you are attractive and your background was supportive, and if you were raised on the principle that families are parts of dynasties, you have an in-built self-confidence that allows you to see husbands as both *hommes d'affaires* and small boys at the same time. Her husband had told her only that Anders had had a rough time on an assignment and that he was coming for a couple of days rest.

'Is he married yet, Peter?'

'No.'

'Has he got a girlfriend he'd like to bring?'

'I want him to come alone.'

'What about asking your father and mother for Saturday?'

'Good idea if they can make it.'

'Luther Meynell and Patsy?'

'Yes. But keep it small and low-key.'

'Oh, Peter. This stupid jargon. What is low-key, for God's sake? Your father, Luther Meynell – are they low-key?'

Nicholson smiled. 'I mean relaxed and intimate. No climbers, no mixers, no talented queers.'

'You are an idiot. An English idiot.' But she kissed him.

He sat watching them playing tennis. Nicholson and his father, Luther Meynell and his Patsy, Anders wondered how you got to be like them. Taking the big house and its two acres of garden and servants in your stride. It wasn't just a case of money. If he himself were rich he wouldn't live like this. He wouldn't know how to. He didn't know the rules. The Nicholsons were wealthy, but not the Meynells, yet Luther and Patsy Meynell fitted into all this. They belonged. As if belonging was all decided genetically the day you were conceived. He wasn't ill at ease. They seemed to take for granted that he was part of their scene. And they certainly weren't snobs. Maybe Fleur was a bit of a snob, but that was a left-over from the Paris background. A touch of the 16th arrondissement. They talked to their servants as if they were friends, and there was no ostentation. No Bentleys. Not even Jaguars. Rovers for the Nicholsons and a well-cared-for Morris Minor for the Meynells. And yet he wasn't a humble man and on a smaller scale he could have lived this sort of life. So why didn't he?

'Are you warm enough, Tad?'

He looked up. It was Fleur and she was putting up the deckchair beside him.

'I'm fine, thanks. What are the girls doing?'

'Sabine is doing her piano practice, Arlette is counting her pocket-money, and my small namesake is lying on the bed reading a comic instead of tidying her room.' She turned her head to look at him. 'Do you like children, Tad?'

'Yes. But I wouldn't want children of my own.'

'Why not?'

Anders shrugged.

'I'd be scared of not being good for them. Caring too much. Smothering them.'

'My three would love that. Of course it's easier with girls. They like all the loving but they don't inhale all the time.'

He smiled. 'You mean girls are more cynical about loving.'

'They're realistic most of the time. They're a bit like I suspect you are. They lap up the loving but keep in the back of their minds that maybe it's flattery and anyway it won't last for ever.'

'Is that how you see me?'

'Yes. Am I wrong?'

'I've no idea. I don't know what I'm like.'

'You're a nice man, Tad Anders, and that's all that matters. Here's Olga with the drinks, and here come the others.'

It was a calm, restful weekend for Anders. He slept well and the easy-going relationships had taken his thoughts away from Moscow and Berlin. Only when he was alone did he have fleeting visions of the house, the cell, Burinski and Kalin. The atmosphere at the Nicholson's was almost Victorian. The three pretty young girls were like models from some Pre-Raphaelite painting. He was left to join or leave the family circle and either way he felt at home.

In his room in the house in Tunbridge Wells were two piles of mail for him. He saw that there were three letters addressed to the PO Box number and seven or eight addressed to him at the club.

He opened the PO Box number letters first. The bulky envelope was a coded statement of payments into his account at a private bank used by SIS and a sheet showing the state of the loan from SIS when he set up the club. The original £8,000 indebtedness was now reduced to £400 and when that was paid, the commentary noted that the lease and small balance of shares would revert to him. He put it to one side and opened the next letter. He didn't recognize the handwriting on the envelope. The letter was quite brief.

Dear Mr Anders,

I shall be visiting London for a month from the last week in May. I should like to take the opportunity to meet you. I shall be the guest of His Excellency the French Ambassador. Perhaps you would kindly let me know if and when it would be convenient for you.

Yours sincerely,

Julia Crawley (Judy's mother)

Anders read it through a second time before he opened the third envelope. It was a bulky packet. There was no covering note but it contained the documents and the watch that the KGB had taken from him. He knew that it wasn't some burst of generosity or honesty on the part of the men in Dzerdzhinski Square but to let him know that they knew enough about him to be able to use his personal PO Box number.

In the larger pile there was a tart letter from Westminster Council reminding him that he had not reapplied for his permit to operate a private club. Unless ... etc., etc. There was a letter in green ink from Baldy Morton giving a month's notice. A bill for repairs and garaging of the MGC. A telephone bill for £185.00. There was a long letter from an SIS colleague in Estoril retailing local gossip and wondering if Anders could put him up in June for a seven day leave. A few personal bills. A statement from Barclays of the two club accounts.

Perhaps because the envelope was pink and faintly perfumed he left that letter to the end.

Dearest Tad,

It seems silly to write you at the club when I know you aren't there. But I'm so worried about you. Jacko and Hawks have tried to find out for me what has happened, but there has been no news. I've phoned hospitals and police stations but there was nothing.

I'm so worried about you and I miss you so much. If you ever read this note will you let me know somehow that you're all right. You needn't speak to me if you don't want. Just let me know you're OK.

Your ever loving, (I mean it!!!)

Candy

Anders walked over to the phone and the signal sergeant on the exchange answered.

'Where's Mr Nicholson?'

'I believe he's in Room seven, sir.'

'Can you give me a line.'

'Compliments of Mr Nicholson, sir, can you check with him first?'

Anders hung up and wandered slowly down the landing to Room seven. He knocked on the door and walked in. Nicholson was talking on the telephone but he waved Anders to a seat. When he hung up he turned in his seat.

'You want a call, Tad. Is it urgent?'

Anders passed him Candy's note and sat silently as Nicholson read it. Nicholson looked up smiling and handed it back.

'She's a real sweetie, that kid. Let me contact the club with a message for her. Shall I say you'll be back on Wednesday?'

'That's up to you.'

'We haven't got much more have we?'

Anders shrugged and said nothing.

They had spent another full day going over what had happened. Checking on maps. Filling in descriptions and going over every word he could remember of what had been said to him.

Nicholson had stayed overnight on the Tuesday and had driven him up to London. He had chosen to go on his own to the club.

As he walked through the familiar streets from Leicester Square he felt suddenly happy. Everything was like it always had been. Lively, cheerful and tatty, and he remembered that Burinski's wife had said that Moscow was like someone had switched all the lights off. And for him the lights had just come on again.

As he walked into the club Joey was behind the counter. He looked up, his mouth agape.

'Boss! Mr Anders! We got a message you'd be back tonight, but I didn't believe it. I thought it was a cod. Are you OK?'

'I'm fine, Joey. Did someone pass on a message to Miss Price?'

Joey smiled. 'You bet. She's been in twice. Like a whirling bloody dervish. Half a tick.'

He reached under the counter and brought out a small package and then another. A long tubular something in gift wrapping.

'She brought that in for you. Said she'd be in at seven prompt.'

'What about Baldy? Is he coming in?'

Joey shuffled uncomfortably. 'Yes. He's been in every night. But he don't get on with your friend Mr Travers.'

Anders smiled. 'What happened?'

'Mr Travers tells him what he's got to play. Baldy didn't like that. And he didn't like what he had to play. I don't think the members were too cheerful either.'

'What kind of things?'

'Military marches and rock and roll.'

Anders laughed, picked up his parcels and went to the head of the stairs.

'I'll be in my place, Joey, if there are any calls.'

'Right, sir. Glad to see you back.'

His room looked just as he had left it except for a layer of dust everywhere. Travers obviously hadn't used it. If he had spent his time down in the club it was a wonder that only Baldy had put in his notice. Joe Travers had obviously run a tight ship.

The barman and two of the girls had blitzed through his room with duster and vacuum cleaner and in half an hour it looked reasonably civilized. Somebody had phoned Baldy, and as Anders walked into the club-room he was grinning over the top of the Bechstein as he played a lazy version of 'You were never lovelier'.

When Anders leaned on the lid of the piano Baldy Morton stopped playing.

'Where you been, boss? We all missed you.'

'Missed you too, Baldy.' He pulled a sheet of paper out of his pocket and slid it across the polished lid. It was Baldy Morton's resignation.

'Couldn't read your writing so you'd better keep it.'

The black man grinned and stuffed it into his pocket.

'Just so long as I don't have to play "Ol' man river" again.'

Anders laughed. 'Is that what he wanted?'

'Jesus no. He used to say, "And now one for you, Baldy. Let's have Ol' Man River." He was serious. Trying to be nice.'

Baldy looked past Anders and said quietly, 'Here's Candy. She's been like a ghost since you went away. Real bad, she's been.'

Anders stood up and turned, and she was hurrying through the chairs and tables to him, laughing and crying. And then her arms were round his neck and her wet mouth on his, her hand stroking the back of his neck. She pulled back her head and looked up at him.

'Oh, Tad. I couldn't wait till seven. I had to see you.' Her eyes were on his face. 'You've been ill, haven't you. What was it? You're so thin. Are you really better?'

'I'm fine, sweetie. And it's good to see you. Can you stay?'

'You bet. Did you like your pressies?'

'I've saved them until you came. Let's go up to my place.'

Baldy Morton played 'Love walked in' as they walked away. But nobody listened.

She sat on the settee, watching as he opened the smaller present. It was a digital watch with a built-in calculator. And the note said: 'I worked it out. It's nearly seven million seconds since I saw you.' The tall tube contained a single long-stemmed red rose and on the heart-shaped card it said, 'I love you so much, Candy,' and there were a lot of scrawled kisses.

The two phones had rung a dozen times before he reached out to the bedside lamp and switched it on. He leaned over her, kissing her gently. And then she frowned and sat up in the bed.

'What on earth are you wearing, Tad?'

And her hand was exploring the bandages round his chest. He pulled her hand gently away.

'It's nothing, sweetie.'

'And you've got a scar with stitch marks on the side of your jaw. Was it a car accident?'

'Something like that. Forget it. Let's go down and say hello to the lads.'

But her eyes were troubled. 'That's not from glass, Tad. It's too neat. That's from a knife, or something sharp.'

'Stop worrying, kid. I'm back, and you're here, and that's all that matters.'

'Can I stay with you tonight?'

'I wish you would. I'd like that.'

Her arms went round him, her head on his shoulder. 'You look ill, Tad. I wish I knew what was the matter.'

'Let's get dressed, honey.'

The club was full, and it was obvious that the word had gone around that the prodigal son was back. Candy's several regular admirers took one look at her happy, smiling face and decided that their propositions would be a waste of time that night. But they were romantic souls and had all sat through TV repeats of *The Sound of Music* at least three times, and knew that love would find a way. And there were, of course, six other pretty girls only too willing to listen to their immodest proposals. There had been champagne toasts from representatives of most criminal activities apart from pushers and ponces. They tended to be foreign and black, and club members were both conservative and prejudiced. Not entirely of course. Jews and Italians rated as true-blue Britishers and shared the same prejudices.

Anders and Candy Price had moved from table to table, sometimes just standing and chatting for a few minutes, sometimes sitting at a table where Anders knew the people well. Nobody asked where he had been and nobody failed to notice the long livid scar on his jaw. Members frequently went absent from time to time and it would have been reckoned as extremely bad form to enquire where they had been.

It was three o'clock before the club eventually closed, and Anders locked the doors and walked with Candy in the early morning street. Across Leicester Square, along Piccadilly and up Park Lane. Leicester Square still had its complement of riff-raff. Drug-pushers and addicts, pimps and their bedraggled girls, meths drinkers and down-and-outs with their bottles, and the cardboard boxes where they slept until the cleaning machines came round in a couple of hours time. But none of them were aggressive, and Piccadilly itself was almost empty except for a cruising taxi or two, and couples in evening dress strolling back to hotels.

Outside the Hilton and around the Dorchester the parking space was crammed with the Rolls Royces and Cadillacs of oil-rich Arabs, and alongside the Playboy an Arab in full regalia was haggling with a couple of teenage scrubbers as his chauffeur stood by the long-bodied Mercedes with its doors open in invitation.

Just before Marble Arch Anders waved down a taxi and back in Charing Cross Road the sky was beginning to show long fingers of light across Trafalgar Square and down towards the river.

Her mother had sent them a carved, peasant cot with rockers and lace frills, and Burinski sat reading *Pravda*, with one carpet-slippered foot gently rocking the baby as he slept. Inge Burinski was folding nappies and listening to the radio. It was tuned to West Berlin's RIAS and a performance of *The Gypsy Princess*. She had another month before she was due back at the office and Burinski himself seemed to be permanently on the supervision of German-speaking suspects held at Normannenstrasse. For both of them it was the happiest time of their lives. Sergei Vasiliyich Burinski was three months old and as he slept in his rustic cot his parents came as near to praying as their programmed minds would let them, that nothing would disturb their happy world.

Meynell had come down to London by train and taken a taxi to the Travellers. Sir Arthur was a member, and had booked them a private room, and Nicholson was to join them.

The skies were grey outside the big windows and as they waited for Meynell to arrive Nicholson sensed that Sir Arthur's mood matched the weather. He stood gazing into space, not noticing the comings and goings of the waiter who was bringing in the cold meats and bowls of salad so that they could eat and talk undisturbed.

Nicholson was relieved when Meynell was eventually shown up to the room but it seemed to do little to alleviate Sir Arthur's air of gloom. In his preoccupation he was a poor host and Meynell and Nicholson exchanged glances as they passed the plates to each other and French waved them aside. It was almost fifteen minutes after they started eating that Sir Arthur told them what he had planned. And when he finished he avoided looking at either of the others and sat in silence as he waited for a response.

In the beginning Meynell and Nicholson were under the impression that they were being asked to comment on a possible operation in its earliest planning stages. They spoke tentatively and negatively, as one in their doubts about the scheme. But as they chipped away at the logic or lack of logic behind the thinking they slowly came to realize that they had not been invited there to evaluate the plan but to give their approval. Not only was the operation already decided but it was operational. A special team had already been assembled and were undergoing intensive training in Northumberland. And its D-day was only twenty days ahead.

When Meynell, as a totally independent outsider, took the onus of criticism from Nicholson and pointed out how disastrous failure could be, Sir Arthur had almost snarled his rebuttal of the criticisms, and when Nicholson had added his own critical comments and tactfully pointed out the fact that the operation was directly inside his area of responsibility French had turned on him angrily for being 'a wet'.

Eventually, when it was obvious that nothing would change Sir Arthur's mind, they had suggested minor alterations to improve the operation's security and he had accepted them with bad grace. There had been a long and uncomfortable silence before Meynell asked in a quiet voice what he felt would be the repercussions inside SIS if the operation failed. Sir Arthur had thrown his unused table napkin on to the table with a theatrical flourish and said that he would resign.

An official car had been waiting for him and he marked his displeasure by not offering Nicholson a lift. In the taxi back to Century House Nicholson closed his eyes and wondered what lay behind the hare-brained scheme. If it failed, the repercussions would be so widespread that it was impossible to assess them. And if it succeeded the prize was not worth the having.

In his train back to Cambridge Meynell leafed through the pile of magazines that he had bought at the station bookstall. Luther Meynell bought magazines for the same reason that other men bought aspirins or double whiskies. The magazines covered yachting, photography, hi-fi and model trains. And the current issue of *Encounter* for reading in bed. Despite his carefully contrived diversions his mind did go back for fleeting moments to the room in the Travellers and French's grim face and grimmer news. But Meynell was older than Nicholson. In one area of life or another he had seen it all before. It was all too often desk-bound men who planned the bloodiest operations. War salved their consciences but in peacetime they paid with neuroses, and if they indulged their frustrations too often the price was psychoses.

Unlike some of his associates Meynell had considerable respect for French's brain. It had been sharp and penetrating in the old days and he had a sense of humour in those days too. Admittedly it was a mordant humour that made more enemies than friends, but it was usually the truth even if it was always so cruelly barbed. It was probably that wretched ex-wife of his who had done the damage. Thank God it had been short and sharp, not one of those long drawn out wars of attrition that bright minds so often indulged in. Maybe the security organizations should look more carefully at a man's private life. Undemocratic, uncivilized, it might be, but at certain levels many men's lives could depend on one man's state of mind. And at other levels years of painstaking diplomacy could be made worthless by the latest outburst of some virago. They checked for homosexuality, gambling, promiscuity and drinking, but they were rare enough or common enough in all men, to be at least visible and capable of being monitored. But how did you monitor the canker in a man's heart or a festering wound in his psyche? French thought that he was taking positive action but he wasn't. It was merely extravagant reaction, and in the Intelligence services more disasters flowed from precipitate reaction than any other cause.

Meynell sighed and turned back to his magazines and picked out the *New Statesman* and *Spectator*. He wondered why he bought the *NS* any longer. Except for Arthur Marshall and Roger Woddis it was virtually unreadable. Just nostalgia, and a trip down Memory Lane.

CHAPTER THIRTEEN

He sat waiting in the residents' lounge at the Connaught for half an hour and he had no doubt that the waiting was intentional. When the meeting had been arranged on the telephone she had told him how to get to the Connaught as if he was unlikely to know where it was.

Then one of the under-managers came up to him. 'Mr Anders?'

'Yes.'

He turned and looked towards a slim blonde woman standing at the entrance to the lounge.

'Mrs Crawley to see you, sir.'

Anders stood up and walked over to the woman. She had sad, haunted eyes and a forced social smile. She moved her handbag from one arm to the other to avoid shaking hands.

'Well, Mr Anders, we meet at last.'

'Would you like a drink or shall we go straight in and have lunch?'

'It's very kind of you but I have a lunch appointment. A drink, perhaps.'

Anders followed her to a table and two chairs in the furthest corner of the room. She asked for a Bloody Mary and he settled for a tomato juice. When he turned to look at her she was already looking at him.

'It was good of you to meet me, Mr Anders.' She paused. 'I'm sure you know that what I have to say will not be agreeable to you.'

Anders looked back at her without comment. A nerve quivered on her cheek and he realized that under the veneer of self-confidence she was, in fact, tense and nervous.

'Judy's very fond of you, I know that. And I know you love her, but it can't go on, Mr Anders. It really can't. She's a very young girl and she's not capable of coping with this sort of situation. She's utterly confused, you know. We've had long talks with her, my husband and I, and we've made quite clear where her duty and her future lie. She must go back to her husband.'

She waited while the glasses were put on the table and when they were alone she turned to look at him again. She managed a weak, mouth-trembling smile. She had said her piece. The worst was over.

'Why did he send you, Mrs Crawley? Why didn't he come himself?'

'He's very busy. Committees and so on. I'm sure you understand.'

'I understand all right, Mrs Crawley. I know from what I've heard that he's a bully, and bullies are always cowards. I'm sorry that you've had to do his dirty work for him. But if Judy agreed with you both, and your advice, you wouldn't be here. So what's the problem?'

She looked away for a moment and there were tears at the edges of her eyes. Then she turned back to look at him.

'You're a very attractive man, Mr Anders. I can understand why Judy wants to run off with you. I really can. But her father would never forgive her. She would be completely cut off from her family. She wouldn't like that, Mr Anders, I assure you.'

'Nobody would, Mrs Crawley. But she's twenty-nine and old enough to decide her own life. My impression is that she doesn't want to go back to her husband. And for the record she didn't run off with me. As you well know she had left her husband long before she even met me.'

'She would go back to him if you were not an alternative. Maybe not for love, but out of duty to us all.'

'So?'

'So we ask that you don't see her again.'

'What do you think that will do for her? To be rejected by someone she relies on.'

She shook her head slowly. 'I don't know, Mr Anders. I really don't know.' She turned her head to look at him, her hand on his arm. 'She would get over it. I know from my own experience. In the end the pain goes and we just live our lives.'

'I haven't seen Judy for over three months. I've been away for some time and I haven't contacted her since I came back. Perhaps she has already made up her mind to go along with your advice.'

She half-smiled. 'You know that isn't true, Mr Anders. Or I should not be here. She has tried to contact you several times but the man said you were away for a long time. If she knew you were back she would contact you.'

'We'd better wait and see if she does.'

'That means you won't cooperate, Mr Anders?'

'No. I won't cooperate.'

She stood up. 'I'd better go. I've done my best.'

He heard the echo of rehearsal in her words. That was what she would say to her husband.

'I'll walk to the door with you and get you a taxi.'

There was no need. There were two taxis waiting and as he opened the door for her she turned and looked at him. She said softly, 'I wish I could run away with you, too.' And she kissed him on the cheek.

It was almost two weeks later that Judy called him. She sounded cheerful enough, almost perky. She didn't ask where he had been or how he was. But she wanted to see him as soon as possible. When he suggested that she came round right away it seemed that it wasn't that urgent. It was Tuesday and could he make it the Thursday evening of the next week? He agreed, and speaking in almost a whisper she told him she loved him, and he said he loved her too.

It was only an hour later that he got the call from Peter Nicholson. They wanted him at a meeting urgently. A private room had been booked at the Hilton; could he be there in half an hour? He said he would be there.

It was raining very slightly as he got out of the taxi and walked towards the big glass doors. A security man at a small table near the entrance checked him perfunctorily and then he walked across the foyer to the lifts. The room number that Nicholson had given him was a suite on the fifth floor and it was Meynell who opened the door when he knocked.

'Come in, Tad. We're all here. A whisky?'

'A malt if you've got one. Neat.'

'Glenlivet or Glen Grant?'

'Glen Grant.'

Sir Arthur French and Nicholson already had drinks and as Anders took the glass it was French who set the ball rolling. Anders thought that he must have been on holiday. His eyes were bright and the pallor had gone from his cheeks. He looked alert and in control. He smiled a tight smile towards Anders who was conscious of the other two watching him intently.

'We've squared the account for you, Tad.'

'What account is that, Sir Arthur?'

'The account with the KGB.'

'I don't understand.'

'We've got Burinski.'

There was a long silence and then Anders said softly, 'How do you mean, you've *got* him?'

'We sent a team in. Picked him up and got him out.'

'When was this?'

'Five days ago. It all went very smoothly.'

'Well . . . congratulations.'

French caught the hesitation and knew that the others would have caught it too. It riled him, but the euphoria from the success of the operation was still pumping the adrenalin into his system when he talked or thought about it.

'We want you to do the interrogation. A thorough debriefing.'

'But after five days, surely you're well into it by now?'

'He's not been well, Tad. We had to get a doctor to him.'

'You mean he was beaten up?'

'Of course not. He's . . . well . . .' he turned to Nicholson who took the hint.

'He just folded, Tad. Shit-scared and shocked. Nobody's laid a finger on him.'

Anders looked from one to the other in disbelief. 'Why was this done?'

Sir Arthur didn't hesitate. 'When your operation failed it didn't remove the original reasons for wanting Burinski. We want to know what the *Spetsburo* are doing and if they're spreading their remit beyond West Germany. We need to know who the staff are and what the general set-up consists of.'

'I see.' Anders sounded unconvinced as he leaned back in his chair.

Meynell took up the threads. 'He's asked a number of times to see you, Tad.

We think he'd talk if you got alongside him.'

'You obviously made an impression on him.' French made it sound as if it were a fault on Anders' part rather than a virtue.

Anders looked at Meynell. 'I'm not a trained interrogator, Luther. It's not my line at all.'

'That doesn't matter. We can have a brief prepared for you to start with and you can be briefed each day after you've done your report. You will just be talking to him. It won't be a formal interrogation. When we see how it's going we'll tell you the areas we want you to explore.'

'Where is he?'

'At the safe-house in Ebury Street,' Nicholson said.

'I'd like to talk to him before I decide.'

'Decide what?' French's voice was sharp.

'Decide whether I want to do it or not.'

'It's an official request, Mr Anders.' French's cheeks were flushed with anger and he leaned forward aggressively. Anders looked back at him.

'So get somebody official to do it, Sir Arthur.'

There were several seconds of silence. Both Nicholson and Meynell would have admitted to themselves that they fleetingly enjoyed Sir Arthur's dilemma but Meynell was too mature to let him flounder even though he deserved it.

'I spoke to Burinski myself. Very briefly. He's very worried about his wife and child and I gathered from what he said that you spent quite a time with her and Burinski. He's certainly got great respect for you, and I think he'd talk to you, Tad. I'd guess he's a bit of a hero-worshipper.'

Anders nodded. 'Maybe. But that's why I want to talk to him before I decide.'

'What doubts have you got about doing it?'

Anders shrugged. 'I don't really know. It isn't a standard relationship.'

Meynell smiled. 'What's worrying you? The Judas factor?'

Anders smiled back. 'Maybe. I just don't know.'

Meynell turned to French. 'Why doesn't Peter take Tad over to see our friend and then we could talk again.'

Sir Arthur obviously resented someone else offering a solution, but it was a solution all the same, and he turned to Nicholson.

'Is that OK with you, Peter?'

'Yes.' Nicholson stood up, aware that French wasn't going to have the courtesy to ask if it was convenient for Anders. 'It won't take long, Tad.'

As they went down in the lift to the Hilton's underground carpark Nicholson said, 'Don't take any notice of French, Tad. Meynell and I were very much against this operation. We thought it would end up as a total disaster. French had got the bit between his teeth so we had no choice. And give him his due it went off exactly to plan. Mind you, it had a cast like Ben-Hur. And we do need to know a hell of a lot more about the *Spetsburo* and what it's up to. We didn't take too much interest when it seemed to be confined to West Germany but now they've started over here we've got to clobber them right at the start.'

'Who was it suggested a trade for me? I bet it wasn't Sir Arthur.'

'It was Luther Meynell, but French went along with it without any great pressure.'

'Why did they abandon the rules?'

'Guilt. They knew they'd not bothered enough. When it was evaluated, Stoppard's report was blistering. Tore it to pieces. Suggested an enquiry to see if undue pressure had been put on you that could explain why you agreed to go.'

He smiled without looking at Anders. 'They're bastards, I know. But not total bastards.'

Burinski was lying on the bed fully clothed. Nicholson left Anders to go in on his own. Anders walked over to the bed, pulled over one of the chairs and sat down.

'You wanted to see me, Vasili.'

The Russian turned his head to look at Anders' face. He looked for several minutes without speaking and then he said, 'I know from your face that you won't help me.'

'What help do you want?'

'I want to go back. I want to be released.'

'You must know that that isn't possible.'

'Why not?'

'You came over here and committed a political murder. You're KGB, and you're a trained assassin.'

'The man was a Jugoslav. He wasn't British.'

'Makes no difference. You know that.'

'You know what will happen to Inge and my child.'

'Tell me.'

'The child will be put in a State orphanage and Inge will be sent to a labour camp.'

'Why should they do that?'

'You know how it works, comrade. You know as well as I do.'

'Maybe they'll offer an exchange for you.'

'Never. Not for a *Spetsburo* man. They don't admit that the *Spetsburo* exists.'

'So what do you want me to do?'

Burinski sat up and swung his legs down to the floor, leaning forward to look at Anders.

'How if I talk with you, answer all your questions? Everything you want to know?'

'Go on.'

'You get my wife and son out, and you let us all live here. I could work for SIS.'

'Is that what you want?'

Burinski shrugged. 'There is nothing else.'

'They will probably say that they will only consider it after you've talked.'

'Then I don't talk.'

'You'll talk in the end, Vasili. People always do.'

'You didn't talk.'

Anders smiled. 'Kalin is an oaf. Beating up professionals doesn't make them talk, it makes them all the more determined not to cooperate. But people always do talk sooner or later. There are other ways than physical violence.'

'Would they have made you talk?'

'Who knows? Maybe in the end. It's possible.'

'So you won't help me?'

'I didn't say that. I told you what the official view might be. That you talk first, and then maybe something could be worked out depending on how cooperative you were.'

Burinski shook his head. 'No. First we make a bargain. Then I will talk.'

'I'll tell them what you've said.'

'You understand, don't you?'

'I understand both sides, Vasili. That's why I'm sure they won't agree.'

'Maybe you can negotiate some compromise for me.'

'Maybe. I'll think about it.'

And then quite suddenly Burinski was sobbing, his hands to his face, his body shivering as if he had an ague. For a few seconds Anders sat there, surprised by the outburst, and then he put his hand on the Russian's bowed shoulder, waiting for the sobs to die away.

He turned as he heard the door open. It was Nicholson, and Anders waved him away. It was a long time before Burinski's sobs died down and he lifted his head, his eyes closed and his face wet with his tears.

'What is it, Vasili?'

'I might just as well have killed them with my own hands. Both of them.' He was shaking his head as he stared at Anders. 'They don't deserve it. They have done nothing. Nothing at all.'

Anders said quietly. 'It's what happens to hundreds of people every day in the Soviet Union. You know that, Vasili. You're part of the system.'

'She had no idea what I did. She knew I was KGB but that was all. She'll die in a labour camp. What can I do? Tell me.'

'I'll talk to my people and see what they say.'

'You'll try very hard?'

'Of course.'

'She liked you so much. She was so impressed that you warned her not to talk in that place. She said you were a very special man.'

The tears were falling again and Anders put his hand on Burinski's knee.

'Have some sleep and I'll see what I can do.'

Burinski nodded, swallowing his tears, unable to speak.

They had been away just over an hour, and Meynell and French were still talking in the suite. They fell silent as Anders sat down.

'He's in a state about his wife and child. Afraid that she'll be sent to the Gulag and the child to an orphanage.'

Sir Arthur shrugged. 'He's probably right.'

'He says that he'll talk with me, answer any questions we ask, provided he can stay here and we get his wife and child out.'

Sir Arthur smiled. 'And if we don't?'

'He says he won't talk at all.'

Meynell stood up. 'D'you think he means it, Tad?'

'I think he meant it but I'd guess that he'll talk in the end. He's not trained as an agent. He's an assassin and nothing more. His victims were unarmed and taken by surprise. You don't need all that much guts to do that. Just a programmed mind. But if he didn't talk voluntarily I'd say it would be a very slow process.'

'How long, Tad?'

'Months. Six or seven. Isolation treatment, and the rest of it. He'd hope that his not talking would filter back to Moscow and might help his wife.'

French leaned back in his chair. 'Well there's no question of getting the wife and child out. They're probably not there now. And if she were I wouldn't authorize it.'

Anders stood up. 'Peter can tell him tomorrow, then. I'd say he needs a psychiatrist right now or he'll be in a hopeless state in a few days.'

As Anders turned to leave French said, 'Mr Anders.'

Anders turned and looked at him. 'Yes?'

'Sit down. Mr Anders, I haven't finished.'

'I have, Sir Arthur. Let someone else deal with him.'

'Tad. Sit down please.' Meynell was looking at him with a quizzical look, his head on one side. 'Let's be sensible, Tad. Let's talk it out.'

Anders sighed, walked back to the chair and sat down.

Meynell said, 'He *is* willing to talk with you.'

'Yes.'

'Everything? Not just answer questions?'

'Yes, he'll cooperate fully.'

'But only if we get out his wife and child?'

'So he says.'

'You think he means it?'

'Yes. He's very dependent on his wife. He loves her. It's as simple as that. He thinks of it as if he had killed them himself.'

'And if we don't do the deal, you think he will talk but it may take months?'

'Yes.'

Meynell looked across at Sir Arthur. 'How urgent is this, Arthur?'

'For heaven's sake, Luther, I got the Minister's agreement to mount this operation because we need to know about the *Spetsburo*. Bonn has been raising hell for months, threatening to go it alone. We need to show results right now.'

'*Could* we get them out?'

'If they're in Berlin it's possible. But they'll be under constant surveillance. They may take them to Moscow. Even in Berlin it would be well nigh impossible without losing lives.'

'We ran that risk to get *him* out.'

Sir Arthur looked up sharply. '*I* ran the risk, Luther. And I ran the risk despite your and Nicholson's wet-blanket attitude because I thought it was necessary. I don't feel this is necessary. Who the hell is this . . . this criminal, to lay down conditions?'

Meynell said softly, 'He's the man who can tell us what we want to know. He's the man who can make your operation a total success.'

Sir Arthur gestured impatiently. 'For God's sake don't butter me up, Luther. I'm too old for that.'

Meynell turned to the other two. 'I wonder if you two would care to leave us for a bit. Say half an hour.'

Anders and Nicholson strolled down to the first floor and ordered a drink. As they sat in the lounge the pianist was playing 'Some Enchanted Evening' but you could barely hear it for the noise. It was louder and shriller than at the club.

They lingered a little longer than the half hour and then walked back up instead of taking the lift. Meynell looked cheerful as he let them in, and after they had sat down French said his piece.

'Luther and I have gone over this wretched situation a dozen times. He's convinced me that we should go along with Burinski's demands. But with one condition.' He wagged a monitory finger at Anders. 'You tell him we will use our best endeavours to get his wife and child out, but there's no guarantee. Is that understood?'

Anders shrugged. 'I'll put it to him and see what he says.'

Sir Arthur opened his mouth to speak and then changed his mind.

Meynell said quickly, 'Why not go back on your way to the club and put him out of his misery?'

Nicholson said, 'I'll drive you, Tad, and then take you on to your place.'

Anders sat without speaking as Nicholson drove him back to Ebury Street. As he got out he looked at his watch and could hardly believe it was only eight-thirty.

Burinski's face was white and drawn as he saw Anders come into the room.

'I've talked to them, Vasili. Provided you cooperate fully, they will agree to what you want. But we want everything you know. Names, backgrounds, organization, everything. You understand?'

He thought for a moment that Burinski was going to faint and then the Russian said, 'My God. My God. I thank you with all my heart. I really do. I'll cooperate any way you want.'

'It will take time to get them out, Vasili. They will be under twenty-four hour surveillance for some time.'

'I understand, comrade. We are professionals, you and I. Your people's word is all I ask.'

'Get some sleep and I'll see you in a couple of days.'

'I'll start making notes right away, and . . . what can I say? I can rest again.'

Nicholson drove Anders to Leicester Square and he walked on his own to the club. He was probably the only man in the world for whom the stretch from Piccadilly Circus to Charing Cross Road was home.

Back at the club he bathed and shaved and changed into shirt and slacks. As he poured himself a whisky he pressed his hand against the pain in his chest. Seeing Burinski had brought all those black thoughts back again. The bastards had thrown him to the wolves unprotected, but when they wanted something it was suddenly possible to mount a full-scale operation. Time and expense no object. But they *had* traded for him. He had to give them that. Why had he joined them and not made it clear to Burinski that if they couldn't get her and the child out he'd have wasted his breath? But that sort of thinking was crazy. The bastard was a KGB man who specialized in political murder. Burinski would spend no time worrying about other people's wives and children. And Burinski himself would be alive and free, and that was a hell of a lot more than he could expect. Then the pain stabbed at the back of his head. He reached for the bottle of pills that the SIS doctor had given him after the check-up. He'd said that he'd have pain for another six months but the attacks would gradually be more spaced out. If they got unbearable despite the pills he'd have to go in and they would do an exploratory operation. He took the two pills with a sip of whisky and then he slowly stood up and stretched his arms. Ignore it and it would go away.

The club was half empty that night and they closed just after midnight. He sat with Candy looking at a late film on TV and they were in bed before one.

When he heard the shouting he jumped out of bed and staggered to the window. But he couldn't find the window and then a light went on and he shielded his eyes. There was sweat pouring down his body but he was cold and shivering as he reached out to steady himself. And there was a naked girl saying something a long way away. As his eyes focused he saw that it was Candy but his eyes still searched for the window. There was no window. He was in his bedroom and it didn't have a window. And the shouting had died away.

'Tad. What's the matter, love? What is it. Come and lie down.'

She led him to the bed and as he sat there she pulled the duvet round his shoulders.

'Shall I phone for a doctor, Tad?'

'It woke me up, the shouting.'

'It was you, Tad. You were talking and shouting.'

He turned his head slowly to look at her. 'What was I on about?'

'I don't know. You weren't speaking English. I couldn't understand. You sounded afraid.'

'I'm OK, sweetie. It must have been a nightmare.'

'You're poorly, Tad. You need a doctor.'

He looked at her pretty face, her big eyes were frightened but full of concern as they looked back at him.

'You know something, kid?'

'No. What?'

'I love you, Candy Price. I certainly do.'

He lay back on the bed and as she covered him up she knew that whatever it was it had passed. His big, deep chest was rising and falling evenly, and he was already asleep.

She let him sleep until ten. The outside phone with the little box beside it rang several times but she didn't answer it.

When she woke him he seemed quite normal but he didn't talk much as he sat drinking the black coffee. As he put the cup and saucer on to the bedside table he turned to look at her.

'What day is it today?'

'Thursday.'

'Are you doing anything special the next few days?'

She smiled. 'I never do anything special, Tad, you know that.'

'How about we go away for a few days. Somewhere quiet.'

'Both of us?'

'Of course.'

'Oh, I'd love that. Where shall we go?'

He smiled. 'It's a surprise.'

'Your phone has rung two or three times.'

He looked alarmed. 'You didn't answer it?'

'Of course not.'

'Good girl. D'you need to get clothes or anything?'

'Of course I do.'

'How long will it take?'

'If I go now I could be back by twelve.'

'OK. You do that.'

Anders put down the hood of the white MGC and they both felt relaxed as they headed down the A21 as far as the turning to Battle where they stopped for lunch. It was mid-afternoon when Anders pulled up outside the cottage in the narrow lane, to open the two gates to the short driveway. When he had parked the car he got their bags out of the boot.

Candy was standing by the car looking at the cottage and when Anders joined her she said, 'Who does it belong to, Tad?'

'Me.'

She turned to look at his face. 'How long have you had it?'

'Six, seven years, I don't remember exactly.'

'Who knows about it?'

'Nobody. Just you and me.'

'It's beautiful, Tad. And it's so quiet here.'

'Let's go in and make ourselves at home. It'll be a bit dusty.'

The cottage was built of local stone with a thatched roof over two dormer windows. On the ground floor there were two small windows set in the whitewashed wall and the door was solid oak with old-fashioned wrought-iron fittings. Inside there was one medium-sized living room with heavy oak beams and alongside was a small modern kitchen and a bathroom. A narrow staircase led to the two bedrooms upstairs.

From the front of the cottage was half-hidden from the lane by a weeping willow on the long narrow lawn. At the back was a sloping lawn with a dozen or so fruit trees; and a white post and rail fence marked off the boundaries from the fields that sloped gradually down to the valley.

Immediately outside the kitchen door was an area of bricks in herring-bone fashion and an old oak bench against the wall. They sat there drinking tea from china mugs, the girl's hand resting on Anders' thigh.

'It's so beautiful, Tad. It's like a cottage from a fairy story.'

'Is it too quiet for you? Too isolated?'

'Of course not. That's what makes it so good.'

'We've got four days, sweetie, before we have to go back.'

'Why didn't you ever tell anyone about it?'

'I didn't want anyone to know about it.'

'And nobody's ever been here before?'

'No. Just me.'

'How often do you come here?'

'Not often. Four or five times a year.'

'What do you do?'

'Nothing much. Read, sleep, eat and think.'

She put her hand up to his cheek and turned his head to look at her. 'Why did you ask me to come with you?'

'I just like being with you.'

'Why?'

He sighed. 'Because you're pretty, because I like making love to you, and because you care about me.'

'I do care about you, Tad. So much.'

'I care about you too, kid. But I'm old enough to be your father.'

'Why should that matter, for God's sake?'

'It doesn't. I don't know why I said it.'

'I do.'

'Why?'

'Because something happened to you while you were away. And you're depressed, and you *should* see a doctor. You're very low, Tad, and you shouldn't be.'

'Why not?'

'Tad, love, you own the club, you make a good living, everybody likes you. You're a special kind of man and you always will be. You'll be fine again when you've had a few days rest.'

Anders stood up. 'Let's go and look at the sea.'

She smiled. 'I'll have to buy you a bucket and spade.'

They ate at small country inns and small cafés on the coast, they made love and slept for long peaceful hours, and as the girl had predicted, Anders recovered his equilibrium. They sat in the sun on their last morning, on the bench outside the kitchen door, Candy reading a Mills and Boon romance and Anders sitting watching her as she turned the pages slowly, intent on the story.

'Candy.'

She put the book on her lap and turned, smiling, to look at him.

'What is it, Tad?'

'Will you marry me, Candy?'

Her smile faded and she looked at him, surprise and disbelief on her face.

'You don't mean that, Tad.'

'I do.'

'Why me?' she said softly.

'Because you care about me, and I care about you.'

She sat looking at his face for a long time. 'Sometimes I wish you weren't such an honest man.'

'Why?'

'I'll tell you some day.'

'You haven't answered me.'

She shook her head. 'What about Judy?'

'What about her?'

'You care about her too.'

'She doesn't care about me. I think she'll go back to her husband sooner or later.'

'Did you ever ask her to marry you?'

He sighed, 'Yes.'

'What did she say?'

'She said yes.'

'But never quite got around to doing anything about it. Like getting a divorce for instance.'

He half-smiled but didn't reply. She saw the dullness come back into his eyes and said quickly, 'So let me be truthful, Tad Anders, just like you are. I'd do anything to be married to you. Absolutely anything. But I happen to love you. Really love you. So I'd want to be sure that I'd make you happy. I'd willingly marry you tomorrow even if I thought that I was going to be unhappy every day of my life, but I wouldn't want that for you. I'd like to walk round Soho right now, shouting out – "Tad Anders has asked me to marry him. The wedding's next Saturday". But I want to be sure, my love, that it's going to be right for you.'

'So?'

'So I'll give you my answer in a few weeks. I desperately want it to be yes. At the worst it'll be "let's wait a bit longer".'

'What do you want to do now?'

She smiled and kissed him on the mouth. 'I'll give you one guess.'

He smiled, stood up, and took her hand.

'Did you ever meet Sudoplatov?'

'I attended lectures by him but I never talked with him as an individual.'

'When did he take over the *Spetsburo*?'

'During the war he was in charge of the Fourth Directorate of the NKVD and when the *Spetsburo* was set up he was in charge from the start.'

'When was that?'

'In 1946.'

'Where does it operate?'

'Mainly Germany, Austria and Switzerland but it's allowed to operate anywhere.'

'Are only Soviets recruited?'

'All supervision is by Soviets but a lot of East Germans and Czechs are recruited for physical violence.'

'How are they recruited?'

'They're almost all criminals and they're recruited from the prisons.'

'What was the Fourth Directorate responsible for in the war?'

'They trained and operated the partisans for espionage and assassination behind the German lines.'

Anders looked at the notes on his clipboard, holding the pause button on the tape-recorder.

'According to our records the *Spetsburo* was disbanded in June 1953. Is that incorrect?'

'Students were not told about that but it was well-known that it was disbanded. It was only for a few months, because Khrushchev decided that he needed it. It became the 9th section of the First Chief Directorate, and when the KGB was founded in 1954 the *Spetsburo* became Department 13 of the First Chief Directorate.'

'Tell me about Kalin. How long has he been *Spetsburo*?'

'He isn't *Spetsburo*. He's 2nd Department of second Chief Directorate. He's a deputy on the British Commonwealth desk.'

'Did you know in advance that I was going to pick you up?'

'Others did. I wasn't told beforehand.'

'How did they know about me?'

'We were using a double-agent. He was told to do surveillance on me by one of your people and he kept the KGB informed. They weren't sure who you were or what you were going to do but they cleared all the taxi stands around the area. You took a taxi that was KGB and you were under surveillance all the time after that.'

'Let's go back to your training period.'

'Can I have a rest, comrade? I find it hard work trying to remember all these details.'

'OK. I'll raise some tea for you.'

Anders took the tape-recorder and the technical sergeant took off the spool and laced up a clean one. The used spool covered fourteen hours of interrogation.

Tape spools were analysed during the night. Sliced into half hour segments they were listened to by a team, and by the following morning a new list of questions or re-checks was ready for Anders. There were few re-checks because it wasn't an interrogation, it was a voluntary debriefing. But despite Burinski's cooperation discrepancies arose and had to be checked because SIS's information on the *Spetsburo* was sparse and the CIA were to be offered the transcript in exchange for their information on both the *Spetsburo* and the *Kamera*.

Anders and Burinski kept at it day after day, four or five hours a day.

It sometimes happens that an interrogating officer who carries out a long interrogation with a subject gradually comes to identify with the man. Their recruitment, training and work was often almost identical. But Anders felt no such identification with Burinski. As a man he despised him, and the total ruthlessness of the *Spetsburo* and its controllers aroused the anti-Soviet, and anti-Russian feelings that most Poles felt for the country that had ravaged Poland so many times in its history.

SIS was ruthless when it needed to be, and Anders was one of its operators, but the *Spetsburo* wasn't the same. SIS operated against the foreign enemies of Britain, but the *Spetsburo* killed and tortured for political reasons just to keep the thugs of the Politburo in power. But Anders was shrewd enough, and professional enough, to keep his distaste for the man well hidden. The West Germans had been placated by the operation that lifted Burinski and had asked for the opportunity of interrogating him themselves, but so far their request had been diplomatically fobbed off, at least until Anders had finished.

CHAPTER FOURTEEN

Luther Meynell sat in the corner seat of the carriage looking out over the flat East Anglian landscape. And as he looked at the peaceful countryside he tried to assemble a rational argument. But there *was* no rational argument. When he and French had talked together that evening at the Hilton they had both known what they were doing. They had never said it out loud even to each other, but they knew it all the same. All that had mattered was getting the Russian to talk. If he didn't, then huge resources in time and money had been wasted. And what also mattered was that they needed the information to head off the West Germans from going it alone. Going it alone would have given Moscow just the excuse it was looking for to try and take over the whole of Berlin. Maybe they wouldn't have done it, but with that sort of provocation they'd have gone on the rampage somewhere. And the Russian would only talk if they agreed to his totally unreasonable demands.

Meynell reached for his copy of *The Times* and opened it, turning to the letters page. Then with a sigh he folded the paper and tossed it on to the empty seat opposite. All that rationalizing was a lot of hogwash. Both he and French had known that there was no question of getting out the woman and the child. Even if the man had come over voluntarily as a defector it wouldn't have been on. And to mount an operation on that scale for such a purpose would have been preposterous. To do it for an assassin who had been picked up and brought over by their own people was out of the question.

Both he and French had been sure that the wife and child would have been moved to Moscow, and nobody would know better than Burinski himself that they would be crazy to try and get her out. And they could have emphasized the risk to the woman's life and the dire punishment she and the child would suffer if the operation went wrong. But she hadn't been removed to Moscow, she was still there with the child in East Berlin. The evaluation team had even put up the theory that the KGB had left them in East Berlin as a bait, and a check on whether Burinski had talked or not. They could have decided that if he talked he may try to make a bargain with SIS about getting them out, and if an attempt was made the trap would close and then there would be yet another set of problems.

But none of it, the rationalizing, the actual facts, could hide the fact that Burinski had talked and they had no intention of lifting a finger to get out his wife and child. What nobody would know, or at least what nobody could prove, was the fact that both he and French had known this when Anders and Nicholson came back that night. Neither he nor French had said it out loud. But both of them had known what was in the other's mind.

Nicholson wouldn't like it, but he would accept the facts of life and console himself that he had been no part of the deception. He had no idea of how Anders would take it. Anders would feel differently because he knew the wife. He had a relationship with both of them. He would probably feel that he had been deceived or exploited. And then that Slav temperament could explode in all directions. On the other hand Burinski had watched the KGB thugs beat up Anders. *He* hadn't offered Anders any helping hand. Anders wouldn't have forgotten that. He could be reminded of it too. Maybe he would take it all in his stride. He doubted it, but it was to give it that chance that French had asked *him* to tell Anders. And Meynell had wrung out of French an assurance that there would be no come-back on Anders. Now that SIS had all the *Spetsburo* information that Burinski could give, French wanted the whole affair forgotten. Burinski wouldn't be tried, he would merely be a prisoner in that grim, silent house on the west coast of Scotland. He'd be there until he died. And as far as Sir Arthur was concerned he could be dead already. He just wanted it all over and done with. Burinski out of the way, the information in the files, and Anders appeased.

At Liverpool Street Meynell walked slowly towards the taxi rank. He looked up at the glassed-in roof but it was too grimy to give any indication of the weather outside. He had slept fitfully for the last half hour of the journey but his mind felt duller rather than brighter. He wondered for a moment why people started campaigns to preserve monstrosities like this station. It was probably because they never used the damn place themselves.

The taxi dropped him at the corner of Great Newport Street and he walked the rest of the way to the club. The doors were open and there was a bucket and vacuum cleaner in the middle of the floor. He reached over to the counter and pressed the bell marked 'Press', and waited. He looked around at the walls with their blistered brown paint, the primitive row of hangers for coats, and an umbrella propped on a saucer in the far corner of the room. It was hard to connect Anders and SIS, and Berlin and Moscow, with this incongruous place. He pressed the bell again and looked at the centrefolds stacked up on the wall behind the counter. They were curling at the bottom edges but the young girls were really beautiful. He wondered if the photographer had sex with the models afterwards. And then a young man wearing an old blue anorak came in from the street.

'You waiting to join, mister? There's a waiting list at the moment nearly . . .'

'Will you tell Mr Anders that his visitor has arrived, please?'

'What name shall I give?'

'Just be kind enough to give him that message.'

The youth picked up one of the phones and pressed one of the square buttons. 'Your visitor's here, boss.'

He listened then put down the phone and looked at Meynell.

'He says to go right up, sir. He's waiting for you.'

Meynell nodded and made his way carefully down the main stairs and then along the corridor that reeked of Lysol and urine and an obnoxious smelling air-freshener.

Anders was waiting for him at the top of the far set of stairs.

Inside the room Anders turned to his visitor.

'A sherry, Luther?'

'I'll have a whisky if I may.'

When they were both sitting Anders said, 'Peter Nicholson said you were down for some academic meeting.'

Meynell shook his head, 'I wish I was. I'm down here to talk with you.'

He saw Anders' eyes narrow like a dog expecting a blow and hated even more what he was about to do. Anders had grown to expect anything from SIS to be unpleasant. Meynell shifted in his chair and drew a deep breath.

'I've got something unpleasant to say, Tad. I've no idea what your reaction will be except that I don't expect you'll like it. All I ask is that you'll think about it as unemotionally as you can before you reach your conclusions.'

'Sounds pretty grim, Luther, you'd better tell me what it is.'

'There's no chance of getting out Burinski's wife and child.'

There was a long silence as they looked at each other.

'Where is she?'

'Still at their flat in East Berlin.'

'So what's the problem?'

Meynell sighed. 'Two problems. We've had an evaluation team report that suggests that she's being left there to see if we try and get her out. If we do, they'll know that we're doing it because Burinski has talked. It's taken for granted that the flat is under continuous surveillance and that any attempt to get them out would fail. Disastrously.'

'You said there were two problems. What's the other?'

'There was never any intention to get them out. We just wanted Burinski to talk.'

Anders poured himself another drink before he looked back at Meynell.

'So you and French lied to me. Deliberately.'

'I'm afraid so, Tad. We didn't discuss it or agree to lie. I think we just both separately knew that it wasn't on, but we needed Burinski's information. And we didn't *promise* to do it.'

'You said we would do our best.'

'I know. I said that myself. It was a lie, and I knew it was a lie. I had a vague hope that things might turn out so that it wasn't a lie but I knew in my mind that it was a vain hope. You must blame me, not French.'

'Why not French?'

'I said the words. He didn't.'

'You were speaking for the two of you. He didn't contradict you.'

'I think maybe he would have told you right out that he wouldn't authorize it. I spoke up because I felt he was in an aggressive mood and I wanted to head him off by saying my piece.'

'Why, Luther?'

'I felt at that moment I was doing the right thing.'

'And what do you feel now?'

'It's probably a terrible thing to say, Tad, but I still think it was the right thing.'

'The end justifies the means? Hitler's old motto.'

Meynell didn't respond although philosophical and historical refutations crowded into his mind. At least Anders was under control so far.

Anders said quietly, 'And when are you going to tell Burinski?'

'Whoever it is, it won't be me, Tad. It has to be somebody official.'

Anders smiled grimly. 'That lets me out, then.'

'I suppose it does.'

Meynell was playing it by ear and he didn't like it. He'd come expecting anger and accusations and all he had hoped for was to damp them down. His scenario had not gone beyond that.

'What will they do with Burinski?'

'He'll go up to the place in Scotland.'

'I suggest that you prepare for a serious psychological shock when he's told.'

'The question of telling him hasn't been discussed with me. Has he finished talking as far as you're concerned?'

'We've covered everything except their communications system.'

'Would you be willing to carry on until you've got that?'

'I'd consider it if I was specifically asked to.'

Meynell looked across at him. 'Would you be prepared to break the news to Burinski instead of it being done formally?'

'And tell him we lied to him?'

'Would you really need to, Tad? Would it do any good? Wouldn't it be better to point out that if we made any attempt even to contact her she'd probably go straight to the Gulag because they'd know he'd talked?'

Anders shrugged. 'Who knows?'

'But you would cooperate?'

'Probably.'

'How about I take you to lunch?'

'I'm taking my girlfriend to lunch, but thanks.'

'How is she? Judy or Julie isn't it? I'm bad with girls' names.'

Anders smiled. 'Her name's Candy.'

'Sounds American.'

'Bethnal Green, actually.'

Anders walked with Meynell to the street door and after Meynell had merged into the crowds Anders walked back to his rooms and poured himself another whisky. He sat in his armchair with his feet up on the coffee table. He sat there composing a dozen variations of a resignation letter as he boiled with anger. Not about Burinski. He had known exactly how he would deal with that from the moment Meynell told him of the lie. His anger was at the indifference and callousness of people like Sir Arthur and Meynell. Especially Sir Arthur. That dried-up old maid, with his cold, venomous little mind. A mind that could throw him away with the same lack of compunction as he threw away Burinski. Not only him and Burinski, but anybody who wasn't needed or didn't fit in. For once he'd teach the bastards a lesson. And he'd do it their way.

French sat listening intently as Meynell reported on his meeting with Anders, and when he had finished he sat silent for several minutes, fiddling with a gilt letter-opener on his desk. When he looked up he said, 'Sounds as though you did surprisingly well, Luther. I'd expected one of those theatrical explosions of Slav temperament. My word is my bond and all that.'

'Not at all. He was calm and sensible, and as cooperative as any man could be in the circumstances.'

'I wonder why?'

'Oh, Arthur, let's not look our gift horse in the mouth. He surely deserves a pat on the back, not suspicion of his motives. He must despise us even if he understands. He could have left us high and dry *and* felt justified in doing so.'

'I expect you're right.' French paused. 'Will you talk to him? Ask him to continue until he's got all we want and then tell Burinski. He's getting off very lightly, is Burinski. Anders wouldn't have ended up in a Russian manor house with hotel food and women and the rest of it.'

'Yes. I'll talk to him.'

'You do whatever you think fit, but let me know if there are any real problems. I'd like to get it all over and done with.'

Meynell phoned Anders and found him still calm if slightly distant. Anders estimated that the rest of the debriefing would take a couple of weeks, maybe three, and had even thought that he might eventually get Burinski to go over the assassination on the spot. Checking the route and the houses where he had stayed. Meynell was relieved that Anders was taking it all in his stride.

Judy phoned and suggest they met in the bar at the Café Royal.

He got there early and ordered a whisky for himself and a Campari and soda for her. She kept him waiting for ten minutes and then swept in through the door, smiling as she hurried towards him. And suddenly he realized why he had always been held by her. She reminded him of Marie-Claire. Not her face, but her style. The clothes she wore, the way she walked and sat, and the movements of her arms. She was wearing a white dress that he guessed was Courrèges, her hair had been styled and set, and her feet in the black, pointed, court shoes looked small and neat. Several heads turned to look as she hurried towards him and then she was putting her mouth up to be kissed in a cloud of Chanel 19. As she sat down she draped a silver fox stole over the next chair, turning quickly to look at his face.

'You look very fit, Charles. Is this mine?' And she sipped the drink and made a smiling moue of disapproval.

'They're slipping Charles, too much soda. Tell me what you've been doing.'

He smiled. 'Nothing much. I was away for some time.'

'What was it? Business?'

'Yes. How about you?'

She looked at him, smiling. 'What on earth did you say to Mama when you two met?'

'Nothing special. Why?'

She laughed. 'You certainly made a hit there. She thinks you're fantastic. Not in front of Daddy, of course. But she didn't entirely desert you. Said you were very presentable. She said dishy to me. Said you looked reliable, and nothing like she had imagined.'

Anders smiled. 'What did he say?'

'Oh, dismissed it of course. Silly, impressionable woman. He should have dealt with you himself and all that sort of guff. What did you think of her?'

He laughed. 'It wasn't quite the sort of meeting where people are at their best. She was obviously scared of the whole thing. She said her piece. I was very uncooperative but when she felt that she had completed her task she was charming.'

'She said it was a pity I hadn't married you in the first place and then there would have been no problems.'

'So now what?'

'Can I have another Campari? So now what? I'm just going to sit it out, Charles. Mama's on my side and she'll keep working on him. She does have some influence. She'll try and find some way of making it all seem more tolerable.' She smiled and reached out to straighten his tie. 'Why the parachutes?'

'It's a club tie. Special Forces Club.'

'D'you like my dress?'

'It's beautiful. Is it Courrèges?'

'Of course. Mama bought it for me. I put it on specially for you. It's only the second time I've worn it.'

'It suits you. You look very pretty.'

'Thank you, kind sir.' She turned to look around. 'They're taking their time with that drink.' She turned back to him. 'Are you going to feed me?'

'I've booked us a table in the Grill.'

'Lovely. By the way, we met some man who knows you. I can't remember his name.'

'Where was it?'

'At the Inn on the Park. Some learned society or other. Frightful bore but good food. Daddy pumped him about you but the old boy wasn't the pumpable kind. A bit old in the tooth but majestic; piercing eyes that kind of looked into you. I think his name was Mendl or maybe Menzies the Scottish way. Although I would have said there was Jewish blood somewhere there. Professor Mendl. Does that ring a bell?'

'Was it Meynell? Professor Luther Meynell.'

'That was it.'

And Anders smiled to himself at the thought of Luther Meynell's reaction to being described as 'an old boy' and 'long in the tooth'.

They ate and enjoyed a long pleasant meal and she retailed the gossip of embassy circles. Who was sleeping with whom, who had been caught out, who was making big money on the side because he could get licences that weren't obtainable, and even the amusing story of a man who loved his wife.

Her parents were still in town, still staying at the French Embassy and she was staying with them. She asked for a brandy, and as she sipped it Anders said, 'When can I see you again?'

Her big brown eyes looked back at him. 'I can't for the next two weeks but I'll phone you as soon as they've gone. I love you, Charles, and I think my Mama loves you too. But I'd better go, honey.'

He walked with her into Regent Street and the doorman waved down a taxi. As Anders opened the taxi door she slid her arms round his neck and put up her mouth to be kissed.

It was almost four in the morning as Anders put the canvas holdall and the case into the boot of the white MGC and turned the key in the lock. He had checked all the things a dozen times. He lifted the bonnet and unclipped the distributor head and slid it into his jacket pocket.

The alarm woke him at eight o'clock and he dressed slowly before he went into the small kitchen and pressed two fresh oranges for a drink. He drove up to the safe-house at Ebury Street just after then, and told Burinski that he was taking him to Hammersmith to go over the details of the assassination. Burinski looked worried.

'Why do we need to do this when I've gone over all the details with you so many times?'

'When you see the various places it might remind you of something, Vasili. Something you'd forgotten.'

'I'm sure it won't.'

'We'll see. Anyway a trip outside might do you good.'

They were almost at Bromley before Burinski turned in his seat. 'Why does it take so long? I don't recognize anywhere. Where are we?'

Anders smiled. 'We're just having a little ride, Vasili. You must be tired of being cooped up in that place for so long.' Burinski looked at him only half-believing, but he settled back in his seat.

As they turned off the Hastings road at the sign for Battle, Anders glanced at Burinski and saw that he was asleep. He woke as Anders drove through the open gates that led up to the cottage garage.

As Anders took the case out of the boot he handed it to Burinski.

'That's yours, my friend.'

He reached for the holdall, pulled down the boot cover, took Burinski's arm and led him to the front door of the cottage.

For a fleeting moment he felt sad as they walked into the sitting room and he remembered his days there with Candy, but he brought his mind back to what he was doing and walked over to the drinks cabinet. He poured them both a large, neat whisky, handed one to Burinski and pointed to one of the chairs and sat in the facing one. He smiled and lifted his glass.

'*Na zdrovye.*'

Burinski smiled. '*Na zdrovye.*'

'I want to talk to you, Burinski. A serious talk. OK?'

Burinski nodded. 'OK.'

'If I hadn't been exchanged what would have happened to me?'

'I guess you'd have ended up in the Gulag.'

'How long for?'

Burinski shrugged. 'Who knows, comrade? Twenty years, thirty years. Maybe for life.'

'Or maybe I would get one of those special injections and then they would bury me in that secret place near Smolensk. Yes?'

'Sometimes that happens.'

'If Moscow had been very generous and allowed me to choose between the injection and the Gulag which do you think I would have chosen?'

Burinski shrugged. 'How should I know that?'

'I said which do you *think* I should have chosen?'

'The Gulag.'

'Why?'

'Because you would think that maybe you could escape.'

'Would you have helped me escape?'

'My God. It would be impossible. How could I do that? Nobody has ever escaped. If they get out of a camp they die of exposure and starvation.'

'If I had talked to Kalin or you, what would have happened to me then?'

Burinski shifted uneasily in his seat and sipped his whisky before he looked back at Anders.

'The same. It would have made no difference.'

'They wouldn't have brought my girlfriend from London and let us live in Moscow?'

'No. That could never happen.'

Anders looked at Burinski's face and said softly, 'So why did you think that we should get your wife and child out and bring them to London?'

All the colour drained from Burinski's face and his hand trembled as he reached out to put his glass on the table.

'You mean you lied to me. And the man Nicholson lied?'

'No. We both told you the truth. Or what we thought was the truth. Other people lied to us.'

He saw the open fear in Burinski's eyes.

'You're going to kill me, comrade, that's why you've brought me here.'

'No. I'm not.'

'What then?'

'I'm going to help you escape.'

Burinski shook his head. 'I don't believe that.'

Anders produced the canvas holdall. 'There are two passports for you in there. There are other documents too, and there's money. Dollars and pounds.' He pointed at the case. 'There are new clothes for you in there.'

Burinski made no move to check what was in the holdall or the case but sat looking at Anders.

'What happens?'

'I'm going to get you out of the country. I'll go with you part of the way, and tonight I'll tell you what you should do when you get to Berlin.'

'Why do they let me go?'

Anders smiled. 'They aren't letting you go, Vasili. *I'm* letting you go.'

'Without permission? Against your orders?'

Anders nodded. 'Yes.'

'And what happens to you?'

'I'll have to wait and see. I don't think anything will happen to me.'

'What news is there of Inge and the baby.'

'They're OK. We'll talk about all that this evening. I want you to change into your new clothes right away so that you'll get used to them.'

Candy's mother sat in the small room in the upright armchair that she had bought for seven shillings just before the war started. Despite the sunshine outside, the room had an air of twilight. A green chenille runner with scallops and bobbles was fastened to the high mantelpiece with big-headed brass tacks. A mahogany clock was in the centre and to the left was a good sized, decorated, japanned tin with 'Biscuits' on the front. Its similiar companion on the right was marked 'Tea'. A low, metal candlestick with half a candle was at the far end, and there were several small photographs in cheap frames at the back of the mantelpiece.

Below was an old-fashioned coal range with an open fire and an oven. There was a trivet for a kettle on the top bar of the fire and on a firebrick lying on its side, the kettle itself in burnished copper.

The wallpaper was faded, but huntsmen, and ladies riding side-saddle were just discernible, and along one angle where the wall met the ceiling were the brown stains of damp above the picture rail.

Candy's mother was knitting, the glossy knitting pattern on her lap, and despite the misshapen joints of her arthritic fingers she knitted easily but slowly. To Victoria Amelia Price and many like her, knitting was more than a way of making sweaters and scarves. It was a therapy that took your mind off poverty and unemployment; and it worked. A cup of tea and a knitting pattern were her generation's equivalents of smoking pot or sniffing glue. Not quite oblivion but a half-way house.

As Candy lifted the teapot her mother said, 'Use the cloth or you'll burn yourself.'

'Do you want some biscuits or a sarnie?'

'No. Just pour the tea and sit down. Put the cosy on the teapot and it won't get cold.'

'Still no sugar?'

'No, not for me.'

Candy put the cup and saucer and a plate of fancy cakes near her mother and sat down.

'Mum.'

'Yes.'

'I've got something to tell you.'

'I know. Get on with it.'

'How did you know?'

Her mother laughed, and without looking up from her knitting she said, 'I know you, my girl. I can read you like a book. Always could. And that's no bad thing either.'

'Tad's asked me to marry him.'

Her mother went on knitting and Candy Price said, 'Why don't you say something?'

'You were telling me something, not asking me a question. If you want to ask me something, ask me.'

'Are you pleased?'

'He hasn't asked me child, he's asked you, and I gather you're pleased enough.'

'Oh I am, Mum. I love him so much.'

The old lady lifted her head and turned it to look at her daughter.

'And what does that mean?'

'What does what mean?'

'You say you love him. What's it mean?'

'You know what it means, and you know what I mean. You're just being awkward.'

'What do you want me to say? That he's attractive, strikes me as reliable and honest and will make you a wonderful husband?'

'No. I want to know if you think I'll make him a wonderful wife.'

'That's the first sensible thing you've said, little girl.'

'So tell me.'

Her mother put her knitting on the floor beside her and leaned back in the chair. She took off her glasses, wiped them on her pinafore and put them back on before she spoke. She smiled at her daughter.

'I'm glad he asked you. He's a nice man. He must think a lot of you to ask you. What did you say to him?'

'I told him I'd think about it before I said either "yes" or "maybe we'll wait for a bit".'

'You've got more sense than I gave you credit for. What about that other girl you told me about?'

'That's Judy. I don't think she would marry him. She's got a rich husband. She wants to leave him but I don't think she's got the guts to go through a divorce. She doesn't love Tad, anyway.'

'How do you know?'

'You can tell. When she's been with him at the club she never looks at him, she just wants to make sure who's looking at her. She puts him down, acts superior.

She won't call him Tad. She thinks it's vulgar. She calls him Charles. That's his second name. And whatever he is Tad ain't a Charles. To my mind she's a real bitch and she'd make him unhappy.'

'Maybe that's what he wants. Those society girls know what the world's all about.'

'Do they hell. They're just the same as the rest of us. They just act like they're different.'

'Some of them *are* different.'

'How for God's sake?'

'They're better educated. Been to good schools and universities.'

'So what?'

Mrs Price reached out and put her hand on her daughter's arm. 'What about his friends, love? They've all been to those Eton and Harrows and universities. How would you get on with them?'

'I'd do my best. They'd have to do their best with me.'

'But you wouldn't like it if they came the old acid with you, would you? You wouldn't keep your temper. There'd be scenes and embarrassment for Tad.'

'He'd stick up for me.'

'I'm sure he would, girl, and in the end he wouldn't see them any more. And he'd end up with no friends.'

'We could make our own friends.'

Her mother didn't answer but when she saw Candy's stricken face she said quietly, 'Why don't you compromise?'

'How?'

'Say yes but you want to wait for a bit. Live with him. See how it develops. Go out of your way to fit in. You and he'll get on fine, I'm sure of that, but you've both got to live in the daily world. If you really love him, see if you can't go a bit towards his sort of people.'

'I love you, Mum. You're always so kind to me. I don't know why you put up with me.'

'I don't, either. Why don't you bring him down for tea one of these days? I'll make a chocolate cake. Men always like those.'

Candy jumped up and rushed round to kiss her mother, and a few minutes later her mother heard her singing as she washed up the crockery in the tiny scullery. She was singing something about "My guy" and her mother shook her head slowly. So much beauty, so much lovingness, all going to waste. If she married Tad Anders it would be cherished and protected. But could she make the effort to fit in? To smile at those chic women and their smooth men? She couldn't have done it herself. All she'd had to get used to was supporting Spurs instead of Fulham, her father's team. The girl would have enough sense to know that there would be no more casual sleeping around. She understood the basics of men and women all right. It was just the glossy bit that might get her down. She sighed as she thought of what her husband would have said if he could hear her persuading her daughter to be nice to the toffs. He'd turn in his grave. His Candy was good enough for the Prince of Wales. He'd said so often enough. If she was going to stay the night she'd better air the bed with a hot-water bottle.

Some people are moved to tears by sunsets or Rachmaninov, and Mrs Price was moved to tears by a hot-water bottle. The new, big, blue one from Boots she put at the foot of the tiny single bed. The one shaped like a rabbit she put near the pillow, and she remembered so many nights when Harry had called her to see the blonde hair on the pillow and a small plump hand just outside the blanket, curved round that same rubber rabbit.

Burinski looked quite smart in his Marks and Spencers two-piece suit. A pale biscuit colour, with a slight flare to the trousers and unmistakeably English. Suede shoes and a cream shirt with a brown tie, and he could have been middle management for any company except IBM. He was obviously pleased with his new image.

There were various documents laid out on the coffee table between them. Anders was pointing at the two passports.

'One's British. The other's West German. Federal Republic. Except for the names they're both genuine. Nobody's going to stop you on suspicion they're forgeries. There's two hundred pounds in Sterling notes. A hundred US dollars and three hundred Deutsche Marks. OK?'

Burinski nodded. 'Yes. OK.'

'I'll be going with you as far as Ostend. We travel separately because they'll be looking for two men together when they do start looking. From Ostend you take a train to Brussels. You speak German when we get to Ostend and once we've landed you use your German passport.

'From Brussels you take a plane to Tegel. You fly only Sabena, Lufthansa or British Airways. No others. From Tegel you take a taxi into the city centre and then you take another taxi to Pension Frohnau. It's not a safe-house nor does it have any Intelligence connections, it's a place that lets out rooms by the hour or the night to prostitutes. Nobody will look at you too carefully.

'There's a guide service in the Kurfürstendamm called Severin and Kühn. They run guided bus tours into East Berlin. For that you use your British passport. After that I can't help you, but I guess you've got your own black-market contacts over the other side.'

Anders picked up an envelope. 'If you get them out or if you decide to settle down on your own in West Berlin, you take this envelope to the address on it and ask for the man named on the envelope. You don't give it to anybody except him. You ask him to read it while you wait. All he can do for you is get you documents so you can rent a room and get a job. You don't ever contact him again. He owes me a favour, but only one. If you play games you'll end up in the river. Understood?'

'Is there any way I can contact you?'

'No. When I've got you back I've done all I'm willing to do.'

Burinski looked at Anders across the table. 'Why are you doing this for me?'

Anders looked back at the Russian. 'You want the truth or a bunch of flowers?'

Burinski smiled. 'The truth of course.'

'I don't give a shit about you, Burinski. I'm doing this for your wife. She's got twice the guts you have. She's unlucky to have got involved with a bastard like you.'

Burinski smiled. A hard-eyed smile. 'You didn't ever bluff me, comrade. You think I don't already realize that this whole thing is set up by SIS. You made a good scenario but you make a mistake. One mistake.'

'Oh. What's that?'

Burinski pointed at the three small piles of money and then looked back at Anders.

'That's your mistake my friend. I make that three hundred and fifty pounds. Fourteen hundred D-marks. Nobody gives a stranger his own personal money to that amount. Why should you?'

Anders looked back at the Russian. 'Why the hell do you think SIS would spend public money on getting you out of the country?'

Burinski saw the barely controlled anger on Anders' face and in his voice. He shrugged.

'What does it matter?'

'You'd better get some sleep, Burinski. We shall be off early tomorrow morning.'

Burinski stood up, pointing at the things on the table. 'Do you want me to take those things?'

'They're all yours, comrade. Unless you'd like to go back to London.'

After Burinski had gone up to the spare bedroom Anders locked the door and went downstairs again. He moved one of the armchairs to the bottom of the stairs, took off his jacket and shoes, loosened his tie and made himself as comfortable as he could. All night he cat-napped in the chair.

CHAPTER FIFTEEN

Nicholson got the call while he was still at the office and he tried to contact Sir Arthur but he was closeted with the Foreign Secretary, briefing him on Tel Aviv and Cairo prior to his Middle East trip. He tried the club but Anders had not been in the previous day or night. He had left no message nor told anyone that he would be away, but they were used to that. He was tempted to try Meynell but that would ruffle Sir Arthur's feathers. And there was nothing that they could say that would alter the facts. Burinski had gone out with Anders and hadn't come back. Anders wasn't at his club. It wasn't very difficult arithmetic.

The routine procedure was quite straightforward. All he had to do was notify Special Branch through MI5 liaison and pass them photographs of Anders and Burinski. And if he did that he might as well write out his resignation at the same time. Once the mincing machine started working it would no longer be in SIS's hands. Anders would be blown; unofficial and even unauthorized operations would be exposed. Not to the general public but to the critical and biased eyes of MI5. As in most countries in the world the Intelligence services were, from time to time, more suspicious of one another than their foreign rivals. But without the resources of Special Branch there was no equivalent in SIS to trace and find the two missing men. And Special Branch belonged to MI5 not SIS.

He phoned Stoppard at liaison and gave him a watered-down briefing on the situation and ordered him to organize his overseas people to drop what they were doing and spend time at ports and railheads looking out for Burinski. He made no mention of Anders and his orders were that if Burinski was identified they should make no contact with him but keep him under surveillance. Stoppard said quite openly that only luck could lead them to Burinski. They were too thin on the ground to do anything beyond going through the motions.

Nicholson phoned home to say that he would either be late or staying in town for the night and then turned back to his work. But his mind kept wandering to Anders. What the hell was he doing? And then Sir Arthur's secretary phoned to say that he was back and wanted to see him.

Sir Arthur was in a good mood, packing his case to take back to his cottage for the weekend.

'Peter. D'you have anything about a KGB man named Kuznetsov? Initials A.V.'

'Where is he?'

French smiled. 'At this moment he's sitting in Saunder's office in the Embassy in Ankara. He's already talking. You'd better contact Saunders and give him your priorities. I gather he can cover Israel, Iran, the Lebanon, Saudi Arabia and Egypt.'

'I'll do that, Sir Arthur. Can you spare me a few minutes?'

'Of course.' French went on putting things down in his case.

'Anders took Burinski out to check the details of the assassination yesterday morning. They left about ten and they haven't come back.'

Sir Arthur stopped fiddling with his clothes in the case but he didn't look at Nicholson.

'What have you done about it, Peter?'

'I've given Stoppard a very bowdlerized scenario, only mentioning Burinski, and told him to put all his men on ports and airports and railheads for a few days.'

'Did you mention Anders?'

'No.'

'Have you informed Five or Special Branch?'

'No, sir.'

'What do you think's going on?'

'I've no idea. It doesn't make sense.'

Sir Arthur turned to look at Nicholson who was amazed by his calmness.

'You're wasting Stoppard's men's time, Peter. Just contact Pritchett in Berlin and tell him to put round-the-clock surveillance on Tegel and when he sees Burinski tell him to contact me personally and I'll deal with it myself.'

'You think that . . .'

'Let's not speculate, Peter. Put your thoughts on the little man in Ankara. He's more important than Burinski.'

'Maybe I should go out for a couple of days and brief Saunders?'

'It's entirely up to you. By the way, I saw your father the other night. He tells me he's thinking of early retirement. I was surprised.'

Nicholson laughed softly. 'He promises or threatens retirement once a year. He's just doing a Sinatra. A last and final appearance every June when he gets his second tax application. I'm sure he doesn't mean it.'

'I must say he sounds very convincing although I'd heard from reliable sources that he was being tapped for the Appeals Court.'

'Did you tell him that?'

'Good God, no. And you musn't either.'

'You'll be at the cottage all the weekend?'

'Yes. I'll take Michelmore as duty officer so the phone will be manned full time.'

'D'you need a lift to Liverpool Street?'

'That's kind of you. No. I'm dining first.'

'Have a good weekend.'

'And you. My regards to all your ladies.'

Nicholson walked slowly back to his own office. He had expected an explosion. Luther Meynell had often said that Sir Arthur was not only unpredictable but that that was one of his virtues. He behaved as if it didn't matter. But he must have at least thought vaguely of the possibility that Anders had lifted Burinski deliberately. And there was only one motive that he could think of for Anders to do that.

Anders washed and shaved and then walked out of the kitchen door. He stood, breathing in the cool, early-morning air. Across the valley the sky was grey, but it was the grey that promised a hot sunny day and a calm flat Channel. He went back into the kitchen and poured the last of the coffee into the china mugs and took one up to Burinski.

At Dover he garaged the car near the ferry terminal and they walked to the embarkation area with half an hour to spare.

Anders kept Burinski in sight for most of the journey and was only a few feet in front of him as he went through customs and immigration at Ostend. But on the cobbled quay-side Burinski was trembling.

'What's the matter, my friend?'

'He asked me the purpose of my visit.'

'They always do that. You'll either say "Business" or "pleasure". He doesn't give a damn which you say.'

'I answered him in Russian. I was tensed up and I'd rehearsed what to say. I'd been thinking in Russian and it just came out.'

'What happened?'

'He went through my passport again. Page by page. And then he took it to another man and they checked in a book. The other man came back with him and asked me what my business was. I told him I was only in transit. That I was going to Düsseldorf via Brussels because I'd never seen Brussels before. He kept looking at me. And he hesitated before he gave me back my passport.'

'Which one did you use?'

'Like you said. The British one.'

'So what's the problem?'

'I'll never make it to Berlin. I nearly ran away.'

'D'you like strawberry tarts, Burinski?'

Burinski looked shocked. 'I don't understand.'

'A simple question. Do you like strawberry tarts?'

'I've never had one.'

'There's a café in the Rue Longue that sells the best strawberry tarts in Europe. We're going to have one each right now.'

Burinski found that he didn't like strawberry tarts and as Anders finished up Burinski's tart he said, 'How are you going to get on in Berlin, comrade?'

'I'll be more at home there. I know my way around.'

'Have you got contacts in West Berlin?'

Burinski nodded. 'One or two.'

'What about East Berlin?'

'Yes, but I shan't use those unless I'm desperate.'

'How are you going to contact Inge?'

'I shall try and contact her parents down south and see what I can find out from them.'

'They'll be watching them too.'

'And there's my father in Moscow.'

Anders shook his head. 'You're playing games with a lot of people's lives, Burinski.'

Burinski shrugged. 'Will you come with me to Berlin? Just to Tegel. That's what scares me most of all. If the West Germans got me . . .' he shrugged and fell silent.

'I'll go with you to Berlin, but after that you're on your own. What you do is up to you. If you take my advice you'll get somewhere to live in West Berlin, and a job and you'll sit the time out. If you really care about your wife you won't go near her. Wait a year or two years until it's almost forgotten.' Anders stood up. 'Let's get to the station.'

They were in Brussels by noon and took a train out to the airport. There was a Lufthansa flight to Düsseldorf in an hour and a connection to Berlin in the late evening.

The DC10 landed at Berlin-Tegel exactly at midnight and was the last scheduled flight of the day. Burinski kept close to him as they walked across the tarmac. Burinski survived the cursory inspection by the immigration officers and they were at the baggage inspection when Anders glanced towards the reception area. There were only half a dozen people there and he didn't recognize any of them. It was only when he turned his back to the customs desk that he saw him. It was Andy Pritchett, standing at the bar with a glass in his hand. For a moment he thought Pritchett had seen him but he had turned to order another drink, chatting up the bar-girl. Anders turned back to the customs officer and said that his other case had not come off the aircraft. He was referred to one of the Lufthansa ground staff.

He took Burinski with him and they sat in the Lufthansa freight office for nearly two hours while the aircraft hold was checked. He was apologetic about his baggage tag being missing but the search had gone on with Lufthansa thoroughness until Anders suggested that he would call back later that day to see if his case had been traced. Lufthansa were going to contact Düsseldorf and Brussels in case it had been misrouted.

Back in the flight reception area Anders could see that the bar and restaurant were in darkness and as they walked out of the big glass doors Anders headed Burinski away from the exit route past the closed airline desks and the shops to the incoming unloading doors.

Outside there were several waiting taxis but the concourse was empty. He looked across at the car park. There were a dozen cars, all empty, and he went straight to the second taxi, and as he pushed Burinski inside he asked for Hotel Windsor in Knesebeckstrasse.

Twenty minutes later Anders paid off the driver and stood talking to Burinski until the taxi had left and then they walked to the other end of the street and Anders rang the night bell of the Plaza.

There were no single rooms so they settled for a double with twin beds. Burinski asked why Anders had gone through the charade about the missing case and Anders merely told him that it was to avoid going through with the other passengers on the flight. Andy Pritchett was too busy with the bar-girl, thank God. She was pretty enough for Pritchett, and he'd probably gone over to chat with her until she was off duty.

Anders was up early the next morning and when he was dressed he left Burinski still asleep and walked to the corner and turned right into the Kurfürstendamm.

Although it was only just 7.30 the broad pavement was already busy with people hurrying to work. Shop windows were being washed down and dustmen were clearing containers of rubbish followed by a street-cleaning team. At Uhlandstrasse he turned right and then another right turn at the end of the block into Lietsenburger Strasse. At the corner of Knesebeckstrasse Anders stopped.

Cars were queuing for the multi-storey carpark, a small post office van was parked just beyond and workmen were digging deep into the road fifty yards further on. There was a smell of stale gas from the red clay soil. There were several people waiting for their employers to open up their shops, and an elderly woman was unloading bunches of flowers from a green van into baskets and pans in the shadow of two plane trees.

Anders walked slowly to stand under the spreading branches of the trees. His eyes were on a dark blue BMW parked on the other side of the street about thirty metres before the hotel. A man sat in the driver's seat, the window was down and his arm rested on the car door. He had a pipe in his mouth but it wasn't lit, and round his thick wrist was a leather band. The kind of wrist-support sometimes worn by men who had to shove their fellow men around. Anders watched for ten minutes as the man sat there unmoving. And he sat with the patience and stillness of a man who was used to sitting and waiting.

Anders walked slowly up to the Ku'damm and stood on the corner. He bought a newspaper and as he turned to walk back down the street the car started up and came towards him. As it passed he saw the man's face. It was round and flabby down to heavy side-burns. Anders had never seen him before and the man didn't even glance at him as he passed.

Anders looked at his watch. The shops would be open and he walked on down the Ku'damm to the travel agency. There was a flight to Brussels leaving at eleven and an onward connection to Ostend half an hour after arrival. They couldn't book him cross-channel but suggested that he check with the Lufthansa desk at Brussels. He paid for his ticket and slid it into his jacket pocket, feeling in reflex for the holster that wasn't there.

Burinski was dressed and waiting, anxious to talk, but Anders had had enough of him and hurried him down to the desk and paid their bill.

There was a taxi off-loading new arrivals at the hotel entrance and Anders gave the address of Pension Frohnau. Burinski seemed to be under control, and with an enthusiasm bordering on euphoria he assured Anders that he had it all worked out in his head. When the taxi stopped Anders pointed out the Pension Frohnau and Burinski picked up his case and got out of the taxi. At the open door he was grinning as he held out his hand. Reluctantly Anders took it, but he neither wished Burinski good luck nor bade him goodbye. He turned to the driver as he closed the car door and told him to take him to Tegel.

At the bookstall he bought copies of *Stern* and *Time* magazines. He sat in the white-tiled toilets until his plane was called.

They were late arriving at Brussels and there was no time to check on the ferries, but at Ostend there was no problem. The ferry was half empty.

At Dover he paid for the garaging of his car and an hour and a half later he pulled up at the cottage. For almost fifteen minutes he sat there, then he started the car again and headed for the A21 and London.

It was 3 a.m. when he turned into the mews at the back of the club. There was the usual array of garbage and overflowing dustbins and a Ford Cortina with a couple in the back seat. Anders wondered what kind of people chose such tatty surroundings for their courting. The man's face was in shadow but the girl looked quite pretty.

He walked round to the entrance to the club. The door was locked and padlocked and as he unlocked he realized how tired he was. The pain in his chest was there again, not severe, but persistent. He locked the doors behind him and switched on the lights as he walked down the stairs and through to his own rooms. He left the lights burning, too tired to close off the control switches.

He was in the bath when the phone rang, his eyes closed and almost asleep. He got out and put his bathrobe over his shoulders as he walked into the sitting room.

'I heard you were back, Tad.'

It was Nicholson, and Anders half-smiled.

'Who was it, Peter? The couple in the Cortina?'

'I'd better come over and see you later today. How about this afternoon at three?'

'That's OK, Peter.'

'Are you all right, Tad?'

'I'm fine.'

'Are you on your own?'

'Yes.'

'You'd better get some sleep in before the balloon goes up.'

'You too, comrade.'

Anders heard Nicholson's quiet laugh and hung up.

Nicholson looked at the wine in his glass as he spoke.

'What do you think Sir Arthur's going to do about it, Tad?'

Anders shrugged. 'I'm not much worried, Peter. I've written out my resignation.'

'You can't resign, Tad, you aren't on the establishment.'

'I've recognized that. I've just said that I've finished working for them.'

'Tell me why? Did you really care all that much about what happened to Burinski?'

'I didn't give a damn about what happened to Burinski.'

'So what was it?'

'French sent me into Berlin with no back-up to get Burinski out. When *he* wanted Burinski out it was a full-scale operation. I've had enough of that kind of thinking.'

'For God's sake, Tad. Sir Arthur authorized the exchange for you. Surely that squares the account?'

'Does it?'

'Why not?'

Anders stood up and slid off his jacket and when he sat down again he slowly unbuttoned his shirt and pulled it open. Nicholson saw the deep well-muscled chest and the white patch on the tanned skin where the rib had pierced the flesh and the long concave recess where half the rib was missing.

He looked back to Anders' face. 'I still don't understand, Tad. It's ghastly, but I don't see the connection with Burinski.'

'It's nothing to do with Burinski. He's just a symbol.'

'Of what?'

'It's a message from me to Sir Arthur. And to you for that matter. A protest, if you like. You two, and others, sit there in your offices and decide what happens to me and other field agents. And when you work it out it's a balance sheet. Debits and credits. But there's something missing in the arithmetic. Nobody takes account of what the man in the trap might want. You salve your consciences by warning us right at the start that you won't lift a finger to help us once we're in the bag. The KGB do more for their agents than you do for us. Just for once your little sums have been spoiled. I spoiled them. Deliberately. And you and French can do what the hell you like about it.'

Nicholson sat in silence for several minutes. Then he looked across at Anders before he spoke.

'Before I say what I really want to say let me make it clear that I've got great respect for you. Not only as an operator but as a man. I haven't got your physical courage. It may seem strange to you but I'm proud of working with you. I may not always show it and for most of the time I'm not even conscious of it. But it's there. I don't have any doubt that Sir Arthur feels much the same. He's older than you and me, so he's less tolerant of some things, but when the chips are down you're one of his men and he'll be on your side, fighting. Not with his fists because it isn't necessary. But with a very bright mind that knows its way around the Whitehall rule-book and cheats when it's necessary.

'However . . .' Nicholson paused and smiled. 'How I hate people who say "however". However, I've never heard such rubbish as in your little homily. It was just hearts and flowers, gypsy violins and bleeding hearts. You make up your mind in absolute ignorance of the facts. You know your side of the story and you're not only ignorant about the other side, but you don't even realize that there *is* another side.'

Nicholson leaned forward and poured himself more wine and when he looked up Anders saw his anger showing in the muscles round his mouth and jaw as he started to speak again.

'Let me give you a few facts, Tad. Do you know what TACFIRE is?'

Anders shook his head.

'TACFIRE is an eyes-only US army system that automates firing instructions for field artillery units. A contract has just been placed with a US company to design digital plotters for TACFIRE. It's worth about 2.4 million dollars. Understand?'

'Yes.'

'Good. We heard rumours that the Soviets had already designed such a system. We weren't sure if the rumours were true but we spent a lot of time and money working on a KGB man who would know. We discovered that they had such a system and we spread a net for the KGB man and we picked him up in Amsterdam. At first he refused to talk, but slowly we were breaking through. We reckoned that in a few weeks he would cooperate. Sir Arthur had this operation very much under his control. If it worked it was going to save maybe two years research and several million dollars. And we should share the technology with the Americans. The name of the Russian was Gorlinski. He was the man Moscow wanted in exchange for you. The decision was entirely Sir Arthur's. He didn't consult anybody or get anybody's permission or suggest to anyone that maybe the exchange should be refused. I told him who they wanted in exchange for you. He just nodded and told me to agree. So much for your martyrdom.

'Next point. Your present little escapade. When I had to report to French that you and Burinski were missing, he didn't panic or call in Special Branch which would have meant real trouble for you. I couldn't understand why he took it so calmly, but he did. And when I phoned him to say that you were back and minus

Burinski he told me to come along and see you. To reassure you that no action was being taken against you. He told me to ask you to stand by for an assignment that's likely to come up in about four weeks. That's your ogre, Tad.'

Anders shrugged. 'That's just *your* gypsy music, Peter.'

Nicholson laughed. 'OK. OK. Maybe I didn't phrase it very well. There's gypsy music on both sides and maybe my side hasn't played you enough music week by week. We do understand, Tad. But there's not all that much we can do. We can't keep saying we love you every day.'

'Just a greetings card a couple of times a year would do.'

Nicholson knew then that Anders had absorbed what he had said. Not convinced, but the feathers had been smoothed down enough for them to gradually get things back to normal. On the whole the life suited Anders and he must know it. And what else would he do?

'Will you come and stay with us for the weekend?'

'I'll be with my girlfriend.'

'Which one?'

'Candy.'

'The smashing blonde from downstairs?'

'That's the one.'

'Why not bring her with you?'

'Are you sure?'

'Of course I'm sure, we'd love to have you both.'

'OK.'

Nicholson smiled. 'Are the back-room boys forgiven?'

'No. But I've taken the point.'

'Fair enough. Are you coming by car to our place?'

'Yes.'

'OK. Friday, any time after lunch.'

They were sitting at the table nearest to the piano. It wasn't a popular table. Members only took it if all the other tables were full. They complained that they had to raise their voices while the piano was playing, and what they were generally talking about wasn't meant to be said that loud. Baldy was singing quite softly, extolling the virtues of Mott Street in July, and Tad Anders was watching the girl's face as she looked up from her drink.

'Did you enjoy the weekend?'

'It was smashing, Tad. They're wonderful people. Not snobby at all.'

Anders smiled. 'Did you think they would be?'

She shrugged. 'I wasn't sure. I thought in little ways they might be. All that jazz about which knife to use and the stuff about wines and vintages. I didn't want to let you down.'

'Who did you like best?'

'I couldn't say. I liked them all for different reasons. I think maybe Peter's mother. She's a toucher. She patted my knee and touched my arm and talked as if she was really interested in me. I liked Peter because he's very dishy but I don't think he knows it. Doesn't cash in on it anyway. And the old judge was marvellous. Sat there with his head on one side, all solemn as I tried to explain the difference between jazz and reggae. Me the expert, him the student. And they're so polite. Even to one another. I loved it.'

'The judge took me on one side and said I ought to have a portrait painted of you in a white dress in a garden. Perhaps sitting on a swing, he said.' He smiled.

'You didn't mention Fleur.'

'I know. She's very beautiful and elegant and chic and she's obviously crazy about Peter but somehow . . . I don't know . . . not my cup of tea.'

'Why not?'

'Reminds me a bit of Judy. A bit self-important. A bit superior. Very much the gracious hostess, the lady of the house, and don't you forget it. Untouched by human hand. Not sure whether she's the fairy princess or the Ice Queen.'

'She said she thought you were an absolute doll.'

'That's exactly what I mean. If you said *she* was an absolute doll she'd take it as an insult. Dolls are in the Third Division at the bottom of the table, struggling against relegation on dumb blondes.'

Anders smiled. 'A bit catty but not a bad assessment, sweetie.'

'It was catty. She was a very good hostess. She came into my bedroom that first evening. Quizzed me a bit about you. Asked if we were going to get married.'

'What did you say?'

She laughed. 'I told her I'd got my eye on Peter.' She smiled at her thoughts. 'For a moment she didn't know what to say and turned the conversation to clothes and perfume. I can hold my corner on those.'

He reached across the table for her hand and looked at her face. 'And are you going to marry me, Candy?'

'I talked about it with Mum, and I've thought about it so much, and I've tried to work out how to say it, but I can't.'

'Why can't you say it?'

'Oh, Tad. I've thought it all out so carefully and I know how it's going to be, but I wish it wasn't.'

'Just tell me, sweetie.'

She sighed. 'The answer's "yes", Tad. I'll marry you. I wish it could be tonight, but I want to suggest something. Let's live for a few months as if we are married and see how it goes. See if I fit in properly.'

'Let's do that, my love. But you don't have to fit in. I'm asking you just as you are right now. There ain't no exams to pass. I'd reckon I was very lucky to get you.'

'D'you mean that, Tad?'

'You bet I mean it.'

'It's a long time – the rest of our lives. And I want to make sure that I'll not spoil your life in any way.'

'In what way?'

'Your friends. People like the Nicholsons.'

'The Nicholsons. Why them?'

'They're well off. Well-educated. Upper class. They'd wonder what you saw in me.'

Anders laughed. 'They've seen you and they'll be quite sure they know why I grabbed you. Of course they'd only be partly right.'

'Tell me.'

'It's impossible to explain. It does matter to me that you're so pretty, but it's much more than that. When I'm with you it's like being in a nice warm bath. I feel much the same about Nicholson as you do. I guess I'm almost as well-off as he is. But because he comes from his sort of background it seems right that he's well-off, but for me it just feels like an accident. Good luck. He's not a snob. He treats me absolutely as an equal. But like you, I don't *feel* an equal. And we're not equal, we're different. He's not better than me, nor am I better than him. I could live much like he does, but I don't want to. It's not sour grapes. You liked his family and his home just as much as I did, but you wouldn't want it. And he doesn't expect me to be like him. You and I are much the same as one another. There's not going to be any problems with other people.'

'Don't tempt me, Tad, don't make me weaken, I need to do it. It's a kind of wedding present from me to you.'

'Speaking of presents, I've got one for you.'

'What is it?'

He fished in his pocket, and brought out a small envelope with the Royal crest on it and put it in front of her.

He smiled at her excitement as she loosened the seal and she looked up at him as she saw the square blue box. And she gasped as she pushed back the hinged lid and looked at the ring in its blue plush fitting. It was gold and there were five diamonds that flared even in the club's dim lighting.

She looked up at him. 'Oh, Tad. It's beautiful. Can I wear it?'

'Of course you can. Try it on.'

And then she turned it. 'There are some words engraved inside.' She smiled. 'I can make out Candy but I can't understand the other words.' She looked at his face. 'What does it say?'

'It says – *Kochana Candy. Ja ciebie kocham.* It's Polish.'

'What does it mean?'

'It means 'Darling Candy, I love you.'

She leaned across the table to kiss him and Joey appeared with an envelope in his hand. She spread out the fingers of her left hand and gave Anders the ring.

'You put it on, Tad.'

He slid it on to the third finger because although it wasn't even the correct hand for Polish custom it was what they did in England.

He turned and looked at Joey who offered him the envelope.

'A taxi-driver brought it, Mr Anders. It's addressed to you.'

There was a scribbled note and a press cutting. The note was hand-written.

TAD,

I thought you should see this. I hope it's not too much of a surprise but I guess you must have known from the start that it wasn't on. I've spoken to A. F. and there'll be no come-back. It looks as if all the accounts are square now.

Fleur and the girls send you their love.

PETER

He unfolded the newspaper cutting. It was from the *Berliner Zeitung*. There was a picture of Burinski's face. The eyes closed. The text covered four columns about four inches deep. The headline was thick and black.

MYSTERY DEATH

West Berlin police are appealing to the public for help in identifying the man in the photograph (inset). At approximately 6 p.m. yesterday evening this man collapsed in Fasanenstrasse about fifty metres from the junction with the Kurfürstendamm. Two onlookers, whose identity has not been disclosed, have made statements to the effect that they saw the man approached by two men who spoke to him briefly and then hurried to a black Volkswagen which was parked in the street nearby. The deceased collapsed and an ambulance was called but the unidentified man was dead on arrival at the hospital.

First indications lead the police to consider that foul play cannot be ruled out. The victim appears to have died from asphyxiation but further medical examinations are due to take place.

The identity papers on the victim were found to be forgeries and it is considered possible that the man may have been involved in black-market or other criminal activities. Extensive checks are being carried out using the newly installed Central Police Records computer based in Wiesbaden.

Any member of the public who believes he has seen the man in the photograph should contact the nearest police station or the Kriminaldirektion (Tel. No. 78 1071).

Anders folded up the newspaper cutting and put it back in the envelope with Peter Nicholson's note. He'd been wrong. Andy Pritchett *had* seen him. He would have contacted London and they would have passed the word to Moscow. And now everybody was happy. Except . . .

Anders looked across at Candy Price. 'Have you got that nice white dress in your case upstairs? The one with the fringe?'

She laughed. 'Yes, I have.'

'Let's go upstairs. You put it on. I'll clean myself up and we'll go out for a meal.'

'Where shall we go?'

'We'll try the Connaught, sweetie. They do a very good steak and kidney pie. Not as good as your mother's, but good enough for us.'

CHILDREN OF TENDER YEARS

This is for Dr Barbara Ansell of Northwick Park Hospital and Great Ormond Street Hospital for Sick Children – with love.

The way we selected our victims was as follows: we had two SS doctors on duty at Auschwitz to examine the incoming transports of prisoners. These would be marched by one of the doctors, who would make spot decisions as they walked by. Those who were fit to work were sent into the camp. Others were sent immediately to the extermination plants. Children of tender years were invariably exterminated since by reason of their youth they were unable to work.

Part of a sworn deposition made at Nuremberg dated 5th April 1946, and signed by SS-Obersturmführer Rudolf Hoess, Commandant of Auschwitz

CHAPTER ONE

The small bedroom window was wide open, the curtain lifting and falling slowly in the breeze. And in the distance the sound of tennis balls on taut-stringed rackets. The sounds of Hampstead on a summer's day. It seemed so senseless, but typical, that the old man had survived the bleak winter and the long drawn-out spring only to die in the first week of summer weather.

He knew it was going to happen. The doctor and the hospital had said that it was only a matter of days. And his father wanted to come home to die. There was no more that they, or he, could do, and he knew somehow that this was to be the day. It was no longer days but hours and minutes.

The old man lay with his head in the soft valley of the pillow, spots of bright red blood speckling his chest and his pyjama jacket. The washed-out blue eyes that dominated the shrunken face stared into the distance as if he were already walking slowly away from the world to some far-distant place. As he held the old man's hand its skin was as dry and fragile as an autumn leaf, and the hand itself was cold and flaccid.

Weeks ago he made out a list of the things he would have to do when his father died. At the time it had seemed just a routine. Notifying a few friends, the death certificate, the funeral arrangements and the sad bureaucratic paraphernalia of death. But now it was so near it seemed too cold, too little, to mark the end of a life that had been so distorted and yet so courageous.

The telephone rang in the hall below but he made no move to answer it. Affection and instinct made him stay, his eyes heavy with sleep as he sat on the edge of the bed.

It was ten minutes later when the racking, gurgling cough made him hurriedly turn his head to stare transfixed at the flood of bright scarlet blood that gushed from the slack mouth to cover the thin arm, the chest and the sheets with its patina of vivid colour. The purpled eyelids were closed over the protruding eyes and when he laid his hand on the old man's chest there was no longer a heartbeat. For long moments he sat there, overcome with inertia, trying not to think of the years of willing sacrifice that had just ended. Sadness borne with few outward signs, with great faith that the best was yet to come. The violin-playing that had earned a living, and a man who shed tears too easily at Puccini love duets, Mendelssohn and Max Bruch. A man who laughed, embarrassed, as he brushed away the tears saying, 'For God's sake – that Bruch wasn't even a Jew. What was "Kol Nidrei" to him?'

They'd lived in Swietokrzyska Street and his father had said that they would be safe now that the wall had been built to mark off the Warsaw ghetto. But two months later they had come in the middle of the night. He was too young to understand who 'they' were, but he knew they were Germans and that they were called the SS.

The shouting and screaming had woken him, and the fear on his parents' faces had frightened him as they stood there trembling. And then the floodlights shining in through the window. His father kissing his mother, tears pouring down his face as he ran from the room. Then his mother had swept him up in her arms and they were going down the stairs. As they turned in the hallway to go to the back-yard he saw an axe-head splitting the wood of the front door.

She ran with him, panting and sobbing as she clutched him to her. Into another house, one that had already been searched. Up the stairs to an empty bedroom. Crouching behind the wreckage of a bed she had put her hand over his mouth as the noise of hob-nailed boots came up the stairs.

They had held their breaths as the two SS men shone torches round the room, and after a few minutes they heard the footsteps going down the stairs. The next morning another patrol had found them and an angry scharführer *had shouted at his mother, calling her a Jewish sow. Then it had been a welter of screaming blows until they were with all the others in the square. He had never seen so many people. There was no shouting, just silence and the stamping of the guards' boots. There were no other people in the Warsaw streets as they were herded like sheep to the train and the night.*

For three days and four nights the waggons had rumbled south, the acrid, sickening stench of urine and excrement saturating the fetid air in the waggon with its freight of eighty or more men, women and children. And day and night he clung to his mother, frightened by the hysterical shouting and screaming of prayers in Polish, German and Yiddish.

Once a day the double doors were swung open, light streamed in and the cries and prayers stopped as they queued for the stale black bread and greasy water.

When the train finally ended its journey the men were separated from the women and children. The big banner across the arched entrance said, 'Arbeit macht frei.' *'Work brings freedom.' He asked his mother what it meant but she just shook her head.*

As he sat there lost in his thoughts the doorbell rang downstairs. He shivered involuntarily as he stood up wearily and went down the stairs into the narrow hall and opened the door.

The man who was standing there was tall and thin. In his late thirties, but looking older because of his old-fashioned moustache. He was smiling.

'Hi, Jake. I've been trying to get you on the phone. They want to have a meeting. Something's coming up. They'd like you to come along.'

'You'd better come in. What time is it?'

'Just after three. You been asleep or something?'

Jacob Malik closed the front door when the man was inside and walked into the sitting room pointing to an armchair.

'Sit down, Arthur.'

As the man sat down he looked up at Malik's face.

'Are you all right?'

'What's it all about, Arthur?'

'Jenkins called a meeting after he'd been to the FO.'

'Go on.'

'There was a report from the West German desk.'

'What about?'

Then Arthur Palmer was staring at Malik's hand.

'Jesus, you've got blood all over your hand. What's happened?'

'My father died. He had a haemorrhage.'

'When? When did it happen?'

'About fifteen minutes ago.'

Palmer stared at him. 'You mean here? In this house?'

'Yes.'

'Oh my God, Jake. Why on earth didn't you say? I didn't even know you had a father. I'm terribly sorry. Is there anything I can do to help you?'

'No.'

'I'll go back at once and tell Jenkins. They can postpone the meeting.' He stood up. 'I'll be in touch in a couple of days . . . are you quite sure I can't help?'

'No, you can't help.'

'Well. You know where I am. I'll let myself out.'

Jake Malik made the phone calls, and all the rituals of bureaucracy and religion were observed. A few old men, friends of his father, came to pay their last respects. No relatives came because there were no relatives still alive. There had been only one small surprise. When he opened the cigar box there was a Will. Witnessed by Hyman Freytag, a friend of his father and a solicitor. Everything the old man had, the Will said, was for his son Jacob. It wasn't that that was the surprise. It was the tattered birth certificate. The name on the paper showed that his father was Jacob Malik, although he had always called himself Abraham Malik. It didn't take all that much working out. He had given his son his own real name and he'd taken Abraham as his own name because it was even more Jewish. It was a badge, a banner against the Germans, and maybe against the world. A small act of defiance? Or was it to mark the change in his life that came when the cattle trucks rattled their way to Auschwitz with his wife and son?

There were two other men at the graveside. Rabbi Rabinowitz said the last prayers and a man he didn't recognize stood there until it was over and then without a word or a glance had hurried away. Malik wanted to get it over but he exchanged a few words with the Rabbi and promised to keep in touch. The old man's days in the Warsaw ghetto with his father deserved whatever courtesies he could muster. Then he walked to Highgate station and bought a ticket to Waterloo. As he sat on the bench waiting for the train he looked across at a poster advertising Cadbury's Milk Chocolate. The blue paper and the silver foil were turned down to display a row of individual pieces. In Auschwitz, just one of those small cubes could have assuaged your terrible hunger, bought you sex if you were a man or saved you a beating from a Kapo. And as the train roared into the station he remembered why he kept thinking of his father's swollen eyelids as he lay dying. They were exactly like the eyes of the first person he had watched as he died. The old Jew in Hut 18, the second day they were in the camp. Sitting like a heap of rags against the wall he had cried out several times as he was dying but nobody had done anything. They just left him there to die. His eyelids had been swollen and red and protruding like his father's.

Jenkins had left a message for him at the security desk and he was escorted up to his office. Jenkins was a dark stocky Welshman. A tough but amiable man in his fifties who had been a department head in SIS for as long as anyone could remember. He was standing, waiting for his visitor after the call from downstairs. He held out his hand and then took Malik's hand in both of his.

'It was good of you to come in, Jake, and I warned the others if you're not up to it we shall postpone the meeting until you are.'

'I'll be all right.'

'I was sorry to hear the news. I remember the few minutes I spent with your father. When was it? Must have been two, maybe three years ago. He was so proud of you, you know. In his modest way. A grand man. You'll miss him, I'm sure.' He paused, head on one side. 'How about you take some of your leave to have a break?'

'No, sir. Maybe I'll take a break later on.'

'It's up to you, my boy. Well, let's go down to the others.'

There was Jenkins; Arthur Palmer, Jenkins' PA; and Truslove from the German (West) desk. A thin, brown file lay in front of Jenkins' place at the table, and it was he who started the meeting. He looked at Jake Malik as he talked, and it was obvious that the others already knew what it was all about.

'As you know, Jake, we've got an arrangement with the West Germans that if they get involved in certain kinds of problems with the KGB, we have the option of dealing with the problem ourselves instead of involving Bonn. They have a similar deal with the Americans. It looks like we've got one of those problems now.' He leaned back in his chair. 'Not a major problem, thank God, but a tricky one.

'There's been an outbreak of anti-Semitism in several West German cities. Anti-Jewish graffiti, daubings on synagogues, graves defiled. The usual sort of hooliganism. But the Germans think that it's KGB-inspired. That's why we're involved.'

Malik frowned. 'What would the KGB gain in supporting anti-Semitism?'

'To create anti-German feeling in the rest of the world. Evidence that the Nazis are still there, biding their time. The Russians are probably reckoning that the West Germans will be more amenable to reviving Soviet-German detente if they feel isolated. That's just speculation. We just don't know.'

'Maybe it was genuine anti-Jewish groups.'

'Could be. That's why you've been brought into it. We want you to check it out, one way or another.'

'What sort of team can I have?'

'None, I'm afraid. You can have all the facilities you need but no bodies. But the Germans have offered one of their men to work with you.'

'You mean just two of us to penetrate all these groups? How many groups are there?'

'We don't know. The estimate is eight or nine. You don't have to do anything about breaking them up, or getting in deep. That can be done later when we know what they're up to.'

'Why the obstacle course?'

Jenkins shrugged. 'It's pretty low-grade stuff, Jake. We're only obliging Bonn so that they don't make things worse by blowing it up into a full-scale diplomatic incident. We just want to know what's going on.'

'Why me, sir?'

'You've got the experience, Jake, and the qualifications. You speak German . . . you know your way around . . .'

'Nothing more than that?'

'No. What had you got in mind?' Jenkins looked mildly irritated.

Malik shrugged. 'Can I see what we've got on file?'

Jenkins pointed to the file on the table. 'It's all there, Jake, and Truslove can fill you in on our talks with Bonn.'

'When do you want me to start?'

'As soon as you're ready. The flap died down once we told the Germans we'd deal with it.'

'Who do I report to?'

'To me. If I'm not around you can contact Palmer and he'll pass it on. I don't need daily reports. Just keep me in the picture when there's anything worthwhile.'

'Who's in charge? Me or the German?'

'You. It's an SIS operation now.'

Jenkins stood up and so did Palmer, and after they had left Truslove leaned back in his chair smiling, and said, 'D'you want me to translate what the Welsh Wizard was saying?'

'I got the message, Tony. Don't make a nuisance of myself. Don't probe too deeply. Don't get exposed, but keep the Germans happy.'

Truslove smiled. 'That's about it. Let's go for a beer and I'll fill you in on the politics.'

It was eleven o'clock when he left the pub in Victoria. The night sky was clear and he decided to walk back to Hampstead. He needed to slow down his mind. He wondered whether Jenkins wasn't right and that it might be wiser to take a few days' leave. He wasn't physically tired but his mind was out of gear and just sleeping might do him good. The black thoughts didn't really start until he got to Mornington Crescent, when he heard the goods waggons being shunted in the sidings outside Euston Station. For a moment he stood still, his eyes closed, his fists clenched and he cried out in the darkness before he shivered and walked on.

Those bloody waggons. The sound of them still made him cold with fear.

'I don't remember the date, Father. I really don't.'

'But the year.'

'I'm not sure; I think it must have been 1944.'

'Why do you think that, son?'

Jake Malik sighed again and shook his head. 'I wasn't old enough to know, Dad. I didn't know about dates.'

'Was it summer?'

'I think so.'

'What happened?'

'I don't know. She just didn't come for me in the hut.'

'Did you ask where she was?'

'Yes.'

'What did they say?'

'Nobody knew. Nobody answered. You know how it was.'

'Did they say she was dead?'

'No, nobody said anything. She just didn't come back.'

The old man's voice trembled. 'I need a date to remember, boy. Just something. Anything.'

'I know, Dad, I'm sorry I can't help you.'

The old man had put his arm round the boy's shoulders.

'I'm sorry, boy. Don't be upset. It's just one of my bad days. I'll be better tomorrow. Have you done your homework?'

'Yes, Dad.'

'You like some warm milk or chocolate drink in bed?'

'Just water, Dad. In a glass.'

And upstairs in the dark, tucked up in his bed, he lay there trying to remember. At first they'd let her take him in the other hut, the guardroom alongside the Lager Kommandant's house. She'd warned him not to talk or move or do anything. And he'd watched her undress and get on the guardroom bed with the SS man. It was always three men. One after the other; and afterwards his mother and he would sit at the table by the telephone and the typewriter and eat the black bread and a bowl of soup. He hadn't known then what they were doing to his mother but he knew now. And he knew that he must never tell his father. And he knew that she had had no choice and that it was to try and keep them both from the gas chambers.

He had no idea what had happened to her. After a time she had started going alone to the hut and she would come back for him every morning. But that day she hadn't come back. And he had never seen her again. An old woman had told him that the guards had grown tired of her and she'd been sent to the ovens. But the old woman was a crazed skeleton, and anyway he hadn't understood what she meant. He understood now. It must have been 1945 when she didn't come back. January or February. Because it was only a few months later that the Russians had come.

He was alseep when his father came up to bed and the old man had switched on the light to look at his son. He stood there silently, his eyes on the boy's face. The long black eyelashes, the neat nose and the soft full lips were just like hers.

CHAPTER TWO

In some musical circles the world divides into devotees of Tchaikowsky or lovers of Mozart, or, on a lower level, between the protagonists of Sinatra and the fans of Bing Crosby. For the young man lying stretched out on the comfortable sofa the separation came from whether, out of the two Schubert Piano Trios, you preferred the one in E flat major to the one in B flat major. If, like him, you preferred the latter, you would admire the cello that was propped in the angle of the piano stool and the pre-war Steinway that took up one corner of the spacious room. The young man was listening to a cassette of the old Casals version of the Trio, smiling to himself from time to time at the maestro's energetic grunting in the second movement.

An accomplished cellist, with callouses on the balls of his spatulate fingers that bespoke long hours of practice, he listened with his eyes closed. His father, mother, and two sisters were all professional musicians. It was a tolerant, civilized family, interested in all the arts, and living in comfort in the fine house on the outskirts of Cologne. The young man, Heinz Fischer, was the odd man out. Not that he didn't play the cello with feeling, and not that any member of the family treated him as an odd man out, despite the fact that he was the only one of them who wasn't a professional musician. But he *was* a professional. Heinz Fischer was a member of an élite group that most Germans refer to as the 'Popos'. Despite the cosy, almost cuddly name, the Popos are, in fact, the *Politscher Polizei.*

Ostensibly the Popos were just a specialist group in the normal German police force. No different in status from the other specialist groups who concerned themselves with vice or fraud. They were frequently to be seen, young men with alert eyes, guarding cabinet ministers and visiting worthies. But the population never believed that these were the Popos' main duties. Their activities were so secret that there were people, mainly dissidents, who swore that the Popos were the modern-day version of the Gestapo. In Berlin they were know as *Abteilung I,* in Bonn as K14, and in Munich as KA III. When, on rare occasions, a spokesman had to respond to media questioning as to their role, they were always described as 'special protectors of order', which, even in German, was virtually meaningless. As it was intended to be. What they could correctly claim was that they were members of the normal West German uniformed police force. The same claim rightfully made about Special Branch officers in the United Kingdom.

Heinz Fischer was almost thirty-two, and because of his fair hair, blue eyes and good physique the Nazis would have claimed that he was typically Geman. He was wearing a light-green corduroy jacket, a check shirt and denim trousers, the universal garb of young men in most countries of the western world. At least of those who didn't work for banks, the big conglomerates and the international fiefdoms of IBM, Siemens and the like. He had joined the *Kriminalpolizei* straight from university, but his talents and languages had led to an early transfer to the Popos. He liked his job and had been promoted twice. And promotion meant that he was seldom part of a team, and spent no time guarding public figures as they hurried from their Mercs, Rolls Royces or Citroens into palaces and parliaments. Although all his family knew that he was a Popo officer they always referred to him as being a police officer, and none of them, not even his father, had much idea of what he did. Some things he did would have shocked them, but most of his work they would have seen as odd but possibly necessary in a wicked world.

When the cassette-player eventually switched itself off Fischer lay there for several minutes in silence before he looked at his watch. Sighing, he swung his long legs off the sofa and stood up. He had to be at Wahn in less than an hour.

Malik checked in his luggage and picked his seat on the Lufthansa flight to Cologne. He sat with a cup of coffee in the cafeteria, his canvas holdall between his feet. Truslove had brought him to Gatwick by car. A generous gesture that made him feel guilty at his lack of response to Truslove's chatter on the journey. When the car pulled up in front of the terminal he had turned to Truslove.

'There's something I'd like to know, Gordon.'

'What's that?'

'Why did they decide to send *me* on this job?'

'Like Jenkins said. You speak perfect German and you're experienced.'

'No other reason?'

'What other reason could there be?'

Malik had seen the embarrassment in Truslove's eyes as he asked the question. Embarrassed because he knew the answer.

'Because I'm a Jew?'

'Oh, for God's sake. What's that got to do with it?'

Malik had reached over onto the back seat for his hand-luggage and he said softly, 'Is the boot unlocked?'

'Yes. Let me help you with your kit.'

'Thanks for the lift, Gordon. I don't need any help.'

They must have known how much he hated dealing direct with Germans. He didn't just hate them. All of them. He was afraid of them. At the monthly conferences in Hamburg he never stayed overnight no matter how long the meeting went on. If there was no convenient direct flight back to London he would fly to Paris or Amsterdam rather than wait around at Fuhlsbüttel. In the early days he had even taken sandwiches and a flask so that there was no need to eat their food. There was nothing about his features or his appearance that indicated that he was a Jew but he was sure that the bastards knew. They had always been amiable and respectful, seldom arguing with his evaluations, accepting his decisions without apparent resentment. But there had been times when he wanted to shout it out loud. 'I am a Jew. You bastards murdered my mamma.' He knew there was no point in doing it, but was ashamed that he had never done it. And now he would be there for weeks, maybe months.

He fetched another coffee but as he got back to the table they were calling his flight. For a split second he closed his eyes and thought of catching the train back to Victoria. Then he reached under the table for his holdall and walked to the loading gate.

It was nearly an hour later when the plane took off. He looked out from his window seat and the houses became smaller as the plane shuddered its way up through the candy-floss clouds. When the warning lights went out he lit a cigarette and reached into his holdall for the paperback copy of Palgrave.

It was dark by the time they swept over the woods on the approach line to Wahn, and it was spitting with rain as he clattered down the metal steps to the tarmac. At the bottom of the steps a Lufthansa ground hostess stopped him. 'Herr Malik?'

He nodded and, smiling, she said, 'Will you follow me, please?'

Malik followed the girl to the main doors and then away from the main processing area, along a corridor to an office marked 'Private'. She opened the door and waved her clipboard to indicate that he should go in.

A young man in a tweed sports coat was sitting on a metal table, one leg swinging until he saw Malik. He stood up and held out his hand. 'Mr Malik. Heinz Fischer. Welcome to Cologne.'

'Good evening.'

'They're putting your bags in my car then I'll take you into town. Would you like a drink while we're waiting?'

'I'd be glad of a coffee.'

'Sugar and cream?'

'Please.'

Fischer picked up the phone, dialled twice and ordered two coffees. He laughed at something that was said and then hung up, turning back to Malik.

'I think you know Cologne quite well. You've been before, I think.'

'A couple of times only, and I didn't leave the hotel.'

'Ah well. We must put that right this time.'

A girl brought the coffees and Malik guessed that Fischer was known at the airport. The coffee was in china cups not plastic. Or maybe it was just that undoubtedly handsome face that did it.

'Do you live in Cologne?'

'I live with my parents in one of the suburbs. Lindenthal. It's very green out there. Woods and lakes and a nature sanctuary. My father sends you an invitation to dine with us tomorrow evening. Just the family.'

'Thank you. Have we got a base, an office or something?'

Fischer smiled. 'They don't want us in Police HQ, that's for sure. It's not that they're uncooperative but I think they want to be able to sweep us under the carpet if anything goes wrong. I've been given funds and I've rented a small apartment in town. There's room for the two of us to live there and two rooms spare for offices.' He smiled. 'I gather you don't want to waste time.'

'Have you got much information already?'

'Not really. A few leads here and there, but I didn't want to do anything much until you came.'

A man in Lufthansa uniform opened the door and nodded to Fischer. 'It's loaded and out front. I've put the parking lights on, so don't be too long.'

Fischer turned to Malik. 'Let's go.'

The apartment was in one of the small streets near the radio station. It had obviously been rebuilt after the war, but although the interior was modern its façade was much the same as it must have been when it was originally built before Germany was a state. The front windows looked down on to a cobbled pedestrians-only shopping precinct and the back windows on to a small public garden with two wooden benches and a few rose bushes just coming into leaf.

The apartment was comfortably furnished with good, solid, German furniture in walnut and mahogany. When Fischer had shown him the layout they both sat together in the main room, and it was Fischer who voiced the first doubts.

'I haven't much background to contribute to this job, you know. It got handed down to me from above as if it were all cut and dried, but as soon as I started looking for real facts – something that would stand up in court – there was very little.' He paused and looked amiably at Malik. 'We could be wasting our time.'

'Where did the information first come from?'

'That's hard to pin down. The first official document is a telephone conversation between a Member of Parliament and the Police Chief in Hamburg. The guy said he had received information that the East Germans were sending agents into the Federal Republic to organize subversion groups. He wouldn't say where he got the information. I don't think it was taken too seriously at first, but a couple of weeks later there was a similar report from Berlin. That was from a journalist who is normally reliable. He had picked it up at a students' meeting at Humboldt University.'

'What party was the Member of Parliament?'

'CDU – a right-winger, but not an extremist by any means. Neither is the journalist, and as his information came via a definitely left-wing source it was treated as a strong indication that there was something in it.'

'Have you been on it full-time?'

'I was for the first couple of weeks, but I was put onto another case and after that I've only put in a day or two here and there. For the last month Bonn have been negotiating with London about our agreement, and since SIS agreed to take it over there's been very little done. Everybody seemed to lose interest.'

'Do you think there's anything in it?'

Fischer smiled. 'Officially I've got no idea. Nothing concrete one way or another. Unofficially . . . yes, I do think there's something in it.'

'What makes you think that?'

'God knows. Just instinct. It sounds right somehow.'

'How long have you been in the racket?'

'Just over eight years, including a year in the *Kriminal polizei*.'

'Maybe we should start by having a word with the politician in Hamburg and see if we can trace his source.'

'I went up to Hamburg to interview him. When I phoned his office for an interview he said he'd check with Bonn. His secretary phoned back and said he regretted that it wasn't possible.'

'Who did he check with in Bonn?'

'He implied that he was checking with the Ministry but I suspect he was actually checking with CDU headquarters.'

'Why shouldn't they want him to cooperate?'

Fischer shrugged. 'Politics. They wouldn't shed any tears if it was discovered that the government had been warned of left-wing subversives and had done nothing about it. They can claim they did their bit by reporting it, and it was up to the government to do the rest. Willy Brandt went down the river because of weak security and KGB infiltration, Schmidt has only been Chancellor for a few weeks, and the CDU would be happy for him to be shown as yet another security risk right now.'

'So why don't the Government pursue this more actively?'

'The agreement with London that we don't act unilaterally against the KGB, for one thing. And the fact that KGB stooges in West Germany are more than we can cope with. At the last count the estimate was 15,000. Give or take a thousand or two I'd say that's about right. And we haven't got resources to cope with that. The CIA are only interested in information about Soviet Intelligence, and your people . . . well, we're never quite sure what they *are* interested in.'

'Are you married, Heinz?'

'No. Are you?'

'No.'

'Steady girlfriend?'

'Girlfriends, but not steady.'

Fischer laughed. 'I've got a steady but I can't see any girl putting up with my sort of life. Or me for that matter. She says she wouldn't mind, but I'm not so sure that she really knows what it would be like.'

'What does she do?'

'She's a musician. Teaches harmony at the School of Music. My whole background is music. All my family are musicians.'

'A large family?'

'Mother, father, two sisters and me. I guess that's large these days.'

'You don't look like a policeman.'

Fischer smiled. 'Why not?'

'You look too happy.'

'I am happy.' Fischer shrugged. 'I've got my family, music, my girl, a job I like, and reasonable pay and conditions. What more could a man want?'

'How old are you?'

'Thirty-one. Thirty-two next month. I guess you're a little older.'

'I'm thirty-eight.'

'Tell me about your family.'

Malik stood up and Fischer was momentarily shocked by the look on his face, but the young German was too sophisticated to linger with what was obviously a gaffe. He stood up too and said, 'There's food in the refrigerator. I'll move in with you tomorrow and we'll get down to it. If you don't mind I'll stay at home tonight.'

Malik's face was taut and grim as he shrugged. 'It's up to you, Fischer. Do whatever you want.'

After Fischer had gone Malik walked over to the window. He could see the lights of the main railway station and the massive silhouette of the cathedral and very faintly from below he heard men shouting. He looked down and saw a policeman struggling with a belligerent drunk as a crowd of youths stood watching. At the far end of the shopping precinct the blue light of a police car was flashing as a police driver opened the doors at the rear. Malik turned away and walked to the bedroom where Fischer had put his bags. All his life when he heard people shouting in anger they seemed to be shouting in German. German was the language for shouting.

He undressed slowly and lay with the bedside light on, looking up at the ceiling. It stayed on all night as he slept.

Day after day, Abraham Malik's group had fought back against the Germans. Both the Germans and the Polish Resistance had expected the Red Army to come to Warsaw's rescue, but day after day they just sat there on the other side of the river, waiting and watching. A few aircraft parachuted food and medical supplies to the beleaguered fighters but they were only token supplies.

As the days went by and the numbers of Polish dead mounted, the Nazis reinforced their troops. Berlin had realized before the Poles that the Resistance fighters were going to be sacrificed by Moscow. The Red Army had no doubts about its ability to crush the SS forces around Warsaw, but Stalin was looking ahead. Resistance fighters could harass occupying armies no matter whether they were Russian or German. Let the Nazis do the dirty work of wiping them out. Forty thousand Poles died in those last few days of fighting the Nazis.

Abraham Malik was thirty-two the day the Red Army tanks rolled into Warsaw. Rabbi Rabinowitz lay with him in the rubble that had been the basement of the telephone exchange. Malik had a long, pus-filled gash, that spread from his ribs to his thigh, from an SS grenade, but as Rabbi Rabinowitz tried to comfort him it seemed certain that he only had a few hours to live. And again and again Malik had wept for his wife and son. He was obsessed by the thought that they might think he had deserted them. She had known that he was one of the Jewish Underground leaders but maybe she would feel that his duty should have been to her and their child. And maybe she was right. They had failed. They had fought against the Nazi occupiers only to exchange them for the Red Army. The Rabbi had feared that Malik's depression would only hasten his death. But when a Red Army medical team took Malik to the tented field hospital the obsession became an advantage. It seemed to give the Jew the reason he needed for living. He would find them and explain. And they would understand.

He had not been discharged from the hospital for two months and it took fourteen soul-destroying, frustrating months of bribery and persuasion before he eventually found his son in a Displaced Persons Camp near the Polish-Russian border. He was just ten years old.

The Rabbi came round to the Maliks most Sunday evenings to play chess with Abraham Malik and it was on one of those nights that Jake Malik had first learned of his father's life in the ghetto.

The Rabbi had just won a long-drawn-out game and as he sat sipping his coffee he turned smiling to the boy.

'Your father had more courage against the SS than he has playing chess.' He turned to look at the older man. 'Remember what you used to say, my friend? He who has nothing to lose can try anything.'

Jake remembered the look on his father's face as he looked up from rearranging the chessboard.

'I was a fool, Leo. We all had things to lose if only we had realized it. And what did we gain? Nothing. Thousands dead who could still be alive. Poland exchanged one tyrant for another. We were all fools, Leo. Especially me. I had a wife and son to lose, and it haunts me that I was wrong.

'How were you wrong, my friend?'

'I sacrificed her for a cause. A cause that was doomed to failure. I curse myself every day. It

doesn't bear thinking about.'

The Rabbi sighed. 'Remember the words in the Talmud, my friend. "When a young man's wife dies, the altar of God is draped in mourning."'

Abraham Malik shook his head. 'There's another line, Leo, that's more real for me – "There is a substitute for everything except the wife of your youth."'

Rabinowitz leaned forward to put his hand on Malik's knee as he turned to look at the boy.

'One of these days I will tell you about those times. He was a brave man, your father. There were many brave men and women in those terrible years.' He turned his head to look at Malik. 'Have you shown him your medal, Abraham?'

Malik's father shook his head. 'It's rubbish, Leo. Rubbish.'

Jake Malik said, 'Show me the medal, Father, please.'

His father stood up slowly and walked over to the small desk in the corner of the room. He came back with a case of dark red leather in the palm of his hand, offering it without looking at it to his son.

Jake Malik opened the case. On a bed of white silk was a red ribbon with narrow blue stripes at each edge, and a gold cross below. It looked pristine, as if the case had never been opened before. As he looked the Rabbi spoke.

'The Cross of Merit, Jacob. First class. In gold.'

The boy looked at his father, embarrassed, not knowing what to say and his father said softly, 'Keep it, boy. I meant to throw it away long ago.' Then he turned to look at the Rabbi. 'I hate them, Leo. I always will. It haunts me. For her to die would be bad enough but to die in that hell-hole . . .' He shook his head slowly. '. . . what can her last moments have been like . . .?' And tears flowed down his cheeks before he put his head in his hands and the Rabbi signalled for the boy to leave them.

CHAPTER THREE

Heinz Fischer let himself into the apartment just before ten o'clock, carrying two small cases. He opened one of them, took out a dark red file cover and placed it carefully on the table.

'Pretty thin, but it's all we've got. Have you eaten yet?'

'I don't eat breakfast but I've had an orange juice.'

Fischer looked at him. 'What's your first name?'

'Jacob. People generally call me Jake.'

Fischer smiled. 'Was it Jacob in the Bible who worked all those years to marry Ruth?'

Malik half-smiled. 'It was Rachel and Leah. Seven years hard labour for each.'

'A pity. My girl's named Ruth, and I've always connected her with that story.'

'Ruth was the grandmother of David. That's even more romantic. Anyway, we'd better get down to work.'

'OK. Let me go over the file.'

They went through it item by item. No matter how routine or apparently insignificant the document, Malik read it carefully before going to the next, asking questions as he went along and making notes on a small pad from time to time. When they were through he looked back at his notes.

'I think the first thing is to interview the guy in Hamburg. Whatever he knows we need to know.'

'Then what?'

'We check whoever his source was.' He looked across the table at Fischer. 'Are your suspect records computerized?'

'Yes. But I haven't got authority to access them except with written permission.'

'So we get written permission or I get London to do it. No problem.'

'There might be, Jake.'

'Why.'

'Inter-party politics.'

'This is an SIS operation, Heinz. German politics don't come into it.'

'You know that's not true, my friend. If London wasn't going along with Bonn you and I wouldn't be sitting here.'

'What's that mean?'

'I think you know already.'

Malik smiled. 'Maybe I do, but you tell me.'

'These groups are all over the country. They must be. When they did the anti-Jewish stuff it was on the same night in ten or eleven different cities. All far apart from one another except for Cologne and Düsseldorf. The slogans in every town were in several places. That meant a lot of groups and several people in each group. And there's just you and me on this operation. Whichever way you look at it it doesn't make sense. Not unless they either don't want us to succeed or they just don't give a damn one way or another.'

'How frankly do we talk to each other, Heinz?'

'For me, as frankly as you like. We're on the same side. Officially and any other way as far as I'm concerned.'

'You aren't going to wear a German hat to protect the national interest?'

'No. If I was told to hold back or my people started playing games I should tell you.'

'OK. How do we get to see the guy in Hamburg?'

Fischer shrugged. 'Let's play it the usual way. I'll phone him for an appointment.'

It was ten minutes before Fischer came back, looking pleased with himself. 'It was like getting through to the Pope. He said he was a very busy man but he can give us a few minutes tomorrow and we won't have to go up to Hamburg. He's going to be in Bonn for a few days.'

'Where are we meeting him?'

'He's got a suite at the Königshof and has granted us audience at eleven o'clock. He sounds a pompous bastard.'

'Can you contact the journalist in Berlin? Then we can book a flight for Friday.'

'I think we'd do better to go there and contact him on the spot. If I phone him he'll want to know why we want to talk with him, and they always have this thing about never revealing their sources. Face to face he'll probably do a deal.'

'Will you book the flight, then?'

'OK. Leave it to me. By the way, you're dining with us tonight, remember.

They all want to meet you.'

'That's very kind of you.'

Fischer called for him at seven o'clock, and twenty minutes later they turned into the drive of a handsome house. The whole of the outside was white, and in the pale, evening sunshine of the spring day it looked peaceful and calm, with the wide lawns and tall yew trees. It looked like the kind of house that was advertised in *Country Life*.

There were lights on despite the sunshine, and a tall, thin man in a dark suit stood on the wide steps of the portico. As Heinz introduced him to his father the grey-haired man took his hand.

'My son tells me you're in Cologne for some time, Herr Malik. You must come and see us often while you're here. Despite your work you might be lonely.'

He took Malik's arm and led him into the house. He was introduced to Frau Fischer and Heinz's two pretty sisters, Heidi, aged twenty, and Lisa, who was a few years older. And then they went straight into the dining room to eat. The conversation was mainly about music. Even the news that the Chinese had launched their first satellite quickly strayed into a discussion on modern Chinese violin-playing techniques. They had almost finished the meal when Heidi said, 'Let's play favourites, Papa.'

Herr Fischer smiled. 'We mustn't bore our guests with nothing but talk of music, my dear.'

The girl turned her blue eyes on Malik. 'You start us off, Herr Malik. What's your favourite piece of music?'

Malik smiled. 'How about you guess?'

Heidi laughed and clapped her hands. 'A clue first. Just one.'

'It's cello music.'

'Ah, as you're English it's going to be the Elgar, yes?'

Heinz grinned across the table. 'The Brahms. I'm sure it's the Brahms.'

Malik shook his head. 'I didn't say it was a concerto – maybe it is, but maybe not.'

'The Bach Partitas?' Herr Fischer said, eyebrows raised.

'No. I'm afraid not.'

Frau Fischer laughed and shrugged. 'One of the Mendelssohn Sonatas.'

Malik looked smiling at Lisa and she frowned. 'Can I have two guesses? I'm sure it's one of them.'

'Go on then.'

'It's either the Tchaikowsky Rococo Variations or it's the Max Bruch setting of "Kol Nidrei".'

Malik smiled. 'Yes. The Bruch setting. But I could easily have chosen the Variations if I'd remembered them.'

Frau Fischer leaned forward to look down the table at her daugher and then at Malik. 'You know, she worries me sometimes, that girl. If we lived in the Middle Ages I think she'd have been in danger of being burnt as a witch. She's got second sight. She knows things she couldn't possibly know.'

As if she were embarrassed, Lisa stood up. 'I'm going into town, Mama. I'll be back about eleven.' She turned to look at Malik. 'Goodnight, Herr Malik. Don't let them bore you with too much music.'

Malik stood up, knocking the table so that the china rattled. 'Goodnight, Fräulein Fischer.'

There were a few moments silence as the girl walked from the room, and then

Herr Fischer said, 'Let's take our coffee in the other room. And you play to us, Heidi. Something gentle. Brahms, perhaps. Or something French.'

Heidi sat down at the piano and they listened in silence as she played a Ballade and the Rhapsody in G major. Then Heinz drove him back into the city. As they walked together up the shopping precinct and stood at the door of the apartment house, Heinz said, 'I hope we didn't bore you too much. We are bores with our music. We know it, but we can't help it. That's why we seldom invite anyone who isn't a musician.'

'I wasn't bored, Heinz. I enjoyed it all very much. It was very thoughtful of you all. I appreciate it.'

'Tomorrow I'll move in properly.'

'OK. Drive carefully.'

Malik stood in the shadow of the building watching Fischer walk away. He looked much younger than his age and he wondered if it was the music that made them such an attractive family. It was hard to believe that they were German. He wouldn't want too much of them. They *were* bores about music. They couldn't just enjoy it. All that talk of performances, and comparisons of one soloist with another. Arguments about tempi and treatment. Why was Toscanini always so fast? Was Karajan's Beethoven really definitive? He wondered if they ever just sat back and listened without analysing every bar. He wondered how the girl Lisa had guessed the Bruch. So few people had ever heard of it. And he'd been going to choose the Mendelssohn fiddle concerto but the lush setting of the Jewish hymn had come into his mind, because he had thought of how much his father would have enjoyed the talk of music and the enthusiasm.

For five days he had hidden between the bottom bunk and the floor. On the fifth day the Kapo had dragged him out by his feet and flung him against the wall. He tried to get back on his feet but there was no power in his skinny legs. He was surprised to see a woman with the Kapo. She had a lean Jewish face and piercing dark eyes as she looked down at him.

'What's your name, boy?' she said.

'Jacob Malik.'

'You mother's name?'

'Rebecca Maria Malik.'

The woman turned to look at the Kapo. 'You bring him tonight, Ganiek, and you get the watch. Understand. If you try playing games there'll be no more Kanada or women's camp for you. I'll see to that.'

The Kapo shrugged, pretending indifference, but the boy could see that he was scared of the woman despite the fact that there was a yellow Jewish triangle on her dress.

When the woman had gone, the Kapo made him get back under the tiered bunk. He had stayed there trembling for another two hours until the Kapo dragged him out again, shoving him past the rows of bunks to the door.

In the dusk they walked across the two sets of railway lines that divided Auschwitz camp from Birkenau, and by the first row of huts inside the wire the woman was waiting.

For just over two months he had never left the hut where the girls sat sewing at the long wooden tables. The woman who had come for him was in charge of them. At the far end of the room was a tailor's dummy. One of the girls had whispered to him that it was the dummy for Frau Hoess, the Camp Commandant's wife, for whom most of the sewing was done. The clothes were of high fashion and the woman in charge had been the owner of an haute-couture *house in Warsaw before the war.*

He was fed and given odd jobs to do, and at night he slept in the locked workroom. He had overheard two of the girls talking about him, discussing why the woman was taking the risk of protecting him. They were sure that his mother must have paid her.

Sometimes in the early morning before the workshop was open he would stand on a wooden box and look out of the windows. Beyond the barbed wire fence was a plantation of silver birches before the outer perimeter fence and the electrified wire. From the window he could see four of the guardtowers with searchlights on their roofs and machine guns mounted on three sides pointing inside the camp.

It was on one of those mornings that the woman had come into the room, so quietly that he had not even heard the key turn in the lock on the door. She was standing beside him before he realized she was there.

'Well, Master Jacob, and what can you see?'

When he jumped violently and she saw the fear on his face she put her hand on his shoulder. She said softly, 'Do you know my name?'

He nodded and she said, 'What is it?'

'You're Panna Felinska.'

For the first time since he had seen her he saw her smile.

'That's very formal, little boy. What else do you know about me?'

He shrugged. 'They say my mother gave you gold to save me, and you made ladies' dresses before the Germans came.'

For long minutes she looked at his face and he saw tears on the edges of her eyes. Then she slowly shook her head. 'They are just stupid . . . no, that's not fair . . . they are just victims. Victims of this hell-hole.' She nodded towards the window. 'Even the animals know what goes on. There are no birds, no squirrels, nothing, in those trees inside the camp.' She turned back to look at his face. 'Where is your father now?'

'I don't know, Panna Felinska.'

'Was he brought to the camp?'

'No. He went before they got us.'

She nodded and sighed. 'He always was a fool. He'll be fighting with the others. All men are fools. Especially if they're Polish Jews.' She sighed again. 'Why should they die for Poland? The Poles are just as bad. They hate us just as the Germans do.'

He stood silent and obviously embarrassed. Not knowing what to say. Not understanding what she said. She smiled at him.

'Will you do something for me one day?'

'Yes, Panna Felinska.'

'If ever you see your father again will you tell him that you met Grazyna Felinska?'

'Yes. I'll tell him when I see him.'

She shook her head slowly. 'Don't say it like that, little Jacob. Not when *you see him.* If *you see him.'*

CHAPTER FOUR

The white Merc had its hood down as Fischer drove them down the main road alongside the Rhine; they were out of the city just after nine o'clock, and in Bonn by ten. They parked the car in the hotel carpark and ordered coffee and toast in the breakfast room.

'Do you want me to introduce you as another Popo or as SIS?'

'He'll tell from my accent that I'm not German.'

'I doubt it. You've only got a very slight accent and it's not English. What is it, by the way?'

'Polish.'

'Were you born in Poland?'

'Yes.'

Fischer waited for Malik to say more but when he didn't he went back to his question.

'Popo or SIS?'

'I'd say at this stage, Popo. You be sweetheart.'

Fischer smiled. 'I don't understand.'

'You be the nice guy. Reasonable, and on his side if he argues. I'll be the nasty.'

Fischer shrugged, smiling, 'OK. If that's how you want it.'

'Don't go along with him too far. You gradually begin to see my point.'

'More coffee?'

'Yes. We've still got twenty minutes.'

Fischer waved to a waiter and he poured them more coffee. When he had gone Fischer said, 'My father was very impressed with you. Said we were all uncivilized hogging away about music all the time. Complained that we hadn't asked you about your family and your interests.'

'I enjoyed it, Heinz. It made me seem one of the family and not just a guest.'

'Tell me about your family. They wanted to know.'

'I don't have any family. My father died a month ago. He was the only relative still alive.'

'You must be rather lonely.'

'I don't think about it, Heinz. I just get on with being alive. Surviving.'

'You're obviously interested in music. Do you play anything?'

'A bit of piano. A bit of violin. I'm mainly a listener.'

'The family are performing next month. Would you care to go if we're here?'

'I'd like to very much. Did you do anything about booking a flight to Berlin?'

'Yes. Typical German efficiency. Provisional bookings for five o'clock today and ten tomorrow morning.'

'Does Lufthansa allow provisional bookings?'

Fischer laughed. 'They do if you're a Popo officer. We'd better pay the bill and go on up.'

Herr Doktor Fassbinder's secretary said that he would be only a few minutes and maybe they would like to take a seat. There was a copy of *Die Welt* and the *Frankfurter Allgemeine* if they wished.

The Herr Doktor kept them waiting for ten minutes which Malik guessed was about par for the course. He came through the big double doors from another room. A large stout man with a shiny, smooth, red face, rubbing his hands together as if they were cold. Bustling towards them with an electioneering smile on his face.

'Which one of you is Fischer?'

Heinz Fischer put out his hand 'I am, Herr Doktor.'

'And your colleague?'

'Herr Malik.'

Fassbinder turned his big body and looked at Malik like a general inspecting the guard, and then turned away dismissively. He didn't seem impressed. He pointed to two chairs and drew up a third for himself.

'What can I do for you, gentlemen?'

Fischer started them off. 'You spoke to the chief of the *Kriminalpolizei* in Hamburg some months ago about the possibility of the East Germans setting up subversion groups in the Federal Republic. We'd like to pursue that.'

'Pursue it? There's nothing to pursue. I assume that whatever needed to be done has been done.'

'Of course. But we are taking it very seriously, and we should appreciate your help.'

The Herr Doktor spread his fat hands like a Frenchman denying guilt. 'What possible help could I give?'

Malik said quietly, 'Who gave *you* the information, Herr Doktor?'

Fassbinder turned his head slowly to look at Malik, the folds of fat at his neck compressing as he turned. His eyes were half closed with overdone disdain.

'What I was told I was told in confidence, young man.'

Malik nodded. 'Of course. And we want you to tell us in confidence who gave you the information.'

Fassbinder shook his head. 'Impossible. Unthinkable.'

Malik sniffed. 'You realize that would mean you were obstructing the police in their inquiries.'

'Who, may I ask, is your superior officer?'

Malik smiled. 'Let's not play games, Herr Fassbinder.'

'D'you realize you are talking to a Member of Parliament? Perhaps you hadn't been told?'

'Yes, I have been told, Herr Doktor. And I checked your file. You were elected seven years ago with a big majority. Your Communist Party opponent withdrew at the last minute but you'd have probably won anyway.'

'This is preposterous.' And Fassbinder looked back at Heinz Fischer for support.

But Malik went on. 'Are you going to tell us who gave you the information?'

'Certainly not. And I shall raise this matter with your senior officers.'

'That's OK with me, Herr Fassbinder. By the way, I saw that on the British de-nazification report on your case that you claimed you joined the Nazi party in 1937. But they had the originals of the party documents and in fact you joined in 1933. Right at the start, when there was no pressure on anyone to join. And in your election address you claimed that you had never been a member of the party at any time. You're a capable politician, Fassbinder, and I could never understand why you had left yourself wide open in that way.'

Fassbinder heaved himself out of his chair and walked over to where a white telephone stood alongside a bowl of anemones on a small table. As he picked up the phone Malik said, 'You're being very unwise, Fassbinder. They don't know in Bonn what's on your file.'

Fassbinder's fat finger dialled once and then stopped, turning to look at Malik.

'What the hell do you mean?'

'I mean that you're giving yourself away. Nobody in Bonn has seen this file. But I imagine that the SDP would be delighted to use it if it came out.'

Fassbinder slowly replaced the receiver.

'Who the hell are you?'

'I'm a policeman.'

'You're a blackmailer, Herr Malik, and you could get yourself into deep trouble. I warn you.'

'Sit down, Herr Fassbinder. Just sit down.'

For a moment Fassbinder hesitated, and then compromised by sitting only on the arm of the chair. Malik looked at him amiably.

'I suggest you help me with my inquiry and that we forget the rest of our talk.'

Fassbinder looked towards the window for several moments and they could hear the typewriter clacking in the outer room. Without turning his head Fassbinder said, 'Where is this so-called file?'

'It's in the Central Archives at Century House in London. Or it was last night.'

Fassbinder turned his head quickly. 'What the hell is Century House?'

'It's the headquarters of MI6. I'm the MI6 officer in charge of this investigation. And I've no wish or intention to embarrass you. But I've every intention of finding out who told you about these groups.'

'You think they exist?' And the voice was suddenly conciliatory.

'I'm sure they do. Don't you?'

'And they're a danger to the State?'

'Any clandestine organization is a danger to the State.'

The fingers of Fassbinder's plump right hand played clumsy arpeggios on the arm of the chair by his leg.

'That puts a different face on this matter. Let me think about it. Call me tomorrow morning about this time.'

'I need to know now, Herr Doktor. We've got a lot of other inquiries to pursue.'

Fassbinder smiled. An ingratiating smile. 'You must be a very good investigator, Herr Malik. You're a very determined man.'

Malik said nothing, and eventually, looking down at his jacket and picking a non-existent speck from his lapel, Fassbinder said, 'This will have to be in confidence, of course.'

'Of course,' Malik said.

Fassbinder smiled at him. 'We're men of the world you and I, Herr Malik, so I know you'll appreciate my concern for complete . . . er . . . confidence.' He paused and then went on. 'I meet all kinds of people in my political life. I have to. I need to know what all levels of society are thinking in my constituency. Of course I have helpers – a trade unionist, a church official, several leading businessmen and of course . . . er . . . young people . . . Why don't we all have a drink?'

Fassbinder walked over to a cupboard, opened its doors to reveal several shelves of bottles and turned towards his guests.

'Schnapps, whisky, vodka . . . what'll you have?'

'Have you got a dryish sherry?' Fischer asked.

'Of course. And you, Herr Malik?'

'Nothing for me, thank you. I've got an internal problem.'

'Nothing serious I hope,' Fassbinder said, with obvious indifference, as he poured the sherry for Fischer and a large whisky for himself before coming back to sit in the armchair. He unbuttoned his jacket, loosened his tie and patted his fat belly. He smiled.

'Too many official dinners. They ought to pay us danger money . . . Cheers.' He took a generous swig of his whisky. 'Now, where was I . . . ah, yes . . . the young people. That's where all the trouble comes from these days . . . drugs . . . protest marches . . . demonstrations against authority and all that bloody nonsense.' He waved his hand dismissively. It was a standard litany and a standard gesture, like the unbuttoned jacket and the loosened tie. It showed that his audience were specially favoured. Intimates of the great man in his moments of relaxation from the cares of State. 'There was one of them . . . one of the young people . . . I took a special interest in . . . insecure, bad home background, wrong set of friends, but intelligent in her own way . . . and talented. A lovely voice.' He sighed. 'She was a singer in one of the clubs . . . I was able to help here and there . . . a word in the right ear. I suppose she saw it as more than it was . . . mind you, I was very fond of her, very fond . . . I helped her get the lease of a small flat . . . saw her from time to time . . . there was a fellow in the background . . . there always is with a pretty girl . . . played in a group at another club . . . a bad influence, drugs and all that . . . she told me he got money from some political source. And he boasted that he was more important than she thought he was. One day she'd see how important he was. Said that "detente" was just a cover-up and when the time came he and his group would be on the winning side. She hadn't told him about her knowing me and it seems one day he looked in her handbag and found a watch I'd given her for her birthday . . . raised hell about it and she told him . . . no reason why she shouldn't, of course . . . anyway the long and short of it was that he forbade her to see me again. Threatened her, said he'd have her beaten up, disfigured. I told her it was a lot of poppycock but there was no convincing her. She was shit-scared and didn't want to see me any more. That's more or less it. I told my friend at the *Kriminalpolizei* but I heard no more of it.'

'What was the girl's name?' Malik's voice was barely audible.

Fassbinder closed his eyes as if he were trying hard to remember, but Malik knew that he didn't need to.

'Maria something or other. Yes. Maria Hauser.'

'Is she still at the flat?'

'Yes. He'll be there too.'

'Can I have the address?'

'You won't mention my name?'

'Herr Fassbinder, as far as I am concerned, when I leave this room I shall forget the whole of our conversation except that man's name and address. Our conversation this morning was concerned with getting your views on Federal police budgets.'

Fassbinder nodded. 'The apartment is at 17 Monkedamm. The name on the door is Hauser.'

Malik stood up. 'Thanks for your help, Herr Fassbinder.'

Fassbinder was relieved and jovial as he walked with them through the outer room and opened the door to the corridor to let them out. 'Good hunting,' he said, and Malik nodded and smiled.

Heinz Fischer reached forward to switch on the ignition and then stopped, leaning back in his seat, turning to look at Malik.

'How the hell did you get that stuff about Fassbinder?'

'I phoned London last night. They phoned me back about one o'clock this morning.'

'But what made you think there might be something compromising in his record?'

'I didn't, I just wanted to check.'

'It was virtually blackmail.'

'Nonsense. Just a bit of pressure to make the bastard tell the truth. He was withholding information about internal security.'

'What would you have done if he had phoned headquarters?'

Malik laughed. 'I knew he wouldn't. There was a lot more on the file than I said.'

'D'you think there's anything in what the girl told him?'

'God knows. He may have been lying, using his position to get his own back on the man who'd taken over the girl.' Malik looked at his watch. 'We could catch the evening flight.'

CHAPTER FIVE

It took them two days to trace the girl. She had moved out of the apartment the day before they arrived and had left no forwarding address, but a cleaning woman was able to tell them the name of the club where the girl worked.

The club was in St Pauli in the basement of a warehouse in Erichstrasse. Its unoriginal name, Klub Eros, was in red neon above the door and a man just inside the door asked for five marks each as a membership fee. The decor inside paid its tribute to the river a hundred yards away. Teak steps down from the street door and ships' barometers and compasses on the mock walnut walls. There were twenty or so tables and the soft pink lighting made both patrons and girls look healthy and glamorous.

A topless waitress led them to a table and they looked carefully at the price list and ordered two beers. Along the furthest wall was a long bench where half a dozen girls sat chatting. A pianist on a slightly raised dais was playing old-fashioned rock and boogie. About half the tables were occupied and the men looked prosperous. The two girls who came over to join them were quite pretty and they settled themselves at the table and started their traditional patter. Names, where do you two boys come from, how long are you staying and a desperate thirst that only champagne could quench. After about twenty minutes Malik asked where Maria was.

'Which one, honey? We've got two Marias.'

'Maria Hauser or is it Haufer?'

'She's gone to change. She sings as well.'

'As well as what?'

The girl giggled. 'There's a room at the back if you want to find out. We could have a foursome.'

Malik smiled back at her. 'Somebody recommended that I should have a look at Maria.'

'Well here she comes, mister.'

The dim lights were dimmed even further, and a spotlight came on to one side of the piano as a girl came on the stage. She was young, pretty and blonde, and she was wearing a white bikini so skimpy that she might just as well have been naked. She was obviously popular because there was some desultory clapping as soon as she appeared. She smiled and nodded to the pianist and after a few chords she started singing. It wasn't a good voice but it was distinctive. Girlish and clear with an attractive catch of the breath as she sang 'Falling in love again'. She was pretty, and her body was attractive, but not enough to explain the obvious sexuality of her performance. Malik guessed that it was her youth, her appeal to masculine protectiveness. The thing that made some men pay for whores to dress up as schoolgirls. A mixture of innocence and complaisance.

She sang again; this time it was 'Where have all the flowers gone?' The two Marlene Dietrich hits were both incongruous yet appealing when sung so differently from the original sultry versions. None of Dietrich's worldly knowingness and yet more sexual.

There was considerable applause and then the spotlight went out and seconds later the lights on the dais went up as the pianist started playing his version of Scott Joplin.

The hostess sitting beside Malik said, 'D'you want to meet her?'

'Is she a hostess as well?'

'Of course she is. But she'll cost you more than I would, honey.'

'Like how much?'

The girl shrugged. 'At least a hundred marks. I'll give you an hour for eighty.'

Malik opened his wallet under the table and passed the girl a ten-mark note. 'You fix it for me, pussy-cat. And maybe you and I can get together tomorrow night.'

The girl shrugged, looked across at her companion and they pushed back their chairs and walked away.

Fischer said, smiling. 'All this on taxpayers' money, Jake. "To surveillance of possible informant – a hundred marks."'

'It's going to cost more than that, Heinz. I want her to take me to her place. How about you leave if she comes out, and check where we go?'

'OK. Here's your one coming back again.'

The girl bent down and said softly, 'She's waiting for you. Go through the curtains where I went. The room's got a red door, it's just past the toilets.'

As Malik stood up Heinz Fischer said, 'I'll settle the bill. See you later.'

Malik nodded and then turned to thread his way past the tables. Dust rose in clouds from the red velvet curtains as he pushed them aside and he found himself in a long corridor that stank of urine and disinfectant. The urine was a clear winner. He knocked on the red door and a girl's voice said, 'Come in.'

She was smiling as he closed the door and she was prettier than he had expected.

'Gerda said you wanted to spend some time with me. Did she tell you how much it is?'

'No.'

'It's one hundred for half an hour.'

'Can I pay for a longer time than that?'

She shook her head, still smiling. 'I can't. I sing every hour after ten until we close.'

He took out his wallet and slowly picked out a hundred-mark note. When he looked up at her he said, 'If I pay you now can I see you tomorrow afternoon?'

She laughed softly, 'You're a funny man.'

'Why?'

She shrugged. 'Most men can't even wait till I get my pants off.'

'You're too pretty to rush it.'

'OK. That's a hundred now and we'll see how long you want tomorrow.'

'What time can I see you?'

She pursed her lips. 'How about two o'clock?'

'Where?'

'D'you know Venusberg?'

'Where that garden is?'

'That's it. There's a paper shop on the corner. My door is next to their door. There's a card over my bell with my name on. Maria Hauser. Ring one long and one short and I'll know it's you.'

'I'll look forward to that.'

She laughed. 'So shall I.'

They had taken adjoining rooms at a *pension* in Grossneumarkt and ordered a meal in their shared lounge.

'How are you going to get the fellow's name out of her?'

'I don't know. I'll just have to keep fishing around. And now we know where she lives we can watch it until we spot him. He's sure to be shacked up with her.'

'Then what?'

Malik seemed intent on cutting his steak and then he looked up. 'What do you suggest?'

'I could maybe persuade the Kripo to arrest him on some charge or other and you and I could interrogate him.'

Malik shook his head. 'If he's what we think he is, he wouldn't talk. Why should he? He'd know the charge was phoney. He'd just wait us out.'

'What else is there?'

'We could keep him on ice until we've talked with the fellow in Berlin.'

'That's a possibility.'

'Or we could do a private job on him.'

'What's that mean?' Fischer looked genuinely surprised.

'Pick him up. Stash him away some place and put him through the mincer.'

'And afterwards, what do we do with him?'

'Get rid of him.'

'You mean kill him?' Fischer's whisper emphasized his disbelief.

'Yes. If it's necessary.'

'You're joking.'

Malik sat back in his chair, chewing slowly as he looked across at Fischer.

'You needn't get involved.'

'But I am involved.'

'I'll send you down to Bonn. That'd give you an alibi.'

'You'd really do this, Jake?'

Malik nodded. 'Sure I would. Why not?'

'You'd get a life sentence if they caught you.'

'They wouldn't get me, and if they did they'd just do a deal with SIS and bundle me back to London.'

'I can't believe you mean it.'

'Why not?'

'You aren't that sort of man.'

'Don't kid yourself, Heinz. I am.' But Malik could see how much the conversation had disturbed the German and he said, 'Let's forget about it until we've had a look at him. Then we can decide whether he looks like a real suspect or not.'

Fischer seemed relieved, but then, looking slightly embarrassed, he said, 'Have you done that kind of thing before?'

Malik pushed aside his plate and grinned. 'Forget it. Leave it to me.'

'But I want to know.'

'Why?'

Fischer shrugged. 'If I'm working with you I want to know what I'm in for.'

'You aren't just working with me, Heinz. You're working *for* me. I give the orders.' Malik smiled but it wasn't a friendly smile. 'I'm sure your people get tough at times.'

'Sure they do. But the guys who do that sort of thing are different. They're thugs, not intelligence men.'

Malik shrugged. 'Maybe you've got a bigger budget than we have. We do our own dirty work.'

'Do you actually get training for this . . .'

'Not everybody. We all get training in self-defence. Even those who are going to end up behind desks. But field agents get further training.'

'To kill innocent people?'

'No. To kill people who might kill us, or want to destroy the State.'

'But this man may know nothing. Or what he knows may be unimportant.'

'If he knows nothing then I'll let him go.' Malik paused then went on. 'You know the problem with people like you, Heinz? You don't like what's done in abattoirs, but you like juicy steaks.'

Fischer said softly, 'Or maybe we learned some lessons from the war.'

'What lessons?'

'That a senior officer's order doesn't have to be obeyed if it's a criminal order.'

Malik shrugged. 'Maybe you should just go back to Cologne right now, and wait until I get back.'

'I'll hang around for now. Let's see what happens.'

Malik nodded and stood up. 'OK,' he said.

As they lay naked on the bed she looked at his face, smiling up at him. 'D'you want to do it again?'

'Can I come back tonight and stay the night?'

She shook her head, still smiling. 'I can't do that.'

'Why not?'

'I've got a boyfriend.'

'Where is he now?'

'God knows. But he'll be back here just before one and I don't leave the club until half past one.'

'What does he do?'

'Plays guitar in a group at another club.'

'You could come to my place.'

'He'd raise hell if I didn't come straight back here. He's very jealous.'

'What's his name?'

'Karl. Anyway, why bother about him now? We've got half an hour left yet.'

'What club does he play at?'

She smiled. 'You wouldn't be interested. They're all queers. Not the group. They're straight.'

'Is he any good?'

She laughed softly and pulled him to her. 'Not as good as you, honey. Do it to me again.'

'Does he know you sleep with other men?'

She kissed him. 'Of course he does. Do it to me now. Come on, honey.'

Ten minutes later, as she was dressing and he was sitting on the edge of the bed, he said, 'You didn't tell me where he plays.'

'It's a dump called The Caliph but you won't like it.'

'Can I have your phone number?'

'Sure. It's on the phone, there. But don't call before eleven in the morning or you'll wake me.'

He took a taxi back to the *pension*. Fischer was out and he'd checked for the address of The Caliph in the telephone directory and with telephone inquiries. Neither was any help. He was coming out of the old-fashioned lift into the hall when Fischer came in, and they went back to their rooms upstairs, as Malik told Fischer what had happened.

'With a name like that it'll be in St Pauli somewhere. I'll get on the phone and check with the police.'

Five minutes later he walked into Malik's room. 'It's down by the Fishmarket. There's no proper address but I know how to find it.' He looked at Malik. 'The inspector said it's a dangerous place if you're not a genuine queer.'

'We'll have to risk that.'

'There is another way.'

'Tell me.'

'I could get the St Pauli police to find out who he is. They could find out more in a couple of hours than we could in days.'

'We couldn't do that.'

'Why not?'

'If I had to pick him up they'd connect it with us straight away.'

'I thought you might say that. There's an alternative but it's not so easy.'

'What's that?'

'I could go with one of the vice officers who cover the clubs. I could say I was doing a general security check-up on homosexuals. And I could ask him to identify various people. Including our friend Karl.'

'Why you?'

Fischer grinned. 'I could try and look at least neutral. Nobody's ever going to take you for anything but a raving hetero.'

Malik closed his eyes for a moment as he sat in the chair. When he opened them he looked at Fischer. 'It's a good idea. Go ahead and fix it.'

'Let me phone St Pauli and then we'll eat.'

It was four o'clock in the morning when Fischer came back. Malik was fast asleep, still sitting in the armchair, the dot on the TV screen still flickering. But as Fischer closed the door gently behind him Malik's eyes opened.

'It worked, Jake. It really worked. Are you too tired to hear it now?'

'I'm not tired, friend. Just cat-napping. What time is it?'

'Ten pas four.'

'Jesus. I must have really slept.' He stood up and walked over to the TV set to switch it off. He turned, smiling, to look at the German.

'You look like Miss World just before they stick the tiara on her head. Shall I ring for some coffee?'

'There's nobody about. It's like a morgue downstairs.'

'OK. Tell me how you were belle of the ball.'

Fischer sat down facing him in the other armchair.

'I went with the sergeant who covers male prostitutes and homosexual brothels and clubs. I learnt more about queers tonight than I did at police school. It's a fantastic world and you don't know whether to be sad or disgusted. That club's like a volcano waiting to erupt.'

Malik smiled. 'What about our Karl?'

'I asked the sergeant who various people were. He knew the life-stories of most of them. Some of them were household names, looking quite at home in that sleazy dump. Wearing lipstick and rouge and eyeshadow. The lot. I got round to the group and he told me that the singer was a queer and told me a bit about him. He was a local. He didn't know anything about the others, but they introduced the group one by one over the microphone when they did solo pieces. Karl Loeb was one of them.'

'What's he look like?'

'About twenty-seven or twenty-eight. Tall, skinny and foxy-looking. Plays guitar well. It was all hard rock. Old stuff and loud.'

'What time did he leave?'

'The group played on right until they closed at about 3.45.'

'Did he leave alone?'

'Yes.'

'Car or walking?'

'Walking. It's only about fifteen minutes to the girl's place.'

'Sounds easy. Well done. Let's get some sleep.'

Fischer grinned. 'It's better than that. They've got files on all the members, including the group.'

'Have you got access to them without showing any interest in them?'

'I've already arranged to look through the tomorrow.'

'What excuse did you use?'

Fischer shrugged. 'Just general interest. Background for experience.'

Malik nodded. 'That's a good start, Heinz. Maybe it won't take as long as we thought.'

Fischer smiled. 'You sound eager to get back to London.'

'No. Just eager to get the job done.'

Malik lay back on top of the bed, his arms behind his head, as Fischer arranged the papers.

'You ready, Jake?'

'Yep.'

'Right. Here goes. Name . . . Karl Loeb, born 1945 in Kottbus . . . father was officer in Waffen SS, rank unknown. Notified killed outskirts of Berlin February 1945 . . . mother fled to relative in Brunswick with child . . . poor scholastic record . . . didn't make High School. National service in signals unit. Then worked as electronics repair man for radio and TV dealer for two years in Wolfenbüttel. Sacked for indiscipline. Loeb claims employer was slave-driver . . . got employment with electronics company working on computer servicing in Rhine area . . . Düsseldorf and Essen . . . self-taught guitar, played in clubs after work . . . now full-time . . . has played with groups in Brunswick, Berlin and other towns. Moved to Hamburg thirteen months ago . . . earns one thousand marks a month with group . . . admits making no tax returns on earnings for approximately three years . . . denies poncing for girl. Flat in her name and she pays all rent but he buys all food etcetera . . . away large part of the day and has no control over what she does when he is away. Told he could still be charged with living beneficially off immoral earnings . . . became violent then verbally aggressive . . . made threats that influential friends would get charges dropped. Full face and profile photographs in green envelope addresses missing . . . police file numbers quoted where applicable.'

Malik lay with his eyes closed.

'That's it, Jake. That's all I got.'

'Sounds beautiful to me, Heinz. Better even than Brahms.'

Malik sat up, his eyes focused far away.

'It doesn't sound all that good to me,' Fischer said.

Malik turned to look at him and smiled.

'Kottbus . . . East Germany . . . relatives still there maybe . . . electronics . . . communications . . . radio network. He obviously isn't the mastermind, but he's one of them. And that's a good start.'

'What now?'

'Can you get the local Kripo to give you details on all the people on that known associates list? Names and addresses.'

'Yes. Some will be on the computer, but it'll probably take a week to cover the lot.'

'That's OK. You fix that. We'll go back to Cologne. Get it all down on paper. Then we'll go to Berlin and fish around there.'

They spent three weeks checking out all the names in the German police file, particularly where the addresses were in Cologne and Düsseldorf. They were mostly drifters, unemployed youths and so-called dropouts. Some of them had been prosecuted for petty theft and two or three had been involved in minor assaults. But there seemed to be no connection between them. They didn't appear to contact one another and some were untraceable.

CHAPTER SIX

During the weeks in Cologne Malik was a frequent visitor to the Fischer house. There were few days when he and Heinz did not drop in for a coffee or a meal and it was obvious that Malik had become Lisa's protegé. They sometimes went out as a foursome, Heinz and his girl, and Lisa and Malik, and Malik took Lisa to the cinema and on picnics in the nearby countryside when the other two wanted to be on their own.

There was no emotional involvement on Malik's side but he came to look forward to their meetings and was conscious of being lonely when she wasn't available. He made no special efforts to please her but it didn't seem necessary. She obviously cared about him, but he counted it as the affection of a favourite sister, even when it became obvious that it was possibly more than just friendliness. And she was understanding. She didn't probe about his background or why he was working with her brother. The talk was always of music and life in general but there were other things that he noticed. When he ate with the family it was Lisa who saw that he was well looked after and when she was asked her opinion about something her reply was often prefaced by 'Jake and I think . . .'

Because she didn't probe he put up no defences against her. He felt relaxed in her company and even her family vaguely treated them as a pair. He was relieved that her family seemed to accept their relationship without comment.

The phone was ringing as they got back to the flat and Fischer moved over to answer it. When he walked into Malik's room he said, 'That was Heidi. It's their concert tonight. They want us to have an early dinner with them and go on to the concert afterwards. What do you think?'

'Are you going anyway?'

'Yes. I'll take my girlfriend. She's invited too, of course.'

'So you go on your own. I'll be in the way. I'll have an early night.'

'They'll be very disappointed if you don't come.'

Malik smiled. 'You're a kind man, Heinz Fischer. And a very polite one. I don't mean anything to your family, and why the hell should I? I'm a foreigner who happens to be working with their son. They're kind, hospitable people so I'm invited along too.'

Fischer stood looking at Malik. 'You're a strange man, Jake.'

'In what way?'

'I'm not sure. I can't really make you out. You choose a piece of cello music as your favourite. A piece that is lush and sad, almost a rhapsody. That's one part of you. Another part contemplates beating up a man, maybe killing him, as if we were discussing the pros and cons of a bottle of wine. And then . . .' He shrugged and let his arms fall to his sides.

'Go on, Heinz. You'd got to "and then . . .".'

'I don't know how to say it.'

'Try.'

'You're obviously a senior SIS man. You're obviously very capable and experienced. But away from the work you seem kind of lost. Right now you can't believe that my family actually like you. That they enjoy having you around. That they'd like you to come tonight. They talk about you after you've been over. Saying how refreshing it is to have someone to talk to about music who is a listener not a professional. You don't seem to believe that anybody can actually like you.' He paused and sighed. 'You don't even seem to like yourself, and that's terrible.' He looked at Malik's drawn face and said, 'And now I've offended you.'

Malik exhaled a cloud of smoke then stubbed out his cigarette on an ashtray on the bedside table before he looked back at him.

'What time do we have to leave for dinner, Heinz?'

'About five.'

'What are they playing?' Malik's voice was very flat.

'It's a varied programme. I can't remember all of it. The family are playing one of the Mozart string quartets. I think it's K387.'

'I'd better have a bath and get ready.'

'Mother wanted to know if you'd drive their car. My father drives terribly badly and he's worse when they're going to play themselves.'

'What is it?'

'A Merc automatic.'

'OK. That's no problem.'

The hall was full and the audience enthusiastic. And the playing had deserved their applause. Heinz Fischer took Malik to the Green Room under the stage where the players and their friends were celebrating with champagne and Rheinwein. Malik was introduced to friends and friends of friends. But eventually he was standing alone, his hands defensively in his pockets. It was then that a slim hand gently touched his arm. It was Ruth, Heinz's girlfriend.

'Will you do me a favour, Jake?'

'Sure. What is it?'

'Heinz was taking me to dinner, but the family have been invited to a friend's house and Lisa doesn't want to go. So we've got a transport problem. Heinz has got his car and the friends will drive the family back. Would it be asking you too much to drive Lisa home and then keep the car yourself until tomorrow at your place?'

Malik smiled. 'What's the matter with Lisa?'

Ruth frowned. 'It's a bit complicated. The friend's daughter is engaged to a boy that Lisa used to go out with. It wasn't ever going to work out and it was all pretty cool. But she's embarrassed about going in case he's there. I think they'd be a bit relieved, too, if she stayed away.'

'OK. Where is she?'

'I don't know. I'll find her and bring her over. She's not in a rush to go or anything.'

Ruth brought Lisa over five minutes later and he said his thanks to the family before they left. It was still light as they walked out of the hall towards the carpark.

'Can you remember where we parked, Jake?'

'Yes. It's in the far corner by the trees. Would you like to wait here, and I'll bring it over?'

She laughed. 'Good heavens no. A bit of fresh air will do me good.'

'You'll have to tell me the way back to your house. I've no idea how to get there from this place. I just followed your father's directions on the way here.'

'It's not difficult. I'll tell you where to go.'

Twenty minutes later they pulled up in front of the house. She turned to look at him. 'Come in for a drink or a coffee. It's early yet.'

'Are you sure?'

'Of course I'm sure. Put the car in the garage and I'll make the drinks. Or would you prefer coffee?'

'Yes. I'd like coffee. With everything.'

She smiled. 'Don't be long.'

The front door was left open for him and as he closed it behind him she called out, 'Come in, Jake. I'm in the music room.'

She was pouring coffee for them both and she patted the seat beside her on the big tapestried sofa.

'Come and sit down. Help yourself to sugar.'

As he stirred his coffee she said, 'How do you think it went?'

'They loved every minute of it. And your quartet was fine.'

'Did you know it already?'

'Yes. I've got it on cassette.'

'Who's playing it?'

'The Melos.'

'Oh, lovely. How often do *you* play?'

'Not often. I can't read music. I play by ear and that drives the other players crazy. I can't count the stops accurately so I tend to come in too early or too late.'

She laughed. 'Why don't you learn to read?'

'Partly laziness, I suppose. But if I had to learn I'd have to go back to exercises and pieces like "The fairies in the glen". I couldn't stick that.'

'Play something for me.'

'I haven't brought my fiddle.'

'For heaven's sake. This house is full of fiddles, cellos, violas, mandolins – everything. Let me get one.'

Without waiting she jumped up and went over to a tall cupboard and a few seconds later she came back with a violin, a bow and a block of resin. She handed them to him and he put them on the seat beside him.

'You play for me first. A nice piano piece.'

'And then you'll play for me?'

'Yes.'

She walked slowly to the piano, smoothing her skirt as she sat down. She opened the lid and put her hands on the keys. Then she played. Soft, major chords, transposing the key as the simple melody developed. It was like a wind blowing over a mountain meadow, and heavy rolling clouds. She was wearing a black silk dress and her blonde hair was done up in a chignon so that her slender neck was emphasized. They looked very much alike, the two sisters. Very pretty, but their personalities somehow made their good looks less obvious. Heidi was the cooler one. Or perhaps more sophisticated, and Lisa, despite being a few years older, was livelier, more extrovert and more impetuous.

'What are you thinking about, Jake?'

She sat on the piano stool, smiling at him, the music ended.

'I was thinking about you and Heidi.'

'And what were you thinking?'

He smiled. 'Nice thoughts.'

'And what did you think of my music?'

'It was beautiful. What was it?'

'Guess.'

'Could have been Brahms . . . or Schubert, even . . . but I think it was more modern.'

'You're right, my boy. It's by Lisa Gertrud Fischer. Now come and play for me. You'd better check the tuning. I'll give you an A.'

He stood beside her at the piano and tightened the nut on the bow before he wiped it slowly with the resin. She gave him an A and he tuned the two strings that were out. Then he tucked the violin under his chin and played. And the girl looked up at him, watching his face. It was an odd face she thought. Strong and dark-skinned like an Italian. High, prominent cheek-bones, and muscles at the corners of his mouth. But the long black lashes that lay curved on his cheek made him seem vulnerable. Younger than his years, though it wasn't a young face. It was too lived-in for that. He was playing the Beethoven Romance. Lingering too long on the bits he liked but playing with feeling. More feeling that she would have expected.

She watched his fingers on the strings. They moved surely and accurately but the vibrato was slightly overdone. His fingers on the bow were out of balance, too close together and his wrist was too stiff. And then she was staring at his wrist where it disappeared into his sleeve. She closed her eyes for a moment but it was still there when she looked again.

And then he stopped playing, smiling at her. 'I can't remember any more.' Then he saw her face and was shocked. 'What's the matter, Lisa?'

She reached out her hand and took his arm and turned it over. The numbers were strangely distorted. Elongated, but still readable. She could make out the first three numbers in the faded bluish-purple. They were 493. And she knew that she'd never forget them.

She looked up at his face, but he looked puzzled. He was looking at her face, not at where her eyes had been.

'What is it, Lisa? Tell me.'

'When did it happen, Jake?'

'What?'

'The numbers on your wrist.'

For a moment he didn't understand, then his eyes went to her hand on his wrist and he pulled it angrily away. Throwing the bow roughly onto the polished top of the grand piano. Pushing the violin towards her.

'Take it, Lisa. I've got to go now.'

'Don't be angry, Jake. Tell me. Tell me what happened.'

He saw the tears brimming at the edge of her eyes and taking a deep breath to get himself under control he said quietly, 'You know how it happened, Lisa. Everybody knows. I don't want to talk about it.'

'But you weren't old enough, Jake.'

And then she saw him trembling, his whole body shaking; and she stood up, putting her arms around him, and like a child he put his head on her shoulder. Slowly and gently she stroked his hair and his neck. For long minutes they stood there until he raised his head, averting his face as he wiped the tears from his face with his hands. When he turned his face to look at her she bitterly regretted that she had spoken at all. It was gaunt, like a corpse, the brown skin grey, the eyes protruding and the mouth helplessly agape.

She said softly, 'I'm so sorry, Jake. I was stupid. I shouldn't have said anything. But don't go. Sit with me until you've recovered. I couldn't bear to be alone until they come back. Please forgive me.'

He went with her, unresisting, to the big sofa, and as they sat there he turned his face to look at her. He opened his mouth to speak but then closed it tight so that the muscles showed at the side of his mouth.

'Don't talk, Jake. Just rest. Shall I get you a whisky?'

He nodded, and she left to pour the drink. When she came back he looked more composed and the colour was coming back into his face.

'I brought you a brandy. Brandy will be better.'

He took a sip and made a face, leaning forward to put the glass on the low table in front of them. He sat looking at the girl.

'You knew I'm a Jew didn't you? That's why you guessed the Max Bruch.'

'No, Jake. I didn't know. I never thought about it. You were just Jake Malik, a nice man who knows my brother and who likes music.'

'You knew when you saw the tattoo on my wrist.' His voice was harsh.

'Jake, my love. Calm down. No. Even then I didn't think about it. All I thought of was how the hell it got there. How you could have been in one of those camps. That you must have been a child.'

'I was a child. But there were hundreds of children in the camps. They killed the children first. Some adults were Germans but all the children were Jews. They only gassed Jew children.'

She sat there in silence. Not knowing what to say. She wanted to say that at least half the musicians they played with were Jews but it sounded too much like that terrible joke.

'I'd better go, Lisa. Will you be OK?'

'No. Don't go. And I won't be OK. I don't think I'll ever be OK again.'

He reached out his hand for hers and she held it tightly as she looked at him.

'Will you forgive me, Jake?'

'There's nothing to forgive. It's not you. It's not even me.' He sighed. 'It was other people. Animals.'

'I was so happy playing to you, Jake. And so pleased when you played for me. It all seemed so right. And then in one thoughtless second I brought it all crashing down. And it won't ever be the same again.'

'Not the same maybe. But better in other ways.'

'What other ways?'

He sighed. 'You know me better. I know you better. For a moment you cared about me.' He shrugged. 'And that means something to me.'

'Will you walk me in the garden, Jake? I hate this room.'

'A good idea. Do you need a jacket or anything?'

She shook her head and they walked to the french windows, opened them wide and walked into the garden.

In the moonlight they could see the blossom on the apple tree, and Malik looked up at the moon. And as he looked she put her arm round his waist, her hand resting on his hip. He turned to look at her. She was looking up at his face and she said softly, 'Don't be unhappy, Jake. And don't be lonely. I care about you.'

He smiled back at her and said, 'I sometimes have nightmares. And those few minutes in there were like one of those nightmares. Or they would have been except for one thing.'

'What was that?' she said softly.

'You called me "my love".' He shrugged, embarrassed.

For a moment she looked away and then she turned her head and put her mouth up to his. He kissed her gently. Lovingly, but without passion. And his arm went round her waist as they walked slowly across the lawn back to the house.

As she closed the door behind them she turned to look at him.

'I do care about you, Jake. I really care.'

'And I care about you too, Lisa Gertrud Fischer. Very much.'

She smiled. 'You must make a very good policeman.'

'Why?'

'You notice everything and you remember everything.'

'Shall I take you out to dinner or the cinema tomorrow night?'

'I've got rehearsals until six-thirty. I could be back here ready by say seven-thirty. So yes, Jacob Malik, the answer is yes.'

And Malik smiled as she laughed up at him. He said, 'Will you be all right now?'

She nodded. 'Yes. They'll be back soon. Drive carefully. Do you know the way?'

'I think so. No problem.'

She laughed. 'You're always saying "no problem".'

'And you're always saying "good heavens".'

'On your way, policeman. Sleep well.'

'And you.'

She was still standing at the door when he drove past and he flashed the headlights as she waved to him.

It was a door closing that woke him and he turned his head to look at the luminous fingers of his travelling alarm clock. It was just past three. And then his bedroom door opened and the light went on. Heinz Fischer stood there staring at him, his fair hair ruffled, a woollen scarf looped round his neck.

'What is it, Heinz?'

'Lisa told me about what happened. She's terribly upset about it.'

'She seemed all right when I left.'

'Oh, *she's* OK. She's worried about you being on your own. Are you OK?'

Malik nodded. 'Yes. I'm OK.'

Fischer sat down on the edge of the bed. 'I'm terribly sorry about what happened, Jake. I really am.'

'We're both OK now. Forget it.'

'I don't mean that. I mean what must have happened in that bloody camp.'

Malik closed his eyes and shook his head. 'Forget it. I don't want to talk about it.'

'I understand. Will you do me a favour?'

'The car's parked in the usual place.'

Fischer smiled. 'It's not that. But I was going to use you as an alibi tonight. I was going to Ruth's place but telling the family I was here. Lisa made me promise I'd come back here. Word of honour and all that. The lovely Ruth is sitting down below in a taxi with its meter running. Would you mind if she stayed here tonight?'

Malik grinned. 'Not at all. She can have my bed and you and I can sleep in your room.'

Fischer stood up smiling. 'Thanks, Sir Galahad.'

CHAPTER SEVEN

The plane came in low over Berlin, sweeping over the forest and lakes, banking and levelling onto the flight path for Tegel. When it had landed and taxied to the terminal stand, there was the usual Gadarene rush to the exit doors, but Malik and Fischer stayed in their seats. It was ten minutes before the steps were latched in place and the door opened, and five minutes later they reached for their hand luggage and left the plane.

Fischer showed his ID card at Immigration and vouched for Malik, and the Customs man recognized Fischer and waved them through. The flight had come through from Madrid but there was only a handful of passengers.

They took a taxi to Fasanenstrasse and booked into the hotel. Fifteen minutes later, they were walking down the Kurfürstendamm towards the number shown on Paul Radtke's union card as his permanent address.

It was over a travel agency and there was a grilled loudspeaker alongside the doorbell. When Fischer pressed the bell a garbled voice said something that they couldn't understand. Fischer gave his name and police rank and the door buzzed and opened to a push.

A man of about thirty was standing at the top of the stairs watching them as they went up towards him. He was dressed in a red shirt and blue denims and his feet were bare.

Fischer went up first and held out his hand. 'Herr Radtke?'

'That's me. I didn't get your name.'

'Fischer, and this is my colleague Herr Malik.'

'Did you say something about the police down there? This goddamn speaker's hopeless.'

'Yes. We're both police officers. We wanted to have a word with you.'

'OK. Come in.'

It was a small office with a door leading into another room that looked like a bed-sitter. The walls were lined with shelves, and the shelves were packed with box files. A cheap office desk was against the window with a typewriter, a phone and a pile of telephone directories.

There were only two office chairs and Radtke waved towards them and perched himself on the edge of his desk.

'What can I do for the *Bundespolizei* today?'

'A couple of months back we had a report through from Berlin that you'd picked up a rumour about the East Germans sending people over to organize subversion groups in the Federal Republic.'

'Christ. Which one was this? I'm always picking up rumours about infiltration and terrorist groups.'

'This was from Humboldt University.'

'Ah yes. I remember that.'

'Can you tell us what was said?'

'Not unless I kept my notes.'

'But you do remember it?'

Radtke laughed. 'All I remember is that the chick who told me had got real big tits.' He stood up and walked to one of the shelves, touching the labels on files as he went along the row. He pulled one out and carried it to his desk.

'If it's anywhere, it's in here.'

He leafed through a pile of papers and newspaper cuttings then pulled out a shorthand notebook, flipping the cover open and slowly turning the pages.

'Yeah. Here we are. It's not much. I went over because there was a debate between students from the Free University and students from Humboldt. Subject was . . . I can't read it . . . yes – "The dangers of the proliferation of nuclear weapons to world peace".' He looked up and shrugged, smiling. 'All the usual crap. Both sides doing their standard pieces. Their lot better informed. Our lot better debaters. There were about sixty people there, and coffee and sandwiches afterwards, courtesy of the Faculty of Political History.' He laughed. 'They used to serve Beluga caviar at these things until some stupid bastard got up and asked where they got caviar from in East Germany. A lot of laughter but some quiet grinding of teeth.

'Anyway, this bird latched on to me. Very pretty, tight sweater and all that. Bent my ear about how many countries were developing or trying to develop nuclear weapons. Egypt, India, Pakistan, Israel, our old friend China, and the usual list.

'She seemed to know quite a lot about what was going on. Things that journalists hear about that don't get printed in the papers. I asked her why it was necessary for the KGB to ruin Willy Brandt's career by planting a spy on his personal staff. He'd been working hard for detente between Moscow and Bonn, and with the East Germans. I asked her if they would prefer dealing with Franz-Josef instead. She huffed and puffed a bit and then came out with this comment. I couldn't make notes at the time but I did when I came back. As near as I can remember, she said . . . quote . . . true detente isn't possible and never was . . . and that one of these days Bonn would realize that playing double games didn't pay off. But Moscow was well aware of what the revanchists in West Germany were trying to do and they had people there who would rise up and expose them when the time was ripe . . . unquote. I genuinely didn't understand what she was getting at so I asked her what she meant and she went on . . . quote . . . there'll be a day of reckoning and we've got the people there who would bring down the war-mongers of Bonn . . . unquote. It didn't seem all that startling, but she seemed to want to take back what she'd said. Said it was off the record, unofficial. Only her own thoughts. She went on so much I thought I should report it and I did.

'I told the police I was going to try and date her and see if there was anything more. They said it was a good idea.' He grinned. 'I was looking forward to it but they phoned me in the afternoon and said maybe it wasn't such a good idea as she was being screwed by a KGB officer based at Karlshorst. I agreed it wasn't a good idea.'

'Did you get her name?'

'I never record informants' names in my notes. I've put an A in a circle and I think her first name was Anna. She was a student, so you should be able to check her out.'

Fischer stood up. 'Thanks for your help, Herr Radtke.'

'Are you people taking this seriously?'

'Not particularly. We do what we can to check these things, but they generally end up in a cloud of smoke.'

Radtke laughed. 'Too true. Anyway, remember me if there is anything. First call so that I can earn an honest buck.'

'We will. Thanks again. We'll let ourselves out.'

'OK. All the best.'

They stood in the sunshine looking in the travel agent's window. Malik said, 'More than I expected, but nothing of any use except the girl's name.'

'Let's walk along to Kempinski's and have a coffee.'

'OK. Let's do that.'

They sat at one of the outside tables and when the waiter had brought the coffee Malik said, 'Is it likely the West Berlin police could trace this girl?'

'I'd say it was certain. They wouldn't have been able to tell Radtke that she was being screwed by a KGB man if they hadn't identified her.'

'Of course.' Malik nodded, thinking. 'You're absolutely right. Can you contact them?'

'I'm not allowed to contact them direct. I have to go through *Abteilung I*.'

'How long will it take?'

'I don't know. There's friction between them and the Kripo.'

'There always is. I think governments like it that way.'

'I'll go along and see them.'

'Where are they?'

Fischer looked embarrassed. 'I'm not allowed to tell you.'

'Ah well. It doesn't matter unless they take too long. If they do, I'll put London onto Bonn.'

'Have another coffee and I'll get on my way and we'll meet back at the hotel.'

'When?'

'God knows. I'll have to do some bowing and scraping first.'

Malik phoned the Fischers' number in Cologne but Lisa was out and he was embarrassed at her father's friendliness and having to hedge about giving his phone number so that she could call him back. He left a message that he would call her again.

Ten minutes later the phone rang and it was Lisa.

'How did you know the number?'

'Heinz scribbled it on the pad by the telephone. Said he'd give the room number when he called.'

He laughed. 'So much for security.'

'Hang security. Are you OK, Jake?'

'I'm OK. How're you?'

'Fine. I played tennis this morning as it's Saturday.'

'Is it Saturday? I'd lost track of the days.'

'When will you be back?'

'I don't really know. Soon, I hope.'

'Try and get back for the Sunday concert.'

'I'll do my best.'

'We must . . . aren't telephone conversations terrible? I'd hoped you'd phone me and now I've got nothing to say . . . Mama has just gone past. Says she sends you her love and say the same to Heinzl. OK. I'd better go.'

'I'll call you again tomorrow.'

'Bye.'

'Bye.'

He waited until she had hung up before he put down the receiver.

For several minutes he sat there thinking about the Fischers. The old man reminded him of his father, with his sudden enthusiasms and the loving way he tucked his violin under his cheek. And his insistence on not using a chin-rest. Tuning by ear and that last minute swish of his bow which they both claimed settled the horsehair into its proper place.

Heidi, despite being the younger sister, was more serious and reserved than Lisa, and their mother tended to keep to the background until there were decisions to be made. Almost like any Jewish matriarch. Lisa was the emotional one. Pretty, impetuous, enthusiastic like her father and easy to get on with. He wondered what they all thought of him now that they knew that he was a Jew.

Fischer looked pleased with himself when he came in, a brown envelope in his hand. He was smiling.

'I got photocopies of the whole file.'

'Is it useful?'

'In a way.' Fischer sat down at the small table. 'Plenty of names, but no common thread that I can see. Maybe you can see something.' He shoved the envelope across to Malik.

'Lisa phoned. Your mother sends you her love.'

'Thanks. I'll give them a ring later. I'm going to get a haircut. I'm beginning to look like a policeman trying not to look like a policeman.'

Malik nodded without looking up as he opened the file. The pretence that they were policemen was beginning to irritate him. Fischer was more of a policeman than he was, but to keep up the public pretence between themselves was pointless. And he had a suspicion that Fischer was emphasizing it so that he could play it by the rules. There was a strong element of the Boy Scout in Fischer. Or was it just the German instinct for bureaucracy? *Befehl ist Befehl*. He turned to the first sheet in the file.

There was half an hour's reading and then he went through it again. Despite his dislike of the policeman attitude the file showed one of the advantages of playing it that way. It was typical police work and typically thorough. It must have taken a lot of man-hours to put it together.

Anna Bauer was twenty years old and a student at Humboldt University, the crown jewel in East Berlin's educational system. She was in her second year and unlike most students she had a room of her own not far from the University buildings. There were a dozen or so photographs. Grainy and contrasty because they were taken undercover and with long lenses. They still showed a girl who looked more like a beauty queen than a political agitator. Some of them were taken in the street as she left her flat, but most of them were in cafés or clubs and the captions on the back of the prints gave details of the place and sometimes the names of the people she was with. There were two photographs of the KGB man, Anatoli Simenov. Malik knew more about him than was on the report. He was in his early fifties and one of the more sophisticated KGB operators. He had started in the 9th Directorate as one of the special guards protecting top Party leaders and their families, but nowadays he was used on special assignments. He'd worked in the United States, had a short stint in Paris and a year in London.

The girl's recorded contacts were on both sides of the Wall, and there were two or three lines of background description when the contact was apparently more than social. The East Berlin contacts were mainly Party officials. Two of them, apart from Simenov, were Russians. One was a Red Army major who was unidentified apart from his artillery insignia and the other was a town-planning expert on loan to the East German government.

In West Berlin her contacts were almost all non-political. Several businessmen. A photographer. A radio announcer from RIAS Berlin and a magazine features writer. And the contacts were evaluated as being social and sexual, typical of the contacts a pretty girl would have. But not if she was from East Berlin. That made all her West Berlin contacts suspect. The mere fact that she could come through the Wall so easily and so often made her suspect. What was more significant was that several of her businessmen contacts were from outside Berlin. One was from Hamburg, another from Munich, one from Cologne and one from Frankfurt. And according to the surveillance she saw them every time they came to Berlin and they were always there at the same time, staying at the same hotel.

The surveillance had been for five months and had been intensified since the journalist's report to the police. The evaluation was non-committal and went no further than the suggestion that the KGB man was using her for gathering bits and pieces of industrial and economic information that would help pad out his reports to Moscow. It was a traditional method for agents of most Intelligence services to finance a mistress, but the evaluation classified the girl and her contacts as of only average security interest. Which was fair enough. They would have thousands of similar files in their Registry.

'What about the Cologne guy, have you ever heard of him?'

Fischer looked embarrassed. 'Yes I have. As a matter of fact I've met him several times. He's a friend of my father. Well, perhaps not a friend, but a close acquaintance.'

'What's he like?'

'Nothing like what we are looking for. Right-wing and ultra-conservative. Sponsors concerts. Happily married so far as I know. He's got a piano factory. Turns out pianos for schools and clubs. They're not Steinways but they're pretty good.'

'Doesn't sound a likely target for us, but nevertheless he does come up to Berlin to see our little Anna.'

'He may come up for business and she's secondary.'

'Is he the kind who screws on the side?'

'Who knows? I suppose nobody's past doing that if they get the chance, and she's very attractive.'

'But why should she let him?'

'I don't know. Money, maybe.'

'If she was doing it for money she'd move into West Berlin and make a fortune.'

'So what next?'

'I think we go back to base and then maybe we have a good look at our friend in Hamburg. We've got a lot of data but no clues. It needs digesting.'

For a few moments Malik looked at Fischer as if he were trying to make up his mind about something.

'Sit down, Heinz.' Malik said quietly and pointed to the chair at the other side of the table. Fischer sat down and waited for Malik to speak.

'Has anything struck you as odd about this operation, Heinz?'

'Apart from the fact that we don't seem to be making much progress – no.'

Malik smiled. 'Just do the sums, Heinz. There are at least six cities that may have these groups. A group is going to be eight or ten people. So we're talking about fifty to sixty people who are involved. SIS have put me on to checking it out. And Bonn have given me you as an assistant and as a means of liaison. That's what's odd.'

'I don't understand.'

'Let's go back to square one. Bonn hears from two sources, the Member of Parliament from Hamburg, and the journalist here in Berlin, about possible subversive groups. But they must get that sort of information week after week. Then there are the anti-Jewish activities and Bonn suddenly get agitated. They assume that the people being planted in the Federal Republic are East Germans controlled by the KGB. It's a possibility, of course, but there could be lots of other solutions. They may be neo-Fascists, or old Nazis, or just anti-Semitic Germans. A dozen scenarios. But if it was any of those then Bonn would just deal with it. That's what the Popos are for. But they stick to the KGB angle and that means referring to London and Washington. So SIS take it over to avoid diplomatic problems with the Soviet Union. But after all this nail-biting and discussion all that happens is that two people are put on to it. You and me. Nobody's pressing us. Nobody's phoning every hour asking what we've got or done. Why?'

'Because they don't really care what happens.'

'That's one possibility, but I don't think it's the real one. Maybe London and Bonn do know what these people are up to and see it as harmless or even useful.'

'And we're being used just to keep the record straight. Someone to blame if something happens they don't like.'

'There's one other possibility.'

'Tell me.'

'That they think they know what's going on but they're wrong.'

'So what do we do?'

'The first thing we do is to check how serious they are about the operation. Both of us contact our seniors and say that we think it's a waste of time. If they agree then that's that. If they disagree and order us to carry on, we ask for additional man-power.' Malik smiled. 'We'll talk about it again when we've had their answers. Meantime we'll have another look at our friend in Hamburg.'

CHAPTER EIGHT

'Where are you speaking from, Jake?'

'Police HQ in Cologne.'

'Have you got a scrambler?'

'Yes.'

'Let's go over to scrambler then.'

Malik pressed the red button on the black box and Jenkins was already speaking. '. . . getting on?'

'Slowly, I'm afraid. There are only vague leads to follow. That's why I called you. I think there's something going on but I'm not sure what. I need more bodies but I wanted to check that you thought it was worthwhile.'

There was a long silence at the other end and Malik said, 'Are you there?'

'Yes, I'm here, Jake. We can't spare any more bodies but we do want you to carry on.'

'But if you . . .'

'Jake. We've had a tip-off from Berlin that seems to link up with your operation. It gives weight to your feeling that something's going on. But we want to keep it low-key in case we're being conned.'

'What was the tip-off?'

'One of our chaps there is playing footsie with an East German KGB man. He's been hinting to us that the KGB are interested in a group of Germans who he thinks are up to something. He talked vaguely of some sort of high technology device.'

'What's the KGB man's name?'

'Hold on . . . I'll have to check the file . . . here we are . . . Simenov. Anatoli Simenov. He's based at Karlshorst.'

'What kind of device is he on about?'

'We don't know. Our chap couldn't look too interested. The implication was that a group of Germans were involved in the development of some piece of high technology. They might be official for all we know. Or a figment of the Russian's imagination. Or some little game the KGB have worked out. The impression was that he genuinely didn't know much and was fishing to see if we knew anything.'

'What makes you think that?'

'He offered a trade. Jake. A name we would very much like, if we could put his mind at rest as he phrased it. Which probably means no more than that he can close the file on some rumour they've made him check up on.'

'What makes you think his little gang are anything to do with my lot?'

'Instinct. Experience. A feeling in my water. How about you?'

'Yes. It fits the timing. Anyway, you want me to keep plugging away?'

'Yes.'

'Can I use SIS facilities at our embassy and the consulates?'

'Yes. But not Berlin.'

'Why not?'

'Just not Berlin, Jake.'

'One last point. I haven't had any mail since I got here.'

'I'll check with Gordon Truslove and liven him up. I know we've been paying the standing orders, I saw the paper-work go through the other day. The mortgage, an insurance or two and I think it was HP on the car, so don't worry about those. I'll see about the mail, though. Anything else?'

'No thanks.'

Fischer looked gloomy as he let himself into the flat.

'How'd you get on, Heinz?'

'You know it's crazy, Jake, but I don't know. The best of German bureaucracy at work. Agreed that we haven't made much progress. Yes, they want the operation to continue. And no, I can't have any help. Facilities yes. Bodies no. Keep at it but don't bother them with too many written reports.' Fischer spread his hands. 'They're not interested, Jake.' He sighed. 'How did your people react?'

Malik told him briefly of his telephone conversation with Jenkins but he didn't mention the information from Berlin. He wasn't sure why he kept that back but he rationalized on the basis that he could always mention it later if it seemed relevant.

'So what do we do next, Jake?'

'We go up to Hamburg again and fish around. If we draw a blank we'll take Loeb for a long weekend.'

They watched the girl's flat for two days. Her name was still on the card over the bell. Different men were there during the day when Loeb was out. Fischer followed Loeb several times but he spent most of his time with other members of the club group in bars and cafés. Both nights he had left the flat carrying his guitar in its case and both nights he had returned in the early hours of the morning.

Back at the hotel Malik sat at the table looking through his notes. Eventually he closed the notebook and looked across at Fischer.

'Any suggestions?'

Fischer sighed. 'None that are worthwhile making.'

'Let's hear them all the same.'

'We can check on all those contacts of the girl in Berlin. We can keep a watch on all Loeb's contacts here. And maybe you could contact the girl again and see her a few times. Gain her confidence and see what you could get from her.'

'And by the time we'd finished we'd be ready for our pensions.'

'I know.'

'How do we go about renting a house?'

'We could do it through an agent.'

'Do they have lists of places to rent?'

'Of course. And photographs.'

'That's our first job tomorrow.'

Fischer didn't reply but Malik was aware that he hadn't said no. And he would have realized what it meant.

They sat at the table looking at the details of the houses.

'Where's Harvestehude?'

'It's the other side of the Alster. The radio station's there.'

'Heavily populated?'

'Yes. It's a major suburb.'

'Which of these houses is likely to be isolated?'

'You'd have to go east towards the East Zone. This one at Gross Hansdorf is a possible and this one at Rausdorf's another.'

'How long do we have to take it for?'

'They wouldn't be interested in less than a month.'

'Let's hire a car and go and look at them.'

'If we want to go inside they'll want to send someone with us.'

Malik smiled. 'We don't need any company, Heinz. You go off and hire us a car.'

'I'll be about an hour.'

'OK.'

As Malik waited he wondered what to do about Fischer. The German knew, all right, what he was intending to do, even though he didn't acknowledge it. For the first time he was going to have to give the German an order. An order to go back to Cologne, or an order to join him in what he intended doing. He hoped there would be some sign, some indication of what would be best.

He had no doubt about doing it. They would sit around for months doing fruitless surveillance of a dozen or more people and at the end of it they would have to make one of them reveal what the groups were doing. It would take a team of eight or nine to penetrate even one or two groups, and even that would take several months. And his orders had been clear. He was to discover what they were doing and who they were. He was not required to penetrate them or round them up.

As soon as the Volkswagen pulled up at the house in Rausdorf he knew it was the one. With high brick walls, it stood back from the road, its garden a jungle of weeds, its wrought-iron gates leaning half open because the bottom hinges had rusted away. They wrenched the gates further apart and drove the car up to the house. The gravel drive itself was thick with cow parsley and plantain but the house itself looked solid and substantial.

They walked round the house, clearing the ivy and bindweed from the windows and peering inside, and Fischer stood looking slightly disapproving as Malik took out the soft chamois wallet and tried the skeleton keys. Water ran freely when Malik turned on the taps and when he pulled down the meter switch the lights functioned in most of the rooms, and the big refrigerator in the kitchen hummed satisfactorily as he opened its door.

As they stood again in the garden he said softly, 'Well, Heinz. This is the one. Let's go back. Pay them two months in advance, book yourself a flight to Cologne and bring the keys back to me in the hotel. Give a false name to the estate agent.'

'I'll stick around, Jake. You're going to need some help.'

'It's an order, Heinz. You don't need to be involved.'

'I'm already involved, Jake. Nobody will believe I didn't know what was going on.'

'They will if I say so.'

Fischer put his hand on Malik's shoulder. 'Forget it, Jake. There's more chance of success if there's two of us.'

Malik knew that was true. And Malik was a professional. 'We'll talk about it when you've got the keys.'

Fischer was already at the hotel waiting for him when Malik got back from the shops with a cardboard box full of food and a cheap canvas holdall that he didn't open. The keys to the house lay on the table, tied together with a shoe-lace that was knotted to a wooden tag. Malik picked up the tag and looked at the letters that had been crudely burned onto the wood. It spelt out *Das Waldhaus*.

They went out for a meal and then rested on their beds until ten o'clock, when Malik made coffee and they sat at the table.

'Can I ask you something, Jake? Something personal.'

'Try me.'

'Do you hate all Germans?'

It was a long time before Malik answered and then he said quietly, 'If you'd asked me that a month ago the answer would have been yes. Even now, when I think of Germans *en masse* the answer would be yes. But I don't hate the Fischer family. I like you all. I seldom think of you as Germans, though. I think maybe hate is the wrong word. Germans scare me. Really scare me.'

'But you're so tough, Jake. I can't imagine you being afraid of anybody.'

'It's not that kind of afraid, Heinz. I'm not afraid of men, just Germans. Sometimes on a TV documentary I see an old newsreel of a Nazi rally, or hear the bastards singing the Horst Wessel Lied and I almost pass out. They put men, women and children in chambers and gassed them. Millions of them. Some bastard supplied the pipes and built the ovens and put up the barbed wire. And everybody for miles around could smell the smoke. It's a smell of burning pork, Heinz. Except that it wasn't pork, it was people. And one of them was my mother.'

'Lisa thinks about it all the time. She told me she didn't know what to say. She asked me what we could say or do.'

'And what did you tell her?'

'I told her that there was nothing we could say, beyond how ashamed or angry we feel. But what we could do is remember. And see that others remembered. She said that at least we could try and help you.'

'Only a frontal lobotomy could do that, my friend.'

Fischer nodded. 'All I really want to say is that we do care, and we do understand. All the family. Not just Lisa and me.'

Malik nodded. 'We'll leave here at one. Is it too late to change the car for a four-door model?'

'We can change it tomorrow. They'll be closed by now.'

'We'll leave it. Let's put our stuff in the car.'

Malik stood in the shadows of the derelict warehouse waiting for Loeb to come out. He could see the lights of a freighter tied up at the dockside and there were lights at the head of a gantry. Far down the river he heard the wistful moan of a ship's siren. And it was beginning to rain.

In the next hour men left the club in twos and threes and then he saw Loeb standing in the doorway looking up at the night sky, turning up his jacket collar against the rain.

Malik let him go under the archway onto the cobbles and then he was alongside him.

'Loeb.'

Loeb turned to glance at him and walked on. Malik realized that the German thought he was a homosexual looking for a partner. Malik's hand went to the back of Loeb's collar, pulling it back until the buttons were at his throat. Loeb jerked his head as he heard the click, and opened his mouth to shout as he saw the long thin blade of the knife. And then Malik's hard fingers were over his mouth.

'Don't make a noise, little boy. Just keep walking. That's it. Keep going. Get in the car. Now.'

Malik bundled the German roughly into the back of the car, clambering over the angled front seat to follow him. As Malik leaned over to swing the door to, Fischer started the car and headed back towards the town centre. Ten minutes later they were on Federal Highway 435, Loeb crouching in the corner of the back seat, still clutching his guitar case, the glint of Malik's knife blade reflected in the rear mirror. As they got to the bridge over the E4 Loeb tried to stand up and Fischer heard him scream, 'For Christ's sake you've cut my hand.'

He heard Malik say, 'I'll cut your face next time, sweetheart.'

As they made their bumpy way up the drive to the house Fischer glanced at his watch. It was less than an hour since Malik had shoved Loeb into the car.

They took Loeb round the house to the back door. He put up no resistance, and Fischer prayed silently that he would stay that way.

Malik had led the way upstairs to the main bedroom and stood aside as Fischer followed Loeb inside. Malik pointed to a worn armchair.

'Sit down, Loeb.'

Loeb turned to put his guitar case on the foot of the bed and for an instant the blade of the knife flickered before Malik realized what Loeb was doing. As Loeb sat down Fischer saw how pale and gaunt the man's face was. His pale blue eyes were red-rimmed, his fair hair spiky and unwashed. His mouth was small and girlish, and his unshaven chin was covered with a fuzz of downy hair.

Malik sat on the edge of the bed looking at Loeb, and Loeb turned his head cautiously to look back at him.

'I don't have money, if that's what you want.' Loeb's voice quavered as he spoke.

'Tell me about the group.' Malik's voice was soft.

Loeb shrugged. 'It's just a group. Drums, vibes and two guitars.'

'I mean the other group. The political group who pay you. You told your girlfriend that you were more important than she thought. Tell me all about it.'

'I was just kidding her.'

'Tell me, Loeb.'

'There's nothing to . . .'

The sound of Malik's fist on Loeb's face echoed round the room. Dull, fleshy and sickening. The German had both hands up to his face and bright red blood trickled through his fingers to run down his arm. He was shaking his head in pain, gasping for breath, rocking backwards and forwards in agony. He screamed as Malik reached out, grabbed his hair and wrenched back his head.

'Tell me about the group.'

'Don't hurt me any more. Please . . . don't . . . I'll tell you.'

'Who's your contact?'

'The Herr Baron, and the boss.'

'Where do you meet?'

'At the Herr Baron's estate.'

'Where's that?'

'At Lauenburg.'

Fischer was frowning as he listened. 'Are you talking about von Busch?'

Loeb nodded, and Malik saw the doubt on Fischer's face.

'Is von Busch the man you called the boss?'

'No. That's Herr Meyer. Amos Meyer.'

Malik looked at Fischer to see if he recognized the name but Fischer shook his head.

'Where does Meyer live?'

'I don't know.'

'Where do you meet him?'

'At the Herr Baron's estate or at a hotel. Wherever they tell me to go.'

'How many are in the group?'

'I don't know. I've only met the two of them.'

'Why do you call it a group, then?'

'That's what they said. A group of patriots.'

'How much do they pay you?'

'Two hundred DM a month and then for the work.'

'Tell me about the work,' Malik said softly.

'It's just electronics, printed-circuit boards, decoders, pulse modulators . . .' Loeb shrugged. 'All kinds of stuff. Whatever they want.'

'What do you do for them?'

'Test the sample and then make repeats.'

'Where do you do this?'

'I've got a lab and workshop at the Herr Baron's place.'

'What are these things used for?'

'God knows. All sorts of things.'

'Like what?'

'Computers, measuring systems. It's impossible to tell from the bits and pieces.'

'What did they tell you they were for?'

'They didn't tell me anything.'

'And what do they pay you for the work?'

'Depends on how long. They pay well. Maybe four times the going rate. I've made ten thousand DM in three weeks sometimes.'

'Why is it all so secret?'

'I don't know, but they told me if I breathed a word to anyone about it they'd finish me off.'

'Why did you go on playing at the club?'

'I like it. And they told me to.'

'How long has this been going on?'

'About six or seven months.'

'How did he first contact you?'

'There was a note for me one night at the club. It said ring the telephone number it gave. And it gave a time and a day when I should do it. When I rang it was a woman's voice and she just gave me another number to phone, and said I would be paid for meeting someone.

'I rang the other number and I was told to go to the Botanical Gardens, by the cafeteria, and someone would contact me. That was for the next day. It was von Busch and he asked me about where I was born and my parents and my background. And then he said there were groups of people in Germany who were concerned that German politicians were leading the country astray. He wanted my help and he'd pay me two hundred DM every month.'

'Did he say what you had to do?'

'No. But he asked me a lot of questions about when I did my army service.'

'What were you in the army?'

'I was on electronics, radar equipment and computers and control systems.'

'But he never said that was how you would help him?'

'No. Whenever I asked what I had to do he just said that it wasn't dangerous and I would be told when it was necessary.'

'Where did he say the other groups were?'

'He said they were all over Germany.'

'How many?'

'He didn't say.'

'Did he mention any places or names?'

'Cologne was one and he mentioned somewhere in the Harz area. I think it was Goslar. He said the leader in Cologne was a business man named Reichardt, or maybe the name was Rechmann, and the man in Goslar was a retired judge. And I think he said the boss of the Hanover group was a retired general named Lomke, or maybe that was the judge's name. I can't remember. It didn't interest me.'

'Any other names?'

'I think there was a Weiss, but I don't really remember.'

'Why did he give you their names?'

'I think it was to impress me. I guess I looked doubtful and he mentioned them to convince me that it was serious.'

'What did you think about it all?'

'I didn't really believe it. You get to meet a lot of odd people in my sort of life. Important men, but real kinky in all sorts of ways.'

'Have you told anybody else about any of this?'

'God, no. He said I would be watched all the time and if I talked I'd get it.' And Loeb pulled a bloody finger across his throat. 'And they meant it, all right.'

Malik looked at Fischer and then reached for the canvas holdall and took out several lengths of rope. Loeb flinched as Malik stood over him, tying him to the chair and his ankles to the chair legs. When he stood up Malik looked at the German and said, 'Don't try any games or you'll be in trouble again.'

Malik nodded to Fischer who followed him out of the room. Malik went down the stairs, along the hall and into the kitchen, switching on the light. Inside the room he turned to look at Fischer.

'What do you think? Does he know any more?'

'I doubt it. But he's obviously met or seen Meyer. You could ask him about that.'

'Good point. Anything else?'

'I don't think so. He's obviously not part of the real group.'

'Is the guy in Cologne he mentioned the piano maker?'

'It's possible. It could be any businessman. It's not an uncommon name. And it depends on what you call a businessman.'

'What's the earliest flight we can get to Cologne?'

'We won't make the first flight. I guess we could make the nine-thirty one. What are you going to do with Loeb?'

'Leave him here. Don't worry about that. I'll deal with him.'

'But he'll talk.'

'He won't,' Malik said brusquely. 'Get the car ready. When we get to Hamburg, check it in and pay, and we'll take a taxi to the airport. Do you need any cash?'

'No. I've got plenty. What about the food you brought?'

'I'll bring that out when I've finished upstairs.'

Fischer nodded and walked out of the kitchen. Malik switched off the light and walked back up the stairs to the bedroom. Loeb was sitting just as they had left him but with his head back and his eyes closed.

Malik stood in front of him. 'Loeb.'

The German opened his eyes, shivering as he looked at Malik.

'Tell me about Meyer. What does he look like? What is he?'

'He's some kind of businessman. He's getting on. In his sixties. Biggish, dark hair, he's got a deep tan. Could be an Arab, or even a Jew. He was the one who told me what to do. He understood electronics, von Busch didn't.'

'What makes you think he could be a Jew?'

Loeb shrugged. 'He looks like one, and sometimes he used Yiddish slang words.'

Malik hesitated and then said, 'Were any of the groups responsible for the anti-Semitic things that have been going on recently? The synagogue daubings, and the slogans?'

'I don't know. I shouldn't think so.'

'Why not?'

'Well, a Jew wouldn't be doing that, and von Busch wouldn't get mixed up with that sort of thing. He's an aristocrat.'

Malik walked over to the window and stood there silently for several minutes. Then he put his thumb over the back of the blade of the knife to soften the sound as he pressed the button and the long thin blade flicked up.

The plane back to Cologne was full of business people and Fischer felt disturbed that he was almost glad that he and Malik hadn't been able to sit together. He hadn't asked Malik what had happened to Loeb but he was certain that he was dead. As he sat in the car he had watched Malik shove the keys through the letterbox after closing the door. There was no reason why anyone should visit the house for days or weeks. The rent had been paid for two months and he realized now why Malik had insisted on two months instead of one.

Fischer was well aware that killings and brutality were weapons in the armoury of all intelligence services but he had never met a man who actually did such things. It seemed strange, uncomfortable, almost eerie, to realize that a man you knew well, a man who liked music, had eaten with you and joked with you, could kill, not in passion but coldly and efficiently because it was expedient. From the moment he decided to pick up Loeb, Malik must have known that it was almost certain that he would kill him. Even the blow with Malik's fist was so professional. Malik knew exactly how to hurt people. Not in anger. Coldly and precisely Malik's fist had smashed the man's nose. No build-up of persuasion to answer the questions. A few uncooperative replies and then that crunch of bone and gristle. Even when he started the questions again there was no anger in his voice. It was almost as if the blow hadn't happened. He had heard no scream, no cry, as he waited in the car and Malik had closed the door behind him, walking to the car carrying the holdall as casually as a housewife going shopping. He hadn't looked back at the house and he had sat with his eyes closed as they drove back into Hamburg. For a few fleeting moments he wondered if there was any element of revenge in killing a German in Malik's mind. He tried not to dwell on it. It didn't bear thinking about.

He could see the back of Malik's head as he sat in an aisle seat a few rows forward. The thick, curly black hair, the tanned skin on the cheek bone and the slightly misshapen ear. He wondered what it was that so attracted his sister to this man. Despite the closed-in face and the cautious eyes, there was an awareness in Malik's face. He listened, and seemed to take in everything that was said to him. He seldom indicated agreement or disagreement but you knew that what you said was weighed and considered. There was a safeness about Malik that would appeal to women. An obvious strength and self-assuredness that had nothing to do with "machismo". But for all the understanding, the man inside Malik never came out. Whatever it was it stayed inside, looking out at people and the world through those soft brown eyes. Was it likely that that carapace of solitariness would crack or melt for a twenty-three-year-old girl? A German? He had gave doubts that it would.

There was no doubt that Malik had freed the log-jam in the operation. They now had definite leads to follow instead of casting around aimlessly in all directions. And when he thought it through he knew that if Loeb had been freed he would certainly have alerted von Busch. Maybe there really had been no choice. If they were to find out anything, somebody in one of the groups would have had to talk, and it was highly unlikely that they would have talked without being threatened. And after they had talked you couldn't put them back in circulation. His own instinct would have been to suborn the talker with money or whatever and turn him back to inform on the group. But that had sometimes proved risky. When it had been done in other operations four out of five had reneged. Maybe it was he who was the hypocrite and Malik merely rational.

Rain was beating against the windows as they banked over Wahn, the raindrops creeping like glass beads across the plexiglass from the wind against the fuselage. The plane was bumping and lurching as it circled the airport and the warning lights were on. Malik turned in his seat to look at Fischer, giving him a brief smile before looking away.

Malik sat on his bed looking at the envelopes of the mail that the consulate had delivered for him. There was nothing that looked interesting, at least half of them were obviously bills and he threw them all carelessly onto the bedside table.

He stretched and stood up, walking over to the window to look down at the small gardens. The rain had stopped and the old lady with the two little girls was there again. She was there most days, sitting on the wooden bench as the children played on the grass. She was always doing something, never just sitting there; today she was knitting, and from time to time she called the taller of the two girls over to measure her work against the plump little body. Both little girls had straw-blonde hair, plaited and tied with ribbon, and despite the fact that it was the start of summer they wore typical German boots rather than shoes. They were both very pretty, but what moved Malik most were their slender necks that looked like the stalks of flowers. Malik had always felt great sympathy for small children.

The phone ringing interrupted his thoughts. It was Lisa wanting to know how he was and inviting him to dinner that night. Ruth and Heinz would be there, she said.

CHAPTER NINE

The lawns had been cut and the smell of mown grass hung in the air as they sat on the bench under the weeping willow, her head resting on his shoulder.

'How much longer will you be staying in Germany, Jake?'

'At least a month, probably longer.'

'You said something nice today when I phoned you.'

'What was that?'

'You said "We got home about two o'clock."'

He turned to look at her. 'We did. What's nice about that?'

She smiled up at him. 'You said "home" not Cologne.'

Malik looked away from her, across towards the house. She was right. He *had* said "home". And that was what it had felt like.

'Tell me about your house in London, Jake.'

'It's nothing special. Victorian. Solidly built. A distant view across Hampstead Heath. That's about it.'

'Are you fond of it?'

'I never think about it. I guess that means I'm not all that fond of it.'

'Heinz seemed very . . . I don't know what . . . edgy when he came home. A bit short-tempered with everybody.'

'He seemed all right at dinner.'

'Ruth always puts him in a good mood. Do you ever go to church . . . to synagogue?'

'No.'

'Don't Jews *have* to go?'

Malik turned to look at her, smiling, 'No more than Catholics or Protestants have to. I was born a Jew and nothing's going to alter that. But it doesn't mean that I do anything about it.'

'Aren't you proud of being a Jew? I would be if I was a Jew.'

Malik shook his head. 'I'm not proud of being a Jew. Nor of being born a Pole and naturalized as British. No more than I would be proud of being French or Italian or American. Whatever nationality you are it's an accident. Where your mother was when you were born, who she was married to and where some politicians drew lines on a map. There are people I admire who happen to be Jews. But there are Frenchmen and Italians I admire too. The individuals, not their nationality.'

'But you must feel proud of the Jews in the camps.'

'Why, for God's sake? They didn't go there voluntarily. They didn't go into the gas chambers singing hymns or chanting prayers. They thought they were going to be deloused. They were victims, not heroes. Being proud of race or nationality is what Hitler wanted. The master race.'

'But the whole world except the Arabs admire the Israelis.'

'Don't kid yourself, Lisa. The whole world just shouts for winners. Wait until the Israelis lose some war and see what the world says then. The people who praise the Israelis see them like their favourite football or baseball team. The boys who bring home the trophies and give the Arabs a bloody nose. Some day the Arabs won't just use the price of their oil as a weapon – they'll stop all supplies and the Israelis won't be the heroes then. Arabs are perfectly capable of cutting off their noses to spite their faces.' Malik turned to look at the girl. 'Are you proud of being a German?'

'How could I be, Jake, after what they did to you and your people?'

'You have to remember that there are Jews who are proud of being Jews because of what happened to us in the camps. They are stupid, too. What did we do? We died or we survived. Those who died didn't all die bravely. Some died without knowing what was happening and some screamed their way to heaven. I wasn't brave. I was scared all the time, and I didn't even know what was going on.'

'But you hate Germans.'

'Yes. I do. It's not logical but it's a fact. I can't help it, Germans scare me. I think they could do it again if they got the chance.'

'I pray for you, Jake.'

Malik smiled. 'Tell me.'

'I pray that some day you can forget. God must think I'm crazy. I pray that you can forget, but not forget your mother and your father. I pray that good things will happen to you.'

Malik put his arm round her shoulders and pulled her gently to him. 'You're a good thing that has happened to me.'

'I wish that was true.'

'It is, sweetie. You may not know it, but it's true all right.'

She sighed, and as she looked up at his face he kissed her.

'These are the newspaper cuttings. That's him presenting a cup to the headmistress. And this one is the panel judging a schools music competition. He's the one in the middle.'

'How can I get a look at him?'

'We could invite him home and you could meet him there.'

Malik shook his head. 'No. We won't do that.'

'Why not?'

'I don't want your family dragged into all this. It would be abusing their kindness. And it's not necessary. I can get to look at him some other way.'

'Why do you want to look at him?'

'It can tell you a lot, actually seeing a man's face and how he talks and looks. Have you got any background notes on him?'

'Yes. There's not much, though.'

'Let's have a look at it.'

Fischer pulled a file out of his brief case and passed a single sheet to Malik.

Franz Rechmann had been born on November 11th, 1918. And that was almost the only item of interest in the details of his life. His father had been the founder of the piano-making business. Well off, but not wealthy, he had never held any official post. He hadn't joined the Nazi Party until 1938 which meant he had held out as long as possible. During the war the factory had been turned over to making artificial limbs. The father had been killed in an RAF raid in January 1945. There was no mention of what Rechmann himself had done during the war. He had two daughters. One was married to a Frenchman and lived in Paris. The other still lived at home. Malik shoved the sheet to one side.

'Nothing much there, Heinz. Has he got any enemies?'

'Not that I know of. He's quite a nice guy.'

'How about you run me out to look at the works.'

'OK. Let's go now.'

They drove up the main river road and turned off to cross the Mülheimer bridge. The plant was far bigger and more modern than Malik had expected. It was on the edge of an industrial estate, and the buildings were well-designed and efficient looking. From where they sat on the service road he could see a brightly painted crane loading huge wooden crates into a container lorry. There were thirty or forty well-made crates waiting to be loaded.

'He must be making a lot of bread, Heinz. Is he very rich?'

'A millionaire.'

'In what? D-marks?'

'Anything you care to name. Dollars, yen, sterling, D-marks. Don't forget that it's not only the pianos with his own name that he makes. There's dozens of well-known names in pianos all round the world that are in fact made here. He's considering making electronic organs in a deal with one of the Japanese manufacturers. Another two hundred jobs.'

'Where does he live?'

'He's got a big estate on the edge of the Königsforst.'

'Let's have a look at it.'

It took them half an hour to get to the edge of the estate and another fifteen minutes to find a vantage point so that they could see the house.

But it wasn't a house. It was a mansion, a *château*, a *schloss*. It was too far away to see any detail without binoculars, but visible enough to see that it was both imposing and vaguely menacing.

'Can we go round the whole perimeter of the estate?'

'Yes. But it's over five hundred acres and this is the only place you can see the house from.'

'Let's just take in the main entrance and then we'll get some large-scale maps.'

The main entrance looked normal enough. Two big wrought-iron gates and a pretty lodge-house with a small herbaceous border along the drive. The gates stood open and there were no obvious guards or security precautions. As they drove slowly past nobody came out of the lodge.

The concert ended and the family had come back home for drinks and a sandwich. Heinz's father and mother were with a neighbour in the music room and Heinz and Malik were playing Scrabble with Lisa and Ruth in the sitting room. Heidi had gone up to bed with the portable TV to watch a play.

Ruth was checking a spelling in the *Langenscheidt*.

'He's right, Lisa.' She looked at Malik. 'Heinz is always right, Jake. It's a waste of time challenging him.'

Malik smiled and Heinz said, 'There ought to be a penalty for wrong challenges.'

Lisa laughed. 'And there ought to be a penalty for anyone who cramps up all the corners with two-letter words. It's your turn, Jake.'

As Malik looked from his tiles to the board Heinz walked over to the TV. The picture was on but the sound was turned down. As he turned the sound up there was a shot of a house on the screen and the newsreader said, '. . . on the outskirts of Hamburg. The body was discovered early today. The Hamburg police authorities are not prepared to comment until further enquiries have been made but a police spokesman said that they were treating it as a case of murder . . . In Paris today there were . . .'

Fischer turned off the set and turned slowly to look at Malik. Malik was arranging his tiles on the board and counting out his score.

'Eleven to us, Lisa.'

'Heinz says you've bought a car. What is it?'

'A five-year-old BMW.'

'Did you bring it tonight?'

'Yes. It's by the garage.'

'Can I see it before you go?'

'Sure you can. It's your go.'

They had played for another half hour and then Lisa had gone with Ruth to get her coat.

Fischer said tensely, 'Did you hear the TV news item?'

'Yes. Interesting.'

'It's going to mean trouble.'

'No, it isn't. Forget it.'

And then the girls were back. The four of them went into the music room to say goodnight and then walked in the warm summer night to where the cars were parked. Malik stood with Lisa, his arm round her waist watching the others get into Heinz's car and they waved as they turned and drove away down the drive.

Malik held the door open for her and then slid into the driving seat.

'What do you want to know about the car?'

She smiled, turning her face to look at him. 'Nothing. I just wanted an excuse to be alone with you.' She reached out and took his hand in hers. 'Tell me about your father.'

Malik leaned back and thought before he spoke. Then he said, 'He was tall and thin, perhaps fragile is more the word. When we first came to England he worked as a clerk in a dress factory in the East End. After a couple of years he became the manager because the old man who owned the place fell ill and the only person he trusted was my father.

'A Pole he knew from Warsaw got him a part-time job playing his fiddle in dance-bands for recording sessions in the evenings and the weekends. He saved the deposit for the house and we moved in about 1952 or '53 and we've been there ever since.'

'What was he like – himself, and with you?'

'He was a very gentle man, but scared. Afraid of people, afraid of losing his job, afraid that something might happen to me. He was delighted when I got a university place, and in a way I think he was relieved when I was away. I know he was lonely without me there, but I think he felt that all those smart professors would make sure that I was safe. When I joined the service he was very agitated at first, but he got used to it. And I think about that time we changed roles. I seemed older and more capable of dealing with the world than he was. In a way I became the father and he was the child.'

'Was *he* proud of being a Jew?'

Malik smiled. 'Yes. He kept up the rituals, but because I wouldn't go along with it he treated it like it was some hidden vice. Not to be flaunted. You've got to realize that he never really belonged there. He admired the English but he belonged back in Warsaw. In a way he didn't live there, he just existed. Looking after me. Caring about me. And then when it wasn't necessary any more he was relieved, but he seemed to lose interest in all outside things. He had a pension, and he still played in orchestras and bands, but he was exhausted. He'd had enough of being alive. He never got over my mother's death. He didn't really believe she was dead. He imagined that one of these days she'd appear at the door and the clock would go back and we'd all start all over again where we left off.'

For a long time they sat there without speaking and then he said, 'You'd better go in, sweetie. They'll wonder where you are. Wave to me when I go by.'

He kissed her gently and watched her walk back to the house. She waved as he drove slowly past.

Malik hadn't realized how the time had gone by. It was past twelve o'clock when he parked the car and walked along the cobbled deserted passage to the door.

Heinz Fischer was waiting for him in a bathrobe.

'The Hamburg police have been on the phone. Said they'd been ringing all evening.'

'Was it the Kripo or the Popo man?'

'Aren't you worried, Jake?'

'No. Why should I be?'

'The piece on the TV news.'

'That doesn't worry me.'

'Not even when the local police phone a few hours later?'

'No. What did they say, anyway?'

Fischer shook his head in slow amazement. 'You really are a cool bastard, Jake. I was shit-scared.'

Malik smiled. 'What did they want?'

'It was Lauterbacher, the Popo man. I phoned him this morning and asked what they knew about a man named Amos Meyer. He was phoning to say that they know where he is.'

'Don't tease, Heinz. Where is he?'

'He's in hospital in Hamburg. In a private room. He was hit by a car.'

'Sounds interesting. Was it an accident or deliberate?'

'An accident.'

'How can they be so sure?'

'It was a police car that hit him. They were chasing a hit-and-run driver.'

'How seriously is he hurt?'

'They don't think it's more than superficial scrapes and shock.'

'Can we see him?'

'I didn't ask. There was no need to. He's just a guy in hospital. It's nothing to do with the police who sees him.'

'We'll fly up tomorrow.'

'I've already booked us on the ten o'clock but we'll have to drive up to Düsseldorf. The morning flights from Wahn are all booked.'

'Well done.'

'I've put in an alarm call for seven o'clock, so we'd better get some sleep.'

The other children were watching him. Standing silently. One of the little girls was crying as he threw the last of the dolls into the hole in the ground. The eldest boy had gone, leaving him to do the digging alone.

He hadn't heard the woman as she hurried down the garden path and her voice made him jump.

'What on earth are you doing, Jake?'

The boy looked up at her from the pile of loamy earth.

'It's for the bodies, Mrs Manson,' and he pointed tentatively at the pile of dolls and soft toy animals heaped in the shallow pit. He saw the look of incomprehension on the woman's face turn to fear and revulsion.

'How dare you frighten the girls like this? Give me that spade at once.'

The boy handed over the toy spade with its bright red-painted blade. 'They weren't frightened, Mrs Manson.'

'For heaven's sake look at Debbie, she's crying her eyes out. You wicked boy. Just you go right back home. Go on.' Her voice was shrill. 'I shall speak to your father when I see him . . . and don't you come round here again . . . whatever next?'

Jake Malik looked at the woman's face. She was shaking with anger as he stepped out of the mock grave, and he couldn't understand what the fuss was all about. But it would be a lonely holiday without the children to play with. They said they wanted a new game and they had joined in enthusiastically at first. It was when he'd taken the clothes off Debbie's doll and tossed it onto the heap with the others that the tears had started. But they were interested, he could tell that. His father would be cross. He had told him never to talk about it to anyone. It would turn them against him, he said.

In Hamburg they booked into a small hotel near the Binnen-Alster and Fischer phoned Lauterbacher to see if he had any further information. A lawyer had contacted the police lawyers regarding compensation and to the police lawyer's surprise and satisfaction it seemed that Meyer was not intending to make allegations of careless driving or to claim damages beyond his medical and hospital expenses plus an amount to cover day-to-day expenses. Fischer guessed that Meyer didn't want to draw attention to himself. Von Busch had been his only visitor apart from an unidentified business friend from Cologne. Meyer was expected to be discharged from the hospital in the next two days.

When Fischer told him this, Malik asked him to see if he could sit in on the discussions between Meyer's lawyer and the police legal department. Fischer was able to arrange this for what was hoped to be the final meeting the following day, and Malik made out a short list of questions that he hoped the police lawyer could get answered.

Malik decided that they would go to the hospital after they had eaten, just for the opportunity of looking at Meyer. The police driver was in the general ward with a broken arm and they would use seeing him as their excuse for visiting the hospital.

They took a taxi to the hospital and the reception desk gave them directions to get to the police driver's ward. They had already checked and found that Meyer's private room was on the same floor.

Malik stayed chatting with the police driver for ten minutes, checking on the details of the accident. It seemed that it had just started to rain and Meyer had been struggling into a plastic mac as he stepped off the pavement without looking; the front wing of the car had caught his thigh, turning him so that he lost his balance and rolled into the gutter. As was normal, the police driver had been suspended until the legalities were concluded.

Malik left Fischer with the driver and walked down the long corridor to Room 734. He knocked, and without waiting for an answer he walked inside the room.

The man in the bed was balding and dark-skinned with heavy-lidded brown eyes, and he put down the magazine he was reading as he looked at Malik.

'Is there anything you want, Herr Meyer? Reading matter or toilet stuff? I'm just going out to get some things for the police driver.'

'You're a policeman?'

Malik nodded. 'Yes.'

'How's the driver?'

'Waiting for his arm to set. The X-rays indicate that it's healing OK.'

'Thanks for the offer, but I've got everything I need. And I'm expecting friends – they will be bringing me today's papers and a few magazines.'

There was a knock on the door and a man put his head in.

'Amos, I didn't know you had a visitor. We'll wait outside.'

'No. Come in. This gentleman is a police officer who offered to get me anything I needed. He's just leaving. I didn't get your name, officer.'

'Malik, Herr Meyer.'

The man at the door nodded. 'Von Busch. Glad to meet you.' He opened the door and another man came in, ignoring Malik and walking over to the bed.

'Amos, it's good to see you. I was worried.'

'I'm fine, Franz. I'll be out in a couple of days they tell me.'

Von Busch moved to one side as Malik bowed slightly to the three of them and headed for the door.

Two things puzzled him. The first was the Israeli passport lying beside the watch and the coins on the bedside table, and the second was the man called Franz. He had seen him somewhere before, but he couldn't think where.

When he went back to the police driver, Fischer had gone. He had left a message that he was going straight back to the hotel and would wait there for Malik.

Fischer had left a note at the hotel reception desk that he was in the hotel's coffee bar, and Malik joined him there.

As he sat down at the table, Malik said, 'Why did you disappear?'

'I had to. I recognized somebody and I was scared he would see me.'

'Who?'

'I saw these two guys walking down the ward and I recognized von Busch. He's well known. I recognized him from newspaper pictures when he used to ride for our Olympic equestrian team. And then the other guy turned to speak to him, and it was Rechmann. Franz Rechmann.'

'The guy with the piano factory we looked at?'

'Yes.'

'Did he see you?'

'No. He was too intent on whatever he was saying to von Busch.'

'The two of them came into Meyer's room while I was there. I thought I'd seen him somewhere before. When could it have been?'

'He was in the Green Room that night when the family played at the concert. You might have seen him there. And you saw the press pictures too.'

'Of course.'

'What excuse did you give when you went in?'

'I told him I was a cop visiting the driver. Just being helpful.'

'So von Busch and Rechmann will know you're a cop.'

'Sure. But that's fine. No need to pretend I'm anything else. They'll connect me with the accident rather than the groups. It won't matter if I meet him with you.'

'What was Meyer like?'

'Polite enough. He uses an Israeli passport.'

Fischer frowned. 'That doesn't fit in, Jake. You wouldn't have an Israeli connected with anti-Jewish groups.'

'So we think again about what the groups are up to. Apart from daubing swastikas on synagogue doors.'

'It rules out the KGB.'

'Not necessarily.'

'What's that mean?'

'A cover for a cover for whatever the real thing is. The KGB like playing these very convoluted games. Let's not cross anything out until we've got some hard facts. Can you find out when Rechmann will be back?'

'I should think so. I'll phone when we get back.'

The police lawyer's meeting with Meyer's lawyer had been brief and amiable. And all Malik had learned, despite his list of questions, was that Meyer was an Israeli citizen and the wealthy and influential owner of a group of companies based in Israel with its headquarters in Tel Aviv. The companies included insurance, engineering, a cotton mill, a freight company, a small shipping line and minority holdings in a variety of small local enterprises. He was sixty-one, he had no family, and he travelled a lot. The German Embassy in Tel Aviv had confirmed that he was well respected and had influence in all the places that mattered. He was much respected, both as a man and as a businessman.

CHAPTER TEN

'There must be somebody who hates his guts. You don't get to be a millionaire without making enemies on the way.'

'I'll phone my father and see if he's got any ideas.'

'What about journalists? They always know the skeletons in the cupboards.'

'There's a freelance guy named Otto Prahl. He'd be worth talking to.'

'How old is he? How far back can he go?'

'He's in his early sixties and he's worked for US magazines, South American newspapers, and most of the European press services take bits and pieces from him. He knows what the dirt is if there is any.'

'What's he go for, money or booze?'

'Both, I should think.'

'Have you got anything you can trade him?'

'I can find something, I guess.'

'Where can we meet without being noticed too much?'

'Let's take a private room at the *Dom* and give him a good dinner.'

'Fine. You can introduce me as British police and that will get him interested.'

Fischer looked up Prahl's telephone number in the directory and rang the number. Prahl accepted the invitation for that evening but couldn't meet them until nine o'clock.

Otto Prahl was nothing like the traditional newsman. He was tall and elegant with a bush of wiry grey hair and a lean ascetic face. He wore a tweed suit that was well cut, and an old-fashioned cravat with an opal pin. He carried an ebony walking-stick with an ivory handle. He was obviously used to meeting people and used to assessing them quickly, and after they had discussed European politics over their meal he sat in the armchair with his glass of neat whisky, looking across at Malik.

'Am I allowed to ask what you're doing in our fair city, Herr Malik, or is that going too far?'

'Are we on or off the record, Herr Prahl?'

'It's up to you, my friend.'

'How about we talk off the record first, and then maybe we can go on the record later.'

'Why not?'

'I'm seconded to the Federal police for a few months to compare notes on various matters of mutual interest.'

Prahl smiled. 'You sound like Helmut Schmidt on his first day as Chancellor.' He waved his hand. 'I mean that as a compliment of course.'

Malik didn't smile. 'One of the things that concerns us is this latest rash of anti-Jewish outrages. Paris, Nice, London, and now it's happening in the Federal Republic. Why?'

Prahl shrugged. 'The wicked Germans at it again, I suppose.'

'So why doesn't it happen in East Germany too?'

'There's no need to daub synagogues over there. You've got an anti-Semitic government to do it for you.'

'So you think it's genuine, anti-Jewish Nazis?'

Prahl shook his head. 'No. I shouldn't think so. Things are never as simple as that. It could be people organizing a few louts to do these things to make those governments that find the new Germany an acceptable partner think again. Once a Nazi always a Nazi, or better still, once a German always a German. The Soviet Union would benefit from that. They would like to see us isolated from NATO and the Common Market. We might turn to them. They have prizes to dangle. Even a vague hint of a unified Germany would keep any Federal Chancellor in power for decades. Even discussions about discussions would be a prize.'

'What about the Israelis?'

'I don't understand, my friend.'

'How does it affect Bonn's relationship with the Israelis?'

'For public consumption Tel Aviv will raise hell, and Bonn will make soothing noises. Underneath it will make no difference. We have paid every pfennig of the agreed reparations. We cooperate with them economically, politically and militarily. A few swastikas or even a bomb or two aren't going to shake that for a moment.'

'You don't see any benefit to the Israelis in these attacks?'

'None. Absolutely none. What benefit could there be?'

'Maybe Israeli domestic politics. The opposition blaming the government for what goes on. Or die-hard anti-Germans trying to break the link.'

Prahl shook his head. 'The Israeli politicians, government and opposition, have got more problems than they can handle, sitting all round their borders. Nobody's going to get any mileage out of finding a new one. Of course there are plenty of Jews who still hate the Nazis, maybe all Germans, but they aren't going to rock the boat for Israel. There's nothing in it for anybody.'

'So who does benefit?'

Prahl pursed his lips. 'The Soviet Union, marginally the East Germans. Nobody else.'

'So you think they could be behind these attacks?'

'Quite frankly I haven't given it much thought. It isn't really important.' He shrugged. 'Violence is an everyday symptom of the whole world today. Maybe it always was, and we are merely better informed now.'

Malik nodded. 'It's your turn now, Herr Prahl. What can I answer that would help you?'

Prahl raised his eyebrows and smiled. 'Two questions, if I might be greedy.'

'Carry on.'

'Are you a Jew, Herr Malik?'

'Yes.'

'How many Germans have noticed the tattoo on your wrist?'

'I don't know. Only one other person has commented on it. It's quite faint by now.'

'You must have been very young at that time.'

'I was seven when they tattooed me.'

'You seem a rather special sort of man, Herr Malik. Very analytical, very observant, but underlying all that I sense something else. You're not just a policeman are you?'

'Technically I am.'

Prahl smiled. 'Of course. I'll say no more, except to ask if I may put one more question?'

'Go ahead.'

'Do you think Englishmen could have behaved like the Nazis?'

Malik smiled, looked at Fischer, then away towards the picture hanging over the fireplace. He looked at it for a long time and shifted uneasily in his seat as he turned his head to look at Prahl as he started to talk.

'I know Englishmen who could behave like the Nazis. I can think of at least half a dozen who could murder innocent women and children because somebody ordered them to. But on the whole, no, they wouldn't behave like the Nazis. There wouldn't be enough thugs to go round to do it on a big enough scale.'

'Why not?'

'For an odd sort of reason, Herr Prahl. The English don't really respect the law. They are all half-anarchists but would be shocked if you told them that. They don't respect politicians or governments or bureaucrats, they despise them. Even if they voted for them. I think there's a difference, too, that Germans admire winners and the English have a soft spot for the underdog. And the English hate obeying orders. Even sensible ones.'

Prahl raised his eyebrows. 'What about the innocent women and children who died in their thousands when the RAF wiped out Dresden in one night?'

'I'm not defending that, Otto, but there is a difference. First of all it was the Germans who started that game. It was the *Luftwaffe* that started bombing cities rather than military targets. Coventry, Liverpool, Birmingham, London. And secondly, the concentration camps were nothing to do with the war. They existed long before the war, so did the campaign against the Jews. No other nation on earth has built gas ovens to kill millions of civilians because they were Jews, or anything else. It wasn't done in the heat of war, it was done in cold blood by barbarians.'

Prahl had noticed Malik's use of his first name and reached for his glass when Malik stopped talking. He lifted it towards Malik.

'*Shalom*, Herr Malik.'

'*Shalom*.'

Malik put down his glass and leaned forward. 'I met a man in Hamburg. He comes from Cologne. I'm told he's a millionaire. How do you get to be a millionaire in post-war Germany, Otto?'

'Who is he?'

'He was introduced to me as Rechmann. Franz Rechmann. He's got a factory or something.'

Prahl leaned back in his chair. 'Well I guess it helps if you start off with a few hundred thousand from your father, and a business that's a going concern. When the old man died there were no other shareholders. Franz inherited the whole of the stock. He turned out the old plant, put in the latest equipment, took on bright people and spent money on promotion. And now he exports to over thirty countries.'

'He must have some skeleton in his cupboard. All millionaires have.'

Prahl smiled. 'Of course. Our dear Franz is no exception. Mind you, it's a comparatively small skeleton compared with some of them.'

'What is it?'

Prahl looked at Fischer. 'Do we tell him, Heinz? Or do we keep it in the family?'

'I don't know of any skeleton, Otto. I really don't.'

'But Rechmann is a friend of your parents.'

'They might know, but I certainly don't.'

'How do you find him? What do you think of him?'

'He's hard-working, amiable, mildly interested in music. Seems an OK guy to me.'

'Paul Rechmann was a major in the *Wehrmacht* but nobody ever mentions it now.'

'Why not? That's nothing to be ashamed of.'

'It depends on what you were up to of course.'

'Like what?'

'Rechmann was one of von Gehlen's men in *Fremde Heere Ost*. Working against the Russians. In charge of the groups operating against the so-called partisans. I'm told that Rechmann was a bitter Russian-hater. And still is.'

'There are plenty of those around, Otto. Anyone who was in Berlin when the Red Army came in has things to remember.'

'Agreed. But if your trade is international it's better to have been a simple soldier than the man in charge of the thugs who killed Russian patriots. It gets in the way. It confuses the issue. It's better to lock it in the closet and keep it locked. With Bonn playing footsie with Moscow it's best to keep the temperature down.'

'Was he a party member?'

'No but there are rumours that the company paid tens of thousands into local party funds. The old man was made a *Wehrwirtschaftsführer* and you didn't get that for spitting in Adolf's eye.' Prahl looked at his watch. 'Gentlemen, it's after midnight and I need my sleep.'

After he had left the two of them sat there finishing the whisky.

'Was it any help, Jake?'

'What do you think?'

Fischer shrugged, his face despondent. 'Another piece in the jigsaw puzzle, but no use to us.'

'It's that kind of operation, Heinz. Just plugging away.'

'What next?'

'See what you can find out about the chap in Goslar. The retired judge.'

Heinz Fischer phoned from Goslar. He had traced the judge. His name was Lemke. Gustav Lemke. He had retired from the *Landesgericht* a year ago. He was a widower with no children.

'What is he, Heinz? Left wing or right wing?'

'Doesn't belong to any party, Jake. And he wasn't a member of the Nazi party, either.'

'That's not possible, Heinz. He could never have had the education and training to be a lawyer without being a member.'

'He wasn't, Jake,' Heinz said softly. 'He was in a camp for six years.'

'Which camp?'

'Sachsenhausen.'

'Is he a Jew?'

'No.'

'Do you know why he was in the camp?'

'Yes. I've got a press cutting. He announced in open court that he would not accept the Nuremberg Race Laws in his court. That was in November 1938. He was arrested as he left the court and went first to Buchenwald and ended up in Sachsenhausen. Refused any post-war compensation on the grounds that he was only doing his duty as a German citizen. He was offered an Order of Merit by Bonn in 1951 and refused that too.'

'Sounds incredible. But he doesn't seem to fit in these groups in any way. A man like that wouldn't be seen dead with synagogue daubers.'

'There is a connection, believe it or not. I showed the local police a photograph of Amos Meyer. He has stayed in a local hotel a number of times. I've checked at the hotel and they confirmed this. I also checked with the taxi driver who does most of the hotel work. He remembers taking Meyer to see the judge a couple of times in the last few weeks.'

'Anything else?'

'Yes. Lauterbacher from Hamburg telexed me at HQ to say that Meyer had booked a suite at the Atlantic. He's due to arrive on Friday morning.'

'You'd better come back, Heinz, and we'll fly up to Hamburg tomorrow.'

They took a taxi from the airport to Lauterbacher's office. He gave them the number of Meyer's suite at the hotel and they booked the double room adjoining. But when Malik asked for Meyer's suite to be bugged, Lauterbacher was adamant. If they wanted that they would have to apply for a warrant and give a judge in chambers good reason. Or get the BKA to sponsor their application.

In the hotel Malik checked the lock on their door and opened the soft brown leather wallet that Fischer had seen at the *Waldhaus*. One after the other he tried the odd-shaped bits of steel until one turned the heavy spring bolt of the lock.

Then as Fischer watched, Malik slid a small metal sleeve along the steel rod and walked into the corridor. Slowly and carefully he slid the rod into the lock of Meyer's suite and turned it slowly. Fischer heard the soft thud as the bolt turned back into the lock. With his free hand Malik turned the knob and slightly opened the heavy door. A few seconds later the lock was closed again and Fischer followed Malik back into their own room.

'Check what time the plane from London gets in, Heinz. If it's after midday try the Paris one. And check if Meyer's on the passenger list.'

The airport had refused to give the information and Malik had to wait until Fischer contacted Lauterbacher to find out for them. He came back in ten minutes. Amos Meyer was a passenger on the London plane and his point of departure was Tel Aviv. The London plane had landed on time twenty minutes earlier.

At two-fifteen Meyer was let into his suite and Malik waited anxiously, looking at his watch from time to time. If Meyer was a practising Jew he would go to the synagogue soon so that he could be back in his rooms before dusk.

'When he leaves his room, Heinz, you follow him. Check that he actually leaves the hotel and then phone me from the lobby. Then stay down there and wait until he comes back. As soon as you see him, ring *his* room number. Let it ring just twice. Even if I'm still in there I shan't answer. Then ring our number and check with me.'

'What do you expect to find?'

Malik shrugged. 'God knows. It's just a fishing expedition.'

And as he spoke they heard Meyer's door slam to and the rattle of keys. Fischer opened their door carefully, looked out, nodded to Malik and closed the door behind him as he walked into the corridor. Ten minutes later Fischer phoned. Meyer had left the hotel.

There was a large sitting room to Meyer's suite and a double bedroom with two single beds. One tan leather case lay open on one of the beds and a black briefcase with a brass zip was on the bedside table. In an old-fashioned silver frame propped up against the bedside lamp was a faded photograph of a pretty girl holding a cat cradled in her arms as she smiled into the camera.

He checked the wardrobe first. There was one blue suit on a hanger and nothing in any of its pockets. There were four white shirts with Marks and Spencer's labels in the top drawer. Three pairs of cotton pants and several pairs of socks in the second drawer, and the third drawer was empty.

In the case there were several magazines. A paperback in Hebrew and two in English. One was the Penguin edition of Montaigne's *Essays* and the other was Lionel Davidson's *A Long Way to Shiloh*. A plastic bag held an electric razor, a bottle of pre-shave, a pack of tissues and an unused flannel. There were two blue denim shirts and a pair of faded khaki shorts wrapped round a pair of well-worn sandals.

Malik picked up the black briefcase and unzipped it. There was Meyer's Israeli passport. A first-class El Al return ticket: Tel Aviv–London–Hamburg–Berlin–Brussels–Tel Aviv. A small diary with few entries, and all of them in Hebrew, an American Express card, and a Timex stop-watch. In a plastic folder were half a dozen business letters and memos, all concerning expenditure on engineering equipment and buildings. Inside an inner flap was a hand-written letter in German. Malik read it several times.

DEAR M

When one sees what has happened in only the last few months, I feel we must hasten our programme. With Nixon sent packing, Mozambique, Angola, the Russians in Ethiopia, Greece pulling out of NATO; it's a catalogue of turmoil that sadly confirms our worst fears.

What is, perhaps, even more concern to us, is that instead of one of our two interests supporting the other we may both be involved at the same time. That would weaken our position tactically if not practically.

The four of us should meet quite quickly. We have the funds, the plan, and the facilities, but our time schedule was wrong. If we have to take risks we should do so. Unless we are *all* in place soon we could be too late. We must look to your people. Remember Judges 20 verse 1 and Judges 21 verse 25.

VON B.

Then the phone rang twice. Malik put everything back in its place, locked the outer door and went back to their room. The phone was already ringing.

'He's just waiting for the lift, Jake. Von Busch is with him. He's been waiting for him down here in the foyer.'

'OK. Watch him into the lift and come up in about five minutes.'

Back in their room Malik scribbled down the chapters and verses and then opened the drawer. A red-bound Gideon Bible was in the drawer of the bedside table with the local telephone directory.

He leafed through for Judges and read both references carefully, and wrote them out.

Judges Chapter 20, verse 1

Then all the children of Israel went out, and the congregation was gathered together as one man, from Dan even to Beer-sheba, with the land of Gilead, unto the Lord in Mizpeh.

Judges Chapter 21, verse 25

In those days there was no king in Israel: every man did that which was right in his own eyes.

When Fischer came into the room he said, 'Anything interesting?'

'I've got his address in Tel Aviv and the name of his main company. I think that we ought to have a look at his set-up in Israel.'

'I wouldn't be allowed to go.'

'Why not?'

'There's an unofficial agreement between Bonn and the Israelis. Political police and intelligence people only go there at the Israelis' specfic request.' He smiled. 'They've never requested anyone yet. Mossad don't like German secret service people in Israel.'

'But I've met Mossad liaison officers at joint intelligence meetings here in Hamburg. Several times.'

'It's a one-way traffic, Jake. We don't object to *them*, but they do object to us. They cooperate in most ways but they won't have us on the ground. I guess it's understandable.'

'Can you apply for leave and we could go as tourists?'

Fischer smiled. 'West Germans have to apply for visas at the point of entry. I'd never be given one. They'll have my name on some file or other. If you're German and born before 1928 you won't get a visa whoever you are. Unless you're a Jew, of course.'

Malik stood up and walked over to the window. There were pleasure boats tied up at the marina on the far side of the Alster and dinghies racing a course round a dozen orange buoys. He had known that Heinz Fischer would never be allowed into Israel but he didn't want to make his move too obvious. And if he were truthful there was just the faintest touch of *schadenfreude* from the fact that he would be welcome while Fischer was banned. He could fix Lisa's visa himself.

He turned, smiling. 'Maybe a week's leave would do me good. Lisa might like to come too. It would give me a chance to do a bit of checking on our friend Meyer.'

'See what she says, Jake. She'd probably jump at the chance.'

And Malik was momentarily ashamed at his deception in the face of such an amiable and trusting response from the man he was deceiving. Because he knew now that he was deceiving Fischer. And meant to go on deceiving him until he had cleared the doubt in his own mind. One thing he knew now for certain. They had been piecing together the wrong pieces for the wrong jigsaw. They were way off beam. Not that he knew where they should be, but at least he could go back to square one and start again with an open mind. There were ominous warning bells ringing in his mind but they were very faint and far away.

CHAPTER ELEVEN

As the taxi drove off Lisa stood looking at the house. Malik had never described it to her but in some strange way it was exactly what she had imagined. Not in any particular detail, but in its aura. It reminded her of the houses in novels by Thomas Mann. Old-fashioned and solid, as if its red bricks had absorbed the warmth and strength of decades of summer sun. Not a warmth of the spirit, but the russet-faced self-assurance that country people have. The stained-glass panels above the front door, the elongated, square-edged bays with their net curtains and stone lintels had a kind of mild aggression that could have come from the Bauhaus; and the worn concave centres to the three stone steps to the front door looked better for not having been levelled.

Malik picked up their bags and they walked together up the short garden path. Tall thistles almost up to their shoulders and bindweed everywhere.

As Malik unlocked the door and she walked inside, the close, hot air was overwhelming, and there was an odour of floor-polish and dust. And as he walked through the house with her, showing her the rooms, she knew exactly what it would have been like to grow up in that house. All it needed was a vignetted sepia portrait of the Kaiser or Pilsudski, and the sound of a child practising scales on a piano and it could have been in Europe rather than Hampstead. It was the kind of house the Maliks would have had in Warsaw once

Abraham Malik had established himself.

They went out that evening to eat at a small local restaurant and when they got back to the house she made them coffee, and as they sat drinking it she said, 'What kind of people do you like, Jake?'

He leaned forward and put his empty cup on the table before he spoke.

'I think I ought to do what the Mafia do and plead the Fifth Amendment.'

'Why?'

'Present company and your family excepted I don't think I like people at all.'

'No heroes?'

'No, none.'

'Nobody you've ever loved?'

'Just my father, but even that was more affection than love.'

'But you read poetry and like music.'

Malik shrugged and smiled. 'I like flowers, too, and sunsets. But none of those things are people.'

'But you're very perceptive about people.'

'That doesn't make me like them.' He sighed and shrugged. 'I don't belong, Lisa. There's me and there's the rest of the world. I just want to survive.'

'And you're never lonely?'

'No. Nobody can hurt me that way.'

'What way?'

'By leaving me, turning me down.' Malik looked at her half-smiling. 'Tell me what you don't like about me.'

She frowned. 'I don't understand.'

'Tell me something bad about me. Something that irritates you. Or embarrasses you.'

'There isn't anything, Jake.'

'Nothing at all?'

'No. Nothing at all.'

'So what do you like about me?'

'Everything.'

He laughed. 'That's impossible.'

'What don't you like about *me*?'

He turned away from her, towards the window. For long minutes he sat there in silence and then he turned to look at her face again.

'There's nothing I don't like about you.'

'Is that because you don't think about me much?'

He sighed. 'No. I think about you a lot.'

'Nice thoughts?'

'Always.'

'I love you, Jake,' she said softly.

He opened his mouth to speak, hesitated and then closed it and she said, 'Say it Jake. Whatever it was.'

He turned in his chair to face her. 'It's just that it's terribly complicated. I don't know how to explain it. I don't understand it myself, so I don't know how to say it.'

'Tell me, Jake. Try. Please.'

He sat with his head back in the chair, his eyes closed.

'I would like to say that I love you too, Lisa. But I don't really know what love is. My father loved me, but that's a different kind of love. One or two girls . . . women . . . have liked me but I didn't feel any involvement with them. None at all. I've always taken for granted that my background from when I was a child would always get in the way. I've wondered sometimes if I'm not actually mad, insane. And my thoughts about those days, my nightmares, are always there in the background, like wild animals in a forest waiting to come out and devour me. I never deliberately think about those days, but now and again something will remind me and trigger it off. Small things, ridiculous things. I used to think it would go, but it doesn't. Sometimes I think it gets worse. Because you're a very kind and gentle person, you sympathize with me, but I'd always be afraid that in the end the sympathy would be worn out. You'd get tired of it, bored with it. You'd wonder why loving you and being loved by you didn't compensate for all that. It would always seem like I had a separate part of my life away from you. And because of my job it would seem even worse.'

He opened his eyes and looked at her face. He saw the tears on her cheeks. 'And now I've made you unhappy.'

'You haven't, Jake. The tears are for you. I understand very well what you mean, but there's no way I can prove to you that I would rather be with you, exactly as you are, than anyone else. Even my family.'

Malik looked at the girl's face for a long time and she saw him take a deep breath before he spoke.

'My momma was twenty-six or seven when we went in the camp. She was very pretty. Every night she was taken to the guard hut, and I went with her. I guess I was about seven then, and she was afraid that something would happen to me if she left me in the big hut. And every night I sat there and watched. There were always three SS guards on standby, and the three of them would have her. Have sex with her. And when they'd finished we sat at the guard room table and we had a plate of soup and some bread. I didn't know then what they were doing to her but I know now. So I hate Germans. I haven't ever eaten soup since, wooden huts frighten me, and I disappointed my father because I refused to believe in the One True God who could let those things happen. And I could never tell him why.'

'What happened to your Momma?'

'They got tired of her and put her in the gas chambers.'

'I could help you, Jake,' she said softly.

'How?'

'I'll remember those things with you. It won't be just you on your own.'

'You won't tell your family or Heinz about my momma, will you?'

She shook her head. 'No.' She paused. 'You've got a paperback book you read. Palgrave's *Golden Treasury*. Have you read all of it?'

'A lot. But not all.'

'You left it in the house one night and I read it in bed and there was a verse in a poem that made me think of you and me.'

'What was it? Shakespeare?'

'No. It was by a poet I've never heard of. The Earl of Stirling and it was called "To Aurora".'

'Can you remember it?'

She nodded, and said softly,

'Then all my thoughts should in thy visage shine,
And if that aught mischanced thou shouldst not moan
Nor bear the burden of thy griefs alone;
No, I would have my share in what were thine:

And whilst we thus should make our sorrows one,
This happy harmony would make them none.'

He reached over and pulled her to him, his mouth on hers, passionately at first, and then gently. Then putting his cheek against hers he said, 'I love you, Lisa. I hope it's going to be all right.'

She reached out and touched his hand. 'It'll be all right, Jake. I do understand. Nobody could survive all that without being affected.'

She saw from the look on Malik's face that it was time to change the subject. But he interrupted her thought.

'I'll be going in to town tomorrow. Provided they can fix it we could fly to Israel on Monday.'

'Does it excite you, the thought of being in Israel?'

'No. And don't you run away with the idea that the streets of Tel Aviv are crowded with Jews playing fiddles and cellos.'

She laughed. 'You try to sound like a hardened cynic, my love, but you're not. You've just got a better disguise than most people.'

Malik stood up, taking her hand as she stood up too.

'I'll put your bags in the back bedroom. It's quieter in there.'

'Was that your bedroom?'

'Yes. I'll do you some hot chocolate to relax you. I'll bring it up.'

When Malik came in with the glass of hot chocolate and a biscuit on an old-fashioned tray it was like being a child again for the girl.

She patted the bed beside her and, smiling, she said, 'Are you going to tell me a story?'

'It was good of your parents to let you come with me.'

'I'm twenty-three, Jake, nearly twenty-four. I'm glad they said yes but I should have come anyway, if that was what you wanted.'

'I want it to work, Lisa, so much.'

Her blue eyes looked at him. 'D'you want to sleep with me, Jake?'

'Of course I do. But I'm not going to. Not until we're married.'

'Why not? Is it because of what those animals did to your mother?'

'Partly. There's several reasons. And that's the least part of what you mean to me.'

'What *do* I mean to you, Jake?' she said quietly.

He looked away from her face towards the window, and for several moments he sat in silence, her hand in his, before he turned his head to look at her again.

'You mean a great change in my life. I feel you have quietly opened a door for me that had always been closed. You've put a third dimension in my life because you're gentle and understanding. And beautiful. You understand me and I think I understand you. I just love you, Lisa.'

He bent to kiss her gently and her arms went round him. It was a long time before he stood up and left her.

Some sound woke her early, and when she looked at her watch she saw that it was barely five o'clock. She slipped out of bed and walked over to the window.

The ground fell away sharply so that all she could see were the tops of the trees and, in the far distance, what she guessed must be Hampstead Heath. She turned and looked around the room. Jake Malik's room.

It was a strange room, lacking any indication of its owner. The walls were papered with a heavy flock paper of plum-red, unidentifiable flowers, the furniture solid but old-fashioned. There were no pictures or photographs, no decorative objects. It was almost monastic. More impersonal than the bedroom of a cheap hotel. The rest of the house was much the same. It was the home of two men who didn't want to remember, anything. It wasn't just Abraham Malik who existed rather than lived. Jacob Malik was just the same. For a brief moment before she got back into bed she closed her eyes and prayed that she really could make a difference.

CHAPTER TWELVE

Jenkins seemed barely to conceal his impatience and indifference as Malik told him briefly of what he and Fischer had done. He gave no details or names, and refrained from any speculation.

'Is your German cooperating, Jake?'

'Yes.'

'No other problems?'

'Just the lack of anything positive.'

Jenkins stood up. 'It's probably some low-key group of cranks. Just keep plugging away.'

'You got my application for leave, sir?'

'Your what . . . ah yes . . . application for leave. Of course. How long would you like?'

'Up to three weeks if I may, but I may come back earlier.'

'Of course. You need a rest, my boy. Where are you going?'

'To Israel.'

'Ah, yes. I see. Good idea.'

Jenkins could barely conceal his embarrassment. He was in no way anti-Jewish. He just wished that they'd keep it to themselves. He felt exactly the same way about homosexuals. He wouldn't ever knowingly employ them, because it made them doubly vulnerable, but he accepted their existence. Providing they didn't flaunt it. All this 'coming out' business was just self-indulgent exhibitionism. There were excellent Jews, but there was no need to emphasize one's religion. To Jenkins it was just bad taste. A lack of feeling for others.

He walked with Malik to the door. 'Gordon can help you with flights and that sort of thing. Don't hesitate to use him.'

The security check had been time-consuming and thorough. Lisa, with her BRD passport, had taken even longer, but when they were together again there was still half an hour before their flight call was due.

They bought cigarettes and soap at the duty-free shop, half a dozen magazines and a couple of paperbacks each.

'I don't think I'll be able to read, Jake, I'm so excited. I feel I ought to have a bucket and spade.'

Malik smiled. 'Let's have a coffee while we're waiting.'

As they sat at the table sipping the scalding coffee she said, 'Mama told me to give you her love when I phoned. She's trying not to be worried.'

'About what?'

'Me, a German, going to Israel.'

He laughed. 'At least ten per cent of the population were Germans before they became Israelis.' And it was the first time she had seen him laugh.

'What are you looking forward to most?'

'Some sunshine. And you?'

'Oh, meeting people who care about music and literature, and seeing all the things they've done. Making a country out of a desert.'

Malik turned his head, listening. 'That's us, sweetie. They're calling us early. You take the boarding cards and tickets and I'll take our hand-luggage.'

They were lucky and had been able to arrange double seats together on the starboard aisle. Lisa had the window seat and Malik passed her a couple of the magazines. But she ignored them, watching intently as the ground staff rolled the passenger steps away and the hoses were stowed away on the drinking-water truck. And then they were taxiing slowly along the feeder, the wide wings undulating as the plane rolled forward. Ten minutes later the undercarriages thudded into place and the billowing cumulus clouds were awash with the vivid colours of the midday sun.

Malik had been amused when the girl insisted on the kosher meals, but even before they were crossing the Swiss Alps he was asleep. And as he slept she looked at his face. There was nothing Jewish about it except the tanned skin, and that could have been Spanish or Italian. He didn't gesticulate as Jews were supposed to do and he never used those Yiddish or Hebrew words that even Germans sometimes used. But she suspected that inside was a flood of Jewish emotion waiting to be released. Even in the time she had known him he had changed a lot. He actually smiled sometimes, and he was prepared to talk to her about his father and himself. Something that would have been impossible when she first knew him. And the music he liked was all hearts-on-the-sleeve music. Violins and cellos, from Bach Partitas to Viennese schmaltz.

Heinz had warned her not to expect too much and had hinted gently that there was a danger that she could be indulging in wishful thinking. Heinz was often right about people, but she had wondered sometimes if there wasn't just a faint touch of jealousy in his warnings about Jake. Heinz was so obviously the junior in whatever it was they were doing together. And Jake Malik was like rock to her brother's crystal glass.

Her father liked Malik, although he was not the kind of man he would normally take to. Malik was too masculine in many ways. Too tough, too sure of himself in physical ways, to appeal to Helmut Fischer. She wasn't sure of her mother's opinion. She seldom passed comments on other people, even to her family. She had seen her mother smiling affectionately sometimes as she looked at Malik when he was unaware of her glance. When she asked her mother what she thought of him she had been noncommittal. 'Everybody has problems. Your Jake has more than most. But you seem to be doing him good.' Lisa had glowed at 'your Jake' and dismissed the rest as mere motherly caution. Of course he had problems, but she would help him get rid of them.

She slept soundly until Malik woke her to say that they were landing in fifteen minutes, and even as he spoke the warning lights went on and she felt the jolt as the undercarriages came down.

As they walked from the plane to the terminal she was thrilled to see the sign that said: Ben Gurion International Airport – Welcome to Israel.

The welcome started right at at the airport when Malik managed to get them a taxi to themselves. The driver was a New York Jew who had lived in Israel for ten years. They heard the whole family saga. He had owned his own garage and workshop in the Bronx and was making twenty grand a year clear. But always there had been the pull of Israel. There had been family meetings every few weeks. Everybody over eighteen was for going. Everybody under eighteen was for staying. Boyfriends, girlfriends, football teams, drama classes and even New York itself suddenly became beautiful and desirable. Grandmothers, as always, had made the decision. When there was twenty-five grand in the bank on top of fares and moving expenses they would go. And a year after the money was there they had booked their passages for two months later after the youngest boy had been bar-mitzvahed. Never a day's regret. Driving a cab in Tel Aviv produced nothing much in the way of extras but all the children were doing well. All of them earning except the boy in the army.

He dropped them at the Tourist Information Service and as Malik gave him the fare the man saw the tattoo on his wrist. He looked at Malik's face, and waved the money away.

'No way, pal. I'm not taking no bread from you. That number on your arm beats twenty Purple Hearts as far as I'm concerned. Where you going now?'

'We're going to find a hotel at the Tourist Office.'

'Forget it. I'm taking you to the City. It's not too expensive, it's clean, it's got decent food. Near the beach and right in town. Let's go.'

Smiling, they got back into the taxi and minutes later they were at the hotel. The driver insisted that he carried in their bags and launched into an energetic dialogue in Hebrew with the receptionist. He stood waiting until they had their rooms and waved peremptorily to the bell-hop to take their luggage.

He held out his hand. 'Tonight at nine o'clock I'm coming back here for you and you're eating with my family.'

Despite Malik's protestations he brushed aside all excuses. He phoned his wife from the reception desk as if he owned the place.

The Brodskys, mother, father, two grandmothers and two daughters kept them amused for the whole of the meal with the gossip of Tel Aviv. Politicians, the more extreme religious groups, rabbis and business were all fair game, and it was obvious that if there was an Israeli style of humour it had been transplanted from New York. They made a special fuss of Lisa. Praising her good looks, agreeing with everything she said. The last half hour was spent with a street map on the dining-room table while Brodsky laid out a programme of sightseeing that would have taken a year.

When he eventually drove them back to the hotel he told them that he was at their disposal. Anytime, every day. It was an honour to please them, he said.

It was the same everywhere they went. Helpful directions when they lost their way, and mild-looking ladies breaking out into tirades when they were being over-charged by the peddlers in the market at Shuk Hacarmel.

They spent most of their mornings on the beach. Lisa swimming and Malik just watching. In the afternoon they explored the city. Malik was amazed at its size and the traffic. It was easier and quicker to walk than take a taxi. Even the loyal Brodsky admitted that.

On the evening of the third day they were discussing the others they had met. A journalist who had talked to them in the bank when they were changing traveller's cheques and had had a coffee with them afterwards, and the businessman who had insisted on escorting them when they asked the way to the old City Hall. Not only walk there with them but show them and explain the exhibits that were housed there now that it was a museum.

'I've never seen you looking so relaxed, Jake.'

Malik smiled. 'I guess I am relaxed. I don't know what it is.'

Lisa laughed softly. 'You do know. You're at home here. You like it, don't you?'

'Yes I do, but I still don't know why. How about you? Are you disappointed that everybody isn't playing violins in the street?'

'I love it, but it *is* funny about the music.'

'In what way?'

'I always felt that because my favourite performers are all Jews, that every Jew was musical. But they're not. A lot of people we've met aren't the slightest bit interested in music, and they'd never heard of some internationally famous Jewish performers. It was only Menuhin, Ashkenazy and Perlman they knew of. And even then they saw them more as show-biz stars than musicians. It's their success they admire rather than their playing. And I find that sad.'

Malik shrugged. 'It just means that Jews are much the same as everyone else. If the experts say it's good, applaud it. And if it's a Jew who's doing it then you pay good money to see him do his stuff. And you cheer like mad because he's a Jew and the rest of the world are impressed, so he's making being a Jew OK.'

'But Jews aren't ordinary. They really are special.'

'What *don't* you like about Israel?'

'Nothing. But I think I'd prefer Jerusalem to Tel Aviv. Tel Aviv is fine for a visit but it's a bit too American for me. Maybe Joppa would be ideal. Not Tel Aviv proper, but near. What do you like about Israel?'

'Like I said. I don't really know. But for the first time in my life I feel that being a Jew does matter.' Smiling he held up his hand. 'No. I *don't* mean I'm proud of being a Jew. That's racism or nationalism. I'm suddenly aware of all the sad sacrifices that have been made for centuries just so that this small country can exist. A sanctuary for Jews.' He laughed. 'Somebody once said that home is the place where, when you go there, they have to take you in. I guess this is home.'

By the fifth day he had brought himself out of his Israeli mental warm bath and had checked Amos Meyer's number in the directory. There was no company listed under that name and when he phoned the home number a servant told him that Mr Meyer was at his office and gave him the number.

When he rang the number the telephonist had replied, 'Litvak Enterprises Holdings,' and he had hung up.

Only because he spoke Polish had they been able to book a table at Lipski's for the last day of Lisa's stay. He had told her before they came that he would have to stay on for some days on things connected with his work.

They walked along the sea road to Joppa and kept straight on to Yefet Street and Lipski's. As so often in Israel the tattoo had been noticed but not remarked on, except by Mrs Lipski herself, who did the cooking for the five tables, coming over to talk to them as her husband served the *krupnik* soup. They lingered over the *pierogi* and finished with lemon sorbet and real coffee. And when they left

Lipski produced from somewhere a red rose for Lisa. They walked back to the hotel through the soft night air.

Malik hadn't used Brodsky to take them to Ben Gurion. He didn't want to explain why he was staying on alone. When her flight was called he walked with her to the door and handed her the small leather box that was not to be opened until she was airborne. The elaborate security checks had meant a long wait in the visitors' lounge, but eventually she was walking across the tarmac with the others. She stopped and turned to look for him and when she saw him she waved and blew him a kiss. He waved back and smiled. His little *shiksa* was more Jewish than he was. He waited until the plane took off and wondered if she was already opening the small box. It was a gold medallion on a fine gold necklace, and on its face was the Hebrew for Joppa, and his note that said, "Yafo is the Hebrew for Jaffa – Yafo means beautiful. I love you. J.M."

Malik rented a car at the airport and drove back into the city to the Embassy on Ha-yarqon. He sat in the information room and noted down all the details given in their commercial review of Israeli companies. Litvak Enterprises Holdings controlled nine companies and had minority shareholdings in half a dozen others. The holding company was registered in Vaduz, and the issued capital of the group companies was seventeen million dollars.

He wrote down the addresses and telephone numbers of all the companies actually in Israel. There were only two that really interested him: one was called Precision Products with an address at Bat Yam just outside Joppa, the other was Project Engineering which had no telephone number given, and just Beersheba as its address. It was a Friday and Malik was sure that Meyer would keep the Sabbath.

Meyer's home address was on the hill near the park at Gan Ha'atzmaut on the other side of the road from the big hotels; Malik parked his car and waited.

Half an hour later he saw the black Mercedes turn into the drive of Meyer's fine house. And Meyer was at the wheel. Malik noted its registration number and then went back to the hotel.

He drove out that evening to Bat Yam. Apart from its beautiful beach and the giant new hotel there was nothing, certainly nothing that looked like a small engineering plant. But a barman told him of an industrial estate at Holon and it was there that he found it. It was small and surrounded by other small industrial plants, too small to be what he vaguely had in mind. But what he had in mind didn't fit most of the established facts. He would have to check out the place at Beersheba the following day.

As Malik drove down the coast road to Beersheba he thought of all those times his father had talked about the city. His father had never been there but he never tired of talking about it because it had been the home of Isaac, Jacob and Abraham. And the long arguments with his father's friends about its name. The Well of the Seven; some said, because Abraham took an oath there to set aside the seven ewe lambs. But the Hebrew word for seven was virtually the same as the word for oath and the scholars had argued ever since. Malik parked his car near the empty camel market. And as he stood there for a moment in the blazing sun he realized for the first time that Israel was the Middle East. Tel Aviv was Europe and it gave the wrong impression. This was the Old Testament. All of them, Arabs and Jews, were Semites. The acrid stench of the camels, the rotting fruit, the raised voices of the Bedouin. No wonder people said that the Jews wore their hearts on their sleeves. Like the Arabs they were easy to rouse. It didn't take much to strip off the European veneer and make them tribesmen again.

As Malik walked around the town he was aware of its strong contrasts. The beautiful new campus of the University of the Negev and a few miles away the desert. That bland-looking grave of the Bedouin; the grim acres of sand where so many Israeli soldiers had died. The heat was almost unbearable in the midday sun and the air was so dry that his throat was parched in minutes. He went to one of the smaller cafés and sipped slowly at a long glass of iced orange juice. He asked the Arab proprietor if he knew where Project Engineering was located. He had never heard of it. Shrugging, he said that Beersheba was a place for university people, desalination experts and the Bedouin. There were a few struggling kibbutzim just off the desert road but engineering workers he had never heard of. But when Malik ordered another drink the man sent his young son to talk to the Bedouin who were loading a ramshackle truck with unsold goods for the journey back to the desert.

The boy came back fifteen minutes later and stood talking volubly to his father who eventually brought him across to Malik at his table. The Bedouin had seen a place in the desert where a track had been established. It was to the east of the road between Tel Malha and Mishlat Ma'ahaz. They were scared to talk about it because they thought it was something to do with *Chail Avir*, the Israeli Air Force.

The Bedouin said it was built out of sand and was protected with barbed wire. They had seen trucks there and sometimes a helicopter. And a bus which took workers home at night and brought them back in the morning. They had not seen men in uniform and that was why they thought it was a secret armed forces installation.

Malik gave the boy a small tip and ordered another drink as he looked at his map. He set off back again the way he had come, driving slowly as he watched for a track leading off the road that was worn enough and wide enough to be the one the Bedouin had described.

He almost missed it. It was just past the third kilometre stone from Tel Malha and as he turned off he could see the tyre marks of heavy vehicles, but a few kilometres from the road the ruts in the sand were too deep for the wheels of his car to take. The steering wheel fought his hands and the car slowly juddered to a halt. It was like driving in deep hard-packed snow, and it took him an hour to turn the car and get back to the road.

As soon as he was back in Tel Aviv he checked in the car and rented an ancient Willys-Knight jeep complete with spare petrol container and sand grids. The hotel made up a basket of food for him and he bought a pair of second-hand Leitz field-glasses in the Shuk.

He was on the road at four o'clock the next morning, and thirty metres north of the track he stopped the jeep and jacked up the rear axle and took off the nearside wheel. As the sun came up there were a few trucks from the fruit farms heading north with their scarce products, and one or two military vehicles.

The bus had taken him by surprise. He had expected it to come from the south, from Beersheba, but it came from the north, a sand-coloured diesel bus carrying a dozen or so passengers. As far as he could see they were all men, and all Israelis.

He bolted on the wheel again and waited another ten minutes to let the bus get well ahead. He would be able to see its dust trail for miles across the desert.

As he drove from the road on to the track, the hard springing in the jeep kept it high off the ground but it was an uncomfortable ride. In places the ruts and tyre marks were packed as hard as rocks, and after fifteen minutes every muscle in his body ached from the pounding and bouncing of the jeep. Everything metallic was too hot to touch and his blue denim shirt was black with sweat.

But way ahead he could see the dust cloud from the bus. The glare from the sand strained his eyes and ten minutes later he realized that he had lost sight of the tell-tale dust clouds. And he discovered too that deserts are not all flat. Not even rolling sensual dunes. No more than a kilometre ahead of him was a range of rocky hills. Red in the morning sun. When he came to the fork in the tracks he took the one that was marked with stones, and minutes later he was in the cool shadow of the sandstone hills.

After two kilometres he stopped and got out to look at the tracks. The sand was looser and the tyre marks were no more than light trucks would make. He realized that he had taken the wrong fork. The stones had been put there by the Bedouin for their truck drivers at night.

He stood there looking up at the hill and guessed that from the top he could probably see for miles. He slung his field glasses round his neck and tucked them inside his shirt, buttoning it to keep them from swinging.

It was easier to climb to the top than he had expected, and as he straightened up at the top of the ridge he crouched down immediately. It was there, in sight, and no more than half a kilometre away. He unbuttoned his shirt and slid out the binoculars, pulling out the matt-black lens hoods.

As far as he could see the desert shimmered in the heat until it met the grey blue mountains in the far distance. Small bushes of camel-thorn were dotted sparsely across the landscape and only the vehicle tracks led his eyes to the buildings.

They were perfectly camouflaged, the flat roofs covered with sand, and the sloping sides were so widely raked that they cast no shadow. As he looked through the glasses he could just make out the shape of vehicles under camouflage nets that were near perfect. There was no sign of people. He lay there in the rocks until the heat of the sun was too great to bear and then moved to the shadow of a cave to recover. At ten-minute intervals he went back to watch the buildings and after half an hour he stumbled back down the rocks to the jeep. The water from the can was hot and acrid, too foul to swallow but enough to ease the burning in his throat and mouth.

He drove the jeep into the shadow of an overhanging rock and slowly ate a couple of sandwiches from the hotel pack. Even in the shadows the heat was almost unbearable. And the silence was total. As he wondered if it might not be a wild goose chase and more sensible to go back to Tel Aviv some instinct or stubborness made him stay, and he stumbled back up to the crest of the ridge and lay down.

For three hours the silence was only broken once. By a trio of Israeli Air Force jets streaking northwards across the sky. Just once he thought he heard the faint sound of artillery fire from the distant hills. When dark came it came quickly.

As the sun went down he could see faint shadows from the buildings, and the ruts left by the vehicles looked black from the oblique angle of the setting sun, and here and there the wind was beginning to stir the sand in small spirals. Twenty minutes later he could see nothing. The deep blue of the night-sky glittered with stars, but the moon was still behind the mountains. And now he was shivering with cold. He went back to the jeep for his anorak and the blankets, and settled as best he could on the outcrop of rock.

He was half asleep when he heard the noise of the truck and as he lifted his head he saw that it was at least a mile away, its headlights shafting through the darkness. As it approached the site it turned slowly, and as it pulled up Malik could see the orange light at the head of a mobile crane. A door opened, flooding the sand with a long tapering rectangle of light, and a tractor came out towing a flat-bed carrier. And on the flat-bed were two large wooden crates. Malik lifted the glasses to his eyes and focused on the crates, and the short hairs on the back of his neck rose as he saw the shape and size of the wooden packing cases. He had seen cases like those before. Outside the piano factory in Cologne.

Malik watched as they hooked up the chains, and one after the other the two crates were swung up onto the articulated lorry. Four men covered them with canvas covers before they were chained and roped to the truck. It was barely half an hour before the lorry moved off, turning in a narrow half-cirle back to the track from where it had come. The moon was up now and Malik stayed to watch as the light on the crane was doused and the door in the huge building was shut. And in the stillness of the night he could just hear the beat of a generator. Like a submarine, they used the night to clear the air. And very faintly he could hear the sound of metal on metal. A ringing sound like a hammer on a pipe.

He stood up slowly and awkwardly, suddenly aware of the stiffness of his joints. For a few moments he stood there looking through the glasses, but there was nothing to be seen. The desert looked white in the moonlight as if it were frost or snow rather than the yellow sand.

Malik climbed back into the jeep, switched on the sidelights and started the engine. As he came out of the rocky mountain track towards the main truck road northwards he felt the steering behaving oddly and clouds of sand rose up around the jeep, the canvas hood billowing madly, straining at the ropes that held it to the body. When he could no longer see the track for the swirling dust he stopped the jeep and switched off the lights. And only then did he hear the noise of the helicopter. He got out of the cab and looked up to where it swung in slow circles above him. He could see two faces at the lighted windows, both peering down at him, one of them with binoculars. And as he looked, a searchlight in the chopper's belly came on, blinding him momentarily, and as he shaded his eyes to look up again the helicopter lifted and swung, turning slowly on its own axis and heading back towards the camouflaged site. It was one of Aerospatiale's Alouette IIIs. One of the 1964 all-weather models with its Doppler radar clearly visible at the rear of the cabin. It was camouflaged in sand and dark green but he hadn't been able to make out its markings.

As he climbed back in the jeep he guessed that somewhere there had been a look-out, but they hadn't spotted him until he stood up on the rock as the truck left. He had had the shades pulled forward on the binoculars but maybe even they had not prevented a reflection from the moon. It had been a stupid thing to do. But they couldn't possibly have identified him from that height nor have read the numberplate on the jeep.

He switched on the headlights and started the engine. He could go flat out now with the headlights on, and he could probably catch up with the articulated before it got to the main road at Kiryat Gat. He held the wheel loosely as the jeep juddered its way along the stone-littered track. It took nearly twenty minutes to reach the main road, a distance of little more than seven kilometres, but there had been no sign of the articulated. He stopped short of the main road and knelt down to check the tyres. They were as hard as iron because of the build up of air pressure from the heat and the rough going. He unscrewed the caps and pressed the valves to release the excess pressure, and the stench of the hot rubber smell was overwhelming. He walked away from the jeep and took deep breaths of the cold night air.

Just past Kiryat Mal'akhi there was a road-block, red and white poles across the road. An Israeli sergeant walked over to him and asked him for his identity card. He showed his passport and the sergeant looked at every page before handing it back. And then he saw the reason for the road-block. Soldiers were removing the poles and he saw the lights of vehicles. A long line of them moving quite slowly. Tanks and armoured fighting vehicles, two staff cars and then a dozen or more troop carriers. It took twenty minutes for them to pass and he knew then that there was no chance of catching up with the articulated. All he could do was to head straight back for Tel-Aviv.

Malik turned off the road at the junction before Bene Re'em and took the road to Gedeva, and it was beginning to get light as he approached Rehovot. As he went through the town people were already at work. There were workers spraying in the orange groves and men were filling farm lorries at a petrol station. It looked peaceful and pastoral in the early morning light. Chaim Weizmann had worked and died there.

It was twenty-three kilometres to Tel Aviv, and by the time he got into the outskirts the roads were busy with cars and buses, and he pulled up at a stall for a fruit drink. He stood sipping the drink and watching the stream of cars. The crates had been export crates. Too elaborate and too expensive for domestic use and that must mean Haifa. He would hand over the jeep and hire a car. He could be there before midday.

Malik stopped for a break just outside Haifa, stretching his arms and legs as he looked across to Mount Carmel. He took off his shirt and laid it on the bonnet of the car to dry out the black patches of sweat, and five minutes later it was dry. He drove the rest of the way to the city in just his shorts; he wanted to save his dry shirt for when he walked round the docks.

In Ha'atzma'uth Road he was stuck in a long line of lorries queueing for the docks, and it was half an hour before he turned into the dock road itself.

He parked the BMW between the first and second warehouses. There were two big merchant ships tied up alongside. One was discharging and the other was loading. The one discharging was French and the other was Greek. He walked slowly down to where the lorries were parked. There were just over twenty but none of them was the yellow articulated. Slowly and meticulously he checked each of the warehouses. There were sacks of grain, drums of chemicals, forty-gallon drums of petrol, wooden crates, hundreds of tins of paint, stacks of timber, and all the things that you could expect at an international port. But there were no signs of the two crates.

Malik called in at one of the shipping offices and asked how he could trace a consignment of pianos and was told that unless he knew who was consigning them or where they were going there was no way to trace them.

He sat on a bollard on the dock side and lit a cigarette. There was no way the crates could have been loaded on a boat before he arrived. They had told him that the average clearing time was eight hours and that loading could be another day or two. The ship that was loading was only taking on ballast. The only other place he could think of was Joppa and that didn't make sense. Whatever was in those crates wasn't pianos. You don't make pianos in camouflaged buildings in the middle of a desert in Israel. And to unload them and load them onto a ship at Joppa would pull as many spectators as a football match. But Malik was a professional and he walked back to the car and headed back down the coast road to Tel Aviv and Joppa.

On Japhet Street he turned down to the jetty and slowly cruised along. There was no boat there larger than a pleasure boat, no crane and no trucks. He was on his way back up Eilat Street when he noticed the El Al poster in a travel agency window and he cursed softly, turned into a side street and stopped the car. He reached into the glove shelf for the street map.

It took him two hours and a lot of lies to get what he wanted at the airport and he walked slowly back from the Freight Office to the cafeteria. As he sat drinking his grape juice he made notes of the details stencilled on the two crates. Instinct and experience were telling him that it wasn't what it seemed. There was no logic to it. Something they were doing was wrong. In some way he and Fischer were kidding themselves. They were listening to the music and ignoring the words.

There was always a point in any operation when it seemed to hang in the balance. A time when the team got together and looked at what they'd got. And inevitably they plodded on. And equally inevitably, in weeks or months, and sometimes years, something happened. Just one thing that pulled aside the curtain and they knew what had to be done. But there was no team. Just him and Heinz Fischer. And no operations director who could keep out of the detail and look down dispassionately from above and help them to avoid every blind alley in the maze.

He walked back to the security hut and one of the guards unlocked the small door to the car park and let him in. At the main guardhouse they checked him and the car again thoroughly. Taking their time with probes and stethoscopes, leaving nothing unchecked. Even if he had been an Israeli they would have done exactly the same.

As he drove back to Tel Aviv he realized what a burden it must be that these hard-working, lively people should have to live under such conditions. Surely to God the gas chambers had been enough. Did they still have to face the threat of bombs and war and terrorists every day of their lives? They had been given so little and they had made it so much. Their supporters were unreliable and the United Nations who had given them back their land now saw world events through Arab eyes. Dependent on Gulf oil and eager to supply their enemies with modern weapons, Israel's 'allies' were politically inept, and their minds more on catching the Jewish vote than on the facts of Middle East life. Claiming to have been horrified by the Holocaust they didn't mind when the slaughter was just a dozen a day. The same victims, just a different generation. Almost every day innocent women and children were blown to pieces somewhere in the country, and forgotten by the world the next day. Israelis were fair game, they were tough, they could look after themselves and there was no close season. Shooting sitting ducks was bad form. Shooting women and children was OK. Maybe Lisa was right and they should live here and be part of it. He felt at home here. He never needed to think about being a Jew. There was nothing to explain. Not even Auschwitz. There were hundreds of others with numbers tattooed on their arms or shiny pink scars where the tattoos had been surgically removed. You didn't need to talk about it. They already knew. Even those who had not been in camps understood by a kind of osmosis. No longer would he have to try to fit in or be the department's statutory Jew. And Tel Aviv was too urgent and too alive to let those skeleton memories parade through his skull at night.

'British Embassy.'

'I want to speak to Mr Morris.'

'Which Mr Morris is that?'

'John Morris.'

'Can I ask what it's about?'

'Just put me through, please.'

'Just a moment.'

It was a couple of minutes before the clicks came and he was put through.

'Johnny. This is Malik. I'd like to see you.'

'Jake. Fine. How about you come in for lunch tomorrow?'

'I need to see you right away.'

'Business or pleasure?'

'Business.'

'We're closed officially and the front's locked up. I'll wait outside for you. Better still, do you know Café Rowal in Rehov Dizengoff?'

'Yes.'

'I'll go over there now and wait for you.'

'OK. See you.'

Morris was sitting at a table already when Malik arrived, four glasses of orange juice arrayed on the table.

'*Shalom*,' Morris said.

'*Shalom*.'

'What's eating you, pal?'

'Technically I'm on holiday, Johnny.'

'Of course. Of course. And technically I'm Embassy librarian, I'll have you know.'

'There are two crates going out from the airport tomorrow afternoon. I need to know where they're going. I think it's Germany. It's a private air-freight company and I need to know where the crates end up, and any stops the plane makes on the way. Authorized and unauthorized stops.'

'What do you mean by unauthorized?'

'Stops that aren't on the normal route and landings on private airstrips. That sort of thing.'

'Have you got details of the consignor and details of the crates?'

Malik pulled out a sheet of paper and passed it to Morris who sat reading it, slowly sipping his orange juice. Then he folded it up and slid it into the pocket of his shirt.

'How Brit is this?'

'What do you mean?'

'Can I use Interpol Air Liaison?'

'What do you have to tell them?'

'Nothing that matters. Any cover story you like. Drugs, old masters, fraud. You name it.'

'If we say terrorism will they want to probe?'

'God. No. It's too common to raise any interest. They're bureaucrats. As long as they aren't heading your way you wave it on. As long as it's not PLO, of course.'

'It's not PLO.'

'What are you doing tonight?'

'I'll just get some sleep. I'm flying out tomorrow provided you can lay on the surveillance.'

'Don't worry about that. When you called I asked over a couple of friends for dinner tonight. I'll go back to the Embassy and fix this thing for you and then I'll pick you up and you can eat with us. No suits. No ties. Just a snack and some chit-chat. OK?'

'OK.'

Johnny Morris left his car at the bottom of the drive and they walked together slowly up the steep incline to the house. Morris turned to look back towards Tel Aviv and the setting sun. He and his wife had rented the house at Ramat Gan rather than take one of the Embassy houses. Ambassadors and senior Embassy staff seldom accepted their SIS man as part of the family. They too often caused diplomatic disturbances – that was the general reason given; but nearer the truth was the fact that His Excellency was not privy to their reports to London and all too often the SIS man's report on local current affairs was at odds with the official version.

The house at Ramat Gan was set on the hillside that gave the suburb its name. It was as isolated as a house in the city could be but still within easy commuting distance of the Embassy by car.

The garden, like most of the gardens on the hill, was flooded with bougainvillea, and there was a sweet heavy smell from a long herbaceous border.

'Do you grow oranges here, Johnny?'

'No. Why?'

'I thought I could smell oranges.'

Morris laughed. 'That's different. And we don't call it a smell in these parts. It's a fragrance. It comes from the Assis processing plant, and we rather like it. Let's go in. The Levys are already here, I can see their car by the garage. You'll like them, they're a nice couple.'

There were lights on in the house already and Adele Morris stood at the door.

'It's lovely to see you, Jake. Come in.'

She kissed his cheek and turned to the couple who were standing, glasses in hand, by the big fireplace.

'Helen and David Levy . . . Jacob Malik.'

They shook hands and said their '*shaloms*' and Johnny Morris led them all to the comfortable armchairs ranged around a low, circular, glass-topped table. There were cold meats and fish, and salad and fruit, and as she handed round the plates Adele Morris looked at Malik.

'Are you here for business or pleasure? Or shouldn't I ask?'

'A bit of both. My girlfriend was with me for the first week but she's gone back now.'

Adele Morris leaned back, smiling. 'A girlfriend. Jake Malik with a girlfriend. I can't believe it. Tell me more.'

'There's nothing to tell. I'm going to ask her to marry me when my present assignment's finished.'

'What's her name? Come on. Don't be a tease.'

'Her name's Lisa Fischer. She's twenty-three and she's a musician. And she's German.'

Adele Morris noticed the faint touch of defiance in Malik's voice.

'You should have called us and brought her up for a meal.' She turned to look at the Levys. 'You've heard of guys who love them and leave them, well this fellow just leaves them.'

David Levy smiled and said quietly, 'We're dark horses, us Jews.'

Adele Morris smiled. 'But Jake isn't . . .' and she turned to look at Malik who said, 'I am, Adele. The only Jew in SIS. They're still looking round for the statutory negro.'

Adele looked at her husband. 'Did you know, Johnny?'

'No. And I don't know who's a Catholic and who isn't.' He stood up to break up the talk. 'I'm famished, kid. What have we got?'

Adele Morris recovered quickly, standing up, smiling at Malik.

'Do you keep to *kashrut*, Jake?'

'I'm happy to, Adele, whatever you've done will do me.'

She nodded and turned to the Levys. 'Help yourselves, you two.'

As they sat eating and the others chatted Malik looked at David Levy. He was in his late thirties, well-built and quite handsome. But what was probably most attractive was his smile. He was a ready smiler and the big strong white teeth under the black moustache gave him a faintly swashbuckling air that matched his broad shoulders and well-muscled legs and arms. And as he was watching him Levy turned and looked at him.

'Is this your first trip to Israel, Jake?'

'Yes.'

'How do you like it?'

'It's strange in a way.'

'How come?'

'I was born a Jew, but I don't live as a Jew. I'm not proud of being a Jew, or ashamed of it for that matter. I'm just me. Jacob Malik. To me Israel was a place for fanatics and refugees. But there's something odd about this place. I feel more alive here. Almost glad to be a Jew.'

'Do you get hassled much as a Jew in London?'

'Very few people know that I am a Jew. And there's no hassle that I've noticed.'

'So why do you feel different here?'

'I honestly don't know. Maybe in a way it's that things that used to put me down don't have any effect on me here. Other people have had what I had. Lots of them. It helps somehow.'

Levy said quietly. 'Do you mean things to do with that number on your arm?'

'Yes.'

Levy leaned forward. 'Try and think, Jake, what's different? It matters, you know, to us Israelis. We forget what it was like outside.'

Malik sighed. 'It will sound crazy. You won't understand. But if I heard a band playing the Horst Wessel Lied in Tel Aviv I don't think it would affect me.'

Levy looked at Johnny Morris. 'You know, that's one of the oddest compliments this country's ever had. But to me it's better than a poem.' He turned to Malik again. 'How long are you staying?'

'I'm leaving tomorrow morning.'

'Have you thought of coming back here?'

'My girlfriend would like us to live here. She was in love with the place before we came.'

'Where's she from?'

'Like I said. She's German, and she's not Jewish.'

Levy laughed. 'You'd better marry before you get here. The Rabbis are hell on mixed marriages. Thank God I married this *shiksa* of mine in Sydney before we came over.' Levy smiled at Morris and Malik. 'I got into a terrible argument with Rabbi Letz about mixed marriages and conversions and all that. He said how can Helen want to become a Jew just to marry me. It can't be genuine, he said. I asked him why not, and he said, "If you were an Arab, my son, then she'd have become a Muslim to marry you. Who do you think you are – Jehovah?" There's something in it of course. Those old boys know most of the answers.'

Morris, eager to change the subject, said softly, looking at Levy, 'What's going to happen on the West Bank, David?'

'We shall keep it, I've no doubt of that.'

'And colonize it?'

'That's not the word I would have used. But yes.'

'Wouldn't it be better to hand it back, so that it's out of the way once and for all? A gesture to the Arabs, for peace, that the whole world can see.'

Levy sighed and glanced at his wife. 'They don't understand, do they? I don't think you people ever will. Because you never listen to what's said. It doesn't matter *what* we give the Arabs. Land, money, economic or industrial help, it would make no difference. They will never recognize Israel. They have said so, in public, a dozen times. They have said that they will sweep us into the sea. Kill us, every man, woman, and child. But you don't believe it. You think that people don't really do those things. But they do, my friend. Hitler said what he was going to do. You had the warning but you didn't believe it. But he did it. By God, he did it. Six million Jews were exterminated for this. For Israel. And nobody, Arab, American, French or whatever, is going to make us give up one grain of sand. No matter who promises what. The Americans won't risk their oil supplies for us despite the Jewish vote in New York. The UN is a paper tiger and Europe just wants a quiet life to sell arms to Israel and arms to the Arabs.'

Morris raised his eyebrows. 'I'm sorry, David. I obviously touched a raw nerve.'

'Forget it, Johnny. You're in good company. Even Kissinger would sell us down the Jordan if it won the next election for his lot.'

Malik diverted the lightning. 'How much would a house cost me in Tel Aviv? Or an apartment?'

The big brown eyes looked at him. 'Are you serious?'

'Yes.'

Levy said, 'What would you do for work?'

'We can both play the fiddle. Lisa's a professional performer and teacher.'

Levy laughed. 'You could get a place in Jaffa. You have to be an artist of some kind or they won't let you buy anything down there. It would still cost, mind you. At least forty thousand sterling. And you wouldn't get much for that.'

It was just before midnight when Johnny Morris drove him back to the hotel.

As they sat in the car at the bottom of Mapu Street, Morris said, 'I fixed what you wanted. They just called me back. On the manifest it says the crates are going to Hamburg and they're down as upright pianos for repair. What's it all about, Jake?'

'I'm not sure, Johnny. It's just part of an operation.'

'OK. Have a good flight and let me know if I can help at this end.'

In his room he put a call through to Heinz Fischer and told him what he wanted him to do. Suddenly Malik's hunter instinct was working. He had been aware for the past weeks that his mind had only been partially engaged by the investigation. With no pressure or apparent interest from Century House, no pattern to the sparse information they had gathered, the operation had become unreal. They needed all the resources of men and facilities that one or both of the two Intelligence services would normally have made available to weave together the hundreds of threads that such operations always revealed. What they had been doing had irked Malik; it fitted neither his character nor his experience. He realized that without his relationship with Lisa Fischer he would probably have asked London to replace him. But instinct told him that the operation was beginning to harden.

He phoned the airport and booked himself a flight for the next morning. When he looked at his watch he was surprised that it was already one o'clock. For a moment he hesitated, and then he put on his jacket and walked down to the street. There were still people about as he headed for the beach. An army jeep patrol stopped him as he crossed the main road. They checked his passport and warned him not to go down on to the beach itself.

He stayed on the promenade, leaning against the balustrade looking out towards the sea. On the horizon he could see an Aldis light blinking a Morse message to the shore, and away to the north he could see a haze of light where Haifa jutted into the Mediterranean. And from one of the big hotels behind him he could hear, faintly, the strains of a dance band. They were playing 'Somewhere over the rainbow', and it seemed oddly appropriate. For several million people Israel *was* the mythical country over the rainbow. Maybe even for Lisa and himself.

He closed his eyes. Trying once again to decide whether they really should settle in Israel. He felt strangely at home. For the first time in his life it didn't matter that he was a Jew. He was quite honest when he said that he was neither proud nor ashamed of being a Jew. It was other people who seemed to think it mattered. One way or the other. It was other people who reminded him that he was a Jew. He had met older survivors from concentration camps who were more deeply religious because of the experience. Seeing their survival as one more proof that the One True God existed. But for Malik the things he had seen made the idea of God controlling men's destinies anathema. It wasn't reasons of religion that would make him live in Israel, but almost the opposite. In Israel he could relax and just be a man.

CHAPTER THIRTEEN

The flat in Cologne had become just a place to live in. He put his bags alongside his bed and reached for the telephone. It was Frau Fischer who answered. Lisa was giving a music lesson at one of the schools. She'd be back at five in the evening. Frau Fischer was as friendly and welcoming as always but he thought he detected just a shade of distance in her voice. But he was tired and on the edge of one of his moods. Maybe he had imagined it. She didn't know where Heinz was.

Malik was dialling the police number when Heinz came in. He looked surprised to see Malik.

'What brings you back so early, Jake? I thought you'd be there at least another week.'

'Did you get a report from Interpol?'

'Yes, it came through early this morning. I couldn't understand what it was about.'

'Where is it?'

'On the desk in the other room. By the telephone.'

Malik walked into the small room that served as an office and picked up the two sheets of flimsy paper that were stapled together. It was all in capitals, the original off the police teleprinter.

EX INPOL PARIS. MALIK, KÖLN. INF. MORRIS TEL AVIV. NUMBER 74193 AIRFREIGHTER REG NO. D1047 LANDED APPROX 51 FIGURES DEGREES 8 FIGURES SECONDS BY 7 FIGURES DEGREES 28 FIGURES SECONDS AREA EAST OF KÖLN. AT 21 FIGURES HOURS 15 FIGURES MINUTES SAME DAY STOP. PROCEEDED TO WAHN AIRPORT 2 FIGURES HOURS LATER STOP NO FURTHER MOVEMENT STOP MESSAGE ENDS.

Malik walked back into the sitting room, but Fischer was in the small kitchen making them coffee. Malik leaned against the door.

'Who do you know at the airport, Heinz?'

Fischer shrugged. 'Practically everybody.'

'Who do you know on the freight side?'

'The manager and his two assistants. His secretary. A girl clerk . . .'

Malik smiled. 'OK. I get the message. I want to check two crates that came in early this morning. I want to know what's inside them.'

'I can phone and get Karl to check the manifest.'

'No. I want to actually see inside them. See for myself. A manifest can be phony.'

Fischer looked doubtful. 'They wouldn't do that as a personal favour, Jake. I'd have to use my police authority.'

'But they wouldn't inform the consignee or anyone else?'

'Not if I gave them official instructions not to.'

Malik gave Fischer the telex message and said, 'Have we got a local map that gives latitudes and longitudes? So that we can identify this first landing place?'

'Sure. I'll get it.'

They spread the large scale map on the table and carefully drew the two lines. One vertical and one horizontal. And where they crossed was a big patch of green indicating woodlands and parkland. The intersection was almost exactly the centre-point of Rechmann's estate.

'What's it all about, Jake?'

'I don't know, Heinz. But this plane is owned by a private independent freight company. The crates it was carrying are exactly the same as those we saw coming out of the piano factory. They were sent from overseas. The freight note said they were going to Hamburg. But they end up in Cologne. Why? And why did the plane touch down at Rechmann's place?'

'Maybe he radioed him to land to get instructions about the diversion.'

'Interpol would have recorded that if it had happened.'

'That's not much to go on, Jake.'

'Why use a private freight company when an airline could do it cheaper?'

'Maybe speed, or convenience.'

'What's all the hurry about a couple of pianos? And why are they coming in, not going out?'

'Reconditioning or repairs maybe.'

'Two at once? Why not get them done locally? There's nothing all that technical about repairing a piano.'

'What country did they come from?'

Malik hesitated for only a second. 'I'm not sure. Somewhere in the Middle East I think.'

'Do you want me to try and get them opened?'

'Yes. As soon as possible in case they get shifted somewhere else.'

'OK. Let's go.'

Karl Oetker, the freight manager, sat at his teak desk, his chin cupped in his hand.

'If you want to know what's inside the crates I'll accept your authority, but our insurance wouldn't cover damage caused in these circumstances.'

'We'll accept responsibility for that.'

Oetker frowned. 'I don't like it, Heinz, but if you say it's necessary then you can go ahead. They're due to collect them sometime tomorrow.'

'Can your people open the crates while we watch?'

'If you want it that way, yes.'

Oetker led Malik and Fischer over to the freight bay and signalled to one of his men and told him to open the crates. The man hammered the splayed end of the crowbar under each of the thick planks and eased them away from the main frame. Then after the other end had been prised away he hammered the planks free. Inside was a brand-new upright piano. When the second crate was opened and that too held a piano Malik asked for a screwdriver. He wanted the backs off both pianos. Oetker refused, but agreed that one of his joiners should take them off.

When the backs were removed Malik knelt and went carefully over every part of both pianos, tapping the iron frames, checking each key and its individual action, sniffing, pressing and touching every accessible part. Eventually he stood up and turned to Fischer.

'Do the airport police have dogs for sniffing out drugs?'

'Yes.'

'Can you get one and its handler over here?'

'I'll phone the main office. There shouldn't be a problem.'

Ten minutes later the handler and the dog came over to the warehouse but there was no positive response. The dog sniffed without interest and returned to his handler.

Malik thanked Oetker and he and Fischer walked back to the car. They were on their way back to the flat when Malik said, 'I want to take some photographs, Heinz. I need a chopper and an infra-red camera. How do we get hold of them?'

'We've got the helicopters that do the traffic surveys and any camera will do for infra-red photographs, it's only the film and the focusing that's different. When do you want to do this, and where?'

'As soon as possible, and I want to cover the whole of Rechmann's estate. Where can we get the film processed and printed?'

'The police lab can do it for us.'

'I don't want anyone official to see the results.'

'Let me make some inquiries when I ask for the chopper and the camera.'

'The main thing is to adjust the focusing back to this red mark to allow for infra-red light waves being longer than light in the normal spectrum. And we can only use black and white or this Kodak colour film. Ektachrome X. And we can use either this special infra-red filter over the lens or the orange one if we want to eliminate the colour cast. There are typed recommendations with the camera operating instructions.'

'When can we have the chopper?'

'As soon as they've finished the autobahn control tomorrow morning.'

'Any information on how we can get the film processed?'

'There's a specialist photo-lab in town that can do both black and white and colour the same day. They process most of the scientific stuff for the university.'

'Write down the name and address for me, will you.'

'Do you want me in the chopper with you?'

Malik sat silent for several seconds, and Fischer realized that Malik's face had that closed-in look that it had had when he first came to Cologne.

'I want you to do something else, Heinz.'

'What?'

'I want you to check as far back as you can go on Rechmann's family and see if there is any indication of a Jew among them. And the same for his wife and her family.'

The cups and saucers and glasses had been cleared from the canteen table and Malik showed the pilot the area that he wanted to photograph. He had outlined the squares in red. It was a large area and he asked the pilot how long he would need.

'It depends on how much ground you cover with each frame. I can go as slow as you want.' He smiled. 'What's the focal length of your lens? We can do a bit of elementary trigonometry.'

'Five centimetres.'

'Have you got a motor-drive?'

'Yes.'

'How many frames a second?'

'Five. But I'll only use it at one frame a second.'

The pilot turned over the map and took out a pencil. A few minutes later he said, 'How much detail do you want? What's the size of the smallest object you want to show clearly?'

'About two metres, a car for instance.'

The man went back to his calculations and Malik read through the operational instruction for the Olympus OM2 yet again. Then the pilot straightened up.

'If we go up and down the long axis it will take five sweeps. Say twenty minutes.'

'I'd like to do it twice.'

'That's OK.'

'Are you ready to go now?'

'I'll file my trip with Air Control and come back here for you.'

Ten minutes later the pilot came back into the office. 'Air Control asked me what it was all about. I referred them to Heinz Fischer – is that OK?'

'That's fine.'

As they walked across the helicopter parking area Malik said, 'Is it easy to photograph from the chopper?'

'Yes. The TV stations use it regularly for video stuff. We can keep the sun on my side for three of the sweeps so that there's no risk of flare.'

And then they were at the pad. It was a Fairchild Hiller in white and black police livery. Up-to-date and well stabilized.

The pilot circled the area once so that Malik could focus the camera and stop down the aperture to allow for some fluctuation on infinity, and then he was ready.

The camera held film for 250 frames and there were only two spare packs and half a dozen bulk cassettes of both black and white and Ektachrome X, and Malik had to make quick changes in the loops at the end of each run. Despite the calculations it had only taken twenty-four minutes for the two coverages.

He drove straight from Wahn to the processing laboratory and asked for immediate processing, including contacts of the black and white infra-red film. The colour film would come back as continuous strips of positives. They wanted three hours and he parked the car and walked back to the flat.

The telephone was ringing as he walked in. It was Heinz Fischer.

'I'm at HQ. I've had Traffic on the phone. They put Rechmann's estate manager on to me, Jake, asking about the chopper. I told him they were testing the gyro-compasses. He hinted that Rechmann was likely to lodge a complaint.'

'On what grounds?'

'Disturbing the livestock. He mentioned his pedigree Friesian herd.'

'Can you deal with it if he does complain?'

'I should think so. At least he knows me.'

'Anything else?'

'I'm working on the genealogy stuff for you. It's not easy because so many records were destroyed in the war. There are no indications of what you were looking for so far. But I'll keep trying.'

'There's one other thing I'd like you to check. The airfreight company. Who owns it and any background material you can get.'

'OK.'

On his way back to the photo-lab Malik looked at the diamond rings in a jeweller's windows and spent twenty minutes inside looking at half-a-dozen rings. He couldn't make up his mind between one large solitaire diamond and a setting of five smaller ones. In the end he chose the solitaire.

At the photo-lab he handed in his ticket and a couple of minutes later one of the technicians came from the laboratory to the reception counter.

'We've just finished the contact prints. Have you got any way of examining them? An enlarger maybe?'

'No. Maybe I can hire one.'

'I can put the colour strips through our projector if you've got the time. The black and white stuff will be wrong way round of course but it will give you an idea of whether you've got what you want or not. They're very slightly over-exposed but I doubt if you'll be able to tell with the naked eye.'

Malik sat in the darkness of the projection theatre and watched the colour frames one by one as they came up on the big screen. They had an eerie reddish purple cast but it wasn't until the second roll that he pressed the button and the theatre lights came up and the assistant's voice came over the speaker system.

'Can I help you?'

'Can you hear me?'

'Yes. The seats are wired for sound.'

'What's the red fuzzy line across the last two frames?'

'Drains. What they call mole drains. This looks like farmland and mole drains are common.'

'How deep in the ground are they?'

'Between two and two point five metres usually.'

'Thanks.'

'Shall I carry on?'

'Yes please.'

The lights dimmed and the frames passed through again. And on the third roll of exposures he saw it. Even in the warm theatre he felt suddenly cold. He just sat there repeating the frame number. 139.

On the black and white film it was frame number 141 and even clearer. When the lights finally went up again he asked for half-a-dozen enlargements of both the colour and the black and white frames. They would be available from the overnight shift and could be collected any time after nine the next morning.

Heinz Fischer was waiting for him at the flat.

'I've got something, Jake, on the air-freight company.'

'Tell me.'

'It's not a German company. It just operates here out of Berlin, Cologne and Hamburg. The general manager and the staff are all German. But guess where it's registered?'

'I've no idea.'

'In Israel. In Tel Aviv. And guess who the owner is?'

'Rechmann?'

'No.'

'Tell me.'

'Amos Meyer. It's a subsidiary of his group holding company. Wholly owned. And Amos Meyer holds all the shares in the airline company except one which is owned by von Busch.'

Malik smiled. 'We're beginning to get there, Heinz. Well done.'

'I just did the routine, Jake. How was your trip?'

'Not so interesting as your stuff.'

'I'm going to pick up Ruth if you don't need me right now.'

'That's fine. Where will you be?'

'I'm meeting her at home.'

'Have a good time.'

Malik walked back into the sitting room and ten minutes later the phone rang. It was the Cologne Police HQ. The man wanted to speak to Fischer. He gave him Heinz's home number. Ten minutes later Heinz phoned himself.

'Jake, I've just had the central records guy on the phone. I've been putting all the names we get through central records computer system. They've just come back with something. You remember the girl from Humboldt University, Anna Bauer?'

'Yes?'

'One of the men she meets regularly in West Berlin is an Erich Deissner.'

'Who is he?'

'He's the general manager and senior pilot of the air-freight company.'

'Have they got details of dates and where he sees her?'

'Berlin may have. They'll send them through if we want them.'

'We want them.'

'OK. I'll notify them.'

Lisa's parents were out when he picked her up and they went to the cinema to see a re-run of *Guess Who's Coming to Dinner*. Neither of them had seen it before and after ten minutes Malik looked surreptitiously at Lisa's face. But she was already looking at him and they both laughed softly at the obvious parallel. Change negro to Jew and it was almost their story.

They had a snack in a café afterwards and argued amiably about the two parents in the film and whether the happy ending was justified. They decided it was.

Malik took the small cube from his pocket and put it on the table in front of her. Her fingers trembled as she tore off the paper and when she turned back the lid she gazed at the ring without taking it out of the velvet base.

When she looked up at Malik's face to speak he said, 'Maybe I should ask your father first.' And as he said it he was ashamed that he couldn't say the words he should have said.

She said softly, 'We can tell them when we get back. They'll be happy for me. And for you too . . . if you *are* happy?' She raised her eyebrows as she smiled at him.

'I just don't want to let you down, Lisa.'

'You won't, my love. Why should you?'

'Not the usual ways men let down women. Just that . . .' He shrugged. '. . . I'm not used to permanent relationships with people . . . a girl.'

'Don't worry, Jake. We'll be all right. Just relax.'

Malik nodded. 'We'll have to wait a few weeks until I've finished this assignment.'

'How long will it be, Jake?'

'I don't know, sweetie. A month. Could be longer.'

'Can I tell my parents?'

'We'll both tell them.'

'When?'

'Will they be at home now?'

'I think so.'

'I think they know already. But I want them to be happy about it. Let's go and see them now.'

The Fischers were saying goodbye to one of their friends as Malik and Lisa walked from the garage to the front of the house and they went together into the music room.

'Where did you two go in the end?' Herr Fischer asked.

'We went to the cinema.' Malik paused and took a deep breath. 'We wanted to have a word with you, if it's convenient.'

Herr Fischer pointed to the settee. 'Of course it is. Sit down, both of you. How about a drink?'

'Not for me, thank you.'

'Nor me,' said Lisa quietly.

Herr Fischer poured himself a whisky and sat down by his wife. He smiled and raised his glass.

'The answer, of course, is yes.'

Malik smiled. 'You knew already.'

'We wondered. We should have had to be deaf and blind not to have seen how things are. We both hope you'll be very happy. The pair of you.'

'There is one other thing.'

'What's that?'

'We're probably going to live in Israel.'

Malik saw the smile fade from Herr Fischer's face and then the trembling lips as he gallantly tried to recover and bring back some semblance of a smile. He glanced at his wife but she didn't respond. He turned his head back to look at Malik and his daughter.

'I'm sure you've thought about it very carefully.'

'We have, papa. We both know that we'll be happier there than in London.'

Herr Fischer slowly absorbed the fact that the choice was between London and Israel, not Germany and Israel, and Malik felt a sudden compassion for this man who so loved his daughter that he tried to look cheerful in his unhappiness. As his own father had done.

He said, 'We hope you'll spend all the time you can with us and we shall be back here frequently I'm sure.'

Herr Fischer nodded and stood up. 'We must celebrate. I'll find our one and only bottle of champagne.'

And both Lisa and Malik saw Herr Fischer furtively wipe the tears from his eyes as he walked over to the small drinks cabinet. He slowly arranged the glasses and the bottle on a silver tray and carried it over to the coffee table. His hands trembled as he peeled off the gold foil and the wire cradle over the bulbous cork. As the champagne foamed from the neck of the bottle he filled their glasses.

'Well. Here's to both of you. Every happiness. We will have a real celebration so that all our friends can be there. And Heidi. And Heinz of course. Does he know about all this already?'

Malik shook his head. 'He's probably guessed how it would end but we wanted to tell you first.'

'What date have you got in mind, Lisa?' It was the first time Frau Fischer had spoken, and although her smile was friendly there was an edge to her voice that alerted Malik. And she had obliquely excluded him from the question as if his view was not necessary.

'We haven't decided yet, Mama. It will depend on the work Jake is doing at the moment.'

'You must let us know dear, when you've decided.'

There was some desultory chat about the concert the Fischers had been to and then Lisa walked with Malik to his car. As they stood there in the bright moonlight she said, 'Like you always say. No problem.'

Malik shrugged. 'I thought your mother was a bit subdued.'

'I expect that was for Papa's benefit. She tries to be the practical one who has to worry about dates and arrangements and all that.'

'Are you teaching tomorrow?'

'Only until midday. Phone me when you can and I'll be ready whenever you want.'

He kissed her gently and then got into his car. She stood there in the moonlight and waved back to him as he drove off, and he was depressed enough to wonder if there was any significance in the fact that she hadn't done what she usually did and walk back to the light of the front porch to wave to him. Was staying by the garage a sign that she was identifying with him, or was not walking back to the porch a subconscious exluding of him from her family? And for the first time for weeks he wondered as he wondered so often, if he was insane.

CHAPTER FOURTEEN

Malik drove over the bridge at Marlow and at the end of the High Street he turned onto the Henley road. About five miles out of Marlow he turned off the road to the entrance of the RAF station. A guard stopped him before he got to the concrete guard room.

'I've got an appointment with Squadron Leader Fowler.'

'Can I have your name, sir?'

'Malik. Jacob Malik.'

'Will you switch off your car engine and give me the keys, Mr Malik, and we'll walk over to the guard room.'

Malik switched off, got out of the car and handed over the keys. He was given a striped celluloid card in exchange and he followed the RAF sergeant to the guard room. A flight-lieutenant asked him if he had anything to identify himself with and he handed over his SIS card. The officer looked at the photograph and back at Malik's face as he reached for a telephone that had a bank of fifty or more touch-buttons. He tapped five of them and waited, then two more.

'Tideway, this is Phantom. I have an MI6 card with serial number 4791032. I'd like a trace.' He looked at Malik as he listened. Then nodded to himself and hung up.

'I'll keep the card, Mr Malik, and issue you an internal pass.'

As he handed Malik a second plastic card the officer reached for the blue phone and dialled four numbers.

'Squadron Leader Fowler? I see . . . will you tell him his visitor is in the guard room . . . thanks.'

A few minutes later Fowler drew up in a Range Rover with RAF roundels on the side and waved Malik over.

'Jump in, Jake. I'm over the other side.'

Fowler turned the vehicle and they followed a tarmac road past a series of buildings; a hangar, a couple of Westland helicopters and then they were at a small concrete building.

They had to use both their passes for Malik to enter, and inside the lighting was artificial but bright and almost like sunshine.

Fowler led him to his own room which was a mass of electronics and photographic equipment. Fowler took off his cap, smiling.

'Sorry about all the bullshit but you're probably used to it. Nice to see you again.'

'Nice to see you too, and thanks for finding time to see me.'

'Not at all. What can I do for you?'

Malik reached into his jacket pocket, took out a plain brown envelope and handed it to Fowler.

'Have a look at that. And tell me what it is.'

Fowler tapped the photograph out of the envelope and held it carefully by its edges. He looked at it, holding it so that it caught the light, and then he looked at Malik before he walked with the print over to a white topped desk.

'Is the scale correct, Jake, or just a guess?'

'The scale was built in on the camera.'

Fowler put it down on the inspection desk and swung over a magnifying lens. Then he reached up and directed a circle of light onto the photograph. For long minutes he looked through the lens, then he turned to look at Malik.

'Where did you get this, Jake?' he asked softly.

Malik shook his head. 'Tell me what it is.'

Fowler frowned. 'You must know roughly what it is.'

Malik half-smiled. 'It's a weapon. I want you to tell me exactly what it is.'

'Can I keep a copy?'

'Afraid not.'

'Can I put in an official request? We haven't got an actual record of one on a site.'

Malik shook his head. 'You'd be told we didn't know what you're on about. Maybe in a few weeks time you can have that print provided you leave it at that for now and don't ask for any more information. Anyway, what the hell is it?'

'I can't give you a precise answer because I don't know. But I can give you a fair idea of what it is. It's a bastard version of a Soviet IRBM that NATO calls Scapegoat. Its proper designation is the SS-14. We know very little about SS-14s and it's too mobile to even appear on satellite pictures.'

'Tell me more.'

'What can I tell you? It's just over thirty-five feet long and it's got a range of just under 2500 miles. It's solid fuel and can be launched easily from an IS-3 chassis.'

'Where have they been used?'

'That I can't tell you. Apart from test launches we've never had evidence that they have been used operationally. But they've been deployed all over the place. You can put them in silos but they're so flexible you don't really need to. The launchers are totally mobile. You can plant one in woods, in buildings, you can trundle it away in a matter of minutes and deploy it somewhere else. It's almost as mobile as a heavy-goods vehicle.'

'What makes you think this is a bastardized version?'

'There's what looks like an extra body unit.'

'What would that do?'

'The only thing I can think of was that they wanted to try making them in smaller plants where the equipment had to produce shorter lengths. It won't affect the performance one way or another.'

'And the warhead?'

'Oh, nuclear.'

'Accurate?'

'Yes. Inertial guidance system. They could MIRV it at some stage and give it two or three warheads.'

'A big bang when it lands?'

Fowler shrugged. 'They're all big bangs these days, Jake. This would be Hiroshima times four or five I'd guess.'

'What kind of crews do they have?'

'God knows. The only sightings have been by the Americans. They saw two SS-14s at the Soviet test centre for ICBMs at Tyuratim. It was a verbal report. Their camera was out of action. I'd guess maybe a technician and a driver would do. They would vector on instructions from a command post. They could be linked in clusters of course if they were permanent sites and the targets weren't changed.'

'What does that mean – linked?'

'You could fire them by remote control in pairs or clusters from a single control point. They would be fired like that, by radio, at Tyuratim.

Malik held out his hand for the photograph but Fowler was reluctant to hand it over.

'How the hell did the reconnaisance plane get so low, Jake?'

'Who says it was low?'

'If this was satellite or even a U2 the grain would be far worse. This must have been taken at under a thousand feet. And there's almost no atmospheric interference.'

Malik waved his hand for the photograph and Fowler handed it back.

Malik smiled. 'I'll have it nicely framed and you can have it for Christmas.'

Fowler wasn't amused. 'Let's go over to the Mess for a drink.'

'I haven't got time, Freddy.'

'OK. Let me take you back to the gate.'

The applause went on long after the lights had gone up in the concert hall and Ashkenazy came back for the sixth and seventh time. It was rapturous to the point of embarrassment, and Malik did not notice Heinz Fischer standing a few feet away at the end of the row vainly trying to attract his attention. It was Lisa who noticed him; she tugged at Malik's arm.

'Heinz wants you, Jake.'

Malik made his apologies as he pushed his way past the rapt faces to the aisle.

'I've just had a call from Lauterbacher. He seems to be doing his stuff for us. He says Meyer is booked into the same hotel in Hamburg the day after tomorrow if we're still interested.'

'Have you tried to book us on a flight yet?'

'No.'

'See what you can do. As early as possible.'

'Are you taking Lisa home after this?'

'Yes.'

'I'll phone you there.'

It was nearly midnight when Heinz Fischer phoned. He had been unable to get them on the early morning flight but using his police muscle he had arranged for them to fly up on a freighter that was leaving at five a.m.

They were at the hotel in Hamburg by seven-thirty but they had not been able to book into the suite next door to Meyer. The best they could do was to be on the same corridor on the same floor.

When they were in their suite Malik said, 'I'm going to pick up Meyer, Heinz. I don't have any choice, and there's no time to play it slowly even if I knew how to go about it. D'you want to stay out of it?'

'Does he end up the same way as Loeb?'

Malik half-smiled. 'I shouldn't think so. Meyer isn't stupid, and I know a hell of a lot more about the background this time.'

'When do *I* get to know about the background?'

'I'd rather you heard it as it comes out. Anyway I don't really know all that much. And I could be way off beam. But I *do* know that it's far and away more serious than we thought. Just how serious remains to be seen.'

'OK. I'll stay.'

'Rent me another house then, Heinz. Somewhere really isolated and not too big.'

'How long for?'

'Same as before. A couple of months.'

In the late afternoon Malik went with Fischer to see the house he had rented deep in the forest of Sachsenwald. He checked it over thoroughly, room by room. It was well furnished and of a size that would be reasonably easy to control.

Back at the hotel Malik rehearsed his plan with Fischer, checking again and again the timings from their suite to Meyer's suite, and then the long journey down the stairs to the last section of the fire escape and the emergency doors that led to the yard serving the kitchens and boiler-house. Malik tested the lock a dozen times. There was no way to drug Meyer and remove him once he was insensible. He either cooperated or they had to guard him in his suite and then take him by force in the early hours of the morning. They covered variations on both methods until Malik was satisfied that both plans could work unless something totally unexpected happened.

Heinz phoned Ruth, and Malik phoned Lisa. She had heard from one of her old schoolfriends that another girl in their class was now a teacher at a kibbutz near Ramla. She had also told the principal at the music school where she taught that she would be leaving before the end of the year. He was giving her a glowing reference and two introductions that could be helpful in getting a job. She was quite sure that those were all obvious signals from the good Lord that everything was going to be fine.

They ate together in their suite and went early to bed. As Malik lay quietly in the darkness his mind went over the things he knew. Remembering the small clues that had been there all the while like minute specks of gold in a prospector's sludge. Loeb and his electronics experience with army control systems. The girl from Humboldt and her talk with the journalist that had wandered off into nuclear missiles and the Israelis. The camouflaged place in the Negev. The crates that he now knew had brought a missile or parts of a missile to Rechmann's estate where they had been unloaded and the pianos substituted. The infra-red photography of that pencil shape that was a missile in an underground silo. But what the hell were they going to do with a missile? And what in God's name could have brought Jews and Germans together in such an unholy alliance? There was no sense in it. Was there a chance that one or both governments were involved? And if so, why? And what kind of crazy set-up brought together a German piano manufacturer, and a wealthy Israeli industrialist? And why was Meyer's airline chief pilot sleeping with the pretty blonde from East Berlin who was also sleeping with a KGB man? Nothing about it gave off the smell of a KGB operation, but it was the KGB bit that had brought MI6 into it in the first place. And as the flotsam swirled in his mind he realized that he had missed an elementary point. In what direction was Rechmann's missile pointing? He had completely overlooked the obvious fact that missiles on fixed sites have a permanent target. And the photographs wouldn't help unless they were all accurately pasted down and orientated on a smaller scale map. He could get it done if necessary but it would take a couple of days.

In the darkness he pressed the light button on his watch. It was past one o'clock. He closed his eyes and pulled the blanket over his head.

The old crone was like the witch in his story book of Hansel and Gretel. She had a shrunken face, the skin like parchment stretched over a skull, yellow and mottled with suppurating patches of eczema. She was sitting on the bottom bunk, her wiry grey hair like a roughly made bird's nest, the whites of her eyes stained with brown patches, her hands trembling as they rested on her bony legs. It was their third day in Auschwitz.

The old woman's voice quavered as she spoke, her eyes intent on his mother's face.

'You need trousers for the boy, missus. I tell you how to get them.'

'But he's got trousers.'

The old witch cackled. 'With short trousers they say he is a child and then in two days he is in the gas chamber. With long trousers he is a man. A small man. But they want men to work before they die.'

'You mean they kill children without reason?'

The old woman made strange, horrifying noises as she laughed. 'He's a Jew, you stupid cow. That is *a reason to them. Where you been all these years?'*

'Where can I get long trousers for him?'

The old woman leaned forward, cupping her bony hands round her mouth as she whispered.

'The Kapo in hut thirty-one has seen the boy. He wants him for himself. He's in for hundred and sixty-five. Done four years already.'

'I don't understand. What's hundred and sixty-five?'

The old woman smiled, her mouth quite toothless.

'He's a homo. He fancies him.'

For a moment his mother sat there paralysed and then she reached for his hand as she stood up unsteadily. The old woman clawed at her dress, holding her there.

'There's another way, sweetheart, an easier way.'

'What's that?'

'Old Schmidt.' She pointed to the man on the bunk in the corner. He wore a kapo's armband. He was an old man, with a beard and whiskers like a rabbi, but he wasn't a rabbi. He was one of the early inmates from when the prisoners were actual criminals. The old woman was stroking his mother's leg. 'He can still get it hard, missus. You open your legs for him and he'll get you the trousers. You tell him I told you. Tell him to remember old Friedl.'

He looked up at his mother's face. Her eyes were closed and her hands were clasped, and as he saw her lips moving he knew she was praying. She had told him to sit on the bunk and wait for her.

He had been asleep when she came back but he woke, trembling as she stuffed the filthy pair of cut-down long trousers under his blanket. He pulled the thin blanket over his head to hide from the world of grown-ups.

CHAPTER FIFTEEN

Malik sent Heinz Fischer to buy food and take it to the house at Sachsenwald. Meyer was not due at the airport until midday. When Fischer got back they checked the stairways and the fire-escape again, and at one o'clock, just before Meyer was due at the hotel, Fischer drove the car round to the hotel's service area at the back and parked it alongside the boiler-room. The only eventuality that he couldn't plan for was if Meyer was not alone when he booked in at the hotel. Malik was afraid that if they weren't able to pick up Meyer quickly he might have visitors or phone someone so that his disappearance would be noticed too quickly.

Fischer moved down the lobby so that he could phone up when Meyer arrived. When Meyer had not arrived by three o'clock Malik gave it another ten minutes. He was just reaching to telephone the lobby when Fischer rang. Meyer had booked in and was just walking over to the lift with the porter.

Malik walked into the corridor and saw the porter standing to one side as Meyer walked into his suite. He saw Fischer come out of the furthest lift and hold the gates as the porter came out of Meyer's door, and then they were alone in the corridor. He waited for a couple of minutes.

Fischer held his breath as Malik slid the skeleton key into the lock and quietly turned the knob. The sitting room was empty and Fischer closed the door carefully as Malik walked across to the half-open bedroom door.

Meyer was sitting on his bed, loosening his tie, his jacket on the bed beside him. He half-smiled as Malik walked into the bedroom.

'You've got the wrong room, I'm afraid. The porter must have left the door open by mistake.'

'Amos Meyer?'

The half-smile faded but Meyer didn't look alarmed.

'Why yes. Who are you? I don't understand.'

'I want you to come with me, Herr Meyer. I want to talk to you. You won't get hurt if you do as I ask.'

Meyer was reaching for the bedside phone when Malik pulled out the Walther. Meyer withdrew his hand from the telephone but he looked quite composed.

'I don't know who you are, but you're being very silly. Now what is it you want?'

'My name is Malik, Herr Meyer, and I told you what I want. I want you to come with me and answer some questions.'

'Are you some sort of policeman, or what?'

'Put your jacket on, Meyer. I have a colleague in the other room. He'll bring your bags.'

'If it's money you want, it's in my wallet.'

Malik waved the pistol. 'Come on, Meyer, you're wasting time,' he said sharply.

Then, as Meyer's hand darted towards the room-service call-button, Malik chopped at Meyer's neck with his hand. The blow knocked him sideways on the bed but its force had been relieved by his collar and tie. He was still conscious, his eyes turned sideways to look at Malik. He sat up slowly and tentatively, as if half-expecting another blow. He opened his mouth to speak but Malik cut in.

'Stand up, Meyer, and put on your jacket.'

Meyer stood up, and his hand shook as he pulled on his jacket. Malik guessed that the trembling was more from shock than actual fear. Meyer looked cautious but not scared.

'Now walk out into the sitting room.'

Malik nodded to Fischer who went into the bedroom and came out a couple of minutes later with Meyer's bag and briefcase. He opened the outer door, looked out and nodded. Malik slid the pistol into his jacket pocket and motioned to Meyer to follow Fischer into the corridor.

They passed an elderly couple heading for the lifts. The man nodded in their general direction as they passed by. Fischer led the way and they walked down ten double flights of carpeted stairs to the emergency door on the mezzanine floor. Fischer pushed on the metal roller and the two doors grated open. There was nobody in the yard as they walked down the iron fire-escape and Malik kept close to Meyer as they made their way through the hotel staff's cars to the BMW. As Malik bent to open the passenger door he saw Meyer turn and he stood up, ramming the pistol hard into Meyer's kidneys. The man's angry eyes looked for a moment at Malik's grim face and then he bent to get into the passenger seat. Malik pushed the door to, waited until Fischer had started the car then slid quickly into the rear seat and the car jerked forward as he was closing the door.

Malik took the pistol out of his pocket. 'Don't do anything stupid, Meyer,' and he reached forward, the nose of the pistol just touching Meyer's neck as they made their way through the city traffic towards the autobahn.

There was heavy traffic until they got to the city boundary just beyond the Youth Hostel at Horn. Fischer took them off the highway at Öjendorf Park and by the time they were passing through Oststeinbrek the traffic was lighter, and by Schönningstedt they were alone. At the Friedrich's Museum Fischer switched on the sidelights as they turned onto the forest road. Ten minutes later the car turned off the road down the hard, rutted track that led to the house.

Malik got out and opened the white wooden gates and Fischer drove up to the small garage. Meyer looked around as they stood waiting for Malik to come. Once they were all inside the house Malik switched on the lights and drew the curtains. He turned to look at Meyer and pointed to one of the armchairs.

'Sit down, Herr Meyer.'

Meyer sat down awkwardly. His face was impassive and he sat there without speaking. Almost dignified.

'Tell me about it, Meyer. All of it.'

'I don't know who you are, or what you want. But I'd better warn you that I have meetings arranged with important people. When I don't arrive there will be immediate inquiries.'

'Who are the important meetings with, Meyer?'

'That's my business.'

'I don't want to hurt you, Meyer.'

Meyer half-smiled. 'You won't hurt me, my friend. I spent two years in one of your concentration camps. There's nothing you can do that will frighten me.'

'Which concentration camp was that?'

'Sachsenhausen.'

'Show me your mark.'

Meyer pushed forward his hands and Malik saw where the tattoo had been removed. There was just a patch of shiny tissue, wrinkled and raw.

He leaned forward and unlocked the handcuffs, sliding them into his jacket pocket. Then he sat back in his chair.

'My name is Malik, Herr Meyer, Jacob Malik. I am a British Intelligence officer and I'm investigating, in conjunction with the German Political Police, the outbreaks of anti-Semitic daubings on synagogues and other Jewish buildings. I believe you are connected with those groups. I don't understand why. Maybe you could tell me.'

'I'm a Jew, Herr Malik, an Israeli citizen. I'm hardly likely to be connected with that sort of activity.'

Malik sighed. 'Neither is Baron von Busch, or Herr Rechmann in Cologne, or the judge in Goslar. Nevertheless they are connected with these groups and you know it.'

For the first time Meyer looked agitated. His hand went to his shirt collar, unbuttoning it and loosening his tie. Then, looking at Malik he said, 'I'm afraid I can't help you.'

'Would you rather I filed my report with Bonn and London?'

'That's up to you.'

Malik reached inside his jacket and pulled out one of the postcard-sized colour prints, handing it to Meyer.

'Are you sure you mean that?'

Meyer looked at the photograph and his hand trembled as he handed it back to Malik. For a moment or two Meyer sat with his eyes closed as if he were praying, then lifting his eyes slowly to look at Malik he said, 'I'll talk to you alone, Herr Malik.'

Malik looked across at Fischer and nodded, and the German stood up and walked out of the room. Malik turned his head to look back at Meyer.

'You realize that if you try to get away not only are you likely to get hurt but everything you've been doing will be exposed.'

'You are a Jew, aren't you, Herr Malik?'

'Yes.'

'How much do you know already?'

Malik shook his head. 'Just tell me your story. I'm not here to answer your questions.'

'How many people have you informed?'

'None. Neither London nor Bonn know yet what I have discovered.'

'But Herr Fischer knows?'

'No. Just me.'

'We could cause another Holocaust, you and I, if we are not very wise.'

'Maybe you should have thought of that before you started.'

'Do you care about what happened to us Jews, Herr Malik?' Meyer saw the anger in Malik's eyes but he went on. 'Everything I have planned, everything I have done, has been to protect my country. I beg of you to believe me.'

'If I believed you, Meyer, I should think you ought to be in a mental hospital.'

'Let me explain and you will understand.'

'That's what I've been asking you to do.'

'It's going to take a long time.'

Malik shrugged and sat down. Meyer leaned forward.

'Maybe it'll be easier if I just answer your questions.'

'OK. Who's in with you apart from von Busch, Rechmann and the old judge?'

'There's two Israelis. Halberstein and Cohen. And one other German.'

'Is there anybody above you?'

'No. I put it together and I run it.'

'How many missiles are there?'

'Ten.'

'Where are they?'

'Five in Germany and five in Israel.'

'Are they armed?'

'Yes.'

'What with?'

'Single nuclear warheads.'

'How are they controlled?'

'Electronic synchronizer and radio.'

'The missile at Rechmann's place. Where is it aimed? And the others.'

'I'll give you a list. They're all aimed at Soviet cities.'

'Who controls the firing?'

'I do, but von Busch could too if I passed him the code.'

'Does he know it?'

'No.'

Malik stood up, looking at Meyer's face. He said softly, 'You must be out of your mind.'

He walked to the door and turned to look at Meyer. 'Don't move, Meyer. If you make any move you'll get hurt.'

Malik walked into the hall and called out.

'Heinz.'

Fischer came out of the kitchen, a half-eaten sandwich in his hand.

'What is it, Jake? Is he talking?'

'Can you put a round-the-clock surveillance on Rechmann and von Busch?'

'I'd have to give a damn good reason. They're both important men in their communities. That wouldn't stop a surveillance, but I'd have to give chapter and verse.'

'I can't do that.'

'Why not?'

Malik shook his head. 'It's better you don't know.' He looked at Heinz Fischer's face. 'You probably wouldn't believe it anyway.'

'What do you want me to do?'

'What time is it?'

Fischer looked at his watch. 'Just past ten.'

'Forget the surveillance. Get some sleep, Heinz. I'll wake you about three. I want you to watch Meyer when he's sleeping. I'll relieve you about seven.'

'Do you want something to eat?'

'What have you got?'

'I can do beef sandwiches, cheese, tomatoes and apples.'

'Bring in a few beef sandwiches and tomatoes. And a flask of coffee.'

'Milk and sugar in the coffee?'

'No milk. He's kosher. And no cheese either for the same reason.'

'I'll be about fifteen minutes.'

'OK. Knock before you come in.'

'Is he likely to try and do a bolt?'

'No. More likely to cut his throat.'

Malik turned and walked back into the sitting room. Meyer was sitting with his head in his hands but he looked up as soon as Malik walked in.

'I don't think you understand, Herr Malik. You've got the wrong impression. This is for defence, not attack.'

'What was a man like Loeb used for?'

'Loeb?' Meyer looked puzzled.

'He worked for von Busch. Played guitar in a club.'

'He was killed.'

'I know. What was he used for?'

'I think he knew about electronics. He was controlled by von Busch.'

'Why the swastikas on the synagogues?'

Meyer sighed and shrugged. 'We thought that the KGB had information about our intentions. We wanted to provide a cover. A diversion. Something to put them off our tracks. We paid a few hooligans to do all that.'

'How many people are in your groups?'

'There are no groups. Just the four of us in Germany. Two in Israel and myself. We have used people for certain things but they didn't know anything about what we were doing.'

'And what the hell *were* you doing?'

'Were you German originally, Herr Malik?'

'No. I was born in Poland.'

Meyer frowned. 'How did you . . .' He stopped as Malik uncovered his wrist for a moment. He looked amazed. 'You were in a camp.'

Malik nodded and Meyer sighed. 'Thank God. Thank God. At least you'll understand.'

Malik shook his head. 'I won't, Meyer. I assure you I won't. I'm not just a Jew, I'm also an intelligence officer and I don't give a damn whether criminals are Jews, Catholics or atheists.'

'Do you care about being a Jew? Do you care about us? Do you care about Israel and all it means?'

Malik took off his jacket and Meyer heard the metallic thud of the gun in the jacket pocket as Malik dropped it onto the floor as he sat down facing Meyer.

'Let me warn you, Herr Meyer, that you have committed a dozen or more criminal acts. Criminal offences under German law, Israeli law and the laws of every civilized country in the world. You must consider yourself as already being under arrest. Anything you tell me I shall report to the authorities, and what you tell me will be used in evidence when you come to trial. Do not, I repeat, do not, imagine for a moment that because I am a Jew, or because I was in Auschwitz, or that because you are a Jew and an Israeli, that it will make any difference. There are Jews in jail tonight in Tel Aviv and Jerusalem because they are criminals as well as Jews. You are a criminal too. Don't make any mistake about that.'

'Are your father and mother still living, Herr Malik?'

'Forget my father and mother. Tell me what you were planning.'

'What do you want to know?'

'For Christ's sake, Meyer. What were you trying to do?'

'To save the peace.'

'Cut out the bullshit. What were you trying to do with ten atomic missiles?'

Meyer opened his mouth to speak and then closed it as Fischer came in with a tray and put it down on the low table between Meyer and Malik.

'You know where I am if you want me, Jake.'

'OK. I'll be around for some time.'

Malik waved towards the sandwiches and Meyer.

'Help yourself. It's not kosher but it's all we've got.'

Meyer shook his head, taking a deep breath as he leaned back in his chair. His mottled hands were clasped together and a nerve quivered at one side of his mouth. And there were beads of perspiration on his forehead and his upper lip.

'It's difficult, Herr Malik, to explain in a few minutes something that I have thought about for years. Especially something as complex as this.'

Meyer waited for a response but when Malik ignored the pause Meyer shrugged and went on.

'I tried to plan for the day when our enemies attacked us and our allies deserted us. I feared that that day would come. I fear now that it is very near. The Soviet Union is openly anti-Semitic. It persecutes our people and supports the Arabs who want to wipe out Israel.

'Because of the Jewish vote and natural generosity the United States has helped us with money, arms, technology, and in the United Nations. But when God gave us Israel he forgot to give us oil. And the Americans need oil. Only the Arabs have oil. Before long the Americans will be forced into deciding whether they want oil or Israel. I fear that they will choose oil. I don't criticize them for that. Without enough oil their whole economy would disintegrate.

'When this happens we shall be open to attack from all sides. Egypt, the Lebanon, Syria, Iran, Iraq, Jordan . . . all the quarrelling Arabs will suddenly be allies. We should fight, of course, but in the end we should be wiped out. All of us. Men, women and children. Just like they always said they would do. The Soviet Union would encourage and assist them. Our friends in America would be shocked and angry. They would raise hell in the Security Council and when we were all dead the United Nations would pass a vote of censure on the Soviet Union. But the Cadillacs and the trucks would still have gas.'

Meyer waited for Malik to respond. But there was no response.

'Germany is in the same position as Israel. They have allies too. NATO and the United States. They have the same old enemy . . . the Soviet Union. And just as the Russians can use their Arab stooges to attack Israel the Russians have their Warsaw Pact stooges to attack West Germany. NATO couldn't stop the Warsaw Pact forces. They may not even try. Especially if the Russians declare on day one that they undertake to go no further than the Rhine. The French and the British are not going to declare war on the Soviet Union for the sake of half of Germany. It would be all over in three or four days. By the time the Americans had called on the UN it would be all over. This is the scenario I imagined, and every week in the last two years has seen it become more likely. When I originally explained it to my colleagues they agreed with its logic but couldn't believe that it would happen. When they saw what was happening, they believed, and we went ahead.' Meyer looked at Malik's grim face and said, hesitantly, 'And I guess you know the rest.'

'You tell me, Meyer. You tell me.'

'We made a pact, the seven of us. We accepted that if either Israel or West Germany was attacked, no government action, no diplomacy, no United Nations would be able to stop the attack. While presidents and prime ministers were consulting their experts, and the diplomats were beating on the doors of the UN, it would be half over, and by the time they decided what to do it would be too late.

'My plan is – was – that on the first move over the frontiers of either country we should inform the media all over the world by anonymous phone calls that somewhere in the world, within striking distance of ten named Soviet cities, are nuclear missiles trained on those cities which would be launched within six hours of our statement.

'We should not announce who we are, our motives, or nationalities . . . absolutely nothing. We should make clear that no organization or government on either side was responsible. There would be nobody for the Russians to negotiate with, and no time for us to be discovered. We could be in South America, anywhere, for all they knew. They would not be able to accuse any country. Their own citizens would know that they were being sacrificed because their leaders were trying to destroy West Germany or Israel. They would have a simple choice. No ifs and buts. They would withdraw within the six hours or their cities would be destroyed. The messages to all the media would be given in Spanish, and no Spanish-speaking country has a nuclear missile capacity.'

Meyer spread his arms in a typically resigned Jewish gesture and said, 'They wouldn't have risked it. Who would they retaliate against? You only start a world war when you've planned it. Not on the spur of the moment, under pressure. They would have withdrawn. The missiles would not have been fired and the world would have been warned of Soviet intentions.'

'And if they *had* ignored the threat?'

Meyer shook his head. 'You're going back into the thinking of planners. What will *they* do if we do this? What shall we do if they do that? They are all hamstrung. They have to go on looking in crystal balls and playing never-ending guessing games. All their thinking is based on "We'll press the button as soon as they attack us. But we press no buttons for other countries." And that's why they are weak. The Russians don't want a world war. There would be nothing left for the winners. Just a heap of radioactive rubble. You don't imagine Brezhnev wants to spend two years down an underground shelter from the moment when the KGB man comes in to tell him that they've won but there's nothing left, anywhere, including the Soviet Union. They want their cars and the pretty girls from the Bolshoi, and all the rest of it. They want power over people, not over cinders and corpses. And what do they lose by withdrawing from inside Israel or West Germany? Nothing. The prize isn't worth the risk. They'll withdraw, Herr Malik. They have no choice.' Meyer leaned forward, looking intently at Malik's face. 'They couldn't withdraw so readily if the threat was from a government. But from an anonymous, independent, uncaring and indifferent source. That's different.'

Malik stood up and walked slowly over to the window, pulling the curtains to one side, looking out to where the half-moon hung in the sky just above the tops of the forest trees. He could see the dark patches on the moon's surface that made it look much like the earth, and even its emptiness gave it a peace and serenity that its companion planet, Earth, seemed to lack. And intentionally or unintentionally Meyer had now handed over to him his can of writhing worms.

He would need time to sort out in his mind what to do. If Meyer's plan was exposed the Germans and the Israelis would be pariahs in the eyes of the whole world. Nobody would believe that they hadn't some knowledge of what was going on. But how did you get ten nuclear missiles into launching sites without anyone knowing? How did you get ten nuclear missiles, period? London, Bonn and Tel Aviv thought they had problems, but this thing was in a league of its own. Each would blame the other for lack of control and security. Each would suspect the other of knowing something. And each would certainly blame the other. London would blame both Bonn and Tel Aviv. After all, the missiles were on their territory.

And yet there was a real validity to Meyer's crazy thinking. It could have worked. But it wouldn't work now and it wouldn't ever be possible to try it again. He tried to imagine Jenkins' reaction when he told him. The hand reaching for the red phone marked 'Foreign Secretary', then the hesitation and withdrawal as he worked out the effect on his inevitable knighthood of being the bearer of such disastrous news. All that diplomatic dancing around in the cause of 'detente' would have been proved to be wasted effort. Down the pan with all the rest of the diplomatic charades that keep ordinary Russians, Britishers, and Israelis from knowing what was really going on behind the scenes. And Washington would go berserk at the thought of its two protegés, West Germany and Israel, going it alone and asking a cynical world to believe that the United States didn't know a thing about it. The words 'trust' and 'loyalty' would be in every White House statement for years. And after that the New York bar-mitzvahs would have to be held behind locked doors.

Malik turned to look at Meyer.

'Where did you get the missiles, Meyer?'

'They were missiles left behind awaiting transport when the Russians were kicked out of Egypt. The warheads were intact but parts of the guidance and firing equipment had been removed. They came under control of an Israeli army unit during the 1973 war. I bought them clandestinely. I implied that I was acting for the government for special security reasons. We made the missing equipment parts ourselves. And the launchers.'

'Where, for God's sake?'

'When you break them all down into bits and pieces nobody except an expert could recognize what they are. The electronics were done at Rechmann's factory and the other parts were made all over Europe.'

'And you assembled them at the place in the Negev?'

'How did you know about that?' Then he nodded. 'You must have been the man in the jeep.'

'But who assembled them?'

'Engineers. They are used to working in odd places on secret devices for *Tsahal* . . . the army. We don't have to explain.'

'Have you got map references for the ten sites?'

'Yes.'

Malik took a deep breath. 'You'd better get some sleep, Meyer. You're going to have a busy time.'

'It will destroy West Germany and Israel if this comes out, Herr Malik. Nobody will believe that Bonn and Tel Aviv were not involved.'

Malik watched Meyer's face as he spoke. 'Maybe they are.'

'I swear to you that they are not. I swear on my life, on my loved ones who were murdered in the camps. Nobody knew but the seven of us.'

'I'll take you up to your room.'

Malik sat staring with his red-rimmed, tired eyes at the picture on the wall, trying to collect his thoughts. It was a painting of some mediaeval Geman town. He guessed it was either Göttingen or Hildesheim. He shook his head to clear it from such distractions.

There was a variety of moves he could make. He could take Meyer to London, report what he knew and leave them to sort it out. He could tell Fischer and let Bonn sort it out, and leave London clean-handed. Or he could tell the Israelis and they could bring their guile to the problem. He tried not to let the other alternative gel in his mind.

If he landed the shambles in London's lap they would think he was out of his mind. And they would be right. The responsibility lay anywhere but in London. But hand it over to Bonn or Israel and it would be disaster. Once the bureaucrats were involved it would be leaked by somebody. Any newspaper in the Western world would pay a fortune for the story. And Moscow would pay even more. It would be the end of all credibility that Israel and West Germany could be trusted as responsible states. It could lead to the very situation that Meyer had forecast.

Malik put his head back in the armchair and closed his eyes to think. Two minutes later he was asleep.

From far away Malik could her Fischer's voice and he clawed his way painfully out of the long tunnel of sleep. His eyes focused slowly on Fischer's face.

'Jake. Wake up, Jake.'

'What is it, Heinz? What time is it?'

'Drink this coffee; it'll help you wake up.'

Malik wiped his face and eyes with his hands then reached for the mug of coffee that Fischer held out for him. He had drunk half of it when Fischer said, 'We've got a problem, Jake.'

Malik didn't look up. 'What is it?'

'A man came to the door and asked for you.'

Malik frowned as he looked up at Fischer's face.

'But nobody knows I'm here.'

'This guy does, he asked for you by name. Jake Malik.'

'Who is he? What did you say?'

'I told him that he'd made a mistake and that there was nobody here of that name.'

'Then what?'

'He just said, "Tell him I'm waiting for him in my car." And he walked away. He's sitting in a white BMW outside the gate.'

'What does he look like?'

'Big-built. Tanned. He said his name was Johnny Morris.'

'Jesus. What the hell's he doing here?'

'Who is he?'

'He's the SIS guy in Tel Aviv. But how can he know I'm here?'

'Do you want me to get him in?'

'What's Meyer doing?'

'He's asleep. He's been tossing and turning but he isn't going to wake for a long while.'

Malik took a deep breath and struggled out of the armchair.

'Go and watch Meyer, Heinz. If he wakes and I'm still outside, keep him in his room . . . in fact keep him in his room anyway. I'll call you when I need you.'

Malik looked at his watch as he opened the door of the cottage. It was ten-fifteen and a sunny morning. He could just see the top of the white BMW as he walked down the flagged pathway to the wicket gate. He wondered how Johnny Morris could have traced him. How could he have known that he was in

Germany, let alone Hamburg? Nobody knew but himself and Heinz.

As he walked across the grass verge to the car he saw the window being wound down and when he bent down to speak to Morris the shock was almost like a physical blow. It wasn't Johnny Morris. He recognized the face but he couldn't place it. The man in the driving seat had a Luger resting on his arm, its muzzle only just visible against his rough tweed jacket.

'Get in the back, Jake. It's loaded, and the safety catch is off.'

And then the voice, added to the face, took him back. Back to Johnny Morris's house that last night in Tel Aviv. And David Levy. The smiling, amiable David Levy. But his face looked grim enough now.

As Malik opened the rear door and clambered into the car Levy stepped out and joined him on the back seat, pulling the door to behind him.

'D'you remember me, Jake?'

'Yes.'

'Can we talk?'

'I guess I'm not in a position to stop you.'

Levy nodded. 'Where's Meyer? Is he in the house?'

'Who's Meyer?'

Levy's big brown eyes looked at Malik. 'We haven't got time for bullshit, Jake. You'd better level with me.'

'About what?'

'Jake. I'm liaison officer between Mossad and *Shin Beth*. Israel's a small country. You came in as a tourist and you had your girlfriend with you. Maybe you *were* on holiday but you were doing some ferreting at the same time. We picked up your name when you came through immigration. We did a bit of quick checking in London and confirmed that you had applied for leave and had been granted leave. But that could have been just SIS being efficiently deceptive. So we kept an eye on you.

'We watched you tagging Meyer and we watched you drive in the jeep off the Beersheba road into the desert. There was no way we could follow you without either you seeing us, or Meyer seeing both vehicles, so we waited for you to come back. Air Force electronic surveillance saw a chopper go up and land but that was about all we got.

'We also found out that Johnny Morris had been doing some prowling for you at the airport. We've been keeping close tabs on Amos Meyer ourselves, and lo and behold he pays a visit to Hamburg and books in at the Atlantic. And you and the German book in on the same floor. I took it you must be in cahoots with him on whatever he was up to. But no. An unhappy-looking Meyer, and you and your Kraut, troop out of the hotel and end up in this little hideaway.' Levy smiled grimly. 'I just want to know what's going on.'

'What else do you know?'

'A bit. Not much.'

'Tell me the bit.'

'Later my friend. You tell me your bit first.'

'What makes you think I should discuss anything I'm doing with a Mossad officer. What's it got to do with you?'

'Anything that involves an intelligence officer of another country stalking an important Israeli citizen inside Israel and eventually kidnapping him in Germany concerns me.'

'Your superiors wouldn't be very happy if I told you what it's all about.'

'They'll be a damn sight more unhappy if you don't, my friend.'

'You said that Meyer is an important citizen. In what way is he important?'

'In one company or another he employs nearly a thousand people. Apart from that he has given money generously to a number of government sponsored projects. He has contacts with most of the top brass in government and politics. They wouldn't like him to get lost in the wash.'

'Can I ask you what rank you have in Mossad?'

'Yes. *Sgan Aloof*. Lieutenant Colonel.'

'What have you reported to your people?'

'Very little. There was nothing worth reporting until you laid hands on Meyer. Maybe you were both just old friends.'

'It wasn't an accident that you were at the Morrises' that night?'

'Not exactly. But Johnny knows I'm Mossad and we cooperate whenever we can. I'd told him we knew of an SIS guy on holiday in Tel Aviv. I told him your name. He said he knew you well and I said I'd like to meet you. He invited us over and said he'd try and contact you. It turned out that you contacted him first. So we met. He doesn't know that it was anything more than just me wanting to get to know one more SIS officer. He told me later that he wasn't even sure that you were a Jew, and he definitely didn't know that you'd been in a camp.'

'Would it be possible for you and me to talk off the record? Genuinely and permanently off the record?'

'It depends on what it's about, Jake.'

'What would make it possible?'

Levy shrugged. 'If it was some purely commercial jiggery-pokery that you were up to. Something that doesn't affect security. I'd even go as far as ignoring something that was more the concern of the police than Mossad.'

'What if it was political but it would be more embarrassing for Tel Aviv to know than not know?'

'There ain't no such scenario, Jake. We're used to being embarrassed. Everything we do or say angers somebody somewhere.'

'Tell me the other bit you know.'

'OK. We ran a photographic reconnaisance over the desert area we reckoned you'd been to. We discovered there was a secret plant there that we hadn't been informed about.'

'Making what?'

'High technology electronics for weapons and control systems.'

'What did you do about it?'

Levy shrugged. 'Nothing. We checked with the Defence Ministry. The plant was authorized by a senior official who had omitted to notify us. There are dozens of plants like that.'

'Who was the authorizing official?'

'I don't remember.'

'Would you recognize the name if you heard it?'

'I guess so.'

'Was it Cohen?'

'No.'

'Was it Halberstein?'

'Yes. It was.' Levy looked at Malik. 'You'd better tell me what's going on, Jake.'

'Let's go back to the cottage.'

Levy smiled. 'No way, sweetheart. I didn't sit out here for the fresh air and the view.'

Malik turned away and looked out of the car windows. It was close and hot inside the car, and outside the tall trees of the forest looked cool in the hot summer sun. Two girls rode by on sleek ponies, an elderly German Shepherd tagging along behind them, and wood-pigeons cooed in the quiet of the forest. Malik turned to Levy.

'I've got a problem, Levy. If I do the wrong thing, your people in Tel Aviv are going to curse the day I was born. If I tell *you* it could maybe help avoid the problem. But if you were stupid it could make it even worse.'

'Maybe you've got an inflated idea of your own importance, my friend. One SIS man and one Israeli businessman couldn't do anything that would make the Cabinet lose five minutes sleep.'

'What about five nuclear missiles in Israel and five in West Germany? All vectored on Soviet cities and all armed. And all in private hands.'

Levy's face showed first disbelief and then caution. He shook his head slowly. 'It's not possible.' But there was doubt in his eyes. 'You don't mean this, Jake. You're talking about some wild plan.'

'I'm not. They're in place. In secret, and in certain circumstances they'll be fired.'

'You're kidding.'

Malik shook his head. 'I'll do a deal with you, Levy. I'll tell you the whole thing provided that you guarantee that it's off the record. I'll tell you how I intend dealing with it. If you don't agree with my plan I'll come back with you to Tel Aviv and tell your people myself. And leave them to sort it out. They'll curse us both for telling them but there's no other way.'

'Who knows about all this?'

'I do. Fischer, my German; Amos Meyer; three other Germans and two other Israelis.'

'Who's in charge of your investigation? You or the Kraut?'

'Me.'

'How did you get involved in it?'

'The Germans in this crazy group used anti-Semitic daubings on synagogues to put up a smokescreen. I came here because London thought it was genuine.'

'Do London know what you've just told me?'

'No.'

'Why not?'

'I've only just discovered what it's all about.'

'When are you reporting to them?'

'Providing you'll cooperate I don't intend telling them. And I'd be grateful if you'd put that catch back on safety.'

Levy pushed the catch back to 'safety' and slid the Luger into his jacket pocket, butt first. For a few moments he sat thinking with his eyes closed. Then, sighing, he said, 'OK. I'll go along with your deal. I guess I don't have much choice. But if half what you say is true I don't think you and I can solve the problem.'

And as they sat there Malik told him everything he had learned that was relevant.

'How reliable is your Kraut?' Levy asked.

'He's a nice enough guy. Lisa, my girlfriend, is his sister. We're getting married when this lot's over.'

'He'll want to play it by the book. Germans always do. Orders are orders and all that crap.'

'Not these days. He's a very sensible guy.'

'What were you planning to do?'

'I've changed my thinking now you're here. Let's go back in the cottage and I'll put Heinz in the picture and we'll discuss my ideas.'

Heinz Fischer sat in silence while Malik told him what he had discovered, and what Meyer had told him. He saw the same look of disbelief and doubt give way to concern and anxiety. Fischer had asked sensible questions and when Malik had answered his questions Fischer asked what Malik was going to do next. Malik looked first at Levy and then back to Fischer.

'If we tell London or Bonn or Tel Aviv it will be a disaster for West Germany and for Israel. Do you both agree with that? Nobody would believe their denials of responsiblity. It would seem too much, too outlandish, for them to have know nothing. Do you agree?'

'If you missed London out, maybe Bonn and Tel Aviv could bury it together,' said Levy.

'How? They've got to locate and destroy the missiles. Fill in the sites. And then they've got four Germans and three Israelis who still know all about it. And us of course. And who do they use to dismantle the weapons and fill the sites? It's going to take dozens of men. Men who'll talk. And the experts who disarm the missiles, they'll talk too.'

Fischer shrugged. 'Meyer's people did it, Jake.'

'It was done over many months, Heinz. Pieces were made all over Europe, not recognizable as to what they were or what they would be. The sites would be dug by farm hands as underground stores. Maybe even casual labourers who didn't know or care why or what they were digging. Maybe one other person saw the final results and that was Loeb. And he's dead.

'If we tell Bonn and Tel Aviv it also means that it's on the record. It's official. It's recorded. There will be minutes of meetings. It will be there for all time.'

Fischer looked at Malik. 'So you mean we tell London only?'

'No. We don't tell London.'

Fischer frowned. 'So who do we tell?'

'We don't tell anybody.'

'You mean we leave these madmen to get on with it?'

'No. We make them undo what they've done.'

The two others sat digesting what Malik had said. Fischer looking unimpressed and Levy's face impassive. And as Malik sat watching them, waiting for an answer, the door opened and Meyer walked in, dishevelled and pale, his sparse hair askew, and his pale eyes trying to take in what he saw. Instinctively he looked at Malik and said, like a child. 'I've only just woken up.'

Malik nodded to Fischer. 'Take him, Heinz. Fix him something to eat and stick with him.'

Fischer led Meyer away and Malik realized that Meyer no longer looked like the wealthy and successful businessman, but just an old and weary Jew with bent shoulders and stumbling feet. When the door closed behind them Levy stood up.

'How about we walk out to the garden. We can talk easier there.'

'OK. Are you hungry?'

Levy shrugged. 'I was, but I'm not now.'

There was a wrought-iron garden bench painted white. Its decorations and curlicues uncomfortable to sit on but it was under a willow tree in the far corner of the lawn and they sat there together.

'I'd go along with some of your thinking, Jake. Not all of it.'

'What would you go along with?'

'That we don't tell London, Bonn or Tel Aviv. You're right about it leaking. It's inevitable. But I wouldn't leave it to these people to do it.'

'Why not?'

'It's a weak move. It leaves them in a morally strong position. It's kind of putting ourselves in with them. I wouldn't go along with that. And it leaves too many loose ends.'

'So who disposes of the hardware and fills in the sites?'

'The sites don't matter; they're just holes in the bloody ground. We can fill those in if we've got time but it's the missiles that have to be removed. Every trace of them.'

'And how do we do that?'

'Would you trust me to put a team together to do that?'

'I'd trust you, David. But how would we trust your team?'

'My people are used to doing as they're told without knowing what it's all about. It's the way we operate and the way we live. They wouldn't know the background. They wouldn't know a damn thing. I'd plan it with you and they'd do it. And that would be the end of it.'

'How long would it take?'

Levy closed his eyes and was silent for a few moments and then he said. 'The rest of today for you and me to work out the basics. A night for me to get back. A day or maybe two to bring my people together. A day to get back and say four days or five to do it. How long's that?'

'Say ten days.'

Levy sighed. 'It's too long, but that's it. How about it?'

'I wonder if Fischer will agree?'

'To hell with Fischer. You're in charge of your end, I'm in charge of mine. You don't ask him, you tell him.'

'But he's the one who's got to guarantee that the three Germans keep quiet.'

'I can deal with that too. If you want me to.'

'What do you mean?'

'You know what I mean, fella. You and I don't need to play games with one another. I'll deal with the two Israelis as well.'

'These people had the right idea you know, David. They may be crazy but it could have worked. The idea wasn't crazy, it was putting it into practice that made it crazy. It was Meyer's idea. He talked the others into it. Would you kill Meyer too?'

'Sure I would. And I don't give a damn whether it would have worked or not. If it had been exposed by the KGB or anyone else you could have said "*shalom*", and our allies would have been among the first to send us down the pike. They may not be brilliant but it's for governments to decide about how we defend ourselves. It can be as dirty as you like and I'll do it. But it's not for private enterprise. That's anarchy gone mad.'

'I need time to think about it, David. But we haven't got time. How about we do it in stages. Deal with the hardware first and then work out what we do with the people.'

Levy shrugged. 'OK. If that's how you want it, I'll go along with it. But I shan't alter my views.'

'But I get final say on the people.'

'OK. Now let's talk about the first part. I think we've got to dump the stuff at sea. Somewhere pretty deep. Take them out whole, not in bits and pieces.'

'That means a ship or a plane.'

'It means a plane. It would take too long to get a ship up here. Where are the bloody things anyway?'

'Meyer has got a list of map references. One will be in Cologne, I guess, one in Hamburg, and I've no idea about the others.'

'Doesn't matter. The next thing is a place we can land a plane. A big one.'

'I'll have to get Heinz Fischer on to that. Maybe we could use a normal airport and crate the stuff like they did. But we don't have time to do it in pieces which was how they did it. Fischer could probably fiddle us through Customs.'

'OK. I'll give you three numbers where you can contact me in Israel. You'll have two days to fix something before I need to know. D'you speak Hebrew?'

'No.'

'We'll use English then, not German. And talk about pianos. And when you've settled on a place or an airport give me the map reference. Give it me the wrong way round. Eastings first and northings second. Minutes first degrees second. OK?'

'OK.'

'I'll get on my way. Give me some paper and I'll write out the phone numbers. And give me your number here and the number in Cologne. And don't tell Fischer more than you need to. He may be a lovely guy but he's still a Kraut, and now the chips are down he'll be looking out for them not us.'

CHAPTER SIXTEEN

Heinz Fischer had reservations about the plan. But when Malik pressed him about which of the alternatives he preferred he shrugged hopelessly and agreed that Malik's was the only way. Malik gave him a list of things to check on while he talked to Meyer.

Meyer had shaved and tidied himself up and he looked in control of himself again as Malik pointed to a chair. When he had sat down Malik started.

'I want your cooperation, Meyer. I'm arranging for the missiles you and your collaborators have collected to be removed and destroyed. I'm doing this so that neither Bonn nor Tel Aviv learn of your crazy scheme, and are not involved. If you cooperate fully I shall bear that in mind when I consider how to deal with you and your colleagues. Do you understand?'

'I assure you that I only had . . .'

Malik held up his hand. 'Do you understand, Meyer?'

Meyer nodded, and said quietly, 'Yes, I understand. And I'll cooperate any way you want.'

Malik reached for the pad on the coffee table.

'Write down this list of questions I want answered.' He waited for Meyer to take a pen from his inside pocket. 'The map references of all the missiles. Dimensions and weight. The basic operations code and any relevant pre-firing procedures. Any code words you have with your friends. Any details necessary for disarming the missiles. And the names, addresses and telephone numbers of your group. All of them, Israelis and Germans. When you've done that, come and see me. I'll be with Herr Fischer in the next room.'

Meyer nodded and set the pad in front of him, sighing as he looked at the blank page.

It was almost an hour later when Meyer knocked on the door and came into the side room that Malik and Fischer were using as an office. Malik took the pages and said, 'Sit down, Meyer,' as he read the careful old-fashioned Gothic script. At the top of the second page was one heart-stopping figure and he closed his eyes for a moment before he read on. When he had read every page he turned to Meyer.

'The weight you give . . . twelve thousand kilos. That's for a single missile?'

'Yes. That's the loaded weight.'

'About ten tons?'

'Yes.'

Malik moved to stand up and then relaxed back onto the chair.

'Will your people carry out your orders?'

'Of course.'

'Without argument?'

'Will you let me explain it to them?'

'We'll see. Are they expecting to see you?'

'They were expecting me but I hadn't contacted them. They don't know I'm in Hamburg yet.'

'What about the two in Israel?'

'We don't have much contact unless we have a reason.'

'Is there anyone expecting to hear from you? Your family or business associates, maybe?'

'No. I often go away on business trips. I contact them when I get there.'

'Are you sure?'

'Yes. Why do you ask if I'm sure?'

'There was a photograph of a young woman in your room at the hotel. What about her?'

Meyer shook his head. 'There's no problem there.'

'Who is she?'

'She's dead. She was my wife. She died in Ravensbrück.'

Malik looked at Meyer's drawn face, at the trembling lips, and tried to think of something to say. Something real. But he knew there wasn't anything to say. Or maybe not enough time to say it in.

'You know that there's no point in trying to get away or anything stupid like that? You know it's all over and finished?'

Meyer nodded. 'I recognize that.'

'I won't put you under guard then, Meyer. But keep to the house.'

'You think it was a mistake, my scheme?'

'It was crazy, my friend, not just a mistake.'

'But you understand?'

For a moment Malik hesitated, then, sighing deeply, he said softly, 'Yes. I understand.'

He phoned the Tel Aviv number that Levy had given him and left his name, and asked for Levy to phone him as soon as he arrived. It was four o'clock in the morning when Levy called.

'What's the matter, Jake?'

'We can forget the plane. Those things weigh ten tons.'

'That's OK.'

'Each.'

'Jesus. That's different.'

'Have you got a boat up this way?'

'I've no idea. I'll have to check. But even if there is it won't be easy.

'Why not?'

'Too many documents, too many formalities.'

'We can cope with those at this end.'

'Let me do some checking first. I'll phone you back.'

Fischer had shaken him awake and it was ten o'clock.

'Tel Aviv on the phone for you, Jake. They're hanging on.'

Levy had sounded dog-tired but he had done his checking. There were two Israeli merchant ships in dock at Hamburg. One waiting for a cargo of steel tubing and engineering spares, the other looking for a cargo before taking on ballast. They were negotiating a mixed cargo from Rotterdam. He was going to have a couple of hours' sleep and then fly straight back to Hamburg.

CHAPTER SEVENTEEN

They sat at the table looking at the maps. Large scale maps of Hamburg, Hanover and Cologne, a map covering the whole of northern Germany, and a map of the Harz mountains.

Malik looked at Levy and Fischer. 'Any views on where we go first?'

Levy shrugged. 'I don't think it matters. Maybe Hamburg last because we've got two to deal with here. I think it's more a matter of choosing the right site to do our first lift. It'll be experience for the others. The easiest one first, I'd say.'

'Heinz?'

Fischer looked embarrassed. 'I'd like to leave the Cologne one way down the list because so many people could recognize me. And Rechmann's going to be a permanent problem if he knows I know what he's been up to.'

'Maybe it's better if you don't get involved in Cologne. Or maybe best of all if you leave it to me and Jake,' said Levy.

Fischer's face was impassive but his voice was harsh and touched with suppressed anger. 'It's up to Jake.'

Malik shook his head. 'We're going to need your help, Heinz. I'll want you riding with every load. We could be stopped by the transport police. But we can keep you away from Rechmann. He doesn't ever need to know that you were involved.'

Levy looked directly at Fischer. 'How about you check on Meyer for ten minutes or so and let Jake and me have a chat?'

Fischer's face was flushed with anger as he turned to look at Malik. 'Is that what you want?'

Malik nodded. 'Maybe. Ten minutes will be long enough.'

As the heavy door slammed to behind Fischer, Malik said, 'You seem to go out of your way to antagonize him, David. He's part of the operation. He's entitled to be in on our discussions.'

'He's not, Jake. Your operation is over. We're in a different ball-game now and the less he knows the better.'

'Why?'

'He's a German, for God's sake. I wouldn't trust any German as far as I could chuck one of Rechmann's pianos. What he doesn't know he can't talk about.'

'But his country is just as much involved as yours.'

'That's rubbish, Jake. The West Germans are vulnerable to the Soviets but they're not surrounded by fanatical enemies. France and Holland and Austria aren't just waiting for the moment when they can slaughter every German. Even the bloody Russians are more interested in territory than killing Germans.' He banged his fist on the table. 'The Arabs don't just want territory and you know it. They want to kill the lot of us. I don't want to let the bastards have even the slightest excuse. And I don't want Israel left without a friend in the world because a stupid oaf like Meyer fancies playing God. He may be a Jew and an Israeli, but for me he's an enemy, whatever his motives were. All I care about is putting the clock back so that it can be as if this crazy dream of Meyer's had never happened.'

'Antagonizing Fischer won't help do that.'

Levy sighed. 'Maybe you're right, but I want you to know how I stand on all this.'

'OK, David, but don't rock the boat. Until this is all cleared up I'm still in charge.'

Malik was well aware that Levy's shrug cancelled out his nod and that he had only reluctantly gone along with his attitude.

Fischer had not come back after half an hour and Malik had found him playing chess with Meyer and ostentatiously more interested in the game than in joining him and Levy.

When the three of them were round the table again Malik reckoned it was time to make it clear that he was in charge.

'We'll do the site at Hildesheim first. Then Goslar.' He looked at Levy. 'Do you think we could risk doing two at the same time?'

Levy shook his head. 'No. It's too risky. We need to be in and out of each site as quickly as possible.'

'OK. After Goslar, Cologne; and then we come up to Hamburg.'

Fischer said, 'Where are we going to store the first three while we are getting the last two?'

'We can rent warehouse space at the docks.'

Fischer shook his head. 'No way. There are regular checks of all cargo left in store, by the dock police and the Kripo anti-terrorist squads.'

Malik half-smiled at Fischer's proof of them needing him.

'Where do you suggest?'

'Hire warehouse space outside the city. A furniture depository or maybe an outbuilding on a farm. There are plenty of empty barns at this time of the year before they get the harvest in. We aren't even concerned with protection against the weather. We can just tarpaulin them.'

Levy nodded. 'Could you recce a place for us, Heinz?'

'Yes. How soon and for how long, and what cover story? What do we say is in them?'

Malik shrugged. 'Just heavy machinery. Printing machinery would do fine.' He turned to look at Levy. 'What sort of people have you got in your team?'

'Two carpenters. Two electronics experts. A welder. Four precision engineering experts. An armourer. And the rest are just strong lads.'

'How many altogether?'

'Twenty-two. And one girl. A radio expert. I've borrowed four sets from our people in . . .' Both Malik and Fischer noticed the hiatus. '. . . our people who are over here for other reasons.'

Malik smiled. 'OK. Heinz, you get moving on storage, and maybe before that you could hire the transporters and the hoists.' Malik turned to Levy. 'Have your men got licences to drive articulateds and operate hoists?'

Levy nodded. 'German documents. Current, and almost genuine.'

Malik turned to Fischer. 'How long will it take you, Heinz?'

'The rest of today. Maybe tomorrow. Depends on what luck I have.'

'I want you to go over all our documents before we start. Check that we've got everything we need, and that it's in order.'

Fischer stood up, nodded to the other two and left them.

They started just after midnight and were on the autobahn in less than half an hour. Levy was in the white Mercedes convertible with two of his men, behind the BMW driven by Fischer with Meyer, Malik and the Israeli signals girl as passengers. Next came the two long mobile homes, and they were followed by the two yellow articulated transporters and finally the two mobile hoists, lagging well behind because of their speed restrictions.

They pulled into the lay-by just before Fallingbostel to wait for the hoists to catch up. By the time they were at the northern outskirts of Hanover the dawn clouds were lifting and there was a pale hint of sun on the horizon. There was a heat mist rising from the fields as they turned off the autobahn for Hildesheim, and when they pulled into the lay-by just outside the town the sun was hot on Malik's back as he stood beside the road drinking coffee from one of the big flasks. Levy and Fischer were with him and Meyer stood alone a few yards away. As Malik tossed away the last drops of coffee from the enamelled mug he beckoned to Meyer who hurried over.

'You're quite sure that he'll be there, Meyer?'

'Quite sure. I told him it was vitally important.'

'Where are we meeting him?'

'At the brickworks.'

'What time?'

'I told him to be there at eight o'clock.'

'Alone?'

'Yes. The workpeople are not there on Saturdays. Just a watchman and a dog. Herr Hoffman will have dismissed him for the day.'

'You remember what you tell him?'

'Yes. I understand. I shan't give any explanation.'

'And you make clear to him that if he talks to anyone his life is in danger.'

'He won't talk, I assure you. None of them will. They trust me.' He looked with his pale blue eyes at Malik's face. 'Even when I am betraying them they trust me.'

Malik opened his mouth to reply but decided to stay silent. They drove through Hildesheim and took the road to Bad Salzdetfurth, but after two kilometres they turned into a side road and the BMW left the main convoy and went on for another two kilometres. And then they saw the buildings, and the big sign that said: *Siegelei und Baustoff Werke Hoffman.*

Malik got out with Meyer and they walked across the dusty area in front of the big double gates. As they approached the long brick building a door opened and a small man came out. His head almost completely bald but held stiffly erect. He wore a formal black suit, and despite the heat of the day, a waistcoat with a gold chain looped across its front.

He held out his hand to Meyer. 'Good to see you, Amos. You've brought a fine day with you. Let's go inside.'

Hoffman glanced at Malik then turned and led them into a narrow corridor. There was a small office at the far end and when they were all inside Meyer wasted no time.

'I've had to alter our plans, Johann. I've brought my people to remove our . . . our weapon.'

Hoffman frowned. 'But why, Amos, why?'

'It's only a temporary move, my friend. I can't say more at the moment.'

Hoffman half turned, shoving some papers aside on his desk before he sat on it. He pulled out a handkerchief and wiped the sweat from his brow.

'I don't understand, Amos. The calculations, the fine adjustments . . . all wasted. Are you sure it's necessary?'

'Quite sure. We can't waste time, my friend. My companion here is responsible for the removal operation. Take us over to the site.'

Hoffman shrugged submissively and raised himself from the desk. 'I'll open the gates and we can go in your car.'

'Open them both, Johann, so that the other vehicles can come inside.'

When both the big gates had been pushed aside Malik told Fischer to walk back to the convoy, get them inside the plant and close the gates.

Malik drove the BMW. Past row on row of circular kilns and tall chimneys. Hoffman gave him new directions from time to time until they were almost a kilometre from the entrance. They came to a fence of tall wooden posts with barbed wire laced between them. Long, close horizontal strands carefully criss-crossed up to a wide metal gate.

Hoffman got out and they watched as he unlocked a series of locks and bolts, struggling to open the heavy gate. A notice said simply: *Forschungs Zone – Eintritt Verboten.*

As they walked inside Malik could hear the rumble of the convoy in the distance. A hundred metres or so from the metal gates were three low structures. Too low for a man to enter. They followed Hoffman to the furthest of the three and then Malik saw the metal steps leading down into the ground.

The locks on the steel door were not elaborate, just two long metal bars with hasps and padlocks. As he walked down the steps and through the open door Malik felt the cool draught from an air-conditioner and then Hoffman switched on the fluorescent lights.

It was an almost incredible sight. The long, comparatively narrow underground room. Tiled like a hospital operating theatre. Dustless, stark and silent, except for the faint beat of an electric motor. And the missile itself looked no more elaborate or dangerous than some giant cigar as it lay cradled in the launcher.

The casing of the missile was olive-green except for the final stage at its tip which was matt black. At its base were the three funnelled exhausts all set at the same angle, but slightly splayed; their metal shrouds looked like untreated gun-metal. The launching cradle went from a large tripod-like front structure to a channel just wide enough to hold the last stage of the rocket. Behind was a huge pit, whose outer face seemed to be clad with baked clay or firebrick, and on a metal trolley linked with heavy cables was a panel of instruments, with a red-figured digital display, its last two digits moving so fast that they were almost unreadable. And two raised buttons. One white and one red.

Then David Levy and two of his men in white overalls clambered down into the chamber. Levy tried to hide his reaction but it wasn't easy. The rocket had a kind of beauty. In its shape, in its size and its inevitability. It was hard to actually encompass its destructive power.

Meyer took Levy and his two men to the control panel and they stood there talking, nodding and pointing until eventually Levy turned and nodded to Malik who walked out of the emplacement back to the BMW and poured himself another coffee. As he stood there, mug in hand, he looked across the flat landscape of the brick-field. It stretched out on every side as far as the eye could see. Still and silent, small wisps of blue-grey smoke winding from the cones of the drying-kilns to be quickly lost in the hazy blue of the summer sky.

It was like the landscape on another planet, a setting for some science-fiction film. And in that vault-like underground emplacement, that smooth surrealist tube, so beautifully made, so precisely engineered. The piece of weaponry they called an SS-14. He had seen the designation in reports and evaluations, and had read details of its destructive power; but weaponry and war were not part of his service life. But there was something especially horrific about a nuclear missile and he wondered if that was the reason that NATO always gave them those jolly code names that they normally gave to Soviet nuclear weapons. Names like Scapegoat, Scamp; Scarp and Scrooge; Sand and Frog. Surface-to-surface nuclear missile number 14. Just two letters and a number, in a combination that made even the missile experts lower their voices. It was like a rare stamp whose reproduction every philatelist knew by heart but had never seen. A Shakespeare Folio, too precious in its air-conditioned vault to be seen by others than its guardian. And all you had to do was press the white button and the red button at the same time. And minutes later, in this particular case, the city of Kiev would shudder for a micro-second in silence before one glowing mushroom cloud grew out of another, again and again as the molecules of half a million human bodies mingled with the molecules of the Cinerama on Rustaveli Ulitsa and Yaroslav the Wise's Golden Gate.

It was an hour before Levy came out, and as he stood with Malik, smoking a cigarette, he seemed full of confidence.

'We've got all the electrical connections unhooked and they're dismantling the guidance system and that's the whole damn thing disarmed.' He turned to look back at the equipment. 'We're going to have to take the roof off. It won't be too bad here but it's going to mean hiring a digger for the others if there's ten foot of earth on top.'

'How long will it take to finish this one?'

Levy looked at his watch. 'We'll have it out in three hours, maybe four. But my carpenters will need at least five hours to crate it.'

'Would it help to dismantle one of the stages?'

'Yes. But we don't know enough to risk it. Meyer destroyed the drawings that were made and the circuit diagrams. I'd rather take it as it is.'

'Is there anything I can do to help?'

Levy smiled. 'Yes. Look like you think I know what I'm doing . . . but say a little prayer as well.'

As Levy walked over to his men Malik knew that although the Israeli was no diplomat he was as much on top of the removal operation as any layman could be.

He turned the car so that he could sit and watch Levy's men hacking at the roof and sides of the emplacement. Despite their overalls they still looked like soldiers, and Malik wondered how Levy could lay his hands on so many men at such short notice. But that was typically Mossad. SIS would have needed God knows how many committee meetings to get a couple of men let alone a couple of dozen.

There had been no break for a meal. Fischer had driven to Hildesheim and come back with the big coffee flasks refilled and boxes of sandwiches. The men ate as they worked.

The shadows were long when Levy walked over to the car and bent down to talk to Malik.

'We're practically finished, Jake, but I don't want to take the last layer off while it's still light. There are too many planes going over. The crates are ready except for fitting up so I'm going to stand my boys down for a couple of hours sleep. Then we can work through the night at Goslar if it looks like being necessary. OK?'

'That's fine, David. They're a good team.'

Levy smiled. 'These guys have just come back from putting a tunnel under the Nile. Half-way across.'

'What's it for?'

'An electronic listening post. We can even pick up the sound of a rubber dinghy on the far side. Even a swimmer. I'd better go and stand them down.'

Before the team was stood down the two mobile hoists had been manoeuvred into place alongside the emplacement, and alongside them was one of the transporters with the framework of the crate already in place.

Meyer came back to sit in the car with Malik. Subdued and unhappy as he saw his handiwork reduced almost to rubble. Ten minutes later the older man was asleep, his head back on the seat of the car, his hand supporting his cheek, the tattoo scar clearly visible, the skin puckered like a deflated child's balloon. Despite the tan his face looked older than his actual years, and it reminded Malik of his father's face when he was dying. All hope gone, all courage gone, the open, wet-lipped mouth, the hollow cheeks and the ragged breathing. He shuddered at the memory and got quickly out of the car.

It was after midnight when they were finished and Malik decided that it was better to leave the loaded transporter inside the locked gates of the brickfield rather than take it on to Goslar. A driver was left with it and one of the radios. The rest of the convoy headed for Goslar, just over 50 kilometres to the south-east of Hildesheim.

Malik stopped the convoy ten kilometres before Goslar and checked the map with Meyer. A string of heavy vehicles rumbling through the mediaeval town in the early hours of a Sunday morning would fetch out half the population to check that it wasn't the East Germans coming over the border. But there was no way of avoiding the town completely. They took the outer road and went through two at a time at ten-minute intervals and turned up the steep road to Ramseck.

The gate in the stone wall was already wide open but although it was wide Malik guessed that the bigger vehicles would find it difficult to turn in because the road was too narrow to allow a wide turn to the gate.

Gerichtspräsident Gustav Lemke owned an 800-acre estate on the stark mountainside. Farmers had long ago given up trying to eke out a living with sheep on the craggy outcrops of granite with its thin bracken-covered top-soil. But its woods and streams could support roe deer and rabbits and a host of game birds which enabled the judge to indulge in his favourite sport, and to glean a regular addition to his State pension by letting the estate to a sporting syndicate for half the year. The big house that had once been the owner's home stood gaunt, its empty windows sprouting willow-herb, its walls half collapsed, covered in lichen and mosses. The retired judge lived in the stone-built lodge just inside the gate.

At three in the morning the old man was sleeping soundly and the convoy passed the lodge without waking him. It was seven-thirty before Malik and Meyer saw the closed curtains pulled aside as the judge looked down, surprised, at the BMW parked in his drive.

As he stood at the open door in his dressing-gown Malik was aware of the man's inherent dignity. He was tall and thin, his feet in sandals and for a moment he didn't seem to recognize Amos Meyer.

'Amos, my boy, what brings you here?'

'Can I come inside, Gustav, with my friend?'

'Of course. Come along in.'

They followed him into a pleasant room. Flowers in brass vases, chintz-covered armchairs and a cat asleep on the windowsill.

'Shall I make us all some coffee, Amos? Or do you want to talk first?'

'I've come to remove the . . . apparatus, Gustav. There is a problem. It will have to be postponed.'

'What kind of problem could make that necessary, Amos?'

'I don't feel it would be wise to explain. I just wanted to let you know.'

Lemke pointed a long finger at Malik.

'Who is this? Is he your problem?'

'His name is Jacob. No, he's not the problem. He is a friend.'

'But how on earth can you remove our little thing. It would take dozens of men. And machinery.'

'We have that, Gustav. I've sent them up to the old house. We've been here for some time. I've told them what to do. They will have already started work.'

'So much effort, so much money, all gone to waste, my old friend?'

'Let's leave it, Gustav. I want you to forget all about it, as if it never happened.'

The old man leaned back in his chair. 'It seems a long time ago when you first came to see me. All those long talks and subtle questions to test me out. And then our meetings. You and the others. Seven men for peace. To prevent another holocaust. What will prevent it now?'

Malik said softly. 'The weapons, all of them, *are* the holocaust, Judge. The new holocaust. First the millions of Jews were killed. Coldly, economically by the standards of the day. Some buildings, a bit of barbed wire, a few sub-machine guns and just a little Zyclon B gas. Only three minutes of gas because prussic acid crystals are expensive. And those who aren't dead in three minutes will be dead in ten.

'And now we have nuclear weapons. They have no point except to kill hundreds of thousands of people in a second or two. If that wasn't their only purpose they might just as well be filled with ice cream. They are not even weapons of war. They won't kill soldiers. They can only be used to kill innocent people, civilians. In their beds, sleeping or making love, shopping, playing music, playing with children. People are the targets, not tanks and guns. The only difference this time is that they won't only be Jews.'

The old man pursed his lips, looking down at his gnarled bony hands as he held them together, then he looked at Malik.

'I'm afraid I've forgotten your name.'

'Jacob. Jake.'

'I gather that you're a pacifist, Jake? Anti-war?'

Malik smiled. 'Even Brezhnev is anti-war. No, I'm not a pacifist. Just a war-preventer if it's possible.'

The old man's hand slapped his bony knee.

'Exactly. That's exactly what we were too. Preventers. Not aggressors.'

Malik shook his head slowly. 'I want you to forget all about it, Judge. Your friends' lives could be in danger.'

'You mean that seriously?'

'Indeed I do.'

Lemke sighed and looked at Meyer. 'Let me get us some coffee.'

Half an hour later Malik and Meyer were standing with Levy and Fischer. Great mounds of earth rose up the stone sides of the building and a dozen men were smashing concrete with huge sledgehammers.

Levy wiped the sweat from his eyes. 'We could have done with pneumatic drills but it's going to be easier than the first one. We disarmed it in twenty minutes and it suddenly dawned on me that after that we don't need to give it cotton-wool treatment. We'll have it uncovered and out in a couple of hours. But I think my guys are gonna need a day's rest before we tackle the next one.'

'We'll all go back to Hamburg. Store the two crates and leave one of your men to keep an eye on them. Then Heinz and Meyer and I will go down to Cologne and get things ready.'

'They can take my electronics guys and the armourer. They can disarm it, and then all we'll have to do is get the bastard out.' Levy looked at Meyer. 'What's the construction in Cologne, Meyer?'

'The same as here. Earth over concrete. It's the same in Hamburg.'

'Great. We know what we're doing now. If we had to preserve them it would have taken at least three days apiece.'

But Levy had been over-optimistic. It was eleven o'clock that night before the crate was on the transporter. The weight of one of the hoists under load had caused it to break through the foundations of the derelict house so that its rear wheels were wedged into a cellar in the basement. It had taken careful manoeuvring with the second transporter to tow it out without collapsing the hoist completely.

Fischer had driven down to Goslar for extra food but the best he had been able to do on a Sunday was cartons of cold cooked sausages and two dozen loaves of bread with two kilos of butter. But there had been no complaints from the hungry men.

They had to back all the vehicles down the steep path as there was no room for even the cars to turn, and it had taken two hours before they were heading back to Hildesheim and the autobahn.

Fischer had gone with Levy to guide them to the warehouse he had rented for them just outside Hamburg at Lohbrügge.

It was dawn when they arrived but the sky was overcast and as Fischer took the padlocks off the high wooden doors it was beginning to drizzle. The ramshackle building had lain empty for two years but it was high enough and big enough to take all the vehicles. Levy had insisted that the crates were unloaded before they left for the city centre. He was sending his men to a hotel to make sure they were properly rested for the longer journey down to Cologne. Fischer, Meyer and Malik were flying down on the early plane.

Fischer had taken a taxi home and Malik had taken a bus to the city centre and walked to the flat with Amos Meyer. Meyer was no problem now, he wouldn't do anything stupid, and he needed all the sleep he could get. He looked exhausted and near the end of his tether.

CHAPTER EIGHTEEN

Malik had sat with Meyer as he phoned Rechmann's home but was told that he was already at the works. An hour later they drove into the works and the doorkeeper pointed to the visitors' parking spaces. Malik parked alongside a big black Mercedes that he guessed was Rechmann's.

The receptionist phoned through Meyer's name to Rechmann's secretary and almost immediately Rechmann himself came into the reception area. The smile fading from his face as he saw that Meyer was not alone. But his outstretched hand was too far committed to withdraw.

'Well this is a surprise, Herr Meyer.' Rechmann turned to look at Malik. 'Franz Rechmann, glad to meet you.'

'This is my friend Jacob, Franz. Could you spare us a little of your time?'

'Certainly. Let's go into the boardroom – or would you prefer my office?'

'I think your office, Franz.'

As they walked down the corridor Rechmann glanced at Malik. 'You know, I'm sure I've met you before. Are you musical at all?'

'I'm afraid not.'

'You live in Cologne?'

'No. I spend most of my time overseas.'

'Ah well. It's a small world,' he said briskly. 'And getting smaller every day.'

Malik remembered what Lisa had once said about Rechmann. That despite the fact that he had made a fortune from making pianos he couldn't tell Tchaikowsky from Delibes unless it was printed in the programme, and that she and her friends sometimes had small bets on how many clichés he would use in an hour.

Rechmann's office was modern and well-furnished, Swedish style, and he sat down briskly at his desk pointing to the two green leather chairs in front of him.

'Now, Amos. What can I do for you?'

'I need to go to your estate, Franz. It may take a couple of days, starting tomorrow. Can you keep your people away for that time?'

Rechmann leaned back in his chair. The astonished businessman, thought Malik. The negotiator doing his stuff. Shocked at the suggestion of an extra discount. He looked as though he had done it a hundred times before. He glanced briefly at Malik and then back at Meyer.

'I've misunderstood, Amos. Obviously I've misunderstood.'

'No, Franz. You haven't.'

'Isn't this something you and I should discuss in private?'

'I'm afraid there's nothing to discuss. The decision has been taken. I can't delay.'

'Has it been . . .' He looked at Malik. He smiled a businessman's smile. Mouth but not eyes. 'I wonder if I could ask you to step outside for a couple of minutes while two old friends have a chat?'

'I'm afraid not, Herr Rechmann. Herr Meyer is acting under my orders.'

Rechmann leaned forward his elbows on his desk with overtly feigned deference.

'Tell me more. Who *are* you, for instance?'

'You don't need to know who I am, Herr Rechmann, and this is not a business negotiation, it's a matter of life and death. It could be *your* death if you waste time.'

Rechmann shifted the leather blotter to one side, trying not to look concerned about the threat. Malik could see that he was concerned all right. But he'd got the problem of how to back down and not lose face.

Malik said softly, 'Herr Meyer assured me that you were entirely reliable, Herr Rechmann, and entirely loyal to your friends. They have cooperated with him without question. He is relying on you for all the assistance he needs.'

Rechmann stared back at Malik, his fingers drumming on the blotter. His head nodding as if he were digesting and agreeing with Malik's comments. Finally he turned to Meyer.

'Just tell me how I can help, Amos. I'm at your disposal.'

'I need the combination, Franz, and nobody in that area for tomorrow and the next day.'

Rechmann smiled benignly. 'It's a letter combination-lock, my friend. A five-letter word dear to my heart.' He smiled. 'And to yours.'

Malik guessed what it was immediately. With a mind like Rechmann's it was obvious. But he sat silently. To say it would rob the actor of his punch-line.

Meyer shook his head. 'Tell me, Franz.'

'M-E-Y-E-R. A good Jewish name, eh?' He smacked his hand on his desk, beaming. Then he stood up and walked round his desk, putting an arm round Meyer's shoulders. 'And as from six o'clock this evening the whole area will be clear of staff. For two whole days. How's that?'

'Thank you, Franz. That's fine.'

Rechmann walked with them back to reception. The businessman once more. An awkward negotiation successfully concluded. Nothing given away that didn't have to be given, and now back to the grindstone. Or words to that effect, thought Malik.

They went out to Wahn in the afternoon to pick up Levy's three men, and hired them a car at the airport. Meyer was going with them out to Rechmann's place at seven and Levy would book them into the Dom.

Malik phoned Lisa and Heinz answered the phone. He said that Lisa was not at home. Almost peremptorily he had suggested that Malik phone the music school. He hadn't bothered to give Malik the number and had hung up before he could ask.

He eventually contacted her at the school and arranged to pick her up at six o'clock when her classes finished.

'Why didn't you want to see me at home, Jake?'

'No particular reason, I just wanted to be on our own.'

And her heart sank because she knew instinctively that for the first time since she had known him he had told her a half-truth or maybe a lie. Suddenly she was an outsider, kept out of his private thoughts.

'How's your work going?'

'What made you ask that?'

She smiled. 'Mainly because I wondered how long it would be before we are married.'

'You said "mainly". What was the other reason?'

She reached out and picked a daisy, looking at it before she looked back at Malik.

'Heinz seems terribly on edge since you both got back. I asked him how you were and he just snapped my head off and told me to ask you myself. I asked him if anything was wrong between you two and he said something odd.'

'What did he say?'

'He said, "Jake's treating me as a German; maybe he'll do the same to you one day."'

Malik sighed and was silent for a moment, then he said, 'It isn't that, Lisa. It's just that I'm in charge of this particular operation and Heinz doesn't like some of my decisions. I think he resents that it's got to a stage when I have to give orders and he has to carry them out whether he agrees or not.'

'It's not like Heinz.'

'It will be over soon; meantime he'll just have to put up with it like the rest of us.'

'Even you sound cross with me, Jake.'

He smiled. 'I'm sorry, sweetie. I don't mean to. I was looking forward to seeing you.'

'Let's forget about Heinz and his problems and enjoy the nice evening.'

'Tell me what you've been doing.'

'Practising, giving some lessons. We had a musical evening you would have liked. Brahms and Schubert. We went over to the Rechmann's one evening to hear his new hi-fi.'

Malik looked away. 'What's he like . . . Rechmann?'

'I like him. He's a bit stiff. Very much the gentleman. He ought to have lived in the Weimar Republic. I don't think he likes the modern world too much.'

'What's his family like?'

'His wife's very different. A great charmer. She sings very well – musical comedy stuff. She's old-fashioned too in a different sort of way. Mildly flirtatious and she must have been terribly pretty when they married.'

'Children?'

'Two daughters. One married and very happy. And one unmarried and very happy. Daddy's girl.' She laughed. 'No. That's a bit unfair. She just gets more attention because she's still at home. They were both very good parents. Kind, and sensibly indulgent. You must meet them.'

'What would you have done if you hadn't met me?'

'How do you mean? I don't understand.'

'What kind of man would you have married? What would you have done with your life?'

She sat in silence, one slim finger probing at the buckle on her shoe.

'I don't know, Jake. I didn't have any sort of plans. Life just went on. I guess things happened to me rather than me making them happen. Somebody might have come eventually whom I'd marry, but it wouldn't have been like with us.'

'What would be different?'

'Oh everything. He would have been somebody from the family's sort of background. Pleasant and routine would have been the best I could hope for.'

'And now?'

She smiled. 'My love, even you must know in your heart that you're one of a kind. You landed on me like an unexploded bomb that not only exploded but has kept on exploding. And I guess you'll go on being like that. It will take longer than we both live for me to peel all the onion skins off you and find what's really inside. When I first knew you that's what I wanted to do. But not any more. I'm just happy to be with you however you are and whatever you do.'

'What would I have to do to stop you loving me?'

'There isn't anything. If you did something I would know that it had to be done.'

'If I say I love you more than I've ever loved anyone it's not much of a compliment because you know that I've never loved anyone even slightly, ever. Except for my father, and that was a poor sort of love when I look back on it.'

She reached out her hand for his. 'I feel so safe and secure with you, Jake. Even my father doesn't seem quite the same since you came along.'

Malik leaned back, resting his head on her shoulder.

'What shall I do for work when we're married?'

'Won't you carry on with your police job?'

Malik turned up his face to look at Lisa. 'I'm not a policeman, Lisa. I'm an Intelligence officer. I work for MI6. I wouldn't be able to stay on.'

'Why not?' She said softly.

'If we're going to live in Israel there's no chance of me getting a posting there. They wouldn't say so but they wouldn't trust a Jew doing their work in Israel. And if MI6 people marry foreigners there's always a suspicion about them. Put those two factors together and I might as well resign. I'd get a bit more than half-pension so we wouldn't starve.'

'How would you feel about giving up your work?'

He smiled up at her. 'Perfectly happy provided I had you.'

She kissed him gently on the forehead, one hand touching his cheek.

'What would you like to do in Israel?'

'I've no idea. I've no qualifications.'

'You could teach violin, you could teach English.'

'I'm not a musician, honey. I can play the fiddle but it's by ear not from music and I've no teaching qualifications for either music or English. Let's not worry about it. I'll get something.'

'When do you think we shall be able to get married?'

'I'd guess in a month. Six weeks at the outside.'

'Will I be able to see you tomorrow?'

'I don't think so, I think I may have to go back to Hamburg. Wherever I am I'll phone you as often as I can. Let's go and eat somewhere, it's getting late.'

When they were driving back towards the city she put her hand on his leg. 'Heinz told me you'd had one of your nightmares again. Was it because of your work?'

'I guess so. It's hard to say.'

'I love you, Jake. I love you so much.'

He smiled. 'I love you too, sweetie.'

David Levy had had a brainwave and hired a 35-mm film camera, an Arriflex with a lighting set-up, and when the convoy rolled through the gates at Rechmann's estate and up to the site at the edge of the woods they had some semblance of a film unit on location. It also gave them an excuse for using lights if they needed to work in the dark.

Rechmann himself drove up to the site to watch. He didn't stay long and he didn't speak to any of them, not even Meyer. He just watched, his face disapproving, his hands in his pockets as he rocked gently on his heels as the mounds of rich soil built up around the pit. He shook his head slowly as he walked back to his car. A sane man witnessing lunatics at their work, vandals destroying a work of art.

Levy was standing with Malik as Rechmann watched the work going on, and when Rechmann went back to his car Levy said, 'How have these birds been taking it, Jake?'

Malik shrugged. 'Mild protests but not for long. Meyer was obviously the organizer. They were willing collaborators but I'd guess that now the chips are down they're glad to be out of it. They're not young and they've got other things to put their minds to.'

'How did Rechmann behave?'

'He was the toughest so far. Not really tough. Just self-important and faintly bloody-minded.' Malik smiled. 'Nothing to worry about. He took maybe ten minutes where the others took five.'

'Do you think they'll talk?'

'God knows. That's the thing that worries me. It's why I want the bloody things out of the way quickly. A hole in the ground doesn't prove anything and we could deny the whole thing. Anyway there's no reason for them to talk. They've nothing to gain.'

'I wouldn't trust Rechmann, he looks a tricky bastard.'

'How long will you need here, David?'

'I'd say we could be gone soon after lunch. We know what we're doing now so it's much easier. And it's good loam here, none of those bloody rocks. Do you want us to go straight back to Hamburg?'

'Yes. The sooner the better.'

Levy smiled. 'You're getting edgy, my boy.'

Malik shrugged. 'No wonder. If something went wrong now it would be worse than if we had just left the damn things under the ground. Nobody outside would have known anything about them. But if we were exposed right now I can't bear to think of the shambles there'd be.'

'Don't worry. Another two or three days and we'll be done.'

CHAPTER NINETEEN

They set off for Hamburg just on midnight and drove for five hours with only two short breaks. They were just over half way but it was obvious that the pace was beginning to tell even on Levy's tough men, and they decided to rest until they could drive in daylight. It was late the next morning when they pulled up outside the warehouse at Lohbrügge.

Malik went with David Levy to look over the ship in the afternoon. She was moored down-river at Schulau, a drab-looking vessel with her name painted in white on her heavy bows – *Maresha.* The birthplace of the prophet Micah.

She was riding high in the water, tugging sporadically at her warps around the bollards on the quayside. A ladder with several missing rungs was the only access, and it shifted uncertainly as the ship rose and fell from the wash of passing boats.

Levy stood looking up, his hands on his hips, but there was nobody in sight. He cupped his hands and shouted.

'*Shalom!*'

A few minutes later a figure appeared. A heavily bearded man who rested his elbows on the ship's side and looked down at them.

Levy shouted again. '*Shalom, Maresha!*'

The man smiled and waved, then pointed to the ladder, and they made their way cautiously and awkwardly up the precarious structure. The man was the captain, a Jewish Arab from Joppa and he took them to the small saloon behind the wheelhouse.

The sat around the small mahogany table and Levy talked to the sailor. He could speak only a bastard mixture of Hebrew and Arabic so Malik had to sit in silence as they talked. There was much nodding of heads, and once or twice the Arab pointed through the saloon window towards the city. Finally he got three glasses and poured them each a large measure of *arak*. The captain grinned as he held up his glass, saying, '*l'chayeem.*'

After they had clambered down the rickety ladder to the quayside, Levy turned and waved to the captain before they walked to the car.

'What was all that, David?'

'We were just going over the loading procedures. When we give him the word he'll move up-river and tie up so that we can use the big quayside hoists, and he says we can have everything loaded inside a couple of hours.'

'What about when we're dumping them?'

'It'll have to be one at a time – his deck cranes aren't built to take more than twelve tons, and by now he reckons that even a crate of ten tons might be pushing them hard.'

'What's he getting out of it?'

'We'll find him his next half-dozen cargoes and he'll get paid the normal rate.'

'Is that enough?'

Levy smiled. 'More than enough, Jake. He's an Israeli. He was skipper of one of the small boats that ran the British blockade to get immigrants into Palestine before the mandate ended. When he's asked by Mossad to help he's proud to be asked.'

'It would save time if we loaded the crates in the warehouse onto the boat now, and then we could bring the transporters with the last two crates direct to the docks.'

Levy stopped walking. 'Why not? Let me go back and tell him. He can move-up river right now. Wait for me in the car.'

Malik watched as Levy hurried back to the boat, breaking into a trot in his eagerness to get things moving. Typical Israeli. Totally involved and totally committed. No fears, no doubts.

With two weapons to remove, the visit to von Busch was inevitably going to take longer, and Meyer had hinted that von Busch might be more resistant than the others.

Malik had gone with Levy to see the first three crates loaded onto the *Maresha*. The ease and speed of the loading had been almost incredible. The chain slings were hooked up and five minutes later the crate had disappeared into the hold. The whole operation took just under twenty minutes. It made their previous laborious efforts seem crude and amateurish. And the big wooden crates swinging in the air no longer held any menace, they were just crates, part of a ship's cargo. Malik, watching them being lowered into the hold, felt for the first time that the disjointed operation was beginning to come under control. He and Levy had taken time off on the way back to the hotel to have a coffee together in a restaurant by the Alster. Levy looked once more like the smiling, amiable man that he had met at Morris's house.

'Have you contacted your family, David?'

'No. I never do when I'm away. It's best that nobody knows where I am. They understand. Well my wife does, and the kids are used to me appearing and disappearing like the Cheshire Cat. What about your girlfriend?'

'I saw her when we were in Cologne.'

'Do you miss her?'

'Yes. Too much.'

Levy smiled. 'Like Kipling said: "Down to Gehenna or up to the Throne, he travels the fastest who travels alone."'

Malik laughed softly. 'It depends where you're going.'

'When's the big day?'

'As soon as this lot's over and finished.' For a moment Malik hesitated. 'We're definitely going to live in Israel when we're married.'

'My God. Why are we drinking coffee? Let's have a real drink to celebrate.'

'Let's wait until it happens.' But Malik was smiling.

'Have your people agreed to a posting to Tel Aviv?'

'No. There's no point in asking.'

'Why not?'

Malik smiled. 'I'm a Jew, David. They wouldn't trust me.'

For a moment Levy glanced away, his fingers screwing up the paper from his sugar cube, then he looked back at Malik.

'My people would take you and be delighted at the chance.'

'I'm grateful for the thought, but I think I've had enough of this game.'

'Rubbish, you're just exhausted by this bloody shambles. I've seen your record on our files. You're just what we need. Experienced and capable. You're ideal for Mossad.'

Malik shook his head slowly. 'No. I've genuinely had enough. If I'd not met Lisa I'd have just gone on. There was nothing better to do. In an odd kind of way it was a natural progression from Auschwitz.' Malik smiled wryly. 'It sounds odd, but it's true. In Israel, with Lisa, I knew I'd escaped. From Auschwitz and all the seamy side of my life. I felt totally different. Like an animal let out of a cage. I can't wait to get there, and Lisa is the one who made it possible.'

'She must be quite a gal.'

Malik smiled. 'She's much younger than me. She's almost more Jewish than me, despite the fact that she's one hundred per cent *shiksa*. She's beautiful and gentle, and she loves me. Without her I might as well have died in that bloody camp.'

'When you come over, Jake, contact me in the first hour. I know lots of people who can help you both. Nothing to do with Mossad. Just ordinary people, but influential people. They'll see you get the breaks.'

'Thanks, David. We'd better go.'

An agitated Heinz Fischer was waiting for them in the foyer of the hotel. He sprang up from his chair as soon as he saw them.

'We've got a problem, Jake. I thought you'd better know before you saw Meyer.'

'Go on. What is it?'

Fischer sighed. 'It's probably my fault. I thought it might save time if Meyer phoned von Busch to check that he would be at his place tonight and tomorrow. When Meyer phoned, von Busch told him that he wouldn't cooperate. He wouldn't agree to the removal.'

'When was this?'

'About ten minutes ago.'

'Why did Meyer tell him on the phone what it was about?'

'He didn't, Jake. Rechmann had already phoned von Busch and talked to him. Warning him what was happening.'

'The bastard,' Levy said softly.

Malik stood there thinking for a moment. Then he looked at Fischer.

'Get Meyer down here. I'll bring the car round.'

Malik stopped the car after twenty-five kilometres and turned to look at Meyer in the back.

'You'd better give us some background on von Busch.'

Meyer shrugged his shoulders. 'He's Baron Theodore von Busch. Sixty-two years old. Widower. No children. Very rich and very influential.'

'Where does the money come from?'

'It was always a very wealthy family. He has substantial shares in many companies. Not just in Germany, but in the United States, France and England. And South America too.'

'What sort of place has he got?'

'It's about five hundred hectares. More than half is forest. A big timber mill and a small furniture-making concern. Too near the East German border to spend much on development.'

'What's he done apart from making money?'

'He rides well. Was in the pre-war Olympics team. Skis. Was an officer in the Wehrmacht. Good record. Served in North Africa, Italy and on the Russian front. Was a colonel when the surrender came.'

'What sort of character?'

'Who knows? I would have said completely loyal before today. He is used to giving orders, of course, not taking them. Nobody's fool, I would say.'

'What sort of security has he got?'

'I don't know. Nothing more than a couple of servants apart from the estate workers of course. That's all, so far as I know. Security precautions draw attention.'

'And the site?'

'In a clearing in the forest.'

Malik started the car. 'When we get there, Meyer, I'll do the talking, but if he tried to appeal to you, you lay it on the line. He does what he's told or he's in real trouble. Understand?'

'Yes, Herr Malik.'

Lauenburg on the Elbe had once been the seat of an independent duchy but now it was little more than a pretty tourist centre on the river.

Malik followed Meyer's directions and turned off the main road where a signpost said *Haus Vierlande*. For a few kilometres the narrow road was flanked by orchards and fields of beans and peas, and then as the ground rose and levelled out, there on the right was a pair of high stone pillars, their large wrought-iron gates wide open. As they drove in Malik saw fleetingly the big armorial shield on one of the gates. He noticed a coronet and an eagle, and a pair of crossed swords.

The road wound slowly uphill until they saw the house. It was built on a spur of the hill, a background of firs and cypress washing down from the steep hill behind. The house was built in stone, and its proportions were timelessly perfect. The main door stood open, a black and gold German Shepherd lay beside the steps, unmoving, but its brown eyes watching them as they got out of the car. It stood up slowly, its head thrust out, as they approached the door, but it neither growled nor made any move towards them.

Malik pressed the bell-button beside one of the Palladian pillars alongside the door. They could see inside the large hall. Glistening wood floor, oil paintings on the wall and small display cabinets holding pieces of porcelain.

The man who walked towards them was obviously von Busch. Thick white hair brushed back from his forehead. Hard grey eyes and a thin wide mouth. Tall and elegant, he looked a typical Prussian aristocrat. As he reached the door he raised his eyebrows as he looked at Meyer.

'So, Herr Meyer. You've brought your entourage with you. I expected you despite our telephone conversation. You'd better all come in, gentlemen.'

He turned, and they followed him across the hall, down a small corridor where he opened a door and stood aside for them to go in. He moved towards half-a-dozen *bergère* armchairs set round a long, low, glass table.

'Sit down, gentlemen.'

And when they were seated he sat down himself, pulling at his trousers to avoid stretching the cloth at his knees. He leaned back comfortably in his high-backed chair.

'Let me tell you, Herr Meyer, that your visit is in vain. I told you so on the telephone, but maybe you are entitled to hear it to your face. I have no idea who your companions are but I gather from Rechmann that one of them is called Jacob.' He turned to look at Malik. 'I think from his description that that must be you, sir.'

Malik nodded. 'Herr Baron. None of us wishes to be discourteous but I have to make clear that asking your agreement was solely a courtesy.'

'On whose part may I ask?'

'Mine.'

'And who might you be, my friend?'

'That's not important, von Busch. It's for your benefit that you shouldn't know.'

'Von Busch, eh? We shall be on Christian name terms before long.'

Malik sighed with impatience. 'I'm afraid I haven't got time for the niceties, von Busch. You're in great danger of going to jail, or even losing your life.'

'It would not be the first time that I've been threatened, my friend. So let us put aside your threats.'

Malik leaned back in his chair his hands in his jacket pockets.

'Have you got a man who can pack a bag for you, von Busch?'

'Is that a gun in your right-hand pocket, Herr Jacob?'

'Yes.'

Von Busch smiled. 'D'you intend shooting me?'

Malik stood up and looked from Fischer to Meyer.

'Go outside, both of you.'

When they had left Malik was still standing. Levy was sprawled casually in his chair. Watching and alert, but not moving.

Malik walked slowly round the table and stood looking down at von Busch.

'Baron von Busch. I know that what you did was done with good intentions. I accept all that. But it's over now. It was anarchy and treason, not patriotism. Nobody official will ever know what was done or planned. I give you my word. All I ask is your cooperation.'

The pale, hollow-cheeked death's-head face looked up at Malik's face.

'Go to hell.'

Malik turned to look at David Levy, who nodded almost imperceptibly. Malik's hand grabbed the bush of white hair and forced von Busch's head back over the edge of the chair. He could see the tracery of red veins in the German's protruding eyes.

'Are you going to cooperate, von Busch?'

The German nodded as best he could and Malik withdrew his hand from the bush of hair. Slowly von Busch arranged himself back to a sitting position. His chest heaving to get back his breath, his hand trembling as he wiped the saliva from his thin lips.

Very softly he said, 'You would have made a splendid Nazi, my friend.'

Levy stood up slowly. 'You're a fool, von Busch. A dangerous fool.' He turned to Malik. 'I'll take the car and get my people, OK?'

'OK.'

'You hang on here with the other two.'

As Levy walked into the hall he beckoned to Fischer who hurried over.

'I'm going to get my team. You and Meyer stay here. Don't let von Busch out of your sight and don't let him near a phone.'

It was two hours later when Levy came back with his convoy and he picked up Meyer and von Busch, taking them up to the site in the woods. Malik followed in the car.

The clearing in the woods was strangely quiet despite the presence of the men.

The late sun touched the tops of the pine trees and left long shafts of light angled down between the trees. Woodpigeons cooed, and he heard the broken call of a late cuckoo. Even when the generator started up it sounded muffled in the cathedral-like enclosure in the woods.

The raised top of the emplacement had been turfed over, and already it supported small clusters of knapweed and ragwort with a sprinkling of daisies and purple saxifrage. Its surface sloped from back to front and a long swath had been cut in the woods facing the centre of the emplacement.

Malik stood on his own, watching Levy's team at work. There were two men he hadn't seen before, sitting in Levy's car. One was reading a newspaper, the other was asleep with his head back on the seat.

Half an hour later Levy came up out of the emplacement and walked over to his own car, tapped on the window and the two men got out. The three of them were talking as they walked over to Malik.

'Jake, meet a couple of friends of mine.' He pointed first to the taller man. 'Niko Bergman and Ben Goldberg. Meet Jake Malik. He's in charge here. My people are just doing the washing-up.'

Malik shook hands with both men but they didn't say anything. Levy turned to them. 'I'll join you later. Just keep watching.'

The two nodded briefly and walked back to Levy's car. Levy turned to look at Malik.

'What do you feel about von Busch?'

'He's a problem. And he'll be more of a problem when we leave.'

'And Rechmann?'

'I'm going to deal with Rechmann myself as soon as we've finished here.'

'How?'

Levy's eyes were intent on Malik's face.

'Don't ask, David, then it stays my problem alone and not yours as well.'

'Are you going to tell Fischer?'

'No. Rechmann's a friend of his family. It wouldn't be fair to saddle him with that.'

'He'll guess, of course.'

'Sure he will. But guessing ain't knowing. And guessing doesn't make you an accessory.'

'This is why I called up Bergman and his friend.'

'Tell me.'

'Let *them* deal with Rechmann and von Busch.'

'Why?'

'They've got resources and experience you haven't got. They've got time which you haven't got. They're not connected with the operation. Nobody's seen them, nobody knows them. It's safer, Jake.'

'What about the other two? The judge and the brick-field man?'

'I reckon they're safe enough. Especially when they hear what's happened to the other two. I'll send Bergman to let them know they're safe provided they don't talk.'

'I think I'd better do that.'

'Forget it, Jake. Twelve hours from now we'll have these two crates on the boat. My people will be on the first available plane to anywhere in Europe and you and I will be on that boat. After we've dumped the crates she'll take us back to Rotterdam or Copenhagen and that's it.'

'What about the missiles in Israel?'

'They'll be somewhere in the Med three days from now.'

'Why did you jump the gun? Why not leave it to me to decide?'

'If you're going to live in Israel I didn't want there to be any chance of you being connected with it. Israel's not Germany. It's a small country and you could be noticed and remembered if anything went wrong. There was only the one site, Jake, and you can shift sand quicker than earth and concrete.'

'They've actually been removed?'

'They're at sea right now.' He smiled. 'They'll be dropped off Gaddafi's coast the day after tomorrow. A present from Jerusalem to the gallant colonel.'

Malik half-smiled. 'What reasons did you give your people for all this?'

Levy shrugged and smiled. 'Mossad spends most of its time not letting the right hand know what the left hand doeth. We get crossed lines now and again. My job is to prevent that happening too often. The team I'm using here are from Section Three . . . *Modi'in*. The team in Israel are *Shin Beth*. I don't have a problem.' Levy paused. 'What are you telling your people?'

Malik looked away. 'Nothing. They weren't all that interested in synagogue-daubers and the like. It's not really our kind of job. We only got stuck with it because there might be a KGB connection. I'm going to leave the impression that it wasn't worth pursuing.'

'What about your Kraut?'

'Fischer?'

'Yes.'

'What about him?'

'Can you trust him?'

Malik smiled. 'He's going to be my brother-in-law.'

'He's still a Kraut.'

'He'll be no problem. Forget him.'

'OK. I hope you're right. I'll go and start Bergman on his way to Cologne.'

As Malik watched the convoy moving out of the clearing in the woods he looked back for a moment at Levy's car. Ben Goldberg sat at the wheel with von Busch sitting beside him. Goldberg flashed his headlights and Malik waved and got into the BMW. Fischer was in the passenger seat and Levy was sprawled on the back seat already asleep.

The caught up with the convoy well before Hamburg and where the E4 ended at Horn the two hoists headed north, back to the hire company. The mobile homes forked away a few minutes later, heading for the airport. The BMW followed behind the two transporters towards the docks.

The *Maresha* had had to move up two berths but the captain and two of his men were already on deck and they called out to the foreman of one of the gangs on the quayside as they saw the transporters manoeuvring alongside.

An hour later the crew were battening down the hatches. Fischer had handled clearance with Customs and the captain had gone to the harbour-master's office with the *zollpapier* and been issued with a *verkehrserlaubnis*. The pilot had complained about the state of the boarding ladder as he came on board. Six hours later they hove-to and the pilots' launch from Cuxhaven had pulled alonside to take off the pilot and Heinz Fischer.

All night and all the next morning they followed the Dutch coastline. Past the necklace of off-shore islands to Den Helder. Then they headed WSW until the sun went down. Levy and Malik slept all day on the floor of the saloon and it was the captain's high-pitched voice talking to Levy that woke Malik. As he sat up rubbing his eyes, Levy said, 'He says we're there. They've opened the hatches and hooked up the first crate. He wants us to go on deck and check that he does it OK.'

There was an almost full moon apart from the two lights on the top of the wheelhouse and Levy and Malik stood watching as the gears on the hoists turned slowly and noisily. Slowly the crate came up, and when it was clear of the deck the hoists slowly turned and the crate swung out over the sea. There was a crew-man holding each of the long warps to the shackles and when the captain raised his hand they pulled in unison. For a moment nothing happened and then the shackles opened and the crate plunged nose-first into the sea. Cleanly and smoothly like an Olympic diver. For a moment the sea foamed and lifted and then there was nothing.

The crew-men were greasing the gears at the base of the hoists as the men in the hold slung the chains on the next crate. One after the other, at twenty-minute intervals, three more crates went into the sea. Then there was a long wait. The heavy loads were distorting some of the metal links on the sling chains and two men were trying to hammer them back into shape.

Eventually the last crate was in the slings. Twice one of the hoists had seized from the excessive loads it had taken, and the crate hung askew over the deck until they had poured oil over the hot gears that were clamped together from friction heat and physical distortion. Finally it was over the sea, the men on the release ropes awaiting the captain's signal. As his hand came down they heard the grunts of the men as they heaved against the ropes. And then the ship shuddered and listed as one sling came free and the huge crate hung, swinging in long pendulum arcs as the second sling held its grip on one end of the crate. Slowly the swings decreased until the crate hung vertically down, ten feet or so above the sea. The boat's list had slightly eased, but Malik was scared that they would be seen by some passing ship. They had chosen this spot because it was marked on the charts as an official dumping ground for ammunition.

Levy was talking to the captain who was shrugging and shaking his head.

'What does he say, David?'

'He says it's locked because the chain rings have been distorted, and he's scared that the dead weight could drag the hoist out of the deck.'

'What does he suggest?'

'He suggests he wishes he'd never heard of us.'

'Ask him if a man climbed up the hoist could he file through one of the links at the top. He'd lose the sling and half the chain but we could pay for a replacement.'

Levy talked to the captain. It sounded as though they were haggling and finally Levy turned to him.

'He says it would work but it's too dangerous. His men wouldn't do it.'

'Tell him to get a file and I'll do it.'

'You must be out of your mind, Jake.'

'Somebody's got to do it.'

Levy turned to the captain, anger on his face. Hands on hips, his head thrust forward aggressively, he shouted and raved, barely heeding the captain's replies. Five minutes later Levy was calm, nodding his head as the captain spoke slowly and deliberately. Then Levy turned to Malik.

'Forty Israeli lira, the bastard wants. But I've told him to go ahead. So much for Israeli loyalty, the shits.'

'It's cheap enough, David. I get dizzy standing on a chair.'

'Would you have done it?'

'Of course I would.'

'You're a better man than I am, my friend. There he goes.'

There was complete silence except for the wind across the deck and in the rigging as they watched the man slowly hauling his way up the steel lattice-work of the arm of the hoist. Several times he rested, his feet splayed out and one arm hooked over a strut. The crew-man perched on the wheel-house followed him with the light, and then, very faintly, they could hear the rasping of a file on metal. It came in snatches on the wind. Twenty minutes later there was the rattle of the freed chain and the crate plummeted down to the sea. A spume of water rose four or five feet in the air and then fell back into the seething foam that was the only remaining sign of the crate's existence.

Malik shook the captain's hand and waited until the crew-man came down. He was a Polish Jew from Cracow and they chatted for an hour before Malik went back to the saloon.

They anchored in the roads at Rotterdam midday the next day. And two hours later they were signalled permission to enter.

Malik pushed his plate aside and stirred his coffee.

'What are you going to do now, David?'

'Are you going back to Cologne?'

'Yes. I'll have to pick up my things and work out a phony joint report with Heinz Fischer.'

'I'll come back with you and check that there's no untidy ends from Bergman and Goldberg. Then I'll go back to Tel Aviv.'

Malik called to the waiter and paid for their meal and they took a taxi to the main station. They had booked on a flight from Schipol at six o'clock that evening and they spent a few hours in Amsterdam. Malik bought a record of the Finzi cello concerto for Lisa, and a small bottle of perfume for Heinz to give to Ruth. There was an hour's delay at the airport and they touched down at Wahn just after eight o'clock. They shared a taxi into town, dropping Malik near the flat and Levy carrying on to book himself a room at the Dom.

The flat seemed cold despite the warm day and it looked deserted. The recording and projection equipment had gone and Heinz had cleared his things from his bedroom. Malik sat on the bed and dialled Lisa's home number. It was Heinz's voice that answered and when he had asked for Lisa the phone had been hung up. He dialled again with the receiver to his ear. He heard the ringing tone at the other end and the phone was lifted and replaced straight away. He realized then that he must have annoyed Heinz Fischer more than he had thought.

He looked at his watch. It was nine-thirty, and he was too scruffy to go out to see her without bathing and shaving, and that would make it too late. He would have to wait until the next day. He was lying in the bath, his feet on the taps, steam condensing on his face, and his eyes closed, when he heard the key in the outer door. For a moment he hoped it might be Lisa. He called out.

'Is that you, Lisa?'

But there was no answer. And no sound of movement. He climbed out of the bath, put on his bathrobe and walked through to the sitting room. Heinz Fischer was sitting at the table but he didn't turn to look at Malik.

'I thought it must be you, or Lisa. I called out but I guess you can't hear from the bathroom.' He paused, towelling his wet hair. 'There was something wrong with your phone earlier on.'

Fischer turned to look at him and Malik was shocked by the look on his face.

'What on earth's the matter, Heinz?'

'You're what's the matter, Malik. You don't suppose I thought it was accidental, do you?'

Malik shrugged. 'I don't understand.'

'Rechmann was killed this morning. Shot by a marksman as he came out of the office at the factory to get in his car.'

Malik sat down at the table. 'What did you expect to happen, Heinz? That we leave him running around to spill the beans? He was warned. I warned him myself. But he's an arrogant bastard. Self-important. He talked to von Busch and told him to ignore us. And that wouldn't have been the last one he would have talked to. Especially when he discovered that his chat with von Busch didn't work. He endangered the whole operation.'

'You know what happened to von Busch?'

'Tell me,' Malik said quietly.

'I phoned his place this morning when I heard what had happened to Rechmann. Von Busch was found drowned in the lake on his estate. There was a rowing-boat floating upside down. A stupid old man drowns himself. No suspicious circumstances.'

'What would you have done, Heinz? Let it all come out despite the consequences?'

'You knew that Levy was going to kill those two?'

'Yes.'

'But you didn't know they were already dead?'

'No.'

'It didn't matter to you. You weren't all that interested in when and how.' Fischer's voice broke with anger, bubbles of saliva on his lips.

'Calm down, Heinz. If Rechmann hadn't played the fool it wouldn't have been necessary.'

'You could have tried to convince him. Threaten him, even.'

Malik looked at Fischer, his anger beginning to override his wish to be friendly.

'Heinz, you're talking about two men who were so stupid, so arrogant, that they were ready to start a world war. What about the Russians in those cities? Innocent people who would die in a holocaust without any choice.'

'The Soviets could pull back. The choice would be theirs.'

'You surely don't think that the Politburo would back down under a threat like that? They would have answered that it was organized by the Americans or the Chinese and they would have struck back immediately. A pre-emptive strike. That would give the Americans no choice. The result doesn't bear thinking about.'

'So if the Soviets or their stooges invade West Germany or Israel you give them away? And don't think I didn't notice the subtle difference about the sites.'

'What difference was that?'

'The sites in Germany are all near big cities. Those in Israel are in the desert.'

'I hadn't noticed that. But Israel's a much smaller country, you couldn't have hidden them in a city.'

'And that justifies the Red Army invading West Germany, yes?'

'That's up to the governments of the countries concerned. It's not for you or me to play God. Nor Meyer and the others.'

'The Rechmann family would have been guests at your wedding.'

'What's the point you're making, Heinz?'

'He was a friend of my family. He was a good man.'

Malik shook his head. 'The men who ran Auschwitz and the other concentration camps had wives and children, and they all sang *Stille Nacht* with tears on their faces at Christmas. But they weren't good men, Heinz. They were animals.'

'Like you, Malik, they would claim that they didn't actually kill. They just turned a blind eye to what others did.'

'Don't kid yourself, Heinz. If it had been necessary I would have killed Rechmann and von Busch myself.'

'Lisa and my mother have gone over to the Rechmanns' to comfort the widow and the two girls. How do you think they would feel if they knew that you were responsible?'

'They won't know, Heinz. Lisa will never know.'

'She will, my friend. Because I shall tell her.'

Malik looked for long moments at the German's face. Then he said softly. 'You would destroy her if you did that. Give me one reason why you should.'

'So that she doesn't marry you, Malik. That would destroy her too. Your hatred of Germans will be used on her some day if you get the chance.'

'You'd better justify that, Fischer.'

'There are only two people dead from this. They're both Germans. The Jews just live happily ever after.'

Malik shook his head slowly. 'You're letting *your* prejudices show, Fischer. You know why those two had to go but you choose to ignore it. You'd better go before I get really angry.'

Fischer stood up. 'Just keep away from my family, Malik. You're not welcome any more. You're mad. You ought to be put away.'

'D'you mean that, Heinz?'

'I swear I mean it.'

Malik took a deep breath. 'We have to discuss our joint report about the operation.'

'There's no need to, Malik. It was your operation. You do the report. Just send a copy to police headquarters here in Cologne. I shan't expose it. I'll sign it, whatever it says.'

Fischer stood up clumsily, knocking his chair over. As he bent down to pick it up he was trembling and when he stood up he stared at Malik for long moments.

'I'm glad I'm not you, Malik. You said something in the first days we met that I never understood, but I understand it now.'

'What was that?'

'You said you envied people who had the chance to be innocent. I know now why you envy them.'

Fischer turned and slammed the outer door as he left the flat.

Malik sat there for almost an hour until the cold finally made him shiver and he wrapped the bathrobe closely round his body. It was just before midnight when the phone rang. It was Levy.

'Hi, Jake. Our friends dealt with both parties.'

Malik couldn't bring himself to reply. He sat there as if he were paralyzed. Unable to speak.

'Jake. Are you there, Jake?'

He put the phone to his mouth. So close that it knocked against his teeth.

'What the hell's the matter, Jake? Stay put. I'm coming right over.' And the phone went dead.

Malik stood up slowly and shuffled towards the outer door. He opened it and left it ajar, leaning back against the wall, his arms wrapped round himself, shaking as if he had an ague. It seemed hours before he heard Levy's steps hurrying up the stairs from the street. For a moment Levy just stood there looking at him.

'For Christ's sake, what's happened? Are you ill?'

But Malik's eyes were closed and his mouth hung open, his head back against the wall. For a few seconds Levy hesitated, not knowing what to do. Then he bent and took Malik's arm and lifted him on his shoulder, carrying him through to the sitting room, looking desperately for the bedroom. He laid Malik gently on the bed and hurried to the bathroom.

Slowly and gently he wiped Malik's face with the warm, wet cloth, and then he took his hand.

'Tell me what happened, Jake. Please.'

Malik turned his head on the pillow and opened his eyes. He said softly, 'Fischer came. He told me about Rechmann and von Busch.' He sighed and closed his eyes. 'He says that if I see Lisa again he'll tell her what has happened. That I'm a murderer and a German-hater.'

'So let the bastard tell her. She knows you better than that.'

Malik's eyes fluttered open. 'Her mother once asked me if I hated Germans enough to end up hating Lisa.'

'Then she's a stupid old bitch.'

'She's not, David. She's an ordinary woman. And remember what von Busch said. He said I would have made a good Nazi.'

'Who the hell are these bastards to say what you are? They all watched the Nazis shovelling our kids into the gas chambers and they didn't holler then, by God.' Levy paused. 'Anyway, you didn't kill those two.'

'No. But I would have done if your people hadn't done it for me.'

'D'you want me to fetch Lisa?'

Malik slowly shook his head. 'No.' Tears ran slowly down his cheeks as his eyes looked up at the ceiling. 'That's all over, David. It's all over.'

'We'll see. We'll see,' Levy said softly. But he knew it was true.

He sat with Malik all night, watching him as he slept, shifting and moving restlessly in his sleep, mouthing in whispers words Levy couldn't understand because they were in Polish.

Early next morning he called the hotel and spoke to Bergman. Then he asked the porter to send over his things and his bill. He booked Malik and himself on to a flight for London later that day.

CHAPTER TWENTY

Levy hired a car at Gatwick and drove them up to the house at Hampstead. He had phoned his wife asking her to come over. He found the house sad and soulless and not likely to help Malik recover.

There was an Israeli Embassy house in Wimbledon for transient diplomats and when Helen Levy arrived Levy arranged for them all to move in. The improvement in Malik's condition was rapid and obvious. Slowly Levy realized what sort of life Malik normally led. He was a loner. Asking and getting nothing from anybody, and Levy realized then what a difference the German girl must have made to him. What she supplied was ordinary enough. Other men might have been bored by it. It was no more than any normal couple would take for granted. And it was well inside what a man could expect from a girl. She didn't need to make him feel special to succeed. She just made him a normal man. With hopes and expectations, and someone to love and be loved by.

He talked it over for hours with Helen, as to whether he should contact the girl, tell her what had happened and suggest that she came over. But Helen Levy was a woman and a realist. She had no doubt that the girl would rush straight over, but she equally had no doubt that the shambles that followed would ruin them both. The fact that he was a Jew would suddenly have significance. The fact that she was a German would be a constant threat. She would not only have to abandon a protective and loving family but would have to cut herself off completely. She would be utterly dependent on Malik, who would be utterly dependent on her. They would make friends of their own as time went by but always in the background would be those accusing ghosts. The ghosts who hated her husband. For being a Jew, for being himself, and for taking her away from them all. Two normal people could work hard at a marriage and keep it alive despite those disadvantages. But these two wouldn't stand a chance. Cut off from her family the guilt and estrangement would take away the girl's confidence. And the time in Auschwitz had ensured that Malik would never have any real self-confidence. In a strange way the camp might have given him the toughness and determination that made him good at his job. Ideal for MI6, but far from ideal for Lisa Gertrud Fischer. A natural loner and an enforced loner were not the basis for a happy marriage. And running like a thread through their discussions was David Levy's awareness that on his part, his argument, although valid and the facts true, was all a polemic. For David Levy knew another reason why it could never be. A reason that he was never going to be able to tell to his wife.

Levy helped Malik put together his phony report. It gave a long list of names that had been built up during the early stages of the investigation. Names that had eventually proved to have no relevance or significance. It attributed the swastika-daubing to being no more than the irrational actions of juvenile malcontents. Students, foreign workers, the less well-off and the usual spectrum of non-political hooligans with some complaint against society or authority in general. It concluded that they were not organized and not politically motivated, and could be dealt with, as and when required, by the normal action of local police. They were neither funded, influenced nor controlled by any political party or any foreign Intelligence service.

Malik eventually phoned Jenkins and made an appointment to see him the following day. He went to Heathrow with Helen and David Levy to see them off, and when their flight was called and they walked through the glass doors to Immigration and Customs, Helen Levy turned and waved, and her lips silently shaped the word '*Shalom*'. But Malik's face was impassive.

He walked slowly to the cigarette kiosk, bought three packets of cigarettes and then walked to the cafeteria.

As he sat at the metal table with its used crockery, greasy bottles of ketchup and pools of spilled tea he slowly stirred his cup of coffee. While the Levys were with him he had tried to think what he would do. But no thoughts would stay in his mind for more than a few seconds. Levy had looked after the sale of the house and the money was in the bank. He could do whatever he wanted. But he knew as he sat there that there was nothing he wanted to do.

For four months, or was it five, he had lived in a different world. For the first time in his life the perspective had been reversed. But nothing had really changed. He was in exactly the same situation now as if he had never met her. He had come back from an assignment and would be given a new one, and life would go on the same as it had always gone on. He stood up slowly and carefully and walked to the front of the terminal and waved for a taxi.

He had know as he listened to the sour words of Heinz Fischer that it was over. By the time Fischer had told her and her parents, no matter how guardedly, she would be left with making a choice. Her family or him. He had little doubt that she would choose him, but he had too little to offer to let her pay the price. She would have no idea what the price really was. He wished that he could see her to explain, but he doubted if he could explain. There was nothing to say that could override her loyalty to him. Only time would teach her how much she would be throwing away.

He told the taxi-driver to take him to the Hilton.

Jenkins spent twenty minutes or so expounding to Malik the problems that SIS were facing in Washington now that Nixon had gone and the CIA was taking the blame for every misdeed that could legitimately or otherwise be laid at its door. Laidlaw as SIS liaison with the CIA had done an excellent job. As things had turned out, too good a job. He was too closely identified as a CIA sympathizer. Even our Embassy was giving him the cold shoulder.

Malik took it all as social chit-chat before his report was discussed. When Jenkins ran out of steam on the problems of Washington, Malik took the plunge.

'You got my report on the operation in the Federal Republic?'

'What? Oh yes. The usual mountain out of a molehill, but we've done our bit of cooperation. Should keep us in Bonn's good books for a few months anyway.' Jenkins looked at Malik. 'How do you feel about an overseas posting, Jake?'

'Where?'

'There are several places where we need an experienced finger stuck in a hole in a local dyke. I haven't decided. Hong Kong is one of them but there's so much going on at the moment that there are other places that are more important. But in principle you've no objection?'

'No. None at all.'

'How soon could you be ready?'

'An hour.'

Jenkins looked at him sharply. Despite his faintly Dickensian air, he was a perceptive man.

'Nothing wrong, is there?'

'No.'

Jenkins sighed and stood up, walking with Malik to the door. As he stood with his hand on the brass door knob he said, 'A pity about the German.'

'What German?'

Jenkins looked embarrassed. 'I'm afraid I can't remember his name. The German who was working with you.'

'You mean Heinz Fischer?'

'Yes. I think that *was* his name.'

'What's the problem with him?'

'They notified us that he wasn't able to co-sign your report until he came out of hospital.'

'Why was he in hospital?'

'Knocked down by a hit-and-run driver. He hung on for a day or two but the injuries were too severe. But they're willing to accept the report on your signature only.'

'You mean he's dead?'

'I'm afraid so. I sent our routine condolences.'

Malik stood silent for a few moments, his eyes closed. And then he said in a flat voice, 'When shall I hear from you about my posting?'

'I'll phone you later today or early tomorrow.'

She stood looking at the front of the house, her heart beating wildly, and she tried to think of a prayer as she opened the gate and walked up to the door. She could hardly breathe as she pressed the china doorbell.

A woman in her late thirties answered the door. She was wearing a dressing gown and green leather slippers.

'Can I help you?'

'I came to see Jake.'

The woman smiled. 'And who's Jake?'

'Jacob Malik.'

'I don't know him, I'm afraid. Try next door.'

'This is Jake's house.'

'It's . . . I see. I'm afraid the house has been sold. We moved in two weeks ago. Maybe he was the previous owner.'

'Is there any forwarding address for him?'

'I expect he made arrangements with the GPO and his mail is re-directed.'

'You didn't meet him?'

'No. We dealt with the estate agents.'

'Can you give me their address?'

'Yes. It was Billings in the High Street.' She paused. 'You go across the green. It's about ten minutes' walk.'

'Thank you.'

She turned and walked down the garden path and across the triangle of grass to where the road forked up to Hampstead village.

The estate agents were obliging enough but they had no forwarding address.

They hadn't met Mr Malik. A Mr David Levy had had power of attorney for the sale of the house.

She went to the Post Office but they couldn't help her. They were not allowed to divulge forwarding addresses even when they existed. She could write to the old address and then it would be automatically re-directed. The woman behind the counter was a kindly person and she noticed the tears brimming in the girl's eyes as Lisa said softly, 'Can I ask if the new address is in Israel?'

For a moment the woman hesitated, and then she hurriedly jerked open the deep wooden drawer and looked through twenty or thirty dog-eared cards. She stopped at one of them and read it carefully. She looked back at Lisa's face, shaking her head.

'I'm afraid not, love. I can't say more than that.'

She stood outside the Post Office, trying to think what else she could do. She could see the small restaurant where they had eaten, and the shop where he had bought the electric light bulbs. It had been a sunny day and the world had seemed so wonderful. It was a sunny day today but everything was so terribly wrong. She couldn't think of any reason why he hadn't contacted her. And the last two weeks had been like a nightmare. The night of Heinz's accident. He had said that morning that he wanted to talk to her. Something serious, he said. And Malik gone. No letter, no explanation. It was a terrible nightmare. The two days while Heinz was dying. Watching her parents hope against hope until their spirits disintegrated. The funeral and Ruth, and her guilt that her thoughts were still about Jake. The two days of terrible arguments with her parents when she had said she was going to London to see him, despite his silence.

The overwhelming silence of her parents' disapproval. A disapproval that finally became a tirade against Jake Malik rather than against herself or fate. And overlying it all, her own pain that he had just left, knowing what grief it would bring her. She could think of no possible reason why it should have happened. Jake Malik wasn't that kind of man. She remembered that he had once asked her what he could do that would cause her to stop loving him. And she remembered her answer, that nothing could do that, because if he did something she would know that it had to be done. Nothing would change her mind about Jake Malik. She knew by instinct that she would never be happy again. But there was nothing she could do. Except write the letter and see what happened. But she knew in her heart that nothing would happen. If he had wanted her he would have contacted her. She wished that he had slept with her and that she was carrying their child. She could have . . . She sighed and turned on her heel, asking the first woman she met where she could find a taxi.

There were two vacant seats next to Malik and when the film started he tried to read, but his mind wouldn't absorb the words.

He took the envelope out of his pocket and slid out the single buff page and read it again.

Memo to Malik J.
From Dpy. H of D III

Your posting to Washington as liaison officer SIS-CIA is now operational.

You are required to effect takeover as quickly as possible, as your predecessor is required for urgent duties elsewhere.

It has been laid down that in future SIS LO is not accommodated at the Embassy and you should rent suitable accommodation on Washington Grade 3 scale. Authorization 19074 applies.

You will report directly to London using the diplomatic bag but in future no copies of your report will be provided for Embassy archives.

Funds are available on existing imprest account but with no increase in scale, until the present Review Board has reported.

We expect you to improve on the existing SIS/CIA relationship as quickly as possible. There is much ground to be made up, as you know.

C. Jenkins

Malik stretched out on the vacant seats and pulled the airline blanket over his body, covering his head. As he closed his eyes, the noise of the aircraft as it strained through the night sky was almost welcome. For five more hours he wasn't even on Planet Earth. He wished that he had learned at least one Jewish prayer. Just one. He had been going to when they got to Israel, but . . .

The plane to Cologne was half-empty and she sat looking out at the moonlight on the thick cumulus clouds. Far away there was a flicker of summer lightning and she turned back to the open pages of the book on her lap. She read the line of the Shakespeare sonnet again and again – 'Love is not love that alters when it alteration finds . . .'

She put back her head and closed her eyes, the paperback copy of Palgrave's *Golden Treasury* held tightly in both hands. It was all she had left of Jacob Malik.

Jenkins shook the rain of the sudden storm from his umbrella on the steps of the Reform Club. Closing it carefully and giving it two last decisive swishes he saw Howarth step out of the taxi and hurry towards the steps.

'Let's go in the bar before it starts filling up, Jenkins. Leave your brolly with the porter . . . That's right, Mason, put it on my hanger, there's a good chap. Number thirty-two.'

Howarth chose two leather armchairs in the far corner of the room. Shoving away the third chair to join several others around an empty table.

'Wettest September for forty years, they say. The buggers have always got some story. Three weeks' time they'll be telling us not to use hoses in the garden. You see if they don't.' He turned to look at the waiter. 'Right. Put them down there. Leave the soda water . . . that's fine. Thank you, Fletcher.'

Howarth raised his glass. 'Cheers.' He took a sip, considered the taste and then put down the glass, satisfied that it really was Bell's. He looked at Jenkins. 'I got your message. What's the news?'

Jenkins looked around but the room was quite empty. Despite that he leaned forward as he spoke. 'It's finished. All wrapped up and no problems.'

'Are you sure about that, Jenkins? Quite sure?'

'Yes, sir.'

'What about your chap, Marples, or whatever his name is?'

'Malik. He's been posted to Washington. He's already on his way there.'

'You mentioned that he'd put in a very low-key report. What do you feel about that?'

'I don't understand, sir.'

Howarth shrugged. 'It shows he's unreliable.'

'But we intended that. We hedged him round so that he'd react that way. I chose him right at the beginning because I knew how he would react.'

'Fair enough, Jenkins. First-class thinking on your part. But the fact remains . . . he went his own way . . . not only made unorthodox decisions but kept us out of the picture.'

'But that was my intention, sir. Like I said, we had a problem and I chose him as the man who would solve it the way we wanted. We can hardly criticize him for doing what we intended him to do.'

'We can, my friend. I can, anyway.' Howarth leaned back in his chair. 'We can expect a lot of cooperation from Bonn and Tel Aviv from now on. Bloody amateurs despite their reputations. You'd better give me a note on what you'd like from them.'

'I'll do that, sir. There's two or three items I'd like to have the files on.'

'You're happy to leave your chap and the Israeli running around loose?'

'Tel Aviv are happy about their man, and I'm perfectly happy about Malik, my chap.'

'Well don't be. Keep a monthly check on him. In my book he's not to be trusted.' Howarth shrugged. 'However, it's your head, my boy, your head.' He raised his eyebrows. 'I'm having lunch with His Nibs. Another drink before you get back to the grindstone?'

Jenkins took the hint. 'No thank you, sir. I've had my ration.'

Howarth nodded as he took out a cigar from a leather case. 'Remember what I've said. It's not a criticism, mind you, just a sensible precaution.' He nodded slowly to mark his words. 'I shouldn't be surprised to see your name in *The Times* on New Years Day. Have a good weekend.'

'And you, sir.'

THE SEEDS OF TREASON

To Julian and Carole – with love

Go search for people who are hurt by fate or nature – the ugly, those suffering from an inferiority complex, craving power and influence but defeated by unfavourable circumstances . . . The sense of belonging to an influential, powerful organization will give them a feeling of superiority over the handsome and prosperous people around them. For the first time in their lives they will experience a sense of importance . . . It is sad indeed, and humanly shallow – but we are obliged to profit from it.

FROM A LECTURE TO KGB OFFICERS BY
KGB GENERAL PAVL ANATOLEVICH SUDOPLATOV

CHAPTER ONE

He had always known at the back of his mind that they would come sooner or later, but he hadn't expected that it would be quite so soon. There had only been a couple of paragraphs in one of those pieces on the security services in the *Daily Telegraph*, and there had been no name given. Just a brief reference to a former officer of MI6. There had been no follow-up story but it would have gone over the wires from the press services, and that would have set people ferreting through the records. The story had appeared in the paper a week ago.

They had bought the farmhouse when they moved to Spain and they had chosen it because of its remoteness and inaccessibility. The plaque over the door said *Hacienda di Santa Anna – 1872* and it was much the same now as when it had first been built. It was on the *sierra*, the mountain ridge behind Malaga, about two miles up the pot-holed mountain road from El Palo to Olias.

There were two cars and a small white van and he could see them pulled up on the lower ridge by the village of Jarazmin. By the time they had made their inquiries about his house it would be another fifteen minutes before they arrived. There was still light, but there was the tell-tale pink of sunset across the Bay of Malaga towards Torremolinos, and the glowing red heads of the geraniums were already taking on the shades of mauve and purple that came with the evening.

It looked as if it was a TV team. He'd always imagined that if it ever happened it would be with a journalist, quietly and in his control. But TV interviews were never like that. They were brash and short, with every second significant. He could refuse to see them. Send them packing. But if he turned them away there would be others. And if he didn't say anything to any of them they would just put the Establishment point of view plus the usual speculation and distortion. Chambers would have a field-day with noncommittal statements that hinted without saying anything out loud. And Paula would loom out of the past to cash in on it without needing too much encouragement from 'investigative' reporters. All the venom of the years unleashed as at long last she could try to even the score. He shivered despite the warm air, and turned, walking back through the big, double front doors to warn Anna. It was cool in the house as he stood at the foot of the stairs and called up to her.

She wasn't upstairs and as she came through from the kitchen she stood in the archway that led to the dining-room and he realized that that was almost exactly how he had seen her that first time. All those years ago. Before it all began. Standing under the wide archway of one of the reception rooms at the hotel in Berlin. She looked no older now. Calmer perhaps, less tension in that slender neck and large brown eyes. But her mouth was the same, wide, and the dimples ready to deepen when she smiled. That first time she had been wearing a black silk dress and her dark hair had been swept up into a chignon held by a tortoiseshell comb. Neither of them knew the other but for a moment their eyes had met and held before he was past her. It could only be hindsight but he was sure that at that moment he had known that their lives would be entangled somehow. She was much younger than he was and she was very beautiful, but it wasn't just that. In those days he went in more for long-legged blondes with well-filled sweaters.

'They're almost here, my love. It looks like a TV crew.'

'This is very soon, Jan, isn't it?'

'Yes, but I suppose it doesn't matter. Shall I send them away? Refuse to be interviewed?'

She walked across to him and put her hands on his shoulders as she looked up at his face. 'What do you want to do?'

'I want to be left alone. With you.'

'But what . . .?'

'I don't understand.'

She smiled. 'If that was exactly what you wanted you wouldn't have asked me what you should do.'

'I'd just like people to understand how these things happen.'

'It might be good for you to talk it out. Good for you, I mean.' She paused. 'But don't expect people to understand. They won't.'

'Are you sure?'

'Quite, quite sure.'

He heard the car engines and then Jackie, their German Shepherd bitch, barking at the strangers at the gate. He turned to go outside but she held him, kissing him gently on the mouth. 'Don't get upset, Jan, if they don't understand. You don't have to explain.'

He sighed. 'There may be somebody else some day. It could help them.'

She smiled and shook her head. 'They wouldn't be like you, Jan. You're just a shade too much Polish for the British to understand.'

As he walked across the patio he could smell the jasmine and the mimosa. The cars were drawn up in a line on the rough track outside. A man stood in shirt-sleeves and denims on the other side of the big wrought-iron gates. He had seen him somewhere before. On *Panorama* or some such programme.

He didn't open the gates and as they faced each other he noticed the TV man put his hands on his hips. The small action of readiness for an aggressive move was revealing. He smiled. 'Mr Massey? Jan Massey?'

'What do you want?'

'My name's Bartram. Tom Bartram. We met briefly when British Forces Network Berlin opened their new studios. It must have been five or six years ago. BBC television have sent me over to interview you.' He paused. 'I expect you've seen the papers.'

'I don't wish to be interviewed. I have nothing to say.'

The man shrugged. 'I could save you a lot of hassle. We've got here several days before anybody else is likely to find you. Give me an exclusive and we'll sell it to all the others. It would save you having to deal with anybody else. You could tell them that this is the only interview you will give. I'm authorized to offer you a fee of £5000. We could double that for an exclusive.'

'What sort of questions have you got in mind?'

For a moment the man hesitated and then, looking at Massey's face, he said quietly, 'Only one.'

'What's that?'

'Just tell me how it all happened.'

'That would take days, not ten minutes.'

'So I'll stay for days, if you'll allow me to.'

There was something about the choice of the word 'allow'. He could have said 'if you'll *let* me'. But 'allow' was different somehow. It acknowledged that Massey had a choice, and control over the situation.

'I don't want my wife disturbed by all your crew and lights and the rest of their paraphernalia.'

Bartram smiled. An amiable smile. 'Its odd. I only learned the real meaning of that word paraphernalia about ten days ago. Maybe you already know the real meaning. The legal meaning?'

'No.'

'Paraphernalia is the old legal description for the things that a husband gives to his wife before and during the marriage that can never be taken from her by him or the courts.'

Massey looked at the TV man's face and then said quietly, 'OK. I'll talk to you, Mr Bartram. I'll see how it goes. Just you and me. Not an interview at this stage. Just a chat. Off the record.' He paused. 'Provided you send your crew away and they don't talk. To anyone.'

Bartram nodded. 'That's OK. I'll take them off now. What time could I come up myself in the morning?'

'Let's make it ten. But if I'm not happy about how it goes there'll be no cameras.'

'It'll be up to you, Mr Massey. I assure you it will be played straight down the middle.'

'And no long lenses or hidden cameras?'

'None. I promise.'

As if it were quite normal they shook hands through the iron-work scrolls of the gates and the BBC man turned and walked over to the cars. Massey watched him bend over, talking at one of the lowered car windows, and then the cars backed to the edge of the track, turned and drove away down towards Malaga.

Massey turned, and looked across the valley. There were lights on in the cluster of houses in Jarazmin below, and the sunset was, as always, theatrical almost to the point of vulgarity. A range of reds, mauves and purples that shaded through that end of the spectrum and touched the creases and folds of the mountains. Around the bay the lights of Torremolinos and Marbella danced and twinkled on the dark waters of the Mediterranean. And everywhere was so still and quiet that he could hear the cassette that Anna must have put on. It was Victoria de los Angeles singing the 'Baïléro' from *Les Chants d'Auvergne*.

They sat on the patio. A bottle of local white wine and glasses on the marble table between them. He had put out the upright cane chairs for them so that he could be continuously reminded that it wasn't a friend he was talking to. It was almost half an hour later when Bartram got round to the first question.

'You were in Berlin for nearly six years according to what I could find out. Isn't that longer than SIS usually leave their agents . . . their officers, in one place?'

Massey looked at him and smiled. 'I signed the Official Secrets Act a long time ago, Mr Bartram. They never release you from that. There's very little I can actually tell you. Nothing that would interest the public.'

'Could we talk about the more personal aspects of what happened? Your feelings and your wife's feelings. Your present wife, that is.'

Massey smiled. 'You'd end up with a sort of *This Is Your Life* piece. You wouldn't want that, would you?'

Bartram shrugged. 'I just want to understand. To show people how these things happen. That it isn't all as black and white and cut and dried as it seems.'

'You really mean that?'

'Of course. Why shouldn't I?'

'The Establishment wouldn't like that very much. They might stop you showing it anyway if it doesn't go along with the official point of view.'

'To hell with them. They wouldn't stop me. I'm a freelance. And as a matter of fact I don't think they'd try.'

'What makes you think that?'

'I talked briefly to several people before I left. They didn't put up any barriers. On the contrary.'

'Who told you where to find me?'

The TV man didn't avoid his eyes. 'Does it really matter? We knew you had been in France and that you had recently moved to somewhere in Spain. It wouldn't have taken long.'

'Was it someone in MI6 who told you where to find me?'

'Yes.'

'Chambers?'

'Yes. But I don't think he told me out of spite.'

Massey laughed. 'Chambers never does things out of spite. None of them do. It's either in the line of duty or in the public interest.'

'It didn't sound like that.'

'Of course not. That's why he's in SIS. They're not the fools that you journalists try to make them out to be. They know how to put the words together. And they're used to dealing with much more cynical people than even journalists are supposed to be.'

'You don't like the people in MI6?'

It was almost impossible to explain to an outsider. Massey shrugged. 'Like any other organization there are people you admire and like, and people who you don't like. People who care more about the rules than human beings. People who are more active against their colleagues than against our enemies.'

'You think Chambers is one of those?'

'I didn't say that.'

Tom Bartram smiled. 'How do you want to do this?'

'I'm not a TV man. You tell me how you want to do it and I'll see if I can co-operate.'

'OK. Let's play it very loosely. How about you give me two or three days of your time? No recordings, no filming. Just you and me on our own. You tell me what you choose to tell me. Just as background material for me. Then, if I feel I can make a worthwhile programme from it, we'll go over it again. On camera. The parts that really tell the story.'

'Will it be a sympathetic treatment?'

'It'll be honest and balanced, but that won't necessarily make it sympathetic. How it comes out depends on the facts.'

'And when I've talked and you've filmed it I can have the final say about what goes in?'

'No. But after we've talked privately you can say an absolute no. And when we film, if you don't want to answer a question you don't have to. But the viewers would see that you hadn't answered.'

'Let's just talk and see how it goes. Where do you want me to start?'

'Back on square one. Tell me about when you were a child. Your parents. Your life. Anything that you can remember.'

CHAPTER TWO

Jan Massey's father, Adrian James Massey, had qualified as a doctor in 1940. He was then twenty-four. He was called up by the army immediately after qualifying and was commissioned in the Royal Army Medical Corps.

Other people had told Jan Massey that his father was a very lively man in those days. A good sportsman and, despite that, something of a scholar. Because of his fluent French he was transferred into Special Operations Executive where he eventually became part of a network on the outskirts of Paris. When the Paris networks began to fall apart he was brought back to England with several other officers and given a refresher course before being sent back to lead an SOE network in the Angoulême area.

It was during his refresher course at Beaulieu that he met Jan's mother. She was being trained by SOE as a radio operator and was eventually parachuted into France as his father's operator three months after he took over the network. She was then twenty-one years old.

Her name was Grazyna Maria Felinska and she had been born in Warsaw. Her parents had sent her to Paris before the Germans invaded Poland in 1939. She had been in England when war was declared, and had been recruited for SOE.

Long after the war was over Jan Massey had spent a sad afternoon shortly after he had joined SIS, looking through their old SOE files. Most SOE files had been destroyed within weeks of the war ending but about a hundred or so had been preserved. Nobody could tell him why those particular files had been kept. It could well have been no more than chance. His father's file read like his school reports. Everything he did he did with enthusiasm. He was commended for his bravery and his inspired leadership of his group in the Dordogne.

His mother's file was very different. The training staff at Beaulieu found her defiant, reckless and disobedient. They conceded that she was courageous and an efficient operator, but they saw her as a liability to any unit in the field. In addition they noted that she was far too attractive not to cause trouble in a network and almost certainly too noticeable to Germans as well as Frenchmen.

No reason was given in her file as to why, after all these negatives, she was posted to his father's network, but his reports on her work made clear that she was a valuable member of the network who cooperated well.

They were married by a local priest in Brantôme in the summer of 1943, and Jan's mother was obligingly brought back by an SOE Lysander in February 1944 so that her child could be born in England. He was, in fact, born in

Edinburgh, where his grandparents lived.

Two weeks after D-Day his father was shot in the chest by a German patrol. His men carried him to a farmhouse where he was treated by a local doctor. It was at a time when the Gestapo and the *Sicherheitsdienst* were reacting ruthlessly against the Resistance, and his father, despite his condition, had to be constantly on the move. Reports came back to Baker Street that Adrian Massey's health was deteriorating and that he was in a state of deep depression. He was considered too vital to the network's morale to be brought back to England.

In defiance of contrary advice from all quarters his mother insisted on being dropped back into France so that she could care for her husband, and in the end a reluctant SOE agreed.

In July 1944 his mother was parachuted back into France with new drugs that could help heal his father's lung. Nobody ever established whether it was through inefficiency or because of a leak, but the Gestapo from Angoulême were waiting for her. The pilot reported later that the guiding lights had been correctly placed and the signal had been in code with the correct password. The only evidence as to what happened to her after her capture was the camp records at Mauthausen concentration camp. His mother and two other SOE girls had been burnt in the ovens at the camp some time in February 1945.

A month before the German surrender Adrian Massey was brought back to England. Even with proper medical treatment it took a year before he was fit to be discharged.

With his savings and his service gratuity he bought a half share in a general practice in the small town of Tenterden in Kent. His son stayed with his grandparents until he was five, and then went to live with his father.

Dr Massey was a lonely man. A sad man, despite his obvious efforts to cope with a child and only a modest income. As the years went by their relationship became close. The boy seemed to recognize that he was much loved, and accepted the lack of any social life for what it was. The residue of sadness, not indifference.

There was a photograph of Jan's mother, in a silver frame on the mahogany table beside the fireplace in their home and a similar one on the tiled window-ledge in his father's bedroom. Even as a small boy he could recognize that she was very beautiful.

He frequently asked his father to tell him about his mother. The things she had said and what they had done. He was about ten years old before he realized that although his father obviously liked talking about her it always made him quiet and withdrawn for several days afterwards. It was then that he stopped asking about her. Looking back he thought that it would have been better if there had been some churchyard, some grave that his father could visit and tend. To be with her or feel that he was with her. His father often walked to the parish church in the High Street on summer evenings, to sit on one of the benches in the churchyard and read. It was generally the blue-bound Oxford version of Palgrave that he took with him. But they had no church and no grave for a pilgrimage. Not even a date that they could hold for remembrance. He couldn't recall his father actually saying it in so many words but he got the impression that his father felt that the British hadn't appreciated her enough because she was a foreigner. And these days his father defiantly wore a cheap metal badge, white with *Solidarnosc* in red script across its face. He was still strongly pro-Poland and the Poles.

Jan Massey identified early with his mother. He supposed that originally it was just a child's wish to be different from other children. He boasted about her and her courage, and got beaten for it by other boys. When he was old enough to fight back and do real damage he imagined himself as a knight in armour defending his lady's honour.

There were several Polish families in the town and on Saturdays and Sundays he was taken to one of the houses and was taught Polish. He learned quickly, and was treated by the Polish families as if he too were Polish. To them his mother was a heroine. A Polish heroine. For years he assumed that all heroines were Polish, and that all beautiful Poles were heroines.

They had a housekeeper who came in every day to cook and clean. She was from one of the Polish families at the far end of the High Street and his father was always mildly amused that she fussed far more over the boy than over him. He said it was because the boy was half Polish while he was just a 'foreigner'.

When Jan was twelve years old his father's partner died and Adrian Massey was able to take over the whole practice. His income was much improved and they were able to spend most of their evenings together. Walking over the marshes on spring and summer evenings, playing chess or reading in the winter months. Jan tried to teach his father Polish but although he spoke fluent French and German he absorbed very little Polish.

At eighteen Jan had the chance of going to university but decided that he would rather join the army. He was accepted for a short-service commission in the Intelligence Corps, and for the few days before he was due to report to the depot in Sussex his father talked to him as if they were contemporaries. It was in those talks that Jan realized the dichotomy in his father's ideas about Poles and Poland. And the Polish temperament. He was worried that his son was so like his mother. Impetuous, over-romantic, defiant of authority when it was unimaginatively applied and, as he put it, 'always ready to cut off her nose to spite her face'. His father warned that what was just tolerable in a pretty girl who was a foreigner would not be tolerated in a young man who was British and in Britain. He seemed to take comfort from the possibility that the army would knock off some of the young man's rough edges.

The army, and particularly the Intelligence Corps, is less clumsy and heavy-footed than civilians and the media imagine. It looks its new boys over with a quite benign eye. Both their faults and their virtues. The Intelligence Corps is flexible enough, and shrewd enough, to use its member's vices as well as their virtues, and Jan Massey enjoyed his time in the army. He served in counter-intelligence in Germany, France and Hong Kong. A few months into his fourth year he was offered a permanent career in the Foreign Office – the euphemism that the Establishment sometimes uses for describing MI6 or SIS, the Secret Intelligence Service. His command of Polish, Russian and German was the attraction.

He served the statutory two years in Moscow as assistant military attaché before being posted back to London. His paper on the structure and organization of the KGB impressed his superiors with its insight into Soviet thinking and attitudes, and under an assumed name he spent a year at Oxford at St Anthony's College studying the history of the Soviet Union. Back to normal duties, he was posted to the special unit that dealt with Soviet and Warsaw Pact defectors. There were one or two senior people who felt that his understanding of the Slav mind was based not only on understanding the Soviet system but on at least a mild sympathy with the system itself. But his success in the initial contacts with potential defectors was too good to be ignored. His amiable and seemingly relaxed debriefing of turned agents seemed to produce more information than the usual more formal methods.

In the aftermath of the arrest and exposure of George Blake, the whole of SIS's organization in Berlin had to be torn apart and put together again. Jan Massey was responsible for the evaluation of and proposals for the new set-up. Most of his recommendations on both organization and personnel were accepted. A year later he was promoted and sent to Berlin to take charge of the organization he had himself devised.

For two years Jan Massey controlled the SIS operations in Berlin with skill and success. The Berlin appointment was one of SIS's key posts. With the KGB and the Soviet military intelligence organization, the GRU, just across the Wall, and the East Germans' security service, the HVA, encircling the city, it was a hotbed of espionage and counter-espionage not only for the British but for other European countries and the USA. It was also a diplomatic minefield where a wrong move could give the Soviets an excuse for another move to oust the Allied occupying forces. But Massey's reading of the Russians' minds proved successful in sending back a flow of vital information and controlling the KGB's crude efforts in West Berlin. Century House congratulated themselves on their shrewd appointment.

The only black mark on his record was in his private life, and his record was enough for it to be overlooked at the time. It wasn't forgotten, because it showed that there were areas where his judgement was all too obviously unsound. But there were no security aspects to the personal disaster and it didn't affect his standing. At least not his official standing. There were even critics who saw it as a sign that Massey's Slav mind was human after all.

In 1976 he was on leave in England. He'd gone to a night-club. It was either the Embassy Club or Churchill's. He couldn't remember which. He met a girl there who was with an old friend of his, an officer in naval intelligence. The old friend was already well away when he waved Jan over to their table. Just before midnight they had to half-carry, half-drag, his naval friend out to a taxi and take him back to the man's flat in Holland Park. She was very efficient and very pretty and as they tucked him into bed she offered to do the Florence Nightingale bit and keep an eye on him until the morning.

He had tried a hundred times since then to try and work out why he did it and still hadn't found a satisfactory answer. The bald fact was that the girl and he married a month later. People tended to smile and say that it was just because she was very pretty and good in bed. Whatever it was it was total disaster. Not a gradual deterioration but right from the very first day.

One of the first precepts of intelligence training is that everybody tells lies about something and it pays to find out as quickly as possible what area of life your particular adversary tells lies about. It's not difficult. You dig a few verbal pits and wait to see which particular one they fall into. If it's done skilfully they don't even notice they've fallen. If you're wise you try to avoid doing this in your private life. If you're unwise, as he was, you ignore the signals even when you see through the lies without digging a pit. It had started on the day they married and went on right into the divorce court. Pointless lies. Lies just for the hell of it. And lies to cover up the liaisons with other men. It wasn't a marriage, it was a mental hurricane that bent the mind and depressed the spirit if you were on the receiving end.

The Polish bit was dragged out by both sides in the divorce court. Her counsel did a smarmy piece about the problems of mixed marriages and what he called the explosive Slav temperament. Suggesting that the 'brutal assaults' on his client's adulterous lovers were all part of that unfortunate temperament. Jan's own chap did an impassioned five minutes agreeing that even a thrice-cuckolded husband should not take the law into his own hands, but suggesting that where honour and the sanctity of the marriage bed were concerned the Poles were second to none in their respect for the law of the land. It was a cross-petition case and he won that round. But the financial settlement was bitter and long-fought. To Jan Massey it seemed typically crazy and typically British that a woman who admitted three separate adulteries and was perfectly capable of earning her own living, should be able to consider the wronged man as a lifetime meal-ticket. Fortunately she married another sucker before it was settled, but he got landed with her lawyer's fees as well as his own. He sometimes wondered if the British divorce laws weren't intended to cloak the fact that Brits don't really like women but try to make up for it when they get rid of them. Professor Higgins's little ditty about women in *My Fair Lady* wasn't all that far from the Brits' ideas about women.

He knew it was a waste of time thinking about all that. It wasn't significant. It had got nothing to do with Anna and him. But the newspapers would dredge it all up and he was sure that Chambers wouldn't have forgotten it either.

CHAPTER THREE

It was still only the last week in February but there was an indefinable feeling of spring in the Berlin air. There were no buds as yet on the trees in the Kurfürstendamm but the sky was cloudless and blue. And the sunshine was bright enough to cast gaunt shadows from the ruins of the Gadächtniskirche and light up the windows of its modern replacement.

But it was the people who made it seem suddenly spring. As if, after a dreary winter, the Berliners' natural optimism was beginning to come back. There were small grey heaps of snow still edging the bases of the trees, and a drift of thin snow on the spoil from the excavations in the road. But there were girls without coats, stopping to look at the new season's fashions in the shop windows. It looked as if people might buy china and jewellery again. Or Hermès scarves and Gucci shoes.

It was the day that would change Massey's life, although he didn't know it at the time. Even looking back on it, it seemed an ordinary enough day.

He stopped the taxi outside the travel agency and when he'd lifted out his case he paid the driver and walked across to the door next to the travel agency's entrance.

His flat was on the top floor, the fourth, and when he had let himself in he dumped his case on the bed and looked at his watch. The flight from London had been half an hour late arriving at Tegel but there was time for a wash and a shave before he needed to start for the meeting.

He washed, plugged in the shaver, staring at his reflection in the mirror. He seldom noticed his reflection in the mirror but that day he was aware that he looked older than he actually was. He had had a birthday while he was away, his thirty-eighth, but the face in the mirror looked much older. His mouth looked set and grim, the muscles each side contracted, giving an impression of aggression. He remembered that his lawyer had nudged him as they sat in the judge's chambers. He'd whispered to him to relax and not look so aggressive. The hearing was going his way, don't spoil it. It was her obvious vindictiveness that was creating a bad impression. Keep calm. And look calm. He switched off the shaver and tried to bring his mind back to Berlin.

There would be time to phone through to the house in Grunewald before he went to the meeting at Spandau. It was a meeting he didn't want to miss. A chance to look over the new Russian.

They met only when one of the occupying powers had a complaint to lodge, so most meetings, including this one, were called by the Russians. Although the meeting were solely concerned with the Spandau prison the representatives of the four powers were, in fact, career intelligence officers. Except Maguire, the American. He was a US Army major, a couple of years from his army pension, who'd been given the post as a well-earned sinecure. Bourget, the Frenchman, was SDECE, the Russian was always KGB, and himself SIS.

According to the files the Russian new boy was Alexei Andreyevich Kholkov. Aged twenty-eight. Newly promoted to captain in the KGB. No previous record of contact with any Western intelligence agency. Believed to have been mainly occupied on training case officers on the handling of agents, couriers and cut-outs. Married. No children. His name corresponded with one on central archives giving details of a man previously employed by the Bolshoi reserve theatre group, and suspected of being a KGB informer. No photographs available. No further information.

Sitting on the edge of the leather couch he reached for the telephone and dialled a local number. It was Howard who answered.

'Signals Security.'

'It's Jan. I'm back. I'll be over to see you early this evening. Tell Cohen and the others, will you?'

'How did it go in London?'

'Fair to bloody.'

'But you won?'

'Kind of. I'll tell you when I see you.'

'OK. And welcome back.'

'OK. See you.'

'Cheers.'

As he drove to the prison in Spandau he wondered what the Russians would be complaining about this time. The elderly Nazi in Spandau, its solitary prisoner, had long been a bone of contention with the Russians who insisted that despite his senility and sickness he should stay there until he died. It wasn't just a question of revenge. It gave them one more access to West Berlin and one more chance to create dissension among the allies. That was why, except for the American, the representatives were intellligence officers not administrators. It gave them opportunities for meeting their opposite numbers, and sometimes a chance to test the water for minor deals and cooperation.

He parked his car in the courtyard and the security sergeant checked his card carefully before opening the side gate to the governor's office.

Maguire and Bourget were already there, drinking coffee from a Thermos on a silver salver. They chatted as he poured himself a coffee, and then the Russian arrived. The escorting officer introduced him.

'Gentlemen. The Soviet representative. Mr Kholkov.'

There had been a brief bow or two but no handshaking as the Russian was waved to a seat at the table. Maguire did the basic courtesy of offering the Russian a coffee which he declined.

They briefly discussed the first of the two items on the agenda. As Maguire read out the MO's report on Hess's deteriorating health Massey looked at the Russian.

He was tall and good-looking. Almost elegant in his Italian silk suit and his Hardy Amies tie. The fingers on the notepad were long, tapering and well manicured. Massey guessed that he must be one of the KGB's new-look officers. The old-time thugs had had their uses but they didn't blend well into Western civilian communities. But Alexei Kholkov could get by successfully in Paris, London or Washington. Even Berlin.

Indifferent to the prisoner's state of health, the Russian sat ostentatiously not listening to Maguire reading out the medical report, his eyes on some distant horizon. When he caught Massey's eye, he hesitated and then nodded an acknowledgment.

Maguire passed on to item two. A complaint from the Soviet representative. The American nodded towards the Russian.

'What's on your mind, Mr Kholkov?'

The Russian turned towards Massey. 'My superiors wish to lodge a formal complaint against the British authorities concerning a grossly defamatory article in the *Sunday Times* regarding the Soviet attitude to the Nazi prisoner, Rudolf Hess. We wish to remind the parties concerned that Soviet Union suffered twenty million dead in the Great Patriotic War and . . .'

Maguire interrupted. 'Mr Kholkov, don't let's go through all that jazz once again. We don't indulge in that sort of propaganda at these meetings. I'm sure Mr Massey will deal with your problem if you say what it is.'

Massey saw the flush of anger on Kholkov's cheeks as he leaned forward aggressively.

'Is it the official view of the United States that twenty million Russians killed fighting the Nazis are of no significance?'

Massey intervened and said quickly, 'Mr Kholkov, we are solely concerned here with Rudolf Hess and the conditions of his imprisonment. And maybe it would put your mind at rest if I remind you that when Rudolf Hess flew to Scotland in 1941 the Soviet Union and Nazi Germany were allies.' He leaned back in his chair. 'Perhaps you could bear that in mind when you frame your complaint.'

He saw the mixture of embarrassment and frustration on Kholkov's face. His mouth half-open to speak but no words emerging. Then the Russian took a deep breath and launched into his well-rehearsed party piece.

'The newspaper article was aimed solely at discrediting the Soviet people by suggesting that our insistence on complying with the sentence passed on this leading Nazi is inhuman, unjust and vindictive.'

As Kholkov paused Maguire said, 'It bloody well *is* inhuman, unjust and vindictive.'

Kholkov's anger broke, his frustration desperate and obvious. He wagged an inappropriately elegant finger at Maguire and said, 'You remember that statement, Mr Maguire, when your Secretary of State next complains about articles in *Pravda* or *Izvestia* criticizing the United States' warmongers.'

Maguire smiled, but not benevolently. 'Just go back, Mr Kholkov, and tell your masters that you delivered their complaint and it was duly noted.'

'And what action will be taken?'

Maguire was lighting a cigar and waved the lighted match towards Massey who said, 'We have a free press, Mr Kholkov. If you want to put your own views forward I suggest that somebody in Moscow sends a letter to the *Sunday Times* making out the Soviet case.'

Kholkov's anger betrayed him. His fist beat on the table as he looked at each one of them in turn. 'Our people are right, you bastards don't give a shit for our people.'

There was a moment's silence and then Maguire said amiably, 'I must congratulate you, Mr Kholkov, on your command of the English language.' He looked around the table. 'Gentlemen. Is there any other business?'

There was none, and the meeting broke up.

As he walked back towards the guardhouse Massey found himself alongside the Russian. 'Have you got time for a cup of coffee, Mr Kholkov?'

Kholkov turned to look at him, the surprise obvious on his face. He shrugged. 'Time, yes. But I'm not allowed to move around in West Berlin. I have to go directly to our liaison unit or your people will arrest me for breaking the rules.'

The SIS man smiled. 'Phone your people or give your driver a message. Tell them you're with me. I'll take full responsibility for returning you in an hour or so.'

'Why do you suggest this?'

Massey shrugged. 'We're going to cross paths quite a few times, Mr Kholkov. It could be sensible for our masters if we had reasonable communications.'

'You call it reasonable communications what you did in there?'

'It should be a lesson to you.'

'How?'

'That you need to do your homework before you put your case.'

'Homework? I don't understand.'

'You need to prepare your case, not just bounce it on the table. That might work in Moscow, but not here.'

Kholkov looked at his watch. 'OK. I'll tell my driver.'

Ten minutes later they were in Kempinski's and as Massey stirred his coffee he said, 'I let you off lightly today, my friend.'

'In what way?'

'I could have pointed out that Stalin murdered as many Russians as the Nazis did. Not only before the war, but while it was still going on.' He paused. 'Thats why you had no experienced commanders when the Nazis invaded you. He'd had them executed because he was scared. Scared of the Soviet people turning on him. And it was that that made it possible for the Finns to give you a bloody nose when you invaded them.'

'Why should you care what Stalin did?'

'Because the present men in the Kremlin would do it again if they needed to.'

'Why are you saying all this?'

'Some day you might come to one of the meetings with a genuine complaint. Something that could be worked out. But if you don't recognize that cheap propaganda and table-thumping doesn't work with experienced people, then you'll never stand a chance of putting things right.'

'But you and the Americans never would put anything right. If you knew something angered us you'd be delighted.'

'What did you do before you were KGB?'

The Russian's dark eyes looked at his face and he said softly, 'Who said I was KGB?'

'The Soviet liaison officer is always KGB. You were promoted to captain before they posted you to this job.'

Kholkov shrugged. 'So why ask about me if you know already, Major Massey, SIS?'

Massey was amused at the knowing schoolboy retort.

'It's Alexei, isn't it?'

'Yes.'

'Where did you learn such good English?'

'At Moscow University.'

'Did you know Yuri Rostov, your predecessor?'

'I met him briefly.'

'He took the hard Moscow line in our meetings but it got him nowhere in three years. But he was a peasant, you're not.'

'So?'

'I imagine that if Moscow had wanted another hardliner in Berlin they wouldn't have chosen you. So maybe it would pay you to prepare your case better when you have a complaint. Especially if it's genuine and not just propaganda.'

'I still don't understand, Mr Massey. Why are you telling me all this? Why should you care whether I succeed or fail?'

'It's part of my job.'

Kholkov laughed. 'What? To train the new KGB man in how to succeed?'

'In a way. It helps keep things from boiling over. The more we understand one another the less tension there will be. Unless one side or another actually wants the tension.'

'And the American? Maguire?'

'He was fighting the Nazis before you were born, my friend.'

'And hates the Russians.'

'Only the nasty ones.'

'Like KGB captains.'

Massey smiled. 'Try some charm next time. It may not work but it won't make things worse like you did today.'

'You think Hess should be released?'

'I'm not sure. I could be persuaded either way. But not by propaganda.' He paused. 'Is this your first posting that gives you direct contact with the West?'

Kholkov hesitated, then nodded. 'Maybe you really know already. But yes, I've been outside the Soviet Union but only inside Warsaw Pact countries.' He shrugged. 'And to answer your other question, I was an actor before I was recruited. With the Bolshoi company.'

Massey smiled. 'Don't you wish you were still an actor?'

'No. I was only in the reserve company. My wife wishes I was still an actor, of course. But she's an intellectual. Are you married?'

'I was. We got a divorce.'

'It's not easy to keep a wife happy in this sort of job.'

Massey smiled and shrugged. 'I guess it depends on the wife. Anyway, I'd better take you back or your people will be getting worried.'

Kholkov smiled. 'I don't think so. Actually talking with the opposition will improve my status.'

Massey said in Russian, 'They're not fools, your bosses.'

Kholkov looked amazed. 'You speak Russian?'

'Why not?'

'So few foriegners speak Russian. It's very rare. And you speak without an accent. Or very little. You could be Ukrainian.'

'More a Georgian by temperament, Alexei.'

Kholkov laughed as he stood up. Georgians were the hot-blooded men of the Soviet Union. 'We must cooperate where we can.'

Massey phoned Max Cohen and told him that he'd leave their meeting until the morning. He read his mail and went early to bed.

CHAPTER FOUR

The sign said simply, and deceptively, BRITISH FORCES COMMUNICATIONS UNIT BERLIN. The Counter Intelligence sergeant checked his pass and identity card and the big gates were swung open. He had done it hundreds of times before but it made no difference.

There was coiled Dannert wire and a net of electric fencing on each side of the drive until he came to the second guardbox. His documents were checked again and a message phoned through to the house.

The house had once been the home of a furniture manufacturer. Built of stone it sprawled over a vast area where wings had been added over the years, and now there were raw, new, windowless concrete blocks that had been added for its present occupants. There were ten acres of parkland to guard, with their complex of aerials. Long criss-crossed wires of antennas, an enormous radome, parabolic microwave dishes and a group of high, slender pylons that were strung with wires like giant birdcages.

Below ground was a vast complex of rooms spreading beyond the foundations of the buildings above ground. Living quarters, working areas, offices, generating plant, air-conditioning and a computer room. And several million dollars' worth of state-of-the-art electronic surveillance and decrypting devices. Most of the gathered information went straight to GCHQ at Cheltenham, and a lesser amount to London Communications Security Agency. A separate section covered the local surveillance and communications needed for local intelligence operations.

Jan Massey, as Head of Station, was responsible for all its activities, not just the GCHQ outstation. He was not involved in the day-to-day operations of the electronic surveillance unit; that was the responsibility of Max Cohen. Massey was much more involved with the convoluted and complex espionage and counter-espionage operations that were run by Gordon Harper. His deputy and personal assistant, Howard Fielding, was responsible for keeping him informed and updated on problem areas and planning.

He had his own quarters on the top floor of the house, the small flat on the Kurfürstendamm and another larger official apartment near Checkpoint Charlie in a block off Wilhelmstrasse. None of his people knew of the place on the Ku'damm. He paid the rental himself and the name on the door was J. Felinski. There were times when he needed to be alone. To spend a night or a couple of days away from the pressures of the house in Grunewald.

Massey walked up the wide staircase to the first floor and along the corridor to Max Cohen's office.

Max Cohen had no known living relatives. At the nearest Cohen could assess, twenty-seven of his family, including both his parents, had been gassed or burnt in one concentration camp or another. That was also the reason why he had never married.

He had been a brilliant science student at Cambridge and a total failure as a don at his own college. He walked out one morning and few days later took a job at a small firm making advanced aircraft communication systems. He was spotted a year later and recruited by GCHQ. He had specified and partly designed the total radio surveillance system that was installed in Berlin, supervised its installation and was then put in charge of the operation. He and Massey got on well with each other without any undue effort on either side. They recognized and tolerated each other's idiosyncrasies and found common ground in their resistance to being moulded into the typical Brit character. The Jew and the Pole, who might well have been antagonistic in any other European community, exchanged their sly but amiable jokes at their British colleagues' expense. It defused their antagonisms and afforded them a small enclave of relief when stiff upper lips or some routine Brit hypocrisy set their pulses pounding in frustrated anger.

Max Cohen's hatred for Germans was controlled but chronic, and active enough for him to feel guilty when he slept with German girls or listened furtively to almost any Wagner music from *Tristan* to *Parsifal*. He loved it all.

Cohen was talking on the phone and Massey stood looking at the bunch of sit-reps clipped to the white board on the wall. Status reports on equipment. Changes of personnel on listening shifts. A list of current names and words to be alerted to the evaluation section. A leave roster for Russian speakers and a similar one for German speakers. A list of four new Red Army units which had moved into Leipzig in the previous twenty-four hours, with their current frequencies in brackets, and a reference number of the files that would give all recorded information about their status and function.

When Cohen hung up Massey sat down on the chair in front of the trestle table that Cohen used as a desk.

'Any new problems, Max?'

'No. Some old ones getting worse.'

'Which ones?'

'The shortage of KG4 microchips for upgrading the special tape recorders. We're ten days behind schedule. And we had a break in recording GRU traffic yesterday. One of the Racal 6790s was on the blink. The RAM "keep alive" memory on one band went down. We lost about an hour.'

'Did you miss anything important?'

Cohen shrugged. 'Who knows, Jan? Probably not.'

'Any problems in Harper's area?'

Cohen smiled. 'That's the only part you really care about, isn't it?'

'It's the only part where people who work for me can get killed because of mistakes.' Massey smiled. 'And it's the part I understand. Anyway you keep your end up pretty well without me. Your friends at Cheltenham were full of praise at the Joint Intelligence meeting last week. There was talk about an MBE or some such thing in the next honours list – services to industry.'

'I'd rather get a guaranteed supply of microchips.'

'So what about Harper and his boys?'

'Which do you want first – the good or the bad?'

'The bad.'

'I want to sack one of your radio operators for bad on-air discipline and I want you to discipline one of Harper's men for the same thing.'

'What happened?'

'Malins had sent a surveillance team into East Berlin to take a look at the KGB HQ in Normanenallee. He'd heard that there was building work going on there and London wanted them to see what it was in aid of. We gave them a frequency and a code and they were warned to use it only in an emergency. One of them, a chap named Rawlins, came on air – in clear – and asked the operator to tell his girlfriend he'd be an hour late. The operator responded – also in clear – and contacted the girl by phone. It was irresponsible, Jan. Harper's people see themselves as being above rules and regulations and it's going to cost you dear one of these days if we don't stop it. I've sent you a memo about it. '

'OK. I'll deal with it.'

'Toughly? No excuses.'

'Exactly how you want, Max. I agree that there are no excuses but there are reasons why they behave like idiots.'

'Tell me. I'd like to hear them.'

For a few seconds Massey was silent. 'When they go through the Wall into East Berlin or over the frontier into the GDR it takes a lot of guts, Max. If they're caught they know what'll happen to them, so there's a lot of adrenalin flowing. What they're doing is illegal and dangerous, and they're on their own with every man's hand turned against them. This place seems a long way away. And the routine rules and regulations are far away too. They've got an in-built disrespect for the law. We train them that way. They're special – and they know it. And sometimes they act irresponsibly. Not excusable, I agree. But just about understandable.'

'You don't need to do a hearts-and-flowers job on me, Jan. I can imagine what it's like, but if they want to end up in a KGB cell at Karlshorst, bad radio security is a quick way of getting there. My boys aren't the only ones with headphones on, twiddling the knobs up and down the short wave frequencies.'

'I'll deal with them, Max. Don't worry.' Massey paused. 'What's the good news?'

Cohen picked up a transparent plastic folder and tossed it across the table. There were half a dozen A4 pages inside it.

'We've broken the new Moscow code in record time. They changed it a day early and in the middle of a transmission. We only missed seven minutes. It's interesting stuff. I wasn't going to pass it to Evaluation until you'd seen it. It looks like a major reshuffle of KGB staff in East Berlin.' He shrugged. 'Anyway. See what you think of it.'

'Thanks. Did Loftus cooperate on the courier problem you had?'

'Yes. He moaned a bit, but he's increased our nominal roll by two extra couriers for the next six months.'

'No other problems?'

'Dozens, but none that you need to worry about.'

'I'll see you at the meeting this afternoon.'

'OK.'

In his own suite of office and living quarters Massey went through the various piles of accumulated memos and reports. A mass of information on what was going on in the city of Berlin, both East and West. Reports on living conditions and morale in East Germany and the GDR. Transcripts of selected intercepts of Soviet military and civilian telephone and radio cummunications. The operations covered not only the Russians and East Germans but all diplomatic establishments in Berlin including its German government and all the representives of other countries' intelligence and diplomatic services.

There was a single-page daily summary of items drawn to his attention and compiled by his assistant, Howard Fielding. Fielding was thirty, a history graduate from Aston University who had specialized in Soviet studies. A calm, unflappable academic who had learned how to act as a safety net and defender of his sometimes over-emotional boss.

Harper had stayed behind after the general meeting and filled him in on the details of a few operations that were too confidential to be discussed in front of other section heads. Massey ordered him to downgrade the two offenders mentioned by Cohen and transfer them back to London without waiting for replacements. Harper saw the look of Massey's face and abandoned the defence he had prepared for the field agent. Massey in that mood wouldn't be impressed by the fact that the man's girlfriend was pregnant.

'I think Bourget is anxious to speak to you. He's mentioned it to me a couple of times. I told him you were in London.'

'What does he want?'

'I've no idea.'

'What are the French up to at the moment?'

'The Mission is buttering up the Germans on orders from Paris. The Mitterand – Kohl axis. And the SDECE – well, you know them as well as I do. Rushing off in all directions to no particular purpose – apart from impressing Paris.'

'Are they operating in East Berlin at all?'

'Just casual line-crossers. In and out the same day.'

'How do they go in?'

'They use the usual tourist coach trips.' Harper smiled. 'They check the prices of fruit and vegetables and few household goods and call it economic intelligence. They chat up a waitress or a barman and that's evaluating public morale.'

'How does Bourget stand with Paris these days?'

'OK, so far as I know.'

'I'll let you know what he's got to say when I've spoken to him.'

'Don't forget I'm in London for two days next week.'

'What for?'

'Routine medical.'

CHAPTER FIVE

Heidi Fischer walked back slowly from the Justiz Palast in Vienna towards the History of Art Museum, her backside rolling provocatively and her blue eyes alert and vigilant for any sign of interest from the few men who passed by in the narrow back streets. She was eighteen and well built, with long legs and firm breasts. She wasn't pretty but she was attractive with a neat turned-up nose and pouting, almost petulant lips. She was Viennese but looked German. Solid, and without the chic that most Viennese girls managed to contrive with a scarf or a belt or even a smile. But the rather stolid farmgirl appearance seemed somehow to emphasize her obvious sexual attraction. There would be no swinging from chandeliers but she looked as if those long legs would open eagerly enough to satisfy a man's lust.

Despite its being the middle of summer a slight drizzle began to fall and that gave her an excuse to stand in the shelter of the shop doorway of Apotheke Ludke. Twenty minutes later a US army jeep slowed down as the driver looked her over and then stopped. A few minutes' bargaining and she climbed in over the tailboard and the canvas flapped to behind her. Arthur was never worried about the men but he objected to her taking them back to the room when he was there.

An hour later her high heels were clattering up the stone steps to the fourth-floor room in the old house in a cobbled alley off Breitegasse. He was sitting there smoking, his battledress blouse hung over the back of the chair. Signalman Arthur Johnson was twenty-three, with a raw, fleshy face and a body already showing a tendency to flabbiness. He glanced at her as she came into the room and then looked back at the black-and-white TV. The sound was turned down because he couldn't speak German and the football game had a German commentary. While he was watching she made coffee for them both and a plateful of corned-beef sandwiches from an army ration tin.

When the match was over he said, 'How did you get on?'

She smiled. 'OK. Thirty marks.'

'How many fellows?'

'Two. One British and one Yank.'

He watched as she counted out the money before putting it in a china vase on the small table under the window.

'I got news for you, Heidi. I've been posted.'

She turned quickly. 'Where to?'

'Berlin.'

'When?'

'The day after tomorrow. Friday.'

'Can I go with you?'

He shook his head slowly, 'I shouldn't think so. You're not even proper German.'

The girl's eyes blazed with anger and her voice was shrill. 'Is that all you care? You said you'd marry me. You said we'd have a proper life. No more street work for me. I'd be your wife. We'd have a place of our own. And now you just sit there calmly and say you're off to Berlin without me.'

'Calm down, for Christ's sake. I'll just have to work out how to get you there when I've settled in and know how to do it.'

He pulled her onto his lap and kissed her avidly as his hand went under her skirt. It was several minutes later when she struggled and took her mouth from his. 'You bastard. You're just like the others. You just want to screw me and you . . .'

Her words were smothered by his mouth on hers and five minutes later they were both naked on the ramshackle bed.

Signalman Arthur Johnson sat in the underground room and checked the computer print-out of incoming stores against the print-out of the official order. He didn't know what most of the items were, and nobody explained them to him because he didn't need to know. And 'need to know' was paramount in the house in Grunewald. He had never been beyond these rooms apart from his shared room in the big house upstairs. It took several minutes of elaborate electronic games to get into or out of his small office. He had only the vaguest idea of what went on in the labyrinth of rooms and cubicles beyond the metal door. Nobody would ever tell him, and part of the reason why he'd been posted to the unit was that he was too oafish to care but bright enough to do several of the routine jobs that had to be done. The fact that he didn't know or care what the difference was between gallium arsenide and recrystallized polysilicon was, to the man who had recruited him, a virtue in itself.

Arthur Johnson was born in Handsworth, a suburb of Birmingham that had once been a cut above its neighbouring district, Aston. Handsworth had then been a place for the upper working class – skilled craftsmen and foremen, many from Scotland and Wales, who worked in the nearby foundries and big industrial plants and saw it as proof of their status that they could move to Handsworth and bring up their families in such a pleasant environment. Flower shows and bands in the local park, a good tram service to other parts of the city, and a quiet respectability that suited their temperaments. But the trams went and soon the respectability went. And Handsworth became the fief of immigrants and the unemployed. Nobody knew why they had chosen Handsworth but in five years they had taken over.

He never knew who his father was apart from the fact that his name was Joe and that his mother hated him. She hated him. She hated her son too. Inevitably he did badly at school but that wasn't unusual by local standards. By the time he was fifteen he seldom went to school and spent his time running errands for local bookmakers and prostitutes. He lacked the street-smartness of his contemporaries and that was an advantage. As it turned out, this lack of enterprise continued to stand him in good stead in the future. He seemed too dull and too stupid to be mistrusted.

When Arthur was sixteen he had gone home one night to find his few possessions in a cardboard box on the front steps. There was a note from his mother telling him that she had given up the house. It was being sold by the landlord and he'd have to find somewhere else to live. She wouldn't be back. She wished him luck and there were two pound-notes in the envelope.

He had picked up the cardboard box and walked round to Johnny's place.

Johnny had been an all-in wrestler using the name Tarzan but now he was keeper for two girls who plied their trade up near the recreation ground. Arthur wasn't actually made welcome but he wasn't turned away. He cleaned the house, ran messages and chatted with the girls when they weren't occupied with their trade. And in their own odd way they became surrogate sisters and mothers to him, and shared their innermost thoughts with the young man: ambitions for hairdressing salons or smart boutiques, and their anecdotes of customers and their funny ways. The older of the two girls granted him her standard favours a few times but it was always her initiative, not his. He was energetic but undemanding.

It was Johnny who fixed him up with the job at the radio shop. Customers bringing in their radios and TVs for repair mistook his silence for hostility and eventually the boss put him out of sight in the small back room to help the repairman. By the time Arthur Johnson was eighteen he could fix most of the routine breakdowns himself. He could even use the test instruments without understanding even the rudiments of electricity.

He saw the display in the window of the recruiting office in the city centre but only stopped to read the noticeboard after he spotted the chassis of a radio set and a television. It happened to be a recruiting campaign for the Royal Corps of Signals and he went inside. After half an hour of questions and chat he signed the papers and was given a travel warrant to Catterick Camp. At the end of the course he wasn't surprised when he failed. The technical stuff was far beyond him and the practical side little better. He was used to domestic appliances, not the high-flown electronics that the army used.

But he was in the army and somehow a job had to be found for him. He had a few virtues that could be of use: he did what he was told, he was uncomplaining, and he could read and write. Signalman Johnson was trained as a clerk and was posted to a small specialist unit in Cumbria. After several other postings he was eventually sent to what was called the Composite Signals Unit in Vienna. One of the small but vital links in a chain that led back to GCHQ in Cheltenham.

The Kit-Kat Club in Berlin's Uhlandstrasse has no pretensions. Dimly lit, to hide its tattiness and the identity of its habitués, it offers expensive drinks and cheap food and a harbour for petty criminals and prostitutes. Arthur Johnson had tried most of the clubs in the area and found the Kit-Kat less of a rip-off than its neighbours. And the girls were pretty and uninhibited.

He had never had a relationship with a girl other than a prostitute. Not that he was either a pervert or particularly sex driven. But, perhaps due to his earlier experiences, he was drawn towards prostitutes because it avioded responsibility. They had their own places and they earned their own money. And in their turn the girls, recognizing his weak but amiable character, found him an undemanding companion. He didn't want to take any of their earnings, his sexual demands were normal and intermittent. And he was male, and someone to talk to.

Johnson's new girlfriend was a twenty-seven-year-old blonde who earned a living between performing an uninspired strip act and casual prostitution. Being both several years older and far more wordly than Johnson, she was aware that she was less a mistress than a mother substitute for him. She listened to his complaints about how the army treated him and he brought her cartons of cigarettes and tins of coffee from the NAAFI. And on Sundays, if he was off duty, he had her for ten minutes of crude urgent lust before they went to a cinema or for a meal in a restaurant. Otherwise, he spent his off-duty evenings with her as if they were brother and sister.

Signalman Johnson would watch her act as he waited for her on his free nights with the feeling that he was part of show business. An impresario, or perhaps a talent spotter for some Hollywood studio. That particular night she was doing the coy version of her act. Twirling the paper parasol as the tape played 'Raindrops keep falling on my head' and undoing the buttons on the yellow plastic raincoat with her free hand.

He was sitting sipping a beer when a shadow fell across the table and a girl's voice said, 'Hello, Arthur.' He didn't look up at the girl, assuming that she was one of the other regulars. But when she pulled out a chair and sat down he turned briefly to see who it was. For long moments he just stared, his mouth open, his eyes screwed up in disbelief.

'Heidi. What the hell are you doing here?'

'You said you'd send for me.'

'I tried, Heidi. I couldn't get anywhere. It's bloody difficult.'

'You glad to see me?'

'Of course I am. Where're you staying?'

'I've got a room near Checkpoint Charlie. I've been here two weeks. Looking for you.'

'Let's go there. It'll be easier to talk.'

She smiled. A knowing, experienced smile. 'Saves paying thirty marks for screwing one of these chicks, you mean.'

'Come on, Heidi, you know it's not just that.'

She shrugged. 'OK. Let's go.'

Heidi Fischer had slept with four different officials to acquire the permits and documents she needed to get to West Berlin. Two in Vienna. One in Bonn. And one in West Berlin who was ready to keep her documents up to date in return for more sex. An impartial observer might wonder if Signalman Johnson was worth all the trouble. He was neither handsome nor wealthy, nor did he have the affection or charm that most girls would consider worth competing for. But he was British and a soldier and he had one unique virtue so far as Heidi Fischer was concerned: he was the only man who had ever, no matter how obliquely, hinted that he might marry her. With a large surplus of women in both Austria and Germany, men who mentioned marriage were rare. And with such a marriage she would become a British citizen with a legal passport of her own. A British subject, not an ex-enemy alien.

As she undressed slowly and professionally she could tell that he wanted her and that was a relief. Although he was never demanding, when they had sex he was crude and clumsy. But her attractive face and the thing between her legs were the only assets she had.

When it was over and he lay smoking a cigarette beside her on the bed she said, 'How've you been getting on?'

He leaned up, reaching over her to stub out the Lucky Strike in the metal ashtray. 'Still the same old grind. Three chaps been promoted over my head. I been thinking of getting out. Going back to civvy street.'

'Why didn't they promote you?'

'Christ knows. They think I'm just a zombie.'

'What's a zombie?'

'A mad person. Crazy.'

'Poor old Arthur.'

'I'll get my own back on the bastards one of these days. You mark my words.'

'How would you do that?'

'I've got ideas, girl. I'm not just bluffing. Maybe you could help me.'

'Oh, Arthur. I'll help you. You know I will. Any way you want.'

Johnson looked at his watch. 'I'll have to go, Heidi. There's a service bus back to the unit at midnight.'

'Can you see me tomorrow?'

'I ain't sure. I'll try. It'd be about eight if I can make it.'

It had been a bad day for Johnson. A document wrongly registered, a rollocking from the CSM, and a snotty interview with Meyer. Just one bloody document and all that fuss. And the same question again and again. Why had he registered it under Karlshorst intercepts instead of GRU? Why keep on asking him? If he could have told them why it had happened he wouldn't have done it in the first place. He'd just mistaken the network coding index, but they behaved like he'd started World War III. They always had to have somebody to blame for their cock-ups and it was always him.

He was still in a bad mood by the time he got to Heidi's rooms. But as she cooked him a meal and he sat drinking a coffee, the first glimmerings of how to strike back at the bastards filtered slowly into his mind.

As Heidi placed the plate of sausages and potato in front of him she noticed the change of mood.

'What have you been up to, Authur?'

'I've had enough of the army, Heidi. I'll never make enough for us to get married. They don't give a damn about me.'

'What you got in mind?'

'You and me are going to Moscow, kid.'

She looked amazed. 'Moscow? What the hell for?'

'I'll do broadcasts against the British and the Yanks. Tell the world how they really treat people. I can tell the Russians how to do it. Propaganda. I'll give press conferences, go on radio and TV. Write for the newspapers, the lot.'

'D'you know any Russians?'

'No. That's where you can help me.'

'How?'

'Go through the checkpoint. Find a Russian officer and tell him I'm ready to come over.'

She looked shocked. 'I couldn't do that. I don't speak Russian. How would I find a Russian officer?'

'They're all over the place, girl. Just give one the eye and tell him the tale. We could make a fortune. I'd be like Philby and what's-his-name, the queer. Questions in Parliament. God, they'd see I wasn't just a dumb cluck after all. I'd show the bastards.'

She shook her head in disbelief. 'I couldn't do it, Arthur. I wouldn't know how to go about it. I wouldn't dare.'

Johnson looked at her. 'If you want to marry me, kid, you'll do it. It's the only way.'

Heidi Fischer shook her head. 'I'll think about it. But I don't fancy it. It's scary.'

'Try. Just try. See what happens. There's no harm in trying.'

'What if they don't believe me?'

'They'll give it a go, girl. They want people to go over to them. They make them into heroes. They do.'

'And if it works we'd get married?'

'Why not, kid? Why not?'

CHAPTER SIX

Massey had slept that night at the flat in the Ku'damm and drove back to the house in Grunewald the next morning.

There was a note on his desk that there had been another call for him from Bourget. The Frenchman had left a number for him to call. It wasn't the usual SDECE number.

Like most British and American intelligence officers he walked very cautiously when he was dealing with the SDECE. They were tough and energetic but in Berlin they were riddled with KGB plants. There had been scandal after scandal ever since SDECE had been founded in the early 1960s. Narcotics dealing, counterfeiting and particularly bloody assassinations. And on top of all that they were unreliable, disreputable and, from an intelligence point of view, insecure.

He dialled the number that Bourget had left and a girl answered. A sleepy bedroom voice in German not French. He had to wait a couple of minutes before Bourget came on the line.

'Jan?' His voice sounded like she'd had to wake him up.

'Yes, Pierre. What can I do for you?'

'What time is it?'

'Nine thirty.'

'Do you know Au Bon Bistroquet?'

'On the Ku'damm?'

'Yes. How about we meet there in an hour? Say a quarter after eleven?'

'OK. But I can't stay long.'

'Just a coffee, my friend, or a bowl of soup.'

'OK.'

Bourget had booked a table but when Massey got there the Frenchman hadn't arrived. They showed him to the table and brought him a glass of red wine. He guessed that that bedroomy voice had held things up.

Bourget came in looking as villainous and attractive as ever. It was one of those very lived-in faces. Tanned, heavily pock-marked, but undoubtedly attractive to women. He was a Hemingway man, strong, energetic and hairy. Massey didn't like the type though he quite liked Bourget. But he suspected that sooner or later the Frenchman would end up on Devil's Island or wherever the French put their naughty boys these days.

'Well, my friend, I made it,' Bourget said, as if being late was some special achievement.

'I've got twenty minutes, Pierre. No longer.'

'Bouillabaisse?'

'Fine.'

Until the girl brought the soup he was given the benefit of Bourget's views on Berlin and the Germans. Bourget wasn't a fan either. Then, hunching his shoulders as if that gave them greater privacy, he got down to business.

'Got a problem, old friend. Think you could help.'

'What is it?'

'What KGB have you got at the moment? Not defectors I mean.'

Massey smiled. 'You don't expect me to tell you, do you?'

'Why not?'

'It'd be in the local papers in two days. Your outfit leaks all over the place.'

'No way. Just between you and me.'

'Why do you want to know?'

'I think I got somebody from the other side.'

'Who?'

Bourget shrugged. 'I can't say you. Is not finished yet.'

'So let's wait. We can talk when you've got him.'

'He's more important to you than to me. Maybe we can cooperate. You went to the meeting in Paris, yes?'

'Yes.'

'So we can cooperate.'

'It doesn't need a meeting in Paris to make us cooperate, Pierre. But I can't do a deal about some unknown man who might defect but hasn't as yet done so.'

Bourget looked troubled. 'You want to know who he is?'

'It's up to you, Pierre.'

'Is Kuznetsov.'

Massey hesitated. 'Tell me more.' He paused. 'Are you sure he's not a plant?'

'No. I'm not sure. That's why I like cooperate with you.'

'Why does he say he wants to defect?'

'He don't say.'

'What's he want?'

'Wants to go to your people or CIA. New identity, cash and pension.'

'So why didn't he approach me or Autenowski at CIA?'

'He got no choice, my friend.' Bourget smiled. 'He talk with me or nothing.'

'When are you meeting him again?'

'Any time you want.'

'Where can we meet him?'

'My villa.'

'He'd never go there. There's people watching your place all the time.'

Bourget grinned. 'I got him there now. We picked him up two days ago. We been working on him.'

'Why don't you just pass him over to me?'

Bourget grinned. 'No way, Jan, no way.' He paused. 'Maybe I sell him to you. A private deal.'

He didn't like the sound of it but it was typical SDECE. 'How much do you want?'

'Fifteen thousand US dollars in cash.'

'London would never agree to that.'

Bourget smiled. 'I can get more than that from others.'

'Who?'

The Frenchman shook his head. 'You think about it, my friend. Let me know when you want to do a deal.'

'Let me talk to London and see what their reaction is.'

'They don't let you decide these things here on the spot?'

Massey smiled because the jibe was so obvious and naïve. 'I like to keep them in the picture, Pierre. By the way, who's the girl with the sexy voice?'

The Frenchman grinned, his strong uneven teeth gleaming. 'You want to try her, my old friend. Leni. Blonde, not yet twenty. Long legs, beautiful big tits. I make you a present of her if we do a deal, yes? What do they call it? A goodwill gesture, yes?'

'You're a thoughtful, wonderful man, Pierre, but I'm too old for young blondes.'

Bourget was looking down at the table crumbling the remains of a *brioche*, and without looking up he said, 'What d'you think of Kholkov?'

'He's hard-working. He knows what he's doing.'

'Would you trust him?'

'I'd never put myself in a position where I needed to trust him. One way or another.'

'Would you trust him in an exchange deal?'

'Provided all the t's were crossed and the i's were dotted, yes.'

'What does it mean, the t's crossed and dotted?'

'It means that I'd want to go over every possible detail and angle first. The Russians usually deliver when they've made a deal but they drive a hard bargain first.'

Bourget shrugged. 'Is best you think seriously about what I say, my friend.'

Massey stood up, 'I'll think about it, Pierre, and I'll be in touch. *Soyez sage*.'

Bourget nodded and turned away to beckon to the waitress.

As Massey walked back to the flat he thought of what Bourget had said about Kholkov. He had met Kholkov three or four times since that first meeting six months earlier. They had been routine meetings at the Kommandatura but he had had a meal with Kholkov after one of the meetings. He had felt then that there was something odd about the Russian. He was cool and sophisticated and he talked fairly freely for a KGB man. But Kholkov's operation in West Berlin was hopelessly inefficient. His people were being pulled in by Harper's men at a rate of almost one a week. He might have been good as an instructor but it was different doing it in the real world. In the real world sex, money and fear were factors that lectures and training manuals only mentioned as hazards. In the real world they were a large part of life itself.

He wondered why Bourget had Kholkov in mind as a contact for some exchange deal. Maybe Bourget knew something about Kholkov that he didn't know. But Bourget's story of having picked up Kuznetsov must be a figment of the Frenchman's imagination. Kuznetsov never ventured into West Berlin. He didn't need to and his KGB bosses wouldn't have let him.

Massey breathed a sigh of relief as he let himself into his flat in the Ku'damm.

He switched on the hi-fi. There was a programme of Viennese songs on RIAS Berlin FM and he hummed along with '*Sag beim Abschied*' as he stood looking out of the window.

The British and the Americans were putting on a cocktail and buffet party that night at the Hilton. He had often tried to remember afterwards what it was in aid of. He thought it was to commemorate the anniversary of the Potsdam Conference, but it could have been something quite different.

He disliked parties of any kind but there were some he couldn't avoid without causing real offence. Twenty minutes of doing his duty then maybe a phone call to the pretty young blonde at the art school. She was American, very young and very pretty and she was having a year in Berlin before heading back to Chicago and the graphics department of her father's advertising agency. She was collecting scalps on the way in case she never got to Europe again. Berlin in the 'eighties had become like Paris in the 'twenties for Americans.

He switched off the radio, passed the Hilton telephone number to Cohen and Moore, then walked a few yards down the Ku'damm until he found a taxi.

When he got to the Hilton he was glad he hadn't backed out. His absence would have been noted. Consular staffs, military missions, NATO and visiting brass from Paris, London and Washington were there in force. There was too much of a crush for any serious talking but Massey dutifully did the rounds. When eventually he made for one of the exits he saw Kholkov talking to Bourget and the Frenchman's current girlfriend. He nodded to them as he passed, smiling to himself at the brashness of the Frenchman who defied the ban on Germans at the party by bringing a German girl – and a callgirl at that.

It was then that he noticed the girl in the black dress. She was standing alone as if she was waiting for someone. He registered that she was beautiful before he passed her.

He was almost at the cloakroom when Kholkov caught up with him.

'Massey. Jan. Come and meet my wife. She's with me tonight.' He smiled. 'Special dispensation from the Kommandatura.'

Massey hesitated for a moment but was aware of the Russian's enthusiasm. 'Of course, Alexei. I'd very much like to meet her.'

She was still standing there, just outside the crowded room, and she definitely was beautiful. Stunningly, breathtakingly beautiful. Almost as tall as her husband. Black hair in a chignon, heavy-lidded brown eyes, and a wide, sensuous mouth. She was wearing a black silk cocktail dress that emphasized her slender, elegant neck.

She put out her hand, smiling as Kholkov said, 'Anna, this is Jan Massey.'

'*Kak pozywacie.*'

'*Jak pozywacie.*'

They both laughed at the Englishness of the greeting and response and then Kholkov said, 'You two talk while I go and say my bread-and-butter thank-yous.'

They stood silent for a moment and then she said, 'Alexei told me that you're English.' She smiled. 'I would have said that you were a Pole.'

He smiled back. 'Why would you say that?'

'You speak very good Russian but you said *jak* instead of *kak* so you must be more used to speaking Polish. And nobody actually bothers to learn Polish.'

'Do you speak Polish?'

She laughed. 'I *am* Polish.' Then she shrugged. 'Or I was Polish. My mother was Polish.'

'My mother was Polish too.'

She lifted her eyebrows. 'Was?'

'She's dead.'

'Oh. I'm sorry.' She paused. 'My momma's dead too. Four years ago. In a car accident in Leningrad when the roads were icy.' Then she said softly. 'When did your mother die?'

'A long time ago. In the last few months of the war.'

'What happened? Was she ill?'

'The Nazis killed her in one of their camps.'

'Was she Jewish?'

'No. She was in the Resistance.'

'Is your father still alive?'

'Yes, he's a doctor in a small town in England. And yours?'

'He teaches music at the Conservatory in Moscow.'

Then Kholkov was back, smiling amiably, 'We'd better go, Anna.'

Massey hesitated for a moment, then said, 'Why don't you both have dinner with me some time next week?'

Kholkov looked at his wife. 'OK, Anna?' She nodded and Massey said, 'How about next Friday? Seven o'clock at Café Wien?'

'Fine. We'll look forward to that.'

They said their goodbyes and after they had left Massey went to the bar for a drink before he walked to the foyer and stood waiting for a taxi. He didn't phone the blonde but went straight back to his flat.

The dinner was not a success despite the good food. Even the traditional questions asked of new acquaintances were taboo. No questions on background, previous life, work politics, relationships but could be seen as probing for information for a dossier.

They talked about music and art, but even in those areas Massey was conscious of the fact that in the Soviet Union the Politburo could decide that a painting or a symphony were anti-Soviet propaganda.

They ended up talking about ice-skating, athletics and gymnastics. Sports where the Russians were world leaders without controversy. Subjects that not one of them cared about but were acceptable for their neutrality.

Anna Kholkov did her best to make it seem normal and less tense. She had been a ballet dancer before they were married and she was able to amuse them with anecdotes about dragon-like wardrobe mistresses and autocratic directors.

Massey drove them back to Checkpoint Charlie just after eleven and watched them pass through the barriers on both sides. A car was waiting for them on the East German side and the girl turned and waved to him as the driver opened the door for her.

He stood for several minutes, looking but not seeing, before he got back into his car and headed for Grunewald.

CHAPTER SEVEN

Massey waved Harper to one of the leather armchairs in his office and pulled its twin to face his visitor.

'Have you had anything out of SDECE recently, Gordon?'

Harper looked surprised. 'Nothing but the usual gossip.'

'Personal gossip or business gossip?'

'Personal. They've been playing footsie with one of my chaps recently but it's only a mild fishing expedition. Hoping to get something they can use to pad out their reports to Paris.' He smiled. 'We feed them a scrap or two to keep them happy and a bit of disinformation to keep the boys in Paris on the hop.' He paused. 'Have you heard something?'

'Nothing that I could believe . . . but I heard a rumour that a Russian had come over and was holed up with Bourget.'

Harper shook his head. 'I don't believe it. Any Russian would come to the CIA or us. Any Russian who knew the business, anyway.'

'Could you get your people to do a little sniffing around?'

'Of course. Anything more to go on? Name, when, how, et cetera?'

'I'm afraid not.'

'Any priority?'

'Days, not weeks. A nil report could be as useful as anything else for my purposes.'

'Can you tell me your source?'

'I could but I'd rather leave it.'

'A classification, maybe?'

Massey smiled at Harper's persistence. 'Let's say . . . unreliable but close. OK?'

Harper laughed softly. 'Sounds like Bourget to me. And he was trying to contact you for some weeks. I passed the messages to Howard Fielding as they came in.'

'No comment.' Massey smiled. 'Any new problems?'

Harper looked quizzically at Massey. 'Are you sure you want to hear?'

'Of course.'

'I need another evaluator, preferably two. Mason's team can't cope with the traffic now we're getting all the transcript summaries.'

'You asked for it that way . . . and you were right . . . it saves thirty-six hours on anything you need.'

'I know but –'

'I'll get you one – let me know if you need another. Evaluators are in short supply and you'll need to spend at least a month before the new one's any use to you'

'Can I tell Mason?'

'Sure. I'll speak to London today.'

When Harper had left, Massey still sat on in the armchair. He couldn't stop thinking about what Bourget had said about Kuznetsov. He didn't believe it, but it worried him that the Frenchman's lie had been based on Kuznetsov. There were dozens of other Russians he could have picked on. Was it some sort of hint? Or a threat? Not even Harper knew about Kuznetsov. Only Chambers and himself. He couldn't mention it to Chambers at this stage. He looked at his watch. It was time to go to the CIA meeting, the Joint Intelligence Liaison Committee where SIS and the CIA exchanged as little information of their operations as diplomacy would allow. If there was anything important that one side had to tell the other it would be done in Washington or London, not in West Berlin.

The Kholkovs had invited him to dinner that evening and they were waiting for him at the barrier on the East Berlin side of the checkpoint.

It was a warm, pleasant evening and they walked to the Café Warschau on Karl Marx Allee.

Anna ordered the meal for the three of them, choosing only Polish dishes – *barszcz, kotlet, nalesniki,* no wine but two bottles of *sliwowica.* She had teased her husband because she had to translate for him.

As they ate, Massey was constantly aware that Kholkov was watching him and he wondered if the Russian was more suspicious and less friendly now that he had had time to absorb what went on between the two sides in Berlin. When the girl photographer was doing the rounds of the guests at the tables, Anna Kholkov angrily waved her away when she attempted to take a photograph of them. He felt grateful to her for the partisanship but he knew that there would be plenty of photographs of him already on the KGB files.

A small orchestra was playing for dancing and he watched as Kholkov danced with his wife. They looked a handsome pair. It passed through his mind that it must be very nice to have a wife who was so beautiful and so intelligent. He asked her to dance with him when they came back to the table. When they were on the small dance floor she said, 'I apologize about the photographer. I don't think Alexei had arranged it.'

Massey smiled. 'It doesn't matter, they'll have dozens on the files already. But thanks all the same.'

She smiled up at him. 'Do you recognize what they're playing?'

'I recognize the tune. It was on one of my mother's old gramophone records. What's it called?'

She sang very softly, '*Płynie Wisła, płynie. Po Polskiej krajinie – Po Polskiej . . .*'

And then he remembered it. The gentle little ballad that said that while the Vistula river still flowed Poland would always be free.

He smiled. 'Are they allowed to play such songs now?'

She shrugged. 'This place is mainly for Poles. I doubt if the Russians know what the words mean. I'm sure they'd stop it if they knew.'

'Any news from your father?'

'Are you trying to change the subject?'

Massey laughed. 'Yes. But for your sake, not mine.'

'My father disapproved of my marriage. I never hear from him. He's cut me out of his life.'

'What did he object to?'

'Oh, two things. The main one was Alexei himself. He didn't like him.'

'And the second?'

'The fact that Alexei is KGB. My father despises them. All of them.'

'But your father's Russian not Polish.'

'All Russians don't go along with the system.' She shrugged. 'But I guess I don't need to tell *you* that.'

'Does Alexei know his views?'

'I'm afraid he does.'

'Maybe your father's attitude to you is to protect you from being associated with his views.'

'That's what I tell myself when I'm lonely and unhappy.'

'You don't look unhappy – ever.'

She sighed. 'That's part of the system, Jan. You know that. That's how one survives.'

'What are you unhappy about?'

'Just being alive.'

'Oh, Anna. Don't say that.'

'Why not?'

'Because you're young and beautiful and far too intelligent to despair like that.'

'I heard a song by Frank Sinatra once – called "Come fly with me". I wish I could just fly away like it says in the song.'

'Where would you fly to?'

'Anywhere. Somewhere quiet and peaceful. A small village. In France maybe.'

'We'll have to see what we can do.'

'We?' And her brown eyes were on his face.

'I'll think of something to cheer you up.'

She smiled but said nothing, and when the music stopped he walked her back to the table.

They both walked back with him to the checkpoint and when he turned on the Allied side to look back she waved to him and he waved back. He saw a big black Merc pull up behind them and he stood watching until its tail-lights faded as it drove away.

In the flat on the Ku'damm he poured himself a whisky and switched on the radio for the news from the Voice of America. But he didn't listen. He was thinking of the car's red lights disappearing into the grim darkness of East Berlin. And of Anna Kholkov. She must trust him implicitly to have been so outspoken. And he wondered what was the root of her unhappiness. Living under the Soviet system was depressing enough. Especially for a Pole. But people did live under that system and survive. Without feeling such despair. It must be more than that.

The Joint Allied Intelligence meeting in Paris had been much as usual. The French pressing for a free exchange of intelligence from Berlin and he and the American choosing their words carefully so that their evasions gave the least possible offence. When the meeting closed in the early evening Massey had strolled back to the hotel with Maguire.

As they walked down the Faubourg Saint-Honoré he saw something in a jeweller's shop window that made him stop and look. It was a model made in plaster displaying a pearl necklace. The slender neck of the model reminded him of another neck. Maguire stood a few paces away. Hands in pockets, watching him. When Massey joined the American again, Maguire said, 'Who's the lucky lady, Jan?'

Massey smiled. 'Nobody. I was just interested by the display.'

'It's about time you got yourself a girlfriend, anyway.'

'I've got several girlfriends already.'

'I mean a real one.'

'You mean a good Irish-American?'

'You could do a lot worse at that.'

'How long before you get back to Boston?'

'Ten months four days.'

Massey laughed. 'You must have found our games in Berlin a bit of a contrast to the US Army.'

'Not really. I did a stint in the Pentagon. That's a bit like Berlin when you get behind the scenes.'

'How do you get on with Bourget?'

Maguire laughed softly. 'I hit the town with him now and again just to look friendly. He's OK. A bit of a bull in a china shop, but he's got guts.'

'Do you exchange much with him?'

'Just penny-ante stuff to keep him happy. He couldn't offer us anything we don't know already.'

'And what's the official attitude to cooperating with the Brits these days?'

'The official attitude is that that's for Washington and London. But I've always had the green light to cooperate with you personally on Berlin matters.'

'Any problems with my people at the moment?'

'None. My guy keeps in touch with Harper and Mason and I leave it to Fort Meade to liaise with Max Cohen. No, no problems – you want a drink?'

'Just a quick one. I've got somebody over here from London and I want to leave before midday tomorrow.'

'To London or Berlin?'

'Berlin.' Massey grinned. 'I don't go to London unless I'm called for.'

CHAPTER EIGHT

Eric Mayhew was forty-eight. A shortish, slightly built man of a usually mild disposition. Acquaintances and colleagues at work had sometimes been surprised by his reaction to a casual and not ill-meant joke about his size or his intelligence. The response was never open anger but he harboured grudges permanently. With a sharp, almost vindictive, tongue he harassed offenders long after they had forgotton the original cause.

He had been routinely bullied at school, but his teachers' praise for his skill in mathematics had compensated for most of it. His career had been a matter of steady and continuous progress. Appreciated by his superiors, almost unknown to his colleagues, he was considered as a solid, respectable, middle-class man of reasonable means and reasonable views. His salary was well above average but his bungalow home was of modest size, furnished in the tradition of three-piece suites and Athena prints. The few visitors were mainly fellow members of the local short wave radio club of which Mayhew had been honorary secretary for almost ten years.

With the pattern of his life so uniform, he had grown into his new role with some confidence. Readier to speak up for himself and less willing to be put upon. Normally mild, he could show sudden bursts of defiance or anger if someone attempted to take advantage of his placid nature.

Everybody who knew him was amazed when he first announced that he was about to marry. And even more amazed when he showed them photographs of his bride-to-be. Young and pretty with a figure to match. Male acquaintances began to see Eric Mayhew as something of a dark horse, and their wives exchanged significant looks and murmured about still waters running deep.

Eric Mayhew was proud of his pretty, young wife but permanently conscious that he was twenty-four years older than her. When she had her birthday in two weeks' time he would be only twenty-three years older. He was well aware that in fact she liked him being older. She had told him that she liked his maturity. He knew what to do about everything. Arguing about the price of things, sending food back in restaurants when it wasn't properly cooked. Jenny Mayhew had been brought up in a Bristol orphanage. She had been on the cosmetics counter at the local Boots' store when he first met her, and for her, Eric Mayhew was her rock and salvation. To outsiders it was obvious, but the man himself lived on a permanent rack of self-doubt. Were younger men staring at her well-filled sweater as they walked together down the street? Were people ignoring them because they were such a mis-matched couple? Were other men trying to make him look small in front of her? It was a constant torment, no less tormenting because it was unfounded.

Jenny Mayhew had seen a pair of second-hand Parker Knoll chairs in the furniture shop. They had paid for them and today was the day they were to collect them. It would save £4 to pick them up in their own car.

The small bungalow, which the previous elderly owner had called The Cottage, was in a close near the grammar school in Cheltenham. Ten minutes' walk from Eric Mayhew's place of work.

PC Brian Bull was hooker for the police rugby football team and built accordingly. He was also a fine cricketer with an excellent eye and a pair of shoulders that could clout a short ball over the pavilion. And he had a temperament that matched his physique.

That Saturday morning two things had happened that set his mood for the day. At breakfast he had quarrelled with his wife about the housekeeping allowance he gave her, and, although he had passed his exam for promotion to sergeant two years earlier, he had learned after inspection parade that a fellow constable had been promoted over his head and out of turn.

When he saw the small car parked outside a shop on double yellow lines he didn't hesitate. He leaned down at the open window, but noticing that the girl in the passenger seat was very pretty told her politely enough that she had to move the car. When she said she couldn't drive, he straightened up and as he turned to look in the shop for the driver a man hurried out.

'What is it, Officer?'

'Is this your car?'

'Yes.'

'It's parked on double yellow lines.'

'I'm loading some furniture.'

'You should know better than that. It's illegal. An offence. You've gotta move it. Loading or no loading.'

'It'll be a couple of minutes. No more. I promise.'

'You'll move it now, mate, or I'll book you.'

'How can I carry two big chairs down to the car park, tell me that?'

'Better do some press-ups, Dad. Anyway, move the banger off the yellow lines.'

'I could have moved the chairs while we've been talking, for heaven's sake.'

PC Bull reached in his pocket. 'OK, mister, if that's the way you want it, I'll book you. Name and address.'

Being called Dad in front of his young wife, and the two-year-old car being dismissed as a banger was too much for Eric Mayhew. Quivering with anger he said, 'Go to hell,' jumped in the car and drove off. PC Bull lifted his mobile radio and pressed Speak.

At three o'clock that afternoon a patrol car pulled up at The Cottage. A policeman delivered the summons which would be heard in the magistrates' court in ten days' time.

In that ten days, Eric Mayhew rehearsed the courtroom scene a dozen times. It was a subtle mixture of Henry Fonda in *Twelve Angry Men* and Winston Churchill's 'Some chicken, some neck' speech in Canada. And all the time he seethed with anger at the policeman's bullying arrogance. He longed for his chance in court to square the account, and was sufficiently convinced of the rightness of his case to ignore a friend's advice to hire a solicitor.

His hour of drama turned out to be ten minutes in front of three magistrates. The policeman didn't need to exaggerate his case. Mr Mayhew had parked his car illegally on double yellow lines, and been warned twice. He then became abusive, had attempted to avoid the proper procedures and had been traced to his present address.

The senior magistrate looked at Eric Mayhew.

'Do you dispute any of those facts, Mr Mayhew?'

'I was only going to load –'

'Do you dispute any of the facts, Mr Mayhew? Please answer me, yes or no.'

'I want to explain –'

'Mr Mayhew, if you refuse to answer I shall take a very serious view of your behaviour in court. Are the facts as stated correct? Yes or no?'

'I didn't say "for Christ's sake", I said "for heaven's sake". He said that just to –'

'Is that the only point you disagree with?'

'I want to make a statement to the court –'

'Twenty pounds fine for the traffic offence and ten pounds for attempting to avoid a summons.' He paused. 'I am sorely tempted to fine you for abuse of a police officer in the course of his duty but in view of your previous good record I shall treat it as no more than a display of that behaviour towards law and order which is becoming so common today among certain hooligan elements in society. Step down, Mr . . .' he looked at his pad '. . . Mayhew.' He turned to the clerk. 'Call the next case, please.'

A more balanced man would have said his piece to his friends about the law having nothing to do with justice, paid his fine and perhaps hoped that the policeman would be thumped in some back-street riot sustaining severe fractures to the jaw. But for Eric Mayhew, the humiliating scene in court only added to the policeman's humiliation of him in front of his young wife. The phrases 'previous good character', and 'certain hooligan elements' echoed in his mind like a mad tape recorder. It was a month before he calmed down at the thought of how he could take his justifiable revenge on the Establishment of phoney law and order which had treated him so grossly unfairly. He wasn't sure how to go about it but he knew quite definitely what he was going to do. A short, sharp lesson was what they needed.

He found the address and telephone number that he wanted on a card on the information board in the public library.

The small room stank of cats and stale food and the elderly man in the wicker chair looked pale and emaciated but he listened intently as Mayhew said his piece. When Mayhew was finished the man turned his head stiffly and with a grimace of pain to look at Mayhew.

'I don't see the connection, my friend.'

'You people want to change society. Make it fair and just for everybody. I'll help you to do it.'

'How?'

'I'll join the party and help you fight the Establishment.'

The old man's watery blue eyes looked at him. 'What do you do, Mr Mayhew? What's your job?'

'I work at GCHQ.'

'At Oakley?'

'No. At Benhall.'

'Doing what?'

'Cryptology. I'm a mathematician.'

'Can I give you some advice, Mr Mayhew?'

'Of course.'

'Go back to your home and your young wife. Get on with your job and forget all about politics, whether it's Tory, Labour or Marxist.'

'Does that mean you don't want me in the party?'

'I'm afraid it does.'

'But I want to help. I want to help people change society.'

The old man sighed. 'And so you shall. We all play our small parts and in the end we shall succeed. Meanwhile, be patient. It takes time.'

Mayhew thought that it was just one more symptom of the crazy world that they didn't want him. He'd expected to be welcomed with open arms. He had a brain. He was a thinker. And had put himself at their service. It was ridiculous. Like when they did those psychology studies where people in the street were offered genuine pound-notes for fifty pence and they wouldn't buy them.

It was almost six months later when Mayhew's wife told him one evening that a man had been asking about him at the paper shop. The shopkeeper had told her himself.

'What did he want to know?'

'Did you pay your paper bill promptly. Did you have any money problems.' She smiled. 'He asked if you were interested in girls or fellas.'

Mayhew shrugged. 'You know what he is?'

'No. What is he?'

'He's doing a positive vetting. They never warn you.'

'Can I tell them that at the shop?'

'Yes, if you want to.'

The man who spoke to him two weeks later had a foreign accent. Mayhew had just backed the car into the concrete driveway when the man came up to him.

'Mr Mayhew?'

'That's me. And who are you?'

'Some friends suggested we spoke together.'

'What about?'

'Is perhaps more private in your car. We go for a spin, yes?'

It was a long time since Eric Mayhew had heard anyone talk of 'going for a spin' but he shrugged and said, 'You can come in the house.'

'I don't want to disturb your wife.'

'She's at my mother's.'

'OK. We speak in your house.'

She was back just before eight and he took her to the cinema to see *The Sting*, but he said nothing to her about his caller. He would have to make some excuse to go to London when they told him the date. He could always say no, but there was no reason why he should. It was everyone for himself in this world. At least somebody appreciated that he really was prepared to help alter the way things were done. There would be some risk, of course, but it was easy enough if you knew how. People nicked old reels of tape to record pop music. They would only be scrapped anyway.

CHAPTER NINE

Lieutenant Barakov was not amused at having his free evening interrupted by such trivialities, and it showed in his brusque questions and his dismissive reactions to the replies. He stared implacably at the man sitting facing him on the other side of the desk.

'But I don't understand, Mr Johnson, why you want to come over.'

Johnson shifted uneasily in his chair. 'But I told you. I hate the army. They don't give me a break. Nothing.'

'Many soldiers don't like being in the army. They'd rather be sitting on their backsides playing cards and drinking vodka. How do you think you could help us, anyway?'

'I could go on TV and radio and denounce them. The British and Americans. Tell the world what they're really like.'

'You think the world would be interested in the grievances of a private in the British Army?'

The telephone rang on Barakov's desk. He reached for it, said his name, listened for several minutes and then hung up without speaking. As he turned to look at Johnson, the signalman sensed a change in the lieutenant's attitude.

Barakov said, 'Of course we appreciate your willingness to help us, comrade.' He shrugged. 'But maybe there are other ways, better ways, that you could help us and we could help you.'

'I don't understand.'

'You're at the house in Grunewald aren't you?'

'How did you know that? I didn't say where I worked.'

Barakov smiled. 'We have to know these things. We have to check. You could have been sent to trick us by the British. We have to be cautious.'

'They didn't send me, mate, that's for sure.'

'Tell me about your work. The kind of things you do.'

'I register the transcripts and route them to the data base.'

'Do you read them?'

'Jesus, no. There's thousands of them pouring in. Hundreds a day. And they're in code anyway.'

'Do you know what they're about?'

'They're the transcripts taken down by the monitors in the listening-room.'

'Do you know what they listen to?'

'It's radio and telephones.'

'What radio and telephones?'

'I don't know . . . everything . . . you people.'

'You've no idea?'

'No.'

'How many people work at the house?'

'There's four shifts working round the clock. About a hundred. Maybe more.'

'How long can you stay with us?'

'I've got to be on duty on Sunday night.'

'I'd like to put you and your girlfriend up for a couple of nights at one of our best hotels. You and I can talk tomorrow. There are other officers who would like to talk to you. We'll see how we can help each other. Yes?'

'My girlfriend didn't come with me.'

'We'll contact her and get her over here for you. Meantime, you must be hungry, why don't we have a meal together?'

Johnson tried not to be openly impressed by the magnificent suite on the top floor of the Berolina but Heidi had no such inhibitions. There was a magnificent sitting-room, a large bedroom and a palatial bathroom. The KGB girl who had contacted her had taken her to a shop on the Ku'damm and bought her a dress, shoes, and underwear.

She lay with her eyes closed in the marble bath and hoped that it would last.

Later that evening, Barakov took Johnson to a house in the suburbs by the river and they talked with two other Russians. They were friendly, treating him as an equal, discussing every detail of what he knew of the operation in Grunewald. And back at the hotel another KGB man talked with Heidi. She could be paid a hundred marks a week for acting as a courier for them and sometimes accommodating someone at her rooms for a night. He was young and good-looking and his eyes wandered from time to time to her legs with obvious interest. She was used to that but was flattered all the same, and readily agreed to his proposals. He made it seem like she was part of a team and she liked the feeling of belonging.

Although his first contact was, in ignorance, with the GRU, Johnson had been passed over to the KGB. He got on well with Kholkov who had taken him over as Johnson worked for Massey's organization. Johnson had only vaguely heard of Massey but Kholkov found it amusing to have contact with both ends of the spectrum at the house in Grunewald. Whenever possible he met Johnson in West Berlin in case the British security men at the checkpoint should notice Johnson's frequent crossings. Numbers of Allied troops crossed the border to buy fresh fruit and vegetables in East Berlin but Johnson had no such excuse as he was fed at his place of work.

They met that night in a club near the Brandenburg Gate. Johnson had passed the three rolls of exposed microfilm in a packet of Benson & Hedges cigarettes, but Kholkov seemed in no hurry to leave.

'Does the code RA 4901 mean anything to you, Arthur?'

'We get a few registrations under that code. Not much.'

'Where do you route it?'

'It goes to Mr Howard's people. And then it goes to London. Not from me but from them.'

'I've got good news for you, Arthur. They're very pleased with what you're doing for us. Moscow have given orders that if the good work continues you'll be officially recognized in a couple of months' time.'

'What's that mean?'

'It means you'll be an officer in the KGB. A lieutenant.'

Kholkov saw the mixture of disbelief and pleasure on Johnson's face as he said, 'You mean for real?'

'Of course. Next time you're over here I'll show you your uniform and insignia. You can wear it inside our HQ whenever you are on our side of the wall.'

'That's great!'

'One other thing. You seem to be giving us material that's always from the same code sectors. Why is that?'

'It depends on what shift I'm on. But it's quieter at night and I can hear them unlocking the doors to come down the stairs if anyone's coming down. I take night shifts when I can and those are the sectors that come through at night most of the time.'

'OK. Leave things as they are for the moment. How are things with you and Heidi?'

'What made you ask?'

'She's been complaining to her contact. He's a little worried about the situation.'

'What's she complaining about?'

'Says you promised to marry her if she made contact with us for you.'

'That was a long time ago.'

'Can't be more than a year, comrade.'

'I'm not interested in marrying her. Nor anyone else for that matter.'

'She's a valuable operator, Arthur. We'd like to keep her happy.'

'What about keeping me happy?'

'We want to do that too.'

'How?'

'She wants a British passport and British citizenship. We could provide the necessary documents for her but they'd have to be in your name as if she was married to you. You won't actually be married to her, of course, but she doesn't need to know that.'

'How would you do all that? It would need birth certificates, marriage certificates . . .'

Kholkov smiled. 'Leave that to us, comrade. But it would help us if you co-operated.'

'OK.' Johnson shrugged. 'If that's what you want.'

She was in her late fifties and she had obviously once been handsome rather than pretty. Grey-haired and well dressed, with a beige jacket and skirt and a brown felt hat, she could well have been one of those ladies the TV cameras pan across at Tory Party conferences. She had an air, not perhaps of authority, but of expecting immediate cooperation from public employees. And she had found a young assistant at the Registrar General's office in St Catherine's House to lift down the heavy leatherbound volumes for her and carry them to the nearby table.

Slowly and carefully she went through the register of deaths for the months of June and July in 1949. An hour later she paid £8.25 for copies of three certificates and the clerk slid them into a stiff brown envelope.

During the next two weeks the lady drove in her well-preserved Rover 105 to the small town of Dorchester, the village of Wadhurst in Sussex, and Richmond in Yorkshire. When she returned to London she revisited the Registrar General's office and paid for a photocopy of the birth certificate of Agnes Mary Andrews, infant, born May 19th, 1948, died June 6th, 1949.

Heidi Fischer, now Heidi Johnson, and her new husband had four days' honeymoon in the luxury suite at the Berolina Hotel in East Berlin and Arthur Johnson wore his KGB lieutenant's uniform. Not out in the street but in their suite of rooms at the hotel. There had been no ceremony but she had the documents. The British passport. The birth certificate in what was supposed to be in her maiden name and a marriage certificate as Mrs Agnes Johnson, née Andrews.

Eric Mayhew had lied to his department head and lied to his young wife. He had claimed four days of accumulated leave from his boss and that had been willingly agreed to. And to Jenny Mayhew he had said that he was being sent away for four days on an assignment in Northumberland.

When the plane touched down at the airport in Vienna he had done exactly what they had told him to do. First buying the copy of *Stern* at the bookstall, then walking over to stand under the departures information board. It was almost ten minutes before he saw the man with the meerschaum pipe and the copy of *Railway Modeller*. Mayhew followed the man to the car park until he stopped at a grey Volkswagen. The car door opened and he got into the passenger seat alongside a tall man in a blue suit who took his bag and reached over to put it carefully on the back seat.

'A good journey, friend?'

'The plane was crowded but it was OK.'

'I'll take you to the house and hand you over to my colleagues. They're looking forward to meeting you.'

Half an hour later he was being introduced to an elderly man who spoke excellent English and reminded Mayhew of his old headmaster. He was shown to the small bedroom but the instruction started straight away. The training programme was modular and reminded Mayhew of the style of some of the Open University programmes he had seen on TV. No previous knowledge was assumed, and the man he knew as Josef never moved on to the next step until the previous section had been mastered.

First came the use of the pads of stationery with specially treated carbons for invisible writing on top of a normally written letter; then the more complicated instruction on the preparation of microdots using the miniature Minox camera and the microscope with its reversed lenses. The technical process he grasped quickly, but he had to practise again and again, using the hypodermic needle to lift the dot out of the emulsion and place it as a full stop on a typed letter, until the KGB man was satisfied. Mayhew was not good with his hands.

The next morning Josef made him go over the whole process a dozen more times before he was satisfied. The afternoon was spent on the less complicated use of one-time pads.

Two whole days were spent on radio procedures, frequencies, transmission timetables and tape recording. The decrypting of the transmissions was no problem for Mayhew – he had listened to those monotonous voices reading out the five-digit groups for hours on end in his job at Cheltenham. He was amused at the simplicity of two codes that GCHQ had not yet broken. A neat, elegant piece of mathematics that used a combination of a log-table and a fourteen-hour day as its variable.

He was shown the equipment that would be provided for him in England. The camera, the reverse microscope, the stationery, the modified Sony tape recorder and the black leather attaché case and its secret hiding-places. He was left to buy the ICOM IC-R70 himself in London as they were in short supply in Moscow.

The final day was spent with a different Russian who gave his name as Max. Mayhew never really understood what he was there for. Just chatting, amiable and joking. Admittedly there were questions about security routines at Cheltenham, and questions about heads of sections and divisions, but it was fairly obvious that he already knew the answers. For most of the time it was just gossip about the people who worked with him. The Russians asked about his childhood, his hobbies and his possibilities of promotion.

Max offered to take him to the Opera House or a cinema, and when he declined, the Russian smiled and asked him if maybe he'd like a pretty girl. He was taken for a meal at a small restaurant that evening and Max offered him a sightseeing tour of Vienna to round off his visit. He said that he'd rather not see the city so that he could never be trapped into talking about it. The Russians complimented him on his foresight.

The whole time he was treated as an important and valuable member of a team. It was the first time in his life that he felt an accepted member of a group. Accepted and respected. Praised, and not derided, for his cautious virtues.

John Hooton was thirty-five and Tony Moore, his boss, was forty-nine; Massey looked at them both from his side of the table.

'Who's their cut-out this side of the Wall, Johnny?'

'The butcher by the station. Franz Lauterbacher, they use the code-name Emil for him.'

'And on their side?'

'A girl who works as an assistant in the KO store.'

'Are you sure of that?' Massey asked.

'Pretty sure.'

'How many sources confirmed it?'

'Only one.'

'You know it's a favourite ploy of agents who haven't got any real lead to pick on somebody at the KO. It's the main place in East Berlin where Allied servicemen go. It looks a suitable place to provide cover for a cut-out but we've never had a confirmed target yet.' Massey paused and looked at the older man, 'What do you think, Tony?'

'I've got a hunch she really is a cut-out, sir. She's always on the counter for fresh fruit and that's where most servicemen go. She seems to work at odd times. Sometimes not more than an hour a day and sometimes she's not there for several days. Works like she's there by arrangement.'

'Any signs of anything being handed over?'

'It's impossible to tell. It could be put in a bag or coded on a receipt. There's hundreds of ways something could be passed over.'

'Why don't you pull in the butcher and see if you can squeeze anything out of him?'

'It would mean pulling in the whole of his network.'

'How many?'

'Five.'

'Who are they working to?'

'We think it's Kholkov.'

'What are they covering?'

'Only low-grade stuff so far. HQ telephone directories. The Oberbürgermeister's clerical staff. And US Army Air Force people.'

'Have you kept CIA informed?'

'No. That's up to Mr Harper. But we think they know at least two of the agents.'

'Any photographs?'

Hooton pushed two ten-by-eight glossy prints across the table and Massey glanced at them. It was a young face although the girl was very plain. A tense mouth and alert eyes. The second photograph was very grainy and it showed the girl handing change to a British captain. He pushed them back across the table to Hooton.

'What do you want to do, Tony?'

'I'm inclined to do as you said. Pull in Emil and the rest of them and see what we can get.'

'And you, Johnny?'

'If we pull them in, then they'll just send new boys over and I've got to go through the jazz all over again to find them from scratch.'

'So leave one of them free. Somebody fairly bright. And they'll form the new network around that one. It's the lazy way, but that's how Kholkov works.'

'OK, sir. I'll do that.'

'Tony, you'd better decide the timing. OK?'

'OK. I'll fix it with the team.'

Massey sat there after the two had left. His office at the house in Grunewald was modern but windowless, and unlike his subordinates' offices there were no personal touches. No photographs of families or Sussex cottages, no holiday postcards tacked to the cork board spreading across one wall. No flowers in looted KPM vases. There was nothing that gave a hint of Massey's private life or interests. Not even a paperback on the double bookshelf. Just dictionaries and other reference books, a microfiche reader and a grey plastic box of fiches, while a crude, metal MOD-issue bookend underlined the reticence.

He realized as he sat there that with the expansion of Max Cohen's division he was being drawn away from the day-to-day SIS operations that were his normal work. He was becoming more and more an administrator, less and less involved in the long-running contest with the Russians and East Germans. In fact, he had more free time than ever before – but he was too used to having a heavy workload to use it creatively. He was on the edge of boredom.

CHAPTER TEN

The KO stores, Kaufhaus des Ostens, were the showpiece of East Berlin and most British and Americans wives, encouraged by both the Allied and West Berlin authorities, went there once a week for the top-class fruit and vegetables that were always available and cheaper than in West Berlin.

He had bought oranges, lemons, potatoes and lettuce, and had recognized the girl who served him as the suspect girl in the photographs. There was nothing suspicious about her apart from the fact that the other girls who laughed and joked among themselves seemed to ignore her. He walked to the cheese counter and as he looked at the array of cheeses and yoghurts a quiet voice said, 'Hello, Jan.'

He turned to look and it was Anna Kholkov.

'Hello, Anna. How nice to see you.'

She smiled and said in Polish, 'Buying the wicked Marxist fruit, I see.'

He smiled. 'Pleasing both sides at the same time. Saving the West Germans freight charges and providing hard currency for the proletariat.' He paused. 'Anyway. How are you? How's Alexei? Or shouldn't I ask?'

'He's busy and fine. I'm bored and fine.'

'Have you got time for a coffee?'

She smiled. 'I'm afraid that on this side of the Wall with you in uniform that could be a problem.'

'Have you got your Kommandatura pass with you?'

She nodded. 'Yes.'

'How about I meet you in half an hour on the Allied side of the checkpoint at Brandenburger Tor.'

For a moment she hesitated, her eyes on his face, and then she said quietly, 'Why not? In half an hour.'

'I'll be there.'

He saw her come through the Allied control post and hesitate until she spotted him when he waved.

She hesitated again for a moment when he opened the door of the taxi for her, but then got in. She turned to look at him as he climbed in and sat beside her. 'Where are we going?'

He put a finger to his lips and she obviously understood. They talked about the weather, and the taxi stopped for them at the junction of the Ku'damm with Lietzenburger Strasse. As he turned from paying the driver he said, 'Follow behind me. Wait until I've unlocked the door.'

She stayed a few yards behind him, watched him unlock a door and then followed him through the doorway. He closed it behind her and stood there looking at her.

'I hope you don't mind me bringing you here. I thought it might be . . .' he hesitated '. . . better if we weren't seen together by too many people.'

She smiled and said softly, 'No, I don't mind. You were going to say safer not better, weren't you?'

'Yes.'

'And the only one of us in danger is me.'

'I'm afraid so.'

'Won't people be watching this place just because it's yours?'

'Nobody knows about it. Not even my own people.'

'Is this what they call a safe-house?'

'No. A safe-house is official. This is mine. I pay the rental and my mother's name – Felinska – is on the contract and on the door. I've never mentioned this place to anyone nor brought anyone here.'

'You must trust me a lot.'

'I do.'

'Why?'

'I don't know exactly. Experience? That you're a Pole? And the usual reason.'

'What's that?'

'I want to trust you.' He paused. 'Let's go up and have that coffee.'

She looked around the living-room as they walked into the flat, and while he made the coffee she looked at the cassettes and records. When he brought in the tray she turned, smiling.

'All jazz and German schmaltz. No Chopin. I'm surprised.'

She shrugged and smiled. 'I always think of you as being so very Polish.'

As his brain absorbed the words 'I always think of you' he looked into her face.

'I always think of you just as you. Not Polish. Not Russian.'

'Is that good or bad?'

He shrugged. 'Neither. Just human and normal.'

'Not me as the wife of a KGB man?'

'No. Never.'

She was standing very close to him, the big brown eyes looking up into his own, and she said softly, 'I'm glad. Very glad.'

He looked back at her. 'You said you always think of me as a Pole.'

'I do.'

'Not as a man?'

'Oh, yes. Very much as a man.'

Then his arms went round her, his mouth on hers, her warm body clinging to his. When eventually she drew back her head to look at him, she said, 'Do you think of me often, Jan?'

He sighed. 'A dozen times a day, every day.'

'Tell me what you think when you think of me.'

'I think of you that night at the Hilton. Your lovely face and your beautiful neck. Your eyes and your mouth.'

'Do you want to make love to me?'

'I do. But that wasn't why I brought you here.'

'Why did you bring me here?'

'So that I had seen you here and I could think of you in these rooms with me when I'm alone.'

'Were you going to tell me that?'

'No.'

'Why not?'

He shrugged. 'How could I?'

'Why not? Because I'm a KGB man's wife?'

'No. Just because you're another man's wife. It would have been the same if he was English.'

'I've imagined this so many times, my Jan.'

'Tell me.'

'You with your arms round me. Then both of us naked. Making love.'

'And where was all this happening?'

She smiled. 'In Lazienki Park by the Chopin monument.'

He laughed softly. 'That's a bit public, isn't it? But very romantic.'

'Have you ever been to Warsaw?'

'No.'

'Will you go there with me one day?'

'I'm not allowed to, honey.'

She smiled. 'Call me honey again.'

'I love you, honey.'

'You don't have to say that.'

'I mean it.'

'How can you mean it? You don't know me.'

'It's got nothing to do with knowing you. I love you, and that's a simple, truthful fact.'

'But why?'

'I don't know. I just do.'

'I know why I love you.'

'Tell me.'

'Take me to bed and I'll tell you.'

As they lay naked an hour later on his bed, he leaned up on one elbow and said softly, 'You said you'd tell me why you love me.'

'So I did.'

'Tell me.'

'Say honey to me again.'

He smiled. 'I love you, honey. But you're a tease.'

She shook her head. 'That first time we met at the hotel I knew you were attracted by me. And I knew that it was because of me you asked us to dinner. I liked that but I'm used to that. But two people said nice things about you. So I looked at you that night at dinner, and listened. I thought they were right in what they said. Not everything, but in the things that mattered. And you're handsome. And you're Polish. I found I couldn't stop thinking about you. Hoping we should meet again. Hoping something might happen.'

'Who were the two people?'

'One a man. One a girl.'

'Who was the man?'

'Alexei.'

'I don't believe it, you're joking.'

'I'm not. He'd already told me what you said the first time he met you. The meeting about Hess. He said you were either very foolish or very kind. When I saw you I knew you weren't foolish. Weak men sometimes see gentleness as weakness. Alexei is a weak man.'

'And who was the other one? The girl?'

'She's a friend of mine. An American. You know her. Judy Campbell. She studies at the Kunstschule here in West Berlin. She came to a seminar at

Humboldt University. She painted me.' She smiled. 'And one day I looked through some of her canvases in her flat and there was a face I knew – you, my love. So I interrogated her about you.'

Massey smiled. 'What did she say?'

'Nice things. All of them nice. They fitted the picture I had in my mind.'

'Tell me.'

She laughed. 'You have a very strong Polish ego under that simple outward appearance of yours. I shall say no more. Ask *her* if you want.'

'We can use her as an excuse for you coming into our zone.'

She nodded. 'Yes. But we must tell her. She knows Alexei too.'

'Does she like him?'

'You must ask her yourself.'

'How long can you stay?'

She looked at her wrist-watch and then at his face.'Another hour.'

'Can I see you tomorrow?'

'You can see me any day for the next ten days. Alexei is in Moscow.'

'Can I see you every day?'

She smiled. 'Yes, please.'

'Let's talk about Alexei.'

She closed her eyes and said, 'OK. You talk.'

'I know what he does and he knows what I do. That gives us an extra problem. So I suggest that we do a deal. I will never ask you anything about him that has anything to do with his work. And we won't ever talk about my work. OK?'

'Of course. You're very honest.'

'Only with you, Anna.'

'Love me again.'

'Can I say something else about us?'

'Yes, of course.'

'I don't know what's going to happen to us. But for me this isn't an *affaire*. I won't say that I never had fantasies about you. Not in the park in Warsaw. Here, on this bed. But if it made any difference to you or to us I'd be happy to do nothing more than hold your hand.'

The brown eyes looked up at his face and she said softly, 'It's not an *affaire* for me, Jan. Not even my fantasies. We have to wait and see what happens with us both. But I'm happy to wait. Afraid, but happy.'

'Why afraid?'

'Afraid because my husband is a KGB man.'

'That's all?'

She shook her head. 'It must be comforting to be so . . . so self-assured.'

'I love you so, Anna. I won't let you come to any harm.'

Judy Campbell was twenty-two. She was a painter, and she already knew that she wasn't an artist. She painted well and several people had bought canvases from her, and she got more commissions for portraits than she could produce. She looked a typical dumb American blonde but like most dumb-looking American blondes she wasn't at all dumb. She was easygoing and good company, and seemed to have a knack for being at home with all the different kinds of people she spent her time with. She never disguised the fact that she liked men and liked sex. But she wasn't promiscuous. She did the choosing and there were no smooth words or pressures that could get her into bed if she didn't want to. The men she slept with mattered. They were usually good-looking but that wasn't the only criterion. They tended to be creative rather than football players, although they could all be classified as mildly macho. There had, in fact only been six altogether in her life. Only the first was a real dud and that had taught her a lesson. It only worked out at 0.75 of a man a year. It seemed more to onlookers merely because she had the rare talent of retaining the friendship of men who had once been lovers. They didn't come back for 'afters' because they weren't available; it was genuine friendship because Judy was loyal and likeable.

She wondered why Jan Massey had been so insistent that he should see her that evening. She'd had a cocktail-party date which she'd cancelled and she'd promised to phone a major in the US Marines later to let him know if he could take her out for the rest of the evening.

She poured them both a whisky and grinned as she raised the glass. 'What the hell is it you say, Jan? *Naz* . . . something or other?'

'Na zdrowie.'

'And the same to you, lover boy.' She looked at him over her glass. 'Why so serious, Jan?'

'Because I've got something serious to say . . . and I don't know how to say it.'

She shrugged. 'Better just say it right out.'

'You know what I do in Berlin?'

'Your job, you mean?'

'Yes.'

'People have told me that you're the top guy in the British spy set-up. Like the CIA.'

He nodded. 'That's more or less right. And you know who we're mainly concerned with?'

She rolled her eyes, smiling. 'The wicked Reds. The boys from Moscow.'

For a moment Massey wondered if he wasn't foolish to go on.

'You know some of them, don't you?'

'Not really. A few Russians, but I wouldn't think many of them are spies.'

'You know one Russian who's a very senior KGB man.'

'Have you been spying on me?'

'No way. But I'm sure the CIA keeps tabs on you.'

'Who's this mystery guy?'

'Kholkov. Alexei Kholkov.'

'You mean *he's* a spy. I can't believe it.'

'He is, Judy. He's quite senior.'

'And you're going to ask me not to see him any more.'

'No. It's not that.'

'What is it? You want me to lure him into bed and ask him for the secret code.' She saw the look on his face and she said quietly, 'I'm sorry, Jan. I don't mean to be flippant. Tell me what you want.'

'I want to tell you something. Something confidential. Something personal. But if you passed it on to anyone else, accidentally or otherwise, it would be a disaster for someone we both know.'

'You mean Alexei?'

'No.'

'Who then?'

'Anna. His wife.'

'You're in love with her and she's in love with you.'

'What made you say that?'

'The penny just dropped. Two pennies. I can remember how she looked at the portrait I painted of you. And the questions she asked about you.'

'What was the other penny?'

'I just realized. You're both Polish and you're very like one another.'

'In what way?'

'Now I come to think of it . . . except that she's a girl and you're a man, you're the same in every way. She's beautiful, you're handsome. She's quiet and calm on the outside but inside there's a volcano. And the same with you.' She shrugged. 'So how do I come into it?'

'She needs to be able to say she's coming over to see you when we meet.'

'Is this for real, my love?'

'Yes. For both of us.'

She stared at him for several moments. And then said softly, 'What the hell are you both gonna do about it?'

'We're going to work this out. That's partly why we need your help. To give us time.'

'Is she KGB?'

Massey smiled. 'Of course not. She's just Kholkov's wife. She was a ballet dancer before they were married.'

'I know. She told me. OK. Let me be your auntie.'

'Do you mind about deceiving Kholkov? I know you've met him.'

'Good God, no.'

'Why so sure?'

'Feminine intuition.'

'What's that mean?'

'I already knew they didn't love one another.'

'How did you know? They've always behaved amicably enough when I've seen them together.'

'You can often tell what a man is like if you watch the expression on a wife's face when her husband's talking. Try it some time. It works.'

'Anything else?'

'Yes,' she said slowly. 'I'd say he was queer. He puts on a good act but most of that charm is because he isn't after the girls. It works because women know instinctively that he's not looking for a prize. Not the one that most men are looking for anyway.'

'Thanks for saying you'll help.'

'I'm not just saying it. I will help. Any way I can.'

'If anyone over there found out, she'd be in a Gulag camp two days later.'

'Do they really do that?'

'They really do. She'd be dead in months.'

'I won't talk, Jan. You can rely on that. I like your Anna.'

'Can I take you for a meal or a drink somewhere?'

She smiled and shook her head. 'I've got a US Marine major jumping up and down waiting for a call to say tonight's the big night.' She stood up and walked across to a stack of canvases. She bent over, looking through them. She came back with two. She handed them to him. 'With love from me to you.' One was the portrait of him, the other was an almost finished portrait of Anna.

CHAPTER ELEVEN

Nobody could actually recall when James Vick was first called Jimbo but it was agreed that that was what his family called him before he was five years old. There is a wide variety of diminutives that derive from the name James, and each has its own particular aura. Jimbo carries implications of bounce and youth that need living up to. Jimbo Vick had lived up to them to such an extent that at thirty-two years old he still had the looks of a quite handsome all-American boy complete with freckles, and chestnut hair that was the envy of every girl who noticed him.

Jimbo was born and brought up in the small town of Montpelier on the edge of the Napa Valley. The town was small but not because it lacked attraction; it was, in fact, a fine example of what purposeful planning could do when combined with utter selfishness. The seven men who were the original founders of the town would have been surprised but not disconcerted by an accusation of selfishness. They saw themselves as no more then a group of like-minded men who wanted to live in a certain way. A way that nobody could describe as ostentatious – two of them were Quakers. But they wanted to maintain what they always referred to as 'certain standards'. None of them would have been able to put in words what they meant by the phrase, but they all knew instinctively exactly what they meant. They had never discussed the exclusion of Jews. There was no need to. No more than the question of blacks or Hispanics at a later stage in the town's development. Even today money alone would not buy you a place in Montpelier. It would be difficult to advise a potential newcomer of the criteria that applied. But the say-so of the present head of any one of those founding families would mean that you were half-way there. One more nod of approval would be enough. But apart from descendants of the founding families the nods had not been given to more than three or four suppliants a year so the town was still small enough to be manageable to the unspoken ethos of its founders.

The Vick property was on Prospect Avenue which in most other towns would be reckoned to be the best road in town. In Montpelier it was merely typical of that far-sighted original planning and no finer than most of the other avenues in town. The house itself had originally been mostly Gothic, but over the years it had been transformed into honest and quite awe-inspiring Colonial, while the remains of the original Gothic building had been converted into servants' quarters and indoor pool with facilities for squash, tennis and gymnastics.

The Vicks had always been bankers and Joss Vick, Jimbo's father, was both respected and liked. Gregarious and given to acts of careful generosity, he was popular not only in Montpelier but in San Francisco, Los Angeles and New York. There was a touch of the 'twenties and Scott Fitzgerald in both his dress and his attitudes. Athletically built and handsome, it was accepted that he had both charm and style enough to make women adore him and men eager for his company. The charm was natural and genuine, the envy of his menfriends and the delight of most of the women he met.

Joan Vick had been the belle of Montpelier, a Hudson from one of the founding families. Intelligent and beautiful though she was, their circle had not expected the marriage to last. They were both too attractive to be left in wedded bliss. But despite both gallant and cruder attempts at seduction they had remained an inviolate pair. Neither lechers nor charmers could make any headway with Joan Vick and, although obviously appreciative of pretty faces and nubile young bodies, Joss Vick admired without wanting to touch. Men gave up trying for Joan Vick and only the very young females still dreamed of luring Joss from the strait and narrow. They had looked a pair on the day that they married and they had stayed a pair. Seemingly without effort or temptation. Joan and Joss, referred to by their friends as the Jaybirds. They were envied by everyone who knew them.

By the time that Jimbo Vick was sixteen the envy had become substantially diluted. Jimbo was a classic example of the spoiled brat. Clever at school but a natural cheat. Leader of a group of middle-class kids from the next town who were mesmerized by his audacity and his money. Worldy wise far beyond his years and detested by the school staff. Openly defiant of all authority from his parents to the police who knew him as Smart-ass and avoided him whenever possible. Two psychiatrists had given up the unequal struggle, confirming as they did so that he was intelligent, clever and uncontrollable. Jimbo had offered to help the second psychiatrist with his own emotional problems.

He was eighteen when it all came to a head in a meeting with his father and the family lawyer, when Jimbo had finally tried the patience of the local police once too often and had been arrested for drug peddling. The ten-thousand-dollar bail had been no problem; his father had not only paid up willingly but had made a contribution to the hospital funds for an additional dialysis machine. The police captain's wife ran that particular appeal. But Joss Vick knew by instinct that this was a time when his local esteem and popularity would not be enough. He phoned Jackson in LA to arrange a meeting.

Jackson was a senior partner in a large and successful Los Angeles law firm. Despite Los Angeles's reputation his knowledge of drug offences was limited to a mere knowledge of the law and procedures. His speciality was high-stake divorce and, for a few special clients, tax avoidance. Joss Vick fell into neither category. Jackson was the son of Joss's father's lawyer and was called on solely for matters concerning the various family trusts and Joss Vick's estate.

The meeting took place in Joss Vick's study. It was more a personal museum than a study. The walls were lined with photographs of various Vicks in the company of politicians, diplomats and captains of industry. Those of Joss Vick were all informal, featuring him with the Beautiful People on yachts, at polo matches, the races and social functions.

'Where did you get the stuff, Jimbo?'

'What is this, Dad, a courtroom?'

Jackson said crisply, 'These are the sort of questions you'll be asked in court, Mr Vick.'

The youth turned a languid look on the lawyer. 'You don't say? And what do you know about drugs, mister?'

'I know about courts and the law,' Jackson said quietly.

'You'd better pay attention to all this, Jimbo. Or you'll end up in jail.'

The boy shrugged. 'So what?'

Joss Vick sighed heavily. 'So I don't want my son in jail. If I can prevent it.'

Jimbo grinned. 'Would you and Ma visit me?'

Jackson intervened. 'Even as a first offence you'd get a very long sentence if you were found guilty. I think you should bear that in mind.'

'Oh, I have, old friend. I have. But you're being paid to keep me out. The family's expecting a lot from you, old sport.'

'Jimbo. Mr Jackson isn't to be talked to like that. I won't have it.'

'You're paying this guy, Dad,' Jimbo shouted angrily. 'He wants me to plead guilty. No way do I do that.'

Joss Vick shrugged helplessly, 'It could help when you're sentenced.'

'You take it I'm guilty, then?'

'I'm goddam sure you are. The police showed me the evidence that they've passed to the DA.'

'Those creeps have been trying to frame me for years. I know enough about Captain O'Keefe to put *him* behind bars for years.'

'Is there some other attorney you'd prefer?'

'No. I'll handle my own case. My own way.'

Joss Vick stared at his son for long moments before he spoke.

'When this business is over, Jimbo, I'll make you a reasonable allowance and you can go your own way. I've had enough of getting you out of trouble. You're just a spoiled brat.'

'How much allowance?'

'We'll talk about it some other time.'

'Why not now? Are you embarrassed because of this guy hearing?'

'Just leave the room, boy, before I lose my temper.'

Jimbo grinned. 'Make it a thousand bucks a month and I'll leave this dump today.'

'I'll make it two. Don't come back.'

Jimbo stood up, grinning. 'I'd like it in writing. Jackson could draw it up while I'm packing.'

As the boy left the room with a swagger, Jackson was aware of the tears at the edges of Joss Vick's eyes.

Jimbo Vick drove off in the Mustang convertible that afternoon, its rear seat and trunk piled high with leather cases. His thinking was too superficial to have any regrets about leaving his home and he had no sense of obligation or affection towards his parents. When cornered in some minor delinquency he had always weaseled out by saying, 'I didn't ask to be born, folks. You had me so you owe me. That's what parents are for.'

From a ten-year-old the apparent logic had amused Joss Vick, but as the years went by it was too obviously specious to be amusing any longer. It wasn't the plaintive protest of a child but the cold, selfish shrugging-off of personal responsibility by a teenager and then a youth.

So many people had longed to see Jimbo Vick get his come-uppance that when he left home they saw it as the beginning of the end of his reign of defiance of both the law and decent behaviour. Unfortunately it was no such thing. Jimbo Vick's defiance of the way things were was without any element of bluff. Getting what you wanted was just a question of working out how easiest to get it. Unlike most upper-class kids he was not only street-smart but extremely shrewd, resourceful and intelligent. The fact that these qualities were misapplied made no difference to their effectiveness.

The charges for drug peddling were never pressed and his card in the local police records was inexplicably mislaid. The new card gave no details of the previous reports of vandalism, drunken driving or participating in the gang-bang of an out-of-town negro girl.

His father knew nothing of all this, neither did he ever discover how his son managed to become a student at UCLA. While he was still at university Jimbo had a small but elegant pad in a good block in Marina del Rey. One of the two girls who lived with him was also at UCLA but Jimbo was quite impartial in fixing them both up with local businessmen who wanted discreet services from pretty, young call girls. They paid him half their earnings towards the cost of running the apartment and they were available for sex whenever he wanted. It was one of Jimbo's repeated boasts that from the age of fifteen he'd never paid for sex. Most of those who heard the boast assumed that he had been sexually precocious to have such experience so early, but in fact it was merely accurate as he had paid for even earlier experience at the rate of a dollar a time with the daughter of the school janitor. Jimbo Vick always impressed some small group of his contemporaries. He knew what he wanted and took it one way or another. His self-confidence was infectious and half a gram of 'smack' between friends always helped.

At UCLA he took mathematics and electronics, and was hard-working far beyond what was necessary for a pass. He was seen as an achiever and encouraged by the staff. After graduating, he was invited to join a team that was financed by one of the newly arrived computer companies in Silicon Valley. A year later he was recruited by the company for its own research department. Much of the equipment that they designed and manufactured was for government departments, and he spent a lot of his time briefing the ultimate users of the high-technology equipment. When he was sent to Washington he assumed it was one of those routine briefing sessions.

There was a message for him when he booked in at the hotel, welcoming him and telling him that a car would call for him the next morning.

The car pulled up at what looked like a private house in Georgetown, and in a sparsely furnished room two men interviewed him. The questions were mainly technical but the older man chatted with him while they were eating lunch alone, about his friends and how he lived, his interests and his ambitions. He slept in the house that night, on a small camp bed with a man sitting outside his room in the corridor.

The following day they gave him a variety of tests. Mainly mathematical problems with a smattering of questions on advanced electronics. Late on the second evening they invited him to join the National Security Agency at Fort George Meade. He smiled at them both as he refused, a smile that was almost a sneer. When they asked him why he refused, he laughed derisively and shrugged, saying that he wasn't interested. He added gratuitously that if he *had* been interested he would have gone to someone at the top not half-way down.

Back at his normal job he was outraged when he was made redundant at the end of the month. He had several interviews for other senior jobs in the area, interviews where the selection panels were obviously impressed. Three of the panels informally told him that he would be appointed. None of the seven companies eventually pursued his application. Two that he phoned were curt to the point of rudeness. When one of the two NSA men who had originally interviewed him called at his apartment one evening, saying that he was just passing through and had wondered how he was getting on, Jimbo finally got the message.

'You creeps have fingered me, haven't you? You told them to shove me out, and you've warned all the others not to give me a job.'

The man smiled amiably, 'Between you and me, why *did* you turn down our offer in Washington?'

'Because I don't like being questioned. Who the hell do you people think you are? I've got a private income, and there's no way I'm going to be cross-questioned by two jerks who think they're doing a favour to some small-town hick.'

'Is that what is seemed like to you?'

'It sure did.'

Hank Lodrick was a trained and experienced psychologist and he had picked up the vibes from Jimbo Vick as soon as they had started talking. It hadn't been so obvious at the original interview. The juvenile aggression, the need to be offensive and derogatory to prove that he resented any kind of evaluation. He was still the boy gang-leader despite his age. But he was what they needed and there was no doubt that he could be tamed. Apologies and some show of deference were called for. As between equals.

'In that case, my apologies. That wasn't what we intended. We thought that you would have realized that just the fact that we spent so much time with you and tested you so thoroughly must mean that you were potentially very important to the Agency.'

'You could have fooled me, buddy.'

'Why don't we go back to square one? No more questions from us, we'll tell you what we had in mind for you. It's a very important and senior assignment.' He paused. 'Especially for a man of your age. We should normally have been looking at professors, maybe heads of faculties, for a post of this nature.' He paused as he looked at Jimbo's face. 'You'd be leading a team of specialist code-breakers on top-secret work.'

He saw the instant response in the young man's eyes to the phrase 'leading a team'.

'How many bosses would I have?'

'Two. The director of Signals Intelligence Operations, a civilian, and beyond that the director of the National Security Agency himself.'

'What would be my title?'

'Officer in charge of Special Cryptanalytic Mathematics.'

'Sounds not bad. How much does it pay?'

Lodrick talked for another hour and arranged for Jimbo Vick to spend a week in Washington at the Agency's expense after he had signed the appropriate documentation. It was almost midnight when Lodrick sat on the edge of the hotel bed and dialled the Washington number. There was no rejoicing; it was just one more assignment dealt with. Another note to add to Vick, J.'s file. Lodrick hesitated between the descriptions 'immature' and 'unstable' and felt that the latter word might be going too far. Among the thousands of men and women who were employed by the NSA there were representatives of most of humanity's frailties. What mattered was knowing that the weakness existed.

CHAPTER TWELVE

He had arranged to meet her by the Kongresshalle in the Tiergarten. The sky was overcast as he waited for her. For a moment he wondered if there was some restriction on her Soviet pass that could prevent her from coming. But exactly on ten he saw her walking towards him. He checked automatically to see if anyone was following her but they seemed to be the only people in sight.

As she stopped in front of him, smiling, he sat quietly, still looking over her shoulder, 'How long can you stay?'

'As long as you want.'

'I'm going to give you an envelope. There's money for a taxi and two keys. Ask the driver to take you to Steiner Travel on the Ku'damm. On the left of their entrance is another door. You'll recognize it. It's my place. The big key is for that door. Go to the top floor and you'll see my name, Felinski, on the door. Let yourself in with the other key. Make yourself at home. I'll be there soon after. OK?'

'OK.'

'Just look at your watch and than shake my hand and walk away.'

She was standing by the window untying the red ribbon, peeling away the flower-patterned wrapping-paper, lifting out the long, narrow, blue-leather box. It was embossed with some coat of arms in gold and the words Étienne et Cie, Paris, Faubourg Saint-Honoré. He watched her open the box and look at the pearl necklace. The three strands of pearls. Then she looked up quickly as if she had only just realized that he was there.

He smiled, 'Do you like them?'

'Oh Jan, they're beautiful. But they're from Paris. How could you have known? When did you get them?'

'I had to go to Paris for a meeting a few months after I first met you. I saw them and they made me think of you. I bought them for you then.'

'But that was a long time ago. How could you have known . . . about us?'

He smiled. 'I didn't know about us. But I knew about me. I just hoped that one day I would have some excuse to give them to you.'

She smiled. 'You really are a Pole, Jan. Not at all English.'

He reached in his pocket, pulled out a thick envelope and handed it to her.

'There's a British passport in there. In the name of Anna Taylor. The photograph is not you but it's good enough to pass. There's also a security card in the same name. If ever you need help this side of the Wall just show that and they'll contact me.' He paused. 'You'll need to keep them hidden very carefully.'

'Is all this a problem for you, Jan?'

'No. No problem at all.'

The clear brown eyes looked intently at him. 'Are you sure it's worth it? There are bound to be problems. Maybe more than just problems.'

'Sit down, honey. Let's talk about it.'

She sat beside him on the leather couch and he took her hand. 'It's easier for me,' he said, 'because I've imagined all this many times before. I'm more prepared for it than you are. And I've no ties. I'm not married to someone else, and my movements aren't restricted as yours are. There's no danger for me. But there is for you. I want to make sure that you have time to think about it. The sacrifices are all yours and I want to be sure that you understand what they are.'

'What are the sacrifices, Jan?'

'Sooner or later it should mean that you leave him. It means the end of all your contacts in the Soviet Union. Your father. Other relatives and friends. You'd be in a strange country. A different way of life. Once you've come over, there could be no going back.' He paused. 'And . . . I'm not sure that I'm worth it.'

'Would you do it for me?' she said softly.

He nodded. 'Yes. But that's different. I know you're worth it.'

'So what do we do?'

'How easy it is for you to come through the Wall?'

'It's not difficult if I have an excuse. I've got my Kommandatura pass.'

'What sort of excuse?'

'Shopping, sightseeing, concerts.' She smiled. 'But I have to notify the Allied Control Authority through the guard at this side of the checkpoint.'

'Do they ever stop you going where you want?'

'Not so far.'

'I'll check on that and see that it doesn't happen. If you use the British passport they'll know you're OK.'

'How?'

'There's something in the number.'

'Sounds just like the KGB.'

'Yes, it does.' He paused, 'That brings me to the last problem. How much do you care about Kholkov?'

She sighed. 'If you mean do I love him, then no, I don't. I don't hate him. There are good things about him. But not good things for me.'

'You won't regret leaving him some day?'

She smiled and shook her head. 'No. Not at all.'

'If we didn't have these problems I guess I'd ask a lot more about him. But because of what he is, and what I am, I won't.' He looked at her face. 'Is what I have said good sense?'

She nodded, smiling. 'You're a good man, Jan Massey.'

'Why do you say that?'

'Because for my sake you're prepared to be British and cautious and patient. And in your Polish heart you'd rather I just stayed here now and never went back. And to the devil with all the problems.'

He laughed. 'You seem to know me very well.'

'I told you. I've thought about you a lot, my Jan. Every day.'

'Since when?'

'Like I said. Since the three of us had dinner together the first time.'

'Why then?'

She smiled. 'Because I wished that it was you that I had come with, and you that I was going home with.' She looked at his face. 'How can I contact you?'

'You can phone me here. But not from your home. That will be monitored. Use a call box. I'll give you the number.' For a moment he hesitated, then he said, 'D'you know the bookshop on Unter den Linden?'

'The one that sells old books?'

'Yes. If you want to write to me you can take it there. Ask for the old man, then ask him for a first edition of *War and Peace* in Russian. He'll tell you they haven't got one and then you hand over the letter. I'll get it about four hours later up to midnight. Then the checkpoint is closed. After midnight I'll get it early the next morning.'

She put her hands on his shoulders. 'Do you like your work, Jan?'

'Most of the time. Not always.' He looked at her lovely face. 'I've told Judy Campbell. You can use her any time as an excuse.'

'Is she safe?'

'Yes. I'm sure she is. I told her how serious it would be if anyone at all ever had a vague thought about us.'

She shivered as she looked at him. 'What shall we do today, Jan?'

'I'm going to take you to a lake in the forest. There's a nature reserve there and we can have a meal and I'll row you on the lake.'

She smiled. 'It will be like being a little girl again. I'll like that.' She kissed him gently. 'Can I see you tomorrow?'

'Of course. What time?'

'Shall I come here about two?'

'I'll be waiting for you.'

Maybe they had got too used to meeting every day, for when they met on the last day before Kholkov was due back they stayed at the flat. Most days they had made love but on that day they just talked and listened to records until it was almost time for her to go. There were tears in her eyes as she stood at the door.

'When shall I see you again, Jan?'

'Whenever you can. You can pick up the keys at the cigarette shop. If ever I'm going to be away I'll leave a note for you here. You've got the phone number where you can always get me. Just say the name on your British passport and they'll get to me and I'll come here.'

'I feel terribly sad today.'

'So do I. But I'll be waiting and thinking about you all the time.'

CHAPTER THIRTEEN

Harper had stayed behind after the weekly heads-of-sections meeting had finished.

'About Bourget, Jan. You asked me to check on their comings and goings.'

'What did you get?'

'There's been no evidence of anybody there permanently apart from the French. But there have been a number of visitors. We've identified most of them. The majority are Germans. Maguire of CIA had been there a couple of times but it always looked like a social visit. A few girls have been there, all Germans. Two of them known prostitutes but the others were just party girls.'

'You sound like that's not the end of the story.'

'It's not. There have been two visitors who we haven't been able to identify. One is about forty and we covered him back through Checkpoint Charlie. He lives in a flat near Humboldt University. He seems to be a free-lance journalist named Hans Bayer. That's the name he uses anyway. We've found pieces in two East German newspapers with that by-line. He's a sports writer.'

'And the other one?'

'There's a guy who's been there three times. Always at night. We can't identify him.'

'Does he matter that much?'

'I think he does.'

'Why?'

'Because all three times we've had him under observation, when he left Bourget's place we lost him. The first time could have been carelessness on the part of Ridge's men. The second time it was a two-man team and he lost them after fifteen minutes. The third time they deliberately set a trailing pattern that would indicate whether he was deliberately avoiding a trail or not. He was. They lost him.' He paused. 'A man who can lose professionals three times is a professional himself.' He paused again. 'Even their descriptions of his appearance are almost useless. They never got a good look at his face.'

'What description have they got?'

'About five eleven tall. Dark complexion. Dark eyes. Hollow cheeks. Thin but with broad shoulders. Age about mid-fifties – but that's a very crude guess.'

'Are Ridge's men still watching the place?'

'Yes.'

'You'd better boost the team for at least the next two weeks. I want to know who that man is. It's important.'

'Can I be frank, Jan?'

'Of course.'

'You obviously had some tip-off that something was going on at Bourget's HQ. Why can't I be told what you know?'

Massey stared back at Harper, his face impassive, his eyes hard and his mouth set aggressively. 'Just do what I want, Gordon.'

For a moment Harper hesitated and then he nodded, stood up and walked out of Massey's office without speaking again.

Five minutes later Massey locked his office and walked down the corridor and the stairs to the front entrance of the house. The CI sergeant handed him the book and he signed it before he stepped out into the garden.

He walked away from the main house past the new blocks to where a group of apple trees clustered together where the grass was not mown. The ground under the trees was covered with the pale pink petals of apple blossom. There were daisies and dandelions and a clump of thin-stemmed field poppies. Behind the trees was a wide tall sweep of rhododendrons in full bloom and at the edge of the orchard was a small pool with a paved surround. Its surface was green from a dense mass of oxygenating plants, and at its fringes were irises and a kind of water celandine. A black and gold fish nosed at the pads of the lilies and a dragon-fly danced and hovered low over the still, dark water. There was a white painted bench angled across the paving stones facing a small marble statue of a young girl. Massey brushed a few stray blossoms from the bench and sat down.

The description was too general to be significant. Only one thing definitely fitted Kuznetsov – the hollow cheeks. The rest could describe thousands of men.

But the hollow cheeks and the expertise made Kuznetsov a possible. Except that he could think of no possible scenario that could link Kuznetsov with Bourget. Unless something had gone wrong. Terribly wrong. He would have to be really desperate to have anything to do with Bourget. Massey closed his eyes for a moment to help him concentrate, but all he was aware of was the sound of the birds and the peacefulness of that almost wild section of the gardens. There were two things he could do. Contact Bourget and fish around, or contact Kuznetsov using the emergency plan. He stood up slowly and walked back to the house, still thinking about Kuznetsov.

Aleksandr Dmitrevich Kuznetsov was born in October 1930 and now, in his early fifties, he was a senior officer in the First Chief Directorate of the KGB. There are five sub-directorates and twenty departments in the First Chief Directorate and all of them specialize in the penetration of foreign intelligence services including those of fellow members of the Warsaw Pact. The Directorate's responsibilities also include the control of KGB agents in all parts of the world outside the Soviet Union.

The administration and control of such a tangled web requires liaison between departments that jealously protect their fiefdoms and bitterly resent any interference in or control of their operations. Kuznetsov had previously been responsible for liaison between Directorate S and three of the departments – the First, Third and Fourth Departments. Between them, these covered KGB operations against the USA and Canada; the United Kingdom, Australia, New Zealand and Scandinavia; and the Federal Republic of Germany and Austria.

It is inevitable that operations of departments can leak into areas where others are both responsible and jealous of their responsibility. Kuznetsov had been responsible for minimizing the conflicts of interest. He was part of Directorate S and not answerable to any of the chiefs of departments which he observed. He had powers of inspection that overrode all security and was responsible only to Moscow and the five controllers of the First Directorate.

Kuznetsov was born and brought up in the city of Yaroslavl on the banks of the Volga River. His mother was a professional violinist and his father a foreman at the local factory which produced heavy lorries. About a hundred and sixty miles from Moscow, the city had stubbornly stayed provincial despite the industry that developed in the mid-'twenties. People still made the journey to see its beautiful old churches. Those that were damaged during the war were eventually restored.

It was said afterwards that the bombing raid which killed his parents had been a mistake. The Junkers had been intended to bomb Rostov but a new deception device had put them far north of their target. Four hundred and seventy-five people died that night. His parents and many others at the works' social club, more in a tenement block building near Professor Pavlov's old house.

Aleksandr was adopted by the family of one of the brass players in the local orchestra, a man who had once been in love with Aleksandr's mother. It was they who changed his name from Davidov to Kuznetsov and registered themselves formally as his parents. They had no children of their own.

In later life he realized how much he owed them. Not just the care and affection that they gave him but his new identity. His mother had been Jewish and there would have been no career with prospects open to the son of a Jew. Especially in the KGB. He was well on in his career before he first understood the significance of the change of name. His new parents had thought neither of deception nor protection any more than he did himself in always proffering the registration papers to any authority concerned. It was only when he heard a lecture about dissidents and Jews on his initial training course with the KGB that he remembered about his real mother. He decided that even his life might be in danger, not just his career, if he revealed his true origins. However, there was virtually no chance of his secret being discovered as the documentation in cities like Yaroslavl had all been destroyed in the fighting.

Kuznetsov studied foreign languages at Moscow University and like many linguist graduates he was offered a job as a reader of foreign publications for an organization that appeared to be part of a publishing house. It was in fact part of the KGB, and in due course he was recruited openly by a KGB colonel into a special unit that was responsible for providing cover stories for KGB illegals in Germany and Britain.

For the first year he was part of Line N, briefing Illegal Support Officers who were responsible for recruiting low-grade agents in Germany and Britain. He was sent on a course and then posted to the Soviet Trade Mission in London to operate a group of agents previously handled by a KGB man who had been recalled to Moscow. His next move, after nearly two years in London, was to Directorate K, known to field agents as Line K. He was based in Paris at the Soviet Embassy but his responsibilities were still concerned with operations in London, those of the KGB's top field agents in Britain and the Republic of Ireland.

Kuznetsov showed a resourcefulness and leadership that almost led to his undoing. The internal rivalries of the First Chief Directorate led to a bitter battle for his services between Directorate S and Directorate K and the eventual compromise saw him promoted to lieutenant-colonel and made deputy head of a new directorate to be called Directorate R, with responsibility for analysing all KGB field operations in Europe, Canada and the USA. The huge and unwieldy overseas operations had become almost uncontrollable. Kuznetsov was to sort them out and control them, discarding hundreds of agents who no longer produced useful material or no longer had access to target intelligence. Poor planning, carelessness, lack of training and lack of imagination had taken its toll of once effective networks. Kuznetsov was feared and resented but his backing from Moscow was always unequivocal, and instant.

KGB officers meeting Kuznetsov for the first time were always surprised. The man who had been nicknamed the Moscow Tiger was nothing like they had expected. He spoke very quietly and was a patient listener. He wore rather old-fashioned clothes, was polite and persuasive rather than belligerent, and his questions and responses showed that he was both well trained and very experienced. The senior KGB officers whom he caused to be dismissed or demoted were given state pensions or distant postings and were careful to voice no criticism of Kuznetsov or his decisions.

During his career there were three major checks on his own security. There had been no negative aspects in the reports. No evidence of financial chicanery, not even the slightest indication of nepotism, and no evidence of deviation from the rules governing all senior KGB officers. He took almost no advantage of the quite normal and legitimate privileges accorded his rank, buying little from the privileged shops and warehouses, refusing the services of permanent servants and declining the luxury flat that was his rank's due. He lived alone in a large but one-roomed flat not far from his office in Dzerdzhinski Square.

There was one aspect of his life that had briefly concerned the investigators.

Kuznetsov had never married nor had he ever had a long-term girlfriend. The possibility of homosexuality had obviously arisen. But with their usual thoroughness, they discovered that Kuznetsov regulary used the resident girls employed by the KGB. The KGB girls, nicknamed the Swallows, were mainly concerned with the entrapment and blackmail of foreign diplomats and businessmen. The investigators interrogated the girls thoroughly on Kuznetsov's sexual behaviour and even tried to find some common factor as to why particular girls were chosen. His sexual behaviour appeared to be quite normal but indicated a taste for a few pleasures that were not usual in the Soviet Union. It was assumed that they were evidence of Kuznetsov having used prostitutes in other countries.

He had no hobbies, but he played the piano well and was friendly with a number of professional musicians who played in the prestige Moscow orchestras. He also frequently used his privilege ticket when Moscow Dynamo were playing at home.

Women liked him, not only because he had a quiet charm and none of the usual sexual aggression that important men seemed prone to, but because his lean frame, large brown eyes and hollow cheeks made them eager to mother him.

Kuznetsov saw his parents very infrequently. Once he became a KGB officer the relationship diminished. He no longer lived with them, and although in a way they were proud of his success and independence the pride was tinged with a mixture of awe bordering on fear. He was no longer the boy or young man they once knew. He always showed concern for their welfare and often brought small gifts when he had been to a foreign country.

They were surprised when he once asked them about his mother. He had never seemed interested before. They told him how beautiful she was. A happy young woman with a talent for music that was well above average. There seemed little else to tell him and he asked no direct questions. They didn't mention that she was Jewish because it had never even entered their heads to do so. It was possible that they didn't even remember. But they had given him a postcard-sized photograph of a quintet. They were not actually playing and his mother was talking to the cellist, her violin and bow in one hand. Her face was in profile and barely discernible, but it was obvious that she was smiling. He had kept the photograph though he seldom looked at it. But he sometimes thought about the pretty girl who was really his mother and he wished that he knew more about her.

As Massey walked back to the house he was tempted to phone Chambers. But he couldn't discuss it even on the top-security circuit. It would be too dangerous. And what could Chambers say, except that he should use his own judgement?

When he was alone in his sitting-room next to his office his thoughts went back to that night so many years before when he had first met Kuznetsov. He had been to a concert at the Festival Hall. Rostropovich had played the *Rococo Variations* and in the interval Massey had walked out to the upper foyer and stood looking across the river at the floodlights on the Houses of Parliament. His eye had been taken by a pleasure steamer all lit up, and he wondered if the passengers ever thought about the things that went on in their names. The answer would have been yes if they had been Europeans, but the British weren't really interested in politics, indifferent to what the rest of the world was up to unless it concerned sport or the cost of food. He had been vaguely conscious of the soft mellow warning bells for the second half of the concert but he had gone on standing there, looking across the river.

Suddenly, he had heard a woman cry out and turning quickly he saw one of the attendants helping a man to a chair. The man was gasping for air, his chest heaving and his face almost purple. Massey turned to the nearest window, forced it open and the cold night air came in with a rush. He pulled the man and the chair nearer the window, loosened the man's tie and said, 'Don't panic. Relax. You're going to be OK. Relax . . . it'll go.' The man's head was thrown back, his chest heaving and he tried to stand. The rasping hoarse sounds were longer and less frequent, and slowly the spasms subsided. When he opened his eyes there were tears pouring down his cheeks and he was trembling, a ring on one of his fingers knocking against the leg of the chair.

'The man had some kind of bronchial attack. He's recovering OK.'

'Should I get a doctor for him?'

'I don't think it will be necessary.'

The man in the chair tried to stand but fell back weakly into the chair again, and Massey realized that the man had cursed in Russian, softly but audibly.

Massey said quietly, in Russian, 'Are you feeling better?'

The man nodded and asked him to call a taxi. Massey asked the assistant manager to get a taxi and he left hurriedly, only too anxious to be relieved of further responsibility.

As Massey stood alone, looking at the man, he wondered who he was. He could be a diplomat, someone from the Trade Mission, a journalist or even a KGB man. There was a time, when he was first in SIS, when he thought he could tell a KGB man from his face and appearance, but he'd learned how wrong that theory could be.

The man had been ashen-faced but he was able to make his way, with Massey's arm round him, down the stairs, across the foyer and through the doors to the waiting taxi. He stood with one hand against the taxi door his head bowed. Massey asked him in Russian where he wanted to go. He groaned, and Massey could just hear him say that he wanted to go to the Soviet Trade Mission.

Massey stopped the taxi several hundred yards before the house, paid the driver and stood in the cold night air, lightly supporting the man.

'Walk around for a few minutes. Get some fresh air.'

The man took deep lungfuls of air and after a few minutes he seemed almost normal again, apart from the beads of sweat on his forehead.

'It happens sometimes,' the Russian said. 'Once or twice a year.'

'Don't worry. You don't have to explain.'

'There's nothing to explain. It just happens.'

Massey nodded as he looked at the man's face. 'Of course not.'

'Why do you look at me like that?'

For a moment Massey didn't reply and then he said quietly, 'Because I know what causes it. But just forget it.'

'How is it you speak such good Russian?'

'I was at the Embassy in Moscow for some time.'

'What's your name?'

'Jan Massey. I was deputy military attaché. Nobody important.'

But Massey had seen the recognition of his name on the Russian's face.

The Russian nodded. 'And my name's Karelin. I'm at the Trade Mission.'

Massey smiled and said quietly, 'You're Kuznetsov and you're KGB.'

'Were you trailing me tonight?'

'No. I booked a ticket for the concert weeks ago.'

'Why did you help me?'

'For the same reasons that I would help anyone. I didn't know then who you were. I didn't even know you were Russian until you spoke.'

'How did you recognize me?'

'I've seen photographs of you on the files.' He smiled. 'And you remembered my name too.'

'It's strange. You and I talking together, and yet we are enemies.'

'Are we enemies?'

The Russian's brown eyes were intent on Massey's face.

'What do we have in common?'

Massey shrugged. 'We're men. We breathe, we eat, we sleep.'

'You're a very strange man, Mr Massey.'

'Why?'

'I guess you're SIS. I don't remember what the files said. SIS or MI5, or some such organization. You could have walked away and raised a laugh or two back at Century House or wherever, about the KGB man gasping like a dying fish in public. But you stayed behind and talked. Am I supposed to say thank you by giving you some information?'

Massey laughed softly. 'You're being naïve. Or pretending to be. I shall report that we met and the circumstances. But nobody will laugh. We have people with the same problem.' He paused. 'And for the same reasons.'

'What reason?' the Russian said softly.

'They've had the same treatment. The water treatment. They live it over again. Once or twice a year. When they're under pressure.'

'I'm not under pressure of any kind.'

Massey shrugged. 'You'd better get back to the Mission and sleep it off.'

'Will this . . . episode . . . be reported in the press?'

'Good God, no. People are frequently taken ill at the Festival Hall and other public places.'

'But not KGB officers.'

'Nobody knew you were a KGB officer. They didn't even know you were Russian. The British aren't natural linguists.'

'But *you* know now.'

'So?'

'So you could inform the news agencies.'

'Why the hell should I?'

'To ridicule the Soviet Union.'

'How long have you been in London?'

'About five months.'

Massey smiled. 'If the incident was reported in the British press, readers would wonder why it was even mentioned. And they'd probably start a fund for underfed KGB men. And sweet old ladies would send the Embassy herbal remedies. You've got a lot to learn about the British, my friend.'

Kuznetsov shrugged. 'Maybe you're right.' He paused. 'Thanks for your help. It was very kind of you.'

'Forget it.' Massey smiled. 'Take care of yourself and don't get into mischief.'

The Russian smiled wanly as he turned and walked slowly away.

It was almost two years later when Chambers got him out of bed at two in the morning. A car was on its way to take Massey to a meeting. No hint of where the meeting was to be or what it was about. As the car went over Putney Bridge, up the hill, to turn right by the common, Massey guessed that it must be the safe-house.

As the car turned into the gardens of the block of flats it swept past the unlit caretaker's kiosk, to the central block of flats. It stopped at the side of the building where the internal road led down to the garage block. Chambers was waiting for him there at the end of the narrow central pathway that ran along the back of the building giving access to the flats through their kitchens. A fir tree and a cupressus cast shadows in the moonlight where Chambers was standing.

'Sorry about this, Massey. But it's important. I'd better put you in the picture before we go inside.' He paused. 'A KGB man has made contact with us. Not a defector exactly, but a potential collaborator.' Chambers coughed. 'But he'll only cooperate if he can deal with you.'

'Why me?'

'He knows you. Says he's willing to trust you.'

'Who is he?'

'Goes under the name of Karelin. Used to be attached to the Soviet Trade Mission in Highgate. He's an accredited diplomat at the Soviet Embassy at the moment. Third Secretary.'

'You mean Kuznetsov? Is he still here?'

'That's the chap. He is here for another month. Then he's being promoted and sent to Paris.'

'Why's he offering to collaborate?'

'I don't know. He refused to give a reason. Said it was a personal decision, not ideological. Maybe he'll tell you more.'

'What is he offering us?'

'He offered to act as a contact for what he described as crisis situations.'

'What the hell does that mean?'

'I think it's some kind of rationalization. Squaring the old conscience. If he feels that things have reached a crisis point and could boil over, or we do, he'll assist us.'

'Sounds a bit naïve, doesn't it? We need the tip-off before it's a crisis.' He paused. 'What's he expect in return?'

'A safety net. If he ever needs to get out we help him and give him protection. The usual stuff. Pension, new identity and so on.'

Massey looked at Chambers's face in the dim light. 'Sounds a real dog's breakfast to me.'

'You think he could be a plant?'

'No way. Not with a pathetic story like that. It's all too vague. No explanation of why he's suddenly decided to help us. No reality to the help he will actually give. He's selling smoke.'

'I'd like you to pick up the pieces all the same, Jan. He could be very important, even if he only acts as some sort of reference point for us.'

'OK. It's up to you . . . where is he?'

'He's in the bottom flat here. Number thirty-nine. I'll take you in. He's got to be back at his place by eight o'clock and it's nearly three now so there's not much time.'

Elaborate arrangements were made for Massey to meet Kuznetsov during the following three months, at first in England and later in a small town on the Seine just outside Paris.

They were difficult meetings because, although he got on well personally with the Russian, he remained unclear about what the Russian was offering. But Kuznetsov made clear that he was prepared to pass on information that would prevent SIS from making substantial errors in combating KGB operations in Britain and the Republic of Ireland. Like most directors he ran the operations in one country while being based in a neighbouring country. It was normal KGB practice.

The first sign of Kuznetsov's cooperation came after six months. He advised SIS to remove one of its agents from Warsaw where he worked as a librarian at the British Embassy, but was in fact organizer of a sensitive network and about to be arrested by the Poles. And a few days later he gave Massey the name of a KGB man at the Soviet Embassy in London who was successfully manipulating a top MP with the objective of a well-publicized defection to Moscow.

Kuznetsov insisted that his only contact with SIS was through Massey by a complex but efficient system devised for immediate contact at any time. But the system had been almost a one-way system for nearly two years. The information passed by the Russian had become more important as time went by and he was more ready to provide answers or guidance on specific items that were put to him. His good faith had been proved on a number of occasions and at no time had he asked for information in return. But on two occasions Massey had passed on warnings that gave Kuznetsov the chance to avoid danger to his own operations from other countries' intelligence organizations. By then the information the Russian was passing had become important enough to warrant sacrificing minor SIS operations, and even their less important operators.

When both Massey and Kuznetsov ended up on different sides of the Berlin Wall in direct opposition it had been entirely fortuitous, both sides having a urgent need for experienced men in the area at the same time. But from London's point of view it was also extremely convenient.

For Kuznetsov and Massey, however, the locality provided additional hazards in their contacts. It was easy enough for Kuznetsov. A call from any phone box to the tobacconist's shop in West Berlin would indicate a meeting, a seemingly innocuous conversation supplying coded details of time and place. But to protect Kuznetsov, Massey's contacts had to be far more cautious and complex. There was no possibility of using cut-outs or any of the usual procedures. Kuznetsov was on his own, on the other side of the Wall. The Moscow Tiger who didn't know how to handle his own problem. He'd never said what the problem was and Massey hadn't probed beyond a friendly and genuine interest and a wish to help.

Massey had respected Kuznetsov from the start. Aware of the danger to himself the Russian had guided them away from some irretrievable mistakes. His advice was always negative advice. He had never supplied them with top-security information. Just warned them against following some route that would lead them to disaster. He gave no explanation but the warnings had saved lives and on some occasions had prevented disasters that might have caused a heightening of East – West tensions that could have led to serious consequences. Massey had never got close enough to him to like Kuznetsov but he admired him and was concerned to make sure that he was never endangered through carelessness on his part. He was the only contact with the Russian. Nobody else in Berlin knew of the relationship, and it was accepted that Massey would only contact Kuznetsov at the Russian's request. There would be no contacts initiated by Massey except in a crisis situation.

If Kuznetsov *had* visited Bourget, then something was seriously wrong. His responsibilities no longer covered France but the Russian would know all about Bourget. It seemed strange. But Bourget could have been lying. The unidentified visitor to the SDECE house could be anybody. There was nothing to go on. And nothing concrete to concern him. He and his staff had to evaluate a dozen rumours a week and assess their likely truth. Most of them were gossip, a few were disinformation put out by the Russians or the East Germans, and maybe one a month had some substance. The rules they usually applied were a mixture of the likelihood of the rumour being true and any supporting facts. If there were no actual facts to support the story it was discounted for the time being.

In this instance there was neither likelihood nor a single actual fact confirming the reality. But Massey's success had often come from intuition. A bell ringing in his mind hinted at some long-forgotten incident of fact, a red light flashing that said that something was wrong. And this was one of those occasions. Massey felt deeply uneasy about Kuznetsov. Should he risk endangering the Russian by using their crisis contact arrangements? And on such a slender basis? He knew that such a move was unjustifiable by any normal standards. He decided that he would have to wait and see what happened.

Most intelligence officers – particularly Massey – hated indecision, but it was part of Massey's responsibilities to resist his inbuilt urge for action, or even reaction. It was a burden for which there was no training; expected of him but not openly acknowledged.

Massey found it haunting his mind through the rest of the day's activities. That one doubt. There could be something wrong and he was doing nothing about it.

CHAPTER FOURTEEN

Massey walked through the series of basement security checks to Cohen's office. Cohen's secretary showed him on the ground plan where he could find him.

Max Cohen was sitting beside an operator in front of a VDU, his eyes intent on the screen. Lines of coded text rolled slowly up the screen, the speed responding to the control button on the computer. The lines were sixty-four characters wide in five-figure groups, alpha-numeric with one digit in each group of lines. A line came up to central screen and the text stopped rolling. One of the groups of figures was flashing slowly and the operator noted the line number. As the text rolled again, Cohen reached over and speeded it up. A few seconds later the scrolling stopped again and another group was flashing. Cohen turned to Massey.

'D'you want me, Jan?'

'I can wait.'

'No need.' Cohen stood up and turned to the operator. 'Warn the cryppies and Evaluation and tell them I want it quickly.' He paused. 'An hour. Not longer . . . in my office.'

'Yes, sir.' The operator nodded and turned back to the VDU.

When they got back to Cohen's office he sat down and reached for the phone, pressing two of the buttons as he put it to his ear.

'Is Mr Mason there . . . Cohen . . . yes.' He put his hand over the mouthpiece and looked at Massey. 'It's urgent, Jan. I'll only be a moment.' His hand uncovered the mouthpiece. 'Joe . . . I've just come from thirty-nine . . . there's a whole lot of traffic coming over to you from there . . . it's got both the key-words you were alerting for . . . yeah . . . OK . . . We'll put it on the fast decoder and printer . . . say fifteen minutes . . . OK.'

Cohen hung up and looked at Massey. 'London's not gonna like this little lot.'

'What is it?'

'We had a warning to keep close check on the traffic of three particular Red Army divisions stationed near Magdeburg. They moved overnight to about twenty kilometres from the border at Helmstedt.'

'Could be unannounced manoeuvres.'

'They leave a whole lot of admin staff behind for manoeuvres. They've taken everything with them. Those were the orders from Thirty Army and we're just deciphering the orders from Moscow to Thirty Army.'

'Won't Cheltenham and Fort Meade have picked it up as well?'

'Probably. I don't know. They always make us work as if we're the only listening-post so far as East Berlin and East Germany are concerned. I suspect that we're just part of a belt-and-braces system but Mason's going to alert Cheltenham right now.'

'But they're always shifting units around, Max. Why is this so significant?'

'Who knows? But if it wasn't significant we shouldn't have had prior warning from London and Cheltenham. Anyway . . .' Cohen shrugged. 'Thank God I'm only the messenger boy.' He paused. 'What can I do for you, Jan?'

'How long would it take to bug the SDECE house?'

'Is that the one by the zoo?'

'Yes.'

'One room or the lot?'

'The lot.'

'Telephone, normal speech and what else?'

'The radio traffic.'

'We've got that. It's on the files. There's nothing on it that matters so it probably doesn't get to your summaries. But you should get a routine "nil report".'

'I probably do. I haven't checked.'

'So speech and telephones.' Cohen closed his eyes. 'Remind me. Garden front and right-hand side. What about the back?'

'It backs onto a block of flats.'

'Back to back? Party wall?'

'Yes.'

'I'd guess a week to do a recce and another week before we'd be operational. Could be three weeks. Anything special you're after?'

'Not that you need to know.'

Cohen half-smiled and shrugged. 'OK. Do you want it?'

'Not yet. But think about it, Max. And just you. It's not for discussion.'

'Leave it with me.'

The internal phone buzzed and Cohen reached for it. He looked at Massey as he listened. When he had hung up he smiled.

'Evaluation . . . panic over. The buggers were playing radio games – they hadn't moved, just put on a radio exercise.'

'For our benefit?'

'Not entirely. They know it causes pandemonium on our side but they do it from time to time to practise deception. Apart from keeping their own radio people up to scratch they get a chance to see if anything appears in the Western press and it gives them a clue to where the leaks might be. We do it to them sometimes. And the Russians do it because they know that it worries our Germans. Makes them realize how close they are across the border.'

'Going by the report from my people, they couldn't have shifted artillery and tanks without months of preparation.'

'Why not?'

'Lack of spares. Bad servicing. And most units at less than half strength.'

'You didn't seem much concerned anyway.'

'If it was likely to be for real I'd have had orders from London to go on standby for disrupting their plans.'

'I thought the experts at NATO estimated that they'd be at the Channel ports a week after they started.'

Massey smiled. 'They used to say that when the Pentagon was on the trail of more cash. They've realized that is isn't worth scaring the Europeans for the sake of a few billion dollars.'

'You think it wouldn't happen that fast?'

'No way. They wouldn't get far in a week if they tried it. And they know it.'

Cohen sighed. 'I'm glad to hear it.'

'You get asked to the top-secret briefing sessions. You should go sometimes.' Massey smiled. 'It'd counteract all that Wagner.'

Massey had checked every day at the Ku'damm flat. It was three weeks since he had heard from her and he was getting anxious. He had known that it would be difficult but he regretted not having made some simple arrangement that could let her indicate that all was well with her.

He was relieved to find a note from her that morning at the flat. She would be there at three o'clock the next day. That was today. For a moment he was tempted to just stay there and wait for her, but he drove back to the Grunewald house and worked until two, driving back into the city centre. It had been difficult in the routine meeting to hide his good mood.

Dead on three the doorbell went and she was standing there, smiling and beautiful.

It must have been just after four as they lay on his bed looking up at the ceiling that she said, 'Tell me about your wife.'

'I don't have a wife, sweetie.'

'Your old wife. How is it said? Your past wife.'

'My ex-wife. She was a bitch, that's all there is to say.'

'Was she beautiful?'

'Pretty.'

'How is the difference between pretty and beautiful?'

'Blondes are pretty, brunettes are beautiful.'

He leaned up on one elbow and looked at her. She was naked except for the pearl necklace and when he looked back at her face she was smiling. 'I like when you look at me like that.'

'Like what?'

She laughed. 'Like you're not really looking but you look all the same.'

He smiled and kissed her, and said, 'How about a coffee?'

She shook her head. 'Tell me about your momma. I think she must have been very pretty to give you your nice face.'

'I've only seen photographs of her. But she *was* pretty. Very pretty.'

'Tell me of her.'

'She was Polish, the same as your mother. Born in Warsaw. Went to Paris just before the war started. Early in the war she was in England, joined the British Army and was transferred into SOE, Special Operations Executive, because of her languages. She was trained as a radio operator. Dropped in France. Married my father who was head of her network. Came back six months later. Left the army to have me. In 1944 my father was back in France and was seriously ill. She insisted she should be dropped back to care for him. He was badly depressed. She was caught by the Germans before she even saw my father. They sent her to a concentration camp. Mauthausen. With two other captured SOE girls. They burnt them in the ovens.'

She lay silent and when he looked at her he saw that her big brown eyes were closed and her cheeks were wet.

He said softly, 'Tell me about your mother.'

'Give me a paper, a tissue thing.'

He wiped her cheeks with a Kleenex and she opened her eyes, still swimming with tears. As she took the tissue she said, 'My mother was born in Lwów . . .' she shrugged '. . . in 1939 it became part of the Soviet Union. She hated not to be Polish and she hated all Russians . . .' she smiled '. . . all except one. My father. And she loved him very much. It was like Chekhov. He teaches music and he teaches her piano. She falls in love with him and they marry. You know the rest. She was killed in a car because of the ice.'

'Is your father still teaching?'

'Yes. He is professor of composition at the Conservatory.'

'Do you see him?'

'Not very often. I told you. He didn't approve of my marriage.'

'Tell me again why he didn't like Kholkov.'

She shrugged. 'Nobody likes KGB men. Especially creative people.'

'No more than that?'

She sighed. 'He disliked him as a man . . .' she smiled '. . . too much charm, he said, not enough substance.'

He was tempted to pursue it but he wasn't sure that he would like the outcome. 'When can I see you again?'

'He goes to somewhere . . . I think Dresden . . . on Saturday. So I could see you on Saturday or Sunday. Or both if you want.'

He smiled. 'I want. You know that.'

She looked at his face and said, 'Can I ask you something? Something we both may not like.'

'Yes.'

She said softly, 'Where do we end, the two of us?'

'Would you leave him and marry me?'

'For me, yes. For him it would be terrible.'

'In what way?'

'He would be disgraced in the KGB. That his wife defects to marry an English

KGB man.' She paused. 'And there is another reason.'

'Tell me.'

'It would be like a traitor. Some day I tell you. It's not important to you and me.'

'Do you love him?'

She shook her head decisively. 'I am sorry for him and that is all I feel.'

'Does he love you?'

'Not love. Not love. Maybe he likes me. Not more.'

'D'you love me?'

'I love you. All my heart. All my body. All my soul. I love you. Always.'

'You know I love you?'

She nodded. 'Oh yes. I know.' And her arms went round his shoulders as she kissed him, moving her mouth slowly on his.

CHAPTER FIFTEEN

It was ten days since they had the weekend together and already he had decided that they must plan her final break with Kholkov and then she would come over for good. There should be no problems. He had ready access to everything they would need. Documents, transport and protection until she was safe in England.

It had seemed just one more day. He had slept that night at the house in Grunewald and had just coffee and toast for breakfast before going along to his office.

He buzzed for Howard Fielding who brought in the previous day's SIS reports. Fielding sat opposite him at his desk, leafing through the typed slips of paper, putting the routine dross into a separate pile before handing Massey the items he thought he should see. He glanced at two sheets stapled together and handed them across.

'You'd better see that, skipper. A new list of staff at the Soviet Embassy in London. The asterisks are suspected KGB.'

When Massey had read the sheets and handed them back Fielding was smiling as he read a teleprinter slip.

'Looks like your friend Kholkov's in trouble.'

'What kind of trouble?'

'They arrested his missus yesterday. Took her to Karlshorst. Wonder what she's been up to.'

For a moment the room, the building, the whole world seemed to be silent, the air shimmering as if an atomic bomb had exploded on a grainy newsreel film. And then the sweat broke out on his face. He reached out for the slip.

'Let me see that.'

Fielding smiled as he handed it over and reached for the next message slip on the pile. Massey was aware that his hand was shaking as he looked at the few lines of type.

SOURCE ZO–17
ITEM 4304/2

ANNA KATERINA KHOLKOV WIFE OF KHOLKOV A.V.
ARRESTED BY KGB AND TRANSPORTED ZIL NO
809741 TO MAIN ENTRANCE KARLSHORST HQ AT
APPROX 0230 HRS TODAYS DATE. ENDS.

He heard Fielding talking but he didn't hear what he was saying. Then Fielding was reaching across the desk, touching Massey's hand.

'What is it, Jan? Are you OK?'

He shook his head because he couldn't speak, and stood up clumsily, heading for the door. The corridor seemed to be pitching and rolling like a ship at sea as he made for his bedroom.

As he sat on his bed he felt icy cold as the sweat poured down his face. It couldn't be true. But he knew it was. And he couldn't bear to think of what was happening to her in those grim buildings in Karlshorst. He tried desperately to think what he could do, but his mind wouldn't get into gear. It was turning in frantic circles like a rat on a laboratory treadmill. All he wanted at that moment was to be in Karlshorst with a gun, and kill everything that moved before they got him.

Then Andrews came into his room. He didn't hear him knock and he was holding his little black bag. Andrews was the unit's doctor.

'Fielding says you're not feeling too good.'

Massey took a deep breath and from somewhere far away he heard his own voice saying, 'I'm OK. I'm OK. Just leave me.'

The MO put his fingers around Massey's wrist and with his other hand the doctor held a flat metal disc against Massey's forehead to read off the temperature on the digital thermometer. What seemed a long time later he said quietly, 'Have you eaten any shellfish in the last forty-eight hours?'

Massey shook his head and the doctor put his hand on Massey's shoulder. 'What have you been up to, Jan?'

'I'm OK, doc. Just leave me.'

'I'll give you a shot that will calm you down.'

'Not a sleep drug.'

'No. Something to counteract all that adrenalin rushing round your system. Have you got any cramp in your legs?'

Massey shook his head.

'Stand up, Jan. Let me see you stand.'

He tried to stand but his legs seemed like lead. Andrews took off Massey's jacket, rolled up his shirt sleeve and dabbed his upper arm with cotton-wool swab. Then he stuck in the syringe and pressed the plunger and Massey felt his muscles relaxing so that he could move his legs. Andrews stood looking at him: he was used to dealing with emergencies where he was never told what had happened. Cracked skulls, bullets in stomachs and the ravings of men or women who had been tortured or brutalized. He had grudgingly grown to accept that his questions wouldn't be answered.

'You'll feel OK in about ten minutes. Whatever caused it, don't do it again. And thank the good Lord that you're fit.'

Massey wiped his face with the edge of the bedsheet as Andrews packed his bag. The MO glanced back at Massey for a moment as he stood at the door, then, shaking his head slowly he walked out of the room.

Instinct had driven him to the Ku'damm flat but as he paced around the room he found no peace from the turmoil in his mind. It was crazy. He was the head of British Intelligence in Berlin and he had no idea what he should do. The wife of a senior KGB officer had been arrested and taken to the Soviet military and intelligence HQ in East Berlin. Why? There was an obvious possibility but he couldn't believe that they knew. He hadn't been careless. He had taken all the precautions he would have taken if she had been a highly valued agent. But what other reason could there be for arresting her? If she had offended against some point of KGB protocol she would just have been sent back home to Moscow. A black mark in Kholkov's record, but nothing more. The wives of KGB men and Soviet diplomats did overstep some ideological mark or diplomatic nicety from time to time but he had never heard of a wife being arrested for that. Not even in the Soviet Union, let alone in a Warsaw Pact country.

Massey stared out of the window, unseeing. What would he do if a top agent had been arrested? He knew what the answer was. Clean out their network in twenty-four hours and wait to see what happened. A new file would be opened and a damage control evaluation would be mounted. But nothing more. And this time he had no back-up resources. He was on his own. Even if he could use every resource he had there was nothing he could do. He didn't know enough. He didn't know anything.

An hour later he drove to the Olympiad offices and sent for several files including Kholkov's. The others were only so that it wasn't obvious from the records what he was looking at. But there was very little in Kholkov's file that he didn't already know. What a fool he had been not to put a special team on Kholkov right from the start. Like the army always said, 'Time spent in reconnaissance is seldom wasted.' But it was too late now. Or was it? He felt a sudden relief from the tension as the idea flowered in his mind.

He checked the address in the file and walked over to the map of West and East Berlin that covered one wall. The curtains glided back as he pressed the red button. It was down by the river. One of those pre-war middle-class suburbs that had been left intact by the Red Army, so that it could provide housing for occupation troops. It was still an area where Soviet and East German officials tended to live. And near enough to the Karlshorst HQ to give easy access.

With the Falk street-plan for Berlin he sat at his desk checking and memorizing the area of Kholkov's house. Just doing something had begun to relieve the terrible tension, and his mind pushed away the doubts that crept in as he looked at the map. It was the kind of thinking that he would have dismissed as futile in his official capacity. Dismissed on the grounds that it had no objective. What could he possibly learn from looking at the house when he already knew that she wasn't there? His mind clung desperately to a thin thread of rational thinking. If he could find out why she had been arrested and it was not because they had discovered her relationship with him, then there were things that he could do. Unofficially and, perhaps, even officially.

The need to do something, anything, was overwhelming. He left messages for Cohen and Fielding that he wouldn't be available for a few days. He left no contact number and the messages left it unclear whether he was on duty or taking a few days' leave. He could be in East Berlin by mid-afternoon and back in West Berlin tomorrow morning.

He emptied all his pockets and took the Canadian passport and documents from the small wall safe together with a wad of US and Canadian dollars. He parked his car in the Hilton car park and took a taxi to Kochstrasse and walked to the Friedrichstrasse checkpoint.

He walked twice past the house. It was a pre-war villa still covered with Virginia creeper, its pale blue shutters newly painted, its garden neat and well cared-for.

As he approached the house a third time, he opened the wooden gate and walked up the gravel path to the porch. There was a large terracotta pot in the porch, filled with trailing pelargoniums and lobelia, but the bell inside the house rang with that hollowness that bells have in an empty house. He walked onto the small lawn in front of the house and looked through the window.

There was a dining-table with six chairs placed round it, a long walnut sideboard, a food trolley, and in the far corner a glass-fronted cabinet housing china plates, dishes and bowls. On the dining-table was a place-setting for one. Salad still on a side-plate, a dinner-plate with a slice of ham and two boiled potatoes. Several dishes with lids on and a silver coffee-set with a coffee-cup and saucer. It was obvious that somebody had left in a hurry before the meal was even started.

There were only small stained-glass windows along the side of the house and at the back he looked into a living-room that was elegant and well furnished but with no sign of life. The top segment of one of the kitchen windows was at an angle, held open by a simple window-latch. He could reach down easily and open the main window over the plastic work-surface. For a moment he hesitated, than walked slowly round the house again, back down the front path to the gate and the street.

At the row of small shops he bought a small pocket torch and then walked back to the café by the bridge. He had a coffee and slowly ate a ham sandwich, and when he eventually paid his bill it was already dusk, but still too light for what he had in mind. He checked that he was not being followed and then walked slowly towards the river.

The houses along the river had been very little damaged in the war. They looked well cared for and inside there were lights going on in the ground-floor rooms as he strolled past them. He was already aware that he had reacted too hastily. There must be other ways, more subtle ways, that he could have tackled the problem. But subtlety takes time, and his need for action was overwhelming. It left him wandering around in East Berlin with little thought of what he was going to do next. Even at that moment he needed to *do* something rather than think things out, and he turned impatiently to walk back towards the house.

As he strolled past the house there was nobody in sight and no traffic in the street. He turned back quickly and went through the garden gate, down the side passage to the back of the house.

The catch on the main kitchen window was stiff but he levered it up slowly and the window finally came free. There was crockery and cooking utensils on the work-surface and he carefully moved them aside before climbing through into the kitchen. He closed the window carefully behind him.

He walked slowly and cautiously to the front room. There was only one thing he wanted to check in there. The food. For a brief moment he shone the torch as he stood by the single place-setting. The smell was almost enough but in the brief light he could see the actual putrefaction of the vegetables.

In the living-room he drew the curtains and switched on the lights. There was a pile of magazines on the settee and a sewing-basket on an embroidered footstool. A bunch of dahlias in a vase was brown and wilting and the telephone receiver was off its hook, lying beside the instrument on a table by the teak desk. The desk was locked. He picked up the phone carefully and put it to his ear. It had the silence of disconnection.

As he left the room he switched off the lights and shone his torch in the hallway. The stairs were on his left and he went up them slowly and tried a door at the top of the stairs. The door was locked and he moved along the carpeted landing to the next bedroom. It faced the street and he didn't want to switch on the lights. But if someone saw even his torch light they would almost certainly phone the police. He made his way cautiously to the windows and closed the curtains.

As he turned, the beam of a powerful light almost blinded him and as he put up his hand to shield his eyes the room lights came on.

There was a man standing by the light switch at the door. Leaning there, smiling. Another man was sitting on the bed, a Kalashnikov resting across his knees, and a few feet away perched on a dressing-table was a man pointing a Walther.

The man by the door he recognized, and it was he who spoke in excellent English.

'Welcome to the German Democratic Republic, comrade.'

Massey said nothing. There was nothing he could say. The Russian was Major Panov, KGB. He was based in Moscow normally and was responsible for some of the operations against the British and Americans in Europe. He had heard about him from Kuznetsov.

He looked at Massey with his eyebrows raised in query. 'Shall we go?'

Massey sat in silence as the big black Mercedes drove to the Karlshorst compound. And for the first time he wondered if all this had some connection with Kuznetsov. Had the Russian's contacts been uncovered? Or, even worse, had Kuznetsov found out somehow about him and Anna and decided to expose him because he saw it as a danger to himself? Panov escorted him to a long, low building that was white in the moonlight.

Inside the building was a long corridor with a dozen doors leading off it and Panov led him to a room at the far end that ran the width of the building. It was furnished as living quarters for some senior official and Panov seemed very much at home as he waved Massey to one of the armchairs as he poured two whiskies from a bottle of Glenlivet.

Panov put the drink for Massey on the low table between them before he sat down himself. Smiling, he raised his glass.

'Your good health, Mr Massey.'

Massey ignored both the drink and the salutation, but Panov was very much at ease as he leaned back in his chair.

'And now what am I going to do about you, Mr Massey? Not the sort of fish I usually catch. What exactly were you after?'

'Just get on with it, Panov. Do whatever you're going to do and cut out the chat.'

'Tell me,' Panov said, 'was it all just a passing fancy or was she more than that?'

'Where is she? Why was she arrested?'

'Oh, come on, Massey. If one of my chaps was having a relationship with one of your officer's wives, wouldn't you take some action? Why be so hypocritical about it? You got her into trouble, my friend, and you must have known that it was possible.'

'You haven't answered my question.'

Panov pursed his lips. 'Where is she? She's in safe custody. Why was she arrested? Because she was having an adulterous relationship with an enemy of the State. To wit, Jan Massey. Officer of SIS.'

'What do you intend doing with her?'

'She'll face a court trial. Probably ten years in a Gulag. The wife of a serving KGB officer can hardly pretend she didn't realize the significance of what she was up to.'

'Is Kholkov himself in custody then?'

Panov smiled. 'Oh, come now, don't let's play games. You've done him enough harm already.'

'So get on with whatever you're planning to do.'

'What do you think we're going to do with you?'

'The usual press conference to announce the arrest of a British intelligence man. A trial in Moscow for the publicity. A hoped-for confession from me. And then a heavy prison sentence. Twenty years and up.'

'And for the girl?'

'Much the same. Enemy of the State. The usual crap.'

Panov sat looking at Massey for long moment. 'What would you do with me if I'd slept with young Fielding's wife – I know he hasn't got one . . . but if he had, and you'd caught me in one of the flats you people have in West Berlin.'

'You've missed something out.'

'What's that, my friend?'

'We shouldn't have arrested Fielding's mythical wife just because she was fond of you.'

Panov raised his eyebrows. 'Is Anna Kholkov fond of you?'

'Of course not. We were just friendly.' And Massey lied unhappily to help her.

'And were you fond of Anna Kholkov?'

'Forget it, Panov. My feelings are none of your business.'

'Why do you think we are talking here together?'

'You've made a good arrest. You're enjoying the feeling, and you're trying me out to see if I'm scared and I'll talk. I'm not scared. And I shall not talk. To you or anybody else.'

'Not even for the sake of the girl?'

Massey hesitated and then said softly, 'Not even for the girl.'

'You wouldn't lift a finger to help her?'

'How could I help her, for God's sake? You'd do whatever you've already planned to both of us. Whether I talk or not. But I repeat . . . I shall not talk.'

'D'you think it is at all possible that you and I could speak the truth to one another?'

Massey shrugged. 'It's unlikely, but possible.'

'Would you answer me just one question truthfully if I offered to release the girl tomorrow?'

Panov saw the immediate response in Massey's eyes and he followed up his question. 'A question about your feelings, nothing to do with your work and mine.'

'Ask me the question.'

'Do you love Anna Kholkov? Genuinely love her?'

'Why do you want to know?'

'If you really do love her I'll set her free.'

'Why would you do that?'

'I'd count it as inexperience and foolishness on her part. She's young and she's not in our business. I could see why she falls for you. You're an attractive man.' Panov paused. 'I can even see how you could love her.' He paused again. 'If it was not love on your part, then your relationship with a KGB officer's wife had another purpose. A professional purpose.'

Massey sat silently trying to sort out the turmoil of his thoughts but Panov leaned forward.

'Do you love her, my friend? If you do, say so now.'

Massey took a deep breath and said quietly, 'Yes, I love her. It was not a professional relationship in any way. Apart from the fact that we only met because she happens to be Kholkov's wife.'

Panov stood up slowly and walked over to the red telephone on the bottom shelf of the bookshelves. He spoke in Russian and Massey listened. Surprised, relieved, but uncomprehending.

'Polyakov? . . . yes . . . Panov. The girl Anna Kholkov . . . yes . . . Release her now if you please . . . yes . . . of course . . . So bring it over and I'll sign the release form. No, no restrictions . . . that's not necessary . . . Leave it to her . . . yes . . . In my room.'

Panov hung up and turned, leaning back against the shelves looking at Massey.

'Does that please you, my friend?'

'Why did you do it?'

'I wanted to –' Panov stopped and shouted, 'Come in' as someone knocked on the door.

A lieutenant in KGB uniform came in and stood to attention. Panov held out his hand, took the printed form and read it slowly. He took a pen from his jacket pocket and signed the paper. He held it out for Massey to read. It was an official prison release form made out in Anna's name and with Panov's signature authorizing her immediate release.

When the lieutenant had left and they were alone, Panov walked to a small alcove and brought back a plate of sandwiches and a bowl of fruit, placing them on the low table before he sat down.

'I don't have plates. These were intended just for me. Help yourself.'

Massey shook his head and Panov smiled. 'Don't be so British stiff-upper-lip, comrade. Just eat, for God's sake. We're not children. There's chicken and there's cheese.'

Massey made no move but Panov helped himself to a sandwich.

'You don't look like the photographs of you, Massey, that we have on our files. They make you look older.' He leaned back in his chair. 'And what are we going to do about you, my friend?'

Massey shrugged. 'Put me through the mincing machine I expect. Hoping you'll make me talk. And then the Moscow trial and the propaganda rubbish. And then the Lubyanka or the Gulag.'

'A bit old-fashioned, Massey. We're not all dinosaurs in the KGB now.'

Massey's eyes showed his disbelief and he asked ironically, 'When did you all change?'

Panov laughed softly. 'We didn't all change. Just some of us. There were cunning minds in Dzerdzhinski Square who thought that we needed a few more . . . what shall I say? . . . sophisticated? . . . sophisticated minds. Subtle rather than crafty.' Panov tapped his chest, smiling. 'I'm one of the new boys.' He spread his arms, shrugging like a Frenchman. 'Not an angel maybe, but different.'

'Why are you telling me all this? It won't make me go soft under interrogation.'

Panov shook his head slowly. 'Your file says you're half Polish. Is that why you are so prejudiced?'

Massey smiled. 'I've been working against the KGB and the GRU for years, Panov. That's why I'm prejudiced.'

'And you don't believe that a KGB officer could be human, too? Just SIS and the CIA are the nice guys, forced to do dirty tricks by the wicked Russians.'

'Tell me why you really let Anna go free?'

Panov shrugged. 'No point in holding her. She's no risk if she loved you and you loved her.'

'You could have used her to bring pressure on me.'

'Would it have worked?'

'Who knows?'

'But you don't feel it was . . .' he shrugged '. . . kind, let us say. You don't feel grateful or anything like that?'

'Very cautiously, a little.'

'But back to you. What should I do with you? What would you like me to do?'

'You could drive me back to Checkpoint Charlie and see me through the barrier.'

'Is that what you would like?'

'Why not?'

'Don't dodge, Massey. Is that what you would like? Yes or no?'

'Yes.'

'You would consider it civilized if I did that?'

'Miraculous.'

'But not civilized?'

'OK. Civilized too.'

Panov leaned forward, his face close to Massey's. 'Let me be frank with you, Massey. Moscow don't particularly want to raise hell with the British at the moment for various reasons. I'm prepared to do a deal with you. No trouble for the girl. I'll let you go back. But I want a small piece of cooperation from you.'

Massey shook his head. 'No way, Panov. No way.'

'You don't even know what I'm asking.'

'I won't talk, Panov. That's final.'

'I'm not asking you to talk.'

'What is it then?'

Panov stood up and walked over to the bookshelves, took down a large format book and walked back to his chair, putting the book on the table. Massey could see a colour picture on the jacket. A close-up shot of a mountainside covered with wild flowers and snow-capped peaks in the distance. The title was *Frühling im Gebirge* – Spring in the Mountains. Panov pointed to the book. 'I just ask that you take that back with you and put it somewhere on the shelves in the library at the house in Grunewald when you get back.'

'And if I don't?'

'Then you stay here and we have to go through the usual ritual. Just like you described.'

'With Anna involved.'

Panov shrugged. 'Inevitably.'

'Can I talk to Anna?'

'No.'

'How do I know that she won't be harassed?'

And in that question Panov knew he had won.

'You have my word, Massey. And there's no advantage for me in harassing the wife of a brother officer.' He paused. 'But you must not contact her again. I'm sure you understand that.'

Massey understood all too well. He had no cards in his hand. Nothing to negotiate with. He would have to go along with them for Anna's sake. He wondered what significance the book had, and why they should want it in the library of the house in Grunewald. Maybe some code. But it looked just like a normally printed book. And who at the house would use it? He could check on the register the name of anyone borrowing it. There was no point in bluffing. In fact there was no bluff he could even try.

Panov interrupted his thoughts. 'Did any of your people know you had come over today?'

'Why do you want to know?'

'It's not quite midnight. I could have you back on the other side in half an hour. You can't go through Charlie because it's closed but I can see you over through the Brandenburg crossing. You wouldn't need to explain where you have been provided you went back to the house tonight.'

Massey stood up slowly and reached for the book. He found it hard to speak at all, but he said quietly, 'OK, Panov, let's go.'

CHAPTER SIXTEEN

Massey walked back through the empty streets to the flat on the Ku'damm. He phoned Fielding who had to be fetched from his bed by the duty officer. He chatted for a few moments, but Fielding had nothing special to report. But he had established that he was around in case it was ever queried.

The book lay on the duvet on his bed and it was almost an hour before he could bring himself to look through it. There was nothing suspicious about the text or the pictures. What he was looking for was taped onto the back cover under the paper jacket. It was just over five inches across. What looked like a thin flexible gramophone record with an extra large hole in its centre. In its top left-hand corner was a normal, white label with four lines of typing.

CP/M-861(tm) VER 1.0 (BRITISH)
SERIAL 3 C86-336-5904
(C) 1982 SIRIUS SYSTEMS TECH.
(C) 1981 DIGITAL RESEARCH.

Although he wasn't in any way a technician he recognized what it was. It was a floppy disk of the kind that Meyer's people used on the Sirius computers. There were a dozen of them always at the side of each computer. Four in use and two sets on standby and they were in use twenty-four hours a day. There were long shelves from floor to ceiling in the computer-room and the disks were filed in slim, grey, plastic cartons of ten. Thousands of them. Maybe tens of thousands. Copies of them were kept at Cheltenham and the NSA's installation at Fort George Meade. Some controlled the functions of the computer and some stored information. Over a million characters on each slim disk. He had no idea of what the function of the disk was that he held in his hand. He folded the illustrated cover back over it and put the book on the table beside the bed.

He lay back on the bed and closed his eyes. What a fool he had been. An unprofessional fool. Just like the new boys who charged into some operation like stampeding elephants. Panov sitting there, suave and cool, watching the worm wriggling on the hook. He had taken for granted that neither Kholkov nor the rest of them knew about his relationship with Anna just because Kholkov had never given even the smallest sign of knowing. He had been amiable and normal every time they met, whether it was on business or privately. But once they had known, then he had been a sitting duck.

They had worked out that it wasn't just sex, it was for real, and they had just sat there, waiting for him to come. And breaking into the house would have been enough to bring a holding charge while they sorted out what to do with him. But they had sorted out what they really wanted long before he arrived. Long before they arrested Anna. And whichever option he chose they were winners. A propaganda victory or the five-inch piece of plastic that did something or other that they wanted. And Anna, although they had released her, was their permanent hold on him so that he couldn't just destroy the disk or pass it to Cohen for comment. The bastards had got him, tied and well knotted. Because he had been Polish, impetuous and stupid.

But as Massey lay there he knew that those thoughts were only to block out the other thoughts. The thought that he would never see her again. Ever. Two days ago it had all seemed so decisive and inevitable, and then, in just thirty-six hours, it had ended. Finally and inexorably. Not even loving last words. Just a void. She must have been terribly scared when they drove her away in the dark, early hours of the morning and put her in a prison cell. He wondered if they had told her why she was arrested. She didn't belong in the world of cells and prisons and it was he who had put her there. He had been careless and irresponsible. He had judged it from Western standards. At the worst, they were committing adultery. But to the KGB it would have seemed incredible. As incredible as if he had just walked through Checkpoint Charlie and given himself up. He felt the salt of his tears as they trickled slowly down his cheeks to the corners of his mouth. If only he were a proper Brit so that he could adopt that stiff-upper-lip approach. He remembered seeing the first light of the false dawn before he slept.

'That's about the lot, Jan.'

Leeming gathered up his files and shoved back his chair. He sat down again slowly as Massey spoke.

'I want a list of all withdrawals from the library, Peter.'

'You mean the technical reference library?'

'No. The general library.'

'We don't keep a record, Jan. It's not worth the time and effort. It's cheaper to risk losing a book or two.'

'I want it done for the next month at least. Name of book. Name of borrower. Date out and date returned.'

'Any particular reason, Jan?'

'Just something I want to check.'

'OK. Will do. How often do you want to see the register?'

'Every day. After the shifts have changed.'

Still looking vaguely mystified, Leeming nodded and stood up.

When Leeming left, Massey walked down to the library and put the book on the new books shelf. And for the first time he let the thought gel in his mind that there was a traitor in the SIGINT organization despite all the vetting procedures and the constant checks. He had known it when Panov gave him the book but he had closed it all out of his mind. Filed it away for another time. And the other time was now.

There were just over two hundred people who worked at the Signals Intelligence installation. Not more than twenty or so worked on the Sirius computers. But that wouldn't really narrow down the suspects. The disk could be filed by one of the non-technical clerks. What puzzled him was its function. What could it do that wouldn't be noticed and lead to its discovery?

Panov went over the instructions again and again, brushing aside Johnson's questions as to what it was all about. He said that it was too technologically complex for him to understand himself let alone explain it. All Johnson had to do was take the disk from the book, transfer it to the file marked K109-1704, remove the first disk from that file, destroy it and return the book to the library. He would be given two days' notice before the exchange had to be made. They would notify him when to do it. And he would then get further instructions. Johnson complained that it was difficult for him to get access to the room where the Sirius computers were housed but Panov brushed his protests aside. An officer of the KGB, Panov said, as Johnson now was, would be capable of working out some means of doing what was necessary. There would be a substantial financial reward if he carried out this small operation successfully. When Johnson asked how much he would be paid and Panov indicated that it could be between four and five thousand US dollars Johnson was obviously impressed.

Although Heidi Fischer's reasons for wanting to be married to Arthur Johnson had been realistic and practical, she had, nevertheless, vaguely imagined that her married life would bring security and some sort of domesticity. But in fact the relationship had deteriorated. He gave her money spasmodically, barely enough to feed them and pay the rent of their rooms, and most nights he slept at his billet or was on night duty. And his ruttish acts of sex were infrequent. But Heidi Fischer had been a survivor and she was still a survivor. She was young and attractive and there were thousands of British and US servicemen in West Berlin. She was naturally promiscuous and she enjoyed the casual pick-ups and the torrid couplings in cars and deserted alleyways. She kept her earnings in a Sparkasse account in her old name.

It rang four o'clock on the Wednesday when the doorbell rang and she slipped on the towelling bathrobe to answer it. It was the young man named Klaus. Panov's messenger boy. He was young and good-looking and cheeky. And he was fantastic in bed.

'Is he here, Heidi?'

'No. You know he's not here in the daytime.'

Klaus grinned. 'I brought you the record you wanted.'

'The Viennese songs?'

'Yeah. "*Dr'unt in der Lobau*", and "*Kleines Hotel*". All the songs you wanted.'

She put her mouth to be kissed and her arms went round him as he slid his hand inside the bathrobe. For long moments his hand fondled her breasts and then he drew back his hand.

'Business first, kid. Important business. Get a pencil and paper.'

'Can't it wait, Klaus? I'm all turned on.'

'Get the paper and pencil. Get a move on.'

She watched as he scrawled on the paper, Friday Sept 12th. Earliest.

He folded the paper, walked over to the fireplace and put the paper under the china dog on the mantelpiece.

'Give it to him the minute he arrives.'

'He might not come here tonight.'

'So give it him tomorrow, you silly bitch.'

As he walked into the bedroom he was unbuttoning his shirt and minutes later they were both naked on her bed.

He left two hours later and stopped at the door to remind her about the message on the mantelpiece.

Johnson phoned her that evening but she forgot to mention the message. He discovered it himself on the Friday evening, asking her what it was. When she told him, he went white with anger, cursing her obscenely as he reached for his jacket. As the outer door slammed to behind him she went to the wardrobe to find the half-empty bottle of whisky that a sergeant had given her. It was the second bottle she had opened that week. An hour later the bottle was empty, the radio still playing as she staggered to the unmade bed in the alcove. She had had enough of Arthur Johnson. She'd got her passport and could leave whenever she wanted. That dark blue passport with its gold coat of arms that meant that she could be in London in a few hours. All she would need was new clothes, a room where she could take the men and she'd be free of the bastard and independent.

As Johnson reported back at the security checkpoint at the house in Grunewald he looked at his watch. It was ten o'clock already. Two hours instead of two days to carry out his instructions.

He wasn't allowed to go down to the underground section unless he was on duty but he phoned through to Corporal Malins offering to take over his shift. Malins was delighted and ten minutes later Johnson was alone in his office.

The only way he could get through to the maze of inner rooms was with an officer on duty. He checked through the day's duty-roster and the roster for the following day. The fourth shift would come off duty just before midnight and the relief shift would be going through in ones and twos from eleven thirty onwards. Lieutenant Strauss was duty change-over officer. He was an American on secondment from Fort Meade, the USA's own electronic surveillance installation. He was a scientist, not a soldier, and was easygoing and amiable. He could probably be conned into letting him through. He wasn't security minded and often forgot his own pass and had to go back and search for it in his room.

In the end, it was incredibly easy. Just like Panov had said. Behave like you're entitled to be wherever you are. He asked Strauss if he could suggest the title of a book that would explain simply how microchips work and Strauss put his plastic card into the security lock and walked with him to the library and showed him four or five suitable books. When Strauss left, Johnson took two and the picture book and sat at one of the reading-desks for a few minutes looking through the books. He was alone in the library, and when he had removed the disk he replaced the books on the shelves. He went into the computer-room with three men from the new shift. Nobody stopped him when he walked over to the files and looked for the number he'd been given. He sweated a little as he exchanged the two disks. He put the original disk from the file inside his battledress blouse.

It was Meyer himself who held the security door open for Johnson to go back into his own office as Meyer come through to check the new shift.

He phoned Heidi on the Saturday evening but there was no reply. On the Sunday he had a twenty-four-hour pass and took the unit bus into Berlin. He walked to her room and let himself in with the key. She was out and the place was a shambles. Two glasses on the table that stank of neat whisky, a half-burned cigar stub in a saucer, the radio babbling away in German and the sink piled high with dirty crockery.

As he stood there he heard the key in the lock and he watched her come in. Swaying a little as she stood there, looking at him.

'What the hell's going on, you stupid bitch?'

She reached out with her hand behind her and steadied herself against the door.

'They sent a message for you.'

'Where is it?'

'It wasn't written down. The chap just told me.'

'What did he say?'

'He said . . .' and she closed her eyes '. . . he said to get rid of the disk.'

'Nothing else?'

'No.' She opened her eyes and saw that he wasn't angry, and leaning back against the door she did the only thing that always worked and pulled up her skirt so that he could see the dark triangle between her legs. He grinned and carried her to the unkempt bed.

CHAPTER SEVENTEEN

For two months Jan Massey had done his best to disguise his deep distress. He had worked long hours trying to concentrate his thoughts on his work but he spent most nights sleeping only fitfully. Hundreds of times he had told himself that there was nothing he could do. And even more times he had recognized that once Anna had been arrested what he had done was the best within his power. But he knew it was a poor best. Somehow he had been careless. He could have sworn that they had not been seen. And if they *had* been seen then the other side must have known from the start that he and both the Kholkovs sometimes met socially from time to time.

There were moments when, on the edge of sleep, he had visions of it all, like brief flashes from some film that he had seen. The uneaten food on the table. The house that she had lived in. Panov's smooth, well worked-out proposition. He would lie there bathed in sweat, angered by his impotence and lost in a sea of misery by his thoughts of Anna, trying not to imagine what repercussions it had had for her. And more anger at his misreading of Kholkov's awareness of what was going on.

His senior colleagues had noticed his withdrawal. There were no longer the informal chats after meetings. When a meeting was over he always left immediately. They frequently saw him walking on his own in the gardens. Shoulders hunched and head down, walking but not looking. Oblivious to the rest of the world. Both Max Cohen and Howard Fielding had tried, tactfully, to discover what was wrong but their tentative enquiries had been brushed aside with obvious resentment.

Massey had seen the weekly status report on the KGB units in East Berlin and when he saw that Alexei Kholkov had been promoted to major and transferred back to Moscow it had seemed like the final act that irrevocably closed the drama. A few days later he decided to take a week's leave and spend it with his father.

The main street of Tenterden is one of the most picturesque streets in southern England. Wide and tree-lined with most of its houses and shops genuine Georgian. The others are mainly typical Kentish ship-lapped timber houses. Even on gloomy days, Tenterden has an air of smiling lightness and summer that lifts the spirits of its visitors from the marshlands and the flat, featureless acres reclaimed from the sea that constitute the Romney Marshes. Dr Massey's surgery was the front room of one of the Georgian houses.

He could have lived well enough on his pension and savings but so many of his patients were old friends. His list had fewer than two thousand names on it and most evenings he had not more than half a dozen people in the small waiting-room. He had several virtues that were much prized by his patients. He had time to listen and time to talk. He was always there, and anxious mothers knew that he could be called out in the middle of the night. And middle-aged patients knew that he would only smile when the dreaded heart attack turned out to be no more than indigestion. Old people found comfort from him because he had the strange habit of sometimes holding their hands as they unfolded their troubles. It was not a working method that he had deliberately devised. It was instinctive. The need had always been there and slowly over the years he had recognized it and satisfied it.

Jan Massey was sitting in the armchair opposite his father, his arm stretched out in front of him, a slice of bread held on an old-fashioned brass toasting-fork in front of the glowing, coal fire.

The old man watched him and then said softly, 'You're burning it, lad.'

Jan Massey sighed, turned the bread and held it back in front of the fire.

The older man waited until they were sipping their second cups of coffee before he said, 'Tell me about it, Jan.'

'Tell you what, Father?'

'Tell me what's troubling you.'

'There's nothing troubling me.'

'You don't *have* to tell me. You know that. I'm not prying. But you *are* my son and I wouldn't need to be a doctor to know that you're unhappy. Is it your work?'

'No, Father.'

'Is there anything I could do to help you?'

Jan leaned forward and put his hand on his father's knee.

'Don't worry about me, Papa. There's nothing that anyone can do.'

'There is always something that can be done. No matter what the problem, there's a solution. Sometimes more than one.'

Jan looked at his father's face and said quietly, 'I fell in love with someone, Papa. I loved her very much and she loved me. It didn't work out. It did her harm. It was my fault. But now it's over. Gone.'

'Have you got a photograph of her?'

'No. An oil-painting. A portrait.'

'Where is it?'

'It's on the dressing-table in my bedroom.'

'Here or in Berlin?'

'Here.'

'Is she in Berlin?'

'I don't know. I don't know where she is.'

'Were you happy with her before it ended?'

'Very happy.'

'What kind of happiness?'

'Just glad to be alive in the same world with her. Glad of every day.'

'Can I recommend a medicine to you?'

'I don't need one of your bottles or a box of pills.'

'That wasn't what I had in mind.'

'Tell me.'

'It's medicine I've used for many years. It's called love. It can sometimes have a bitter taste but it works. I know it can work because it works for me. When I knew that your mother was dead, and how she died, it was a very dark, cold world for me. I think if I hadn't had you to care for and love I might have decided to die myself. Do you remember when I used to walk up to the parish church here and sit in the churchyard?'

'Yes. I remember.'

'There was a book I read. Palgrave. There were two lines of a Shakespeare sonnet that made me realize that my love for your mother had become an inferior love. Maybe you know them:

Love is not love which alters when it alteration finds, or bends with the remover to remove . . .

It goes on in the same vein. It made me realize that my thinking was both selfish and negative. I could love my girl the same way I had always loved her . . . if I chose to. And if it was real love. And if I didn't, then the sick ghouls in Mauthausen had won. Maybe you could find some kind of solace that way?'

Massey half-smiled. 'You're a good man, Father. And a good doctor.'

'Will you try it? Just look up at the sky sometimes. Day or night. It gives us new dimensions.'

'Maybe, Father. Thanks for understanding.'

The old man reached for the tuner on the hi-fi and the music was the Barenboim recording of Fauré's *Requiem*.

Massey walked over to the window to draw the curtains. There was a light scatter of snow on the garden and he shivered involuntarily as the bare branches of the apple trees swung and tossed in the first harsh winds of winter. There would be four or five inches of snow in Moscow already.

CHAPTER EIGHTEEN

There was heavy snow as the plane came in to land at Tegel and Howard Fielding had come to the airport with a car to meet him in.

Fielding watched Massey as he passed through Immigration and stood waiting for his bag from the carousel. He didn't look any more amiable than when he had left. It was going to be back to 'sir' again, not Jan, and Fielding was disappointed. He was a young man and Massey was his idea of what he'd like to be in a few years' time. It was a mixture of affection, respect and young man's hero-worship. He had seen Massey listening to a report of a failure of some operation. The brown eyes as hard as glass, those muscles tense at the side of his mouth and the deep lines from his nose almost to the stubborn chin. And seconds later calmly telling them all what had to be done next. No apportioning of blame, no apparent anger, just cool, calm professionalism. Fielding had lost none of the respect or affection over the last few months but he was ill at ease in the cold, aloof relationship that now existed. He had discussed his feelings unofficially with both Cohen and Harper who obviously shared his views but were not prepared to comment or criticize. Massey was the boss and his aloofness was his privilege. It was up to them all to get on with their jobs.

When Bourget phoned, the Frenchman insisted that Massey met him somewhere where they couldn't be seen in public. Massey suggested Club Chérie and Bourget had agreed.

Despite the great urgency when Bourget had phoned, the Frenchman, as usual, arrived half an hour late at Club Chérie. Massey was playing chess with one of the girls, a pretty young blonde who said she was an artist but obviously earned more money obliging the customers at Club Chérie than she did from the sale of her paintings. But she really did paint. She had shown him one of her paintings that Karl, who owned the club, had hung on one of the walls. It was a mixture of Dali and Picasso. The kind of picture that needs a long and explanatory title. She dragged Bourget over to see it and he admired it loudly and fulsomely without taking his eyes from the young blonde's fantastic breasts.

But he came back to the table alone, staring at the pieces on the chessboard as if he were trying to work up some deep and significant comment relating chess to the 'game of life' or maybe, espionage. Either way he gave up the struggle and came down to earth.

'How much they charge, these little whores?'

'It used to be a hundred and fifty D-marks, Pierre, room extra, but that was a few years ago and inflation may have crept in.'

'What's her name, that one?'

'She didn't tell me. Do you want me to ask?'

Bourget shook his head vigorously. A bit too vigorously to be convincing. 'We talk about Kuznetsov, yes?'

Massey hesitated and said quietly, 'OK. But I'm not really interested.'

'You're not interested, or London are not interested?'

Massey smiled. 'Same thing, Pierre.'

'How much you know of him in, say, last two years?'

'He's in charge of operations against SIS and CIA in Berlin. Mainly NATO and United States stuff.'

'For last two years, maybe a little less, that was only his cover. He specializes in other direction.'

Bourget's big brown eyes were full of significance and fatherly concern for a wayward son.

'Tell me more,' Massey said.

The Frenchman's big, thick forefinger tapped the table slowly, like the hammer of a piano. 'He is concerned now with your people. SIS. He builds a big dossier on all your people in Berlin and the Federal Republic.'

'They've always done that, Pierre. They do it automatically.'

'He says he knows of top-secret operations. And more.'

'What more?'

'He knows of traitor in your organization. Maybe two traitors. They not even know of each other. Not even work to same KGB man.'

'Do you believe him?'

'Yes.'

'Have you really got Kuznetsov, or are you just dreaming dreams?'

'I swear on my mother's grave, Jan.'

'Your mother's still alive, you bastard. Lives in Lyon.'

'Is just a turn of phrase. I swear I got him.'

'You mean that he's physically held at your place right now?'

Bourget shrugged. 'He come to me whenever I say the word.'

'When did he approach you first?'

'Two months ago. Maybe three.'

'He's just visited you and then gone back to the other side?'

'Who knows where he goes?'

'What did he say when he approached you?'

'He identified himself. He says he wants to make a deal.'

'What's the deal?'

'He gives us information and in return we talk with CIA for him to go to United States.'

'Why doesn't he go direct to the CIA?'

Bourget grinned. 'He don't trust them. Wants us to find out which way they jump.'

'So why are you talking with me?'

'Two reasons. First is, Paris don't like CIA, and second is, Kuznetsov talks about your people . . . SIS.' Bourget grinned. 'You not want that he talks to Washington about English traitors, yes.'

'No. We shouldn't like that too much.' Massey turned and looked directly at the Frenchman's face. 'What was the other reason, Pierre?'

'Which other reason?'

'The one you haven't told me?'

'Who say there is another reason?'

'You're wasting my time, Pierre. And yours.'

Bourget sighed theatrically. 'OK. I tell you. Last time I meet with Kholkov he tell me that if ever we are approached by Soviet intelligence defector he would pay cash to know and more cash if I return him. The cash for me personally. In Swiss bank in code-name. They would pay plenty for Kuznetsov, my friend. He's more important than Kholkov himself.'

'They do that sometimes, Pierre, if they've planted some guy on you. They want to make it look like they're desperate to get him back. It's an old trick to divert suspicion and make you feel you've got a really hot guy.'

'He talked of a hundred and fifty thousand D-marks.'

'Jesus. No. Are you sure you heard him right?'

'I hear him OK.' He paused. 'I go fifty-fifty with you.'

'Was the conversation recorded?'

'No.'

'He could be trying to frame you, Pierre. It's been done before. *He* could have recorded it. Have you been doing much against them in the last few months? Anything I might not know about?'

'Maybe. How do I know what you know? You tell *me*.'

Massey closed his eyes, trying to remember the French summaries. There never was much worth reporting about the SDECE. They didn't do all that much. West Berlin didn't interest them really except for political things.

'I can't remember much, Pierre. I'd need to check the records. There was that homosexual thing involving one of your Berlin Mission. Then the French girl clerk at NATO Brussels. The cipher clerk at your Embassy in Bonn who was getting drugs paid for by the KGB man through SDECE in Marseilles, or Nice was it? That's all I can remember off-hand.'

Bourget nodded. 'Is plenty more but nothing special. So what do we do?'

'Have you told Kholkov that we're interested and that I'm going to London soon and I'll talk about it while I'm there. He'll have to wait until I get back. Maybe another twelve days. I'm not going until Saturday week.'

'He will want sooner than that.'

'So tell Kuznetsov that we are interested in principle. And tell Kholkov to get stuffed. He's laying a trap for you.'

'So I sell Kuznetsov to you people. You pay instead of Kholkov. I need money, my friend. So do you.'

'I don't, Pierre. The money's all yours. I don't want to know about it. London might be interested but I doubt if they'd pay forty thousand pounds. For me it's just business. We either want Kuznetsov or we don't. Simple as that. We shall thank SDECE officially for your cooperation whether we take him or pass.'

'And if you take him what do I get? Me personally?'

'I'll pay for a night with that pretty blonde.'

'Nothing more? No money?'

'Not forty thousand pounds, that's for sure.' Massey smiled. 'I doubt if we'd pay that for Andropov himself.'

'Maybe a retainer. Monthly.'

'If Kuznetsov really has what he says he has, then London might authorize me to do something, but I couldn't promise anything.'

Bourget sighed. 'OK. I leave in your hands.'

Without looking at Massey, Bourget said, 'One of my guys says he see you twice with a dark-haired girl. Who is she?' And he looked up smiling, but his eyes were intent on Massey's face.

'How should I know? All the girls I know are either dark-haired or blonde. I've never gone for redheads.'

'They say she not your type.'

Massey shrugged. 'What's my type?'

'They say you like pretty ones, long legs, big tits, like my Leni. They say this one is beautiful, not pretty. Walks like a dancer and looks at you like she marry you some day.'

'I'm not the marrying kind, Pierre. And I must get on my way. Thanks for the drink. I'll be in touch.'

As Massey stood up the Frenchman looked at him from under the black bushy eyebrows. But he said nothing. Just nodding as Massey walked away.

He walked back to the flat on the Ku'damm and let himself in. It was nearly midnight and he ran himself a bath. As he lay in the warm soapy water he tried to remember the exact words that Bourget had used. He'd mentioned Kholkov first and then the dark-haired girl, or did he say black-haired girl? Was it a crude attempt at pressuring him about Kuznetsov? It was almost impossible that he should know who she was. Bourget could have put a routine surveillance on him just for the hell of it, but Ridge's people would have spotted them. The SDECE boys in Berlin weren't well trained. But Bourget was obsessed by girls. Maybe he just wanted to know who she was and get an introduction to try his luck. But if it was that, he would have pursued it. He wasn't a romantic, just a lecher.

It looked as if Kuznetsov *had* actually contacted Bourget. He could think of no reason why he should; and a dozen reasons why it was highly dangerous for the Russian to do so. His status in the KGB made any movement by him into West Berlin virtually impossible. Did that mean that Moscow had authorized or even initiated his contact with Bourget? It seemed highly unlikely. But the whole thing was unlikely.

It was a relief to know that the Russian was not with Bourget and Massey decided once more that he could only wait and see what developed.

CHAPTER NINETEEN

Massey looked through the pages of the SIGINT summary. A clandestine transmitter was operating out of the French sector, using a code generally used by the PLO; an extract from the transcription of a telephone conversation that indicated that a CDU politician in Bonn was asking for money for supporting the request for a grant to a West Berlin electronics company. A French diplomat in a French Mission car had given a frank view of his opposite number on a Franco-German committee; the Soviet HQ at Karlshorst had circulated the description of a Red Army major who was suspected of having defected to the West through Helmstedt some time over the weekend. A KGB detachment in Dresden was complaining to Moscow of lack of funds. A West German trade union leader had had three telephone conversations with a number suspected of being a cut-out for a group of low-grade KGB agents fomenting trouble among West Berlin civil servants.

Day after day the pages of two-line summaries came to Massey, Harper and Mason. Mason and his team were responsible for evaluating each item, checking the traffic against previous reports, seeing how they fitted into the general intelligence jigsaw and sometimes warning that the material was deliberate disinformation put out by some section of the Soviet intelligence services.

Harper was responsible for the gathering of intelligence by other means than monitoring and responsible for countering KGB and the Red Army's GRU attempts at penetrating the British and West German intelligence services. All information gathered by technical rather than human means was passed back to GCHQ within hours. For Massey it was a sign of the times that SIGINT, the monitoring service, was more highly valued than HUMINT, the intelligence gathered by Harper's team. It was the official view that HUMINT was subject to all the mental and psychological vagaries of the human source and the human evaluator. SIGINT was fact. It had been transmitted by phone, radio or computer. Sometimes it was false but Mason's evaluation team could spot the phoney material in minutes. Others back at Cheltenham could provide an even finer safety net. And the NSA at Fort George Meade provided one more filter in the assessment of much of the SIGINT information.

Massey turned to the surveillance reports on Bourget's place but there was nothing significant. The mystery visitor had not appeared again. Their telephone and radio traffic gave no mention of Kuznetsov nor any other Russian name of significance. Bourget's chatter still disturbed Massey but it looked as if it had been nothing more than a crude attempt to get money. And Bourget had talked as if he were still in touch with Kholkov who had been posted back to Moscow weeks ago.

He strolled down to Cohen's office and saw him through the glass partitions at one of the Evaluation work-stations bending over to look at the screen of a VDU. When Cohen showed no sign of returning to his office Massey threaded his way through the rows of work stations until he was standing behind Cohen. As his shadow fell across the screen Cohen turned irritably, and then relaxed as he saw it was Massey.

'We're getting an interesting batch from the Soviet Mission HQ. We don't know what it's about but it's showing checkwords we've had on our priority list and have never come up before.'

'What does it indicate?'

'Some sort of major event in the Kremlin and with top KGB people involved.'

'Who provided the checkwords list in the first place?'

'It's coded as a Foreign Office request. Top priority if more than five of the checkwords come up in the same four-hour shift.'

'Any guesses of what it's about?'

Cohen frowned, a meaningful, warning frown. 'Not beyond what I've told you.' He turned to the operator. 'Warn Evaluation that there's top priority material coming their way and get the emergency cryppies on it right away.' Cohen turned back to Massey. 'Let's go to my office, Jan.'

In the security of his office Cohen stood looking at Massey. 'It means that either Brezhnev is dying or dead or that they've eased him out. And he's being replaced by Andropov.'

'Our Andropov?'

'Yes. One big step for mankind. From head of the KGB to President.'

'How can you tell?'

'Sit down and I'll explain.'

When they were both seated Cohen said, 'We have checkword lists from all sorts of people. SIS, NSA, GCHQ, special units, the Foreign Office and a good number of government departments. We get so much material when we're monitoring, either in code or clear, that if we transcribed it all it would be months out of date by the time anyone saw it. So we have the checkword lists and if those words, in code or clear, come up on the screens, then we transcribe that section of our traffic. Sometimes it has to be a combination of words before we transcribe. One of the words could be somebody's name. The American President for instance. Too common in the traffic if it's standing alone, but if certain other words on the list come up in the same text then we transcribe.

'The Foreign Office checklist had nineteen words on it. Four were names of Politburo members. Actual names, and the KGB code-names for them. This batch was from the Politburo to the head of the Soviet Mission in East Berlin and the head of the KGB at Karlshorst. The other checkwords had no significance for me but when the list came through I was told – well, it was hinted – that this would cover an upheaval at the top in Moscow, or Brezhnev's death. Andropov's code-name was the only other name in the whole piece.' Cohen shrugged. 'We shan't be the only station to have picked it up. It'll have gone to all Soviet ambassadors, warning them. But I want to get our stuff back to London inside the hour.'

Massey stood up. 'I'll let you get on with it, Max.'

'Was there something you wanted to talk to me about?'

'Nothing that can't wait.'

That night Massey went to the Ku'damm flat. There were days when no matter how hard he tried he couldn't keep her out of his mind. He wandered from the sitting-room to the bedroom to the kitchen. There were the two coffee-cups on the draining board alongside the sink. Unwashed, the dark stains dry and reticulated, a spoon covered with crystals of brown sugar. The air in the rooms was still dry and he tried to think of what he had wanted when he had decided to go there again. It had seemed possible that some of the pleasure of his days with her could still linger there and, by some kind of osmosis, make his heart lighter. But it did nothing. He had a small photograph copy of her portrait that he had brought framed to place on the bedside table. He stared at it, on the edge of tears. Her eyes were still big and beautiful, the neck still slender and graceful. He turned away suddenly. That beautiful face still existed somewhere. In Moscow or Warsaw or maybe Prague. He could find out from Central Archives where Kholkov was. Just a phone call or a single-line routine request. But he was not sure that he could bear knowing. It would be so much better if he could wipe it out as if it had never happened.

He walked to the window and looked across the city. The blue sky was reflected on the snow on the roofs of the buildings. They had never seen snow together. He walked slowly to the bed and lay there, his eyes closed, his cheeks wet.

When he eventually stood up it was dark, and, despite the heating, he shivered as he walked to the door and let himself out.

Signalman Johnson let himself into the flat. It was untidy as always. Clothes on the floor and on the bed, a pile of dirty crockery in the sink and fag-ends everywhere. He hadn't seen her for a week and he wondered what she'd been up to. The Russkis giving her the fake passport and marriage certificate had calmed her down for six months or so but for the past year she'd grown more and more cantankerous. She shouted back at him now whenever she was displeased and once or twice she'd threatened to leave him. But what was worse was her putting in the dirt about him to the Russians. He wasn't sure what she was telling them but both his usual contact and the major above him had been a bit offhand the last two times that they'd met. Urging him to keep her happy because she was very useful to them.

He'd had a meeting with them that evening and Levchenko had finished up talking about her again. Stressing the importance of keeping her happy.

'For Christ's sake,' Johnson shouted. 'Whose side are you on? Her's or mine?'

Levchenko touched his shoulder with a friendly gesture. 'It's for you as much as for us, comrade. We want to protect you. An angry wife is a danger in this business.'

'So what do you suggest I do? I don't start the rows.'

Levchenko shrugged and smiled. 'A box of chocolates sometimes. Or a bunch of red roses. Women like these little signs of affection.'

'You mean when she calls me dirty names I run out and buy her a bunch of flowers? Not bloody likely.'

Levchenko sighed and involuntarily glanced at the chandelier where the microphones were hidden. He hoped that the surveillance people were listening to what he had to put up with. 'How about you take her on a few days' holiday in London? Show her the sights. She'd like that.' He paused. 'We could arrange funds for you . . . say, five hundred sterling pounds.'

Levchenko was satisfied by the obvious greed on Johnson's face as he said, 'If that's what you want, OK then.'

'Tell me,' Levchenko said, 'tell me what you know about Mr Massey.'

Johnson shrugged. 'He's the head guy. That's all I know.'

'You see him around the place?'

'Not very often. He spends his time with the big white chiefs. The section bosses like Cohen and Harper. Not with the likes of me.'

'Is he popular? Do the staff like him?'

'No idea. The people in London must like him or they wouldn't have given him such a top job.'

'Who are his friends?'

'I've no idea. How should I know?'

'Has he got a girlfriend?'

'God knows. I don't. He ain't gonna tell me if he has.'

'There must be gossip about him. There always is about the top man. What do people say about him?'

'We don't spend our time talking about the nobs. They don't interest us.'

'The nobs?' Levchenko looked confused.

'Yeah. The nobs. The bosses.'

'What are his interests? His hobbies?'

'I've no idea. I told you. He's way above people like me.' With sudden inspiration Johnson said, 'Maybe he likes gardening. He spends a lot of time in the grounds of the house. Just walking around, sitting by the pond. Maybe gardening's his hobby.'

'I've arranged for you to be given a camera. A little Minox. One of my men is going to show you how to use it. There's some things we want you to photograph.'

'I'd never get through the metal detectors.'

'You will. It won't register. We've made it so that it won't show up. There's no metal in it.'

'What d'you want me to photograph?'

'I'll tell you later.' Levchenko paused. 'By the way, how did you get the tape out?'

Johnson smiled. 'That's a trade secret, comrade.'

'Tell me how you did it.'

Johnson heard the quiet voice but he saw the hardness in the Russian's eyes.

'Tell me why you want to know.'

'I'll tell you when you've told me how you got it out.'

'I wrapped the tape round my arm in the toilet and then put a piece of medical plaster round it.'

'Why didn't they pick up the metal reel on the detector?'

'The tape wasn't on the reel. I've got empty reels at my place in town. I put it on there.'

Levchenko smiled. 'Clever thinking, my friend. You're learning the business fast.'

'So why did you want to know how I did it? So you can show other guys, yes?'

Levchenko saw the pleasure in Johnson's eyes. He was pathetic, but they needed him. If he wanted a phoney ego trip let him have it.

'Exactly. Now, let's eat before you go over the camera instructions.'

As Johnson walked around the living-room at the flat he opened drawers and looked inside. But it was a piece of paper on the bedside table that he looked at longest. He sat on the bed and stared at the figures. They were in pencil and there was the number 31287 followed by a division sign and the figures 3.50. Eventually he screwed up the paper and tossed it towards the paper basket. It missed and fell to the floor. Three fifty was at that time the current exchange rate for changing D-marks into sterling. But he didn't connect it.

He waited around for twenty minutes, switching on the small colour TV they had just bought, but there was only some sort of quiz programme in German and a fuzzy picture on the other channel. Finally he yawned, looked at his watch and left. He wondered what she was doing. Not that he cared, but she ought to be there. He wondered if she was screwing for money again on the side.

Mayhew always followed the instructions precisely but he sometimes wondered why they made it all so complicated. He could have put the stuff in a Jiffy bag and posted it and they'd have got it sooner. It was raining as he parked the car and he put up his umbrella before he walked on up the lane. He could hear the water running in the ditch below the hedge. He wasn't a countryman and he found the unlit lane, the darkness and the night rustlings of birds and animals quite frightening. It was almost half a mile to the cottage and they'd told him never to use a torch.

He was panting and sweating despite the cold night air when he went through the rickety gate and up the short path to the door. There were no lights on at the front of the stone cottage but he felt for the bell and pressed the button exactly as they had said. He walked back down the path and on up the lane to the telephone kiosk. There was no light inside but he lifted the receiver and dialled the ten digits carefully and accurately. He pushed in the 10p coin and heard the three rings before the phone was picked up at the other end.

'Can I speak to Mr Jamieson, please?'

'Of course.'

Then the phone was hung up at the other end and the dialling tone came back. He hung up his receiver and stood outside the kiosk. Five minutes later the man came, and stood there in silence.

Mayhew felt slightly embarrassed as he said softly, 'The red poppies are blooming.'

The man said, 'All's well that ends well.'

They walked back together in silence to the cottage. The door was ajar, the man went inside and Mayhew followed. There was an oil-lamp burning now in the small parlour and Mayhew waited as the man pulled back the worn carpet and lifted the hinged cover that revealed the wooden steps that led down to the brightly lit cellar.

The cement walls were painted white and the plasterboard ceiling supported two strip lights. A strip of chipboard covered with black Formica served as a work-bench. Mayhew recognized the Japanese NRD-515 short wave receiver but the small transmitter had no name badge and was not a model he had seen before. There was a simple microscope under a plastic cover and a pile of notepads. On the wall above the bench were two digital display clocks. One showed local time and the other, he realized, showed Moscow time.

On a small shelf under the clocks were a few books. Mayhew recognized the faded red-covered copy of *The Town that was Murdered* by Ellen Wilkinson. It was the old Left Book Club edition. The *World Radio and TV Handbook*, 36th edition was between the Penguin *Decline and Fall* and a Russian – English dictionary. The Berlitz *Russian for Travellers* was alongside Bertrand Russell's *History of Western Philosophy*.

There were two folding canvas chairs and Rose pointed to one of them and settled in the other himself.

'I hear you've been promoted, comrade.' He smiled. 'The people at Cheltenham must be pleased with your work.'

'How did you hear that? It was only a couple of weeks ago.' Mayhew was smiling and relaxed. He liked being called comrade. It was a sign that he belonged.

Rose half-smiled. 'I hear. Anyway, how did you get on with the project?'

'The Watch List has been extended very considerably. That's the main thing. The new numbers and frequencies are on my tape.'

'Good. Are any of them significant?'

Mayhew shrugged. 'How should I know?'

Rose nodded. 'Any news on Rhyolite?'

'It's very difficult for me. It's nothing to do with my work but I've heard that there have been two new launchings. One seems to be a back-up on an existing orbit and I've heard gossip that the other is to concentrate on transmissions from the Soviet base at Kabkan.'

'Is it now? And what about new helpers?'

Mayhew looked surprised. 'You told me not to try any contacts.'

'Absolutely. But I asked for details of possible targets.'

'I see. Well, there's a couple of people you might look at.'

'Go on.'

'There's a chap named Smallwood. He's due to retire in two years' time. He's a technician but he's not done long enough for a decent pension. He's worried about how he'll manage on what he'll get.'

'What does he do?'

'He services the decoding machines.'

'Which ones?'

'The American ones – I think they're called Pyramiders.'

'They're not decoding machines, they're frequency hoppers for communicating with agents in "denied areas". Tell me more about him. Everything you know.'

The two had talked until well after midnight and then Rose had walked back down the lane with Mayhew to where he had parked his car. He watched as its red tail-lights faded into the distance and then walked slowly back to the cottage. The quiet, modest little man, Mayhew, was worth an armoured division. He seemed to have an instinct for the kind of information that they wanted. He kept him on simple gleanings of information; most of it was no more than double-checking on what they already knew. It was the gossip, those diffident asides, that were so valuable. A man who had serviced Pyramiders was an incredible find. It was almost unbelievable that the British would let a man with knowledge and experience retire on an inadequate pension and social security handouts. But that was the sort of thing they let happen. Bureaucracy was seldom tempered with imagination.

Jack Rose always said, with a grin, that he was a member of the Bristol Conservative Club only because they had three full-size billiards tables. He was the owner of successful antiques shops in Cheltenham and Bristol. He had never married despite his obvious charm and was much in demand at local dinner parties. He had been a JP for ten years but had declined several invitations to stand for mayor. It was well known that he had no interest in politics. He gave a £50 cheque to both the local Tories and the Labour Party at election times and both felt that he was more on their side than the opposition's.

CHAPTER TWENTY

Signalman Johnson had never taken to Fomenko. He'd only been dealt with by him two or three times but he didn't like the Russian's attitude. The other Russians were always ready to put an arm round his shoulder, to crack a joke and show their appreciation of what he was doing for them. But not Fomenko. He was never impolite but he was impassive and only concerned himself with the business in hand.

Johnson had gone through Checkpoint Charlie and walked on as they had instructed to Karl Marx Platz where a black Mercedes had picked him up and taken him to the small office at the back of the hospital where Fomenko was waiting.

The Russian shook hands briefly and motioned Johnson to a chair on the opposite side of the small table.

'Your trip to England, comrade.' He handed over an envelope. 'Five hundred pounds. Half in sterling, half in dollars.' He pushed across a white envelope. 'Two British Airways tickets Berlin – Gatwick and return. Seats have been booked on both flights. Return flight eight days later as you asked for. Any questions so far?'

Johnson shook his head. 'No.'

'Right. Now, a few words of warning. The lady's documentation. Apart from the name the passport is genuine. The marriage certificate is a high-grade forgery . . . not genuine, but it will pass all normal visual scrutiny. It's in your interest, comrade, that it's not genuine. It keeps the lady happy, but as you wished, it does not make her legally your wife. As the same time I want to warn you to be very careful while you are in England. A driving offence, a drinking offence . . . anything of that sort could bring you in contact with the police. If they had reason to examine the marriage certificate carefully you could be in trouble. Serious trouble. Remember that, please.'

Johnson bridled. 'And you remember, mate, it was your people wanted me to take her to England in the first place . . . not me, comrade.' And Johnson jabbed his finger at his chest in emphasis. 'I didn't want no holiday in the first place. You people wanted to please *her*, not me. I take the bloody risks but she's the one you always want to please.'

Fomenko sat in silence, looking at Johnson's face. He said quietly, 'Is that what you really think, Mr Johnson?'

'For Christ's sake . . . it's not a question of what I think . . . it's facts. Just facts.'

Fomenko stood up and held out his hand. As Johnson responded, the Russian held Johnson's hand in both of his as he spoke. 'When you come back, comrade Johnson, we will talk about your feelings again. Meantime I must make it clear that you are the one who matters to us – not the girl. Our only reason to please her is to make sure that there is no trouble for you with her. Do I make myself clear? You are the one who matters. That, too, is a question of fact.'

Fomenko knew from Johnson's face that he was not merely mollified by what he had said but pleased, and flattered.

He walked with Johnson to the car that was waiting and stood, watching, as he was driven off.

Back in the small office he gathered up his papers, phoned Grushko and arranged to see him at Karlshorst.

Fomenko signed in at the desk, showed his pass and walked down the main corridor to Grushko's office. Grushko was his boss.

Grushko was listening to the radio news from Moscow and he waved Fomenko to a chair and went on listening. He was using headphones, and when he took them off and switched off the set he turned to Fomenko. 'His death's official. Andropov will take over in a few days.' As he sat down he said, 'No comment outside.' He paused. 'And none inside if you're as sensible as I think you are.' He reached for a packet of cigarettes and his lighter. 'What's your problem?'

'The man Johnson.'

'Johnson . . .' Grushko frowned. 'Is he the British SIGINT man or the American sergeant?'

'He's the British SIGINT man.'

'And what's the problem?'

Fomenko outlined almost verbatim his conversation with Johnson, and Grushko leaned back in his chair and was silent for several minutes. Then he said, 'What do we use the girl for?'

'She does courier work for us. She lets us use their room as an emergency safe house. And she keeps an eye on Johnson.' Fomenko shrugged. 'That's about it.'

'The room, we don't need – we've got plenty of safe-houses that are properly organized. So we can discount that. So far as keeping an eye on Johnson is concerned – I don't like that at all. When I interviewed the girl she struck me as being of low intelligence, cunning but not intelligent. She was – maybe still is – a prostitute, and she had the arrogance that those women have. They are used to being abused by men and that often means they despise not only the men who use them, but all men. Maybe she behaves with Johnson as if she controls his relationship with us. He might have sensed this. The psychiatrist's report said he was of low intelligence but simple in his outlook. Neither clever nor cunning. Naïve even. So I discount her value in that respect. What courier work has she done?'

'Various officers have used her. Taking written messages and money. Person to person where any other type of communication would be dangerous.'

'How often is she used?'

'About once a week. Sometimes more often if it's urgent.'

'Who's her contact on this side of the Wall?'

'Usually the KGB girl at Kaufhaus der Osten. Sometimes we have to use the tobacconist shop by the zoo.'

'And who is her contact on the other side?'

'The man at *Postamt* 301.'

'Any complaints?'

'None.'

Grushko leaned forward, his arms on the table. 'OK. When they get back from this trip you go on paying her the weekly amount – but you don't use her. Nothing.' He looked across at Fomenko. 'I don't want anything to disturb our relationship with Johnson. We've got a number of special operations we want to use him for in the future. He may be a sheep but he's a useful sheep so far as we are concerned. Understood?'

'Yes, comrade.'

'And in future you alone will handle him. It's got very untidy over the months. Stick to the rulebook, comrade, and you won't go wrong. Handle him like he is a prize. Maybe he is.'

'Yes, comrade General.'

Signalman Johnson and Heidi had two days in London. They did all the usual sightseeing from Buckingham Palace to the Tower of London, and then he had taken her to Birmingham and back to his old stamping-ground in Handsworth.

All his old friends had disappeared. Three were in Winson Green prison and one was dead, killed in a knife fight. The only contact with the old days was an ex all-in wrestler named Tony. He hadn't known him well but he'd been a regular at the betting shop and a regular client of one of the girls Johnson had run messages for.

Tony was now running six girls of his own and had offered Johnson and Heidi the use of one of the rooms in the house where he and one of the girls lived.

Johnson and Tony visited the local pubs together, and when she wasn't busy, the girl, who called herself Diana, and Heidi compared notes on their profession. Services, the law, prices and accommodation.

Diana was amazed at what the girl from Berlin told her.

'So how much is thrity D-marks in real money?'

'You divide by three point five.'

'I'm no good at that sort of stuff.' She laughed. 'I can add up and do takeaways but not no more than that. What is it in pounds?'

'Just under nine pounds.'

'You mean you do it for nine quid?'

'Yes. But they have to pay for the room.'

'And how much is that?'

'Say three pounds for an hour.'

'You mean you give them an hour for nine quid?'

Heidi shrugged. 'That's how it is for street girls.'

'But you've got a place.'

'He don't let me take them there. So it's hotels or the backs of cars.'

'You could get thirty quid for an hour over here. And they'll have finished in twenty minutes anyway if you help things along. Why don't you move over here? Tony'd take you on if I talk to him.'

'He's in the army, we have to stay where he's sent.'

'Look, honey. You could be clearing a hundred quid a day here. No trouble at all. *After* Tony's cut. You could rent a room and then buy a house. I've got two houses. All mine. No mortgage on one and only a few thousand on the other. Talk to your fella. He wouldn't need to work. You could both live good on your money alone. He's not daft, surely. Let me talk to him.'

Heidi looked towards the window and then back at the girl. 'If he said no but I came here on my own, would Tony look after me the same?'

Diana looked at the girl. 'Like that is it?'

'Maybe.'

'I wondered how you got stuck with him. Looks a right dummy to me. Yeah, Tony'd look after you. How about I tell him in confidence?'

'He'll tell Arthur. They're friends and they're men.'

'They're not friends. Tony wouldn't have a dimwit like him for a friend. I'll tell him and then you can have a talk with him, private like.' She grinned. 'You know how to handle him. He's a pushover when he's not drunk.'

'I'll phone you from Berlin when I'm ready.'

'OK.' Diana looked at her watch. 'Let's go to town. Buy a dress or something.'

They spent two hours in the city and Heidi noticed the bank in the first big street they walked along. She made an excuse in the tearoom to go to the toilets and using her passport as proof of identity she deposited what now amounted to £9537·64 in her own name.

CHAPTER TWENTY-ONE

Jimbo Vick didn't like New York. He didn't like Chicago or San Francisco either. He was ill at ease in big cities. He maintained that big cities gave out bad vibes. He would have found incredible and laughable the suggestion that his unease was because he was born to be a big fish in only quite small ponds, and that in big cities nobody was impressed by anything he'd got. His money was peanuts compared with the wealth of big cities and his talents were of no interest either to those who were the society trendsetters or the young swingers who were his usual companions.

He spent his free evenings in Baltimore, driving the red Ferrari up Interstate-95, parking it at the Baltimore Hilton on West Fayette. Sometimes he ate at the Hilton but it was generally a few drinks at the bar with that night's lucky girl and then a move to the China Doll for a meal, or the Peabody in North Charles Street if she was more that kind of girl. He had a small but luxurious apartment over a delicatessen in a side street off Saratoga, and that's where most evenings became nights.

Everybody in Baltimore knew what went on at Fort George Meade. They knew it was the HQ of the National Security Agency. A listening-post that could eavesdrop on Soviet generals issuing orders to tank commanders in Smolensk or Siberia and on Politburo members whispering state secrets to their mistresses as they drove out from Moscow to their *dachas* in the pine forests. And they knew that a lot of the money earned by the thousands who worked at NSA was spent in Baltimore. NSA people were given the respect that would be given by any civilian population to occupying troops who behaved well and spent money locally.

Jimbo had been more successful as the leader of his small group than even those who had recruited him had expected. The notice on the outer office of the suite of rooms in which they worked merely said Math 190. But their work was both exotic and creative in its area of mathematics. Jimbo had never been told what the reports and experiments that they produced were used for or even that they were used at all.

His team were all young and highly committed. They were mathematics glamour boys and they knew it. And although Jimbo Vick could turn nasty if anyone tried to challenge his authority, most of the time he treated them as equals, relaxed and ready to kid along with them. But they grew to realize that the camaraderie was not between equals but a gesture from the leader to his troops. They respected his skill at their speciality and his tiger-like defence of their status and privileges. He took no nonsense from the bureaucrats, fighting their corner with what was frequently considered as insubordination and impertinence by senior administrators. But Jimbo generally got his way. He worked conscientiously and over long hours and his speciality was of prime importance far beyond the thousand acres of Fort George Meade.

When he was told to prepare a paper to read to a seminar in Washington he resented the wasted time, but when he found that the seminar was restricted and that his paper was only one of four to be presented to an audience of only ten top mathematicians who were working on allied areas of mathematical problem-solving, he realized that he was being honoured, not relegated.

The seminar was to last for three days and was held in a suite of rooms at the Sheraton Carlton and there were a dozen or more plain-clothes security men providing discreet but efficient round-the-clock surveillance.

Jimbo had noticed the blonde the first time the group had assembled. He had assumed that she was somebody's secretary but she had been introduced by the convener as Miss Swenson. She looked more like a Las Vegas showgirl than a mathematician but in the discussion after the first paper had been read, her questions had been searching and she was obviously well informed.

The convener had said that it would be appreciated if the group stayed together during the three days. Eating together in the dining-room provided.

He also pointed out that he had not given any details of their jobs and would prefer that such matters were not pursued in private. The seminar was intended to provide the members with a broad picture of how the frontiers of mathematics were being extended by various government agencies. The other members of the group were older than Jimbo and he guessed that at least half of them were academics. At least one he recognized as a professor from MIT who had written a piece for one of the scientific journals on the mathematics of chance as applied to contract bridge.

There were no real contenders for the blonde, and from the familiarity between most of the men he surmized that many of them knew one another and had academic and private reputations to preserve.

Three tables had been set out for meals in the private dining-room, and name-cards had been placed so that the seating could be varied from meal to meal and day to day.

The need to avoid talking about their jobs made conversation difficult, especially for Jimbo. The older men had private lives and interests that could be discussed but Jimbo Vick's private life was limited and, after the necessary expurgation, boring. He was included in the general conversation but was aware that they saw him as young enough, and perhaps naïve enough, to warrant a touch of condescension.

The blonde was at another table and went to her room as the meal was over.

On the second morning Jimbo was reintroduced to the others and presented his paper. During the question period the convener intervened several times to prevent answers on security grounds but Jimbo was aware that the blonde was obviously impressed too. She asked no questions but Jimbo recognized the universal vibes. On that subjecct he was even more of an expert.

They were at the same table for the evening meal that night, but he had little chance of talking to her because he was constantly answering questions about his paper. There was no longer any condescension. He was the expert and they were the tyros in his area.

He walked over to the table laid out as a bar after the meal was over and the girl walked over a few minutes later.

'Can I get you a drink?'

'Thanks, a tomato juice. No sauce, just the juice.'

As he handed her the juice he smiled. His little boy smile. 'Are you anti-alcohol?'

'No way. I'm not anti-anything. I just don't like the taste of the stuff.'

'What about beer?'

'I don't like that either.'

'Well, whatever you drink it's obviously good for you.'

The girl smiled and shrugged. 'Thanks. I was impressed by your paper. Is it going to be published?'

'I shouldn't think so.'

'Why not.'

He smiled. 'The usual reasons. Security.'

'How long have you been working on those theories?'

'Just over a year.'

'You've done a hell of a lot of research for just a year.'

'I've got a team working with me.'

'You're very young to be heading a team on that kind of material.'

'How about you? What's your speciality?'

She grinned. 'Nobody here admires my work, that's for sure. I specialize in knocking down mathematical theories. Creative negativity my bosses call it.' She laughed. 'Others are less polite.'

'Have you knocked down any theories of any of the people here?'

She laughed again. 'At least two of them.'

'It must help that you're so pretty. Softens the blow a bit.'

'I've always suspected that that's why I was given the job. But I don't think it works.'

'It would work with me. Definitely.'

The girl laughed. 'Let's hope you don't have to test that theory.'

'Am I allowed to ask where you are based?'

'Why not? I live in Washington.'

'Did you understand my presentation?'

She smiled. 'If I say no, then it confirms the dumb blonde theory. If I say yes, then it confirms the theory that all women are liars.'

'Typical Women's Lib evasion. There were several men here who obviously only had the vaguest idea of what I was talking about. It's a very narrow area of mathematics.'

'I got the general idea. What's your name by the way? Your first name.'

'James, but my friends and family call me Jimbo.'

She looked at his face, laughing. 'They're right. You are a Jimbo.'

'Meaning?'

'Bouncy, macho and – shall we say? – young.'

'And your name?'

'Kirsten. Kirsten Swenson.'

'A nice name. Very Swedish. Very glamorous. Like its owner.'

'Thank you, kind sir. Now I'm off to bed.'

'How about I take you out to dinner tomorrow night?'

For a moment she hesitated. 'OK. But I'm catching a plane at eleven thirty. I need to be at the airport by eleven.'

'Which airport – Dulles?'

'Yes.'

'No problem. I'll drive you there after dinner.'

'OK. It's a deal.'

Jimbo was aware that by meeting him at the restaurant she had avoided letting him know where she lived. But she wasn't one of his usual teenyboppers, she was big game and well worth stalking slowly and carefully.

He had booked a table at the Montpelier restaurant at the Madison Hotel and Kirsten Swenson had looked stunning in a pale blue linen suit. Jimbo Vick was aware of the heads that turned to follow them as they made their way to the corner table. She had let him choose the food for both of them. Calf's liver with a good year's Chambertin after a superb soufflé, followed by fresh raspberries and cream. As the meal progressed, he realized more and more that she was definitely very special. Obviously used to Washington society, with friends on Capitol Hill and at several of the embassies, she chatted amusingly of the latest scandals, and seemed well informed on what was going on in the White House.

'Tell me about you, Jimbo. What do you do when you're not beating a path through stochastic math theories?'

Jimbo shrugged. 'Nothing much.'

'I'd have thought you were a bit of a swinger.' She smiled. 'And a bit of a ladies' man.'

'Why that?'

'You're good-looking, lively, young and active, that's what most guys are who meet that description.'

'And you don't like swingers and ladies' men.'

'They're fine in their place?'

'And what's their place?'

She smiled and reached forward, putting her hand on his as it lay on the table. 'Don't take it so seriously, Jimbo. I'm only teasing.' She paused. 'How about you meet me from the plane on Sunday night? Arrives at six fifteen.'

'And I can take you out for the evening?'

She smiled. 'We'll see.'

'Say yes.'

'Maybe.'

Long after she had gone through the checkin and the door to the boarding gate he still stood there. Looking into space and thinking about her. Jimbo Vick was smitten and it was a new and not entirely pleasant experience. Why was she going to Chicago? Who was she seeing there? Where did she work and what did she do?

On Sunday night Jimbo had been at the airport half an hour before the plane was due, feeling faintly embarrassed at the bunch of long-stemmed red roses in the Cellophane wrapping and a small decorated message ticket that said, 'Welcome back – Jimbo'.

She was wearing a black silk dress that clung to her beautiful body like a second skin, and she had obviously been surprised and delighted at the roses.

They had had a drink at the airport bar and she had left him for a few minutes to make a telephone call. When she came back she'd invited him back to her apartment with the offer to grill them a steak.

Her apartment was in one of the old brick townhouses in Foggy Bottom. A top-floor attic studio with polished wood floors and chintzy décor and furnishings.

Jimbo was on his best behaviour and distinctly ill at ease. For once in his life he was trying to look like an upright citizen. A reliable, intelligent and responsible adult. The role sat on him like a suit two sizes too large and the girl was obviously aware of his efforts – and amused.

He made no pass at her as they sat having a final drink on the divan-settee but she'd let him kiss her good night at the doorway and she had responded, as his tongue explored her mouth, out of habit. When his breathing became heavy she moved out of his arms and said that she had tickets for a jazz concert the following Wednesday if he'd like to take her. He accepted eagerly and she laughed at his boyishness as she kissed his cheek before letting him out.

At the end of two weeks Jimbo Vick was in love. Desperately and painfully in love. Wishing that he had told her about his previous rip-roaring life so that he could lay his reformed character at her feet like a dog bringing a bone. He seemed to have nothing to tell her about his life since leaving home that wouldn't destroy his new image. He had already told her that he worked for NSA. And she had told him that she worked for a high-technology consultancy in downtown Washington that was part-funded by government departments who required independent assessments of high-technology projects.

He dated her two or three times a week and it would have been every night if she had agreed. It was six weeks before he had sex with her. He was careful not to indulge in any fancy stuff and the missionary position became the norm. Just once in the first three months he had been tempted to phone one of his teenage swingers and make a wild night of it. But after much pacing and indecision he stuck to the straight and narrow. He even phoned his home and made it up with them so that he could go through the ritual of her meeting his parents before he asked her to marry him. They were delighted to hear from him and said that any friend of his was welcome any time. He suggested the following weekend and they readily agreed.

But Kirsten Swenson didn't agree. Lying there naked and beautiful she shook her head slowly but emphatically. Long before that night he had told her that he loved her.

'Why do you shake you head so angrily?'

'I'm not angry, Jimbo. I just don't want to be married. Not to anybody. It isn't just you.'

'I'll go on asking you until you say yes.'

'Don't, Jimbo. Don't spoil it. I like you a lot but I'm not the marrying kind.'

'Is there anything I could do to make you change your mind?'

She swung her long legs off the bed and sat looking at his face. There were tears of disappointment in his eyes and she said quickly, 'I'll see you whenever you want to see me. You can make love to me. But if you pressure me about marriage I'd want to walk away, Jimbo. Don't ask me. Let's talk about something else.'

'Like what?'

She screwed up her eyes, thinking. Then she said, 'There's something you could help me with.'

'What?' he said eagerly.

'The office want me to do a consultancy job in San Francisco. I'd have to be away for three months and I don't want to go.' She turned her head and the big, heavy-lidded blue eyes were intent on his face. 'I thought I could get out of it if I could offer some speciality that I needed to work on.' She paused. 'Can I heist your subject? Will you tutor me a bit? Just enough to make me look like I know what I'm at?'

'Of course I will.'

'Has it got any practical uses or is it just pure mathematics?'

'Of course it has practical uses or I wouldn't be paid for doing it.'

'How can I sell the idea to my people? We only deal with practical applications. What kind of client could use your work?'

'How much did you understand of my paper?'

She laughed as she looked at his face. 'Not much. It sounded like the mathematics of guessing to me.'

'That's not a bad description actually. The word stochastic comes from a Greek word, *Stokhastikos*, capable of guessing. Have you ever used decision tables?'

'Yes. We use them a lot for our clients. More or less standard practice.'

'Well, the two main definitions of stochastic math theory would be . . .' he hesitated then went on '. . . statistically, a random variable with zero mean and infinite variance. In a process, it could be summarized as involving a random variable whose successive values are not independent. Say of a matrix that it was square with non-negative elements that add to the unity of each row.' He smiled.

'Like you said, it's the mathematics of conjecture, of guessing.'

She shook her head, smiling. 'Now come down to earth. What can I read that will give me enough to sound convincing when I do my pitch for being left in place in Washington?'

'How long have you got?'

'Three weeks, maybe a month.'

'There are no books that could help you in that time.' He turned to look at her. She was so beautiful. 'I'll tutor you. I'll bring you some of our concept work and we'll go over it piece by piece. It'll only be a veneer of knowledge.'

'That's all I need, Jimbo. Just enough to impress them.'

He laughed softly. 'In the country of the blind the one-eyed man is king.'

'Who said that?'

'I'm not sure, it sounds like Huxley.'

'It was Erasmus. Desiderius Erasmus, 1508.'

'My God, what a memory.'

She smiled. 'Make love to me, Jimbo.'

Night after night Jimbo tutored his girl. She was obviously not going to grasp much beyond the application of existing theory but that was all she needed. The consultancy accepted her alternative proposal and that night, for the first time, she let Jimbo stay at her place all night.

CHAPTER TWENTY-TWO

Chambers's phone call had been brief. He was coming to Berlin the following day with an official of GCHQ. He asked that nobody should be given prior notice of the visit. And that was to include Max Cohen.

Massey met them both at the airport and then drove them to the house in Grunewald. They were intending to fly back to London the same day. Chambers took Massey to one side.

'There's a technical problem come up, Jan. Not on your side but on Cohen's operation. It may be serious, it may not.' He paused. 'It could even be no problem at all, just a routine cock-up. Listen to what Phillips from GCHQ has to say and listen to Cohen's explanations. I'd like your opinion afterwards. Not in front of Phillips, just for my ears only. OK?'

'Of course.'

'What's your present assessment of Cohen?'

'He's enthusiastic, puts in far more hours than he should and he's kept his people happy in substandard conditions. About his technical ability my views would be useless. I'm not qualified to comment.'

'What about his loyalty?'

Massey frowned. 'A hundred per cent. No doubts at all.'

'What about his attitude to routine security?'

'As far as I know he sticks to the procedures I originally laid down.'

'How do you know he does?'

'There's no way anyone could be a hundred per cent certain. If there was a lapse it would almost certainly be picked up at Cheltenham or London. Or by the NSA.' Massey shrugged. 'There's no such thing as absolute security. You know that better than I do.'

'OK. I just wanted to hear your views before we start. Shall we go in?'

Chambers sat with Massey on one side of the mahogany table, Cohen and Phillips on the other.

Chambers leaned forward as he spoke. 'A problem, gentlemen. Or to be strictly accurate, maybe a problem. I'll leave it to Mr Phillips from GCHQ to explain.' Chambers turned to Phillips. 'It's all yours, Mr Phillips.'

Phillips wasted no time. 'The problem concerns traffic on July 3rd of last year. It was the section covering Soviet Army and Air Force traffic from Karlshorst for the period . . ' Phillips looked at a small notebook and then back at Cohen and Massey '. . . thirteen-hundred hours to sixteen-hundred hours.' He looked at Max Cohen. 'That doesn't have any significance for you, Mr Cohen?'

'Not until I've checked. Was it garbled transmissions or what?'

'No. Transmission was OK. Reception was OK. The codes used were all routine and standard codes that we broke when they originally started using them.'

Cohen shrugged. 'If reception was OK what was wrong? Did we misroute it, or what?'

'No. It wasn't misrouted. It went to Evaluation, was extracted for the Ia summary and was passed to Cheltenham about . . .' again Phillips looked at his notes ' . . . about sixteen minutes after decoding.'

Cohen smiled. 'So what's wrong with it?'

Phillips didn't look amused. 'We don't know.'

Cohen leaned back in his chair. 'So why are we here?'

'Because NSA were monitoring that traffic that day and they didn't record the same traffic.'

'What did they get?'

'Perfectly routine traffic from Karlshorst. Nothing exceptional. But entirely different from our stuff.'

'You mean we both monitored the same wavelengths, at the same time, on the same day and they both recorded different transmissions?'

'Yes.'

'That's technically impossible. It doesn't make sense.'

Phillip's eyes were intent on Cohen's face. 'It happened, Mr Cohen,' he said quietly. 'It happened.'

Massey intervened. 'Could it be wrong labelling or incorrect filing? Some office routine cock-up?'

'No, sir. It went straight on disk in both cases and the timing and monitoring details are computer-recorded on the disk. The software does that automatically.'

Cohen said, 'Have you examined the original disks? Both of them? And have you checked the print-out?'

'I've done all that. The timing and the rest of it is recorded in both cases. Identical. But the traffic is different.'

'Substantially different?'

'No part of it is the same. The same codes from the same units but different text.'

Massey looked at Chambers. 'Maybe we should get Evaluation to look at both texts and see if there is any significance in the two texts.'

Phillips interrupted. 'Evaluation at GCHQ and Fort Meade have already done that. They've found no significance in either text. It's humdrum routine stuff. Indents for pay, rations and medical supplies. Leave-rosters. Weapon and ammunition returns. Minor movements of troops and armour. The usual sort of stuff. But differing between the two.'

'Not one single item the same?'

'On your disk there were details of a promotion that didn't fit. A routine promotion from captain to major of an artillery officer.'

'Why didn't it fit?'

'He'd already been promoted. Six months earlier and the words and details were exactly the same as in the original notification.'

Massey shrugged. 'Could be some admin balls up. Their second echelon is notoriously inefficient.'

Phillips didn't respond. He just sat there looking from one to the other. Eventually he said, 'We'd be glad of any explanations anybody could offer.'

Cohen smiled. 'Me too.'

The man from Cheltenham was not amused. 'We're taking it seriously, Mr Cohen. It's not a light matter.'

Massey moved in. 'Tell us exactly what you want us to do, Mr Phillips.'

'We want your people to come up with an explanation, sir.'

'And what are Fort Meade doing about it?'

'Checking it out the same as us.'

'No suggestions from them?'

'Not so far, sir. But I'm in touch with them daily.'

'And GCHQ at Cheltenham? What are they doing about it?'

'They sent me over here, sir.'

Massey was mildly irritated at Phillips's manner. 'Nothing more than that? What is this – a buck-passing exercise?'

'You'd have to suggest that to the director, sir. He approved my visit.'

'Is there anything else you'd like to do while you're here?'

'I'd like to interrogate the operator concerned.'

Cohen barely kept the anger from his voice but he said quietly, 'I think you mean interview, Mr Phillips, not interrogate.'

'Call it what you like, Mr Cohen.'

'Have you got the operator's name to save checking the records?'

Phillips looked at his notebook. 'It was a Sergeant Turnbull. Reginald Turnbull. Royal Corps of Signals.'

'You could talk with him in my office. I'll be interested to hear if he's got any suggestions.'

'I'd prefer to see him alone.'

Cohen smiled frostily. 'I'll pretend I didn't hear that, Mr Phillips.' He looked at Massey. 'Can I fall out, Mr Massey, and get on with this?'

'Yes. Let me know what happens.'

Phillips's meeting with Cohen and his operator had provided nothing apart from irritation to both parties, and Cohen had not done his colleague from Cheltenham the courtesy of driving him back to the airport. He had arranged for a pool car to take him. Chambers had dinner with Massey, after Cohen had reported the essence of the interview to them. Chambers appeared to have lost interest in the problem. He and Massey ate at Kempinski's.

When the coffee had been poured, Chambers said, 'How're things in general?'

'We've got seven networks the other side. We seem to be getting what your people want.'

'Any problems?'

'No. I thought I had a problem a few months back but it's died down.'

'What was that?'

'I had an approach from the top Frenchman. Wanted to sell me a Russian defector.'

'Sell?'

'Yes.'

'What was the prize?'

'He said he'd got K holed up at his place. Ready to come over to the CIA.'

'You mean our K?'

'That's what he said.'

'Why didn't you tell me?'

'Because I didn't believe it. I had the French place under intensive surveillance. They hadn't got any Russian there.'

'You're sure of that?'

'Quite sure.'

'What was the object of the approach?'

'Cash. Personal cash.'

'How did you react?'

'Mildly interested. Argued about the amount. Said I'd see what London had to say.'

'Has he been back to you again?'

'No.'

'And you think it was just a bluff?'

'I'm sure it was.'

'Why did he pick on that name, d'you think?'

'K's name sometimes appears in top-secret NATO reports. I didn't want to use the emergency system if I could avoid it. It's not that safe from K's point of view.'

'Maybe we should review it. One of the P19 radios might be more efficient.'

'They listen just as hard as we do.'

'I'll talk to Facilities when I get back.'

Heidi had made her plans carefully. She had the money in the bank in Birmingham. She had phoned the girl and spoken to Tony. He would take care of her and get her started. All she had to do was plan her departure. She had no intention of even hinting to Johnson that she was leaving. But she wished she could be there to see his face when he came back to the empty rooms. She would have loved to leave him a note telling him what she thought of him but she knew that it didn't matter. Her new life would make up for all of it. Some time in the future she'd find out how to divorce him. There were things that she had to leave. The big stuff like the bed, the table and chairs and the old-fashioned wardrobe, but the rest she would take.

There had been no problem getting the plane ticket and booking a seat, but as the day for leaving approached her apprehension grew. He would really beat her up if he found out what she was up to, she had no doubt about that. He could even destroy her passport and the Russians were unlikely to give her another. Especially if Johnson told them what she had been planning to do.

She left the rooms in the early morning and took a taxi to the airport with her three heavy cases. Her passport, a plane ticket and her bankbook were in her new Italian handbag.

There was an hour's wait at the airport which she spent in the toilets until the flight was called. She neither ate nor drank anything during the flight. Immobile in her seat she tried not to think about what she was doing.

There was no problems at Gatwick and she took a taxi to Euston where she phoned Tony who said he would meet her at New Street station.

The three of them, Tony, Diana and Heidi, went to a local club that night to celebrate her new freedom.

'What would happen if he came over and found me here?'

Tony shrugged. 'Nothing. What *could* he do? You can live where the hell you like. He wouldn't do anything anyway.'

'He might beat me up.'

'Then you go to the cops. That'll stop him. They won't do anything, but it could go on his army record if they called in the military police.'

'When can I start earning, Tony?'

Tony grinned. 'Tonight if you want. I can make a phone call and the chap'll pay for your taxi.'

'How much do I charge him?'

'Make it fifteen. Give him an hour. And ask for the taxi fare. I can lend you a quid or two if you're broke.'

She shook her head. 'It's OK. I just want to start building up a few clients.'

Tony smiled. 'You'll be all right, kid. Don't worry.'

'Phone the guy now,' she said softly.

CHAPTER TWENTY-THREE

Chambers stood up and walked over to the window, opening it to let out the cigarette smoke. And to collect his thoughts. He looked out of the open window for a few moments, watching one of the pleasure steamers heading up the Thames towards Chelsea Bridge.

Walking back to the table he took off his jacket and hung it over the back of his chair. Harris from GCHQ sat facing him. Balding and rosy-faced, Harris looked like a cherub from some medieval Italian painting. His pale blue eyes were emphasized by his gold-rimmed glasses. But Harris was the hatchet-man who dealt with GCHQ's major problems.

Casey was NSA. A deputy director of long-standing more used to the buffetings and changes of mind of successive administrations and their committees than his British colleagues. The NSA's secrecy had to be guarded and preserved by top men willing to put their careers at stake to preserve the Agency's privileges and responsibilities. In his own opinion the British lived a charmed life with their D-Notices and the Official Secrets Act.

It was Casey whom Chambers turned to. 'Tell me what you think, Casey. No tact, no diplomacy, no bullshit.'

'Well, sir . . .' he paused '. . . if you put it that way I can only repeat the Agency's attitude. We think that heads should roll.'

'Why exactly?'

'Just to show we take a real poor view of what's happened.'

'What *has* happened, Joe? Exactly what?' Harris's voice was high-pitched and querulous. 'There's something happened that we can't explain. Not yet, anyway. So we chuck out a top man just to show we care?'

'You don't have to lose him, just put him out to grass for a couple of years. Then think again. The same will apply to one of our top guys.'

'We virtually accuse a man of treason without any grounds whatsoever? Not a shred of evidence?'

Casey shook his head emphatically. 'No way. Treason doesn't even get mentioned. Administrative inefficiency is all. Just like a senior guy in a big public company. He doesn't cut the mustard so he gets the chop or demotion. Nothing against his character.'

Chambers leaned forward to look at Casey. 'Do *you* think it was administrative inefficiency?'

'No. I'm darn sure it's not. And our internal security people will stay on it until we find out what happened.'

Harris said smoothly, 'Who's going to get the chop at your end?'

'D'you know Altieri?'

'Yes.'

'D'you think he's good?'

'First-rate.'

'Well, he's the boy. He's heading for somewhere quiet and unimportant as soon as I get back.'

'You've met Max Cohen?'

'Yeah. Several times. Looks a good guy.'

Chambers sighed. 'What reasons will you give your chap?'

'Somewhere near the truth. Why not? He isn't going to be surprised. He knows his job's on the table.'

Harris said, 'Cohen will be shocked. Really shocked.'

Casey shrugged. 'Well, he shouldn't be. He's a top guy. Somebody makes a balls-up in his area . . . so he carries the can.'

Chambers leaned back in his chair. 'Your people really think that this is the answer, Casey?'

'It's not the answer, Mr Chambers. Finding out what happened is the answer. This is just a gesture to show that when such things happen the guy responsible gets the chopper.'

'Which version of the traffic do your people find more credible?'

Casey turned to look at Harris. 'They're both credible. Both versions are typical. Nothing to choose between them. But they're different. So one of 'em's a phoney. It's as simple as that.'

Chambers pushed back his chair. 'Let's think about it overnight, yes?'

Casey shook his head. 'I've got a plane to catch tonight.'

Chambers looked at Harris's grim face. 'I think we'd better agree, Harris. Reluctantly.' He sighed and looked at Casey. 'But our cooperation with NSA is more important than any individual.'

'More important than justice, Mr Chambers?' Chambers tried to ignore Harris's question.

Casey stood up tucking his shirt back in his trousers. 'I'll leave you two gentlemen to philosophize and get on my way. If we find the answer be sure we'll contact you right away.'

At first Johnson hadn't realized what had happened. He had assumed that she had gone out for cigarettes or a pack of beer and he had taken off his jacket and settled down in the wicker chair. It was when he went to switch on the TV that he realized that something was wrong. There was no TV. And as he looked around the room he saw that there was no clock on the mantelpiece and no china vase. The place had been stripped. But only when he went in the bedroom did he realize that she'd gone. The wardrobe doors stood open and the rails were bare. There was none of the usual jumble of cosmetics and trinkets on the rickety dressing-table and the bedclothes had been thrown in a heap in a corner of the room. The bed had been stripped down to its mattress.

The bitch had gone. Done a moonlight flit. But where? He wondered if it was something to do with the Russians. But surely they'd have warned him.

For two weeks Johnson checked the clubs and massage parlours almost every night. But there was no sign of her. And nobody had seen her. They could be covering up for her, but not all of them. Some of the girls didn't like her but they hadn't seen her either.

It was the first thing he asked Fomenko at the next meeting.

The Russian frowned. 'I don't understand, comrade. Why do you ask me where she is?'

'Because she's gone, mate, scarpered, flown the coop.'

'How long has she been gone?'

'Just over two weeks.'

'She didn't leave a note?'

'Nothing.'

'And you had no idea she was going to leave?'

'If I'd known I'd have stopped her.'

'Had you quarrelled at all?'

'No. I hadn't seen her for nearly a week. I was doing extra half-shifts.'

Fomenko looked away towards the door and then back at Johnson.

'We've been paying her regularly but after our talk a few months ago we haven't used her for anything. Did she say anything about that? Did she complain?'

'No. Never said a word.'

'Do you want her back?'

'Not particularly.'

'We'd better find her, comrade. She knows too much.'

'She's too stupid to talk. Nobody'd believe her anyway.'

'They would if they questioned her. We couldn't risk that.'

'So what do we do?'

'Leave it with me.' He paused. 'Did you get the list we wanted?'

Johnson reached inside his jacket and took out a narrow strip of paper that he handed to Fomenko who looked at it before looking back at Johnson.

'How did you get this stuff?'

'I did the extra half-shifts. I worked in Central Registry. I wrote the frequencies in Biro on my arm. The code programmes I memorized over two nights.' He reached inside his jacket again and took out what looked like a folded magazine. He handed it to Fomenko, smiling as he said, 'A little present from the West, comrade.'

As Fomenko opened it he saw that it was a copy of the German edition of *Playboy*. He put it on his desk and turned back to Johnson.

Johnson grinned. 'Have a look inside, mate.'

'I'll look some other time, comrade.'

'Look now. Don't be so bloody obstinate.'

Fomenko sighed with exasperation and reached for the magazine. As it fell open he saw the printed cover of the booklet. It was the internal telephone directory of all the SIS set-ups in West Berlin, Cologne and Bonn. When Fomenko looked up Johnson said, 'Thought you might find it useful.'

'Good initiative, my friend. I'll see that other people are told.' He paused for a moment. 'Do you know any of the men who service the microcomputers?'

'Are those the ones with the TV screens?'

'Yes. There's an octagonal metal badge on the printers with the letters ACT in the centre.'

'I don't remember that. I don't go in there except to deliver urgent print-outs.'

'What about the service men?'

'I don't know who they are. We aren't allowed to talk about what we do except to chaps in our own sections.'

'Maybe you could find out. Just gossip around.'

'I'll see what I can do. What if I get information?'

'Just give us the name and anything you get to know about him.' Fomenko turned to the papers on the bedside table and picked up an envelope. 'There's four hundred D-marks. There'll be more next time.'

It was only eleven days until Johnson's next meeting with Fomenko. The Russian had taken a suite at the Berolina and after they had dealt with their routine talk they had eaten together. A meal to meet Johnson's taste. Sausage and chips with baked beans and a fried egg. Fomenko stuck to trout garnished with almonds.

'We've traced the girl, comrade.'

'Jesus. That's quick. Where is she?'

'She's left the country.'

'Where's she gone – Vienna?'

'She's in England. In Birmingham. A place called Handsworth.'

Johnson put down his knife and fork. 'The cheeky cow. That's my home place. What made her go there?'

'She's set up as a call girl. She works for a man named Tony. Tony Morello.'

'I know him. He's an old mate of mine. The bastard. The two-timing bastard.'

'Maybe it's best to just leave her there. What do you think?'

'She could tell Tony and his girl what we've been doing. Everything. Just to make herself more important. Sell her story to one of the newspapers.'

D'you think she would?'

'I don't know.'

'Maybe you should go over. Be friendly. Talk to her so that she isn't tempted to be aggressive towards you. She can live her life and you can lead yours and everybody can be happy.'

Johnson didn't reply. He was more in the mood for knocking hell out of her.

'What do you think, Arthur?'

'I'll have to think about it.'

'We'd pay for the trip and some cash for her or a present of some kind.'

'I'll let you know.'

'See me in a couple of days' time. At the garage office. D'you remember it?'

'Yeah, of course.'

He wore his uniform to give him confidence but as he got in the taxi at New Street station his anger came back. She'd got British nationality out of him, and she'd strung him along. She'd been going with men on the quiet. He realized that now.

Probably even used the rooms and done it on their bed. She'd put the poison down with the Russkis and now he was supposed to pretend to be all friendly and nice when he felt more like beating the living daylights out of her. The lying little cow. Calling herself a call girl. A ten-quid whore more like. But the Russkis had been insistent that he should make peace with her, as Fomenko put it.

Tony answered his knock on the door. His surprise and embarrassment were obvious.

'Hi, pal. What are you doin' in wonderful downtown Brummagem?'

'Where is she?'

'Where's who?'

'Heidi.'

'How should I know?'

'Don't bullshit me, Tony, or I'll go to the police and tell them you're running a knocking-shop here.'

'You'd better watch your words, big-mouth.'

'So where is she?'

'She ain't here, sunbeam.'

'I said where is she?'

'What do you want with her anyway?'

'I just want to talk to her.'

'She won't go back if that's what you're after.'

'I don't want her to go back. If this is what she wants it's OK by me.'

'D'you mean that?'

'Of course I do.'

For a moment Tony Morello hesitated, then he opened the door wide and beckoned Johnson inside.

'Are you on the level, mate?'

'Yeah. I just want to talk to her.'

'She's at the club.'

'Which club?'

'The White Rabbit. It's in the basement of the dry cleaners by the recreation grounds. D'you remember it?'

'I'll find it. Thanks.'

'She may be with a chap, I ain't sure.'

Johnson shrugged. 'Makes no odds to me.'

'Of course it don't. You're dead right. Live and let live, that's what I always say.'

The White Rabbit Club was down a flight of cement stairs and an orange light glowed over the door. Johnson pressed the bell and a small hatch opened. A pair of smoky eyes examined him. The door opened slightly, still held by a chain. A tall, thin West Indian looked him over.

'What you wantin', man?'

'I've come to see a girl here.'

'What's she calling herself?'

'Heidi. She's tall and blonde. Got an accent.'

The man nodded, unlatched the chain and opened the door.

There were four steps down to the club area and he saw her on her own at a table in the far corner. She was lighting a cigarette and she didn't see him until he was standing in front of her.

'Hello, Heidi. How're you doin'?'

She looked up startled and then recognized him.

'Piss off,' she said and he saw the anger and defiance in her eyes.

'I'm not here to make trouble, honey. I brought you a present.'

'I don't want a present from you, you bastard.'

Johnson's anger flared. 'You stupid cow, who the hell do you think you're talking to?'

She called out, leaning to one side to look past him, 'Tiger. This creep's insulting me.'

A big negro and the tall West Indian walked over and each took one of Johnson's arms. 'Come on, lover boy. Let's cool it, eh?'

Johnson turned as they frogmarched him, he saw her contorted face and heard her screaming out, 'He's a fucking spy. He's a Russian spy.'

As the West Indian closed the door behind him Johnson stood at the bottom of the steps trembling. Not with fear but with anger and frustration. He slammed the side of his fist against the iron railings that led up to the street. It was their idea not his. He knew her. Knew she'd not cooperate. That bitch who'd pounded the pavements of Vienna screwing for six quid a go. All comers welcome. Sitting there insulting him. Degrading him in front of the niggers. The Russkis may know about spying but they knew fuck-all about hookers. But the bit that mattered was the shout as he left. That was really asking for it. No way was she going to get away with that. Even the bloody Russians would go along with him on that.

CHAPTER TWENTY-FOUR

They were walking back over the bridge from Theodore Roosevelt Island to the parking lot off the Memorial Parkway and she turned quickly to look at Jimbo.

'Say that again.'

He smiled. 'I asked if you'd like to drive the Ferrari back to your place.'

'My God, Jimbo,' she said softly, 'I never thought I'd live to hear those words.'

'So, how about it? Do you want to have a go?'

She shook her head, smiling, 'No, *sir*. That would be going too far. It would be like you moving all the furniture around in my place.'

'You mean you wouldn't let me do that?'

She pursed her lips, smiling. 'If I did, I'd put it right back in its proper place the moment you'd gone.'

'But you like the car?'

She shrugged. 'Cars I can take or leave. They don't do anything for me. Not even bright red Ferraris. It suits you but it's definitely not me. Not me at all. They're just little boys' toys.'

'What turns *you* on?'

She stood still, her eyes closed, thinking. And then she said, 'I suppose in a way your darned math turns me on. It's kind of spooky. Mysterious. Forbidden territory.'

Almost an hour later they were both naked on her bed. They had made love and she was smoking a cigarette. 'What kind of people d'you have in your team? Are they old, young or what?'

'They're all about my age. A couple two years older and three younger.'

'Are they all oddballs?'

'No way. They're all prefectly normal. Fanatics, maybe, but not crazy. They're just hooked on being right out there on the frontiers of science.'

'Tell me about them. What they're like.'

'The youngest is Billy Myers. He's twenty-four. Got a PhD in math at Berkeley. Born in San Francisco. Got a stack of girlfriends. All teenagers. Spends money like a drunken sailor. The oldest is Bert Sayer. He's thirty-eight or -nine. Pillar of the church. Pretty wife. Three kids. Keen photographer. Quiet. Calm. And a brilliant mathematician.' He smiled. 'Any more?'

She laughed and shook her head. 'Do you have to justify what you all do?'

'I don't understand.'

'Don't you have to find a use for it? To justify the time and money and talent?'

'The use is in-built in NSA's function.'

'I don't see how.'

'Well, there are two obvious applications. We can crack complex codes using stochastic theory in hours instead of months and we can use the theory in voice recognition. Even word recognition.' He paused. 'There are dozens of other uses too.'

'Could your work be used in industry?'

'Technically, yes. There's hundreds of applications. Thousands maybe.'

'So why aren't you making a fortune with IBM?'

'Because what we do is totally restricted. People outside don't have any access to what we do and few of them realize what stochastic math theory could do for them.'

'But you could just leave and you'd be a millionaire inside a year.'

He smiled. 'Would you marry me if I was a millionaire?'

She laughed and took his hand. 'Maybe. Let's make love again.'

And as he rolled on top of her Jimbo wondered if that 'maybe' was for real.

Howard Fielding had stopped Massey in the corridor.

'Max Cohen's very upset by the news.' He paused. 'He could do with a kind word.'

'What news? What happened?'

'You don't know, sir?' Fielding looked surprised.

'Just tell me what it is,' Massey said brusquely.

'He's just heard from GCHQ that he's being moved. Being sent to some outpost on one of the Scottish islands.

'Any reason given?'

'Bad security in his operation here.'

'Where is he?'

'In his room.'

'I'll be there if anyone wants me.'

'Right, sir.'

After talking with an indignant and depressed Cohen, Massey had phoned Chambers using the scrambler but had got no joy out of him. He was adamant. Cohen's opposite number at NSA was getting the same treatment. There had been lax security and heads were going to roll.

The following day Chambers phoned and told him in guarded words that he should expect a visitor from Special Branch. It was implied that there was more trouble on the way. Chambers hinted that Max Cohen was probably involved again.

The Special Branch man arrived early that evening and Cohen and Massey took him into Massey's private quarters. He was a sergeant, middle-aged and obviously experienced. Calm, and no sign of panic stations as he accepted a neat whisky.

'The name's Lowther. Jimmy Lowther. Sergeant . . . Special Branch. Got a small problem. Thought maybe you could help me.' He looked amiably at them both, waited for a response, noted the grim faces and pulled out his small white notebook with the royal cipher on the cover. He turned over a few pages and then looked up.

'It's a case of elimination, gentlemen. Not much to go on.' He paused. 'Have you got any Signals chaps on leave in the UK at the moment?'

Cohen shrugged. 'Probably got half a dozen. Do you want me to check?'

'I'd be very grateful, sir. Maybe I could have names as well.'

Massey and Lowther sat in silence as Max Cohen talked on the phone and wrote out the details he was given. He turned to Lowther. 'Do you know what rank? Do you want officers as well as NCOs?'

'The description says no stripes. I've taken it as being a private.'

'Signalman,' Cohen corrected pedantically, then turned back to the phone. A few moments later he rejoined them.

'Only two. One warrant officer, a sergeant-major, is on a seven-day pass. He left here two days ago. And one signalman. Also on seven days.'

'His name, Mr Cohen?'

'Signalman Johnson.'

'When did he leave?'

'On the fourth.'

'And it's the thirteenth today.' He paused. 'Could I have a word with him, Mr Cohen?'

'I'm afraid not. He's not yet returned. He was posted AWOL this morning.'

'I see . . . Has there been any attempt to contact him?'

'Not as yet.'

'I read your standing orders and they lay down that you notify local police in their UK town in case of absence without leave. Am I right?'

'That's so.'

'So the local police have been notified.'

Cohen looked embarrassed. 'We generally wait for twenty-four hours before we do that. Sometimes travel to Berlin creates problems.'

'I see.' Sergeant Lowther looked very much the policeman. Noncommittal but faintly disapproving. 'It's Arthur Johnson, isn't it, sir?'

Cohen looked surprised. 'How the hell did you know that?'

'Just hearsay, sir. We get a lot of hearsay.'

'Has he done something?'

'The local police in Birmingham found a body, sir. A young women. Was identified as Mrs Heidi Johnson. The chap who identified her said she was German, married to this Signalman Johnson. Seems she'd left him. Didn't care for his ways. He came over to see her. Seems they had a disagreement and she was found dead in the early hours of the morning. The parties said Johnson was wearing battledress with Royal Corps of Signals insignia. White-on-blue arm flashes and the badge on the hat. The local police in Birmingham got in touch with the Provost Marshal in London and he was traced as being posted to this unit. That's why it was handed over to Special Branch.' He nodded. 'That's why I'm here.'

Massey said quietly, 'And now you'll be handing it over to Homicide.'

'I'm afraid not. Wish I could do that.' He sighed. 'Seems like this quarrel was in public. In one of these tatty drinking-clubs. The girl was on the game and when the husband appeared she called the bouncer to put him out. And as he was leaving she shouted out . . .' Lowther looked at his notebook as he read out the words '. . . "He's a fucking spy. He's a spy for the Russians".' He looked up impassively. 'They don't always get the words exactly right. But that was the gist of it.'

Cohen shook his head in disbelief. 'If he was a spy, sergeant, then I'm Mata Hari. He was as thick as they come. He could read and write and that was about all.'

Sergeant Lowther half-smiled. 'Mr Massey'll tell you that they come in all shapes and sizes. There's no A levels for spies. They're not all Philbys, you know. They also serve who only stamp the pieces of paper.'

Cohen looked at Massey. 'What do you think, Jan?'

'Sergeant Lowther's quite right, I'm afraid. The KGB want any information they can get about establishments like this. They can get a lot even from the low-level peole like Johnson.' Massey turned to Lowther. 'What can we do to help you, sergeant?'

'I'd like to look over his quarters and talk to some of the people who knew him.'

Massey turned to Cohen. 'Let me hand Sergeant Lowther over to you, Max. Any problems just contact me.'

Even in the first few minutes of the meeting with Chambers, Cohen and the man from GCHQ, Massey had realized that the disk in the book was involved. He had checked the library list for two months before he called off the check. Nobody had withdrawn the book. But it was obvious now that the disk had been removed. As they were talking he was trying to work out how he could identify who had taken it, though he was reluctant to pursue anyone who might be able to identify him as the man who had made it possible. Although they probably wouldn't know that. He had had no qualms of conscience about what he had done.

It was something that had to be done to save Anna. If it had turned out to be more serious than it now appeared, and he had been suspected, he would have lied to cover up. He would do nothing voluntarily that would cause her further harassment. He had done too much damage to her already. He had paid the debt as best he could, and he had no regrets.

The only guilt he ever felt was that Max Cohen was being removed for poor security. But even then some self-justifying mechanism made him rationalize that Cohen's security *had* been inefficient or none of it could have happened. When remorse or guilt seeped into the edges of his thoughts he pictured Anna in the KGB cell at Karlshorst. Terrified, trembling, knowing full well what they could do to her. Sometimes when he was alone with these thoughts he would shake his head angrily to dismiss them and groan aloud at what he had done to her.

The meeting had reinforced his attitude. Whichever day's traffic was the true version, it made little apparent difference. Both days were routine typical transmissions of no interest to SIGINT in any way.

What didn't fit was the Russians using him as the carrier. That presupposed that whoever they had inside was not sufficiently senior to have taken it unexamined through the usual security checks. But a man without that status would also not have had clearance to visit the disk library unless he was operational and involved in monitoring Red Army signals. And somebody at that level would surely have been able to find some way of smuggling in the substitute disk himself. The metal detectors would not have shown it. The disk was plastic.

CHAPTER TWENTY-FIVE

Sir Peter Tovey had arranged a private room for the meeting at the Reform Club. He had taken over as head of SIS five years before at a difficult time, and times had not changed much. The intelligence services were never praised by the opposition and the media when some Russian mole or active spy was caught, more likely they were blamed for the fact that such traitors existed. But Sir Peter was now reconciled to the vagaries of his career. Balding, with a froth of white hair like a cloud around his head, he had a face like those on Roman coins. An aquiline nose, hooked eyes, furrows on cheeks and brows that had grown deeper from maintaining a passive demeanour, he seldom looked directly at those he was conversing with. He chose his words carefully and listened alertly to what was said to him. Chambers had never decided whether Tovey actually approved of him or not. In fact he wasn't sure that Tovey even approved in general of SIS. It was known that Tovey got on well with the Prime Minister who made no secret of her dislike of the whole of the Foreign Office establishment.

When the coffee had been brought Tovey nodded to the waiter. 'Tell the club servants I don't want to be disturbed.'

'Right, Sir Peter.'

When the waiter had gone, closing the door firmly behind him, Sir Peter said,

'How long is this going to take, Chambers?'

'Not long, Sir Peter.'

'What's the problem?'

'Massey. Jan Massey.'

'I thought he was one of your prize specimens. That's what you always said.'

'That's true. But time moves on and circumstances change. I'd like to move him.'

'You don't need to ask me. He's your chap. Move him where you like.' He paused and blinked. 'I assume you've got good reasons for doing it.'

'There's the problem of our top Russian. He won't work with anyone but Massey.'

'Got more faith in Massey than you have, what?' Sir Peter smiled. He knew it annoyed Chambers when he made light of any of his problems.

'We haven't had any contact with the Russian for nearly a year.'

'Why do you think that is?'

'He's too important to them not to be carefully monitored. Contact has always been difficult. But the kind of information he has given us in the past has been absolutely invaluable.'

'So why the rush to move Massey if he's the only pipeline?'

'I'm a little uneasy about Berlin. Several security breakdowns. Massey seems to be very distant from day-to-day operations these days. I've heard talk that he's become aloof. Remote. Disengaged. Not got the spirit he used to have.'

'Happens to all of us, Humphrey, from time to time.'

'But you've no views on a move.'

Sir Peter blinked the hooded eyes as he always did when he was being less than frank. 'I'd go slowly if I were you. Let things ride a bit. Haste was never a virtue in this business. I see examples of it every day. A rush of blood to the head, and then months of shambles.'

'I'll remember that, sir.'

Sir Peter laughed and coughed. 'You mean you'll remember it if I'm proved wrong, eh?'

'I wouldn't dream of it, Sir Peter.'

'A cognac or something before you go?'

The hint was broad enough and Chambers left a few minutes later.

It was a phone call from the Berlin city police which had uncovered Johnson's room in the city. The new tenant had cleared out the old furniture and had found an envelope behind the sideboard in the sitting-room. It had obviously fallen down the narrow gap between the wall and the plywood back of the sideboard.

The envelope had faded edges but the contents were well preserved. A list of addresses written in pencil. A plastic card with Cyrillic lettering and a handwritten signature. A menu from the Berolina Hotel and a horoscope for Scorpios torn from an English newspaper.

The plastic card was a Soviet Kommandatura pass valid for any Berlin checkpoint giving the bearer top priority. And it was that that made the new tenant ring the police. The list of addresses was written in ill-formed capitals and one of them was a known KGB dead-letter drop. Signalman Johnson was only just a Scorpio. One day inside, Twenty-fourth of October.

Sergeant Lowther phoned London and he was instructed to hand over his notes concerning Johnson to Massey to pursue if he thought necessary. His companion on the flight back to Heathrow was an unhappy and silent Max Cohen.

The short inquest on Heidi Johnson found that she had been murdered by a person or persons unknown. The following day she was buried in Witton cemetery and the ceremony was paid for by Tony Morello from the substantial bundle of cash that he had found under the mattress in her room. He was praised as a generous and public-spirited citizen by his friends at the local pub.

The girl and the man stood side by side in Arlington cemetery, looking at the graves of President Kennedy and his brother. It had been raining and they were the only people in that part of the cemetery that afternoon. Already a heat mist was beginning to rise and the man said quietly, 'I read your report. It's getting near the time. What do you think?'

'It's up to you, Zak. I don't seem to be making much progress.'

'You've done fine, honey. Real fine. It's the relationship that matters right now, not the information. We've got two more names to work on now. Maybe a month from now. What d'you think? Maybe a couple of months?'

The girl sighed. 'He's such a pain in the ass. Just a grown-up juvenile delinquent.'

The man laughed softly. 'A guy named John Turnbull in 1782 said, "From dunghills deep of blackest hue, your dirt-bred patriots spring to view." You just keep that in mind.'

The girl pointed her shoe and jabbed angrily at the gravel on the path. 'Shall I leave first or you?'

'Did you bring your car?'

'Of course.'

'It's starting to rain again. You go first and take the umbrella.'

He passed the umbrella to the girl and she said softly, '*Do svedanya*' as she walked away.

Bourget had been brusque to the point of rudeness on the telephone. Demanding a meeting with him. Insisting it was held that day. Massey had placated the Frenchman by agreeing to go the SDECE house, something that he had always avoided.

The house was still and quiet as he walked into the tiled hallway through the open door. Bourget came out of one of the rooms, standing in the doorway beckoning him inside.

The furniture and décor were surprisingly tasteful. Bergère armchairs and sofas, and modern paintings on the walls. He had little time to look around before Bourget waved him to one of the armchairs and sat down himself in another, facing Massey.

'What was the big idea, my friend? To go behind my back to Paris?'

'I don't know what you're talking about, Pierre. I haven't been to Paris for over a year.'

'Don't play the innocent, Massey. You could have cost me my career. As it is, I'm being recalled.'

'You'd better tell me what it's all about.'

'You told them about the Russian. And the deal. You made me a crook. Why? I ask myself, why?'

'I haven't told Paris anything, Pierre. I haven't been in contact with Paris at all.'

'They knew the name – Kuznetsov. They knew the amount of money. How did they know? Only you and I knew about the deal.'

'Maybe London discussed it with Paris.'

'For God's sake. You told those idiots in London?'

'I told you that I'd have to discuss it with them.'

'You told them the whole story?'

'More or less.'

'But you didn't come back to me. Why not?'

'For several reasons. Mainly because London weren't interested.'

'What were the other reasons?'

'Only one. I didn't believe you'd been in contact with Kuznetsov.'

'Why you not believe?'

'You told me at our first meeting that Kuznetsov was here at your place. That he'd defected and you'd got him.' Massey paused, and then said quietly, 'You never had him, Pierre. You were bluffing. You were trying to con me.'

'Con you? What is that?'

'You were trying to deceive me. I checked up and you hadn't got any Russian here. I wasn't interested any more. Neither was London.'

'So if they were not interested why did they talk to Paris about it?'

'I don't know. I don't know that they did talk to Paris. I'll find out if they did if you want me to.'

Bourget drew a deep breath. 'You're a fool, Massey. You play the upright Englishman, the man of honour. But you sell your friends down the river.'

Massey stood up slowly and Bourget stood up too, his face suffused with anger. He said deliberately, small bubbles of saliva on his lips, 'I won't forget this, Massey. I promise you. Don't ever come to me for help. And . . .' he clenched his big fist '. . . you just watch your step. One day I'm going to settle with you. I swear it.'

Massey swallowed his anger and said quietly, 'Is there anything I can do to help you, Pierre?'

The Frenchman shrugged angrily. 'You've done enough damage to me, Massey. Just get out of my sight before I go too far.'

As Massey drove back to Grunewald he wondered why Chambers had passed on the information about Bourget to Paris. Chambers would never have let it come out accidentally. And he wouldn't even have talked inside SIS about anything that so much as vaguely touched on Kuznetsov. Kuznetsov was their pipeline, not only to the very top of the KGB but to the Politburo itself. The kind of information that he contributed was far from the normal grist of intelligence. What he gave them was the most valuable intelligence of all – the intelligence of intention. Both he and Chambers had spent hours analysing the warnings that Kuznetsov gave them, looking for some factor, some rationale in what he chose to pass on. His hints, his warnings had never proved wrong. On two occasions in the early days they had deliberately ignored his advice. On the first occasion it had led to eighteen months when West Germans were not allowed to visit East Berlin or the GDR. The second occasion, concerning the stationing of nuclear-armed warships in the South Pacific, had been 'punished' as Kuznetsov had said it would be, by providing the Argentines with satellite intelligence. London had assumed that the Soviets would never assist the fascist Junta in Buenos Aires. They were mortal enemies of the Soviet Union on a dozen major counts, but the aid had been given as Kuznetsov had said it would be.

If there was no movement from Kuznetsov on the next few weeks he would have to take the risk of activating the contact mechanism himself.

He read the investigation reports on Johnson before he went to bed. There had been no trace of him despite extensive enquiries by the Birmingham police and Special Branch at Massey's request. Neither had he been seen in West Berlin. None of his working colleagues knew much about him and none of them even knew that he was married. Superficial examination of Heidi's passport and marriage and birth certificates indicated that they were genuine. Massey passed an instruction for them to be sent to Forensic for a full check.

CHAPTER TWENTY-SIX

He couldn't understand why she was so aloof and indifferent. She didn't want to go out for a meal, she didn't want to go to the jazz club and she wasn't interested in them driving out of town for the weekend. He'd ended up watching yet another rerun of *Casablanca* on TV while she just sat in the armchair smoking one cigarette after the other, her long legs draped over the arm of the chair, her eyes closed. Finally he got up, switched off the TV and stood looking at her.

'What's wrong, honey?'

'Nothing's wrong, Jimbo.'

'It is. I can tell it is. Are you down with something?'

'Why don't you go if you're not satisfied?'

'It's only nine o'clock.'

'So what? Have an early night.'

She swung her legs down and stood up, frowning. She pushed him away when he reached out towards her.

'Tell me what's wrong, babe.'

'For Christ's sake don't call me babe.'

'OK. Tell me what's wrong, ma'am.'

For a moment she hesitated, then she said quietly, 'I'm sorry if I'm being a bitch . . .' she looked at his face '. . . they fired me today. Two months' pay and out. Some bastard even stood there watching as I cleared out my desk.'

'Why did they fire you?'

'They said that I was wasting their time and money and stochastic math theories were mathematicians' pipe dreams.'

'They must be out of their minds. In two years' time anybody who's worked on stochastic math will be worth their weight in gold bars.'

She sighed. 'I'm sure you're right, Jimbo. But meantime I've got to earn a living.'

'Let me see what I can do. There's a computer outfit I know who could be interested.'

Slowly, he cheered her up and the next day he phoned his contact at the computer company and arranged an interview for her that afternoon.

When they met in the evening she was despondent again.

'What happened at the interview?'

She shrugged. 'He talked about a job as a systems analyst and when there was a commercial use of stochastic math I could take over in their software section.'

'Maybe that's better than nothing while you look around. Maybe I sent you off in the wrong direction way back and I *was* wasting your time suggesting you moved over to experimental math.'

She looked at him for long moments and then she said, 'Would the Agency take me on?'

He looked surprised and then pleased. 'Of course they would. I could hire you myself.' He paused. 'I always imagined that you thought the Agency was a bit . . . well . . . not your style.'

She half-smiled and shrugged. 'I did at first . . . the spook stuff . . . but I guess I've got used to it knowing you.'

'There'll be some security checking but if you don't mind working for me . . . then that's it. I'll leave it to Personnel to fix your pay and conditions. You'll have to sign a "Conditions for retention of employment" agreement and you'll be employed in a special section of the NCS. And you may be sent on a course before you work for me.'

'What's the NCS?'

'The National Cryptological School.' He smiled. 'We think it's the jewel in NSA's crown.'

'And the course.'

'I'd guess they'd put you on CY-001 which is an indoctrination course and then I guess you'd go on a course titled Intensive Program in General Analysis.' He smiled. 'That's the equivalent of a PhD in codebreaking.'

She looked up at his face. 'You're really very good to me, Jimbo. I appreciate it. I really do.'

He grinned. 'Will you . . .' he shook his head '. . . no, forget it.'

'Go on . . . ask me whatever it was.'

He sighed and looked very much the small boy as he said, shrugging, 'The same old question – will you marry me?'

She looked away for a few moments and then back to his face. 'Would it really make all that much difference to you, Jimbo? Is it really what you want?'

'It's what I very definitely want.'

'Tell me why.'

He sat down on the floor beside the chair and she slid down beside him. 'Tell me, Jimbo. Tell me why it matters.'

'I don't know. It just does. I was wild when I was a kid. Got into scrapes. And in the end my folks had had enough. I felt they were ready to sell me down the river. I hated them for that. They wanted me to do what they wanted and I left home. More to prove them wrong than anything else, I got myself to university and without intending to I got myself hooked on this math thing. Till I met you I guess I was a sort of Jekyll and Hyde character. Conforming in the daytime. The wild swinger at night. It pleased me to be defying the Establishment, deceiving them. And in the circles I mixed with at night I was the leader. The guy with money and a special talent . . .' he smiled '. . . and a red Ferrari.' He paused. 'And then I met you and it all changed.'

'Why did it change?'

'I don't know. You just seemed right for me. You were impressed by the Dr Jekyll bit – the math bit – and you obviously weren't impressed by the swinger stuff nor the money. I guess you were the first person I had a real feeling for. The first person I had a real relationship with. I felt at home with you. I always have done.' He smiled. 'And you're beautiful. Really beautiful.'

'And me marrying you would make you happy?'

'Nothing could make me happier.'

'Would you agree to wait until I've done my courses and then we get married?'

He laughed. 'I'd agree to anything, believe me. Do you mean it?'

'Yes.' She nodded. 'I mean it.'

They went out that night for a celebratory meal and he stayed at her apartment for the rest of the night.

He saw little of her during the day but while she was on her courses he went over her work with her night after night. Her security clearance had gone through smoothly and she was on a probationary pay scale that paid her $25,000 a year. It would be almost doubled after she had worked at NSA for a year.

Six months after her start at the Agency they were married. Jimbo's family had come up for the weekend and there were a dozen guests from NSA. Most of those who attended the ceremony were touched by a feeling of sadness for the stunningly pretty girl whose parents had been killed in the car crash so many years ago, and had no family to enjoy the obviously happy occasion.

As a gesture of forgiveness and relief, Joss Vick bought them a house in Georgetown not far from the girl's old apartment. Jimbo was happy. He was also pleased and proud that she was as bright and creative as any other member of his team of fanatics.

Chambers wasn't sure why he chose the zoo for the meeting with Redway. It provided good security among the crowds of visitors and nobody could overhear their conversation. And it was a fine day, and he was sick of the sight of Century House and its problems. It was like a marshalling yard for problems, particularly those that had no final answer. And he was tired of problems. They flowed over his desk in a neverending stream. Was the hint from the Czech minister at the congress in Paris for real or just a veiled threat? Was the monitored telephone conversation between the importer of Russian magazines and the Soviet trade attaché an invitation to launder money for dissidents in the UK? And was Kuznetsov's prolonged silence because he distrusted Massey's security in Berlin? He had looked through his checklist that morning. There were thirty-seven specific problems on which somebody expected his views and on fourteen of them it wasn't just his views they wanted, but his final decision.

Massey had certainly changed in the last year or eighteen months. He worked long hours. Chambers had checked on that. But the fire had gone. The inspiration and enthusiasm. For years he had told Massey to be less involved in actual operations. That his talents were best used in directing others. Maybe it was his fault, for that was exactly what Massey had done. But he'd drawn back too far. He might just as well be operating from a desk in London. Was it that? Or could there be something in what that bloody Frenchman had said to his bosses in Paris? Some high-up Russian in the KGB who had hinted to the Frenchman that there was a traitor in the Berlin SIS station. Even two, they'd said. And some gossip about Massey and a girl.

Redway was waiting for him, sitting at one of the outside tables at the cafeteria near the parrot house. He'd waved to Redway, bought two coffees and carried them over to the table. As he sat down it all seemed so normal and ordinary that he was faintly embarrassed at making this rendezvous so artificial. But he'd been brought up on the tradition of open-air meetings when possible. St James's Park if you were in a hurry. The zoo if it was a fine day and the Festival Hall cafeteria if the weather was bad.

Redway was his opposite number, responsible for operations in the USA and South America. He had been Chambers's predecessor at the European desk.

'Thanks for coming along, Joe. I need the benefit of a good, experienced mind. Yours.'

'What's the problem?'

'D'you remember Massey?'

'You mean Jan Massey – West Berlin?'

'That's the one.'

'And now he wants New York or Washington and you're softening me up.' He shook his head, smiling. 'No way, old friend. I wanna let my sleeping dogs lie.'

'I wish it were that, Joe. No, it's more complex than that.'

'You look worried. Tell me what's worrying you.'

For twenty minutes Chambers detailed his doubts, and even as he was speaking he realized how flimsy it all seemed. Rumour, gossip, hunches, vague doubts. But flimsy or not, they were the only grounds he had for discussing the soundness of a senior man.

Redway pursed his lips. He wasn't surprised by the sparse information that had created the doubts. He had had plenty of such crises to cope with in his time at SIS.

'Nothing more?' he asked, when Chambers had finished.

'No.'

'We all come up against these situations but when they land on my desk I've got a rule I always stick to. When in doubt – do something. If you don't and you just leave it and it goes wrong, then you carry the can. I don't mind carrying the can when I haven't seen it coming, but I don't like it at all if I've had fair warning and then done nothing.'

'What would you do in this case?'

'I'd move friend Massey. No. Let me go back to square one. I'd have a week off. A break. Just to make sure it's not me that's causing the problem. If it isn't me, on reflection, then I'd move Massey away from Berlin. And I'd *promote* him. Up a grade or two and I'd create some little problem area for him to deal with. No criticism, plenty of pats on the back. His talents being wasted in Berlin and all that crap. And give him a task where he's totally involved. Nothing vital but something needing a lot of ferreting and some opportunity for initiative and creative thinking.' He paused. 'How's that strike you?'

'It's more or less what I had in mind, Joe.'

'Of course,' Redway said diplomatically. 'Have you got something specific in mind?'

'Vaguely. I'll work on it.'

'How about we get out of this dump and you treat me to a wonderful lunch at your club?'

Chambers smiled. 'They've got the decorators in. What about the Savoy?'

'That'll do.' Redway slapped Chambers's thigh and stood up. 'Come on. Cheer up. This place would give anyone the heebie-jeebies. I was in a jail in La Paz once that looked exactly like these bloody birdcages. Brings it all back.'

Chambers didn't take a week's holiday but he took a long weekend up at St Andrews with his wife who was also an enthusiastic golfer. And when he came back he had spent a week thinking how he could create a place for Massey that fulfilled the conditions that Joe Redway had prescribed.

His solution wasn't ideal but it had the benefits of solving the immediate problem and being actually useful, but a little too obviously contrived. He took another week to embellish a little and devise a suitable scenario to placate Jan Massey. He thanked the Lord that there was still just enough time to work an MBE into the Birthday Honours list. The citation would have to read as 'services to industry and commerce', but those who mattered would know what it really meant. An open pat on the back. He had still had enough doubts, though, to leave it for a further month before he put the personal call through to Jan Massey in Berlin.

It was another week before they were due to meet and in that week he swung between determination and indecision. But it was too late now to stop the internal machinery that the change had activated. Fortunately GCHQ had been eager to cooperate with his initiative, suggesting that GCHQ themselves took over the surveillance part of the operation in Berlin. It was a sacrifice that he'd had to make to provide the main reason for the reorganization. It wasn't only Massey he had to convince but others inside SIS. Any hint of his doubts on the grounds of security could lead to another of those ghastly witch-hunts that had haunted the intelligence services from the days of Philby, and more recently, Blunt.

Chambers's office was panelled in bird's-eye maple with ornate brass light fittings and a desk big enough to accommodate six people for a meeting. But there were four leather armchairs arranged round the wide, open fireplace and it was these that Chambers thought more fitting for his meeting with Massey. After a few minutes' social chit-chat Chambers came to the point.

He was smiling as he started his party piece. 'I've got a pleasant surprise for you, Jan. Two in fact.' He paused and laughed. 'I could even claim three.' He leaned forward towards Massey. 'There's been much talk in the last six months that we were wasting your talents in Berlin. You've got it all bedded down and you've ironed out the initial snags in the system so . . . why shouldn't the organization have the benefit of those talents elsewhere?

'I also wanted to make sure that if we moved you your successor wouldn't be overburdened with the joint responsibilities of Berlin. Then out of the blue – mainly because of the removal of Max Cohen – Cheltenham put up the proposal that GCHQ should take over the SIGINT responsibilities and leave SIS to get on with its normal job. We had a number of meetings about it and it was obviously a little incongruous that an SIS officer should have charge of the Signals section which is not normally an SIS responsibility. They agreed that by good luck you fitted the dual role well but they pointed out that you were an exception.' Chambers paused. 'So . . .' he went on enthusiastically '. . . it gave us back our man.

'Almost at the same time we became aware of a lack that we had in Paris. A touchy Embassy staff – particularly His Excellency – a poor liaison with French intelligence, and not much idea of how we could improve things.' Chambers smiled broadly. 'That's what we want to use you for, Jan.'

Massey's face was impassive as he said quietly, 'When do you want me to hand over?'

Chambers looked as if he were only just considering when it should be. But he said quite quickly, 'How about we make it the end of July and you take up the Paris problem late August – early September?'

'Whenever you want. Was there anything else?'

Chambers beamed. 'There's a little something coming your way in the Birthday Honours list. We're all delighted.'

Massey frowned for a moment and then said, 'My father will be pleased.'

As Massey stood up to leave, Chambers stood up too and walked with him to the door. 'How is your father?'

'He jogs along.'

'Give him my regards, Jan, when you see him. They were a great bunch, SOE. A great bunch.'

'I'll be flying back tonight if you don't need me any more.'

'By all means. It's been good to see you again.'

CHAPTER TWENTY-SEVEN

They had bought two copper casseroles on the far side of the square and had walked back with the white plastic bag to have a coffee at one of the tables outside the café. It was the first time that Jenny Mayhew had been outside Britain and she loved every moment of it. Albufeira was her idea of heaven. The sunshine, the long golden beach, the awesome rocks and caves, and the people. Men from Manchester wearing Bermuda shorts as if all this were their usual lifestyle. Men who owned garages in Liverpool who smiled as they raked their teeth with gold toothpicks. Men who ordered wine by the bottle, not by the glass. Teenage girls from the Midlands who wore daring swimsuits that had been featured in the *Mirror* or the *Sun*. Blue-rinsed wives of peeling men who sat reading the *News of the World*, their lips moving slowly as the front page kept them in touch with vicars and scoutmasters who had surprised the whole village by running off with bellringers and cub-mistresses. They accepted her, the women nodding and smiling at breakfast, the men having a good look at her sweater.

'We must come here again next year, Eric. If we can afford it.'

He was gratified that she was so pleased with their holiday, and she had taken to the foreign ways so easily. Saying *obrigada* and *por favor* like a seasoned traveller.

'I'd thought of giving Rome the once-over next year. But they tell me it's no good in August. Far too hot. I'll think about it.' And, leaving Rome to its uncertainty, he said, 'Better get back to the condominium.'

She frowned and said softly, 'What *is* a condominium, Eric? I know they call it that but what is it?'

'They have 'em in the States, love. Apartments grouped together or villas, just a block of flats, really, or a small housing estate.'

'You seem to know everything, Eric. It's wonderful being with you.'

For a moment he was worried. Why did she say it was wonderful *being* with him? Why not *married* to him? Was she telling people he was just her boyfriend, as if they were just having a dirty weekend at Brighton?

'I love you, Jenny. There's never been anyone but you and there never will be.'

She smiled fondly. 'Me too neither.'

Chambers had been surprised at Massey's apparent indifference to his posting to Paris. If there was any security problem about Massey, his move to Paris would neutralize it. The Russians had almost no interest in the activities of the SDECE and Massey in Paris would be of little use to them. And surely if Massey had been involved with the KGB he would have put up at least some sort of argument for being left *en poste* in Berlin.

He had a twinge of conscience about having given any credence to the gossip of a Frenchman who had been trying to line his own pockets by abusing his official position. But the gossip had had to go down on the confidential file. It had been said, and it had to be recorded. The fact that he had taken swift action would be on the record too. Action that had not prejudiced Massey's career if he were innocent. And action that was not officially recorded as being based on any security doubts could not be used in years to come to earn a fat fee from some newspaper by implying that everybody knew that 'X' was a Russian mole but the head of the department had stopped the official inquiry because he was a Russian mole too. Old rivalries and jealousies could be raked up again and again to add a little jam to the meagre pension. All in the name of democracy and patriotism, of course.

They were undressing to go to bed and he watched her as she sat naked at the dressing-table wiping off her makeup. She was so young and pretty it didn't seem true that she was his wife. But she was.

As he lay in bed with his arm around her, she said, 'There was a chap watching us today. I wonder what he was up to.'

'What man? Where?'

'He came in the shop when we were buying the cooking pots, and when we were having our coffees he was sitting on a bench by the fountain. He was pretending to read a paper but he was looking at us. And when we were on the beach this afternoon he walked past us twice.'

'What's he look like?'

'Fair-haired. A bit like Robert Redford but sort of more podgy.'

'How old was he?'

'In his thirties. Thirty-six or -seven.'

'Maybe he was looking at you?'

'No. It wasn't that kind of look. It was more like he was keeping an eye on us.'

'What was he wearing?'

'Marks and Spencer's plaid shirt, and grey trousers. They looked like Marks and Sparks as well.'

'If you see him again point him out to me. I'll soon settle him. Cheeky bugger.'

'Maybe I just imagined he was looking at us. It's hard to tell. On holiday people are sitting looking at other people all the time. Just passing the time. Anyway . . .' she turned and smiled at him as his arms went round her, then leaned over and switched off the bedside lamp.

Massey had gone up to London from Tenterden for two meetings with Chambers. At the first he had been briefed on the information currently available on SDECE and its top personnel. And he had been introduced to the

London-based SIS officers specializing in French intelligence, and counter-intelligence officers in both Metropolitan France and the French overseas possessions.

At the second meeting Chambers was outlining his briefing for the new posting to Paris.

He stood looking out of the window while Chambers talked on the phone. He had never really understood why he didn't like Chambers. He was urbane and tactful, amiable and efficient, but there was a smoothness about him that Massey had never trusted. Even his calm, pale face was smooth, and his black hair was smoothed back as if Brylcreem was still in fashion. But he knew that if he were honest, what he disliked was that Chambers was such a typical Brit. An Establishment Brit who wore three-piece suits to the office and gear from the via Veneto when he was relaxing at home. He belonged in a Dormeuil advertisement in *Punch* or the *Sunday Times* magazine.

Looking from the window on the fourteenth floor he could see the grey outlines of the Houses of Parliament and Westminster Bridge in the early morning mist of what looked as if it were going to be another typically English autumn day. It was a relief from the stark modernity of Berlin but it was part of the Establishment that he disliked, despite having served it dutifully for over twelve years. For he was at least half British and he owed them that.

Chambers waved to him to take a chair as he went on talking. A few minutes later he hung up and turned, smiling, to Massey.

'Sorry, Jan. But it's budget time and that always means panic stations all round.' He paused. 'Are you having a good leave?'

Massey shrugged. 'Quiet, anyway.'

'You're staying with your father?'

'Yes.'

Chambers took a deep breath and leaned forward to indicate that the social chit-chat was over.

'Well now, Paris.' He leaned back in his chair until it creaked, fiddling with a gilt letter-opener in the shape of a Spanish sword. 'It's more a monitoring job than anything else. And full of pitfalls. Ever since they flounced out of NATO, the French have been very touchy about any kind of cooperation.

'They're barely on speaking terms with the Americans and we've become sort of honest brokers between the two of them. It's a röle we don't really want. The CIA trample everywhere in Europe with hob-nailed boots and the SDECE are so corrupt and infiltrated that the CIA treat them as if they were an enemy operation rather than allies. So there's quite a task ahead of you.'

'What's our set-up at the moment?'

'Very thin on the ground. Morrow at the Embassy, who loathe having him there. Plumpton at the Consulate, and a string of informers.'

'Do they produce anything?'

'Not much more than top-echelon gossip. Most of our information comes from other sources. Mainly NATO itself. It's mainly about SDECE cock-ups. But don't kid yourself about the SDECE and the DST; they treat us like we were enemies too. They'd cut our throats as happily as if we were KGB.' He smiled. 'Maybe even more so.'

'What about offices?'

'No office, Jan. Take a decent apartment. Use the embassy radio set-up. Use Morrow and Plumpton. They are directly under you. When you want to interfere, then interfere. Otherwise just keep us informed. Weekly sit-rep. No copy to the Embassy, no internal copies. We'll give you a PO box number. Post it or use the diplomatic bag if it's urgent or necessary.'

'Budget?'

'There's an existing budget and we're prepared to increase it by up to fifty per cent. If you think that's necessary.'

'When do you want me to start?'

'No mad hurry. Next month perhaps. There's no rush.' He stood up. 'Congratulations on the promotion by the way. Well deserved.' Chambers looked at his watch then back at Massey's face. 'Have lunch with me?' And Chambers smiled at the defensive look on Massey's face. 'We needn't go to White's. Why not a sandwich at the Special Forces Club? Say, one o'clock?'

Massey smiled. 'OK. I'll meet you there.'

As they walked slowly up the High Street in Tenterden and turned into the churchyard he realized that his father had suddenly grown old. No longer standing so upright, he walked with a stoop, and his walking stick was no longer just a decoration or a pointer.

They sat on the bench and russet leaves blew into small heaps at the edges of the larger graves, but there was still a pale blue sky and trailing white mares'-tails that signalled the fact that though autumn might have been late it was here now and making up for lost time.

The old man coughed and put a white handkerchief to his mouth. 'I still come here, Jan. After all these years. No justification for it. She'd never heard of Tenterden, I'm sure.'

'But it's been a comfort all the same.'

'Yes. Stupid, isn't it? Just the habit and the years have made it our place. I used to talk to her when I was alone and there was nobody around. Tell her what I'd been doing.' He laughed briefly without humour. 'Hernias, hysterectomies, and the gossip. The babies, wanted and unwanted. Nothing more interesting to say, I'm afraid. And now . . .' he waved the stick towards the moss-covered headstones '. . . and now it's just thoughts. Waiting until I see her again.' He turned sharply to look at Massey's face. 'D'you believe in anything, Jan? God, religion and all that? D'you think I shall see her again?'

'I'm sure you will, Father. You see her every day in your mind.'

'What about your girl? Ever see her again?'

'I'm afraid not.'

'No chance of putting it right?'

'No.'

'I'll be interested to hear what you think of Paris.' He smiled. 'It will be very different from the old days. The Gestapo and the *Sicherheitsdienst*. The rumours and the rationing.' He sighed. 'Your mama loved Paris. We were never there together, but I think we might have lived there, or somewhere in France, if it had turned out differently. She liked the country and she liked the people. They were very brave, the French. Nobody who wasn't there could know what it was like. The humiliation, the fear, the shortages. It seemed as if it would go on for ever.'

'What about the collaborators?'

'There were very few real collaborators. Despite wars, despite occupation, life goes on for ordinary people. A girl sleeps with a German soldier. But what does it matter? She was probably very young and very lonely. He was probably the same.' He shook his head. 'I see it in the surgery every day. People can't think about the dangers of nuclear bombs every hour of the day. Nor the class struggle or political parties. A few fanatics have nothing better to do, but people get on with their daily lives. All over the world it's the same. We should be sparing with our criticisms.' He turned to look at his son. 'Where are you going to stay? Do you have an official place?'

'No. I get an allowance to rent an apartment.'

'That's good, my boy. A new life. A new start. Where will you live?'

'I don't know. I'll spend a week or so looking around.'

'In my days it had to be Montmartre or Montparnasse. Even in wartime, they were the only places to live.'

Jan Massey smiled. 'I'll remember that.' He gently touched the old man's knee. 'We ought to go. It's getting cold.'

The old man sighed. 'I love talking to you, Jan. It's a great comfort. You were a good boy, really. And you've grown into a fine man. An MBE. Your mother would have been so pleased, despite not liking authority.' He sighed. 'You lead the way.'

CHAPTER TWENTY-EIGHT

Chez Raymond on West 56th Street was never a place to patronize when you were in a hurry, but the onion soup was topped with excellent Swiss cheese and nicely browned. But what he went for was the guinea fowl and the delicious wild mushrooms called *chanterelles*. He finished his meal with an excellent Brie. The coffee was the only drink he ordered. No aperitif and no wine. He checked the bill meticulously, paid on his American Express card and tipped the waiter in cash.

As he walked into the street he looked at his watch. It was later than he thought and he waved down a cab. On West End Avenue he asked the driver to drop him just past 72nd Street and he walked the rest of the way.

It was a tall block, offices and shops in the lower half and residential above. There were five penthouse suites and his was on the corner so that he had the fine view across the Hudson river.

He looked at his watch again as he walked from the elevator along the carpeted corridor. It was nine thirty-five, and he had cut it rather fine. Ten o'clock local time was the scheduled time.

As he slid his key into the security lock and pressed down the two retaining clips he wondered what the response would be to tonight's information. He opened the heavy door, carefully took out the key and slid it back in his coat pocket. It was only when he turned that he saw the two men. One, with an old-fashioned crewcut who was about fifty, was sitting in the armchair which had been turned to face the door. The younger man was standing at the side of the door and he reached out and pushed the door to.

The older man said, 'Good evening, Mr Swartski.'

'Who are you? What are you doing here? How did you get in my apartment?'

'The porter let me in.'

'That's impossible, the house regulations say –'

He stopped as the man held up a small, black-leather folder displaying an identity card. There was a photograph and a white diagonal line from corner to corner.

Swartski leaned forward to look more closely and the man said, 'My name's Logan, Mr Swartski. And my colleague is Mr Curtis. We're both FBI. We want to ask you some questions.'

'I want to call my attorney. That's part of my rights.'

'You can phone him when we've charged you. Meantime –'

'Charged me with what?'

Logan smiled. 'Depends on how cooperative you are. Take your coat off, Mr Swartski, and sit down.'

'Do you have a warrant to enter this apartment?'

'No. We didn't want to attract attention to our visit at this stage. We can get one if you wish.'

Swartski hesitated then took off his coat and sat on an upright chair alongside the small desk.

'Tell me what it is you want to know.'

'I want you to tell me what you've been doing in the United States with a forged passport, a forged residence permit and using a false name.'

Swartski stood up slowly. 'In that case, mister, either get your warrant or charge me with whatever you've got in mind.'

Logan nodded amiably, 'Sit down, Swartski, and we can get down to business. Go on. Sit down.' Swartski sat down reluctantly and Logan said, 'We've taken your radio and various documents. They're at the DA's office.' He paused. 'We've also arrested Lipski and Saanen.' He looked across at Swartski. 'Do you want to cooperate or do you want us to do it the hard way?' Logan reached inside his jacket and pulled out a folded paper. 'I have got a warrant. It's signed and dated but I haven't filled in the charges yet. It could mean the difference between five and twenty years.'

Swartski was silent for several minutes and then he said quietly, 'What do you mean by cooperate?'

'I mean exactly what you think I mean. I want the lot. Names, places, controls, payments. The whole bag of tricks.'

'You'd better charge me.'

'That's OK by me if that's how you want to play it.'

Logan stood up and Curtis took the handcuffs out of his jacket pocket. As Swartski held out his hands he said, 'Can I make a phone call to my sister?'

Logan smiled. 'Your only sister's in Dublin, my friend. And she doesn't want to know you. The man at the United Nations won't want to know you. You won't get any help from the Embassy either. You're on your own now.'

Swartski shrugged. 'Just charge me or get the hell out of my apartment.'

Logan turned to Curtis. 'Take him in and book him.'

Curtis had booked Swartski in at one of the downtown precincts and had made sure that Swartski was put in with the drunks and drug addicts. The police captain had been warned earlier of the scenario and didn't like it. He liked it less as the hours passed. He had phoned City headquarters and they'd told him to cooperate but not to get involved. It was six a.m. when Swartski had had enough and asked for Curtis.

Curtis didn't go in the cage. Swartski was standing there, his clothes covered with vomit and his jacket sleeve torn from the shoulder.

'What is it, Swartski?'

'I want my rights. I want an attorney.'

Curtis said, 'No way,' and turned to walk away. Swartski shouted to him, his hands on the bars, shaking them. 'Let me out of here.' Curtis stopped and turned. 'Are you ready to answer our questions?'

'Not here. I'm not a criminal. You know that.'

'I'll take you to our offices provided you cooperate.'

'Answer questions, yes. Cooperate, I don't have to.'

A police car took them both to the underground garage of the block and they went up to the top floor in the service elevator. Logan was waiting for them in the outside office and he took over, leading Swartski into a small room. The room was comfortably furnished and Logan pointed at an armchair. When Swartski was sitting, Logan pulled up a chair facing him.

'Mr Swartski,' he said quietly, 'I've been through this situation dozens of times. It's like seeing reruns of old films on TV for me.' He paused. 'But for you it's different. I'd like you to have the benefit of my experience. There's only two ways these things can end. The first way you get yourself an attorney. Then you go on trial. You get sentenced and you appeal. The appeal is rejected and you do fifteen, twenty years depending on the judge's views as to the extent of your guilt and the consequences to national security of what you've done. Right?' He paused again for several moments. 'The second way, you cooperate. And when it comes to the indictment we remember that. You go on trial. You get five to seven and that's the end of it.

'Now you might wonder why we ask you to cooperate. If we've got enough evidence to indict you – and I assure you we have – why not just go ahead and get the maximum sentence the law provides? Well, let's just say we do that. You'll rot in jail but that won't help or hinder me.

'But if you cooperate I've benefited, the Agency has benefited. We've filled in the little holes in the fabric. We can repair some of the damage. If we can do that with your help then we bear it in mind. Whatever happens you can do no more harm to this country. Your thing is over – finished. It doesn't help the Agency that you spend fifteen years in jail. Maybe it discourages a few of your friends from trying the same game. But nothing more than that. Do you understand?'

Swartski nodded. 'You ask that I implicate other people, is that it?'

'You'll find that most of them are already implicated. We know who they are. What they've been doing. They will be arrested too. Some of them are already in custody as of last night. The ones who matter we know already. There may be minor figures we don't know. They are not all that important. But it helps us complete the picture.'

'How long will it take?'

'If you cooperate, Mr Swartski, we're in a different ballgame. We shall be *talking* to you, very different from interrogating you.'

'What kind of things do you want to know?'

Logan knew it was the breakthrough. 'Before we talk let me have my people get you a change of clothes. And we can get you a drink and a meal. I'll send in Mr Curtis. Tell him what clothes you want from your apartment.'

The two seven-storey blocks were officially known as FANX I and II. Friendship Annex I and II. So called because they were so close to the Washington–Baltimore Friendship International Airport. To their disgruntled occupants they were known as the Friendship Leper Colony because of their physical separation from the main NSA complex and their lack of facilities.

One of the most constant complaints was the state of the parking lot, known as Cardiac Hill. It was frequently ankle deep in water because of an inefficient drainage system.

It was seven p.m. when Jimbo and Kirsten walked gingerly between the night shift's cars to the red Ferrari. Jimbo was just unlocking the car doors when the two men walked over from the grey Mustang. Jimbo nodded to them and flattened himself against the car to let them pass. But they didn't pass, and one of them moved round to the other side of the car where Kirsten was standing.

The older man on Jimbo's side said, 'Are you Mr Vick? Mr James Vick?'

'Yeah,' Jimbo nodded, 'do I know you?'

'I guess not. I'm FBI. I'd be grateful if you and your wife would come with me and my colleague.'

'What is this – a security check?'

'Kind of. We'll go back in the building if you'll both follow me.'

Jimbo looked at Kirsten and shrugged. They walked together, the FBI man leading the way, the other FBI man following.

They were shown into an office at the far end of one of the corridors and when they were inside the older man introduced himself and his colleague. 'I'm Rademacher and that's Mr Pekkanan.' Rademacher smiled amiably at Kirsten and said, 'He speaks Finnish if that might help you, ma'am.'

Jimbo said aggressively, 'My wife's family are from Sweden not Finland.'

Rademacher nodded and smiled. 'You don't say. They all sound the same to me.'

Jimbo was surprised at the anger in Kirsten's voice when she said sharply, 'I'd like to see your documents. Both of you.'

They both held out their identity cards and Kirsten looked at them carefully. Not the quick glance that most people gave them. She looked up at Rademacher. 'What's the big idea? This isn't a routine check, is it?'

'What makes you think that, ma'am?'

'Routine checks are done by Agency security men. Not FBI.'

'Well, we had a few questions we wanted to put to you both. Is that agreeable to you, ma'am?'

'I want to have my attorney here. I want to phone him. Now. Before I answer any questions.'

Rademacher raised his eyebrows. 'D'you think that's really necessary, ma'am?' He added slowly, 'At this stage?'

'Yes I do. Where is the nearest phone?'

'Well, now,' Rademacher said, 'how about you take the lady to the phone, Pekkanan, and I'll talk to Mr Vick while we're waiting. No hurry.'

Jimbo said, 'My wife stays here. Let's get that clear.'

'I'll go with him, Jimbo. You stay here.'

'Who're you gonna phone? Do you want my guy's number? He's in Baltimore.'

'No. Leave it to me.'

She turned, and Jimbo watched her walk back down the corridor with the FBI man. Then he turned to look at Rademacher. 'I'm going to lodge a strong complaint with the director himself first thing tomorrow morning. Nobody has to put up with this sort of thing.'

'How about we both sit down, Mr Vick? Let's have a quiet word together.'

'About what? If it's my work, you should know that it can't be discussed with anyone who hasn't been specially cleared.'

'It's not directly your work, Mr Vick.' He paused. 'I'm afraid it's going to be something of a shock to you.' He looked at Jimbo's face intently as he said quietly, 'We're arresting your wife on charges of espionage, Mr Vick. And I'm holding you on suspicion as an accessory. Does that surprise you?'

'No way. I think you're out of your fucking minds. I'm going to call the director right now.'

As Jimbo stood up Rademacher pushed him gently back onto his chair.

'I know how you must feel, young man. I'd better tell you that your wife has been under surveillance for some time. Long before you came in contact with her. She's not Swedish, she's Finnish. And both her parents are still alive. They live in Helsinki. They're both active communists and her name isn't Swenson, it's Vaara. Kirsten Vaara. She's been working for the KGB ever since she came to the States.'

Jimbo sat stunned. 'I don't believe it,' he said, shaking his head.

'You had no idea of all this? Not even a faint suspicion?'

'I told you. I don't believe it.'

'She never mentioned the name Zak or Zacharia? Or Swartski?'

'No, never. Who are they?'

'He's the next one up the line. He's her controller. Bureau officers arrested him in New York last night.' He paused. 'He's cooperating.' He paused again. 'I think you should too, Mr Vick. It isn't pleasant. But it wasn't very pleasant what they did to you. Stringing you along and all that. We see a lot of it. We get hardened to it. But it's not very nice for the people who've been deceived.' He paused. '*If* they've been deceived.'

'Can I speak to her, alone?' He shrugged helplessly. 'Please.'

'I'm afraid not. She'll be already on her way to our place in Washington. She is under arrest. You're only detained for questioning.'

'You'll be wasting your time questioning me. I don't know anything, and if I did I wouldn't tell you bastards.'

'Let's go, Mr Vick. We've got some paperwork to do before I've finished with you.'

It was the third day of Logan's questioning of Swartski.

'Why did you pick on Vick as the target?'

'We'd only got details of three people working in that area at NSA. He looked the obvious one.'

'Why?'

'The life he led. The teenage chicks. The need to impress women. No relatives in the immediate background to get in the way. No close relationships with other people.'

'Nothing more than that?'

'No. He just looked a suitable target.'

'Where did the girl get her math training?'

'At the university in Helsinki and later at Moscow University.'

'And what was the brief? What were they after?'

'Anything on the use of stochastic math theory as applied to cryptology. How NSA were using it. Their attitude to it. Was it important? Did they see it as a real tool? How far had they got? Applications and results.' Swartski shrugged. 'And after that any information from inside NSA. Names, routines – anything.'

'I couldn't understand why you let it get out of hand and you let her marry Jimbo Vick. Why that?'

'Because a husband doesn't have to testify against a wife.'

'But she married on false pretences. The marriage can be annulled. It's void.'

Swartski shrugged. 'Moscow wanted it that way.'

'Who put together her cover story?'

'Moscow.'

'And her documentation?'

'Moscow, Ottawa and the Embassy in Washington.'

'Who did you pass it on to?'

'Tell me who you think it was and I'll nod if you're right.'

Logan shrugged. 'Let's come back to you. How long have you been working for them?'

'Since Abel set up in New York. After he was arrested I was on my own for a couple of years.'

'And your jewellery business, did they fund that?'

'No way. I built it up myself.'

'Where did you get your radio training?'

'In Toronto.'

'The place over the newspaper shop on Yonge Street?'

'You know about that?'

'Of course.'

Swartski shrugged. 'The radio was only for emergencies. I didn't use it much. I never really mastered it.'

'What other training did you get?'

'I had a few weeks' general training. Surveillance, codes, inks, photographs and procedures.'

'Where was that?'

'In Dresden. I went there to a trade fair. Buying jewellery.'

'What made you offer your services way back?'

'The Rosenberg case.'

'Why that?'

'I thought they had a raw deal. I thought they were framed.'

Logan smiled. 'Another sucker for Moscow's propaganda machine.' He sighed. 'You weren't the only one, my friend. The bleeding hearts department did a good job.'

'You think they were guilty?'

'I know damn well they were.'

'When do we talk about me? What's going to happen to me?'

'The way we've been progressing, Mr Swartski, is going to make a lot of difference to our attitude.'

'What's that mean?'

Logan looked at Swartski's pale face for several moments before he spoke. 'I'm considering asking the Justice Department to offer you immunity if you'd become a State witness. How would you feel about that?' He paused. 'Not that I'm sure they would agree.'

'You mean testifying in open court against them?'

'If we needed it – yes. But it wouldn't just be the Vick couple. It would have to cover your whole operation. The people in New Jersey and San Francisco.' Logan smiled. 'And the girl who works for the AFSAC committee.'

Swartski shifted uneasily in his seat. 'How long have you people been on to me?'

'Right from when you first contacted the KGB man at the Soviet Mission to the UN.'

'So why wait all this time to do something?'

'We wanted to know what they were interested in. If we'd pulled you in before you got going we may not have uncovered your replacement so easily.'

'So you know who my controller is?'

Logan smiled. 'Was, Mr Swartski. Yes, we know. He was deported a few days ago.' Logan stood up. 'Are you comfortable here? Anything you want – magazines, cigarettes or the like?'

Swartski shook his head. 'If I testify what happens to me?'

'We'd take care of you and you would be given a short sentence. A couple of years. But you wouldn't serve any of it.'

'How long have I got to decide?'

'A couple of weeks.'

CHAPTER TWENTY-NINE

They had bundled him through the checkpoint in the Wall at Bornholmer Strasse just after three o'clock in the morning. He had staggered as far as the patch of grass about a hundred and fifty yards away. A railwayman coming off the night shift had found him lying with his head hanging over the gutter. When the police came they assumed he was drunk, but in the van one of them noticed that the man's eyes were wide open but obviously unseeing. They radioed that they were diverting to the emergency service at the hospital.

The young doctor on the emergency detail had checked the man over. He wasn't drunk as they had assumed. The man had been drugged but some sort of alcohol had been poured over his shirt and jacket; there was no alcohol in the blood sample.

They searched the man's clothing and all the pockets were empty. But when they took off his shoes and socks they found a five-pound note and a British Army identity card taped to the sole of his left foot. They phoned the police liaison squad, and an hour later the one remaining German policeman was joined by a uniformed sergeant from the military police SIB detachment.

It was ten o'clock that morning before the man stirred in the hospital bed and an hour later he tried to sit up.

The sergeant leaned over and looked at the man's pale face.

'What's your name, sunbeam?'

The man closed his eyes and shook his head. When he opened his eyes again the sergeant said, 'What you been up to, mate?' He paused. 'You been and gone AWOL, ain't you? Been naughty, eh?'

'Where am I?'

'You're in dock, mate. You been sniffing coke, ain't you?'

The man sat up, running his hands through his lank greasy hair. He looked at the sergeant's face. 'What you done to me?'

'Nothing, mate. I just been playing Florence Nightingale.'

'What happened?'

'You tell me.'

'I don't know what happened. I can't remember.'

A nurse told the sergeant that there was a phone call for him. She plugged in the telephone and he lifted the receiver. 'Turnbull . . . yeah . . . yeah . . . OK.' He replaced the receiver and turned to the man in the bed.

'I'm taking you to the nick, mate. Seems like you've been a very naughty boy. They wanna talk to you.'

'Who?'

'The security boys.'

'I'm a civilian. I'm not in the army.'

The sergeant grinned. ''Course not. You tell 'em.' He paused and looked at the German policeman.

'*Ich* will take him *mit*. To the *Britische polizei*. *Ja*.'

The policeman shrugged. 'He's one of yours, yes?'

The sergeant laughed. 'Yeah. He's one of ours all right.'

Lieutenant O'Hara was twenty-six with red hair and freckles that made him look even younger. His pale blue eyes looked at the notes on his pad and then back at the face of the man sitting on the wooden chair.

'How about we cut out the bullshit? What were you doing in the last six months?'

'I told you. I was working on the black market.'

'What were you flogging?'

'Coffee, cigarettes, blankets. The usual stuff.'

'Tell me your name.'

'I told you twice already.'

'Tell me again.'

'Joseph Steel.'

'Is that the name they told you to use?'

'Who?'

'The Russians.'

'I don't know any Russians.'

The lieutenant slid the greasy ID card from under his pad and handed it to the man on the chair.

'What's that?'

The man looked at it for several seconds and his hand trembled as he handed it back.

'What's gonna happen to me?'

'Depends on how you cooperate.'

'What's that mean?'

'Your name is Arthur Johnson, yes?'

'Yeah.'

'Signalman Johnson?'

'Yes.'

'You went on leave to the UK and you went AWOL and didn't return to your unit?'

'OK.'

'Signalman Johnson. As of now, you are under arrest for the murder of a woman known as Heidi Fischer. Also known as Heidi Johnson. Your common-law wife. You will be taken back to Birmingham and handed over to the civilian police. Do you understand?'

Johnson sighed and nodded. 'Can't we do a deal?'

'About what?'

'I been working for the Russkis. The KGB.'

'Don't come the old soldier with me, Johnson. You're facing a charge of murder. Telling more lies isn't going to help you.'

'I'm an officer of the KGB. Same as you, a lieutenant. Phone 'em up and ask 'em if you don't believe me.'

Lieutenant O'Hara stood up. 'You're out of your fucking mind, Johnson. That's what's wrong with you.'

The Birmingham City police had questioned Johnson for days and on the fifth day they had called in their Special Branch officer. And Johnson had been transferred from Winson Green prison to Wormwood Scrubs and a top security cell. The interrogations were patient, meticulous and probing. Hipwell, the SB interrogator, was an experienced officer and he slowly drew the threads together.

'When you got back to Berlin after your trip to Birmingham, you went through Charlie and contacted your controller. What was his reaction?'

'He was angry. Said I'd no business to make decisions like that without their approval.'

'Then what happened?'

'Two of them interrogated me for weeks. They seemed to think I'd been caught by our lot and sent back in to spy on them.'

'Go on.'

'When they found out about Heidi they seemed satisfied I was OK. But they said I was no use to them any more. They found me a job repairing TV sets. I got me a girlfriend and they found out she was on the game. The police took her and after that I got no protection from the Russians. The chap at the repair shop cut my wages and I told him I'd had enough hassle from all of 'em.'

'Let's go back over when you were at the house in Grunewald. What kind of things did they want from you?'

'Almost anything. Like I told you, even gossip about people interested them. Names and ranks. Home addresses. Jobs. Equipment and routines.'

'Apart from that sort of information, you gave them tapes and other things. What was on the tapes?'

'No idea. I just took anything that was easy to take. They wanted anything.'

'Did anybody help you to do this? Anyone else at the house?'

'No. I never told a soul.'

'The disk you changed. How did it get inside? Did you take the book in?'

'No way. I wouldn't have dared. They just told me it was in the book in the library – and it was there. I changed it over and destroyed the old one.'

'How did you destroy it?'

'I burned it in the toilet and flushed it down the bog.'

'Have you any idea who put the disk in the book?'

'No.'

Johnson shrugged as if he thought it was stupid to think he might know. But it was one of the many things that Hipwell went back to again and again.

CHAPTER THIRTY

Apart from the centre of the city, Massey knew little of Paris but his father had often talked about the rue Mouffetard where he had lived for a short time during the war, before the Paris networks had been broken up. His father had made it seem a romantic street and enthused about its raffish inhabitants as being the only real French people in the city.

When he asked at the patisserie the old lady told him of two apartments that were available in the vicinity, one in rue Mouffetard itself.

He walked from the bottom of the hill by the church, up the steep incline of the narrow bustling street until it became the rue Descartes. The rows of stalls made the street even narrower. He turned back and walked slowly down the hill turning into the passage des Patriarches where the landlord had a workshop near the public baths. The old man had looked him over and only reluctantly agreed to show him the rooms he had to rent.

Massey followed the old man to a doorway between an ironmongery and a dilapidated hotel. The wooden door had to be lifted on its hinges before it would open. The rooms were on the top floor and were better than he had expected. There was one large living-room lit by two mansard windows. The floor was polished wood and the furnishings were sparse but sufficient. A low divan bed, a wardrobe, a variety of mahogany cupboards, wicker chairs and a circular table. The bathroom and kitchen were small but clean. The old man explained that the room had been used as a studio by a painter who had moved to the Midi. The rent was reasonable and when Massey had offered three months' rent in advance the old man had accepted.

For several days he spent his mornings making notes of the things he planned to do and lists of the kind of contacts that he wanted. In the afternoons he explored the area where he lived, and checked the locations of various government offices in the city itself. At night, he ate locally in small restaurants and went early to bed. It was a week before he contacted the Embassy.

For a week he read batches of files from the Embassy on their last twelve months' work. Compared with his operation in Berlin it was a shambles. Not much more than the kind of gossip to be picked up at the usual rounds of Embassy cocktail parties. It was almost all political with very little about the French intelligence services. There were the minutes of monthly liaison meetings with NATO intelligence representatives that all too obviously showed that nobody divulged any information to anyone else. The only original information concerned French military intelligence which was only barely the province of SIS. The military attaché at the Embassy was responsible for armed forces' intelligence.

There was only one really experienced SIS man at the Embassy. An old hand named Morrow who was obviously trying to ride out his last couple of years before retirement without rocking any boats. And that meant keeping on the right side of His Excellency. Not sending in reports that conflicted with the Embassy's own evaluations. Not offending the French. Not offending anybody. Not doing the job. Maybe it was time to get him transferred back to London.

What surprised Massey most was the lack of information on the French intelligence service, SDECE. Its official title – Service de Documentation Extérieure et de Contre-Espionage – was typical of its obscurity. There seemed little information on its staff and even less on where it was housed and how it operated. He decided that his best source of useful information was the Americans.

The senior CIA man in Paris was Autenowski and the Polish connection had worked its usual magic. They had met the second time in the bar at the Ritz.

'Tell me what you want to know, Jan.'

'Anything about SDECE.'

'Anything?' The American looked surprised.

'Yes.'

The CIA man smiled. 'Well, first it's not called the SDECE any more. There was a big shake-up when Mitterand became president. They call it the DGSE these days – Direction Générale de la Securité Extérieure.'

'How long ago was the change?'

'Six weeks, seven weeks, something like that.'

'What else has changed?'

Autenowski grinned. 'Nothing. Absolutely nothing. Sometimes they report to the Minister of Defence, sometimes the Interior, and in some cases direct to the President.'

'Is Bourget still with them?'

'You bet. Bourget's a survivor. He applied for a transfer to internal security – DST – but they wouldn't have him.'

'What's he doing?'

'Taking bribes, screwing young girls – same as he always did.' The CIA man laughed. 'I'm only kidding. He's working in their Soviet section. God knows why. He doesn't speak Russian or have any other qualfications that I know of.'

'Where does he work?'

'They've got a floor at one of the buildings belonging to the Ministry of Agriculture. Supposed to be a secret cover but when the buses stop there the ticket guy calls out, "Spy palace". Everybody knows so it doesn't matter.'

'Can I trade with you for a few months?'

Autenowski shrugged. 'Depends what you want and what you've got.'

'I want to start building up a detailed picture. Names, ranks, responsibilities. Who matters. What kind of current operations they have. Names of informants.'

The American smiled. 'Names of informants you won't get. You know that. The rest I can give you.' He paused. 'What do I get?'

'What do you want?'

'Your assessment of our operation in Berlin. An indication of what your mission is over here and . . . let's call it . . . future cooperation.'

'That's OK by me.'

'How about we meet in ten days' time? You've got my home address. Let's have lunch together. Say a week from Wednesday. The twelfth. Noon at my place.'

Massey had sent a note to Chambers on the change of name of the SDECE and had received a memo back in the bag asking if he was sure of the information. He had ignored it. Bit it angered him that they hadn't known of the change much earlier.

For a week he had worked on his assessment of the CIA operation in Berlin. He typed it out slowly on a portable borrowed from the Embassy. He had no intention of using Embassy facilities. He was going to build up his own efficient unit as soon as he could justify it. The indifference of London to intelligence out of Paris amazed him. There were Caribbean islands that got more attention.

Rademacher stood to one side as the warder unlocked the cell door. As he went inside he turned and said, 'I'll buzz you when I want you. On Channel 16. OK?'

The warder nodded and Rademacher turned to look at Jimbo Vick as the key turned in the lock behind him.

The young man was sitting on the edge of the regulation bed, his arms folded, his elbows on his thighs, his head bowed.

'How are you this morning?'

Jimbo made no reply. Rademacher pulled up the wooden chair and sat down, putting the newspaper he was carrying on the floor beside his feet.

'I phoned your father, Jimbo. Like you asked. He's fixing a lawyer for you. A local guy. He's pretty good.'

Jimbo looked up and Rademacher noticed the pale, drawn face and the bloodshot eyes.

'Is the lawyer going to act for Kirsten as well?'

'She's got her own lawyer.'

'Who is he?'

'His name's Theodore S. Lewin. You ever heard of him?'

Jimbo shook his head. 'No.'

'He's from New York.'

'Is he any good?'

'Yeah. He's a very tricky operator. Specializes in defending people facing espionage and treason charges.'

'Have you seen her recently?'

'I saw her this morning.'

'Did she send any message for me?'

'I'm afraid not.'

'Did you give her my message?'

'I certainly did.'

'What did she say?'

'I'm afraid her mind's pretty occupied at the moment.'

'Why are you doing this to us? Just tell me why.'

'Have you got any idea why we should be doing anything?'

'None. I swear it. Neither of us has done a goddamn thing.'

'You thought she was a nice Swedish girl?'

'She was.' He paused. 'She is.'

'And like all pretty Swedish girls she just happened to be a very talented mathematician?'

Jimbo shrugged. 'Why not, for God's sake? You don't have to be a Plain Jane these days to have a talent.'

'Why do you think she told you – and everyone else – that she was Swedish when in fact she's Finnish?'

'It's academic. She's an American citizen. Where she comes from doesn't matter.'

'She's not an American citizen, and she never was.'

'She is now. She's my wife.'

'She's not, Jimbo. She used forged and fraudulent documents. She was never given citizenship and she never applied for it. The papers she used were made in Moscow.'

'You can prove that? Because you'll have to. Not just speculate. Not just fish around.'

Rademacher sighed. 'I'm not fishing around, Jimbo. Forensic have established the forgery. So has an independent expert. The DA's office has accepted it.'

'And what does that prove? There's thousands of spics with no documents at all coming over every week. Are *they* all spies?'

'Some of them are.' He paused. 'What would you have done if you'd found out yourself that she was spying for the Russians?'

'I'd have told her she was crazy.'

'Would you have reported it to the FBI or NSA security?'

'No way. She's my wife and I love her.'

'Despite how she's used you?'

'How has she used me?'

'Deceived you about her nationality and her background. Persuaded you to employ her on highly secret work. Married you to make sure she's going to keep her job at NSA. What more do you want?'

'She married me because I love her and she loves me.'

'Are you sure she loves you, Jimbo?'

There were tears on Jimbo's cheeks and his voice faltered as he said, 'You're a real bastard, Rademacher. A real bastard.'

Rademacher bent down, picked up the newspaper and handed it to Jimbo Vick.

'Read that, Jimbo.'

The headline said, 'Blonde held as Red spy', and alongside was a picture of Kirsten that he had never seen before. It appeared to have been taken by the Kennedy Memorial in the cemetery at Arlington. There were three columns of copy under the photograph, starting off in bold type.

> Acting district director of the Immigration Service Joseph H. Ryan issued the following statement from his office yesterday evening. 'Whereas from evidence submitted to me, it appears that the alien Kirsten Vaara alias Kirsten Swenson or Kirsten Vick who entered this country from an unknown point from Canada during 1980, is within the United States in violation of the immigration laws thereof, and is therefore being taken into custody as authorized by section 242 of the Immigration and Nationality Act.' When asked if other charges were to be brought ADD Ryan indicated that the arrest had been made by special agents of the FBI and that further charges were imminent.
>
> The beautiful young blonde woman was arrested as she left her place of employment which is believed to be the NSA HQ at Fort Meade. Inquiries indicate that the young woman was employed on highly secret mathematical research in a high security section headed by James Vick, the son of Joshua Vick of. . .

Jimbo threw down the paper angrily. 'I'll sue those bastards – and you, Rademacher. It's time somebody taught you zombies a lesson.'

Rademacher stood up, pressing the alert button on his radio timer.

'Is there anything you want, Jimbo?'

'I want to see Kirsten. Alone.'

Rademacher hesitated and then, as the warder unlocked the door, he said quietly, 'I'll see what I can do.'

Pekkanan reached over and took the sachet of sugar from the saucer of Rademacher's cup, tore it open and emptied the brown crystals into his coffee. As he stirred it slowly he said, 'She's a real tough cookie, Pete. Cold as ice. She's a real Soviet. Well trained, well motivated and ready to open those long legs for Moscow.'

'What makes you say that?'

Pekkanan shrugged. 'She made the offer. That and a life pension and a *dacha* at Peredelkino.'

'Was it recorded what she said?'

'I assume so. No reason why they should have switched off.' He grinned. 'I played along with it for a bit. It'll liven up the court when they play the tapes.'

'He wants to see her.'

'Why, for Christ's sake?'

'He loves her. And he thinks she loves him.'

'How can a guy who understands all that way-out math be so stupid? That little gal has never loved anybody in her life.'

'He's not the first man to be fooled by a pretty girl.'

'Just tell him he's wasting his time. She's never mentioned him. Remember when you gave her that message from him that he loves her? She just rolled her eyes up to heaven and went on talking.'

'Maybe he'd cooperate if he knew she didn't love him. That she'd fooled him deliberately.'

'I think the poor bastard knows in his heart that she fooled him. If he wasn't party to it the only help he can give us is on dates and times when she was out of town.'

'He's going to take it bad. Real bad.'

'So what? Shouldn't have been such a sucker in the first place.'

'How could he have known?'

'What made him think a dame like that was interested in him. What the hell's he got that she'd want?' He grinned. 'She'd have made Miss Universe if she'd tried. She could have had some millionaire if she'd been straight. Not a little hick like Jimbo Vick.'

'What do you think?'

'Let him see her and we can record it. She might give something away. Let me work something out.'

They had blindfolded Jimbo for the journey. It took about an hour and he had no idea where they were taking him. But all that mattered was that he was going to see her. He felt loose gravel under his feet as he got out of the car and the two agents took an arm each, warning him of three steps. He thought he heard the click of a magazine being clipped into a gun. They walked him slowly and carefully down a long corridor and he stood, held by Rademacher, as a metal door was unlocked.

He was trembling as the FBI man untied the blindfold and he blinked in the bright lights as Rademacher said, 'You've got fifteen minutes, Mr Vick. If you want to leave before then just press the bell on the table.'

As the door clanged to he looked around the room, and then he saw her. She was sitting in an armchair in the linen suit they had bought in Washington, her long legs crossed, her blonde hair tied in a ponytail with a wide black ribbon. And he felt paralyzed at the look on her face. She pointed to a chair facing her. 'Do sit down, Jimbo. You can take it that everything we say is being recorded.'

His throat was dry as he swallowed with difficulty. 'It isn't, Kirsten, they gave me their word.'

The blue eyes looked at him as she said, 'Don't be such a fool, man. Why do you think the lights are so bright? There'll be a video camera as well as a recorder.'

His eyes were on her face, pleading. 'Just tell me you love me, Kirstie. You don't need to say anything else.'

'Jimbo. Just listen to what I say.' She looked up at the light fitting on the ceiling. 'And you bastards listen too.' She turned and looked at him again. 'You don't know anything, you weren't involved in anything. We are not married. I don't love you.' She nodded and said, 'Now you can just press that bell.'

There were tears streaming down his face. 'You did love me, Kirsten, you did, didn't you?'

The blue eyes looked at him coldly, 'I don't love you, man. And I never loved you. Now just leave me alone. Just get out of my life.'

'Why, Kirstie? Why did you do it to me?'

'Piss off, for Christ's sake. You make me sick. You creep.' She leaned forward and pressed the bell on the table.

On the journey back Jimbo Vick sat bent forward, his face in his hands, sobbing as if he would never stop.

Jimbo Vick had refused to see his parents and refused to see the lawyer his father had provided to defend him.

Rademacher intended to give him a few days to settle down and then go over the dates and times when Kirsten had been meeting Swartski and the Russian.

Two days after Jimbo's meeting with Kirsten, there was a call for Rademacher at two in the morning. Jimbo Vick had tried to kill himself, slashing both his wrists. But the medics said that he was OK. He'd recover.

Pekkanan and another Finnish-speaking FBI man interrogated Kirsten Vaara for hours every day for seven weeks, aware that their time was running out. The girl was aware of it too. More acid in her replies, more defiant in her attitude as the days went by.

Rademacher had warned Pekkanan of his suspicions right from the start. What made him suspicious was the fact that the actual arrest of the girl was made by the Immigration and Nationality Service and the indictment made under the IN Act. Why hadn't she been charged with the capital offence of Soviet espionage? Rademacher had his suspicions confirmed when the girl was flown without any publicity to Hanover and taken by car to the border control point at Helmstedt. Only a handful of people would have heard of the man who was exchanged for her but both the Russians and the Americans reckoned that they had the better bargain in the deal. Kirsten Vaara, with a new identity and background and using the name Susie McCarthy, is now working in Perth, Australia, as personal assistant to the president of an electronics firm. Her boyfriend is a middle-aged officer in the Perth office of ASIO, Australia's security service.

CHAPTER THIRTY-ONE

They had met at a café near the St-Michel Metro station and as Autenowski went off to make a telephone call Massey leafed through the file of papers that the CIA man had handed to him.

When Autenowski came back, he gave the American his evaluation of their operation in West Berlin.

'I'll look at it later, Jan. But, briefly, what was your opinion?'

'They do a good job, Bill. No doubt about that.'

'No criticisms?'

'Not criticism exactly, but I think they're overexposed so far as the public is concerned.'

'In what way?'

Massey smiled. 'They're a bit too American. They behave like they're at home in the States where you have at least a public face.'

'What's wrong with that?'

'Well, it's OK in your own country where, on the whole, the public support you. But it makes for problems in Europe, especially Berlin, where all other intelligence services are very much hidden.' Massey paused. 'It makes your guys very easy targets. Not just physical targets but too easily identified by people who are up to no good.'

Autenowski smiled. 'I'll read your papers and maybe we can talk again.'

'Thanks for your material. It looks very generous.'

'It's not. It's just routine stuff.'

'We've got so little it'll help me get a grip on things.'

'You asked about informants. Are you interested still?'

'Very interested.'

'OK. Let's put the cards on the table face up. I've got a girlfriend. She's a reporter. She's just lost her job. She's been covering the Paris scene – politics, scandals and all that for a couple of years. I'd gladly employ her if she wasn't my girlfriend. She'll keep you far better informed than your Embassy people can do. She knows the inside stuff, not just the gossip.' He paused. 'If you're interested, I'll set up a meeting.'

'How soon?'

'This evening if you want.'

'Where? When?'

Autenowski smiled. 'Ritz bar at seven, OK?'

'Fine. I'll be there.'

If he hadn't already been told that Anne-Marie Loussier was a journalist, Massey would never have guessed. In her late twenties she was both pretty and elegant. As Massey and Autenowski talked Massey was aware of the girl's grey eyes studying his face, and when she joined in the discussion her voice was as quiet as her views were forthright. Mitterand had come in like a lion but the facts of life and the French were going to turn him into a lamb. She quoted current policies and compared them with the last time they had been attempted by a socialist government. They hadn't worked in the old days, they would be even less effective now.

She knew all the section and department heads of French intelligence personally. Their backgrounds, their responsibilities, and their capabilities. She judged them to be more efficient than they were painted. At least in certain areas.

She met him the next day and he hired her. No contract, no specific duties beyond keeping him informed of the actualities of French policies. He phoned or met her briefly most days and the reports that he was sending back to London were received in silence. But from time to time he was asked for further information on various points and it became obvious that his reports were at least being studied.

She joked with him about his own indifference to Paris outside the fifth *arrondissement* and his lack of knowledge of French people in general. She and Autenowski took him to La Madeleine and the Louvre and were embarrassed and almost amused by his lack of interest. He sat bored for an hour at a nightclub that Autenowski took him to one evening.

It was Anne-Marie who first found something that impressed him – a Polish pâté at Michael Guérard's shop in the place de la Madeleine. In the glamorous shop's cafeteria, Massey came alive as he talked with the Polish waiter.

Morrow from the Embassy brought round the sealed message and handed it to Massey together with the special receipt book. Massey had been about to leave and after he had signed the book he walked back into his rooms.

The message was so cryptic and uninformative that it seemed hardly to warrant the top diplomatic code that had been used. He was to get back to London immediately and contact Chambers. He was not to communicate by any means until he was in London. Just go.

He telephoned Chambers from the immigration office at Gatwick and his call was diverted to the duty officer. He was to go straight to the safe-house in Ebury Street.

An hour later he checked that the small light was on over the bottom bellpush and when he pressed the upper button the door opened immediately. The thin middle-aged woman who everybody knew as Amelia nodded to him without smiling and stood aside to let him into the narrow hallway. Amelia pointed to the stairs and Chambers was waiting for him on the top landing. He looked relieved to see Massey who followed him into the sitting-room with its old-fashioned, chintz-covered three-piece suite.

'Have you eaten, Jan?'

'I ate on the plane.'

Chambers sighed. 'Let's sit down.' When they were seated Chambers said, 'I apologize for all the mystery but . . .' he waved a hand dismisively '. . . I'd better explain straight away.' Chambers looked intently at Massey's face. 'Have you got any idea what it's all about?'

'Not the slightest idea. Should I have?'

'No, of course not.' He paused before he said quietly, 'It's Kuznetsov. He wants to see you. Urgently. I think he's in trouble.'

'How did he contact you?'

'A call-box phone call to my home. Late last night.'

'How do you know it was K?'

'He used your code-phrase. The emergency one.'

'What did he say?'

'As near as I can remember he gave me the code-phrase twice and when I responded he just said, "Stockholm. Amarantan Hotel. Urgent. Must be my friend."'

'What makes you think he's in trouble?'

'The crude contact and the fact that he contacted me not you. He probably didn't know where you were and was desperate.'

'Is your home traffic still monitored and taped?'

'Yes. I had the voice print cleared. It was K all right.'

Massey shrugged. 'I'd better get on my way then.'

'I've brought you a passport and Swedish kroner and I've had our people book you a room in the passport name at the hotel. We paid a week in advance and they'll hold the room for the week. I had to leave it loose in case you were out of touch in Paris.'

'Who's "we"?'

'I don't understand.'

'Who's the "we" who paid the hotel and booked the room?'

'The travel company.'

'Our own one?'

'Of course.'

'Has there been anything strange out of Berlin in the last few weeks?'

'No. Nothing.'

'What about Moscow?'

'The usual stuff about internal tensions in the Politburo but nothing really new.'

'And the KGB?'

'No personnel upheavals so far as we know. And nothing at K's level or in his sphere of interest.'

'Have we got any anti-KGB operations going on against the KGB that could affect the top boys?'

'Nothing in Europe. Something rather touchy in the Middle East and something in South America – a bit of leftover business from the Falklands days. But none of them in K's manor.'

'How can I contact you from Stockholm?'

'D'you know Marsden?'

'Vaguely.'

'You can contact him through the Embassy. Ask for the cultural attaché's office. I'll warn him but I'll use the name on your passport.'

'What is it?'

'Mathews. Edward Mathews. Ted Mathews.'

'Are there any flights tonight?'

'There's a Scandinavian Air Services flight to Copenhagen and you could go over on the ferry to Malmö and take an internal flight to Stockholm. There's a shuttle that calls at Göteborg and goes on to Stockholm. I can get a car to take you to Gatwick.'

'OK. I'll do that. Where's the passport and the cash?'

'It's on the little table. And there's an American Express card in the passport name. Check it all over while I phone Facilities.'

Most of the passenger facilities at Kastrup airport were closed, but it was two hours before the first ferry left Copenhagen for Malmö and Massey decided to stay at the airport while he was waiting. He could take an SAS bus into the city and a taxi to the ferry and allow an hour for the journey.

He put a 10 kroner coin into the machine, opened the door, took out the Fanta and the 3 kroner change, and walked over to the almost empty café area. He wondered afterwards if it was the near-medical cleanliness of the airport building that had started his train of thought. Floors, shops, toilets, ticket counters, everything was spotless, and he wondered how Scandinavian governments had managed to instil this orderliness and cleanliness into their people. Or maybe it was the other way around. But whatever its roots the impression it created on foreigners was of orderliness. Not just in outward and physical things, but an orderliness of mind and character. They were sane, stable people, and it showed.

As he sipped the drink and absorbed the atmosphere he started thinking about his own life. There was no orderliness there. For the first time in a long time he looked at his life from the outside and there was nothing about it that he liked. He had no roots. He belonged nowhere. He had no home or relationship to which he could retreat from his work as other men did. His mind went to Chambers and others like him. They kept office hours, they had homes and families. And they used men like him as if they were born to wander rootless from place to place, relying on the initial glamour of the job. The knowing what went on in the world behind the scenes. The follies and greed of well-known people. The machinations of statesmen and governments. The unexpurgated history of the times that would never appear on the record. The feeling of power and superiority. And when all that became no more than routine, there were the incentives of promotion and approval, and the self-assurance that came from experience.

Massey had never been prone to hero worship but he had respected the experience and knowledge of the top men like Chambers who headed the various sections of SIS. Yet there was something about their meeting at the safe-house that he resented. He had been vaguely conscious of the resentment at the time, but in the brightly lit, clinical atmosphere of Kastrup it seemed suddenly of prime importance. It was, perhaps, the taking for granted that he could be pulled out of Paris at a moment's notice and shuffled off to Stockholm without any thought of whether it was convenient to him. Chambers knew, of course, that he had no wife, no family, so it was rational enough for him to assume that he was mobile and constantly available. But what Massey suddenly resented was that Chambers and the rest of them didn't care that he had no background. Never wondered if he was happy or unhappy with his lot. He was just Massey, a senior man who could be moved around the chessboard to cover any emergency that arose. No problems of wife, children and schools, houses and mortgages. If they thought of him in personal terms it would be as their wild half-Slav, footloose and fancy-free, living the life of Riley and always a blonde in tow. There were some who actually envied him his freedom from emotional ties.

He heard a call on the loudspeaker system asking for an official to go to see the Met officer, and looked at his watch. He gathered up his canvas holdall and walked down to the bus stop. The indicator showed a bus leaving in ten minutes and he bought a ticket and took a seat at the back of the bus. He wondered what Kuznetsov wanted and his mind switched back to his work. He smiled to himself as he thought of what must have been Chambers's embarrassment as he responded to the emergency code-phrase. Using Kuznetsov's nickname, the Moscow Tiger, as a base, Massey had chosen two lines from William Blake's poem as code and response. Kuznetsov's line, 'What immortal hand or eye', was mild enough, but the awkward, non-rhyming 'Dare frame thy fearful symmetry' would not have come easily to Chambers's lips.

They had booked the room at the Amarantan in Massey's own name but he had not been asked for his passport. At the reception desk he filled in his real name and the cover address that he had been given in London and was given a room in the executive tower. There was a punched-hole coded plastic card instead of a key and he let himself into his room. It was just ten o'clock.

When he had unpacked his holdall he walked down to the hotel foyer and checked the message board. There were no messages for anyone with the initial M. He bought a couple of English paperbacks and went back to his room.

It was almost six o'clock when the telephone rang. No code-word but he recognized Kuznetsov's voice. He sounded breathless, as if he had been running.

'There's a gas station opposite the Soviet Embassy. Ten o'clock tonight . . . yes?'

'OK. I'll be there.'

And Kuznetsov had hung up.

Most of the embassies were clustered together in the same area but the Soviet Embassy was well away from the centre of Stockholm. It stood back from the main road, just visible through the big wrought-iron gates, half hidden by tall trees and a grassy mound that had been thrown up on the right-hand side and hid most of the building itself. There were lights on behind the glass façade but none of the social bustle of cars and visitors that usually went on at other embassies.

Massey slowed the hire car, saw the gas station and turned right towards a tall tower block and a block of offices or flats. There were empty parking spaces and he backed the Volvo in carefully and switched off the lights. It was nine forty-five p.m.

At nine fifty-five Massey walked towards the gas station. He didn't know whether Kuznetsov would be arriving by car or on foot but whichever way he came he would be visible from the glass-fronted kiosk at the side of the petrol pumps. The long yellow fascia board above the kiosk carried the Shell logo and the door was half open as he walked inside. He bought a packet of cigarettes and used up time choosing one of the cheap lighters from a display board. As he paid for the goods he saw the grey Mercedes draw up at the pumps. The driver got out. He was alone and it was Kuznetsov. He heard him ask in German for the car to be filled and Massey walked slowly down the side street to stand, lighting a cigarette, beside a large white concrete tub overflowing with geraniums.

A few minutes later the Mercedes drew away from the pumps heading towards him. It stopped in the shadows about twenty yards away. Massey walked slowly towards the car and when the passenger door opened he slid inside.

The Russian spoke very quietly. 'I'm in trouble, Massey. I need to talk to you.'

'Where can we meet?'

'I'm at a meeting with Swedish officials at the offices of the security services tomorrow. The meeting should finish at lunchtime. I could come to your room at the hotel at about half-past one.'

'That's OK. I'll be waiting for you.'

Kuznetsov had not looked at Massey while he was speaking, he just stared ahead into the darkness. But Massey could see the tension on the Russian's face.

'It's not that simple, Massey. I may need more than just talking.'

'Tell me what you need and you'll get it.'

The Russian was silent for several seconds and then he said softly, 'I may need to get away. Tomorrow or the next day.'

'You mean . . .' Massey hesitated, choosing his words carefully '. . . you mean, leave permanently?'

'Better to say what you were going to say – defect.'

'Whatever it is you want, it will be done.'

'Is that a promise?'

'Absolutely.'

'No matter what my reason is for leaving?'

'No matter what.'

'Even murder?'

'No matter what. That's a promise.'

'I must go. They'll be timing me.'

'I'll be in my room all morning. Waiting for you.'

Massey got out of the car and pushed the door to quietly. The Russian backed the car and Massey stood watching as it crossed the main road and waited for the uniformed guard to open the Embassy gates.

It was just after one o'clock when the knock came at his door. Massey jumped up from his chair and opened the door. Kuznetsov's face was pale with the skin drawn tight over his prominent cheekbones, but his eyes looked calmer than they had the previous evening.

There was only one armchair in the room and Massey pointed to it and sat on the edge of the bed.

'How long have you got?'

Kuznetsov shrugged. 'Several hours. Whatever it takes.'

'What's the problem?'

'There's a lot of problems, Jan.'

'Tell me.'

'What do you know about Bourget?'

Massey shrugged. 'French intelligence. Wild. Not very efficient. He was in Berlin when I was there.'

'Do you think he would use blackmail?'

'I'm sure he would.'

'He was blackmailing me. Threatening to expose me unless I became a double agent for him.'

'He knew nothing about your relationship with us. I swear it. Only Chambers and I know anything.'

'I know. He wasn't blackmailing me about that.'

'What was he using?'

'D'you remember about a year ago the Moscow Symphony Orchestra visited Paris to give four concerts and one of their players asked the French for asylum?'

'No. I don't remember it.'

'The man's name was Abramov. The leader of the orchestra. One of the finest violinists in the Soviet Union.'

'Why did he defect?'

'He was a man in his sixties. While they were in Paris he met a very pretty young French girl. He fell in love with her. Wanted to marry her. He spoke to friends. The friends contacted the authorities and eventually he was interviewed by a security officer. The officer happened to be Bourget. The French Foreign Ministry had already decided to give asylum to Abramov and the interview with Bourget was really a formality, for the sake of diplomatic protocol.

'But Bourget isn't a diplomat. He's a lout. And he asked Abramov what he could offer in return for asylum. The Russian protested that he was a musician and knew nothing of politics or state secrets. Bourget told him to go away and think about it overnight and see him again the next day. Abramov was panic-stricken and didn't sleep at all that night.

'When he saw Bourget the next day, he told him that he only knew one KGB officer but he did know something about the man that was compromising. To Abramov's surprise Bourget was delighted with his offering. It seemed that the KGB officer was the son of a couple Abramov had known years ago. They had played music together before Abramov became well known. The compromising information was that the KGB man's mother was a Jewess. This was something that the man had never revealed to the authorities. There were reasons why it was possible for them not to know. Innocent reasons. Stemming from ignorance, not deceit.'

'Who was the KGB man?'

Kuznetsov shrugged. 'The KGB man was me.'

For long moments Massey sat in silence then he said quietly, 'What did Bourget do about it?'

'It took him a long time but eventually he contacted me when I was on a visit to East Berlin. A message hinting that he knew something that could ruin my career, and a place and time to contact him. The message scared me. Not just what was in it but the fact that it was in plain language, no code, in French.'

'Was the rendezvous his place in West Berlin?'

Kuznetsov looked surprised. 'How did you know?'

'I'll tell you later. What happened when you met him?'

'I met him three times. The first time I told him he was bluffing, that he had no proof of his wild statements. The second time he showed me a notarized statement from Abramov about my parents. The third time was to tell me what he wanted.'

'Was it money or information?'

'Money. I think he'd realized that there was not only no chance of me defecting or turning but that I might take steps to have him eliminated. He was happy to settle for money.'

'Did you pay him?'

'I told him I'd think about it and pointed out there were things I knew about him that would interest his superiors in Paris.'

'How much did he want?'

'Thirty thousand US dollars.' The Russian smiled wryly. 'He was kind enough to offer to let me pay it in four equal quarterly payments over a year.'

Massey smiled. 'Always a gentleman was Bourget.' He looked at Kuznetsov. 'So what else has happened to worry you?'

The Russian took a deep breath. 'Do you remember Kholkov? Alexei Kholkov.'

'Yes, I do,' Massey said quietly.

'When he was in Berlin he had some kind of deal going with Bourget. They exchanged bits of information. Nothing of any importance. But it was paid for in US dollars both ways. And the payments were far too high for the information supplied. I found out about it a couple of weeks ago and interrogated Kholkov. He didn't admit that he and Bourget were lining one another's pockets but I scared the wits out of him all the same. Bourget's back in Paris now, and the day before I was due to come to this meeting in Stockholm Kholkov phoned me. He didn't say it in so many words but he made clear that Bourget had told him about my Jewish mother.' Kuznetsov paused. 'I wouldn't trust Kholkov an inch. It's just a question of time before he tries to put the bite on me. He wouldn't be able to resist it. He's greedy, ambitious and ruthless as you know. To have a top man in his hands would be irresistible. So I want to get out before I'm on the train to some Gulag labour camp.'

'Would they really do that, Aleksandr?'

The Russian nodded his head emphatically. 'There's never been such anti-semitic feeling in Moscow for years as there is now. I'd be accused of God knows how many offences against the State. They would assume that everything was deliberate, right from the start.'

'When do you want to come over?'

'Your people will agree?'

'Yes.'

'Just like that? No bargaining about what I'll bring with me? Documents? Information and the rest of it?'

'No. No bargaining. So – when do you come over?'

'How long do you need?'

'No time at all. You can leave with me tonight if you want.'

'It would be easier tomorrow.'

'Why?'

'I've got another meeting with the Swedes in the morning. I can leave there after half an hour and be here by ten thirty.'

'Won't the Swedes notify the Embassy that you've disappeared in the middle of a meeting?'

'I'll tell them the truth.'

'They might not like that.'

Kuznetsov shrugged. 'They'll like it better than me asking them for political asylum in Sweden.'

'What's the meeting about?'

The Russian smiled. 'I've been supplying them with evidence that at least half the suspect submarines bumping along the bottom of the Gulf of Bothnia are NATO not Soviet.'

'Did they believe it?'

'Of course. They already suspected it.'

'How long can you stay now?'

Kuznetsov looked at his watch. 'Another hour.'

'Let's have something to eat up here.'

'OK.'

When Massey had phoned room service, he chatted to the Russian until the food was delivered and served. And then he said quietly, 'When you said that

Kholkov was ambitious and ruthless you said "as you know". What made you say that?'

For a moment Kuznetsov looked at Massey's face then he turned to look at the window before slowly turning back to look at Massey again. 'I heard about the mistake you made in Berlin.'

'What mistake was that?'

'I mean Kholkov's wife. That was an example of his ruthlessness and ambition.'

'What did you hear?'

'Very little. It wasn't my area of responsibility. I heard only gossip.'

'What was the gossip?'

Kuznetsov shrugged uncomfortably. 'I heard that you had been trapped into a liaison with Kholkov's wife and then forced to agree to do something rather than be exposed.'

'Nobody suggested that the pressure was applied because I loved his wife and she loved me?'

The Russian shook his head. 'No. Nobody could possibly think that.'

'Why not? If not that, why the relationship?'

'One assumed it was a matter of sex.'

'Why not affection or love?'

'A member of the KGB would not have been allowed such feelings.'

'I'm not talking about Kholkov. I'm talking about Anna, his wife.'

'What is the difference?'

'Only Kholkov was a member of the KGB.'

'That's not what I heard.'

'What did you hear?'

'That she too was KGB and a party to the deception.'

'I don't believe that.'

Kuznetsov sighed. 'How could she have gone through the Wall to see you without their agreement? She would be under surveillance just because she was the wife of a middle-seniority KGB man. Wives are not trusted.' He smiled. 'KGB men themselves are not trusted. It is part of my own responsibilities not to trust even the most senior people.' He paused. 'I'm sorry to have to tell you this, Jan. But I had to answer your question.'

'Would you have told me anyway?'

'No. I assumed that you had already worked it out for yourself.'

Kuznetsov looked at his watch. 'I must leave, Jan.' He stood up. 'Will you still help me?'

'Of course. Why shouldn't I?'

'You might have wondered if, when they were sounding me out in London, that I might mention that event.'

'Will you?'

'Of course not. It isn't important. And it did no harm to anyone but you.' He sighed. 'Was it real on your side. Did you love her?'

Massey nodded and said softly, 'Yes, I loved her. I still do.' He shrugged. 'I'll make all the arrangements tonight for tomorrow. I'll wait for you and we'll leave straight away.' He smiled. 'There'll be no problems.'

CHAPTER THIRTY-TWO

When Massey phoned Chambers, guardedly describing the situation, Chambers sounded incredulous.

'You mean it's all done and decided?'

'Yes.'

'For tomorrow?'

'Yes.'

'I can hardly believe it.'

'It's a fact.'

'What's he offering?'

'Nothing.'

'You mean he won't cooperate?'

'He didn't say so. We didn't discuss it. I'm sure he'll help where he can.'

'And there's no alternative?'

'Sure there is.'

'What is it?'

'The CIA would be delighted to have him, I'm sure.'

There was a long pause at Chambers's end and then he said, 'Anything else?'

'No. I guess we'll be back in a couple of days.'

'You'd better take him to the place at Ashford. You know where I mean?'

'Yes. I'll do that.'

When Massey hung up he wasn't sure whether he was angry or amused. Angry that the defection of a top man in the KGB's hierarchy should be treated as if it needed justification. And amused at Chambers's obvious pique that the issue had not been left for him to decide.

His mind went over the clothes that Kuznetsov had been wearing. A dark grey two-piece suit, Moscow cut and poor cloth, a white shirt and a black tie. Massey took a taxi to Kungsgatan and bought a cotton, zip-up, showerproof jacket and a pair of jeans. He bought a plastic airline holdall and put in two cotton shirts, a brush and comb, a packet of Bic razors and a tube of shaving cream. Back at the hotel he had asked for a wake-up call at seven o'clock.

He had breakfast in his room and had told the desk that he would be checking out mid-morning and to send up his bill. He checked the items and used his American Express card to pay. After that it was just waiting. The offices of the Swedish security services were at Polhelmsgatan and it wouldn't take Kuznetsov more than a five- or six-minute walk to get to the hotel. He was tempted to take the two bags and wait for him in the foyer but he daren't be away from the phone in case there was some change in Kuznetsov's movements.

And as he sat there waiting, he could feel his heartbeat increasing as the thoughts he had been avoiding seeped back into his mind. He took several deep breaths to calm himself. What Kuznetsov had said about Anna made logical, realistic sense. If she was KGB and part of a set-up with Kholkov, it would explain a lot of things that seemed odd in retrospect. The convenient absences of Kholkov. The coincidence of meeting her in the KO store. And other more intangible things. But he still didn't believe it. A girl can fake sexual pleasure but she can't fake love and loving words.

It reminded him of times when he had had to break the news of an agent's death to his wife. So many of them said the same thing. They accepted that he was dead, but they wished that they could see him just once more. Just two minutes. Just time enough to say how much they loved him. He accepted that he wouldn't ever see Anna again but he would gladly give several years of his life, and everything he possessed, just to be able to ask her if it had been real or only a KGB exercise.

The knock came on his door just before ten o'clock. He made the Russian change into the jacket and jeans as he stuffed his suit into the holdall. Fifteen minutes later they were in a taxi to Arlander. Massey bought two tickets for the domestic SAS flight to Malmö which was already boarding at gate 21. Any Russians looking for Kuznetsov would concentrate on flights from Stockholm to London and the USA. Their resources would be limited and it was highly unlikely that they would check flights from Copenhagen or Helsinki.

At Malmö they had taken a taxi from the airport to the ferry ticket office and an hour and a half later they were in a taxi on their way to Kastrup. Massey booked them on to the Amsterdam plane but they had missed the London connection. After a two-hour wait at Schiphol they landed at Gatwick just before six o'clock local time. There had been no problems at Immigration. Massey had used his own passport, and Kuznetsov the one in the name of Mathews.

As they walked through the green customs section Massey was being paged to go to Airport Information. At the information counter a girl gave him an envelope. His name was typed and it had URGENT in capitals below his name. The note inside told him to go to the Spa Hotel in Tunbridge Wells where a suite for them both had been booked in his own name.

Just over an hour later the taxi dropped them at the hotel entrance. Massey signed in for both of them and they were shown to their suite. He dialled Century House and the duty officer told him that Chambers would be down to see them the next morning at about ten o'clock.

They ate together in the restaurant, took a brief walk in the parklike grounds and then went up to the sitting-room of their suite.

'What was Chambers's reaction?'

'Surprised, of course. I couldn't go into any detail with him on an insecure phone, of course.' Massey smiled. 'He'll be used to the idea by the time he gets here tomorrow.'

'I have to make quite clear to him my position.'

'What, in particular?'

'Your people have to understand that I am not a defector. I'm a refugee.'

'In terms of your cooperation with them, what is the difference?'

'All the difference in the world. I have no intention of committing treason. No intention of damaging my countrymen.'

Massey raised his eyebrows. 'Your reason for coming here was that your countrymen might send you to a labour camp because your mother was Jewish.'

'The men who would do that are not Russians. They're Bolsheviks. I'm a Russian. I have no wish to die to please such men.'

'Was it that certain do you think?'

'There were four pages in *Krasnaya Zvezda* last month, the official Red Army newspaper. The article was as anti-Semitic as anything the Nazis ever wrote. It suggested that Jews were not only not Russian and non-Soviets but that no Jews should be allowed in any position of authority or decision. It went on to point out how skilful Jews were in hiding their Jewish backgrounds and that it should be the task of a special committee to uncover them, remove them from their posts, and, if necessary, punish them.' Kuznetsov sighed deeply. 'That piece was a warning. It wouldn't have been printed if it wasn't instigated by the Kremlin.'

Massey smiled. 'It didn't mention Marx or Lenin I suppose?'

'It's not a joke, Jan, when you are on the receiving end.'

'Do you have any living relatives, Aleksandr?'

'None, thank God. There were times when I wished that I had. But now I am glad.'

'It seems a long time ago that we met, that night at the Festival Hall.'

'It is a long time.' Kuznetsov paused. 'I'm sorry I had to tell you about the girl.'

'It was just gossip, Aleksandr. Just gossip. One should never believe gossip.'

'How could you have imagined that she would not be under surveillance?'

'I'm sure she wasn't. I was very careful.'

'When you walk into a trap it makes no difference how careful you are. It's all fixed and arranged before your foot crosses the line.'

'You believe Anna was KGB?'

'I do.'

'Have you any evidence that she was? Did the people who gossiped say that she was?'

'No. No evidence. Like everybody else I took it for granted that she was KGB.'

'Did you hear what they asked me to do?'

'You helped exchange some radio traffic disks.'

'Why did they want them changed?'

'We were launching a booster system MHV. It was just possible that your radio surveillance that day could pick it up.'

'What's an MHV?'

'A miniature homing vehicle. An anti-satellite missile. It's the main area of space friction between the Americans and the USSR. One MHV costs about four million US dollars. You have to get your missile up twenty-two thousand miles to hit a satellite parked in its geosynchronous orbit. But if you hit it then you've wiped out most of your enemy's military control system.'

'Was it a successful launch?'

'No. It didn't get beyond one thousand miles.'

'So exchanging the disks was of no real value.'

'It had some value. It kept the West from knowing that we had not succeeded. Its failure allows the Soviet negotiators to claim that the Americans are the sole aggressors in that particular high-technology area. Andropov had instructed our people to make every effort to get the Americans to agree to ban the use of anti-satellite weapons.' Kuznetsov shrugged. 'You carry more weight if you say you come to the negotiating table with clean hands. If you come having failed, and your opponents know that, you might as well have stayed in Moscow.'

'I expect the Americans have a good idea of what the Soviets are up to.'

Kuznetsov shrugged. 'Having a good idea of what they're doing cuts no ice in Geneva or the UN or on the TV screens. Having proof of an attempt that failed is something else.' He paused. 'The Americans are working on what's called an EMP – an electromagnetic pulse that would destroy all satellites for thousands of miles.'

'They're a mad lot – both of them.'

'We're part of it, Jan.'

'What do you want to do now you're here?'

'Will there be a debriefing?'

'I should imagine so.'

'Will it be you?'

'I've no idea. I'm in Paris now.'

Kuznetsov looked quickly at Massey's face, frowning as he said, 'How long have you been there?'

'A few months.'

Kuznetsov went on staring at Massey's face. He opened his mouth to speak, then closed it and stood up, walking towards the window. He stood there, drawing aside the curtains to look outside.

'What time did you say Chambers was coming tomorrow?'

'Ten.'

'What sort of man is he?'

'He's very experienced. Well educated. Cool and calm. A desk man. Quietly spoken. Professionally charming and diplomatic. Privately rather withdrawn and reserved. Very Brit. And not given to displays of emotion.' He paused. 'Probably because there isn't much emotion to display.'

'Is he a friend of yours?'

'He's my boss.'

'Yes. I know. But does he like you? Is he sympathetic towards you?'

'I've no idea. I think he values my experience and is satisfied with my work. More than that, I don't know.' Massey stood up. 'He won't be unreasonable with you, Alex, you can be sure of that.' He looked at his watch. 'I'm going to turn in.'

'Does Chambers speak Russian?'

'I'm afraid not. He's not a linguist.'

Chambers had talked with Massey alone after having a few polite words with Kuznetsov. Chambers had seemed ill at ease with the Russian. SIS were used to handling the problems of defectors, but the decisions were normally expected and arranged, and it seemed as if the sudden appearance of Kuznetsov was an embarrassment. He was undoubtedly the most important defector they had ever had but Chambers's approach was so low-key that Massey wondered what was behind it. Maybe it was just because Chambers spoke no Russian and Kuznetsov's English was very limited.

'Did he give any indication of how he'll cooperate, Jan?'

Massey shrugged. 'He made clear that he considered himself a refugee, not a defector.'

'That doesn't sound too promising.'

'He'll probably prove more amenable when he's settled down.'

'When are you planning to get back to Paris?'

'Do you want me for debriefing Kuznetsov?'

Chambers hesitated. 'I think not, Jan. I think somebody neutral would be better. Someone who's less involved. D'you agree?'

Massey shrugged. 'I don't know. It's up to you. You can always involve me later on if it doesn't work out.'

'I hope he's not going to be a problem.'

'No reason why he should be. Is there?'

Chambers drew a slow deep breath. 'Seems to be taking rather a lot for granted.'

'We gave him our word way back. He's just taking for granted that we meant it.'

'No sign of gratitude that I've detected so far.'

'Why should there be? He's given us far more than we could have hoped for. He's just cashing in on our IOU.'

Chambers nodded, but without conviction. 'Maybe. We'll see.' He stood up. 'I'll take him back with me.'

CHAPTER THIRTY-THREE

After months of interrogation it had been decided that Arthur Johnson should be removed from Wormwood Scrubs and taken to a special safe-house in the Midlands. Arthur Johnson had become a problem. He had not been charged with the murder of his common-law wife although he had eventually confessed to killing her. And apart from his own admissions, which were extremely vague they had no evidence to charge him with offences against national security that would be acceptable by a court. He himself was not aware of what he had passed to the Russians apart from gossip and a few minor documents. The items that he had photographed and the tapes that he had passed to them were unidentifiable.

What made things more difficult was that if he was charged with the murder of Heidi Fischer his lawyers would inevitably, and justifiably, drag in the security aspects.

Those concerned were thankful that he had no relations or friends who could start quoting habeas corpus and ask by what law he was being detained without being charged with any offence, and without at least being brought in front of a magistrate.

Inspector Hipwell of Special Branch visited him once a week at the special safe-house on Cannock Chase. Like many tenacious interrogators he was loth to give up at least until he had discovered what had been passed to the KGB. Johnson's motives had easily been established but he was puzzled about why they had pushed Johnson back into West Berlin. Their whole relationship with Johnson seemed tatty and disorganized and that wasn't typical of the KGB. It could have been that they were making the best of a bad job, taking what was offered in the hope that it would be useful. And almost anything had some use. But why push him back through the Wall and risk him being picked up?

Hipwell had a sneaking sympathy for Johnson. His upbringing and his lack of education had made him what he was, and his tawdry ambitions and lifestyle were part of the pathetic picture. It was after one of their rather inconclusive chats that Johnson had hinted that he would like a night with a girl. Hipwell had made arrangements with the staff that a girl should be provided. Johnson seemed to be becoming more distant and withdrawn as the weeks went by and Hipwell thought that maybe a session with a girl would help. Johnson seemed not only to be withdrawn but incapable of recalling things that had happened only in the last few months. He was never bright or even alert, but what had been merely a doltish response to questions became an inability even to understand the questions. Johnson and his fate were already a problem and if he became antagonistic it would make things worse. Nobody quite knew what to do with their moronic captive.

The girl who was provided had, oddly enough, been brought from Johnson's old haunts in Handsworth, Birmingham. Nobody had realized the connection with his past and it played no part in the final outcome. The girl's reaction would have been the same no matter where she came from.

The girl was in her mid-twenties and attractive enough for the guard to wonder if she might be willing to engage in a little extra-curricular activity after Johnson was through. But it was not to be. She was only in Johnson's room for five or six minutes before she rushed out angrily.

'You bastards,' she shouted. 'What do you think I am? Where's the bloody driver? I'm off.'

'What's the matter, honey? What is it?'

'Don't you fuckin' honey me, you creep. You know what the matter is.'

The guard's surprise was just enough to convince her when he said, 'Honest, kid, I don't know what you're on about.'

'Have you seen him? Have you seen his crotch?'

'Of course I haven't. Why should I?'

'He's got syph up to his eyeballs. Don't tell me you didn't know.'

'Are you sure? Maybe it's a rash or something. Been scratching it.'

'Jesus wept! You must be off your bloody head. Anyway it's your worry, mate. I'm off.'

The duty guard phoned Hipwell at his home.

The Special Branch man thought long and hard before he took what he later referred to as appropriate action.

Appropriate action meant accompanying an Army doctor to the safe-house and waiting for his diagnosis in the sitting-room. It was an hour before the doctor came back to him.

'Who is he, Mr Hipwell?'

'He's . . .' Hipwell shrugged '. . . let's say he's a detainee. Sort of awaiting Her Majesty's pleasure as they call it.'

'Well, he's not got long to wait, and Her Majesty's not going to get much pleasure from him. Why didn't anybody notice it before?'

'I don't know. He never complained. It *is* syph, is it?'

'Too bloody true. *Dementia paralytica.* I wouldn't give him more than two months at the outside.'

'No cure?'

'No. The tissues are destroyed. I can ease pain but he isn't complaining of pain. He's past it. He's only half in this world anyway.'

'You're sure he's not curable?'

'If I could cure that poor bastard I could be a millionaire by Christmas.'

'And he's only got another couple of months left?'

'If he's lucky. Could be less. He's beyond anything that medicine can do. If he was a dog I'd have him put down.'

Hipwell had had a long think about the situation. He didn't want to stick his neck out but there was a solution to all their problems. There was a device in the intelligence services called talking in parables. It consisted of talking about hypothetical situations. What could we do 'if'? It was recognized that the situation being described was real rather than imaginary and it allowed questions to be asked and answers given that were official but to all intents and purposes had never been asked or answered.

The inspector talked in parables to Chambers, who suggested that in the circumstances that the Special Branch officer described perhaps no action at all would be best for all concerned. But added a codicil that in those circumstances the doctor who signed the death certificate should be a member of the organization.

Obstinate and anti-Establishment to the last, Arthur Johnson had survived for three months and two days before he finally expired. And Arthur Johnson, neglected child, eager youth, ineffectual protester against fate, mild fornicator, traitor and honorary lieutenant in the KGB, was buried, unmourned by anyone, in Witton cemetery in Birmingham. Not far from where he was born. The only witness to the event was Inspector Hipwell who rationalized what was really quite a soft heart as merely being the official closing of a file.

Massey settled back into his Paris routine, sending back far more information to London that they had received for years, getting in return unofficial praise and thanks from officers on the French desk, but only silence from Chambers.

He enjoyed his meetings with both Autenowski and Anne-Marie, and after that first visit to Michael Guérard's shop and cafeteria they went two or three times a week. Either the three of them or just him and the French girl.

That day they were lunching alone and discussing a report she had done for him on the DGSE's operations in French territories overseas. He was stirring his coffee when she spoke. She was looking over his shoulder.

She said softly, 'I think you've made a hit, Jan. There's a very pretty lady been looking at the back of your head for the last five minutes as if you were Yves Montand or Robert Redford.'

Massey smiled. 'I'm flattered. If you're not kidding that is.'

'I'm not, my friend. Have a look. She's just got up from her table and she's heading for the door.'

Massey turned, reluctantly, to look and for a moment he seemed paralyzed. Then he stood up clumsily, knocking the table so that the crockery rattled.

Anne-Marie saw his face, the perspiration on his forehead, and heard the quick shallow breathing.

'What is it, Jan? What's the matter?'

He looked at her for a moment, unseeing; then he turned and threaded his way through the tables to the door. She saw him looking both ways outside in the street. Hesitating, then breaking into a run as he headed towards the boulevard des Capucines.

He saw her, in the black silk summer coat, walking slowly down the street. Many times he had walked behind girls who looked like her from the back but this time it *was* her. For a moment their eyes had met in the cafeteria as she stood at the door.

She looked over her shoulder and he shouted her name. He saw her looking, then her eyes closed for a moment as she stopped.

Then their arms were round each other, her head on his shoulder, and for long moments neither of them spoke. Then she drew back her head and looked up at his face.

'I used to dream about this, Jan. Night after night. But it wasn't in Paris.'

'What are you doing here?'

She shrugged. 'He's at a meeting at the Embassy. Tomorrow's my last day.'

'Are you being followed?'

'Me? No. They're not interested in small fry like me.'

'I've got a room. Can we go there and talk?'

For a moment she hesitated and then said softly, 'Of course.'

In the taxi they didn't speak but her hand reached out. She was wearing a glove but he could feel the warmth of her hand in his. He told the driver to drop them at the church and he felt his composure returning as he paid the fare and waited for the change. She slid her arm in his and they walked up the hill. A few minutes later as she looked around his room she was immediately aware of its bleakness. It had an air of human despair and loneliness. She had already noticed the tension in his eyes and around his mouth. They stood in the middle of the room looking at each other's faces, each searching for clues or answers to their unspoken questions. Her hands on his shoulders, his arms around her. It was Anna who spoke first.

'I've missed you so much, Jan.' Her eyes searched his face. 'Tell me what happened.'

For a moment or so he was silent, then he said quietly, 'Let's sit on the bed.'

As he settled down beside her she reached out for his hand. As she laced her fingers through his he said, 'Tell me what you think happened.'

'Nothing happened. I just never saw you again. I got no answer to my messages.' She shrugged. 'Just nothing.'

'How did you send the messages?'

'Like you said, through the bookshop.'

'Where were you living at that time?'

'In the first week I was at the house. I sent one message in that week. Then I had to leave in a hurry to go to Moscow. They said my father was ill.'

'Was he ill when you got there?'

'They told me he was in an isolation ward. That he had an infectious fever but he would be OK.'

'How long before you saw him?'

'Nearly a month.'

'Had he been ill?'

'Yes. He didn't know what it was but he had had a terrible fever.'

'Then what?'

'I stayed with him for another ten days or so, then I went back to East Berlin. They had found us a new house because Alexei had been promoted. I sent two more messages to say I was back and giving the new address but there was no reply. About two weeks later Alexei was moved to Moscow and then to Budapest. That's where we are now.'

Massey looked at her face. 'When you married Kholkov did they make any attempt to recruit you into the KGB?'

'No. Never. I had the usual lecture about supporting my husband but all new wives get that.' She paused. 'What made you ask that?'

As coherently and carefully as he could, Massey told her what had happened. It was almost dark in the room as he finished, but he could see the pale face and the dark eyes as she looked back at him.

'Did you ever think I was part of it, Jan?'

'No, never.'

'I'm glad in a way that I didn't know. It would have driven me mad. It must have been terrible for you.'

'What shall we do?'

For a moment she was silent and then she said, 'Do you still love me?'

'Of course I do. I've never stopped loving you. What about you?'

She smiled wanly. 'You don't need to ask, do you?'

'So what do we do?'

She shrugged and said quietly, 'We should do what we ought to have done in Berlin.'

'What's that?'

'D'you want me to stay, now, this minute?'

'I didn't dare ask you so soon. The answer is yes. But what about you – your life with Kholkov, Moscow and your father?'

'I always accepted the break with my father. I never owed Kholkov anything. I will sacrifice the pleasure I would have in telling him what I think of what he's done. To me and to you.'

'Don't think about him, my love. To him it's just part of his work. They don't have scruples about what they do to people.'

'Do you know what I wish this moment?'

'No. Tell me.'

'I wish I was twenty years older and we were sitting here remembering the twenty years we had had together. I can't wait to get on with my life with you.'

'Have you got your passport with you?'

'Yes, it's in my handbag.'

'Let me see it.'

Massey looked at it page by page. There was no indication that she was connected with any Soviet organization and there was a year of validity still left.

'Are you hungry?'

'No. I had a snack at the cafeteria.'

'I'll pack a bag and we'll go tonight. Where's Kholkov staying?'

'They've got an apartment near the place Vendôme.'

'Has it got a telephone number?'

'Yes.'

'OK. I'll pack a few things.'

'Where are we going?'

'We're going to do the grand tour, honey.'

She laughed, 'I've been waiting for that.'

'For what?'

'For you to call me honey again. I'm so happy, Jan. So happy.'

'So am I.'

'Where are we going?'

'To Amsterdam, then Copenhagen. And from there to Sweden. When I've found us somewhere in Sweden I'll have to do some work on getting documents for you. Then we'll go to England and get married.

'Will it be legal?'

'Not entirely, but enough for us. Nobody will know anyway. You'll have a different name on the passport and after that it will be my name.'

Anna had nothing but the contents of her handbag and the clothes she was wearing. Massey had little more. Only enough to fill his canvas holdall. He left one suit hanging in the wardrobe.

They took a taxi to de Gaulle and there was less than a half-hour wait for the KLM flight to Amsterdam. The plane was half empty and there was no problem about getting seats.

At Amsterdam there was a two-hour wait before a flight to Copenhagen. As they sat in the restaurant Massey asked her to write down Kholkov's number. When she passed him the paper he looked at her face. 'You said "they've" got an apartment near the place Vendôme. Who's "they"?'

'Another man.'

'KGB?'

'No.'

'Who is he?'

'His name is Antonov. He's just a young man. About twenty years old.'

'What's he doing there?'

For a moment she hesitated, then she said, 'He's Alexei's boyfriend. Why do you want the number?'

'I'm going to phone him.'

'But why? He could try and have the call traced.'

'He might think you're missing for some other reason and notify the police. I want him to know you're with me and if he raises a hue and cry the Soviet Embassy won't like it. He won't be able to trace the call. It wouldn't matter if he did. That's why we're not going a direct route to anywhere.' He stood up. 'Stay here, order some more coffee and I'll be back in five or ten miunutes.'

In the kiosk he checked the dialling code for France and put a small pile of guilders on top of the box. Slowly and carefully he dialled the codes and the number. It rang several times before the phone was picked up.

'Who are you calling?'

He recognized Kholkov's voice.

'Is that Alexei Kholkov?'

'Who is that speaking?'

'Massey. Jan Massey.'

There were several seconds of silence and then the Russian said, 'I wondered if it was you. It's time she was back.'

'Have you told the Embassy that she's missing?'

'Missing? What do you mean?'

'She's with me, Kholkov. And she won't be coming back.'

'You mean -'

'I mean she's left you for good. If you make a nuisance of yourself there's going to be a lot of scandal for the Embassy. And for Moscow too. Even comrade Antonov won't like it.'

There was a long silence and then the phone was hung up at the other end.

It was past midnight when they landed at Kastrup and the tourist desk was closed. The taxi driver had taken them to a small hotel in one of the small streets near the Tivoli. They weren't asked for passports and he signed them in as Mr and Mrs Mortimer.

There were no problems in getting seats on the mid-morning ferry from Copenhagen to Malmö and no passport check at either end.

The Royal Hotel in Malmö was within walking distance of the ferry terminal and Massey booked a small suite with a living-room on the fifth floor.

After a bath they took a meal in their suite and as Anna poured out their coffee from a Thermos she said, 'What are we going to do, Jan? Have you decided?'

'We'll rent some rooms here in Malmö for a few weeks.' He looked at her face. 'I'm sorry it's so messy but I've got to cover our tracks as well as finding us a way to live. And I'll have to go to Berlin. It's the only place where I can get you the documents you need.'

'What do I need?'

'A passport. A forged passport won't be too difficult but we shall need a birth certificate for the marriage registrar, so the passport has to be in that name.' He smiled. 'I'll sort it out, don't worry.'

'Will you have to explain why you left Paris so suddenly?'

'No. I doubt if London will notice that I'm away.'

'Do you think Alexei will do anything?'

'I'm sure he won't. Nothing publicly anyway.'

'Will it be illegal for us to marry?'

'Technically, yes. But in normal circumstances you could have divorced him on the grounds that he's a homosexual. Nobody has an interest in exposing us.'

'What about your people – the men in London?'

'As far as they are concerned you'll be British and of no interest to them. I shan't notify them anyway.'

'But my bad English?'

He smiled. 'It's not that bad and people will love the accent.' He stood up, reaching out for her hand. 'Let's go and look for our rooms.'

They moved into the furnished apartment over one of the shops in Södergatan the next day. It was bright and spotlessly clean with well-made wooden furnishings and it was the first bright omen in their disjointed and unplanned flight from Paris.

As they ate their first meal in the apartment that night, Massey suddenly felt relieved. The hurried departure, the disjointed journey had depressed him. He was worried about what they were doing. Not about its rightness, but the way they had moved without a plan, improvising as they went along. His other concern was about the consequences of what they were doing. Despite what he had said to Anna and Kholkov, he knew that he was vulnerable now. He could see nothing rational that could be done against him, but he knew that he had made them both hostages to fate. He wasn't sure what fate had in mind. It was no more than an all-pervading uneasiness. All his experience told him that such spur of the moment adventures were generally doomed to failure. It was time to do some thinking and planning but somehow his mind was confused. Anna seemed to be taking it all in her stride but he was apprehensive. He'd reacted in exactly the same way as when he'd gone into East Berlin to find out what had happened to her. Not the cool experienced intelligence officer, just the traditional bull in a china shop. All brawn and no brain.

But the neat white rooms lifted his spirits, and he sat down after they had eaten, with a pad and pencil and started listing the things he had to do.

CHAPTER THIRTY-FOUR

Chambers was disturbed enough to fly to Hong Kong himself to interview Max Cohen, who was now second in command of the GCHQ operations in that area. Cohen was resentful of his transfer from Berlin and his attitude to Chambers was guarded to the point of open hostility. He was no longer under any control from SIS and had no intention of becoming involved with them in any way.

As they sat on the verandah of the government guesthouse that Chambers was using, Cohen closed his eyes as Chambers talked.

'You don't remember Arthur Johnson by any chance? Signalman Johnson?'

'No. I don't. And I don't remember the name of the guy who ran the cafeteria.'

'It's a serious matter, Max. He not only murdered his wife but he was working for the Russians for most of the time that you were in charge of the operation.'

'At no time was I responsible for any security aspects of the unit. That was your people's responsibility, not mine.'

Cohen's voice rose ominously as he spoke and Chambers tried another tack.

'I'm not trying to establish responsibility, Max. I'm just trying to find out what actually happened.' He paused. 'We need to know if this is one isolated incident or just the tip of the iceberg.'

'I'm not stopping you, Chambers. You managed to cast some of the blame onto me in Berlin and you sure ain't going to do that again.'

'Johnson said that he got the substitute disk from inside the jacket of a book in the library. Could you suggest how it might have got there?'

'How the hell should I know?' Cohen banged down his glass and swore as the drink spilt over the back of his hand. He looked at Chambers as he dried his hand. 'Why don't you ask Jan Massey? He was responsible for security – not me. I ran the electronic surveillance operation. I didn't run agents into East Berlin. I didn't evaluate the signals traffic – and I didn't put the books on the shelves in that fucking library!' Cohen emphasized his words, his finger jabbing in Chambers's direction. 'Don't try and get the buck off your desk and stick it on mine. Don't try and involve me or GCHQ. It's your worry, not ours.'

Chambers shook his head in mock despair. 'Are you telling me, Max Cohen, that the Russians can penetrate a top security installation where you work and you don't give a damn?'

'What you've just said is typical of what's wrong, Chambers. They're just weasel words. Have you stopped beating your wife? If you want to ask me straightforward questions, ask me. But don't, repeat don't, ask me if I know who did it. If I knew, he'd have been in the nick a long time ago.'

'OK, Max. Just let me ask for your help. Just your opinion. If the Russians had got into the operation why all the palaver with putting the disk in the book? Why didn't they just do a straight swap in the disk file?'

'Maybe whoever they used couldn't get into the main operation. Maybe – I don't know – why didn't they get Johnson to do a straight swap at the disk-file shelves? Maybe they didn't trust Johnson? There's a dozen possibilities.'

'Who could get into the library and put the disk there, or the book and the disk, but not carry on and do the whole exchange?'

'Anybody who could get as far as the library could go the rest of the way. The real tight security was getting past the inner door.'

'Why two people to carry out such a simple operation?'

'There's one explanation. But you won't like it.'

'Try me.'

'All signals people, every one of them except me, go through the X-ray machine and at random times during the day there's a full strip search. None of that applied to SIS people. Or me.'

'What reason would SIS people have for going into the signals installation?'

'None. And they never did go in. They got their paperwork by individual despatch clerks and the clerks were all my people. Checked in and out every time. I don't think I've ever seen an SIS type in my area, ever. Ask Massey if he agrees.'

Chambers looked out towards the bay and then back at Cohen.

'Does that mean Massey was in your area sometimes?'

'Yes, of course. We had frequent meetings in my office.' Then he looked quickly at Chambers's face and said softly, 'Whoever it is, it isn't Jan Massey.'

'Why not, Max? Tell me why not.'

'For a dozen reasons. First of all, he knows more than anybody about what the Soviets are up to. There's no persuasion and no bribe they could offer Massey that would turn him. He knows the bastards too well.'

'You couldn't have a better cover than what you've just described.'

Cohen laughed. 'For God's sake. OK, let's pursue that scenario. What the hell do they offer him to make him go over? It's going to need to be something fantastic. So let's say they offer him a million dollars in a deposit box in Basle. Yes? And then we come to what they want him to do. Kidnap Sir Peter? Microdots of the most confidential files in Berlin or Century House?' Cohen smiled. 'No. They want him to put a floppy disk inside a book in the reading library. A floppy disk that covers all the usual traffic you get on a couple of routine frequencies. So we are brought to our knees by not realizing that the leave schedule for some clapped-out Red Army unit is incorrect. Or that they ain't got any pull-throughs for their Kalashnikovs. No way, Chambers. Whoever it is, it's not our friend. I'd bet my last dollar on that.'

Chambers nodded amiably. 'Can I take you for a meal, Max?'

'I've got somebody here from Cheltenham. I've got to look after him this evening.'

'Top brass?'

'No. A cryppie.' Smiling at Chambers's confusion. 'A code-breaker.'

'What kind of chap goes in for that sort of stuff?'

'Oh, they come in all shapes and sizes. This one's tame enough. He's just comparing notes with his opposite number over here. The routine's the same but pulling in the Chinese dialects isn't as easy as pulling in the Russian stuff. There's God knows how many dialects.'

'How wide do you cover?'

'The whole area. We just suck in everything like a giant vacuum cleaner. Private stuff, commercial and official. After that we've got to chew it and spit it out. Phones, radio, telegraphy – the lot.'

'How do you get on with the SIS people here?'

'OK. We don't see much of them.' He smiled. 'What happened to me was a lesson to all of us.'

'I'm sorry about that, Max. It was unfair in retrospect.'

'It was unfair to Massey too, so I suppose honour was served all round.'

'All the same – it was unfortunate.'

Max Cohen had not been entirely truthful about his responsibilities for entertaining the man from Cheltenham. The man from GCHQ was neither on Cohen's level nor did he have a personality that would make him good company for an evening out. He looked a bit of a stick-in-the-mud, and Cohen had too many of those in his working life to want them in his free time too.

So Tony Lucas, one of Cohen's juniors, prepared himself for a dull evening with his colleague from Cheltenham. As they stood on the hotel steps he said, 'What d'you fancy, Eric, beans on toast or the bright lights?'

'What do you prefer yourself?'

Lucas laughed. 'It's on the old firm tonight. How about a bit of fun?'

'It's your town, Tony. You lead the way.'

The garish neon lights of Wanchai winked their various invitations to the strolling tourists but the entrance to the club was discreet, and the sign that said Lola's Club was bathed in a soft pink glow.

The food had been well prepared and Eric Mayhew had gradually got used to having his glass refilled regularly by a topless bar-girl. When they got to the coffee stage Lucas leaned forward across the table and said quietly, 'You can screw any of the girls, you know.'

Mayhew shrugged. 'You carry on. I'll wait for you. No problem. I can listen to the music.'

'Can't afford it on my money, old chap. Wish I could.'

'Are they very expensive?'

'No, about twenty quid. It's the end of the month though – the old till's a bit empty.'

Mayhew smiled. 'Let me finance you. I've hardly spent any of my overseas allowance. And you've been very helpful the last couple of days.'

Lucas laughed. 'You're a real sport, Eric. How about we take a couple of them upstairs.' He winked. 'We could swap at half-time.'

Mayhew smiled and passed a bundle of HK dollars under the table to Lucas who slid them into his pocket.

'I'll sit this one out, Tony. Maybe I'll join you tomorrow.'

'You sure?'

'Of course I am. I'll wait for you. No hurry.'

Lucas disappeared with one of the girls and he was obviously a regular: a couple of other girls had stood laughing with him trying to persuade him to take them too.

Fifteen minutes later, Mayhew had found the payphone near the entrance and with his diary open at the page for Christmas week he dialled the number written there, reversing the digits and adding a zero at the end. When the call was answered, he listened carefully and then hung up without speaking.

Half an hour later Tony Lucas joined him at the table, smiling as he poured himself a coffee.

Mayhew smiled, 'Everything OK, Tony?'

'Fantastic, old boy. She's really something, that kid.'

'What's Max Cohen like, Tony?'

'Very efficient. Shit hot.'

'I mean, as a man. Is he a family man?'

'No. He's a Jew. All his folk were put in the ovens in one of those Nazi camps. Never married.'

'Girlfriends?'

'No steady, but he screws on the side. I know that.'

'How do you know?'

'I've screwed his favourite. A Vietnamese girl. A real goer. Uses this place at weekends.'

'They're very pretty I understand, the Vietnamese girls?'

'You'd go for May Lai.'

'Who's in charge of your maintenance? Is it a chap named Wright?'

'No. I don't know a Wright. Our chap's Helliwell. Came to us from NCR.'

'Is he good?'

Lucas shrugged. 'So-so. Nobody likes him . . .' he smiled '. . . maybe because he leans on us. Who knows.'

'A family man?'

'Yes, but the family's in the UK. Two kids at private schools. Keeps to himself. I'd guess he's stretched pretty tight for cash.'

'Must be lonely out here if you're a family man.'

'Yeah, I guess so. Most people make the best of it.'

'Do you operate the key changes on the coding machines yourself?'

'Yes. Even when I'm on forty-eight-hour leave I come in at seven in the morning and turn the key.'

'How long will you be serving here?'

'Another three years, I guess.'

'I think I ought to be getting back to the hotel, Tony. I'm a bit tired and we've got a long day tomorrow.'

'Fine. Let's get the cloakroom girl to call us a taxi.'

Eric Mayhew had absentmindedly slipped the internal telephone directory from Lucas's desk into his case along with his own papers when he was clearing up to go back to his hotel after the meeting.

That evening, he walked a hundred yards up the hill to the telephone kiosk. On the wooden frame behind the kiosk he saw the blue chalk mark. Just a short vertical stroke about four inches long. Early the next morning he took the train to Sha Tin and a few yards from the station the man was waiting. He was smoking a pipe like they had said and he took the packet from Mayhew without turning his head and without speaking.

Mayhew caught the next train back to Hong Kong Central and was at the airport two hours later. He phoned Jenny the next morning from Heathrow and was back home late that afternoon. She was delighted with the embroidered silk blouse that he had brought back for her.

CHAPTER THIRTY-FIVE

Before SIS had moved from its old headquarters at Broadway House, the pubs in the vicinity could have provided a useful order of battle for the KGB. Top men were more likely to be seen at some Whitehall club or St Ermin's Hotel. But lesser lights frequented the local pubs at lunchtimes and, on occasion, in mid-evening when there was a crisis.

One of the most popular was the Ironmonger's Arms where the brewers had shrewdly put in a retired ex-SIS man as its landlord. Jack McAvoy had started his working life as a Shanghai policeman. When he was exposed as the owner of three brothels and their twenty-five inmates he had been discreetly posted back to England where, at one of SIS's stately mansions on the Welsh borders, he taught SIS officers the noble art of self defence and unarmed combat. Most of them never needed to put any of it into practice but even the academics found him a useful and amiable contact. A blind eye was turned to the obvious fact that Jack McAvoy had connections with the criminal world that from time to time produced items that were otherwise impossible to obtain. Items that ranged from half-price but brand-new washing machines to the as-yet-unmarketed latest version of Ortofon's record-player cartridge and stylus.

Massey had known McAvoy for years and they were mutual admirers despite the fact that Massey never drank in McAvoy's pub. But in the small back parlour in his early days he had sat talking with his informants, patient and persistent as they drank pint after pint or their cocktail equivalents. Bloody Marys had not surfaced in London in those days but there were Pink Ladies and port-and-lemons. Jack McAvoy had admired the tough young man who sat defiantly with a glass of milk.

Massey's one-day trip to Berlin had shown that there was no longer any chance of him getting fake documents from those sources. On the flight back to Copenhagen he had thought of Jack McAvoy and wondered why he hadn't thought of him first.

Massey had done exactly what the KGB were used to doing – checking cemeteries and graveyards for a suitable name and date. He had found two Annas born in the right year and had paid for copy birth certificates in both names. English bureaucracy unwittingly assisted several foreign intelligence services by not linking death certificates with birth certificates.

As he sat in his bedroom at the Park Lane Hotel he realized that he didn't know Anna's unmarried name. He chose the certificate of Anna Lovegrove for no better reason than that he liked the soft name. It was Anna Mary Lovegrove, her father's occupation was registered as Teacher (Grammar School) and the birth had been registered at Keighley in Yorkshire. Anna Mary Lovegrove had died, according to the gravestone in the churchyard in Tooting, when she was two years and seven months old.

Massey had waited until a few minutes before closing time before he went in the Ironmonger's Arms. McAvoy had taken him into his own room behind the bar and had left to lock up. As he sat waiting he looked around the room. Nothing seemed to have changed. The photographs of McAvoy in fake leopard-skin briefs, lifting weights, demonstrating wrestling holds, and the centrepiece over the fireplace that showed a smiling Jack in evening dress with a member of the Royal Family on one side and a well-known criminal on the other. There were a few medals in a glass case hanging on the wall and a framed letter from the royal patron of an orphanage thanking John Kevin McAvoy for the cheque for £500 sent on behalf of his customers. It was an entirely masculine room and as dreary as the public bar outside. It was ten minutes before McAvoy came back. He sat down smiling in the worn armchair alongside his visitor.

'You on leave, Jan?'

'Kind of.'

'Still in Berlin?'

'I was posted to Paris a few months ago.'

'You buggers certainly get around.' He grinned. 'Still plenty of crumpet in the gay city?'

'I imagine so.'

'What can I do for you?'

'I want a passport, Jack.'

'What country?'

'British.'

McAvoy looked surprised. 'Why me? Your pals down the road at Petty France can do that easier than me.'

'I don't want to use them.' Massey paused. 'Can you do it?'

McAvoy laughed. 'I can do anything, mate, you know that. But it'll cost a packet if you want something authentic.'

'I want something as near perfect as you can get.'

'Visas?'

'No. Just a straight passport.'

'Used or new?'

'Brand new if possible. How long will it take?'

McAvoy shrugged. 'A couple of weeks.'

'I need it in two days, Jack. But I'll pay whatever it takes.'

'Jesus wept! You must be joking. Let me make a phone call.'

'OK.'

It was twenty minutes before McAvoy put his head round the door.

'Will you go up to a thousand quid?'

Massey nodded. 'Yes. But two days.'

'They say a week. Can we offer them an incentive?'

'It's up to you. I'll pay whatever it takes.'

'Let me talk to them.'

When McAvoy came back he nodded. 'Twelve fifty but it'll be late on Wednesday night. You can pick it up here. They want the details and the photo tonight.'

Massey took out an envelope from his jacket pocket.

'They're all in there, Jack. How are you going to get them to your people?'

'I'll take 'em myself.'

'Is it far?'

McAvoy smiled. 'Never you mind. Have you got a place to kip tonight?

There's a camp bed here if you want it.'

'I'm OK. When do they want the cash?'

'I told 'em cash on delivery.'

Massey stood up. 'I'll come here at closing time on Wednesday night. I'll phone you tomorrow to check there are no snags.'

'There won't be any snags. These guys are the best.' He smiled. 'It'll be better than out of the basement at Petty France if I know 'em.'

Anna had met him at the airport and they took a taxi back into Malmö. Relieved that she now had all the documentation she was likely to need, Massey knew that he would have to go back to Paris alone. Somehow the small Swedish town had begun to feel like their home. They had found real peace there, walking through the Old Town along the canals, exploring the parks and drinking coffee in the square at Stortorget and Gustav Adolf's Torg. Anna spent hours every day in the Lundgren bookshop near their apartment. After two days Massey took a flight back to Paris, and a week later they both flew to Gatwick and drove to Tunbridge Wells.

Dr Massey sat listening to the cassette on his hi-fi equipment. He was smiling to himself as he listened to Jack Buchanan singing 'And her mother comes too'. When Jan Massey drew up his chair the old man leaned sideways to switch off the machine.

'Did you find what you wanted in Tunbridge Wells, my boy?'

'I did, Father.'

'You look better than the last time I saw you.'

'I am, Father. I'm fine.' He paused. 'Can I talk to you about something?'

'You don't have to ask, boy. You know better than that. What is it?'

'I'm going to get married, Father. A week on Friday. I'd very much like for you to be there.'

'And I will be, but that isn't what's making you look so . . . tense. Is it?'

'D'you remember me telling you about a girl I loved and it all fell through?'

'Yes. I remember very well.'

'That's the girl I'm marrying. But there are problems. I'd like your comments.'

'What are the problems?'

For well over an hour Massey talked to his father and the old man listened without comment or questions. When eventually Massey finished the old man said, 'What do you want me to comment on?'

'Am I doing the wrong thing for Anna? She's nobody to turn to for advice except me. I'm not impartial.'

'What kind of wrong did you have in mind?'

'Have I rushed her into something she'll regret?'

'It sounds as if you did your rushing a long time ago. When you got yourself arrested in East Berlin. And she seems to be as much inclined to be rushing as you are.' He sighed. 'You seemed to have a very finite amount of calmness and patience all your life, boy. And then you'd be off like a wild thing. It seems a little late in the day to have doubts now. You wonder if she might regret this. Why should she? The worst thing that could happen for her is that you stop loving her. Knowing you, I'd say that's very unlikely. You sacrificed your career when you thought it would get her out of prison.'

'And a technically illegal marriage.'

'The marriage isn't a necessity. Just a formality. If that's what you both want, then get on with it.'

'Anything else?'

'If they threaten to harm her, those people. What would you do?'

'Protect her.'

The old man shook his head. 'That's foolish thinking, Jan. You'd better face the reality.'

'And what's that?'

'You'd have to do whatever they wanted. Just like you did the first time.'

'We could move. There are places I know where we could go where they would never find us. Contacts I have.'

'Think about it, Jan. Think about it.'

'Will you be a witness for us at the registrar's office?'

'Of course I will. Where is she now?'

'We're both staying at a hotel just outside Tunbridge Wells to establish our local address.'

The old man smiled. 'I'll be there, boy.' He paused. 'How about you bring her down here for tea tomorrow? Mrs Hargreaves'll be around.'

Dr Massey had put on his best suit and as he walked her round the small garden he realized what appeal she must have for his son. That calm beautiful face and the lithe young body. Gentle and intelligent, and an obvious strength of character behind the outward diffidence.

He brushed a scatter of leaves from the bench under the apple tree, and as they sat there he said quietly, 'Are you happy, Anna?'

'Very happy. The happiest I've ever been in my life.'

'No regrets? Your father?'

She sighed and shrugged. 'I've seen very little of him in the last few years.'

'You'll need to be very strong.'

'She smiled. 'Jan is strong enough for both of us. But I will be strong if it's necessary.'

'It will be necessary. You can be sure of that.'

'Why do you think that?'

'Those people will come back to him. Will want him to commit real treason not just changing some disk.'

'What makes you think that?'

'I can remember him explaining to me – years ago – when he had been on a training course – that when they wanted to use someone they asked for something very minor the first time. Just borrowing a passport maybe. Something illegal but not very important. And once you had done *anything* illegal, you were committed. They had a hold on you. What they asked for next time would be more important.'

'You think they will do that with Jan?'

'I'm sure they will.'

'But he knows those things better than we do.'

'Of course he does. But he's capable of ignoring them if it suits him. Especially where you are involved.'

'So what should we do?'

'I don't know, my love. I don't know. Only he can decide when it happens. But it's best you should know that some day it will happen. They are evil people and they already have a hold on him, whatever he thinks.'

She walked back to the house with the old man, thoughtful and concerned because she had seen the tears in his eyes.

It had moved her to see where Jan had been a boy. To think of him with his father. Just the two of them. And the influence of those conflicting genes. The reserved, stoical Englishman and the beautiful, impetuous Pole. All influencing the life of the man who looked so controlled and capable but who, she knew, had that gap in his armour. His own people didn't recognize it, but the KGB had seen it and used it. Maybe it took a Slav to recognize that fatal flaw. The impetuous heart that could overrule the head without a moment's hesitation. His father's warning had been perceptive and wise, and she would bear it in mind. When it happened she must be calm, not join him in the turmoil. For both their sakes she must be just a little bit English.

CHAPTER THIRTY-SIX

Chambers needed time to sort out his thoughts about Massey and he'd booked himself in for a couple of nights at the Compleat Angler in Marlow.

As he sat on the riverbank he watched the tip of the float curve round in the swirl of the tail of the weir. He'd baited the hook with weed from the stone steps and there were roach under the elderberry on the far bank. But the roach, like his thoughts, had been elusive. As he reeled in his line he checked the hook and stuck it into the cork handle, laying the rod alongside him on the grass. It was time to face the thinking.

Why had Kuznetsov been so determined in his refusal to be debriefed by Massey? He'd tried to get some explanation no matter how vague. But the Russian had just smiled faintly and shaken his head. Then the odd comment from the French way back. A hint about Massey and some girl. When the French gave sly hints about relations with a girl they must really be scraping the bottom of the barrel. And when he'd pressed them for details, the knowing smiles but no more. And then that chat with Max Cohen in Hong Kong. Massey was the only SIS man who had unchecked access into Cohen's operation. And Cohen's vigorous defence of Massey. That was all very well as the attitude of a chap concerned with signals, but in SIS nobody was taken at face value. Burgess, Maclean and Philby had wiped out any lingering temptation to count background, upbringing or outward appearance as proof of loyalty and integrity. Even a man's record of efficiency could be a cover for treason. Loyalty was no longer taken for granted. Civil servants leaked documents to the media and self-publicizing politicians on the grounds that it was in the public interest. People signed their acceptance of the Official Secrets Act and then justified leaking State secrets with no more excuse than that they thought it should be done. Politics, and even government, were now part of an unstable Establishment built on the shifting sands of some clerk's whim of the moment. He had thought that when he used the excuse of GCHQ deciding to move Cohen and posted Massey to Paris, he would have put him in baulk.

Massey being in baulk meant avoiding another of those dreadful departmental investigations, and the settling of old scores concerning rivalries of decades long past. The near impossibility of finding positive evidence that would satisfy a High Court judge. And then the traditional media outcry, harking back forty years and more to the shortcomings of people long dead. What possible justification did he have for unleashing such chaos on a hard-working and conscientious group of people? People who knew that there would never be any public kudos for their years of loyalty. And others who continuously risked their lives?

Chambers, after two days' thinking, decided to wait. There was far too little to justify any action against Jan Massey. Instinct, or maybe wishful thinking, told him that something would happen that would resolve the problem. He was sufficiently on edge to wonder if it was significant that in the two days he had spent fishing, he had not taken a single roach. He needed a sign. From God, or somewhere.

In Paris Massey, too, was looking for a sign. For two months he had spent five days a week in Paris on his own, flying back to Malmö on Fridays.

He never went straight to their apartment from the airport and he never allowed Anna to meet him when he flew in. The airport buildings were quite sparse and open and gave him plenty of opportunity to check if he was being followed. He waited for the other passengers on the flight to take the airport bus or drive off in waiting cars and there was never a sign of anyone watching him.

He had apologized to Anne-Marie for his sudden disappearance from the cafeteria and although she had smiled she had made no comment nor asked any questions.

The material that he was sending back to London came partly from Autenowski but mainly from Anne-Marie. He had repeatedly asked the French-desk officer for some indication of what areas particularly interested them, but there was very little response.

Massey was aware that his role had changed substantially. What was expected of him was no more than top-grade hack work. The kind of work that old faithfuls of SIS were given when they were working out their last couple of years before retirement. But he was too much the professional to just coast along, and through Anne-Marie he had built up a small network of useful informers who provided a wide spectrum of information that could be expanded easily into a well-based intelligence network. He had sent a memo and report to Chambers showing what could be done if the budget was quite modestly increased. There had been no reply beyond an acknowledgement that his report had been received.

Autenowski had obviously sensed that he was frustrated and had made a discreet and tentative suggestion that he might like to join the CIA. There were top jobs that he could be offered and it was clear that Autenowski had discussed the possibility with CIA headquarters at Langley before sounding him out. But the complications of Anna virtually ruled it out, and Massey settled down to accepting that he was being made to work his passage back into SIS's favour. He wasn't sure why he had to do it but was well aware that such things were not uncommon.

He also had Anna for consolation. He telephoned her daily and their weekends together made up for his arid existence in Paris. She was well aware of his desperate need for the calm, peaceful routine of their weekends. She asked no questions about his work but knew instinctively that he was in a state of uncertainty and turmoil. Although it was in her life that the greater upheaval had taken place, she had coped with it more easily. Even before she met Jan Massey she had considered leaving Kholkov. She wondered sometimes why she had married him. He had not been KGB when she first knew him: he had been a not-very-successful actor with the Bolshoi reserve group. She wondered later if perhaps he had been KGB even then. Maybe just an informer on his colleagues. He had been charming and diffident and undemanding. They had been married for three months before she discovered that he was homosexual. She had been resigned to her situation and her acceptance had, in fact, made their relationship more relaxed. She no longer saw him as a husband but merely a man whose career would be jeopardized if she broke off their relationship. She neither sought or expected to find another man to share her life. When she first met Jan Massey it was like being a teenager again. He was handsome and intelligent, and she was conscious of him being an exceptional man. A big, calm, quiet man, who was too sure of himself to need the macho devices that most men adopted. And right from the first words they exchanged she had sensed the great depths of his emotions. Bottled up, as hers were.

When she lost touch with him after her visit to Moscow she had been hurt at first and confused. But gradually she had grown to accept that because of his work something serious could have happened to cause him to cut off the contact with her. She was quite sure that it was not a question of him ceasing to love her. But as the months went by she found herself more often daydreaming about him, wondering if perhaps she had done something or said something that had caused him to have doubts. But the daydreams just as often involved imaginary scenarios of them meeting. The meeting was always in a wood, sunshine slanting through the trees. Jan walking towards her down a narrow track in the slender birch trees, unaware that she was waiting for him at the end of the path. The daydreams always ended at the moment when their eyes first met. She never knew what happened after that.

The actual meeting with him in Paris was nothing like her daydreams. Nothing like anything she had imagined. It was so ordinary that it seemed as if they had arranged it beforehand. She had needed no time to think about staying with him. It was no more than putting the clock back to the time in Berlin when they were so near to grasping the nettle but had waited for a sign. For her the lesson had been painfully learned and she didn't hesitate. She knew instinctively that he loved her and she believed implicitly what he had told her of what had happened. Apart from believing him, it all fitted in with what had happened to her. Despite her knowledge of the KGB, she was shocked at what they had done and angry with Kholkov's duplicity. But it didn't matter any more to her. She was with Jan and that was enough.

She had known that it would create problems for him but she knew that he would be able to cope with them. But as the weeks went by, she realized that despite his obvious pleasure in their being together he was tense and uncertain about what they should do. She made no suggestions, just following his lead without question, and as the weeks went by he seemed to regain his old confidence. On the telephone during the week his voice was always tense despite his reassuring words but at the weekends he relaxed as soon as he was with her. They were both used to a rootless existence and they found the small Swedish city friendly and civilized.

Their weekends together were no more than most couples could take for granted, but for both of them their pleasure in the ordinariness and routine of their weekend lives was almost the first real pleasure that they had ever experienced. It was as if they had both come in from the cold.

CHAPTER THIRTY-SEVEN

Massey had given up his room in the rue Mouffetard and had taken two rooms at a small hotel near the place Vendôme. He was putting on his bathrobe when he heard the knock on the door and he walked across the room slowly as he tied the belt. When he opened the door he saw a man in a well-cut dark blue suit. Tall and slim with a tanned, smiling face that for a moment Massey couldn't place. As the man smiled at Massey he said softly, in Russian, 'Fomenko, comrade . . . may I come in?'

For a moment Massey hesitated, and then he stood aside to let the Russian into the room.

Fomenko stood in the centre of the room. 'I apologize for coming unannounced . . . but I thought it might be more tactful this way . . .' he shrugged. 'And easier, of course.'

'What do you want, Fomenko?' Massey said quietly.

Fomenko smiled, his eyes amused, his head slightly tilted as if he were interviewing Massey for a job. 'Could we sit and talk for a few moments, do you think?'

Massey nodded and pointed to an armchair, seating himself on the arm of a chair facing the Russian. Fomenko made himself comfortable before looking up at Massey.

'It seems a long time since we last met. I was looking forward to seeing you again as soon as I got the news.'

'What news?'

Fomenko smiled broadly, 'Kholkov's news . . . you really do provoke our little friend.' He smiled. 'A touch of Oscar Wilde – losing your wife once is unfortunate, but losing her twice is just careless.' He paused. 'Anyway – I thought we should talk.'

'What about? Get on with it.'

Fomenko waved towards the other armchair. 'Do make yourself comfortable, my friend. You look so tense perched up there.'

'Just say what you've got to say, Fomenko.'

'Well, I'm really more concerned to hear what you've got to say to me.'

'About what?'

'Oh, Massey, be a good chap. You ride off into the sunset like young Lochinvar with a senior KGB man's wife and you wonder what there is to talk about.' He leaned forward. 'You don't imagine that we shall just let you walk away with it, do you?'

'Do what you like, Fomenko. Moscow would be the laughing-stock of the world if you publicize that the wife of a KGB officer prefers an SIS officer instead.'

'Of course. I can visualize the cartoons right now. Even our Warsaw Pact colleagues might manage a smile at our expense. But I wasn't thinking along those lines.' Fomenko flicked a nonexistent speck from his immaculate lapel. 'I was thinking more about the very, very senior SIS man in Berlin who co-operated with the KGB.' Fomenko paused. 'Some misguided people might see it as treason, might wonder what kind of men they were who chose, as head of a vital intelligence operation, a man who is prepared to commit treason for the sake of a pretty girl.' Fomenko sighed, taking a deep breath. 'So what do we do about it, my friend? Do we lash out at one another in public, or do we find some way to avoid this? Compromise?'

'Go on.'

'You told me . . . that night in Berlin . . . that you loved Anna Kholkov . . . Do you still love her . . . Or are you just paying off an old debt . . . a debt of honour, let us say? What is it?'

'Forget the questions, just say what you want.'

'Do I detect a hint of willingness to cooperate, my friend?'

'If you do you'd be wrong, Fomenko. You've got no hostage now. No phoney scenario of a young girl held in prison on fake charges as a trade for what you want.'

Fomenko said softly, 'We've got two hostages this time, Massey. The two of you.' His face was grim as he looked back at Massey. 'I give you fair warning, my friend. No matter how long it takes, we'd find her. And when we find her we'll settle the score. I'm not bluffing, Massey, I mean it. I want you to believe me. We'll get her wherever she is. We've got all the time in the world. And every time you kiss her goodbye you'll wonder if that's the last time you'll see her alive.' He shrugged. 'If that's what you prefer to co-operation just say so and I'll walk away right now.'

'What is it you want?'

'Right now, nothing. I just want to establish that when we call for your co-operation again we shall get it.'

'What kind of cooperation?'

Fomenko shrugged. 'Who knows? It's not been thought about. Maybe we never ask you for anything.'

'You just wanted to make the threat.'

'Put it like that if you wish. Let us say that I'm pointing out that you can't play games with us without paying the entrance fee. If you put your hand in our mincing machine don't complain when we turn the handle.'

'So. You've made your point. You'd better go.'

'You sure you've got the message, my friend? If you want her to stay alive. If you want to live undisturbed you toe the line. It's a kind of insurance policy, Massey. And it doesn't cost you a cent. *You* cooperate with us if we ask you to and . . .' he shrugged '. . . you both live happy ever after.'

Fomenko stood up, walking slowly to the door. As he put his hand on the lock to open it he turned and said, 'If you wonder if we could find her, just work out how I traced you here. Think about it.'

The Russian nodded and then let himself out, closing the heavy door quietly. Massey walked to the door and pushed down the catch on the lock, and then, realizing how pointless it was, pushed it back up again.

In a strange way Fomenko's visit had cleared his mind. He was a professional, back in the world he understood. It was part of the card game that he had been playing for years. Not the classic bridge game that top desk men played, but poker, where temperament was almost as important as the cards you held. Up to now there had been an unacknowledged deadlock. They had taken the kitty in Berlin and now, with Anna, he'd just got his money back. So they were dealing the cards again. He had little doubt that they would be prepared to wait for years if necessary to carry out their threats, either against Anna or by exposing him. But they were aware that if he chose he could retaliate by embarrassing them – by exposing the pressures they had brought to bear on him with all the charade they had gone through in Berlin.

Fomenko and others would have worked out the play quite carefully. Branding him as a traitor would mean being exposed themselves. His downfall wasn't worth that to them. So they had raised the stakes. Not exposure but a death threat. So it must matter to them not to be exposed. The move to involve him further was probably no more than a pre-emptive upping of the stakes just to see how he responded. A fishing expedition, to which he had no need to respond. There was a vague feeling at the back of his mind that there was another card in his hand to play, but he couldn't, at that moment, recognize what it was. In a way Fomenko's visit had cleared the air. He hadn't been sure what their reactions would be to Anna's departure, but now he knew. She was back in her original role as a useful pressure point. But it had been threats, not action.

There had been no signs of his being followed in Paris or on his weekend journeys. He recognized that this pattern of life could only be temporary but he had doubts about how to solve the problem.

He had his sign when he walked through Customs and Immigration at de Gaulle on a Monday morning a few weeks later. Two men had closed in on him as he walked through to the taxi rank, one on each side. The jab in his back unmistakably from a silencer. When he stopped, the man on his right said, 'There's a white Citroën just ahead. Comrade Fomenko just wants to talk to you. If you make trouble I'll shoot. Those are my orders.'

For a moment Massey was tempted to lash out but he took a deep breath and walked to the car. The rear door opened as he got there and Fomenko beckoned him inside. When the other two were in the car and the doors closed, Fomenko nodded to the driver.

He turned to Massey. 'I must apologize for the crudity but it seemed the only way.'

Massey said nothing as the car was driven towards the city. When they turned right at place de Colombie into boulevard Lannes he guessed where they were going and was amazed at their arrogance.

The gates of the Soviet Embassy stood open and the car swept inside and down to the far end of the building.

Fomenko led the way through a small door in a stone wall, along a short corridor to a room that was furnished as a living-room. He held the door open for Massey and pointed to one of the leather armchairs.

'Do sit down, my friend.'

Fomenko nodded to the two other men to leave and as they closed the door behind them he turned to Massey.

'Please believe me when I say I don't wish to harm you or disturb you in any way. But we need your help.' As Massey opened his mouth to speak the Russian held up his hand. 'Let me finish, comrade.' He paused. 'If you would assist us on this occasion I have been authorized to tell you that we give a solemn undertaking that we shall never ask for any assistance from you again. We should leave you and Anna in peace. You may not like us but you know enough to know that when we make a bargain we keep our word. Always.' He paused again. 'As an indication of our attitude, let me say that we learned only by accident of your flight back this morning from Sweden. You have not been under any surveillance by us and . . .' he smiled '. . . perhaps more important to you . . . let me say we have no idea where Anna is. We have not tried to trace her.'

'So why today's little show?'

Fomenko smiled and shrugged. 'Forgive me. It was the only way I could be sure of being able to talk to you.'

'I'm not going to help you, Fomenko. You're wasting your time.'

The Russian's brown eyes looked at Massey's face as he said quietly, 'Would you really like her to be killed? I can't believe that.'

He saw the anger on Massey's face, the white knuckles and the deep breath to control himself. Fomenko went on.

'We've been putting together one of our jigsaw puzzles. It's taken us quite a time and a lot of work. We've only just begun to see the picture. And the picture's very disturbing. A very senior KGB officer disappeared while he was at meetings in Stockholm. You may have heard of him. Aleksandr Dmitrevich Kuznetsov. There seemed to be no reason why he defected. He was not under suspicion. In fact he was due for yet another promotion. Now, in our investigations there are two threads. Threads that lead to two different men. One is a Frenchman – Bourget. A man who you knew in Berlin. The other is you.' Fomenko waited for a moment and then went on. 'All I want to know is which one of you it was. We've traced contacts by Kuznetsov with both of you. You and the Frenchman.' Fomenko spoke very quietly, 'Which one of you made him defect? And how did you do it?'

'Have you asked Bourget?'

'No. We don't trust Bourget. Maybe we shall talk to him but either way he would say it was you.' He paused. 'This is a serious matter for us and for you too. We are prepared to give you time to think it over.'

'I'm not going to answer your question, Fomenko. You're wasting your time.'

'You will, Massey. Because if you don't the girl will die. Wherever she is we will find her. It would be just a question of time. It didn't take us long to trace you to the hotel or to check that you would be landing at de Gaulle this morning.'

'You're not on your home ground this time, Fomenko. We're not in East Berlin now.'

'Oh, come, Massey. You know us better than that.' He looked at Massey's face. 'Let's leave it for a week, yes? You think it over and we meet again.' Fomenko smiled. 'I'll contact you.'

'If I told you it was Bourget what would you do?'

'I'd believe you,' the Russian said softly.

'Why?'

'Because you might as well kill the girl yourself if you told me a lie.' Fomenko stood up. 'You have nothing to lose provided you tell the truth. If it was Bourget, then that is the end of the matter for you. If it was you it is still the end of the matter for you. Either answer and our account is squared. All we want is the answer.' He paused. 'You're free to leave – there are no guards on the door.'

Massey bent to pick up his bag and was tempted to wreak his anger on the Russian, but there was no point and he straightened up and walked to the door.

Outside he let the first empty taxi pass and hailed the second. He had no doubt what he must do. He must warn Kuznetsov.

Massey phoned Chambers as soon as he got back to the hotel and was taken aback by Chambers's reaction when he said that he wanted to talk to Kuznetsov. He thought at first that Chambers didn't understand who he meant because when referring to the Russian he used just the initial letter, but it became clear that Chambers knew exactly who he meant but was reluctant to agree to a meeting. When he asked why he shouldn't talk with the Russian, Chambers asked him what he wanted to talk about. Massey said that he had heard several pieces of gossip concerning the KGB that he would like to discuss with Kuznetsov, and Chambers grudgingly agreed. He would like a meeting himself with Massey before Massey saw the Russian. Massey suggested that he would fly over straight away and they could meet that evening, but Chambers said it was not convenient, suggesting the afternoon flight the next day and adding that he would meet Massey at Gatwick.

As the plane started its descent to Gatwick Massey went over in his mind again how he would pass the warning to Kuznetsov. He took it for granted that there was a strong possibility that wherever they met would be bugged. Chambers's reluctance to agree to the meeting could only mean that they were still debriefing Kuznetsov. The Russian was an experienced professional who would need the truth of what had happened to convince him. It would be up to Kuznetsov to demand even higher security protection without revealing why. It had got to be between Kuznetsov and himself. There mustn't be the vaguest hint that the request for higher security came from anything that he had said.

CHAPTER THIRTY-EIGHT

Chambers, looking tired and pale faced, was waiting on the tarmac and had walked him through Immigration and Customs with a familiar nod to the officials. As they were going towards the exit they passed a small crowd of people waiting for passengers. A young woman with a scarf round her head stared at them, checked something in her handbag and walked towards the public telephones.

As they got in the car Chambers said, 'I've arranged for us to go to one of the safe-houses. It's not far.'

'Which one is it?'

'I don't think you know it. It's just outside East Grinstead. It's a pleasant little place and we should be comfortable there.'

'Is K there?'

'We're bringing him down from St Albans. Tomorrow.'

Chambers didn't respond to his attempts at conversation but was friendly enough once they were at the house. He showed Massey to a pleasant room and left him to settle in while he went to check if there were any messages for him.

There were only two for Chambers. One from his wife and one to phone the duty officer at Century House immediately he arrived.

He dialled the CH number.

'Duty officer.'

'Chambers. I got a message to phone you.'

'Ah, yes, sir. I took a phone call about fifteen minutes ago. The caller asked for you and I said you were not available. They asked for a message to be passed to you urgently. Do you want to go over to a scrambler?'

'Is it necessary?'

'I don't think so.'

'Go on then.'

'The message was quote tell Mr Chambers to ask Massey about Anna Kholkov unquote. End of message.'

'Is that all?'

'Yes, sir.'

'Any name given?'

'No. None, sir. It was a foreign accent.'

'A recognizable accent?'

'I'd say it was Russian, sir.'

'Do you speak Russian?'

'Yes, sir. I was at St Anthony's.'

'OK. Thank you.'

Chambers hung up and stood in the panelled hall. He'd been waiting for a sign. This looked like the sign. He sighed and picked up the phone again. Radford would be down in about an hour.

They had dinner together in the annexe and Chambers talked about his recent visit to Buenos Aires. As they got up from the table Chambers said, 'Let's go up to my room and talk about things.'

As Chambers opened the door of his suite Massey saw a man sitting there. He recognized the face but couldn't remember who he was.

Chambers said, 'Let me introduce you. Jimmy Radford, Jan Massey.'

Radford didn't get up but he smiled as he put out his hand. 'You won't remember me but I took over a defector named Kinsky from you about six or seven years ago.'

Massey nodded as he shook Radford's hand and sat down as Chambers pointed to one of the chairs. It was Chambers who started them off.

'I've been worried about several things recently, Jan. All of them concerning you. I thought it was time to get them off my chest.' He waved towards Radford. 'I thought it might be sensible for Jimmy Radford to be here too. Any objections?'

Massey shook his head. 'No. None at all. Is this an official inquiry?'

Chambers shrugged. 'Not quite, but it could turn into that.'

Massey nodded and said quietly, 'Please go ahead.'

'I'd like to go back to when Kuznetsov came over.' Chambers paused and looked at Massey's face. 'I suggested to him that as he knew you for so long that you should debrief him. He was adamant that he wouldn't be debriefed by you. I asked him why not you, and he wouldn't answer. Just shook his head and smiled. Why do you think he didn't want you to debrief him, Jan?'

'I've no idea. I'm surprised to hear it.'

'Any suggestions why he took that attitude?'

'Could be several reasons. Maybe he preferred to start fresh with somebody different.'

'Go on.'

'How should I know why? Maybe he doesn't like me, or remembers how we first met. He was embarrassed about that at the time. Thought he'd lost face.'

'Could it be that he doesn't trust you?' Radford said quietly.

'If he didn't trust me why did he want me to help him defect?'

'You and I were his only contacts, Jan,' Chambers said. 'And I don't speak Russian.'

'He speaks good enough English to make contact with you.'

Radford said, 'Is there any possible reason why he shouldn't trust you? Maybe a misunderstanding?'

'Not that I know of.'

Chambers said, 'Let's go back to when you were in Berlin and we had that trouble about the disks . . .'

They questioned him for three hours. Politely, persistently, going back over his answers again and again, but they got nowhere. Jan Massey was a professional and he knew more about interrogation than the two of them would ever know. He guessed right from the start that they were fishing. They had nothing to go on and they got nothing from him. It was one in the morning when the confrontation broke up. The atmosphere was strained but no direct accusation had been made. They agreed to talk again the following morning at eleven.

Neither Chambers nor Radford slept that night. They had a lot to do.

Massey sat in his room going over what had obviously become an interrogation. He had no intention of giving them an inch. He was aware that he was now under pressure from both sides. From the KGB and SIS.

In Paris, Fomenko had fumed when he got the message that Massey had flown to London and that the man who had met him at Gatwick was Chambers. He assumed that Massey had gone to report the Russian offer in the hope that it would give him SIS protection. He also assumed that Massey would not divulge past events or his relationship with the girl. But there was no hope now, Fomenko assumed, of getting what they wanted from Massey. His sudden flight to London was answer enough. And now all he could do was finish Massey off as an SIS officer.

Chambers had driven back to London and the name Kholkov had been run through Central Archives's computer. It had thrown up two Kholkovs. One at the Soviet Embassy in Cairo and the other a KGB officer who had been in Berlin and was now in Budapest. It had not taken long for Berlin to confirm that an Anna Kholkov was the KGB man's wife. There was no photograph on file but there was a detailed description.

Kuznetsov was roused from his sleep at the safe-house in Kensington and led to believe that Massey had told SIS of his relationship with Anna Kholkov, and asked what he knew. Kuznetsov was suspicious and refused to go beyond the fact that he knew that the girl and Massey had had an *affaire*.

Massey walked round the garden of the safe-house that had once been a vicarage and saw Chambers drive his car through the guarded gates and park it at the front of the house.

At a few minutes before eleven he knocked on Chambers's door and walked in. Chambers was alone and on the telephone, nodding as he listened to what was being said at the other end. Finally he said he had a meeting and hung up. He turned to look at Massey and Massey took some comfort from the troubled look in Chambers's eyes.

Chambers pointed to the chair and sat opposite, his hand reaching up to loosen the knot of his tie.

'How did you sleep, Jan?'

Massey shrugged. 'Not too well.'

Chambers sighed. 'I thought it would be better . . . more constructive . . . if we talked alone.'

Massey nodded but said nothing, his face impassive.

Then Chambers said quietly, 'Tell me about Anna Kholkov.'

There was a long silence. Two or three minutes. And then Massey said quietly, 'I want to resign from SIS. As of today. And I refuse to answer any more questions.'

Chambers shook his head slowly and emphatically. 'Jan, Jan. It's gone too far to be that simple. You know that. Please talk with me. I'll do all I can to help.'

'And if I don't?'

'I'll have to charge you and take you to a magistrates' court. You know the drill. You've done it enough times yourself. But, I beg of you, don't . . . just once in your life . . . think before you jump. There are compromises that can be arranged. You know that too.'

'You mean you want me to do a Blunt?'

'Yes. If that's how you want to describe it.'

'It's a game I've not played. Tell me the rules.' Massey saw the relief on Chambers's face.

'Let me tell you the reasons so that you'll understand that it's not some device to incriminate you. We strongly suspect that you have worked with or for the Russians. With the KGB. There is a lot of circumstantial evidence pointing that way. Given time we could almost certainly come up with enough evidence to convince a court.

'It is more use to us to know exactly what has been going on than to have you sitting in a cell for the rest of your life in Wormwood Scrubs. And you don't need me to tell you that the media and the politicians would have a field day at SIS's expense if you went on trial. We've had a bellyful of them the last few years. We've been whipping-boys for so-called investigative journalists and the militant left doing Moscow's bidding.' He paused. 'What do you say, Jan?'

'Just let's assume that I cooperate. *If* I do – how do I come out of it?'

'Early retirement on health grounds. Full pension but no gratuity. And we'll leave you in peace. No messing about.'

'What protection would I get?'

Chambers looked surprised. 'Is it that bad, Jan?'

'It could be. I don't know.'

'Let's say that if you cooperate and it looks like we need to warn off Moscow, we'll do it.'

Massey knew already that he had no choice. His career would limp on if he didn't cooperate, but Anna and he would live like nomads, constantly under tension as they waited for the blow to fall.

'OK, Chambers. I'll tell you what's happened. It started in Berlin . . .'

They had hired a car and driven out to Skanör and then walked down to the shore. The beach was almost completely deserted, just two anglers casting for bass.

They found a sheltered inlet in the bank and opened the haversack with their Thermos and sandwiches. There were small flocks of sandpipers at the edge of the sea and snipe on the bank behind them. Great clusters of willow-herb covered the sheltered side of the bank, its fluffy seeds already visible where the long thin seedpods had begun to split. It reminded Massey of his walks on Romney Marshes with his father. Almost as if she had read his thoughts she handed him a sandwich and said, 'Have you told your father?'

'I told him about you and me and what had happened but I haven't told him about the present situation.'

'Why not?'

'It would depress him and he's too old to face this kind of thing. He was always afraid that I should do something hotheaded and land myself in trouble. He'd start thinking that he is in some way responsible for letting what he calls the Polish influence affect me.

'He never knew what I was actually doing and as far as he's concerned he'll assume that I'm still doing the same job but somewhere else.'

'And what about you?'

Massey turned to look at her face. 'All I want is to buy us some peace.'

'What do you have to pay for peace?'

'I've told them what they wanted to know. They've given me most of what I asked for.'

'What did you ask for?'

'Guaranteed permanent immunity to prosecution. Full pension. No disclosure internally or externally. No harassment of any kind.'

'Why should they do a deal, Jan?'

Massey shrugged. 'A lot of reasons. First of all, despite what they said, they couldn't have provided anywhere near enough evidence against me to satisfy a court. In fact they didn't have a shred of evidence. Just a few shrewd guesses. Nothing a court would accept for a moment. And exposing me would have been an embarrassment. For the department and for the government.

'And it means they can do what they call a "damage limitation" exercise. They can go back to the moment when the disk was changed and look at all the decisions that were made subsequently and check whether they were influenced by the changeover.' Massey shrugged impatiently. 'It hasn't affected anything really. It was out of the mainstream of intelligence.'

'Why did the KGB go to such elaborate lengths to trap you if it wasn't important?'

Massey shrugged. 'That was only the beginning. Once you've committed an illegal act on behalf of the KGB they've got a hold on you. The first time can be some very small offence. But once you've committed *any* offence, that gives them an extra hold on you. Next time it's something more important.'

'And Fomenko and the KGB?'

'Well, they refused to give any guarantee when Chambers first contacted them but he had obviously made his point. They came back a week later and said they'd reconsidered and they would agree to leave us alone provided I was no longer active in SIS.' He smiled. 'They really wouldn't have liked their part of the game to be published in the press. It was in the KGB's interest to call it a day. And in Moscow's interest too.'

'What *didn't* you get that you asked for?'

'I asked for genuine British citizenship for you. They agreed to that, and I asked that our marriage was made legal. They wouldn't agree to that unless Moscow agreed to allow you a legal Soviet divorce. Moscow would never agree to that because it would provide documentary evidence of what had happened if it was ever investigated. That's the only thing I couldn't get.'

Anna looked at his face and said softly, 'Do you ever wish you'd never met me?'

'Of course I don't. The unpleasant things that happened were nothing to do with us. I behaved very stupidly and they cashed in on it.'

'Where shall we live when it's over?'

'I'd got in mind New Zealand or Spain.'

'Why New Zealand?'

'It's a long way from Europe. They're nice people and it's a lovely country. The only snag is they speak English and still have some ties with London. People over there could look into my background and start putting two and two together. In Spain we could lose ourselves. They wouldn't care enough to check on me. Why should they? Even if they found out that I was once SIS I doubt if they'd care. There are scores of British criminals there. One British traitor wouldn't matter.'

'You're not a traitor, Jan. Nobody could say that.'

'I am, my love. I'm afraid I am.'

'And all those years of service in SIS count for nothing?'

'I'm afraid not. To everybody except us, I'm a traitor. That's how they would see me. The government, politicians, the media have a vested interest in ignoring any human factor. Loving you would be no excuse. It would be misrepresented. Deliberately. It would be in their interest to make it a question of sex not love.'

'But why? Why couldn't it be for love?'

Massey smiled. 'Because some people, some of the public, would feel sympathy for you and me if it was a question of love. When a man is exposed as a traitor he must be shown to be *all* bad. Not just a traitor but a pervert, a bad father and husband. A man whose friends always found him strange and aloof. A man who cheated at school. If possible a homosexual or a child molester. And a man who was motivated by hatred for his country and his countrymen. Whatever you do you mustn't let a traitor look human. If he is intelligent you must make his intelligence mere cunning, any qualities or virtues he has as a human being must be made to seem malevolent. Otherwise some people might sympathize with him, even identify with him. He must be a monster not a man.

'And this is not just the attitude of the Soviet Union or Britain, but every country in the world. Even a spy can be allowed admirers. Provided that he's working for his own country. The KGB's Abel in the United States, Sorge in the Far East – they have their admirers. But not Philby or Alger Hiss, or Gouzenko.'

'And you think that nobody would say good things about you? Not even Chambers and the others who knew you well?'

Massey laughed, shaking his head. 'They would say that they hardly knew me. If they wanted to be kind. If not, they would recall some incident that showed them I was always ruthless or maybe mentally sick.'

She shivered despite the sunshine. 'When can we go to Spain?'

'I think it will be all over in about ten days. You could go ahead if you like and start looking for a house.'

She shook her head. "I'm not going anywhere without you.'

CHAPTER THIRTY-NINE

It was only twenty-four hours after Tom Bartram arrived that the first piece appeared. Just a few lines in the *Standard*'s gossip column.

> Yet another mystery in the ongoing troubles of BBC TV's Current Affairs department. It seems that a project being worked on by top interviewer Tom Bartram has been stopped in its tracks by the new Head of Current Affairs Stanley 'The Knife' Dillon. It seems that several thousand pounds have already been spent on planning an investigation into the perennial problems of the security services. We understand that an Opposition MP is to raise the matter with the Home Secretary next week. Supporters of veteran Tom Bartram at the BBC TV Centre hint that this is, in fact, just one more shot from Dillon at his old rival Bartram, and that the programme was, in fact, a light-hearted look at how some of the alleged British criminals are now living it up on the Costa del Sol.

The *Daily Express* carried the follow-up the next day.

> Members of the opposition are suggesting that a new *Belgrano*-type campaign is to be expected soon, raising doubts about some of the activities of MI6, the Secret Intelligence Service. Since the Blunt affair the Foreign Office has constantly denied that any similar deals have been done with Moscow's moles and sleepers. But at least one Opposition MP is convinced that both MI5 and MI6 are riddled with what he calls the 'Cambridge closet communists.'

The next day's *Times* parliamentary report recorded an exchange at Prime Minister's Question Time.

> Mr Paul Schubert (Lab. Otterly West) asked the Prime Minister if it was true that an immunity-from-prosecution deal had recently been offered to an officer of MI5 or MI6 suspected of passing top-secret information to the Soviet Union or one of the Warsaw Pact countries.
>
> The Prime Minister said that no such deal had been done or contemplated.
>
> Several Opposition MPs indicated dissatisfaction with the Prime Minister's reply and said the matter would be pursued through other channels.

It was a typed slip pushed in front of the late-night ITN newsreader that started the next phase.

Tomorrow's *Sunday Express* carries a report on an investigation that a team of reporters has compiled on a man who is alleged to have been a senior officer of MI6 who was working at the same time for the Russian intelligence service, the KGB.

The report in the *Sunday Express* covered two pages except for a few advertisements. There was a large photograph of the Foreign Office and a large and grainy photograph of a man who had once been head of MI6. He had been dead for almost ten years. He stood awkwardly in the bright summer sunlight, facing the camera, a tennis racket in his hand, a cocker spaniel at his feet and a mass of hydrangeas just visible in the background.

The piece was by-lined to Jason Armitage and Ruby Edwards, and a few short sentences claimed a long history of investigative successes to the pair.

The headline was heavy and across the two pages. 'Is the Fifth Man still doing Moscow's work?' A boxed paragraph explained in bold type.

Due to the protection given by our ridiculous libel laws we have been advised not to publish the name of the MI6 suspect. Neither are we allowed to give a description that would lead to his being identified. We ask – why not? Moscow knows who he is. The Cabinet knows who he is. MI6 knows who he is. We know who he is. But under our archaic laws, you – the public – are not allowed to know.

The first two columns of the report were in heavy type.

We have talked with ex-officers of the security services and the Secret Intelligence Services and there is no doubt in their minds that Burgess, Maclean, Philby and Blunt were only the tip of the iceberg of the Soviet penetration of these two services on which our national security depends.

The more we talked to these experienced officers, now in honourable retirement, the more disturbing was the picture that emerged. To prevent accusations of bias or misunderstanding we asked for the name of one such suspect who we could investigate ourselves. The man whose name was given to us was given the code-name Lucifer for our investigation.

We have visited several European countries during our investigation of Lucifer and interviewed literally scores of people who knew the man concerned. At no time did we divulge why we were making our inquiries. What we have discovered makes a horrifying story of incompetence and falsification. We asked for interviews with the present bosses of both services. And were refused. We asked for various pieces of information to be confirmed or denied. All our requests were refused. It seems that the intelligence services are better at keeping their own guilty secrets than defending our national interests. Ex-members of SIS refer to the department as the Firm. We would call it, more appropriately, the Club.

Let us look at this one single case. The man concerned was a senior officer in SIS. His mother was born a national of a Warsaw Pact country and was at one time an intelligence agent for one of the British wartime espionage and sabotage departments. We were not able to trace her present whereabouts. The man concerned had frequent meetings with KGB officers using his official position as a cover. He speaks fluent Russian.

In an interview with his ex-wife she told us something of his character.

She described him as ruthless and aggressive. In several interviews with a psychiatrist, when we described details of some of the incidents in his married life, the psychiatrist, who has appeared as an expert witness in several court cases, confirmed that the behaviour described was typical of some kinds of psychopath. In the divorce proceedings it was admitted by Lucifer's counsel that he had, on three separate occasions, brutally attacked his wife's friends. It was suggested in court that this was due to his 'Slav temperament'.

As head of station for SIS in a key European city he was in a position to pass to the Russians every detail of the massive radio surveillance organization under his control. There was recently a token clean-up of our intelligence operations in this important city and the man concerned was removed virtually overnight and posted elsewhere to a different country where there was no possibility of his gaining top-secret information of interest to his paymasters in the KGB. Why, if this man was not suspect, was this hurried move necessary?

One of the men previously under his command was later found to be a double agent for the KGB with the rank of lieutenant in that élite Soviet organization. There is little doubt that the protection provided by his commander gave the best possible cover that a double agent could wish for.

There were unconfirmed suggestions, from the intelligence organization of another country operating in the same city at the same time, that our suspect was involved in offers of money bribes for the release of KGB agents under arrest.

Any one of these revelations should have been enough to alert our security forces. And even now they should be investigating this man and others like him. 'No comment' is not good enough.

The stone-walling by the Establishment is not confined to us. Members of Parliament, alarmed by the state of affairs, have raised questions in Parliament about this specific case. The government's replies have been devious to the extent of denying all knowledge of the circumstances.

Few people realize the powers and responsibilities of the two organizations still known as MI5 and MI6 and the following section of our report gives a complete summary of both intelligence departments.

The rest of the article consisted of charts showing the chain of command from the Home Secretary to MI5 and the Foreign Secretary to MI6. And then the internal chain of command of both organizations. There was nothing that had not appeared in a dozen or more books over the years. The exploration of the two organizations' responsibilities and history repeated what was already on the public record, including the usual errors.

The subheadings on the rest of the article promised more than the text delivered. Facts went unsubstantiated and where the omissions were too obvious it was implied that proof would be given later in the piece. The proof never quite caught up with the allegations.

People long dead, unable to defend themselves, were accused of treason and conspiracy on no more grounds than having been at a school or university which some renegade had attended years before or after them. Their motives were impugned without a shred of evidence, their characters assassinated because they had once lived in the same city as some communist suspect. They might never have met but the implication was that they could have.

Nowhere in the article was there a word of praise for men who risked their lives, saw little of their families and who knew enough to expose a score of public figures as hypocrites or worse, yet kept silent.

Jan Massey, despite his long experience, found the media hunt and its distortions only confirmed his dislike of the British Establishment. But Tom Bartram knew that Massey's defiant attitude hid real wounds.

CHAPTER FORTY

A report on the mounting media coverage had been phoned through to Tom Bartram twice a day. His instructions fluctuated, from advice to be very cautious to insistence that he should get as much material as possible and try and ensure that it was all exclusive.

His talks with Massey had been extended over ten days and his outside broadcast team had been sent to fill in their time getting stock film of the Costa del Sol from the gates of Gibraltar to Malaga and on up the coast to Nerja.

On the tenth day Tom Bartram had been told by BBC TV Features that he had only three days left in which to film or call it a day.

He stood with Massey at the side of the house as Massey turned on the pump to fill the water tanks from the well, and Bartram turned to look again across the bay. It was a view he had seen so many times now but the lushness of the flowers, red, purple, bright orange and white marguerites, still held his eye. And the blue of the Mediterranean was a perfect backgroud for an opening shot. You could pull back from the long-shot and fill the lens with a single bloom. A marigold, the ornate head of a geranium or the purple bracts of bougainvillaea.

He turned slowly to look at Massey's face. For long moments his eyes travelled over it. The strong bones, the brown eyes, the full sensual mouth would look marvellous in close-up. And he knew in that moment that he wouldn't do it.

'When can I fetch the team up, Jan?'

Massey shrugged. 'It's up to you.' He turned off the pump switch. 'Let's go back on the patio.'

When they were sitting, drinks in hand, in the wicker chairs, Bartram turned to Massey and held up his glass. 'What is it you and Anna say?'

Massey smiled. '*Na zdrowie.*'

'*Na zdrowie.*' He paused. 'I'm going to leave you two in peace, Jan.'

'What's that mean?'

'I'm going to pass. I'm not going to finish the assignment. No filming.'

'Why not?'

'I just don't want to.'

'Tell me why.'

'I'm not sure it would end up as good material.'

'I don't believe that. You asked me a few minutes ago if you could bring your chaps up to start filming.'

'I wanted to see if you'd refuse.'

'Why?'

'Then I could have justified myself in persuading you to let me do it.'

'And?'

'And I would have done it.'

'So why *didn't* you do it?'

'Because you so obviously trust me.'

'Is that a bad thing?'

'It is for me. I don't want to be trusted.' Bartram looked at Massey. 'You're going to get a rough ride, Jan. I think you know that already. You're a professional, and you know how these things go.' He paused. 'I don't want to be the guy who puts the first boot in. I made a tactical mistake when I started chatting with you. I ought to have stayed at arm's length. I've got involved with you both.'

'Or do you mean your bosses wouldn't give your stuff screen time if it didn't point an accusing finger at me?'

'No. It's more than that. They'd probably accept whatever I did. But I *would* have to point an accusing finger at you. You did what you did. There's no use pretending you didn't. The reasons why you did it won't be acceptable to the Establishment. They'll make them seem tawdry if they let them get mentioned at all. If I hadn't got to know you so well they wouldn't be acceptable to me either.' He sighed. 'But I *have* got to know you and that rules me out.' He shrugged. '*Tout comprendre c'est tout pardonner*. I'd either end up as a bad reporter or a bad friend.' He paused. 'And I don't want to be either.'

Massey smiled. 'I understand. I'm sorry for your sake.'

'Can I give you some advice, Jan? Professional advice.'

'By all means.'

'Nobody else seems to have tracked you down yet. But they will. Don't talk to them as you have talked with me. Refuse to be interviewed. Refuse to answer any questions. Just give them the old "no comment" routine. And stick to it.'

'Why do you say that?'

Bartram turned to look over the bay before he turned back to look at Massey. 'You know why, Jan, as well as I do. They'll all have a vested interest in destroying you. No editor will give them orders to do it and no cabinet minister will threaten to reduce the BBC's licence fee. But the media will know by a kind of osmosis what's expected of them.'

'A hatchet job?'

'No . . . well, I can think of a couple who might do a hatchet job, but the majority will just make you look like a first-class bastard.'

'Won't it be even worse if I refuse to talk at all?'

'It'll be speculation then, Jan. That's different. It's mere gossip-column stuff. A few paras here and there. They'll have difficulty getting their libel lawyers to let them mention your name if there's no official statement implicating you.' He smiled. 'It'll be a thing that so-called investigative journalists ferret away at for years. Long double-page spreads in the heavies – all hints but no facts – no facts that prove anything, anyway. You'll just have to sit tight, both of you, and let it wash over you. Get yourself a good lawyer right away.' Bartram grinned. 'You might even end up with a nice libel settlement out of court.'

Bartram stood up and held out his hand. As Massey took it he said, 'Did *you* understand, Tom?'

Bartram nodded. 'Yes, I understood, Jan. But don't be tempted. Stay silent. Give my love to Anna when she gets back from the market.'

'She'll be disappointed.'

'She won't. Your Anna may be a romantic but she's also a realist.'

Bartram waved from the wrought-iron gates, closing them carefully and snapping the padlock closed on the links of the chain.

CHAPTER FORTY-ONE

The court case against Jimbo Vick had dragged on for several months. He refused to go into the witness box himself. His attorney argued that he was not avoiding cross-examination but was not prepared to give evidence that could affect his wife's reputation. The prosecution claimed that there was no valid marriage and that Jimbo Vick had no wife and was unmarried. They produced all the necessary documentation to substantiate their claim. And day after day Jimbo Vick sat at the table, his wrists still strapped, staring into space as if he was oblivious to everything that was going on around him.

When eventually he was sentenced to ten years he showed no emotion as he was led away, and refused to let his counsel mount an appeal. There were the usual background reports on his life in the media, with emphasis on the wilder episodes. A few newspapers suggested that it was an injustice that allowed a proven spy, a foreigner, to be deported while an American citizen got a long prison sentence as a mere accessory.

Jimbo refused to see his parents both during the trial and after sentencing. He was given a cell on his own and was under more or less constant supervision.

It was over six months after he had started his sentence before Katy Holland and her editor were able to get permission for Katy to interview Jimbo Vick, and over a dozen letters to him before he agreed to see her.

As he sat opposite Katy Holland in the interview cell that was provided for lawyers to meet their clients, she knew that she would have to tread very carefully with her questions. Jimbo Vick's mind was a long way away. But he made no move to stop her as she pressed the record button on the small Sony tape recorder.

'Do you mind if I call you Jimbo, Mr Vick?'

He didn't reply, just a shrug of his shoulders that she treated as assent. She glanced at her shorthand notes and then back at his face.

'Did you feel your sentence was rather harsh, Jimbo? A bit unfair in the circumstances?'

'No.'

'Why not?'

'It was the price that had to be paid.'

He spoke slowly and quietly.

'For what?'

'If I'd defended myself it could only be at the expense of Kirstie. That's what the bastards wanted me to do.'

'Did you never have even the slightest suspicion of what she was doing?'

'No. Never. You don't have suspicions about somebody you love.'

'You must have loved her a lot.'

'I did. I still do.'

'Despite what she did and despite her attitude to you?'

'If an American had done what she did about some Soviet secrets, she'd have been praised as a heroine.'

'And her attitude to you after you were both arrested?'

'If you love somebody, they don't necessarily have to love you in return.'

'What was it about her that made you love her so much?'

'That's a very perceptive question, you know?'

'So tell me.'

He took a deep breath and then sighed. 'I've no idea. No idea at all. I just loved her.'

'Do you ever wish you hadn't met her?'

'No. Never. She was my fate. Nothing else could explain it.' He sighed. 'Despite what happened, we were a pair. A rather odd pair – but a pair all the same.'

'Your answers are unusually honest and frank. Why?'

'You think you're using me, don't you? But you're not. I'm using you.'

'How come?'

'When your paper, magazine, whatever, prints this interview she'll see it eventually. This is my way of telling her that I really did love her.'

'Let's go back to the beginning. How did you first meet her?'

He smiled very faintly. 'It was at a seminar in Washington, she was there too and . . .'

THE CROSSING

This is for Phyl and Ted Davies – with love

PART ONE

CHAPTER ONE

The boy and the young man were the only people on board the ship. They stood leaning over rails looking at the crowd around the man standing on the wooden box, waving his arms and shouting, but the sharp wind carried his words away.

'What's he saying, Boris?'

'He's from the Military Revolutionary Committee from the Petrograd Soviet. He's telling them that the workers, the peasants, and the soldiers are in charge now in Russia. All peasants will be given land, the soldiers will be paid and the people will be fed and given jobs.'

'Are they pleased about that?'

The young man laughed. 'They've heard it too many times, boy, from too many people. They don't believe him. They say they want deeds not words.'

The boy looked at the young man's face, tanned and lined from wind and sun. He had strange eyes. Old, sad eyes that never blinked.

'Somebody told me that hundreds of people have been killed, maybe thousands,' the boy said.

The young man nodded. 'And many more thousands will die before this is over.'

'Why do they kill working people if they want to give them freedom?'

The young man spat over the side of the ship. 'They don't intend to give them freedom, Josef. This is just a struggle for power. Revolutionaries against revolutionaries. Old allies facing the final truth. Which pigs will have their snouts in the trough for the next hundred years. Bolsheviks or Mensheviks.'

'Whose side are you on? Who do you want to win?'

'I'm on the side of whoever wins, boy. And that will be the Bolsheviks. Nobody wants them to win but they will, because they know what they want and they'll kill anyone who stands in their way.'

'Who are these Bolsheviks?'

'Who knows? Here in Petrograd it's Trotsky, Stalin, Sverdlov, Dzerzhinski, Latsis and Peters.'

'How do you know so much about them?'

'I live here. This is my home town. I read the papers and listen to the talk in the bars.'

'Will there be another revolution like they had before?'

'A revolution, yes. But not like we've had before. This time it is power-hungry men at each other's throats. The people will be safe until it's over.'

'When will it be decided who's won?'

'Tonight, at the meeting of the MRC. Tomorrow we shall have new Tsars, in the pay of the Germans this time.'

It was October 25, 1917.

Misha had been a worker in one of the iron-foundries. He was one of Zagorsky's friends and the young man let him on board once or twice a week so that he could have a meal. There was neither bread nor vegetables any longer in the whole of Petrograd despite the promises of commissars from the revolutionary committees.

Even on the ship there were only the standard tins of bully-beef and not enough of those to offer to anybody who wasn't a member of the crew. The meal the three of them ate was boiled potatoes in a thin Oxo cube gravy. Misha ate it with obvious relish, Zagorsky ate it without noticing and young Josef was too busy talking to notice what he was eating.

'Tell me what else they're going to do, Misha.'

'Every man will be free. No more serfs. No more peasants. Every farmer with his own land. No Cossacks to ride down the people. No policeman can arrest a worker without a reason. Laws that protect every citizen.

'We shall share everything; food, housing, work, goods. Every man will care for his neighbour, and all will be equal. No Tsars. No more Rasputins. No priests. For us we work today for our children's tomorrow. And our children's children.' He waved his arms. 'A workers' paradise, young Josef.'

The boy smiled. 'You really think they will do all these things, Misha?'

'I swear it, boy. On my heart and on my soul. It will take time to sort out the past but they are making the laws now.' He tapped the table with his spoon. 'At this minute Lenin is planning Russia's wonderful future. We are a great people. They have freed our greatness. It will happen.'

Zagorsky grinned. 'That's what they said when the women came out in 1905 in Vyborg District, shouting for bread. Kerensky said it years ago. Mentov wrote it in *Iskra* six months ago.'

'That's the point, my friend. The Military Revolutionary Committee was split between the Mensheviks and the Bolsheviks. The Mensheviks promised but did nothing, the Bolsheviks are not afraid. They fought for us. They organized the revolution.'

Zagorsky laughed. 'All the pigs are fighting for power. We'll see. You'd better get back to your place or they might give it to some deserving Bolshevik.'

Misha rose easily to the taunt, beating his fist against his thin chest. 'I am a Bolshevik, my friend.'

The boy walked to the companionway with Misha and pulled aside the rough gate that kept unauthorized people off the boat.

The Russian turned to the boy. 'You care, don't you, Josef? You understand our joy.'

The boy smiled. 'Yes, I understand, Misha. Zag just likes teasing you.'

'He is no fool, that fellow. He knows a lot. He listens and watches. He knows much more than he says. But he has no heart.' Misha smiled. 'Not like us, my friend. We are comrades, yes?'

'Of course, Misha.'

Back in the saloon the boy collected up the dishes and took them to the small galley. As he dried the last enamel plate Zagorsky walked in and sat on the small box that held the cleaning materials.

'Did you believe what Misha said?'

The boy hesitated, blushing. 'Why not? What he says makes sense.'

'They will work harder than they've ever worked in their lazy lives and for no more money. It will take years before any of it comes true.'

'So? What does it matter? They make sacrifices for their children's sake. It's like planting seeds. You have to wait for the corn to grow.'

Zagorsky laughed. 'Who said that, boy?'

'Said what?'

'About planting seeds.'

'I said it. It's true.'

'Would you do all that if there was a revolution in England.'

'Of course I would. All workers would.' He frowned. 'But there's no chance of a revolution in England.'

'Maybe one day you'll have the chance. You'd fight with the workers, would you?'

'Of course.'

Zagorsky said softly, 'Why don't you stay here in Petrograd and help? It would be a good experience for when your time comes.'

'I've signed on, Zag; I'd go to prison if I jumped ship.'

'They'll never have the chance, boy, if you stay. You could walk off now and nobody could stop you.'

'There's Royal Navy ratings at the dockyard gates.'

'So we don't go out through the gates.'

'But you don't believe in it, Zag. You think they won't do it.'

The young man looked at the boy a long time before he spoke, and then he said. 'Never believe what a man says, no matter who he is. Listen, but don't believe. Listen for what's believed in, what's in his mind. That's *all* that matters.' He paused. 'Do you want to stay and help? It will be hard work, with lots of disappointments.'

'Would I be with you and Misha?'

'Maybe. But you've got to learn the language first. Not many Russians speak English, especially the kind you'd be working with.'

'Would they have me?'

Zagorsky nodded. 'Yes. They'd have you. We need all the help we can get. Think about it tonight. If tomorrow you still want to help I'll take you to see the right people.'

'But what good will I be? I can't do anything.'

'I've watched you, Josef. You are a good organizer – and you're honest. That's enough.'

After three months the boy they called Josef could speak enough Russian to understand the orders he got and to hold a reasonable conversation. The Russian he learned was crude and ungrammatical, like the speech of his fellow workers. He saw Misha most days but seldom saw Zagorsky. He realized from what people said that the young man he called Zag so familiarly was important. Zag went to meetings of the Council of the People's Commissars, the *sovnavkom*, and mixed with the leaders like Lenin and Dzerzhinski, who was the head of the newly formed Committee for Struggle Against the Counter-Revolution. The committee that became what people called the *Cheka*.

The boy learned his way around the backstreets of Petrograd, carrying messages and delivering batches of the latest issue of *Pravda*. At night he sat listening to the heated discussions on how long the Bolsheviks would last. Some gave them only a few days, others a month or two and a few, very few, said that the Bolsheviks would be the final victors in the ruthless struggle for power that was being waged in the Duma.

By December 1917 the Bolsheviks had taken control. Arrests, confiscations and house searches were common and there were numerous cases of violence by self-appointed bandit-revolutionaries. Drunkenness and disorder were widespread in the city and rumour had it that it was much the same in all big cities. A newspaper published a speech by Maxim Gorky which said openly that the Bolsheviks were already showing how they meant to rule the country. His final sentence was, 'Does not Lenin's government, as the Romanov government did, seize and drag off to prison all those who think differently?' But no figure arose who could successfully stop the ruthless surge to power of Lenin's men. Resistance from any quarter was met by bringing out the workers on the streets. They seldom knew what they were demonstrating about but it had become part of their daily lives. For the Bolsheviks it was a warning to all those who opposed them that 'power lay in the streets'.

There was a wide spectrum of resistance to the Bolsheviks, including many workers' groups and political parties; almost all left-wing political parties were sworn enemies who recognized that the Bolsheviks' struggle for power was just that, and no more. It was like a juggernaut out of control, its only policy repression of the opposition.

Josef saw Misha almost every evening. Misha liked the long rambling discussions that the group fell into every night. Analyses of personalities and policies, forecasts of a golden future or prophecies that nothing would change except a different group of despots who would behave like any Tsar. The boy always remembered Zagorsky's advice. He listened and said nothing, watching their faces, sometimes recognizing the false ring of praise for the new leaders from some obviously ambitious man. And sometimes he heard the echo of the deliberate incitement of an *agent provocateur*.

It was a hot summer evening when he had to deliver a letter to Zagorsky and he had been invited in, the Russian pointing to a wooden box that was used as a chair.

'Sit down, Josef. I want to talk to you.'

When Josef was perched on the box Zagorsky looked at his face.

'Are you busy with your errands?'

'Yes.'

'They tell me you can write Russian now.'

'Not very well.'

'Well enough to make notes of the decisions at the committee meetings, yes?'

'Yes, I do that.'

'Misha thinks you should be made secretary of the committee. Official secretary. How do you feel about that?'

'What would the older men think?'

'What they think doesn't matter. What about you? Do you want to do it?'

'Yes, if it will help.'

'Help what?'

'The revolution. The workers' new freedom.'

Zagorsky half-smiled. 'What do they think of Comrade Lenin down there?'

'Some say he is the only leader who will do what he says. Others that he is as bad as the Tsar. Some say he is worse.'

'And you? What do you think?'

'I don't know, Comrade Zagorsky. I only hear what others say about him.'

'Comrade, eh? A Bolshevik already?'

The boy smiled, embarrassed. 'At least they are doing things, not just talking about it.'

'Before you are appointed as secretary you will have some training on how to run meetings and control events. It will be in Moscow and it will take about four months. Come and see me tomorrow at ten o'clock, ready to leave.'

'Yes, comrade.'

Josef had had his seventeenth birthday while he was on the training course. Despite being a foreigner he was very popular with the other students. Their ages ranged from eighteen to the mid-fifties and they came from all parts of the Soviet Union. On his birthday they threw a party to celebrate. It was at the party that he met Anna, an eighteen-year-old from Warsaw. Polish and proud of it, her father had been a party worker for many years. She too was going to be secretary to a committee in Moscow.

They were housed in an old warehouse just across the Moscow River in Kuncevo. The building was divided up into classrooms, sleeping accommodation and a canteen that provided only very basic meals of vegetable soup and bread. Twice a week there were special rations of potatoes.

Josef found some of the people on the course strange to the point of being mentally unbalanced. Men who were fanatics, constantly leaping to their feet and quoting from Marx and Lenin. Arguing with the instructors at every opportunity. Smug and self-satisfied, pleased with the devisiveness of their disruption. But most of the students were working-class men and women whose only concern was to learn how to be competent leaders in some small committee and help their fellow workers improve their standards of living.

Josef and Anna were both model students, but on fine evenings they walked along the river bank and stared across the island and Terechovo. They were cautious at first about what they said but as time went by they talked, guardedly but honestly.

'Why is an Englishman interested in a revolution in Russia?'

'Because I'm working-class and I think workers get a poor deal all over the world. I wish there could be a revolution in England.'

'You could go back and start one yourself.'

'Things aren't as bad there for workers as they are here. They're not ready for a revolution.'

'Levkin the instructor said that you had the right kind of mind to be an organizer. He said you were to be trusted and you learned quickly.'

'Did you ask him about me?'

'Yes.'

'Why?'

'Because I'm staying on for another month of training. I suggested that you should stay on too.'

'I've got work to do when I get back to Petrograd.'

'This is special training. Only for trusted people. Comrade Zagorsky had recommended you for further training.'

'Why do you want me to stay on here?'

'Because I shall miss you. I like being with you.'

He smiled and reached for her hand. 'I like being with you but I didn't have the courage to tell you.'

'You didn't need to tell me. I knew.'

'How could you tell?'

'When you talk to me your voice is different. It's gentle and deep. You don't paw me like other men try to do.'

'Which men?'

'Don't be angry, Josef. And don't be jealous. I can look after myself.' She paused. 'So will you stay if they want you to?'

'If Zag wants me to and if you want me to then I'll stay.'

'You shouldn't call him Zag. He's a very important man now. He's a commissar at the new Ministry of Foreign Affairs.'

He laughed. 'He won't mind what I call him.'

'How did you get to know him so well?'

'I was a cabin-boy on a British boat that was tied up in Petrograd when the Revolution started. People came to arrest the crew in case they were spies. I was left with Zag to guard the ship against looters.'

'Did he talk you into staying?'

'No. He was very critical of . . .' He shrugged. '. . . no, I wanted to stay.'

Josef never went back to his old committee in Petrograd. After the extension course he was sent as secretary to a committee in one of the Moscow suburbs. Anna went as an administrator to the security organization, the Ve-Cheka, which controlled all local Chekas throughout the Soviet Union. Its chief was Feliks Edmundovich Dzerzhinski, an austere and ruthless man who came from an aristocratic Polish family.

Josef and Anna saw one another regularly during the following six months. They recognized the dangers of talking about their work even to one another. Zagorsky was now even more important and he seemed to go out of his way to encourage their relationship. When they decided they wanted to live together it was Zagorsky who used his influence to get them a room in a new block of workers' flats.

It was in August 1918 that Josef was called to the building that had once been the offices of the All-Russia Insurance Company and had now been taken over by the Party. Three men interviewed him. One of them was Zagorsky. They asked him question after question about his background in England and his work in Petrograd and Moscow. When he left he had no idea what the purpose of the meeting had been. It was two months later that he heard he was being transferred as an administrator to the Cheka division which Zagorsky controlled. The Secret Political Department.

By that time the Cheka was quite plainly an instrument of brutal power which was outside any legal control, and was used openly to suppress even the mildest resistance to the regime. Imprisonment without trial, on speculation alone, and liquidation when necessary, were its normal weapons against the people. Apart from political suppression, personal rivalries and old scores were being settled by the newcomers to power.

It was a stifling summer evening in their small room when Anna told him that she was pregnant. As soon as she saw that Josef was delighted with the news she was happy too. They had a state wedding a month later. Zagorsky had smiled and said that they were two little bourgeois, not real Bolsheviks, but he had come to the brief ceremony together with half a dozen of their friends. Afterwards they had all had tea and cakes in their room.

When Anna stopped working, a month before their child was due, it gave them more time together and they walked everyday to the local park and watched the mothers with their babies and the old *babushkas* who looked after toddlers while their mothers were at work.

One day they sat for ten minutes without speaking and then Josef said, 'Are you feeling all right?'

'Yes.'

She smiled. 'I'm fine. I can't wait for it to arrive.'

'You seem very quiet these last few days.'

'Do I?'

Josef noticed the evasion. 'Is there anything else troubling you?'

She nodded as she looked at his face. 'I don't want to go back to that place.'

'Why not?'

'I don't like the things they do.'

'What kind of things?'

'You must know what they do, Josef, you work there too.'

'What things do you dislike?'

'They treat the people like they were enemies. Not just the counter-revolutionaries but ordinary people. There are thousands of people being arrested every month.'

'There's a constitution now, Anna. State laws that govern what can be done.'

'They're not interested in the constitution. They don't care about the laws. Most people arrested never get to a court. And if they do then the Cheka tell the judge what his verdict has to be.'

'They just want to make sure that the revolution is not destroyed by counter-revolutionaries. It will get back to normal when things have settled down.'

'But it's been almost two years now, Josef, and it's getting worse not better. They haven't done the things they promised. None of them.'

'It has taken longer to remove the kulaks than anybody expected. Until that's done there is no land to give to the peasants.'

She shook her head slowly. 'They've taken tens of thousands of hectares from the kulaks in the Ukraine alone. The peasants have been given none of it. They work on collective farms owned by the State. They've just exchanged one set of masters for another.'

'You don't say those kinds of things to other people, do you, Anna?'

'Of course I don't. I'm not a fool.'

'Is there anything else that worries you?'

'I want to go back to Poland, Josef. I can feel at home there. There aren't the same problems.'

'There are plenty of problems in Poland, my love.'

'I know, but they're only the problems that all countries have.'

'They'd never let us go to Poland, Anna. We know too much.'

She looked at his face. 'And what we know is bad for the Bolsheviks, isn't it?'

Josef sighed and looked towards the children playing by the small ornamental lake. 'I'm afraid you're right.'

'You feel the same way I do, don't you?'

'Not really. There's a difference. This isn't my country. I don't feel responsible for what they do.'

'But you know that these people are evil men?'

'Not even that, Anna. I know that they are ruthless and unjust in many ways. But I've felt that they mean well. They will carry out their promises when the big country is organized, settled down. The problems are so big, Anna. Even the fact that they are trying to put things right means that they deserve our sympathy and our support.'

'You must decide what you think, Jo-jo. As long as I don't have to go back to that dreadful place.'

'I'll think of some story, Anna, and I'll see what I can do with Zagorsky.'

'You won't tell him what I've said, will you?'

'Of course I won't.' He smiled and took her arm. 'Let's go back and I'll make us a meal.'

Zagorsky had arranged for her to have the baby in hospital. A rare privilege but one that Josef's hard work justified.

Josef took flowers to her and was allowed to hold the baby who lay contentedly in his father's arms, the big, pale blue eyes like his father's eyes, his neat nose like his mother's.

For several months the new baby had occupied their minds and then Anna's official maternity leave came to an end.

Zagorsky listened in silence as Josef explained that Anna wanted to stay on leave for another six months to be with their child. When his lame explanation was finished Zagorsky looked at him.

'Why do you lie to me, Josef?'

'It's not a lie, Comrade Zagorsky. She wants to be at home.'

'That's just another way of saying that she doesn't want to be here. She is more interested in the child than her work.'

'I think there is that too.'

'So why didn't you say so?'

'I didn't want you or the Party to feel that she was discontented.'

'Josef, she has been discontented for the last six months.'

'You mean she has said so?'

'No.'

'Her work is not the standard you expect?'

'Her work is well done, she is conscientious and she carries out her orders meticulously.'

'So what is wrong?'

'I didn't say anthing was wrong.' Zagorsky shifted in his chair and looked back at Josef. 'I told you a long time ago not to believe men's words. With some people they show their discontent or unhappiness by working harder and longer than anyone could reasonably expect. Over-compensation for inner feelings of guilt.'

'Guilt of what?'

'Their lack of faith. In this case, lack of faith in the correctness of what she is doing. Or maybe the correctness of what others are doing with whom she is connected.'

'I don't think . . .'

Zagorsky waved his hand to silence him.

'There is another thing, isn't there. Another thing that occupies her mind, not just the child.'

'I don't think so.'

'You've not heard her when she's bouncing the boy on her knee? Crooning away in Polish – "*Jedzie, jedzie, pan, pan – Na koniku, sam, sam . . .*".' He shrugged. 'She even has the boldness to address me at the office in Polish. And that doesn't do her a lot of good with senior people. Nor me either.'

'There's no law against speaking Polish as far as I know.'

The aggressive defence of the girl confirmed Zagorsky's guess that Josef knew all about Anna's attitude to Moscow and the Party.

'Don't play the committee secretary with me, my friend. It won't work.'

Zagorsky slammed his fist on the table. 'I want her back here in the department no later than next week. You understand?'

'Yes, Comrade Zagorsky.'

'She is entitled to use the crèche. The child will be properly cared for while she is working.'

Two months later they were notified that both of them were being transferred to Warsaw to work with the Polish Bolsheviks, Josef as liaison with the Polish section in Moscow and Anna as secretary to the Commissar for Internal Affairs.

Josef's liaison point in Moscow was Zagorsky. It was not an easy relationship and Zagorsky seemed to go out of his way to keep their meetings formal; showing no signs of any personal friendship. Although it was obviously he who had arranged their assignment to Warsaw. The years of struggle and imprisonment were finally beginning to take their toll on him. He was only five years older than Josef but he looked much older.

They had the top floor of a small house in the centre of Warsaw and Anna had time to make it comfortable and there was room for a small bed for the toddler.

Their lives were very different from their time in Moscow. They had few contacts away from the Party and they were part of an underground movement that was being constantly harrassed by the Polish government whose hatred for Moscow was traditional and bitter.

There were new problems for Anna who daily recorded the Bolshevik plans for the overthrow of the Polish government. Meetings where men coldly and calmly discussed the assassination of the President of Poland, Pilsudski, and the planning to turn Poland into another Soviet state disturbed her. She found herself suddenly more patriotic and nationalist than she had ever thought possible in her first upsurge of enthusiasm for the reforms of Russia. What was good for the virtual slave population of that sprawling continent seemed obscenely inappropriate to a civilized culture that was determinedly western not Slav. Even in Russia there were still large armed forces actively fighting Moscow for the independence of the Baltic States and the Ukraine and Transcaucasia. And when in the spring of 1920 Moscow offered Poland a peace treaty, the Polish government saw it as a sign of Moscow's weakness and a chance to ensure Polish independence by fostering the independence of Lithuanian, Belorussian and Ukrainian states.

On April 25, 1920, in agreement with the weak government in Kiev, Polish forces launched a surprise attack into the Ukraine. It met little resistance and by May 6 Kiev was occupied by Polish forces.

But the foreign invasion invoked a patriotic upsurge against the Polish invaders and in the space of a month the Polish forces were pushed back to their own borders and beyond. Moscow saw its success as the herald of a communist Poland and in a small town in occupied Poland Feliks Dzerzhinski was set up as the supreme Bolshevik authority in Poland. But the spread of Communism in Poland was a dismal failure and in Moscow the blame for its lack of success had to be allotted, not only for that failure but for the lack of warning about the Polish invasion of the Ukraine. It was easier, and to some extent logical, to heap blame onto the shoulders of Moscow's Poles rather than its Russians.

When Josef opened the envelope that one of the committee had brought from Moscow the message inside was chilling. It said briefly that they were both wanted urgently in Moscow for discussions. His hands trembled as he folded the half-sheet of paper and tucked it into his jacket pocket. They made arrangements to leave the next day and arrived in Moscow that night. An official from the Internal Affairs department met them at the station, and from him they learned that Zagorsky had been arrested. When they asked what he had been charged with the man merely shrugged. They were taken to a hostel and given a room. There was just a mattress on the floor.

They were careful to say nothing to each other of any significance and they lay with their son between them. It was already getting light the next morning before either of them slept.

Josef sat with their son on a bench outside the room where Anna had been taken and it was three hours before she came out, her face white and tear-stained. A Cheka officer stopped them from speaking to one another and pushed Josef roughly to the door of the room, knocked and waved him inside. There was a militiaman on each side of him as he stood facing the three men sitting at the trestle table. The man in the centre looked down at his papers and then at Josef.

'You are a friend of Boris Zagorsky?'

'Yes.'

'How long have you known him?'

'Since October 1917.'

'How did you meet him?'

'I was cabin-boy on a British ship berthed in the docks at Petrograd. The crew had been arrested by the docks committee; Comrade Zagorsky and I were left to guard the ship.'

'Did he talk politics with you?'

'Yes.'

'Tell us what he said. An overall impression.'

'He was very pro-Bolshevik. He said that the Bolsheviks would take over and put the country right.'

'Why did you join the Party?'

'Because Comrade Zagorsky said I could help in the struggle.'

The man looked down at his papers and then back at Josef.

'When did he start criticizing the Party?'

'I never heard him criticize the Party.'

'How did you come to work for him?'

'I was ordered to by the Party.'

'Your wife is Polish?'

'Yes. She is also a member of the Party.'

'You knew that Zagorsky was Polish?'

'I heard that he was. He didn't mention it himself.'

'Why did you stay in this country?'

'I told you. Comrade Zagorsky said I would be of use and I wanted to help, so I stayed.'

'Why did you continue to stay? Why are you still here?'

'Because this is where I belong.'

'What about your family in England?'

'I have no family in England. I was an orphan. I lived in an orphanage.'

'When do you intend to return to England?'

Josef shrugged. 'I had never thought of returning to England.'

'Who gave you permission to stay here?'

'Nobody. I joined the Party and I was given work to do.'

'Do you share your wife's views on political matters?'

'We are both Bolsheviks, we have no need to discuss our views.'

'But she defends Zagorsky's actions.'

'I don't know what actions you refer to.'

'You mean that after all your training you were not able to recognize that Zagorsky was a counter-revolutionary? A traitor, more concerned with the politics of Poland than the security of the Soviet Union?'

'I have seen no evidence that would suggest that he was anything but a loyal Party member.'

'Are you a loyal Party member?'

'Of course.'

'Can you prove that?'

'I don't know any way of proving it. But it's a fact.'

'Would you work for the Party in England?'

For only a moment he hesitated and then his training took over.

'I would do anything to establish a fair distribution of work and wealth for the proletariat in Britain.'

'Zagorsky will be tried by the People's Court tomorrow. Both you and your wife will attend. We may need you as witnesses. If not you will do well to observe what happens to enemies of the people.'

They said nothing to each other about the interviews while they were in the hostel but as they walked the next day to the Cheka building he said softly, 'Did you make any mistakes at your interview?'

'Only one I think.'

'What was that?'

'I said that Poland was my country even if I was a Bolshevik. I said that it was possible to be a loyal Bolshevik and a loyal Pole as well.'

'That was stupid, Anna.'

'They provoked me. They referred to Poles as savages. I couldn't let them get away with that.'

'You should let them get away with anything. It's just words. And words don't matter.' He paused. 'If they make us witnesses, don't say anything like that in court.'

'You want me to act like a coward, for God's sake?'

'No. Not for God's sake. For our sake and the boy's sake. We can think of what to do when this is all over.'

The panelled room held no more than two dozen people, and most of those were officials. Josef was surprised to see that the five judges were all in army officers' uniform. So was the prosecutor. The defence lawyer, a civilian, was sitting at a small table, his arms folded across his chest, his eyes closed. There were several policemen and soldiers in the court and on a bench below the tall windows were several civilians. Josef recognized two of them from the committee in Petrograd.

The senior of the judges rapped the gavel on the block and the prosecutor stood up, a sheaf of papers in his hand. And only then did the door at the back of the hall open and Zagorsky was led through to the witness box by a uniformed policeman.

The charge was read out. It merely accused him of being an enemy of the State. There were no specific examples or indications of what sort of evidence would be offered to the court.

As Josef looked across the courtroom at Zagorsky he saw him standing there, one hand pressed to his back as if to relieve a pain and Josef guessed that they'd beaten him across his kidneys. It didn't make too much of a visible bruise but the damage inside was always extreme. Zagorsky stood bent as if he were unable to stand up straight, and his left hand clutched the rail of the witness stand as if to keep himself from falling forward.

The prosecutor made no attempt to establish a coherent case; witnesses were called who quoted what seemed to be quite innocuous criticism of Party officials who were not meeting Zagorsky's high standards of performance. His Polish origins were established but not emphasized, and the status of the five witnesses was no more than routine clerks and minor administrators in Zagorsky's department. The Polish invasion of Kiev was mentioned but not dwelt on, and an hour after he had started the prosecuting lawyer sat down. He had demanded the death penalty for persistent and secret subversion of the security of the State.

When the defence lawyer rose to his feet Zagorsky's voice rang out surprisingly loud.

'Dismiss this man. I am defending myself.'

There was a whispered conversation among the judges and the senior officer said that the court would note that Zagorsky had refused the legal aid provided by the State. But if Zagorsky wished to conduct his own case the court would hear him.

Josef had noticed that like the men who had interrogated him they referred to him as Zagorsky not as Comrade Zagorsky or Commissar Zagorsky which was his actual status. They were already distancing him from the Party.

Zagorsky took a deep breath and his voice was clear although he spoke very slowly.

'I quote from the rules of the Communist Party of the Soviet Union. Paragraph four – I quote – "the promotion, in every possible way, of inner-party democracy, the activity and initiative of the Communists, criticism and self-criticism".

'I quote from the same document Part One clause three sub-clauses b and c. I quote – "A party member has the right to discuss freely questions of the Party's policies and practical activities at Party meetings, conferences and congresses, at the meetings of Party committees and in the Party press; to table motions; openly to express and uphold his opinion as long as the Party organization concerned has not adopted a decision; to criticize any Communist, irrespective of the position he holds, at Party meetings, conferences and congresses, and at the full meetings of Party committees. Those who commit the offence of suppressing criticism or victimizing anyone for criticism are responsible to and will be penalized by the Party, to the point of explusion from the CPSU".'

He paused and he was shaking visibly, his whole body trembling as if tormented by an ague.

'That is all I have to say. That is all that needs to be said. This trial is a farce and the laws of the Soviet Union are being abused in this process. The evidence of the poltroons you bring as witnesses shows how hopeless this prosecution must be.' He paused and closed his eyes. When he opened them again he said, 'You will see that I am trembling, comrades. Make no mistake. I do not tremble from fear. Not even from illness. Oh, no. I tremble because I have been beaten near to death to make me give false evidence that would incriminate me. All my life I have worked loyally for the Party. I ask that those who know me and know my record will step in and punish those people who have so infamously brought this case to court. I ask not for mercy but for justice. The justice that I sought for all of us when I first walked with my fellow-workers holding that beautiful red flag above our heads. You may cause my death but it will not be execution – it will be murder. Murder from others' greed, jealousy and ambition.' He seemed to hesitate before his final words, gulping for air before he said, 'People in the pay of our enemies, the Germans.'

There was a sudden murmur in the courtroom, quickly stopped by the angry face of the senior judge. He kept his eyes away from Zagorsky as he said, 'The judgement of the People's Court will be promulgated after due consideration.'

The officers stood up and filed to the door and Josef and Anna saw two policemen carry Zagorsky from the witness box. They handled him quite gently.

Outside it was beginning to rain and Josef was glad that it was, so the rain could hide the tears on Anna's face.

Despite her anxiety to get back to their son she had insisted that they went to the church at the back of the museum. And there she prayed and wept, with Josef standing awkwardly beside her, his hand just touching her shoulder.

They went back to Warsaw and they heard rumours that Zagorsky had been sent to one of the Siberian labour-camps and other rumours that he had been shot the same day, after the trial, at the Lubyanka building.

The treatment meted out to Zagorsky and the totally spurious trial frightened and angered them both. They said nothing to anybody of their feelings. Even between themselves there was a reluctance to admit their disillusion with the Party.

The breaking point came when Anna had to take notes of a meeting where the annexation of Poland was being recommended. Half of Poland would become the Polish Soviet State and a rump would be left that the planners were willing to leave to be annexed in due course by Germany. Hearing Poles describe the annexation of their own country, and listening to the details of how its industry and agriculture would serve the Soviet Union had sickened her.

They walked the streets of Warsaw that night, Josef carrying the small boy in his arms as they talked. Anna wanted to get away, anywhere, and quickly. Josef knew that there was no chance of planning their escape. Anna wouldn't be able to dissemble her feelings long enough. She was ready to carry on for a few days, but no longer. He told her that they would leave at the weekend, starting their journey on the Friday night. If anyone saw them they would say they were having a weekend break in the country.

There was little preparation that Josef could make. They would have to leave their few possessions behind them. But fortunately, like most underground party members, he had always kept their meagre savings in cash, and they both had Soviet passports. He still had his British passport and he tucked their marriage certificate inside it.

Josef brought tickets for only the journey from Warsaw to Łodz. And there he booked them onto the night train to Berlin. At the German frontier there were no problems when they presented their USSR passports. In Berlin they found a cheap lodging house. Josef calculated that he had enough money for them to live frugally for six weeks while they decided what to do.

After a few days Josef realized that because he didn't speak German it was going to be difficult to find work. His Russian and smattering of Polish he was afraid to use in case there were local Party members who would check up on him and cause trouble. Having worked in the Cheka he knew that it had its people in every big European city. As the days went by he became desperate for anything that would provide some income. It was then that he took the job as a dish-washer in the kitchens of a night club on the Kurfürstendamm. He worked long hours and the wages were just enough to pay for their room and food, and his share of the tips went on clothes and other necessities. After six months he was promoted to serving drinks in the bar, where his English was useful with American and English tourists.

The club's main business came from foreigners. Businessmen on a night out, looking for a girl, and long-term visitors like reporters and a sprinkling of writers and painters.

He had heard nothing about how the news of their escape had been received in Warsaw and Moscow because he had no contacts back there and had no intention of trying to find out.

It was two weeks before their first Christmas in Berlin and he had bought cakes and a bunch of flowers on the way home as an early treat. When he saw the police-car and the ambulance and the small crowd of people outside the building he knew at once it was Anna. He didn't know what had happened but he knew it was her.

They had let him travel in the ambulance with her body. They had driven straight to the morgue and he had officially identified her body. And then at the police station there had been the questions. The detectives had been sympathetic and considerate. Almost as if they knew or guessed why she had been murdered. Garotting was generally confined to assassins and professional criminals. There were more questions about his son. Why did he think that he'd been taken rather than killed with his mother? What kind of people did he know who were so ruthless? Had he met any people at the club where he worked who might have had a grudge against him? But after a couple of hours they had let him go. It was obvious that they would not spend much time looking for the boy. They acted as if they were aware that he knew who had committed both crimes. The inquest would be held in two days' time.

He never went back to the rooms. For two days and nights he wandered the streets of Berlin like a lost soul. Oblivious of his surroundings, his mind a turmoil of grief and hatred.

The inquest gave a verdict of murder by strangulation by a person or persons unknown. The coroner had commented on the fact that nothing appeared to have been stolen or even disturbed. But Josef had seen the small red star stamped on the inside of her wrist and for him it was not murder by a person or persons unknown. He knew all too well who had murdered her. Half demented, Josef had gone back to his job that night. There had been a great deal of sympathy for him. Staff and customers had seen the two small photographs in the evening paper.

Just on midnight he was serving a drink to a man he had seen several times before. He had been told that he was a journalist for one of the press agencies. When he had poured the double whisky the man looked at Josef's face, lifted his glass and said in Russian, 'To the dead, Josef. The living should remember it and learn the lesson.'

Josef felt the room spin and the man said quickly in English, 'My friend, I'm on your side. Make no mistake. I'll help you all I can.'

'Who are you, mister?'

The man half-smiled. 'Just call me Johnny.' He paused and said softly, 'I saw the red star before they took her downstairs.'

'You were there?'

'I was with the police inspector when they got the phone call.'

'What phone call? They never mentioned a phone call to me or at the inquest.'

'Somebody phoned in to the police HQ. They said she had been executed and gave the address. Then they just said – "The red flag will fly all over the world." They said it first in Russian and then in heavily accented German.'

'Why didn't the police mention it at the inquest?'

The man took a sip of whisky. 'Who knows, Josef? Who knows?'

'How is it you speak Russian?'

The man shrugged but didn't reply.

'You're a reporter, yes?'

'A foreign correspondent. Much the same thing.'

'You knew what the red star meant?'

'Of course I did.' He paused. 'What are you going to do about it, my friend?'

Josef looked down at the bar-counter and wiped a damp patch with his cloth before he looked back at the man's face. 'I'm going to make those bastards pay a thousand times. I don't know how. But I'll do it if it takes the rest of my life.'

'Were you one of them way back?'

'Not way back. Six months ago I was one of them. I was a fool.'

'You're in good company, Josef. There are a lot of people being fooled by the thought of the brotherhood of man. They'll learn in due course.' He paused. 'I could help you do a lot to hurt them. Could we talk some time?'

'Prove to me that it'll hurt them and I'll talk all you want.'

'Are you staying at the same place?'

'No. I sleep here at nights.'

'How about three o'clock tomorrow afternoon.'

'OK.'

Almost every day for three weeks Johnny asked questions and listened. Josef was surprised at the reporter's interest in the people in the Cheka International Affairs section. Names and personal details, their families, their vices, favourite foods, their houses and their office responsibilities. It was five weeks after Anna's death when the journalist asked if Josef would like to go back to England.

'They wouldn't let me back in.'

'I think it could be arranged if you went about it the right way. There's always people who are interested in what goes on in Moscow.'

Josef shrugged. 'They'd think I was a stooge sent in by the Cheka.'

'I know a lot of people in London. Would you like me to talk to them?'

'Yes. If you think it'd do any good. But don't get into trouble for my sake.'

'Look. Do you want to go back?'

'Yes.'

'Well, just leave it to me to see what I can do.'

The meeting with the British Consul had gone smoothly enough. After it had all been arranged the journalist asked for the Soviet passports that Josef and Anna had held, as souvenirs of their getting to know one another.

Josef disembarked from the boat at Newcastle, on January 22, 1924. He was twenty-two years old. There were two main items on the front page of the

Evening Chronicle that night. Ramsay MacDonald had formed the first Labour Government that day, and Lenin had died in Moscow the previous day. Neither Josef, nor even the man who called himself Johnny, who spoke to him in the bar at the Railway Hotel later that evening, could have imagined the strange life that was starting for him that day.

CHAPTER TWO

The man who sometimes called himself Emil Goldfus and other times Martin Collins was nearly fifty when he signed the lease for premises at 216 West 99th Street in New York. His birth certificate gave his age as fifty-three and no casual observer was likely to doubt it. He had the air of a European refugee academic. Rather old-fashioned but charming. Some of the people he met thought he looked rather sad. A sad man who put a brave face on life.

He banked a few hundred dollars a month at the 96th Street branch of the East River Savings Bank. And like any other customer there were small withdrawals from time to time. But unlike most other customers Emil Goldfus had similar accounts at banks all over the city. And at all of them, Emil Goldfus, retired photographer, was a respected client.

When he had first come to New York in 1950 he had spent his days studying the city. Riding the bus and subway routes, getting himself established locally with the neighbourhood shopkeepers, eating simple meals in the local cafeterias. He knew how long the express train took to get from his nearest station to Times Square and how to change lines for the Bronx or connect with Lexington Avenue. He never owned a car and seldom took taxis. There were two cinemas that he visited regularly. One he particularly favoured. Many people would have seen it as a mildly idyllic existence. Sitting on the park benches reading a paper, strolling along unfrequented streets, standing and staring sometimes at derelict buildings and weed-ridden plots of waste-land. But there was no observer of the quiet unobtrusive oldish man.

There were two or three people who lived on East 71st Street who knew him. But they knew him as Milton, an Englishman.

Later in 1953 Goldfus moved to Brooklyn and rented studio space in a drab seven-storey building that flattered itself by having the name of the Ovington Building. The Ovington Building was on the outskirts of Brooklyn Heights and, in addition to the fifth-floor studio, Goldfus also took a room in a boarding house on Hicks Street.

It was a more expansive time in his life. He painted and sketched and slowly got to know a number of the artists who worked in the building. He was quite liked, the old-world charm and wry humour made him pleasant company. He made friends with several of the struggling artists who occupied the studios.

The couple he knew on East 71st Street were Mona and Morris Cohen, and he had been in touch with them from his first days in New York.

There were other people whom he met regularly on his strolls in the parks, or at the cinema. Some knew him as Emil Goldfus, others as Martin Collins or Milton. Some years earlier there were people who knew him as Andrew Kayotis.

He became an accepted and well-liked neighbour to several of the artists who shared the rooms in the building. His paintings were amateurish but he accepted criticism with good grace and seemed eager and determined to improve his painting skills. One of his neighbours even gave up a little of his time to teaching Emil Goldfus to play classical guitar. He joined in their late-night discussions and they came to the conclusion that Emil was no intellectual and marked him down as an elderly Socialist whose vaguely liberal views belonged more to the pre-war thirties than the late fifties.

PART TWO

CHAPTER THREE

Despite its name, the Canadian township of Cobalt was better known for its silver mining, and in 1920 its population of just over a thousand was what you could expect in a boom town. Wildcat prospectors, surveyors, a handful of officials from Toronto and Ottawa, and the suppliers of goods and services that batten on such communities. Three hundred and thirty miles by rail from Toronto it was one of the richest silver deposits in the world.

Jack Emmanuel Lonsdale was a half-breed who found his life in Cobalt rewarding and congenial, and he reckoned he had made a good move when he married the immigrant Finnish girl. Their son Gordon was born four years later in 1924. But instead of cementing the marriage it marked the beginning of the end. Only a special kind of woman thrives in boom towns and even they see it as a place and a time to make your pile and then get out. The girl from Karelia saw no future for a family in the rough and tumble of Cobalt and the couple slowly drifted apart.

The half-breed couldn't understand why the woman hated what to him seemed a veritable paradise of money, booze, and girls on the make. It was not so much a difference of opinion as a total inability to comprehend the woman's objections. When she eventually left, taking the boy with her, there was no rancour from the man. She wanted to go back to Karelia, to Finland, where she was born.

He gave her cash for the journey and enough for a few month's keep. He was neither angry or hurt. It was just beyond his understanding. He never heard again from his wife or son and when, in 1940, the Soviet Union invaded Finland through Karelia he neither heard nor knew of the world's praise for the gallant Finns who fought back against overwhelming odds for over a month. So he never knew that his son was sixteen years old when he was killed or that his wife died in a Soviet slave-labour camp a few years later. He had long forgotten them both and had no idea where Finland was. He had only the vaguest idea where Toronto was.

In the late spring of 1940 as the snows were beginning to melt in the forests of Karelia the special document unit of the NKVD had the unpleasant but routine job of checking the corpses that had been buried in the snow, and the log cabins, the homes that had been pounded by Soviet artillery. Documents of any kind were bundled up carefully and despatched to the NKVD's new Finnish headquarters in Helsinki for the central document unit to process and send on to Moscow.

CHAPTER FOUR

The woman stood in the small sunlit kitchen watching the boy as he ate his Jell-o and ice-cream. He was her sister's son and she had been pleased to have him. He was a bright cheerful boy and had done well in his first year at the school. He was no trouble, he did as he was told and the Californian sunshine suited him. The chronic cough had disappeared after a couple of months.

When she reached for his empty plate she said, 'D'you want some more, boy?'

He shook his head. 'No more thank you, aunt.'

'I had a letter from your mother today. She sends you her love and told me to tell you that she's very pleased that you're doing so well at school.'

'Why isn't she write to me?'

'Why *doesn't* she write to me.'

'Why doesn't she write to me?'

'There are problems, boy. Government regulations and so on. It's not her wish, you can be sure of that.'

'What else she say?'

'She says there's still snow in Moscow and she's sending you photographs of the new apartment. Two rooms she says. She's very lucky.'

'Why doesn't she come and live here too?'

She walked into the small kitchen with the empty dishes. 'They wouldn't allow that.'

'Why do they allow it for me then?'

'I don't know, boy. All I know is the people in Moscow gave permission and here you are. What homework have you got?'

'Not much. Can I play with the Carter boys first?'

'Where?'

'In the park.'

'OK. But you've got to be back by seven.'

'Thanks. What does goose mean, aunt?'

'It's a bird. You had goose at Christmas.'

'Tom Carter said old man Field had goosed Jenny and he was reporting him to the sherrif.'

'That's a vulgar word, boy. Not a word you should be using nor young Carter neither.'

'But what's it mean?'

'I guess in that case it means grabbing a girl's backside. Now run on with you or you'll be back before you've started.'

It wasn't until 1938 and Konrad Molody was sixteen that he eventually went back to Moscow. It took him a few weeks to settle down. He missed the San Francisco sunshine and his friends, and Moscow seemed grim after the free and easy time in Berkeley with his aunt. But there were compensations. He spoke fluent and almost perfect English, and he had been given a place at Moscow University and that meant a sure career in some government department.

At the end of his first year at university he had been interviewed by two men. They were both Red Army officers. One a major, the other a lieutenant-colonel. They both spoke excellent English and they had talked English for most of the time, asking him about his five years in the United States. They obviously knew the United States better than he did but they talked as if he were the expert, especially on the details of everyday life. They were unlike any army officers he had talked with before. They were almost like Americans. Easy-going, amused and amusing, and no hint of using their rank. They seemed to know quite a lot about him and his background, but they gave no hint as to why they had talked with him.

When he saw one of them again, the colonel, the Germans were already into the Ukraine. Five hundred thousand Russians had been killed or captured when they took Kiev. And now an army of a million men, seventy-seven German divisions under Field Marshal Bock, were heading up the open road to Moscow. Molody had been recruited into the Red Army and was driving an ammunition truck for an artillery battery. He had no uniform, just a band round his arm with a red star. A despatch rider had brought him a message to report back to the temporary headquarters in a bombed-out shop by the railway station at Volchonka-zil, one of the southern suburbs of Moscow.

Molody stood there in the flickering light of a paraffin lamp, his civilian clothes in tatters and his face pale and drawn with hunger and exhaustion.

'D'you remember me?'

'Yes, Comrade Colonel.'

'Have you kept up your English?'

'Yes, comrade.'

'Where are you parents?'

'My father died a long time ago. I don't know where my mother is. Our block was shelled but I heard that she survived.'

'I'm sending you on a training course. You'll be leaving Moscow tomorrow.' He looked at the youth's ragged figure. 'Have you got any other clothes?'

'No, Comrade Colonel.'

'You'd better come back with me. My car's outside.'

'I'll have to report to my officer.'

'Don't bother. He knows. Let's go before they start the night barrage.'

The colonel drove him to a villa way out of Moscow on the road to Vladimir. The rooms had been turned into offices and an officers' mess. He was given a meal and then told to be ready at six o'clock the next morning. He slept on a mattress on the floor of an empty room.

It was still dark at five o'clock but he was up and waiting. He was driven to an airstrip near Yaroslav. It took ten days by plane and trains to get to Sverdlovsk.

The training school was outside the city in a clearing in the forest. Rows on rows of wooden huts behind a ten-foot stockade with an outer perimeter of barbed wire. It was to be his home for almost five years. The training he received as a future intelligence officer was thorough and comprehensive, and the extra year had been because he spoke fluent English. He attended lectures with four others on Canadian, US and British history, politics and armed forces. He himself gave several talks on his boyhood in California.

During all the remaining years of the Great Patriotic War he lived at the training school. Well fed, healthy and cut off from any aspect of the war. The war might not have existed for the students at the school. When he had completed the course Molody was made a captain in the MVD, the Soviet secret service. He was one of the youngest men ever to hold that rank.

In the aftermath of the war he was sent back to Moscow and in 1949 he married. She was a pretty girl named Galyusha, uncomplicated, amiable and affectionate. He was working in the directorate responsible for controlling and supporting MVD agents in overseas countries, and his own work was in the department responsible for espionage in the USA and Britain.

In 1953 he was sent to the MVD special training school at Gaczyna. He was away from his wife for six months. There were facilities for wives at Gaczyna but his applications for Galyusha to join him were refused. Moscow wanted him to get used to being away from his wife.

He was told things at Gaczyna about the MVD's operations in Britain that made him realize that even though Britain had been an important part of his control area there were many things he hadn't been told before.

There were half a dozen pretty girls on the staff of the training school working as waitresses and housekeepers for the living quarters. Nobody said they were available. Nobody needed to. Molody had regular sex with two of them. He knew it would go down on his file because they wouldn't have been there if they weren't already trained MVD operators. But they were there for sex as well as security and Molody liked pretty girls.

All the time he was at Gaczyna he was allowed to listen to the BBC. News, entertainment and music. And his newspapers were the London nationals. Two days old. He lived in a single, isolated hut that was furnished with G-plan furniture with a typically English lower middle-class, suburban decor.

When he returned to Moscow he was given a month's leave and he and Galyusha went down to the sunshine of the Black Sea, using an MVD rest-house in Sochi as their base.

Galyusha was conscious of the benefits they got from her husband's privileged position. 'Hard' roubles, shopping privileges and a superior apartment in the centre of Moscow overlooking the river. She was allowed to go with him for the month he had in Leningrad. He spent long hours at the Red Navy base every day but she had been taken around the city by an Intourist girl who showed her the sights, and took her to good restaurants and cafés to eat. Galyusha was not much interested in galleries and museums but she loved the city itself. A few weeks after they went back to Moscow the doctor confirmed that she was pregnant.

Molody leaned over the rails of the boat where it lay at anchor in Kolsky Bay and looked across to the grey buildings on the dockside. There were nine months of winter in Murmansk and from November to mid-January there were no daylight hours. There were still old people in Murmansk who spoke the ancient local language, Saami. And in the Saami language Murmansk means 'the edge of the earth'. Already the town was shrouded in mist and it was still only July. He wondered why they had insisted that he travel by sea and he wondered too why he had to leave from Murmansk. Maybe they thought that if his last memories were of this grim town he wouldn't feel homesick. He wouldn't feel homesick anyway. He was a professional and what he was being sent to do was important. He was now a key agent and his new rank of major marked their recognition of his past work and their confidence in him in his new role. It was 1954 and there had been the big purge in the MVD and he had not only survived but benefited.

It was now the KGB and its reponsibilities were even greater than before.

He turned and looked at the seamen who were battening down the last of the hatches. It was a grain transporter and there were only three other passengers.

The ship docked at Vancouver in the late afternoon and the Canadian excise rummage crew came straight on board. Molody made himself scarce and the crew-list for Immigration showed only three passengers. The three legitimate passengers had been cleared through Immigration in twenty minutes.

It was ten o'clock when Molody and one of the crew showed their shore passes to the security guards at the gate. They were warned that they had to be back by midnight. Molody had talked in broken English with a thick Russian accent and it had been all too easy. He handed over the pass he had used to the crewman and without a word he had walked off alone. A small, worn, cardboard attaché case in his hand.

Once he was away from the dock area he asked the way to the YMCA. They found him a bed for the night. He joined and stayed for another two weeks, and in that time he found himself an inexpensive one-room apartment and a job as a salesman in a radio shop.

In the next few weeks he used the genuine birth certificate that he had been given in Moscow and obtained what he most wanted, a genuine Canadian passport. He got a driving licence and a YMCA membership card and several other minor pieces of documentation that provided him with background material.

He changed jobs twice during the winter. Both moves got him increased pay. He had several girlfriends and his colleagues at work liked his easy-going ways. But behind the casual façade he worked hard, and the shop owner recognized that he was not only a good salesman but ambitious. He made several suggestions at the last shop that increased their turnover and profits and the owner seriously considered giving him a small stake in the business. But before he had formulated a suggestion the young man took a week's holiday and never came back.

Molody stood looking across towards Goat Island where the falls were split in two. The American Falls and Horseshoe Falls. Most residents on the American side of the Niagara would reluctantly admit that the Canadian side was the pleasanter: commercialization was not so all-pervading.

The two governments cooperated to make the formalities of crossing the border from one side to the other as easy as possible, and when Molody presented his Canadian birth certificate and his return bus ticket to Toronto he was passed through without query.

He didn't hurry, he joined the crowds and looked at the sights before he caught a bus to Buffalo and found lodgings for the night.

The following day he took a train to New York. He walked from the station to Fifth Avenue and the New York Public Library. He immediately recognized the girl at the inquiry desk from the description they had given him. When he asked her where he could find biographical material on John Dos Passos she turned to one of the huge reference books before she realized the significance of what he had said. Then she walked from behind the counter and he followed her to the far end of the library.

She turned to look at him, and said softly, 'Doris Hart,' and he said, 'Victor Seixus Junior.'

When he left he had the bundle of money and the key to the luggage locker at Grand Central. In the locker there was just the coded message.

He booked a room at the YMCA on West 34th Street and sat in the small room and decoded the message. He wondered what Alec would be like. He took a meal at a nearby automat and the evening paper headlined the news that Gromyko had taken over from Shepilov as Foreign Minister. It was February 15, 1957.

CHAPTER FIVE

There were a few villas still standing near Łazienki Park. A dozen or so which had escaped both the German and the Russian onslaughts on Warsaw. Some people said that they had been deliberately preserved for the Russian officials to use when it was all over. But in the event they had been used by Polish officials of the new communist regime and one of them had been divided up into ten flats for junior staff who worked for the newly established foreign embassies.

Harry Houghton had one such flat. A small living room, a bedroom and kitchen and bathroom. Its furnishings were sparse and primitive but despite its size and starkness the minute apartment provided the best accommodation he had had in his life.

Born in Lincoln he had run away from home at sixteen and joined the Royal Navy. Obsequious and ingratiating, he had made little progress until war broke out. By the end of the war he had become a chief petty officer. A reasonably efficient clerk, he had legitimately used Admiralty regulations to get his officers their marginal extra service payments and had kept the messes supplied with black-market booze. Not liked, but tolerated for his ability to bend and manipulate service regulations on rations and supplies, he had never experienced a day's service in a battle zone until 1942 when he was assigned to merchant protection vessels on convoys to Malta and Russia.

He was demobilized in 1945 and joined the civil service as a clerk. For four years he served as an Admiralty clerk in the minor Navy port of Gosport near the big Royal Navy base at Portsmouth. At the end of four years he was assigned as clerk to the British naval attaché in Warsaw.

A line-shooter and a drunk, Harry Houghton was detested by the rest of the embassy staff. But it was in Warsaw that he spent the best time of his life.

Harry Houghton sat sprawled on the leather settee in the soft, pink light from the silk-shaded lamp which he had bought on the black market. With an unsteady hand he poured vodka into the deep glass and passed it to the girl on the settee beside him. Then he reached for the empty glass on the table and filled it slowly and carefully.

The girl was in her late twenties, dark-haired and attractive. Her face was flushed from drinking and as the Englishman lifted his glass to her she touched it with hers and said '*Na zdrowie.*' She laughed when he tried to respond in Polish.

'Is easier I say "cheers" for you, Harry.'

'Cheers, sweetheart. Did you sell the stuff OK?'

'Yes. No problems at all. They want all you can get.'

'What do they want?'

'Any drugs at all. But they pay most for penicillin and sulfa drugs.'

'How much will they pay?'

'Fifty US dollars for a tablet.'

'Jesus. That's good. How much have we got?'

She reached over for her worn leather handbag, took out a fat brown envelope and handed it to him.

'I haven't counted it yet.'

He looked at her, his eyes alert. 'Can you stay the night?'

She laughed and nodded. 'Is OK, Harry. If you want that I stay.'

He grinned. 'Let's count the cash first.'

For ten minutes he counted the notes. There were $4,450 in used notes. He counted out a hundred and fifty and handed them to the girl.

'OK, Krissie?'

'You're very good to me, Harry.'

He smiled. 'It's your turn to be good to me now. Let's finish the bottle first.' He reached for the bottle and held it up. 'Bloody thing's empty.'

He stood up unsteadily and lurched across to the shelf of bottles and glasses and the framed photograph that showed him in uniform, grinning, with a glass of beer in his hand. He swore as the corkscrew split the cork and he shoved the cork into the bottle.

Back at the settee he poured another glass for each of them and drank his down and poured again. With his free hand he leaned over and pulled the girl to him, his mouth on hers, his hand pulling the strap of her dress from her shoulder.

Despite negative reports from the embassy and strongly critical reports from his immediate superior, Harry Houghton survived two years in Warsaw from 1949 to 1951 and in that time he had accumulated several thousand pounds in his bank account in England. He had lived an extraordinary life in the post-war ruins of Warsaw. Kristina had introduced him to some of the richest people in Warsaw. The black-market operators and the collaborators with the Soviet occupation controllers. Notorious for his crude behaviour at embassy social events, he was frequently seen drunk in broad daylight on the city streets.

After he was back in England he still sent a few cheap cosmetics to Kristina, but without the diplomatic bag there was no possibility of sending more antibiotics. Despite the fact that he was sent home for chronic drunkenness he was given security clearance and a job at the Underwater Weapons Establishment at Portland naval base, a secret installation employing over 20,000 people and concerned only with submarine and anti-submarine research. When Harry Houghton joined the establishment, HMS *Dreadnought*, the Royal Navy's first atomic submarine, was being fitted out with its American atomic plant. But Portland's main task was to improve NATO's underwater defence programme in detecting and destroying enemy submarines. He joined the base in 1951, and lived in a village just outside Portland itself with his wife Peggy.

CHAPTER SIX

Molody stood looking across the street at the hotel. Somehow it didn't look like the photographs he had been shown. But it was the right name and the right address: Hotel Latham E. 28th Street. He couldn't remember what made it seem different and he walked across the road, into the hotel lobby and took the elevator to the seventh floor. And then walked up the stairs to the eighth.

For a moment he hesitated as he looked at the number on the door. 839. That was the room number all right. And the name on the card was the name he expected – Martin Collins. He looked both ways up the corridor and then pressed the bell.

The man who opened the door was thin-faced and balding and he recognized him straightaway. He had been shown photographs of the man in Moscow. The man recognized him too, nodded impassively and stood aside to let him in.

For a moment, after the door was closed, they stood looking at each other. They had never met before or communicated in any way, but they were Russians in a strange, dangerous country and instinctively their arms went round each other and they kissed cheeks like old friends meeting.

Collins looked at the younger man, his observant eyes taking in the details of his face, his hands still on the young man's shoulders.

'How long are you staying in New York, my friend?'

'As long as necessary, as short as possible.'

'There are a few people I want you to meet while you are here. They could be useful to you some day if things go wrong over here.'

'Are you expecting trouble?'

'No,' Collins smiled. 'But after ten years you bear it in mind. Have you eaten today?'

'Yes, comrade, but I'd appreciate a drink.'

Collins would have preferred vodka but he always kept to whisky, Jamiesons, to go with his Irish name. He poured them generous glasses before he sat down.

Molody looked around the large almost empty room. A single bed, a heavy, wooden artist's easel alongside a small table and a stool and canvases leaning against the walls.

Molody looked back at his companion. 'Does it make you a living?'

Collins frowned. 'It *is* my living, comrade, I'm an artist. Anything else I forget. My name is Collins, my father was Irish and I'm a New Yorker.' He shrugged. 'You have to be convinced. If I don't believe it why should others believe it? It's the most important thing you can remember.'

'You mean having a good cover?'

'No. I mean never having a cover.' He waved his hand at the room. 'This is not cover. This is me. It's real. Neither you nor anybody else could convince me otherwise. This is reality. If there is anything else then it is a small secret in my mind. Like a married man with a mistress or a man who likes being whipped. Anything else is a small secret vice in the back of my mind. You must work out for yourself what you want to be and then *be* it. Every minute of every day.' He put down his glass. 'What do you want to be?' He smiled. 'Fulfil your dreams my friend.'

Molody laughed. 'A millionaire.'

'So be it, comrade, make money, be a businessman. It's no more difficult than being an artist. Do it as if that is the only thing you care about. Don't pretend. Be a tycoon.'

'Who are the people you want me to meet?'

'Do you know Jack Sobell?'

'I don't know him. I've seen his file.'

'And?'

'Moscow instructed me to avoid him. He's under suspicion.'

'So I understand. But he had two people working for him before he fell out of favour. A married couple. The Cohens. First-class agents. Experienced, disciplined and committed. The man was a teacher here in New York. Had an excellent record, but Moscow moved them from Sobell's control to another ring that was eventually exposed. When the Rosenbergs were betrayed I managed to warn the Cohens in time for them to go underground. They are intending to go to England. I've kept them back so that you could meet them.'

'Would Moscow approve?'

Collins smiled. 'You are independent now, comrade. It is up to you to decide. All that Moscow wants from you is results. How you get them is up to you. Who you use is up to you. You cut the cord with the Centre when you boarded the ship in Murmansk.'

'When can I meet them?'

Collins looked at his watch. 'In an hour. You know the zoo in Central Park?'

'No. But I can find it.'

'Fine.'

Collins gave him a password, pointed out the meeting point on a large-scale map and instructions on how he should be contacted again if the chalk mark was on the wall of the toilet at the cinema. He was to check for the mark every day.

CHAPTER SEVEN

Sir Peter Clark's office was the only deliberate reminder in the building of their connection with the mandarins of Whitehall and the Foreign Office. Panelled and finished in the highest Civil Service good taste it acknowledged that the Director-General of MI6 was still a servant of the Foreign Secretary despite his privilege of direct contact with the Prime Minister if he felt it necessary. And 'necessary' usually meant when some MP was heading for something worse than a domestic scandal, something that could affect national security. The old-fashioned and rather ornate office was neither typical of the man's character nor a sign of self-importance but an overt symbol of the D-G's awareness of his political masters.

Once a top Civil Servant himself in the Ministry of Defence when it was called more frankly the War Office, Sir Peter knew where the levers of Whitehall lay and how to operate them. Tall and lean, he looked like something out of P. G. Wodehouse but it was totally deceptive. A double-first at Balliol, a blue for boxing and a brain that had won him the respect of both the soldiers and the politicians.

He looked across at his deputy, Hugh Morton, one of the organization's old China hands who had survived the swings and roundabouts of MI6's turbulent fortunes because he was a wise assessor of both men and situations. Sir Peter pointed at the file that lay on his desk between them.

'What did you think of that little lot?'

Morton shrugged. 'Looks more like a job for Five and Special Branch to me.'

'Why? Because Maguire-Barton's an MP?'

'Yes.' He had smiled. 'And a government MP to boot.'

'Maybe that's why Five have suggested that we handle it.'

'Did they give any reason why they suggested that?'

'Yes. They see Grushko, the Russian as the one who really matters. Not Maguire-Barton. They think he's just a stooge.'

'I'd agree that Grushko is the one who really matters but I don't see Maguire-Barton as a stooge. He's too fly and too ambitious for that.'

'What's his rôle then?'

'Who knows? Agent of influence maybe.'

'Influence in what area?'

'We'll know more when we've looked them over. He's got influence in the House. Cultivates journalists. Appears on chat shows and TV. He's got plenty of opportunities for pushing the Soviet view either openly or covertly.'

'Who'll you get to handle this?'

'Shapiro.'

Sir Peter pursed his lips. 'Is it important enough for Shapiro to handle?'

Morton smiled. 'You don't like him do you?'

Sir Peter shrugged. 'Like, maybe not. Admire, yes. He knows the Soviets inside out, but when an MP's involved I wonder if somebody less obssessed might not be more suitable.' Sir Peter paused. 'But I leave it to you.'

'Any comments on our submission for an increased budget?'

'Plenty. Most of them unfavourable. The opposition hate our guts and there are plenty on the government side who'd like to cut us down to size. The only consolation I ever have at the budget meetings is that they give Five even more stick than they give us.'

'Why do you think this is?'

'It's a combination of two things in my opinion. It's popular with the media to denigrate our intelligence services and on the other hand they're scared of what we know about them.' He laughed softly. 'Of what they think we know about them. When I hear them talking on the budget committee I can hear the skeletons rattling in their cupboards.' He shrugged and stood up slowly. 'Thank God it's only once a year. I don't mind the criticism but the sheer hypocrisy angers me.' He paused. 'Keep me in touch from time to time about Maguire-Barton.'

'Is it urgent?'

'I don't know, Hughie. We won't know that until Shapiro and his chaps have found out a bit more.'

Harris, sitting at his desk, wore a faded blue denim shirt and twill slacks to mark the fact that it was Saturday morning. Chapman wore a light-weight grey suit and a dark blue cravat instead of a tie. There was some sort of emblem or coat of arms on the cravat. Hand-embroidered.

'Tell me what you've been doing since you came into SIS.'

'All the way back?'

Harris nodded. 'It's not all that way back. But yes.'

'I did the basic three-month training course and then six months at St Anthony's on the history of the Soviet Union and the organization of the KGB and the GRU. I got Beta-minus on both. Then I worked for Lowrey for a few months on surveillance.'

'What kind of surveillance?'

'The Oxford Group and Jehovah's Witnesses.'

'On your own or with Lowrey?'

'Both. About half and half.'

'Go on.'

'I did surveillance as part of a team on the Czech Embassy and then I did solo on two suspected KGB safe-houses.'

'Which ones?'

'The small one in Highgate and one in Kensington.'

'Who did you report to?'

'Joe Shapiro.'

'Tell me about Joe Shapiro. What kind of man do you think he is?'

'I didn't really get to know him. He's a bit high up for me.'

'You must have got some sort of an impression. What was it?'

Chapman hesitated. 'He won't be told what I say, will he?'

Harris raised his eyebrows in obvious disapproval of the question. 'No. And I doubt that he'd be interested anyway.'

'I found him a very strange man. Absolutely dedicated. Any crumb of information about the KGB or the Soviet Union was pounced on as if it might be vitally important. He wanted to know every detail. What they wore. Did they look pleased or unhappy. Had they had their hair cut short since I last saw them. If they ate out he expected to know everything they ate.' Chapman paused, hesitating. Then he went on. 'He made me feel that he was very like a KGB man himself. More than just dedicated . . . fanatical.'

Harris's face was non-committal. 'Go on.'

'I guess that's about it. I admire him. His knowledge and his expertise. But . . . you know, when he was de-briefing me I felt that he got a kick out of knowing every little detail. I'd talked to men who he knew all about. He didn't seem much concerned that I'd made a cock-up of the surveillance or that I'd blown my cover-story.' He hesitated. 'I found him a bit odd.'

'Did they brief you on what you might be doing with me?'

'No. They said you'd tell me.'

'Tell me about yourself.'

Chapman smiled. 'I'm sure you've checked my "P" file.'

'Maybe. But you tell me.'

'I'm thirty next October. I went to Eton and Oxford. Played a bit of tennis. Messed about in France and Germany for a couple of years. Doing odd jobs. Tour agency's courier and that sort of thing.' He shrugged. 'I guess that's about it.'

'Tell me about your father.'

Chapman looked uneasy for the first time. 'He runs an engineering outfit in Stafford. He's pretty good at it.'

'Why don't you work for him?'

Chapman smiled. Rather wanly. 'He's never asked me to.'

'Why not? Your brother works for him.'

Chapman looked away towards the window and when he looked back at Harris he said quietly, 'He doesn't think much of me.'

'Why not?'

'I'm not sure. I think he thinks I'm rather feckless, and not commercially minded.'

'What did he say when you told him you were in SIS?'

Chapman laughed softly. 'He wasn't impressed. Said it was a bunch of academics and queers.'

'Sounds quite a charmer.'

'He had to fight his way up the ladder. He's not so bad.'

Harris reached for the two files. 'I've got them to free an office for you. Number 431, two doors down the corridor. Read these and come and see me at three.'

When Chapman had left, Harris sat thinking about what Chapman had said. His assessment of Joe Shapiro had been very perceptive for someone who couldn't know anything about his background. Not that he knew all that much himself.

And Chapman hadn't mentioned that his father had a knighthood and he hadn't mentioned that he was Chairman of Carlson Engineering who employed about eight thousand people and was the biggest firm of its kind in the north Midlands. Maybe it wasn't modesty, maybe he took it for granted that everyone knew that he was the son of Sir Arthur Chapman, who paused grim-faced for TV cameras as he walked into some Ministry or harangued some meeting of the CBI on how the country should be run. His donations to the Liberal Party were as acceptable as his membership was frequently an embarrassment. Nobody could understand why he had joined the party when he was so obviously a right-wing Tory in word and deed. But he added a touch of reality to party conferences and committees, and at election times canvassers discovered that his views were shared by many old-fashioned working people. They too thought that taxes were too high and that blacks should go home unless they played for Arsenal or Lancashire County Cricket Club.

There was one other thing that Chapman had said that registered with Harris, but he didn't recall it when he was going over the conversation in his mind. But subconsciously it made him change his attitude to taking on Chapman. He'd at least give him a fair run for his money.

CHAPTER EIGHT

A lot of people thought that Shapiro looked remarkably like Spencer Tracy in *Guess Who's Coming to Dinner*. His face had the same topography and his hair was white and luxuriant. His eyes too had that same speculative, disbelieving, wary look. Only a handful of people knew what his responsibilities were, and any questions on the subject were treated with evasion or outright condemnation of the questioner for indulging in idle curiosity. But everyone knew that he had been with MI6 for longer than any serving officer could remember. Joe Shapiro was part of the fabric of the organization. They knew he had been an officer in MI6 well before World War II. And they knew that he had a hand in almost all operations concerning the KGB. But that was all. There were rumours of an unhappy marriage that surfaced from time to time but there was virtually nothing known of his domestic life.

He was talking on the phone when Harris knocked and came in and Shapiro pointed to one of the chairs in front of his desk. When Shapiro finished talking he hung up and turned to look at Harris.

'I've told Morton that if we're to do this job properly we're going to need at least four or five more bodies.'

'Did he agree?'

Shapiro shrugged. 'He agreed. But that doesn't mean we'll get 'em. I gather you've taken on young Chapman.'

'Yes. There wasn't a great deal of choice.'

'Any suggestions of how to tackle this thing?'

'I thought maybe I should cover Grushko and let Chapman cover Maguire-Barton. Until we get more people.'

'There's not much in either file that's of any real use. Gossip column stuff about Maguire-Barton and four or five days of random surveillance of Grushko. But they've met on a dozen or more occasions in the last twelve months. Not always in this country. Two so-called parliamentary visits to Prague, one to Sofia. A trade fair in Dresden and a few sponsored jaunts to East Berlin. Ostensibly exchanges of views on East-West relations and general arms reductions. The usual crap.'

'How often do you want me to report?'

'Every day. A written summary once a week.'

'Can I use your secretary?'

'You're out of date, laddie. I haven't had a secretary for two years. Use the pool and if there's any delay I'll deal with it. You just let me know.'

Three days after seeing Shapiro, Harris met Chapman at Victoria Station and they walked together to Harris's rooms.

'Tell me what you've got.'

'I've divided my time between Maguire-Barton and Grushko. But I haven't got much.'

'Tell me about Grushko. I'll be taking him over myself and you can concentrate on Maguire-Barton.'

'Grushko's got a flat off Kensington High Street in Adam and Eve Mews. It's over a garage where an antique dealer keeps some of his stock. He's got a special lock on the door and a rather primitive light-cell and an old-fashioned pressure alarm under the mat inside the door. It's quite a pleasant flat and a woman from the embassy cleans it every other day. A good collection of classical cassettes and a Jap hi-fi. A lot of books. A few Russian but mainly English and American. Novels, poetry, social history. I've made a list.'

'Any correspondence or files?'

'No. Absolutely nothing. The postman hasn't made a delivery there since he took over six months ago. His mail must go to the embassy. None of them have much mail even at the Press Centre. And that's all official stuff from UK sources. Invitations, press releases. That sort of stuff. But there is one thing. He's got a bird he sees regularly. A real doll. Looks Russian or Italian. Very dark, flashing eyes and rather sultry.'

'Who is she?'

'I haven't found out anything about her except that she doesn't live permanently in London. She generally spends the night with Grushko when they meet and she takes the Cardiff train home but I don't know where she gets off. Once or twice she's stayed at a flat in Hammersmith after meeting Grushko. I'm checking on whose flat it is.'

'Is she anything more than a girlfriend?'

'I think she is. I'm not sure.'

'Why do you think that?'

'They're obviously fond of one another. But they look like conspirators.' He laughed. 'They seem to talk almost too much and too earnestly for just lovers.'

'What about Maguire-Barton?'

'He's got a pad in Pimlico. A conversion. Three bedrooms. Quite swish. And it's paid for by a public relations company. Lobbyists. It's pretty exhausting following him, he's a real busy bee. Goes to everything he's invited to. Especially embassy parties. Mainly eastern bloc ones but to others as well. And what's even more interesting is that our friend Grushko is nearly always at the communist receptions, at the same time. But they never leave together. And . . .' he paused smiling, '. . . the most interesting thing is that Grushko's girlfriend has been escorted by Maguire-Barton on two occasions. Once to the Italian Embassy and once to the Dutch Embassy. Grushko wasn't there on either occasion.'

'Anything else?'

'Maguire-Barton has two or three girls he sees regularly. All-night jobs. Sometimes his place, sometimes theirs. Seems to be a lavish spender. I asked for permission to check his bank account but Painter says he needs more grounds before he could authorize it.'

'Have you checked over Maguire-Barton's file in the Archives?'

'It doesn't go back very far. They've not been checking him for long, and before the surveillance started there's very little if anything of interest to us.'

On the tenth day Chapman followed Maguire-Barton's taxi to the Embankment on the south side of the river and walked behind him as the MP strolled past County Hall towards the Festival Hall.

Chapman hung back as Maguire-Barton walked into the Festival Hall and across to the cafeteria. He saw him standing with a tray in the short queue for tea and then Chapman saw Grushko sitting at one of the window tables alone.

Grushko and Maguire-Barton sat at separate tables but after ten minutes Grushko stood up, walked to Maguire-Barton's table and bent over for a light for his cigarette. Smiling his thanks the Russian picked up the folded newspaper from the table beside Maguire-Barton's arm and walked back to his seat. Maguire-Barton left five minutes later and Chapman followed him back to the flat in Pimlico. It was the first time that they had established a positive and covert connection between the KGB man and the MP. Harris confirmed later that Grushko had met his dark-haired girlfriend at the Golden Egg in Leicester Square. They had gone to the Zoo and then back to his Kensington flat. He left alone at eight o'clock the next morning and later the girl had taken the Cardiff train.

CHAPTER NINE

The cabin on the SS *America* was small, with two berths, one over the other, and two small lockers for clothes and hand luggage. But Molody had slipped the steward ten dollars and he had got the cabin to himself. As he sat on the lower berth he wondered why Collins had ordered him to leave the United States within forty-eight hours. The orders came from Moscow and he was to go to London and be prepared to stay there indefinitely. It didn't seem like a routine posting. He had been doing a good job for Collins in the United States but Collins had seemed tense and apprehensive. He had been given the London address of the Cohens who had apparently already moved to England. But Molody wasn't a man who indulged in doubts and introspection.

For the first two days he had been mildly seasick but by the third day he had recovered. He spent a lot of time playing cards with some of the stewards and it was from them he learned about the Overseas Club which provided cheap accommodation in London. He learned too about the various rackets the crewmen ran to augment their earnings, and he realized that there were going to be even more opportunities for earning quick easy money in London than he had had in Canada and New York.

He found the crewmen impressed by his story of his wealthy Canadian father with the huge estate in Vancouver, and he regaled them with stories of how, despite the money his father gave him, he had worked as a cook in a labour camp, as a gold prospector, a long-haul truck driver and a gas-station attendant. By the time the ship docked at Southampton he had added to his legend a nagging wife who he had walked out on. It seemed to go down well and bit by bit he had fabricated a past that explained and fitted his present life and character.

At the Royal Overseas League off St James's Street he only added to his story that he had been given a Canadian government grant to study Chinese at London University's School of Oriental and African Studies. A far-seeing government was anticipating a relaxation of contacts that could lead to trade with Red China.

Two weeks later he had a job as a second-hand car salesman in Clapham. He was successful from the first day and although he was only paid commission he was earning reasonable money. But not enough to justify the flat he took in the White House, a residential hotel in Regent's Park. But the legend of the wealthy father covered that, and his fellows at the car showrooms were impressed by his constant flow of anecdotes about his life in Canada. He found that, like Collins had said, he already believed his own story. He could bring himself to raging anger at the indignities heaped on him by his imaginary wife and could bring tears to his own eyes as he reluctantly revealed the unhappiness of his childhood. Neglected by his frivolous mother, his wealthy father too often away abroad on business trips.

The advertisement in the *Evening Standard* offered the opportunity for investors to get into the vending machine business and Molody had telephoned the next morning.

He'd spent an hour with the two men talking about their proposition. They wanted £500 down and he'd be given a small territory to sell machines in. To offices, canteens and clubs. But there was no chance of him having a stake in the business. He had offered up to £1,000 for a five per cent shareholding but they'd refused. Molody was impressed by the two Jaguars in the tatty yard outside. And he was impressed by their refusal of an offer that valued their business at £20,000. There was only one room and the two lock-up garages that housed the vending machines. He got on well with both men, they were amiable rogues, as talkative and confident as he was and they finally gave him the telephone number of a firm that handled juke-boxes.

The man with the juke-boxes was an altogether different sort of man. Big and rough, he was obviously not interested in Molody's amiable chat. If Molody paid a hundred-pound deposit in cash on each machine he could have up to five. Take it or leave it. There were no exclusive territories and no sales leads. It was all up to him. He paid the deposit on five machines and stood watching as the man counted every note.

In six days of tramping the streets of Clapham Molody had placed seven juke-boxes, and by the end of two months had a regular income of over two hundred pounds a week in cash. An income on which he would pay no tax and was therefore worth more than double what it netted him.

In his journeys he heard of a syndicate in another district selling and renting one-armed bandits that was looking for an additional partner. They were in Peckham, and Molody invested several hundred pounds and became a substantial shareholder and a director.

From the office he set up in Rye Lane Molody worked from early morning until late at night. Gradually his partners let him take over and he became managing director. He was then planning how to make extra profits by setting up a plant to manufacture machines for them to sell. He had already started exporting machines. There was only one condition he laid down and that was that he was to have all weekends free.

The girls who phoned and called for him at the small offices were much admired by his colleagues and when he came in on Mondays looking tired he made no protest when they made their schoolboy jokes about why he always wanted his weekends free.

CHAPTER TEN

Alongside Portland is the small seaside town of Weymouth. Its harbour has provided safe anchorage for invading Saxons, Romans and Normans. But when it became a favourite resort of George III it became better known for its sandy beach and old-world peace.

The Old Elm Tree public house in Weymouth had Harry Houghton as one of its regulars. Night after night he regaled the other regulars with stories of his war-time exploits. They listened with amusement, exchanging winks, because they were well aware that his tales were often self-contradictory, manning naval guns in Mediterranean convoys at the same time that he had been twenty below zero on an ice-gripped convoy to Murmansk. But with his mottled, red-veined face and his pointed nose he was harmless enough. He was a bullshitter but he livened up the bar-room chat. He was always there promptly at opening time and he seldom left before the bar closed. It was well known that he did not get on with his wife.

It was in May 1958 when his wife contacted the probation service in Bournemouth and arranged an interview. Probation officers are reluctant to hear complaints about third parties who have not been put under their control by the courts, and it often turns out that their informants are more in need of help than the alleged offenders. But listening is part of their official therapy.

Mrs Houghton's interviewer was a cautious man and he listened without comment to her litany of her husband's drunkenness, neglect, unfaithfulness, and his determination to get his own back on the Admiralty who had ruined his career prospects. It was an old, old story that had been retailed with variations on the theme hundreds of times in every social service office in the kingdom and when all this seemed to rouse no indignation Mrs Houghton played her trump card. She claimed that her husband regularly brought home classified documents from the naval bases. When even that brought no response she gave up.

The probation officer thought vaguely of passing the information to naval intelligence but decided against it. The woman was almost certainly lying, from spite against her husband. And if he passed on such information and it turned out to be a pack of lies God knows what repercussions there could be. Actions for defamation, libel and all the rest of it. Anyway, none of her problems concerned the probation service. It was the Marriage Guidance Council she needed or Special Branch. Or, more likely, a psychiatrist.

Ethel Elizabeth Gee was forty-six, and a temporary clerk at the Portland navy base. With small features and a clear complexion she looked younger than her years but very plain. Expecting little or nothing from life, she was surprised and flattered when Harry Houghton started paying court to her. Even when it had matured their relationship was far short of a romance but in some odd way it satisfied them both. The meek timid woman saw the man as a protector; not quite a hero, but a man who had seen something of the world. He spent money freely, took her on trips to London, and everywhere he went he seemed to get to know people easily and quickly. And for the man, he had a sympathetic listener and a woman who didn't despise him, who mended his clothes and cared about whether he had eaten enough.

'Call for you, Harry.'

'Who is it?'

'Don't know, mate. A fella – he said it was personal.'

Harry Houghton reached across the desk for the receiver and put it to his ear.

'Houghton. Who is it?'

'I've got news of Kristina for you, Mr Houghton.' The voice was soft and had a slight foreign accent.

'Who are you?'

'A friend of Kristina. She asked me to talk to you.'

'Is she coming over then?'

'Maybe we should meet and I can give you her news.'

'Where do you want to meet?'

'I suggest you come up to London and we meet outside Drury Lane theatre on Saturday next. About twelve o'clock mid-day.'

'How shall I recognize you?'

'I'll recognize you, Harry. Don't worry.'

And the caller hung up. Houghton reached for his mug of tea. It was cold but he sipped it slowly as he thought about the call. Kristina had always said that she wanted to get out of Poland and come to England. It would complicate things but by God it would be worth it to have a girl like that to show off to his friends.

He found it hard to concentrate on his work for the next two days. And in the evenings when he and Ethel were decorating the empty cottage that he had bought in Portland he wondered how she'd take it when the time came. She was a dignified woman so she'd probably not make a fuss. And that bitch Peggy would have finished divorcing him and it would be one in the eye when she heard he'd got a pretty young girl as his new wife.

Houghton stood in front of the theatre looking at the front page of the early edition of the *Evening Standard*. There was a picture of the President of Italy in London on a State visit. He looked up from the paper. There were plenty of people about but nobody who seemed to be looking for someone. He turned to the stop-press. Chelsea were playing at home. He'd just be able to make it to Stamford Bridge if the chap on the phone didn't turn up.

And then a hand touched his arm. 'Glad to meet you, Harry.'

The man was tall. Younger than he had expected.

'Glad to meet you too.'

'Where can we have a coffee and talk?'

'There's a place round the corner.'

'You lead the way, my friend.'

When the waitress had brought the tea and coffee and the buttered toast Houghton couldn't wait any longer.

'How is she? How's Krissie?'

'She's got problems, Harry. She needs your help.'

'I'm nothing to do with the embassy now you know.'

'I know that, comrade.'

'What's the problem anyway?'

'She's got problems with the police. They know about the drugs and the black market. It's a very serious offence you know in Poland.'

'Who says she did such things?'

The man smiled. 'They've got statements from the buyers. Dates. Places. And she's confessed, so they have a clear court case.'

'How can I do anything?'

'Well, Harry, she feels she's only in this mess because she wanted to help you. She thinks that the police might be more lenient if you cooperated.'

'Cooperated. How?'

'There are things the authorities would like to know. If you helped them I'm sure things would go better for Kristina.'

'There's nothing I can tell them that Kris couldn't tell them. I just brought the stuff over.'

'I'm not thinking of that business, Harry, I'm thinking about your present work. There are small bits of information that we should like to know.'

Houghton looked at the man's face. 'You mean tell you things about Portland?'

'Yes.'

'I couldn't do that. I'm not allowed to. You ought to know that.'

The man shrugged. 'It could be very bad for you if you don't, Harry. Bad for your lady-friend too.'

'You mean they'd . . .'

The man held up his hand. 'Let's not talk about that. We both know the facts of life. And nothing will happen if you cooperate.'

'I'll think about it.'

The man shook his head, dismissively. 'In future when we are to meet you will receive a brochure in the mail offering you a Hoover vacuum cleaner. When you receive this you will phone this number and ask for Andrew.' He pushed a scrap of paper across the table. 'When you phone you say your name and you will be given a time and date. Nothing more. No talk. At the time and on the day given you go to a public house called the Toby Jug. You already know it, don't you.'

Houghton nodded. 'Yes.'

'Anything else, my friend?'

'What the hell do I get out of this?'

The man reached inside his jacket for his wallet and below the table he counted out eight pound notes, folded them over and then passed them over the table to Houghton. 'That's for your expenses, Harry.'

The man stood up, put a pound note on the table alongside the bill, gave Houghton a brief cold smile and left.

It was beginning to snow as Houghton walked into Covent Garden, and he walked down into the Strand and across to Charing Cross Station and changed trains at Waterloo.

The train was almost empty and he sat alone in the second-class carriage thinking about the man. They were bluffing, of course. They could play their games in Russia and Poland but not in England. He would ignore the whole thing. Put it out of his mind and forget it. He picked up his copy of *Reveille* and leafed through, glancing at the pictures. At no time did it occur to him to report the matter to the police or the security officer at Portland. It was just a try-on that hadn't worked.

And as the days went by he *did* forget about the meeting and the threats. And he was all the more shocked when a month later he got a brochure through the post offering a special deal on Hoover vacuum cleaners. He was shocked but not scared. He hadn't enough imagination to be scared. But he phoned the number the following day and he was given a time and a date.

The man came into the Toby Jug five minutes after Houghton sat down at one of the tables. He wasted no time after he had ordered two beers.

'What have you brought?'

Houghton passed him half a dozen back copies of the *Hampshire Telegraph and Post*. He pointed to one of the back pages, to a regular column headed 'Naval and Dockyard Notes'.

'That's all very useful stuff.'

The man read the column that consisted of nothing more than routine published information on ship movements and naval promotions and postings. He pushed the newspaper to one side and turned in his seat to look at Houghton.

'Is this meant to be some sort of joke?'

Houghton shrugged. 'That's all I can do for you, mate.'

'Maybe you don't believe my warning about what could happen to you and your woman.'

'You can't do anything in this country. You'd never get away with it.'

The man looked at him with half-closed eyes as he spoke. 'I'm going to give you one more chance, comrade. If you don't respond sensibly you're going to be in very deep trouble.'

And without further words the man pushed aside the table and walked out of the pub.

For the first time Harry Houghton wondered if they really would dare to try something. For a couple of days he thought about it from time to time. But he was getting ready to move his belongings from the repository and the trailer he had moved into while he and Ethel decorated the cottage. It had taken months but it would be ready for Christmas and there was a lot to sort out now that he was on his own.

But when another Hoover brochure arrived in the post the first week in December he decided to ignore it. When in doubt do nothing was Harry Houghton's motto.

CHAPTER ELEVEN

The small shop in a side-street just off the Strand had shelves from floor to ceiling with row on row of books. Books were piled high on half a dozen tables and books were stacked on shelves up the stairs to the small second storey. In the small untidy inner office a glass-fronted bookcase held the really expensive volumes.

They were books of all kinds except fiction and the majority were about the Americas. The United States, Canada, South America and the Polar Regions. History, geography, economics, politics, flora and fauna, the arts, anything related to the Americas.

When the bell on the street door clanged a small white-haired man came down the rickety stairs and walked over to the man who had come in.

'Don't let me disturb you if you want to browse. You're very welcome to look around but if I can help you . . .'

'Maybe you can. Have you ever heard of a guy named Moore, a poet?'

'You must mean Clement C. Moore, died about 1860 or thereabouts.'

'That's pretty good. Yes, he's the guy. He had a book published called *Saint Nicholas*, something like that.'

'Ah, yes. Actually *A Visit from Saint Nicholas*.'

'That's the one. You got it by any chance?'

'No. I could get you a copy maybe, if you're not in a hurry.'

'How long would it take?'

'Oh, that's very hard to say. Months rather than weeks, I'm afraid. Especially if you wanted the original edition.'

'Yep. That's what I wanted. Well maybe I'll leave you my card. I'm at the US Embassy. I'll give you a call in a few months' time.'

'I'll see what I can do, sir.'

When the customer had left the white-haired man went back up to his small office and sat looking at the visiting card. The American was the naval attaché at the US Embassy. He reached for the telephone, hesitated, then slid the card into the drawer of his desk. He was fifty, a spry, healthy-looking man with a ready smile and already well-respected in London's antiquarian book world. It was known that he was a New Zealander and only just established, but he knew his subject and had a reputation for fair dealing. He didn't deal in the areas that most dealers covered, he was a genuine specialist and he passed on leads to other booksellers for a small commission. And even apart from business he was a likeable man. He didn't talk about his past but that was understandable. He was a Jew and he had been in Europe before he became a refugee to New Zealand. People assumed that he had a background of persecution and concentration camps as many others did who were now in London. Nobody wanted to open old wounds, neither his nor theirs.

He and his wife lived in a typical London suburb in a modest bungalow. 45 Cranley Drive, Ruislip, was quite small. Mock Tudor with white-washed walls and fake beams with a small front garden and a drive up to the garage. His wife, Helen, was forty-seven, also white-haired and with alert eyes that were always on the edge of a smile. Obviously well-educated and capable she looked a very compatible wife for her bookseller husband.

The bookshop didn't open on Saturdays. It wasn't worth it, and apart from that he needed his weekends free.

He was up in the attic when his wife called up to him.

'The phone, Peter. For you.'

'Who is it?'

'Our friend.'

He clambered down the ladder, brushing the dust from his clothes and in the hall he picked up the phone. It was only a short conversation and then he walked into the kitchen.

'He'll be here at mid-day. I'd better finish the attic. I'll need the vacuum cleaner.'

The three of them ate together. *Borsch* and *pirozhki* followed by lemon sorbet.

When the woman left the two men together they got straight down to business.

'When can you take the radio?'

'Now if you want.'

'Where are you putting it?'

'Under the kitchen floor.'

'Isn't that risky?'

'No. It's the last place anyone would look.'

'And the aerial?'

'I've already fitted one in the attic.'

'Don't forget to give me that American's visiting card. That could be very useful.'

He smiled, patting his jacket pocket. 'I haven't forgotten it.'

CHAPTER TWELVE

There had been a Hipcress farming on the Romney Marshes long before Napoleon contemplated invasion, and one of the early Hipcresses had helped dig out the channel for the Military Canal. They were none of them good farmers although they were financially quite successful. They had a hunger for land that outran their husbandry. All farmers complain about the weather and the crops but Albert Hipcress didn't complain. He seethed silently with anger against the government, the tax office, the National Farmers' Union and neighbours with more than his five hundred acres.

Hipcress was a bachelor of forty-five, and with his unprepossessing appearance and his country bumpkin manners seemed likely to remain one. But he assumed that every woman on the marshes, single or otherwise saw him as a prime target because of his five hundred acres. His farming was simple and primitive. Potatoes, beans, and sheep. His lambing record was poor, but his feed costs were minimal.

The farmhouse itself was a pleasant, rambling old house alongside two disused oasts, and beyond the oasts were two large metal-clad barns. The shepherd's cottage was a hundred yards away, barely visible from the farmhouse itself.

Albert Hipcress sat in the farm kitchen next to the Rayburn solid-fuel cooker, reading a week old copy of the *Kent Messenger*. He wore a pair of old felt slippers and a pair of shiny blue serge trousers held up by a pair of army braces. He looked up at the old clock on the mantlepiece. There was half an hour yet. He used the tool to lift the hotplate, spat into the fire and wiped his mouth on the back of his hand. He walked through to his tiny office that had once been a larder and switched on the light. Taking a bunch of keys from his trouser pocket he unlocked the bottom drawer in the ancient roll-topped desk, took out a blue folder and turned over the pages until he came to the balance sheet. He had not only read it many times before in the past month but he could have recited the figures blindfolded. The farm itself was valued at £672,000. The stock was written down to £7,000 and the plant and machinery at £24,000. Albert Hipcress used contractors to avoid capital expenditure. But the last figure was the one that pleased him most. Cash at bank. £943 on current account and £34,000 on deposit. The scattered cottages that he owned were not included in the farm accounts.

He walked through to the bedroom. The light at the side of the bed was already on, the bottle of whisky and the two glasses were on the cast-iron mantlepiece over the gas-fire. The corner of the sheets was turned down neatly on the bed. And then he saw the lights of the car as it went over the hump-backed bridge across the feeder to the canal. He was downstairs, waiting at the back door as it swept in to draw up between the oasts where nobody could see it. He heard her high heels as she hurried across the concrete yard. Then he saw her and she was the one he'd asked for.

'Hello, Mr H. How are you?'

He nodded. 'Not bad. How are you?'

The girl laughed softly. 'Rarin' to go, honey.'

Upstairs he sat on the edge of the bed watching as she took off her sweater, chatting to him, her firm young breasts swinging and bouncing as she struggled with the zip of her skirt. And then she was naked, standing smiling at him as he stared at her body.

'There you are, Mr H. That's what you've been waiting for all the week isn't it?'

It was seven o'clock the next morning when she left the farmhouse and hurried over to the cottage.

The Romney Marshes are not dairy country, its bleakness and its terrain can only support sheep, and the Romney Marsh sheep were bred to withstand the biting winds and the soggy marshland. On the marshes shepherds had always been known as 'lookers' and on the Hipcress farm the 'looker's' cottage was almost hidden from the farmhouse by a mild slope of the ground and a small copse of beech trees.

There had been no 'looker' on the Hipcress farm for the last twenty years and the cottage had stood empty for most of the time. Albert Hipcress had often wondered if there wasn't some way he could make some cash out of the 'looker's' cottage. He spoke to the estate agents in Rye and a few weeks later they had sent a man to see him. The estate agents suggested that he could possibly get seven to ten pounds a week rent for the cottage provided it was tidied up a bit.

Hipcress took an instant dislike to the man the agents sent to look at the cottage. He was a city man, smiling, confident and condescending. But when Hipcress said ten pounds a week the man had accepted. When they looked over the cottage together Hipcress said that it was up to the tenant to put it in order and bear the cost. The man had agreed to this too and Hipcress took him back to the farmhouse and wrote out a rental agreement from a tattered copy of *Every Man His Own Lawyer*. He asked for three months' rent in advance and was amazed when the man not only agreed but paid in cash.

He had watched the 'looker's' cottage being cleared out and furnished and wondered why a man would go to so much trouble when he only used the place at weekends and once or twice a month on weekdays just for the night. Slowly he changed his opinion of the man who was always so amiable and who frequently brought him a few bottles of beer. Two or three times on Saturday nights the man walked over to the farmhouse and chatted with him in the kitchen. He couldn't remember how they'd got on to the subject of girls and sex. From the way the man talked he obviously expected that Hipcress had a girl now and again. He seemed amazed when Hipcress said that he'd never been able to find a girl to oblige him in that way.

The following weekend the man had shown him photographs of two girls and asked him which he liked best. Albert Hipcress studied the two photographs as carefully as if he were judging the Miss World contest and finally pointed at the picture of the young blonde. The man smiled. 'You've got a good eye for a girl, Albert. She's a real goer that one.' He looked at the farmer. 'She's a friend of mine. How about I fix for her to come down with me in the week and give you a nice time?' Albert Hipcress was torn between the embarrassment of letting an outsider know his innermost thoughts and his desire for the girl. 'Just try her, Albert. I'd like to know what you think of her.' Albert Hipcress put up only token resistance and it was obvious that he was eager to take advantage of the man's offer.

Twice a month the girl had been brought down to the farmhouse. It cost Hipcress nothing and he was an enthusiastic and willing learner. When a visit was due, his mind as he worked around the farm was obsessed by thoughts of what they would do on the ramshackle bed in his room upstairs. His tenant never asked him if he liked the sessions with the girl and he never mentioned them himself. But he wondered how the man persuaded the girl to do it. He guessed it must be money. It wasn't the man's looks. His face had not even one good feature and his sallow complexion was especially unattractive. His eyes were always half-closed as if he was watching carefully; his nose was shapeless and his small mouth was mean. When Hipcress had asked him what he did he'd said that he was a businessman but he didn't say what business he was in. Most men would have wondered why, if it was money that made it possible, a stranger should spend money on him. But Albert Hipcress never wondered what the man's motive might be.

CHAPTER THIRTEEN

When the reception clerk phoned through to Joe Kimber he listened with no great interest. At least once a week some nutter came into the US Embassay in Paris, offering the innermost secrets of the Politburo or his services to the CIA.

'Can he hear you talking to me now?'

'No. I've shoved him in the annexe.'

'What's he look like?'

'Pretty rough. Tensed up and tanked up.'

'Did he speak French or English?'

'English. But real bad English. A heavy accent.'

'Tell me again what he said?'

'He said he was an officer in the KGB. He'd just come from his assignment in the US and he wants to defect.'

Kimber sighed. 'OK. I'd better have a look at him. Tell one of the guards to bring him in.' He cleared everything off his desk except the two telephones and drew the curtains over the map on the wall. He didn't get up from his desk when the Marine brought in the visitor. He pointed to the single chair.

'Sit down, Mister . . . I didn't get your name.'

The man shrugged. 'Is Maki or Hayhanen – whichever you like.'

The American smiled. 'Which one do you like?'

'My real name is Hayhanen but I use Maki name in New York.'

'Tell me about New York.'

'I work there for KGB.'

'So what are you doing in Paris?'

'I was recalled by Moscow. I don't wish to go. I am afraid.'

'Why are you afraid?'

'I think they discipline me. Punish me.'

'Why should they do that?'

'I don't know. I think the man in New York gives bad report on me.'

'Which man is that?'

'Is two men. Sivrin at United Nations and an older man named Mark. He never liked me from the beginning.'

'Why not?'

'He was old-fashioned. No friendliness. Just orders. All the time he criticize everything I do.'

'And who is this Mark fellow?'

'He is top illegal in United States.'

'Where did you have meetings with him?'

'All over. Central Park; RKO Keith's Theatre in Flushing, a cinema; Riverside Park; a place in Bergen Street in Newark.' He paused and shrugged. 'Many places.'

'What nationality are you?'

'Russian-Finnish.'

'You speak Russian?'

'Of course?'

'What about Sivrin?'

'I work first for Sivrin. Then Mark.'

'Where did you meet Sivrin?'

'Was not meeting – was mainly drops.'

'Where were the drops?'

'A hole in the wall in Jerome Avenue in the Bronx, a bridge over a path in Central Park and a lamp-post in Fort Tryon Park.'

'What was your address in New York?'

'We've got a cottage at Peekskill.'

'You mean Peekskill up the Hudson?'

'Yes.'

'Who's we?'

'I don't understand?'

'You said *we've* got a cottage. Who else is involved?'

'Just my wife. She lives there with me.'

'You mean she's still living there?'

'Of course.'

Kimber sat looking at his visitor, uncertain how to deal with him. He needed to check on at least some of the items in his story before he decided what to do with him. It was such a ragbag of a story but it had that faint smell of truth. There was one fact he could check on easily. And it was worth a call to the States.

Kimber looked across the desk. 'I'm going to get one of our people to take you to have a meal downstairs. He'll bring you back to me when you've finished. OK?'

Hayhanen nodded and stood up. Reaching into his jacket pocket he took out a Finnish five-mark coin and, as Kimber watched, the man prised the coin open with the nail of his thumb. The coin was hollowed out to take a single-frame negative from a Minox camera.

Half an hour later, after Kimber had phoned New York for a check on Sivrin and the cottage in Peekskill, it was Washington who came back to him. Seats had been booked on the night-flight from Paris for him and his visitor. He was not to interrogate him further himself. Just deliver him safely at Idlewild. He was to stay behind on the plane with Hayhanen until all the other passengers had left and a CIA deep interrogation team would come on board and take over.

When they arrived at Idlewild Kimber was amazed at the group that poured into the empty aircraft. Six or seven top men and Allan Dulles himself in the private room in the terminal building. It seemed that Hayhanen was the break they had been looking for the last four years. He was congratulated as if it were some skill on his part that had pulled in the KGB man. There was apparently no doubt in their minds that Hayhanen really *was* genuinely KGB.

Two hours after his arrival in New York Hayhanen was officially handed over to the FBI and four Special Agents had interrogated him through the night to mid-afternoon. By that time he had signed a document giving his permission for the house in Peekskill to be searched.

They had to use Russian-speaking agents in the following days because Hayhanen's poor English became unintelligible under pressure. Apart from the language problem it became obvious that Hayhanen had a very disturbed personality as well as being a heavy drinker. Questioning Hanna his wife and several local tradesmen who knew him was like cleaning an old painting. As a layer of paint or varnish came off a different picture was revealed, and another and another. Hayhanen's life had been a strange, wild nightmare of drunken wife-beating, bizarre outbursts of public violence and then the secret life controlled by the man called Mark.

The interrogators gradually realized why Moscow had recalled him. Apart from keeping their appointments with his controller, Hayhanen had been totally indifferent to his mission. Using the money he was paid for his own purposes, unscrupulous in his demands for more funds and, as far as they could tell, never carrying out even the minor tasks that he had been ordered to undertake. But what they got from him that really mattered was the description of Mark, the places where they met and the various addresses in New York where he lived or appeared to live. As often happened when a man really hates another, Hayhanen could describe Mark in great detail.

It was the studio in the Ovington Building that they were able to identify most accurately despite the vague, rambling description, and a twenty-four-hour surveillance of the building was mounted by the FBI even before the interrogation of Hayhanen was completed. The interrogation team were going back into his recruitment and training in the Soviet Union but Hayhanen was slowly disintegrating, becoming fearful of KGB retribution for what he had done. Nervous and excitable he refused to sign statements and insisted that even if they were able to trace the man named Mark, he would not appear personally in court as a witness to Mark's activities.

His description of Mark had portrayed an elderly man, bald with a fringe of grey hair, a narrow face with a prominent nose and a receding chin; he thought that maybe Mark was Jewish. And always the dark straw hat with the broad white band around it.

CHAPTER FOURTEEN

Bert Harris stirred his coffee slowly as he watched the two men at the table near the service counter. One of the men was Grigor Grushko and he had no idea who the other man was. It was the second time they had met in the last two weeks. The first time they had met at a pub, the Bricklayer's Arms near Victoria Station, and this time they were in the cafeteria on the main concourse at Euston Station.

They were talking earnestly, with Grushko tapping his finger on the table as if to emphasize some point. They weren't quarrelling but it looked as they were disagreeing about something. Ten minutes later Grushko stood up, standing still for a moment, still speaking as if he was trying to convince the other man of something.

Harris looked at his watch. It was four-thirty and he decided, for no particular reason, to stay with the second man. But he watched as Grushko walked across the concourse and down the steps to the underground taxi rank.

Ten minutes later the second man looked around the cafeteria slowly, and Harris was sure that the man had had anti-surveillance training. It had been done too methodically, despite the casualness. The man stood up, patted his jacket as if to check that something was there, and then he walked across to the bookstall and bought a copy of the *Evening Standard*. He turned it sideways to look at the stop-press column on the back page, folded it slowly and strolled across to the exit to Euston Road. He stood outside, looking at the passing traffic. Harris watched him from just inside the station.

When the man walked to the line of taxis Harris was close behind him. After the man closed the door of the taxi Harris let one taxi go and took the second. He flashed his ID card at the driver and pointed to the taxi he wanted followed.

They were held up by the lights in Regent Street but the target taxi had turned into Beak Street and was heading for Golden Square where it stopped by the Dormeuil building and the man got out. Harris waited in the taxi for a few moments watching the man walk across the gardens towards Berwick Street. Then he paid off the cabbie and followed the man into Brewer Street. In Old Compton Street the man turned into an open doorway leading to a flight of stairs. A handwritten postcard tacked to the door merely said. 'Sunshine Escort Agency.'

Harris crossed the street and looked up at the dusty windows of the agency above the newspaper shop and couldn't for the moment think of anything positive he could do. So he waited. Fifteen minutes later the man came out with a young girl. He guessed she was about eighteen. She was very pretty. He followed them both to Cambridge Circus where the man waved down a taxi. It had circled the roundabout before there was another empty taxi and he'd told the driver to go down Charing Cross Road and they caught up with the other taxi as it turned into Charing Cross Station.

He heard the man ask for two tickets to Folkestone and the clerk said that a train was due to leave in twelve minutes which had given Harris time to buy a ticket and phone through to Shapiro for some assistance. No assistance was available.

Just over an hour later the man and girl got off the train at Ashford in Kent. Harris walked ahead of them and took the first taxi, telling the driver to wait. It was nearly five minutes later when the man and the girl came out of the station and Harris breathed a sigh of relief as they got into a taxi themselves. He had to use his ID card again but the driver cooperated well. Harris asked him to check with the taxi company's despatcher where the white Granada was going. The reply was that it was going to Stone-cum-Ebony to Cooper's Farm. The driver said he'd been there himself a month before with a fellow and a girl. It was old man Hipcress's farm. When Harris asked him to describe the male passenger he knew it was the same man. The driver also volunteered that when he had done the trip he'd been told to pick them both up at the farm the following morning in time to catch the 9.15 from Ashford to London.

The white Granada was already heading back for Ashford as they turned into the lane that led past the farm. The driver slowed and stopped, winding down his window to talk to his colleague. He was going straight home. He'd got to pick up his fare at 8.15 the next morning. Harris paid off his driver a hundred yards past the farmhouse and asked him where was the nearest telephone box. It was half a mile away at the bend in the lane, where it joined the main road to Rye.

The farmhouse was reached by a gravel drive, there was one light on downstairs and one light upstairs in the gable end and Harris stood in the darkness, listening and watching. Apart from the distant bleating of sheep and the sound of water running in the ditches everywhere was silent. When his eyes were accustomed to the darkness he made his way cautiously up the drive.

When he was about twenty yards from the farmhouse he saw that the gravel drive gave way to a cinder track rutted from farm vehicles. As his eyes followed the ruts he saw the lights in the 'looker's' cottage by the trees. There were two cars parked by the cottage. A Mini and a Rover 90.

Harris waited for ten minutes before he approached the farmhouse. As he edged his way along the wall towards the lighted window he could see that the curtains were open and when he looked inside he saw that there was nobody in the room. It was a farmhouse kitchen. Quarry-tiled floor, a solid fuel cooker, big oak table and old-fashioned chairs. The sink and cupboard were modern and cheap. From the overhead beams the old hooks for carcasses still hung down. On one of them was a oil-lamp, its glass shade cracked and dusty.

The 'looker's' cottage was not so easy. There were lights on all over but the curtains had been drawn. There was a small gap in the curtains at one end of the downstairs window but the view of the inside of the room was blocked by a man standing with his back to the window. He could hear voices but not the words. He had a feeling they were talking in a foreign language. The rhythms were not English.

Then the man moved away and he saw that it was the man he had been following. He was offering sandwiches to a white-haired man, a man in his fifties, and a woman who was a little younger. They were talking animatedly, shrugging and shaking their heads. Then they laughed at something the man had said.

Harris made his way cautiously back to the lane. He had no idea where it led but he followed it to the telephone kiosk and phoned the duty officer. Fifteen minutes later a police car picked him up and drove him back to Ashford Station.

The Vice Squad from West End Central applied some discreet pressure to the agency's proprietor. The girl's name was Judy Manners, she was twenty-two and she had a room in Islington. The client was a Mr Gordon. He always paid cash and they had no address for him. He paid £80 and the girl got half.

A plain-clothes policewoman from the Vice Squad picked up the girl and brought her in to West End Central for Harris to interview. The three of them sat around the table in the stark interview room. The girl defiant but obviously scared.

'What are you charging me with?'

'Nobody's charging you with anything – yet,' the policewoman said.

'So why am I here?'

'The gentleman wants to talk to you.'

The girl glanced at Harris. 'Go on then – talk.'

'You went with a man a few days ago to a farmhouse in Kent. Yes?'

'So what?'

'What was the name of the man who took you there?'

'You'd better ask the agency, mate.'

'They said his name was Mr Gordon. Is that correct as far as you know?'

'Yeah.'

'How many times have you been to the farm with him?'

'Three times – maybe four – I don't remember.'

'Always with Mr Gordon?'

'Yes.'

'And what happens at the farm?'

'You know bloody well what happens.'

'I want you to tell me.'

'It's none of your business.'

'I can make it my business if you like it that way.' The girl turned to look at the policewoman.

'You can't touch me. Everything I do is legal.'

'So tell the gentleman what you do.'

The girl turned her head to look at Harris. She shrugged. 'OK. He screws me.'

'Who? Mr Gordon?'

'No. For Christ's sake. The old man, Hipcress or whatever his name is.'

'What about Mr Gordon? What does he do?'

'God knows. He goes off to the cottage. He meets his friends – I go over there in the morning and Mr Gordon takes me back to London.'

'Is it straight sex with the old man?'

'More or less. He plays around for a bit but there's nothing out of the ordinary.'

'Have you ever had sex with Mr Gordon?'

'No.'

'Does Mr Gordon talk about himself at all?'

'He chats. He obviously fancies himself with girls but he never makes a pass.'

'What does he chat about?'

'Nothing special. Football sometimes – I think he said he's a Portsmouth supporter. I think his friends come from Portsmouth or it could be Plymouth. I don't remember which. He's obviously got plenty of money.'

'What does he do?'

She laughed. 'At first he used to give me this spiel about being in entertainment. He sounded off like he was running the Palladium or at least a club.' She laughed again. 'It turns out that he flogs one-armed bandits.' She shrugged. 'He obviously makes a lot of dough but it sure ain't showbusiness.'

'Have you got any idea where he lives?'

'No.' She hesitated. 'It's near Regent's Park I know that – and it's posh. He showed me a photo of his main room. Some sort of party for his friends.'

'Is he English?'

'No – he's Canadian.'

'Did he seem to be on good terms with the farmer?'

She shrugged. 'He thinks he is. But the old man told me on the quiet that he didn't really like him. Thought he was too full of his own importance.'

'What do you make of him?'

'I never made me mind up about him. He wasn't mean or anything like that. But there was something odd about him. I don't know what it was. A bit scary.'

'What did you think about the farmer?'

She laughed. 'He's all right – just a dirty old man.'

Harris stood up. 'You've been very helpful, Miss Manners. We much appreciate it. I'd like you not to talk about our conversation with anybody. Especially Mr Gordon. Is that understood?'

'Yes.' She nodded. 'Is that all?'

'Yes. Can we give you a lift somewhere?'

'You're not doing the agency for anything?'

Harris smiled. 'Of course not. Not so long as you don't talk with *anybody* about being here today. I'm sure the agency is a very well-run business concern.'

'Well,' she said, 'you know where to come if you want to find me.'

A routine check on the two cars at the cottage had been inconclusive. The Mini belonged to a middle-aged spinster in Weymouth and the Rover 90 was registered in the name of Peter John Kroger at an address in one of the outer London suburbs. A check with the local police showed that Peter Kroger was a dealer in antiquarian books. Married, the couple lived a quiet middle-class life and were regarded well by their neighbours. A check on the bookshop indicated that the man was considered an expert in his field by other booksellers and the business was modestly successful. A contrived inspection of the house by Chapman posing as a Ratings Assessment Officer from the local council proved negative. It was a typical suburban house and there were no signs of anything suspicious.

Harris applied for a specialist search team to check the cottage at the farm but it took two weeks before it was available and a pattern of the farmer's daily movements had been established. The only opportunity seemed to be his regular visit to Ashford Market on Wednesdays, and the search team were assembled and briefed the evening before. They estimated that they would need three hours for a Class A search but would only need half an hour for a routine check.

Harris decided on a Class A and the team moved in when the radio link confirmed that the farmer's Landrover had gone through Appledore village.

A Class A search was based on the assumption that the target site was operated by a trained agent and where security precautions might have been taken either to prevent search or merely to reveal that a search had taken place. The team made their entry from an upstairs window and neither the front nor rear door of the cottage were opened. They were the most likely places for check-traps to have been laid.

Before the search team started the photographer, with a Polaroid camera, photographed every wall and feature of every room. And as the search started he recorded the layout of every drawer as it was opened, and nothing on any surface was moved until its position had been recorded.

The technicians applied stethoscopes and thermocouples to the walls and floors of every room to check for cavities, and a two-man team checked all the inside and outside dimensions of the whole building room by room. There were two bedrooms upstairs, one living room below, a good-sized kitchen and what had once been a pantry. As soon as they saw the two elaborate locks on the pantry door they guessed that the search was going to be worth while.

Everything was neatly laid out. A small pile of one-time pads, a Minox camera, a photo-copying stand, a standard KGB micro-dot reader, photographic paper and chemicals, plastic trays, a Durst enlarger, an almost new ICOM transceiver, and a label with transmission and reception times and frequencies pasted on its case. It was the first of the missing jig-saw pieces, and there was only one snag. There wasn't a single clue as to who Mr Gordon was. But they were justified now in extending the surveillance on the cottage as well as on Mr Gordon and Grushko.

CHAPTER FIFTEEN

The FBI's surveillance team's first sighting of Mark was on May 23. He paid a brief visit to the studio late in the evening and with the aid of a radio-link a team of two agents followed him when he left. Along Fulton Street to Clinton through to Montague and down to the Borough Hall subway station. He was followed to the City Hall stop where he got off, walking north on Broadway to the corner of Chambers Street, where he took a bus and got off at 27th Street. Up Fifth Avenue the FBI man followed as his quarry walked the block to 28th Street and turned the corner. But when Special Agent McDonald reached the corner of 28th Street and Fifth Avenue there was no sign of his man.

It was three weeks before they saw him again, and once more it was late at night when the lights went on in Studio 505 in the Ovington Building. It was ten minutes before midnight when he left and although the route was different this time the journey still ended at 28th Street, and this time they watched him enter the Hotel Latham. It was just past midnight on June 13 and the report of the sighting went back to FBI headquarters. The hotel register showed that the man

Hayhanen called Mark had booked in under the name of Emil Goldfus. The FBI notified the New York director of the Immigration and Naturalization Service, and from there a report on Hayhanen and the surveillance operation was passed to the Internal Security Division of the US Attorney's office.

What could seem to outsiders as an exercise in passing the buck was, in fact, the reverse. When espionage is involved and the suspect is not a citizen, either born or naturalized, Federal Law require legal procedures to be followed meticulously. If the accused come to trial on charges of espionage the evidence has to be concrete and conclusive or any experienced defence lawyer can reduce the prosecution case to one where nothing more than deportation can be the outcome. When prosecuting foreigners or illegal immigrants every step of the legal process has to be observed. If, as now seemed possible, Goldfus was an illegal immigrant, he would have to be brought to justice by the INS, but that would not give powers to the FBI or the CIA to use the arrest to obtain evidence of espionage.

The head of Internal Security Services decided that without Hayhanen giving evidence in public, in court, they had too little evidence to bring a charge of espionage. He sent two of his attorneys to talk to the only witness – Hayhanen.

For two days and nights they talked, argued, pressured and persuaded but Hayhanen adamantly and angrily refused to go beyond just talking. He said he was afraid of reprisals by the KGB against his family in the Soviet Union. They also realized that he was genuinely afraid that the long arm of the KGB could reach out for him, even in the United States. He would go on answering their questions but he would never testify in court.

Nielson turned in his chair to look at the CIA man standing at the end of his desk.

'Nowak, I warn you. If you people – and the FBI – don't get your asses out of this operation this guy may never come to trial. We won't even be able to hold him for more than a week.'

'This is crazy – this guy is . . .'

Nielson cut him short. 'I don't care whether it's crazy or not. We have a warrant and a show cause order drawn up in Washington and that's enough for us to pull him in. But if you people try to ride in on the back of these, nothing you uncover or find will have any legal standing in a charge of espionage and will never – I repeat, never – stand up in court. Without Hayhanen giving evidence in court and subject to cross-examination you haven't got a leg to stand on. Even with Hayhanen testifying in court you may not make it anyway.'

'For Chrissake, man, this guy is . . .'

Nielson stood up waving his hand dismissively in front of him.

'Don't shout at me, Paul. The law is the law. I don't make it, I just administer it.'

Nowak shrugged. 'Can I ask you something off the record?'

Nielson relaxed and said quietly, 'OK. Go ahead.'

'Is somebody protecting this bastard behind the scenes?'

Nielson looked surprised. 'I've seen nothing that would make me think that. Why do you ask?'

'We know this guy has been the principal KGB man in the whole of the USA. For years. He's been running a network of agents very efficiently from what we've learned. Why has he never been picked up before? And why is everybody so anxious to protect him now?'

Nielson shrugged. 'The first question I can't answer, Paul. The United States is a big place. It's easy to disappear if you want to. About people protecting him – there's no one protecting him in my department. It's you people we're protecting. Warning you that you'll come to grief if you don't stick to the rules.' He paused. 'It's a simple as that.'

'If we risk it – what then?'

'You'd be gambling. If you didn't get a confession from him you'd be put through the mincer by the defence attorneys.' He shook his head. 'I wouldn't want to see that happen.'

CHAPTER SIXTEEN

On June 21, 1957, despite the warnings of legal complications, there were a dozen FBI agents in or near the Hotel Latham. Two officers from the INS were waiting in Room 841.

Just after 7 a.m. an FBI agent knocked on the door of Room 839, and a few moments later the man who called himself Martin Collins and Emil Goldfus, naked and still half-asleep, had opened the door, and as they walked into the room the two FBI men had showed their indentification cards to him. Then a third man joined the two agents and stood by the open door.

Nobody was sure who had actually authorized the operation in that form but they knew very well what their instructions were. They could question the suspect for up to half an hour. They could tell him that he was suspected of espionage but not charge him. He was to be given every encouragement to 'co-operate' and that meant indicating that he was willing to give them details of his activities and maybe offer to 'come over'. The possibility of him becoming a double-agent was the prize, but any kind of cooperation could be considered a victory. If neither outcome seemed possible he was to be arrested by the two INS agents under section 242 of the Immigration and Nationality Act.

By the time the half-hour was up he had given his name as Martin Collins and admitted the obvious – that he resided at the Hotel Latham. And nothing more. He seemed subdued but not scared and he remained silent to all other questions.

When INS agent Boyle read out the warrant for arrest it was in the name of Martin Collins a.k.a. Emil Goldfus. He had been given the routine caution that he was entitled to consult a lawyer and had a constitutional right to remain silent.

At INS headquarters he was fingerprinted, photographed and searched. And for hours he was questioned, the INS agents asking him again and again to co-operate. But he consistently refused.

Back at the Latham Hotel, the FBI search team was checking the room thoroughly. They had been amazed that a professional spy should have left around so much incriminating evidence of his trade. And there was still the studio to be searched if they could get a judge to sign a search warrant.

A few days later three affidavits were presented to a district judge in Brooklyn and after checking the statements he had agreed that sufficient cause had been shown to allow the studio search to take place. The warrant listed specific items but included wording that covered almost anything they might find that could be connected with espionage. The last sentence of the warrant seemed innocuous enough, but it marked a major change in the official attitude to the case. It said – '... which material is fitted and intended to be used in furtherance of a conspiracy to violate the provisions of 18 USC 793, 794 and 951.'

The charge of being an 'illegal alien' carried a maximum penalty of deportation. The conspiracy charge could lead to a death sentence.

It looked as if someone of the government side had decided to go for broke, because making that charge involved considerable risks for the prosecution. It was feared that the switch could be challenged in court on grounds that it was unconstitutional. In addition, the conspiracy charge entitled Goldfus to a hearing without delay, and without the evidence of Hayhanen in court whatever they found, in itself would definitely not be considered as proving a conspiracy.

By the end of the day two things happened that made it look as if the gamble had succeeded. Between the hotel room and the studio they had amassed a wide selection of espionage material. One-time pads, hollowed out nails, nuts, bolts and pencils, cryptic messages, a Hallicrafter short-wave radio, bank books and microfilms. And in mid-afternoon Reino Hayhanen had agreed to testify in court. June 28, 1957, suddenly seemed a very good day.

CHAPTER SEVENTEEN

They were only half a dozen people in the Warsaw LOT office on Ulica Warynskiego. He gave the girl five złotys for the airport bus ticket. Five minutes later they boarded the bus and the man took a window seat. He was tall and well-built, in his mid-thirties, his black hair cut very short. His right hand guarded the worn black leather briefcase on the seat beside him.

With the darkness came the rain, sweeping across the fields and the blocks of flats that lined the road to the airport. He guessed it would be snow by the time they got to Moscow.

At Okecie airport there was time for a coffee. He bought a copy of *Pravda* and settled down at the table, lighting a cigarette, his arm resting protectively across the black briefcase on the table. It was half an hour before he heard the airline announcement.

'*Uprzejmie prosimy pasażerów odlatujących rejsem 207 do Moskwy o zgłoszenie się do wyjścia numer 3.*'

He stood up and joined the queue at Gate 3. He could see the plane on the feeder runway, an old Antonov AN24. It looked as if it would be a crowded flight. It was generally full on the Friday evening flight to Moscow. Solemn-looking Soviets going back to spend the weekend with their families, hoping that their pretty Polish girlfriends were not being too blatantly unfaithful while they were away. And, of course one or two upper-echelon Polish *apparatchiki* heading for a few sybaritic days in Sivtsev Vrazhek and a walletful of privilege roubles for purchases at the discreet place on Granovsky Street that went under the name of 'The Building of Passes' but was really the treasure-trove of the *nachaltsvo*, the Kremlin élite.

They had been airborne for nearly half an hour when the stewardess announced that owing to technical difficulties on the ground the flight was being diverted and would not be landing at Moscow's main airport, Sheremetyevo, but at Vnukovo II. Vnukovo was the almost secret airport used only by top Soviet officials and never the general public. Kretski wondered what difficulties could have caused such an extraordinary diversion. He checked his watch. They were already ten minutes overdue. There seemed to be some consternation among the other passengers, and a man whose face he recognized as a senior Russian official had beckoned to the stewardess. And when she leaned over to listen to him Kretski could hear that his voice was raised in anger as he pointed at his watch. The stewardess nodded and left and a few minutes later the co-pilot came back to talk to the man, obviously anxious to placate him.

There was a long wait on the ground before they disembarked, and as Kretski walked across the tarmac the snow was swirling and already thick on the ground.

As he gave up his boarding card at the desk two men walked out from behind the metal screen. He didn't know them but he knew instantly that they were KGB. The older man said in Russian, 'Mr Kretski, I'd like you to come to my office.'

'What's the problem, comrade?'

The man smiled. 'No problem at all.' He nodded towards the white-walled corridor and the smaller man led the way, opening the door at the far end. And Kretski noticed the security locks and the bars on the windows.

The older man pointed to a plain wooden chair by the small bare table and drew up a similar chair on the other side. Kretski was aware that the second man was leaning back against the door, lighting a cigar.

'My name is Pomerenko, Comrade Kretski. Would you prefer to talk in Russian or Polish?'

Kretski shrugged. 'It's up to you.'

'You are Jan Kretski, yes?'

'Correct.'

'Deputy chief liaison officer between KGB and Polish Z-1?'

'That's right.'

'And you must know why you are here?'

'Not until you tell me, comrade.'

'Maybe it would be easier for you if we spoke English.'

'I can speak English if you prefer it.'

Pomerenko smiled. 'I am KGB, Comrade Colonel, Directorate Four. You have been under surveillance for two months and two days. And you are now under arrest.'

'On what charges may I ask?'

Pomerenko leaned back slowly, his hand reaching into an inside pocket, taking out an envelope, looking at it for a moment before he pulled out a photograph and laid it, facing Kretski on the table.

'Tell me, comrade – who is that?'

It was a grainy black-and-white photograph, obviously blown up from the original, but he knew all right who it was. He wondered who had taken it, and when. He could just make out the archway at the back of Horse Guards Parade. He made sure that his hand didn't shake as he put the photograph back on the table.

'Who is it, Comrade Kretski?' Pomerenko said softly.

'You tell me.'

Pomerenko pointed. 'The name is on the back – look at it.'

As Kretski leaned forward for the photograph Pomerenko clamped his big paw down on Kretski's hand.

'You looked very pleased with yourself that day in the sunshine, didn't you?'

Pomerenko released Kretski's hand and as he turned over the photograph Kretski leaned forward. There was a typed label on the back. Just two lines in Cyrillic script.

Captain John Summers. Intelligence Corps.
10350556. See file D4/9074/GB/ 94–105.

Kretski looked up at Pomerenko. 'I don't understand.'

Pomerenko laughed. 'It's taken a long time, comrade.' He looked at his watch. 'We'd better go.'

They had taken his briefcase and in the black *Chaika* that took them back to Moscow nobody spoke a word.

He sat with his eyes closed, his head resting back on the seat and only stirred as they swept into Dzerzhinski Square.

CHAPTER EIGHTEEN

'Tell us about the Malta convoys, Harry.'

The group of men were grinning but Harry Houghton had turned to call for another pint. When it came he turned towards them, glass in hand.

'It was air-cover that was the problem in the Med. We was doing double watches on the guns. Officers and men all had . . .'

'What guns were they, Harry?'

'Oerlikons. Twin turrets fore and aft. We had DEMS gunners. When we got to Valletta they had the Royal Marines band lined up on the harbour to play us in. "White Cliffs of Dover" they played and "Auld Lang Syne".'

'I thought you said last time it was the Black Watch played you in. A piper and "Flowers of the Forest".'

'That was another time, Lofty.'

'Tell us about the Maltese girls, Harry. When you went to the party the day you tied up.'

'They were fantastic those Maltese birds. You had to watch your step, mind you. Try it on the wrong one and you'd have her brothers sticking knives in you. But there was girls. Kids of fourteen and fifteen, real pretty ones. You could have 'em all night for a quid. But if you came in on the relief convoys it was all free. We was heroes to those poor bastards. Starving they was and we brought the food to them through thick and thin. I went to this party and Jesus they were all over me. Took me in the back room. Two of 'em. We was at it all night.'

The men laughed and one of them said, 'Have another pint on me, Harry, you old bullshitter.'

'I'm not bullshitting, I swear. You ask the others.'

'What others?'

'The lads on the Malta convoys. They didn't give Malta the George Cross for nothing, mate.'

The man grinned. 'And no bloody sailor ever got it for free off a Maltese bird neither.'

Houghton grinned. 'Depends on who you are, mate. Anyway, I gotta be on my way.'

'Your divorce come through yet, Harry?'

'Two months ago, skipper. Foot-loose and fancy free. That's me.'

As he stood outside the pub he turned up his coat collar. It was beginning to snow. He put his head down and walked slowly down the empty promenade. He could hear the waves crashing slowly and heavily on the shingle on the beach. The wind caught his face as he turned into a side road, and five minutes later he passed the permanently open gates to the plot of waste land where his trailer was parked.

He pulled out his keys and turned towards the faint light from the street lamps to sort out the key to the trailer door. He turned to put the key in the door and a hand clamped round his wrist. He turned quickly and saw the man. He looked a real thug and when he spoke he had a Cockney accent.

'Are you Houghton?'

'Yes. Who are you?'

The man put his big leather-gloved fist in front of Houghton's face, and as Houghton instinctively backed away a pair of strong arms went around him from the other side and he realized that there were two of them.

'What the hell's going on?'

'Open the trailer door. Look slippy.'

Houghton's hand shook as he fitted the key into the lock and then one of them opened the door and shoved him up the steps and inside.

'Put the light on.'

Houghton switched the light on and turned to face the two men. The tall one said, 'Why didn't you telephone when you got the Hoover leaflet?'

'I don't understand. Who are you?'

'We brought you a message, sonny boy?'

'What . . .'

And he groaned as the knee went into his crotch. And then the two of them worked him over. Carefully, professionally, leaving his face unmarked as the blows thudded into his stomach and kidneys. Even after they had finished and they stood panting, looking down at his body on the floor, he was still half-conscious and he heard one of them say, 'Next time we'll do your old woman as well. The new one. So watch it, mate.'

It was four o'clock when he came to. The light was still on inside the trailer but the streetlights were out. They had left the door open and snow had drifted onto the shabby linoleum. He groaned as he slowly picked himself up.

He made himself a hot whisky and stirred in a spoonful of sugar and lay down in his clothes on the bunk. The light still on, the door of the trailer still open and swinging in the wind.

CHAPTER NINETEEN

When Shapiro got the news he had called Morton immediately and they were still in Morton's smoke-filled office at four the following morning. Ashtrays full of cigarette ends and cigar butts, trays full of coffee cups, two jugs of cold coffee and several plates with a variety of curling sandwiches.

They had talked for hours, sat silent for minutes at a time and they were no nearer to a solution and no nearer to deciding what to do. They were sprawled in the leather armchairs around a low glass-topped table.

Morton started them off again. 'Let's go over it again, Joe. Piece by piece. Agreed?'

Shapiro nodded and shifted in his seat to try and get comfortable again.

Morton sighed. 'So. Back to square one, Joe. Are they absolutely certain that he's been picked up?'

'He was supposed to ring the Moscow number that evening at nine local time. Just ring and they would give the password. Just that one word and then they'd both hang up. He didn't ring.'

'What about the Warsaw end?'

'We know he got on the airport bus. We know he was at the airport. The girl was watching him and when the call came he went to the correct boarding gate. That was the last time he was seen.'

'What happened at Sheremetyevo?'

'Our guy watched for the plane. Just as a routine check. There was no contact intended.' He paused. 'The flight number was never called and there was no flight from Warsaw announced or accounted for until the following morning. And that was the normal 9 a.m. flight from Paris and Warsaw.'

'So not only our boy missing but a whole planeload of passengers missing?'

'Yes.'

'Any indications of a crash anywhere on that route?'

'No. But you know what they're like about air disasters.'

'Could it have been diverted because of bad weather?'

'I got Met to check. They say there was heavy snow and some wind but nothing that wasn't normal for the time of year.'

'Where would they have to divert to if there had been a problem?'

'God knows. There are a dozen or more airfields around Moscow that could take an old Antonov. And they could have diverted to some place way out of Moscow.'

'No way of checking if there was a diversion?'

'RAF intelligence say no. Even internal domestic flights in Warsaw Pact countries are classified. And we haven't got good enough contacts anyway.'

Morton nodded. 'There's one good indication.'

'Tell me.'

'If they'd picked him up and he'd talked they would have tried phoning that number – and they didn't.'

'It was a bit early for that.'

'Agreed, but it weighs against any thoughts he might have defected.'

Shapiro shrugged without speaking and Morton said, 'Was he in Moscow to do anything top-grade?'

'No. Not as far as I know. It was just a routine visit as liaison officer.'

'So why the telephone contact?'

'Routine. Another precaution.'

There was another long silence and then Morton said, 'So we're left with deciding whether we do nothing – or something – and if something – what?'

'There are only two things we can do. We can't make an official diplomatic complaint. He's officially – genuinely – a Polish national. We've got no diplomatic standing in the case. We could try an official deal and admit that he was ours. Or we could offer an exchange.'

Morton shook his head. 'We haven't got anybody in the bag who's anywhere near equivalent. Put half a dozen together and they aren't worth offering to Moscow. They'd just laugh at us.'

'Diplomatic pressure?'

Morton laughed harshly. 'Our masters wouldn't go along with it. Détente is the reigning policy. The FO were never informed about the operation in the first place.' He shrugged. 'But they were bloody glad to get the stuff he provided.' He shook his head, sighing. 'Forget 'em, they wouldn't lift a finger to help us.

'Apart from that we can't really make any move until we know that he's in the bag, and that they've broken him. We could be confirming their suspicions if he hasn't talked already. I recommend that we do nothing except keep a close monitoring of the situation.'

When Morton finished Shapiro looked at him. 'What do you think?'

'How many people know about Phoenix?'

'You, me, Sir Peter and FO liaison, Saunders.'

'Nobody in the FO. Not the Foreign Secretary?'

'No. Nobody. There's been a change of government since we launched Phoenix and the previous Foreign Secretary's dead. We've always tried to treat it as just a piece of routine operations.'

'What about CIA?'

'We share out material with them and they value it highly – but they've no idea of the source. When they've pressed to know we've always implied that it was a Polish national.'

Morton sighed and said, 'So I still recommend we do nothing until we know more. A lot more.'

'I agree.'

Morton looked across at Shapiro. 'I understand your concern, Joe, but we could easily make things worse for him.'

Shapiro shook his head slowly. 'It haunts me, Hughie. Right this minute he could be lying in a cell in the Lubyanka after the first beating-up. Hoping against hope that we can do something.'

'You warned him I assume?'

'Of course. All the usual crap. But no matter what we say they never really believe that we'll leave them to rot. Others, yes. Them, no. They're special.' He sighed. 'They never really grasp that once they're in the bag they're not special. Just an embarrassment. Not even a problem. You just forget 'em. At least that's how it supposed to be.' Shapiro looked at Morton. 'He was so brave, Hughie. All the guts in the world. I'd give everything I've got in the world to get him out. Ten years of his life. Taking risks every day. For us. And it ends like this. No medals, no bloody anything.'

'Take consolation where you can. He may not be in the bag at all. Just some aviation cock-up.'

'I wish I could think that, Hughie. But I can't.' Shapiro stood up, sighing. 'We'd better get on our way. I need some sleep to clear my mind.' But Morton noticed the tear in Shapiro's pale blue eyes. He made a mental note to keep close to Shapiro until things were sorted out. Deep concern was one thing. Tears were something else. And with a temperament like his there was no knowing what he could get up to.

CHAPTER TWENTY

Having been charged with being an illegal alien Emil Goldfus was flown down to McAllen Alien Detention Facility in Texas. All concerned had recognized that it was only luck that had allowed them to wriggle off the horns of a legal dilemma. If Goldfus had been arrested for espionage he would have been entitled to an almost immediate hearing on that charge and with Reino Hayhanen refusing to testify in court the government had no case. But having arrested him as an illegal alien it meant that the evidence of espionage found in his room was inadmissible. The search was out of bounds for a mere illegal entry charge. Fortunately by the time the judge issued the warrant to search Goldfus's studio Hayhanen had changed his mind.

As the investigators and the prosecution lawyers again went over Hayhanen's statements and questioned every statement as rigorously as he would be questioned by defence counsel in court, the exact location of every 'drop' was established and photographed. Their main difficulty was Hayhanen's desperately poor English.

At first they saw him as just being of low intelligence but they realized as the days passed that in fact he had an excellent memory and was quite astute. What concerned them subconsciously was that despite his vices of drink and women and his total lack of interest in the mission he had been sent on, the United States security services had known nothing about him nor his organizer, Emil Goldfus.

By midsummer the man who now officially admitted to being Rudolph Ivanovich Abel, colonel, KGB, was brought before the grand jury. The main evidence was given by Reino Hayhanen, with other testimony from people who had just happened to be neighbours or acquaintances of Abel.

Finally came the indictment. It charged Rudolph Ivanovich Abel, also known as Mark and Martin Collins and Emil R. Goldfus, of conspiracy on three counts. The first count was conspiring to transmit information relating to the national defence of the USA, particularly arms, equipment and disposition of the armed forces, and the atomic energy programme. The second count was conspiring to gather that information, and the third count was that he had remained in the country without registering as a foreign agent. The third count sounded both strange and faintly ridiculous to the public, but it had its purpose. The penalty for failing to register is five years in prison. To be classed as a foreign agent did not necessarily imply that a person was an intelligence agent. They may merely represent some foreign company or interest and only have as their objective the lobbying of some influential group in government or politics generally. But in the case of Colonel Abel the media made clear that they, at least, had no doubt as to what sort of 'foreign agent' Abel was. The second count could mean ten years' imprisonment and the first count carried the death penalty.

The afternoon newspapers and TV were grateful for such a story in the dog days of summer and the headlines left their readers in no doubt that this was the spy capture of all time. The probability that the colonel would be executed if convicted was also emphasized. The vigilance of the security services was highly recommended.

When Abel told the court that he had no lawyer Judge Abruzzo said a lawyer should be appointed and the trial was set for September 16, to be held in the Brooklyn Federal Court before Judge Mortimer W. Byers.

The Bar Association chose wisely. James B. Donovan, an alumnus of Harvard Law School, had been an intelligence officer of the US Navy during World War II, and a member of OSS. He had also been on the staff of the US prosecutor at the Nuremberg Trials. Arnold Fraiman and Tom Dibevoise were appointed as his assistants.

They set out to examine everything that had happened between June 21, the day of Abel's arrest and August 7, when he was indicted by the grand jury. They immediately moved to have everything that had been taken from the hotel declared inadmissible at the trial on the grounds that it had been illegally seized, contrary to the Fourth and Fifth Amendments to the Constitution. An inept statement to the press just after the arrest, by the Commissioner of Immigration, stating that the arrest was made at the specific request of 'several government agencies', added weight to their submission.

The defence was also entitled to all the evidence that the prosecution would be offering and that included an interview with the prosecution's 'mystery man' – Reino Hayhanen. At the interview with the defence lawyers Hayhanen quoted, and insisted on sticking to, his legal rights not to talk until the trial.

The hearing of the motion submitted by the defence was to reveal the main thrust of the case against Abel, but when it came to identification of the items from the hotel room that the defence wanted excluded, Judge Byers had been irritated by both sides' fencing in their approach. When Donovan asked a prosecution witness, 'And did you find any documentary evidence of his status as an alien?', prosecution counsel interrupted, 'I think he should just ask what was found in the hotel room.'

Judge Byers. 'I agree.' He looked down at Donovan. 'The witness doesn't need to give his opinion as to the nature of the papers in the evidentiary sense. Ask him what he found.'

'Your honour, this is extremely important.'

Judge Byers shrugged, his irritation all too obvious.

'All right, *don't* ask him what he found. I am telling you what I would like to have you do. Of course, you can disregard my instructions: I realize that.'

Donovan turned again to the witness. 'What did you find in the room that confirmed the information that the FBI had given you?'

Judge Byers intervened. 'The witness does not need to characterize the probative nature of the documents.'

'Agreed, Your Honour, but he did make the statement.'

'I know you like to argue, we all like to argue. Will you just move along.'

Donovan tried to put the question to the witness again and Judge Byers cut him off.

'I am not going to listen to the witness's opinion as to what those documents show. Now take that from me.'

Eventually Donovan argued that the arrest was not made in good faith and that the search and seizure were illegal.

Judge Byers told him bluntly that it was not part of the court's duty to tell the FBI how they should function.

On October 11, Donovan's motion to suppress the evidence was denied. The case could go to trial.

One of the strange features behind the legal wrangling was that Abel was liked, and in some cases admired, by all those who came in contact with him. Prisoners, officials and lawyers found him both mild in manner and extremely intelligent. Their reaction to the man accused of being a Soviet spy was much the same as his friends and neighbours at the Ovington Building.

Tomkins, the prosecutor, was happy about the evidence but was worried about how Reino Hayhanen would react under interrogation and coming face to face with Abel and identifying him as a Soviet spy. But Tomkins made his opening speech to the jury with confidence and authority.

Later he listened to Donovan's speech for the defence and it confirmed his expectation that Donovan would try to discredit Hayhanen's evidence. He closed his eyes and listened intently as Donovan stated the defence case.

'The defendant is a *man*, a man named Abel,' Donovan said. 'It is important that you keep that fact uppermost in your mind throughout the days to come. This is not a case against Communism. It is not a case against Soviet Russia. Our grievances against Russia have been voiced every day in the United Nations and other forums. But the sole issues in this case . . . whether or not Abel has been proved guilty beyond reasonable doubt of the specific crimes with which he is now charged.'

Half an hour later Tomkins was listening intently as Donovan started his attack on Hayhanen.

'The prosecution has told you that among the principal witnesses against the defendant will be a man whose name is Hayhanen, who claims that he helped the defendant to spy against the United States . . . I want you to observe his demeanour very carefully when he takes the stand.

'Bear in mind that if what the government says is true, it means that this man has been here for some years, living among us, spying on behalf of Soviet Russia . . . It means that he entered the United States on false papers . . . that he has lived here every day only by lying about his true identity, about his background, about every fact of his everyday life . . . He was trained in the art of deception . . . He was trained to lie. In short, assuming that what the government say is true, this man is a professional liar.'

Some observers thought it was odd that neither the prosecution or the media pointed out that every word of Donovan's derogatory references to Hayhanen applied equally to Rudolph Abel. Tomkins was saving the point for a more effective stage in the proceedings.

When Hayhanen took the stand the courtroom and the media listened to the details of 'drops' and secret signs in places they knew well. It was an amalgam of every spy story they had read and every spy film they had seen. A lamp-post in Riverside Park at 74th Street, another lamp-post near 80th Street. A cinema in Flushing. Drawing-pins in the slat of a park bench. Mail boxes on Central Park West in the upper 70s used for magnetic containers, others on every street corner between 74th and 79th Streets. A fence around the Museum of Natural History and a 'drop' at a 95th Street subway station. Meetings and journeys with Abel. Abortive attempts to trace and contact American citizens named by Moscow as potential collaborators.

Then followed the descriptions of meetings of conversations with Abel about his links with Americans already serving prison sentences for passing information to the Soviet Union. Information concerning atomic and military secrets. Day after day the jury listened to the paraphernalia of espionage. Impressed but confused. Amazed that it could have gone on for so many years apparently without detection.

For four days Donovan, for the defence, cross-examined Hayhanen, trying to discredit his evidence, but Hayhanen was immovable. He insisted vehemently that everything he had said had happened. In one last effort Donovan sought to discredit Hayhanen himself. Questioning him about his lies to Abel about his work, his lies about the money he received, and his lies to get more. But Hayhanen just admitted quite openly to it all. Unabashed and unashamed.

When Donovan referred to the fact that Hayhanen had a wife in Russia but had married another woman, a church marriage, Hayhanen was riled to the point of complaining to the judge about Donovan's questions. It seemed that he didn't care about being accused as a liar, a thief, a coward and a drunkard, but Donovan's smug hypocrisy about his morals clearly enraged him.

On the last day but one of the trial Donovan made his summation. He had one last card to play. He went back over the trial item by item. Then he paused for a moment before looking at the jury.

'What evidence of national defence information or atomic information has been put before you in this case? When you and I commenced this case, certainly we expected evidence that this man is shown to have stolen great military secrets, secrets of atomic energy and so on . . .'

Judge Byers interrupted to point out that the charge was only conspiracy to get such information. He turned to Donovan and said, 'The charge doesn't involve a substantial offence. When you undertake to tell the jury what the law is, be accurate in your statements please.'

Donovan turned to a comparison of the characters of Abel and Hayhanen. The dissolute, dishonest drunkard and Abel, the devoted husband, the family man . . . a very brave patriotic man serving his country. He ended his summation with a warning to the jury.

'You are not serving your country and you are not fighting Communism to convict a man on insufficient evidence.' He paused and went on. 'Ladies and gentlemen if you will resolve this case on that higher level so that you can leave it with a clear conscience, I have no question but that certainly on counts one and two of this indictment, you must bring in a verdict of not guilty.'

Then Donovan sat down. His reference to Abel as a family man had some effect. During the trial letters had been read from his wife and family that had been enlarged from micro-dots found in his studio. They could possibly have been coded messages but they had an authenticity that was convincing. They seemed to be letters from a wife and daughter to an obviously much-loved father. They described the humdrum incidents of domestic life and emphasized how much he was missed. Several observant people had noticed that when the letters were read out there were tears in Abel's eyes. The only indication of any emotion by the prisoner during the whole trial.

Tomkins was aware of the sympathy that the letters might arouse and covered it in his final speech. He reminded the jury of the many items of evidence and then went on to remind them of the significance of conspiracy.

'If we agree – if two persons agree, to assassinate the President, and one of them procures a gun, that would be all you needed to complete the crime of conspiracy, and it does not need to be completed to be a crime.' He paused to emphasize his next words. 'In other words, we don't have to stand idly by and permit an individual to commit espionage, to get our secrets. We are not powerless in that case. We can intervene. We can prevent the consummation of the crime.'

Tomkins then referred to Donovan's disparaging description of Hayhanen as 'bum', 'renegade', 'liar', and 'thief' and used it to counter the letters from Abel's family.

'The witness had the same training as the defendant . . .' He went on to point out the difference in their backgrounds, the hapless Hayhanen left to scavenge as best he could, and then reminded them that it appeared from the letters read out in court that Abel's family lived very well in Moscow, with a second home in the country, and servants. He went on to say, 'The defendant is a professional, a highly trained espionage agent . . . a master spy, a real pro . . . Just remember this was the man's chosen career. He knows the rules of the game and so do his family. He is entitled to no sympathy.'

Tomkins looked down at his papers for a moment as he collected his thoughts for his final comment. He looked at the jury for several seconds before he spoke.

'I simply say this: this is a serious case. This is a serious offence. This is an offence directed at our very existence and through us at the free world and civilization itself, particularly in the light of the times.' He paused. 'And I say this, and I don't believe I have ever said anything with more sincerity or more seriously: I am convinced that the government has proven its case, not only beyond a reasonable doubt as required, but beyond all possible doubt.'

Tomkins sat down with his face still turned to the jury.

On the Friday morning Judge Byers went over again the difference between conspiracy to commit a substantive crime and the crime itself.

At mid-day the jury and the US marshals in charge of them left for the jury room.

It was almost five o'clock when the jury filed back to their seats in the courtroom. The clerk of the court rose, and the foreman of the jury looked back at him.

'Members of the jury, have you agreed upon a verdict?'

'We have.'

'In the case of the United States of America against Rudolph Abel, how do you find the defendant, guilty or not guilty on count one?'

'Guilty.'

'How do you find the defendant, guilty or not guilty on count two?'

'Guilty.'

'How do you find the defendant, guilty or not guilty on count three?'

'Guilty.'

Rudolph Abel was taken to West Street jail to wait for sentencing.

Inevitably Donovan and his team put in a carefully considered submission to the Court of Appeals contending that there were aspects of law that had been ignored at the trial. On July 11, 1958 Judge Watkinson, in a written opinion, rejected the appeal. But not without praising Donovan and his team for 'having represented the appellant with rare ability and in the highest tradition of their profession.'

There was one last weapon in the defence's armoury and Donovan filed a petition for *certiorari* to the Supreme Court. It listed six points of law which Donovan suggested had been ignored or avoided in the trial. He asked that the Supreme Court should grant a hearing for those points to be argued. In October the Supreme Court announced that it would grant a hearing on two points. Both points covered the old original problem of the search and seizure of evidence when Abel was arrested.

In prison in Atlanta, Georgia, Abel was a model prisoner. At that time Joseph Valachi, Vito Genovese and other figures from the Mafia were also serving sentences of various lengths in the same prison. The prison Warden had no problems with Abel, who behaved like the senior officer that he was, and the Warden assumed that Abel had been trained in methods of survival in case he was captured. Both mental and physical survival.

Meanwhile in New York, both sides filed arguments and counter-arguments. Towards the end of February Donovan presented his case and a month later the Supreme Court handed down its decision. Everybody on the defence and Abel himself were surprised by the decision. It seemed to bode well for the prisoner in Atlanta. The court ordered a re-argument and asked each side to appear on October 12.

More briefs were fired back and forth by both the government and the defence. What the Supreme Court wanted to hear were both sides' arguments on those aspects of Constitutional protection that affected not only the present case but the future interpretation of the current law.

The law gave every citizen 'the right to be secure from searches for evidence to be used in *criminal proceedings*'. Nine eminent judges of the Supreme Court listened to the arguments from both sides.

It was not until March 28, 1960, the following year, that the Supreme Court gave its ruling. The Supreme Court upheld the conviction of Rudolph Ivanovich Abel. But what surprised all concerned was that five judges had upheld the conviction but four had given dissenting opinions. And one of the four dissenters was Chief Justice Warren himself.

After two and a half years in prison in Atlanta Abel himself had changed. People who had known him for a long time said that he had become frail and sick, consumed by tension as if he had been waiting for something that he no longer expected to happen.

CHAPTER TWENTY-ONE

The plane stood on the tarmac of the parking bay at the airfield in Peshawar, Pakistan, half concealed in its enormous hangar. With its long body, high tail and unusually wide wings its elegance was not obvious because it was painted black. On the drawing board at Lockheed it looked like a smooth, sleek flying fish, but on the ground, in its strange livery, it looked more like a killer shark. It carried no guns, but a mass of infra-red cameras and electronics.

It could photograph a section of the earth's surface 125 miles wide and 3,000 miles long. And photo-interpreters looking at the huge enlargements of the 40,000 paired frames could read the headlines of a newspaper taken from ten miles above the earth. It was believed to be beyond the reach of even the most sophisticated attack planes available to the Soviet Union. It was one of three identical planes used in Operation Overflight, an operation that had already been working successfully and fruitfully for almost four years.

The only unusual feature of the flight that day – May 1, 1960 – was that it was the first flight which would cross the whole of the Soviet Union. Taking off from Peshawar and landing almost 4,000 miles away at Bod in Norway, it would pass over important targets that had never been photographed before.

Rumour had it that the flight was to ensure that when President Eisenhower met President Khrushchev shortly he would be fully up-to-date on Soviet military dispositions.

Inevitably, USAF intelligence officers had considered what routines should apply if a pilot was shot down or force landed in Soviet territory. The plane itself was protected by a timed destruction system. The pilots were offered a cyanide tablet and a silver dollar with a small metal loop so that it could be fastened to a key chain or a chain around the wrist or neck. If the loop was unscrewed it revealed a thin needle whose minute grooves were laced with curare, an instant killer. Taking and using either or both was entirely the pilot's option. They were merely available. Most pilots carried neither but on that particular morning the young, crew-cut pilot when asked if he wanted the silver dollar had taken it, seeing it as a useful weapon rather than a means of committing suicide.

That morning the pilot stood at the table in the hangar with the intelligence officer as he was handed the various standard items for a flight. Shaving kit, civilian clothes, a packet of filter cigarettes, pictures of his wife, some German marks, Turkish lira, Russian roubles, gold coins, watches and rings for barter, a hundred US dollars, US postage stamps, a Defense Department ID card, a NASA certificate, instrument rating cards, US and International driving licences, a Selective Service card, a social security card, and an American flag poster that said in fourteen different languages "I am an American".

For the last time they traced his route on the maps. From Peshawar he would cross Afghanistan and the Hindu Kush and enter Soviet airspace near Stalinabad. Then over the Aral Sea, the Turyatam missile testing base,

Chelyabinsk, Sverdlovsk, Kirov, Archangel, Kandalaksha and Murmansk on the Kola peninsula, then across the Barents Sea to the north coast of Norway and Bod. The flight would take nine hours, and for three-quarters of the time would be inside the USSR. During the nine-hour flight there would be complete radio silence.

The only qualms the twenty-seven-year-old pilot had were about the plane itself. The plane which had previously been reserved for the flight had been grounded at the last moment for a maintenance check, and its substitute, Number 360, was what the pilots referred to as a 'dog'. There was always something going wrong with it, most recently its fuel tanks had malfunctioned and wouldn't feed fuel to the engine. It was a single-engined turbojet.

May 1, 1960 was a Sunday and the pilot got into the plane at 5.30 a.m. for the pre-flight check. The scheduled take-off time was 6 a.m. but it came and went without the signal to go.

The cockpit was like a furnace and the pilot sat with his long underwear drenched in perspiration as he waited. A senior officer came over to apologize for the delay and to explain that they were awaiting final approval for the flight from the White House. Presidential approval normally came through well before the pilot was locked in his seat.

It was twenty minutes later when the plane took off and when it was at flight altitude the pilot completed his flight log entries: aircraft number 360, sortie number 4154 and the time was 6.26 a.m. local time, 1.26 Greenwich Mean Time, 8.26 p.m. in Washington and 3.26 a.m. in Moscow.

As he crossed into Soviet territory he saw several con trails of aircraft way below him but he knew they wouldn't even be able to get near him. He guessed the Soviet radar might have picked him up on their screen and were sending up scouts. A waste of time at his altitude.

Some thirty miles east he could see the launching pads of the Turyatam Cosmodrome where they launched the Soviet Sputniks and ICBMs. He flipped the camera switches to 'on' and only switched them off when the cloud cover thickened again. Fifty miles south of Chelyabinsk the skies cleared and he got a wonderful view of the snow-capped Urals.

It was then that the trouble started; the auto-pilot seemed to have gone berserk and the plane was pitching and yawing nose-up. He switched off the auto-pilot and drove the plane manually for twenty minutes before he switched to auto-pilot again. And again the plane was pitching nose-up. He tried it again at intervals and always with the same result. He decided to stay on manual and make long zigs and zags. He was making notes in his log of the engine and instrument behaviour when he felt a dull thud. The plane bucked forward and a blinding flash of orange light flooded the cockpit.

He reached for the destruction switches and then decided to get into position to use the ejection seat first, but the metal canopy rail was trapping his legs. Ejecting in those conditions would slice off both his legs about three inches above the knee. The plane was already down to 30,000 feet when he released his seat belt. The force of gravity snatched him half out of his seat, only his oxygen hoses were holding him back. He had forgotten to release them. He kicked and wrestled in panic until he was sucked out of the cockpit and found himself floating free. At the moment when he realized that he had not pulled the ripcord his body jerked as, at 15,000 feet, his parachute opened automatically. At that moment he saw his plane hurtling past him, intact, towards the earth.

The following Thursday Nikita Khrushchev showed all the peasant cunning that had been rather admired in the West. He addressed the Supreme Soviet for over three hours during which he announced that Soviet gunners had shot down a US plane violating Soviet airspace. He went on to denounce the United States in aggressive abuse, accusing them of deliberately trying to wreck the forthcoming summit conference between the four heads of government.

The following day, to the delight of the Kremlin, Lincoln White, the State Department's spokesman, announced to crowds of journalists in Washington, that 'There was absolutely no – N – O – no deliberate intention to violate Soviet airspace, and there never had been.' President Eisenhower confirmed the statement later the same day.

The next day Khrushchev told the Supreme Soviet what some of them already knew – a Soviet rocket had brought down the plane from an altitude of 65,000 feet. And then the final blow for the White House, the US pilot had been taken prisoner 'alive and kicking' and had made a complete confession about his spying mission.

A few days later Khrushchev said, at a display of the U-2 wreckage, 'The Russian people would say I was mad to negotiate with a man who sends spy planes over here.'

The turmoil and embarrassment in the White House and the State Department were there for all to see. Not only had they put the summit conference at risk but had been caught out in a flagrant lie. And the President of the United States had himself lied in public.

Nevertheless, on May 14 Khrushchev arrived in Paris. His first move was to announce that he would not participate in the summit unless the United States stopped all U-2 flights, apologized for past aggressions and punished those responsible for the flight.

President Eisenhower said in public that the flights had been suspended and would not be resumed. But even the humbling of the President was not enough for Khrushchev. At the opening session of the conference at the Elysée Palace with President Eisenhower, President de Gaulle and Prime Minister Harold Macmillan, Khrushchev suggested that the conference should be postponed for six months and accused the President of the United States of 'treachery' and 'acts of banditry', and announced the cancellation of the arranged visit of Eisenhower to the USSR.

A grim-faced Eisenhower replied that the over-flights were over but that Khrushchev's ultimatum was unacceptable to the United States. And at that point Khrushchev stormed out of the conference. Eisenhower went back into the US Embassy trembling with rage.

Eisenhower, de Gaulle and Macmillan held an informal, broken-backed meeting the next day, and the summit was over.

But Khrushchev's revenge was far from over. Three thousand journalists and broadcasters attended a chaotic press conference the next day when Khrushchev denounced the United States as 'piratical', 'thief-like', and 'cowardly'. He followed this diatribe by announcing that the Soviet Union would now solve the Berlin problem by signing a separate treaty with communist East Germany.

CHAPTER TWENTY-TWO

The long line of cattle-trucks stretched right across the horizon, silhouetted by the setting sun and black against the first scattering of the coming winter's snow.

In one of the tail-end wagons a man sat hunched up in a corner, his legs drawn up, his head resting on his knees, his dark hair lank and long, his cheeks flushed with fever. There were forty other prisoners in the wagon. Five of them frozen stiff, to be thrown out by the guards the next time they checked the prisoners.

The train had been on its journey for two weeks already and of the 1,650 who had started the journey 60 had already died.

Five days later the prisoners were herded onto the steamer *Dzhurma* for the voyage across the Sea of Okhotsk. If they were lucky they would complete the voyage before the pack-ice closed in around Wrangel Island. If the transport authorities guessed wrong and the ice closed in, that would mean that there would be no prisoner survivors from that shipment. The Gulag authorities in Moscow and Kolyma considered it a worthwhile risk. Once the pack-ice formed, the steamer would be locked-in until the spring thaw. But Gulag labour camps needed their new replacements if they were to meet their norms. Leaving it late could generally mean pushing through four extra shipments, and even with the chance of a twenty-five per cent loss that was a reasonable return.

The man in the corner was going through the litany that had kept him alive and as near to sanity as he could hope for. Amid the stench of excreta and urine he went again and again through the Lord's Prayer, half a dozen hymns, Gray's 'Elegy in a Country Churchyard' and Wordsworth's 'Daffodils', the names of the home grounds of every first-class football club that he could remember, the instructions for clearing a blockage on a Bren gun, odd bits of the Bible and Shakespeare, Boyle's Law on expansion of gases and the names of the girls he had slept with. Sometimes he thought of the password, but he never said it, or even let it linger in his mind. It was best forgotten, but you can't forget just because you want to.

He could smell the pus from the weals on his back and ribs. They'd offered him a course of antibiotics in return for what he knew about Mark Wheeler and Tony Craddock. The instructors had always said that beating-up and torture never produced useful information and that the beatings and pain only stiffened a prisoner's resistance. He had smiled when he had heard it and hadn't believed a word of it. A broken finger or two, a rough hand round your scrotum or even the bath treatment, and you'd be singing like a nightingale. Maybe it applied to ex-Shanghai police instructors but not to ordinary mortals. But the bastards were right. Once you got over the shock of being caught it wasn't the pain that counted but the fact that they were doing it to you that sat in the front of your mind. It was a fight even though you couldn't move. You could hit back by saying nothing. Screaming maybe but not talking. Name, rank and number stuff taken to ridiculous extremes. Just hate the bastards and shout obscenities in their own language. And it wouldn't take long before they went too far and you were out. Sailing on white cumulus clouds in a summer sky, the wolves below snapping at your gliding body until you floated past the cliff and out over the sea.

There was a week in the transit camp at Vladivostok before the sea voyage to the horror camp at Kolyma, where tens of thousands laboured in the gold mines. Men, women and children were the victims of disease and a regime of systematic cruelty that rivalled the worst excesses of the Nazi concentration camps. Three million of the stream of hopeless prisoners had died in Kolyma, their graves unmarked because there were no graves. A tractor gouged out a few feet of frozen earth and then shovelled the daily quota of corpses into the pit, skeletal hands, feet and sometimes heads were left projecting when the permafrost set the earth iron-hard, chopped off later by a mechanical grader.

John Summers had been put in a separate enclosure with three other special grade prisoners. Two of them had no legs and the third was blind. At night the barbed-wire compound was permanently floodlit. Day after day Summers was detailed to collect all the new corpses and deliver them on a flat barrow to the guardroom for registration. The routine was simple. The name and prison number were recorded with the date of death, the duty guard thrust his bayonet into the silent heart of the already dead prisoner and the corpse was stripped and thrown onto the pile of other bodies to await the next mass-burial.

CHAPTER TWENTY-THREE

Harris was in a hurry but he went into the information room and signed that he had checked the weekly information files laid out on the table. As he headed for the door he stopped, hesitating, and then, sighing, he walked back to the table and sat down. No responsible officer signed that he had read his obligatory files when he hadn't done so. Out of the dozen or so files there were only three obligatory files for him. One marked 'USSR', one marked 'CIA/FBI' and a third, a thin file marked 'Australasia'.

There were two file number references in the Soviet file that he noted and then he reached for the CIA/FBI file. He had virtually no current contacts with the United States security services but he read through the two-line references to other files as he slowly turned the pages. It was on the third page of photographs that he stopped. Despite the grainy blow-ups he recognized both faces immediately. It just said: 'Morris Cohen and Laura Teresa Cohen. Associate of the Rosenbergs, David Greenglass, Harry Gold and others. Disappeared from their address in New York immediately prior to the arrest of Julius Rosenberg. Present whereabouts unknown. Possible locations, Australia, New Zealand, West or East Germany, United Kingdom. See Washington file 70410/04/3466. Restricted.'

He was looking at photographs of Peter John Kroger and Helen Joyce Kroger, antiquarian bookseller and his quiet surburban wife. The owners of the

Rover car that had been parked at the 'looker's' cottage. Associates of the mysterious Mr Gordon and the middle-aged woman from Weymouth and Portland who had owned the cream-coloured Mini.

For ten minutes Harris sat there, collecting his thoughts. He knew by instinct that they were no longer just thrashing about. They were in business at last and it meant a radical change in the operation. This latest piece in the jig-saw would warrant a full surveillance organization. It could mean thirty or more trained people. And that could mean the operation being taken over by Shapiro himself or someone else equally senior. He reached for the internal telephone and dialled Shapiro's number. Shapiro had already left the office but he had left a number where he could be contacted. He dialled the number and Shapiro answered.

'Shapiro. Who is it?'

'It's Harris, sir. I've just come across something that alters my opinion.'

'Oh, what is it?'

'A connection, sir. A CIA/FBI connection.'

'Why can't you deal with it?'

'I think it's more your level.'

'Can it wait until the morning? I'll be in early. About eight.'

'I'd rather deal with it tonight if I can.'

He heard the impatience in Shapiro's voice as he said, 'Are you at the office?'

'Yes.'

'I'll be there in fifteen minutes.'

'I can come to you if that's more convenient.'

'I'll be there in fifteen minutes.'

Shapiro was in evening dress: dinner jacket, black tie and four miniature medals. He took Harris's arm and walked to the far side of the reception area. When he came to a halt he said, 'Right, what is it?' He sounded as if he resented being disturbed. He frowned as if whatever he was going to be told was unwelcome.

Harris told him of the CIA/FBI photographs.

Shapiro said sharply, 'Are you quite sure? Those photographs are never good quality.'

'Yes, I'm quite sure.'

'We'd better go up to my office.'

As they went up in the lift Harris said, 'I'm sorry I've had to disturb your evening.'

Shapiro didn't respond but in his office he took off his dinner jacket. 'Show me your photographs and the file photographs.'

It was ten minutes before Harris came back with the material and Shapiro looked at both sets of photographs for several minutes before he looked up at Harris.

'Yes. You're right.' He paused and leaned back in his chair, closing his eyes. 'We'll need a twenty-four-hour team for the Cohen's place in Ruislip and the bookshop. Another team for the Gordon chap and the spinster at Weymouth. We'll have to think about Grushko. Has Grushko got diplomatic status?'

'No. It wasn't requested for him either.'

'We'll pull him in when we pick up the others.'

'What about the MP – Maguire-Barton?'

'Go on checking on him and keep me informed – but leave him for me to deal with.'

'Do you want me to stay in charge of the operation?'

Shapiro looked surprised. 'Do you know of any reason why you shouldn't?'

'I thought that as it was getting bigger you might . . .'

'How many bodies do you want?'

'On my calculations I could get by with thirty. I might need more if it takes long.'

'We might have to call in some outside help if it's a long term job. Special Branch and Five.' He stopped and looked at Harris's face. 'You'd better leave this to me. Go home and get some sleep. You look as if you need it.'

Shapiro was on the phone even before Harris got to the door and he called out, 'Be here at eight, Mr Harris. There'll be people to brief.'

'Yes, sir.'

Harris applied for, and got, an incident room and two clerks to record and collate the information coming in from the surveillance team and other sources. Like most surveillance operations whole days could go by with nothing suspicious reported, but when there were contacts every detail had to be noted. Locations, time, photography where possible, identification, description of the meeting, weather conditions, light conditions and all the rest of the information to rebut defending counsels' insistence in court that the meeting never took place or that the light conditions were too bad for accurate observation.

Harris reported daily to Shapiro who seemed anxious to hurry things along. But there was always one major problem with this kind of surveillance and investigation: they were founded on little more than suspicion, and courts were not interested in suspicion, neither was the Director of Public Prosecutions.

What they wanted was evidence, and, so far as English law was concerned, it had to be evidence not merely of intent to spy but proof of actual espionage. If Soviet diplomats were concerned then suspicion could be enough. They could be declared '*personae non gratae*' and sent packing. But 'illegals', who had to come before the courts, were given all the benefits that any other defendant could expect.

CHAPTER TWENTY-FOUR

Once Shapiro had arranged for full surveillance teams Harris deployed them quickly and right at the start they had a lucky break. Farrance, one of the new men, had followed Mr Gordon to a block of luxury flats, the White House, in Regent's Park. And from there to his workplace in Peckham.

Both places had been subjected to covert searches but the searchers found nothing suspicious apart from large sums of money in cash in a false ceiling in the toilet at the flat. The money was sterling and dollars to the value of just over three thousand pounds. But the search revealed that Mr Gordon was, in fact, a Mr Gordon Arnold Lonsdale. Discreet enquiries among some of the customers of the business only confirmed that the business was both successful and efficient.

The company had a substantial share of the London gambling machine market, and Mr Lonsdale's partners seemed to be no more than normal businessmen.

A request was sent to the Royal Canadian Mounted Police in Canada for any information on a Gordon Arnold Lonsdale. Suspected of espionage. Two weeks later a report came back that at least established that Lonsdale was travelling on a fake passport. With espionage suspected, the RCMP implemented a routine check on driving licence applications. A Gordon Arnold Lonsdale had applied for one in 1954 giving his address at No. 1527 Burnaby Street, Vancouver. From there he was traced to the address of a boarding house in Toronto. And it was at that point they discovered that he had a Canadian passport.

Corporal Jack Carroll of the RCMP had landed from a British Viscount plane at a snow-covered landing-strip in northern Ontario to check the details of Gordon Arnold Lonsdale in his birthplace – Cobalt, Ontario. It took only three days to reveal that the real Gordon Lonsdale had been taken back to Finland by his mother when he was only three years old. The rest was surmise, but for experienced intelligence officers it wasn't difficult to imagine what had happened. The boy's genuine documents would have been taken by the KGB and used to provide cover for the man calling himself Lonsdale. It was normal KGB practice. But above all they now had legitimate grounds for picking up Lonsdale and charging him, any time they wanted. But they wanted to challenge him with a lot more than using a false passport.

The check on Ethel Gee showed that she had started work at the Underwater Weapons Establishment at Portland in 1950, and she had signed the Official Secrets Act document that all civil servants have to sign if they are engaged on any secret work. She was forty-six and she lived in Hambro Road, Portland, Devon.

Her boy-friend was fifty-five. He was Henry Frederick Houghton and he lived not far from Gee in Meadow View Road, Broadway, a suburb of Weymouth. He was employed at the same establishment as Gee and was responsible for the distribution and filing of all papers and documents, including Admiralty Fleet Orders and Admiralty charts. His salary was £741 a year.

The first meeting of all three of them that the surveillance team had covered was on July 9, 1960.

Lukas had followed Houghton to the Cumberland Hotel. Ethel Gee had walked into the foyer through the Oxford Street entrance a few minutes later. She and Houghton had talked for a few moments and then left the hotel taking the Underground to Waterloo Station. Lukas asked for assistance on his pocket radio and Ivan Beech and Lukas followed the couple out of the station. As they approached the Old Vic they were joined by Lonsdale. They obviously knew one another well. Lonsdale gave Houghton an envelope. A few moments later Houghton left Lonsdale and Gee talking together. When he returned he was carrying a blue paper bag. He took a parcel out of the bag and gave it to Lonsdale.

About five minutes later they split up. Lukas followed Lonsdale, and Beech followed the couple.

Lonsdale had walked to where he had parked his car, frequently looking over his shoulder to see if he was being followed. Twice he had walked past his car before doubling back and driving to his flat.

Houghton and Gee had gone to the Albert Hall for a performance by the Bolshoi Ballet.

The surveillance was stepped up when the evaluation showed that the first Saturday in the month seemed to be a permanent rendezvous for the three of them.

Farrance had been trailing Lonsdale on August 26 when he followed him to Great Portland Street where Lonsdale parked his car and went into the Midland Bank. A few minutes later he came back to his car and took out a brown attaché case and several small packages which he took back into the bank and left with the clerk for safe custody.

Harris had applied for, and got, a search warrant for the attaché case, and the contents had been listed and photographed before the case was returned to the bank.

In the case was a Ronson table-lighter, a Praktica camera, two film cassettes and a bunch of seven keys.

It wasn't until October 24 that Lonsdale reclaimed the case from the bank. He walked to an address in Wardour Street and when he left he was carrying a different brown leather briefcase. Lukas had followed him when he went by Underground from Piccadilly and got off at Ruislip Manor station. From the station he walked to 45, Cranley Drive and at last there was further confirmation implicating the bookseller.

On Saturday November 5 Houghton was under surveillance in Puddletown in Dorset. When Houghton entered a hotel Farrance saw a large cardboard box and a leather briefcase on the back seat of Houghton's Renault car. Beech and Farrance followed him as he drove to London where he parked his car near a pub called the Maypole. Ten minutes later Lonsdale joined him there carrying a briefcase. A few minutes later Houghton and Lonsdale were driving slowly in Houghton's car. They stopped in the shadows of a group of trees and then drove back to the Maypole. When they left, Lonsdale was carrying a black document case which was not the case he had arrived with. They drove off in Houghton's car and were lost in the traffic at Marble Arch.

Saturday, December 10 linked both sides of Lonsdale's network. In the early afternoon Lonsdale had met Houghton and Gee at their old rendezvous in Waterloo Road and in the early evening Lonsdale had parked his car about twenty-five yards from the Kroger's home in Cranley Drive. It had stayed there until just before noon the following day.

It was decided at a meeting between Morton and MI5 liaison that the arrest of the five suspects and the subsequent handling of the case should revert to MI5 and Special Branch who had been kept informed of the last six months' surveillance.

Shapiro's meeting with Harris had not been smooth.

'You'll be required to give evidence and so will your team but the rest is out of our hands now.'

'But why? They're there for the taking.'

'And Special Branch will take them.'

'But we've done the hard grafting all the way.'

'Which was what you were told to do.'

'How do I explain all this to my chaps who've sweated their guts out for months?'

'You don't explain. You send them back to the pool with your congratulations and praise them for a job well done.'

'Can I ask you a very frank question, sir?'

'Yes – but I might not answer it.'

'Was there ever a reason why we – SIS – were told to take on this operation?'

'Yes – a very good reason.'

'You know the reason?'

'Yes. I was one of the three people who made the decision.'

'But *I* can't be told what the reason was?'

'I'm afraid not.'

For a moment Harris locked eyes with his senior and then he turned and headed for the door. As he opened the door Shapiro called out.

'Harris.'

'Sir.'

Shapiro nodded. 'Well done. Keep at it.'

Harris was plainly neither amused nor mollified by the official pat on the back.

The spy network's regular, first Saturday in the month meeting on January 7 was the last. Houghton had deviated from his usual routine and had parked his car at Salisbury Station and he and Ethel Gee had caught the 12.32 train to Waterloo. The train arrived at 3.20 p.m. At 4.30 Lonsdale arrived outside the Old Vic Theatre, parked his car and stood on the corner of the street. Houghton and Gee crossed from Lower Marsh to where Lonsdale was standing. They walked past him without acknowledging him and he turned and followed them, catching up with them a few moments later.

Gee was carrying a shopping basket and Lonsdale took a parcel from it. It was then that a Special Branch officer walked past them, turning to face them as he said, 'You are under arrest.' The parcel was found to contain four Admiralty Test reports and a cassette of undeveloped film. When it had been processed it was of 230 pages of an Admiralty book entitled 'Particulars of War Vessels'.

At 6.30 p.m. that evening SB officers knocked on the door of 45 Cranley Drive and the Krogers were arrested.

CHAPTER TWENTY-FIVE

When the brief radio message came through that Lonsdale and the others had been arrested and that there was hard evidence of espionage, Shapiro checked with the teams still covering Grushko and Maguire-Barton. Grushko was at his flat and alone.

When Shapiro rang the bell it was a couple of minutes before Grushko opened the door. Shapiro held up his ID card and Grushko shrugged and looked back at him.

'What is it you want?'

'I'd like to come in and talk to you.' And there was real surprise on Grushko's face when Shapiro responded in Russian. For a moment he hesitated and then he opened the door wider and Shapiro walked in. He had seen photographs of the room way back and it looked much the same.

Grushko said, 'I'll have to leave in ten minutes. What is it you want?'

Shapiro smiled and sat down on the couch as he pointed at an armchair. 'Let's make ourselves comfortable, comrade.'

Grushko sat reluctantly. 'I haven't got much time.'

'It's going to take quite a time, Comrade Grushko, so you might as well relax.'

'What is this all about?'

'Well now. We've got a problem. You've been rather a naughty boy and we're not sure yet what we're going to do about you. You haven't any diplomatic immunity so we could put you on trial, or we could ship you back to Moscow. Or we could just talk – and cooperate – and leave it at that.' Shapiro smiled. 'We don't have a lot of evidence to put before a court. But enough. Enough to show that you've been involved in espionage. You've not been all that successful I'll admit, but it's enough to get you two or three years in prison.' He paused. 'And when we eventually send you back to Moscow they wouldn't be very happy with your performance here. If we just send you back without taking you to court they'll be even more unhappy with your operation in London. We'd just have to let them know that you'd been so amateurish, so inept, that we just smiled at your efforts and sent you back.' He looked at Grushko. 'You do understand what I mean, don't you?'

'What the hell is it you want from me? I don't understand all this . . .' he waved his arm dismissively '. . . all this rubbish.'

'Oh, but you do, Grigor. You know that I'm being very generous with you. Giving you a chance to just go about your journalistic work on Monday morning as if nothing had happened. No trouble from Moscow and no trouble from us.' He paused. 'That is, if you behave yourself in future.'

'What is it you want to know?'

'Let's start with Maguire-Barton. Tell me about him and his relationship with you.'

Grushko shrugged. 'He just wanted a few free trips abroad.'

'So why did he use a faked passport?'

'He thought he might be criticized for taking too many journeys to Warsaw Pact countries.'

'He could have avoided such criticism by not going. So why was it so important to him?'

For long moments Grushko was silent and then he said, 'If I tell you everything do you promise that I'll not be drawn into it and nothing will go back to Moscow?'

'If you cooperate – really cooperate. We're prepared to let you carry on as a journalist for six months. After six months you will tell Moscow that you think that you're under surveillance and you think you should be withdrawn back to Moscow. Tell them that you've had enough of the West and you want to be back in Moscow.'

Grushko seemed to be considering what Shapiro had said and then he took a deep breath. 'Maguire-Barton gave me profiles of Members of Parliament. Their life-styles, their finances, their sexual habits – the usual stuff. And he gave me reports on his colleagues' attitudes to the Soviet Union. Who might be influenced or bribed with money or sex. Nothing more than that. I passed the information to the embassy KGB so that certain MPs could be recruited as agents of influence.'

'Tell me about Lonsdale.'

The Russian looked back at Shapiro, shaking his head. 'I daren't. If I talked about him they'd know that you people could only have got it from me.'

Shapiro said quietly, 'We arrested Lonsdale today. About an hour ago. We've arrested his network too.'

Shapiro could see that the news of Lonsdale's arrest had really shaken the Russian. It was best to let the news sink in.

'When were you recruited to the KGB?'

'I never was.'

'Was it GRU then?'

'I was never a member of either organization. I genuinely am a journalist.' He shrugged. 'But as you know we get used by the KGB for odd jobs from time to time.'

'What did you think of Maguire-Barton?'

'As a man you mean?'

'Yes.'

'He's what we call in Moscow "a skater". A chap who just skates on the surface. Likes to be seen around but no real interest in anything. He's a kind of playboy. A political playboy. Likes publicity. Likes women of course. Especially if they help in getting his picture in the papers. He'd like to be a TV personality doing chat-shows. Recognized wherever he goes but not needing any real talent. I think he knows he's second-rate. He's not really ambitious. Just wants the good life. Or what he thinks is the good life.'

'What kind of money did he take?'

'A few thousands a year. Not a lot.' He shrugged and smiled. 'He didn't do a lot either.'

'Did you get receipts for the money?'

'Yes. Moscow wanted to have a hold on him.'

'Have you got them?'

'I've got photocopies.'

Shapiro looked at Grushko's face. 'Anything else you think I should know?'

'You're not bluffing about Lonsdale being arrested?'

'No way.'

'What were the names of the others who were taken?'

'Do you know their names?'

'Yes.'

'OK. They were Harry Houghton, Ethel Gee and a married couple named Kroger.'

Grushko sighed. 'Lonsdale is KGB. I'm not sure what his rank is but it's senior, major or lieutenant-colonel.'

'What was your rôle in the network?'

'I was just a post-box for his material. He's an illegal alien so he has no contact with our embassy. Not even a KGB contact. He was mainly responsible for getting naval information.'

'What kind of naval information?'

'I've no idea. I should imagine anything he could get.'

'Who ordered you to cooperate with him?'

Our embassy in Ottawa briefed me. Told me to assist him in any way he needed so long as it didn't compromise my position here.'

'And what did you do for him?'

'I took his material and passed it to the embassy and they forwarded it in the diplomatic bag. They thought it was mine. I arranged meeting places and drops.' He shrugged, 'That's about it.'

'Tell me about him. What sort of fellow is he?'

'He's an arrogant bastard. Sees himself as the master-spy. The spider at the centre of the web and all that rubbish.' When Shapiro smiled Grushko said, 'I mean it. I got the impression that Moscow didn't like him much either, so he must have been useful. Women go for him. God knows why. He's an ugly bastard. You've only got to look at his eyes and you'd know that he's a crook. He was a born capitalist. Fancied himself as a tycoon with his tatty little business. He told Moscow it was just as a cover for his movements but it wasn't. He told me he was aiming to be a millionaire. He'd have probably ended up staying here permanently if you hadn't spotted him.'

'Who's your girlfriend? The dark-haired one. Lives in Cardiff.'

'I don't know who you mean. I've never been to Cardiff nor had a girlfriend who lives there.'

'You've been seen with her and she's been to embassy receptions with both you and Maguire-Barton.'

Grushko smiled. 'I know who you mean now. Do trains to Cardiff stop at Birmingham?'

'Most of them do.'

'She's the girlfriend of a Party member who lives in Birmingham. She brings material from him for me and takes instructions back to him.'

'What's his name?'

'Holloway. Jake Holloway.'

'And what does he do?'

'He's a left-wing activist, a lecturer in Birmingham at the university.'

'Tell me about him.'

'I don't remember much about him. He's a friend of Maguire-Barton. He put me in touch with Holloway. Said he was a Marxist activist. I had brief contacts with a lot of these grass-roots types.'

'What sort of contacts?'

Grushko shrugged. 'Sometimes they needed aid but usually they wanted to talk politics.' He half-smiled. 'Wanting to tell Moscow how to run our foreign policy.' He paused. 'Was this fellow bald with a beard?'

'Yes.'

'I remember him now. He saw himself as the leader of the revolution in Britain. Used to give me messages to Gromyko and the Politburo. When was the revolution going to start? Had they forgotten Marx's article in 1855 about tearing off the mask of the bourgeoisie in England? The usual crap these people go in for.'

'Did you pass money to Holloway?'

'I don't remember. I never met one of them who didn't want funds for some wildcat scheme. I gave them small amounts and just kept them happy.'

'Is that all Moscow wanted?'

'Moscow was happy to keep them on the boil. They had a nuisance value.'

'Does Moscow give you leads to these people?'

'With people like Maguire-Barton – yes. But people like Holloway they get in touch with the embassy and if they're not interested they pass them on to me.'

'What do they expect from you?'

Grushko sighed. 'Free trips to Moscow, cash, moral support – whatever feeds their little power struggles.'

'Would Lonsdale be interested in coming over to us?'

'I don't know. I don't know him all that well. I shouldn't think so. He's got a family. And he'd rather play the hero. If you put him in court he'll love it. Every minute of it.'

'Did he have contact with Maguire-Barton?'

'I'm not sure. They're rather like one another in a lot of ways so they disliked each other.'

Shapiro said quietly, 'Find a reason for going back to Moscow in about six months, Grigor. You'll be quite safe. There'll be no leaks from us. But no more silly games. Stick to the journalism.'

'You give me your word there will be no leaks?'

'Absolutely. Only two other people in SIS even know that I've been here. There will be no written record.'

'And you've not bugged this place?'

Shapiro smiled. 'Grigor. What a thing to say.'

Sir Peter interviewed Maguire-Barton personally. There was just about enough on the MP for the DPP to mount a court case against him but it was not much more than a long list of contacts with suspected people. Courts didn't like circumstantial evidence in treason charges unless there was at least an attempt to provide actual hard evidence of information being passed that could be considered to endanger the security of the State. A nod from certain quarters of the Establishment was as good as a wink even in the High Court, but there had to be some underlying evidence especially when the MP concerned was a member of the Labour Party, whose left-wing militants would claim that one of the brotherhood was being deliberately harassed in carrying out his normal parliamentary duties.

It was an occasion for the black jacket, pin-striped trousers and a black tie. And the panelled office.

Maguire-Barton was tall, with a quite handsome face, sallow complexion, soft brown eyes and considerable charm. The kind of charm that most men instinctively dislike. Professional and indiscriminate charm. He was mentioned frequently in the gossip diaries, generally as the escort of some minor film actress or débutante. Like any other minor public figure who was unmarried, there were rumours of homosexuality and hints of unprintable predilections, but nobody had ever provided even the faintest substance for such rumours. He was adored by the female contingent who dominated his constituency party and disliked and envied by most of his colleagues in the House of Commons. Disliked by Tories as a social-climbing, self-publicizing nonentity, and envied by his fellow Labour MPs for much the same reasons. For a short period he had been the opposition's spokesman on trade and industry but his ill-concealed indifference to the subject had made it a short-lived appointment.

Sir Peter had long years of experience in putting quite senior civil servants and administrators in their place. And he knew from experience that it was the lightweights who were always the most difficult to deal with. The heavyweights mounted a well-argued defence that he was capable of destroying piece by piece, but lightweights blustered or were indifferent because they didn't know any other way.

When Maguire-Barton was shown in Sir Peter walked from his desk to greet him and show him to the armchair by the marble fireplace. He settled himself comfortably into its twin and looked across at the MP, taking an instant dislike to the brown suit and the flamboyant MCC tie.

'Mr Maguire-Barton. I thought we should have a chat.'

Maguire-Barton smiled. 'Honoured, I'm sure. Please make it Jack. I hate formality.'

'Don't we all. But although this is an informal chat it nevertheless has some formal aspects.'

'Sounds ominous, Sir Peter.'

'Let's talk first about Mr Grushko.'

'Mr Grushko?'

'Yes. Grigor Grushko. A Russian. Calls himself a freelance journalist.'

'Ah yes. A very talented man. And with considerable influence in Moscow I understand.'

'You see a lot of him, don't you?'

'I see him from time to time, as I do a number of members of the press.'

'What other members of the press have you met a couple of dozen times in the last six months.'

The spaniel eyes looked at Sir Peter for several moments before Maguire-Barton replied. 'Are you telling me that I've been watched?' he said softly.

'Observed, let us say.'

'You mean that your people have been checking on the comings and goings of a Member of Parliament?'

'Yes. We keep a protective eye on any MP who has regular contacts with Russians or any other Warsaw Pact people.'

'Have you received any authorization to do this in my case?'

'I don't need any authorization to do this, it's part of our standard practice.'

'You mean you waste your people's time on watching an MP who in the normal course of his duties happens to meet foreigners?'

'Depends on the foreigners, Mr Maguire-Barton. And on what they're up to.'

'I shall have to report this to the Prime Minister and I shall certainly ask questions in the House.'

'The Foreign Secretary and the PM already know that I'm interviewing you. And why. And you would be very unwise to raise any questions in Parliament.'

'It happens to be one of my privileges as an MP, Sir Peter.'

'Are you suggesting that regular meetings, both public and private, with a Russian who is a close working associate and collaborator of a senior KGB in this country, are the privilege of a man just because he's an MP? And that such meetings should be treated differently than they would be if they were by a member of the public?'

'Who says he's anything to do with the KGB?'

'I say so, Mr Maguire-Barton.'

'You'd have to prove that.'

'I wouldn't. My opinion would be enough.'

'Not for me it wouldn't.'

Sir Peter smiled acidly and said quietly, 'Grushko has already been interviewed. We should be happy to publish the statement he's made concerning his relationship with you.'

'The word of a Russian agent against the word of an MP?'

'You could hardly cast doubt on the veracity of a man with whom you admit that you had such a close and continuous relationship.' He paused. 'And why do you assume that you would want to cast doubt on what he has told us?'

'When was he arrested?'

'I'm afraid I can't discuss such matters with you.' He paused. 'Then there is your relationship with Mr Holloway, a lecturer at Aston University.'

'And what is wrong with that may I ask?'

Sir Peter saw the relief in Maguire-Barton's eyes at the change of direction of the interview. 'Mr Holloway is also a contact of Mr Grushko and has received certain benefits from him that would take a lot of explaining.'

'What kind of benefits?'

'Much the same as you received yourself from the same source. All-expenses-paid trips to Warsaw Pact capitals for instance.'

'I was a member of a parliamentary group.'

'You've had four trips to Prague, one to Warsaw, two to Sofia and two to Moscow which were all private trips. And on at least three of those trips you used a passport that was not your own.'

'Whose passport was it?'

'That would be given in evidence if the matter came before a court. It's hard evidence, on the record.'

Maguire-Barton frowned. 'What court case are you on about?'

'Mr Maguire-Barton, you don't seem to appreciate that you might well be prosecuted for endangering the security of the State.'

'But that's preposterous.'

Now that it had got to the bluster and indignation stage Sir Peter had had enough.

'Preposterous or not, that is what will inevitably happen if you don't heed my advice.'

'What advice, for Christ's sake. I haven't had any advice.'

'I'm about to give you my advice, Maguire-Barton. It would be to your benefit if you not only listened, but listened carefully.'

'Don't sermonize – just say what you've got to say.'

For long moments Sir Peter looked at Maguire-Barton without speaking and he was aware of the white knuckles and the small vein that had come up on Maguire-Barton's forehead.

'I'm not sure in the light of your attitude that I want to give you advice. Maybe you'll learn quicker the hard way.'

'OK,' Maguire-Barton said quietly. 'Tell me what you want.'

'First of all I want you to understand that a record of our discussion will go on the files. I told you that this meeting had its formalities. That's one of them.' He paused. 'My advice is quite simple, Maguire-Barton. Stop playing games with Moscow. No more contacts with them, official or unofficial. And stop assisting or advising the people or groups who are trying to infiltrate your own Party.'

Maguire-Barton shrugged. 'And what if I don't go along with your advice?'

'Then we'll throw the book at you.'

'You haven't got a shred of evidence that a court would accept.'

'I won't comment on that piece of wishful thinking but you might care to reflect on what your position will be in the Party and outside when what we have is pinned on you in open court.'

'Are you threatening me?'

'Yes.'

'In that case . . .'

Sir Peter held up his hand. 'Don't go on, Maguire-Barton. I've had enough of you. But I warn you. One wrong move and your feet won't touch, you'll be at the Old Bailey before you can draw breath. And whether you're found guilty or not you'll be finished, in public life and in private too.'

'You bastards should be controlled and I'll bloody well see that you are.'

Sir Peter stood up and said quietly, 'Don't tempt me, Maguire-Barton. You've had your little fling. Don't push your luck.' He walked to the desk and pressed one of the buttons on a panel. One of the juniors came in almost immediately.

'Jonathan, please show Mr Maguire-Barton the way out.' He turned to Maguire-Barton and said, 'Thank you so much for your cooperation Mr Maguire-Barton. You've been a great help.'

Maguire-Barton opened his mouth to speak, saw the look on Sir Peter's face, and then changed his mind, heading for the open door.

CHAPTER TWENTY-SIX

Macleod and Shapiro had always got on well despite the rifts that sometimes disturbed the various levels of relationships between SIS and the CIA. Macleod was in his middle-fifties, experienced, a good negotiator and always amiable and relaxed. And always used the opportunity of the liaison meeting to get Shapiro's views on current CIA problems concerning the KGB. On several occasions tentative offers had been made to the Brit to recruit him to the CIA. But Shapiro knew that his almost unlimited brief on combatting the KGB in SIS would not be possible in the much larger organization in the USA. In London he was three thousand miles nearer the Soviet Union. They were almost at the end of the agenda of their routine Washington liaison meeting when Macleod raised the point under 'Any other business.'

He looked at Shapiro. 'Have you got any points?'

'Nothing official.'

'What unofficial?'

'There was a question raised at my last liaison meeting with GCHQ. They queried whether Fort George Meade ever passed on commercial surveillance material to US companies that could disadvantage British industry or commerce.'

'What did you say to them?'

'I assured them that it didn't happen and would never happen but I promised to raise the point either with NSA or you guys on a semi-official basis.'

'Well let's put the cards on the table. The National Security Agency, as you know, carries out radio and telephonic surveillance on everything. Specific targets are the main traffic but their listening facilities are non-specific. They sweep the whole world like a damn great vacuum cleaner and suck in everything. Radio at all levels, satellites, telephones – the lot. And that includes commercial stuff. Foreign and domestic. Indiscriminately. The censorship comes at evaluation level.

'There's no way we can handle all we get but some commercial stuff has a security element in it. High-tech and weaponry for instance. Also the movement of large sums of cash here and overseas. That stuff's pulled out with check-words. The rest is retained on tape for two months and then wiped clean. It's treated as highly confidential before it's destroyed and that's because we recognize that that information could make a guy a fortune or even destroy an industry.' He paused. 'So we care, Joe, we really do. If it was leaked, which would be very difficult because of our cut-out systems, we should treat it internally as a criminal offence and any outsiders involved would be treated the same.'

'Have you ever uncovered a leak, Robert?'

'Yes. Two. Both way back. They were picked up in hours. The NSA employee concerned has spent the last two years manning a dish aerial on some lonely rock in the Pacific, and the guy who suborned him never worked out how his company went bust inside six months. In the second case we intercepted the whole deal at an early stage and the information passed on was both spurious and damaging to the company that received it. The NSA person concerned not only was dismissed without a reference but never quite understood why she was called in by the IRS to look at her tax returns for the previous eight years. It cost her seventeen thousand bucks.' He shrugged. 'So that's the picture. Cards on the table. Not even the President could ask for that stuff without authentication of grounds. It's dynamite and we know it. OK?'

'I'll pass it on. But I guess they'll raise it again from time to time. Any points from you?'

Macleod smiled. 'Yes. Same sort of query. Our Polish and Soviet people think you've been holding back on them in the last few months.'

'What grounds to they give?'

Macleod pulled out a slip of paper from the inside pocket of his jacket and read it before he looked back at Shapiro.

'They say that the exchange of information shows a very obvious deterioration. Routine stuff OK but your usual top-level stuff has been missing. Seems they set great value on that information.'

'How great a value?'

'My impression was that they consider that that "special source" material is vital.'

'They're right in saying that. It's dried up I'm afraid.'

'They told me that they've put a lot of cash and effort into supporting that operation. They're not pleased. I need to give them a convincing explanation or I think it can mean a high-level hassle. Way above you and me. And the possible withdrawal of reciprocal information.'

'The explanation's simple, Jake. Our man disappeared some months back. We assume that he's in the bag.'

'Oh. I'm sorry to hear that. Why weren't we told?'

'Because we don't know what's happened. He may not have been picked up. He boarded a scheduled domestic flight from Warsaw to Moscow. The plane never landed at Sheremetyevo. We've cast around a bit but we've drawn a complete blank and we don't want to indicate an interest that would blow his cover if it isn't already blown.'

'Can I tell my people this?'

'We'd rather you didn't.'

'Why? Don't you trust our people?'

'We just don't want to stir the pool. He may be in the Lubyanka but not talking. He may be dead. He may have been involved in an air-crash that they have never publicized.'

'We've got people in both Warsaw and Moscow who could keep their ears to the ground if they knew more.'

Shapiro shrugged but didn't reply, and Macleod said, 'Would you talk to my guys?'

'If London clear it – yes.'

Macleod pointed to the red phone on his desk. 'Call 'em, Joe. I'll leave you alone.' He smiled. 'It's auto-scrambler. And it's not monitored.'

Shapiro talked with London for nearly an hour and it was only his suggestion that if they came clean with the CIA they might cooperate on an exchange that made London agree to him going ahead. A meeting was arranged by Macleod for the following day in Washington.

Macleod walked with Shapiro from his hotel to the meeting in the private house in Foggy Bottom. It was a modest town house on 24th Street not far from the Washington Circle. There was a small, neat front-garden and a white picket fence and a paved pathway that led to the front door.

Macleod made the introductions and Shapiro noticed that he only introduced two of the three men. The third had nodded and half-smiled but had not been named or introduced.

Goldsmith and Merrick were typical of the broad spectrum of American society from which the CIA recruited its officers. Goldsmith was tall and lean and in his early fifties. He had taught history at Berkeley, specializing in the history of revolution. Merrick was in his thirties, heavily built and already showing a tendency to pudginess, but he had a sharp mind and a forceful personality. Son of a California fruit farmer he had surprised his contemporaries by his success at Yale. And surprised them even more when he was invited to join a well-established law firm in Washington. When he had successfully represented various interests of the CIA he had been recruited, not as a legal adviser, but as a clear-minded situation evaluator.

They listened attentively to Shapiro's report on the disappearance of Phoenix. He had not been entirely candid about all of the operation, particularly in its early days, and he had said nothing that would enable them or their colleagues in Warsaw to pinpoint Phoenix's identity or official position in the Polish security service. When he finished it was Merrick who started the questions.

'This guy, Phoenix, how good was his Russian?'

'At least as good as his English. He was bi-lingual and Russian was his first language.'

'And his Polish?'

'Fluent but not perfect.'

Goldsmith said, 'Have you considered that he may have gone over – defected?'

'Of course.'

'And your evaluation?'

'Unlikely to the point of not worth considering seriously.'

'And how likely is it he would talk under pressure?'

Shapiro shrugged. 'Who can tell? He had the usual training but our experience is that you can never tell until it happens. Sometimes it's the tough macho who's spilling the beans after ten minutes and your ivory tower intellectual who goes silent to the Gulag.'

'If you had a bet, which way would it go?'

'Not talking.'

Goldsmith looked at Shapiro. 'Was he the source of the material we got on the inside of the KGB HQ?'

'Yes.'

'And on the Polish Politburo?'

'It's fair to say that any top-level inside stuff concerning the Warsaw government and the KGB came from Phoenix.'

Merrick nodded. 'Could you give us a brief picture of his activities?' When he saw Shapiro hesitate he went on. 'You can rely on anything you say staying inside this room, Joe. We appreciate how delicate the situation is for you people.'

Shapiro looked away for a moment towards the window and then at his clasped hands on the table. Then he raised his head and looked at Merrick.

'He spoke English, and fluent Russian and Polish. He was recruited by SIS from the Army. He was intensively trained to go back to Poland and infiltrate inside any government establishment that could give us an inside picture of what was going on inside the regime.

'For five years he had been Deputy Chief Liaison Officer between Polish Intelligence and the KGB in Warsaw and Moscow. He fed us information on the Soviet internal rivalries, the organization and personnel of the KGB in Moscow and Warsaw, especially those who were active against Britain and the United States.

'He prevented both Langley and London from making several major mistakes in our operations and it's fair to say that there was little that they planned against either of us that we were not warned about. Not always in precise detail but enough to allow us to take general precautions.'

Macleod intervened, looking at his two colleagues. 'The Agency's considered comment to me was that the material provided by SIS from this agent was the only reliable material that we have received in the last four years. I understand that it is the wish of the Director himself that we furnish any help we can to assist SIS.'

Goldsmith said softly, 'What help do they need that we can provide?'

Shapiro shrugged. 'There is nothing that could help us at the moment. The reason why Robert Macleod wanted this meeting was so that I could clear up your doubts that we were deliberately holding back information from you. I hope I have convinced you on that score.' He paused. 'But if I could move to the future for a moment – maybe our friends in CIA could help. I'm hypothesizing that we discover that Phoenix has been taken. Whether he's talked or not doesn't really matter. We should want to get him out. We have nobody of theirs at the moment who would make the Soviets interested in an exchange. If we put all our Warsaw Pact prisoners together Moscow wouldn't be interested for a moment.' Shapiro paused again. 'Have you got anybody?'

Goldsmith and Merrick looked at Macleod, who looked across at the man who had not been introduced and who had contributed nothing to the conversation. He in turn looked at Shapiro for several moments before he spoke.

He said very quietly, 'My name's Paul Nowak. I'm also CIA. We don't have anybody who would constitute a likely exchange for Phoenix.'

Shapiro nodded. 'Can I ask why you are here at this meeting, Mr Nowak?'

'I'm just an observer.'

'Why is that necessary? Does somebody not trust your colleagues here?'

'I don't have to give a reason.'

'Only three or four people in Britain know about Phoenix. I've talked to your colleagues as a courtesy, I don't appreciate having somebody else in the picture without it being established that they have a need to know. A man's life is at stake.'

'I came because I was invited to come. It's not just curiosity I assure you.'

Shapiro looked at Macleod who looked across at Nowak. 'I trust Joe Shapiro implicitly, Paul. So does the Director. Are you going to tell him or shall I?'

Nowak stood up and walked to the door. Before he opened it he looked at Macleod. 'I won't tell him. If you do . . .' He shrugged. '. . . then it's your responsibility.'

Macleod nodded, his face calm and showing no concern at the apparent threat. When Nowak had left Macleod said, 'Nowak's under a lot of stress at the moment. I won't go into the details.' He paused. 'What matters is what he said is quite correct. At the moment we have no suitable body for exchange. But it is possible that that could change in the next couple of months.'

'Can I be told the basics?'

'OK. But just the basics. We have man in custody. An important Soviet. He'll be coming to the final stages of the legal battle in the next few weeks. Nowak was in charge of the operation. There may be a legal cock-up. Nowak is obsessed by getting him the death sentence or at least life. When it all eventually gets untangled there's just the possibility that the best solution would be an exchange. Nowak knows this but doesn't want to admit it so that an exchange doesn't become an alternative in the legal people's minds and they hold back from making a one hundred per cent effort to nail this guy.'

'Is this Sivrin at the UN, or is it Colonel Abel?'

Macleod shook his head. 'I can't answer any more questions, Joe. But it's not Sivrin.'

'Can I keep in touch with you on this?'

'By all means. But remember – it's vague on both sides. On your side you don't even know that you need an exchange. And on our side we don't know if it's a possibility.'

'Is your guy in the same league as Phoenix?'

'Maybe higher. Even more important. We think. Do you want me to book you a flight? I'll take you to the airport myself.'

'That would be fine, Robert.'

CHAPTER TWENTY-SEVEN

The trial of Lonsdale and his network was set for March 13, 1961, only narrowly depriving the press of the chance to quote Shakespeare and the Ides of March. By then the media knew quite a lot about the private lives of the accused but nothing of their alleged activities. The original formal charge gave no details. But they had to restrain their eagerness to unveil glowing statements from Lonsdale's discarded girlfriends, the love-life of Houghton and Gee and the middle-class normality of the Krogers. It was all *sub judice* until the verdict had been given.

So the personal stories were of the barristers who were to prosecute or defend.

The Attorney-General, Sir Reginald Manningham-Buller headed the prosecution, and four leading counsel were to appear for the defence, one each for Houghton, Gee, the Krogers and Lonsdale.

Sir Reginald was already quite well known to the public. Bespectacled, fifty-five, testy in public but kindly and witty in private, he had a reputation for crushing his opponents like a legalistic steamroller. Living in the market town of Towcester, he was inevitably pictured as a man of the rolling acres despite the fact that his house and gardens barely made up to six acres. Word pictures were painted in the Sunday press before the trial of Sir Reginald pruning his floribunda roses to soothe his nerves before rising in court next day for what seemed to be Britain's most important spy-trial.

Baron Parker of Waddington, the Lord Chief Justice, was to preside at the trial. A gentle, moderate and modest man. Against the death penalty, but for corporal punishment. A man who had had to give up his rare hobby on appointment as Lord Chief Justice. The study of genetics applied to the breeding of high butter-fat dairy cattle.

The barrister defending Lonsdale was the grandson of an admiral and the son of a naval officer killed in the war. Born in Guernsey in the Channel Islands Mr W.M.F. Hudson was well aware of the significance of the charges against his client.

Two barristers from the same chambers were to defend Houghton and Gee. Mr Henry Palmer was to defend Houghton, and his equally young colleague Mr James Dunlop was to defend Gee.

The heavyweight of the defence team was Mr Victor Durand QC, a tough, able barrister who was to defend Peter and Helen Kroger.

When the trial started the defence objected to twelve of the jurors. Nine men and three women. It was finally an all-male jury.

Lonsdale sat in the dock, smartly dressed in a light grey suit. Ethel Gee wore a dark blue dress and Helen Kroger wore a heather mixture costume.

The Attorney-General opened the case, describing the circumstances of the arrests of the accused and the details of what had been discovered in the parcel handed by Ethel Gee to Lonsdale. And then he went meticulously through the espionage material found at Lonsdale's flat, the farm cottage, Houghton's home and the Krogers' bungalow.

It became obvious that the Krogers' bungalow was the hub of the network. The searchers had found a microscope that could be used for reading micro-dots, a list of radio call-signs using the names of Russian rivers, a high-powered radio transmitter hidden under a trapdoor in the kitchen, one-time code pads and several letters in Russian. There were two New Zealand passports in the Krogers' names, a Ronson table lighter with a concealed cavity in its base which contained film; the camera that had been in Lonsdale's briefcase deposited in the Midland Bank was in the study.

The Attorney-General showed the jury a tin of well-known talcum powder which had a special compartment with a standard KGB micro-dot reader. There were black-painted boards in the loft to cover the bathroom windows so that the bathroom could be used for enlarging or reducing photographed material. Also in the loft was 74 feet of aerial which led to a radiogram in the sitting room. Under the loft insulation were several thousand US dollars, and American and British travellers' cheques.

At Houghton's semi-detached cottage was a list of the Admiralty Test pamphlets that had been passed to Lonsdale. Further Test pamphlets were found hidden in Houghton's radiogram. There were Admiralty charts with pencil markings of secret submarine exercise areas, others had pencil marks pinpointing the site of suitable pieces of equipment for sabotage. £500 in Premium Bonds and a camera were found in a drawer with what looked like a box of normal Swan matches. Under the base of the match-box was a paper which registered dates for meetings and codes if a meeting had to be called off. In an empty tin of Snowcem paint in a garden shed was £650 in pound and ten shilling notes.

In Lonsdale's flat there was another Ronson lighter with a concealed cavity holding radio signal plans similar to those found at the Krogers' place. There was a similar tin of talcum powder with its hidden micro-dot reader, and a large amount of money in US dollars and sterling.

Nowak listened with envy as the prosecution established the evidence and its significance in carrying out espionage. The Attorney-General established the connections between them that constituted a conspiracy. Compared with the legal circus that they had to go through in New York it all looked so simple.

Witnesses gave evidence of how the various espionage items were used and others gave details of dates, times and locations of meetings.

Houghton had offered to turn Queen's Evidence against the other four if the charges against him could be dropped but the prosecution had refused the offer. They were confident that they didn't need his testimony.

A Special Branch officer explained how the false passport had been obtained but there was no way that the prosecution could prove that Lonsdale was a Russian. They read out letters translated from Russian that were from a woman named Galyusha who wrote as if she were his wife. But the jury, the court, and the general public got the message, and the prosecution would have gained little even if they had been able to prove that he was Russian.

On the second day of the trial the Attorney-General established in considerable detail the evidence that had only been touched on in the first day, and defence counsel queried as best they could the significance and accuracy of the evidence given by witnesses whose names were not given for security reasons.

Some embarrassment to the security services arose on the third day when a witness who had been instructed by a solicitor to sort through the possessions of the Krogers at their bungalow in Cranley Drive gave his evidence. Despite the previous searches by Special Branch, the witness had discovered two passports concealed in the cover and lining of a writing case. The witness had also discovered $4,000 concealed in a pair of bookends.

A specialist naval officer gave evidence that the transmitter found in the Krogers' house was amply capable of transmitting to Moscow and beyond. A Russian-language expert confirmed that the signal schedules found in the Krogers' Ronson lighter and the lighter from Lonsdale's flat were similar, and included coded transmission details under the headings 'transmission blind' and 'transmissions on orders of centre'.

The next day included the evidence of a communications expert from the HQ of the British monitoring services. Using the signals plan found in the Krogers' bungalow he had plotted the bearings and confirmed that the transmitter covered was sited in Moscow.

Towards the end of the day the defence began calling witnesses. When the trial resumed on the following Monday most of the court's time was taken up with defence counsel's attempt to establish that Houghton had acted only under threat and that Gee had been a reluctant partner.

By the Wednesday it was the Krogers' turn. Their several changes of name was touched on. The Attorney-General also brought out their connection with the Rosenbergs in the USA and their connections with Colonel Abel.

On Wednesday March 22, 1961 the Lord Chief Justice said of Lonsdale: 'You are clearly a professional spy. It is a dangerous career and one in which you must be prepared – and no doubt *are* prepared – to suffer if you are caught.'

He passed sentence of 25 years' imprisonment.

Of the Krogers he said: 'I cannot distinguish between either of you – you are both in this up to the hilt. You are both professional spies.'

They received sentences of 20 years each.

Houghton and Gee were both given sentences of 15 years and Lord Parker condemned them as traitors to their country whose motive was sheer greed.

With the trial over the press gave itself up to an orgy of revelation. Houghton's ex-wife described a marriage of physical cruelty and meanness. Lonsdale's ex-girlfriends and mistresses described in vivid detail his charm and generosity and hinted that his prowess as a lover was incredible. Those who studied the simian features of Lonsdale's photographs wondered if that mean-eyed face was really that of the man the women had described. A couple of newspapers mounted the usual campaign that the secret service was inefficient and a few MPs called for an enquiry.

Media interest in the case was short-lived. The new E-type Jaguar was more interesting at £1,480 plus purchase tax and it still wasn't easy to get tickets for *Mr Fair Lady* at Drury Lane.

CHAPTER TWENTY-EIGHT

The house in Georgetown had been converted from a derelict warehouse with great skill and taste. Two teams of CIA electronics engineers had swept it thoroughly and declared it clean. It was used as a safe-house by the CIA for top-secret meetings. As added security, there were no telephones. Communication with the outside world was by messenger or radio.

Six places had been arranged around a glass-topped table for the meeting, but there were none of the usual scrap-pads or writing materials that went with normal meetings for note-taking. It had been agreed beforehand that there would be no record of the meeting.

The three Americans chatted about the weather, the new CIA pay-scales and their views on Allen Drury's *Advise and Consent*, anything except the matter that had brought them there.

When the two Britishers arrived, Shapiro from SIS and Andrews from CIA-SIS liaison, there were handshakes all round and introductions to the two Americans they had not already met.

It was Macleod who started them off, smiling as he pushed an ash-tray towards Andrews.

'Apologies for the formal arrangements.' He laughed. 'Unfortunately, we don't have furniture for a more informal layout.' He paused. 'However, we all know why we are here and we all know that this meeting is informal and off-the-record.' He nodded towards Shapiro.'I'll leave it to Mr Shapiro to start the ball rolling.'

Shapiro took a deep breath. 'As you know, I've come to ask for help from the CIA.' He looked at the three Americans' faces but there was no response. 'For many years we have passed on to the CIA almost all the information from one of our top agents. I think it's fair to say that most of the CIA's information on both the internal politics of the KGB and Polish intelligence came solely from this source. I'm authorized to tell you now that the man concerned was in fact the liaison officer between the Polish security service and the KGB. But he is actually an Englishman.' Shapiro paused and looked around the table. 'You can imagine the courage it took to maintain that cover. And you can imagine the importance to both SIS and CIA of having that level of information.' He paused and then said quietly. 'At the moment that man is in a special punishment section of a Gulag labour-camp. Perhaps I should add that he is a commissioned officer in the Intelligence Corps with the rank of captain. We understand from two sources that he has been very badly treated and is unlikely to survive more than three or four months.' Shapiro paused again. 'We have nobody of similar importance to offer as an exchange. I should like to ask officially – if you would consider offering Moscow an exchange for this officer.' Shapiro took a deep breath. 'Maybe I ought to declare an interest. I recruited this man myself. We had a very special relationship. I explained the risks but he went ahead willingly.' He paused and his voice quavered slightly as he said, 'I feel personally responsible for his terrible situation.'

For several moments there was silence around the table and then Macleod said, 'Have you any indication that Moscow would agree to such an exchange?'

'We have nothing comparable to offer so we haven't made any approach, either unofficial or official.'

Macleod said quietly, 'What made you come to us at this particular moment?'

Shapiro shrugged. 'Two reasons only. Firstly because you've got Abel, and secondly we only heard two days ago that our man was alive and in the Kolyma Gulag.'

'Did you know that Abel and Gary Powers's parents are trying to persuade Moscow to do an exchange for Gary Powers, the U-2 pilot?'

'Yes I knew that from your weekly sitrep.'

Da Costa chipped in. 'You're asking us to leave one of our own citizens in a Soviet prison for the sake of your own man.'

'He was hardly our *own* man. He was virtually working for you as well. He was under our control but you got almost everything that we got.'

Macleod turned to look at da Costa. 'We contributed funds to this operation, Ray. And it wasn't just a hand-out. It was on the Director's instructions.'

Nowak said, 'There are already rumours in the press about an exchange for Powers. There'd by hell to pay if we ended up leaving Powers to rot in the Lubyanka and brought back a Brit instead.'

Macleod looked at Shapiro. 'What do you say to that?'

'It's undoubtedly a problem.' For a moment he looked uncomfortable. 'I don't like saying this but isn't our man more important than Gary Powers?'

Da Costa half-smiled. 'D'you mean more important or more deserving?'

Shapiro shrugged. 'I wouldn't dream of passing any comment about what your guy deserves. I just claim that our man is worth exchanging for anybody we've got. Either of us.'

'Why don't you offer them Lonsdale?'

'We're quite prepared to do that but we don't think that they set as much value on him as they do on Abel. And they'd certainly want the Krogers as well. The couple who worked for Abel in New York – the Cohens.'

Da Costa said quietly, 'So why don't you try them first and maybe have Abel as a fall-back position. If our people agreed.'

'We've had indications that there's a batting order of people who Moscow want and Lonsdale is at best about third on the list. Maybe not even that high.'

'And Abel is number one in your opinion?'

'No. Abel is number two on their list.'

'So who's their number one?'

'The defector. Hayhanen.'

There was a chorus of protest but Macleod held up a silencing hand as he looked at his colleagues. 'Nobody's suggesting that we trade Hayhanen, but Joe Shapiro's right in his assessment.' He turned to look at Shapiro. 'What is it you want us to go with?'

'A flat refusal on Hayhanen. Try offering Lonsdale – with the Krogers thrown in if necessary. And if that doesn't work I'd like to be able to offer Abel, as a last resort.'

There was a long silence and then Macleod said, 'How about we break for half an hour and I'll walk around the block with Joe while you guys think about it.'

Nobody dissented and as they walked slowly round the block Shapiro said, 'Are your people in a mood to help, Robert?'

'Well, they're on your side, that's for sure. It's the problem of leaving Powers to rot that worries them. The public won't like that. They won't understand. And none of us – FBI and CIA – is anybody's favourite son at the moment.'

'I think there is a solution that could avoid any problem about Gary Powers.'

'You're a cunning old fox, Joe Shapiro. You'd better tell them what you've got in mind.'

When they got back to the house the others settled back round the table and Macleod said, 'Joe's got some thoughts on this situation.' He paused and looked at Shapiro. 'Tell us what you've got in mind, Joe.'

Joe looked around the table at each of them. 'Let me tell you first how I think those guys in Dzerzhinski Square will be thinking.

'Their guy Abel is a sick man according to what I've heard. A disappointed man too. Disappointed that Moscow haven't raised a finger so far to get him released. He was their top guy in New York – maybe in the States for that matter. And he'll have expected that they'd at least try for a deal. But they ain't tried – have they?

'So when they're forced to consider a deal about him they'll know that we'll have tipped him off that we're offering Moscow a deal. If they refuse they'll know that he'll be a very bitter man. He's kept silent so far – and they'll know that too. But if they refuse a deal then maybe his attitude would change. He's had some years in prison but he won't have contemplated actually spending the last years of his life in jail. Dying in jail. The KGB will assume that if he was left to rot by them he could well feel that he's done his bit and with a nice offer from you guys he might jump at the chance of cooperating. If Moscow don't care about him why should he tough it out?

'Now we come to our guy – code-name Phoenix. He won't ever talk – no matter what they do to him – no matter what they offer him. I've had word that he's a very sick man. Physically and mentally. They've put him through the mincing machine, that's for sure.' He shrugged. 'He's of no use to them and they will know it.'

As he paused da Costa interrupted. 'That sounds like a stand-off, Joe.'

Shapiro shook his head. 'No. It's not. There's two things to bear in mind. Firstly, Abel will know he's going to spend the rest of his life in jail. Abel has hopes, our man has none.' He paused. 'There's one other plus factor on our side. The Russians have never publicized the capture of our man – no show-trial for the world's press – the usual scenario. Why?'

Macleod said softly, 'They don't want to lose face. They don't want the world to know they were fooled by your man. That a top KGB liaison man with the Poles was a mole for the West.'

Shapiro nodded. 'And they wouldn't dare put him on show in court after they'd beaten him up and he still wasn't admitting to anything.'

Da Costa said, 'That still leaves the problem of Powers, Joe.'

Shapiro shook his head slowly. 'Powers isn't a problem. He's our ace in the hole.'

'How come?'

'We do the deal with Moscow so that as far as the rest of the world is concerned we exchange Abel for Powers. The deal for Phoenix is a secret deal. Never to be revealed by either side. And he doesn't come over at Check-point Charlie or any of the usual Berlin crossing points.'

Macleod nodded. 'And if the Russians say no?'

'We stick to our position. No deal for our guy means no deal for Abel.'

Nowak said, 'And what if Langley or the White House say "no"?'

'And you trade Abel just for Powers?'

'Yep.'

Shapiro pursed his lips reflectively. 'Well, apart from the whole of the western world thinking you were either very naive or very weak to trade a top Soviet spy for a run-of-the-mill pilot, I'd say you would be wise to reflect on what effect it would have on your relationship with SIS.'

Da Costa said quickly, 'Are you talking with official backing when you say that, Joe?'

'Not at all. I'm not even suggesting that it would be official government policy or even official SIS policy. But a lot of top people in SIS would have very hard feelings about working with CIA or the FBI in future.'

Da Costa said, 'That's blackmail, Joe.'

Shapiro shook his head vigorously. 'It's not, Mr da Costa. And let me assure you that if I thought that blackmail was the only way then I'd resort to blackmail. All I am asking is help and consideration from my colleagues. You people.'

Macleod raised his eyebrows. 'It's rather more than help and consideration, Joe.'

'It's very urgent, Robbie. Desperately urgent. I need a quick reaction.'

Macleod nodded and looked at the others. 'I'll take our friends back to their hotel. I'll be back in about an hour. Kick it around while I'm away.'

Da Costa stood up. 'Before you go, what's your view, Robbie?'

'I go for it. But with a proviso. It has to be approved by State and the Director

CIA.' Macleod turned to the two Britishers. 'Let's go.'

When Macleod and the Englishmen had gone da Costa walked over to the window. For a few minutes he stood there and then turned to look at Nowak.

'What d'you think?'

'You're against it, aren't you?'

'Not really. But I don't think it'll work.'

'Why not?'

'I don't think the KGB will play ball. Not two for one.'

'They've had all they want out of Powers. A trial, a public confrontation, an abject apology for being a naughty boy. What more can they get out of him? And the world won't know it's two for one.'

'It'll take weeks to negotiate. According to what Shapiro said their chap could be dead by then.'

'All the more reason for the Russians to get their fingers out.'

'And we give up any chance we've got of getting Abel to come over to us and spill the beans.'

'He won't come over. They've tried everything they know. He just smiles and shakes his head. He's built up this image of himself now. The friendly, intelligent and patriotic soldier who bears his punishment with dignity and courage. He'd never abandon that for being a defector.'

'What will the brass say d'you reckon?'

'The Director CIA will say "yes". The Secretary of State will say "no".'

'And then?'

'It'll be up to the President. I'd guess he'll say "yes".'

Late the same evening Macleod drove Shapiro out to CIA HQ at Langley and they sat in a small office with a microfiche reader and a small bundle of fiches, marking the CIA references of typical material that had come from Phoenix.

It was 4 a.m. when they finished and a secretary had typed up the list. The information concerned had been collated onto two fiches while Macleod and Shapiro slept in a couple of small duty officers' bunks. Macleod woke Shapiro at 8 a.m. with shaving kit and talked to him as he washed and shaved.

As Nowak had forecast, the response from the CIA Director had been positive, and from the State Department negative. The President would make the decision. He would be at his desk by 8.30, would sample the information on the fiches and make his decision. He might ask to see Shapiro and ask some questions. Macleod was to put the facts to the President verbally.

It was 11 a.m. when Macleod returned. The President had agreed after seeing the representative samples of the kind of information that Phoenix had been supplying. He had even wished them luck and had asked to be kept informed.

CHAPTER TWENTY-NINE

Although Nowak had been so determined to get a conviction against Colonel Abel he was aware that the prosecution had sailed very near the wind to get that conviction. And he was aware too that they had not been able to establish even one actual act of espionage against the Russian. Now it was all over he felt a sneaking respect for the man who had refused to talk or cooperate in any way, and he was pleased to be the bearer of good news.

He sat at the plain wooden table in the prison office block waiting for the Russian to be shown in. A week-old copy of *Pravda* which he had brought with him lay on the table alongside a carton of Marlboros. When he heard the footsteps in the corridor outside he stood up and faced the door. He was shocked by the Russian's appearance. He was much thinner, his clothes hanging loose on his gaunt frame and his steps unsteady. He waved the old man to the chair and sat down facing him.

'I've got some good news for you, Colonel.'

The old man nodded but said nothing.

'We're trying to negotiate an exchange with Moscow. You for one of our own men.'

When Abel still made no reply Nowak said, 'Are you OK, Colonel? Are you feeling alright?'

The old man looked at the American. 'I saw a few reports of this in the newspapers some weeks ago.' He half smiled. 'The young pilot was mentioned. A Mr Powers, yes?'

'Yes.'

The old man shrugged. 'I didn't believe it. I still don't believe it.'

'Why not?'

The Russian pursed his lips. 'Experience. Experience of Moscow and experience of Washington. It's a piece of propaganda.'

'How do you make that out?'

'Moscow have made no move to suggest an exchange. Why should they? I have kept silent. And I shall remain silent. So what do they gain?'

'That's a bit cynical isn't it?'

'Not cynical. Just realistic.'

'And Washington?'

The old man sighed. 'You think after all the trouble you people went to to have me convicted that they're going to trade me for a pilot who embarrassed you all from Eisenhower down?' He shook his head. 'No way, my friend, no way.'

Nowak smiled. 'I think you're going to be surprised, Colonel.'

'No, sir. It's you people who are going to be surprised.'

'How come?'

'Because I won't agree to the exchange myself.'

Abel saw the shock and surprise on the American's face and despised him for his naivety.

'And one more thing, my friend. The pieces in the newspapers. The pleading by the pilot's parents are propaganda too. One more stick to beat the Soviets with. The hard-hearted men in the Kremlin.' He shook his head. 'You won't get me to join in the charade.'

'I swear to you – there's no charade. It's a genuine attempt to release you and Gary Powers.'

'Whatever it is – count me out. I shall not cooperate.'

'You don't have any choice, Colonel,' Nowak said quietly.

Abel smiled coldly. 'Even your own media will condemn you and the European press will have a field day. The American State Department sending back a Russian who asks for asylum.'

'You mean you would actually do that?'

'You can rely on it, my friend.'

'But why?'

'Think about it. Work it out very carefully. And remember what we tell our new KGB recruits: when you've looked at every possibility and it still won't fit – then try the impossibilities.' Abel stood up. 'I'd like to go back to my cell.'

Shapiro and Macleod were sitting in the VIP lounge at the airport when the girl came over to say that Macleod was wanted on the phone. He was away for about ten minutes and when he came back he told Shapiro of Nowak's meeting with Abel.

'Would you people let me talk to him?'

'Why? Do you think you could make him change his mind?'

'I'd like the chance to try.'

'We'd better tell the desk that you're not taking this flight.'

Back at CIA'S HQ at Langley, Shapiro hung around trying to hide his tension as Macleod consulted his colleagues. It was almost an hour before Macleod came back.

It had been agreed that he could interview Abel, but it was obvious that it had been a reluctant agreement. It was conditional on him not mentioning or even hinting at the inclusion of Phoenix in the proposed exchange. He would be flown to the Atlanta Penitentiary by military plane the next day. Nowak would go with him but they had agreed that he could see Abel alone.

A local CIA officer had driven them to the prison and Nowak had introduced Shapiro to the Prison Warden and then left him.

'He's got a cell of his own, Mr Shapiro. You could talk to him there or in the visitors' room. You'd be alone in either place.'

'Would you have any objections to me talking to him in the open air, the recreation area maybe?'

'Can I ask you why?'

Shapiro sighed. 'You know his background, Warden. He'll take it for granted that any inside place is bugged. I'd like him to feel free to talk. It could be important.'

'We've got a sports area. You could talk to him there. He's not violent and he's a bit too old and too rational to try and escape. How long do you think you'll need?'

'About a couple of hours maybe.'

'I'll get one of my men to take you there and somebody will bring him out to you.'

'Thanks for your cooperation.'

'You're welcome.'

Shapiro sat on a wooden bench at the far side of the sports field and took off his jacket as the sun beat down. He had tried to make notes the previous evening of what he would say to the KGB colonel but there was nothing to write down. He had no idea of what he should say. And why should the Russian be more influenced by talking to him rather than Nowak? But the thought of the man in the Gulag camp haunted him. He had had no peace of mind from the first moment when he learned that Phoenix was missing. It was as if history was repeating itself. Then he saw a uniformed prison officer open the wire-mesh door at the far end of the sports field. Shapiro watched as the tall lean figure of the man in the outsize suit came through the open gate. He was almost a hundred yards away. It wasn't until he was twenty feet away that Abel recognized the man who was sitting on the bench.

CHAPTER THIRTY

Sir Peter Clark's cottage was on the outskirts of Petersfield. Its grounds were no more than one acre but they gave onto the village cricket ground which in turn sloped upwards to a wooded hillside lined with beech and oak. Shapiro and Morton had been waved to wicker armchairs with cushions while Sir Peter sat on a rustic bench that was green with age and weathering. In an odd way their chosen drinks expressed much of their individual characters. Shapiro was drinking whisky, Morton locally brewed beer and Sir Peter was sipping from a glass of milk.

'Tell me again, Joe. It was before my time. Why did you think . . .' He paused, sensing that he was beginning to build a sentence that implied either blame or criticism, '. . . remind me of the circumstances.'

Morton, sensing Shapiro's confusion said, 'We had to make sure that the minimum number of people knew of what was planned. The only people involved in the decision were Joe, myself and Sir Mortimer who was D-G at the time. And even he was told only of the general outline. We gave him no details of names or background on the plan itself. All we were concerned with was that if things went wrong at some stage – and there was a political rumpus – at least he would be forewarned.'

'Did he tell the PM?'

'He didn't tell us. My belief is he did.'

'And there was no come-back from him?'

'Not that we knew of.'

'Go on . . .' Sir Peter nodded towards Shapiro as he looked at Morton, '. . . let

Joe speak for himself, Hughie. It's only between the three of us even now.'

'The Americans have made a big gesture, Sir Peter.' Shapiro shrugged. 'In appreciation of the past information that has come from Phoenix. They have authorized me to negotiate an exchange – Colonel Abel for Phoenix. But that exchange will be top-secret. So far as the public are concerned Abel will be exchanged for the U-2 pilot, Gary Powers. I'd like your authority to go ahead with this.'

Sir Peter looked towards the village cricket field, then at Morton, and finally at Shapiro.

'You've been almost obsessed about this problem of Phoenix, ever since the news first came through. Why, Joe?'

'Because I'm responsible for what has happened to him. I recruited him. I planned his training and his whole set-up. I owe it to him to do anything – anything I can to get him back.'

'You explained to him the risks honestly and fairly?'

'Yes.'

'And you told him what we always tell undercover people, that we should not be able to help them if they were caught. That we should deny their existence and any knowledge of them?'

'Yes.'

'And this kind of situation has happened before. A dozen times even in my time as D-G, yes?'

'And in half those cases we played it by the book and in time we got them back.'

'It took years in every case. The information we have is that Phoenix is seriously ill in Kolyma Camp. One of the worst of the Gulag camps. He'll just die there if we don't do something positive.'

'Do you feel even the smallest suspicion of guilt that you may not have really laid it on the line with Phoenix?'

'No. But I feel a hell of a lot of guilt that I recruited him in the first place.'

'You've recruited scores of men in your time, Joe. You always took it in your stride. Why this sudden concern for one man?'

Shapiro looked exasperated. 'I can't understand why this offer by the Americans isn't being grabbed with both hands.'

'Oh, but it is. You have my authority right now to go ahead in an attempt to negotiate an exchange. All that concerns me is that you seem to be rushing things. You're always so careful, so professional. I don't want you to risk making things worse than they already are.' He paused. 'And I'm concerned about you too.'

'In what way, Sir Peter?'

'We'll have a talk when this is over. Meantime – use any resources or help that you need. And the best of luck.'

When Shapiro had left, Morton said quietly, 'What's worrying you, Peter?'

Sir Peter shrugged. 'I don't know, Hughie. Just things that don't hang together properly.'

'Like what?'

'With hindsight it seems to me that when we decided to hand over the Lonsdale business to Five that Shapiro didn't mind. Normally he'd have fought like a tiger to keep it. I think that was because this Phoenix business was on his mind.' He looked at Morton for a moment. 'He went off to New York without mentioning what he had in mind – about the exchange I mean. Just gave the impression that it was a routine liaison meeting. That's not like Shapiro. I didn't say anything just now, but I didn't like it.'

'Anything else?'

'There's something that's changed Shapiro in the last few months. It reminds me of a report I saw on him when he was in Germany after the war. Said he was a loner and not suitable for high-level direction.'

'But that's exactly what he's been doing for the last ten years – coordinating our activities against the KGB. And he's done it very well.'

'Remind me – how old is he?'

'This is his last year. He retires at the end of December.'

Sir Peter stood up, stretching his arms. 'I'll put him up for something in the New Year's list. Forget what I've been waffling about. It's probably me, not him, that's out of step.'

CHAPTER THIRTY-ONE

Max Lutz was the Berlin lawyer who always negotiated exchanges on behalf of the Soviet Union. He was in his early sixties. Wealthy, successful and sophisticated, he had acted for the Russians for twenty years. Apart from being a very successful lawyer he was a shrewd negotiator and had been a colonel in the Wehrmacht who had served in the Afrika Korps under Rommel, and later, in Europe, on the staff of Army Group 'B' under Field Marshal Modl.

One of the advantages of indirect negotiations had been that Lutz had established himself as an intermediary rather than a negotiator. This meant that bluffing and haggling were totally unacceptable. If either party turned down an original proposal then both parties were given one more opportunity to make a fresh proposal. If either party declined the second proposal the negotiations were over. There was no third chance. And Lutz would never participate in the future in any negotiation concerning any of the prisoners named in a rejected proposal. He maintained that men's freedom and lives were at stake and he would not be party to anything that could be construed as raising the hopes of a man or woman and their families and deliberately dashing these hopes. He was not a member of the Communist Party nor any other political party or group. He genuinely had no interest in politics. SIS had negotiated with Lutz half a dozen times over the years and respected the German's honesty and impartiality. Lutz was seldom told by either side the importance or otherwise, or the significance, of the prisoners concerned. They were names on a list and their priorities were not his concern. That was for their captors and countrymen to decide.

Two telephone calls to Berlin and a couple of days waiting and the call had come back setting up a meeting. The first meeting was to be at Shapiro's hotel.

It was raining when Shapiro landed at Tegel. There was nobody to meet him and not even the head of station in Berlin had been informed of his visit. He took a taxi to Kempinski's and booked in under the name of Macnay with a Canadian passport.

The desk phoned him a hour later. There was a Herr Lutz to see him. He asked them to send him up.

Herr Lutz was tall and thin and elegant. And he shook hands as if he really meant it before sitting down in the profferred armchair.

'So, Mr Macnay. A good journey, I hope.'

'Fine, thank you. Would you like a drink?'

'Maybe after we talk, yes. First business and then the schnapps.' He shrugged and smiled. 'As my countrymen always say, "*Schnapps ist Schnapps und Arbeit ist Arbeit*".'

'How do we start?'

'Perhaps you show me some identification first?'

Shapiro got up and walked over to the briefcase on the bed. He handed Lutz an SIS ID card and a letter that stated that he was authorized to discuss the possible exchange of prisoners on behalf of Washington and London.

Lutz studied them carefully and as he handed them back he reached in his pocket with his other hand and offered Shapiro a photostatted page which included his photograph and a statement in Russian, German and English that confirmed that he was authorized to discuss all matters concerning exchanges of prisoners with foreigners on behalf of Moscow. Lutz smiled as he slipped the paper back in his pocket.

'My clients in Moscow were surprised that you had contacted me.'

'Why is that?'

'They wonder who you have who is sufficiently important to warrant a meeting.'

Shapiro smiled. 'That sounds like the opening move of a professional negotiator decrying the other party's goods.'

Lutz looked shocked. 'I assure you, Mr Shapiro . . .' He smiled. 'I can call you Mr Shapiro I hope . . .' Lutz paused until Shapiro nodded and then went on. 'It is no such thing. There is no question of bargaining in these cases. If my clients are interested they will say so immediately. I assure you. We talk as intermediaries with the possibility of arranging something to both of our clients' mutual advantages.'

'So why are you surprised at our request for a meeting?'

'As you know, I am only called upon to act when the negotiations are . . . shall we say . . . concerning significant exchanges. There are other contacts and other systems for discussing the exchange of people of less significance.'

'So why the surprise?'

'Quite genuinely my clients know of nobody in your hands, either officially or unofficially, who they could classify as being of high significance.'

'I'm representing United States interests as well as British interests.'

'Ah, yes – of course.' Lutz leaned back in the armchair, relaxed and satisfied. 'Tell me who you had in mind to offer my clients.'

'I'd like to do it the other way around. May I?'

'By all means.'

'You have an Englishman named Summers. Captain John Summers. He is in a special section in one of the Gulag camps.' Shapiro looked at a card he took from his jacket pocket. 'Gulag number 704913.' Shapiro watched Lutz's face carefully as he said, 'We had in mind suggesting an exchange with a man who calls himself Gordon Arnold Lonsdale. We believe that he is a Soviet citizen. It seems that his wife might be named Galyusha and that she lives in Moscow with their two children.'

Lutz put on his glasses and looked at his list again. After a few moments he said, 'He is in Wormwood Scrubs prison, yes?' He looked up at Shapiro. 'Sentenced to twenty-five years' imprisonment.'

'That's the one.'

'He had two associates. They call themselves Kroger or Cohen. Would they be included?'

'I'm quite sure that they could be part of a deal.'

Lutz shifted in the chair and looked towards the window then back at Shapiro.

'This is the first of these exchanges that you've been involved with, Mr Shapiro, is it not? At least, the first when you did the negotiating.'

'Yes.'

'But they briefed you on how we go about it?'

'What particular aspect were you thinking of?'

'Long long ago, nineteen forty-seven or thereabouts, we did the first deal. We took nearly a year and by the time the year was up your man – an American – had died. And Moscow's man – a Czech – had escaped.' He sighed. 'Both sides agreed that if exchanges were to be made in the future we didn't haggle like Armenian carpet-dealers. We said, right from the start, what we wanted and what we would offer in return. If that was not possible then one further offer. If that was not acceptable we shook hands and it was over. We never discuss those people again. Ever. It became an unwritten, unofficial rule of the game. We could tell our superiors or not, as we chose. They would learn one way or another that we were not hagglers, not stooges. But intermediaries. You understand?'

'I think so.'

'So we stop playing games with one another . . .' He paused, '. . . and I set a good example, yes?'

Shapiro half-smiled. 'Please do.'

'OK. The man my friends in Moscow would like to exchange for your man calls himself Reino Hayhanen. His real name is something else. He is half-Finnish, half-Russian and at the moment he is protected by the CIA.'

Shapiro sat down facing Lutz. 'OK. No bargaining, Herr Lutz. The CIA will not exchange Hayhanen for anybody. That is absolutely certain.' Shapiro paused for a moment. 'Is there anyone else that your friends have in mind?'

'Make me an offer, Mr Shapiro. Show me that you understand what we are here for. Tell me who you put on offer for your man.'

'Colonel Rudolph Abel. He is serving a thirty-year sentence in jail in Atlanta, Georgia.'

For a few moments Lutz was silent, then he said, 'Quite frankly, you surprise me.'

'Why?'

'I seem to remember reading that the parents of the young pilot had been in contact with the Soviet Embassy in Washington to suggest an exchange. Their son for Colonel Abel.'

'I don't think the American government feel that that is a fair exchange.'

'But why should they prefer an Englishman instead of an American?'

'We have asked for their collaboration and they have agreed.'

Lutz smiled and stood up. 'You must be very tired after your journey or I'd suggest that I go to my office a couple of blocks away and talk with my clients. And then come back and talk with you.'

'I'd be very happy to do that. I'd like to get it settled, one way or another.'

Lutz stopped with his hand on the doorknob. 'That's something we didn't discuss, Mr Shapiro. What if my clients can't find their way to cooperate?'

Shapiro shrugged. 'That would be the end of the matter so far as we were concerned.'

'You wouldn't be prepared to go ahead with the rumoured exchange of Abel for the American pilot?'

'No.'

'May I ask why not?' Lutz said softly.

'As I said earlier. It's a grossly uneven exchange – a senior KGB officer for a young plane pilot. It's not on, Mr Lutz. I'm sure your clients will realize that.'

It was almost midnight when Lutz returned. He wasted no time. As he sat down he said, 'My people's reaction was not entirely what I hoped for.' As he saw the grim look on Shapiro's face he shook his head. 'No great problem, Mr Shapiro. In fact, general agreement but with two sets of conditions. Conditions that I think you will find acceptable.'

'What are the conditions?'

'Let me give you the situation as it now is. The case of your man Kretski – Summers – there is no problem. He can be exchanged.' Lutz shrugged. 'The problem of course was Hayhanen. The hard-liners in the KGB would obviously like to get their hands on such a man. A man who has betrayed his trust in every possible way.

'Then we come to Powers, the pilot. He is no longer of any interest to Moscow. He was tried and sentenced publicly. He confessed. He served his purpose. He can be released too. That would allow the exchange to be made public.

'So we come to Colonel Abel. An honourable man who has behaved as we should expect a Soviet citizen to behave who fell foul of – shall we say – antagonistic authority.'

Lutz leaned back in the chair. 'So, reluctantly, the exchange you ask for will be accepted. Provided . . .' and Lutz wagged a monitory finger, '. . . provided we can agree on two sets of conditions. Condition number one I imagine is no real problem. It is what you want as much as my friends do. I refer to complete secrecy. Not just at the time of exchange, but permanently. No hints in the press. No books, no articles about a spy who came in from the cold. You know what I mean?'

'Of course. Both sides have a vested interest in keeping it secret.'

'And complete denial if there should ever be questions from the media or in Parliament or Congress?'

'Definitely. No problem. What's the second condition?'

'The second condition is just an act to show good faith.' He paused. 'If at some time in the future we should want an exchange for Gordon Lonsdale and the Krogers it would be seriously considered.'

'You know the problem that arises from that?'

'I can think of one – but you tell me.'

'My people could perhaps visualize some innocent British subject being arrested in Moscow and accused of espionage just to effect an exchange for Lonsdale and the Krogers.'

Lutz shrugged. 'I can only assure you, my friend, that that is not likely to happen. My people are not all that concerned about Lonsdale's fate – or the Krogers' for that matter.'

'OK.' Shapiro nodded. 'I agree to both conditions.' He paused. 'How can we arrange the details of the exchanges? Dates, locations, et cetera.'

'How long are you prepared to stay on in Berlin, Mr Shapiro?'

'If it pushes things along I'll stay however long it takes.'

CHAPTER THIRTY-TWO

Soon after the midnight head count at the Atlanta prison two men showed the release note to the Warden. Half an hour later prisoner number 80016–A was roused from his sleep and told to dress. Rudolph Abel dressed slowly and meticulously and then walked with the two FBI agents to the waiting car.

The Delta jet took off promptly at 2 a.m. and at 5.30 a.m. Abel was taken into the federal detention house on West Street, New York. Throughout the next day, Wednesday, the prisoner was kept out of the way of anyone who could possibly recognize him, apart from the agents guarding him.

Twice, a time was set for his departure, and twice it was cancelled, but on the Thursday afternoon the clearance came through. The car holding Abel was the middle car in a three-car convoy heading for McGuire Air Force Base. When they drove into the base Abel and the two agents transferred into a station wagon which drove down the runway right up to the waiting plane.

It was a big Super-Constellation transport plane usually at the disposal of a USAAF general. Spacious and comfortable, its curtains drawn. The crew waited confined in the cockpit until 6 p.m., when they were given orders to take off. Neither the captain or the navigator had any idea where they were heading for. But once they were air-borne they were told that they were on a secret mission and their destination was Wiesbaden. But they were not told who they were carrying on board or any details apart from their destination.

Just the fact that Moscow had agreed to Abel's return made the controllers of the operation especially cautious. With the cynicism of their trade they had considered the possibility that Moscow's previous indifference to having Abel back could be because he was out of favour. The possibility that Abel's restlessness could be because he was, in fact, apprehensive as to his fate now he was on his way back made them search him again thoroughly to make sure that he had no means in his clothes or on his body of committing suicide.

It was six o'clock the next morning when the plane landed at Wiesbaden. There was a technicians' meeting because of a fault in the aircraft's radio system that required servicing. The curtains around the passenger seats were drawn so that the repairman could not see Abel and his guards.

The repairman reported that the radio wasn't serviceable, it would have to be replaced. Just over two hours later the plane was edging into the control pattern of the Berlin Air Corridor. For the last half-hour of the two-and-a-half-hour flight to Berlin the plane was under surveillance by three squadrons of MiG fighters. It was 3 p.m. when the plane landed at Tempelhof. The US Provost Marshal was there and one of the military police cars drove Abel and his escort to the US Army Base.

Abel spent the night in a small, grim cell clad only in pyjamas, watched over continuously by a double guard who were changed every two hours. His escorts slept as badly as Abel did but in the comparative comfort of a private house.

At 7.30 the next morning, Saturday February 10, Abel was driven to the Glienicke bridge. The car and its escorting vehicles pulled up at the entrance to Schloss Glienicke and there were officials already there, including two men busy with walkie-talkies. Then, on a signal from one of the men with radios, the two CIA men walked with Abel to the bridge itself. At the bridge they stopped and Abel was handed a document signed by Robert Kennedy as US Attorney-General and John F. Kennedy as President. The document commuted Colonel Abel's sentence and granted him an official pardon on condition that he never re-entered the United States.

The Glienicke Bridge, with its sandstone piers and approaches, spans two small lakes, and is used solely as a crossing-point for the occupation forces. At the other side of the bridge Gary Powers stood with his KGB guard. Abel was asked to take off his glasses so that the other side could confirm his identity. When both sides had signalled their satisfaction that the man displayed by the other side was their man, Abel was told he was free to cross the bridge.

Picking up his two cases he walked forward, passed Gary Powers just before the demarcation line. Neither acknowledged the other and the transaction was over.

In Washington the lawns of the White House were sprinkled with snow. In the Blue Room Lester Lanin and his orchestra were playing for the guests at a going-away party for the President's brother-in-law and sister. At two o'clock several top government officials discreetly left the room and an hour later Pierre Salinger, the President's press secretary, announced the rapatriation of Abel to the Soviet Union and Gary Powers' release to the US authorities. Neither at the party nor in the press room was any great interest aroused by the event.

Joe Shapiro climbed awkwardly into the front passenger seat of the ambulance and told the driver to start. The streets of Brunswick were already crowded with people going to work and traffic, and it was almost an hour before they were approaching the border-crossing at Helmstedt. Trails of mist swirled across from the woods on each side of the road.

Already there was a long queue of cars. Not at the usual crossing-point barriers but nearly a quarter of a mile from the frontier post. At the temporary pole barrier Shapiro showed his ID card and the operational order to the Field Security sergeant. The sergeant checked them carefully and then waved to the military policeman who raised the counter-weighted pole.

At the normal control point the ambulance stopped again and Shapiro climbed down. He could see the grey Soviet Army field ambulance at the pole on the far side. From the back of the British ambulance two men got down. One was an SIS doctor and the other was Hugh Morton.

The three men walked to the white painted control post and Shapiro lifted the phone, speaking slowly and distinctly in Russian. He listened for a moment and then hung up. He nodded to the other two and the barriers of both sides of the crossing control lifted slowly.

The two ambulances rolled forward and stopped. The rear doors of both vehicles were opened and latched and two Soviets in civilian clothes eased a stretcher down the sloping metal runners. A KGB man in major's uniform waved Shapiro over. Shapiro looked at the face of the man on the stretcher then back at the KGB man. They exchanged a few words, the officer nodded and Shapiro signalled to the doctor to come over. They rolled the stretcher to the British ambulance and waited for the ramp to lift it into the back of the ambulance. When it had been latched in place, Shapiro spoke to the driver then got in the back of the ambulance, followed by the doctor and Morton. As the rear doors were closed Shapiro looked at the doctor.

'Well?'

'He looks in a pretty bad way but I'd need to examine him before I pass any comment.' He paused. 'Will you pass me that clamp?'

The doctor adjusted the drip and then Shapiro banged on the back of the driver's cab and the ambulance turned slowly and headed back up the road to Brunswick.

Shapiro looked across at the doctor. 'Is what you've got at the house enough? Or should he go to hospital?'

The doctor shrugged. 'Joe. If what I've got at the house isn't enough there's nothing else at the hospital that can do better. Not at this stage, anyway.'

The big house was in five acres of its own grounds and a room on the ground floor was equipped with all the paraphernalia of a mobile operating theatre and pharmacy.

The doctor and his assistant, masked and sterile, cut the sweat-sodden clothing from the man's shrunken body. No attempt had been made by the Russians to alleviate or hide his condition. Not even a wash or a bandage to give a better impression.

Slowly and gently the doctor checked over the body and the head of the man who lay there with his eyes closed, barely breathing, his teeth clenched tight as if he were resisting pain. Twenty minutes later the doctor gave his instructions to his two assistants and left them to their work.

In the small ante-room he joined Shapiro and Morton. He pulled up a chair and sat down looking at them both.

'In lay terms he's suffering from exhaustion, starvation and various wounds. He may have broken bones or internal injuries but until he's in a suitable condition for a proper examination I can't be certain.'

'What's it add up to, James?' Shapiro's face was grim.

'Now I've looked him over, I'm more hopeful. With a transfusion, a clean-up and a controlled feeding regime a week will make a big difference so far as his body is concerned.'

'What's that mean?'

'It means that I've no way of diagnosing what his mental state might be.' He paused. 'It doesn't look good. He's in coma and shows little or no response to the preliminary neural tests – I'm afraid you'll have to be patient and I'll keep you in touch with his condition.'

Shapiro looked at Morton. 'I'll stay here with him, Hughie. You get back to London. They need you and there's nothing you can do here that I can't do.'

The doctor interrupted. 'If you'll excuse me I'll get on with my job.'

When the doctor had left Morton said, 'What do you think? Will he make it?'

Shapiro sighed heavily. 'If you mean will he live – yes. I'd put my last dollar on it. But if you mean more than that –' Shapiro shook his head. 'I don't know. He looks bad to me. He's going to need a lot of psychiatric help. You'd better warn them back in London.'

Morton stood up. 'Get some rest, Joe. Get some sleep. Don't dwell on it. Give it time. You've got to be patient.'

By the end of a week Shapiro was really worried and had asked for a second opinion and Morton sent over a neuro-surgeon who checked over the doctor's notes and examined the patient. When he saw Shapiro afterwards he confirmed that the physical diagnosis was correct.

'Physically he's recovered remarkably well. The broken ribs and the bones in his hands we can deal with in a few weeks' time. But the central nervous system has taken a lot of punishment.' He paused. 'As you know he's no longer in coma. But his hearing is negligible and although there seems to be no damage to the vocal chords he doesn't speak. He can see all right but at the moment he is literally both deaf and dumb. And I suspect that that is psychological – trauma. That's going to take quite a time to treat. And it may or may not be curable. I just don't know.'

'How long will it take to find out?'

'Months rather than weeks.'

'And to cure?'

The surgeon shrugged. 'I've no idea. It could take years. But on the other hand he could recover overnight. Not from anything we can do. Just mother nature doing her stuff. Spontaneous healing.'

'And that's all you can say?'

'I'm afraid so. But if it's any consolation I should think that he will be fit enough to get up and walk around – with help – in a matter of days. He's got an amazing constitution, that chap.'

Five days later there was a vast physical improvement. The man called Phoenix had put on weight and his ribs and hands had been strapped and the X-rays showed that the bones were knitting together satisfactorily. He walked slowly and uncertainly but without a stick or any other aid. The washed-out pale blue eyes stared rather than looked, and his mouth was always shut tight, the teeth clenched and the muscles taut at the sides of his mouth. But there was no visible response to the words or sounds. Sometimes Joe Shapiro reached out and gripped the man's heavy forearm as they sat in the spring sunshine in the garden. The flesh was firm and warm but there was never any reaction.

PART THREE

CHAPTER THIRTY-THREE

The man named Johnny had paid for a meal for them both and Josef felt uncomfortable in the hotel restaurant in his cheap, drab clothing, but Johnny didn't seem to notice. They were drinking their coffee when Johnny said, 'Did you see in the paper that Lenin died yesterday?'

Josef nodded. 'Yes, I saw it.'

'What difference will it make?'

The young man shrugged. 'The fight will be out in the open now.'

'Between who?'

'Stalin, Trotsky, Zinoviev and maybe Rykov.'

'And who will come out on top?'

Josef laughed. 'Lenin?'

'I don't understand. Lenin's dead.'

'Trotsky is finished, Stalin will cash in on Lenin's reputation, Lenin will become a kind of Bolshevik saint, and the others will go along with Stalin.'

'I heard rumours that Lenin had recommended that Stalin had become too powerful and should be removed from the Central Committee.'

The young man looked at him for long moments before he replied. 'You're not a journalist are you?'

'What makes you say that?'

'Only people right inside the Party know anything about rumours like that.'

'There are a lot of rumours going around about the Bolsheviks. Lenin was poisoned was one I heard. There were plenty of others too.'

'Yeah. But yours wasn't a rumour. It was the real thing. And you know it was. A journalist isn't going to get information like that.'

Johnny smiled. 'You've got a sharp mind Josef. They must have taught you well in Moscow.'

'Maybe.'

'What are you going to do now you're back?'

'Anything that will keep me alive and let me spend my free time making them pay for what they have done to me and my family.'

'How are you going to do that?'

Josef shrugged helplessly. 'I've no idea. But I'll find some way.'

'It won't be easy, Josef. There are a lot of people in this country who believe in Communism. Not just workers but influential people.'

Josef half-smiled. 'You don't understand do you?'

'Understand what?'

'I'm not against Communism. Communism would work. What they've got in Moscow isn't Communism. It's Bolshevism. And that's a very different thing.'

'Was it what they did to your family that disillusioned you?'

'No. I was disillusioned before. I was on the inside. I knew what they were doing. At first I thought it was just a temporary thing that would be over in a few months. But it wasn't. It was obscene. The Party philosophers writing pamphlets and theses about a brave new world and behind them groups of men fighting like savages for power.' He shook his head sadly. 'Nobody could believe or understand what went on unless they were on the inside and saw it happening.'

'Where are you going to live?'

'I'll probably stay here if I can find work. It doesn't matter to me where I live.'

'Would you consider moving to London if there was work for you there?'

'I'd move to Land's End. It makes no odds to me where I live.'

'I know people who could give you work.'

'Doing what?'

'Translating.'

'Translating what?'

'Newspapers, documents – that sort of thing. From Russian into English.'

'How much would I get?'

'Five pounds a week.'

Josef shook his head, smiling. 'I'm twenty-two and nobody's gonna pay somebody of that age five quid a week.'

'Why don't you put it to the test?'

'What sort of firm is this we're talking about?'

'It's a small government department but you'd work at home.'

'Do you work for this place?'

'I work for the department that is setting up this new service.'

'You know that I've got no education, no qualifications.'

'You may have no formal qualifications but you've got all the qualifications we're looking for.' The man leaned forward and put his hand gently on Josef's leg. 'We'll look after you.'

And those words to the orphanage boy meant more than the man who called himself Johnny could have known. After a lifetime of looking after himself the words were like balm to his raw, wounded mind. They travelled together to London the following day.

CHAPTER THIRTY-FOUR

Johnny had found him a small flat in one of the rows of Victorian houses on the south side of the river at Putney. It turned out that Johnny was Major Johnson. But he could tell that he wasn't a normal soldier. He never wore uniform and seemed to be able to come and go as he pleased. But he was obviously a man with considerable authority. He made instant personal decisions when it was necessary. To his surprise his wages were paid promptly, and in cash, every Friday afternoon.

Johnny had bought him dictionaries and a supply of paper for the typewriter, and the material he had to translate was varied. Sometimes an article from *Pravda*, sometimes the minutes of a Party committee meeting in Moscow or

Leningrad. There were frequent reports of the organization of secret Party cells in other European countries, and confidential reports on industry and agriculture in various parts of the Soviet Union. He was not allowed to keep copies and sometimes a woman's voice on the telephone would raise queries about some point of English in his translation. He apologized for his poor English but she never commented back.

They had asked him to change his name to Smith and had given him a back-dated insurance card in that name. And his wages came in a plain brown envelope marked 'S' and he was asked to sign for them just with the letter 'S'. He had been given no special working hours nor was pressure put on him to get work done in a hurry, but he worked a full nine-hour day every day of the week including weekends.

It was almost nine months after he had started work for Johnny Johnson that he was asked if he would deliver a small package to a man in Paris. The address was in the rue Mouffetard, two room over at *pâtisserie* and a man who looked as if he was dying, his face was so gaunt and pale. He was invited inside and he went in reluctantly. But inside, although it was incredibly untidy, it was like so many of those small rooms that he had delivered messages to in Moscow. Even an icon set in a space on the crowded bookshelves and an etching of Karl Marx in a wooden frame on the wall.

The old man pointed to a box with a blanket folded on top of it and when Josef sat down he was handed a small glass of vodka. The old man sat on the ramshackle bed and looked at his messenger.

'What's your name, young man?'

'I don't give my name to strangers, mister.'

'And quite right too.' He paused. 'When are you going back to London?'

'That's my business.'

The old man cackled. 'You sound like one of those bastards from the Cheka.' He paused. 'You ever heard of the Cheka?'

'Yes. I've heard of it.'

'I got something for you to take back with you to London.' He paused. 'You want it now?'

'Is it small?'

'Yeah. But I'll have to wrap it for you.' The old man stood up and walked awkwardly to the bookshelves and took down a thin yellow book. As he walked back Josef noticed the old man's strenuous efforts to walk and for the first time noticed his mis-shapen leg. When the man stumbled he jumped up to save him from falling. As his arms went round the man's frail body he saw the man's teeth as he fought against the pain.

'Are you OK, Mr Lukas? Shall I get you some help? A doctor maybe.'

Lukas shook his head. 'No. It will go. Just let me sit down.' When he was seated Lukas looked at Josef and said, 'When people talk about the brave new world in Moscow just think of my leg, my friend. A present from the comrades.'

'What happened?'

'I had a small printing business. A man asked me to print something for him. I never read it. I was too busy. It was a resolution to the Politburo by Trotsky. They beat me up in the old insurance office in Dzerzhinski Square that the Ve-Cheka have taken over. The doctors say I'll have to put up with it or have my leg taken off.'

'Are you a White Russian?'

For the first time Josef saw Lukas laugh. 'Me? I'm not White nor Red nor any other bloody colour. I'm just a Russian who hates those bastards who broke up my body.'

Josef glanced at the paper cover of the yellow book that Lukas had handed to him. The legend on the cover, in Russian, described the contents as a résumé of the Twelfth Congress of the CPSU. He looked up at Lukas and said, 'You'd better cover it up. Have you got some paper we can wrap it in?'

Lukas smiled and said quietly, 'So you can read Russian, my friend?'

Josef shrugged. 'Perhaps. What about the wrapping paper?'

Ten minutes later, with the document wrapped, Josef stood at the door and turned to look at the old man. He said in Russian, 'You're working against them, aren't you?' When the old man nodded Josef said, 'I'm sorry about what they did to you. Some day it will change.'

'Goodbye, young man. But stop dreaming dreams. Nothing will change. But we can hurt them by letting the world know what they do to their own working-people.'

Major Johnson had asked him about the hour or so that he spent with Lukas. He listened as Josef told him what had been said, but he asked no more questions and had not pursued the matter. But when Josef was leaving Johnson said, 'What did you think of Lukas?'

'He's very lonely. And very sick.'

Johnson nodded but said nothing more.

It was almost four months later when Major Johnson asked him if he would be prepared to go to Paris for a few months to help Lukas, who found it more difficult to get around. Josef had pointed out that he spoke no French but Johnson said it didn't matter. The only people he would be dealing with were Russians. It never entered his mind to refuse and he had left for Paris a week later.

But in that week Johnson had briefed him carefully about his new duties in Paris. His job would be to liaise with groups of Russians who were anti-Bolshevik. In some cases anti-Revolution as well. He was to pass funds and messages to them and tell them what London wanted in return. He was warned that they were not easy to deal with. Not only differing convictions and objectives but forceful, independent leaders who quarrelled bitterly among themselves. He was to keep an eye on what they were doing, interpret their usefulness to London and try and hold the peace between them.

Before he left for Paris a meeting had been arranged by Major Johnson. It was at the St Ermin's Hotel and the man's name was Mason. Just the two of them. He was about the same age as Johnson but not so easy-going. He had asked Josef about his time in Moscow and Leningrad. He talked slowly as if he was slow in absorbing what was said, digesting it before he asked the next question. But as the chat went on Josef realized that Mason wasn't slow-minded or stupid, he was just a very clever interrogator. Never asking the same question twice as if he doubted the truth of what Josef said, but frequently crossing the tracks of what had been said, checking obliquely but with that innocent country-bumpkin look of trying hard to understand what he was being told. What also seemed odd was that, unlike this man, Major Johnson had never asked him about his time in Russia.

Johnson had seen him off on the boat-train at Victoria and had said that Mason was much impressed by Josef's attitude. Josef had no idea what he meant. He hadn't had an attitude. He'd just answered some questions. He'd been given a hundred pounds for his expenses in Paris, in cash. More money than he had ever handled in his life before.

The old man, Lukas, had helped him find a room himself in the rue Mouffetard at the back of a butcher's shop. He had paid for Lukas to see a doctor and had gone with him to the surgery. The doctor had come out of his small office and told Josef that Lukas was terminally ill. He had no more than a few months to live.

But it was nearly two years later when the old man died and in the meantime Josef had consolidated his relationships with the various groups in contact with Lukas. It was all a vivid reminder of his early days in Moscow. The committees, the resolutions, the speeches and pamphlets and the rivalries. Nevertheless, the contacts those groups had in the Soviet Union were widespread and in all walks of life. Josef talked and listened and painstakingly typed out his reports and delivered them in sealed envelopes to a man at the British Embassy, to be forwarded to London via the diplomatic bag. From time to time London asked him to pursue certain items but there was no pressure of any kind. His wages had been increased to ten pounds a week when he moved to Paris and they paid the rent for his room in Putney while he was away.

Lukas died in the summer of 1927 and there was only Josef and Major Johnson at his funeral. The people in London had paid for everything. After it was over they went back to Josef's room. Johnson said they should have a talk.

He was to be given a new name – Sanders, and he was to have new responsibilities. He would take over Lukas's job and also be responsible for maintaining contact with anti-Bolshevik groups in Berlin.

Two years later he was pulled back to London with the suggestion that he should have formal education in the Russian language. He never saw himself as having a choice in how his life should be. He counted himself lucky to be so well-paid. The Russian course took a year and then he was interviewed by Mason again. This time in a private room at the Reform Club.

'Remind me,' Mason said. 'What do we call you these days?'

'Sanders, sir. Josef Sanders.'

'Yes, of course. You did very well on your Russian course. Your tutor says you speak more fluently than he does.'

'He kept telling me that I'd never learn the grammar of Russian because I didn't know the grammar of my own language.' Josef smiled. 'I never could work out the difference between accusative and dative.'

'Ah, yes.' Mason looked embarrassed at the frankness, or the ignorance. It was hard to tell which. He shifted uneasily in the big leather armchair. 'I'd like to put a suggestion to you if I may.'

'Whatever you want is OK with me, Mr Mason.'

'Kind of you, I'm sure. Let me explain first before you agree. I – we – would like you to be put on a more official, more substantial footing. You have done valuable work for us in your own modest way and there is much else that we would like you to do that could not be done by a civilian.' He paused and shuffled his body again. 'Briefly I am authorized to offer you a commission as a full lieutenant in the army.' He sat back slapping his thighs with both hands as if he was glad to get done with a rather dubious proposition.

'I don't know anything about soldiering, Mr Mason.'

'Of course not. Of course not. You wouldn't have to do any of that. It's just a device – a way – of making you official, giving you some proper standing in the service.'

'I don't understand, Mr Mason. What service are we talking about?'

'Who do you think you're working for?'

'Major Johnson said it was a small government department that was interested in what is going on in the Soviet Union.'

'And you didn't wonder why a government department should be interested in those things?'

Josef shrugged. 'No. It's not my business.'

'Well. I suppose that's a point of view.' He paused. 'A very practical point of view if I may say so.' Mason leaned forward awkwardly. 'We're a department that is responsible for collecting intelligence about the Soviet Union.'

'You mean research?'

'It's rather more that that, Josef. The government doesn't like what's happening in Russia.'

Josef laughed sharply. 'A lot of Russians don't like it either.'

'Exactly,' Mason said. 'And I understand from the major that you don't like it either. The things they did to your family. Is that so?'

Josef nodded. 'Yes.'

'There are others involved in this but you've got an advantage over them. You know all about it from the inside. You're a very valuable man to us and we want to make you even more valuable.'

'Like I said, Mr Mason. I'll do whatever you want. You don't need to persuade me.'

When Johnson talked to him about his meeting with Mason he had obviously been amused at Josef's description of the encounter. He sat down heavily in the cane chair and looked at Josef.

'You know, my friend, it's time you changed.'

'Changed what?'

'Every bloody thing. You're not a cabin-boy on an old tub of a boat now. What old Mason said is right. You're a valuable man.' When he saw the smile of Josef's face he said sharply. 'Grow up, Josef. This isn't just a job, this is a career. Make something of it. Don't be so bloody humble. You said you wanted to fight those bastards who killed your wife and you just go on like a maiden aunt.'

When Josef didn't reply Johnson said, 'I've recommended that you should do three months' basic training in the army before you're commissioned.'

Josef just shrugged.

Johnson's hunch about how to stiffen up his protégé was not arrived at without a lot of thought. He knew too much of Josef's background not to realise that you don't come out of an orphanage to being a cabin-boy on an old tramp steamer with any great confidence in yourself or the world. And what had happened after must have been like a dream turning into a nightmare. But his ploy worked. Josef came out of his three months' training a different man. A new self-confidence, no longer the humble orphanage boy. Johnson had given him a copy of the official warrant for the King's Commission. He was now, despite his civilian clothes, Lieutenant Josef Sanders, General Service.

Lieutenant Sanders tackled his work with the groups with authority when he went back to Paris, and his instructions from London were now more demanding. It was no longer just a matter of listening to the information that came out of the groups' contacts in Russia but passing on demands for specific information. Gradually the groups were turned into cells of actual intelligence gathering. The information that they produced was low-level but it covered a wide spectrum of the political and economic life in the Soviet Union. And it was almost the only intelligence available to London.

His visits to Berlin became more frequent and more important. By 1933 the rise of the Nazi Party had made Moscow put pressure on the Cheka to try and recruit the Russian counter-revolutionaries in Germany with pardons for past defections. Sanders worked actively against the Cheka recruitment of any of his contacts and was largely successful. Both in Paris and Berlin his guidance was respected and he was seen as a man of authority. And although his new official status was never revealed it was taken for granted that his authority flowed from official sources in London.

When it became obvious that the Berlin groups were more active and purposeful than those in Paris Josef was moved to Berlin. Johnson had wondered if past events in Berlin would lead to objections from Josef but when he put the suggestion of the move to him it was clear that Josef welcomed the challenge.

By 1938 Josef was a major in the Intelligence Corps and was now spending more time in London. SIS was now trying desperately to reorganize itself to meet the demands of the war with Germany that was obviously coming. He was put in charge of intelligence aimed at the Soviet Union and his advice was frequently sought on matters concerning the Soviet attempts to penetrate British life.

On the Sunday morning of September 3, 1939, when war was declared on Nazi Germany, Major Sanders's identity was changed once again. He was now, officially, Major Joseph Shapiro, thirty-seven years old, and a long-serving and senior officer of MI6.

CHAPTER THIRTY-FIVE

When Hitler gave the order to launch Operation Barbarossa on June 22, 1941 the Soviet Union and Great Britain became allies. Uncomfortable allies.

In the next six months the Nazi hordes took city after city. Brest-Litovsk, Kiev, Kharkov, Rostov and Smolensk. And in mid-October the Soviet Government left Moscow in what looked like the last few days before the Nazis took the city. In North Africa Rommel had taken over the Afrika Corps. Joseph Kennedy, the United States Ambassador to Britain, counselled his government to abandon the British to their fate.

Then in December 1941 two things happened. It was obvious that the Germans were not able to take Moscow against its grim defence. At the end of the first week the Japanese attacked Pearl Harbour and the United States was reluctantly in the war.

In was in December that the British allowed the Soviet Union to set up a liaison unit in London. Member of the Red Army gave speeches to workers in munitions factories, negotiators pleaded for more and more supplies of medicines, medical equipment and arms, and propagandists urged an Allied invasion of France. Inevitably there were members of the Soviet liaison unit whose objectives were subversive.

A separate entity was the Soviet Military Mission. And it was the mission that came under the closest scrutiny of the British intelligence services. The mission consisted of representatives of the Soviet Army, Navy and Airforce and they were responsible for exchanging information about their mutual Axis enemies. Orders of Battle, captured documents and military intelligence. The exchanges were so cautious and the two sides so suspicious of each other that little of real help came from the meetings for either side. The fact that the Soviets were willing to maintain the mission in London despite its ineffectiveness was the basis for the British suspicion that some members of the mission had more covert functions. There were seven members of the mission who were suspected of being NKVD officers. The files on the suspects were passed to Joe Shapiro.

Each file had photographs of the suspect and brief details of his movements and contacts during his time in London. It was the file marked Abromov, Nikolai, that had Shapiro's attention. Not the report itself which had nothing of any real significance. Contacts with journalists, minor politicians and visits to art galleries. It was the photographs that made him stop. Photographs of Abromov with various people. Some identified, some not. But it was the Russian's face that stayed in his mind. He had seen him somewhere before. His mind went back over his counter-revolutionary groups in Berlin. There was a connection with Berlin. He was almost certain it was Berlin.

Shapiro decided that he should find some excuse for meeting the man casually, with other people rather than alone, so that his intent was not obvious. It was a week before there was a suitable occasion. An informal get-together so that the mission could meet some of the Eighth Army officers who had started the defeat of Rommel in the desert. The reception was in one of the conference rooms at the War Office, and Shapiro had gone with Johnson and two of Johnson's colleagues from his old regiment.

The high-ceilinged, panelled room with ornate chandeliers was crowded when they arrived, with much laughter and the usual rounds of toasts already livening things up as the various victories of the two allies were being celebrated in vodka and whisky, one by one. After fifteen minutes slowly circulating among the groups of people Shapiro had not seen the man named Nikolai Abromov. He was thinking of leaving when he saw him. They saw each other in the same moment and neither of them could believe what he saw. Shapiro was in battledress with Intelligence Corps' green-based major's crowns on his shoulder straps and the man going under the name of Abromov was wearing his duty green uniform, jacket, breeches and black boots with a full colonel's three stars on his shoulder bands. But they had both seen the recognition in the other's eyes.

Shapiro nodded towards the door and the Russian acknowledged the indication. In the empty corridor they stood facing one another.

Shapiro took the proferred hand. 'Nice to see you, Zag.'

Zagorsky smiled. 'Nice to see you too, young Josef.' He paused. 'Can we talk?'

'Of course. Let's go to my place. It's not far away.'

As Shapiro brewed them some tea Zagorsky looked around the room. The white walls bare of any kind of relief or decoration except for three shelves of books.

Books in Russian, French, German and English but almost every one covering the history of Russia, from the days of the Tsars to the first year of the war.

When they were sitting in the only two chairs in the room Shapiro said quietly. 'Who talks first?'

Zagorsky smiled. 'It might as well be me. Or you'll think I've risen from the dead.'

Shapiro said softly, 'And I believe you could if you wanted to enough. When I saw you being almost carried out of that court-room I thought it was all over for you. What the hell happened?'

Zagorsky said, 'Your Russian is really excellent, how did you get that good?'

'They sent me to university. Anyway, tell me what happened.'

'What did you think had happened?'

'I only heard rumours. Rumours that you had been shot the same day, rumours that you were in Siberia in a labour-camp. The usual rumours one hears in these cases.'

'They *were* going to shoot me. The next day. And then, late that night Dzerzhinski sent for me. He saw me himself. He had the transcript of my trial in front of him, including my rather emotional outburst in court.

'He said that he had been impressed by my work at Ve-Cheka and because he himself was originally a Pole he was aware of the harassment of Poles by certain Soviets. He said too that the military judge had been angered by being dragged into what was essentially political harassment and had spoken to him angrily.

'He said that he could offer me a way out. If I agreed to going underground as a Cheka officer my sentence would be struck out. The record would be wiped clean.'

'Did you accept?'

Zagorsky smiled. 'Of course I did. I told him to let the trial and the verdict stand. It would provide me with perfect cover. Like you, everybody would assume that I was dead.' He laughed. 'You couldn't have better cover than that.'

'Can I ask you what you've been doing since then?'

'You can ask, but that uniform you're wearing means that the answers will be cautious.'

'Tell me what you can.'

'I went down to Samarkand and ran a network of illegals into Iran and Afghanistan. Then like you I went to university to improve my foreign languages. Mainly my English.' He smiled. 'And now I'm here.'

'Spying on us.'

'Collecting information let us say. And what about you. How is the family?'

For long moments Shapiro looked at Zagorsky and then said softly, 'Are you kidding?'

The Russian looked genuinely surprised. 'I don't understand.'

'You mean you never asked what had happened to us?'

'I went straight down to Samarkand the next day. I was there for two years. A lot had changed by the time I got back to Moscow. A lot of people were no longer there. One didn't ask what had happened to them or where they'd gone.'

'What was the last you heard of me?'

'As I remember it you were in Warsaw with your wife and child. A son wasn't it?'

'Yes. It was a son. When you were put on trial we were in court. They forced us to go. My wife, Anna, was Polish and she was very upset. Not only about you but what the Polish Bolsheviks were planning to do in Poland. We escaped to

Berlin. I got a job in a bar. Washing-up at first and later as a barman.

'I came back one night and found that my wife had been murdered. Garotted. And they stamped a red star on her wrist. They took my small son away. I don't know what happened to him.'

For several minutes Zagorsky just sat there and Shapiro could see that he was genuinely shocked. Then the Russian took a deep breath.

'Saying I'm sorry won't help, Josef. Nevertheless I am sorry. I can't bear to think about it happening. It sickens me.'

'All for the good of the Party, comrade?'

Zagorsky shook his head. 'I won't attempt to make excuses. There are no excuses that would satisfy me. And there are none that would satisfy you.' He paused and sighed. 'And that's why you're wearing that uniform.'

'I never needed a uniform, Zag. It's my life's work to fight you people.'

'We're not all murderers, Josef. You know better than that.'

'You're all part of it. You know it goes on but you never raise a voice to stop it. You may not be a murderer, Zag. But you're an accessory to murder. And in my book the one is as evil as the other.'

'Do you include yourself in that? You must have known a lot of what was going on when you and Anna were working for me.'

'I don't excuse myself but I take comfort from the fact that I was very young. I thought it would change and when it didn't I escaped.' He paused. 'I'd rather be a coward than a murderer, Zag.'

'When did this happen in Berlin?'

'About twenty years ago.'

'And you've hated Russians for nearly twenty years.'

'No. I loved the Russians. I just hate Bolsheviks.'

'Including me?'

'No. You didn't have any part in murdering my wife. They were ready to murder you if it had suited them. I'm just sorry for you.'

'Is there any way – short of treason – that I can try and make up for that terrible thing?'

'Yeah, come over to us and work against them.'

'I said short of treason.'

'Are you married Zag?'

'No. I don't live the kind of life that goes with marriage.'

'How long are you staying in London with the mission?'

'I was posted here permanently. But I shall put in for a transfer now.'

'Why?'

'It would be pointless for me to stay. You know too much about me and I wouldn't relish working against you.'

'Can I ask you something personal?'

'Of course.'

'Did you ever really believe in the Bolsheviks? Especially way back when we were on that boat?'

Zagorsky closed his eyes, his face turned up towards the ceiling as he thought. Then he opened his eyes and looked at Shapiro.

'It's a tough question to answer, Josef. I need to search my heart. On the boat I think the answer has to be "yes". I believed in Communism, especially Lenin's version of it. Not Trotsky's and not Stalin's – although he wasn't all that important in those days. So Communism I believed in, but Bolshevism I wasn't sure about. Let's say I gave it the benefit of the doubt. There were harsh things to be done to organize our country. At least the Bolsheviks were determined enough and ruthless enough to do what was necessary.'

'How long did you go on believing in them?'

'Until my trial. I knew then that one didn't have to be guilty of anything beyond the greed and envy of rivals to lose one's freedom or one's life. After the deal was done with Dzerzhinski I just switched off my mind so far as politics were concerned. I made my work, my life.' He shrugged. 'Maybe not my life – more an existence.' He sighed. 'Not a hero's story, my friend. But the truth.'

It was too near the pattern of Shapiro's own life for him not to recognize its truth. He looked at Zagorsky's gaunt face and was sorry for him.

'Are you going to tell them of our meeting?'

'Of our meeting, yes. Your name, no. What we have talked about, no. You were a friendly officer who invited me home for a drink, and following our orders to make contacts with any friendly Englishman, I went to your home. I don't know where it was. You talked on and on about Montgomery and I talked on and on about Timoshenko.'

'So how do you get them to withdraw you?'

'That's no problem. I volunteer for more active duties. The mission is a privileged posting with a long, long waiting list. And the war won't last much longer. Two years perhaps and then we'll all have to pay the bill.'

'What bill is that?'

'The cost of the sacrifices, the price of victory. The Soviet Union having flexed its muscles and found that they work will be ready to advance on the world.'

'Which part of the world?'

Zagorsky stood up slowly, 'Where can I get a taxi?'

'On the corner.' He paused. 'You didn't answer my question.'

Zagorsky picked up his white gloves and his cap and as he stood at the door he said quietly, 'You know the answer, Josef, as well as I do. Not a part of the world. Just the world.'

CHAPTER THIRTY-SIX

When the war in Europe ended Shapiro was posted to 21 Army Group at its HQ in Bad Oynhausen. It was only a few months since the Soviet Union and Britain had been genuine allies, but by the end of 1945 the Red Army was deploying overwhelming forces of infantry and armoured divisions on their side of the Occupation Zone border.

Shapiro's first task was to set up line-crossing operations into the Russian Zone of occupied Germany. Each line-crossing unit was run by a British intelligence officer but the line-crossers were Germans or German-speaking displaced persons. Where possible the crossers were sent to areas that they already knew well. The local hatred of the Red Army's ruthless occupation made it easy to recruit local informants who could supply information on almost any aspect of the occupying forces.

It was in the summer of 1947 when Shapiro got a telephone call from the CO of 70 Field Security Unit in Hildesheim. Line-crossers worked both sides of the zone borders but the Russians had more difficulty in recruiting volunteers from a hostile population. From time to time Field Security Units picked up a line-crosser working for the Russians in the British Zone. A Russian line-crosser had been caught by a detachment of 70 FSU in Göttingen.

'Why are you calling me, Captain?'

'This chap we picked up refuses to talk except to you.'

'To me. Did he know my name?'

'Yes. He gave your name, your rank and he knew that you were at 21 AG headquarters in Bad Oynhausen.'

'Did he say why he wanted to talk to me?'

'No, sir.'

'What's his name?'

'I don't know. He won't talk.'

'How do you know he's working for the other side?'

'He was with a fellow who admitted under interrogation that he was a line-crosser. They both had the same type of forged papers.'

'What's he like?'

'Mid-twenties, well-built, educated. We think he speaks English as well as German.'

'OK. I'll come down in a couple of days. Where are you holding him?'

'In the local prison in Hildesheim.'

'OK. I'll see you on Wednesday.'

It was a pleasant drive down to Hildesheim in the confiscated Mercedes. The old town itself was still largely rubble. For some strange reason or blunder the quiet medieval town had been almost completely wiped out by the US Air Force in the last few weeks of the war. Centuries-old buildings had been reduced to rubble and dust in less than an hour.

70 Field Security's HQ was in a large house on the edge of the town and when Shapiro had been shown around he was offered a room where he could talk to the prisoner from the jail.

An hour later a young man was shown into the room by a sergeant who took off the handcuffs and left. Shapiro sat on the edge of the camp bed looking at the young man.

'What's your name, young man?' he said in German.

'My field name is Lemke,' the young man said and to Shapiro's surprise he spoke in Russian.

'Why do you want to speak to me?'

'I was told to speak to you.'

'By whom?'

'A man whose real name is Zagorsky. He uses other names but he told me to tell you his real name.'

There was a long pause before Shapiro spoke.

'Do you work for him?'

'No. He contacted me about a month ago. He gave me orders to cross the border in this area and to ask to speak to you.'

'You'd better tell me what it's all about.'

'He told me to tell you that it was payment of a debt.'

'A debt. What debt?'

'I don't know. He said to tell you about my family and you would understand.'

Shapiro pointed at a chair. 'Sit down.' When the young man was sitting down Shapiro said, 'OK. Tell me about your family.'

'I never knew my family. All I can tell you is what Zagorsky told me.'

'Go on.'

'My mother was Polish, my father was English. They married in Moscow but went to work for the Party in Warsaw. Something happened and they fled to Berlin. My mother died a short time after and I was taken away by strangers. I was only two or three years old. I was put in an orphanage near Leningrad.' The young man shrugged.'That's what he told me to tell you.'

Shapiro sat looking at his son, but all he could think of was Anna. He wished that he could tell her that the boy was safe. To tell her that his hair was as black as hers, his eyes as blue as his father's and his fingers long and slender. And she would say that the boy's firm mouth and strong jaw were all his. It had been twenty four years since the small boy had been taken away and in his mind's eye he had never changed. Despite the lapse of time he had always thought of his son as a small child in a woollen jersey and leggings and a red knitted hat with a white bobble on top of it. He had no doubt that the young man sitting there was his son. He felt relief to know that he was alive and well but he felt no sudden surge of love and affection. There were things that had to be done. And he would do them, but time and life had ground away his capacity to feel an upsurge of emotion. He should be calling for champagne, telling the world that his long-lost son was found, flinging his arms about those strong shoulders. But he couldn't bring himself to do it. Maybe in time he could feel that way and do those things. But right now, despite the heavy thumping of his heart, he felt no such emotion.

'Did Zagorsky say anything more to you?'

'He just gave me the instructions on how to come over the Zone border and told me about my family.' The young man smiled diffidently. 'He said that you were a man to be trusted.'

Shapiro stood up. 'Where are your belongings?'

'I only had the papers and a little money. I expected to be caught quite quickly.'

'You say your mother was Polish, do you speak Polish?'

'It's not bad.' He smiled. 'Poles tell me it's very old-fashioned. Out of date slang. But the orphans were mainly Poles.'

Shapiro stood looking at his son. 'I'll take you back with me to my house, and I'll get proper documentation for you.'

'Did this message from Zagorsky make any sense to you?'

'Yes it did. Apart from anything else it means you're under my protection now but you're not under arrest.'

Shapiro had spoken to the Field Security captain and the arrest sheet had been torn up and Shapiro had signed for the take-over of the prisoner. Shapiro had asked for the receipt to be endorsed to establish that the prisoner had not been charged with any offence.

As they got into the car the young man said quietly, 'Can I ask you what this is all about?'

Shapiro started the car as he said. 'I'll tell you later.'

PART FOUR

CHAPTER THIRTY-SEVEN

Sir Peter came in from the garden when he heard Shapiro's car pull into the drive. It didn't really fit the organization's protocol to be seeing Shapiro without the request coming through Morton and it was even less palatable that Shapiro had made clear that he didn't want Hugh Morton to know about his visit. But Joe Shapiro was MI6's longest serving officer and Sir Peter was sure that whatever it was all about Shapiro would have good reasons for his request. He glanced in the hall mirror as he walked to the front door. Untidy but clean was his verdict.

The handshakes and greetings were warm and genuine and when they were seated he looked at Shapiro.

'You look tired, Joe. It's time you took some leave.'

'That's what I came to see you about. One of the things anyway.'

'You don't need to see me about that, for heaven's sake. Take what leave you want. When did you last have leave? Must be two years at least. Or is it more?'

'About six years, Sir Peter.' He looked towards the window on the garden and then back at his boss.

'I'm due to retire next June. I wondered if there was any chance of retiring early without my pension being reduced?'

'Of course. No problem at all. Is there some other problem, Joe? You don't look your usual energetic self.'

'Not a problem. But there's something I want to tell you. But I need your assurance that it will stay between you and me.'

'Is this a personal thing or work?'

'Both.'

'I don't like open-ended promises, Joe. What's the general area of what we are talking about?'

'Would you rather I didn't raise the matter with you?'

'Not at all, Joe. I just don't want to be giving promises that I'll do or not do something without knowing what I'm committing myself to.' He paused. 'I've known you too long not to realize that you wouldn't be here unless you thought it was necessary.'

'It's a matter of putting a certain part of the record straight.'

'Part of your record . . .?'

'Mine and one other person's record.'

'To that person's disadvantage?'

'No. Just to my disadvantage.'

'Joe, I don't want to play twenty questions. What are we talking about?'

'I did something way back that I've come to regret. I put the organization above human relationships. I wish today that I had acted differently.'

'Does anybody else know about this?'

'Only the other person concerned.'

'Is he gunning for you now?'

'No. He knew what I was doing at the time and he agreed to do it. There's no come-back of any kind. Except my conscience.'

Sir Peter looked at Shapiro's solid, four-square face and saw the anguish in the eyes.

'OK, Joe. It's just between you and me.'

'It's about Phoenix. Summers.' He paused. 'He's my son.'

For several minutes Sir Peter was silent and then he said quietly, 'Tell me all about it, Joe. I don't understand yet but I understand well enough how tormented you must be. Just take your time. There's no hurry.'

'When I was a kid in Moscow my protector was a man named Zagorsky. He was tried for treason and I thought he was dead. About nineteen forty-three or forty-four we met accidentally, in London. He was an officer at the Soviet Military Mission under an assumed name. We talked for a couple of hours that night. He didn't know that the Bolsheviks had murdered my wife and abducted my son. He was genuinely upset about it.'

'Did you report any of this?'

'Major Johnson knew about my wife and son. No I didn't mention our talk. He was going to leave the Mission. It wasn't significant.'

'Carry on.'

'In nineteen forty-seven when I was at 21 AG I got a message that a line-crosser was asking to see me. When I talked with him he said Zagorsky had sent him to me to pay off a debt. He had told the young man, who was brought up in a Soviet orphanage, just enough about his background to tell me. The young man had no idea of the significance of what he was telling me. But I did. He was my son.'

'That must have been quite a shock, Joe.'

'It was. I'd always had him in my mind as a baby. It sounds terrible but I found I didn't have the right feeling for him. He was a real nice fellow – but that was all.'

'What happened?'

'I never told him he was my son. I got false papers for him and he joined the British Army. Because of his intelligence and his languages he was transferred to the Intelligence Corps. Then, as you know, he was transferred to us, to SIS, because he was a fluent Russian speaker. When Hodgkins was looking for a volunteer to be infiltrated into Poland he volunteered. I'd not seen him more than half a dozen times in all that time but it fell to me to provide his legend and documentation. I did it all very, very carefully. The only thing I did that was out of line was to tell him that I knew that his mother had been murdered by Bolsheviks. I showed him the old cuttings from the Berlin newspaper.' He paused. 'I shouldn't have done that. Not as a father. It was unforgivable. It was baiting a trap. And it wasn't even necessary. He'd got all the guts you needed. I put the Polish documents in his mother's family name – Kretski. His British passport and his papers were in my real name of Summers.' Shapiro took a deep breath. 'That's it, Peter. That's about it. I might as well have cut his throat.'

'There's nothing more than that?'

'Maybe just one last thing for the record.'

'Tell me.'

'When I went to Washington to try and persuade them to exchange Abel for Phoenix there was a problem. The CIA had discussed a possible exchange with Abel and he said he would refuse to be part of an exchange. I asked if I could talk to Abel. I'm not sure why but I thought I could persuade him.' Shapiro took a deep breath. 'When we met at the prison it was unbelievable. Colonel Abel was my old friend Zagorsky. That's how he came to agree to the exchange.'

'How is your son now?'

'Physically he's not too bad. They say he'll improve. But mentally he's in a bad way. The quacks say there's nothing clinically or surgically they can do.'

'Don't they hold out any hope?'

'You know doctors, Peter. Yes. Plenty of hope. Could come all right in a few years. Even over-night. But the prognosis is pessimistic.'

'And you feel obliged to take him over?'

'I've no doubt about that. He's my son. It may not feel like it. But he is. That's the least I can do for him.'

'What can you do?'

'Just be around. Wake when he has his nightmares. Hold his hand when he starts screaming. Pray for his soul. And mine.'

Sir Peter noticed the quaver in Shapiro's voice and decided that practicalities were the best cure.

'Let's deal with the practicalities first, Joe. You can leave the service in two month's time. I say two months so that we can put you up to full colonel in Part Two orders and your pension will go up accordingly. Early retirement will not affect your pension. It amounts to taking years of accrued leave. I'll see to that.

'So far as your son is concerned, he can be back-dated as a major from when he was caught. His disabilities came on active service so there will be an increased pension for him. His medical bills will be paid by the department and I'll arrange a bounty payment so that there will be enough to buy a house.

'I hope that will relieve you of the day-to-day worries we all have. But I'm worried about you.'

'In what way?'

'You've got a guilt complex, my friend. And like all those things they're never founded on fact but on fantasy. The more rational the man is normally, the wider and deeper the complex.'

'So?'

'Let's look at the chicken's entrails, Joe. Your son was forcibly taken away and there's nothing you could have done to get him back.'

'I could have offered to go back to Moscow if he was released.'

'And who would have cared for him after you'd died in a Gulag camp? Nobody. And then when you saw him again after over twenty years you couldn't relate to a healthy young man when all those years in your mind he was a baby. Irrational maybe but I suspect it's par for the course. And you had no family or anyone else around you to support you and take some of the load. So you did what you could for him.'

'And they sent him to his death.'

'Did you know that Hodgkins was looking for a volunteer?'

'No.'

'Did you suggest to your boy that he should volunteer?'

'No.'

'And when it was all cut and dried and put on your plate to provide his cover did you do it to the best of your ability?'

'Of course I did.'

'And is it fair to say that if you had not been his father and an old friend of Abel Zagorsky he would still be in the labour camp or in his grave?'

'It's possible.'

'Joe. Don't be so stupid. You know it is so. When you were that small boy, a cabin-boy on a broken-down merchant ship, you were about to be sucked up by a whirlwind that was sweeping over Europe. Was that the fault of a teenage boy, for God's sake?'

'I appreciate what you've said. I know that it's meant to be helpful but it still leaves me as a very poor specimen of a man.'

'Oh, for Christ's sake, Joe. With a mind like yours, how can you twist the facts so remorselessly? If you were my father I should be very proud of you. And I mean that. Wipe this blackness out of your mind. You've got much to do for that young man. Don't give up your strength to this ridiculous farrago of guilt. If you still feel you have a debt to pay then for God's sake pay it the only way you can. Your usual way, with guts and self-confidence.'

It was Gavrilov from Special Service-I who de-briefed the man whom the world knew as Colonel Abel. They got on well together. Much the same age as one another, worldly-wise so far as Soviets can be, they met almost every day for nearly two years. There was no hidden recorder. It was lying there, turning slowly, quite openly on the table, the latest Uher, bought in West Berlin.

Reel after reel went to the evaluation unit who sent copies of significant sections to other departments and sections of the KGB.

Zagorsky had been given a pleasant apartment overlooking the river. Two rooms and the usual facilities, and a middle-aged lady who cleaned up the place every day. It wasn't an onerous duty but she did sometimes complain about the tangle of wires that sprawled onto the floor from his hi-fi and short-wave receiver.

His wants were not extravagant and most of them were easily and willingly provided. In the first summer Zagorsky and Gavrilov took a simple meal every day in a small restaurant within sight of the KGB HQ. They played middle-grade chess and exchanged reminiscences of other cities they had both known in the Soviet Union and abroad. They both confessed to a liking for Paris as a permanent home but neither of them had ever been there.

It was after one of those protracted meals that Gavrilov said, with a smile, 'We were amused when we saw the newspaper cuttings about your trial and it mentioned the coded messages that were supposed to be letters from your loving wife and daughter.'

Zagorsky shrugged. 'Who wrote those damn things?'

'There was a team. When it was decided to use that format for coded messages we got in a lady novelist and we created this little family for you, like a radio serial.'

Zagorsky smiled. 'It was well done. It influenced people. It even made me feel homesick when they read them out in court.'

'We heard that when the pilot's family were pressing for an exchange that you weren't very happy about it. Why was that?'

Zagorsky looked for a few moments at the people walking in the sunshine and he looked at Gavrilov.

'Off the record or on the record?'

'Off. Nobody's ever raised the point. I was just curious, that's all.'

'First of all I was disappointed that Moscow hadn't offered an exchange for me. The embassy didn't contact me. Nobody. I was just left to rot. I hadn't talked to the Americans. The press made that clear. So I took it as a sign.'

'A sign of what?'

'That Moscow didn't particularly want me to come back so long as I wasn't talking to the CIA. Then out of the blue is the stuff in the newspapers about an exchange with young Powers.' Zagorsky shrugged. 'You get rather paranoid when you've been in prison for years. Years with no contact with my own people and my own country. Virtually the only friendly contacts I had were from the people who had put me in jail.

'So when there is a suggestion about an exchange I am well aware that the initiative did not come from Moscow but from the pilot's parents and I asked myself what sort of reception I would get when I returned to Moscow.' Zagorsky smiled at Gavrilov. 'As you know, with a few exceptions it was not a very enthusiastic welcome.' He sighed. 'After all those years of risks and difficulties I have heard people suggest that my mission to the USA was a failure.' Zagorsky shook his head. 'It no longer angers me. It no longer disappoints me. All I ask . . . is to be left in peace.'

'That's no problem, Zag. When the de-briefing is over you'll have your apartment and the *dacha* and all the privileges you're entitled to.'

'We'll see, comrade. We'll see.'

'You don't trust them, do you?'

Zagorsky just smiled as he waved to the waiter for more coffee.

The de-briefing was virtually completed by mid-April and Gavrilov was no longer a daily visitor. Perhaps one short visit a week to tidy up loose ends in his de-briefing, but no more. Zagorsky still went to the same restaurant for lunch but it wasn't the same on his own. From time to time he saw KGB officers whom he knew from the old days. They waved and smiled but they never stopped to talk or join him at his table. And being long experienced in the ways of the KGB he knew that it would always be like that. He had spent years in the West, virtually unsupervised, independent and surviving. And that made him suspect. To the KGB he was contaminated. It wasn't personal. It applied to anybody who had lived independently in the West. Who knew what they might have been up to? And in any case they were men who now knew about the West. Knew the Soviet lies and knew what freedom was like. The experience didn't necessarily make them pro-Western. There were many things about life in the West that they found abhorrent. But whatever their feelings they knew too much about the lies and fake promises to the people that kept the Bolshevik machine in power. They were not officially ostracised. Nobody was ordered to avoid them. But people knew the system and they didn't need to be told. There was a KGB word for it. Sanitization.

Zagorsky knew the system too and he didn't resent his treatment. He understood the motives, but it didn't stop him from being lonely. Gradually his outside forays were reduced to a brief daily walk for exercise and then back to his rooms. It was not unlike his life in New York. But he missed the people and he missed the talk. Being a patriot he spent no time wondering if his life was just reward for his services to his country. He left no will or last testament and it was the cleaning lady who found his body one morning. He was still sitting crouched in the leather armchair and there was jazz coming from the short-wave receiver which was tuned to 'The Voice of America'.

The meeting between Volnov and Gavrilov about the man who had used the name of Gordon Lonsdale took place in a *dacha* about ten miles east of Moscow. It was held at the *dacha*, not for any security reason but merely because Volnov didn't want to spoil his weekend in the country. He was in his sixties and he didn't like his routine being disturbed. Especially for a man he positively disliked. Gavrilov too disliked Lonsdale but he was stuck with the responsibility of deciding what should be done with him. He sensed that his compromise proposal was not going to be acceptable to the older man. But he could see no alternative that would be tolerable to those who wanted Lonsdale to be given public honours.

Volnov folded his arms and leaned back against the cushions on the couch. 'Why all the fuss about the man? He was never in danger. The worst that could happen to him was a prison sentence. We exchanged him for the Englishman Lynne or Wynne, whatever his name was. He's back here without a hair of his head disturbed. So why the circus?'

'He did a good job for us.'

'Rubbish. The fool was caught. His network in London was handed to him on a plate from Moscow. He was just a glorified messenger-boy.'

'It would help with his family problems.'

'That woman's right – his wife. I saw all that translation of the English newspapers. "I was spy's mistress says Natasha something or other".' His face was flushed as he looked at Gavrilov. 'All those foreign whores he slept with. She should be allowed to divorce him if that's what she wants.'

'Then we have another scandal on our hands.'

'No need to announce it. It can be kept quiet. You can warn the woman not to talk.'

'It's not as easy as that, Comrade Volnov.'

'Why not?'

'It would be bad for the morale of others we send overseas if we didn't support Konrad Molody.'

'Let it be a lesson to them. Don't screw foreign tarts. They expect their wives to be faithful but they live like brothel-keepers themselves.'

'The woman herself did not live an entirely blameless life while he was away.'

'So. Let them stew in their own juice, the two of them.'

'The naval intelligence people were very pleased with what he sent back.'

'So. It was the others who took the risk. The Cohens and the English couple. They did the work and they're still in jail. Molody just passed it on.'

'That's all most of them do.'

'Rubbish.' He paused. 'Anyway, what is it you want to do?'

'I've suggested that he writes a book. An autobiography. In English so that it can be sold in the West.'

'For what purpose?'

'So that the English and American public can see how inefficient their intelligence services are.'

'They don't give a damn one way or another.'

'The propaganda section say that it could cause a lot of embarrassment for London and Washington.'

'And Molody is the master-spy who deceives them all. The gallant hero.'

'Of course.'

'And that would keep him happy? And feed his ego?'

'Yes. We should control every word of it of course.'

Volnov shrugged, impatiently. 'Do it then, if that's what you want. But mark my words. There are to be no flags and no heroics in Moscow for Molody.'

'Right, comrade.'

'Don't look so pleased with yourself, Gavrilov. You're wasting your time bothering with that arrogant little kulak.'

Reino Hayhanen died in an unexplained car-crash on the Pennsylvania Turnpike.

Joe Shapiro bought a cottage in Northumberland. Near Bamburgh, within sight of the sea and within easy walking distance of the long sandy beaches. Except for a few weeks in summer the beautiful beaches were deserted and Shapiro and his son walked daily along the coast in all kinds of weather.

Shapiro had chosen that part of the world because he wanted to be away from people. Sir Peter had arranged for medical treatment for John Summers by a Newcastle doctor who was ex-Special Operations Executive and whose discretion could be trusted. He had not been told everything, but enough to understand the background of the man he was treating. When it was impossible to avoid contact with local people they were told that John Summers was a polio victim, an explanation that was readily accepted.

As the months went by the nightmares were less frequent but there was no improvement in speech or hearing. At a two-day check-up just before the Easter holiday Shapiro was told that tests showed that there was a strong indication that his son could now definitely hear sounds at certain frequencies. But what had seemed like good news was dashed by the consultant's opinion that the tests also indicated that there was no likelihood of John Summers ever recognizing speech. There appeared to be some gap in the nervous system that meant that while the ear itself reacted to certain sounds there was no link to the brain itself, and therefore no recognition of the sounds. Although it was cautiously and considerately put it was made clear that Shapiro could expect no improvement. He would best accept that his son's life would continue to be physically normal but mentally retarded.

Shapiro's life was devoted entirely to his son. A life of routine drudgery as nurse, guardian and housekeeper that he bore with stoicism that was a mixture of irrational guilt and resignation, and a genuine affection for the human being who had been so ruthlessly destroyed by evil men. There were times when his spirit flagged and he classed himself as one of the evil men.

In January of the second year they had to go for another consultation. This time in London. The journey by train from Newcastle had been such a strain on his son that he decided that it would be better to take a plane back to Newcastle. The short journey had been uneventful despite the take-off being delayed because of bad weather.

When they touched town at Newcastle they were warned about the slippery steps because of the snow, and snow swirled around them as they walked towards the terminal building. They were almost there when his son grabbed his arm trying to stop him from walking into the building. As he turned to look at him his son was shaking his head, grunting as he sometimes did when he was disturbed. And then, as if by some miracle he heard the words. Words in Russian. A jumble of half-finished sentences. Swear words, curses, violent protests and then, his chest heaving, his eyes staring John Summers gasped, 'Where in God's name am I? What am I doing here? Where are the guards?'

Shapiro spoke, also in Russian. 'You're safe, Jan. You're free. There are no guards. We're going home to the cottage.'

'They are waiting for me inside. We didn't land at Sheremetyevo. They know. They've got a photograph.' He looked away, towards the people inside the well-lit terminal building. Then he looked back at Shapiro. 'This isn't Moscow . . .

not . . . I don't feel well.' There were tears coursing down his cheeks and Shapiro put his arm around him. 'We're in England, Jan. There's nothing to worry about. The car is in the car-park. We're going home.'

As Shapiro drove up the A1 to Alnwick he listened to the flow of words from the back seat. Sometimes Russian, sometimes Polish. And finally in English. Strange juxtapositions of the words of hymns, girls' names and endearments, a short burst of laughter and the quiet heavy breathing as John Summers slept.

They sat together in the cottage until it was getting light the next morning. As they talked Shapiro picked his way carefully through the minefield of a brain that had too much to unload. But as he sat there with the man who was his son he knew that the long slog was over. It was going to be alright. His son could hear and speak and sometimes he stopped and replied to a question. All he had to do was help that wounded psyche get back to health and peace and then, by God, he could make amends.